W9-BHZ-527
HARRIS COUNTY PUBLIC LIBRARY

WITHDRAWN

EVERYMAN'S LIBRARY

EVERYMAN,
I WILL GO WITH THEE,
AND BE THY GUIDE,
IN THY MOST NEED
TO GO BY THY SIDE

FYODOR DOSTOEVSKY

THE BROTHERS KARAMAZOV

TRANSLATED FROM THE RUSSIAN
BY RICHARD PEVEAR
AND LARISSA VOLOKHONSKY

WITH AN INTRODUCTION
BY MALCOLM V. JONES

EVERYMAN'S LIBRARY
Alfred A. Knopf New York London Toronto

70

THIS IS A BORZOI BOOK

PUBLISHED BY ALFRED A. KNOPF

First included in Everyman's Library, 1927
This translation first published in Everyman's Library, 1992 (USA), 1997 (UK)

Published in the USA by arrangement with North Point Press
Published in the UK by arrangement with Quartet Books Ltd.

Eleventh printing (US)

This translation has been made from the text of the Soviet Academy of Sciences edition (Leningrad, 1976). Portions of it first appeared in TriQuarterly (#74), a publication of Northwestern University. The preparation of this volume was made possible in part by a grant from the National Endowment for the Humanities, an independent federal agency.
Quotations from Dostoevsky's letters in the introduction have been taken from *Dostoevsky: His Life and Work*, by Konstantin Mochulsky, trans. by Michael A. Minihan (Princeton University Press, Princeton, N.J., 1967).

 Published in the United States by Alfred A. Knopf, a division of Random House, Inc., New York, and in Canada by Random House of Canada Limited, Toronto. Distributed by Random House, Inc., New York. Published in the United Kingdom by Everyman's Library, Northburgh House, 10 Northburgh Street, London EC1V 0AT, and distributed by Random House (UK) Ltd.

US website: www.randomhouse.com/everymans

ISBN 0-679-41003-1 (US)
1-85715-070-8 (UK)

A CIP catalogue record for this book is available from the British Library

Library of Congress Cataloging-in-Publication Data
Dostoevsky, Fyodor, 1821–1881.
[Bra'tiâ Karamazovy. English]
The brothers Karamazov / Fyodor Dostoevsky; [translated by Richard Pevear and Larissa Volokhonsky]
p. cm.—(Everyman's library)
Translation of Bra'tiâ Karamazovy.
ISBN 0-679-41003-1
I. Pevear, Richard, 1943–. II. Volokhonsky, Larissa. III. Title.
PG3326.B7 1992 91-53186
891.73'3—dc20 CIP

Book design by Barbara de Wilde and Carol Devine Carson

Printed and bound in Germany by GGP Media GmbH, Pössneck

THE BROTHERS KARAMAZOV

INTRODUCTION

In one sense the introduction to a classic is superfluous. Having established a claim on our attention, it is for each reader to respond in his or her own way. Yet the very fact that a novel has become a classic suggests that there is more to the claim than immediately meets the eye. Even a vague awareness of the hundreds of books and thousands of articles (or is it now thousands and hundreds of thousands?) on *The Brothers Karamazov* and other works by Dostoevsky may intimidate the scholar and critic, let alone the general reader.

What makes *The Brothers Karamazov* a literary classic? It is easy to list some of the superficial reasons. Over a century after publication it remains a readable, up-to-date, entertaining and thought-provoking novel of action, its plot pivoting on those stand-bys of the best-seller – murder, violence and sexual rivalry.

At a deeper level, its characters and the dramatic events in which they participate continue to agitate the memory long after the book has been put down. Ivan, Dmitri or Alyosha Karamazov, what they say, their emotional torments, their clash of personalities, how they react to dramatic events, readily spring to mind in discussions of the modern condition. Dostoevsky's characters are men and women under stress, victims of modern neuroses, in the grip of modern ideas. Their presentation, while eminently readable in realistic terms, has also provoked comparisons with modernist and post-modernist fiction. Indeed, not least of the novel's claims to classic status is that it has continued, it seems, to stimulate and to find an echo in every significant intellectual development to have gripped the western mind since its appearance.

Yet it is not just that *The Brothers Karamazov* seems contemporary and relevant to every succeeding generation – like that famous portrait whose eyes seem to follow you round the room; it also echoes and develops some of the most ancient paradoxes and preoccupations of humanity and foresees intellectual, social and political developments of our own time. It was the French existentialist Albert Camus who said that Dostoevsky not Karl Marx was the great prophet of the twentieth century. No less interestingly, though more difficult to fathom, Albert Einstein declared that he had learnt more from Dostoevsky than from any other thinker.

Does Dostoevsky then simply use the novel form as a vehicle for his philosophical and religious ideas, for prophecy and psychological experiment? The reactions of some critics, in his own day as much as in ours, might lead one to think so. There they are on the shelves: works on Dostoevsky and theology, psychology, philosophy and so forth. But the important point is that for Dostoevsky himself only imaginative fiction is capable of expressing what matters about the human condition. It does not always do so, especially in the work of the 'realists' of his day at whom he was always having a dig. Yet at its best, it is capable not simply of entertaining, telling a good story or providing a social chronicle, but also of plumbing and illuminating the depths of the human soul. In Dostoevsky, one might say following his own line of thought, the novel finds its true vocation.

The Brothers Karamazov was Dostoevsky's last book, published in serial form in *The Russian Herald* from January 1879 to November 1880, and is generally held to represent the synthesis and culmination of his entire work. It appeared as a single volume almost immediately its serialization was complete, bearing the date 1881. The prefatory note called 'From the author' indicates that there was to be a sequel and it is widely assumed that we were denied this only by Dostoevsky's untimely death on 28 January 1881. (All dates are given according to the pre-revolutionary calendar which was twelve days behind ours in the nineteenth century.) But Dostoevsky could easily have changed his mind. The surviving notebooks for his novels show how often he did this. What we have is a text which, because it claims to be incomplete, stimulates the reader to imagine how it might have continued and that is much more important than any fragmentary evidence of what was in Dostoevsky's mind: for whatever reason *The Brothers Karamazov* is a novel whose story has no definite end.

His last few years, in spite of the fatal illness which would shortly overtake him at the age of fifty-nine, were probably the most stable and relaxed period of Dostoevsky's life, and the notebooks for this novel are the most coherent. He had married Anna Grigorevna, his second wife, in 1867, having employed her in a crisis to take down *The Gambler* in shorthand as he composed it. Thanks to her good housekeeping his financial affairs were in order for the first time in his life. The greater part of the book was written at Staraia Russa, a provincial town about a hundred and fifty miles south-east of St Petersburg, where the Dostoevskys bought a house in 1877, and the novel was completed at Bad Ems, a German spa near Koblenz, to which Dostoevsky repaired from time to time for health reasons. In the summer of 1880 he had been hailed as a great contemporary prophet by representatives of the warring factions in the Russian intelligentsia on the occasion of his famous 'Pushkin Speech', delivered to mark the unveiling of the Pushkin statue in Moscow. Moreover he was now *persona grata* in government and court circles. He was on good personal terms with Konstantin Pobedonostsev, the reactionary and increasingly influential Chief Procurator of the Holy Synod, and corresponded with him about the religious aspects of *The Brothers Karamazov*. Moreover the Emperor had asked him to act as spiritual guide to his younger sons. Still, tragedy haunted him. In May 1878 his little boy Aleksei died and he made a pilgrimage in the company of the young philosopher Vladimir Solovyov to the monastery of Optina Pustyn. Both these events had a profound effect on the writing of the novel.

If Dostoevsky's last days saw increasing acceptance and respectability, it had not always been so. His life story seems to swing backwards and forwards between extremes. His introduction to the great critic Belinsky and the literary circles of St Petersburg in the mid-1840s had, owing to the success of his first novel *Poor Folk*, momentarily turned his head. But hubris invited nemesis: his flirtation with groups of utopian socialists in St Petersburg at the end of the decade led to his arrest, a death-sentence, the commuting of the sentence at the place of execution and eight years in Siberia.

The sixties and seventies, after his return to St Petersburg from exile, did indeed see his transformation into the great

European novelist we know, with the publication of *Notes from Underground* (1864), *Crime and Punishment* (1866), *The Idiot* (1868), and *The Possessed* (1871). But the price in personal terms was considerable. These years also saw him racked by illness, with increasingly severe epileptic fits, by a gambling obsession and consequent debts, which he only began to get on top of with his wife's help in the 1870s. Indeed the tormented character of the novels themselves is evidence enough of his state of mind.

All Dostoevsky's major novels turn on murder. *The Brothers Karamazov* is exceptional in this respect only in the nature of the murder, parricide. In spite of the assurance in 'From the author' that the hero of the novel is Alyosha, the main story line is about his brother Dmitri who has the motive, the means and the opportunity to kill his father and is deeply incriminated by circumstantial evidence. Many readers, when the book first came out in serial form, were held in suspense month by month wondering if he would do it, if he had done it, whether he would be convicted and if so whether he would escape. And this narrative still grips the imagination.

In curious ways the theme of parricide haunted Dostoevsky all his life. As a boy he had been fascinated by Schiller's play *The Robbers*. In 1838 he entered the Engineering Academy in St Petersburg, housed in the building where the Emperor Paul had been murdered, some believed with the collusion of the future Alexander I. In 1839 Dostoevsky's father died, presumed murdered by his serfs, and though Dostoevsky certainly had no hand in it, and there is even doubt about whether it was murder at all, the point is that he always believed in the murder story and perhaps felt guilty about his absence at the time. Freud certainly associates this event with the working out of the Oedipus complex in Dostoevsky's life and work, as also the metaphorical threat to the Tsar implicit in his association with the utopian socialists in the forties, for which Dostoevsky accepted punishment in Siberia. Late in life he returned to *The Robbers* which he read to his young children and to which there are allusions in *The Brothers Karamazov*. Most important of all for the plot of the novel was an encounter in Siberia with a convict called Ilinsky, who served ten years for the murder of his father, before the real murderers confessed and he was exonerated. At the time of his trial he had denied all knowledge of the crime though the evidence was overwhelming. Dostoevsky was convinced of Ilinsky's innocence after meeting him.

Yet in each case one is struck more by the fascination than by the reality, and in each there is a certain distance between Dostoevsky and the act of parricide. Either we are dealing with fiction (*The Robbers* or George Sand's *Mauprat* which also has striking parallels with the plot of Dostoevsky's novel), or doubt and error (Alexander I seems not to have known about the intention of killing his father; Dostoevsky certainly had no hand in his father's death, which may not even have been murder; he never had any intention of assassinating the Tsar; Ilinsky was actually innocent).

So it is with the novel. Guilt and guilt feelings vaguely motivate the action of all rather than focus on the one who physically committed the crime. Is there parricide at all? Assuming Dmitri did not commit the deed and Smerdyakov did: is Dmitri still in some sense morally culpable? Is Smerdyakov definitely Fyodor Karamazov's son? Is not Ivan in some sense to blame? Is not even Alyosha guilty of dereliction? Is not everybody, in Zosima's words, in some sense guilty for everything?

So we find ourselves drawn from our focus on the murder story to questions of moral responsibility and guilt, complicity and collusion. We also find ourselves drawn into Ivan Karamazov's thinking about religion: is his rejection of God not a sort of religious parricide, a killing in his own mind of the Divine Father, reminding us of the nearly contemporaneous claim by Nietzsche that God is dead? Similarly we find ourselves thinking about whether Fyodor Karamazov brought his death upon himself, about his treatment of his wives and the Karamazov children, of innocent suffering (the source of Ivan Karamazov's rebellion and the stories he gathers from the newspapers). The very nature of fatherhood is discussed at the trial itself, reflecting another of Dostoevsky's long-term ambitions, to write a novel about children.

The reader who reads exclusively for the excitement of the

story may of course become impatient with, or even skip, Books Five and Six. But for Dostoevsky they were the heart of the novel. Ivan's rebellion against God and his story 'The Grand Inquisitor' have been widely read as an immensely powerful indictment of Christianity on the one hand and as a uniquely prescient analysis of totalitarianism on the other.

Dostoevsky believed that Ivan's rebellion against God was much more devastating than any case contemporary left-wing intellectuals had managed to assemble. The text speaks for itself. By marshalling a series of anecdotes illustrating the suffering inflicted by adults on innocent children (child abuse as we have come to call it) Ivan reaches the conclusion that he cannot accept God's world and that if such suffering is the price of entry into paradise then (echoing Schiller here) he respectfully returns the entry ticket. He does not at this point deny the existence of God as he does elsewhere in the text; he revolts against the order of the universe out of compassion for the suffering of little children. In letters to N. A. Liubimov, his editor, and to Konstantin Pobedonostsev, Dostoevsky insists that Ivan's blasphemous arguments are to be refuted later in the novel. Clearly, he was anxious that the censor, the publisher (M. N. Katkov) or the editor might refuse publication. But as time went on, Dostoevsky found the task of refuting them through Zosima increasingly taxing.

Meanwhile 'Rebellion' was followed by 'The Grand Inquisitor'. Whole books have been written on this chapter (a reference to Sandoz's book is given below) and indeed it has many enigmatic aspects. For example, the meaning of Jesus' silence and his kiss has generated much discussion, as has the Grand Inquisitor's reading of the Gospel narrative of the temptations in the wilderness, which the novel presents in Matthew's version. Since the story is there to be read in Dostoevsky's text it would be fatuous to repeat it here. Nevertheless it may be worth rehearsing some of its central features. Some modern readers are overwhelmed by its incisiveness, but others labour in vain to discover the point.

The Grand Inquisitor, a Roman Catholic Cardinal, already ninety years old, in charge of the burning of heretics in sixteenth-century Seville, is unexpectedly visited by Jesus in his cell, and attempts to justify himself. It should be noticed that the Grand Inquisitor is actually an atheist. He is also a humanitarian, motivated by a deep love for humanity. His objective is the happiness of mankind and he has devoted his life to organizing society so as to ensure general peace and prosperity. He perceives that humanity's deepest need is not for freedom: moral choice is the gift which Jesus brought to the world, but it is a burden too heavy for all but a very few to bear. Humanity's present lot is conflict, turmoil, confusion, bloodshed and unhappiness, the result of that gift of freedom. Humanity yearns above all not for freedom but for what the Grand Inquisitor calls 'mystery', 'miracle' and 'authority', and he relates these three principles to the three temptations in the wilderness. There the devil tempted Jesus to win people's hearts by turning stones into bread, to test God by leaping from the pinnacle of the temple, and to rule over all the kingdoms of the earth. Jesus was wrong to reject these temptations. The Catholic Church has corrected Jesus' error and accepted them. For eight centuries it has been on the devil's side. Of course this means that for eight centuries the leaders of the Church have been propagating an enormous lie, since they alone know that there is no God and that Christianity is an elaborate myth designed to organize and control people's rebellious imaginations. But they have done so in the interests of humanity and its greater happiness. Freedom is incompatible with happiness.

By adopting these three principles – formulated by the devil in the most penetrating questions ever devised – the Church has furnished all that humanity seeks on earth: someone to bow down to, someone to take over their consciences, and a means for uniting everyone into a common, concordant and incontestable anthill.

Alyosha challenges Ivan's identification of his Grand Inquisitor with the Catholic Church, but of course Ivan's Legend does not have to be taken literally: he is talking about fundamental forces in human history. For him the Grand Inquisitor stands for all totalitarian creeds and ideologies based on an honest desire to save humanity from its own inability to handle freedom without lapsing into bloodshed and chaos. Ivan does not question the Grand Inquisitor's motives: indeed he affirms that he is tormented by great sadness and loves humanity. But until human beings understand the feebleness of their rebellion, the burning of heretics will continue to be necessary.

Readers familar with Dostoevsky's other writings know that Dostoevsky saw socialism as the illegitimate offspring of Catholicism. The 'anthill' and the 'Tower of Babel' which 'The Grand Inquisitor' also mentions are among Dostoevsky's favourite metaphors for socialism. It is for such reasons that the story has frequently been taken from its context in the novel and seen as a powerful allegory of the development of twentieth-century totalitarianism, particularly of the Communist variety. There can be little doubt that with the collapse of the Soviet empire it will take on a potent new force as that country reviews its recent history.

The Legend is but one of four, or possibly five, stages in Ivan's thought recorded in the novel. They span the period between his eighteenth and twenty-fourth year: they are the legend of the philosopher who refused to believe in paradise, the story of the Grand Inquisitor, the article on the ecclesiastical courts, the conversation with Alyosha on rebellion and the theory of 'geological upheaval' set forth by Ivan's hallucinatory devil. Each of them represents a stage in Ivan's wrestling with questions of theodicy, God and the world-order. And they feed back into the plot through the axiom which so impresses Smerdyakov, that 'if there is no God there is no morality'.

It was Dostoevsky's declared intention that the refutation of Ivan's rebellion should find its focus in Zosima's testament in Book Six. The Jesus of 'The Grand Inquisitor' remains entirely silent apart from the Aramaic words 'talitha cumi' ('damsel arise') which he utters as he makes his way through the crowd to meet the Inquisitor. Alyosha concludes that the Legend is in praise of Jesus and does not blaspheme him.

Dostoevsky was, however, very worried by the thought that he might fail to refute Ivan's blasphemy convincingly. In May 1879 he assured Liubimov that he was working on the chapter 'The Russian monk' 'with fear, trepidation and awe'. He had done an enormous amount of background reading of the Bible and works of Russian Orthodox piety; he had briefly met the Elder Amvrosy on his visit to Optina Pustyn. He had read the monk Parfeny's account of a visit to the Elder Leonid. In August 1879 he wrote to Pobedonostsev that he did not intend to refute Ivan 'point by point' but 'indirectly' by means of an 'artistic picture'.

Whether this 'artistic picture' does the work Dostoevsky intended for it has been a matter of intense dispute. His Zosima has been accused of heresy by some; others have simply regarded his image as too weak to overcome the deep emotional impact made by Ivan. Some, though usually those with a pre-existing commitment to Christianity, have been profoundly impressed by him. Yet there remains a lingering doubt that the God whom the Grand Inquisitor failed to take account of is frustratingly elusive in Zosima's religious consciousness as well. One scholar (A. B. Gibson) has referred to 'the combination of the sincerest piety with the apparent absence of its object'.

Alyosha too represents the religious principle in the debate, but for all his allegiance to Zosima and the life of the monastery, his profoundest religious ecstasy has very little about it that is specifically Christian.

> It was as if threads from all those innumerable worlds of God came together in his soul, and it was trembling all over, 'touching other worlds.' He wanted to forgive everyone and for everything, and to ask forgiveness, oh, not for himself! but for all and for everything, 'as others are asking for me,' rang again in his soul. But with each moment he felt clearly and almost tangibly something as firm and immovable as this heavenly vault descend into his soul. Some sort of idea, as it were, was coming to reign in his mind – now for the whole of his life and unto ages of ages. He fell to the earth a weak youth and rose up a fighter, steadfast for the rest of his life, and he knew it and felt it suddenly, in that very moment of his ecstasy. Never, never in all his life would Alyosha forget that moment. 'Someone visited my soul in that hour,' he would say afterwards, with firm belief in his words . . .

Expressions such as 'as if', 'almost', 'some sort of', qualify the description and it is 'someone', not specifically 'God', who visits his soul.

Perhaps to the modern mind, however, this bashfulness about the Christian God is less important than the affirmation of the value of religious experience itself. There is no doubt that Dostoevsky wanted at all costs to escape dry conventionality in the presentation of his answer to Ivan, and to represent religious faith as a synthesis of unique personal experience with the authority of the Scriptures. What he has undoubtedly succeeded in doing is demonstrating a wide variety of religious experience, much of it false (Ivan, Ferapont, Fyodor Karamazov), some of it bearing fruit in richer lives (Zosima, Markel, Alyosha).

As always, ideas are intimately linked with personal feelings in Dostoevsky and the reader is invited to judge the validity of the ideas by the viability of the personality. In that case, Alyosha's spiritual destiny, being more enviable than Ivan's, might incline us in his favour. The Russian scholar Valentina Vetlovskaia has shown, moreover, that Dostoevsky uses various subtle rhetorical devices to predispose us towards Zosima and Alyosha, and against Ivan and characters such as Miusov and Rakitin. Indeed, Zosima's and Alyosha's voices are never presented ironically, whereas the reverse is true to varying degrees of all the other characters.

This runs against what many readers, following the influential Russian critic Mikhail Bakhtin, have seen as the principal distinguishing feature of Dostoevsky's major novels, and *The Brothers Karamazov* in particular. Bakhtin called the Dostoevskian novel 'polyphonic'. One of the things he meant by this is that each voice in the book has equal weight in an ongoing dialogue, including the author's. Nowadays we should be more inclined to say 'including the narrator's' in order not to confuse the voice of Dostoevsky's narrator (itself a fictional construct) with his own. Bakhtin argues that this constitutes a major revolution in the history of the novel. Most other novels are 'monologic' in the sense that the voices of the characters are evidently subordinated to a single consciousness which we usually identify with that of the author. As a matter of fact (as Terras explains), Dostoevsky's narrator himself exhibits here two fundamentally incompatible voices: a local resident who is realistic and sceptical, and an omniscient narrator who is an idealist and a believer, and who knows things about the characters' thoughts which the resident could not possibly know. The reader may notice that in the former mode the narrator displays all sorts of stylistic awkwardness. Although the permissible limits of stylistic awkwardness are not the same in English as in Russian, the translators of this much-acclaimed English version have endeavoured to retain his idiosyncratic prose, thereby preserving much of the humour and distinctive voicing of the novel.

There has of course been much dispute about Bakhtin's thesis, but it has proved a very powerful tool when applied to Dostoevsky's major novels. They do privilege free dialogue in a more radical way than we find in any of Dostoevsky's predecessors or contemporaries. One thing about which there is no doubt is that each of the major characters has a distinct and distinctive personality and with it an individual voice of his or her own. Although it is claimed that each of the brothers has something of the Karamazov inheritance, they are so different from each other that some critics have been tempted to see in them three basic human types, roughly defined as the sensual (Dmitri), the spiritual (Alyosha) and the intellectual (Ivan).

It is true that Dmitri seems to have inherited sensuality from his father, but he has none of his father's low meanness. On the contrary, Dmitri is notable for his idealism, his sense of honour and his wrestling with the idea of two kinds of beauty – the beauty of Sodom and the beauty of the Madonna. He complains that people are so complex that a thirst for both types of beauty can coexist within them.

In spite of his own misgivings, Alyosha appears to have very little of his father's sensuality and what he has seems, as the critic Frank Seeley argues, to have been sublimated: 'Alyosha is predominantly his mother's son.' To the reader of Dostoevsky's earlier novels he follows in that tradition of 'saintly' characters which include Sonya Marmeladova (*Crime and Punishment*), Myshkin (*The Idiot*), Shatov (*The Possessed*) and Makar (*A Raw Youth*). He is, however, healthier and less complicated than any of his predecessors, though he shares with them a certain immediacy and childlikeness of response, insight into the hidden thoughts of others, compassion and humility.

Ivan's relationship to his father is seen differently by different people. Fyodor does not see himself in Ivan and Ivan loathes and rejects the old man. Ivan certainly experiences a love of life but, above all, his energies are channelled into thought, a thought racked with his own inner contradictions based, one would surmise, on his repression of the Karamazov inheritance. However that may be, Ivan is doomed to neurotic inactivity and indecision in the world of action.

Dialogue in Dostoevsky means not just the coexistence of independent and distinctive voices. It means being able to absorb aspects of the voice of another and exerting influence over the other's voice. The examples given show how Fyodor Karamazov's voice is partly absorbed (and modified) in his sons. But we also observe Zosima's influence on Alyosha, Ivan's on Smerdyakov, Alyosha's on Kolya. And we may note that the whole novel can be read as an extension of Ivan's voice (point-of-view), or Alyosha's or Mitya's. In extreme cases (but not unusual ones in Dostoevsky) characters have 'doubles'. This term is sometimes used to denote conflicting 'personalities' in the same character. Sometimes it is used to refer to a projection of some aspect of a character's personality with which the character enters into dialogue. The classic case occurs in Dostoevsky's early novel *The Double* where the hero meets his *Doppelgänger*. The most striking case in this story is, of course, Ivan's conversation with his devil representing aspects of his personality he wants to disown but cannot. The third use of the term 'double' indicates secondary characters who seem to embody one significant aspect of a main character's personality. Such is Smerdyakov's relationship to Ivan.

Dostoevsky often brings divergent and conflicting personalities together in scenes of excruciating embarrassment, variously known as his 'conclaves' or 'scandal scenes'. Possibly the most memorable of these in *The Brothers Karamazov* occurs in the monastery in Part I, Book Two. Typically Dostoevsky sets the scene in a place and on an occasion where a high degree of social decorum is expected. Any breach of it will inevitably cause offence and embarrassment. He places there at least one character who sets great store by the preservation of this decorum but who is on edge in fear of a disaster. He also introduces a number of other characters who in a variety of ways are likely to cause some sort of scandal – perhaps because this kind of decorum goes against their normal inclinations. But they are also predisposed to do things to upset each other; their personalities and interests are bound to clash and since they are all play-acting to some degree, they may try to 'unmask' each other and show up the other's lie. Interestingly, it is not the monks who are embarrassed. Equally interestingly, Zosima accurately diagnoses the source of Fyodor Karamazov's provocative behaviour, advising him not to lie, above all to himself. The victims of the scandal are Miusov and the Karamazovs.

Another memorable scandal scene, though played out on a less public stage, is described in the chapter 'The Two Together', in which Grushenka has lured Katerina into pouring out her heart, only to turn on the girl and humiliate her, finally revealing in a parting taunt that she knows her awful secret. Katerina is devastated in Alyosha's presence, just as Grushenka had planned. At a time when Katerina is emotionally vulnerable she proffers love and then cruelly withdraws it. She calls attention to areas of Katerina's personality of which Katerina is but dimly aware and which she is unwilling to recognize. She stimulates her emotionally in a situation where it is disastrous for her to respond. She exposes her almost simultaneously to stimulation and frustration and switches from one emotional wavelength to another while on the same topic. Finally, she blames Katerina for provoking the scene which she has herself engineered. These are akin to the strategies which the psychologist R. D. Laing has identified as causing the most intense emotional confusion. They can be found at work frequently between Dostoevsky's characters.

But the 'multivoicedness' of Dostoevsky's novel is not restricted to dialogue between and within the characters and the narrator. It has other important functions. One of them involves the constant echoes of other texts. Of course if one actually knows these texts intimately the echoes are richer and more thought-provoking. Otherwise they appear as little more than unfamiliar quotations. Footnotes can do little to repair this deficiency. Still, if one is aware of the precursor voices summoned up through the shared memory of author and reader one still senses that multidimensionality which is one of the glories of *The Brothers Karamazov*. Such awareness may stimulate all sorts of reflections which the author was unaware of, especially if the 'allusions' one detects are to texts which post-date the novel. Some would call such connections misreading. Others would point to them as evidence of Dostoevsky's extraordinary powers of anticipation.

The novel contains over eighty quotations from the Bible alone. Over forty different sources are mentioned or quoted by Ivan in 'The Legend of the Grand Inquisitor'. In addition quotations from hagiography and religious folklore, Pushkin, Schiller, Shakespeare, Nekrasov, Herzen, Pecherin, Polezhaev and others, not to mention contemporary journalism, abound throughout the novel. The end-notes to this edition will indicate the sources of some of them. But, as Nina Perlina has pointed out, their significance does not end with their place in the text or the associations they may have in our memories of their sources. Sometimes, for example, sources are reaccentuated and misquoted, and this may play an important role in characterization. Perlina notes that in his drafts to Part I of the novel, Dostoevsky wrote,

> Most important ... the landowner quotes from the Gospel and makes a crude mistake. Miusov corrects him and he makes even worse errors. Even the scholar makes mistakes. No-one knows the Gospel. 'Blessed is the womb that bore thee,' ... said Christ ... It is not Christ who said that ...

Sometimes, of course, there is no quotation or overt allusion, but the well-read reader will catch the tones of other texts, and the likeness is so compelling one suspects that such texts have served Dostoevsky as models, even unconsciously. Hackel's view that Dostoevsky must have modelled his presentation of Zosima in part on the Bishop Bienvenu in Victor Hugo's novel *Les Misérables* is based partly on such intuitions and partly on Dostoevsky's known admiration for the book.

The result of such techniques is that the reader's mind is

encouraged to stray from the path of the narrative and to reflect on connections, parallels, echoes, both within the text and without. The narrator's own inadequacies and uncertainties also encourage this. But the more one ponders the novel the more one realizes that one is dealing with layer upon layer of text, of voice echoing other voices and not with a single reliable 'true' version of events or of life. The sections of the book which purport to lay bare the truth in one form or other ('The Legend', Zosima's testament, the trial) seem to exhibit this most clearly. 'The Legend of the Grand Inquisitor', for example, that mighty myth of modern times, is presented as a poem, not to be taken literally, never written down, and recalled by one of the characters in conversation with another. How the narrator got hold of it in all its detail is never explained. Zosima's discourse is introduced by the narrator, but it appears to be his account of Alyosha's recollections of fragments of conversations with Zosima over a period of time. This itself contains recollections of fragments of conversations with Markel and the mysterious visitor. The mysterious visitor, in turn, talks about his own past experiences. And so on. As for the trial, the inadequacy of every account – the prosecutor's, the defence counsel's, the witnesses' – to the evidence with which the reader is acquainted simply underlines their provisional nature.

This is why Nathalie Sarraute, an exponent of the French *nouveau roman*, could write,

> The time had long passed when a Proust could believe that 'in pushing his powers of penetration to their limits' he could 'attempt to reach those far depths where truth, the ultimate reality, our authentic experience reside.' Everyone now knew, enlightened by successive deceptions, that there is no such thing as ultimate reality. 'Our authentic experience has been revealed as a multiplicity of depths and these depths go on to infinity.'

It is to this vision that she assimilates Dostoevsky which is not to say, of course, that he was unconcerned with truth to life in the social sphere. That he consulted experts in matters of theology, psychology (Ivan's nightmare) and legal procedure (the trial) is well attested. It does, however, point to the diversity of possible interpretations.

Many of these interpretations can be found in the critical literature on the novel. There are many general books on Dostoevsky's life and work. Konstantin Mochulsky's scholarly but highly readable work is still rightly regarded by many as the classic work of its kind. More recent is Richard Peace's fine book which provides an excellent reading of *The Brothers Karamazov*. It is notable, among other things, for its treatment of the tradition of the Russian Old Believers in Dostoevsky's novel. And, although it certainly cannot be regarded as an introductory study, no list of works on Dostoevsky nowadays should fail to draw attention to Bakhtin's seminal book, which has probably been more influential than any other, not only on Dostoevsky studies but on literary studies in general.

Among books specifically on this novel, Victor Terras' *Karamazov Companion* is an invaluable guide to every student of Russian literature. It has a long introduction which examines virtually every aspect of the novel, thematic and stylistic. Robert Belknap's latest book on the novel displays many remarkable critical insights and is the work of a distinguished and influential scholar who has devoted many years to his subject.

New Essays on Dostoevsky, edited by myself and Garth Terry, contains an excellent psychological study of Ivan Karamazov by F. F. Seeley and an exceptionally knowledgeable and well-presented analysis of Zosima's discourse by Sergei Hackel.

This brings me to the philosophical and religious dimensions of the novel. Sandoz's magnificent book on the 'Legend of the Grand Inquisitor' is required reading. Stewart Sutherland's book brings the insights of an Anglo-Saxon philosopher to bear on the religious philosophy of the novel with some surprisingly positive and fruitful results. Gibson's book, also written by a philosopher, adopts a more conventional, but no less informative approach. In Cambridge, Diane Thompson has recently published a fine and convincing study of the fundamental structuring role of memory in the novel which is sure to stimulate much interesting discussion.

Some readers will be fascinated by Wasiolek's English

translation of the Notebooks for *The Brothers Karamazov*. Notebooks can be very difficult to translate because by their very nature notes are often elliptical and obscure: the associations which they had in the mind of the writer, using another language, are often impossible to capture, especially in translation. Very often too notebooks are distinguished by what the author rejected rather than what leads directly into his text. So they should always be used with caution in interpreting obscure parts of the published work. But with these warnings the enthusiastic reader may find much of interest in them and explore the writer's workshop at leisure. As a matter of fact the drafts that remain are relatively late and close to the text we know.

There are many biographies of Dostoevsky. The most recent, which can be thoroughly recommended, is Geir Kjetsaa's *Fyodor Dostoyevsky: A Writer's Life*.

Last of all (or possibly first of all) some readers may like to explore W. J. Leatherbarrow's magisterial and invaluable *Reference Guide*, which lists, with commentary, over twelve thousand books and articles in many languages by and about Dostoevsky. Many of them are, of course, in English and many of them are relevant to *The Brothers Karamazov*. This is a book above all for the specialist, but for him or her it is indispensable.

So I return to my starting point. That, for better or for worse, is the fate of classics.

Malcolm V. Jones

SELECT BIBLIOGRAPHY

BAKHTIN, MIKHAIL, *Problems of Dostoevsky's Poetics*, University of Manchester Press, Manchester, 1984.

BELKNAP, ROBERT, *The Structure of 'The Brothers Karamazov'*, Northwestern University Press, Evanston, Illinois, 1989.

—*The Genesis of 'The Brothers Karamazov'*, Northwestern University Press, Evanston, Illinois, 1990.

DOSTOEVSKY, FYODOR, *The Notebooks for 'The Brothers Karamazov'*, edited and translated by Edward Wasiolek, Chicago University Press, Chicago and London, 1971.

GIBSON, A. BOYCE, *The Religion of Dostoevsky*, S. C. M. Press, London, 1973.

JONES, MALCOLM V., and TERRY, GARTH M., eds., *New Essays on Dostoyevsky*, Cambridge University Press, Cambridge, 1983.

KJETSAA, GEIR, *Fyodor Dostoyevsky: A Writer's Life*, Macmillan, London, 1987.

LEATHERBARROW, W. J., *Fedor Dostoevsky, a reference guide*, G. K. Hall & Co., Boston, Mass., 1990.

MOCHULSKY, KONSTANTIN, *Dostoevsky*, Princeton University Press, Princeton, N. J., 1967.

PEACE, RICHARD A., *Dostoyevsky, an Examination of the Major Novels*, Cambridge University Press, Cambridge 1971.

SANDOZ, ELLIS, *Political Apocalypse: Dostoevsky's Grand Inquisitor*, Louisiana State University Press, Baton Rouge, 1971.

SUTHERLAND, STEWART R., *Atheism and the Rejection of God: Contemporary Philosophy and 'The Brothers Karamazov'*, Basil Blackwell, Oxford, 1977.

TERRAS, VICTOR, *A Karamazov Companion*, University of Wisconsin Press, Wisconsin, 1981.

THOMPSON, DIANE DENNING, *The Brothers Karamazov and the Poetics of Memory*, Cambridge University Press, Cambridge, 1991.

CHRONOLOGY

DATE	AUTHOR'S LIFE	LITERARY CONTEXT
1821	Born in Moscow	Birth of Flaubert (d. 1880).
1823–31		Pushkin: *Evgenii Onegin.*
1825		
1828		Birth of Tolstoy (d. 1910).
1830		Stendhal: *Le Rouge et le noir.*
1833–7	Studies in Moscow schools.	
1834	Family purchases estate of Darovoe.	Pushkin: *The Queen of Spades.*
1835		Balzac: *Le Père Goriot.*
1836		Gogol: *The Government Inspector.*
1837	Death of mother. Dostoevsky and brother Mikhail move to St Petersburg.	Death of Pushkin (b. 1799). Dickens: *The Pickwick Papers.*
1838–41	Studies at Military Engineering Academy in St Petersburg.	
1839	Death of father, assumed murdered by serfs.	Stendhal: *La Chartreuse de Parme.*
1840		Birth of Zola (d. 1902).
1841	Commissioned as officer.	Death of Lermontov (b. 1814).
1842		Death of Stendhal (b. 1783).
1843	Enrolled in Engineering Corps.	Gogol: *Dead Souls, The Overcoat.*
1845	Completes *Poor Folk* – acclaimed by the critic Belinsky.	
1846	*Poor Folk. The Double.* 'Mr Prokharchin'.	
1847	Breaks with Belinsky; attends meetings of Petrashevsky circle. 'The Landlady', 'A novel in nine letters', 'A Petersburg Chronicle'.	Thackeray: *Vanity Fair.*
1848	'White Nights' and other stories.	Death of Belinsky (b. 1811). Dickens: *Dombey and Son.*
1849	*Netochka Nezvanova.* Attends Speshnev and Durov circles; arrested and imprisoned in Fortress of St Peter and St Paul; sentenced to death; sentence commuted; departs for Siberia.	
1850		Death of Balzac (b. 1799). Dickens: *David Copperfield.*

HISTORICAL EVENTS

Death of Napoleon on St Helena.

Death of Alexander I. Decembrist revolt. Accession of Nicholas I.

Revolutions in Paris and other European cities (to 1849).

DATE	AUTHOR'S LIFE	LITERARY CONTEXT
1850–54	Imprisoned in Fortress of Omsk.	
1851		
1852		Death of Gogol (b. 1809).
1853–6		
1854–9	Army service in Semipalatinsk.	
1855		
1856		Turgenev: *Rudin*. Flaubert: *Madame Bovary*.
1857	Marries Mariia Dmitrievna Isaeva.	
1859	Moves to Tver. Returns to St Petersburg in December. 'Uncle's Dream'. *The Village of Stepanchikovo and its inhabitants*.	
1860	Founds periodical *Time*. *Notes from the House of the Dead*.	Turgenev: *On the Eve*. George Eliot: *The Mill on the Floss*. Dickens: *Great Expectations*.
1861		
1862	First trip abroad – visits Germany, France, England, Switzerland, Italy.	Turgenev: *Fathers and Children*. Hugo: *Les Misérables*.
1863	Second trip abroad – visits Germany, France, Italy. *Winter Notes on Summer Impressions*.	
1864	Founds new journal *The Epoch*. *Notes from Underground*. Death of wife; death of brother Mikhail.	
1865	'Crocodile'. Closure of *The Epoch*. Third trip abroad.	
1865–9		Tolstoy: *War and Peace*.
1866	*Crime and Punishment*.	
1867	Marries Anna Grigorevna Snitkina. *The Gambler*. Fourth trip abroad – visits Germany and Switzerland.	
1868	Birth and death of daughter, Sonya. *Idiot*. Visits Switzerland and Italy.	
1869	Birth of daughter, Liubov.	
1870	*The Eternal Husband*.	Death of Dickens (b. 1812). Death of Herzen (b. 1812).
1871	Birth of son, Fyodor; returns to St Petersburg. *The Possessed*.	
1872	Summer in Staraia Russa – becomes normal summer residence. *A Raw Youth*.	

CHRONOLOGY

HISTORICAL EVENTS

Great Exhibition at Crystal Palace.

Crimean War.

Death of Nicholas; accession of Alexander II.

Emancipation of the serfs in Russia. Outbreak of American Civil War.

Polish uprising. Freeing of American slaves.

Franco-Prussian War.

Proclamation of German Empire. Paris Commune.

DATE	AUTHOR'S LIFE	LITERARY CONTEXT
1873	Becomes editor of *The Citizen*, which includes *The Diary of a Writer*.	
1874	Resigns as editor and publishes *The Diary of a Writer* separately (1876, 1877, 1880, 1881).	
1875	Health visit to Bad Ems.	
1875–8		Tolstoy: *Anna Karenina*.
1876	'The Gentle One'.	
1877	'The Dream of a ridiculous man'.	
1878	Birth and death of son, Aleksei. Visits monastery at Optina Pustyn with Vladimir Solovyov.	
1879	Health visit to Bad Ems.	
1879–80	*The Brothers Karamazov.*	
1880	'Pushkin Speech' delivered at Pushkin celebrations.	Death of Flaubert (b. 1821).
1881	Death. Funeral at Aleksandr Nevsky monastery, St Petersburg.	

CHRONOLOGY

HISTORICAL EVENTS

Assassination of Alexander II; accession of Alexander III.

Contents

Epilogue

List of Characters

The following list comprises the names of the novel's main characters, with variants and pronunciation. Russian names are composed of first name, patronymic (from the father's first name), and family name. Formal address requires the use of first name and patronymic; diminutives are commonly used among family and friends and are for the most part endearing, but in a certain blunt form (Katka, Mitka, Alyoshka, Rakitka) can be insulting and dismissive. Stressed syllables are indicated by italics. N.B. The *z* in Karamazov is pronounced like the *z* in *zoo*, not like the *z* in *Mozart*.

Kara*ma*zov, *Fyo*dor *Pav*lovich
  *Dmi*tri *Fyo*dorovich (*Mi*tya, *Mit*ka, *Mi*tenka, *Mit*ri *Fyo*dorovich)
  I*van* *Fyo*dorovich (*Va*nya, *Van*ka, *Va*nechka)
  Alex*ei* *Fyo*dorovich (Al*yo*sha, Al*yo*shka, Al*yo*shenka, Al*yo*shechka, Alex*ei*chik, L*yo*sha, L*yo*shenka)

Smerdya*kov*, *Pa*vel *Fyo*dorovich

Svet*lov*, Agra*fe*na Alex*an*drovna (*Gru*shenka, *Gru*sha, *Gru*shka)

Ver*khov*tsev, Ka*te*rina I*va*novna (*Ka*tya, *Kat*ka, *Ka*tenka)

Zo*si*ma (Zi*no*vy before he became a monk)

Snegir*yov*, Niko*lai* Il*yich*
  A*ri*na Pet*rov*na
  Var*va*ra Niko*la*evna (*Var*ya)
  *Ni*na Niko*la*evna (*Ni*nochka)
  Il*yu*sha (Il*yu*shechka, Il*yu*shka)

Kra*sot*kin, Niko*lai* I*va*nov (*Ko*lya)

Khokhla*kov*, Ka*te*rina O*si*povna
  *Li*za (*Lise*)

Ku*tu*zov, Gri*go*ry Va*sil*ievich (also Va*sil*iev)
        *Mar*fa Ig*na*tievna (also Ig*na*tieva)

Ra*ki*tin, Mikha*il* *O*sipovich (*Mi*sha, Ra*kit*ka, Ra*ki*tushka)

Paissy

Fera*pont*

Ippo*lit* Ki*ril*lovich (no family name)

Nel*yu*dov, Niko*lai* Par*fe*novich

Fetyu*ko*vich

*Her*zenstube

Ma*xi*mov (Ma*xi*mushka)

Kal*ga*nov, *Pyo*tr Fo*mich* (Pe*tru*sha)

Per*kho*tin, *Pyo*tr Il*yich*

Mi*u*sov, *Pyo*tr Alex*an*drovich

Tri*fon* Bo*ri*sovich (also Bo*ri*sich)

Fe*do*sya *Mar*kovna (*Fe*nya, also Fe*do*sya *Mar*kov)

Sam*so*nov, Kuz*ma* Kuz*mich*

Liza*ve*ta Smerd*yash*chaya (Stinking Lizaveta; no family name)

Ma*ka*rov, Mikhail Ma*ka*rovich (also Ma*ka*rich)

Mussya*lo*vich

Vrub*lev*sky

Ma*ri*a Kon*dra*tievna (no family name)

Var*vin*sky

THE BROTHERS KARAMAZOV

Dedicated to
Anna Grigorievna Dostoevsky

Verily, verily, I say unto you, Except a corn of wheat fall into the ground and die, it abideth alone: but if it die, it bringeth forth much fruit.
John 12:24

From the Author

Starting out on the biography of my hero, Alexei Fyodorovich Karamazov, I find myself in some perplexity. Namely, that while I do call Alexei Fyodorovich my hero, still, I myself know that he is by no means a great man, so that I can foresee the inevitable questions, such as: What is notable about your Alexei Fyodorovich that you should choose him for your hero? What has he really done? To whom is he known, and for what? Why should I, the reader, spend my time studying the facts of his life?

This last question is the most fateful one, for I can only reply: perhaps you will see from the novel. But suppose they read the novel and do not see, do not agree with the noteworthiness of my Alexei Fyodorovich? I say this because, to my sorrow, I foresee it. To me he is noteworthy, but I decidedly doubt that I shall succeed in proving it to the reader. The thing is that he does, perhaps, make a figure, but a figure of an indefinite, indeterminate sort. Though it would be strange to demand clarity from people in a time like ours. One thing, perhaps, is rather doubtless: he is a strange man, even an odd one. But strangeness and oddity will sooner harm than justify any claim to attention, especially when everyone is striving to unite particulars and find at least some general sense in the general senselessness. Whereas an odd man is most often a particular and isolated case. Is that not so?

Now if you do not agree with this last point and reply: "Not so" or "Not always," then perhaps I shall take heart concerning the significance of my hero, Alexei Fyodorovich. For not only is an odd man "not always" a particular and isolated case, but, on the contrary, it sometimes happens that it is precisely he, perhaps, who bears within himself the heart of the whole, while the other people of his epoch have all for some reason been torn away from it for a time by some kind of flooding wind.

I would not, in fact, venture into these rather vague and uninteresting explanations but would simply begin without any introduction—if they like it, they'll read it as it is—but the trouble is that while I have just one biography, I have two novels. The main novel is the second one—about the activities of my hero in our time, that is, in our present, current moment. As for the first novel, it already took place thirteen years ago and is even almost not a novel at all but just one moment from my hero's early youth. It is impossible for me to do without this first novel, or much in the second novel will be incomprehensible. Thus my original difficulty becomes even more complicated: for if I, that is, the biographer himself, think that even one novel may, perhaps, be unwarranted for such a humble and indefinite hero, then how will it look if I appear with two; and what can explain such presumption on my part?

Being at a loss to resolve these questions, I am resolved to leave them without any resolution. To be sure, the keen-sighted reader will already have guessed long ago that that is what I've been getting at from the very beginning and will only be annoyed with me for wasting fruitless words and precious time. To this I have a ready answer: I have been wasting fruitless words and precious time, first, out of politeness, and, second, out of cunning. At least I have given some warning beforehand. In fact, I am even glad that my novel broke itself into two stories "while preserving the essential unity of the whole": having acquainted himself with the first story, the reader can decide for himself whether it is worth his while to begin the second. Of course, no one is bound by anything; he can also drop the book after two pages of the first story and never pick it up again. But still there are readers of such delicacy that they will certainly want to read to the very end so as to make no mistake in their impartial judgment. Such, for instance, are all Russian critics. Faced with these people, I feel easier in my heart: for, in spite of their care and conscientiousness, I am nonetheless providing them with the most valid pretext for dropping the story at the first episode of the novel. Well, that is the end of my introduction. I quite agree that it is superfluous, but since it is already written, let it stand.

And now to business.

PART I

BOOK I: A NICE LITTLE FAMILY

Chapter 1

Fyodor Pavlovich Karamazov

Alexei Fyodorovich Karamazov was the third son of a landowner from our district, Fyodor Pavlovich Karamazov, well known in his own day (and still remembered among us) because of his dark and tragic death, which happened exactly thirteen years ago and which I shall speak of in its proper place. For the moment I will only say of this "landowner" (as we used to call him, though for all his life he hardly ever lived on his estate) that he was a strange type, yet one rather frequently met with, precisely the type of man who is not only worthless and depraved but muddleheaded as well—one of those muddleheaded people who still handle their own little business deals quite skillfully, if nothing else. Fyodor Pavlovich, for instance, started with next to nothing, he was a very small landowner, he ran around having dinner at other men's tables, he tried to foist himself off as a sponger, and yet at his death he was discovered to have as much as a hundred thousand roubles in hard cash. At the same time he remained all his life one of the most muddleheaded madcaps in our district. Again I say it was not stupidity—most of these madcaps are rather clever and shrewd—but precisely muddleheadedness, even a special, national form of it.

He was married twice and had three sons—the eldest, Dmitri Fyodorovich, by his first wife, and the other two, Ivan and Alexei, by his second. Fyodor Pavlovich's first wife belonged to a rather wealthy aristocratic family, the Miusovs, also landowners in our district. Precisely how it happened that a girl with a dowry, a beautiful girl, too, and moreover one of those pert, intelligent girls not uncommon in this generation but sometimes also to be found in the last, could have married such a worthless "runt," as everyone used to call him, I cannot begin to explain. But then, I once knew a young lady still of the last "romantic" generation who, after several years of enigmatic love for a certain gentleman, whom, by the way, she could have married quite easily at any moment, ended up, after inventing all sorts of insurmountable obstacles, by throwing herself on a stormy night into a rather deep and swift river from a high bank somewhat resembling a cliff, and perished there decidedly by her own caprice, only because she wanted to be like Shakespeare's Ophelia. Even then, if the cliff, chosen and cherished from long ago, had not been so picturesque, if it had been merely a flat, prosaic bank, the suicide might not have taken place at all. This is a true fact, and one can assume that in our Russian life of the past two or three generations there have been not a few similar facts. In the same way, the action of Adelaida Ivanovna Miusov was doubtless an echo of foreign influences, the chafings of a mind imprisoned.[1] Perhaps she wanted to assert her feminine independence, to go against social conventions, against the despotism of her relatives and family, and her obliging imagination convinced her, if only briefly, that Fyodor Pavlovich, despite his dignity as a sponger, was still one of the boldest and most sarcastic spirits of that transitional epoch—transitional to everything better—whereas he was simply an evil buffoon and nothing more. The affair gained piquancy from elopement, which strongly appealed to Adelaida Ivanovna. As for Fyodor Pavlovich, his social position at the time made him quite ready for any such venture, for he passionately desired to set himself up by whatever means. To squeeze into a good family and get a dowry was tempting indeed. As for mutual love, it seems there never was any either on the bride's part or on his own, despite the beauty of Adelaida Ivanovna. This was, perhaps, the only case of its kind in Fyodor Pavlovich's life, for he was a great sensualist all his days, always ready to hang onto any skirt that merely beckoned to him. This one woman alone, sensually speaking, made no particular impression on him.

They had no sooner eloped than it became clear to Adelaida Ivanovna that she felt only contempt for her husband and nothing more. Thus the consequences of their marriage revealed themselves extraordinarily quickly. And though her family even accepted the situation fairly soon and allotted the runaway bride her dowry, the married couple began leading a very disorderly life, full of eternal scenes. It was said that in the circumstances the young wife showed far more dignity and high-mindedness than did Fyodor Pavlovich, who, as is now known, filched all her cash from her, as much as twenty-five thousand roubles, the moment she got it, so that from then on as far as she was concerned all those thousands positively vanished, as it were, into thin air. As for the little village and the rather fine town house that came with her dowry, for a long time he tried very hard to have them transferred to his name by means of some appropriate deed, and he would probably have succeeded, merely because of the contempt and loathing, so to speak, that his shameless extortions and entreaties aroused in his wife, merely because of her emotional exhaustion—anything to be rid of him. Fortunately, Adelaida Ivanovna's family intervened and put a stop to his hogging. It is well known that there were frequent fights between husband and wife, but according to tradition it was not Fyodor Pavlovich who did the beating but Adelaida Ivanovna, a hot-tempered lady, bold, dark-skinned, impatient, and endowed with remarkable physical strength. Finally she fled the house and ran away from Fyodor Pavlovich with a destitute seminarian, leaving the three-year-old Mitya in his father's hands. Fyodor Pavlovich immediately set up a regular harem in his house and gave himself to the most unbridled drinking. In the intermissions, he drove over most of the province, tearfully complaining to all and sundry that Adelaida had abandoned him, going into details that any husband ought to have been too ashamed to reveal about his married life. The thing was that he seemed to enjoy and even feel flattered by playing the ludicrous role of the offended husband, embroidering on and embellishing the details of the offense. "One would think you had been promoted, Fyodor Pavlovich," the scoffers used to say, "you're so pleased despite all your woes!" Many even added that he was glad to brush up his old role of buffoon, and that, to make things funnier still, he pretended not to notice his ridiculous position. But who knows, perhaps he was simply naive. At last he managed to find the trail of his runaway wife. The poor woman turned out to be in Petersburg, where she had gone to live with her seminarian and where she had thrown herself wholeheartedly into the most complete emancipation. Fyodor Pavlovich at once began bustling about, making ready to go to Petersburg. Why? He, of course, had no idea. True, he might even have gone; but having undertaken such a decision, he at once felt fully entitled to get up his courage for the journey by throwing himself into more boundless drinking. Just then his wife's family received news of her death in Petersburg. She died somehow suddenly, in some garret, of typhus according to one version, of starvation according to another. Fyodor Pavlovich was drunk when he learned of his wife's death, and the story goes that he ran down the street, lifting his hands to the sky and joyfully shouting: "Now lettest thou thy servant depart in peace."[2] Others say that he wept and sobbed like a little child, so much so that they say he was pitiful to see, however repulsive they found him. Both versions may very well be true—that is, that he rejoiced at his release and wept for her who released him, all at the same time. In most cases, people, even wicked people, are far more naive and simple-hearted than one generally assumes. And so are we.

Chapter 2

The First Son Sent Packing

Of course, one can imagine what sort of father and mentor such a man would be. As a father he did precisely what was expected of him; that is, he totally and utterly abandoned his child by Adelaida Ivanovna, not out of malice towards him and not from any wounded matrimonial feelings, but simply because he totally forgot about him. While he was pestering everyone with his tears and complaints, and turning his house into an iniquitous den, a faithful family servant, Grigory, took the three-year-old Mitya into his care, and if Grigory had not looked after him then, there would perhaps have been no one to change the child's shirt. Moreover, it so happened that the child's relatives on his mother's side also seemed to forget about him at first. His grandfather, that is, Mr. Miusov himself, the father of Adelaida Ivanovna, was no longer living. His widow, Mitya's grandmother, had moved to Moscow and was quite ill, and the sisters were all married, so that Mitya had to spend almost a whole year with the servant Grigory, living in the servants' cottage. But even if his papa had remembered him (indeed, he could not have been unaware of his existence), he would have sent him back to the cottage, for the child would have gotten in the way of his debaucheries. Just then, however, the late Adelaida Ivanovna's cousin, Pyotr Alexandrovich Miusov, happened to return from Paris. Afterwards he lived abroad for many years, but at the time he was still a very young man, and, among the Miusovs, an unusual sort of man—enlightened, metropolitan, cosmopolitan, a lifelong European, and at the end of his life a liberal of the forties and fifties. In the course of his career he had relations with many of the most liberal people of his epoch, both in Russia and abroad; he knew Proudhon and Bakunin personally;[1] and he particularly liked to recall and describe—this was already near his journey's end—the three days of the February revolution in Paris in forty-eight,[2] letting on that he himself had almost taken part in it on the barricades. This was one of the most delightful memories of his youth. He had independent property, valued according to the old system at about a thousand souls.[3] His splendid estate lay just beyond our little town and bordered on the lands of our famous monastery, with which Pyotr Alexandrovich, while still very young, having just come into his inheritance, at once began endless litigation over the rights to some kind of fishing in the river or wood-cutting in the forest—I am not sure which, but to start a lawsuit against the "clericals" was something he even considered his civic and enlightened duty. Hearing all about Adelaida Ivanovna, whom he of course remembered and had once even shown some interest in, and learning of Mitya's existence, he decided, despite his youthful indignation and his contempt for Fyodor Pavlovich, to step into the affair. It was then that he first made the acquaintance of Fyodor Pavlovich. He told him straight off that he wanted to take responsibility for the child's upbringing. Years later he used to recall, as typical of the man, that when he first began speaking about Mitya with Fyodor Pavlovich, the latter looked for a while as if he had no idea what child it was all about, and was even surprised, as it were, to learn that he had a little son somewhere in the house. Though Pyotr Alexandrovich may have exaggerated, still there must have been some semblance of truth in his story. But all his life, as a matter of fact, Fyodor Pavlovich was fond of play-acting, of suddenly taking up some unexpected role right in front of you, often when there was no need for it, and even to his own real disadvantage, as, for instance, in the present case. This trait, however, is characteristic of a great many people, even rather intelligent ones, and not only of Fyodor Pavlovich. Pyotr Alexandrovich hotly pursued the business and even got himself appointed the child's guardian (jointly with Fyodor Pavlovich), since there was, after all, a small property, a house and estate, left by his mother. Mitya did, in fact, go to live with his mother's cousin, but the latter, having no family of his own, and being in a hurry to return to Paris for a long stay as soon as he had arranged and secured the income from his estates, entrusted the child to one of his mother's cousins, a Moscow lady. In the event, having settled himself in Paris, he, too, forgot about the child, especially after the outbreak of the abovementioned February revolution, which so struck his imagination that he was unable to forget it for the rest of his life. The Moscow lady died and Mitya was passed on to one of her married daughters. It seems he later changed homes a fourth time. I won't go into that now, particularly as I shall have much to say later on about this first-born son of Fyodor Pavlovich, and must confine myself here to the most essential facts, without which I could not even begin my novel.

First of all, this Dmitri Fyodorovich was the only one of Fyodor Pavlovich's three sons who grew up in the conviction that he, at any rate, had some property and would be independent when he came of age. He spent a disorderly adolescence and youth: he never finished high school; later he landed in some military school, then turned up in the Caucasus, was promoted, fought a duel, was broken to the ranks, promoted again, led a wild life, and spent, comparatively, a great deal of money. He received nothing from Fyodor Pavlovich before his coming of age, and until then ran into debt. He saw and got to know his father, Fyodor Pavlovich, for the first time only after his coming of age, when he arrived in our parts with the purpose of settling the question of his property with him. It seems that even then he did not like his parent; he stayed only a short time with him and left quickly, as soon as he had managed to obtain a certain sum from him and made a certain deal with him concerning future payments from the estate, without (a fact worth noting) being able to learn from his father either the value of the estate or its yearly income. Fyodor Pavlovich saw at once (and this must be remembered) that Mitya had a false and inflated idea of his property. Fyodor Pavlovich was quite pleased with this, as it suited his own designs. He simply concluded that the young man was frivolous, wild, passionate, impatient, a wastrel who, if he could snatch a little something for a time, would immediately calm down, though of course not for long. And this Fyodor Pavlovich began to exploit; that is, he fobbed him off with small sums, with short-term handouts, until, after four years, Mitya, having run out of patience, came to our town a second time to finish his affairs with his parent, when it suddenly turned out, to his great amazement, that he already had precisely nothing, that it was impossible even to get an accounting, that he had already received the whole value of his property in cash from Fyodor Pavlovich and might even be in debt to him, that in terms of such and such deals that he himself had freely entered into on such and such dates, he had no right to demand anything more, and so on and so forth. The young man was stunned, suspected a lie or a trick, was almost beside himself, and, as it were, lost all reason. This very circumstance led to the catastrophe, an account of which forms the subject of my first introductory novel, or, better, the external side of it. But before I go on to this novel, I must introduce the other two sons of Fyodor Pavlovich, Mitya's brothers, and explain where they came from.

Chapter 3

Second Marriage, Second Children

Fyodor Pavlovich, having packed off the four-year-old Mitya, very soon married for a second time. This second marriage lasted about eight years. He took his second wife, Sofia Ivanovna, also a very young person, from another province, where he happened to have gone for a bit of contracting business in the company of some little Jew. Fyodor Pavlovich, though he led a wild, drunken, and debauched life, still never stopped investing his capital, and always managed his deals successfully, though of course almost always somewhat shabbily. Sofia Ivanovna was one of our "little orphans," left without relations in early childhood, the daughter of some obscure deacon, who grew up in the rich house of her benefactress, mistress, and tormentress, an aristocratic old lady, the widow of General Vorokhov. I do not know the details but have only heard that, it seems, the ward, who was a meek, gentle, uncomplaining girl, was once taken out of a noose that she had hung from a nail in the closet—so hard was it for her to endure the willfulness and eternal nagging of the old woman, who was apparently not wicked but had become a most insufferable crank from sheer idleness. Fyodor Pavlovich offered his hand, inquiries were made, and he was turned away; and then once again, as with his first marriage, he suggested elopement to the little orphan. Most likely she would not have married him for anything if she had learned more about him in time. But she lived in another province, and what could a sixteen-year-old girl understand except that she would rather drown herself than stay with her benefactress. So the poor girl traded a benefactress for a benefactor. Fyodor Pavlovich did not get a penny this time, because the general's widow was furious, refused to give anything, and, moreover, cursed them both; yet this time he did not even count on getting anything, but was tempted only by the innocent girl's remarkable beauty, and above all by her innocent look, which struck the sensualist who until then had been a depraved admirer only of the coarser kind of feminine beauty. "Those innocent eyes cut my soul like a razor," he used to say afterwards with his disgusting little snigger. However, in a depraved man this, too, might be only a sensual attraction. As he had gotten no reward, Fyodor Pavlovich did not stand on ceremony with his wife, and taking advantage of the fact that she was, so to speak, "guilty" before him, and that he had practically "saved her from the noose," taking advantage, besides that, of her phenomenal humility and meekness, he even trampled with both feet on the ordinary decencies of marriage. Loose women would gather in the house right in front of his wife, and orgies took place. I should report, as a characteristic feature, that the servant Grigory, a gloomy, stupid, and obstinate pedant, who had hated his former mistress, Adelaida Ivanovna, this time took the side of the new mistress, defended her, and abused Fyodor Pavlovich because of her in a manner hardly befitting a servant; and on one occasion even broke up the orgy and drove all the scandalous women out of the house. Later this unhappy young woman, who had been terrorized since childhood, came down with something like a kind of feminine nervous disorder, most often found among simple village women, who are known as shriekers because of it. From this disorder, accompanied by terrible hysterical fits, the sick woman would sometimes even lose her reason. Nevertheless she bore Fyodor Pavlovich two sons, Ivan and Alexei, the first in the first year of marriage, the second three years later. When she died, the boy Alexei was in his fourth year, and, though it is strange, I know that he remembered his mother all his life—as if through sleep, of course. After her death, almost exactly the same thing happened with both boys as had happened with the first one, Mitya: they were totally forgotten and forsaken by their father and wound up in the same cottage with the same servant, Grigory. It was in this cottage that they were found by that old crank, the general's widow, their mother's mistress and benefactress. She was still alive, and in all that time, for all those eight years, had not forgotten the injury done her. For all those eight years, she had been receiving underhandedly the most exact information about "her Sofia's" life, and, hearing how ill she was and in what outrageous surroundings, she said aloud two or three times to her lady companions: "It serves her right. God has sent it to her for her ingratitude."

Exactly three months after Sofia Ivanovna's death, the general's widow suddenly appeared in person in our town, right at Fyodor Pavlovich's house. She spent only about half an hour in our little town, but she accomplished a great deal. It was evening. Fyodor Pavlovich, whom she had not seen for all those eight years, was tipsy when he came out to her. They say that the moment she saw him, without any explanations, she at once delivered him two good, resounding slaps and jerked him three times by his forelock; then, without adding a word, she made straight for the cottage and the two boys. Seeing at a glance that they were unwashed and in dirty shirts, she gave one more slap to Grigory himself and announced to him that she was taking both children home with her, then carried them outside just as they were, wrapped them in a plaid, put them in the carriage, and took them to her own town. Grigory bore his slap like a devoted slave, without a word of abuse, and while helping the old lady to her carriage, he bowed low and said imposingly that "God would reward her for the orphans." "And you are a lout all the same!" the general's widow shouted as she drove away. Fyodor Pavlovich, thinking the whole thing over, found that it was a good thing, and in a formal agreement regarding his children's education by the general's widow did not afterwards object to any point. As for the slaps he had gotten, he drove all over town telling the story himself.

It so happened that the general's widow, too, died soon after that. In her will, however, she set aside a thousand roubles for each of the little ones, "for their education, and so that the money will be spent only on them, but in a way that will make it last until their coming of age, for it is quite enough of a handout for such children, and if anyone else wants to, let him loosen his own purse-strings," and so on and so forth. I did not read the will myself, but I've heard that there was indeed something strange of this sort in it, and rather peculiarly expressed. The old woman's principal heir, however, turned out to be an honest man, the provincial marshal of nobility of that province,[1] Yefim Petrovich Polenov. After an exchange of letters with Fyodor Pavlovich, he guessed at once that no one could drag any money out of him even for the education of his own children (though he never refused directly, but in such cases always simply delayed, sometimes even pouring out sentimentalities). He took a personal interest in the orphans, and came especially to love the younger one, Alexei, who for a long time even grew up in his family. I should like the reader to remember that from the very beginning. If there was anyone to whom the brothers were indebted for their upbringing and education for the rest of their lives, it was to this Yefim Petrovich, a most generous and humane man, of a kind rarely found. The thousands left to the little ones by the general's widow he kept intact, so that by the time they came of age, each thousand with interest had grown to two thousand, and meanwhile he educated them at his own expense, certainly spending far more than a thousand on each boy. Again, for the time being, I will not go into a detailed account of their childhood and adolescence, but will note only the most important circumstances. However, of the elder, Ivan, I will only say that as he was growing up he was somehow gloomy and withdrawn, far from timid, but as if he had already perceived by the age of ten that they were indeed living in someone else's family and on someone else's charity, that their father was such that it was a shame to speak of him, and so on and so forth. The boy began very early, almost in infancy (so they say at least), to show some sort of unusual and brilliant aptitude for learning. I do not know exactly how, but it somehow happened that he parted from Yefim Petrovich's family when he was barely thirteen, passing on to one of the Moscow secondary schools and boarding with a certain experienced and then-famous pedagogue, a childhood friend of Yefim Petrovich's. Ivan himself used to say afterwards that it all happened, so to speak, because of the "ardor for good works" of Yefim Petrovich, who was carried away by the idea that a boy of genius must also be educated by an educator of genius. However, neither Yefim Petrovich nor the educator of genius was living when the young man, having finished school, entered university. Yefim Petrovich left his affairs in disarray, and owing to red tape and the various formalities quite unavoidable among us, there was a delay in obtaining the children's own money, left to them by the cranky widow, which had grown from one thousand to two thousand with interest, so that for his first two years at the university the young man found himself in a pickle, since he was forced all the while both to feed and keep himself and to study at the same time. It must be noted that he did not even try at that time to communicate with his father—perhaps out of pride or contempt for him, perhaps because his cold common sense told him that he would not get even the smallest token of support from his papa. Be that as it may, the young man was not at all at a loss, and did succeed in finding work, at first giving lessons at twenty kopecks an hour, and then running around to newspaper publishers, plying them with ten-line articles on street incidents, signed "Eyewitness." These little articles, they say, were always so curiously and quaintly written that they were soon in great demand; and even in this alone the young man demonstrated his practical and intellectual superiority over that eternally needy and miserable mass of our students of both sexes who, in our capitals, from morning till night, habitually haunt the doorways of various newspapers and magazines, unable to invent anything better than the eternal repetition of one and the same plea for copying work or translations from the French. Having made the acquaintance of the editors, Ivan Fyodorovich never broke his connection with them afterwards, and in his later years at the university began to publish rather talented reviews of books on various specific subjects, so that he even became known in some literary circles. However, it was only quite recently that he had succeeded by accident in suddenly attracting to himself the particular attention of a much wider circle of readers, so that a great many people at once noticed and remembered him. The incident was rather curious. Having already graduated from the university, and while preparing to go abroad on his two thousand roubles, Ivan Fyodorovich suddenly published in one of the big newspapers a strange article that attracted the attention even of nonexperts, and above all on a subject apparently altogether foreign to him, since he had graduated in natural science. The article dealt with the issue of ecclesiastical courts, which was then being raised everywhere.[2] While analyzing some already-existing opinions on the subject, he also expressed his own view. The main thing was the tone of the article and its remarkably unexpected conclusion. And yet many churchmen decidedly counted the author as one of their own. Suddenly, however, along with them, not only secularists but even atheists themselves began to applaud from their side. Finally some quick-witted people concluded that the whole article was just a brazen farce and mockery. I mention this incident particularly because the article in time also penetrated our famous neighboring monastery, where there was general interest in the newly emerged issue of ecclesiastical courts—penetrated and produced complete bewilderment. When they learned the author's name, they became interested in the fact that he was a native of our town and a son of "that very same Fyodor Pavlovich." And then suddenly, just at that time, the author himself appeared among us.

Why Ivan Fyodorovich came to us then is a question I even recall asking myself at the time, almost with a certain uneasiness. This so-fateful arrival, which was the start of so many consequences, long afterwards remained almost always unclear to me. Generally considered, it was strange that so learned, so proud, and seemingly so prudent a young man should suddenly appear in such a scandalous house, before such a father, who had ignored him all his life, who did not know or remember him, and who, though if his son had asked, he would certainly not have given him any money for anything in the world or under any circumstances, nonetheless was afraid all his life that his sons Ivan and Alexei, too, would one day come and ask for money. And here the young man comes to live in the house of such a father, lives with him for one month, then for another, and they get along famously. This last fact especially astonished not only me but many others as well. Pyotr Alexandrovich Miusov, whom I have already mentioned, a distant relation of Fyodor Pavlovich's through his first wife, happened to be in the neighborhood again at that time on his nearby estate, paying us a visit from Paris, where he had already settled permanently. I remember it was precisely he who marveled most of all when he got acquainted with the young man, who interested him greatly and with whom he used—not without inner pangs—to have occasional intellectual altercations. "He is proud," he used to say to us about him, "he will always have something in his pocket, and even now he has enough money to go abroad—what does he want here? It's clear to everyone that he did not come to his father for money, because in any case his father won't give it to him. He doesn't like drinking and debauchery, and yet the old man can't do without him, they get along so well!" It was true: the young man even had a noticeable influence over the old man; the latter almost began to listen to him occasionally, though he was extremely and at times even spitefully willful; he even began sometimes to behave more decently.

Only later did we learn that Ivan Fyodorovich had come partly at the request and on the behalf of his elder brother, Dmitri Fyodorovich, whom he met and saw for the first time in his life on this visit, but with whom, however, he had entered into correspondence prior to his arrival from Moscow, on the occasion of a certain important matter of more concern to Dmitri Fyodorovich than to himself. What that matter was, the reader will learn fully and in detail in due time. Nevertheless, even when I already knew about this special circumstance, Ivan Fyodorovich still seemed to me a mysterious person, and his arrival among us still inexplicable.

I will add that Ivan Fyodorovich seemed at the time to be a mediator and conciliator between his father and his elder brother, Dmitri Fyodorovich, who had gotten into a great quarrel with his father and had even started formal proceedings against him.

This nice little family, I repeat, got together then for the first time and some of its members saw each other for the first time in their lives. Only the youngest brother, Alexei Fyodorovich, had been living in our parts already for about a year, and so had come to us before the rest of his brothers. It is about this very Alexei that it is most difficult for me to speak in my introductory story, before bringing him on stage in the novel. Still, I shall have to write an introduction for him as well, if only to give a preliminary explanation of one very strange point—namely, that I must present my future hero to the reader, from the first scene of his novel, dressed in the cassock of a novice. Yes, at that time he had been living for about a year in our monastery, and it seemed he was preparing to shut himself up in it for the rest of his life.

Chapter 4

The Third Son, Alyosha

He was then only twenty years old (his brother Ivan was in his twenty-fourth year, and their elder brother, Dmitri, was going on twenty-eight). First of all I announce that this young man, Alyosha, was not at all a fanatic, and, in my view at least, even not at all a mystic. I will give my full opinion beforehand: he was simply an early lover of mankind,[1] and if he threw himself into the monastery path, it was only because it alone struck him at the time and presented him, so to speak, with an ideal way out for his soul struggling from the darkness of worldly wickedness towards the light of love. And this path struck him only because on it at that time he met a remarkable being, in his opinion, our famous monastery elder Zosima, to whom he became attached with all the ardent first love of his unquenchable heart. However, I do not deny that he was, at that time, already very strange, having been so even from the cradle. Incidentally, I have already mentioned that although he lost his mother in his fourth year, he remembered her afterwards all his life, her face, her caresses, "as if she were standing alive before me." Such memories can be remembered (everyone knows this) even from an earlier age, even from the age of two, but they only emerge throughout one's life as specks of light, as it were, against the darkness, as a corner torn from a huge picture, which has all faded and disappeared except for that little corner . That is exactly how it was with him: he remembered a quiet summer evening, an open window, the slanting rays of the setting sun (these slanting rays he remembered most of all), an icon in the corner of the room, a lighted oil-lamp in front of it, and before the icon, on her knees, his mother, sobbing as if in hysterics, with shrieks and cries, seizing him in her arms, hugging him so tightly that it hurt, and pleading for him to the Mother of God, holding him out from her embrace with both arms towards the icon, as if under the protection of the Mother of God . . . and suddenly a nurse rushes in and snatches him from her in fear. What a picture! Alyosha remembered his mother's face, too, at that moment: he used to say that it was frenzied, but beautiful, as far as he could remember. But he rarely cared to confide this memory to anyone. In his childhood and youth he was not very effusive, not even very talkative, not from mistrust, not from shyness or sullen unsociability, but even quite the contrary, from something different, from some inner preoccupation, as it were, strictly personal, of no concern to others, but so important for him that because of it he would, as it were, forget others. But he did love people; he lived all his life, it seemed, with complete faith in people, and yet no one ever considered him either naive or a simpleton. There was something in him that told one, that convinced one (and it was so all his life afterwards) that he did not want to be a judge of men, that he would not take judgment upon himself and would not condemn anyone for anything. It seemed, even, that he accepted everything without the least condemnation, though often with deep sadness. Moreover, in this sense he even went so far that no one could either surprise or frighten him, and this even in his very early youth. Coming to his father in his twentieth year, precisely into that den of dirty iniquity, he, chaste and pure, would simply retire quietly when it was unbearable to watch, yet without the least expression of contempt or condemnation of anyone at all. His father, a former sponger and therefore touchy and easily offended, and who met him at first with sullen suspicion ("He's too quiet," he said, "and he reasons in himself too much"), soon ended up, nonetheless, in no more than two weeks, by hugging and kissing him terribly often, with drunken tears and tipsy sentimentality, true, but apparently having come to love him sincerely and deeply, more than such a man had, of course, ever managed to love anyone else.

Indeed, everyone loved this young man wherever he appeared, and it was so even in his earliest childhood. When he came to live in the house of his benefactor and guardian, Yefim Petrovich Polenov, he attached everyone in the family to himself so much that they decidedly considered him, as it were, their own child. Yet he entered the house at such an early age that one could hardly expect in a child any calculated cunning, or pushiness, or skill in ingratiating himself, or knowledge of how to please and how to make himself loved. Thus he possessed in himself, in his very nature, so to speak, artlessly and directly, the gift of awakening a special love for himself. It was the same with him at school, too, and yet it would seem that he was exactly the kind of child who awakens mistrust, sometimes mockery, and perhaps also hatred, in his schoolmates. He used, for instance, to lapse into revery and, as it were, set himself apart. Even as a child, he liked to go into a corner and read books, and yet his schoolmates, too, loved him so much that he could decidedly be called everyone's favorite all the while he was at school. He was seldom playful, seldom even merry, but anyone could see at once, at a glance, that this was not from any kind of sullenness, that, on the contrary, he was serene and even-tempered. He never wanted to show off in front of his peers. Maybe for that very reason he was never afraid of anyone, and yet the boys realized at once that he was not at all proud of his fearlessness, but looked as if he did not realize that he was brave and fearless. He never remembered an offense. Sometimes an hour after the offense he would speak to the offender or answer some question with as trustful and serene an expression as though nothing had happened between them at all. And he did not look as if he had accidentally forgotten or intentionally forgiven the offense; he simply did not consider it an offense, and this decidedly captivated the boys and conquered them. There was only one trait in him that in all the grades of his school from the lowest even to the highest awakened in his schoolmates a constant desire to tease him, not out of malicious mockery but simply because they found it funny. This trait was a wild, frantic modesty and chastity. He could not bear to hear certain words and certain conversations about women. These "certain" words and conversations, unfortunately, are ineradicable in schools. Boys, while still almost children, pure in mind and heart, very often like to talk in classes among themselves and even aloud about such things, pictures and images, as even soldiers would not speak of; moreover, many things that soldiers themselves do not know or understand are already familiar to still quite young children of our educated and higher society. There is, perhaps, no moral depravity yet, and no cynicism either of a real, depraved, inner sort, but there is external cynicism, and this is not infrequently regarded among them as something refined, subtle, daring, and worthy of emulation. Seeing that "Alyoshka Karamazov" quickly put his fingers in his ears when they talked "about that," they would sometimes purposely crowd around him, pull his hands away by force, and shout foul things into both his ears, while he struggled, slipped to the floor, lay down, covered his head, all without saying a word to them, without any abuse, silently enduring the offense. In the end, however, they left him alone and no longer teased him with being "a little girl"; moreover, they looked upon him, in this respect, with compassion. Incidentally, he was always among the best of his class in his studies, but was never the first.

After Yefim Petrovich died, Alyosha spent two more years at the local secondary school. Yefim Petrovich's inconsolable spouse left almost immediately after his death for a long visit to Italy with her whole family, which consisted entirely of persons of the female sex, while Alyosha wound up in the house of two ladies he had never even seen before, some distant relations of Yefim Petrovich's, but on what terms he himself did not know. It was characteristic, even highly characteristic of him, that he never worried about who was supporting him. In this he was the complete opposite of his older brother, Ivan Fyodorovich, who lived in poverty for his first two years at the university, supporting himself by his own labor, and who even as a child was bitterly aware that he was eating his benefactor's bread. But it was not possible, it seems, to judge this strange trait in Alexei's character very harshly, for anyone who got to know him a little would immediately be convinced, if the question arose, that Alexei must be one of those youths, like holy fools,[2] as it were, who, if they were to chance upon even a large fortune, would have no trouble giving it away for a good deed to the first asker, or maybe even to some clever swindler who approached them. Generally speaking, he seemed not to know the value of money at all—not, of course, in the literal sense. When he was given pocket money, which he himself never asked for, he either did not know what to do with it for weeks on end, or was so terribly careless with it that it disappeared in a moment. Later, after getting used to Alyosha, Pyotr Alexandrovich Miusov, who was rather ticklish on the subjects of money and bourgeois honesty, once pronounced the following aphorism: "Here, perhaps, is the only man in the world who, were you to leave him alone and without money on the square of some unknown city with a population of a million, would not perish, would not die of cold and hunger, for he would immediately be fed and immediately be taken care of, and if no one else took care of him, he would immediately take care of himself, and it would cost him no effort, and no humiliation, and he would be no burden to those who took care of him, who perhaps, on the contrary, would consider it a pleasure."

He did not complete his studies at school; he had one more year to go when he suddenly announced to his ladies that he had to see his father about a certain matter that had come into his head. They were sorry for him and did not want to let him go. The trip was very inexpensive, and the ladies would not allow him to pawn his watch—a gift from his benefactor's family before they went abroad—but luxuriously provided him with means, and even with new clothes and linen. He, however, returned half the money, announcing that he definitely intended to travel third class. On his arrival in our town, he made no direct reply to the first question of his parent: "And precisely why this visit before you've finished your studies?" but he was, they say, more than usually thoughtful. It soon became clear that he was looking for his mother's grave. He even as much as confessed himself, then, that that was the sole purpose of his coming. But this hardly exhausted the reasons for his visit. Most likely he himself did not know and would not at all have been able to explain what it was precisely that suddenly rose up in his soul and irresistibly drew him onto some sort of new, unknown, but already inevitable path. Fyodor Pavlovich could not show him where he had buried his second wife, because he had never visited her grave after her coffin was covered with earth, and it was all so long ago that he just could not recall where they had buried her . . .

By the way, about Fyodor Pavlovich. For a long time before then, he had not been living in our town. Three or four years after his second wife's death, he set off for the south of Russia and finally wound up in Odessa, where he lived for several years in a row. First, he made the acquaintance, in his own words, of "a lot of Yids, big Yids, little Yids, baby Yids," but he ended up later being received "not just by Yids but by Jews, too." We may assume it was during this period of his life that he developed his special skill at knocking money together, and at knocking it out of other people. He came back to our town again, finally, only three years before Alyosha's arrival. Former acquaintances found him terribly aged, though he was by no means such an old man. He behaved, shall we say, not with more dignity but somehow with more effrontery. There appeared in this old buffoon, for example, an insolent need to make others into buffoons. He now loved to be outrageous with the female sex, not simply as before, but even, somehow, in a more repulsive way. He soon became the founder of a number of new taverns throughout the district. It was apparent that he had maybe as much as a hundred thousand, or perhaps only a little less. Many inhabitants of our town and district immediately got into debt with him, naturally on the best securities. Lately he had somehow become bloated; he began somehow to be erratic, lost his self-control, and even fell into a sort of lightheadedness; he would start one thing and end up with another; he somehow became scattered; and he got drunk more and more often. If it hadn't been for the very same servant Grigory, who by then had also aged considerably, and who looked after him sometimes almost like a tutor, Fyodor Pavlovich would not have gotten away without serious trouble. Alyosha's arrival seemed to affect him even on the moral side, as if something woke up in this untimely old man, something that had long been stifled in his soul. "Do you know," he now often said to Alyosha, studying him intently, "you resemble her, the 'shrieker'?" That was how he referred to his dead wife, Alyosha's mother. The "shrieker's" grave was finally pointed out to Alyosha by the servant Grigory. He took him to our town cemetery, and there, in a remote corner, showed him a cast-iron marker, inexpensive but well tended, on which there was an inscription giving the name, social position, age, and date of death of the deceased woman, and below that even some sort of four-line verse chosen from the old cemetery lore commonly used on middle-class tombs. Surprisingly, this marker turned out to be Grigory's doing. He himself had erected it over the grave of the poor "shrieker" at his own expense, after Fyodor Pavlovich, whom he had already pestered with numberless reminders about the grave, finally went off to Odessa, brushing aside not only graves but all his memories. Alyosha did not show any particular emotion at his mother's grave; he simply listened to a solemn and sensible account of the construction of the marker, stood for a while looking downcast, and walked away without saying a word. After that, perhaps even for a whole year, he did not visit the cemetery. But this little episode also had an effect on Fyodor Pavlovich—and a very original one. He suddenly took a thousand roubles and brought them to our monastery to have memorial services said for the soul of his wife, but not of his second wife, Alyosha's mother, the "shrieker," but of the first, Adelaida Ivanovna, who used to thrash him. In the evening of that day, he got drunk and berated monks to Alyosha. He was far from religious; the man probably had never put a five-kopek candle in front of an icon. Strange fits of sudden feelings and sudden thoughts come over such individuals.

I have already mentioned that he had grown very bloated. His physiognomy by that time presented something that testified acutely to the characteristics and essence of his whole life. Besides the long, fleshy bags under his eternally insolent, suspicious, and leering little eyes, besides the multitude of deep wrinkles on his fat little face, a big Adam's apple, fleshy and oblong like a purse, hung below his sharp chin, giving him a sort of repulsively sensual appearance. Add to that a long, carnivorous mouth with plump lips, behind which could be seen the little stumps of black, almost decayed teeth. He sprayed saliva whenever he spoke. However, he himself liked to make jokes about his own face, although he was apparently pleased with it. He pointed especially to his nose, which was not very big but was very thin and noticeably hooked. "A real Roman one," he used to say. "Along with my Adam's apple, it gives me the real physiognomy of an ancient Roman patrician of the decadent period." He seemed to be proud of it.

And then, quite soon after finding his mother's grave, Alyosha suddenly announced to him that he wanted to enter the monastery and that the monks were prepared to accept him as a novice. He explained further that this was his highest desire and that he was asking for his solemn consent as his father. The old man already knew that the elder Zosima, who was seeking salvation in the monastery hermitage, had made a particular impression on his "quiet boy."

"That elder is, of course, the most honest man there," he remarked, having listened to Alyosha silently and thoughtfully, almost, however, as if he were not at all surprised by his request. "H'm . . . so that's where you want to go, my quiet boy!" He was half drunk, and suddenly smiled his long, half-drunken smile, which was not devoid of cunning and drunken slyness. "H'm . . . I even had a feeling you'd end up with something like that, can you imagine? That's just where you were headed. Well, why not? After all, you do have your little two thousand—there's a dowry for you!—and I, my angel, will never forget you, I'll pay in for you now, too, whatever's due, if they ask. And if they don't ask, well, we can't go pushing ourselves on them, can we? You spend money like a canary, anyway, two little grains a week . . . H'm. You know, there's one monastery that has a little village nearby, and everybody around knows that only 'monastery wives' live there, that's what they call them, about thirty little bits of wives, I'd say . . . I was there, and, you know, it's interesting—in its own way, of course, for the sake of variety. The only trouble is this terrible Russianism, there are no French women at all, not so far, and there could be, the money's there, plenty of it. Once the word gets around, they'll come. Well, there's nothing like that here, no monastery wives, and about two hundred monks. It's honest. They fast. I admit it . . . H'm. So you want to go to the monks? You know, I'm sorry for you, Alyosha, truly, believe me, I've grown to love you . . . However, it's a good opportunity: you can pray for us sinners, we've sat around sinning too much. I keep thinking all the time: who is ever going to pray for me? Is there anyone in the world? My dear boy, you know, I'm terribly stupid about these things, would you believe it? Terribly stupid. You see, stupid as I am, I still keep thinking about it, I keep thinking, every once in a while, of course, not all the time. Surely it's impossible, I think, that the devils will forget to drag me down to their place with their hooks when I die. And then I think: hooks? Where do they get them? What are they made of? Iron? Where do they forge them? Have they got some kind of factory down there? You know, in the monastery the monks probably believe there's a ceiling in hell, for instance. Now me, I'm ready to believe in hell, only there shouldn't be any ceiling; that would be, as it were, more refined, more enlightened, more Lutheran, in other words. Does it really make any difference—with a ceiling or without a ceiling? But that's what the damned question is all about! Because if there's no ceiling, then there are no hooks. And if there are no hooks, the whole thing falls apart, which, again, is unlikely, because then who will drag me down with hooks, because if they don't drag me down, what then, and where is there any justice in the world? *Il faudrait les inventer*,[3] those hooks, just for me, for me alone, because you have no idea, Alyosha, what a stinker I am . . . !"

"No, there are no hooks there," Alyosha said quietly and seriously, studying his father.

"Yes, yes. Only shadows of hooks. I know, I know. That's how one Frenchman described hell: *J'ai vu l'ombre d'un cocher, qui avec l'ombre d'une brosse frottait l'ombre d'une carrosse.*[*] How do you know, my dear, that there are no hooks? When you've been with the monks for a while, you'll sing a different tune. But go, get to the truth there, and come back and tell me: anyway it will be easier to go to the other world knowing for certain what it's like. And it will be more proper for you to live with the monks than with me, a little old drunk man with his young girls . . . though you're like an angel, nothing touches you. Well, maybe nothing will touch you there either, that's why I'm letting you do it, because I hope for that. The devil hasn't made off with your wits. You'll burn and burn out, you'll get cured and come back. And I'll be waiting for you: I really feel you're the only one in the world who hasn't condemned me, you are, my dear boy, I feel it, how can I not feel it . . . !"

He even began to snivel. He was sentimental. He was wicked and sentimental.

Chapter 5

Elders

Perhaps some of my readers will think that my young man was a sickly, ecstatic, poorly developed person, a pale dreamer, a meager, emaciated little fellow. On the contrary, Alyosha was at that time a well-built, red-cheeked nineteen-year-old youth, clear-eyed and bursting with health. He was at that time even quite handsome, slender, of above-average height, with dark brown hair, a regular though slightly elongated face, and bright, deep gray, widely set eyes, rather thoughtful, and apparently rather serene. Some will say, perhaps, that red cheeks are quite compatible with both fanaticism and mysticism, but it seems to me that Alyosha was even more of a realist than the rest of us. Oh, of course, in the monastery he believed absolutely in miracles, but in my opinion miracles will never confound a realist. It is not miracles that bring a realist to faith. A true realist, if he is not a believer, will always find in himself the strength and ability not to believe in miracles as well, and if a miracle stands before him as an irrefutable fact, he will sooner doubt his own senses than admit the fact. And even if he does admit it, he will admit it as a fact of nature that was previously unknown to him. In the realist, faith is not born from miracles, but miracles from faith. Once the realist comes to believe, then, precisely because of his realism, he must also allow for miracles. The Apostle Thomas declared that he would not believe until he saw, and when he saw, he said: "My Lord and my God!"[1] Was it the miracle that made him believe? Most likely not, but he believed first and foremost because he wished to believe, and maybe already fully believed in his secret heart even as he was saying: "I will not believe until I see."

Some will say, perhaps, that Alyosha was slow, undeveloped, had not finished his studies, and so on. That he had not finished his studies is true, but to say that he was slow or stupid would be a great injustice. I will simply repeat what I have already said above: he set out upon this path only because at the time it alone struck him and presented him all at once with the whole ideal way out for his soul struggling from darkness to light. Add to this that he was partly a young man of our time—that is, honest by nature, demanding the truth, seeking it and believing in it, and in that belief demanding immediate participation in it with all the strength of his soul; demanding an immediate deed, with an unfailing desire to sacrifice everything for this deed, even life. Although, unfortunately, these young men do not understand that the sacrifice of life is, perhaps, the easiest of all sacrifices in many cases, while to sacrifice, for example, five or six years of their ebulliently youthful life to hard, difficult studies, to learning, in order to increase tenfold their strength to serve the very truth and the very deed that they loved and set out to accomplish—such sacrifice is quite often almost beyond the strength of many of them. Alyosha simply chose the opposite path from all others, but with the same thirst for an immediate deed. As soon as he reflected seriously and was struck by the conviction that immortality and God exist, he naturally said at once to himself: "I want to live for immortality, and I reject any halfway compromise." In just the same way, if he had decided that immortality and God do not exist, he would immediately have joined the atheists and socialists (for socialism is not only the labor question or the question of the so-called fourth estate, but first of all the question of atheism, the question of the modern embodiment of atheism, the question of the Tower of Babel built precisely without God, not to go from earth to heaven but to bring heaven down to earth).[2] To Alyosha it even seemed strange and impossible to go on living as before. It was said: "If thou wilt be perfect, give all that thou hast to the poor and come and follow me."[3] So Alyosha said to himself: "I cannot give two roubles instead of 'all,' and instead of 'follow me' just go to the Sunday liturgy." Among his early childhood memories, something may have been preserved about our neighboring monastery, where his mother may have taken him to the Sunday liturgy. Perhaps he was also affected by the slanting rays of the setting sun before the icon to which his mother, the "shrieker," held him out. Thoughtful, he came to us, then, maybe only to see if it was "all" here, or if here, too, there were only "two roubles"—and in the monastery he met this elder . . .

This elder was, as I have explained above, the elder Zosima; but I ought to say a few words first about what, generally, the "elders" in our monasteries are, and the pity is that I feel myself not very competent or steady on this path. I shall try, however, to give a superficial account in a few words. First of all, special and competent people maintain that elders and the institution of elders appeared in our country, in our Russian monasteries, only very recently, less than a hundred years ago, whereas in the whole Orthodox East, especially on Sinai and Athos,[4] they have existed for well over a thousand years. Some maintain that the institution of elders also existed in Russia in ancient times, or must have existed, but that owing to national calamities—the Tartar yoke,[5] disorders, the interruption of the former ties with the East after the fall of Constantinople[6]—the institution was forgotten and elders ceased. It was revived again in our country at the end of the last century by one of the great ascetics (as he is known), Paissy Velichkovsky,[7] and his disciples, but even to this day, after almost a hundred years, it exists in rather few monasteries and has sometimes been subjected almost to persecution as an unheard-of innovation in Russia. The institution flourished especially in one celebrated hermitage, Kozelskaya-Optina.[8] When and by whom it was planted in our neighboring monastery I cannot say, but they had already counted a succession of three elders, the latest being the elder Zosima. But he himself was now dying from weakness and disease, and they did not even know whom to replace him with. It was an important question for our monastery, which until then had not been famous for anything in particular: it had no relics of saints, no wonder-working icons, not even any glorious legends connected with its history, nor did it have to its credit any historical deeds or services to the fatherland. It flourished and became famous all over Russia precisely because of the elders, whom crowds of pilgrims from all over Russia, from thousands of miles, came flocking to us to see and hear. What, then, is an elder? An elder is one who takes your soul, your will into his soul and into his will. Having chosen an elder, you renounce your will and give it to him under total obedience and with total self-renunciation. A man who dooms himself to this trial, this terrible school of life, does so voluntarily, in the hope that after the long trial he will achieve self-conquest, self-mastery to such a degree that he will, finally, through a whole life's obedience, attain to perfect freedom—that is, freedom from himself—and avoid the lot of those who live their whole lives without finding themselves in themselves. This invention—that is, the institution of elders—is not a theoretical one, but grew in the East out of a practice that in our time is already more than a thousand years old. The obligations due to an elder are not the same as the ordinary "obedience" that has always existed in our Russian monasteries as well. All disciples accept an eternal confession to the elder, and an indissoluble bond between the one who binds and the one who is bound. They say, for instance, that once in the early days of Christianity there was such a disciple who, having failed to fulfill a certain obedience imposed on him by his elder, left his monastery in Syria and went to another country, to Egypt. There, after a long life of great asceticism, it was finally granted him to suffer torture and die a martyr for the faith. When the Church, already venerating him as a saint, went to bury his body, suddenly, at the deacon's exclamation: "All catechumens, depart,"[9] the coffin containing the martyr's body tore from its place and cast itself out of the church. This happened three times. In the end, it was discovered that this holy martyr had broken his obedience and left his elder, and therefore could not be forgiven without the elder's absolution, even despite his great deeds. The elder was summoned and absolved him of his obedience, and only then could his burial take place. Of course, all that is only ancient legend, but here is a recent fact: one of our contemporary monks was seeking salvation on Mount Athos, and suddenly his elder ordered him to leave Athos, which he loved and adored with all his soul as a haven of peace, and go first to Jerusalem to venerate the holy places, and then back to Russia, to the north, to Siberia: "Your place is there, not here." Stricken and overcome with grief, the monk went to Constantinople, to the Ecumenical Patriarch,[10] and implored him to release him from his obedience, but the Ecumenical bishop replied that not only was he, the Ecumenical Patriarch, unable to release him but there neither was nor could be any power on earth that could release him from his obedience, once it had been imposed by the elder, except the power of the very elder who had imposed it. Thus elders are, in certain cases, granted a boundless and inconceivable power. That is why in many Russian monasteries the institution of elders was first met almost with persecution. Yet elders immediately found great respect among the people. For instance, common people as well as the highest nobility flocked to the elders of our monastery so that, prostrating before them, they could confess to them their doubts, their sins, their sufferings, and ask for advice and admonition. Seeing which, the opponents of the elders shouted, among other accusations, that here the sacrament of confession was being arbitrarily and frivolously degraded, although a disciple's or layman's ceaseless confession of his soul to the elder is not at all sacramental. In the end, however, the institution of elders held out and is being established little by little in Russian monasteries. It is also true, perhaps, that this tested and already thousand-year-old instrument for the moral regeneration of man from slavery to freedom and to moral perfection may turn into a double-edged weapon, which may lead a person not to humility and ultimate self-control but, on the contrary, to the most satanic pride—that is, to fetters and not to freedom.

The elder Zosima was about sixty-five years old, came from a landowning family, had been in the army back in his very early youth, and served in the Caucasus as a commissioned officer. No doubt he struck Alyosha by some special quality of his soul. Alyosha lived in the cell of the elder, who loved him very much and allowed him to stay by him. It should be noted that Alyosha, while living in the monastery at that time, was not yet bound by anything, could go wherever he pleased even for whole days, and if he wore a cassock, it was voluntarily, so as not to be different from anyone else in the monastery. But of course he also liked it. It may be that Alyosha's youthful imagination was deeply affected by the power and fame that constantly surrounded his elder. Many said of the elder Zosima that, having for so many years received all those who came to him to open their hearts, thirsting for advice and for a healing word, having taken into his soul so many confessions, sorrows, confidences, he acquired in the end such fine discernment that he could tell, from the first glance at a visiting stranger's face, what was in his mind, what he needed, and even what kind of suffering tormented his conscience; and he sometimes astonished, perplexed, and almost frightened the visitor by this knowledge of his secret even before he had spoken a word. But at the same time, Alyosha almost always noticed that many people, nearly everyone, who came to the elder for the first time for a private talk, would enter in fear and anxiety and almost always come out bright and joyful, and that the gloomiest face would be transformed into a happy one. Alyosha was remarkably struck by the fact that the elder was not at all stern; that, on the contrary, he was almost always cheerful in manner. The monks used to say of him that he was attached in his soul precisely to those who were the more sinful, and that he who was most sinful the elder loved most of all. There were some among the monks, even towards the very end of the elder's life, who hated and envied him, but they were becoming fewer, and they were silent, although they numbered among themselves several renowned and important persons in the monastery—for instance, one of the most aged monks, famous for his great silence and remarkable fasting. However, the vast majority were already undoubtedly on the elder Zosima's side, and many among them loved him with all their hearts, ardently and sincerely; some were almost fanatically attached to him. These said outright, if not quite aloud, that he was a saint, that there was already no doubt of it, and, foreseeing his near end, even expected immediate miracles from the deceased and, in the nearest future, great glory for the monastery. Alyosha, too, had unquestioning faith in the miraculous power of the elder, just as he had unquestioning faith in the story of the coffin that kept flying out of the church. Many of those who came with sick children or adult relatives and implored the elder to lay his hands on them and say a prayer over them, he saw return soon, some even the next day, and, falling in tears before the elder, thank him for healing their sick. Whether it was a real healing or simply a natural improvement in the course of the disease was a question that did not exist for Alyosha, for he already fully believed in the spiritual power of his teacher, and his glory was, as it were, Alyosha's own triumph. His heart especially throbbed and he became radiant when the elder came out to the crowd of simple pilgrims waiting for him at the gates of the hermitage, who flocked from all over Russia purposely to see the elder and receive his blessing. They prostrated before him, wept, kissed his feet, kissed the ground he stood on, and cried out; women held their children up to him, they brought him the sick "shriekers." The elder spoke to them, read a brief prayer over them, blessed and dismissed them. Recently he sometimes became so weak from the attacks of his illness that he was scarcely able to leave his cell, and the pilgrims sometimes waited in the monastery several days for him to come out. For Alyosha there was no question of why they loved him so much, why they prostrated before him and wept so tenderly just at the sight of his face. Oh, how well he understood that for the humble soul of the simple Russian, worn out by toil and grief, and, above all, by everlasting injustice and everlasting sin, his own and the world's, there is no stronger need and consolation than to find some holy thing or person, to fall down before him and venerate him: "Though with us there is sin, unrighteousness, and temptation, still, all the same, there is on earth, in such and such a place, somewhere, someone holy and exalted; he has the truth; he knows the truth; so the truth does not die on earth, and therefore someday it will come to us and will reign over all the earth, as has been promised." Alyosha knew that this was precisely how the people felt and even reasoned; he understood it; and that the elder Zosima was precisely that very saint, that keeper of God's truth in the eyes of the people—this he himself did not doubt at all, any more than did those weeping peasants and their sick women who held out their children to the elder. The conviction that the elder, after death, would bring remarkable glory to the monastery, reigned in Alyosha's soul perhaps even more strongly than in anyone else's in the monastery. And generally of late a certain deep, flaming inner rapture burned more and more strongly in his heart. He was not at all troubled that the elder, after all, stood solitary before him: "No matter, he is holy, in his heart there is the secret of renewal for all, the power that will finally establish the truth on earth, and all will be holy and will love one another, and there will be neither rich nor poor, neither exalted nor humiliated, but all will be like the children of God, and the true kingdom of Christ will come." That was the dream in Alyosha's heart.

It appears that Alyosha was strongly impressed by the arrival of his two brothers, whom until then he had not known at all. He became friends more quickly and intimately with his half-brother, Dmitri Fyodorovich—though he arrived later—than with his other brother, Ivan Fyodorovich. He was terribly interested in getting to know his brother Ivan, but though the latter had already spent two months in our town, and they met fairly often, they still somehow were not close: Alyosha was reticent himself, and seemed as if he were waiting for something, as if he were ashamed of something; and his brother Ivan, though Alyosha noticed how he looked long and curiously at him at first, soon seemed even to have stopped thinking about him. Alyosha noticed this with some puzzlement. He attributed his brother's indifference to the disparity in their ages and especially in their education. But he also thought that, perhaps, such scant curiosity and interest in him on Ivan's part might be caused by something completely unknown to him. For some reason he kept thinking that Ivan was preoccupied with something, something inward and important, that he was striving towards some goal, possibly a very difficult one, so that he simply could not be bothered with him, and that that was the only reason why he looked at Alyosha so absently. Alyosha also kept wondering whether the learned atheist did not feel some sort of contempt for him, the silly little novice. He knew perfectly well that his brother was an atheist. This contempt, if there were any, could not offend him, but still he was waiting with some sort of anxious puzzlement, which he himself did not understand, waiting for his brother to move closer to him. His brother Dmitri Fyodorovich spoke of their brother Ivan with the deepest respect; he talked about him with a special sort of feeling. It was from him that Alyosha learned all the details of the important affair that had recently joined the two older brothers with such a wonderful and close bond. Dmitri's rapturous words about his brother Ivan were all the more significant in Alyosha's eyes since, compared with Ivan, Dmitri was an almost entirely uneducated man, and the two placed side by side would seem to present so striking a contrast, in personality as well as in character, that it would perhaps be impossible to imagine two men more unlike each other.

It was at that time that the meeting, or one might better say the family gathering, of all the members of this discordant family, which had such an extraordinary influence on Alyosha, took place in the elder's cell. The pretext for the gathering, in reality, was false. Precisely at that time, the disagreements between Dmitri Fyodorovich and his father, Fyodor Pavlovich, over the inheritance and the property accounts had, it seemed, reached an impossible point. Their relations sharpened and became unbearable. Fyodor Pavlovich was apparently the first to suggest, apparently as a joke, that they all get together in the elder Zosima's cell, and, without resorting to his direct mediation, still come to some decent agreement, since the dignity and personality of the elder might be somehow influential and conciliatory. Dmitri Fyodorovich, who had never been at the elder's and had never even seen him, thought, of course, that they wanted to frighten him with the elder, as it were, but since he secretly reproached himself for a number of especially harsh outbursts recently in his arguments with his father, he decided to accept the challenge. Incidentally, he did not live in his father's house, like Ivan Fyodorovich, but by himself at the other end of town. It happened that Pyotr Alexandrovich Miusov, who was living among us at the time, especially seized upon this idea of Fyodor Pavlovich's. A liberal of the forties and fifties, a freethinker and an atheist, Miusov, perhaps out of boredom, or perhaps for some lighthearted sport, enthusiastically took part in the affair. He suddenly wanted to have a look at the monastery and the "saint." Since his old feud with the monastery was still going on, and the lawsuit over the boundaries of their land and some rights for cutting wood in the forest and fishing in the river and so on was still being dragged out, he hastened to take advantage of this meeting under the pretext of an intention to settle everything with the Father Superior and end all their controversies amicably. A visitor with such good intentions would, of course, be received in the monastery more attentively and deferentially than one who was merely curious. All these considerations could result in establishing in the monastery a certain inside influence over the ailing elder, who lately almost never left his cell and refused, because of his illness, to receive even ordinary visitors. In the end, the elder agreed to see them, and the day was fixed. "Who made me a divider over them?"[11] he merely remarked to Alyosha with a smile.

When he heard about this meeting, Alyosha was very disturbed. If any of these quarrelers and litigants could take such a council seriously, it was undoubtedly only his brother Dmitri. The rest would come with frivolous purposes, perhaps offensive to the elder—this Alyosha knew. His brother Ivan and Miusov would come out of curiosity, perhaps of the crudest sort, and his father, perhaps, for some buffoonery or theatrics. Oh, although Alyosha said nothing, he already knew his father through and through. I repeat, this boy was not at all as naive as everyone thought he was. He waited for the appointed day with a heavy heart. No doubt he was concerned within himself, in his heart, that somehow all these family disagreements should end. Nevertheless, his greatest concern was for the elder: he trembled for him, for his glory; he feared any insult to him, especially Miusov's refined, polite jibes and the haughty innuendos of the learned Ivan, as he pictured it all to himself. He even wanted to risk warning the elder, to tell him something about these persons who were soon to arrive, but he thought better of it and kept silent. He only sent word to his brother Dmitri, through an acquaintance, on the eve of the appointed day, that he loved him and expected him to keep his promise. Dmitri thought for a moment, because he could not recall what he had promised, and replied in a letter that he would do his best to restrain himself "in the face of vileness," and that although he deeply respected the elder and their brother Ivan, he was convinced that the whole thing was either some sort of trap, or an unworthy farce. "Nevertheless, I would sooner bite off my own tongue than fail to show respect for the saintly man you esteem so highly," Dmitri concluded his note. Alyosha was not greatly encouraged by it.

Chapter 1

They Arrive at the Monastery

The day was beautiful, warm and clear. It was the end of August. The meeting with the elder had been appointed for immediately after the late liturgy, about half past eleven. Our monastery visitors did not, however, appear at the liturgy, but arrived just as the show was over. They drove up in two carriages: in the first, a jaunty barouche drawn by a pair of expensive horses, sat Pyotr Alexandrovich Miusov with a distant relative of his, a very young man, about twenty years old, Pyotr Fomich Kalganov. This young man was preparing to enter university, whereas Miusov, with whom he was for some reason meanwhile living, was tempting him to go abroad with him, to Zurich or Jena, to enter university and pursue his studies there. The young man was still undecided. He was thoughtful and, as it were, distracted. He had a nice face, was strongly built and rather tall. His gaze sometimes acquired a strange fixity: like all very distracted people, he would sometimes look directly at you, and for a long time, without seeing you at all. He was taciturn and somewhat awkward, but occasionally—only, by the way, when he was alone with someone—he would suddenly become terribly talkative, impulsive, giggly, laughing sometimes for no reason at all. But as quickly and suddenly as his animation was born, it would also quickly and suddenly die out. He was always well and even elegantly dressed; he already possessed some independent means and had expectations of much more. He was friendly with Alyosha.

In a very ancient, rattling, but roomy hired carriage, with a pair of old pinkish gray horses that lagged far behind Miusov's carriage, Fyodor Pavlovich also drove up with his boy Ivan Fyodorovich. Dmitri Fyodorovich had been informed of the time and length of the visit the day before, but he was late. The visitors left their carriages at the guest house outside the walls and entered the gates of the monastery on foot. With the exception of Fyodor Pavlovich, none of the other three seemed ever to have seen any monastery before; as for Miusov, he probably had not even been to church for some thirty years. He looked around with a sort of curiosity that was not without a certain assumed familiarity. But his observant mind was presented with nothing inside the monastery walls except a church and some outbuildings, which were in any case quite ordinary. The last worshippers were leaving the church, taking off their hats and crossing themselves. Among the common people were a few from higher society, two or three ladies, one very old general; they were all staying at the guest house. Beggars immediately surrounded our visitors, but no one gave them anything. Only Petrusha Kalganov took a ten-kopeck piece from his purse and, embarrassed for some reason, hastily shoved it at one woman, saying quickly: "To be shared equally." None of his companions said anything to him, so there was no point in his being embarrassed; which, when he noticed it, made him even more embarrassed.

It was odd, however; they should, in fact, have been met, perhaps even with some sort of honor: one of them had recently donated a thousand roubles, and another was the richest landowner and, so to speak, the best-educated man, on whom everyone there somewhat depended as far as catching fish in the river was concerned, subject to what turn the trial might take. And yet none of the official persons came to meet them. Miusov gazed distractedly at the tombstones near the church, and was on the point of remarking that these tombs must have cost the relatives a pretty penny for the right to bury their dead in such a "holy" place, but he said nothing: mere liberal irony was transforming itself in him almost into wrath.

"But, devil take it, isn't there someone we can ask in all this muddle? Something must be done, we're wasting time," he said suddenly, speaking, as it were, to himself.

Suddenly an elderly, balding gentleman in a loose summer coat, and with sweet little eyes, came up to them. Tipping his hat and speaking in a honeyed lisp, he introduced himself as the Tula landowner, Maximov. He entered at once into our wayfarers' difficulty.

"The elder Zosima lives in the hermitage . . . shut up in the hermitage . . . about four hundred paces from the monastery . . . through the woods . . . through the woods . . ."

"I myself know, sir, that it is through the woods," Fyodor Pavlovich replied. "But we do not quite remember the way, it's a long time since we were here."

"Out the gate here, and straight through the woods, through the woods. Follow me. If I may . . . I myself . . . I, too, am . . . This way, this way . . ."

They went out the gate and through the woods. The landowner Maximov, a man of about sixty, was not so much walking but, more precisely, almost running alongside, staring at them all with contorted, almost impossible curiosity. His eyes had a pop-eyed look.

"You see, we have come to this elder on a private matter," Miusov remarked sternly. "We have, so to speak, been granted an audience with this 'said person,' and therefore, though we thank you for showing us the way, we cannot invite you to go in with us."

"I've been, I've been already . . . *Un chevalier parfait!*"[1] And the landowner loosed a snap of his fingers into the air.

"Who is a *chevalier*?" asked Miusov.

"The elder, the splendid elder, the elder . . . The honor and glory of the monastery. Zosima. Such an elder . . . !"

But his disjointed talk was cut short by a little monk in a cowl, very pale and haggard, who overtook them. Fyodor Pavlovich and Miusov stopped. The monk, with an extremely courteous, deep bow, announced:

"The Father Superior humbly invites you, gentlemen, to dine with him after your visit to the hermitage. In his rooms, at one o'clock, not later. And you, too," he turned to Maximov.

"That I shall certainly do!" cried Fyodor Pavlovich, terribly pleased at the invitation. "Certainly! And you know, we've all given our word to behave properly here . . . And you, Pyotr Alexandrovich, will you go?"

"Why not? Did I not come here precisely to observe all their customs? Only one thing bothers me, and that is being in your company, Fyodor Pavlovich . . ."

"Yes, Dmitri Fyodorovich doesn't exist yet."

"And it would be excellent if he failed to come at all. Do you think I like it, all this mess, and in your company, too? So we shall come to dinner, thank the Father Superior," he turned to the little monk.

"No, it is my duty now to conduct you to the elder," the monk replied.

"In that case, I shall go meanwhile to the Father Superior, straight to the Father Superior," chirped the landowner Maximov.

"The Father Superior is busy at the moment. However, as you please . . . ," the monk said hesitantly.

"A most obnoxious old fellow," Miusov remarked aloud, as the landowner Maximov ran back to the monastery.

"He looks like von Sohn,"[2] Fyodor Pavlovich declared suddenly.

"Is that all you can think of . . . ? Why should he look like von Sohn? Have you ever seen von Sohn?"

"I've seen his photograph. It's not his features, but something inexplicable. He's the spit and image of von Sohn. I can always tell just by the physiognomy."

"Well, maybe so; you're an expert in such things. But see here, Fyodor Pavlovich, you yourself were just pleased to mention that we've given our word to behave properly, remember? I'm telling you—control yourself. If you start any buffoonery, I have no intention of being put on the same level with you here. You see what sort of man he is," he turned to the monk. "I'm afraid to appear among decent people with him."

A thin, silent little smile, not without cunning of a sort, appeared on the pale, bloodless lips of the monk, but he made no reply, and it was all too clear that he remained silent from a sense of his own dignity. Miusov scowled even more.

"Oh, the devil take the lot of them, it's just a front, cultivated for centuries, and underneath nothing but charlatanism and nonsense!" flashed through his head.

"Here's the hermitage, we've arrived!" cried Fyodor Pavlovich. "The fence and gates are shut."

And he started crossing himself energetically before the saints painted above and on the sides of the gates.

"When in Rome, do as the Romans do," he remarked.[3] "Here in the hermitage there are altogether twenty-five saints saving their souls, looking at each other and eating cabbage. And not one woman ever goes through these gates, that's what's so remarkable. And it's really true. Only didn't I hear that the elder receives ladies?" he suddenly addressed the monk.

"There are some peasants of the female sex here even now, over there, lying near the porch, waiting. And for higher ladies two small rooms were built on the porch, but outside the wall—you can see the windows—and the elder comes to them by an inner passage, when he feels well enough, so it is still outside the wall. Right now there is a lady, a landowner from Kharkov, Madame Khokhlakov, waiting there with her paralyzed daughter. Probably he has promised to come out to them, although lately he's been so weak that he's hardly shown himself even to the common people."

"So, after all, a little hole has been made from the hermitage to the ladies. Not that I'm implying anything, holy father, I'm just . . . You know, on Mount Athos—have you heard?—not only are the visits of women not allowed, but no women at all, no female creatures of any kind—no hens, no hen-turkeys, no heifers . . ."

"Fyodor Pavlovich, I shall turn back and leave you here, and without me they will throw you out, I forewarn you!"

"How am I bothering you, Pyotr Alexandrovich? Just look," he cried suddenly, stepping inside the wall of the hermitage, "what a vale of roses they live in!"

Indeed, though there were no roses, there were many rare and beautiful autumn flowers, wherever there was room for them. They were obviously tended by an experienced hand. There were flowerbeds within the church fences and between the graves. The little house where the elder had his cell, wooden, one-storied, with a front porch, was also surrounded with flowers.

"Was it like this in the time of the previous elder, Varsonofy? They say he didn't like such niceties, they say he used to jump up and beat even ladies with a stick," Fyodor Pavlovich remarked as he went up the steps.

"The elder Varsonofy indeed sometimes seemed like a holy fool, but much of what is told about him is nonsense. And he never beat anyone with a stick," replied the little monk. "Now, gentlemen, if you will wait a moment, I will announce you."

"Fyodor Pavlovich, for the last time I give you my conditions, do you hear? Behave yourself, or I will pay you back for it," Miusov had time to mutter once again.

"I don't see why you're so greatly agitated," Fyodor Pavlovich said mockingly. "Are you afraid of your little sins? They say he can tell what's on a man's mind by the look in his eyes. And, anyway, do you value their opinion so highly—you, such a Parisian, such a progressive-minded gentleman? You even surprise me, you really do!"

But Miusov did not have time to reply to this sarcasm. They were invited to come in. He walked in feeling somewhat irritated.

"That's it, I know what will happen, I'm irritated, I'll start arguing . . . lose my temper . . . demean myself and my ideas," flashed through his head.

Chapter 2

The Old Buffoon

They came into the room almost at the same moment as the elder, who emerged from his bedroom just as they appeared. Two hieromonks[1] of the hermitage were already in the cell awaiting the elder, one of them the Father Librarian, and the other Father Paissy, a sick man, though not old, but, it was said, a very learned one. Besides them, there stood in the corner (and remained standing there all the while) a young fellow who looked to be about twenty-two and was dressed in an ordinary frock coat, a seminarian and future theologian, who for some reason enjoyed the patronage of the monastery and the brothers. He was rather tall and had a fresh face, with wide cheekbones and intelligent, attentive, narrow brown eyes. His face expressed complete deference, but decently, with no apparent fawning. He did not even bow to greet the guests as they entered, not being their equal, but, on the contrary, a subordinate and dependent person.

The elder Zosima came out accompanied by a novice and Alyosha. The hieromonks rose and greeted him with a very deep bow, touching the ground with their fingers, and, having received his blessing, kissed his hand. When he had blessed them, the elder returned the same deep bow to each of them, touching the ground with his fingers, and asked a blessing of each of them for himself. The whole ceremony was performed very seriously, not at all like some everyday ritual, but almost with a certain feeling. To Miusov, however, it all seemed done with deliberate suggestion. He stood in front of all his fellow visitors. He ought—and he had even pondered it the previous evening—despite all his ideas, just out of simple courtesy (since it was customary there), to come up and receive the elder's blessing, at least receive his blessing, even if he did not kiss his hand. But now, seeing all this bowing and kissing of the hieromonks, he instantly changed his mind: gravely and with dignity he made a rather deep bow, by worldly standards, and went over to a chair. Fyodor Pavlovich did exactly the same, this time, like an ape, mimicking Miusov perfectly. Ivan Fyodorovich bowed with great dignity and propriety, but he, too, kept his hands at his sides, while Kalganov was so nonplussed that he did not bow at all. The elder let fall the hand he had raised for the blessing and, bowing to them once more, invited them all to sit down. The blood rushed to Alyosha's cheeks; he was ashamed. His forebodings were beginning to come true.

The elder sat down on a very old-fashioned, leather-covered mahogany settee, and placed his guests, except for the two hieromonks, along the opposite wall, all four in a row, on four mahogany chairs with badly worn black leather upholstery. The hieromonks sat at either end of the room, one by the door, the other by the window. The seminarian, Alyosha, and the novice remained standing. The whole cell was hardly very big and looked rather dull. The objects and furniture were crude and poor, and only what was necessary. Two potted plants stood on the windowsill, and there were many icons in the corner—including a huge one of the Mother of God painted, probably, long before the schism.[2] An icon lamp flickered before it. Next to it were two more icons in shiny casings, and next to them some little figurines of cherubs, porcelain eggs, an ivory Catholic crucifix with the Mater Dolorosa embracing it, and several imported engravings from great Italian artists of the past centuries. Next to these fine and expensive prints were displayed several sheets of the commonest Russian lithographs of saints, martyrs, hierarchs, and so on, such as are sold for a few kopecks at any fair. There were several lithographic portraits of Russian bishops, past and present, but these were on other walls.

Miusov glanced at all this "officialism," then fixed the elder intently with his gaze. He esteemed this gaze—a weakness forgivable in him, in any case, considering that he was already fifty years old, the age at which an intelligent and worldly man of means always becomes more respectful of himself, sometimes even against his own will.

He disliked the elder from the first moment. Indeed, there was something in the elder's face that many other people besides Miusov might have disliked. He was a short, bent little man, with very weak legs, who was just sixty-five, but, owing to his illness, appeared much older, by at least ten years. His whole face, which, by the way, was quite withered, was strewn with little wrinkles, especially numerous around his eyes. His eyes themselves were small, pale, quick and bright like two bright points. A few white hairs remained only on his temples, his pointed beard was tiny and sparse, and his often smiling lips were as thin as two threads. His nose was not so much long as sharp, like a little bird's beak.

"To all appearances a malicious and pettily arrogant little soul," flashed through Miusov's head. In general he felt very displeased with himself.

The chiming of the clock helped to start conversation. A cheap little wall clock with weights rapidly struck twelve.

"It's precisely the time," cried Fyodor Pavlovich, "and my son Dmitri Fyodorovich still isn't here! I apologize for him, sacred elder!" (Alyosha cringed all over at this "sacred elder.") "I myself am always very punctual, to the minute, remembering that punctuality is the courtesy of kings."[3]

"Not that you're a king," muttered Miusov, unable to restrain himself in time.

"That's quite true, I'm not a king. And just imagine, Pyotr Alexandrovich, I even knew it myself, by God! You see, I'm always saying something out of place! Your reverence," he exclaimed with a sort of instant pathos, "you see before you a buffoon! Verily, a buffoon! Thus I introduce myself! It's an old habit, alas! And if I sometimes tell lies inappropriately, I do it even on purpose, on purpose to be pleasant and make people laugh. One ought to be pleasant, isn't that so? I came to a little town seven years ago, I had a little business there, and went around with some of their merchants. So we called on the police commissioner, the *ispravnik*, because we wanted to see him about something and invite him to have dinner with us. Out comes the *ispravnik*, a tall man, fat, blond, and gloomy—the most dangerous type in such cases—it's the liver, the liver. I spoke directly with him, you know, with the familiarity of a man of the world: 'Mr. Ispravnik,' I said to him, 'be, so to speak, our Napravnik!'[4] 'What do you mean, your Napravnik?' I can see from the first split second that it's not coming off, that he's standing there seriously, but I keep on: 'I wanted,' I say, 'to make a joke, for our general amusement. Mr. Napravnik is our famous Russian *Kapellmeister*, and we, for the harmony of our enterprise, also precisely need a sort of *Kapellmeister*, as it were . . .' I explained it all and compared it quite reasonably, didn't I? 'I beg your pardon,' he says, 'I am an *ispravnik*, and I will not allow you to use my title for your puns.' He turned around and was about to walk away. I started after him, calling out: 'Yes, yes, you are an *ispravnik*, not Napravnik.' 'No,' he says, 'have it your way. I am Napravnik.' And just imagine, our deal fell through! And that's how I am, it's always like that with me. I'm forever damaging myself with my own courtesy! Once, this was many years ago now, I said to an influential person, 'Your wife, sir, is a ticklish woman,' referring to her honor, her moral qualities, so to speak. And he suddenly retorted, 'Did you tickle her?' I couldn't help myself; why not a little pleasant banter, I thought? 'Yes,' I said, 'I did tickle her, sir.' Well, at that he gave me quite a tickling . . . ! But it was a long time ago, so I'm not even ashamed to tell about it. I'm always damaging myself like that!"

"You're doing it now, too," Miusov muttered in disgust.

The elder silently looked from one to the other.

"Really! Imagine, I knew it all along, Pyotr Alexandrovich, and, you know, I even had a feeling that I was doing it just as I started speaking, and, you know, I even had a feeling that you would be the first to point it out to me. In those seconds when I see that my joke isn't going over, my cheeks, reverend father, begin to stick to my lower gums; it feels almost like a cramp; I've had it since my young days, when I was a sponger on the gentry and made my living by sponging. I'm a natural-born buffoon, I am, reverend father, just like a holy fool; I won't deny that there's maybe an unclean spirit living in me, too, not a very high caliber one, by the way, otherwise he would have chosen grander quarters, only not you, Pyotr Alexandrovich, your quarters are none too grand either. But to make up for it, I believe, I believe in God. It's only lately that I've begun to have doubts, but to make up for it I'm sitting and waiting to hear lofty words. I am, reverend father, like the philosopher Diderot.[5] Do you know, most holy father, how Diderot the philosopher came to see Metropolitan Platon[6] in the time of the empress Catherine? He walks in and says right off: 'There is no God.' To which the great hierarch raises his finger and answers: 'The fool hath said in his heart, There is no God.'[7] Right then and there our man fell at his feet: 'I believe,' he cries, 'I will accept baptism!' And so they baptized him at once. Princess Dashkova was his godmother, and his godfather was Potiomkin . . ."[8]

"Fyodor Pavlovich, this is unbearable! You know yourself that you are lying, that your silly story isn't true. Why are you clowning?" Miusov said in a trembling voice, losing all control of himself.

"All my life I've had a feeling that it wasn't true!" Fyodor Pavlovich cried excitedly. "No, let me tell you the whole truth, gentlemen. Great elder! Forgive me, but that last part, about Diderot's baptism, I invented myself just a moment ago, while I was telling it to you. It never occurred to me before. I made it up for its piquancy. That's why I'm clowning, Pyotr Alexandrovich, to make myself more endearing. Though sometimes I don't know myself why I do it. As for Diderot, I heard this 'the fool hath said' maybe twenty times from local landowners when I was still young and lived with them; by the way, I also heard it, Pyotr Alexandrovich, from your aunt, Mavra Fominishna. They all still believe that the godless Diderot came to Metropolitan Platon to argue about God . . ."

Miusov rose, not only losing patience, but even somehow forgetting himself. He was furious, and realized that this made him ridiculous. Indeed, something altogether impossible was taking place in the cell. For perhaps forty or fifty years, from the time of the former elders, visitors had been coming to this cell, but always with the deepest reverence, not otherwise. Almost all who were admitted entered the cell with the awareness that they were being shown great favor. Many fell to their knees and would not rise for as long as the visit lasted. Even many "higher" persons, even many of the most learned ones, moreover even some of the freethinkers who came out of curiosity, or for some other reason, when entering the cell with others or having obtained a private audience, considered it their foremost duty—to a man—to show the deepest respect and tactfulness throughout the audience, the more so as there was no question of money involved, but only of love and mercy on one side, and on the other of repentance and the desire to resolve some difficult question of the soul or a difficult moment in the life of the heart. So that suddenly this buffoonery displayed by Fyodor Pavlovich, with no respect for the place he was in, produced in the onlookers, at least in some of them, both astonishment and bewilderment. The hieromonks, who incidentally showed no change at all in their physiognomies, were watching with grave attention for what the elder would say, but they seemed as if they were about to stand up, like Miusov. Alyosha was on the verge of tears and stood looking downcast. What seemed strangest of all to him was that his brother, Ivan Fyodorovich, on whom alone he had relied and who alone had enough influence on their father to have been able to stop him, was now sitting quite motionless in his chair, looking down and waiting, apparently with some kind of inquisitive curiosity, to see how it would all end, as if he himself were a complete stranger there. Alyosha could not even look at Rakitin (the seminarian), whom he knew and was almost close with. Alyosha knew his thoughts (though he alone in the whole monastery knew them).

"Forgive me . . . ," Miusov began, addressing the elder, "it may seem to you that I, too, am a participant in this unworthy farce. My mistake was in trusting that even such a man as Fyodor Pavlovich would be willing to recognize his duties when visiting such a venerable person . . . I did not think that I would have to apologize just for the fact of coming with him . . ."

Pyotr Alexandrovich broke off and, completely embarrassed, was about to leave the room.

"Do not upset yourself, I beg you," the elder suddenly rose on his feeble legs, took Pyotr Alexandrovich by both hands, and sat him down again on the chair. "Do not worry, I beg you. I ask you particularly to be my guest." And with a bow, he turned and sat down again on his settee.

"Great elder, speak and tell me whether I offend you with my liveliness or not?" Fyodor Pavlovich suddenly cried, gripping the arms of his chair as if he were about to leap out of it, depending on the answer.

"I earnestly beg you, too, not to worry and not to be uncomfortable," the elder said to him imposingly. "Be at ease, and feel completely at home. And above all do not be so ashamed of yourself, for that is the cause of everything."

"Completely at home? You mean in my natural state? Oh, that is much, too much—but I'm touched, and I accept! You know, blessed father, you shouldn't challenge me to be in my natural state, you shouldn't risk it . . . I myself will not go so far as to be in my natural state. I'm warning you in order to protect you. Well, and the rest is wrapped in the mists of uncertainty; though there are some who would like to paint me in broad strokes. I'm referring to you, Pyotr Alexandrovich; and you, most holy being, here is what I have for you: I pour out my rapture!" He rose slightly and, lifting up his hands, said: " 'Blessed is the womb that bare thee and the paps which thou hast sucked'[9]—the paps especially! That remark you just made: 'Not to be so ashamed of myself, for that is the cause of everything'—it's as if you pierced me right through and read inside me. That is exactly how it all seems to me, when I walk into a room, that I'm lower than anyone else, and that everyone takes me for a buffoon, so 'Why not, indeed, play the buffoon, I'm not afraid of your opinions, because you're all, to a man, lower than me!' That's why I'm a buffoon, I'm a buffoon out of shame, great elder, out of shame. I act up just because I'm insecure. If only I were sure, when I came in, that everyone would take me at once for the most pleasant and intelligent of men—oh, Lord! what a good man I'd be! Teacher!" he suddenly threw himself on his knees, "what should I do to inherit eternal life?"[10] It was hard even now to tell whether he was joking or was indeed greatly moved.

The elder looked up at him and said with a smile:

"You've known for a long time what you should do; you have sense enough: do not give yourself up to drunkenness and verbal incontinence, do not give yourself up to sensuality, and especially to the adoration of money, and close your taverns; if you cannot close all of them then at least two or three. And above all, above everything else—do not lie."

"About Diderot, you mean?"

"No, not exactly about Diderot. Above all, do not lie to yourself. A man who lies to himself and listens to his own lie comes to a point where he does not discern any truth either in himself or anywhere around him, and thus falls into disrespect towards himself and others. Not respecting anyone, he ceases to love, and having no love, he gives himself up to passions and coarse pleasures, in order to occupy and amuse himself, and in his vices reaches complete bestiality, and it all comes from lying continually to others and to himself. A man who lies to himself is often the first to take offense. It sometimes feels very good to take offense, doesn't it? And surely he knows that no one has offended him, and that he himself has invented the offense and told lies just for the beauty of it, that he has exaggerated for the sake of effect, that he has picked on a word and made a mountain out of a pea—he knows all of that, and still he is the first to take offense, he likes feeling offended, it gives him great pleasure, and thus he reaches the point of real hostility . . . Do get up from your knees and sit down, I beg you, these posturings are false, too . . ."

"Blessed man! Let me kiss your hand," Fyodor Pavlovich rushed up to the elder and quickly gave him a smack on his thin hand. "Precisely, precisely, it feels good to be offended. You put it so well, I've never heard it before. Precisely, precisely, all my life I've been getting offended for the pleasure of it, for the aesthetics of it, because it's not only a pleasure, sometimes it's beautiful to be offended—you forgot that, great elder: beautiful! I'll make a note of that! And I've lied, I've lied decidedly all my life, every day and every hour. Verily, I am a lie and the father of a lie! Or maybe not the father of a lie, I always get my texts mixed up; let's say the son of a lie,[11] that will do just as well! Only . . . my angel . . . sometimes Diderot is all right! Diderot won't do any harm, it's some little word that does the harm. Great elder, by the way, I almost forgot, though I did intend, as long as two years ago, to inquire here, to stop by on purpose and insistently make inquiries and to ask—only please tell Pyotr Alexandrovich not to interrupt. This I ask you: is it true, great father, that somewhere in the Lives of the Saints there is a story about some holy wonder-worker who was martyred for his faith, and when they finally cut his head off, he got up, took his head, 'kissed it belovingly,' and walked on for a long time carrying it in his hands and 'kissing it belovingly'?[12] Is this true or not, honored fathers?"

"No, it is not true," said the elder.

"There is nothing like that anywhere in the Lives of the Saints. Which saint did you say the story was about?" asked the Father Librarian.

"I don't know which. I don't know, I have no idea. I was led to believe, I was told. I heard it, and do you know who I heard it from? This same Pyotr Alexandrovich Miusov who just got so angry about Diderot, he told me."

"I never told you that, I never even speak to you at all."

"True, you didn't tell it to me; but you told it in company when I was present; it was three years ago. I mention it because you, Pyotr Alexandrovich, shook my faith with this funny story. You didn't know it, you had no idea, but I went home with my faith shaken, and since then I've been shaking more and more. Yes, Pyotr Alexandrovich, you were the cause of a great fall! Diderot nothing, sir!"

Fyodor Pavlovich was flushed with pathos, though by now it was quite clear to everyone that he was acting again. Even so, Miusov was painfully hurt.

"What nonsense, it's all nonsense," he muttered. "I may actually have told it once . . . but not to you. It was told to me. I heard it in Paris, from a Frenchman. That it is supposedly read from the Lives of the Saints in our liturgy.[13] He was a very learned man, he made a special study of statistics about Russia . . . lived in Russia for a long time . . . I myself have not read the Lives of the Saints . . . and do not intend to read them . . . It was just table talk . . . ! We were having dinner then . . ."

"So you were having dinner then, and I just lost my faith!" Fyodor Pavlovich went on teasing him.

"What do I care about your faith!" Miusov almost shouted, but suddenly checked himself and said with contempt: "You literally befoul everything you touch."

The elder suddenly rose from his seat:

"Excuse me, gentlemen, if I leave you now for just a few minutes," he said, addressing all of his visitors, "but there are people awaiting me who came before you. And you, all the same, do not lie," he added, turning to Fyodor Pavlovich with a cheerful face.

He started to leave the cell. Alyosha and the novice rushed after him to help him down the stairs. Alyosha was breathless, he was glad to get away, but he was also glad that the elder was cheerful and not offended. The elder turned towards the porch in order to bless those who were awaiting him. But Fyodor Pavlovich managed to stop him at the door of the cell.

"Most blessed man!" he cried out with feeling, "let me kiss your dear hand once more. No, still you're a man one can talk to, a man one can get along with. Do you think I always lie like this and play the buffoon? I want you to know that all the while I've been acting on purpose in order to test you. I've been getting the feel of you, seeing whether one can get along with you. Whether there's room for my humility next to your pride. I present you with a certificate of honor: one can get along with you! And now, I am silent, from here on I'll be silent. I'll sit on my chair and be silent. Now it's your turn to speak, Pyotr Alexandrovich, you are the most important man left—for the next ten minutes."

Chapter 3

Women of Faith

Below, crowding near the wooden porch built onto the outside wall, there were only women this time, about twenty of them. They had been informed that the elder would come out at last, and had gathered in anticipation. The Khokhlakov ladies, who were also waiting for the elder, but in quarters set aside for gentlewomen, had come out to the porch as well. There were two of them, mother and daughter. Madame Khokhlakov, the mother, a wealthy woman, always tastefully dressed, was still fairly young and quite attractive, slightly pale, with very lively and almost completely black eyes. She was not more than thirty-three years old and had been a widow for about five years. Her fourteen-year-old daughter suffered from paralysis of the legs. The poor girl had been unable to walk for about half a year already, and was wheeled around in a long, comfortable chair. Hers was a lovely little face, a bit thin from illness, but cheerful. Something mischievous shone in her big, dark eyes with their long lashes. Her mother had been intending to take her abroad since spring, but was detained through the summer by the management of her estate. They had already spent about a week in our town, more for business than on pilgrimage, but had already visited the elder once, three days before. Now they suddenly came again, though they knew that the elder was almost unable to receive anyone at all, and, pleading insistently, begged once again for "the happiness of beholding the great healer."

While awaiting the elder's appearance, the mama sat on a seat next to her daughter's chair, and two steps away from her stood an old monk, not from our monastery, but a visitor from a little-known cloister in the far north. He, too, wanted to receive the elder's blessing. But when the elder appeared on the porch, he first went directly to the people. The crowd started pressing towards the three steps that connected the low porch with the field. The elder stood on the top step, put on his stole, and began to bless the women who crowded towards him. A "shrieker" was pulled up to him by both hands. She no sooner saw the elder than she suddenly began somehow absurdly screeching, hiccuping, and shaking all over as if in convulsions. The elder, having covered her head with the stole, read a short prayer over her, and she at once became quiet and calmed down. I do not know how it is now, but in my childhood I often used to see and hear these "shriekers" in villages and monasteries. Taken to the Sunday liturgy, they would screech or bark like dogs so that the whole church could hear, but when the chalice was brought out, and they were led up to the chalice, the "demonic possession" would immediately cease and the sick ones would always calm down for a time. As a child, I was greatly struck and astonished by this. And it was then that I heard from some landowners and especially from my town teachers, in answer to my questions, that it was all a pretense in order to avoid work, and that it could always be eradicated by the proper severity, which they confirmed by telling various stories. But later on I was surprised to learn from medical experts that there is no pretense in it, that it is a terrible woman's disease that seems to occur predominantly in our Russia, that it is a testimony to the hard lot of our peasant women, caused by exhausting work too soon after difficult, improper birthgiving without any medical help, and, besides that, by desperate grief, beatings, and so on, which the nature of many women, after all, as the general examples show, cannot endure. This strange and instant healing of the frenzied and struggling woman the moment she was brought to the chalice, which used to be explained to me as shamming and, moreover, almost as a trick arranged by the "clericals" themselves—this healing occurred, probably, also in a very natural way: both the women who brought her to the chalice and, above all, the sick woman herself, fully believed, as an unquestionable truth, that the unclean spirit that possessed the sick woman could not possibly endure if she, the sick woman, were brought to the chalice and made to bow before it. And therefore, in a nervous and certainly also mentally ill woman, there always occurred (and had to occur), at the moment of her bowing before the chalice, an inevitable shock, as it were, to her whole body, a shock provoked by expectation of the inevitable miracle of healing and by the most complete faith that it would occur. And it would occur, even if only for a moment. That is just what happened now, as soon as the elder covered the woman with his stole.

Many of the women who pressed towards him were shedding tears of tenderness and rapture, called up by the effect of the moment; others strained to kiss at least the hem of his clothes, and some were murmuring to themselves. He gave blessings to everyone and spoke with several. The "shrieker" he knew already; she came not from far away but from a village only four miles from the monastery, and had been brought to him before.

"But she comes from far away!" He pointed to a woman who was not at all old yet but very thin and haggard, with a face not tanned but, as it were, blackened. She was kneeling and stared at the elder with a fixed gaze. There was something frenzied, as it were, in her eyes.

"From far away, dear father, far away, two hundred miles from here. Far away, father, far away," the woman spoke in a singsong voice, rocking her head gently from side to side with her cheek resting in her hand. She spoke as though she were lamenting. There is among the people a silent, long-suffering grief; it withdraws into itself and is silent. But there is also a grief that is strained; a moment comes when it breaks through with tears, and from that moment on it pours itself out in lamentations. Especially with women. But it is no easier to bear than the silent grief. Lamentations ease the heart only by straining and exacerbating it more and more. Such grief does not even want consolation; it is nourished by the sense of its unquenchableness. Lamentations are simply the need to constantly irritate the wound.

"You must be tradespeople," the elder continued, studying her with curiosity.

"We're townspeople, father, townspeople, we're peasants but we live in town. I've come to see you, father. We heard about you, dear father, we heard about you. I buried my baby son, and went on a pilgrimage. I've been in three monasteries, and then they told me: 'Go to them, too, Nastasia'—meaning to you, my dear, to you. So I came; yesterday I was at vespers, and today I've come to you."

"What are you weeping for?"

"I pity my little son, dear father, he was three years old, just three months short of three years old.[1] I grieve for my little son, father, for my little son. He was the last little son left to us, we had four, Nikitushka and I, but our children didn't stay with us, they didn't stay. When I buried the first three, I wasn't too sorry about them, but this last one I buried and I can't forget him. As if he's just standing right in front of me and won't go away. My soul is wasted over him. I look at his clothes, at his little shirt or his little boots, and start howling. I lay out all that he left behind, all his things, and look at them and howl. Then I say to Nikitushka, that's my husband, let me go on a pilgrimage, master. He's a coachman, we're not poor, father, not poor, we run our own business, everything belongs to us, the horses and the carriages. But who needs all that now? Without me, he's taken to drinking, my Nikitushka, I'm sure he has, even before I left he'd give in to it, the minute I turned my back. And now I don't even think about him. It's three months since I left home. I've forgotten, I've forgotten everything, and I don't want to remember, what can I do with him now? I'm through with him, through, I'm through with everybody. And I don't even want to see my house now, and my things, I don't want to see anything at all!"

"Listen, mother," said the elder. "Once, long ago, a great saint saw a mother in church, weeping just as you are over her child, her only child, whom the Lord had also called to him. 'Do you not know,' the saint said to her, 'how bold these infants are before the throne of God? No one is bolder in the Kingdom of Heaven: Lord, you granted us life, they say to God, and just as we beheld it, you took it back from us. And they beg and plead so boldly that the Lord immediately puts them in the ranks of the angels. And therefore,' said the saint, 'you, too, woman, rejoice and do not weep. Your infant, too, now abides with the Lord in the host of his angels.' That is what a saint said to a weeping woman in ancient times. He was a great saint and would not have told her a lie. Therefore you, too, mother, know that your infant, too, surely now stands before the throne of the Lord, rejoicing and being glad, and praying to God for you. Weep, then, but also rejoice."

The woman listened to him, resting her cheek in her hand, her eyes cast down. She sighed deeply.

"The same way my Nikitushka was comforting me, word for word, like you, he'd say: 'Foolish woman,' he'd say, 'why do you cry so? Our little son is surely with the Lord God now, singing with the angels.' He'd say it to me, and he'd be crying himself, I could see, he'd be crying just like me. 'I know, Nikitushka,' I'd say, 'where else can he be if not with the Lord God, only he isn't here, with us, Nikitushka, he isn't sitting here with us like before!' If only I could just have one more look at him, if I could see him one more time, I wouldn't even go up to him, I wouldn't speak, I'd hide in a corner, only to see him for one little minute, to hear him the way he used to play in the backyard and come in and shout in his little voice: 'Mama, where are you?' Only to hear how he walks across the room, just once, just one time, pat-pat-pat with his little feet, so quick, so quick, the way I remember he used to run up to me, shouting and laughing, if only I could hear his little feet pattering and know it was him! But he's gone, dear father, he's gone and I'll never hear him again! His little belt is here, but he's gone, and I'll never see him, I'll never hear him again . . . !"

She took her boy's little gold-braided belt from her bosom and, at the sight of it, began shaking with sobs, covering her eyes with her hands, through which streamed the tears that suddenly gushed from her eyes.

"This," said the elder, "is Rachel of old 'weeping for her children, and she would not be comforted, because they are not.'[2] This is the lot that befalls you, mothers, on earth. And do not be comforted, you should not be comforted, do not be comforted, but weep. Only each time you weep, do not fail to remember that your little son is one of God's angels, that he looks down at you from there and sees you, and rejoices in your tears and points them out to the Lord God. And you will be filled with this great mother's weeping for a long time, but in the end it will turn into quiet joy for you, and your bitter tears will become tears of quiet tenderness and the heart's purification, which saves from sin. And I will remember your little child in my prayers for the repose of the dead. What was his name?"

"Alexei, dear father."

"A lovely name! After Alexei, the man of God?"[3]

"Of God, dear father, of God. Alexei, the man of God."

"A great saint! I'll remember, mother, I'll remember, and I'll remember your sorrow in my prayers, and I'll remember your husband, too. Only it is a sin for you to desert him. Go to your husband and take care of him. Your little boy will look down and see that you've abandoned his father, and will weep for both of you: why, then, do you trouble his blessedness? He's alive, surely he's alive, for the soul lives forever, and though he's not at home, he is invisibly near you. How, then, can he come to his home if you say you now hate your home? To whom will he go if he does not find you, his father and mother, together? You see him now in your dreams and are tormented, but at home he will send you quiet dreams. Go to your husband, mother, go this very day."

"I will go, my dear, according to your word, I will go. You've touched my heart. Nikitushka, my Nikitushka, you are waiting for me, my dear, waiting for me!" The woman began to murmur, but the elder had already turned to a very old little old lady, dressed not as a pilgrim but in town fashion. One could see by her eyes that she had come for some purpose and had something on her mind. She introduced herself as the widow of a noncommissioned officer, not from far away but from our own town. Her dear son Vasenka had served somewhere in the army commissariat and then gone to Siberia, to Irkutsk. He wrote twice from there, but it had already been a year now since he stopped writing. She made inquiries about him, but to tell the truth she did not even know where to inquire.

"Just the other day, Stepanida Ilyinishna Bedryagin, she's a merchant's wife, a wealthy woman, said to me: 'I tell you what, Prokhorovna, go to church and put your son on a list to be remembered among the dead. His soul,' she says, 'will get troubled, and he'll write to you. It's just the thing to do,' Stepanida Ilyinishna says, 'it's been tested many times.' Only I'm not so sure . . . Dear father, is it right or wrong? Would it be a good thing to do?"

"Do not even think of it. It is shameful even to ask. How is it possible to commemorate a living soul as one of the dead, and his own mother at that! It is a great sin, it is like sorcery, it can be forgiven only because of your ignorance. You had better pray to the Queen of Heaven, our swift intercessor and helper, for his health, and that you be forgiven for your wrong thoughts. And I will tell you something else, Prokhorovna: either he himself, your boy, will soon come back to you, or he will surely send you a letter. I promise you that. Go, and from now on be at peace. Your boy is alive, I tell you."

"Dear father, may God reward you, our benefactor, pray for all of us and for our sins . . ."

But the elder had already noticed in the crowd two burning eyes seeking his, the eyes of a wasted, consumptive-looking, though still young, peasant woman. She stared silently, her eyes pleaded for something, but she seemed afraid to approach.

"What is it, my dear?"

"Absolve my soul, dear father," the woman said softly and unhurriedly, and she knelt and prostrated at his feet.

"I have sinned, dear father, I am afraid of my sin."

The elder sat on the bottom step, and the woman approached him, still on her knees.

"I'm three years a widow," she began in a half-whisper, with a sort of shudder. "My married life was hard, he was old, he beat me badly. Once he was sick in bed; I was looking at him and I thought: what if he recovers, gets up on his feet again, what then? And then the thought came to me . . ."

"Wait," said the elder, and he put his ear right to her lips. The woman continued in a soft whisper, almost inaudibly. She soon finished.

"It's the third year?" the elder asked.

"The third year. At first I didn't think about it, and now I've begun to be ill, grief has caught hold of me."

"Have you come from far away?"

"Over three hundred miles from here."

"Did you tell it at confession?"

"I did. Twice I confessed it."

"Were you allowed to receive communion?"

"I was. I'm afraid, afraid to die."

"Do not be afraid of anything, never be afraid, and do not grieve. Just let repentance not slacken in you, and God will forgive everything. There is not and cannot be in the whole world such a sin that the Lord will not forgive one who truly repents of it. A man even cannot commit so great a sin as would exhaust God's boundless love. How could there be a sin that exceeds God's love? Only take care that you repent without ceasing, and chase away fear altogether. Believe that God loves you so as you cannot conceive of it; even with your sin and in your sin he loves you. And there is more joy in heaven over one repentant sinner than over ten righteous men[4]—that was said long ago. Go, then, and do not be afraid. Do not be upset with people, do not take offense at their wrongs. Forgive the dead man in your heart for all the harm he did you; be reconciled with him truly. If you are repentant, it means that you love. And if you love, you already belong to God . . . With love everything is bought, everything is saved. If even I, a sinful man, just like you, was moved to tenderness and felt pity for you, how much more will God be. Love is such a priceless treasure that you can buy the whole world with it, and redeem not only your own but other people's sins. Go, and do not be afraid."

He blessed her three times, took a little icon from around his neck, and put it on her. She bowed deeply to him without speaking. He stood up and looked cheerfully at a healthy woman with a little baby in her arms.

"I'm from Vyshegorye, dear father."

"Why, you've worn yourself out walking four miles with a baby! What do you want?"

"I came to have a look at you. I was here before, don't you remember? Your memory isn't so good if you've forgotten me! Our people said you were sick, and I thought, well, I'll go and see him myself. So, now I see you, and you don't look sick at all! God be with you, really, you'll live another twenty years! With all the people you've got praying for you, how could you be sick!"

"Thank you for everything, my dear."

"By the way, I have a little favor to ask you: here's sixty kopecks; give them, dear father, to some woman who's poorer than I am. As I was coming here, I thought: better give them through him, he'll know who to give them to."

"Thank you, my dear, thank you, kind woman. I love you. I'll be sure to do it. Is that a little girl in your arms?"

"A little girl, father. Lizaveta."

"The Lord bless you both, you and your baby Lizaveta. You've gladdened my heart, mother. Farewell, my dears, farewell, my dearest ones."

He blessed them all and bowed deeply to them.

Chapter 4

A Lady of Little Faith

The visiting lady landowner, looking upon the whole scene of the conversation with the people and their blessing, shed quiet tears and wiped them away with her handkerchief. She was a sentimental society lady whose inclinations were in many respects genuinely good. When the elder finally came up to her, she met him in raptures.

"I experienced so much, so much, looking on at this moving scene . . . ," she was too excited to finish. "Oh, I understand that the people love you, I myself love the people, I want to love them, and how can one not love them, our beautiful Russian people, so simple in their majesty!"

"How is your daughter's health? Did you want to talk with me again?"

"Oh, I begged insistently, I pleaded, I was ready to go down on my knees and stay kneeling even for three days under your window until you let me in. We have come to you, great healer, to express all our rapturous gratitude. You have surely healed my Liza, healed her completely. And how? By praying over her on Thursday, by laying your hands on her. We have hastened here to kiss those hands, to pour out our feelings and our reverence!"

"What do you mean—healed? Isn't she still lying in her chair?"

"But her night fevers have completely disappeared, for two days now, since Thursday," the lady nervously hurried on. "Besides, her legs have grown stronger. This morning she woke up healthy, she slept through the night, look at her color, at her bright eyes. She used to cry all the time, and now she's laughing, gay, joyful. Today she insisted on being helped to her feet, and she stood for a whole minute by herself, without any support. She wants to make a wager with me that in two weeks she'll be dancing the quadrille. I summoned the local doctor, Herzenstube, and he shrugged and said: amazing, baffling. And you want us not to trouble you, not to fly here and thank you? Thank him, Lise,[1] thank him!"

Lise's pretty, laughing little face suddenly became serious for a moment.

She rose from her chair as much as she could, and, looking at the elder, clasped her hands before him, but she couldn't help herself and suddenly burst out laughing . . .

"It's at him, at him!" she pointed to Alyosha, childishly annoyed with herself because she could not keep from laughing. If anyone had looked at Alyosha, who was standing a step behind the elder, he would have noticed a quick blush momentarily coloring his cheeks. His eyes flashed and he looked down.

"She has a message for you, Alexei Fyodorovich . . . How are you?" the mama continued, suddenly addressing Alyosha and holding out to him an exquisitely gloved hand. The elder turned and suddenly looked at Alyosha attentively. The latter approached Liza and, grinning somehow strangely and awkwardly, held out his hand. Lise put on an important face.

"Katerina Ivanovna sends you this by me." She handed him a small letter. "She especially asks that you come to her soon, soon, and not to disappoint her but to be sure to come."

"She asks me to come? Me . . . to her . . . but why?" Alyosha muttered, deeply astonished. His face suddenly became quite worried.

"Oh, it's all about Dmitri Fyodorovich and . . . all these recent events," her mama explained briefly. "Katerina Ivanovna has now come to a decision . . . but for that she must see you . . . why, of course, I don't know, but she asked that you come as soon as possible. And you will do it, surely you will, even Christian feeling must tell you to do it."

"I've met her only once," Alyosha continued, still puzzled.

"Oh, she is such a lofty, such an unattainable creature . . . ! Only think of her sufferings . . . Consider what she's endured, what she's enduring now, consider what lies ahead of her . . . it's all terrible, terrible!"

"Very well, I'll go," Alyosha decided, glancing through the short and mysterious note, which, apart from an urgent request to come, contained no explanations.

"Ah, how nice and splendid it will be of you," Lise cried with sudden animation. "And I just said to mother: he won't go for anything, he is saving his soul. You're so wonderful, so wonderful! I always did think you were wonderful, and it's so nice to say it to you now!"

"Lise!" her mama said imposingly, though she immediately smiled.

"You've forgotten us, too, Alexei Fyodorovich, you don't care to visit us at all: and yet twice Lise has told me that she feels good only with you." Alyosha raised his downcast eyes, suddenly blushed again, and suddenly grinned again, not knowing why himself. The elder, however, was no longer watching him. He had gotten into conversation with the visiting monk, who, as we have already said, was waiting by Lise's chair for him to come out. He was apparently one of those monks of the humblest sort, that is, from the common people, with a short, unshakable world view, but a believer and, in his own way, a tenacious one. He introduced himself as coming from somewhere in the far north, from Obdorsk, from St. Sylvester's, a poor monastery with only nine monks. The elder gave him his blessing and invited him to visit his cell when he liked.

"How are you so bold as to do such deeds?" the monk suddenly asked, pointing solemnly and imposingly at Lise. He was alluding to her "healing."

"It is, of course, too early to speak of that. Improvement is not yet a complete healing, and might also occur for other reasons. Still, if there was anything, it came about by no one else's power save the divine will. Everything is from God. Visit me, father," he added, addressing the monk, "while I'm still able: I'm ill, and I know that my days are numbered."

"Oh, no, no, God will not take you from us, you will live a long, long time yet," the mama exclaimed. "What's this about being ill? You look so healthy, so cheerful, so happy."

"I feel remarkably better today, but by now I know that it is only for a moment. I've come to understand my illness perfectly. But since I seem so cheerful to you, nothing could ever gladden me more than your saying so. For people are created for happiness, and he who is completely happy can at once be deemed worthy of saying to himself: 'I have fulfilled God's commandment on this earth.' All the righteous, all the saints, all the holy martyrs were happy."

"Oh, how you speak! What brave and lofty words!" the mama exclaimed. "You speak, and it seems to pierce one right through. And yet happiness, happiness—where is it? Who can call himself happy? Oh, since you were already so kind as to allow us to see you once more today, let me tell you everything that I held back last time, that I did not dare to say, everything that I suffer with, and have for so long, so long! I am suffering, forgive me, I am suffering!" And in a sort of hot rush of emotion, she pressed her hands together before him.

"From what precisely?"

"I suffer from . . . lack of faith . . ."

"Lack of faith in God?"

"Oh, no, no, I dare not even think of that, but the life after death—it's such a riddle! And no one, but no one will solve it! Listen, you are a healer, a connoisseur of human souls; of course, I dare not expect you to believe me completely, but I assure you, I give you my greatest word that I am not speaking lightly now, that this thought about a future life after death troubles me to the point of suffering, terror, and fright . . . And I don't know who to turn to, all my life I've never dared . . . And now I'm so bold as to turn to you . . . Oh, God, what will you think of me now!" And she clasped her hands.

"Don't worry about my opinion," the elder answered. "I believe completely in the genuineness of your anguish."

"Oh, how grateful I am to you! You see, I close my eyes and think: if everyone has faith, where does it come from? And then they say that it all came originally from fear of the awesome phenomena of nature, and that there is nothing to it at all. What? I think, all my life I've believed, then I die, and suddenly there's nothing, and only 'burdock will grow on my grave,'[2] as I read in one writer? It's terrible! What, what will give me back my faith? Though I believed only when I was a little child, mechanically, without thinking about anything . . . How, how can it be proved? I've come now to throw myself at your feet and ask you about it. If I miss this chance, too, then surely no one will answer me for the rest of my life. How can it be proved, how can one be convinced? Oh, miserable me! I look around and see that for everyone else, almost everyone, it's all the same, no one worries about it anymore, and I'm the only one who can't bear it. It's devastating, devastating!"

"No doubt it is devastating. One cannot prove anything here, but it is possible to be convinced."

"How? By what?"

"By the experience of active love. Try to love your neighbors actively and tirelessly. The more you succeed in loving, the more you'll be convinced of the existence of God and the immortality of your soul. And if you reach complete selflessness in the love of your neighbor, then undoubtedly you will believe, and no doubt will even be able to enter your soul. This has been tested. It is certain."

"Active love? That's another question, and what a question, what a question! You see, I love mankind so much that—would you believe it?—I sometimes dream of giving up all, all I have, of leaving Lise and going to become a sister of mercy. I close my eyes, I think and dream, and in such moments I feel an invincible strength in myself. No wounds, no festering sores could frighten me. I would bind them and cleanse them with my own hands, I would nurse the suffering, I am ready to kiss those sores . . ."

"It's already a great deal and very well for you that you dream of that in your mind and not of something else. Once in a while, by chance, you may really do some good deed."

"Yes, but could I survive such a life for long?" the lady went on heatedly, almost frantically, as it were. "That's the main question, that's my most tormenting question of all. I close my eyes and ask myself: could you stand it for long on such a path? And if the sick man whose sores you are cleansing does not respond immediately with gratitude but, on the contrary, begins tormenting you with his whims, not appreciating and not noticing your philanthropic ministry, if he begins to shout at you, to make rude demands, even to complain to some sort of superiors (as often happens with people who are in pain)—what then? Will you go on loving, or not? And, imagine, the answer already came to me with a shudder: if there's anything that would immediately cool my 'active' love for mankind, that one thing is ingratitude. In short, I work for pay and demand my pay at once, that is, praise and a return of love for my love. Otherwise I'm unable to love anyone!"

She was in a fit of the most sincere self-castigation, and, having finished, looked with defiant determination at the elder.

"I heard exactly the same thing, a long time ago to be sure, from a doctor," the elder remarked. "He was then an old man, and unquestionably intelligent. He spoke just as frankly as you, humorously, but with a sorrowful humor. 'I love mankind,' he said, 'but I am amazed at myself: the more I love mankind in general, the less I love people in particular, that is, individually, as separate persons. In my dreams,' he said, 'I often went so far as to think passionately of serving mankind, and, it may be, would really have gone to the cross for people if it were somehow suddenly necessary, and yet I am incapable of living in the same room with anyone even for two days, this I know from experience. As soon as someone is there, close to me, his personality oppresses my self-esteem and restricts my freedom. In twenty-four hours I can begin to hate even the best of men: one because he takes too long eating his dinner, another because he has a cold and keeps blowing his nose. I become the enemy of people the moment they touch me,' he said. 'On the other hand, it has always happened that the more I hate people individually, the more ardent becomes my love for humanity as a whole.'"

"But what is to be done, then? What is to be done in such a case? Should one fall into despair?"

"No, for it is enough that you are distressed by it. Do what you can, and it will be reckoned unto you. You have already done much if you can understand yourself so deeply and so sincerely! But if you spoke with me so sincerely just now in order to be praised, as I have praised you, for your truthfulness, then of course you will get nowhere with your efforts at active love; it will all remain merely a dream, and your whole life will flit by like a phantom. Then, naturally, you will forget about the future life, and in the end will somehow calm down by yourself."

"You have crushed me! Only now, this very moment, as you were speaking, did I realize that indeed I was waiting only for you to praise my sincerity, when I told you that I couldn't bear ingratitude. You've brought me back to myself, you've caught me out and explained me to myself!"

"Is it true what you say? Well, now, after such a confession from you, I believe that you are sincere and good at heart. If you do not attain happiness, always remember that you are on a good path, and try not to leave it. Above all, avoid lies, all lies, especially the lie to yourself. Keep watch on your own lie and examine it every hour, every minute. And avoid contempt, both of others and of yourself: what seems bad to you in yourself is purified by the very fact that you have noticed it in yourself. And avoid fear, though fear is simply the consequence of every lie. Never be frightened at your own faintheartedness in attaining love, and meanwhile do not even be very frightened by your own bad acts. I am sorry that I cannot say anything more comforting, for active love is a harsh and fearful thing compared with love in dreams. Love in dreams thirsts for immediate action, quickly performed, and with everyone watching. Indeed, it will go as far as the giving even of one's life, provided it does not take long but is soon over, as on stage, and everyone is looking on and praising. Whereas active love is labor and perseverance, and for some people, perhaps, a whole science. But I predict that even in that very moment when you see with horror that despite all your efforts, you not only have not come nearer your goal but seem to have gotten farther from it, at that very moment—I predict this to you—you will suddenly reach your goal and will clearly behold over you the wonder-working power of the Lord, who all the while has been loving you, and all the while has been mysteriously guiding you. Forgive me for not being able to stay with you longer, but I am expected. Good-bye."

The lady was weeping.

"Lise, Lise, but bless her, bless her!" she suddenly fluttered herself up.

"But does she deserve to be loved? I saw how she was being naughty all this time," the elder said jokingly. "Why have you been laughing at Alexei all this time?"

Lise had, indeed, been busy teasing Alyosha all the time. She had noticed long ago, from their first visit, that Alyosha was shy of her and tried not to look at her, and she found this terribly amusing. She waited purposely to catch his eye: Alyosha, unable to endure her persistent stare, would glance at her from time to time, unwillingly, drawn by an irresistible force, and at once she would grin a triumphant grin right in his face. Alyosha would become embarrassed, and even more annoyed. Finally he turned away from her altogether and hid behind the elder's back. After a few minutes, drawn by the same irresistible force, he turned to see if he was still being looked at or not, and saw Lise, almost hanging out of her chair, peering at him sideways, waiting with all her might for him to look at her. Having caught his eye, she burst into such laughter that even the elder could not help saying:

"Naughty girl, why are you shaming him like that?"

Lise suddenly and quite unexpectedly blushed, her eyes flashed, her face became terribly serious, and with hot indignation she suddenly protested rapidly, nervously:

"And why has he forgotten everything? He carried me in his arms when I was little, we played together. Why, he used to come and teach me to read, do you know that? Two years ago, when we parted, he said he would never forget that we were friends forever, forever and ever! And now all of a sudden he's afraid of me. I'm not going to bite him, am I? Why doesn't he want to come near me? Why doesn't he say anything? Why won't he come to see us? It's not that you won't let him: we know he goes everywhere. It's improper for me to invite him, he should be the first to think of it, if he hasn't forgotten. No, sir, now he's saving his soul! Why did you put those long skirts on him . . . If he runs, he'll trip and fall . . ."

And suddenly, unable to restrain herself, she covered her face with her hand and burst, terribly, uncontrollably, into her prolonged, nervous, shaking, and inaudible laughter. The elder listened to her with a smile and blessed her tenderly. As she kissed his hand, she suddenly pressed it to her eyes and started crying:

"Don't be angry with me, I'm a fool, I'm worthless . . . and maybe Alyosha is right, very right, in not wanting to come and see such a silly girl."

"I'll be sure to send him," the elder decided.

Chapter 5

So Be It! So Be It!

The elder's absence from his cell lasted for about twenty-five minutes. It was already past twelve-thirty, yet Dmitri Fyodorovich, for whose sake everyone had gathered, was still nowhere to be seen. But it was almost as if he had been forgotten, and when the elder stepped into the cell again, he found his guests engaged in a most lively general conversation. Ivan Fyodorovich and the two hieromonks were the main participants. Miusov, too, was trying—very eagerly, it appeared—to get into the conversation, but again he had no luck; he was obviously in the background, and they scarcely even responded to him, which new circumstance only added to his growing irritation. The thing was that he had engaged in some intellectual fencing with Ivan Fyodorovich before, and could not calmly endure this seeming negligence from him: "Up to now, at least, I have stood very high with all that is progressive in Europe, but this new generation is decidedly ignoring us," he thought to himself. Fyodor Pavlovich, who had given his word to sit in his chair and be silent, was indeed silent for a while, but he watched his neighbor, Pyotr Alexandrovich, with a mocking little smile, obviously taking pleasure in his irritation. He had been meaning for a long time to pay back some old scores and now did not want to let his chance slip. Finally, unable to restrain himself, he leaned over his neighbor's shoulder and began taunting him again in a half-whisper.

"And why, instead of going away just now, after my 'kissing it belovingly,' have you consented to remain in such unseemly company? It's because you felt yourself humiliated and insulted, and stayed in order to display your intelligence and get your own back. You won't leave now until you've displayed your intelligence for them."

"What, again? On the contrary, I'll leave at once."

"You'll be the last, the last of all to go!" Fyodor Pavlovich picked at him once more. This was almost the very moment of the elder's return.

The discussion died briefly, but the elder, having sat down in his former place, looked around at them all as if cordially inviting them to continue. Alyosha, who had learned almost every expression of his face, saw clearly that he was terribly tired and was forcing himself. In the recent days of his illness, he had occasionally fainted from exhaustion. Almost the same pallor as before he fainted was now spreading over his face; his lips became white. But he obviously did not want to dismiss the gathering; he seemed, besides, to have some purpose of his own—but what was it? Alyosha watched him intently.

"We are talking about a most curious article by the gentleman," said the hieromonk Iosif, the librarian, addressing the elder and pointing to Ivan Fyodorovich. "There is much that is new in it, but it seems the argument is two-edged. It is a magazine article on the subject of ecclesiastical courts and the scope of their rights, written in reply to a churchman who wrote an entire book on the subject . . ."[1]

"Unfortunately, I have not read your article, but I have heard about it," the elder replied, looking intently and keenly at Ivan Fyodorovich.

"He stands on a most curious point," the Father Librarian went on. "Apparently, on the question of ecclesiastical courts, he completely rejects the separation of Church and state."

"That is curious, but in what sense?" the elder asked Ivan Fyodorovich.

The latter answered at last, not with polite condescension, as Alyosha had feared the day before, but modestly and reservedly, with apparent consideration and, evidently, without the least ulterior motive.

"I start from the proposition that this mixing of elements, that is, of the essences of Church and state taken separately, will of course go on eternally, despite the fact that it is impossible, and that it will never be brought not only to a normal but even to any degree of compatible relationship, because there is a lie at the very basis of the matter. Compromise between the state and the Church on such questions as courts, for example, is, in my opinion, in its perfect and pure essence, impossible. The churchman with whom I argued maintains that the Church occupies a precise and definite place within the state. I objected that, on the contrary, the Church should contain in itself the whole state and not merely occupy a certain corner of it, and that if for some reason that is impossible now, then in the essence of things it undoubtedly should be posited as the direct and chief aim of the whole further development of Christian society."

"Very true!" Father Paissy, the silent and learned hieromonk, said firmly and nervously.

"Sheer Ultramontanism!"[2] Miusov exclaimed, crossing and recrossing his legs in impatience.

"Ah, but we don't even have any mountains!" exclaimed Father Iosif, and turning to the elder, he continued: "Incidentally, he replies to the following 'basic and essential' propositions of his opponent, who, mind you, is a churchman. First, that 'no social organization can or should arrogate to itself the power to dispose of the civil and political rights of its members.' Second, that 'criminal and civil jurisdiction should not belong to the Church and are incompatible with its nature both as divine institution and as an organization of men for religious purposes.' And finally, third, that 'the Church is a kingdom not of this world . . .' "

"A most unworthy play on words for a churchman!" Father Paissy, unable to restrain himself, interrupted again. "I have read this book to which you objected," he addressed Ivan Fyodorovich, "and was astonished by this churchman saying 'the Church is a kingdom not of this world.'[3] If it is not of this world, it follows that it cannot exist on earth at all. In the Holy Gospel, the words 'not of this world' are used in a different sense. To play with such words is impossible. Our Lord Jesus Christ came precisely to establish the Church on earth. The Kingdom of Heaven, of course, is not of this world but in heaven, but it is entered in no other way than through the Church that is founded and established on earth. And therefore to make worldly puns in this sense is impossible and unworthy. The Church is indeed a kingdom and appointed to reign, and in the end must undoubtedly be revealed as a kingdom over all the earth—for which we have a covenant . . ."

He suddenly fell silent, as if checking himself. Ivan Fyodorovich, having listened to him respectfully and attentively, went on with great composure, but, as before, eagerly and openheartedly, addressing the elder.

"The whole point of my article is that in ancient times, during its first three centuries, Christianity was revealed on earth only by the Church, and was only the Church. But when the pagan Roman state desired to become Christian, it inevitably so happened that, having become Christian, it merely included the Church in itself, but itself continued to be, as before, a pagan state in a great many of its functions. Essentially, this is undoubtedly what had to happen. But Rome as a state retained too much of pagan civilization and wisdom—for example, the very aims and basic principles of the state. Whereas Christ's Church, having entered the state, no doubt could give up none of its own basic principles, of that rock on which it stood, and could pursue none but its own aims, once firmly established and shown to it by the Lord himself, among which was the transforming of the whole world, and therefore of the whole ancient pagan state, into the Church. Thus (that is, for future purposes), it is not the Church that should seek a definite place for itself in the state, like 'any social organization' or 'organization of men for religious purposes' (as the author I was objecting to refers to the Church), but, on the contrary, every earthly state must eventually be wholly transformed into the Church and become nothing else but the Church, rejecting whichever of its aims are incompatible with those of the Church. And all of this will in no way demean it, will take away neither its honor nor its glory as a great state, nor the glory of its rulers, but will only turn it from a false, still pagan and erroneous path, onto the right and true path that alone leads to eternal goals. That is why the author of the book on *The Principles of the Ecclesiastical Court* would have judged correctly if, while seeking and presenting these principles, he had looked upon them as a temporary compromise, still necessary in our sinful and unfulfilled times, and nothing more. But as soon as the inventor of these principles makes so bold as to declare the principles he is presenting, some of which Father Iosif has just enumerated, to be immovable, elemental, and eternal, he goes directly against the Church and its holy, eternal, and immovable destiny. That is the whole of my article, a full summary of it."

"In short," Father Paissy said again, stressing each word, "according to certain theories, which have become only too clear in our nineteenth century, the Church ought to be transforming itself into the state, from a lower to a higher species, as it were, so as to disappear into it eventually, making way for science, the spirit of the age, and civilization. And if it does not want that and offers resistance, then as a result it is allotted only a certain corner, as it were, in the state, and even that under control—as is happening in our time everywhere in modern European lands. Yet according to the Russian understanding and hope, it is not the Church that needs to be transformed into the state, as from a lower to a higher type, but, on the contrary, the state should end by being accounted worthy of becoming only the Church alone, and nothing else but that. And so be it, so be it!"

"Well, sir, I confess that you have now reassured me somewhat," Miusov grinned, recrossing his legs again. "So far as I understand it, this, then, would be the realization of some ideal, an infinitely remote one, at the Second Coming. That is as you please. A beautiful utopian dream of the disappearance of wars, diplomats, banks, and so on. Something even resembling socialism. And here I was thinking you meant it all seriously, and that the Church might *now*, for instance, be judging criminals and sentencing them to flogging, hard labor, perhaps even capital punishment."

"But if even now there were only ecclesiastical courts, even now the Church would not sentence criminals to hard labor or capital punishment. Crime and the whole way of looking at it would then undoubtedly have to change, little by little, of course, not all at once, not immediately, but still quite soon . . . ," Ivan Fyodorovich said calmly and without batting an eye.

"Are you serious?" Miusov looked at him intently.

"If everything became the Church, then the Church would excommunicate the criminal and the disobedient and not cut off their heads," Ivan Fyodorovich continued. "Where, I ask you, would the excommunicated man go? He would then have to go away not only from men, as now, but also from Christ. For by his crime he would have rebelled not only against men but also against Christ's Church. That is so now, too, of course, strictly speaking, but it is not avowed, and the criminal of today all too often bargains with his conscience: 'I stole,' he says, 'but I have not gone against the Church, I am not an enemy of Christ.' Time and again that is what the criminal of today says to himself. Well, but when the Church takes the place of the state, it will be very difficult for him to say that, unless he means to reject the Church all over the earth, to say: 'All are mistaken, all are in error, all are a false Church, and I alone, a murderer and thief, am the true Christian Church.' It is very difficult to say this to oneself; it requires formidable conditions, circumstances that do not often occur. Now, on the other hand, take the Church's own view of crime: should it not change from the present, almost pagan view, and from the mechanical cutting off of the infected member, as is done now for the preservation of society, and transform, fully now and not falsely, into the idea of the regeneration of man anew, of his restoration and salvation . . . ?"

"But what are you talking about? Again I cease to understand," Miusov interrupted. "Some kind of dream again. Something shapeless, and impossible to understand as well. Excommunication? What excommunication? I suspect you're simply amusing yourself, Ivan Fyodorovich."

"But, you know, in reality it is so even now," the elder suddenly spoke and everyone turned to him at once. "If it were not for Christ's Church, indeed there would be no restraint on the criminal in his evildoing, and no punishment for it later, real punishment, that is, not a mechanical one such as has just been mentioned, which only chafes the heart in most cases, but a real punishment, the only real, the only frightening and appeasing punishment, which lies in the acknowledgement of one's own conscience."

"How is that, may I ask?" Miusov inquired with the liveliest curiosity.

"Here is how it is," the elder began. "All this exile to hard labor, and formerly with floggings, does not reform anyone, and above all does not even frighten almost any criminal, and the number of crimes not only does not diminish but increases all the more. Surely you will admit that. And it turns out that society, thus, is not protected at all, for although the harmful member is mechanically cut off and sent far away out of sight, another criminal appears at once to take his place, perhaps even two others. If anything protects society even in our time, and even reforms the criminal himself and transforms him into a different person, again it is Christ's law alone, which manifests itself in the acknowledgement of one's own conscience. Only if he acknowledges his guilt as a son of Christ's society—that is, of the Church—will he acknowledge his guilt before society itself—that is, before the Church. Thus, the modern criminal is capable of acknowledging his guilt before the Church alone, and not before the state. If it were so that judgment belonged to society as the Church, then it would know whom to bring back from excommunication and reunite with itself. But now the Church, having no active jurisdiction but merely the possibility of moral condemnation alone, withholds from actively punishing the criminal of its own accord. It does not excommunicate him, but simply does not leave him without paternal guidance. Moreover, it even tries to preserve full Christian communion with the criminal, admitting him to church services, to the holy gifts,[4] giving him alms, and treating him more as a captive than as a wrongdoer. And what would become of the criminal, oh, Lord, if Christian society, too—that is, the Church—rejected him in the same way that civil law rejects him and cuts him off? What would become of him if the Church, too, punished him with excommunication each time immediately after the law of the state has punished him? Surely there could be no greater despair, at least for a Russian criminal, for Russian criminals still have faith. Though who knows: perhaps a terrible thing would happen then—the loss of faith, perhaps, would occur in the desperate heart of the criminal, and what then? But the Church, like a mother, tender and loving, withholds from active punishment, for even without her punishment, the wrongdoer is already too painfully punished by the state court, and at least someone should pity him. And it withholds above all because the judgment of the Church is the only judgment that contains the truth, and for that reason it cannot, essentially and morally, be combined with any other judgment, even in a temporary compromise. Here it is not possible to strike any bargains. The foreign criminal, they say, rarely repents, for even the modern theories themselves confirm in him the idea that his crime is not a crime but only a rebellion against an unjustly oppressive force. Society cuts him off from itself quite mechanically by the force that triumphs over him, and accompanies that excommunication with hatred (so, at least, they say about themselves in Europe)—with hatred and complete indifference and forgetfulness of his subsequent fate as their brother. Thus, all of this goes on without the least compassion of the Church, for in many cases there already are no more churches at all, and what remains are just churchmen and splendid church buildings, while the churches themselves have long been striving to pass from the lower species, the Church, to a higher species, the state, in order to disappear into it completely. So it seems to be, at least, in Lutheran lands. And in Rome it is already a thousand years since the state was proclaimed in place of the Church. And therefore the criminal is not conscious of himself as a member of the Church, and, excommunicated, he sits in despair. And if he returns to society, it is not seldom with such hatred that society itself, as it were, now excommunicates him. What will be the end of it, you may judge for yourselves. In many cases, it would appear to be the same with us; but the point is precisely that, besides the established courts, we have, in addition, the Church as well, which never loses communion with the criminal, as a dear and still beloved son, and above that there is preserved, even if only in thought, the judgment of the Church, not active now but still living for the future, if only as a dream, and unquestionably acknowledged by the criminal himself, by the instinct of his soul. What has just been said here is also true, that if, indeed, the judgment of the Church came, and in its full force—that is, if the whole of society turned into the Church alone—then not only would the judgment of the Church influence the reformation of the criminal as it can never influence it now, but perhaps crimes themselves would indeed diminish at an incredible rate. And the Church, too, no doubt, would understand the future criminal and the future crime in many cases quite differently from now, and would be able to bring the excommunicated back, to deter the plotter, to regenerate the fallen. It is true," the elder smiled, "that now Christian society itself is not yet ready, and stands only on seven righteous men; but as they are never wanting, it abides firmly all the same, awaiting its complete transfiguration from society as still an almost pagan organization, into one universal and sovereign Church. And so be it, so be it, if only at the end of time, for this alone is destined to be fulfilled! And there is no need to trouble oneself with times and seasons, for the mystery of times and seasons is in the wisdom of God, in his foresight, and in his love.[5] And that which by human reckoning may still be rather remote, by divine predestination may already be standing on the eve of its appearance, at the door. And so be that, too! So be it!"

"So be it! So be it!" Father Paissy confirmed with reverence and severity.

"Strange, most strange," Miusov pronounced, not so much fervently as with, so to speak, a sort of repressed indignation.

"What seems so strange to you?" Father Iosif cautiously inquired.

"But, really, what are you talking about?" Miusov exclaimed, as if suddenly bursting out. "The state is abolished on earth, and the Church is raised to the level of the state! It's not even Ultramontanism, it's arch-Ultramontanism! Even Pope Gregory the Seventh never dreamed of such a thing!"[6]

"You have been pleased to understand it in a completely opposite sense," Father Paissy spoke sternly. "It is not the Church that turns into the state, you see. That is Rome and its dream. That is the third temptation of the devil![7] But, on the contrary, the state turns into the Church, it rises up to the Church and becomes the Church over all the earth, which is the complete opposite of Ultramontanism and of Rome, and of your interpretation, and is simply the great destiny of Orthodoxy on earth. This star will show forth from the East."

Miusov was imposingly silent. His whole figure expressed remarkable self-respect. A haughtily condescending smile appeared on his lips. Alyosha followed it all with a pounding heart. The whole conversation stirred him deeply. He happened to glance at Rakitin, who stood motionless in his former place by the door, listening and watching attentively, though with downcast eyes. But by the lively color in his cheeks, Alyosha guessed that Rakitin, too, was stirred, probably no less than he was. Alyosha knew what stirred him.

"Allow me to relate a little anecdote, gentlemen," Miusov suddenly said imposingly and with a sort of especially grand air. "In Paris, several years ago now, soon after the December revolution,[8] I happened once, while visiting an acquaintance, then a very, very important and official person, to meet there a most curious gentleman. This individual was not exactly an undercover agent, but something like the supervisor of an entire team of political agents—rather an influential position in its way. Seizing the chance, out of great curiosity, I struck up a conversation with him; and since he was there not as an acquaintance but as a subordinate official, who had come with a certain kind of report, he, seeing for his part how I was received by his superior, deigned to show me some frankness—well, of course, to a certain extent; that is, he was more polite than frank, precisely as a Frenchman can be polite, the more so because he viewed me as a foreigner. But I well understood him. The topic was socialist revolutionaries, who then, by the way, were being persecuted. Omitting the main essence of the conversation, I shall quote only one most curious remark that this person suddenly let drop: 'We are not, in fact, afraid of all these socialists, anarchists, atheists, and revolutionaries,' he said. 'We keep an eye on them, and their movements are known to us. But there are some special people among them, although not many: these are believers in God and Christians, and at the same time socialists. They are the ones we are most afraid of; they are terrible people! A socialist Christian is more dangerous than a socialist atheist.' His words struck me even then, but now, here, gentlemen, I somehow suddenly recalled them . . ."

"That is, you apply them to us and see us as socialists?" Father Paissy asked directly, without beating around the bush. But before Pyotr Alexandrovich was able to think of a reply, the door opened and in came the long-awaited Dmitri Fyodorovich. Indeed, he was, as it were, no longer expected, and his sudden appearance at first even caused some surprise.

Chapter 6

Why Is Such a Man Alive!

Dmitri Fyodorovich, a young man of twenty-eight, of medium height and agreeable looks, appeared, however, much older than his years. He was muscular and one could tell that he possessed considerable physical strength; nonetheless something sickly, as it were, showed in his face. His face was lean, his cheeks hollow, their color tinged with a sort of unhealthy sallowness. His rather large, dark, prominent eyes had an apparently firm and determined, yet somehow vague, look. Even when he was excited and talking irritably, his look, as it were, did not obey his inner mood but expressed something else, sometimes not at all corresponding to the present moment. "It's hard to know what he's thinking about," those who spoke with him would occasionally say. Others, seeing something pensive and gloomy in his eyes, would suddenly be struck by his unexpected laughter, betraying gay and playful thoughts precisely at the moment when he looked so gloomy. Though his somewhat sickly look at that time could well be understood: everyone knew or had heard about the extremely troubled and "riotous" life he had given himself up to precisely of late, just as they knew about the remarkable irritation he reached in quarrels with his father over the controversial money. Already there were several anecdotes about it going around town. It is true that he was irritable by nature, "abrupt and erratic of mind," as our justice of the peace, Semyon Ivanovich Kachalnikov, characteristically described him at one of our gatherings. He entered, impeccably and smartly dressed, his frock coat buttoned, wearing black gloves and carrying his top hat. As a recently retired military man, he wore a moustache and still shaved his beard. His dark brown hair was cut short and combed somehow forward on his temples. He had a long, resolute military stride. He stopped for a moment on the threshold and, glancing around at everyone, went directly to the elder, guessing him to be the host. He made a low bow to him and asked for his blessing. The elder rose a little in his chair and blessed him; Dmitri Fyodorovich respectfully kissed his hand and with remarkable excitement, almost irritation, said:

"Be so generous as to forgive me for having kept you waiting so long. But the servant Smerdyakov, sent by papa, in reply to my insistent question about the time, told me twice in the most definite tone that the appointment was at one. Now I suddenly find out . . . "

"Don't worry," the elder interrupted, "it's nothing, you're just a bit late, it doesn't matter . . ."

"I am extremely grateful, and could expect no less from your goodness." Having snapped out these words, Dmitri Fyodorovich bowed once again, then, suddenly turning to his "papa," made the same deep and respectful bow to him as well. It was obvious that he had considered this bow beforehand and conceived it sincerely, believing it his duty to express thereby his respect and goodwill. Fyodor Pavlovich, though taken unawares, found the proper reply at once: in response to Dmitri Fyodorovich's bow, he jumped up from his chair and responded to his son with exactly as deep a bow. His face suddenly became solemn and imposing, which gave him, however, a decidedly wicked look. Then, silently, giving a general bow to all those present in the room, Dmitri Fyodorovich, with his big and resolute strides, went over to the window, sat down on the only remaining chair, not far from Father Paissy, and, leaning forward with his whole body, at once prepared to listen to the continuation of the conversation he had interrupted.

Dmitri Fyodorovich's appearance had taken no more than a couple of minutes, and the conversation could not fail to start up again. But this time Pyotr Alexandrovich did not deem it necessary to reply to Father Paissy's persistent and almost irritated question.

"Allow me to dismiss the subject," he said with a certain worldly nonchalance. "Besides, it's a complex one. Ivan Fyodorovich, here, is grinning at us: he must have saved something curious for this occasion as well. Ask him."

"Nothing special, except for a small remark," Ivan Fyodorovich answered at once, "that European liberalism in general, and even our Russian liberal dilettantism, has long and frequently confused the final results of socialism with those of Christianity. This wild conclusion is, of course, typical. Incidentally, it turns out that socialism is confused with Christianity not only by liberals and dilettantes, but along with them, in many cases, by gendarmes as well—I mean foreign ones, of course. Your Parisian anecdote, Pyotr Alexandrovich, is quite typical."

"Generally, again, I ask your permission to drop the subject," Pyotr Alexandrovich repeated, "and instead let me tell you another anecdote, gentlemen, about Ivan Fyodorovich himself, a most typical and interesting one. No more than five days ago, at a local gathering, predominantly of ladies, he solemnly announced in the discussion that there is decidedly nothing in the whole world that would make men love their fellow men; that there exists no law of nature that man should love mankind, and that if there is and has been any love on earth up to now, it has come not from natural law but solely from people's belief in their immortality. Ivan Fyodorovich added parenthetically that that is what all natural law consists of, so that were mankind's belief in its immortality to be destroyed, not only love but also any living power to continue the life of the world would at once dry up in it. Not only that, but then nothing would be immoral any longer, everything would be permitted, even anthropophagy. And even that is not all: he ended with the assertion that for every separate person, like ourselves for instance, who believes neither in God nor in his own immortality, the moral law of nature ought to change immediately into the exact opposite of the former religious law, and that egoism, even to the point of evildoing, should not only be permitted to man but should be acknowledged as the necessary, the most reasonable, and all but the noblest result of his situation. From this paradox, gentlemen, you may deduce what else our dear eccentric and paradoxalist Ivan Fyodorovich may be pleased to proclaim, and perhaps still intends to proclaim."

"Allow me," Dmitri Fyodorovich suddenly cried unexpectedly, "to be sure I've heard correctly: 'Evildoing should not only be permitted but even should be acknowledged as the most necessary and most intelligent solution for the situation of every godless person'! Is that it, or not?"

"Exactly that," said Father Paissy.

"I'll remember."

Having said which, Dmitri Fyodorovich fell silent as unexpectedly as he had unexpectedly flown into the conversation. They all looked at him with curiosity.

"Can it be that you really hold this conviction about the consequences of the exhaustion of men's faith in the immortality of their souls?" the elder suddenly asked Ivan Fyodorovich.

"Yes, it was my contention. There is no virtue if there is no immortality."

"You are blessed if you believe so, or else most unhappy!"

"Why unhappy?" Ivan Fyodorovich smiled.

"Because in all likelihood you yourself do not believe either in the immortality of your soul or even in what you have written about the Church and the Church question."

"Maybe you're right . . . ! But still, I wasn't quite joking either . . . ," Ivan Fyodorovich suddenly and strangely confessed—by the way, with a quick blush.

"You weren't quite joking, that is true. This idea is not yet resolved in your heart and torments it. But a martyr, too, sometimes likes to toy with his despair, also from despair, as it were. For the time being you, too, are toying, out of despair, with your magazine articles and drawing-room discussions, without believing in your own dialectics and smirking at them with your heart aching inside you . . . The question is not resolved in you, and there lies your great grief, for it urgently demands resolution . . ."

"But can it be resolved in myself? Resolved in a positive way?" Ivan Fyodorovich continued asking strangely, still looking at the elder with a certain inexplicable smile.

"Even if it cannot be resolved in a positive way, it will never be resolved in the negative way either—you yourself know this property of your heart, and therein lies the whole of its torment. But thank the Creator that he has given you a lofty heart, capable of being tormented by such a torment, 'to set your mind on things that are above, for our true homeland is in heaven.'[1] May God grant that your heart's decision overtake you still on earth, and may God bless your path!"

The elder raised his hand and was about to give his blessing to Ivan Fyodorovich from where he sat. But the latter suddenly rose from his chair, went over to him, received his blessing, and, having kissed his hand, returned silently to his place. He looked firm and serious. This action, as well as the whole preceding conversation with the elder, so unexpected from Ivan Fyodorovich, somehow struck everyone with its mysteriousness and even a certain solemnity, so that for a moment they all fell silent, and Alyosha looked almost frightened. But Miusov suddenly heaved his shoulders, and at the same moment Fyodor Pavlovich jumped up from his chair.

"Divine and most holy elder!" he cried, pointing at Ivan Fyodorovich, "this is my son, the flesh of my flesh, my own dear flesh! This is my most respectful Karl Moor, so to speak, and this son, the one who just came in, Dmitri Fyodorovich, against whom I am seeking justice from you, is the most disrespectful Franz Moor, both from Schiller's *Robbers*, and I, I myself in that case am the *regierender* Graf von Moor![2] Judge and save us! It's not just your prayers we need, but your prophecies!"

"Speak without foolery, and do not begin by insulting your relations," the elder replied in a weak, exhausted voice. He was clearly getting more and more tired and was visibly losing his strength.

"An unworthy comedy, just as I anticipated on my way here!" Dmitri Fyodorovich exclaimed indignantly, also jumping up from his seat. "Forgive me, reverend father," he turned to the elder, "I am an uneducated man and do not even know how to address you, but you have been deceived, and were too kind in letting us come together here. Papa is only looking for a scandal—who knows for what reason. He always has his reasons. But I think I see now . . ."

"All of them accuse me, all of them!" Fyodor Pavlovich shouted in his turn, "and Pyotr Alexandrovich, here, he accuses me, too. You did accuse me, Pyotr Alexandrovich, you did!" he suddenly turned to Miusov, though the latter had no thought of interrupting him. "They accuse me of pocketing children's money and turning a profit on it, but, I beg your pardon, don't we have courts of law? They'll reckon it up for you, Dmitri Fyodorovich, according to your own receipts, letters, and contracts, how much you had, how much you've destroyed, and how much you've got left! Why does Pyotr Alexandrovich not give us his judgment? Dmitri Fyodorovich is no stranger to him. It's because they're all against me, and Dmitri Fyodorovich in the end owes me money, and not just a trifle but several thousand, sir, I've got it all on paper. The whole town is rattling and banging from his wild parties. And where he used to serve, he paid a thousand if not two thousand for the seduction of honest girls—we know about that, Dmitri Fyodorovich, sir, in all its secret details, and I can prove it, sir . . . Most holy father, would you believe that he got one of the noblest of girls to fall in love with him, a girl from a good family, with a fortune, the daughter of his former superior, a brave colonel, decorated, the Anna with swords on his neck,[3] and then compromised the girl by offering her his hand, and now she's here, now she's an orphan, his fiancée, and he, before her very eyes, keeps visiting one of the local seductresses. But although this seductress has lived, so to speak, in civil marriage with a respected man, yet she is of independent character, an impregnable fortress to all, the same as a lawful wife, for she is virtuous—yes, sir, holy fathers, she is virtuous! And Dmitri Fyodorovich wants to unlock this fortress with a golden key, and that's why he's trying to bully me even now, he wants to get some money out of me, and meanwhile he's already thrown away thousands on this seductress, which is why he's continually borrowing money from me, and, incidentally, from whom else, whom do you think? Shall I tell them, Mitya?"

"Silence!" Dmitri Fyodorovich shouted. "Wait until I'm gone. Do not dare in my presence to sully the noblest of girls . . . That you are even so bold as to mention her is shameful enough . . . I will not allow it!"

He was gasping for breath.

"Mitya! Mitya!" Fyodor Pavlovich cried tremulously, trying to squeeze out a tear. "Don't you care about a father's blessing? And what if I should curse you?"

"Shameless impostor!" Dmitri Fyodorovich roared in fury.

"He says that to his father! His father! Think how he must treat others! Imagine, gentlemen: there's a poor but honorable man living here, a retired captain, fell into misfortune and was retired from service, but not publicly, not by court-martial, he preserved his honor. He's burdened with a large family. And three weeks ago our Dmitri Fyodorovich seized him by the beard in a tavern, dragged him by that same beard into the street, and there in the street publicly thrashed him, and all because he's acted as my agent in a little business of mine."

"That is all a lie! Outwardly it's true, but inwardly it's a lie!" Dmitri Fyodorovich was trembling all over with rage. "My dear papa! I do not justify my actions. Yes, I acknowledge publicly that I behaved like a beast with that captain, and now I'm sorry and loathe myself for my beastly rage, but this captain of yours, your agent, went to that very lady whom you yourself have described as a seductress, and began suggesting to her on your behalf that she should take over my promissory notes that are in your possession, and sue me in order to have me locked up with the help of those notes, in case I pestered you too much for an account of my property. And now you reproach me with having a weakness for this lady, when you yourself were teaching her how to ensnare me! She told me so to my face, she told me herself, and she laughed at you! And you want me locked up only because you're jealous of me, because you yourself have begun approaching this woman with your love, and that, too, I know all about, and she laughed again—do you hear?—she laughed at you as she told me. Here, holy people, is a man for you, a father reproaching his profligate son! Gentlemen witnesses, forgive my wrath, but I anticipated that this perfidious old man had gathered you all here for a scandal. I came intending to forgive, if he held out his hand to me, to forgive and to ask forgiveness! But since he has just now insulted not only me but that most noble girl, whose very name I do not dare to utter in vain out of reverence for her, I am resolved to give away his whole game in public, though he is my father . . . !"

He could not go on. His eyes flashed, he was breathing hard. Everyone else in the cell was excited, too. They all rose anxiously from their chairs, except for the elder. The hieromonks looked stern, but waited, however, to know the elder's will. He sat looking quite pale now, not from excitement but from sickly weakness. An imploring smile shone on his lips; every once in a while he raised his hand as if wishing to stop the two raging men; and, of course, one gesture from him would have been sufficient to end the scene; yet he himself seemed to be waiting for something, and watched intently, as if still trying to understand something, as if still not comprehending something. At last, Pyotr Alexandrovich Miusov finally felt himself humiliated and disgraced.

"We are all to blame for this scandal!" he said hotly. "But all the same, I did not anticipate, on my way here, though I knew whom I was dealing with . . . This must be stopped at once! Your reverence, believe me, I did not know exactly all the details that have just been revealed here, I did not want to believe them, and have only now learned for the first time . . . The father is jealous of his son over a woman of bad behavior, and himself arranges with this creature to lock the son up in prison . . . And this is the company in which I've been forced to come here . . . I have been deceived, I declare to you all that I have been deceived no less than the others . . ."

"Dmitri Fyodorovich!" Fyodor Pavlovich suddenly screamed in a voice not his own, "if only you weren't my son, I would challenge you to a duel this very moment . . . with pistols, at three paces . . . across a handkerchief! across a handkerchief!" he ended, stamping with both feet.[4]

Old liars who have been play-acting all their lives have moments when they get so carried away by their posing that they indeed tremble and weep from excitement, even though at that same moment (or just a second later) they might whisper to themselves: "You're lying, you shameless old man, you're acting even now, despite all your 'holy' wrath and 'holy' moment of wrath."

Dmitri Fyodorovich frowned horribly and looked at his father with inexpressible contempt.

"I thought . . . I thought," he said somehow softly and restrainedly, "that I would come to my birthplace with the angel of my soul, my fiancée, to cherish him in his old age, and all I find is a depraved sensualist and despicable comedian!"

"To a duel!" the old fool screamed again, breathless and spraying saliva with each word. "And you, Pyotr Alexandrovich Miusov, let it be known to you, sir, that in all the generations of your family there is not and maybe never has been a woman loftier or more honorable—more honorable, do you hear?—than this creature, as you have just dared to call her! And you, Dmitri Fyodorovich, traded your fiancée for this very 'creature,' so you yourself have judged that your fiancée isn't worthy to lick her boots—that's the kind of creature she is!"

"Shame!" suddenly escaped from Father Iosif.

"A shame and a disgrace!" Kalganov, who had been silent all the while, suddenly cried in his adolescent voice, trembling with excitement and blushing all over.

"Why is such a man alive!" Dmitri Fyodorovich growled in a muffled voice, now nearly beside himself with fury, somehow raising his shoulders peculiarly so that he looked almost hunchbacked. "No, tell me, can he be allowed to go on dishonoring the earth with himself?" He looked around at everyone, pointing his finger at the old man. His speech was slow and deliberate.

"Do you hear, you monks, do you hear the parricide!" Fyodor Pavlovich flung at Father Iosif. "There is the answer to your 'shame'! What shame? This 'creature,' this 'woman of bad behavior' is perhaps holier than all of you, gentlemen soul-saving hieromonks! Maybe she fell in her youth, being influenced by her environment, but she has 'loved much,' and even Christ forgave her who loved much . . ."[5]

"Christ did not forgive that kind of love . . . ," escaped impatiently from the meek Father Iosif.

"No, that kind, monks, exactly that kind, that kind! You are saving your souls here on cabbage and you think you're righteous! You eat gudgeons, one gudgeon a day, and you think you can buy God with gudgeons!"

"Impossible! Impossible!" came from all sides of the cell.

But the whole scene, which had turned so ugly, was stopped in a most unexpected manner. The elder suddenly rose from his place. Alyosha, who had almost completely lost his head from fear for him and for all of them, had just time enough to support his arm. The elder stepped towards Dmitri Fyodorovich and, having come close to him, knelt before him. Alyosha thought for a moment that he had fallen from weakness, but it was something else. Kneeling in front of Dmitri Fyodorovich, the elder bowed down at his feet with a full, distinct, conscious bow, and even touched the floor with his forehead. Alyosha was so amazed that he failed to support him as he got to his feet. A weak smile barely glimmered on his lips.

"Forgive me! Forgive me, all of you!" he said, bowing on all sides to his guests.

Dmitri Fyodorovich stood dumbstruck for a few moments. Bowing at his feet—what was that? Then suddenly he cried out: "Oh, God!" and, covering his face with his hands, rushed from the room. All the other guests flocked after him, forgetting in their confusion even to say good-bye or bow to their host. Only the hieromonks again came to receive his blessing.

"What's that—bowing at his feet? Is it some sort of emblem?" Fyodor Pavlovich, who for some reason had suddenly grown quiet, tried to start a conversation, not daring, by the way, to address anyone in particular. At that moment they were just passing beyond the walls of the hermitage.

"I cannot answer for a madhouse or for madmen," Miusov at once replied sharply, "but I can and will rid myself of your company, Fyodor Pavlovich, and that, believe me, forever. Where is that monk . . . ?"

However, "that monk"—that is, the one who had invited them to dinner with the Superior—did not keep them waiting. He met the guests immediately, just as they came down the steps from the elder's cell, as if he had been waiting for them all the time.

"Do me a favor, reverend father, convey my deepest respects to the Father Superior, and apologize for me, Miusov, personally to his reverence, that owing to the unexpected occurrence of unforeseen circumstances it is quite impossible for me to have the honor of joining him at his table, despite my most sincere wishes," Pyotr Alexandrovich said irritably to the monk.

"And that unforeseen circumstance is me!" Fyodor Pavlovich immediately put in. "Do you hear, father? Pyotr Alexandrovich, here, doesn't want to be in my company, otherwise he'd be glad to go. And you will go, Pyotr Alexandrovich, be so good as to visit the Father Superior, and—*bon appetit*! You see, it is I who am going to decline, and not you. Home, home—I'll eat at home. Here I just don't feel able, Pyotr Alexandrovich, my dearest relative."

"I am no relative of yours and never have been, you despicable man!"

"I said it on purpose to make you mad, because you disclaim our relation, though you're still my relative no matter how you shuffle, I can prove it by the Church calendar.[6] Stay if you like, Ivan Fyodorovich; I'll send horses for you later. As for you, Pyotr Álexandrovich, even common decency must tell you now to go to the Father Superior, if only to apologize for the mess we made in there."

"Are you really leaving? It's not another lie?"

"Pyotr Alexandrovich, how could I dare stay after what happened? I got carried away, forgive me, gentlemen, I got carried away! And besides, I'm shaken! And ashamed, too! Gentlemen, one man has a heart like Alexander of Macedon and another like little Fido the lapdog. Mine is like little Fido the lapdog's. I turned timid! How, after such an escapade, could I go to dinner and slop up monastery sauces? It's shameful, I can't, excuse me!"

"Devil knows if he means it!" Miusov stood in doubt, following the retreating buffoon with a puzzled look. The latter turned around and, noticing that Pyotr Alexandrovich was watching him, blew him a kiss.

"And you? Are you going to the Superior's?" Miusov curtly asked Ivan Fyodorovich.

"Why not? Besides, I was specially invited by the Superior just yesterday."

"Unfortunately, I do indeed feel almost compelled to go to this damned dinner," Miusov went on with the same bitter irritation, even ignoring the fact that the little monk was listening. "At least we should ask forgiveness for what we've done and explain that it wasn't us . . . What do you think?"

"Yes, we should explain that it wasn't us. Besides, papa won't be there," Ivan Fyodorovich remarked.

"Yes, that would be the last thing . . . ! Damn this dinner!"

Still, they all walked on. The little monk was silent and listened. On the way through the woods, he simply remarked once that the Father Superior had been kept waiting and that they were already more than half an hour late. He got no response. Miusov looked at Ivan Fyodorovich with hatred.

"He goes off to dinner as if nothing had happened!" he thought. "A brazen face and a Karamazov conscience."

Chapter 7

A Seminarist-Careerist

Alyosha brought his elder to the little bedroom and sat him down on the bed. It was a very small room with only the necessary furnishings; the bed was narrow, made of iron, with a piece of thick felt in place of a mattress. In the corner by the icons there was a reading stand, and on it lay a cross and the Gospel. The elder lowered himself weakly onto the bed; his eyes were glazed and he had difficulty breathing. Having sat down, he looked intently at Alyosha, as if he were pondering something.

"Go, my dear, go. Porfiry is enough for me, and you must hurry. They need you there, go to the Father Superior, serve at the table."

"Give me your blessing to stay here," Alyosha spoke in a pleading voice.

"You are more needed there. There is no peace there. You will serve and be of use. If demons raise their heads, recite a prayer. And know, my dear son" (the elder liked to call him that), "that from now on this is not the place for you. Remember that, young man. As soon as God grants me to depart, leave the monastery. Leave it for good."

Alyosha started.

"What's wrong? For the time being your place is not here. I give you my blessing for a great obedience in the world.[1] You still have much journeying before you. And you will have to marry—yes, you will. You will have to endure everything before you come back again. And there will be much work to do. But I have no doubt of you, that is why I am sending you. Christ is with you. Keep him, and he will keep you. You will behold great sorrow, and in this sorrow you will be happy. Here is a commandment for you: seek happiness in sorrow. Work, work tirelessly. Remember my words from now on, for although I shall still talk with you, not only my days but even my hours are numbered."

Strong emotion showed again in Alyosha's face. The corners of his mouth trembled.

"What's wrong now?" the elder smiled gently. "Let worldly men follow their dead with tears; here we rejoice over a departing father. We rejoice and pray for him. Leave me now. It is time to pray. Go, and hurry. Be near your brothers. Not just one, but both of them."

The elder raised his hand in blessing. It was impossible to object, though Alyosha wanted very much to stay. He also wanted to ask, and the question was on the tip of his tongue, what this bow at his brother Dmitri's feet prefigured—but he did not dare ask. He knew that the elder himself would have explained it, if possible, without being asked. Therefore it was not his will to do so. The bow struck Alyosha terribly; he believed blindly that there was a secret meaning in it. Secret, and perhaps also horrible. As he left the hermitage in order to get to the monastery in time for dinner with the Superior (only to serve at the table, of course), his heart suddenly contracted painfully, and he stopped in his tracks: it was as if he heard again the sound of the elder's words foretelling his very near end. What the elder foretold, and with such exactness, would undoubtedly happen, Alyosha piously believed. But how could he be left without him, how could he not see him, not hear him? And where was he to go? He had ordered him not to weep and to leave the monastery—oh, Lord! It was long since Alyosha had felt such anguish. He hastened through the woods that separated the hermitage from the monastery, and being unable to bear his own thoughts, so greatly did they oppress him, he began looking at the ancient pines on both sides of the forest path. The way was not long, about five hundred paces at most; at that hour it should have been impossible to meet anyone, yet suddenly, at the first turning of the path, he noticed Rakitin. He was waiting for someone.

"Is it me you're waiting for?" Alyosha asked, coming up to him.

"Precisely you," Rakitin grinned. "You're hurrying to the Father Superior's. I know; there's a dinner on. Not since he received the Bishop and General Pakhatov—remember?—has there been such a dinner. I won't be there, but you go and serve the sauces. Tell me one thing, Alexei: what's the meaning of this dream?[2] That's what I wanted to ask you."

"What dream?"

"This bowing at the feet of your brother Dmitri Fyodorovich. He even bumped his forehead on the ground."

"You mean Father Zosima?"

"Yes, Father Zosima."

"His forehead . . . ?"

"Ah, I was irreverent! Well, let it be. So, what does this dream signify?"

"I don't know what it means, Misha."

"I knew he wouldn't explain it to you! Of course, there's nothing very subtle about it, just the usual blessed nonsense, it seems. But the trick had its purpose. Now all the pious frauds in town will start talking and spread it over the whole province, wondering 'what is the meaning of this dream?' The old man is really astute, if you ask me: he smelled crime. It stinks in your family."

"What crime?"

Rakitin evidently wanted to speak his mind.

"A crime in your nice little family. It will take place between your dear brothers and your nice, rich papa. So Father Zosima bumps his forehead on the ground, for the future, just in case. Afterwards they'll say, 'Ah, it's what the holy elder foretold, prophesied,' though bumping your forehead on the ground isn't much of a prophecy. No, they'll say, it was an emblem, an allegory, the devil knows what! They'll proclaim it, they'll remember: 'He foresaw the crime and marked the criminal.' It's always like that with holy fools: they cross themselves before a tavern and cast stones at the temple. Your elder is the same: he drives the just man out with a stick and bows at the murderer's feet."

"What crime? What murderer? What are you saying?" Alyosha stopped dead. Rakitin also stopped.

"What murderer? As if you didn't know. I bet you've already thought of it yourself. As a matter of fact, I'm curious. Listen, Alyosha, you always tell the truth, though you always fall between two stools: tell me, did you think of it or not?"

"I did," Alyosha answered softly. Even Rakitin felt embarrassed.

"What? You thought of it, too?" he cried.

"I . . . I didn't really think of it," Alyosha muttered, "but when you began speaking so strangely about it just now, it seemed to me that I had thought of it myself."

"You see? (And how clearly you expressed it!) You see? Today, looking at your papa and your brother Mitenka, you thought about a crime. So I'm not mistaken, then?"

"But wait, wait," Alyosha interrupted uneasily, "where did you get all that . . . ? And why does it concern you so much in the first place?"

"Two different questions, but natural ones. I shall answer them separately. Where did I get it? I'd have gotten nothing if today I hadn't suddenly understood Dmitri Fyodorovich, your brother, fully for what he is, all at once and suddenly, fully for what he is. By one particular trait I grasped him all at once. Such honest but passionate people have a line that must not be crossed. Otherwise—otherwise he'll even put a knife in his own papa. And the papa, a drunken and unbridled libertine, never knew any measure in anything—both of them unable to hold back, and both of them, *plop*, into the ditch . . ."

"No, Misha, no, if that's all it is, then you've reassured me. It won't come to that."

"And why are you shaking all over? I'll tell you one thing: granted he's an honest man, Mitenka, I mean (he's stupid but honest), still he's a sensualist. That is his definition, and his whole inner essence. It's his father who gave him his base sensuality. I'm really surprised at you, Alyosha: how can you be a virgin? You're a Karamazov, too! In your family sensuality is carried to the point of fever. So these three sensualists are now eyeing each other with knives in their boots. The three of them are at loggerheads, and maybe you're the fourth."

"You are mistaken about that woman. Dmitri . . . despises her," Alyosha said, somehow shuddering.

"You mean Grushenka? No, brother, he doesn't despise her. If he's publicly traded his fiancée for her, he doesn't despise her. It's . . . it's something, brother, that you won't understand yet. It's that a man falls in love with some beautiful thing, with a woman's body, or even with just one part of a woman's body (a sensualist will understand that), and is ready to give his own children for it, to sell his father and mother, Russia and his native land, and though he's honest, he'll go and steal; though he's meek, he'll kill; though he's faithful, he'll betray. The singer of women's little feet, Pushkin, sang little feet in verse;[3] others don't sing, but they can't look at little feet without knots in the stomach. But it's not just little feet . . . Here, brother, contempt is no use, even if he does despise Grushenka. He may despise her, but he still can't tear himself away from her."

"I understand that," Alyosha suddenly blurted out.

"Really? No doubt you do, if you blurt it out like that, at the first mention," Rakitin said gleefully. "It escaped you, you just blurted it out inadvertently—which makes the confession all the more valuable. So for you it's already a familiar theme, you've already thought about it—sensuality, I mean. Ah, you virgin! You, Alyoshka, are the quiet type, you're a saint, I admit; you're the quiet type, but the devil knows what hasn't gone through your head, the devil knows what you don't know already! A virgin, and you've already dug so deep—I've been observing you for a long time. You are a Karamazov yourself, a full-fledged Karamazov—so race and selection do mean something. You're a sensualist after your father, and after your mother—a holy fool. Why are you trembling? Am I right? You know, Grushenka said to me: 'Bring him over (meaning you), and I'll pull his little cassock off.' She really asked me: bring him over! bring him over! And I wondered: what interests her so much in you? You know, she's an unusual woman, too!"

"Give her my regards, and tell her I won't come," Alyosha grinned crookedly. "Finish what you were saying, Mikhail, then I'll tell you what I think."

"What is there to finish? It's all clear. It's all the same old tune, brother. If there's a sensualist even in you, then what about your brother Ivan, your full brother? He's a Karamazov, too. The whole question of you Karamazovs comes down to this: you're sensualists, money-grubbers, and holy fools! Right now your brother Ivan is publishing little theological articles as a joke, for some unknown, stupid reason, since he himself is an atheist and admits the baseness of it—that's your brother Ivan. Besides which, he's stealing his dear brother Mitya's fiancée, and it looks like he'll reach that goal. And how? With Mitenka's own consent, because Mitenka himself is giving her up to him, just to get rid of her, so that he can run to Grushenka. All the while being a noble and disinterested man—make note of that. Such people are the most fatal of all! The devil alone can sort you all out after that: he admits his own baseness even while he throws himself into it! But there's more: now dear old papa crosses Mitenka's path. He's lost his mind over Grushenka, starts drooling the moment he sees her. Why do you think he caused such a scandal in the cell just now? Only because of her, because Miusov dared to call her a loose creature. He's worse than a lovesick tomcat. Before, she only served him on salary in his shady tavern business, but now he suddenly sees and realizes, he goes wild, he pesters her with his propositions—not honorable ones, of course. So the papa and his boy will run into each other on that path. And Grushenka takes neither the one nor the other; so far she's still hedging and teasing them both, trying to decide which of them will be more profitable, because while she might be able to grab a lot of money from the papa, still he won't marry her, and maybe in the end he'll get piggish and shut his purse. In which case, Mitenka, too, has his value; he has no money, but he's capable of marrying her. Oh, yes, sir, he's capable of marrying her! Of dropping his fiancée, an incomparable beauty, Katerina Ivanovna, rich, an aristocrat and a colonel's daughter, and marrying Grushenka, formerly the kept woman of an old shopkeeper, a profligate peasant, the town mayor Samsonov. Out of all that some criminal conflict may indeed come. And that is what your brother Ivan is waiting for. He'll be in clover. He'll acquire Katerina Ivanovna, whom he's pining for, and also grab her dowry of sixty thousand roubles. For a poor, bare little fellow like him, that's rather tempting to start with. And note: not only will he not offend Mitya, he'll even be doing him an undying service. Because I know for certain that Mitenka himself, just last week, when he got drunk with some gypsy women, shouted out loud in the tavern that he was not worthy of his fiancée Katenka, but that Ivan, his brother, he was worthy of her. And in the end, Katerina Ivanovna herself will not, of course, reject such a charmer as Ivan Fyodorovich; even now she's already hesitating between the two of them. And how is it that Ivan has seduced you all, that you're all so in awe of him? He's laughing at you: he's sitting there in clover, relishing at your expense!"

"How do you know all that? What makes you speak so certainly?" Alyosha suddenly asked curtly, frowning.

"Why are you asking now, and why are you afraid of my answer beforehand? It means you admit that I'm right."

"You dislike Ivan. Ivan will not be tempted by money."

"Is that so? And what of Katerina Ivanovna's beauty? It's not just a matter of money, though sixty thousand is tempting enough."

"Ivan aims higher than that. Ivan won't be tempted by thousands either. Ivan is not seeking money, or ease. Perhaps he is seeking suffering."

"What sort of dream is that? Oh, you . . . gentry!"

"Ah, Misha, his is a stormy soul. His mind is held captive. There is a great and unresolved thought in him. He's one of those who don't need millions, but need to resolve their thought."

"Literary theft, Alyoshka. You're paraphrasing your elder. Look what a riddle Ivan has set you!" Rakitin shouted with obvious spite. He even lost countenance, and his lips twisted. "And the riddle is a stupid one, there's nothing to solve. Use your head and you'll understand. His article is ridiculous and absurd. And did you hear his stupid theory just now: 'If there is no immortality of the soul, then there is no virtue, and therefore everything is permitted.' (And remember, by the way, how your brother Mitenka shouted, 'I'll remember!') A tempting theory for scoundrels . . . I'm being abusive, which is foolish . . . not for scoundrels, but for boasting schoolboys with 'unresolved depths of thought.' He's just a show-off, and all it amounts to is: 'On the one hand one can't help admitting . . . , on the other hand one can't help confessing . . . !'[4] His whole theory is squalid. Mankind will find strength in itself to live for virtue, even without believing in the immortality of the soul! Find it in the love of liberty, equality, fraternity . . ."

Rakitin became flushed and could hardly contain himself. But suddenly, as if remembering something, he stopped.

"Well, enough," he smiled even more twistedly than before. "Why are you laughing? Do you think it's all just platitudes?"

"No, I didn't even think of thinking they were platitudes. You're intelligent, but . . . forget it, it was just a foolish grin. I understand why you get so flushed, Misha. From your excitement I guessed that you yourself are not indifferent to Katerina Ivanovna. I've long suspected it, brother, and that is why you don't like my brother Ivan. Are you jealous of him?"

"And of her money, too? Go on, say it!"

"No, I won't say anything about money. I'm not going to insult you."

"I'll believe it only because it's you who say it, but still, the devil take you and your brother Ivan! Will no one understand that it's quite possible to dislike him even without Katerina Ivanovna? Why should I like him, damn it? He deigns to abuse me. Don't I have the right to abuse him?"

"I've never heard him say anything about you, good or bad. He never speaks of you at all."

"But I have heard that the day before yesterday, at Katerina Ivanovna's, he was trouncing me right and left—that's how interested he is in your humble servant! And after that, brother, I don't know who is jealous of whom! He was so good as to opine that if, perchance, I do not pursue the career of archimandrite in the very near future and have myself tonsured,[5] then I will most certainly go to Petersburg and join some thick journal, most certainly in the criticism section; I will write for a dozen years and in the end take over the journal. And I will go on publishing it, most certainly with a liberal and atheistic slant, with a socialistic tinge, with even a little gloss of socialism, but with my ears open, that is, essentially, running with the hare and hunting with the hounds, and pulling the wool over the fools' eyes. The aim of my career, according to your kind brother's interpretation, will be not to allow that tinge of socialism to prevent me from laying aside the subscription money in my bank account and investing it occasionally under the guidance of some little Yid, until I've built myself a big town house in Petersburg, to which I can transfer my editorial office, while renting out the rest of the floors to tenants. He has even chosen the place for this house: by the New Stone Bridge over the Neva, which they say is being planned in Petersburg to connect the Liteiny Prospect with the Vyborg side . . ."

"Ah, Misha, maybe it will all be just as he says, to the last word!" Alyosha suddenly cried out, unable to resist and laughing gaily.

"So you, too, are venturing into sarcasm, Alexei Fyodorovich."

"No, no, I'm joking, forgive me. I have something quite different on my mind. However, excuse me, but who could have informed you of all those details, or where could you have heard them? Surely you could not have been present at Katerina Ivanovna's when he was talking about you?"

"I wasn't, but Dmitri Fyodorovich was, and I heard it all with my own ears from the same Dmitri Fyodorovich; that is, if you like, he wasn't telling it to me, but I was eavesdropping, unwillingly of course, because I was sitting at Grushenka's, in her bedroom, and couldn't leave all the while Dmitri Fyodorovich was in the next room."

"Ah, yes, I forgot, she's your relative . . ."

"My relative? Grushenka, my relative?" Rakitin suddenly cried out, blushing all over. "You must be crazy! Sick in the head!"

"What? Isn't she your relative? I heard she was . . ."

"Where could you have heard that? No, you gentleman Karamazovs pose as some sort of great and ancient nobility, when your father played the fool at other men's tables and got fed in the kitchen out of charity. Granted I'm only a priest's son and a worm next to you noblemen, but still don't go offending me so gaily and easily. I, too, have my honor, Alexei Fyodorovich. I could not be the relative of Grushenka, a loose woman, kindly understand that, sir!"

Rakitin was extremely irritated.

"Forgive me, for God's sake, I had no idea, and besides, why is she a loose woman? Is she . . . that sort?" Alyosha suddenly blushed. "I repeat, I heard she was your relative. You visit her often, and told me yourself that you have no amorous relations with her . . . It never occurred to me that you of all people despised her so much! Does she really deserve it?"

"I may have my own reasons for visiting her; let that be enough for you. As for our relations, your good brother or even your own papa himself is more likely to foist her on you than on me. Well, here we are. Better march off to the kitchen. Hah, what's this, what's happening? Are we late? They couldn't have finished dinner so soon! Or is it some more Karamazov mischief? That must be it. There goes your father, with Ivan Fyodorovich after him. They've bolted from the Father Superior's. Look, Father Isidore is shouting something at them from the porch. And your father is shouting, too, and waving his arms—he must be swearing. Hah, and Miusov, too, has left in his carriage, there he goes. And the landowner Maximov is running—we've had a scandal! It means there wasn't any dinner! Maybe they thrashed the Superior? Or got thrashed themselves? That would be a good one . . . !"

Rakitin's exclamations were not without point. There had indeed been a scandal, unheard-of and unexpected. It all happened "by inspiration."

Chapter 8

Scandal

Miusov and Ivan Fyodorovich were already entering the Superior's rooms when a sort of delicate process quickly transpired in Pyotr Alexandrovich, a genuinely decent and delicate man: he felt ashamed of his anger. He felt within himself that, essentially, his contempt for the worthless Fyodor Pavlovich should have been such as to have kept him from losing his composure in the elder's cell and getting as lost as he had done himself. "It was not at all the monks' fault, in any case," he suddenly decided on the Superior's porch, "and if there are decent people here as well (this Father Nikolai, the Superior, seems to be of the gentry, too), then why not be nice, amiable, and courteous with them . . . ? I shan't argue, I shall even yes them in everything, I shall seduce them with amiability, and . . . and . . . finally prove to them that I am not of the same society as that Aesop, that buffoon, that Pierrot, and was taken in just as they all were . . ."

The controversial wood-cutting in the forest and the fishing (where it all went on he himself did not know) he determined to relinquish to them finally, once and for all, that very day, and to stop his court actions against the monastery, the more so since it was all worth very little anyway.

All these good intentions were further strengthened when they entered the Father Superior's dining room. There was no dining room, incidentally, because the entire apartment in fact consisted of two rooms, though indeed far more spacious and comfortable than the elder's. But the furnishings of the rooms were not more distinguished by any special comfort: leather-covered mahogany, in the old fashion of the twenties; the floors were not even painted; yet everything was bright and clean, there were many costly plants in the windows; but the main luxury at the moment was, naturally, the luxuriously laid table—once again, relatively speaking, by the way: a clean table cloth, sparkling dishes, perfectly baked bread of three kinds, two bottles of wine, two bottles of excellent monastery mead, and a big glass jug of monastery kvass, famous throughout the neighborhood. There was no vodka at all. Rakitin recounted afterwards that the dinner this time consisted of five courses: a sturgeon soup with little fish pies; then boiled fish prepared in some particular and perfect way; then salmon cakes, ice cream and fruit compote, and finally a little custard resembling blancmange. Rakitin sniffed it all out, unable to restrain himself, peeking for that purpose into the Superior's kitchen, where he also had his connections. He had connections everywhere and made spies everywhere. He had a restless and covetous heart. He was fully aware of his considerable abilities, but in his conceit he nervously exaggerated them. He knew for certain that he would become a figure of some sort, but Alyosha, who was very attached to him, was tormented that his friend Rakitin was dishonest and was decidedly unaware of it; that, on the contrary, knowing he wouldn't steal money from the table, he ultimately considered himself a man of the highest integrity. Here neither Alyosha nor anyone else could do anything.

Rakitin, as an insignificant person, could not have been invited to dinner, but Father Iosif and Father Paissy, along with another hieromonk, were invited. They were already waiting in the Superior's dining room when Pyotr Alexandrovich, Kalganov, and Ivan Fyodorovich entered. The landowner Maximov was also waiting to one side. The Father Superior stepped forward into the middle of the room to meet his guests. He was a tall, lean, but still vigorous old man, dark-haired with much gray, and with a long, pious, and important face. He bowed silently to his guests, and this time they came up to receive the blessing. Miusov even risked trying to kiss his hand, but the Superior somehow snatched it away just in time, and the kiss did not take place. But Ivan Fyodorovich and Kalganov this time got the full blessing, that is, with the most simple-hearted and ordinary smack on the hand.

"We really must beg your forgiveness, your noble reverence,"[1] Pyotr Alexandrovich began, grinning affably, but still in a solemn and respectful tone, "for arriving by ourselves, without our fellow guest, Fyodor Pavlovich, whom you also invited. He felt obliged to miss your dinner, and not without reason. In the reverend Father Zosima's cell, being carried away by his unfortunate family quarrel with his son, he spoke certain quite inappropriate words . . . quite indecent, that is . . . of which it appears"—he glanced at the hieromonks—"your noble reverence has already been informed. And therefore, aware that he was at fault and sincerely repentant, he felt ashamed, and, unable to overcome it, asked us, myself and his son, Ivan Fyodorovich, to declare before you his sincere regret, remorse, and repentance . . . In a word, he hopes and wishes to make up for it all later, and for now, asking your blessing, he begs you to forget what has happened . . ."

Miusov fell silent. Having spoken the final words of his tirade, he was left feeling thoroughly pleased with himself, so much so that not even a trace of his recent irritation remained in his soul. He again fully and sincerely loved mankind. The Superior, having listened to him with a solemn air, inclined his head slightly and spoke in reply:

"I most sincerely regret our guest's absence. Perhaps over our dinner he would have come to love us, and we him. Gentlemen, welcome to my table."

He stood facing the icon and began to pray aloud. They all bowed their heads respectfully, and the landowner Maximov even edged somehow especially forward, with his palms pressed together in special reverence.

And at that moment Fyodor Pavlovich cut his last caper. It should be noted that he indeed intended to leave and indeed felt the impossibility, after his shameful behavior in the elder's cell, of going to dinner at the Superior's as if nothing had happened. It was not that he was so very much ashamed and blamed himself; perhaps even quite the contrary; but still he felt that to stay for dinner would really be improper. But when his rattling carriage drew up to the porch of the inn, and he was already getting into it, he suddenly stopped. He remembered his own words at the elder's: "It always seems to me, when I go somewhere, that I am lower than everyone else and that they all take me for a buffoon—so let me indeed play the buffoon, because all of you, to a man, are lower and stupider than I am." He wanted to revenge himself on all of them for his own nasty tricks. At the same moment he suddenly remembered being asked once before, at some point: "Why do you hate so-and-so so much?" And he had replied then, in a fit of buffoonish impudence: "I'll tell you why: he never did anything to me, it's true, but I once played a most shameless nasty trick on him, and the moment I did it, I immediately hated him for it." Remembering it now, he sniggered softly and maliciously, in a moment's hesitation. His eyes gleamed, and his lips even trembled. "Since I've started it, I may as well finish it," he decided suddenly. His innermost feeling at that moment might be expressed in the following words: "There is no way to rehabilitate myself now, so why don't I just spit all over them without any shame; tell them, 'You'll never make me ashamed, and that's that!' " He ordered the coachman to wait, and with quick steps went back to the monastery, straight to the Superior's. He did not quite know what he was going to do, but he knew that he was no longer in control of himself—a little push, and in no time he would reach the utmost limits of some abomination—only an abomination, by the way, never anything criminal, never an escapade punishable by law. In that respect he always managed to restrain himself, and even amazed himself in some cases. He appeared in the Superior's dining room precisely at the moment when the prayer was over and everyone was moving to the table. He stopped on the threshold, looked around at the gathering, and laughed his long, insolent, wicked little laugh, staring them all valiantly in the face.

"They thought I was gone, and here I am!" he shouted for all to hear.

For a moment everyone stared straight at him in silence, and then suddenly they all felt that now something revolting, absurd, and undoubtedly scandalous was about to happen. Pyotr Alexandrovich, from a most benign mood, immediately turned ferocious. All that had just died out and grown quiet in his heart instantly resurrected and rose up.

"No! This I cannot bear!" he cried, "I absolutely cannot and . . . I simply cannot!"

The blood rushed to his head. He even stammered, but he could not be bothered about style and grabbed his hat.

"What is it that he cannot," Fyodor Pavlovich cried out, "that he 'absolutely cannot and simply cannot'? Your reverence, may I come in? Will you accept me at your table?"

"You are most cordially welcome," the Superior replied. "Gentlemen!" he added suddenly, "allow me to ask you earnestly to lay aside your incidental quarrels and come together in love and familial harmony, with a prayer to the Lord, over our humble meal . . ."

"No, no, impossible," cried Pyotr Alexandrovich, as if beside himself.

"If it's impossible for Pyotr Alexandrovich, then it's impossible for me—I won't stay either. That is why I came. I will be with Pyotr Alexandrovich wherever he goes: if you leave, I leave, Pyotr Alexandrovich, and if you stay, I stay. You really stung him with that 'familial harmony,' Father Superior: he doesn't consider himself my relative! Am I right, von Sohn? That's von Sohn over there. Greetings, von Sohn!"[2]

"Are you . . . is it me, sir?" muttered the amazed landowner Maximov.

"Of course it's you," Fyodor Pavlovich shouted. "Who else? The Father Superior couldn't be von Sohn!"

"But I am not von Sohn either, I am Maximov."

"No, you're von Sohn. Your reverence, do you know about von Sohn? It was a murder case: he was killed in a house of fornication—is that what you call those places?—they killed him and robbed him and, despite his venerable age, stuffed him into a box, nailed it shut, and sent it from Petersburg to

Moscow in a baggage car, with a label and everything. And as they nailed him up, the dancing harlots were singing songs to the psaltery, I mean the pianoforte. And this is that same von Sohn. He rose from the dead, didn't you, von Sohn?"

"What's that? How can he!" came from the group of hieromonks.

"Let's go!" cried Pyotr Alexandrovich, turning to Kalganov.

"No, sir, allow me!" Fyodor Pavlovich interrupted shrilly, taking another step into the room. "Allow me to finish. You defamed me there in the cell, as if I'd behaved disrespectfully—namely, by shouting about gudgeons. Pyotr Alexandrovich Miusov, my relative, likes it when one speaks with *plus de noblesse que de sincerité*, and I, conversely, like to speak with *plus de sincerité que de noblesse*, and—to hell with *noblesse*![3] Right, von Sohn? Excuse me, Father Superior, although I'm a buffoon and play the buffoon, still I'm an honorable knight and I want to have my say. Yes, I'm an honorable knight, and in Pyotr Alexandrovich there is wounded vanity and nothing more. I came here today, perhaps, to look around and have my say. My son Alexei is saving his soul here; I'm a father, I'm concerned for his future, and I ought to be concerned. I was listening and performing and quietly observing, and now I want to give you the last act of the performance. How is it with us generally? With us, once a thing falls, it lies there. With us, if a thing once falls, it can lie there forever. I won't have it, sirs! I want to rise! Holy fathers, you make me indignant. Confession is a great mystery before which I stand in awe and am ready to bow down, and here suddenly everyone in the cell falls on his knees and confesses out loud. Is it proper to confess out loud? The Holy Fathers instituted whispered confession, only then is there any mystery in it, and that has been so since olden times.[4] Otherwise how am I to explain to him in front of everyone that I did this and that, for instance . . . well, this and that, you know what I mean! Sometimes it's even indecent to say it. There would be a scandal! No, fathers, one might even get drawn into flagellationism with you here . . .[5] I shall write to the Synod the first chance I get,[6] and I shall take my son Alexei home . . ."

Nota bene: Fyodor Pavlovich had heard the ringing of rumor's bells. At one time there had been malicious gossip, which even reached the Bishop (and not only about our monastery but about others where the institution of elders had been established), that the elders seemed to be respected overmuch, to the detriment even of the position of Superior, and that, among other things, the elders allegedly abused the sacrament of confession, and so on and so forth. The accusations were absurd and eventually died down of themselves, both here and everywhere. But the silly devil who had snatched up Fyodor Pavlovich and carried him on his own nerves further and further into the shameful deep prompted him to this former accusation, which Fyodor Pavlovich could not even begin to understand. Nor did he manage to formulate it correctly, the more so since this time no one had knelt down in the elder's cell and confessed aloud, so that Fyodor Pavlovich could have seen nothing of the sort and was simply repeating old rumors and gossip, which he recalled haphazardly. But, having uttered this foolishness, he suddenly felt that he had blurted out some absurd nonsense, and he wanted at once to prove to his listeners and above all to himself that what he had said was not nonsense at all. And though he knew perfectly well that with each word he would be adding more and more absurdities of the same sort to the nonsense he had already spoken, still he could not help himself and plunged headlong off the mountain.

"How vile!" cried Pyotr Alexandrovich.

"Excuse me," the Superior said suddenly. "Of old it was said: 'And they began to speak against me many things and evil things. And I heard it and said within myself: this is the medicine of Jesus, which he has sent me to heal my vain soul.' And therefore we, too, humbly thank you, our precious guest."

And he bowed deeply to Fyodor Pavlovich.

"Tut, tut, tut! Humbug and old phrases! Old phrases and old sentences! Old lies and conventional bows! We know these bows! 'A kiss on the lips and a dagger in the heart,' as in Schiller's *Robbers*.[7] I don't like falseness, fathers, I want the truth! And the truth is not in gudgeons, I've already declared as much! Father monks, why do you fast? Why do you expect a heavenly reward for that? For such a reward, I'll go and start fasting, too! No, holy monk, try being virtuous in life, be useful to society without shutting yourself up in a monastery on other people's bread, and without expecting any reward up there—that's a little more difficult. I, too, can talk sensibly, Father Superior. What have we got here?" He went up to the table. "Old port wine from Factori's, Médoc bottled by Eliseyev Brothers![8] A far cry from gudgeons, eh, fathers? Look at all these bottles the fathers have set out—heh, heh, heh! And who has provided it all? The Russian peasant, the laborer, bringing you the pittance earned by his callused hands, taking it from his family, from the needs of the state! You, holy fathers, are sucking the people's blood!"

"That is altogether unworthy on your part," said Father Iosif. Father Paissy was stubbornly silent. Miusov rushed from the room, with Kalganov behind him.

"Well, fathers, I will follow Pyotr Alexandrovich! And I won't come back again, even if you beg me on bended knee, I won't come back. I sent you a thousand roubles, and now you've got your eyes cocked, heh, heh, heh! No, I won't add any more. I'm taking revenge for my lost youth, for all my humiliations!" He pounded the table with his fist in a fit of sham emotion. "This little monastery has played a big part in my life! I've shed many a bitter tear because of it! You turned my wife, the shrieker, against me. You cursed me at all seven councils,[9] you smeared my name over the whole district! Enough, fathers! This is the age of liberalism, the age of steamships and railways. You'll get nothing from me—not a thousand roubles, not a hundred roubles, not even a hundred kopecks!"

Another *nota bene*: our monastery never meant anything special in his life, and he had never shed any bitter tears because of it. But he was so carried away by his own sham tears that for a moment he almost believed himself; he even as much as wept from self-pity; but at the same moment he felt it was time to rein himself in. In reply to his wicked lie, the Superior inclined his head and again spoke imposingly:

"It is said, again: 'Suffer with joy the dishonor which providentially befalleth thee, and be not troubled, neither hate him who dishonoreth thee.' So shall we do."

"Tut, tut, tut! They will have bethought themselves and the rest of that balderdash! You bethink yourselves, fathers, and I will go. And I'm taking my son Alexei away from here forever, on my parental authority. Ivan Fyodorovich, my most respectful son, allow me to order you to follow me! Von Sohn, why should you stay here? Come home with me now. We'll have fun. It's just a mile away. Instead of lenten oil, I'll serve suckling pig with kasha stuffing; we'll have dinner, then some cognac, and liqueurs, I have a cloudberry liqueur . . . Hey, von Sohn, don't miss your chance!"

He went out shouting and waving his arms. It was at this moment that Rakitin saw him leaving and pointed him out to Alyosha.

"Alexei!" his father cried from far off when he saw him, "move back in with me today, for good, bring your pillow and mattress, don't leave a trace behind!"

Alyosha stopped in his tracks, silently and attentively observing the scene. Fyodor Pavlovich meanwhile got into his carriage, and Ivan Fyodorovich started to get in after him, silently and glumly, without even turning to say good-bye to Alyosha. But at that point one more clownish and almost incredible scene took place, which put the finishing touch to the whole episode. The landowner Maximov suddenly appeared on the step of the carriage. He ran up, panting, afraid of being late. Alyosha and Rakitin saw him running. He was in such a hurry that in his impatience he put his foot on the step where Ivan Fyodorovich's left foot was still standing and, clutching the side, started to jump into the carriage.

"Me, too, I'm coming with you!" he cried, jumping, laughing his merry little laugh, with a blissful look on his face, ready for anything. "Take me, too!"

"Didn't I tell you?" Fyodor Pavlovich cried in delight. "He's von Sohn! He's the real von Sohn, risen from the dead! But how did you get away? What did you vonsohn in there, how did you manage to get out of the dinner? It takes a brazen face! I have one, but I'm still surprised at yours! Jump, jump in quick! Let him in, Vanya, it will be fun. We'll find room for him somewhere at our feet. Will you lie at our feet, von Sohn? Or shall we stick him in the box with the coachman . . . ? Jump up in the box, von Sohn . . . !"

But Ivan Fyodorovich, who had sat down by then, silently and with all his force gave Maximov a sudden shove in the chest that sent him flying for two yards. It was only by chance that he did not fall.

"Drive!" Ivan Fyodorovich shouted angrily to the coachman.

"What's got into you? What's got into you? Why did you do that to him?" Fyodor Pavlovich heaved himself up, but the carriage was already moving. Ivan Fyodorovich did not answer.

"How do you like that?" Fyodor Pavlovich said again after two minutes of silence, looking askance at his boy. "You started this whole monastery business, you urged it, you approved it, why are you angry now?"

"Enough of this drivel. Take a little break, now at least," Ivan Fyodorovich snapped sternly.

Fyodor Pavlovich was again silent for about two minutes.

"Be nice to have some cognac," he remarked sententiously. But Ivan Fyodorovich did not reply.

"You'll have a drink, too, when we get there."

Ivan Fyodorovich still said nothing.

Fyodor Pavlovich waited for about two minutes more.

"I'll still take Alyoshka from the monastery, despite the fact that it will be very unpleasant for you, my most respectful Karl von Moor."

Ivan Fyodorovich shrugged contemptuously and, turning away, began staring at the road. They did not speak again until they reached home.

BOOK III: THE SENSUALISTS

Chapter 1

In the Servants' Quarters

The house of Fyodor Pavlovich Karamazov stood far from in the very center of town, yet not quite on the outskirts. It was rather decrepit, but had a pleasant appearance: one-storied, with an attic, painted a gray color, and with a red iron roof. However, it had many good years left, and was roomy and snug. It had all sorts of closets, all sorts of nooks and unexpected little stairways. There were rats in it, but Fyodor Pavlovich was not altogether angry with them: "Still, it's not so boring in the evenings when one is alone." And indeed he had the custom of dismissing the servants to their cottage for the night and locking himself up in the house alone for the whole night. This cottage stood in the yard. It was spacious and solid; and Fyodor Pavlovich also appointed his kitchen to be there, though there was a kitchen in the main house: he did not like kitchen smells, and food was carried across the yard winter and summer. As a matter of fact, the house had been built for a large family: it could have accommodated five times as many masters and servants. But at the moment of our story, only Fyodor Pavlovich and Ivan Fyodorovich lived in the house, and in the cottage there were just three servants: the old man Grigory, the old woman Marfa, his wife, and the servant Smerdyakov, who was still a young man. We must say a little more in particular about these three auxiliary persons. We have already said enough, however, about old Grigory Vasilievich Kutuzov. He was a firm and unwavering man, who persistently and directly pursued his point, provided that this point for some reason (often surprisingly illogical) stood before him as an immutable truth. Generally speaking, he was honest and incorruptible. His wife, Marfa Ignatievna, despite the fact that she had submitted unquestioningly to her husband's will all her life, pestered him terribly, just after the emancipation of the serfs, for example, to leave Fyodor Pavlovich and move to Moscow to open some sort of little shop there (they had some money); but Grigory then decided once and for all that the woman was talking nonsense, "for every woman is without honor," and that they should not leave their former master, whatever sort he was, "for it was now their duty."

"Do you understand what duty is?" he asked Marfa Ignatievna.

"I understand about duty, Grigory Vasilievich, but why it should be our duty to stay here, that I do not understand at all," Marfa Ignatievna replied firmly.

"Don't understand, then, but that is how it will be. Henceforth hold your tongue."

And so it was: they did not leave, and Fyodor Pavlovich appointed them a salary, a small one, but he paid it. Besides that, Grigory knew that he had an unquestionable influence over his master. He felt it, and he was right. A cunning and obstinate buffoon, Fyodor Pavlovich, while he had a very firm character "in certain things in life," as he himself put it, showed, to his own surprise, even a rather weakish character in certain other "things in life." And he knew which ones, he knew and was afraid of many things. In certain things in life one had to be on one's guard, and that was difficult without a faithful man. And Grigory was a most faithful man. It even so happened that many times in the course of his career, Fyodor Pavlovich might have been beaten, and beaten badly, but Grigory always came to his rescue, though he admonished him each time afterwards. But Fyodor Pavlovich would not have been afraid of beatings alone: there were higher occasions, even rather subtle and complicated ones, when Fyodor Pavlovich himself would have been unable, perhaps, to explain this remarkable need for a close and faithful man that he would sometimes, all of a sudden, momentarily and inconceivably, begin to feel in himself. These occasions were almost morbid: most depraved, and, in his sensuality, often as cruel as a wicked insect, Fyodor Pavlovich at times suddenly felt in himself, in his drunken moments, a spiritual fear, a moral shock, that almost, so to speak, resounded physically in his soul. "On those occasions it's as if my soul were fluttering in my throat," he sometimes used to say. And at such moments he was glad that nearby, close at hand, maybe not in the same room but in the cottage, there was such a man, firm, devoted, not at all like himself, not depraved, who, though he saw all this depravity going on and knew all the secrets, still put up with it all out of devotion, did not protest, and—above all—did not reproach him or threaten him with anything either in this age or in the age to come; and who would defend him if need be—from whom? From someone unknown, but terrible and dangerous. The thing precisely was that there should be *another* man, ancient and amicable, who could be summoned in a morbid moment, so that he could look him in the face and perhaps exchange a few words, even quite irrelevant words, and if it's all right and he does not get angry, then somehow it eases the heart, but if he gets angry, well, then it's a little sadder. It happened (very rarely, however) that Fyodor Pavlovich would even go at night to the cottage to wake Grigory so that Grigory could come to him for a moment. Grigory would come, and Fyodor Pavlovich would begin talking about perfect trifles, and would soon let him go, sometimes even with a little joke or jibe, and would spit and go to bed himself, and sleep the sleep of the blessed. Something of this sort happened to Fyodor Pavlovich when Alyosha arrived. Alyosha "pierced his heart" because he "lived there, saw everything, and condemned nothing." Moreover, he brought something unprecedented with him: a complete lack of contempt for him, the old man, and, on the contrary, an unvarying affection and a perfectly natural, single-hearted attachment to him, little though he deserved it. All of this came as a perfect surprise to the solitary old lecher; it was quite unexpected for him, who until then had loved only "iniquity." When Alyosha left, he admitted to himself that he had understood something that until then he had been unwilling to understand.

I mentioned at the beginning of my story that Grigory hated Adelaida Ivanovna, Fyodor Pavlovich's first wife and the mother of his first son, Dmitri Fyodorovich, and that, on the contrary, he defended his second wife, the shrieker, Sofia Ivanovna, against his master himself and against all who might chance to speak a bad or flippant word about her. His sympathy for the unfortunate woman became something sacred to him, so that even twenty years later he would not suffer a slighting allusion to her from anyone at all, and would at once object to the offender. Outwardly Grigory was a cold and pompous man, taciturn, delivering himself of weighty, unfrivolous words. In the same way, it was impossible to tell at first glance whether he loved his meek, obedient wife or not, and yet he really did love her, and she, of course, knew it. This Marfa Ignatievna not only was not a stupid woman, but was even perhaps more intelligent than her husband, at least more reasonable than he in everyday things, and yet she submitted to him without a murmur and without complaint from the very beginning of their married life, and unquestionably respected his spiritual superiority. It was remarkable that all their life they spoke very little to each other, and then only of the most necessary daily things. Pompous and majestic Grigory always thought through all his affairs and concerns by himself, and Marfa Ignatievna had long ago understood once and for all that he had absolutely no need of her advice. She felt that her husband valued her silence and took it as a sign of her intelligence. He had never beaten her, save only once, and then slightly. In the first year of the marriage of Adelaida Ivanovna and Fyodor Pavlovich, one day in the village, the village girls and women, who were then still serfs, were gathered in the master's yard to sing and dance. They began "In the Meadows," and suddenly Marfa Ignatievna, then still a young woman, leaped out in front of the chorus and performed the "Russian dance" in a special manner, not as village women did it, but as she used to dance when she was a servant of the wealthy Miusovs, in their own household theater, where they were taught to dance by a dancing master invited from Moscow. Grigory saw his wife's performance and, back home, an hour later, taught her a lesson by pulling her hair a little. There the beatings ended forever, and were not repeated even once in the rest of their life, and Marfa Ignatievna also foreswore dancing.

God did not grant them children; there was one baby, but it died. Grigory obviously loved children, and did not even conceal it, that is, he was not ashamed to show it. After Adelaida Ivanovna fled, he took charge of Dmitri Fyodorovich, then a three-year-old boy, and fussed over him for almost a year, combing his hair and even washing him in a tub himself. He took the same trouble over Ivan Fyodorovich, and then over Alyosha, for which he received a slap in the face; but I have already related all that. His own baby gave him only the joy of hope while Marfa Ignatievna was still pregnant. When it was born, it struck his heart with grief and horror. The fact is that the boy was born with six fingers.[1] Seeing this, Grigory was so mortified that he not only kept silent up to the very day of the baptism, but even went out to the garden especially to be silent. It was spring, and he spent all three days digging beds in the vegetable garden. On the third day they were to baptize the infant; by then Grigory had worked something out. Going into the cottage where the clergy and guests had gathered, including, finally, Fyodor Pavlovich himself, who came in person to be the godfather, he suddenly announced that "the baby oughtn't to be baptized at all"—announced it not loudly or in many words, but speaking each word through his teeth, and only gazing dully and intently at the priest.

"Why not?" asked the priest with good-humored astonishment.

"Because . . . it's a dragon . . . ," Grigory muttered.

"A dragon? How is he a dragon?"

Grigory was silent for a while.

"A confusion of natures occurred . . . ," he muttered, rather vaguely but very firmly, apparently unwilling to say more.

There was laughter, and of course the poor baby was baptized. At the font, Grigory prayed zealously, yet he did not change his opinion about the newborn. However, he did not interfere in any way, but for the two weeks that the sickly boy lived, he scarcely ever looked at him, did not even want to notice him, and kept away from the house most of the time. When the child died of thrush two weeks later, he himself put him into the little coffin, looked at him with deep grief, and when his shallow little grave was covered with earth, he knelt and prostrated before it. For many years afterwards he never once mentioned his child, and Marfa Ignatievna never once recalled her child in his presence, and whenever she happened to talk with someone about her "baby," she spoke in a whisper, even if Grigory Vasilievich was not present. As Marfa Ignatievna observed, ever since that little grave, he had mainly concerned himself with "the divine," reading the Lives of the Saints, mostly silently and by himself, and each time putting on his big, round silver spectacles. He rarely read aloud, except during Lent. He loved the Book of Job,[2] and somewhere obtained a copy of the homilies and sermons of "Our God-bearing Father, Isaac the Syrian,"[3] which he read persistently over many years, understanding almost nothing at all of it, but perhaps precisely for that reason prizing and loving it all the more. Of late he had noticed and begun to take an interest in the Flagellants,[4] for which there was an opportunity in the neighborhood; he was apparently shaken, but did not deem it necessary to convert to the new faith. Assiduous reading in "the divine" certainly added to the pomposity of his physiognomy.

He was perhaps inclined to mysticism. And here, as if by design, the occasion of the arrival in the world of his six-fingered baby and its death coincided with another very strange, unexpected, and original occurrence, which left, as he himself once put it later, "a stamp" on his soul. It happened that on the very day when they buried their six-fingered infant, Marfa Ignatievna, awakened during the night, heard what sounded like the cry of a newborn baby. She was frightened and woke her husband. He listened and observed that it was more likely someone groaning, "possibly a woman." He got up and dressed; it was a rather warm May night. Stepping out on the porch, he heard clearly that the groans were coming from the garden. But the garden was always locked from inside for the night, and it was impossible to get in except by that entrance, because the whole garden was surrounded with a high, sturdy fence. Grigory went back in, lighted a lantern, took the garden key, and paying no attention to the hysterical terror of his wife, who kept insisting that she heard a baby crying, and that it could only be her little boy crying and calling her, he silently went out to the garden. There he clearly recognized that the groans were coming from their bathhouse, which stood in the garden not far from the gate, and that they were indeed the groans of a woman. He opened the bathhouse door and was dumbfounded by what he saw: a local girl, a holy fool who roamed the streets and was known to the whole town as Stinking Lizaveta, had gotten into the bathhouse and just given birth to an infant. The infant was lying beside her, and she was dying beside him. She said nothing, for the simple reason that she had never been able to speak. But all this had better be explained separately.

Chapter 2

Stinking Lizaveta

There was one particular circumstance here that deeply shocked Grigory, ultimately strengthening in him an earlier, unpleasant and abhorrent, suspicion. This Stinking Lizaveta was a very short girl, "a wee bit under five feet," as many pious old ladies in our town touchingly recalled after her death. Her twenty-year-old face, healthy, broad, and ruddy, was completely idiotic; and the look in her eyes was fixed and unpleasant, though mild. All her life, both summer and winter, she went barefoot and wore only a hempen shift. Her nearly black hair, extremely thick and as curly as sheep's wool, formed a sort of huge hat on her head. Besides, it was always dirty with earth and mud, and had little leaves, splinters, and shavings stuck to it, because she always slept on the ground and in the mud. Her father was homeless and sickly, a failed tradesman named Ilya, who had fits of heavy drinking and for many years had been sponging off one of our well-to-do middle-class families as some sort of handyman. Lizaveta's mother had long been dead. Eternally ill and angry, Ilya used to beat Lizaveta brutally whenever she came home. But she rarely came home, because she went begging all over town as a holy fool of God. Both Ilya's employers and Ilya himself, and even many compassionate townspeople, mainly merchants and their wives, tried more than once to clothe Lizaveta more decently than in her one shift, and towards winter always put a sheepskin coat and a pair of boots on her; but she, though she let them put everything on her without protesting, usually went away somewhere, most often to the porch of the cathedral church, and took off all they had given her—whether a kerchief, a skirt, or a sheepskin coat and boots—left it there, and went away barefoot, dressed as before only in her shift. It happened once that the new governor of our province, observing our town on a visit, was greatly offended in his noblest feelings when he saw Lizaveta, and though he understood that she was a "holy fool," as had been reported to him, nevertheless pointed out that a young girl wandering around in her shift was an offense to public decency, and that a stop should be put to it. But the governor left and Lizaveta remained as she was. Her father finally died, and she thereby became even dearer, as an orphan, to all the pious people in town. Indeed, everyone seemed to like her, and even the boys did not tease or insult her, though our boys, especially at school, are a mischievous lot. She walked into strangers' houses and no one turned her out; quite the opposite, everyone was nice to her and gave her a kopeck. When she was given a kopeck, she would accept it and at once take it and put it in some poor box in the church or prison. When she was given a roll or a bun in the marketplace, she always went and gave this roll or bun to the first child she met, or else she would stop some one of our wealthiest ladies and give it to her; and the ladies would even gladly accept it. She herself lived only on black bread and water. She would sometimes stop in at an expensive shop and sit down, and though there were costly goods and money lying about, the owners were never wary of her: they knew that even if someone had put thousands down and forgotten them, she would not take a kopeck. She rarely went into a church, but she used to sleep on church porches, or in kitchen gardens, having climbed over someone's wattle fence (we still have many wattle fences instead of real fences, even to this day). She would go home—that is, to the home of those people her late father had lived with—about once a week, every day in winter, but only to spend the night, and she slept either in the hallway or in the barn. People marveled that she could endure such a life, but it was what she was used to; though she was small, she was remarkably sturdy. There were some among our gentry who said she did it all out of pride; but that somehow did not make sense; she could not even speak a word, and would only rarely move her tongue and mumble—how could she have been proud? And so it happened that once (this was quite a while ago), on a bright and warm September night, under a full moon, rather late by our standards, a bunch of drunken gentlemen, five or six hearty fellows, were returning home from their club "by the back way." There were wattle fences on both sides of the lane, behind which lay the kitchen gardens of the adjacent houses; the lane gave onto a plank bridge that crossed the long, stinking puddle it is our custom sometimes to call a stream. Near the wattle fence, among the nettles and burdock, our band discovered Lizaveta sleeping. The tipsy gentlemen looked down at her, laughing loudly, and began producing all sorts of unprintable witticisms. It suddenly occurred to one young sir to pose a completely bizarre question on an impossible subject: "Could anyone possibly regard such an animal as a woman, right now, for instance?" and so on. With lofty disdain, they all declared it impossible. But the group happened to include Fyodor Pavlovich, and he at once popped up and declared that, yes, she could be regarded as a woman, even very much so, and that there was even some piquancy in it of a special sort, and so on and so forth. It's true that at that time he was even overzealously establishing himself as a buffoon, and loved to pop up and amuse the gentlemen, ostensibly as an equal, of course, though in reality he was an absolute boor beside them. It was exactly at the same time that he received the news from Petersburg about the death of his first wife, Adelaida Ivanovna, and, with crêpe on his hat, went drinking and carousing so outrageously that some people in our town, even the most dissolute, cringed at the sight. The bunch, of course, burst out laughing at this unexpected opinion; one of them even began urging Fyodor Pavlovich on, but the rest spat even more disgustedly, though still with the utmost merriment, and finally they all went on their way. Later, Fyodor Pavlovich swore that he, too, had left with everyone else; maybe it was so, no one knows or ever knew for certain, but about five or six months later the whole town began asking, with great and genuine indignation, why Lizaveta was walking around pregnant, and trying to find out: who was the sinner? Who was the offender? And then suddenly a strange rumor spread all over town that the offender was none other than Fyodor Pavlovich. Where did the rumor come from? Of that bunch of drunken gentlemen, only one participant remained in our town by then, and he was an elderly and respectable state councillor,[1] a family man with grown-up daughters, who would by no means have spread anything, even if there were some truth in it. The rest of the participants, about five in all, had left by that time. But the rumor pointed straight at Fyodor Pavlovich, and kept pointing at him. Of course he never owned up to it: he would not even deign to answer such petty merchants and tradesmen. He was proud then, and refused to speak anywhere but in the company of the civil servants and gentlemen whom he entertained so well. This time Grigory stood up for his master energetically and with all his might, and not only defended him against all this slander but even got into arguments and disputes and managed to convince many people. "She herself is to blame, the low creature," he asserted, and the offender was none other than "Karp with the Screw" (this was the nickname of a horrible convict, well known at the time, who had just escaped from the provincial prison and was secretly living in our town). This surmise seemed plausible: Karp was remembered, it was specifically remembered that on those very nights, in autumn, he had been lurking around town and had robbed three people. But the whole affair and all this gossip not only did not turn people's sympathy away from the poor holy fool, but everyone began looking after her and protecting her all the more. The widow of the merchant Kondratiev, a wealthy woman, even arranged it all so that by the end of April she had brought Lizaveta to her house, intending to keep her there until she gave birth. They guarded her vigilantly, but in the end, despite their vigilance, on the very last day, in the evening, Lizaveta suddenly left the widow's house unobserved and turned up in Fyodor Pavlovich's garden. How she managed, in her condition, to climb over the high and sturdy garden fence remained rather a mystery. Some asserted that "someone had lifted her over," others that "it had lifted her over." Most likely everything happened in a natural, if rather tricky, way: Lizaveta, who knew how to climb over wattle fences to spend the night in people's kitchen gardens, somehow also climbed up onto Fyodor Pavlovich's fence and from there jumped down into the garden, despite her condition, though not without harming herself. Grigory rushed to Marfa Ignatievna and sent her to help Lizaveta while he himself ran to bring the midwife, an old tradeswoman who happened to live nearby. The child was saved, but Lizaveta died towards morning. Grigory took the infant, brought him into the house, sat his wife down, and put him in her lap near her breast: "God's orphan child is everyone's kin, all the more so for you and me. Our little dead one sent us this one, who was born of the devil's son and a righteous woman. Nurse him and weep no more." And so Marfa Ignatievna brought the baby up. He was baptized and given the name of Pavel; as for his patronymic, as if by unspoken agreement everyone began calling him Fyodorovich. Fyodor Pavlovich made no objection to anything, and even found it all amusing, though he still vehemently disavowed it all. The townspeople were pleased that he had taken the foundling in. Later on, Fyodor Pavlovich invented a last name for the child: he called him Smerdyakov, after the name of his mother, Lizaveta Smerdyashchaya.[2] This Smerdyakov became Fyodor Pavlovich's second servant, and was living, at the time our story begins, with old Grigory and Marfa in the servants' cottage. He was employed as a cook. I ought to say a little more about him in particular, but I am ashamed to distract my reader's attention for such a long time to such ordinary lackeys, and therefore I shall go back to my narrative, hoping that with regard to Smerdyakov things will somehow work themselves out in the further course of the story.

Chapter 3

The Confession of an Ardent Heart. In Verse

Alyosha, having heard the order his father shouted to him from the carriage as he was leaving the monastery, remained for a while in great perplexity. Not that he stood there like a post—such things did not happen to him. On the contrary, despite all his anxiety, he managed to go at once to the Superior's kitchen and find out what his father had done upstairs. And then he set off for town, hoping that on the way he would somehow succeed in resolving the problem that oppressed him. I hasten to say that he was not in the least afraid of his father's shouts or his order to move home with "pillows and mattress." He understood very well that the order to move, given aloud and with such ostentatious shouting, was given "in passion," even for the beauty of it, so to speak—just as recently in our town a tradesman who got a little too merry at his own birthday party, in front of his guests, became angry when they would not give him more vodka and suddenly began smashing his own dishes, tearing up his and his wife's clothes, breaking his furniture, and, finally, the windows, and all, again, for the beauty of it. The same sort of thing, of course, had now happened with his father. And of course the next day the too-merry tradesman sobered up and was sorry for the broken cups and dishes. Alyosha knew that the old man, too, would surely let him return to the monastery the next day, or perhaps even that same day. He was also quite sure that he was the last person his father would want to offend. Alyosha was sure that no one in the whole world would ever want to offend him, and not only would not want to but even would not be able to. For him this was an axiom, it was given once and for all, without argument, and in that sense he went ahead without any hesitation.

But at that moment another fear was stirring in him, of quite another sort, and all the more tormenting since he himself was unable to define it: namely, the fear of a woman, and, namely, of Katerina Ivanovna, who so insistently pleaded with him, in the note just given him by Madame Khokhlakov, to visit her for some reason. This demand, and the absolute necessity of going, immediately awakened some tormenting feeling in his heart, and all morning as time went on this feeling grew more and more painful, despite all the subsequent scenes and adventures in the monastery, and just now at the Superior's, and so on and so forth. He was afraid not because he did not know what she wanted to talk with him about or what he would answer. And generally it was not the woman in her that he was afraid of: he had little knowledge of women, of course, but still, all his life, from his very infancy right up to the monastery, he had lived only with women. It was this woman he was afraid of, precisely Katerina Ivanovna herself. He had been afraid of her ever since he saw her for the first time. And he had seen her only once or twice, perhaps even three times, and had even chanced to exchange a few words with her once. Her image he recalled as that of a beautiful, proud, and imperious girl. But it was not her beauty that tormented him, it was something else. It was precisely the inexplicable nature of his fear that now added to the fear itself. The girl's aims were the noblest, that he knew; she was striving to save his brother Dmitri, who was already guilty before her, and she was striving solely out of magnanimity. And yet, despite this awareness and the justice he could not fail to do to all these beautiful and magnanimous feelings, a chill ran down his spine the closer he came to her house.

He reckoned that he would not find his brother Ivan Fyodorovich, who was so close with her, at her house: his brother Ivan was certainly with their father now. It was even more certain that he would not find Dmitri there, and he sensed why. So their conversation would be one to one. He would have liked very much to see his brother Dmitri, to run over to him before this fateful conversation. He would have a word with him without showing him the letter. But his brother Dmitri lived far away and most likely was not at home either. He stood still for a moment and at last made a final decision. He crossed himself with an accustomed and hasty cross, at once smiled at something, and firmly went to meet his terrible lady.

He knew her house. But if he were to go to Main Street, then across the square and so on, it would be rather long. Our small town is extremely sprawling, and the distances can sometimes be quite great. Besides, his father was expecting him, had perhaps not yet forgotten his order, and might wax capricious, and therefore Alyosha had to hurry to get to one place and the other. As a result of all these considerations, he decided to cut the distance by going the back way, which he knew like his own hand. That meant passing along deserted fences, almost without a path, sometimes even climbing over other people's fences and past other people's yards, where, by the way, everyone knew him and said hello to him. That way he could get to Main Street twice as soon. In one place he even had to pass very close to his father's house—namely, by the garden adjacent to his father's, which belonged to a decrepit, crooked little house with four windows. The owner of this little house was, as Alyosha knew, a bedridden old woman who lived with her daughter, a former civilized chambermaid from the capital, who until recently had lived in generals' homes, and who now had come home for about a year already, because of the old woman's infirmity, and paraded around in smart dresses. The old woman and her daughter fell into terrible poverty, however, and even went every day to the kitchen of their neighbor, Fyodor Pavlovich, for soup and bread. Marfa Ignatievna gladly ladled out the soup for them. But the daughter, while coming for soup, did not sell a single one of her dresses, one of which even had a very long train. This last circumstance Alyosha had learned—quite accidentally, of course—from his friend Rakitin, who knew decidedly everything in their little town, and having learned it, he naturally forgot it at once. But coming up to the neighbor's garden, he suddenly remembered precisely about the train, quickly raised his downcast and thoughtful head, and . . . stumbled into a most unexpected meeting.

In the neighbors' garden, perched on something on the other side of the wattle fence, and sticking up half over it, stood his brother Dmitri Fyodorovich, wildly gesticulating, waving and beckoning to him, apparently afraid not only to shout but even to speak aloud, for fear of being heard. Alyosha at once ran up to the fence.

"It's a good thing you looked up yourself—I was just about to call out to you," Dmitri Fyodorovich whispered to him joyfully and hurriedly. "Climb up here! Quick! Ah, how good that you've come. I was just thinking about you . . ."

Alyosha was glad himself and was only wondering how to get over the fence. But "Mitya" caught hold of his elbow with his powerful hand and helped him to jump. Alyosha tucked up his cassock and jumped over with the agility of a barefoot street urchin.

"Bravo! Let's go!" Mitya burst out in a delighted whisper.

"Where?" Alyosha also whispered, looking around on all sides and finding himself in a completely deserted garden with no one there but the two of them. The garden was small, but even so the owner's little house stood no less than fifty paces away from them. "Why are you whispering? There's no one here."

"Why am I whispering? Devil take it," Dmitri Fyodorovich suddenly shouted at the top of his lungs, "why am I whispering! You see what jumbles of nature can suddenly happen? I'm here in secret, I'm guarding a secret. Explanation to follow; but knowing it's a secret, I suddenly began to speak secretly, whispering like a fool when there's no need to. Let's go! Over there! Till then, silence. I want to kiss you!

Glory to the Highest in the world,
Glory to the Highest in me . . . ![1]

I was sitting here reciting that just before you came."

The garden was about three acres or a little less, but there were trees planted only around it, along all four fences—apple trees, maples, lindens, birches. The middle of the garden was empty, a meadow that yielded several hundred pounds of hay in the summer. The owner rented the garden out for a few roubles each spring. There were rows of raspberries, gooseberries, currants, all near the fence as well; there was a vegetable garden up next to the house, started, in fact, quite recently. Dmitri Fyodorovich led his guest to the corner of the garden farthest from the house. Suddenly, amid a thicket of lindens and old currant, elder, snow ball, and lilac bushes, something that looked like the ruins of an ancient green gazebo appeared, blackened and lopsided, with lattice sides, but with a roof under which it was still possible to find shelter from the rain. The gazebo had been built God knows when, about fifty years ago according to tradition, by the then owner of the house, Alexander Karlovich von Schmidt, a retired lieutenant colonel. But everything was decayed, the floor was rotted, all the planks were loose, the wood smelled of dampness. Inside the gazebo stood a green wooden table, fixed in the ground, and around it were benches, also green, on which it was still possible to sit. Alyosha had noticed at once his brother's exalted state, but as he entered the gazebo, he saw on the table half a bottle of cognac and a liqueur glass.

"It's cognac!" Mitya laughed loudly. "I see your look: 'He's drinking again!' Do not believe the phantom.

> Do not believe the empty, lying crowd,
> Forget your doubts . . .[2]

I'm not drinking, I'm just relishing, as that pig of yours, Rakitin, says; and he'll become a state councillor and still say 'relishing.' Sit down. I could take you, Alyoshka, and press you to my heart until I crushed you, for in all the world . . . I really . . . re-al-ly . . . (understand?) . . . love only you!"

He spoke this last line almost in a sort of ecstasy.

"Only you, and also one other, a 'low woman' I've fallen in love with and it was the end of me. But to fall in love does not mean to love. One can fall in love and still hate. Remember that! I say it now while there's still joy in it. Sit down here at the table, I'll be right beside you, and I'll look at you and go on talking. You'll keep quiet and I'll keep talking, for the time has come. And by the way, you know, I've decided we really ought to speak softly, because here . . . here . . . the most unexpected ears may turn up. I'll explain everything: sequel to follow, as they say. Why was I longing for you, thirsting for you now, all these days and now? (It's five days since I dropped anchor here.) Why all these days? Because I'll tell everything to you alone, because it's necessary, because you're necessary, because tomorrow I'll fall from the clouds, because tomorrow life will end and begin. Have you ever felt, have you ever dreamed that you were falling off a mountain into a deep pit? Well, I'm falling now, and not in a dream. And I'm not afraid, and don't you be afraid either. That is, I am afraid, but I'm delighted! That is, not delighted, but ecstatic . . . Oh, to hell with it, it's all the same, whatever it is. Strong spirit, weak spirit, woman's spirit—whatever it is! Let us praise nature: see how the sun shines, how clear the sky is, the leaves are all green, it's still summer, four o'clock in the afternoon, so calm! Where were you going?"

"To father's, but first I wanted to stop and see Katerina Ivanovna."

"To her, and to father! Whew! A coincidence! Why was I calling you, wishing for you, why was I longing and thirsting for you with every curve of my soul and even with my ribs? Because I wanted to send you precisely to father, and then to her as well, to Katerina Ivanovna, to have done with her and with father. To send an angel. I could have sent anybody, but I need to send an angel. And here you are going to her and father yourself."

"Did you really want to send me?" Alyosha let fall, with a pained expression on his face.

"Wait! You knew it! And I see that you understood everything at once. But not a word, not a word now. Don't pity me, and don't cry!"

Dmitri Fyodorovich stood up, thought for a moment, and put his finger to his forehead:

"She sent for you herself, she wrote you a letter or something like that, and that's why you were going to see her, otherwise why would you go?"

"Here's the note." Alyosha took it from his pocket. Mitya quickly read it over.

"And you were going the back way! Oh, gods! I thank you that you sent him the back way and he got caught, like the golden fish in the tale who gets caught by an old fool of a fisherman.[3] Listen, Alyosha, listen, brother! Now I'm going to tell you everything. For I surely must tell at least somebody. I've already told it to an angel in heaven, but I must also tell it to an angel on earth. You are the angel on earth. You will listen, you will judge, and you will forgive . . . And that is what I need, that someone higher forgive me. Listen: if two beings suddenly break away from everything earthly and fly off into the extraordinary, or at least one of them does, and before that, as he flies off or perishes, he comes to someone else and says: do this or that for me, something that one would never ask of anybody except on one's deathbed—can that person refuse to do it . . . if he's a friend, a brother?"

"I'll do it, but tell me what it is, and quickly," said Alyosha.

"Quickly . . . Hm. Don't be in a hurry, Alyosha: you hurry and worry. There's no rush now. Now the world has come out onto a new street. Hey, Alyosha, it's a pity you never hit on ecstasy! But what am I saying? As if you hadn't hit on it! What a babbler I am:

O man, be noble!

Whose line is that?"[4]

Alyosha decided to wait. He realized that all his business was now, indeed, perhaps only here. Mitya thought for a moment, leaning his elbow on the table and resting his head in his hand. Both were silent.

"Lyosha," said Mitya, "you alone will not laugh. I wanted to begin . . . my confession . . . with Schiller's hymn to joy. *An die Freude*![5] But I don't know

German, I only know it's *An die Freude*. And don't think this is drunken nonsense. I'm not drunk at all. Cognac is cognac, but I need two bottles to get drunk—

> And a ruddy-mugged Silenus
> Riding a stumbling ass—[6]

and I haven't drunk even a quarter of a bottle, and I'm not Silenus. Not Silenus, but not silent either, because I'm telling you I've made a decision forever. Forgive the pun; you'll have to forgive me a lot more than puns today. Don't worry, I'm not losing the point, I'm talking business, and I'll get to business at once. I won't leave you hanging. Wait, how does it go . . . ?"

He raised his head, thought for a moment, and suddenly began ecstatically:

> Darkly hid in cave and cleft
> Shy, the troglodyte abode;
> Earth a waste was found and left
> Where the wandering nomad strode:
> Deadly with the spear and shaft,
> Prowled the hunter through the land;
> Woe to the stranger waves may waft
> On an ever-fatal strand!
>
> Thus was all to Ceres, when
> Searching for her ravish'd child
> (No green culture smiling then),
> O'er the drear coast bleak and wild,
> Never shelter did she gain,
> Never friendly threshold trod;
> All unbuilded then the fane,
> All unheeded then the god!
>
> Not with golden corn-ears strew'd
> Were the ghastly altar stones;
> Bleaching there, and gore-imbued,
> Lay unhallow'd human bones!
> Wide and far, where'er she roved,
> Still reign'd Misery over all;
> And her mighty soul was moved
> At man's universal fall.[7]

Sobs suddenly burst from Mitya's breast. He seized Alyosha's hand.

"My friend, my friend, still fallen, still fallen even now. There's so terribly much suffering for man on earth, so terribly much grief for him! Don't think

I'm just a brute of an officer who drinks cognac and goes whoring. No, brother, I hardly think of anything else, of anything but that fallen man, if only I'm not lying now. God keep me from lying, and from praising myself! I think about that man, because I myself am such a man.

> That men to man again may soar,
> Let man and Earth with one another
> Make a compact evermore—
> Man the son, and Earth the mother . . .[8]

There's just one thing: how can I make a compact with the earth evermore? I don't kiss the earth, I don't tear open her bosom; what should I do, become a peasant or a shepherd? I keep going, and I don't know: have I gotten into stench and shame, or into light and joy? That's the whole trouble, because everything on earth is a riddle. And whenever I happened to sink into the deepest, the very deepest shame of depravity (and that's all I ever happened to do), I always read that poem about Ceres and man. Did it set me right? Never! Because I'm a Karamazov. Because when I fall into the abyss, I go straight into it, head down and heels up, and I'm even pleased that I'm falling in just such a humiliating position, and for me I find it beautiful. And so in that very shame I suddenly begin a hymn. Let me be cursed, let me be base and vile, but let me also kiss the hem of that garment in which my God is clothed; let me be following the devil at the same time, but still I am also your son, Lord, and I love you, and I feel a joy without which the world cannot stand and be.

> Joy is the mainspring of the whole
> Of endless Nature's calm rotation;
> Joy moves the dazzling wheels that roll
> Within the great heart of creation;
> Joy breathes on buds, and flowers they are;
> Joy beckons, suns come forth from heaven;
> Joy moves the spheres in realms afar,
> Ne'er to thy glass, dim wisdom, given!
>
> All being drinks the mother-dew
> Of joy from Nature's holy bosom;
> And good and evil both pursue
> Her steps that strew the rose's blossom.
> The brimming cup, love's loyalty
> Joy gives to *us*; beneath the sod,
> To insects—sensuality;
> In heaven the cherub looks on God![9]

But enough poetry! I shed tears; well, then, let me cry. Maybe everyone will laugh at this foolishness, but you won't. Your eyes are shining, too. Enough poetry. I want to tell you now about the 'insects,' about those to whom God gave sensuality:

To insects—sensuality!

I am that very insect, brother, and those words are precisely about me. And all of us Karamazovs are like that, and in you, an angel, the same insect lives and stirs up storms in your blood. Storms, because sensuality is a storm, more than a storm! Beauty is a fearful and terrible thing! Fearful because it's undefinable, and it cannot be defined, because here God gave us only riddles. Here the shores converge, here all contradictions live together. I'm a very uneducated man, brother, but I've thought about it a lot. So terribly many mysteries! Too many riddles oppress man on earth. Solve them if you can without getting your feet wet. Beauty! Besides, I can't bear it that some man, even with a lofty heart and the highest mind, should start from the ideal of the Madonna and end with the ideal of Sodom. It's even more fearful when someone who already has the ideal of Sodom in his soul does not deny the ideal of the Madonna either, and his heart burns with it, verily, verily burns, as in his young, blameless years. No, man is broad, even too broad, I would narrow him down. Devil knows even what to make of him, that's the thing! What's shame for the mind is beauty all over for the heart. Can there be beauty in Sodom? Believe me, for the vast majority of people, that's just where beauty lies—did you know that secret? The terrible thing is that beauty is not only fearful but also mysterious. Here the devil is struggling with God, and the battlefield is the human heart. But, anyway, why kick against the pricks? Listen, now to real business."

Chapter 4

The Confession of an Ardent Heart. In Anecdotes

"I was leading a wild life there. Father said I used to pay several thousand to seduce girls. That's a swinish phantom, it never happened, and as for what did happen, 'that,' in fact, never required any money. For me, money is an accessory, a fever of the soul, an ambience. Today, here she is, my lady—tomorrow a little street girl is in her place. I entertained the one and the other. I threw fistfuls of money around—music, noise, gypsy women. If need be, I'd give her something, because they do take it, they take it eagerly, one must admit, and are pleased, and grateful. The ladies used to love me, not all of them, but it happened, it happened; but I always liked the back lanes, dark and remote little crannies, away from the main square—there lay adventure, there lay the unexpected, nuggets in the dirt. I'm speaking allegorically, brother. In that little town there were no such back lanes, physically, but morally there were. If you were the same as me, you'd know what that means. I loved depravity, I also loved the shame of depravity. I loved cruelty: am I not a bedbug, an evil insect? In short—a Karamazov! Once there was a picnic for the whole town; we went in seven troikas; in the darkness, in winter, in the sleigh, I began squeezing a girl's hand, the girl who was next to me, and forced her to kiss me—an official's daughter, a poor, nice, meek, submissive girl. She let me, she let me do a lot in the darkness. She thought, the poor dear, that I would come the next day and propose (I was prized, above all, as an eligible young man); but after that I didn't say a word to her for five months, not even half a word. I'd see her eyes watching me from the corner of the room when we used to dance (in that town they were always having dances), I saw them burning like little flames—flames of meek indignation. This game only amused my insect sensuality, which I was nurturing in myself. After five months she married an official and left . . . angry, and maybe still in love with me. Now they're living happily together. Note that I didn't tell anyone, I didn't defame her; though I have base desires and love baseness, I'm not dishonorable. You're blushing; your eyes flashed. Enough of this filth for you. And it's all nothing yet, just Paul de Kock's little flowers,[1] though the cruel insect was already growing, spreading out in my soul. I have a whole album of memories, brother. God bless the little dears. I preferred not to quarrel when breaking up. And I never gave them away, I never defamed even one of them. But enough. You don't think I called you in here just for this trash, do you? No, I'll tell you something more curious; but don't be surprised that I'm not ashamed before you, but even seem to be glad."

"You say that because I blushed," Alyosha suddenly remarked. "I blushed not at your words, and not at your deeds, but because I'm the same as you."

"You? Well, that's going a bit too far."

"No, not too far," Alyosha said hotly. (Apparently the thought had been with him for some time.) "The steps are all the same. I'm on the lowest, and you are above, somewhere on the thirteenth. That's how I see it, but it's all one and the same, all exactly the same sort of thing. Whoever steps on the lowest step will surely step on the highest."

"So one had better not step at all."

"Not if one can help it."

"Can you?"

"It seems not."

"Stop, Alyosha, stop, my dear, I want to kiss your hand, just out of tenderness. That rogue Grushenka has an eye for men; she once told me she'd eat you up some day. I'll stop, I'll stop! From abominations, from this flyblown margin, let us move on to my tragedy, another flyblown margin, covered with all kinds of baseness. The thing is that though the old man lied about seducing innocence, essentially, in my tragedy, that's how it was, though only once, and even so it never took place. The old man reproached me with a fable, but this fact he doesn't know: I've never told anyone, you'll be the first, except for Ivan, of course, Ivan knows everything. He's known it for a long time before you. But Ivan is a grave."

"Ivan is a grave?"

"Yes."

Alyosha was listening with great attention.

"You see, though I was a lieutenant in a line battalion, even so it was as if I were under observation, like some exile. But that little town received me awfully well. I threw a lot of money around, they thought I was rich, and I thought so myself. However, something else about me must have pleased them as well. Though they wagged their heads, still they really liked me. My colonel, who was an old man, suddenly took a dislike to me. He kept finding fault with me, but I had my connections, and besides the whole town stood up for me, so he couldn't find too much fault. I was partly to blame, too, I deliberately failed to show due respect. I was proud. This old pighead, who was not at all a bad sort, quite good-natured and hospitable, had had two wives at some point, both deceased. One of them, the first, came from some simple family, and left him a daughter, also a simple person. In my time she was already a maiden of about twenty-four, and lived with her father together with an aunt, her dead mother's sister. The aunt was simple and meek; the niece, the colonel's older daughter, was simple and pert. I like to put in a good word for her whenever I think of her: I've never known a lovelier woman's character than in this girl, Agafya was her name, imagine it, Agafya Ivanovna. And she wasn't bad looking either, for Russian taste—tall, buxom, full-figured, with beautiful eyes and, shall we say, a rather coarse face. She wouldn't marry, though two men had proposed to her; she declined without losing her cheerfulness. I became close with her—not in that way, no, it was all pure, we were just friends. I often became close with women, quite sinlessly, as a friend. I used to chat with her in such a frank way—whew!—and she just laughed. Many women like frankness, make a note of that, and besides she was a virgin, which I found very amusing. And another thing: it was quite impossible to call her a young lady. She and her aunt lived with her father in some sort of voluntary humility, not putting themselves on a par with the rest of society. Everyone loved her and needed her, because she was a great dressmaker: she had talent, asked no money for her services, did it all as a favor, but if they gave her presents she wouldn't refuse them. But the colonel was something else again! He was one of the big men of the place. He lived in grand style, entertained the whole town, gave dinners, dances. When I came and joined the battalion, the talk all over the little town was that we were about to have a visitor from the capital, the colonel's second daughter, a beauty of beauties, who had just finished one of the institutes for well-born young ladies there. This second daughter was none other than Katerina Ivanovna, born of the colonel's second wife. And this second wife, already dead, was from the great, noble family of some general, though, by the way, I know for certain that she didn't bring the colonel any money either. So she had her relatives, but that was all; some hopes, maybe, but nothing in her hands. And yet, when the institute girl came (to visit, not to stay), our whole little town seemed to revive: our noblest ladies—two generals' wives, one colonel's wife, and after them everyone, everyone immediately got into it, and kept inviting her right and left, entertaining her, she was the queen of the balls, the picnics, they cooked up *tableaux vivants* for the benefit of some governesses. I kept still. I kept on carousing. Just then I fetched off such a stunt that the whole town was squawking about it. I saw her sizing me up; it was at the battery commander's, but I didn't go up to her then: I scorn your acquaintance, thought I. I went up to her a bit later on, also at a party; I began talking, she barely looked at me, pressed her contemptuous lips together. Well, thought I, just wait, I'll get my revenge! I was a terrible boor then, on most occasions, and I felt it. Mainly I felt that 'Katenka' was not like some innocent institute girl, but a person of character, proud and truly virtuous, and above all intelligent and educated, while I was neither the one nor the other. You think I wanted to propose? Not at all, I simply wanted revenge because I was such a fine fellow and she didn't feel it. Meanwhile, riot and ruin! The colonel finally put me under arrest for three days. It was just then that father sent me six thousand, after I'd sent him a formal renunciation of all and all, that is, saying we were 'quits' and I would make no further demands. I didn't understand a thing then: not until I came here, brother, and even not until these very last present days, maybe even not until today, did I understand anything in all these financial squabbles between me and father. But to hell with it, save that for later. Then, when I received that six, I suddenly learned from a friend's letter something that interested me very much—namely, that there was some dissatisfaction with regard to our colonel, that there was a suspicion that things were not in good order, in short, that his enemies were arranging a little surprise for him. And indeed the division commander came and hauled him over the coals. Then, a little later, he was ordered to apply for retirement. I won't go into detail about how it all went; he certainly had enemies; but suddenly the town became extremely cool towards him and his whole family, everyone suddenly withdrew. It was then that I did my first stunt: I met Agafya Ivanovna, with whom I had always remained friends, and said: 'Your papa, by the way, is short forty-five hundred roubles of government money.' 'What do you mean? Why do you say that? The general came recently and the cash was all there . . .' 'It was there then, but it isn't now.' She was terribly frightened: 'Please don't frighten me! Who told you?' 'Don't worry,' I said, 'I won't tell anyone, and you know that on that account I'm like the grave, but I wanted to say something more on that account, "just in case," as it were: when they ask your papa for the forty-five hundred and he hasn't got it, then instead of having him face court-martial and end up as a foot soldier in his old age, why don't you secretly send me your institute girl? I've just received money; maybe I'll fork out some four thousand to her and keep it a holy secret.' 'Oh, what a scoundrel!' (She actually said that.) 'What a wicked scoundrel!' she said. 'How dare you!' She went away terribly indignant, and I shouted after her once more that I'd keep it a holy and inviolable secret. Both women, that is, Agafya and her aunt, I'll tell you beforehand, turned out to be pure angels in this whole story, and indeed adored this sister, haughty Katya, humbled themselves before her, were like her maids . . . Only Agafya then went and told her all about this stunt, I mean our conversation. I learned that later in full detail. She didn't conceal it, and I . . . well, naturally, that was just what I needed.

"Suddenly a new major arrived to take command of the battalion. He took command. And the old colonel suddenly fell ill, couldn't move, stayed home for two days, did not turn over the government money. Our doctor Kravchenko gave assurances that he really was ill. Only here's what I knew thoroughly and secretly, and for a long time: that for four years in a row, as soon as the authorities finished going over the accounts, the money disappeared for a while. The colonel used to loan it to a most reliable man, a local merchant, the old widower Trifonov, a bearded man with gold spectacles. Trifonov would go to the fair, put the money out as he liked, and return the whole amount to the colonel immediately, with some little presents from the fair besides, and along with the presents a little interest as well. Only this last time (I learned of it quite by chance from a boy, Trifonov's driveling son, his son and heir, one of the most depraved lads the world has yet produced), this time, as I said, when Trifonov returned from the fair, he didn't return anything. The colonel rushed to him. 'I never received anything from you, and could not have received anything,' came the answer. So our colonel sat at home like that, with his head wrapped in a towel, and all three women putting ice to it; suddenly an orderly arrived with the books and an order to turn over the government funds at once, immediately, in two hours. He signed—I saw his signature afterwards in the book—stood up, said he would go and put on his uniform, ran to the bedroom, took his double-barreled shotgun, loaded it, rammed home a service bullet, took off his right boot, propped the gun against his chest, and began feeling for the trigger with his foot. But Agafya was suspicious; she remembered what I had told her, stole over and peeked into the room just in time: she rushed in, threw herself on him from behind, the gun fired into the ceiling, no one was hurt; the others ran in, seized him, took the gun away, held him by the arms . . . All this I learned afterwards to the last detail. I was sitting at home at the time, it was dusk, I was just about to go out, I got dressed, combed my hair, put scent on my handkerchief, picked up my cap, when suddenly the door opened—and there, in my room, stood Katerina Ivanovna.

"Strange things do happen: no one in the street then noticed her coming into my place, so for the town it just vanished. I rented my lodgings from two widows of local officials, two ancient crones, they also served me, respectful women, they obeyed me in everything, and this time, on my orders, they were as silent as iron posts. Of course, I at once understood everything. She came in and looked squarely at me, her dark eyes resolute, defiant even, but on her lips and around her mouth I noticed some irresolution.

"'My sister told me you would give us forty-five hundred roubles if I came . . . to get them myself. I have come . . . give me the money . . . !' She couldn't keep it up, she choked, got frightened, her voice broke off, and the corners of her mouth and the lines around her mouth trembled. Alyoshka, are you listening or sleeping?"

"Mitya, I know you will tell me the whole truth," Alyosha said with emotion.

"So I will. If you want the whole truth, this is it, I won't spare myself. My first thought was a Karamazov thought. Once, brother, I was bitten by a spider, and was laid up with a fever for two weeks; it was the same now, I could feel the spider bite my heart, an evil insect, understand? I sized her up. Have you seen her? A real beauty. And she was beautiful then, but for a different reason. She was beautiful at that moment because she was noble, and I was a scoundrel; she was there in the majesty of her magnanimity and her sacrifice for her father, and I was a bedbug. And on me, a bedbug and a scoundrel, she depended entirely, all of her, all of her entirely, body and soul. No way out. I'll tell you honestly: this thought, this spider's thought, so seized my heart that it almost poured out from the sheer sweetness of it. It seemed there could even be no struggle: I had to act precisely like a bedbug, like an evil tarantula, without any pity . . . I was breathless. Listen: naturally I would come the next day to ask for her hand, so that it would all end, so to speak, in the noblest manner, and no one, therefore, would or could know of it. Because although I'm a man of base desires, I am honest. And then suddenly, at that very second, someone whispered in my ear: 'But tomorrow, when you come to offer your hand, a girl like this will not even see you, she'll have the coachman throw you out: Go cry it all over town, I'm not afraid of you!' I glanced at the girl. The voice was right: that was certainly what she would do. I'd be thrown out, you could see it in the look on her face. Anger boiled up in me. I wanted to pull some mean, piggish, merchant's trick: to give her a sneering look, and right there, as she stood before me, to stun her with the tone of voice you only hear from some petty merchant:

" 'But four thousand is much too much! I was joking, how could you think it? You've been too gullible, madam. Perhaps two hundred, even gladly and with pleasure, but four thousand—it's too much money, miss, to throw away on such trifles. You have gone to all this trouble for nothing.'

"You see, I'd lose everything, of course, she would run away, but on the other hand, such infernal revenge would be worth it all. I might have spent the rest of my life howling with remorse, but right then I just wanted to pull this little stunt. Believe me, never in such a moment have I looked at any woman, not a single one, with hatred—see, I'm making the sign of the cross—but I looked at this one for three or five seconds, then, with terrible hatred—the kind of hatred that is only a hair's breadth from love, the maddest love! I went to the window, leaned my forehead on the frozen glass, and I remember that the ice burned my forehead like fire. I didn't keep her long, don't worry; I turned around, went to the table, opened the drawer and took out a five percent bank note for five thousand roubles, with no name filled in (it was stuck in a French dictionary). I silently showed it to her, folded it, handed it to her, opened the door to the hallway for her, and, stepping back, bowed deeply to her, with a most respectful and heartfelt bow, believe me! She was startled, she looked intently at me for a second, turned terribly pale—white as a sheet—and suddenly, also without saying a word, not impulsively but very gently, deeply, quietly, bent way down and fell right at my feet—with her forehead to the ground, not like an institute girl but like a Russian woman! Then she jumped up and ran away. When she ran out—I was wearing my sword—I drew it and wanted to stab myself right there—why, I don't know, it was terribly foolish, of course, but probably from a certain kind of ecstasy. Do you understand that one can kill oneself from a certain kind of ecstasy? But I didn't stab myself, I only kissed the sword and put it back in the scabbard—which detail, by the way, I needn't have mentioned. And it even seems that while I was telling about all these agonies just now, I must have been filling them out a little, to praise myself. But let it be, let it be so, and to hell with all spies into the human heart! That's the whole of my past 'incident' with Katerina Ivanovna. So now brother Ivan knows about it, and you—and that's all."

Dmitri Fyodorovich got up, took a step, then another in his agitation, pulled out his handkerchief, wiped the sweat from his brow, then sat down again, not in the same place as before, but on another bench against the opposite wall, so that Alyosha had to turn all the way around to face him.

Chapter 5

The Confession of an Ardent Heart. "Heels Up"

"Now," said Alyosha, "I understand the first half of this business."

"You understand the first half: it's a drama, and it took place there. The second half is a tragedy, and will take place here."

"I still don't understand anything of the second half," said Alyosha.

"And I? Do I understand it?"

"Wait, Dmitri, there is one key word here. Tell me: you are her fiancé, aren't you still her fiancé?"

"I became her fiancé, not at once, but only three months after those events. The day after it happened I told myself that the case was closed, done with, there would be no sequel. To come with an offer of my hand seemed a base thing to do. For her part, during all the six weeks she then spent in our town, she never once let me hear a word of herself. Except, indeed, in one instance: on the day after her visit, their maid slipped into my room, and without saying a word handed me an envelope. It was addressed to me. I opened it—there was the change from the five-thousand-rouble bank note. They needed only forty-five hundred, and there was a loss of about two hundred and something on the sale of the note. She sent me back only two hundred and sixty roubles, I think, I don't quite remember, and just the money—no note, no word, no explanation. I looked into the envelope for some mark of a pencil—nothing! So meanwhile I went on a spree with the rest of my roubles, until the new major also finally had to reprimand me. And the colonel did hand over the government funds—satisfactorily and to everyone's surprise, because nobody believed any longer that he had them intact. He handed them over, and came down sick, lay in bed for about three weeks, then suddenly he got a softening of the brain, and in five days he was dead. He was buried with military honors, since his discharge hadn't come through yet. Katerina Ivanovna, her sister, and her aunt, having buried the father, set out for Moscow ten days later. And just before their departure, on the very day they left (I didn't see them or say good-bye), I received a tiny letter, a blue one, on lacy paper, with only one line penciled on it: 'I'll write to you. Wait. K.' That was all.

"I'll explain the rest in two words. Once they were in Moscow, things developed in a flash and as unexpectedly as in an Arabian tale. The widow of the general, her main relative, suddenly lost both of her closest heirs, her two closest nieces, who died of smallpox in one and the same week. The shaken old woman welcomed Katya like her own daughter, like a star of salvation, fell upon her, changed her will at once in her favor, but that was for the future, and meanwhile she gave her eighty thousand roubles outright—here's a dowry for you, she said, do as you like with it. A hysterical woman, I observed her later in Moscow. So then suddenly I received forty-five hundred roubles in the mail; naturally, I was bewildered and struck dumb. Three days later came the promised letter as well. It's here with me now, I always keep it with me, and shall die with it—do you want to see it? You must read it: she offers to be my fiancée, she offers herself, 'I love you madly,' she says, 'even if you do not love me—no matter, only be my husband. Don't be afraid, I shan't hinder you in any way, I'll be your furniture, the rug you walk on . . . I want to love you eternally, I want to save you from yourself . . .' Alyosha, I'm not worthy even to repeat those lines in my mean words and in my mean tone, in my eternally mean tone that I can never be cured of! This letter pierced me even to this day, and is it easy for me now, is it easy for me today? I wrote a reply at once (I couldn't manage to go to Moscow in person). I wrote it in tears. One thing I am eternally ashamed of: I mentioned that she was now rich and had a dowry, and I was just a poverty-stricken boor—I mentioned money! I should have borne it, but it slipped off my pen. Then I wrote at once to Ivan, in Moscow, and explained everything to him, as far as I could in a letter, it was a six-page letter, and sent Ivan to her. Why are you looking, why are you staring at me? So, yes, Ivan fell in love with her, is in love with her still, I know it, I did a foolish thing, in your worldly sense, but maybe just this foolishness will now save us all! Ah! Don't you see how she reveres him, how she respects him? Can she compare the two of us and still love a man like me, especially after all that's happened here?"

"But I'm sure she does love a man like you, and not a man like him."

"She loves her own virtue, not me," the words suddenly escaped, inadvertently and almost maliciously, from Dmitri Fyodorovich. He laughed, but a moment later his eyes flashed, he blushed all over and pounded his fist violently on the table.

"I swear, Alyosha," he exclaimed with terrible and sincere anger at himself, "believe it or not, but I swear as God is holy and Christ is the Lord, that even though I sneered just now at her lofty feelings, still I know that I am a million times more worthless in my soul than she is, and that her lofty feelings—are as sincere as a heavenly angel's! That's the tragedy, that I know it for certain. What's wrong with declaiming a little? Am I not declaiming? But I am sincere, I really am sincere. As for Ivan, I can understand with what a curse he must look at nature now, and with his intelligence, too! To whom, to what has the preference been given? It has been given to a monster, who even here, already a fiancé and with all eyes looking at him, was not able to refrain from debaucheries—and that right in front of his fiancée, right in front of his fiancée! And a man like me is preferred, and he is rejected. Why? Because a girl wants to violate her life and destiny, out of gratitude! Absurd! I've never said anything of the sort to Ivan; Ivan, of course, has never said half a word about it to me either, not the slightest hint; but destiny will be fulfilled, the worthy man will take his place, and the unworthy one will disappear down his back lane—his dirty back lane, his beloved, his befitting back lane, and there, in filth and stench, will perish of his own free will, and revel in it. I seem to be rambling; all my words are worn out, as if I were just joining them at random; but I've determined that it will be so. I'll drown in my back lane, and she will marry Ivan."

"Wait, brother," Alyosha interrupted again, deeply troubled, "you still haven't explained one thing to me: are you her fiancé, are you really her fiancé? How can you want to break it off if she, your fiancée, doesn't want to?"

"I am her fiancé, formally and with blessings; it all happened in Moscow after my arrival, with pomp, with icons, in the proper manner. The general's widow gave the blessing, and—would you believe it?—even congratulated Katya: you have chosen well, she said, I can see inside him. And would you believe that she disliked Ivan and did not congratulate him? In Moscow I talked a lot with Katya, I painted myself in my true colors, nobly, precisely, in all sincerity. She listened to it all.

> There was sweet confusion,
> There were tender words . . .[1]

Well, there were some proud words, too. She extorted from me, then, a great promise to reform. I gave my promise. And now . . ."

"What now?"

"And now I've called you and dragged you here today, this very day—remember that!—in order to send you, again this very day, to Katerina Ivanovna, and . . ."

"And what?"

"And tell her that I shall never come to her again, that I—tell her that I bow to her."

"But is it possible?"

"But that's why I'm sending you instead of going myself, because it's impossible. How could I say that to her myself?"

"But where will you go?"

"To my back lane."

"You mean to Grushenka!" Alyosha exclaimed ruefully, clasping his hands. "Can it be that Rakitin was really speaking the truth? And I thought you just saw her a few times and stopped."

"How can a fiancé just see another woman? And with such a fiancée, and before everyone's eyes? It's impossible! I have my honor, haven't I? As soon as I began seeing Grushenka, I at once ceased to be a fiancé and an honest man, of course I know that. Why do you stare at me? You see, first of all I went to give her a beating. I had heard, and now know for certain, that this Grushenka had gotten from this captain, father's agent, a promissory note in my name, so that she could demand payment and that would stop me and shut me up. They wanted to frighten me. So I set out to give Grushenka a beating. I'd seen her before around town. Nothing striking. I knew about the old merchant, who on top of everything else is lying sick now, paralyzed, but still will leave her a nice sum. I also knew that she likes making money, that she does make it, loans it out at wicked rates of interest, a sly fox, a rogue, merciless. I went to give her a beating, and stayed. A thunderstorm struck, a plague broke out, I got infected and am infected even now, and I know that everything is over and there will never be anything else. The wheel has come full circle. That's how it is for me. And then suddenly, as if on purpose, in my beggar's pocket, three thousand roubles turned up. We went from here to Mokroye, it's fifteen miles away, I got some gypsies to join us, gypsy women, champagne, got all the peasants drunk on champagne, all the village women and girls, thousands were flying around. In three days I was broke, but a hero. And did he get anywhere, this hero? She didn't even show it to him from a distance. A curve, I tell you! That rogue Grushenka has a certain curve to her body, it even shows in her foot, it's even echoed in her little left toe. I saw it and kissed it, but that's all—I swear! She said, 'I'll marry you if you like, though you're a beggar. Tell me you won't beat me and will let me do anything I want, and then maybe I'll marry you,' she laughed. And she's laughing still."

Dmitri Fyodorovich rose from his place, almost in a sort of fury. He seemed suddenly as if he were drunk. His eyes suddenly became bloodshot.

"And do you really want to marry her?"

"At once, if she will, and if she won't, I'll stay anyway, I'll be a caretaker in her yard. You . . . you, Alyosha . . . ," he stopped suddenly in front of him and, grasping his shoulders, suddenly began shaking him violently, "but do you know, you innocent boy, that all of this is raving, impossible raving, because there's a tragedy here! I tell you, Alexei: I can be a mean man, with passions mean and ruinous, but a thief, a pickpocket, a pilferer, that Dmitri Karamazov can never be! And now let me tell you that I am a little thief, a pickpocket and pilferer! Just before I went to give Grushenka a beating, that very morning, Katerina Ivanovna sent for me and, in terrible secrecy, so that for the time being no one would know (I have no idea why, but that's evidently how she wanted it), she asked me to go to the provincial capital and from there post three thousand roubles to Agafya Ivanovna in Moscow, so that nobody here in town would know about it. And with those three thousand roubles in my pocket, I then found myself at Grushenka's, and on them we went to Mokroye. Later I pretended that I had raced to the capital and back, but I didn't present her with a postal receipt; I told her I'd sent the money and would bring her the receipt, but so far I haven't brought it, I've forgotten, if you like. Now, what if you go today and say to her: 'He bows to you,' and she says, 'And the money?' You could tell her: 'He's a base sensualist, a mean creature with irrepressible passions. He did not send your money that time, he spent it, because he couldn't help himself, like an animal,' and then you could add: 'But he is not a thief, here are your three thousand roubles, he returns them to you, send them to Agafya Ivanovna yourself, and he says he bows to you.' But then what if she suddenly says: 'And where is the money?' "

"Mitya, you're unhappy, yes! But not as unhappy as you think. Don't kill yourself with despair, don't do it!"

"What do you think, that I'll shoot myself if I can't find three thousand roubles to give back to her? That's just the thing: I won't shoot myself. It's beyond my strength right now—later, maybe, but right now I'll go to Grushenka . . . Let my flesh rot!"

"And what then?"

"I'll be her husband, I'll have the honor of being her spouse, and if a lover comes, I'll go to another room. I'll clean her friends' dirty galoshes, I'll heat up the samovar, I'll run errands . . ."

"Katerina Ivanovna will understand everything," Alyosha all of a sudden said solemnly. "She will understand all the depths of all this grief and be reconciled. She has a lofty mind, because it's impossible to be unhappier than you are, she will see that."

"She will not be reconciled to everything," Mitya grinned. "There's something here, brother, that no woman can be reconciled to. Do you know what the best thing would be?"

"What?"

"To give her back the three thousand."

"But where can we get it? Listen, I have two thousand, Ivan will give a thousand, that makes three—take it and give it to her."

"And how soon will we get your three thousand? Besides, you're not of age yet, and you must, you must go today and make that bow to her, with the money or without it, because I can't drag on any longer, that's what it's come to. Tomorrow will already be too late, too late. I'll send you to father."

"To father?"

"Yes, to father, and then to her. Ask him for three thousand."

"But, Mitya, he won't give it."

"Of course he won't, I know he won't. Alexei, do you know what despair is?"

"I do."

"Listen: legally he owes me nothing. I've already gotten everything out of him, everything, I know that. But morally he surely owes me something, doesn't he? He started with my mother's twenty-eight thousand and made a hundred thousand out of it. Let him give me only three of those twenty-eight thousands, only three, and bring up my life from the Pit,[2] and it will be reckoned unto him for his many sins! And I'll stop at those three thousands, I give you my solemn word on it, and he'll never hear of me again. For the last time I give him a chance to be my father. Tell him that God himself sends him this chance."

"Mitya, he won't do it for anything."

"I know he won't do it, I know perfectly well he won't. Not now, especially. Moreover, I know something else: recently, only the other day, just yesterday maybe, he learned for the first time *seriously*—underline seriously—that Grushenka indeed may not be joking and could very well up and marry me. He knows her nature, he knows the cat in her. And can he really give me money to help make that happen, when he himself has lost his mind over her? And that's still not all, I can present you with something more: I know that about five days ago he withdrew three thousand roubles in hundred-rouble notes and packed them into a big envelope, sealed with five seals and tied crisscross with a red ribbon. See what detailed knowledge I have! And written on the envelope is: 'To my angel Grushenka, if she wants to come.' He scribbled it himself in silence and secrecy, and no one knows he's keeping the money except the lackey Smerdyakov, whose honesty he trusts like himself. For three or four days now he's been waiting for Grushenka, hoping she'll come for the envelope. He sent her word of it, and she sent word back saying, 'Maybe I'll come.' But if she comes to the old man, could I marry her then? Do you understand, now, why I'm keeping a secret watch here, and what precisely I'm watching for?"

"Her?"

"Her. The sluts who own this house rent out a closet to Foma. Foma is a local man, one of our former soldiers. He does chores for them, guards the house at night, and goes hunting grouse during the day, and that's how he lives. I've set myself up in his place; neither he nor the women of the house know the secret, that is, that I'm keeping watch here."

"Only Smerdyakov knows?"

"Only he. And he'll let me know if she comes to the old man."

"It was he who told you about the envelope?"

"Yes. It's a great secret. Even Ivan knows nothing about the money or anything. And the old man is sending Ivan on a ride to Chermashnya for two or three days: a buyer has turned up for the woodlot, eight thousand to cut down the trees, so the old man is begging Ivan: 'Help me, go by yourself'—which means for two or three days. So that when Grushenka comes, he won't be there."

"So he's expecting her even today?"

"No, she won't come today, there are signs. She surely won't come today!" Mitya suddenly shouted. "And Smerdyakov thinks the same. Father is drinking now, he's sitting at the table with brother Ivan. Go, Alexei, and ask him for the three thousand . . ."

"Mitya, my dear, what's the matter with you!" Alyosha exclaimed, jumping up and staring at the frenzied Dmitri Fyodorovich. For a moment he thought he had gone mad.

"What's wrong? I haven't gone mad," said Dmitri Fyodorovich, looking at him intently and even somehow solemnly. "No, when I tell you to go to father, I know what I'm saying: I believe in a miracle."

"In a miracle?"

"In a miracle of divine Providence. God knows my heart, he sees all my despair. He sees the whole picture. Can he allow horror to happen? Alyosha, I believe in a miracle. Go!"

"I will go. Tell me, will you be waiting here?"

"Yes. I realize it will take some time, you can't just walk in and ask him—bang!—like that. He's drunk now. I'll wait three hours, and four, and five, and six, and seven—only know that you must go to Katerina Ivanovna today, even if it's at midnight, *with the money or without it*, and tell her: 'He says he bows to you.' I want you to say precisely this verse: 'He says he bows to you.'"

"Mitya! What if Grushenka comes today . . . or if not today, then tomorrow, or the day after?"

"Grushenka? I'll spot her, burst in, and stop it . . ."

"And if . . . ?"

"If there's an if, I'll kill. I couldn't endure that."

"Kill whom?"

"The old man. I wouldn't kill her."

"Brother, what are you saying!"

"I don't know, I don't know . . . Maybe I won't kill him, and maybe I will. I'm afraid that at that moment his face will suddenly become hateful to me. I hate his Adam's apple, his nose, his eyes, his shameless sneer. I feel a personal loathing. I'm afraid of that. I may not be able to help myself . . ."

"I'll go, Mitya. I believe God will arrange it as he knows best, so that there will be no horror."

"And I'll sit and wait for a miracle. But if it doesn't happen, then . . ."

Alyosha, in deep thought, went to see his father.

Chapter 6

Smerdyakov

And indeed he found his father still at the table. And the table was laid, as usual, in the drawing room, though the house had an actual dining room. This drawing room was the largest room in the house, furnished with some sort of old-fashioned pretentiousness. The furniture was ancient, white, with threadbare upholstery of red half-silk. Mirrors in fanciful frames with old-fashioned carving, also white and gilt, hung in the spaces between the windows. The walls, covered with white paper, now cracked in many places, were adorned by two large portraits—one of some prince who thirty years before had been governor-general hereabouts, and the other of some bishop, also long since deceased. In the front corner were several icons, before which an oil-lamp burned all night . . . not so much out of veneration as to keep the room lit through the night. Fyodor Pavlovich went to bed very late, at about three or four o'clock in the morning, and until then would pace around the room or sit in his armchair and think. This had become a habit with him. He often spent the night quite alone in the house, after sending the servants to the cottage, but usually the servant Smerdyakov stayed with him, sleeping on a bench in the front hall. The dinner was all finished when Alyosha entered, but they were still having coffee and preserves. Fyodor Pavlovich liked sweets and cognac after dinner. Ivan Fyodorovich was there at the table, also having coffee. The servants Grigory and Smerdyakov stood near the table. Both masters and servants were obviously and unusually animated. Fyodor Pavlovich loudly roared and laughed. From the front hall, Alyosha already heard his shrill laughter, by now so familiar to him, and concluded at once from the sound of it that his father was not yet drunk, but was still only in a benevolent mood.

"Here he is! Here he is!" yelled Fyodor Pavlovich, terribly glad suddenly to see Alyosha. "Join us, sit down, have some coffee—it's lenten fare, lenten fare, and it's hot, it's good! I'm not offering you cognac, you're fasting, but would you like some, would you? No, I'd better give you some liqueur, it's fine stuff! Smerdyakov, go to the cupboard, second shelf on the right, here's the key, get moving!"

Alyosha started to refuse the liqueur.

"We'll serve it anyway, if not for you then for us," Fyodor Pavlovich beamed. "But wait, did you have dinner or not?"

"I did," said Alyosha, who in truth had had only a piece of bread and a glass of kvass in the Superior's kitchen. "But I'd very much like some hot coffee."

"Good for you, my dear! He'll have some coffee. Shall we heat it up? Ah, no, it's already boiling. Fine stuff, this coffee. Smerdyakovian! With coffee and cabbage pies, my Smerdyakov is an artist—yes, and with fish soup, too. Come for fish soup some time, let us know beforehand . . . But wait, wait, didn't I tell you this morning to move back today with your mattress and pillows? Did you bring the mattress, heh, heh, heh?"

"No, I didn't," Alyosha grinned too.

"Ah, but you were scared then—weren't you scared, scared? Ah, my boy, my dear, could I offend you? You know, Ivan, I can't resist it when he looks me in the eyes like that and laughs, I simply can't. My whole insides begin to laugh with him, I love him so! Alyoshka, let me give you my paternal blessing."

Alyosha stood up, but Fyodor Pavlovich had time to think better of it.

"No, no, for now I'll just make a cross over you—so—sit down. Well, now you're going to have some fun, and precisely in your line. You'll laugh your head off. Balaam's ass,[1] here, has started to talk, and what a talker, what a talker!"

Balaam's ass turned out to be the lackey Smerdyakov. Still a young man, only about twenty-four years old, he was terribly unsociable and taciturn. Not that he was shy or ashamed of anything—no, on the contrary, he had an arrogant nature and seemed to despise everyone. But precisely at this point we cannot avoid saying at least a few words about him. He had been raised by Marfa Ignatievna and Grigory Vasilievich, but the boy grew up "without any gratitude," as Grigory put it, solitary, and with a sidelong look in his eye. As a child he was fond of hanging cats and then burying them with ceremony. He would put on a sheet, which served him as a vestment, chant, and swing something over the dead cat as if it were a censer. It was all done on the sly, in great secrecy. Grigory once caught him at this exercise and gave him a painful birching. The boy went into a corner and sat there looking sullen for a week. "He doesn't like us, the monster," Grigory used to say to Marfa Ignatievna, "and he doesn't like anyone. You think you're a human being?" he would suddenly address Smerdyakov directly. "You are not a human being, you were begotten of bathhouse slime, that's who you are . . . " Smerdyakov, it turned out later, never could forgive him these words. Grigory taught him to read and write and, when he was twelve, began teaching him the Scriptures. But that immediately went nowhere. One day, at only the second or third lesson, the boy suddenly grinned.

"What is it?" asked Grigory, looking at him sternly from under his spectacles.

"Nothing, sir. The Lord God created light on the first day, and the sun, moon, and stars on the fourth day.[2] Where did the light shine from on the first day?"

Grigory was dumbfounded. The boy looked derisively at his teacher; there was even something supercilious in his look. Grigory could not help himself. "I'll show you where!" he shouted, and gave his pupil a violent blow on the cheek. The boy suffered the slap without a word, but again hid in the corner for a few days. A week later, as it happened, they discovered for the first time that he had the falling sickness, which never left him for the rest of his life.[3] Having learned of it, Fyodor Pavlovich seemed to change his view of the boy. Formerly he had looked on him somehow indifferently, though he never scolded him and always gave him a kopeck when they met. If he was in a benevolent mood, he sometimes sent the boy some sweets from the table. But now, when he learned of the illness, he decidedly began to worry about him, called in a doctor, began treating him, but a cure turned out to be impossible. The attacks came on the average of once a month, and at various times. They were also of various strength—some were slight, others were extremely severe. Fyodor Pavlovich strictly forbade Grigory any corporal punishment of the boy, and began allowing him upstairs. He also forbade teaching him anything at all for the time being. But once, when the boy was already about fifteen years old, Fyodor Pavlovich noticed him loitering by the bookcase and reading the titles through the glass. There were a fair number of books in the house, more than a hundred volumes, but no one had ever seen Fyodor Pavlovich with a book in his hands. He immediately gave Smerdyakov the key to the bookcase: "Well, read then, you can be my librarian; sit and read, it's better than loafing around the yard. Here, try this one," and Fyodor Pavlovich handed him *Evenings on a Farm near Dikanka*.[4]

The lad read it but with displeasure; he never once smiled, and, on the contrary, finished it with a frown.

"What? Not funny?" asked Fyodor Pavlovich.

Smerdyakov was silent.

"Answer, fool!"

"It's all about lies," Smerdyakov drawled, grinning.

"Well, then, go to the devil with your lackey soul! Wait, here's Smaragdov's *Universal History*,[5] it's all true, read it!"

But Smerdyakov did not get through even ten pages of Smaragdov. He found it boring. So the bookcase was locked again. Soon Marfa and Grigory reported to Fyodor Pavlovich that Smerdyakov suddenly was beginning to show signs of some terrible squeamishness: at supper, he would take his spoon and explore the soup, bend over it, examine it, lift up a spoonful and hold it to the light.

"What is it, a cockroach?" Grigory would ask.

"Maybe a fly," Marfa would suggest. The fastidious boy never answered, but it was the same with the bread, the meat, every dish: he would hold a piece up to the light on his fork, and study it as if through a microscope, sometimes taking a long time to decide, and, finally, would decide to send it into his mouth. "A fine young sir we've got here," Grigory muttered, looking at him. Fyodor Pavlovich, when he heard about this new quality in Smerdyakov, immediately decided that he should be a cook, and sent him to Moscow for training. He spent a few years in training, and came back much changed in appearance. He suddenly became somehow remarkably old, with wrinkles even quite disproportionate to his age, turned sallow, and began to look like a eunuch. But morally he was almost the same when he returned as he had been before his departure for Moscow, was still just as unsociable, and felt not the slightest need for anyone's company. In Moscow, too, as was afterwards reported, he was silent all the time; Moscow itself interested him somehow very little, so that he learned only a few things about it and paid no attention to all the rest. He even went to the theater once, but came home silent and displeased. On the other hand, he returned to us from Moscow very well dressed, in a clean frock coat and linen, scrupulously brushed his clothes twice a day without fail, and was terribly fond of waxing his smart calfskin boots with a special English polish so that they shone like mirrors. He turned out to be a superb cook. Fyodor Pavlovich appointed him a salary, and Smerdyakov spent almost the whole of this salary on clothes, pomade, perfume, and so on. Yet he seemed to despise the female sex as much as the male, and behaved solemnly, almost inaccessibly, with it. Fyodor Pavlovich also began glancing at him from a somewhat different point of view. The thing was that the attacks of his falling sickness became more frequent, and on those days Marfa Ignatievna prepared the meals, which did not suit him at all.

"How come you're having more attacks now?" he sometimes looked askance at the new cook, peering into his face. "I wish you'd marry somebody, do you want me to get you married . . . ?"

But Smerdyakov only turned pale with vexation at such talk, without making any reply. Fyodor Pavlovich would walk off, waving his hand. Above all he was convinced of his honesty, convinced once and for all that he would not take or steal anything. It once happened that Fyodor Pavlovich, being a little drunk, dropped in the mud of his own yard three hundred-rouble bank notes he had just received, and did not notice it until the next day: just as he was rushing to search through all his pockets for them, he suddenly discovered all three bank notes lying on the table. How did they get there? Smerdyakov had picked them up and brought them in the evening before. "Well, my lad, I've never seen the likes of you," Fyodor Pavlovich said brusquely, and gave him ten roubles. It should be added that he was not only convinced of his honesty, but for some reason even loved him, though the fellow looked as askance at him as at others and was always silent. Only rarely did he speak. If at that time it had occurred to someone to ask, looking at him, what this fellow was interested in, and what was most often on his mind, it would really have been impossible to tell from looking at him. Yet he would sometimes stop in the house, or else in the yard or the street, fall into thought, and stand like that even for ten minutes. A physiognomist, studying him, would have said that his face showed neither thought nor reflection, but just some sort of contemplation. The painter Kramskoy has a remarkable painting entitled *The Contemplator*:[6] it depicts a forest in winter, and in the forest, standing all by himself on the road, in deepest solitude, a stray little peasant in a ragged caftan and bast shoes; he stands as if he were lost in thought, but he is not thinking, he is "contemplating" something. If you nudged him, he would give a start and look at you as if he had just woken up, but without understanding anything. It's true that he would come to himself at once, and yet, if he were asked what he had been thinking about while standing there, he would most likely not remember, but would most likely keep hidden away in himself the impression he had been under while contemplating. These impressions are dear to him, and he is most likely storing them up imperceptibly and even without realizing it—why and what for, of course, he does not know either; perhaps suddenly, having stored up his impressions over many years, he will drop everything and wander off to Jerusalem to save his soul, or perhaps he will suddenly burn down his native village, or perhaps he will do both. There are plenty of contemplators among the people. Most likely Smerdyakov, too, was such a contemplator, and most likely he, too, was greedily storing up his impressions, almost without knowing why himself.

Chapter 7

Disputation

But Balaam's ass suddenly spoke. The topic happened to be a strange one: Grigory, while picking up goods that morning at the shop of the merchant Lukyanov, had heard from him about a Russian soldier stationed somewhere far away at the border who was captured by Asians and, being forced by them on pain of agonizing and immediate death to renounce Christianity and convert to Islam, would not agree to change his faith, and endured torture, was flayed alive, and died glorifying and praising Christ—a report of which deed was printed in the newspaper received that day.[1] And this Grigory began speaking about at the table. Fyodor Pavlovich always liked to laugh and talk after dinner, over dessert, even if only with Grigory. This time he was in a light and pleasantly expansive mood. Sipping cognac, he listened to the reported news and remarked that such a soldier ought at once to be promoted to saint, and his flayed skin dispatched to some monastery: "You'll see how people will come pouring in, and money, too." Grigory scowled, seeing that Fyodor Pavlovich was not at all moved but, as usual, was beginning to blaspheme. Then Smerdyakov, who was standing at the door, suddenly grinned. Even before then, Smerdyakov was quite often allowed to stand by the table—that is, at the end of dinner. And since Ivan Fyodorovich arrived in our town, he began appearing at dinner almost every day.

"What is it?" asked Fyodor Pavlovich, noticing his grin at once and understanding, of course, that it referred to Grigory.

"What you're talking about," Smerdyakov suddenly spoke loudly and unexpectedly, "that if the deed of this laudable soldier was so great, sir, there would also have been no sin, in my opinion, if on such an occasion he had even renounced Christ's name and his own baptism in order thereby to save his life for good deeds with which to atone in the course of the years for his faintheartedness."

"How could there be no sin in it? What nonsense! For that you'll go straight to hell and be roasted there like mutton," Fyodor Pavlovich took him up.

And it was here that Alyosha entered. Fyodor Pavlovich, as we have seen, was terribly glad he had come.

"We're on your subject, your subject!" he chuckled gleefully, sitting Alyosha down to listen.

"Concerning mutton, it isn't so, sir, and there will be nothing there for that, sir, and there shouldn't be any such thing, if it's in all fairness," Smerdyakov solemnly observed.

"How do you mean—in all fairness?" Fyodor Pavlovich cried even more merrily, nudging Alyosha with his knee.

"He's a scoundrel, that's who he is!" Grigory suddenly burst out. Angrily he looked Smerdyakov straight in the eye.

"Wait a little with your 'scoundrel,' Grigory Vasilievich, sir," Smerdyakov retorted quietly and with restraint, "and you'd better consider for yourself, that if I am taken captive by the tormentors of Christian people, and they demand that I curse God's name and renounce my holy baptism, then I'm quite authorized to do it by my own reason, because there wouldn't be any sin in it."

"You've already said all that. Don't embroider on it, but prove it!" cried Fyodor Pavlovich.

"Broth-maker!" Grigory whispered scornfully.

"Wait a little with your 'broth-maker,' too, Grigory Vasilievich, and consider for yourself without scolding. Because as soon as I say to my tormentors: 'No, I'm not a Christian and I curse my true God,' then at once, by the highest divine judgment, I immediately and specifically become anathema, I'm cursed and completely excommunicated from the Holy Church like a heathener, as it were, so that even at that very moment, sir, not as soon as I say it, but as soon as I just think of saying it, not even a quarter of a second goes by and I'm excommunicated—is that so or not, Grigory Vasilievich?"

He addressed Grigory with obvious pleasure, though essentially he was answering Fyodor Pavlovich's questions, and was well aware of it, but deliberately pretending that it was Grigory who had asked them.

"Ivan!" Fyodor Pavlovich suddenly shouted, "give me your ear. He arranged all this for you, he wants you to praise him. Go on, praise him!"

Ivan Fyodorovich listened quite seriously to his papa's rapturous communication.

"Wait, Smerdyakov, be still for a minute," Fyodor Pavlovich shouted again. "Ivan, your ear again."

Ivan Fyodorovich leaned over once more with a most serious expression.

"I love you as much as Alyoshka. Don't think that I don't love you. A little cognac?"

"Yes." Ivan Fyodorovich looked intently at his father, thinking, "You're pretty well loaded yourself." As for Smerdyakov, he was watching him with great curiosity.

"You're anathema and cursed even now," Grigory suddenly broke out, "and how dare you reason after that, you scoundrel, if . . ."

"No abuse, Grigory, no abuse!" Fyodor Pavlovich interrupted.

"You wait, Grigory Vasilievich, at least for a very short time, sir, and keep listening, because I haven't finished yet. Because at the very time when I immediately become cursed by God, at that moment, at that highest moment, sir, I become a heathener, as it were, and my baptism is taken off me and counts for nothing—is that so, at least?"

"Come on, lad, get to the point," Fyodor Pavlovich hurried him, sipping with pleasure from his glass.

"And since I'm no longer a Christian, it follows that I'm not lying to my tormentors when they ask am I a Christian or not, since God himself has already deprived me of my Christianity, for the sole reason of my intention and before I even had time to say a word to my tormentors. And if I'm already demoted, then in what way, with what sort of justice can they call me to account in the other world, as if I were a Christian, about my renunciation of Christ, when for the intention alone, even before the renunciation, I was deprived of my baptism? If I'm not a Christian, then I can't renunciate Christ, because I'll have nothing to renounce. Who, even in heaven, Grigory Vasilievich, will ask an unclean Tartar to answer for not being born a Christian, and who is going to punish him for that, considering that you can't skin the same ox twice? And God Almighty himself, even if he does hold the Tartar to account when he dies, I suppose will only give him the smallest punishment (because it's not possible not to punish him at all), considering that it's surely not his fault that he came into the world unclean, and from unclean parents. The Lord God can't take some Tartar by the neck and claim that he, too, was a Christian? That would mean that the Lord Almighty was saying a real untruth. And how can the Almighty Lord of heaven and earth tell a lie, even if it's only one word, sir?"

Grigory was dumbfounded and stared wide-eyed at the orator. Though he did not understand very well what was being said, he did suddenly understand some of all this gibberish, and stood looking like a man who had just run his head into a wall. Fyodor Pavlovich emptied his glass and burst into shrill laughter.

"Alyoshka, Alyoshka, did you hear that? Ah, you casuist! He must have spent some time with the Jesuits, Ivan.[2] Ah, you stinking Jesuit, who taught you all that? But it's lies, casuist, lies, lies, lies. Don't cry, Grigory, we'll grind him to dust and ashes this very minute. Tell me something, ass: before your tormentors you may be right, but you yourself have still renounced your faith within yourself, and you yourself say that in that very hour you became anathema and cursed, and since you're anathema, you won't be patted on the back for that in hell. What do you say to that, my fine young Jesuit?"[3]

"There's no doubt, sir, that I renounced it within myself, but still there wasn't any sin especially, and if there was a little sin, it was a rather ordinary one, sir."

"What do you mean—rather ordinary, sir!"

"You're lying, cursse you!" Grigory hissed.

"Consider for yourself, Grigory Vasilievich," Smerdyakov went on gravely and evenly, conscious of his victory but being magnanimous, as it were, with the vanquished enemy, "consider for yourself: in the Scriptures it is said that if you have faith even as little as the smallest seed and then say unto this mountain that it should go down into the sea, it would go, without the slightest delay, at your first order.[4] Well, then, Grigory Vasilievich, if I'm an unbeliever, and you are such a believer that you're even constantly scolding me, then you, sir, try telling this mountain to go down, not into the sea (because it's far from here to the sea, sir), but even just into our stinking stream, the one beyond our garden, and you'll see for yourself right then that nothing will go down, sir, but everything will remain in its former order and security, no matter how much you shout, sir. And that means that you, too, Grigory Vasilievich, do not believe in a proper manner, and merely scold others for it in every possible way. And then, again, taken also the fact that no one in our time, not only you, sir, but decidedly no one, starting even from the highest persons down to the very last peasant, sir, can shove a mountain into the sea, except maybe one person on the whole earth, two at the most, and even they could be secretly saving their souls somewhere in the Egyptian desert, so they can't even be found—and if that's so, if all the rest come out as unbelievers, can it be that all the rest, that is, the population of the whole earth, sir, except those two desert hermits, will be cursed by the Lord, and in his mercy, which is so famous, he won't forgive a one of them? So I, too, have hopes that though I doubted once, I'll be forgiven if I shed tears of repentance."

"Stop!" shrieked Fyodor Pavlovich in an apotheosis of delight. "So you still suppose that those two, the kind that can move mountains, really exist? Ivan, cut a notch, write it down: here you have the whole Russian man!"

"You are quite right in observing that this is a feature of popular faith," Ivan concurred with an approving smile.

"So you agree! Well, it must be so if even you agree! Alyoshka, it's true, isn't it? Completely Russian faith is like that?"

"No, Smerdyakov's faith is not Russian at all," Alyosha spoke seriously and firmly.

"I don't mean his faith, I mean that feature, those two desert dwellers, just that little detail alone: that is certainly Russian, Russian."

"Yes, that detail is quite Russian," Alyosha smiled.

"Your word, ass, is worth a gold piece, and I'll see that you get it today, but for the rest, it's all still lies, lies, lies; let it be known to you, fool, that we here are unbelievers only out of carelessness, because we don't have time: first, we're too beset with business, and second, God gave us too little time, he only allotted twenty-four hours to a day, so that there isn't even time enough to sleep, let alone repent. And you went and renounced your faith before your tormentors when you had nothing else to think about, and when it was precisely the time to show your faith! And so, my lad, isn't that tantamount?"

"Tantamount, it may be tantamount, but consider for yourself, Grigory Vasilievich, that if it is tantamount, it makes things easier. Because if I then believed in very truth, as one ought to believe, then it would really be sinful if I did not endure torments for my faith but converted to the unclean Mohammedan faith. But then it wouldn't even come to torments, sir, for if at that moment I were to say unto that mountain: 'Move and crush my tormentor,' it would move and in that same moment crush him like a cockroach, and I would go off as if nothing had happened, praising and glorifying God. But if precisely at that moment I tried all that, and deliberately cried unto that mountain: 'Crush my tormentors'—and it didn't crush them, then how, tell me, should I not doubt then, in such a terrible hour of great mortal fear? I'd know even without that that I wasn't going to reach the fullness of the Kingdom of Heaven (because the mountain didn't move at my word, so they must not trust much in my faith there, and no very great reward awaits me in the other world), so why, on top of that, should I let myself be flayed to no purpose? Because even if my back were already half flayed, that mountain still wouldn't move at my word or cry. In such moments, you can not only get overcome by doubt, you can even lose your mind itself from fear, so it would be quite impossible to reason. And so, why should I come out looking so specially to blame, if, seeing no profit or reward either here or there, I at least keep my skin on? And therefore, trusting greatly in the mercy of God, I live in hopes that I'll be completely forgiven, sir."

Chapter 8

Over the Cognac

The dispute was over, but, strangely, Fyodor Pavlovich, who had been laughing so much, in the end suddenly frowned. He frowned and tossed off a glass of cognac, which was quite superfluous.

"Clear out, Jesuits, out!" he shouted at the servants. "Go, Smerdyakov. That gold piece I promised, I'll send you today, but go now. Don't cry, Grigory, go to Marfa, she'll comfort you, she'll put you to bed. *Canaille!* They won't let one sit quietly after dinner," he suddenly snapped in vexation, as the servants at once withdrew on his orders. "Smerdyakov sticks his nose in every time we have dinner now—is it you he's so interested in? What have you done to endear yourself to him?" he added, turning to Ivan Fyodorovich.

"Nothing whatever," the latter replied. "He has taken to respecting me; he's a lackey and a boor. Prime cannon fodder, however, when the time comes."

"Prime?"

"There will be others and better ones, but there will be his kind as well. First his kind, and then the better ones."

"And when will the time come?"

"The rocket will go off, but it may fizzle out. So far the people do not much like listening to these broth-makers."

"That's just it, my friend, a Balaam's ass like him thinks and thinks, and the devil knows what he's going to think up for himself."

"He's storing up his thoughts," Ivan smirked.

"You see, I for one know that he can't stand me, or anybody else, including you, though you imagine he's 'taken to respecting you.' Still less Alyoshka, he despises Alyoshka. Yet he doesn't steal, that's the thing, he's not a gossip, he keeps his mouth shut, he won't wash our dirty linen in public, he makes great cabbage pies, and furthermore to hell with him, really, is he worth talking about?"

"Of course not."

"As to what he's going to think up for himself, generally speaking, the Russian peasant should be whipped. I have always maintained that. Our peasants are cheats, they're not worth our pity, and it's good that they're still sometimes given a birching. The strength of the Russian land is in its birches. If the forests were destroyed, it would be the end of the Russian land. I stand with the men of intelligence. In our great intelligence, we've stopped flogging our peasants, but they go on whipping themselves. And right they are. For as you measure, so it will be measured, or however it goes . . . [1] In short, it will be measured. And Russia is all swinishness. My friend, if only you knew how I hate Russia . . . that is, not Russia, but all this vice . . . and maybe Russia, too. *Tout cela c'est de la cochonnerie.*[2] Do you know what I love? I love wit."

"You've had another glass. That's enough, now."

"Wait, I'll have one more, and then another, and then I'll stop. No, wait, you interrupted me. I was passing through Mokroye, and I asked an old man, and he told me: 'Best of all,' he said, 'we like sentencing the girls to be whipped, and we let the young lads do the whipping.[3] Next day the young lad takes the girl he's whipped for his bride, so you see, our girls themselves go for it.' There's some Marquis de Sades for you, eh? Say what you like, but it's witty. Why don't we go and have a look, eh? Alyoshka, are you blushing? Don't be bashful, child. It's a pity I didn't sit down to the Superior's dinner this afternoon and tell the monks about the Mokroye girls. Alyoshka, don't be angry that I got your Superior all offended this afternoon. It really makes me mad, my friend. Because if there's a God, if he exists, well, then of course I'm guilty and I'll answer for it, but if there's no God at all, then what do those fathers of yours deserve? It's not enough just to cut off their heads—because they hold up progress. Will you believe, Ivan, that it torments me in my feelings? No, you don't believe it, I can see by your eyes. You believe I'm just a buffoon like they say. Alyosha, do you believe that I'm not just a buffoon?"

"I believe that you are not just a buffoon."

"And I believe that you believe it and speak sincerely. You look sincerely and speak sincerely. Not so Ivan. Ivan is haughty . . . But still I'd put an end to that little monastery of yours. Take all this mysticism and abolish it at once all over the Russian land, and finally bring all the fools to reason. And think how much silver, how much gold would come into the mint!"

"But why abolish it?" asked Ivan.

"To let the truth shine forth sooner, that's why."

"But if this truth shines forth, you will be the first to be robbed and then . . . abolished."

"Bah! You're probably right. Ah, what an ass I am!" Fyodor Pavlovich suddenly cried, slapping himself lightly on the forehead. "Well, then, Alyoshka, in that case let your little monastery stand. And we intelligent people will keep warm and sip cognac. You know, Ivan, God himself surely must have set it up this way on purpose. Speak, Ivan: is there a God, or not? Wait: tell me for certain, tell me seriously! Why are you laughing again?"

"I'm laughing at the witty remark you made about Smerdyakov's belief in the existence of two hermits who can move mountains."

"Do I sound like him now?"

"Very much so."

"Well, then I, too, am a Russian man, and have the Russian feature, and you, a philosopher, can also be caught with the same sort of feature yourself. Want me to catch you? I bet you I'll catch you tomorrow. But still, tell me: is there a God or not? But seriously. I want to be serious now."

"No, there is no God."

"Alyoshka, is there a God?"

"There is."

"And is there immortality, Ivan? At least some kind, at least a little, a teeny-tiny one?"

"There is no immortality either."

"Not of any kind?"

"Not of any kind."

"Complete zero? Or is there something? Maybe there's some kind of something? At least not nothing!"

"Complete zero."

"Alyoshka, is there immortality?"

"There is."

"Both God and immortality?"

"Both God and immortality. Immortality is in God."

"Hm. More likely Ivan is right. Lord, just think how much faith, how much energy of all kinds man has spent on this dream, and for so many thousands of years! Who could be laughing at man like that? Ivan? For the last time, definitely: is there a God or not? It's the last time I'll ask."

"For the last time—no."

"Then who is laughing at mankind, Ivan?"

"Must be the devil," Ivan smirked.

"And is there a devil?"

"No, there is no devil, either."

"Too bad. Devil knows, then, what I wouldn't do to the man who first invented God! Hanging from the bitter aspen tree would be too good for him."

"There would be no civilization at all if God had not been invented."

"There wouldn't? Without God?"

"Right. And there would be no cognac either. But even so, we'll have to take your cognac away from you."

"Wait, wait, wait, my dear, one more little glass. I offended Alyosha. You're not angry with me, Alexei? My dear Alexeichik, my Alexeichik!"

"No, I'm not angry. I know your thoughts. Your heart is better than your head."

"My heart is better than my head? Lord, and it's you who say so? Ivan, do you love Alyoshka?"

"I love him."

"Do love him!" (Fyodor Pavlovich was getting very drunk.) "Listen, Alyosha, I committed a rudeness with your elder this afternoon. But I was excited. Say, there's wit in that elder, don't you think so, Ivan?"

"Perhaps so."

"There is, there is, *il y a du Piron là-dedans*.[4] He's a Jesuit, a Russian one, that is. As a noble person, he has this hidden indignation seething in him because he has to pretend . . . to put on all this holiness."

"But he does believe in God."

"Not for a minute. Didn't you know? But he himself says so to everyone, that is, not to everyone, but to all the intelligent people who visit him. With Governor Schultz he came right out and said: *credo*, but I don't know in what."

"He said that?"

"Precisely that. But I respect him. There's something Mephistophelean in him, or, better, from the *Hero of Our Time* . . . Arbenin, or what's his name?[5] . . . you see, I mean, he's a sensualist, he's such a sensualist that even now I'd be afraid for my daughter or my wife if she went to him for confession. You know, when he gets to telling stories . . . The year before last he invited us to tea, with liqueur, too (the ladies send him liqueurs), and he began painting such pictures of the old days that we almost split our sides laughing . . . Especially about how he healed one paralyzed woman. 'If my legs were still good, I'd show you a step or two.' Eh? You see? 'I've done some holy fooling in my day,' he said. He filched sixty thousand from the merchant Demidov."

"What, stole it?"

"Demidov brought it to him as to a decent man: 'Keep it for me, brother, they're going to search my place tomorrow.' Keep it he did. 'You donated it to the Church, didn't you?' he said. I said to him: 'You're a scoundrel,' I said. 'No,' he said, 'I'm not a scoundrel, I'm broad-natured . . .' It wasn't him, though . . . It was someone else. I confused him with someone else . . . and didn't notice. Just one more glass and that's it; take the bottle away, Ivan. I was lying, why didn't you stop me, Ivan . . . why didn't you tell me I was lying?"

"I knew you'd stop by yourself."

"That's a lie! It was out of malice towards me, out of sheer malice. You despise me. You came to me and you despise me in my own house."

"And I'll leave; the drink is acting up in you."

"I asked you for Christ's sake to go to Chermashnya . . . for a day or two, and you don't go."

"I'll go tomorrow, if you're so insistent."

"You won't go. You want to spy on me here, that's what you want, you wicked soul, that's why you won't go."

The old man would not be still. He had reached that level of drunkenness at which some drunkards, who until then have been peaceable, suddenly want to get angry and make a show of themselves.

"What are you staring at me for? What kind of look is that? Your eyes look at me and say: 'You drunken pig!' Suspicious eyes, malicious eyes . . . You came here with something in mind. Alyoshka looks at me and his eyes shine. Alyosha doesn't despise me. Alexei, do not love Ivan . . ."

"Don't be angry with my brother! Stop hurting him," Alyosha all of a sudden said insistently.

"Well, well, maybe I will. Oof, what a headache! Take away the cognac, Ivan, it's the third time I'm telling you." He lapsed into thought and suddenly smiled a long and cunning smile: "Don't be angry with an old runt like me, Ivan. I know you don't love me, but still don't be angry. There's nothing to love me for. You go to Chermashnya, and I'll visit you there, I'll bring presents. I'll show you a young wench there, I've had my eye on her for a long time. She's still barefoot. Don't be afraid of the barefoot ones, don't despise them, they're pearls . . . !"

And he kissed his hand with a smack.

"For me," he suddenly became all animated, as if sobering up for a moment, once he hit on his favorite subject, "for me . . . Ah, you children! My babes, my little piglets, for me . . . even in the whole of my life there has never been an ugly woman, that's my rule! Can you understand that? But how could you understand it? You've still got milk in your veins instead of blood, you're not hatched yet! According to my rule, one can damn well find something extremely interesting in every woman, something that's not to be found in any other—one just has to know how to find it, that's the trick! It's a talent! For me, there's no such thing as an ugly woman: the fact alone that she's a woman, that alone is half the whole thing . . . but how could you understand that? Even old maids, even in them one sometimes finds such a thing that one can only marvel at all the other fools who let her get old and never noticed it before! The barefoot or ugly ones have to be taken by surprise, first of all—that's how one must approach them. Didn't you know that? They must be surprised so that they're enraptured, smitten, ashamed that such a gentleman should have fallen in love with such a grimy creature. It's very nice, indeed, that there have always been and always will be boors and gentlemen in the world, and so there will always be such a little floor scrubber, and there will always be a master over her, and that is all one needs for happiness in life! Wait . . . listen, Alyoshka, I always used to take your late mother by surprise, only it worked out differently. I never used to caress her, but suddenly, when the moment came—suddenly I'd lay myself down before her, crawling on my knees, kissing her feet, and I always, always sent her—I remember it as if it were today—into that little laugh, a showery, tinkling, soft, nervous, peculiar little laugh. It was the only kind she had. I knew that that was how her sickness usually began, that the next day she'd start her shrieking again, and that this present little laugh was no sign of delight—well, it may have been false, but still it was delight. That's what it means to be able to find the right little touch in everything! Once Belyavsky—a handsome man, and a rich one, from these parts; he was chasing after her and had taken to coming for visits—suddenly slapped me in the face, in my own house, right in front of her. And she, sheep though she was, attacked me for that slap so that I thought she was going to give me a thrashing herself: 'You've been beaten now, beaten!' she said. 'You've had your face slapped by him! You were selling me to him . . . ,' she said. 'How dare he strike you in front of me! Don't you dare to come near me again ever, ever! Run right now and challenge him to a duel . . .' I took her to the monastery then, to humble her, the holy fathers reprimanded her. But honest to God, Alyosha, I never offended my little shrieker! Except once only, still in the first year: she was praying too much then, she especially kept the feasts of the Mother of God, and on those days she would drive me away from her to my study. I'd better knock this mysticism out of her, I thought. 'Look,' I said, 'look, here's your icon, here it is, I'm taking it down. Now watch. You think it's a wonder-working icon, and right now, before your eyes, I'm going to spit on it, and nothing will happen to me . . . !' When she saw that, Lord, I thought, now she's going to kill me! But she just jumped up, clasped her hands, then suddenly covered her face with them, shook all over, and fell to the floor . . . just sank down . . . Alyosha! Alyosha! What's wrong? What's wrong?"

The old man jumped up in fright. From the time he began talking about his mother, a change had gradually come over Alyosha's face. He flushed, his eyes burned, his lips trembled . . . The drunken old man went on spluttering and noticed nothing until the moment when something very strange suddenly happened to Alyosha—namely, the very same thing he had just told about the "shrieker" repeated itself with him. He suddenly jumped up from the table, just as his mother was said to have done, clasped his hands, then covered his face with them, fell back in his chair as if he'd been cut down, and suddenly began shaking all over in a hysterical attack of sudden trembling and silent tears. The remarkable resemblance to his mother especially struck the old man.

"Ivan! Ivan! Quick, bring him water! It's like her, it's just like her, his mother did the same thing! Spray him with water from your mouth, that's what I used to do with her. It's on account of his mother, his mother . . . ," he muttered to Ivan.

"But my mother, I think, was also his mother, wouldn't you agree?" Ivan suddenly burst out with irrepressible, angry contempt. The flashing of his eyes startled the old man. But here something very strange happened, if only for a moment. The notion that Alyosha's mother was also Ivan's mother really seemed to have gone clean out of the old man's mind . . .

"What do you mean, your mother?" he muttered, not understanding. "What are you talking about . . . ? Whose mother . . . was she . . . ? Ah, damn! Of course she was yours, too! Damn! You know, my friend, my mind just went blank as never before. Forgive me, Ivan, I was thinking . . . heh, heh, heh!" He stopped. His face split into a long, drunken, half-senseless grin. And suddenly, at that very moment, a terrible noise and clamor came from the front hall, furious shouting was heard, the door was flung open, and Dmitri Fyodorovich flew into the room. The old man rushed to Ivan in terror.

"He'll kill me, he'll kill me! Don't let him get me! Don't let him!" he cried out, clutching at the skirt of Ivan Fyodorovich's coat.

Chapter 9

The Sensualists

On the heels of Dmitri Fyodorovich, Grigory and Smerdyakov also ran into the room. It was they who had struggled with him in the front hall and tried not to let him in (following instructions given them by Fyodor Pavlovich several days earlier). Seizing his chance when Dmitri Fyodorovich stopped for a moment to look about him after bursting into the room, Grigory ran around the table, closed both halves of the door leading to the inner rooms, which was opposite the entrance from the front hall, and stood before the closed door with his arms spread crosswise, ready to defend the entrance, so to speak, to the last drop. Seeing this, Dmitri gave something more like a shriek than a shout and hurled himself at Grigory.

"So she's there! They've hidden her in there! Get away, scoundrel!"

He tried to tear Grigory away, but Grigory pushed him back. Beside himself with rage, Dmitri swung and hit Grigory with all his strength. The old man collapsed as if he had been cut down, and Dmitri jumped over him and smashed through the door. Smerdyakov stayed at the other end of the room, pale and trembling, pressed up close to Fyodor Pavlovich.

"She's here!" cried Dmitri Fyodorovich. "I just saw her turn towards the house, but I couldn't catch up with her. Where is she? Where is she?"

Inconceivable was the effect produced on Fyodor Pavlovich by the cry: "She's here!" All his fright dropped away.

"Catch him! Catch him!" he yelled and dashed after Dmitri Fyodorovich.

Grigory meanwhile had gotten up from the floor but was still beside himself, as it were. Ivan Fyodorovich and Alyosha ran after their father. From the third room came the sound of something falling to the floor with a crash and a tinkle: it was a large glass vase (of the inexpensive sort) on a marble pedestal, which Dmitri Fyodorovich had brushed against as he ran past it.

"Sic him!" yelled the old man. "Help!"

Ivan Fyodorovich and Alyosha finally caught up with the old man and forced him back to the drawing room.

"What are you chasing him for? He really will kill you in there!" Ivan Fyodorovich shouted angrily at his father.

"Vanechka, Lyoshechka, she's here, then, Grushenka is here, he said he saw her . . ."

He was spluttering. He had not expected Grushenka to come this time, and suddenly the news that she was there drove him at once beyond his wits. He was shaking all over. He seemed to have gone mad.

"But you can see for yourself that she hasn't come!" Ivan cried.

"Maybe by the back door."

"But it's locked, the back door is locked, and you have the key . . ."

Dmitri suddenly reappeared in the drawing room. He had of course found that door locked, and the key to the locked door was indeed in Fyodor Pavlovich's pocket. All the windows in all the rooms were locked as well. There was no way Grushenka could have gotten in, then, and no way she could have jumped out.

"Catch him!" shrieked Fyodor Pavlovich the moment he sighted Dmitri again. "He's stolen money in there, from my bedroom!"

And breaking away from Ivan, he again rushed at Dmitri. But Dmitri raised both hands and suddenly seized the old man by the two surviving wisps of hair on his temples, pulled, and smashed him against the floor. He even had time to kick the fallen man in the face two or three times with his heel. The old man let out a shrill moan. Ivan Fyodorovich, though not as strong as his brother Dmitri, grasped him with both arms and tore him with all his might away from the old man. Alyosha, too, helped with his small strength, grasping his brother from the front.

"Madman, you've killed him!" shouted Ivan.

"Serves him right!" Dmitri cried, gasping. "And if I haven't killed him this time, I'll come back and kill him. You can't save him!"

"Dmitri! Get out of here, at once!" Alyosha shouted commandingly.

"Alexei, you tell me, you alone, you're the only one I'll believe: was she here just now or not? I saw her sneaking this way past the fence from the lane. I called out. She ran away . . ."

"I swear to you, she has not been here, and no one here even expected her."

"But I saw her . . . So, she . . . I'll find out where she is . . . Farewell, Alexei! Not a word to Aesop now about money. But go to Katerina Ivanovna at once, and be sure to tell her: 'He says he bows to you, he bows to you, bows!' Precisely that: 'He bows to you—and he bows out!' Describe this scene to her."

Ivan and Grigory had meanwhile lifted the old man up and put him in the armchair. His face was covered with blood, but he was conscious and listened eagerly to Dmitri's shouts. He still imagined that Grushenka was indeed somewhere in the house. Dmitri Fyodorovich gave him a hateful glance as he was leaving.

"I do not repent of your blood!" he exclaimed. "Watch out, old man, watch out for your dream, for I, too, have a dream! I curse you and disown you completely . . ."

He ran out of the room.

"She's here, she must be here! Smerdyakov, Smerdyakov," the old man wheezed almost inaudibly, beckoning to Smerdyakov with his finger.

"She's not here, not here, you crazy old man!" Ivan shouted at him viciously. "Hah, he's fainted! Water, a towel! Move, Smerdyakov!"

Smerdyakov ran to get water. The old man was finally undressed, taken to the bedroom, and put to bed. His head was wrapped with a wet towel. Weakened by cognac, strong sensations, and the beating, he rolled up his eyes as soon as he touched the pillow and at once dozed off. Ivan Fyodorovich and Alyosha went back to the drawing room. Smerdyakov was carrying out the shards of the broken vase, and Grigory was standing by the table looking gloomily at the floor.

"Shouldn't you, too, put something wet on your head and lie down?" Alyosha turned to Grigory. "We will look after him. My brother gave you a terribly painful blow . . . on the head."

"Me he dared . . . !" Grigory uttered gloomily and distinctly.

"He 'dared' father, too, not just you!" Ivan Fyodorovich observed, twisting his mouth.

"I used to wash him in a tub . . . Me he dared . . . !" Grigory kept repeating.

"Devil take it, if I hadn't pulled him away, he might have killed him right there. It wouldn't take much for Aesop," Ivan Fyodorovich whispered to Alyosha.

"God forbid!" exclaimed Alyosha.

"Why 'forbid'?" Ivan continued in the same whisper, his face twisted maliciously. "Viper will eat viper, and it would serve them both right!"

Alyosha started.

"Of course I will not allow murder to be committed, any more than I did just now. Stay here, Alyosha, while I take a walk in the yard. I'm getting a headache."

Alyosha went to his father's bedroom and sat with him behind the screen for about an hour. The old man suddenly opened his eyes and gazed silently at Alyosha for a long time, evidently recollecting and pondering. Suddenly an extraordinary agitation showed on his face.

"Alyosha," he whispered warily, "where is Ivan?"

"Out in the yard. He's got a headache. He's keeping watch for us."

"Bring me the mirror, it's over there, bring it to me!"

Alyosha brought him a small, round folding mirror that stood on the chest of drawers. The old man looked in it: his nose was quite badly swollen, and there was a large purple bruise on his forehead above the left eyebrow.

"What does Ivan say? Alyosha, my dear, my only son, I'm afraid of Ivan; I'm more afraid of Ivan than of the other one. Only you I'm not afraid of . . ."

"Don't be afraid of Ivan either. Ivan is angry, but he'll protect you."

"And what about the other one, Alyosha? He ran to Grushenka! My dear angel, tell me the truth: was Grushenka here just now or not?"

"No one saw her. It's not true, she wasn't here."

"But Mitka, he wants to marry her, marry her!"

"She won't marry him."

"She won't marry him, she won't, she won't, she won't, she won't marry him for anything in the world!" The old man roused himself joyfully, as if nothing more delightful could have been said to him at that moment. Enraptured, he seized Alyosha's hand and firmly pressed it to his heart. Tears even shone in his eyes.

"That little icon, the one of the Mother of God, the one I was just talking about, you can have it, take it with you. And I permit you to go back to the monastery . . . I was joking this morning, don't be cross with me. My head aches, Alyosha . . . Lyosha, ease my heart, be an angel, tell me the truth!"

"You mean whether she was here or not?" Alyosha said ruefully.

"No, no, no, I believe you, but I tell you what: go to Grushenka yourself, or get to see her somehow; find out from her soon, as soon as possible, figure out with your own eyes who she wants to be with, me or him. Eh, what? Can you do it or not?"

"If I see her, I'll ask her," Alyosha murmured in embarrassment.

"No, she won't tell you," the old man interrupted. "She's a fidget. She'll start kissing you and say it's you she wants to marry. She's a cheat, she's shameless. No, you mustn't go to her, you mustn't."

"And it wouldn't be nice either, father, not nice at all."

"Where was he sending you just now when he shouted 'Go!' as he ran out the door?"

"To Katerina Ivanovna."

"For money? To ask for money?"

"No, not for money."

"He has no money, not a drop. Listen, Alyosha, I'll lie in bed all night and think things over. You go now. Maybe you'll meet her . . . Only be sure to stop by tomorrow morning. Be sure to. I'll tell you a little something tomorrow. Will you come?"

"I will."

"When you do, pretend that it was your own idea, that you just came to visit me. Don't tell anyone I asked you to come. Don't say a word to Ivan."

"Very well."

"Good-bye, my angel, you stood up for me today, I won't ever forget it. I'll tell you a little something tomorrow, only I still have to think . . ."

"And how do you feel now?"

"By tomorrow, by tomorrow I'll be up and around. Quite well, quite well, quite well!"

Passing through the yard, Alyosha met his brother Ivan on a bench by the gate. He was sitting and writing something in his notebook with a pencil. Alyosha told Ivan that the old man was awake and conscious and had let him go to spend the night in the monastery.

"Alyosha, it would be my pleasure to meet with you tomorrow morning," Ivan said affably, rising a little. His affability took Alyosha completely by surprise.

"I'll be at the Khokhlakovs' tomorrow," Alyosha replied. "I may be at Katerina Ivanovna's, too, if I don't find her in now . . ."

"So you are going to Katerina Ivanovna's now? 'To bow and bow out'?" Ivan suddenly smiled. Alyosha looked embarrassed.

"I think I understood it all from those exclamations just now, and from certain things that happened before. Dmitri, most likely, has asked you to go to her and tell her that he . . . well . . . well, in a word, that he is 'bowing out'?"

"Brother! What will all this horror between father and Dmitri come to?" Alyosha exclaimed.

"It's impossible to guess for certain. Maybe nothing: the whole affair could just dissolve. That woman is a beast. In any case, the old man must be kept at home, and Dmitri must not be let into the house."

"Brother, let me ask you one more thing: can it be that any man has the right to decide about the rest of mankind, who is worthy to live and who is more unworthy?"

"But why bring worth into it? The question is most often decided in the hearts of men not at all on the basis of worth, but for quite different reasons, much more natural ones. As for rights, tell me, who has no right to wish?"

"But surely not for another's death?"

"Maybe even for another's death. Why lie to yourself when everyone lives like that, and perhaps even cannot live any other way? What are you getting at—what I said about 'two vipers eating each other up'? In that case, let me ask you: do you consider me capable, like Dmitri, of shedding Aesop's blood, well, of killing him? Eh?"

"What are you saying, Ivan! The thought never entered my mind! And I don't consider Dmitri . . ."

"Thanks at least for that," Ivan grinned. "Let it be known to you that I will always protect him. But as for my wishes in the matter, there I reserve complete freedom for myself. I'll see you tomorrow. Don't condemn me, and don't look on me as a villain," he added with a smile.

They shook hands firmly, as they had never done before. Alyosha felt that his brother had stepped a step towards him, and that he must have done so for some reason, with some purpose in mind.

Chapter 10

The Two Together

Yet Alyosha left his father's house even more broken and dejected in spirit than when he had entered it. His mind, too, was splintered and scattered, as it were, while he himself felt at the same time that he was afraid to bring the scattered together and draw a general idea from all the tormenting contradictions he had lived through that day. Something was bordering almost on despair in Alyosha's heart, which had never happened to him before. One main, fateful, and insoluble question towered over everything like a mountain: how would it end between his father and his brother Dmitri with this terrible woman? Now he himself had been a witness. He himself had been there and had seen them face each other. However, only his brother Dmitri could turn out to be unhappy, completely and terribly unhappy: disaster undoubtedly lay in wait for him. Other people also turned out to be concerned in it all, and perhaps far more so than Alyosha could have imagined before. There was something even mysterious in it. His brother Ivan had taken a step towards him, which Alyosha had so long desired, but now for some reason he felt frightened by this step towards intimacy. And those women? It was strange: earlier he had set out to see Katerina Ivanovna in great embarrassment, but now he felt none; on the contrary, he was hurrying to her, as though he expected her to give him guidance. And yet to convey the message to her was now obviously more difficult than before: the matter of the three thousand roubles was decided finally, and his brother Dmitri, now feeling himself dishonest and without any hope, would of course not hesitate at any further fall. Besides, he had ordered him to tell Katerina Ivanovna about the scene that had just taken place at his father's.

It was already seven o'clock and dusk was falling when Alyosha went to see Katerina Ivanovna, who occupied a spacious and comfortable house on Main Street. Alyosha knew that she lived with two aunts. One of them, however, was the aunt only of her sister Agafya Ivanovna; this was that meek person in her father's house who had looked after her together with her sister when she had come from the institute. The other was a stately Moscow grande dame, of the impoverished sort. Rumor had it that they both obeyed Katerina Ivanovna in everything and stayed with her solely for the sake of propriety. And Katerina Ivanovna obeyed only her benefactress, the general's widow, who had remained in Moscow because of her illness, and to whom she was obliged to send two letters every week with detailed news of herself.

When Alyosha entered the front hall and asked the chambermaid who had let him in to announce him, they evidently already knew of his arrival in the drawing room (perhaps they had seen him from the window); in any case Alyosha suddenly heard some noise, some women's running steps, the rustle of skirts: perhaps two or three women had run out. It seemed strange to Alyosha that his arrival could cause such a stir. However, he was at once shown into the drawing room. It was a large room, filled with elegant and abundant furniture, not at all in a provincial manner. There were many sofas, settees, love seats, tables large and small; there were paintings on the walls, vases and lamps on the tables, there were lots of flowers, there was even an aquarium by the window. Twilight made the room somewhat dark. On a sofa where someone had obviously just been sitting, Alyosha noticed a silk mantilla, and on the table in front of the sofa two unfinished cups of chocolate, biscuits, a crystal dish with purple raisins, another with candies. Someone was visiting. Alyosha realized that he had intruded on guests and frowned. But at that very moment the portière was raised and Katerina Ivanovna came in with quick, hurrying steps, and with a joyful, delighted smile held out both hands to Alyosha. At the same moment a maid brought in two lighted candles and set them on the table.

"Thank God it's you at last! All day I've been asking God for no one but you! Sit down."

The beauty of Katerina Ivanovna had struck Alyosha even before, when his brother Dmitri had brought him to her for the first time three weeks earlier, to introduce them and get them acquainted, at Katerina Ivanovna's special request. In that meeting, however, they had failed to strike up any conversation. Supposing Alyosha to be ill at ease, Katerina Ivanovna had spared him, as it were, and spent the whole time talking with Dmitri Fyodorovich. Alyosha had been silent, but had perceived a great deal very clearly. He was struck by the imperiousness, the proud ease, the self-confidence of the arrogant girl. And all that was unquestionable. Alyosha felt that he was not exaggerating. He found her large, black, burning eyes beautiful and especially becoming to her pale, even somewhat pale yellow, oval face. But in those eyes, as well as in the outline of her lovely lips, there was something that his brother certainly might fall terribly in love with, but that it was perhaps impossible to love for long. He almost said so outright to Dmitri, who pestered him after the visit, begging him not to conceal his impressions after seeing his fiancée.

"You will be happy with her, but perhaps . . . not quietly happy."

"That's just it, brother, such women stay as they are, they don't humble themselves before fate. So you think I won't love her eternally?"

"No, maybe you will love her eternally, but maybe you won't always be happy with her . . ."

Alyosha had given his opinion then, blushing and annoyed with himself for having yielded to his brother's entreaties and expressed such "foolish" thoughts. Because his opinion seemed terribly foolish to him as soon as he expressed it. And he felt ashamed at having expressed such an authoritative opinion about a woman. With all the more amazement did he feel now, at the first sight of Katerina Ivanovna as she ran out to him, that perhaps he had been very mistaken then. This time her face shone with unfeigned, openhearted kindness, with direct and ardent sincerity. Of all the former "pride and arrogance" that had so struck Alyosha at first, he now saw only a courageous, noble energy and a certain clear, strong faith in herself. Alyosha realized at the first sight of her, at the first words, that the whole tragedy of her situation with respect to the man she loved so much was no secret to her, that she, perhaps, knew everything already, decidedly everything. And yet, despite that, there was still so much light in her face, so much faith in the future, that Alyosha suddenly felt himself gravely and deliberately guilty before her. He was conquered and attracted at the same time. Besides which he noticed at her first words that she was in some great excitement, perhaps quite unusual for her—an excitement even almost resembling a sort of rapture.

"I've been waiting for you so, because now I can learn the whole truth only from you—and from no one else!"

"I've come . . . ," Alyosha muttered, confused, "I . . . he sent me . . ."

"Ah, he sent you! Well, that is just what I anticipated. Now I know everything, everything!" Katerina Ivanovna exclaimed, her eyes suddenly flashing. "Wait, Alexei Fyodorovich, I shall tell you first of all why I was so anxious for you to come. You see, I know perhaps much more even than you do yourself; it's not news that I need from you. This is what I need from you: I need to know your own personal, last impression of him, I need you to tell me directly, plainly, even coarsely (oh, as coarsely as you like!) how you yourself see him now and how you see his position after your meeting with him today. It will be better, perhaps, than if I myself, whom he no longer wishes to see, were to discuss it with him personally. Do you understand what I want from you? Now, what is it that he sent you to tell me (I just knew he would send you!)—tell me simply, to the very last word . . . !"

"He says that he . . . bows to you, and that he will never come again and . . . that he bows to you."

"Bows? Did he say that, did he put it that way?"

"Yes."

"Just in passing, inadvertently, maybe he made a mistake, maybe he used the wrong word?"

"No, he asked me precisely to give you this word, 'bows.' He asked about three times, so that I wouldn't forget to tell you."

Katerina Ivanovna flushed.

"Help me now, Alexei Fyodorovich, it is now that I need your help. I'll tell you my thought, and you simply tell me whether my thought is right or not. Listen, if he had asked you to bow to me just in passing, without insisting on the word, without underlining the word, that would be it . . . that would be the end! But if he especially insisted on this word, if he especially told you not to forget to convey this *bow* to me, then it means he was agitated, beside himself perhaps. He had made a decision, and was frightened by his decision! He did not walk away from me with a firm step but leaped headlong off the mountain. That he stressed this word may only be a sign of bravado . . ."

"Right, right!" Alyosha ardently agreed, "so it seems to me now."

"And if so, then he hasn't perished yet! He's just in despair, but I can still save him. Wait: did he tell you anything about money, about three thousand roubles?"

"He not only told me, but that is perhaps what was killing him most of all. He said he was now deprived of his honor and nothing mattered anymore," Alyosha ardently replied, feeling with his whole heart that hope was flowing into his heart, and that, indeed, there might be a way out, there might be salvation for his brother. "But do you . . . know about this money?" he added, and suddenly stopped short.

"I've known for a long time, and for certain. I inquired by telegraph in Moscow and have long known that the money was never received. He never sent the money, but I said nothing. Last week I learned how much he needed and still needs money . . . I set myself only one goal in all of this: that he should know who to turn back to, and who is his most faithful friend. No, he does not want to believe that I am his most faithful friend, he has never wanted to know me, he looks on me only as a woman. All week one terrible care has tormented me: how to make it so that he will not be ashamed before me because he spent those three thousand roubles. I mean, let him be ashamed before everyone and before himself, but let him not be ashamed before me. To God he says everything without being ashamed. Why, then, does he still not know how much I can endure for him? Why, why does he not know me, how dare he not know me after all that has happened? I want to save him forever. Let him forget that I am his fiancée! And now he's afraid before me because of his honor! He wasn't afraid to open himself to you, Alexei Fyodorovich. Why haven't I yet deserved the same?"

The last words she spoke in tears; tears gushed from her eyes.

"I must tell you," said Alyosha, also in a trembling voice, "of what took place just now between him and father." And he described the whole scene, described how he had been sent to get money, how Mitya had burst in, beaten their father, and after that specifically and insistently confirmed that he, Alyosha, should go and "bow" . . . "He went to that woman . . . ," Alyosha added softly.

"And do you think that I cannot endure that woman? He thinks that I will not endure her? But he won't marry her," she suddenly gave a nervous laugh. "Can a Karamazov eternally burn with such a passion? It's passion, not love. He won't marry her, because she won't marry him . . . ," again Katerina Ivanovna suddenly laughed strangely.

"He may well marry her," Alyosha said sadly, lowering his eyes.

"He won't marry her, I tell you! That girl—she's an angel, do you know that? Do you know it?" Katerina Ivanovna suddenly exclaimed with remarkable fervor. "The most fantastic of all fantastic beings! I know how bewitching she is, but I also know how kind, firm, noble she is. Why are you looking at me that way, Alexei Fyodorovich? Perhaps you're surprised at my words, perhaps you don't believe me? Agrafena Alexandrovna, my angel!" she suddenly called out to someone, looking into the other room, "come and join us! This is a dear man, this is Alyosha, he knows all about our affairs. Show yourself to him!"

"I've only been waiting behind the curtain for you to call me," said a tender, even somewhat sugary woman's voice.

The portière was raised and . . . Grushenka herself, laughing and joyful, came up to the table. Something seemed to contract in Alyosha. His eyes were glued to her, he couldn't take them off of her. Here she was, that terrible woman, that "beast," as his brother Ivan had let slip half an hour earlier. And yet before him stood what seemed, at first glance, to be a most ordinary and simple being—a kind, nice woman; beautiful, yes, but so much like all other beautiful but "ordinary" women! It's true that she was very good-looking indeed—with that Russian beauty loved so passionately by so many. She was a rather tall woman, slightly shorter, however, than Katerina Ivanovna (who was exceptionally tall), plump, with a soft, even, as it were, inaudible way of moving her body, and delicate as well, as though it were some sort of special sugary confection, like her voice. She came up not like Katerina Ivanovna, with strong, cheerful strides, but, on the contrary, inaudibly. Her step was completely noiseless. Softly she lowered herself into an armchair, softly rustling her ample black silk dress, and delicately wrapping her plump neck, white as foam, and her wide shoulders in an expensive black woolen shawl. She was twenty-two years old, and her face showed exactly that age. Her complexion was very white, with a pale rosy tint high on her cheeks. The shape of her face was too broad, perhaps, and her lower jaw even protruded a bit. Her upper lip was thin, and her more prominent lower lip was twice as full and seemed a little swollen. But the most wonderful, most abundant dark brown hair, dark sable eyebrows, and lovely gray blue eyes with long lashes could not fail to make even the most indifferent and absent-minded man somewhere in the crowd, on market day, in the crush, stop suddenly before this face and remember it afterwards for a long time. What struck Alyosha most of all in this face was its childlike, openhearted expression. Her look was like a child's, her joy was like a child's, she came up to the table precisely "joyfully," as if she were expecting something now with the most childlike, impatient, and trusting curiosity. Her look made the soul glad—Alyosha felt it. But there was something else in her that he could not, and would not have been able to, account for, but which perhaps affected him unconsciously—namely, once again, this softness, this tenderness of her bodily movements, the feline inaudibility of her movements. And yet it was a strong and abundant body. Under the shawl one sensed her broad, full shoulders, her high, still quite youthful bosom. This body perhaps promised the forms of the Venus de Milo, one could sense that—though the proportions must have been and indeed already were somewhat exaggerated. Connoisseurs of Russian feminine beauty could have foretold with certainty, looking at Grushenka, that this fresh, still youthful beauty would lose its harmony towards the age of thirty, would grow shapeless, the face itself would become puffy, wrinkles would very quickly appear around the eyes and on the forehead, the complexion would turn coarser, ruddier perhaps—the beauty of a moment, in short, a passing beauty, such as one so often finds precisely in a Russian woman. Alyosha, of course, was not thinking of that, but, though he was fascinated, he asked himself with a certain unpleasant feeling, and as if regretfully, why she had this manner of drawing out her words instead of speaking naturally. She did it, obviously, because she found this drawn-out and too-sugary enunciation of sounds and syllables beautiful. It was, of course, simply a bad habit, in bad tone, which indicated a low upbringing and a notion of propriety vulgarly adopted in childhood. And yet this manner of speaking and intonation seemed to Alyosha almost an impossible contradiction to the childlike, openhearted, and joyful expression of her face, to the quiet, happy, infant shining of her eyes! Katerina Ivanovna at once sat her down in an armchair facing Alyosha, and delightedly kissed her several times on her smiling lips. She seemed to be in love with her.

"We've met for the first time, Alexei Fyodorovich," she said rapturously. "I wanted to know her, to see her. I would have gone to her, but she came herself as soon as I asked. I knew that we would resolve everything, everything! My heart foresaw it . . . They begged me to abandon this step, but I foresaw the outcome, and I was not mistaken. Grushenka has explained everything to me, all her intentions; like a good angel, she has flown down here and brought peace and joy . . ."

"My dear, worthy young lady did not scorn me," Grushenka drawled in a singsong voice with the same lovely, joyful smile.

"Don't you dare say such a thing to me, you enchantress, you sorceress! Scorn you? I shall kiss your lower lip one more time. It seems a little swollen, then let it be more swollen, and more, and more . . . See how she laughs! Alexei Fyodorovich, it's a joy for the heart just to look at this angel . . ."

Alyosha blushed, and an imperceptible trembling came over him.

"You are too kind to me, dear young lady, and perhaps I am not at all worthy of your caresses."

"Not worthy! She is not worthy!" Katerina Ivanovna again exclaimed with the same fervor. "You know, Alexei Fyodorovich, we have a fantastic little head, we're willful and have a proud, proud little heart! We are noble, Alexei Fyodorovich, we are magnanimous, did you know that? Only we have been so unhappy! We were too ready to make all sorts of sacrifices for an unworthy, perhaps, or frivolous man. There was one man, he was an officer, too, we fell in love with him, we offered him everything, it was long ago, five years ago, and he forgot us, he got married. Now he's a widower, he's written, he's coming here—and, you know, it is only him, only him and no one else that we love now and have loved all our life! He will come, and Grushenka will be happy again, and for all these five years she has been unhappy. But who will reproach her, who will boast of her favors? Only that bedridden old man, a merchant—but he has been more of a father, a friend, a protector to us. He found us in despair, in torment, abandoned by the one we loved so . . . why, she wanted to drown herself then, and this old man saved her, saved her!"

"You defend me too much, dear young lady; you are in too much of a hurry with everything," Grushenka drawled again.

"Defend? Is it for me to defend you? Would we even dare to defend you here? Grushenka, angel, give me your hand. Look at this plump, lovely little hand, Alexei Fyodorovich; do you see it? It brought me happiness and resurrected me, and now I am going to kiss it, back and front, here, here, and here!" And as if in rapture, she kissed the indeed lovely, if perhaps too plump, hand of Grushenka three times. The latter, offering her hand with a nervous, pealing, lovely little laugh, watched the "dear young lady," apparently pleased at having her hand kissed like that. "Maybe a little too much rapture," flashed through Alyosha's mind. He blushed. All the while his heart was somehow peculiarly uneasy.

"Won't you make me ashamed, dear young lady, kissing my hand like that in front of Alexei Fyodorovich!"

"How could I possibly make you ashamed?" said Katerina Ivanovna, somewhat surprised. "Ah, my dear, how poorly you understand me!"

"But perhaps you do not quite understand me either, dear young lady. Perhaps I'm more wicked than you see on the surface. I have a wicked heart, I'm willful. I charmed poor Dmitri Fyodorovich that time only to laugh at him."

"But now it will be you who save him. You gave your word. You will make him listen to reason, you will reveal to him that you love another man, that you have loved him for a long time, and he is now offering you his hand . . ."

"Ah, no, I never gave you my word. It's you who were saying all that, but I didn't give my word."

"Then I must have misunderstood you," Katerina Ivanovna said softly, turning a bit pale, as it were. "You promised . . ."

"Ah, no, my young lady, my angel, I promised nothing," Grushenka interrupted softly and calmly, with the same gay and innocent expression. "Now you see, worthy young lady, how wicked and willful I am next to you. Whatever I want, I will do. Maybe I just promised you something, but now I'm thinking: what if I like him again all of a sudden—Mitya, I mean—because I did like him once very much, I liked him for almost a whole hour. So, maybe I'll go now and tell him to stay with me starting today . . . That's how fickle I am . . ."

"You just said . . . something quite different . . . ," Katerina Ivanovna said faintly.

"Ah, I just said! But I have such a tender, foolish heart. Think what he's suffered because of me! What if I go home and suddenly take pity on him—what then?"

"I didn't expect . . ."

"Eh, young lady, how kind and noble you turn out to be next to me. So now perhaps you'll stop loving such a fool as I am, seeing my character. Give me your little hand, my angel," she asked tenderly, and took Katerina Ivanovna's hand as if in reverence. "Here, dear young lady, I'll take your little hand and kiss it, just as you did to me. You kissed mine three times, and for that I ought to kiss yours three hundred times to be even. And so I shall, and then let it be as God wills; maybe I'll be your complete slave and want to please you in everything like a slave. As God wills, so let it be, with no deals or promises between us. What a hand, what a dear little hand you have, what a hand! My dear young lady, beauty that you are, my impossible beauty!"

She slowly raised this hand to her lips, though with the rather strange purpose of "getting even" in kisses. Katerina Ivanovna did not withdraw her hand: with a timid hope, she listened to Grushenka's last, also rather strangely expressed, promise to please her "like a slave"; she looked tensely into her eyes: she saw in those eyes the same openhearted, trusting expression, the same serene gaiety . . . "Perhaps she is so naive!" a hope flashed in Katerina Ivanovna's heart. Meanwhile Grushenka, as if admiring the "dear little hand," was slowly raising it to her lips. But with the hand just at her lips, she suddenly hesitated for two, maybe three seconds, as if thinking something over.

"Do you know, my angel," she suddenly drawled in the most tender, sugary voice, "do you know? I'm just not going to kiss your hand." And she laughed a gleeful little laugh.

"As you wish . . . What's the matter?" Katerina Ivanovna suddenly started.

"And you can keep this as a memory—that you kissed my hand, and I did not kiss yours." Something suddenly flashed in her eyes. She looked with terrible fixity at Katerina Ivanovna.

"Insolent!" Katerina Ivanovna said suddenly, as if suddenly understanding something. She blushed all over and jumped up from her place. Grushenka, too, got up, without haste.

"So I'll go right now and tell Mitya that you kissed my hand, and I didn't kiss yours at all. How he'll laugh!"

"You slut! Get out!"

"Ah, shame on you, young lady, shame on you! It's really quite indecent for you to use such words, dear young lady."

"Get out, bought woman!" screamed Katerina Ivanovna. Every muscle trembled in her completely distorted face.

"Bought, am I? You yourself as a young girl used to go to your gentlemen at dusk to get money, offering your beauty for sale, and I know it."

Katerina Ivanovna made a cry and was about to leap at her, but Alyosha held her back with all his strength.

"Not a step, not a word! Don't speak, don't answer anything—she'll leave, she'll leave right now!"

At that moment both of Katerina Ivanovna's aunts, having heard her cry, ran into the room; the maid ran in, too. They all rushed to her.

"That I will," said Grushenka, picking up her mantilla from the sofa. "Alyosha, dear, come with me!"

"Go, go quickly," Alyosha pleaded, clasping his hands before her.

"Alyoshenka, dear, come with me! I have something very, very nice to tell you on the way. I performed this scene for you, Alyoshenka. Come with me, darling, you'll be glad you did."

Alyosha turned away, wringing his hands. Grushenka, with a peal of laughter, ran out of the house.

Katerina Ivanovna had a fit. She sobbed, she choked with spasms. Everyone fussed around her.

"I warned you," the elder of the aunts was saying, "I tried to keep you from taking this step . . . You are too passionate . . . How could you think of taking such a step! You do not know these creatures, and this one, they say, is worse than all of them . . . No, you are too willful!"

"She's a tiger!" screamed Katerina Ivanovna. "Why did you hold me back, Alexei Fyodorovich! I'd have beaten her, beaten her!"

She could not restrain herself in front of Alyosha, and perhaps did not want to restrain herself.

"She should be flogged, on a scaffold, by an executioner, with everyone watching!"

Alyosha backed towards the door.

"But, my God!" Katerina Ivanovna suddenly cried out, clasping her hands. "And he! He could be so dishonest, so inhuman! He told this creature what happened then, on that fatal, eternally accursed, accursed day! 'You came to sell your beauty, dear young lady!' She knows! Your brother is a scoundrel, Alexei Fyodorovich!"

Alyosha wanted to say something, but he could not find a single word. His heart ached within him.

"Go away, Alexei Fyodorovich! It's so shameful, so terrible! Tomorrow . . . I beg you on my knees, come tomorrow. Do not condemn me. Forgive me. I don't know what I'll still do to myself!"

Alyosha went outside, staggering, as it were. He, too, felt like crying as she had. Suddenly a maid caught up with him.

"The young lady forgot to give you this letter from Madame Khokhlakov. She's had it since dinnertime."

Alyosha mechanically took the small pink envelope and almost unconsciously put it in his pocket.

Chapter 11

One More Ruined Reputation

From town to the monastery was not more than half a mile or so. Alyosha hurried along the road, which was deserted at that hour. It was already almost night; it was difficult to make out objects thirty paces ahead. There was a crossroads halfway. At the crossroads, under a solitary willow, a figure came into view. Alyosha had just reached the crossroads when the figure tore itself from its place, leaped out at him, and shouted in a wild voice:

"Your money or your life!"

"Ah, it's you, Mitya!" Alyosha, though badly startled, said in surprise.

"Ha, ha, ha! You didn't expect me? I wondered where to wait for you. Near her house? There are three roads from there, and I might have missed you. Finally I decided, I'll wait here, because he'll have to pass here, there's no other way to the monastery. Well, give me the truth, crush me like a cockroach . . . Why, what's the matter?"

"Nothing, brother . . . Just that you startled me. Oh, Dmitri! Father's blood today . . ." Alyosha began to cry. He had been wanting to cry for a long time, and now it was as if something suddenly snapped in his soul. "You all but killed him . . . you cursed him . . . and now . . . here . . . you're making jokes . . . 'Your money or your life!' "

"Well, what of it? Improper, eh? Doesn't fit my position?"

"No . . . I just . . ."

"Wait. Look at the night: see what a gloomy night it is, what clouds, how the wind is rising! I hid myself here, under the willow, waiting for you, and suddenly thought (as God is my witness): why languish any longer, why wait? Here is the willow, there is a handkerchief, a shirt, I can make a rope right now, plus suspenders, and—no longer burden the earth, or dishonor it with my vile presence! And then I heard you coming—Lord, just as if something suddenly flew down on me: ah, so there is a man that I love, here he is, here is that man, my dear little brother, whom I love more than anyone in the world, and who is the only one I love! And I loved you so, I loved you so at that moment that I thought: I'll throw myself on his neck! But then a foolish thought came to me: 'I'll amuse him, I'll give him a scare.' So I yelled: 'Your money!' like a fool. Forgive my foolishness—it's only nonsense, and in my soul . . . it's also fitting . . . Well, damn it, tell me what happened! What did she say? Crush me, strike me down, don't spare me! Was she furious?"

"No, not that . . . It wasn't like that at all, Mitya. It was . . . I found the two of them there together."

"What two?"

"Grushenka and Katerina Ivanovna."

Dmitri Fyodorovich was dumbstruck.

"Impossible!" he cried. "You're raving! Grushenka with her?"

Alyosha told him everything that had happened to him from the very moment he entered Katerina Ivanovna's house. He spoke for about ten minutes, one would not say fluently or coherently, but he seemed to convey it clearly, grasping the main words, the main gestures, and vividly conveying his own feelings, often with a single stroke. His brother Dmitri listened silently, staring point blank at him with horrible fixity, but it was clear to Alyosha that he already understood everything and comprehended the whole fact. But his face, as the story went on, became not merely grim but menacing, as it were. He glowered, clenched his teeth, his fixed stare seemed to become still more fixed, more intent, more terrible . . . Which made it all the more unexpected when, with inconceivable swiftness, his face, until then angry and ferocious, suddenly changed all at once, his compressed lips parted, and Dmitri Fyodorovich suddenly dissolved in the most irrepressible, the most genuine laughter. He literally dissolved in laughter, and for a long time could not even speak for laughing.

"She just didn't kiss her hand! She just didn't, she just ran away!" he exclaimed with some sort of morbid delight—one might have called it insolent delight had it not been so artless. "And the other one shouted that she was a tiger! A tiger she is! And that she deserves the scaffold! Yes, yes, so she does, she does, I agree, she deserves it, she has long deserved it! Let's have that scaffold, brother, but let me recover first. I can see that queen of insolence, the whole of her is there, that hand expresses the whole of her! Infernal woman! She's the queen of all infernal women the world can imagine! Delightful in a way! So she ran home? Then I . . . eh . . . will run to her! Alyoshka, don't blame me, I do agree that throttling's too good for her . . ."

"And Katerina Ivanovna!" Alyosha exclaimed sadly.

"I see her, too, right through her, I see her, I see her better than ever before! It's quite a discovery—all four cardinal points—all five, I mean.[1] What a thing to do! It's the same Katenka, the institute girl, who wasn't afraid to run to an absurd brute of an officer with the generous idea of saving her father, at the risk of being horribly insulted! But what pride, what recklessness, what defiance of fate, what infinite defiance! You say the aunt tried to stop her? That aunt, you know, is a despot herself, she's the sister of the Moscow general's widow, she used to put on even more airs than the other one, but her husband was convicted of embezzlement, lost everything, his estate and everything, and his proud spouse had to pull her head in, and never stuck it out again. So she was holding Katya back, and Katya didn't listen. 'I can conquer all, all is in my power; I can bewitch Grushenka, too, if I like'—and she did believe herself, she was showing off to herself, so whose fault is it? Do you think she first kissed Grushenka's hand with some purpose, out of cunning calculation? No, she really and truly fell in love with Grushenka—that is, not with Grushenka but with her own dream, her own delusion—because it was *her* dream, *her* delusion! My dear Alyosha, how did you manage to save yourself from them, from those women? You must have hitched up your cassock and run! Ha, ha, ha!"

"But Mitya, you don't seem to have noticed how you offended Katerina Ivanovna by telling Grushenka about that day. And she immediately threw it in her face, that she 'went secretly to her gentlemen to sell her beauty'! Could any offense be greater than that, brother?" Alyosha was most tormented by the thought that his brother seemed pleased at Katerina Ivanovna's humiliation, though of course it could not be so.

"Bah!" Dmitri Fyodorovich frowned horribly all of a sudden and slapped himself on the forehead. Only now did he notice it, though Alyosha had just told him both about the offense and about Katerina Ivanovna's cry: "Your brother is a scoundrel!"

"Yes, maybe I really did tell Grushenka about that 'fatal day,' as Katya calls it. Yes, I did, I did tell her, I remember! It was that time in Mokroye, I was drunk, the gypsy women were singing . . . But I was weeping, I myself was weeping, I was on my knees, praying before Katya's image, and Grushenka understood. She understood everything then. I remember, she wept herself . . . Ah, the devil! But it couldn't be otherwise! Then she wept, and now . . . now 'a dagger in the heart.' That's how it is with women."

He looked down and thought for a moment.

"Yes, I am a scoundrel! An unquestionable scoundrel!" he said suddenly in a gloomy voice. "No matter whether I wept or not, I'm still a scoundrel! Tell her I accept the title, if it's any comfort. But enough, farewell, there's no use talking. It's not amusing. You take your road and I'll take mine. And I don't want to see you any more until some last moment. Farewell, Alexei!" He gripped Alyosha's hand, and still looking down, without raising his head, as though tearing himself away, he quickly strode off towards town. Alyosha looked after him, not believing that he was quite so suddenly gone.

"Wait, Alexei, one more confession, to you alone!" Dmitri Fyodorovich suddenly turned back. "Look at me, look closely: right here, do you see, right here a horrible dishonor is being prepared." (As he said "right here," Dmitri Fyodorovich struck himself on the chest with his fist, and with such a strange look as though the dishonor was lying and being kept precisely there on his chest, in some actual place, maybe in a pocket, or sewn up and hanging around his neck.) "You know me by now: a scoundrel, an avowed scoundrel! But know that whatever I have done before or now or may do later—nothing, nothing can compare in baseness with the dishonor I am carrying, precisely now, precisely at this moment, here on my chest, here, right here, which is being enacted and carried out, and which it is fully in my power to stop, I can stop it or carry it out, make a note of that! And know, then, that I will carry it out and will not stop it. I just told you everything, but this I did not tell you, because even I am not so brazen! I could still stop; if I stopped, tomorrow I could recover fully half of my lost honor; but I will not stop, I will carry out my base design, and in the future you can be my witness that I told you beforehand and with aforethought! Darkness and ruin! There's nothing to explain, you'll learn it all in due time. A stinking back lane and an infernal woman! Farewell. Don't pray for me, I'm not worthy of it, and it's unnecessary, quite unnecessary . . . I don't need it at all! Away!"

And suddenly he was gone, this time for good. Alyosha walked towards the monastery. "What does he mean? Why will I not see him anymore? What is he talking about?" went wildly through his head. "Tomorrow I must be sure to see him and find him; I'll make a point of finding him. What is he talking about?"

He skirted the monastery and walked straight to the hermitage through the pine woods. The door was opened for him, though at that hour no one was let in. His heart trembled as he entered the elder's cell: Why, why had he left? Why had the elder sent him "into the world"? Here was quiet, here was holiness, and there—confusion, and a darkness in which one immediately got lost and went astray . . .

In the cell were the novice Porfiry and the hieromonk Father Paissy, who all through the day, every hour, had come to inquire about the health of Father Zosima. Alyosha was alarmed to learn that he was getting worse and worse. This time even the usual evening talk with the brothers could not take place. Ordinarily, each day after the evening service, before going to bed, the monastery brothers gathered in the elder's cell, and everyone confessed aloud to him his transgressions of the day, sinful dreams, thoughts, temptations, even quarrels among themselves if there had been any. Some confessed on their knees. The elder absolved, reconciled, admonished, imposed penance, blessed, and dismissed. It was against these brotherly "confessions" that the opponents of the institution of elders protested, saying that this was a profanation of confession as a sacrament, almost a blasphemy, though it was a matter of something quite different. It was even brought up before the diocesan authorities that such confessions not only do not achieve any good purpose, but really and knowingly lead to sin and temptation; that for many of the brothers it was a burden to go to the elder, and that they went against their will, because everyone went, and to avoid being considered proud and rebellious in thought. It was said that some of the brothers agreed among themselves before going to the evening confession: "I'll say I was angry with you this morning, and you confirm it," so that they could get off with saying something. Alyosha knew that this sometimes really happened. He also knew that there were some among the brothers who were quite indignant at the custom of having even the letters they received from their relatives brought to the elder first, to be opened, before they were delivered to them. It was assumed, of course, that this all should be done freely and sincerely, without reservation, for the sake of free humility and saving instruction, but in reality, as it turned out, it sometimes was also done quite insincerely and, on the contrary, artificially and falsely. Yet the older and more experienced of the brothers stood their ground, arguing that "for those who have sincerely entered these walls in order to be saved, all these obediences and deeds will no doubt work for salvation and be of great benefit; as for those who, on the contrary, find them burdensome and murmur against them, for them it is the same as if they were not monks, and they have come to the monastery in vain, for their place is in the world. And as one cannot protect oneself from sin either in the world or in the Church, so there is no need for indulging sin."

"He's grown weak, overcome by drowsiness," Father Paissy informed Alyosha in a whisper, having given him a blessing. "It is even difficult to rouse him. But there's no need to rouse him. He woke up for about five minutes, asked to send the brothers his blessing, and asked the brothers to mention him in their evening prayers. Tomorrow morning he intends to take communion one more time. He mentioned you, Alexei, asked whether you were away, and was told that you were in town. 'I gave him my blessing for that; his place is there, and not here as yet'—so he spoke of you. He remembered you lovingly, with concern; do you realize what has been granted you? But why did he decide that you should now spend time in the world? It must mean that he foresees something in your destiny! Understand, Alexei, that even if you go back into the world, it will be as though it were an obedience imposed on you by your elder, and not for vain frivolity, not for worldly pleasure . . ."

Father Paissy went out. That the elder was dying, Alyosha did not doubt, though he might still live for another day or two. Alyosha firmly and ardently resolved that, despite the promises he had given to see his father, the Khokhlakovs, his brother, and Katerina Ivanovna, he would not leave the monastery at all the next day, but would stay by his elder until the very end. His heart began burning with love, and he bitterly reproached himself that he had been able, for a moment, there in town, even to forget the one whom he had left in the monastery on his bed of death, and whom he honored above everyone in the world. He went to the elder's little bedroom, knelt, and bowed to the ground before the sleeping man. The latter slept quietly, motionlessly; his faint breath came evenly, almost imperceptibly. His face was peaceful.

When he returned to the other room, the same room in which the elder had received his guests that morning, Alyosha, almost without undressing, taking off only his boots, lay down on the hard, narrow leather divan he always slept on, and had for a long time now, every night, bringing only a pillow. As for the mattress his father had shouted about, he had long ceased sleeping on it. He simply took off his cassock and covered himself with it instead of a blanket. But before going to sleep, he threw himself down on his knees and prayed for a long time. In his ardent prayer, he did not ask God to explain his confusion to him, but only thirsted for joyful tenderness, the same tenderness that always visited his soul after praising and glorifying God, of which his prayer before going to sleep usually consisted. This joy that visited him always drew after it a light and peaceful sleep. Praying now, he suddenly happened to feel in his pocket the little pink envelope that Katerina Ivanovna's maid had given him when she caught up with him in the street. He was troubled, but finished his prayer. Then, after some hesitation, he opened the envelope. It contained a note signed by Lise, the young daughter of Madame Khokhlakov, the one who had laughed at him so much that morning in front of the elder.

"Alexei Fyodorovich," she wrote, "I am writing to you in secret from everyone, from mama, too, and I know how wrong it is. But I cannot live any longer without telling you what has been born in my heart, and this no one but the two of us should know for the time being. But how shall I tell you that which I want so much to tell you? Paper, they say, does not blush, but I assure you that it is not true, and that it is blushing now just as I am blushing all over. Dear Alyosha, I love you, I have loved you ever since childhood, in Moscow, when you were nothing like you are now, and I shall love you all my life. I have chosen you with my heart, to be united with you, and to end our life together in old age. Of course, on the condition that you leave the monastery. As far as our age is concerned, we will wait as long as the law requires. By that time I shall certainly get well, I shall walk and dance. There is no question of it.

"You see how I have thought of everything. There is only one thing I cannot imagine: what will you think when you read this? I am always laughing and being naughty, just today I made you angry, but I assure you that now, before I took up the pen, I prayed to the icon of the Mother of God, and I am praying now and nearly crying.

"My secret is in your hands; tomorrow when you come, I do not know how I shall look at you. Ah, Alexei Fyodorovich, what if I am again unable to help myself and start laughing like a fool, as I did today, when I see you? You will take me for a naughty teaser and will not believe my letter. And so I beg you, my dear one, if you have any compassion for me, when you come in tomorrow, do not look too directly in my eyes, because if I happen to meet yours, perhaps I shall surely burst out laughing, and besides you will be wearing that long dress . . . Even now I feel cold all over when I think of it, and so, when you come in, do not look at me at all for a while, but look at mama, or at the window . . .

"So, I have written you a love letter, oh, my God, what have I done! Alyosha, do not despise me, and if I have done something very bad and upset you, forgive me. Now the secret of my reputation, ruined perhaps forever, is in your hands.

"I shall surely cry today. Till tomorrow, till that *terrible* morrow. Lise.

"P.S. Only, Alyosha, you must, must, must come! Lise."

Alyosha read the note with surprise, read it a second time, thought a moment, and suddenly laughed softly and sweetly. Then he gave a start; this laughter seemed sinful to him. But a moment later he laughed again just as softly and happily. He slowly put the note into the little envelope, crossed himself, and lay down. The confusion in his soul suddenly passed. "Lord have mercy on them all today, unhappy and stormy as they are, preserve and guide them. All ways are yours: save them according to your ways. You are love, you will send joy to all!" Alyosha murmured, crossing himself and falling into a serene sleep.

PART II

BOOK IV: STRAINS

Chapter 1

Father Ferapont

Early in the morning, before dawn, Alyosha was awakened. The elder had gotten up, feeling quite weak, though he still wished to move from his bed to the armchair. He was fully conscious; his face, though quite tired, was bright, almost joyful, and his eyes were merry, cordial, welcoming. "I may not survive this coming day," he said to Alyosha; then he desired to make a confession and receive communion immediately. His confessor had always been Father Paissy. After the completion of both sacraments, the rite of holy unction began.[1] The hieromonks gathered, and the cell gradually filled with monks from the hermitage. Meanwhile day came. Monks began to arrive from the monastery as well. When the service was over, the elder desired to take leave of everyone and kissed them all. As the cell was small, the first visitors went out to make room for others. Alyosha stood near the elder, who had moved back to the armchair. He spoke and taught as much as he could; his voice, though weak, was still quite firm. "I have taught you for so many years, and therefore spoken aloud for so many years, that it has become a habit, as it were, to speak, and, speaking, to teach you, so much so that I would find it almost more difficult to be silent than to speak, my dear fathers and brothers, even now in my weakness," he joked, looking tenderly upon those who crowded around him. Later Alyosha recalled something of what he said then. But though he spoke distinctly and in a sufficiently firm voice, his talk was rather incoherent. He spoke of many things, he seemed to want to say everything, to speak one last time before the moment of death, to say all that had not been said in his life, and not only for the sake of instruction, but as if he wished to share his joy and ecstasy with all, to pour out his heart once more in this life . . .

"Love one another, fathers," the elder taught (as far as Alyosha could recall afterwards). "Love God's people. For we are not holier than those in the world because we have come here and shut ourselves within these walls, but, on the contrary, anyone who comes here, by the very fact that he has come, already knows himself to be worse than all those who are in the world, worse than all on earth . . . And the longer a monk lives within his walls, the more keenly he must be aware of it. For otherwise he had no reason to come here. But when he knows that he is not only worse than all those in the world, but is also guilty before all people, on behalf of all and for all,[2] for all human sins, the world's and each person's, only then will the goal of our unity be achieved. For you must know, my dear ones, that each of us is undoubtedly guilty on behalf of all and for all on earth, not only because of the common guilt of the world, but personally, each one of us, for all people and for each person on this earth. This knowledge is the crown of the monk's path, and of every man's path on earth. For monks are not a different sort of men, but only such as all men on earth ought also to be. Only then will our hearts be moved to a love that is infinite, universal, and that knows no satiety. Then each of us will be able to gain the whole world by love and wash away the world's sins with his tears . . . Let each of you keep close company with his heart, let each of you confess to himself untiringly. Do not be afraid of your sin, even when you perceive it, provided you are repentant, but do not place conditions on God. Again I say, do not be proud. Do not be proud before the lowly, do not be proud before the great either. And do not hate those who reject you, disgrace you, revile you, and slander you. Do not hate atheists, teachers of evil, materialists, not even those among them who are wicked, nor those who are good, for many of them are good, especially in our time. Remember them thus in your prayers: save, Lord, those whom there is no one to pray for, save also those who do not want to pray to you. And add at once: it is not in my pride that I pray for it, Lord, for I myself am more vile than all . . . Love God's people, do not let newcomers draw your flock away, for if in your laziness and disdainful pride, in your self-interest most of all, you fall asleep, they will come from all sides and lead your flock away. Teach the Gospel to the people untiringly . . . Do not engage in usury . . . Do not love silver and gold, do not keep it . . . Believe, and hold fast to the banner. Raise it high . . ."

The elder spoke, however, in a more fragmentary way than has been set forth here or in the notes that Alyosha later wrote down. Sometimes he stopped speaking altogether, as if gathering his strength, and gasped for breath, yet he seemed to be in ecstasy. He was listened to with great feeling, though many wondered at his words and saw darkness in them . . . Afterwards they all remembered these words. When Alyosha happened to leave the cell for a moment, he was struck by the general excitement and anticipation among the brothers crowding in and near the cell. Some were almost anxious in their anticipation, others were solemn. Everyone expected something immediate and great upon the elder's falling asleep.[3] This expectation was, from the one point of view, almost frivolous, as it were, yet even the sternest old monks suffered from it. Sternest of all was the face of the old hieromonk Paissy. Alyosha happened to leave the cell only because he had been mysteriously summoned, through a monk, by Rakitin, who came from town with a strange letter sent to Alyosha by Madame Khokhlakov. She informed Alyosha of a curious piece of news, which came at a highly opportune moment. It so happened that the day before, among the faithful peasant women who had come to venerate the elder and receive his blessing, there was a little old lady from town, Prokhorovna, a noncommissioned officer's widow. She had asked the elder if in a prayer for the dead she could remember her dear son Vasenka, who had gone on official duty far away to Siberia, to Irkutsk, and from whom she had received no news for a year. To which the elder had replied sternly, forbidding it, and likening this sort of commemoration to sorcery. But then, forgiving her because of her ignorance, he had added, "as if looking into the book of the future" (so Madame Khokhlakov put it in her letter), the consolation "that her son Vasya was undoubtedly alive, and that he would either come himself or send a letter shortly, and she should go home and wait for that. And what do you think?" Madame Khokhlakov added ecstatically, "the prophecy came true even literally, and even more than that." The moment the old lady returned home, she was at once handed a letter from Siberia, which was there waiting for her. And that was not all: in this letter, written en route from Ekaterinburg, Vasya informed his mother that he was coming to Russia, that he was returning with some official, and that in about three weeks after she received this letter "he hoped to embrace his mother." Madame Khokhlakov insistently and ardently begged Alyosha to report this newly occurred "miracle of prediction" immediately to the Superior and all the brothers: "It must be made known to everyone, everyone!" she exclaimed in conclusion. Her letter had been written hastily, in a rush; the writer's excitement rang in every line of it. But there was nothing for Alyosha to tell the brothers: everyone already knew everything. Rakitin, as he sent the monk for Alyosha, charged him, besides, "most respectfully to notify his reverence Father Paissy as well, that he, Rakitin, had some business with him, of such importance that he could not postpone informing him of it even for a minute, asking him with a low bow to forgive his boldness." Since the monk had brought Rakitin's request to Father Paissy before finding Alyosha, it only remained for Alyosha, after reading the letter, to hand it over to Father Paissy as a document. And then even that stern and mistrustful man, as he read, frowning, the news of the "miracle," could not quite contain a certain inner emotion. His eyes flashed, and a solemn and knowing smile suddenly came to his lips.

"Shall we not behold greater things?" he suddenly let fall.

"We shall, we shall!" the monks around him repeated, but Father Paissy frowned again and asked them all to tell no one about it for the time being, "not until we have more confirmation, for there is much frivolousness among people in the world, and this incident also may have taken place naturally," he added prudently, as if for the sake of conscience, but almost not believing in his own reservation, as his listeners very well saw. Within an hour, of course, the "miracle" became known to the whole monastery, and even to many of the laymen who had come there for the liturgy. More than anyone else, the new miracle seemed to have struck the little monk "from St. Sylvester's," who had come to the monastery the day before from his small Obdorsk monastery in the far north. The day before, standing near Madame Khokhlakov, he had bowed to the elder and, pointing to that lady's "healed" daughter, had asked him with great feeling: "How do you dare do such deeds?"

He was already in some perplexity as it was, and almost did not know what to believe. The previous evening he had visited the monastery's Father Ferapont in his private cell beyond the apiary, and was struck by this meeting, which had made an extraordinary and terrifying impression on him. This old Father Ferapont was that same aged monk, the great faster and keeper of silence, whom we have already mentioned as an adversary of the elder Zosima, and above all of the institution of elders, which he regarded as a harmful and frivolous innovation. He was an extremely dangerous adversary, even though, as a keeper of silence, he hardly ever spoke a word to anyone. He was dangerous mainly because many brothers fully sympathized with him, and among visiting laymen many honored him as a great ascetic and a righteous man, even though they regarded him as unquestionably a holy fool. Indeed, it was this that fascinated them. Father Ferapont never went to the elder Zosima. Though he lived in the hermitage, he was not much bothered by hermitage rules, again because he behaved like a real holy fool. He was about seventy-five years old, if not more, and lived beyond the hermitage apiary, in a corner of the wall, in an old, half-ruined wooden cell built there in ancient times, back in the last century, for a certain Father Iona, also a great faster and keeper of silence, who had lived to be a hundred and five and of whose deeds many curious stories were still current in the monastery and its environs. Father Ferapont had so succeeded that he, too, was finally placed, about seven years earlier, in this same solitary little cell, really just a simple hut, but which rather resembled a chapel because it housed such a quantity of donative icons with donative icon lamps eternally burning before them, which Father Ferapont was appointed, as it were, to look after and keep lit. He ate, it was said (and in fact it was true), only two pounds of bread in three days, not more; it was brought to him every three days by the beekeeper who lived there in the apiary, but even with this beekeeper who served him, Father Ferapont rarely spoke a word. These four pounds of bread, together with a prosphora,[*] which the Superior regularly sent the blessed man after the late Sunday liturgy,[5] constituted his entire weekly sustenance. The water in his jug was changed every day. He rarely appeared at a liturgy. Visiting admirers sometimes saw him spend the whole day in prayer without rising from his knees or turning around. And even if he occasionally got into conversation with them, he was brief, curt, strange, and almost always rude. There were, however, very rare occasions when he would start talking with visitors, but for the most part he merely uttered some one strange saying, which always posed a great riddle for the visitor, and then, despite all entreaties, would give no further explanation. He was not a priest but just a simple monk. There was, however, a very strange rumor among the most ignorant people that Father Ferapont was in communication with the heavenly spirits and conversed only with them, which was why he was silent with people. The Obdorsk monk found his way to the apiary on directions from the beekeeper, also rather a silent and surly monk, and went to the corner where Father Ferapont's cell stood. "Maybe he'll speak, since you're a visitor, or maybe you'll get nothing out of him," the beekeeper warned him. The monk, as he himself recounted later, approached in great fear. It was already rather late. This time Father Ferapont was sitting by the door of the cell on a low bench. Over him a huge old elm was lightly rustling. The evening was turning cool. The Obdorsk monk prostrated before the holy man and asked for his blessing.

"Do you want me to prostrate in front of you, too, monk?" said Father Ferapont. "Arise!"

The monk stood up.

"Blessing wilt thou bless thyself, have a seat here. Where'd you drop from?"

What struck the poor monk most was that Father Ferapont, with his undoubtedly great fasting, and though he was of such an advanced age, still looked to be a vigorous old man. He was tall, held himself erect, without stooping, and had a fresh face, thin but healthy. He also undoubtedly still preserved considerable strength. And he was of athletic build. Despite his great age, he was not even completely gray yet, and his hair and beard, formerly quite black, were still very thick. His eyes were gray, large, luminous, but extremely bulging, even strikingly so. He spoke with a strong northern accent. He was dressed in a long, reddish peasant coat made from coarse convict broadcloth, as it used to be called, with a thick rope for a belt. His neck and chest were bare. An almost completely blackened shirt of the thickest canvas, which had not been taken off for months, stuck out from under the coat. It was said that underneath he wore thirty pounds of chain. On his bare feet he wore a pair of old shoes, which were almost in pieces.

"From the small Obdorsk monastery of St. Selivester," the visiting monk replied humbly, watching the hermit with his quick, curious, though somewhat frightened eyes.

"I was at your Selivester's. Used to live there. How's Selivester's health?"

The monk faltered.

"Eh, what muddleheads you peoples are! How do you keep Lent?"

"This is the refectory rule, according to the ancient order of the monastery: for all forty days of Lent there are no meals on Monday, Wednesday, and Friday. On Tuesdays and Thursdays we have white bread, stewed fruit with honey, cloudberries or salt cabbage and oatmeal gruel, and on Saturdays white cabbage soup, noodles with peas, and hot kasha, all made with oil. On Sundays we have cabbage soup, dried fish, and kasha. During Holy Week,[6] from Monday until Saturday evening, for six days, we eat only bread and water and uncooked vegetables, and that with restraint; eating is permitted, but not every day, just as in the first week. On Great and Holy Friday we eat nothing, and on Great Saturday, too, we fast until the third hour and then have a little bread and water and one cup of wine. On Great and Holy Thursday we eat uncooked food or boiled food without oil, and drink wine. For the rule of the Council of Laodicea says of Great Thursday: 'It is not worthy during the Great Lent to relax on the Thursday of the last week and so dishonor all forty days.'[7] That's how it is with us. But what's that compared to you, great father," the little monk added, taking courage, "for all year round, and even on Holy Easter, you eat just bread and water, and as much bread as we'd eat in two days lasts you a whole week. Truly marvelous is your great abstinence!"

"And mushrooms?" Father Ferapont suddenly asked.

"Mushrooms?" the surprised monk repeated.

"Right. I can do without their bread, I don't need it at all, I can go to the forest and live on mushrooms and berries, but they can't do without their bread here, that's why they're in bondage to the devil. Nowadays these unclean ones say there's no need to fast so much. Arrogant and unclean is their reasoning."

"Ah, true," sighed the little monk.

"Did you see all the devils around there?" asked Father Ferapont.

"Around where?" the monk timidly inquired.

"I was up at the Superior's last year, at Pentecost,[8] and haven't been back since. I saw one sitting on one monk's chest, hiding under his cassock, with only his little horns sticking out; another monk had one peeking out of his pocket, looking shifty-eyed, because he was afraid of me; another had one living in his stomach, his unclean belly; and there was one who had one hanging on his neck, clinging to him, and he was carrying him around without even seeing him."

"And you . . . could see?" the monk inquired.

"I'm telling you—I see, I see throughout. As I was leaving the Superior's, I looked—there was one hiding from me behind the door, a real beefy one, a yard and a half tall or more, with a thick tail, brown, long, and he happened to stick the tip of it into the doorjamb, and me being no fool, I suddenly slammed the door shut and pinched his tail. He started squealing, struggling, and I crossed him to death with the sign of the Cross, the triple one. He dropped dead on the spot, like a squashed spider. He must be rotten and stinking in that corner now, and they don't see, they don't smell a thing. I haven't gone back for a year. I reveal it to you only because you're a foreigner."

"Terrible are your words! And tell me, great and blessed father," the monk took more and more heart, "is it true, this great fame that has spread even to faraway lands, that you are in constant communication with the Holy Spirit?"

"He flies down. He does."

"How does he fly down? In what form?"

"As a bird."

"The Holy Spirit in the form of a dove?"[9]

"There is the Holy Spirit, and there is the Holispirit. The Holispirit is different, he can descend as some other bird—a swallow, a goldfinch, a tomtit."

"And how can you tell him from a tomtit?"

"He speaks."

"How does he speak? In what language?"

"Human language."

"And what does he tell you?"

"Well, today he announced that a fool would visit me and ask improper questions. You want to know too much, monk."

"Dreadful are your words, most blessed and holy father," the monk shook his head. In his fearful little eyes, however, there seemed to be some doubt.

"And do you see this tree?" asked Father Ferapont, after a short silence.

"I see it, most blessed father."

"For you it's an elm, but for me the picture is different."

"What is it for you?" the little monk asked after pausing in vain expectation.

"It happens during the night. Do you see those two branches? In the night, behold, Christ stretches forth his arms to me, searching for me with those arms, I see it clearly and tremble. Fearsome, oh, fearsome!"

"Why is it fearsome, if it's Christ himself?"

"He may grab hold of me and ascend me."

"Alive?"

"What, haven't you heard of the spirit and power of Elijah?[10] He may seize me and carry me off . . ."

Though following this conversation the Obdorsk monk returned to the cell assigned him with one of the brothers in a state of considerable perplexity, his heart was still undoubtedly inclined more towards Father Ferapont than towards Father Zosima. The Obdorsk monk was above all in favor of fasting, and it was no wonder that such a great faster as Father Ferapont should "behold marvels." Of course, his words were absurd, as it were, but the Lord knew what was hidden in those words, and Father Ferapont's words and even his deeds were no stranger than those of other holy fools. The devil's pinched tail he was ready to believe, sincerely and with pleasure, not only figuratively but literally as well. Besides, even earlier, before coming to the monastery, he had been strongly biased against the institution of elders, which until then he had known only from hearsay, and, along with many others, regarded it as a decidedly harmful innovation. Having spent one day in the monastery, he had already managed to take note of the secret murmuring of some light-minded brothers who were not accepting of elders. Besides, this monk was meddlesome and adroit by nature, and extremely curious about everything. That was why the great news of the new "miracle" performed by the elder Zosima threw him into such perplexity. Alyosha recalled later that among the monks crowding near the elder and around his cell, the little figure of the inquisitive Obdorsk visitor, darting everywhere from group to group, listening to everything, and questioning everyone, kept flashing before him. But at the time he paid little attention to him and only later remembered it all . . . And indeed he could not be bothered with that: the elder Zosima, who felt tired again and went back to bed, suddenly, as he was closing his eyes, remembered him and called him to his side. Alyosha came running at once. Only Father Paissy, Father Iosif, and the novice Porfiry were with the elder then. The elder, opening his tired eyes and glancing attentively at Alyosha, suddenly asked him:

"Are your people expecting you, my son?"

Alyosha hesitated.

"Do they need you? Did you promise anyone yesterday that you would come today?"

"I promised . . . my father . . . my brothers . . . others, too."

"You see, you must go. Do not be sad. I assure you I will not die without saying my last word on earth in your presence. I will say this word to you, my son, to you I will bequeath it. To you, my dear son, because you love me. But for now, go to those you have promised to see."

Alyosha obeyed at once, though it was hard for him to go. But the promise of hearing his last word on earth, and above all that it would be a bequest, as it were, to him, Alyosha, shook his soul with rapture. He hurried so that he could finish everything in town and come back the sooner. And just then Father Paissy, too, spoke some parting words to him, which made a rather strong and unexpected impression on him. They had both just left the elder's cell.

"Remember, young man, unceasingly," Father Paissy began directly, without any preamble, "that the science of this world, having united itself into a great force, has, especially in the past century, examined everything heavenly that has been bequeathed to us in sacred books, and, after hard analysis, the learned ones of this world have absolutely nothing left of what was once holy. But they have examined parts and missed the whole, and their blindness is even worthy of wonder. Meanwhile the whole stands before their eyes as immovably as ever, and the gates of hell shall not prevail against it.[11] Did it not live for nineteen centuries, does it not live even now in the movements of individual souls and in the movements of the popular masses? Even in the movements of the souls of those same all-destroying atheists, it lives, as before, immovably! For those who renounce Christianity and rebel against it are in their essence of the same image of the same Christ, and such they remain, for until now neither their wisdom nor the ardor of their hearts has been able to create another, higher image of man and his dignity than the image shown of old by Christ. And whatever their attempts, the results have been only monstrosities. Remember this especially, young man, since you are being assigned to the world by your departing elder. Perhaps, remembering this great day, you will not forget my words either, given as cordial words of parting for you, because you are young and the temptations of the world are heavy and your strength will not endure them. Well, go now, my orphan."

With these words Father Paissy gave him a blessing. As he was leaving the monastery, thinking over all these unexpected words, Alyosha suddenly understood that in this monk, who had hitherto been stern and severe with him, he had now met a new and unlooked-for friend, a new director who ardently loved him—as if the elder Zosima, in dying, had bequeathed him Paissy. "And perhaps that is indeed what happened between them," Alyosha suddenly thought. The unexpected learned discourse he had just heard, precisely that and not some other sort, testified to the ardor of Father Paissy's heart: he had hastened to arm the young mind as quickly as possible for its struggle with temptations, to surround the young soul bequeathed to him with a wall stronger than any other he could imagine.

Chapter 2

At His Father's

Alyosha went first of all to his father's. As he was nearing the house, he remembered his father insisting very much the day before that he come somehow in secret from his brother Ivan. "I wonder why?" the thought suddenly occurred to Alyosha. "If father wants to say something to me alone, in secret, still why should I have to come secretly? He must have meant to say something else, but in his excitement yesterday he didn't manage to," he decided. Nevertheless he was very glad when Marfa Ignatievna, who opened the gate for him (Grigory, it turned out, had fallen ill and was in bed in the cottage), in answer to his question, informed him that Ivan Fyodorovich had gone out two hours before.

"And father?"

"He's up, he's having his coffee," Marfa Ignatievna answered somehow drily. Alyosha went in. The old man was sitting alone at the table, in his slippers and an old coat, looking through some accounts for diversion, but without much interest. He was quite alone in the house (Smerdyakov, too, had gone out, to buy things for dinner). It was not the accounts that concerned him. Though he had gotten up early in the morning, and was trying to keep himself cheerful, he still looked tired and weak. His forehead, on which huge purple bruises had come out overnight, was wrapped with a red handkerchief. His nose had also become badly swollen overnight, and several patchy bruises had formed on it, insignificant but decidedly giving his whole face an especially wicked and irritated look. The old man was aware of it himself and shot Alyosha an unfriendly glance as he entered.

"The coffee's cold," he cried sharply, "I'm not offering you any. Today, my friend, it's just lenten fish soup for me, and nobody's invited. Why have you come?"

"To ask about your health," said Alyosha.

"Yes. And, besides, yesterday I told you to come. It's all nonsense. You've troubled yourself for nothing. I knew, by the way, that you'd drag yourself here first thing . . ."

He spoke with the most inimical feeling. Meanwhile he got up worriedly and looked in the mirror (perhaps already for the fortieth time that morning) at his nose. He also began to arrange the red handkerchief on his forehead in a more becoming way.

"Red's better; white would be too much like a hospital," he observed sententiously. "Well, what's with you? How is your elder?"

"He's very bad; he may die today," Alyosha replied, but his father did not even hear him, and at once forgot his question as well.

"Ivan left," he said suddenly. "He's doing his best to win over Mitka's fiancée, that's why he's staying here," he added maliciously, and, twisting his mouth, looked at Alyosha.

"Can he have told you so himself?" asked Alyosha.

"Yes, he told me long ago. Three weeks ago, in fact. It can't be that he's come here to put a knife in me, too, can it? So he must have some reason!"

"What? How can you say such things?" Alyosha was terribly dismayed.

"It's true he's never asked for money, and he won't get a fig out of me anyway. I, my dearest Alexei Fyodorovich, plan to live on this earth as long as possible, let it be known to you, and therefore I need every kopeck, and the longer I live, the more I'll need it," he continued, pacing from one corner of the room to the other, keeping his hands in the pockets of his loose, greasy, yellow cotton coat. "At the moment I'm still a man, only fifty-five years old, but I want to occupy that position for about twenty years longer; I'll get old and disgusting and they won't come to me then of their own free will, and that's when I'll need my dear money. So now I'm saving up more and more, for myself alone, sir, my dear son, Alexei Fyodorovich, let it be known to you, because let it be known to you that I want to live in my wickedness to the very end. Wickedness is sweet: everyone denounces it, but everyone lives in it, only they all do it on the sly and I do it openly. And for this ingenuousness of mine, the wicked ones all attack me. And I don't want your paradise, Alexei Fyodorovich, let it be known to you; it's even unfitting for a decent man to go to your paradise, if there really is such a place. I say a man falls asleep and doesn't wake up, and that's all; remember me in your prayers if you want to, and if not, the devil take you. That's my philosophy. Ivan spoke well here yesterday, though we were all drunk. Ivan's a braggart, and he doesn't have so much learning . . . or any special education either; he's silent, and he grins at you silently—that's how he gets by."

Alyosha listened to him in silence.

"He won't even speak to me! And when he does, it's all put on; he's a scoundrel, your Ivan! I could marry Grushka right now if I wanted to. Because with money one only needs to want, Alexei Fyodorovich, sir, and one gets everything. That's just what Ivan is afraid of, and he's keeping an eye on me to see that I don't get married, and that's why he's pushing Mitka to marry Grushka: he wants to keep me from Grushka that way (as if I'd leave him any money even if I don't marry Grushka!), and on the other hand, if Mitka marries Grushka, then Ivan can take his rich fiancée for himself—that's how he figures! He's a scoundrel, your Ivan!"

"How irritable you are. It's because of yesterday. Why don't you go and lie down?" said Alyosha.

"You say that," the old man suddenly remarked, as if it had just entered his head for the first time, "you say that, and it doesn't make me angry, but if Ivan said the same thing to me, I'd get angry. With you alone I have kind moments, otherwise I'm an evil man."

"You're not an evil man, you're just twisted," Alyosha smiled.

"Listen, I was about to have that robber Mitka locked up today, and I still haven't made up my mind. Of course, in these fashionable times it's customary to count fathers and mothers as a prejudice, but the law, it seems, even in our time, does not allow people to pull their old fathers by the hair and kick them in the mug with their heels, on the floor, in their own house, and boast about coming back and killing them completely—and all in the presence of witnesses, sir! I could break him if I wanted, I could have him put away right now for what he did yesterday!"

"But you're not going to make a complaint, are you?"

"Ivan talked me out of it. To hell with Ivan, but one thing I do know . . ." And bending close to Alyosha, he went on in a confidential half-whisper: "If I had him put away, the scoundrel, she'd hear that I had him put away and go running to him at once. But if she hears today that he beat me, a weak old man, within an inch of my life, then maybe she'll drop him and come to visit me . . . We're like that—we do everything contrary. I know her through and through. Say, how about a little cognac? Have some cold coffee and I'll add a little shot of cognac—it improves the taste, my friend."

"No, no, thank you. But I'll take this bread with me, if I may," said Alyosha, and picking up the three-kopeck French loaf, he put it in the pocket of his cassock. "And you'd better not have any cognac either," he advised cautiously, looking intently into the old man's face.

"True enough; the truth hurts, but there it is. Still, maybe just one little glass. From the little cupboard . . ."

He opened the "little cupboard" with a key, poured a glass, drank it off, then locked the cupboard and put the key back in his pocket.

"That's enough. One glass won't do me in."

"You see, you're feeling kinder now," Alyosha smiled.

"Hm. I love you even without cognac, but with scoundrels I'm a scoundrel.

Vanka won't go to Chermashnya—why? He's got to spy on me, to see how much I'll give Grushenka when she comes. They're all scoundrels! I refuse to acknowledge Ivan. Where did he come from? He's not our kind at all. Why should I leave him anything? I won't even leave a will, let it be known to you. And Mitka I'll squash like a cockroach. I squash black cockroaches at night with my slipper: they make a little pop when you step on them. And your Mitka will make a little pop, too. *Your* Mitka, because you love him. You see, you love him, and I'm not afraid that you love him. If Ivan loved him, I'd fear for myself because he loved him. But Ivan loves nobody, Ivan is not one of us; people like Ivan are not our people, my friend, they're a puff of dust . . . The wind blows, and the dust is gone . . . Some foolishness almost came into my head yesterday, when I told you to come today: I wanted to find out through you about Mitka—what if I counted him out a thousand, or maybe two, right now: would he agree, beggar and scoundrel that he is, to clear out altogether, for about five years, or better for thirty-five, without Grushka, and give her up completely, eh, what?"

"I . . . I'll ask him," Alyosha murmured. "If it were all three thousand, then maybe he . . ."

"Lies! There's no need to ask him now, no need at all! I've changed my mind. It was yesterday that this foolishness crept into my noddle, out of foolishness. I'll give him nothing, not a jot, I need my dear money myself," the old man began waving his arm. "I'll squash him like a cockroach even without that. Tell him nothing, or he'll get his hopes up. And you can go, there's absolutely nothing for you to do here. This fiancée, Katerina Ivanovna, that he's been hiding from me so carefully all this time, is she going to marry him or not? You saw her yesterday, didn't you?"

"She won't leave him for anything."

"These delicate young ladies love just his sort, rakes and scoundrels! They're trash, let me tell you, these pale young ladies; a far cry from . . . Ah! With his youth and the looks I had then (I was much better looking than he is at twenty-eight), I'd have just as many conquests. *Canaille!* But he still won't get Grushenka, sir, no, he won't . . . I'll make mud out of him!"

With the last words he got into a rage again.

"And you can go, too, there's nothing for you to do here today," he snapped abruptly.

Alyosha went up to him to say good-bye and kissed him on the shoulder.

"What are you doing?" the old man was slightly astonished. "We'll still see each other. Or do you think we won't?"

"Not at all, I just did it for no reason."

"And me, too, I just did it . . . ," the old man looked at him. "Listen," he called after him, "come sometime soon, do you hear? For fish soup, I'll make fish soup, a special one, not like today. You must come! Listen, come tomorrow, I'll see you tomorrow!"

And as soon as Alyosha stepped out the door, he again went to the little cupboard and tossed off another half-glass.

"No more!" he muttered, grunting, and again locked the cupboard, and again put the key in his pocket. Then he went to the bedroom, lay exhausted on the bed, and the next moment was asleep.

Chapter 3

He Gets Involved with Schoolboys

"Thank God he didn't ask me about Grushenka," Alyosha thought for his part, as he left his father's and headed for Madame Khokhlakov's house, "otherwise I might have had to tell him about meeting Grushenka yesterday." Alyosha felt painfully that the combatants had gathered fresh strength overnight and their hearts had hardened again with the new day: "Father is angry and irritated, he's come up with something and he's sticking to it. And Dmitri? He, too, has gained strength overnight; he, too, must be angry and irritated; and of course he, too, has thought up something . . . Oh, I must find him today at all costs . . ."

But Alyosha did not have a chance to think for long: on the way something suddenly happened to him that, while it did not seem very important, greatly struck him. As soon as he had crossed the square and turned down the lane leading to Mikhailovsky Street, which runs parallel to Main Street but is separated from it by a ditch (the whole town is crisscrossed by ditches), he saw down at the foot of the little bridge a small gang of schoolboys, all young children, from nine to twelve years old, not more. They were going home from school with satchels on their backs, or with leather bags on straps over their shoulders, some wearing jackets, others coats, some even in high leather boots creased around the ankles, in which little boys spoiled by their well-to-do fathers especially like to parade around. The whole group was talking animatedly about something, apparently holding a council. Alyosha could never pass children by with indifference; it had been the same when he was in Moscow, and though he loved children of three or so most of all, he also very much liked ten- or eleven-year-old schoolboys. And so, preoccupied though he was at the moment, he suddenly felt like going over and talking with them.

As he came up, he peered into their rosy, animated faces and suddenly saw that each boy had a stone in his hand, and some had two. Across the ditch, about thirty paces away from the group, near a fence, stood another boy, also a schoolboy with a bag at his side, no more than ten years old, or even less, judging by his height—pale, sickly, with flashing black eyes. He was attentively and keenly watching the group of six schoolboys, obviously his comrades who had just left school with him but with whom he was apparently at odds. Alyosha came up and, addressing one curly, blond, ruddy-cheeked boy in a black jacket, looked him up and down and remarked:

"I used to carry a bag just like yours, but we always wore it on the left side, so that you could get to it quickly with your right hand; if you wear yours on the right like that, it won't be so easy to get to."

Alyosha began with this practical remark, without any premeditated guile, which, incidentally, is the only way for an adult to begin if he wants to gain the immediate confidence of a child, and especially of a whole group of children. One must begin precisely in a serious and practical way so as to be altogether on an equal footing. Alyosha instinctively understood this.

"But he's left-handed," another boy, a cocky and healthy eleven-year-old, answered at once. The other five boys all fixed their eyes on Alyosha.

"He throws stones with his left hand, too," remarked a third. Just then a stone flew into the group, grazed the left-handed boy, and flew by, though it was thrown deftly and forcefully. The boy across the ditch had thrown it.

"Go on, Smurov, give it to him!" they all shouted. But Smurov (the left-handed boy) did not need any encouragement; he retaliated at once and threw a stone at the boy across the ditch, but unsuccessfully. It landed in the dirt. The boy across the ditch immediately threw another stone at the group, this time directly at Alyosha, and hit him rather painfully on the shoulder. The boy across the ditch had a whole pocket full of stones ready. The bulging of his pockets could be seen even from thirty paces away.

"He was aiming at you, he did it on purpose. You're Karamazov, Karamazov, aren't you?" the boys shouted, laughing. "Hey, everybody, fire at once!"

And six stones shot out of the group. One caught the boy on the head and he fell, but he jumped up immediately and in a rage began flinging stones back at them. A steady exchange of fire came from both sides, and many in the group turned out to have stones ready in their pockets.

"What are you doing! Aren't you ashamed, gentlemen? Six against one! Why, you'll kill him!" Alyosha cried.

He leaped forward and faced the flying stones, trying to shield the boy across the ditch with himself. Three or four of them stopped for a moment.

"He started it!" a boy in a red shirt cried in an angry child's voice. "He's a scoundrel, he just stabbed Krasotkin in class with a penknife, he was bleeding. Only Krasotkin didn't want to squeal on him, but he needs to get beaten up . . ."

"But why? I'll bet you tease him."

"Look, he threw another stone at your back! He knows who you are!" the boys shouted. "It's you he's throwing at now, not us. Hey, everybody, at him again! Don't miss, Smurov!"

And another exchange of fire began, this time a very savage one. The boy across the ditch was hit in the chest by a stone; he cried out, burst into tears, and ran up the hill towards Mikhailovsky Street. A clamor came from the group: "Aha, coward! He ran away! Whiskbroom!"

"You still don't know what a scoundrel he is, Karamazov. Killing's too good for him," a boy in a jacket, who seemed to be the oldest of them, repeated with burning eyes.

"What's wrong with him?" asked Alyosha. "Is he a squealer?"

The boys glanced knowingly at one another.

"You're going the same way, to Mikhailovsky?" the boy went on. "Catch up with him, then . . . You see, he's stopped again, he's waiting and looking at you."

"Looking at you, looking at you!" the other boys chimed in.

"Ask him how he likes the whiskbroom, the ratty old whiskbroom. Just go and ask him that!"

They all burst out laughing. Alyosha looked at them and they at him.

"Don't go, he'll hurt you," Smurov cried warningly.

"I will not ask him about the whiskbroom, gentlemen, because I'm sure you tease him with that somehow, but I will find out from him why you hate him so much . . ."

"Go on, find out, find out!" the boys laughed.

Alyosha crossed the bridge and went up the hill, past the fence, straight to the banished boy.

"Watch out," they shouted after him warningly, "he won't be afraid of you, he'll stab you suddenly, on the sly, like he did Krasotkin."

The boy waited for him without moving from the spot. Coming close, Alyosha saw facing him a child not more than nine years old, weak and undersized, with a pale, thin, oblong little face, and large, dark eyes that looked at him angrily. He was dressed in a very threadbare old coat, which he had awkwardly outgrown. His bare arms stuck out of the sleeves. On the right knee of his trousers there was a large patch, and on his right boot, over the big toe, there was a big hole, and one could see that it had been heavily daubed with ink. There were stones in both bulging pockets of his coat. Alyosha stood facing him, two paces away, looking at him questioningly. The boy, guessing at once from Alyosha's eyes that he was not going to beat him, dropped his guard a little and even began speaking first.

"There's one of me and six of them . . . I'll beat them all by myself," he said suddenly, his eyes flashing.

"One of those stones must have hurt you very badly," Alyosha remarked.

"And I got Smurov in the head!" exclaimed the boy.

"They told me that you know me and threw a stone at me for some reason?" Alyosha asked.

The boy gave Alyosha a dark look.

"I don't know you. Do you really know me?" Alyosha kept asking.

"Leave me alone!" the boy suddenly cried irritably, not moving from the spot, however, as if he were waiting for something, and again his eyes flashed angrily.

"Well, then, I'll go," said Alyosha. "Only I don't know you, and I'm not teasing you. They told me how they tease you, but I don't want to tease you. Good-bye!"

"Fancy pants, the monk can dance!" cried the boy, following Alyosha with the same angry and defiant look, and readying himself, besides, expecting that now Alyosha would certainly attack. But Alyosha turned, looked at him, and walked away. He had not gone three steps when he was hit painfully in the back by the biggest stone the boy had in his pocket.

"From behind, eh? So you do attack people on the sly, like they say!" Alyosha turned around to him, but this time the boy, in a rage, threw a stone right at his face. Alyosha had just time to shield himself, and the stone hit him on the elbow.

"Shame on you! What have I done to you?" he cried.

The boy stood silently and defiantly, waiting for one thing only—that now Alyosha would certainly attack him. But, seeing that he did not attack him even now, the boy went wild, like a little beast: he tore from his place and threw himself at Alyosha, and before Alyosha could make a move, the wicked boy bent down, seized his left hand in both hands, and bit his middle finger badly. He sank his teeth into it and would not let go for about ten seconds. Alyosha howled in pain, pulling his finger away with all his might. The boy finally let go and jumped back to his former distance. The finger was badly bitten, near the nail, deeply, to the bone; blood began to flow. Alyosha took his handkerchief and tightly wrapped his wounded hand. He spent almost a whole minute bandaging it. All the while the boy stood waiting. At last Alyosha raised his quiet eyes to him.

"All right," he said, "you see how badly you've bitten me. That's enough, isn't it? Now tell me what I've done to you."

The boy looked at him in surprise.

"Though I don't know you at all, and it's the first time I've seen you," Alyosha went on in the same gentle way, "it must be that I did something to you—you wouldn't have hurt me like this for nothing. What was it that I did, and how have I wronged you, tell me?"

Instead of answering, the boy suddenly burst into loud sobs, and suddenly ran from Alyosha. Alyosha slowly walked after him towards Mikhailovsky Street, and for a long time saw the boy running far ahead, without slowing down, without turning around, and no doubt still crying loudly. He resolved that he must seek the boy out, as soon as he could find time, and clear up this mystery, which greatly struck him. But he had no time now.

Chapter 4

At the Khokhlakovs'

He soon reached the house of Madame Khokhlakov, a stone house, privately owned, two-storied, beautiful, one of the best houses in our town. Although Madame Khokhlakov spent most of her time in another district, where she had an estate, or in Moscow, where she had her own house, she still kept her house in our town, which she had inherited from her fathers and grandfathers. The estate she owned in our district was the largest of her three estates, yet until now she had come to our district quite rarely. She ran out to Alyosha while he was still in the front hall.

"Did you get it, did you get it, my letter about the new miracle?" she began nervously, quickly.

"Yes, I got it."

"Did you spread it around? Did you show everyone? He restored the son to his mother!"

"He will die today," said Alyosha.

"I know, I've heard, oh, how I long to talk with you! With you or with someone about it all. No, with you, with you! And what a pity there's no way I can see him! The whole town is excited, everyone is expecting something. But now . . . do you know that Katerina Ivanovna is here with us now . . . ?"

"Ah, that's lucky!" Alyosha exclaimed. "I can see her here, then. She asked me yesterday to be sure to come and see her today."

"I know everything, everything. I've heard all the details of what happened there yesterday . . . and of all those horrors with that . . . creature. *C'est tragique*, and in her place, I—I don't know what I'd have done in her place! But your brother, too, your Dmitri Fyodorovich is a fine one—oh, God! Alexei Fyodorovich, I'm getting confused, imagine: right now your brother, I mean, not that one, the terrible one yesterday, but the other one, Ivan Fyodorovich, is sitting and talking with her: they're having a solemn conversation . . . And you wouldn't believe what's happening between them now—it's terrible, it's a strain, I'm telling you, it's such a terrible tale that one simply cannot believe it: they're destroying themselves, who knows why, and they know they're doing it, and they're both reveling in it. I've been waiting for you! I've been thirsting for you! The main thing is, I cannot bear it. I'll tell you everything now; but wait, there's something else, and it's really the main thing—ah, I even forgot that this is the main thing: tell me, why is Lise in hysterics? The moment she heard you were coming, she immediately had hysterics!"

"*Maman*, it is you who are having hysterics, not me," Lise's little voice suddenly chirped through the crack of the door to one of the side rooms. The crack was very small, and the voice was strained, exactly as when one wants terribly to laugh but tries hard to suppress it. Alyosha at once noticed the little crack, and Lise was surely peeking at him through it from her chair, but that he could not see.

"And no wonder, Lise, no wonder . . . your caprices will have me in hysterics, too. But anyway, Alexei Fyodorovich, she's so sick, she was sick all night, in a fever, moaning! I could hardly wait for morning and Herzenstube. He says he can make nothing of it and that we should wait. This Herzenstube always comes and says he can make nothing of it. As soon as you neared the house, she screamed and had a fit, and demanded to be taken here to her old room . . ."

"Mama, I had no idea he was coming. It wasn't because of him at all that I wanted to move to this room."

"That is not true, Lise. Yulia ran to tell you that Alexei Fyodorovich was coming; she was keeping watch for you."

"Dear, darling mama, that is terribly unwitty on your part. And if you want to make up for it now and say something very intelligent, dear mama, then please tell my dear sir, the newly arrived Alexei Fyodorovich, that he has shown his complete lack of wit by this alone, that he has ventured to come to us today after what happened yesterday, and despite the fact that everyone is laughing at him."

"Lise, you are going too far, and I assure you that I shall finally take strict measures. Who is laughing at him? I am very glad that he has come, I need him, I cannot do without him. Oh, Alexei Fyodorovich, I'm extremely unhappy!"

"But what is the matter with you, mama darling?"

"Ah, these caprices of yours, Lise, your fickleness, your illness, this terrible night of fever, this terrible and eternal Herzenstube most of all, eternal, eternal, eternal! And, then, everything, everything . . . And then even this miracle! Oh, how it struck me, how it shook me, this miracle, dear Alexei Fyodorovich! And now this tragedy there in the drawing room, which I cannot bear, I cannot, I declare to you beforehand that I cannot! A comedy, perhaps, not a tragedy. Tell me, the elder Zosima will live until tomorrow, won't he? Oh, my God! What is happening to me? I close my eyes every moment and see that it's all nonsense, all nonsense."

"I should like very much to ask you," Alyosha suddenly interrupted, "for a clean rag to wrap my finger with. I injured it badly, and it hurts very much now."

Alyosha unwrapped his bitten finger. The handkerchief was soaked with blood. Madame Khokhlakov screamed and shut her eyes tightly.

"God, what a wound, it's terrible!"

But Lise, as soon as she saw Alyosha's finger through the crack, immediately swung the door open.

"Come in, come in here to me," she cried insistently and commandingly. "And no foolishness now! Oh, Lord, why did you stand there all this time and say nothing? He might have bled to death, mama! Where did you do it? How did you do it? Water, water first of all! The wound should be washed, just put it in cold water to stop the pain, and keep it there, keep it there . . . Water, quick, quick, mama, in a basin. Hurry!" she finished nervously. She was completely frightened. Alyosha's wound struck her terribly.

"Shouldn't we send for Herzenstube?" cried Madame Khokhlakov.

"Mama, you'll be the death of me! Your Herzenstube will come and say he can make nothing of it! Water, water! Mama, for God's sake, go yourself, make Yulia hurry! She's bogged down somewhere, and can never come quickly! Please hurry, mama, or I'll die . . ."

"But it's nothing!" Alyosha exclaimed, frightened by their fright.

Yulia came running in with water. Alyosha put his finger in it.

"Mama, for God's sake, bring some lint; lint and that stingy, muddy lotion—what's it called?—for cuts! We have it, we do, we do . . . Mama, you know where the bottle is, it's in your bedroom, in the little cabinet on the right, a big bottle next to the lint . . ."

"I'll bring everything right away, Lise, only don't shout so, and don't worry.

See how firmly Alexei Fyodorovich endures his misfortune. Where could you have gotten such a terrible wound, Alexei Fyodorovich?"

Madame Khokhlakov hastened from the room. This was just what Lise was waiting for.

"First of all, answer the question," she began talking quickly to Alyosha, "where did you manage to get yourself such a wound? And then I shall speak with you about quite different matters. Well?"

Alyosha, feeling instinctively that the time before her mama's return was precious to her, hastily, with many omissions and abbreviations, but nonetheless precisely and clearly, told her of his mysterious encounter with the schoolboys. Having heard him out, Lise clasped her hands:

"But how could you, how could you get involved with schoolboys—and in that dress, too!" she cried angrily, as if she had some rights over him. "You're just a boy yourself after that, the littlest boy there could be! But you must find out for me somehow about this bad boy, and tell me the whole story, because there's some secret in it. Now for the second thing—but first a question: are you able, Alexei Fyodorovich, despite the pain you are suffering, to speak about perfect trifles, but to speak sensibly?"

"Perfectly able. And there's not so much pain now."

"That's because you've kept your finger in water. It should be changed right now, because it gets warm immediately. Yulia, bring a piece of ice from the cellar at once, and a fresh basin of water. Well, now that she's gone, I'll get to business: this instant, dear Alexei Fyodorovich, be so good as to give me back the letter I sent you yesterday—this instant, because mama may come back any minute, and I don't want . . ."

"I haven't got the letter with me."

"It's not true, you do have it with you. I just knew you'd say that. You have it there in your pocket. I so regretted this silly joke all night! Return the letter to me right now, give it back!"

"I left it there."

"But you must consider me a girl, a little, little girl after such a silly joke as that letter! I ask your forgiveness for the silly joke, but you must bring me the letter, if you really don't have it—bring it today, you must, you must!"

"Today I simply cannot, because I'll be going back to the monastery, and won't be able to visit you for another two, three, maybe four days, because the elder Zosima . . ."

"Four days? What nonsense! Listen, did you laugh at me very much?"

"I didn't laugh a bit."

"Why not?"

"Because I believed everything completely."

"You're insulting me!"

"Not at all. As soon as I read it, I thought at once that that was how everything would be, because as soon as the elder Zosima dies, I must immediately leave the monastery. Then I'll finish my studies and pass the exam, and when the legal time comes, we'll get married. I will love you. Though I haven't had much time to think yet, I don't think I could find a better wife than you, and the elder told me to get married . . ."

"But I'm a freak, I'm driven around in a wheelchair!" Liza laughed, a blush coming to her cheeks.

"I'll wheel you around myself, but I'm sure you'll be well by then."

"But you're crazy," Liza said nervously, "to make such nonsense suddenly out of such a joke! Ah, here's mama, maybe just in time. Mama, you're always late, how can you take so long! Here's Yulia with the ice!"

"Oh, Lise, do not shout—above all, do not shout. All this shouting makes me . . . I cannot help it if you yourself stuck the lint somewhere else . . . I've been hunting and hunting . . . I suspect you did it on purpose."

"But how could I know he'd come with a bitten finger, otherwise maybe I really would have done it on purpose. Angel mama, you're beginning to say extremely witty things."

"They may be witty, Lise, but what a to-do over Alexei Fyodorovich's finger and all that! Oh, my dear Alexei Fyodorovich, it's not the particulars that are killing me, not some Herzenstube, but all of it together, the whole of it, that is what I cannot bear!"

"Enough, mama, enough about Herzenstube," Liza laughed gaily. "Give me the lint quickly, mama, and the lotion. This is just Goulard's water, Alexei Fyodorovich, now I remember the name, but it's wonderful water. Imagine, mama, on his way here he had a fight with some boys and one of the boys bit him, now isn't he a little, little fellow himself, and how can he get married after that, mama, because imagine, mama, he wants to get married! Imagine him married—isn't it funny, isn't it terrible?"

And Lise kept laughing her nervous little laugh, looking coyly at Alyosha.

"Why married, Lise? Why this all of a sudden? And why are you all of a sudden . . . Besides, that boy may be rabid."

"Oh, mama, can there be rabid boys?"

"Why can't there be, Lise? As if I would say something silly! Your boy might have been bitten by a rabid dog, and become a rabid boy, and then he might go and bite someone around him. How well she has bandaged you, Alexei Fyodorovich, I would never have been able to do it. Does it still hurt?"

"Very little now."

"And are you afraid of water?" asked Lise.

"That's enough, Lise. Perhaps I did speak too hastily about the rabid boy, and you have your conclusions ready. Katerina Ivanovna just learned that you are here, Alexei Fyodorovich, and rushed to me, she's thirsting, thirsting to see you."

"Oh, mama! Go and see her yourself, he can't go now, he's suffering too much."

"I'm not suffering at all, I'm quite able to go . . . ," said Alyosha.

"What? You're leaving? So that's how you are! That's how you are!"

"Why not? When I'm through, I'll come back here, and we can talk again as much as you please. But I would like to see Katerina Ivanovna now, because in any event I want very much to return to the monastery as soon as possible today."

"Mama, take him and go at once. Alexei Fyodorovich, you needn't bother to stop and see me after Katerina Ivanovna, but go straight back to your monastery where you belong! And I want to sleep, I didn't sleep all night."

"Oh, Lise, these are more of your jokes, but I wish you really would sleep!" Madame Khokhlakov exclaimed.

"I don't know what I . . . I'll stay for another three minutes if you wish, even five," Alyosha muttered.

"Even five! Take him away, mama! Quickly! He's a monster!"

"Lise, you have lost your mind! Let us go, Alexei Fyodorovich, she is too capricious today, I'm afraid of upsetting her. Oh, what grief a nervous woman is, Alexei Fyodorovich! And maybe she really does want to sleep after seeing you. How quickly you managed to make her sleepy, and how lucky it is!"

"Ah, mama, what a nice thing to say! I kiss you for it, dear mama!"

"And I kiss you, too, Lise. Listen, Alexei Fyodorovich," Madame Khokhlakov began speaking mysteriously and importantly, in a quick whisper, as she left with Alyosha, "I don't want to suggest anything, or to lift the veil, but you go in and you will see for yourself what's going on in there, it's terrible, it's the most fantastic comedy: she loves your brother Ivan Fyodorovich, and is persuading herself as hard as she can that she loves your brother Dmitri Fyodorovich. It's terrible! I'll go in with you, and if they don't send me away, I'll stay to the end."

Chapter 5

Strain in the Drawing Room

But in the drawing room the conversation was already coming to an end. Katerina Ivanovna was greatly excited, though she had a determined look. At the moment when Alyosha and Madame Khokhlakov entered, Ivan Fyodorovich was just getting up to leave. His face was somewhat pale, and Alyosha looked at him anxiously. The thing was that one of Alyosha's doubts, a disturbing mystery that had been tormenting him for some time, was now being resolved. Over the past month it had been suggested to him several times and from different sides that his brother Ivan loved Katerina Ivanovna, and, most important, that he indeed meant to "win her away" from Mitya. Until very recently, this had seemed monstrous to Alyosha, though it troubled him very much. He loved both his brothers and feared such rivalry between them. But meanwhile, Dmitri Fyodorovich himself had suddenly declared outright to him yesterday that he was even glad of this rivalry with his brother Ivan and that it would be a great help to him, Dmitri. In what would it be a help? In marrying Grushenka? But this step Alyosha considered a desperate and last one. Besides all of which, Alyosha had unquestioningly believed until just the evening before that Katerina Ivanovna herself passionately and persistently loved his brother Dmitri—but he had believed it only until the evening before. Besides, he kept imagining for some reason that she could not love a man like Ivan, but loved his brother Dmitri precisely as he was, despite all the monstrosity of such a love. Yesterday, however, in the scene with Grushenka, he suddenly imagined, as it were, something different. The word "strain," just uttered by Madame Khokhlakov, made him almost jump, because precisely that night, half-awake at dawn, probably in response to a dream, he had suddenly said: "Strain, strain!" He had been dreaming all night about yesterday's scene at Katerina Ivanovna's. Now suddenly the direct and persistent assurance of Madame Khokhlakov that Katerina Ivanovna loved his brother Ivan, and deliberately, out of some kind of play, out of "strain," was deceiving herself and tormenting herself with her affected love for Dmitri, out of some kind of supposed gratitude—struck Alyosha: "Yes, perhaps the whole truth indeed is precisely in those words!" But in that case where did his brother Ivan stand? Alyosha sensed by some sort of instinct that a character like Katerina

Ivanovna must rule, and that she could only rule over a man like Dmitri, but by no means over a man like Ivan. For only Dmitri (in the long run, let us say) might finally submit to her "for his own happiness" (which Alyosha even desired), but not Ivan, Ivan could not submit to her, and such submission would not bring him happiness. Such was the notion that Alyosha had somehow involuntarily formed of Ivan. And so all these hesitations and considerations flew and flashed through his mind now, as he was entering the drawing room. And one more thought flashed—suddenly and irrepressibly: "What if she loves no one, neither one nor the other?" I will note that Alyosha was ashamed, as it were, of such thoughts, and had reproached himself for them whenever, during the past month, they had occurred to him. "What do I know of love and of women, and how can I resolve on such conclusions?" he thought in self-reproach after each such thought or conjecture. And yet it was impossible not to think. He understood instinctively that now, for example, this rivalry was all too important a question in the fate of his brothers, and all too much depended on it. "Viper will eat viper," his brother Ivan had said yesterday, speaking with irritation about their father and Dmitri. So in his eyes their brother Dmitri was a viper, and perhaps had long been a viper? Perhaps since Ivan had first met Katerina Ivanovna? These words, of course, had escaped Ivan unwittingly, but they were all the more important for that. If so, what sort of peace could there be? On the contrary, weren't there only new pretexts for hatred and enmity in their family? And, above all, whom should he, Alyosha, feel pity for, and what should he wish for each of them? He loved them both, but what could he wish for each of them amid such terrible contradictions? One could get completely lost in this tangle, and Alyosha's heart could not bear uncertainty, for the nature of his love was always active. He could not love passively; once he loved, he immediately also began to help. And for that one had to have a goal, one had to know firmly what was good and needful for each of them, and becoming firmly convinced of the correctness of the goal, naturally also to help each of them. But instead of a firm goal there was only vagueness and confusion in everything. "Strain" had just been uttered! But what could he understand even of this strain? He did not understand the first thing in all this tangle!

Seeing Alyosha, Katerina Ivanovna quickly and joyfully said to Ivan Fyodorovich, who had already gotten up from his place to leave: "One minute! Stay for just one more minute. I want to hear the opinion of this man, whom I trust with my whole being. Don't you leave either, Katerina Osipovna," she added, addressing Madame Khokhlakov. She sat Alyosha down next to herself, and Khokhlakov sat opposite them next to Ivan Fyodorovich.

"Here are all my friends, the only ones I have in the world, my dear friends," she began ardently, in a voice that trembled with tears of genuine suffering, and again Alyosha's heart went out to her at once. "You, Alexei Fyodorovich, were a witness yesterday to that . . . horror, and you saw how I was. You did not see it, Ivan Fyodorovich, but he did. What he thought of me yesterday I do not know, but one thing I do know—that if the same thing were to repeat itself today, now, I should express the same feelings as yesterday—the same feelings, the same words, and the same movements. You remember my movements, Alexei Fyodorovich, you yourself restrained me in one of them . . ." (saying this, she blushed, and her eyes flashed). "I declare to you, Alexei Fyodorovich, that I cannot be reconciled with anything. Listen, Alexei Fyodorovich, I do not even know whether I love *him* now. He has become *pitiful* to me, which is a poor sign of love. If I loved him, if I still loved him, then perhaps I should not pity him now, but, on the contrary, should hate him . . ."

Her voice trembled, and tears glistened on her eyelashes. Alyosha started inwardly: "This girl is truthful and sincere," he thought, "and . . . and she no longer loves Dmitri!"

"That's right! Right!" Madame Khokhlakov exclaimed.

"Wait, my dear Katerina Osipovna, I haven't said the main thing, I haven't said the final thing that I decided during the night. I feel that my decision, perhaps, is terrible—terrible for me—but I have a feeling that I shall never change it for anything, not for anything, for the rest of my life it will be so. My dear, my kind, my constant and generous advisor and profound reader of hearts, my only friend in the world, Ivan Fyodorovich, approves of me in everything and praises my decision . . . He knows what it is."

"Yes, I approve of it," Ivan Fyodorovich said in a quiet but firm voice.

"But I wish that Alyosha, too (ah, Alexei Fyodorovich, forgive me for calling you simply Alyosha), I wish Alexei Fyodorovich to tell me now, before my two friends, whether I am right or not. I have an instinctive feeling that you, Alyosha, my dear brother (because you are my dear brother)," she said again rapturously, grasping his cold hand with her hot one, "I have a feeling that your decision, your approval, in spite of all my torments, will bring me peace, because after your words I shall calm down and be reconciled—I feel it."

"I don't know what you are going to ask me," Alyosha spoke out, his face burning, "I only know that I love you, and at this moment I wish for your happiness more than for my own . . . ! But I know nothing about these affairs . . . ," he suddenly hastened to add for some reason.

"In these affairs, Alexei Fyodorovich, in these affairs the main thing now is honor and duty, and something else, I don't know what, but something higher, even perhaps higher than duty itself. My heart tells me of this irresistible feeling, and it draws me irresistibly. But it can all be said in two words. I've already made up my mind: even if he marries that . . . creature," she began solemnly, "whom I can never, never forgive, *I still will not leave him*! From now on I will never, never leave him!" she spoke with a sort of strain, in a sort of pale, forced ecstasy. "I do not mean that I shall drag myself after him, trying to throw myself in front of his eyes every minute, tormenting him—oh, no, I shall go to another town, anywhere you like, but I will watch him all my life, all my life, untiringly. And when he becomes unhappy with that woman, and he certainly will and very soon, then let him come to me and he will find a friend, a sister . . . Only a sister, of course, and that will be so forever, but he will finally be convinced that this sister really is his loving sister, who has sacrificed her whole life for him. I will do it, I will insist that he finally know me and tell me everything without being ashamed!" she exclaimed as if in frenzy. "I will be his god, to whom he shall pray—that, at least, he owes me for his betrayal and for what I suffered yesterday because of him. And let him see throughout his whole life, that all my life I will be faithful to him and to the word I once gave, despite the fact that he was faithless and betrayed me. I shall . . . I shall become simply the means of his happiness (or how should I say it?), the instrument, the mechanism of his happiness, and that for my whole life, my whole life, so that he may see it from now on, all his life! That is the whole of my decision. Ivan Fyodorovich approves of me in the highest degree."

She was breathless. She might have wished to express her thought in a more dignified, artful, and natural way, but it came out too hastily and too baldly. There was too much youthful uncontrol, too much that still echoed with yesterday's irritation and the need to show her pride—she felt it herself. Her face suddenly somehow darkened, an ugly look came into her eyes. Alyosha noticed it all immediately, and his heart was moved to compassion. And just then his brother Ivan added to it.

"I only expressed my thought," he said. "In any other woman, all of that would have come out in a broken and forced way—but not so in you. Another woman would be wrong, but you are right. I do not know what is behind it, but I see that you are sincere in the highest degree, and therefore you are right . . ."

"But only for this moment . . . And what is this moment? Just yesterday's insult—that's all it is!" Madame Khokhlakov, though she obviously did not want to interfere, could not contain herself and suddenly spoke this very correct thought.

"Yes, yes," Ivan interrupted, with a sort of sudden passion, clearly angry that he had been interrupted, "yes, and in another woman this moment would be only yesterday's impression, and no more than a moment, but with Katerina Ivanovna's character, this moment will last all her life. What for others would be just a promise, for her is an everlasting, heavy, perhaps grim, but unfailing, duty. And she will be nourished by this feeling of fulfilled duty! Your life, Katerina Ivanovna, will now be spent in the suffering contemplation of your own feelings, of your own high deed and your own grief, but later this suffering will mellow, and your life will then turn into the sweet contemplation of a firm and proud design, fulfilled once and for all, truly proud in its own way, and desperate in any case, but which you have carried through, and this awareness will finally bring you the most complete satisfaction and will reconcile you to all the rest . . ."

He spoke decidedly with a sort of malice, evidently deliberate, and even, perhaps, not wishing to conceal his intentions—that is, that he was speaking deliberately and in mockery.

"Oh God, how all that is wrong!" Madame Khokhlakov again exclaimed.

"You speak, Alexei Fyodorovich! I desperately need to know what you will tell me!" exclaimed Katerina Ivanovna, and she suddenly dissolved in tears. Alyosha got up from the sofa.

"It's nothing, nothing!" she went on crying. "It's because I'm upset, because of last night, but near two such friends as you and your brother, I still feel myself strong . . . for I know . . . you two will never leave me . . ."

"Unfortunately, I must go to Moscow, tomorrow perhaps, and leave you for a long time . . . And that, unfortunately, cannot be changed . . . ," Ivan Fyodorovich suddenly said.

"To Moscow, tomorrow!" suddenly Katerina Ivanovna's whole face became distorted. "But . . . but, my God, how fortunate!" she cried in a voice instantly quite changed and having instantly chased away her tears so that no trace of them was left. Precisely in an instant an astonishing change took place in her, which greatly amazed Alyosha: instead of the poor, insulted girl who had just been crying in a sort of strain of emotion, there suddenly appeared a woman in complete possession of herself and even greatly pleased, as if she were suddenly rejoicing at something.

"Oh, not fortunate that I must abandon you, of course not that," she suddenly corrected herself, as it were, with a charming worldly smile, "a friend like you could not think that; on the contrary, I am only too unhappy to be losing you" (she suddenly dashed impulsively to Ivan Fyodorovich and, grasping both his hands, pressed them with ardent feeling), "but what is fortunate is that you yourself, personally, will now be able to tell auntie and Agasha, in Moscow, of my whole situation, my whole present horror, with complete frankness to Agasha, but sparing dear auntie, as you will know how to do. You cannot imagine how unhappy I was yesterday and this morning, wondering how I could ever write them this terrible letter . . . because there was no way in the world to say it in a letter . . . But now it will be easy for me to write, because you are going to be there in person and will explain it all. Oh, how glad I am! But I am only glad for that, again believe me. You yourself, of course, are irreplaceable for me . . . I'll run at once and write the letter," she suddenly concluded, and even turned to leave the room.

"And what of Alyosha? What of Alexei Fyodorovich's opinion, which it was so necessary for you to hear?" Madame Khokhlakov cried. There was a caustic and angry note in her words.

"I haven't forgotten that," Katerina Ivanovna suddenly halted, "and why are you so hostile to me in such a moment, Katerina Osipovna?" she said with bitter, burning reproach. "What I said before, I will say again: his opinion is necessary to me; moreover, I need his decision! It shall be as he says—that is how much, on the contrary, I thirst for your words, Alexei Fyodorovich . . . But what's wrong?"

"I never thought, I could not have imagined it!" Alyosha suddenly exclaimed ruefully.

"What? What?"

"He is going to Moscow, and you cry that you're glad—you cried it on purpose! And then you immediately started explaining that you are not glad about that, but, on the contrary, are sorry to be . . . losing a friend, but this, too, you acted on purpose . . . acted as if you were in a comedy, in a theater . . . !"

"In a theater? Why? What do you mean?" Katerina Ivanovna exclaimed, deeply astonished, frowning, and blushing all over.

"But no matter how much you assure him that you will miss him as a friend, you still insist right in his face that you are happy he's going away . . . ," Alyosha spoke somehow quite breathlessly now. He was standing at the table and would not sit down.

"What are you saying? I don't understand . . ."

"I don't know myself . . . I suddenly had a sort of illumination. I know I'm not putting it well, but I'll still say everything," Alyosha continued in the same trembling and faltering voice. "My illumination is that you perhaps do not love my brother Dmitri at all . . . from the very beginning . . . And Dmitri perhaps does not love you at all either . . . from the very beginning . . . but only honors you . . . I really don't know how I dare to say all this now, but someone has to speak the truth . . . because no one here wants to speak the truth . . ."

"What truth?" cried Katerina Ivanovna, and something hysterical rang in her voice.

"This truth," Alyosha stammered, as if throwing himself off the roof. "Call Dmitri now—I'll go and find him—and let him come here and take you by the hand, and then take my brother Ivan by the hand, and let him unite your hands. For you are tormenting Ivan only because you love him . . . and you are tormenting him because you love Dmitri from strain . . . not in truth . . . because you've convinced yourself of it . . ."

Alyosha suddenly broke off and fell silent.

"You . . . you . . . you're a little holy fool, that's what you are!" Katerina Ivanovna suddenly snapped, her face pale now and her lips twisted in anger. Ivan Fyodorovich suddenly laughed and got up from his seat. His hat was in his hand.

"You are mistaken, my good Alyosha," he said, with an expression on his face that Alyosha had never seen there before—an expression of some youthful sincerity and strong, irresistibly frank emotion. "Katerina Ivanovna has never loved me! She knew all along that I loved her, though I never said a word to her about my love—she knew, but she did not love me. Nor have I been her friend, not even once, not even for one day; the proud woman did not need my friendship. She kept me near her for constant revenge. She took revenge on me and was revenged through me for all the insults she endured continually and every moment throughout all this time from Dmitri, insults that started with their very first meeting . . . Because their very first meeting, too, remained in her heart as an insult. That is what her heart is like! All I did all the time was listen to her love for him. I am leaving now; but know, Katerina Ivanovna, that you indeed love only him. And the more he insults you, the more you love him. That is your strain. You precisely love him as he is, you love him insulting you. If he reformed, you would drop him at once and stop loving him altogether. But you need him in order to continually contemplate your high deed of faithfulness, and to reproach him for his unfaithfulness. And it all comes from your pride. Oh, there is much humility and humiliation in it, but all of it comes from pride . . . I am too young and loved you too much. I know I shouldn't be telling you this, that it would be more dignified on my part simply to walk out of here; it would not be so insulting to you. But I am going far away and shall never come back. It is forever . . . I do not want to sit next to a strain . . . However, I cannot even speak anymore, I've said everything . . . Farewell, Katerina Ivanovna, you must not be angry with me, because I am punished a hundred times more than you: punished already by this alone, that I shall never see you again. Farewell. I do not want your hand. You've been tormenting me so consciously that I am unable to forgive you at the moment. Later I shall forgive you, but no hand now:

Den Dank, Dame, begehr ich nicht,"[1]

he added with a crooked smile, incidentally proving, quite unexpectedly, that he, too, could read Schiller, enough so as to learn him by heart, which Alyosha would not have believed before. He walked out of the room without even saying good-bye to the hostess, Madame Khokhlakov. Alyosha clasped his hands.

"Ivan," he called after him desperately, "come back, Ivan! No, no, nothing will bring him back now!" he exclaimed again in a rueful illumination; "but it's my fault, mine, I started it! Ivan spoke spitefully, wrongly. Unjustly and spitefully . . . ," Alyosha kept exclaiming like a half-wit.

Katerina Ivanovna suddenly went into the other room.

"You did nothing wrong, you were lovely, like an angel," Madame Khokhlakov whispered quickly and ecstatically to the rueful Alyosha. "I will do all I can to keep Ivan Fyodorovich from leaving . . ."

Joy shone in her face, to Alyosha's great chagrin; but Katerina Ivanovna suddenly returned. In her hands she had two hundred-rouble bills.

"I have a great favor to ask of you, Alexei Fyodorovich," she began, addressing Alyosha directly, in a seemingly calm and level voice, quite as though nothing had just happened. "A week ago—yes, a week, I think—Dmitri Fyodorovich committed a rash and unjust act, a very ugly act. There is a bad place here, a tavern. In it he met that retired officer, that captain, whom your father employed in some business of his. Dmitri Fyodorovich got very angry with this captain for some reason, seized him by the beard in front of everyone, led him outside in that humiliating position, and led him a long way down the street, and they say that the boy, the captain's son, who goes to the local school, just a child, saw it and went running along beside them, crying loudly and begging for his father, and rushing up to everyone asking them to defend him, but everyone laughed. Forgive me, Alexei Fyodorovich, I cannot recall without indignation this shameful act of *his* . . . one of those acts that Dmitri Fyodorovich alone could bring himself to do, in his wrath . . . and in his passions! I cannot even speak of it, I am unable to . . . my words get confused. I made inquiries about this offended man, and found out that he is very poor. His last name is Snegiryov. He did something wrong in the army and was expelled, I can't talk about that, and now he and his family, a wretched family of sick children and a wife—who, it seems, is insane—

have fallen into abject poverty. He has been living in town for a long time, he was doing something, worked somewhere as a scrivener, and now suddenly he's not being paid. I looked at you . . . that is, I thought—I don't know, I'm somehow confused—you see, I wanted to ask you, Alexei Fyodorovich, my kindest Alexei Fyodorovich, to go to him, to find an excuse, to visit them, this captain, I mean—oh, God! I'm so confused—and delicately, carefully—precisely as only you could manage" (Alyosha suddenly blushed)—"manage to give him this assistance, here, two hundred roubles. He will surely accept . . . I mean, persuade him to accept . . . Or, no, what do I mean? You see, it's not a payment to him for conciliation, so that he will not complain (because it seems he wanted to lodge a complaint), but simply compassion, a wish to help, from me, from me, Dmitri Fyodorovich's fiancée, not from him . . . Well, you'll find a way . . . I would go myself, but you will know much better how to do it. He lives on Lake Street, in the house of a woman named Kalmykov . . . For God's sake, Alexei Fyodorovich, do this for me, and now . . . now I'm a little tired. Good-bye . . ."

She suddenly turned and disappeared again behind the portière, so quickly that Alyosha did not have time to say a word—and he wanted to. He wanted to ask forgiveness, to blame himself, to say at least something, because his heart was full, and he decidedly did not want to go from the room without that. But Madame Khokhlakov seized his hand and herself led him out. In the front hall she stopped him again as before.

"She's proud, fighting against herself, but kind, lovely, magnanimous!" exclaimed Madame Khokhlakov in a half-whisper. "Oh, how I love her, especially sometimes, and how glad I am now once more again about everything, everything! Dear Alexei Fyodorovich, you did not know this, but you must know that all of us, all of us—I, and her two aunts—well, all of us, even Lise, for as much as a whole month now, have been wishing and praying for one thing only: that she would break with your beloved Dmitri Fyodorovich, who does not even want to know her and does not love her in the least, and marry Ivan Fyodorovich, an educated and excellent young man, who loves her more than anything in the world. We've joined in a whole conspiracy here, and that is perhaps the only reason I haven't gone away . . ."

"But she was crying, she's been insulted again!" Alyosha exclaimed.

"Don't believe in women's tears, Alexei Fyodorovich—I'm always against the women in such cases, and for the men."

"Mama, you are spoiling and ruining him," Lise's thin little voice came from behind the door.

"No, I was the cause of it all, I am terribly to blame!" the inconsolable Alyosha repeated in a burst of agonizing shame for his escapade, and even covered his face with his hands in shame.

"On the contrary, you acted like an angel, an angel, I will gladly say it a thousand times over."

"Mama, how did he act like an angel?" once more Lise's voice was heard.

"I suddenly fancied for some reason, looking at all that," Alyosha continued as if he hadn't heard Liza, "that she loves Ivan, and so I said that foolishness . . . and now what will happen?"

"To whom, to whom?" Lise exclaimed. "Mama, you really will be the death of me. I'm asking you and you don't even answer."

At that moment the maid ran in.

"Katerina Ivanovna is sick . . . She's crying . . . hysterics, thrashing."

"What is it?" cried Lise, her voice alarmed now. "Mama, it's I who am going to have hysterics, not her!"

"Lise, for God's sake, don't shout, don't destroy me. You are still too young to know everything that grown-ups know. I'll run and tell you everything you ought to know. Oh, my God! I must run, run . . . Hysterics! It's a good sign, Alexei Fyodorovich, it's excellent that she's in hysterics. It's precisely as it should be. In such cases I am always against the women, against all these hysterics and women's tears. Yulia, run and tell her I'm flying. And it's her own fault that Ivan Fyodorovich walked out like that. But he won't go away. Lise, for God's sake, stop shouting! Oh, yes, you're not shouting, it's I who am shouting, forgive your mama, but I'm in ecstasy, ecstasy, ecstasy! And did you notice, Alexei Fyodorovich, what youthfulness came out in Ivan Fyodorovich just now, he said it all and walked out! I thought he was such a scholar, an academician, and he suddenly spoke so ardently—ardently, openly, and youthfully, naively and youthfully, and it was all so beautiful, beautiful, just like you . . . And he recited that little German verse, just like you! But I must run, run. Hurry, Alexei Fyodorovich, do that errand for her quickly and come back soon. Lise, do you need anything? For God's sake don't keep Alexei Fyodorovich for a minute, he will come back to you right away . . ."

Madame Khokhlakov finally ran off. Alyosha, before leaving, was about to open the door to Lise's room.

"No you don't!" Lise cried out. "Not now you don't! Speak like that, through the door. How did you get to be an angel? That's all I want to know."

"For my terrible foolishness, Lise! Good-bye."

"Don't you dare go like that!" cried Lise.

"Lise, I am in real grief! I'll come back right away, but I am in great, great grief!"

And he ran out of the room.

Chapter 6

Strain in the Cottage

He was indeed in real grief, of a kind he had seldom experienced before. He had gone and "put his foot in it"—and in what? An affair of the heart! "But what do I know of that, what kind of judge am I in such matters?" he repeated to himself for the hundredth time, blushing. "Oh, shame would be nothing, shame would be only the punishment I deserve—the trouble is that now I will undoubtedly be the cause of new misfortunes . . . And the elder sent me to reconcile and unite. Is this any way to unite?" Here again he recalled how he had "united" their hands, and again he felt terribly ashamed. "Though I did it all sincerely, I must be smarter in the future," he suddenly concluded, and did not even smile at his conclusion.

For Katerina Ivanovna's errand he had to go to Lake Street, and his brother Dmitri lived just on the way there, not far from Lake Street, in a lane. Alyosha decided to stop at his place in any case, before going to the captain's, though he had a premonition that he would not find him at home. He suspected that his brother would perhaps somehow be deliberately hiding from him now, but he had to find him at all costs. Time was passing: the thought of the dying elder had never left him, not for a minute, not for a second, from the moment he left the monastery.

There was one fleeting detail in Katerina Ivanovna's errand that also interested him greatly: when Katerina Ivanovna mentioned that a little boy, a schoolboy, the captain's son, had run beside his father, crying loudly, the thought flashed through Alyosha's mind even then that this boy must be the same schoolboy who had bitten his finger when he, Alyosha, asked him how he had offended him. Now Alyosha was almost sure of it, though he did not know why. Thus, drawn to other thoughts, he became distracted and decided not to "think" about the "disaster" he had just caused, not to torment himself with remorse, but to go about his business, and let be what came. With that thought, he finally cheered up. Incidentally, as he turned into the lane where his brother Dmitri lived, he felt hungry, pulled from his pocket the loaf he had taken from his father, and ate it as he walked. This fortified him.

Dmitri was not at home. The owners of the little house—an old cabinet-maker, his son, and an old woman, his wife—even looked at Alyosha with suspicion. "It's three days now since he's slept here, maybe he's vacated somewhere," the old man replied to Alyosha's urgent inquiries. Alyosha realized that he was answering on instructions. When he asked whether he might be at Grushenka's, or hiding at Foma's again (Alyosha used these confidences deliberately), the owners all even looked at him with alarm. "So they love him, they're on his side," thought Alyosha, "that's good."

At last he found Mrs. Kalmykov's house on Lake Street, a decrepit, lopsided little house, with only three windows looking out onto the street, and a dirty courtyard, in the middle of which a cow stood solitarily. The entry to the front hall was through the courtyard; on the left side of the hall lived the old landlady with her elderly daughter, both apparently deaf. In reply to his question about the captain, repeated several times, one of them finally understood that he was asking for the tenants and jabbed with her finger across the hall, pointing at the door to the front room. Indeed, the captain's lodgings turned out to be just a peasant cottage. Alyosha already had his hand on the iron door-pull when he was suddenly struck by the unusual silence behind the door. Yet he knew from what Katerina Ivanovna had told him that the retired captain was a family man: "Either they're all asleep, or perhaps they heard me come and are waiting for me to open the door. I'd better knock first," and he knocked. An answer came, though not at once but perhaps even ten seconds later.

"Who are you?" someone shouted in a loud and forcedly angry voice.

Alyosha then opened the door and stepped across the threshold. He found himself in a room that was rather spacious but extremely cluttered both with people and with all kinds of domestic chattels. To the left was a big Russian stove. From the stove to the window on the left, across the entire room, a line was strung, on which all sorts of rags were hanging. Along the two walls to left and right stood beds covered with knitted blankets. On one of them, the left one, was erected a pile of four cotton-covered pillows, each one smaller than the next. On the other bed, to the right, only one very small pillow could be seen. Further, in the front corner, there was a small space closed off by a curtain or a sheet, also thrown over a line stretched across the corner. Behind this curtain could be glimpsed another bed, made up against the wall on a bench with a chair placed beside it. A simple, rectangular wooden peasant table had been moved from the front corner to the middle window. The three windows, each with four small, green, mildewed panes, were very dim and tightly shut, so that the room was rather stuffy and none too bright. On the table sat a frying pan with the remains of some fried eggs in it, a bitten piece of bread, and, in addition, a half-pint bottle with the faint remnants of earthly blessings at the bottom. On a chair by the left bed sat a woman who looked like a lady, wearing a cotton dress. Her face was very thin and yellow; her extremely sunken cheeks betrayed at first glance her sickly condition. But most of all Alyosha was struck by the look in the poor lady's eyes—an intensely questioning, and at the same time terribly haughty, look. And until the moment when the lady herself began to speak, all the while Alyosha was talking with the husband, she kept looking in the same haughty and questioning way, with her large brown eyes, from one speaker to the other. Next to this lady, at the left window, stood a young girl with a rather homely face and thin, reddish hair, poorly, though quite neatly, dressed. She eyed Alyosha with disgust as he came in. To the right, also near the bed, sat yet another female person. This was a very pitiful creature, also a young girl, about twenty years old, but hunchbacked and crippled, with withered legs, as Alyosha was told later. Her crutches stood nearby, in the corner, between the bed and the wall. The remarkably beautiful and kind eyes of the poor girl looked at Alyosha with a sort of quiet meekness. At the table, finishing the fried eggs, sat a gentleman of about forty-five, small, lean, weakly built, with reddish hair, and a thin red beard rather like an old whiskbroom (this comparison, and particularly the word *whiskbroom*, for some reason flashed through Alyosha's mind at first glance, as he later recalled). Obviously it was this same gentleman who had shouted, "Who are you?" from behind the door, since there was no other man in the room. But when Alyosha entered, he all but flew from the bench on which he was sitting at the table, and, hastily wiping his mouth with a tattered napkin, rushed up to Alyosha.

"A monk begging for the monastery—he's come to the right place!" the girl standing in the left corner meanwhile said loudly. But the gentleman who had run up to Alyosha immediately turned on his heel to her, and in an excited, somehow faltering voice, answered her:

"No, ma'am, Varvara Nikolaevna, that's not it, you've got it wrong! Allow me to ask in my turn, sir," he suddenly wheeled around to Alyosha again, "what has urged you, sir, to visit . . . these depths?"

Alyosha looked at him attentively; it was the first time in his life he had seen the man. There was something angular, hurried, and irritable in him. Although he had obviously just been drinking, he was not drunk. His face expressed a sort of extreme insolence, and at the same time—which was strange—an obvious cowardice. He looked like a man who had been submissive for a long time and suffered much, but had suddenly jumped up and tried to assert himself. Or, better still, like a man who wants terribly to hit you, but is terribly afraid that you are going to hit him. In his speech and the intonations of his rather shrill voice could be heard a sort of crack-brained humor, now spiteful, now timid, faltering, and unable to sustain its tone. The question about "depths" he had asked all atremble, as it were, rolling his eyes, and jumping up to Alyosha, so close that Alyosha mechanically took a step back. The gentleman was wearing a coat of some sort of dark, rather shabby nankeen, stained and mended. His trousers were of a sort of extremely light color, such as no one had even been wearing for a long time, checkered, and made of some thin fabric, crumpled at the cuffs and therefore bunched upwards, as if he had outgrown them like a little boy.

"I am . . . Alexei Karamazov . . . ," Alyosha said in reply.

"That I am quite able to understand, sir," the gentleman immediately snapped, letting it be known that he was aware, even without that, of who Alyosha was. "And I am Captain, sir, for my part, Snegiryov, sir; but still it would be desirable to know precisely what has urged you to . . ."

"Oh, I just stopped by. As a matter of fact, I'd like very much to have a word with you . . . if I may . . ."

"In that case, here is a chair, sir, pray be seated, sir. As they used to say in the old comedies: 'Pray be seated . . . ,'" and with a quick gesture the captain seized an empty chair (a simple peasant one, all wood, not upholstered with anything) and placed it almost in the middle of the room; then, seizing another chair, just like the first, for himself, he sat facing Alyosha, as close up to him as before, so that their knees almost touched.

"Nikolai Ilyich Snegiryov, sir, former captain in the Russian infantry, sir, disgraced by his vices, but still a captain. I should have said Captain Yessirov instead of Snegiryov, because it's only in the second half of my life that I've started saying 'Yessir.' 'Yessir' is acquired in humiliation."

"That's very true," Alyosha smiled, "but is it acquired unwillingly or deliberately?"

"Unwillingly, God knows. I never used to say it, all my life I never used to say 'sir.' Suddenly I fell down and got up full of 'sirs.' It's the work of a higher power. I see that you're interested in contemporary problems. Yet how can I have aroused such curiosity, living as I do in conditions that render the exercise of hospitality impossible?"

"I've come . . . about that matter . . ."

"About what matter?" the captain interrupted impatiently.

"Concerning that encounter of yours with my brother, Dmitri Fyodorovich," Alyosha blurted out awkwardly.

"Which encounter, sir? You mean that one, sir? The one concerning the whiskbroom, the old whiskbroom?" he suddenly moved so close that this time he positively hit Alyosha with his knees. His lips somehow peculiarly compressed themselves into a thread.

"What whiskbroom?" Alyosha mumbled.

"He came to complain to you about me, papa!" a boy's voice, already familiar to Alyosha, cried from behind the curtain in the corner. "It was his finger I bit today!"

The curtain was pulled aside, and Alyosha saw his recent enemy, in the corner, under the icons, on the little bed made up on a bench and a chair. The boy was lying under his own coat and an old quilted cotton blanket. He was obviously not well, and, judging by his burning eyes, was in a fever. He looked fearlessly at Alyosha now, unlike the first time: "See, I'm at home now, you can't get me."

"Bit what finger?" the captain jumped up a little from his chair. "Was it your finger he bit, sir?"

"Yes, mine. Today he was throwing stones with some boys in the street; the six of them were throwing at him, and he was alone. I came up to him, and he threw a stone at me, too, then another one, at my head. I asked him what I had done to him. He suddenly rushed at me and bit my finger badly, I don't know why."

"A whipping, right now, sir! A whipping this very minute, sir," the captain now jumped all the way out of his chair.

"But I'm not complaining at all, I was simply telling you . . . I don't want you to whip him at all. Besides, he seems to be ill now . . ."

"And did you think I'd whip him, sir? That I'd take Ilyushechka and whip him right now, in front of you, for your full satisfaction? How soon would you like it done, sir?" said the captain, suddenly turning to Alyosha with such a gesture that he seemed as if he were going to leap at him. "I am sorry, my dear sir, about your poor little finger, but before I go whipping Ilyushechka maybe you'd like me to chop off these four fingers, right here, in front of your eyes, for your righteous satisfaction, with this very knife? Four fingers, I think, should be enough for you, sir, to satisfy your thirst for revenge, you won't demand the fifth one, sir . . . ?" he suddenly stopped as if he were suffocating. Every feature of his face was moving and twitching, and he looked extremely defiant. He was as if in a frenzy.

"I think I understand it all now," Alyosha replied softly and sadly, without getting up. "So your boy is a good boy, he loves his father, and he attacked me as your offender's brother . . . I understand it now," he repeated, pondering. "But my brother, Dmitri Fyodorovich, repents of his act, I know, and if it were only possible for him to come to you, or, best of all, to meet you again in the same place, he would ask your forgiveness in front of everyone . . . if you wish."

"You mean he pulls my beard out and then asks my forgiveness . . . and it's all over and everyone's satisfied, is that it, sir?"

"Oh, no, on the contrary, he will do whatever you want and however you want!"

"So if I asked his excellency to go down on his knees to me in that very tavern, sir—the 'Metropolis' by name—or in the public square, he would do it?"

"Yes, he would even go down on his knees."

"You've pierced me, sir. Pierced me to tears, sir. I'm too inclined to be sensitive. Allow me to make a full introduction: my family, my two daughters and my son—my litter, sir. If I die, who will so love them, sir, and while I live, who will so love me, a little wretch, if not them? This great thing the Lord has provided for every man of my sort, sir. For it's necessary that at least someone should so love a man of my sort, sir . . ."

"Ah, that is perfectly true!" exclaimed Alyosha.

"Enough of this clowning! Some fool comes along and you shame us all," the girl at the window suddenly cried out, addressing her father with a disgusted and contemptuous look.

"Wait a little, Varvara Nikolaevna, allow me to sustain my point," her father cried to her in a peremptory tone, looking at her, however, quite approvingly. "It's our character, sir," he turned again to Alyosha.

> "And in all nature there was nothing
> He would give his blessing to—[1]

only it should be in the feminine: that she would give her blessing to, sir. But allow me to introduce you to my wife: this is Arina Petrovna, sir, a crippled lady, about forty-three years old, she can walk, but very little, sir. From simple people. Arina Petrovna, smooth your brow; this is Alexei Fyodorovich Karamazov. Stand up, Alexei Fyodorovich," he took him by the arm and, with a force one would not have suspected in him, suddenly raised him up. "You are being introduced to a lady, you should stand up, sir. Not that Karamazov, mama, the one who . . . hm, and so on, but his brother, shining with humble virtues. Allow me, Arina Petrovna, allow me, mama, allow me preliminarily to kiss your hand."

And he kissed his wife's hand respectfully and even tenderly. The girl at the window indignantly turned her back on the scene; the haughtily questioning face of the wife suddenly took on a remarkably sweet expression.

"How do you do, sit down, Mr. Chernomazov,"[2] she said.

"Karamazov, mama, Karamazov—we're from simple people, sir," he whispered again.

"Well, Karamazov, or whatever it is, but I always say Chernomazov . . . But sit down, why did he get you up? A crippled lady, he says, but my legs still work, only they're swollen like buckets, and the rest of me is dried up. Once I was good and fat, but now it's as if I swallowed a needle . . ."

"We're from simple people, sir, simple people," the captain prompted once again.

"Papa, oh, papa!" the hunchbacked girl, who until then had been silent on her chair, said suddenly, and suddenly hid her eyes in her handkerchief.

"Buffoon!" the girl at the window flung out.

"You see what sort of news we have," the mother spread her arms, pointing at her daughters, "like clouds coming over; the clouds pass, and we have our music again. Before, when we were military, we had many such guests. I'm not comparing, dear father. If someone loves someone, let him love him. The deacon's wife came once and said: 'Alexander Alexandrovich is a man of excellent soul, but Nastasya,' she said, 'Nastasya Petrovna is a hellcat.' 'Well,' I said, 'we all have our likes, and you're a little pile, but you smell vile.' 'And you need to be kept in your place,' she said. 'Ah, you black sword,' I said to her, 'who are you to teach me?' 'I'm letting in fresh air,' she said, 'yours is foul.' 'Go and ask all the gentlemen officers,' I told her, 'whether the air in me is foul or otherwise.' And from that time on it's been weighing on my heart, and the other day I was sitting here, like now, and saw the same general come in who visited us in Holy Week: 'Tell me, now, Your Excellency,' I said to him, 'can a noble lady let in free air?' 'Yes,' he said to me, 'you should open the window or the door, because that the air in here is not clean.' And it's always like that! What's wrong with my air? The dead smell even worse. 'I'm not spoiling your air,' I tell them, 'I'll order some shoes and go away.' My dear ones, my darlings, don't reproach your own mother! Nikolai Ilyich, dear father, don't I please you? I have only one thing left—that Ilyushechka comes home from school and loves me. Yesterday he brought me an apple. Forgive me, my dears, forgive me, my darlings, forgive your own mother, I'm quite lonely, and why is my air so offensive to you?"

And the poor woman suddenly burst into sobs, tears streamed from her eyes. The captain quickly leaped to her side.

"Mama, mama, darling, enough, enough! You're not lonely. Everyone loves you, everyone adores you!" and he again began kissing both her hands and tenderly caressing her face with his palms; and taking a napkin, he suddenly began wiping the tears from her face. Alyosha even fancied that there were tears shining in his eyes, too. "Well, sir, did you see? Did you hear, sir?" he suddenly turned somehow fiercely to Alyosha, pointing with his hand to the poor, feebleminded woman.

"I see and hear," murmured Alyosha.

"Papa, papa! How can you . . . with him . . . stop it, papa!" the boy suddenly cried, rising in his bed and looking at his father with burning eyes.

"Enough of your clowning, showing off your stupid antics, which never get anywhere . . . !" Varvara Nikolaevna shouted from the same corner, quite furious now, and even stamping her foot.

"You are perfectly justified, this time, to be so good as to lose your temper, Varvara Nikolaevna, and I shall hasten to satisfy you. Put on your hat, Alexei Fyodorovich, and I'll take my cap—and let us go, sir. I have something serious to tell you, only outside these walls. This sitting girl here—she's my daughter, sir, Nina Nikolaevna, I forgot to introduce her to you—is God's angel in the flesh . . . who has flown down to us mortals . . . if you can possibly understand that . . ."

"He's twitching all over, as if he had cramps," Varvara Nikolaevna went on indignantly.

"And this one who is now stamping her little foot and has just denounced me as a clown—she, too, is God's angel in the flesh, sir, and rightly calls me names. Let us go, Alexei Fyodorovich, we must bring this to an end, sir . . ."

And seizing Alyosha's arm, he led him from the room and straight outside.

Chapter 7

And in the Fresh Air

"The air is fresh, sir, and in my castle it is indeed not clean, not in any sense. Let's walk slowly, sir. I should very much like to enlist your interest, sir."

"And I, too, have some extraordinary business with you . . . ," Alyosha remarked, "only I don't know how to begin."

"Didn't I know that you must have some business with me, sir? Without some business, you would never come to call on me. Unless you came, indeed, only to complain about the boy, sir? But that is improbable. By the way, about the boy, sir: I couldn't explain everything in there, but here I will describe that scene to you. You see, the whiskbroom used to be thicker, sir, just a week ago—I'm referring to my beard, sir; my beard is nicknamed a whiskbroom, mostly by the schoolboys, sir. Well, and so, sir, your good brother, Dmitri Fyodorovich, dragged me by my beard that day, he dragged me out of the tavern to the square, and just then the schoolboys were getting out of school, and Ilyusha with them. When he saw me in such a state, sir, he rushed up to me: 'Papa,' he cried, 'papa!' He caught hold of me, hugged me, tried to pull me away, crying to my offender: 'Let go, let go, it's my papa, my papa, forgive him'—that was what he cried: 'Forgive him!' And he took hold of him, too, with his little hands, and kissed his hand, that very hand, sir . . . I remember his face at that moment, I have not forgotten it, sir, and I will not forget it . . . !"

"I swear to you," exclaimed Alyosha, "that my brother will express his repentance in the most sincere, the fullest manner, even if it means going down on his knees in that very square . . . I will make him, or he is no brother of mine!"

"Aha, so it's still in the planning stage! And proceeds not directly from him, but only from the nobility of your fervent heart. Why didn't you say so, sir? No, in that case, allow me to finish telling you about the highly chivalrous and soldierly nobility of your good brother, for he showed it that time, sir. So he finished dragging me by my whiskbroom and set me free: 'You,' he said, 'are an officer, and I am an officer; if you can find a second, a decent man, send him to me—I shall give you satisfaction, though you are a scoundrel!' That is what he said, sir. Truly a chivalrous spirit! Ilyusha and I withdrew then, but this genealogical family picture forever imprinted itself in the memory of Ilyusha's soul. No, it's not for us to stay gentry, sir. And judge for yourself, sir, you were just so good as to visit my castle—what did you see, sir? Three ladies sitting there, sir, one crippled and feebleminded, another crippled and hunchbacked, the third not a cripple, but too smart, sir, a student, longing to go back to Petersburg and search for the rights of the Russian woman, there on the banks of the Neva. Not to mention Ilyusha, sir, he's only nine years old, alone in the world, for if I were to die, what would become of those depths, that's all I ask, sir. And so, if I challenge him to a duel, what if he kills me on the spot—well, what then? Then what will happen to them all, sir? Still worse, if he doesn't kill me but just cripples me: work would be impossible, but there would still be a mouth to feed, and who will feed my mouth then, who will feed them all, sir? Or should I then send Ilyusha out daily to beg instead of going to school? So that's what it means for me to challenge him to a duel, sir. It's foolish talk, sir, and nothing else."

"He will ask your forgiveness, he will bow at your feet in the middle of the square," Alyosha again cried, his eyes glowing.

"I thought of taking him to court," the captain went on, "but open our code of law, how much compensation would I get from the offender for a personal offense, sir? And then suddenly Agrafena Alexandrovna summoned me and shouted: 'Don't you dare think of it! If you take him to court, I'll fix it so that the whole world will publicly know that he beat you for your own cheating, and you'll wind up in the dock yourself.' But the Lord knows who was the source of this cheating, sir, and on whose orders some small fry like me was acting—wasn't it her own orders and Fyodor Pavlovich's? 'And besides,' she added, 'I'll turn you out forever, and you'll never earn anything from me again. And I'll tell my merchant, too'—that's what she calls the old man: 'my merchant'—'and he will turn you out as well.' So I thought to myself, if even the merchant turns me out, then where will I earn any money? Because I only had the two of them left, since your father, Fyodor Pavlovich, not only stopped trusting me for some unrelated reason, sir, but even wants to drag me into court himself, on the strength of some receipts he has from me. As a result of all that, I've kept quiet, sir, and the depths, sir, you've seen for yourself. And now, allow me to ask: did he bite your finger badly, my Ilyusha? Inside my castle, in his presence, I didn't dare go into such details."

"Yes, very badly, and he was very angry. He took revenge for you upon me, as a Karamazov, it's clear to me now. But if you had seen how he was fighting with his schoolmates, throwing stones! It's very dangerous, they might kill him, they're children, stupid, a stone goes flying and could break his head."

"Yes, he got it, sir, not in the head but in the chest, over the heart, a stone hit him today, bruised him, he came home crying, groaning, and now he's fallen sick."

"And you know, he starts it himself, he attacks everyone, he's bitter because of you; they say the other day he stabbed a boy, Krasotkin, in the side with a penknife . . ."

"I heard about that, too, it's dangerous, sir: Krasotkin is a local official, there could still be trouble . . ."

"I would advise you," Alyosha continued fervently, "not to send him to school at all for a while, until he calms down . . . and this wrath in him passes . . ."

"Wrath, sir!" the captain chimed in, "wrath indeed, sir! A small creature, but a great wrath, sir! You don't know all of it. Allow me to explain the story more particularly. The thing is that after that event all the children at school began calling him whiskbroom. Schoolchildren are merciless people: separately they're God's angels, but together, especially in school, they're quite often merciless. They began teasing him, and a noble spirit arose in Ilyusha. An ordinary boy, a weak son, would have given in, would have felt ashamed of his father, but this one stood up for his father, alone against everyone. For his father, and for the truth, sir, for justice, sir. Because what he suffered then, as he kissed your brother's hand and cried to him: 'Forgive my papa, forgive my papa'—that only God alone knows, and I, sir. And that is how our children—I mean, not yours but ours, sir, the children of the despised but noble poor—learn the truth on earth when they're just nine years old, sir. The rich ones—what do they know? In their whole lives they never sound such depths, and my Ilyushka, at that very moment in the square, sir, when he kissed his hand, at that very moment he went through the whole truth, sir. This truth, sir, entered into him and crushed him forever," the captain said fervently, again as if in a frenzy, hitting his left palm with his right fist, as if he wished to show physically how "the truth" had crushed his Ilyusha. "That same day he came down with a fever, he was delirious all night. All that day he hardly spoke to me, he was even quite silent, only I noticed him looking, looking at me from the corner, but he kept leaning more towards the window, pretending he was doing his homework, but I could see that he didn't have homework on his mind. The next day I did some drinking, sir, and forgot a lot, I'm a sinful man, from grief, sir. Mama there also began crying—and I love mama very much, sir—well, from grief I had a drop on my last few kopecks. Don't despise me, my good sir: in Russia, drunks are our kindest people. Our kindest people are also the most drunk. So I was lying there and I didn't much remember Ilyusha that day, and it was precisely that day when the boys started jeering at him in school, that morning, sir: 'Whiskbroom,' they shouted at him, 'your father was dragged out of the tavern by his whiskbroom, and you ran along asking forgiveness.' On the third day he came home from school, and I saw that he looked pale, awful. 'What's wrong?' I asked. Silence. Well, there was no talking about it in our castle, otherwise mama and the girls would immediately take part—and besides, the girls already knew all about it even on the first day. Varvara Nikolaevna was already grumbling: 'Clowns, buffoons, can you never be reasonable?' 'Right,' I said, 'Varvara Nikolaevna, we can never be reasonable.' I got off with that at the time. So, sir, towards evening I took my boy out for a walk. And you should know, sir, that even before that, every evening he and I used to take a walk, just the same way we're going now, from our gate to that big stone over there, standing like an orphan in the road near the wattle fence, where the town common begins: the place is deserted and beautiful, sir. We were walking along, Ilyusha and I, his little hand in my hand, as usual; he has such a tiny hand, his little fingers are so thin and cold—my boy suffers from a weak chest. 'Papa,' he said, 'papa!' 'What?' I said to him, and I could see that his eyes were flashing. 'Papa, the way he treated you, papa!' 'It can't be helped, Ilyusha,' I said. 'Don't make peace with him, papa, don't make peace. The boys say he gave you ten roubles for it.' 'No, Ilyusha,' I said, 'I won't take any money from him, not for anything.' Then he started shaking all over, seized my hand in both his hands, and kissed it again. 'Papa,' he said, 'papa, challenge him to a duel; they tease me at school, they say you're a coward and won't challenge him to a duel, but you'll take his ten roubles.' 'It's not possible for me to challenge him to a duel, Ilyusha,' I answered, and explained to him briefly all that I just explained to you about that. He listened. 'Papa,' he said, 'papa, even so, don't make peace with him: I'll grow up, I'll challenge him myself, and I'll kill him!' And his eyes were flashing and shining. Well, I'm still his father for all that, I had to tell him the right thing. 'It's sinful to kill,' I said, 'even in a duel.' 'Papa,' he said, 'papa, I'll throw him down when I'm big, I'll knock the sword out of his hand with my sword, I'll rush at him, throw him down, hold my sword over him and say: I could kill you now, but I forgive you, so there!' You see, sir, you see what a process went on in his little head over those two days! Day and night he was thinking precisely about that revenge with the sword, and that must have been in his delirium at night, sir. Only he started coming home from school badly beaten up, I learned of it the day before yesterday, and you're right, sir, I won't send him to that school any more. When I learned that he was going alone against the whole class, and was challenging everyone, and that he was so bitter, that his heart was burning—I was afraid for him. Again we went for a walk. 'Papa,' he asked, 'papa, is it true that the rich are stronger than anybody in the world?' 'Yes, Ilyusha,' I said, 'no one in the world is stronger than the rich.' 'Papa,' he said, 'I'll get rich, I'll become an officer, and I'll beat everybody, and the tsar will reward me. Then I'll come back, and nobody will dare . . .' He was silent for a while, then he said, and his little lips were still trembling as before: 'Papa,' he said, 'our town is not a good town, papa!' 'Yes, Ilyushechka,' I said, 'it's really not a very good town.' 'Papa, let's move to another town, a good one,' he said, 'a town where they don't know about us.' 'We will,' I said, 'we will move, Ilyusha, as soon as I save some money.' I was glad to be able to distract him from his dark thoughts, and so we began dreaming of how we'd move to another town, how we'd buy our own horse and cart. 'We'll sit mama and your sisters in the cart and cover them, and we ourselves will walk beside it, and from time to time you'll get in and ride and I'll walk beside, because we must spare our horse, we shouldn't all ride, and so we'll set off.' He was delighted with that, most of all because we'd have our own horse and he could ride it. Everyone knows that a Russian boy is born with a horse. We chattered for a long time: thank God, I thought, I've diverted him, comforted him. That was two days ago, in the evening, but by yesterday evening it all turned out differently. That morning he went to school again and came back gloomy, much too gloomy. In the evening I took him by the hand, we went for a walk; he was silent, he didn't speak. The breeze picked up, the sun clouded over, there was autumn in the air, and dusk was already coming—we walked along, both feeling sad. 'Well, my boy,' I said, 'how are we going to get ourselves ready for the road?'—thinking to bring him around to our conversation of the day before. Silence. But I could feel his little fingers trembling in my hand. Eh, I thought, that's bad, there's something new. We came to this very stone, just as we are now, I sat on the stone, and in the sky there were kites humming and flapping on their strings, about thirty of them. It's the season for kites, sir. 'Look, Ilyusha,' I said, 'it's time we flew our kite from last year. I'll mend it. Where do you keep it?' My boy was silent, he looked away, turned aside from me. And suddenly the wind whistled and blew up some sand . . . He rushed to me suddenly, threw his little arms around my neck, and hugged me. You know, when children are silent and proud, and have been holding back their tears for a long time, when they suddenly burst out, if a great grief comes, the tears don't just flow, sir, they pour out in streams. With these warm streams he suddenly wet my whole face. He suddenly sobbed as if he were in convulsions, and began shaking and pressing me to him as I sat there on the stone. 'Papa,' he cried, 'papa, dear papa, how he humiliated you!' Then I began weeping, too, sir. We were sitting, holding each other, and sobbing. 'Papa,' he said, 'dear papa!' 'Ilyusha,' I said, 'dear Ilyusha!' No one saw us then, sir, only God saw us—let's hope he'll enter it into my record, sir. Thank your good brother, Alexei Fyodorovich. No, sir, I will not whip my boy for your satisfaction, sir!"

He ended on the same note of cracked and spiteful humor. Alyosha felt, however, that he already trusted him, and that if someone else were in his, Alyosha's, place, with someone else the man would not have "talked" as he had, would not have said all that he had just said to him. This encouraged Alyosha, whose soul was trembling with tears.

"Ah, how I wish I could make peace with your boy!" he exclaimed. "If only you could arrange it . . ."

"Right, sir," the captain muttered.

"But something else now, something quite different," Alyosha went on exclaiming. "Listen: I've come with an errand. This same brother of mine, this Dmitri, has also insulted his fiancée, a most noble girl, of whom you've probably heard. I have the right to tell you of this insult, I even must do so, because when she learned of your offense and learned everything about your unfortunate situation, she charged me at once . . . just now . . . to bring you this assistance from her . . . but just from her alone, not from Dmitri, who has abandoned her as well, not at all, and not from me, his brother, or from anyone else, but from her, just from her alone! She entreats you to accept her help . . . you have both been offended by one and the same man . . . She thought of you only when she suffered the same offense from him (the same in intensity) as you! It means that a sister is coming to the aid of a brother . . . She precisely charged me to persuade you to accept these two hundred roubles from her as from a sister. No one will know of it, no unjust gossip will arise from it . . . here are the two hundred roubles, and, I swear, you must accept them, otherwise . . . otherwise it follows that everyone in the world must be enemies of each other! But there are brothers in the world, too . . . You have a noble soul . . . you must understand, you must . . . !"

And Alyosha held out to him two new, iridescent hundred-rouble bills. They were both standing precisely by the big stone near the fence, and there was no one around. The bills seemed to make a terrible impression on the captain: he started, but at first only as if from astonishment; he had not imagined anything of the sort and did not at all expect such an outcome. Even in sleep he did not dream of anyone's help, not to mention so large a sum. He took the bills, and for a moment almost could not reply; something quite new flashed in his face.

"Is this for me, for me, sir, so much money, two hundred roubles? Good heavens! But I haven't seen so much money for the past four years—Lord! And she says that a sister . . . and it's true . . . really true?"

"I swear that everything I told you is true!" Alyosha cried. The captain blushed.

"Listen, sir, my dear, listen, if I do accept it, won't that make me dishonorable? In your eyes, Alexei Fyodorovich, won't it, won't it make me dishonorable? No, Alexei Fyodorovich, listen, listen to me, sir," he was hurrying, touching Alyosha all the time with both hands, "here you are persuading me to accept it, telling me that a 'sister' has sent it, but inside, in your own heart—won't you hold me in contempt if I accept it, sir, eh?"

"But, no, of course not! I swear to you by my own salvation, I will not! And no one will ever know of it but us: you, I, and she, and one other lady, her great friend . . ."

"Forget the lady! Listen, Alexei Fyodorovich, listen to me, sir, because the moment has now come for you to listen, sir, because you cannot even understand what these two hundred roubles can mean for me now," the poor man went on, gradually getting into a sort of confused, almost wild ecstasy. He was befuddled, as it were, and was speaking extremely quickly and hastily, as if he were afraid he might not be allowed to get it all out. "Besides the fact that it has been acquired honestly, from such a respected and holy 'sister,' sir, do you know that I can now get treatment for mama and Ninochka—my hunchbacked angel, my daughter? Dr. Herzenstube came once out of the goodness of his heart, and examined them both for a whole hour. 'I can make nothing of it,' he said, but still, the mineral water they sell at the local pharmacy (he gave a prescription for it) will undoubtedly do her good, and he also prescribed a footbath with medications. The mineral water costs thirty kopecks, and she would have to drink maybe forty jugs of it. So I took the prescription and put it on the shelf under the icons, and it's still there. And for Ninochka he prescribed baths in some solution, hot baths, every day, morning and evening, but how could we dream of such a treatment, sir, in our place, in our castle, with no maid, with no help, with no tub or water, sir? And Ninochka is rheumatic all over, I didn't even tell you that yet, at night her whole right side aches, she suffers, and would you believe it, God's angel, she keeps it in, so as not to disturb us, she doesn't groan, so as not to wake us up. We eat whatever we can get, and she always takes the worst piece, what should only be thrown to a dog: 'I'm not worthy of it,' is what she means, 'I'm taking food from you, I'm just a burden to you.' That's what her angelic eyes mean to say. It weighs on her that we serve her: 'I don't deserve it, I don't deserve it, I'm a worthless cripple, I'm useless,' but I wouldn't say she was worthless, sir, when she's been the salvation of us all with her angelic meekness; without her, without her quiet word, we'd have hell, sir, she's even softened Varya. And don't condemn Varvara Nikolaevna either, sir; she, too, is an angel, she, too, is an offended one. She came home this summer and brought sixteen roubles with her that she'd earned giving lessons and set aside so that in September, now, that is, she could go back to Petersburg. And we took her money and lived on it, and she has nothing to go back with, that's how things are, sir. And she can't go back, because she slaves for us—we've saddled and harnessed her like a nag, she takes care of everything, mends, washes, sweeps the floor, puts mama to bed, and mama is fussy, sir, mama is tearful, sir, and mama is mad, sir . . . But now, with these two hundred roubles, I can hire a maid, sir, do you understand, Alexei Fyodorovich, I can undertake treatment for my dear ones, sir, send the student to Petersburg, sir, and buy beef, and introduce a new diet, sir. Lord, but this is a dream!"

Alyosha was terribly glad that he had caused so much happiness and that the poor man had agreed to be made happy.

"Wait, Alexei Fyodorovich, wait," the captain again seized upon a new dream that had just come to him, and again rattled on in a frenzied patter, "do you know, perhaps now Ilyushka and I will indeed realize our dream: we'll buy a horse and a covered cart, and the horse will be black, he asked that it be black, and we'll set off as we were picturing it two days ago. I know a lawyer in K—— province, my childhood friend, sir, and I was told by a reliable man that if I came he might give me a position as a clerk in his office, and who knows, maybe he would . . . So I could put mama in the cart, and Ninochka in the cart, and let Ilyushechka drive, and I'd go by foot, by foot, and so I'd take them all away, sir . . . Lord, if only I could get one miserable debt paid back to me, then maybe there would even be enough for that, sir!"

"There will be enough, there will be!" Alyosha exclaimed. "Katerina Ivanovna will send you more, as much as you want, and, you know, I have some money, too, take what you need, as you would from a brother, from a friend, you can pay it back later . . . (You'll get rich, you will!) And, you know, you could never have thought of anything better than this move to another province! It will be your salvation, and, above all, your boy's—and, you know, you should hurry, before winter, before the cold, and you will write to us from there, and we will remain brothers . . . No, it's not a dream!"

Alyosha was about to embrace him, he was so pleased. But glancing at him, he suddenly stopped: the man stood, stretching his neck, stretching his lips, with a pale and frenzied face, whispering something with his lips, as if he were trying to utter something; there was no sound, but he kept whispering with his lips. It was somehow strange.

"What's wrong with you?" Alyosha suddenly started for some reason.

"Alexei Fyodorovich . . . I . . . you . . . ," the captain muttered and broke off, staring strangely and wildly straight in his face, with the look of a man who has decided to throw himself off a cliff, and at the same time smiling, as it were, with his lips only. "I, sir . . . you, sir . . . And would you like me to show you a nice little trick, sir?" he suddenly whispered in a quick, firm whisper, his voice no longer faltering.

"What little trick?"

"A little trick, a bit of hocus-pocus," the captain kept whispering; his mouth became twisted to the left side, his left eye squinted, he went on staring at Alyosha as if his eyes were riveted to him.

"But what's wrong with you? What trick?" Alyosha cried, now quite alarmed.

"Watch this!" the captain suddenly shrieked.

And holding up both iridescent bills, which all the while, during the whole conversation, he had been holding by the corner between the thumb and index finger of his right hand, he suddenly seized them in some kind of rage, crumpled them, and clutched them tightly in his right fist.

"See that, sir, see that?" he shrieked to Alyosha, pale and frenzied, and suddenly, raising his fist, he threw both crumpled bills with all his might on the sand. "See that, sir?" he shrieked again, pointing at them with his finger. "Well, so, there, sir . . . !"

And suddenly raising his right foot, he fell to trampling them with his heel, in wild anger, gasping and exclaiming each time his foot struck:

"There's your money, sir! There's your money, sir! There's your money, sir! There's your money, sir!" Suddenly he leaped back and straightened up before Alyosha. His whole figure presented a picture of inexplicable pride.

"Report to those who sent you that the whiskbroom does not sell his honor, sir!" he cried out, raising his arm in the air. Then he quickly turned and broke into a run; but he had not gone even five steps when, turning all the way around, he suddenly made a gesture to Alyosha with his hand. Then, before he had gone even five more steps, he turned around again, this time for the last time, and now there was no twisted laugh on his face, but, on the contrary, it was all shaken with tears. In a weeping, faltering, spluttering patter, he cried out:

"And what would I tell my boy, if I took money from you for our disgrace?" And having said this, he broke into a run, this time without turning around. Alyosha looked after him with inexpressible sadness. Oh, he understood that the captain had not known until the very last moment that he would crumple the bills and fling them down. The running man did not once look back, and Alyosha knew that he would not look back. He did not want to pursue him or call out to him, and he knew why. When the captain was out of sight, Alyosha picked up the two bills. They were just very crumpled, flattened, and pressed into the sand, but were perfectly intact and crisp as new when Alyosha spread them and smoothed them out. Having smoothed them out, he folded them, put them in his pocket, and went to report to Katerina Ivanovna on the success of her errand.

BOOK V: PRO AND CONTRA

Chapter 1

A Betrothal

Madame Khokhlakov was again the first to meet Alyosha. She was in a hurry; something important had happened: Katerina Ivanovna's hysterics had ended in a fainting spell, then she felt "terrible, horrible weakness, she lay down, rolled up her eyes, and became delirious. Now there's fever, we sent for Herzenstube, we sent for her aunts. The aunts are already here, but Herzenstube still isn't. They're all sitting in her room and waiting. Who knows what may come of it? And she's unconscious. What if it's brain fever?"

Exclaiming this, Madame Khokhlakov looked seriously frightened: "Now this is serious, serious!" she added at every word, as if everything that had happened to her before were not serious. Alyosha listened to her with sorrow; he tried to begin telling her of his own adventures, but she interrupted him at the first words: she had no time, she asked him to sit with Lise and wait for her there.

"Lise, my dearest Alexei Fyodorovich," she whispered almost in his ear, "Lise has given me a strange surprise just now, but she has also moved me, and so my heart forgives her everything. Imagine, no sooner had you gone than she suddenly began sincerely regretting that she had supposedly been laughing at you yesterday and today. But she wasn't laughing, she was only joking. Yet she so seriously regretted it, almost to the point of tears, that I was surprised. She has never so seriously regretted laughing at me, she has always made light of it. And you know, she laughs at me all the time. But now she's serious, now everything has become serious. She values your opinion highly, Alexei Fyodorovich, and, if possible, do not be offended, and do not bear her a grudge. I myself am forever sparing her, because she's such a smart little girl—don't you think so? She was saying just now that you were a friend of her childhood—'the most serious friend of my childhood'—imagine that, the most serious—and what about me? In this regard she has the most serious feelings, and even memories, and above all, these phrases and words of hers, the most unexpected little words, that suddenly pop out when you least expect them. Recently, for instance, talking about a pine tree: there was a pine tree standing in our garden when she was very little, maybe it's still standing, so there's no need to speak in the past tense. Pines are not people, Alexei Fyodorovich, they take a long time to change. 'Mama,' she said, 'how I pine for that pine'—you see, 'pine' and 'pine'—but she put it some other way, because something's confused here, *pine* is such a silly word, only she said something so original on the subject that I decidedly cannot begin to repeat it. Besides, I've forgotten it all. Well, good-bye, I am deeply shaken, and am probably losing my mind. Ah, Alexei Fyodorovich, twice in my life I've lost my mind and had to be treated. Go to Lise. Cheer her up, as you always manage to do so charmingly. Lise," she called, going up to her door, "here I've brought you your much-insulted Alexei Fyodorovich, and he's not at all angry, I assure you; quite the opposite, he's surprised you could think so!"

"*Merci, maman.* Come in, Alexei Fyodorovich."

Alyosha went in. Lise looked somehow embarrassed and suddenly blushed all over. She seemed to be ashamed of something, and, as always happens in such cases, she quickly began speaking of something quite unrelated, as if at that moment only this unrelated thing interested her.

"Mama suddenly told me just now, Alexei Fyodorovich, the whole story about the two hundred roubles, and about this errand of yours . . . to that poor officer . . . and the whole awful story, how he was offended, and, you know, though mama gets everything mixed up . . . she keeps jumping all over . . . I still cried when I heard it. Well, what happened? Did you give him the money, and how is the wretched man now . . . ?"

"That's just it—I didn't, but it's a long story," Alyosha replied, as if for his part what concerned him most was precisely that he had not given the money, but at the same time Lise saw perfectly well that he, too, was looking away and was also obviously trying to speak of unrelated matters. Alyosha sat down at the table and began telling his story, but from the first words he lost all his embarrassment and, in turn, carried Lise away. He spoke under the influence of strong emotion and the recent extraordinary impression, and succeeded in telling it well and thoroughly. Earlier, while still in Moscow, still in Lise's childhood, he had enjoyed visiting her and telling her now something that had just happened to him, now something he had read, or again something he remembered from his own childhood. Sometimes they even both daydreamed together and made up long stories between them, mostly gay and amusing ones. Now it was as if they were suddenly transported back to that time in Moscow two years before. Lise was greatly moved by his story. Alyosha managed to paint the image of "Ilyushechka" for her with ardent feeling. And when he finished describing in great detail the scene of the wretched man trampling on the money, Lise clasped her hands and cried out with irrepressible feeling:

"So you didn't give him the money, you just let him run away like that! My God, but you should at least have run after him and caught him . . ."

"No, Lise, it's better that I didn't run after him," Alyosha said, getting up from his chair and anxiously pacing the room.

"How better? Why better? Now they'll die without bread!"

"They won't die, because these two hundred roubles will still catch up with them. He'll take them tomorrow, despite all. Yes, tomorrow he'll certainly take them," Alyosha said, pacing back and forth in thought. "You see, Lise," he went on, suddenly stopping in front of her, "I made a mistake there, but the mistake has turned out for the better."

"What mistake, and why for the better?"

"This is why: he's a cowardly man and has a weak character. He's so worn out, and very kind. And now I keep wondering: why is it that he suddenly got so offended and trampled on the money—because, I assure you, until the very last minute he did not know he was going to trample on it. And it seems to me that he was offended by a number of things . . . in his position it could hardly be otherwise . . . First, he was offended because he had been too glad of the money in front of me, and hadn't concealed it from me. If he had been glad but not overly so, if he hadn't shown it, if he had given himself airs as others do when they're accepting money, making faces, then he might have stood it and accepted, but he was too honestly glad, and that is what was offensive. Ah, Lise, he's an honest and kind man—that's the whole trouble in such cases! All the while he was speaking then, his voice was so weak, weakened, and he spoke so fast, so fast, and he kept laughing with such a little giggle, or else he just wept . . . really, he wept, he was so delighted . . . and he spoke of his daughters . . . and of the position he would find in another town . . . And just when he had poured out his soul, he suddenly became ashamed that he had shown me his whole soul like that. And he immediately began to hate me. He's the sort of man who feels terribly shamed by poverty. But above all he was offended because he had accepted me too quickly as a friend and given in to me too soon; first he attacked me, tried to frighten me, then suddenly, as soon as he saw the money, he began embracing me. Because he did embrace me, and kept touching me with his hands. That is precisely why he came to feel such humiliation, and it was just there that I made that mistake, a very serious one: I suddenly said to him that if he didn't have enough money to move to another town, he would be given more, and that even I myself would give him as much of my own money as he wanted. And that suddenly struck him: why, indeed, should I up and help him? You know, Lise, it's terribly difficult for an offended man when everyone suddenly starts looking like his benefactor . . . I knew that; the elder told me so. I don't know how to put it, but I've noticed it often myself. And I feel exactly the same way. And above all, though he didn't know until the very last minute that he would trample on the bills, he did anticipate it, he must have. That's what made his delight so intense, because he anticipated . . . And so, though this is all so bad, it's still for the better. I even think that it's for the best, that it even could not be better . . ."

"Why, why couldn't it be better?" Lise exclaimed, looking at Alyosha in great astonishment.

"Because, Lise, if he had taken the money instead of trampling on it, he'd have gone home, and within an hour he'd have been weeping over his humiliation—that's certainly what would have happened. He would weep, and perhaps tomorrow, at the first light, he would come to me, and maybe throw the bills at me and trample on them as he did today. But now he's gone off feeling terribly proud and triumphant, though he knows that he's 'ruined himself.' And so nothing could be easier now than to get him to accept these same two hundred roubles, maybe even tomorrow, because he has already proved his honor, thrown down the money, trampled on it . . . He couldn't have known, when he was trampling on it, that I would bring it to him again tomorrow. And at the same time he needs this money terribly. Although he is proud of himself now, even today he'll start thinking about the help he has lost. During the night the thought will become stronger still, he will dream about it, and by tomorrow morning he will perhaps be ready to run to me and ask forgiveness. And at that moment I shall appear: 'Here,' I'll say, 'you are a proud man, you've proved it, take the money now, forgive us.' And this time he will take it!"

Alyosha said in a sort of rapture: "And this time he will take it!" Lise clapped her hands.

"Ah, it's true, ah, I suddenly understand it so terribly well! Ah, Alyosha, how do you know all that? So young, and he already knows what's in the soul . . . I could never have thought that up . . ."

"Now, above all, he must be convinced that he is on an equal footing with all of us, in spite of his taking money from us," Alyosha continued in his rapture, "and not only on an equal but even on a greater footing . . ."

"'On a greater footing'—how charming, Alexei Fyodorovich, but go on, go on!"

"You mean I didn't put it right . . . about a greater footing . . . but no matter, because . . ."

"Oh, no matter, no matter, of course no matter! Forgive me, Alyosha dear . . . You know, until now I almost didn't respect you . . . that is, I respected you, but on an equal footing, and now I shall respect you on a greater footing . . . Dear, don't be angry at my 'witticisms,'" she went on at once with strong feeling, "I'm funny, I'm little, but you, you . . . Listen, Alexei Fyodorovich, isn't there something in all this reasoning of ours, I mean, of yours . . . no, better, of ours . . . isn't there some contempt for him, for this wretched man . . . that we're examining his soul like this, as if we were looking down on him? That we have decided so certainly, now, that he will accept the money?"

"No, Lise, there is no contempt in it," Alyosha answered firmly, as if he were already prepared for the question. "I thought it over myself, on the way here. Consider, what contempt can there be if we ourselves are just the same as he is, if everyone is just the same as he is? Because we are just the same, not better. And even if we were better, we would still be the same in his place . . . I don't know about you, Lise, but for myself I consider that my soul is petty in many ways. And his is not petty, on the contrary, it is very sensitive . . . No, Lise, there is no contempt for him! You know, Lise, my elder said once that most people need to be looked after like children, and some like the sick in hospitals . . ."

"Ah, Alexei Fyodorovich, my darling, let's look after people that way!"

"Yes, let's, Lise, I'm ready—only personally I'm not quite ready. I'm sometimes very impatient, and sometimes I don't see things. With you it's quite different."

"Ah, I don't believe it! Alexei Fyodorovich, how happy I am!"

"How good that you say so, Lise."

"Alexei Fyodorovich, you are wonderfully good, but sometimes it's as if you're a pedant . . . and then one looks, and you're not a pedant at all. Go to the door, open it quietly, and see whether mama is eavesdropping," Lise suddenly whispered in a sort of nervous, hurried whisper.

Alyosha went, opened the door a little, and reported that no one was eavesdropping.

"Come here, Alexei Fyodorovich," Lise went on, blushing more and more, "give me your hand, so. Listen, I must make you a great confession: yesterday's letter was not a joke, it was serious . . ."

And she hid her eyes with her hand. One could see that she was very ashamed to be making this confession. Suddenly she seized his hand and impetuously kissed it three times.

"Ah, Lise, isn't that wonderful," Alyosha exclaimed joyfully. "And I was completely sure that you wrote it seriously."

"He was sure—just imagine!" she suddenly pushed his hand aside, without, however, letting go of it, blushing terribly and laughing a little happy laugh, "I kiss his hand and he says 'how wonderful.'" But her reproach was unjust: Alyosha, too, was in great confusion.

"I wish you would always like me, Lise, but I don't know how to do it," he barely murmured, blushing himself.

"Alyosha, dear, you are cold and impudent. Just look at him! He was so good as to choose me for his spouse, and left it at that! He was quite sure I wrote to him seriously—how nice! It's impudence, that's what it is!"

"Why, is it bad that I was sure?" Alyosha suddenly laughed.

"Ah, Alyosha, on the contrary, it is terribly good," Lise looked at him tenderly and with happiness. Alyosha stood still holding her hand in his. Suddenly he leaned forward and kissed her full on the lips.

"What's this now? What are you doing?" Lise cried. Alyosha was quite lost.

"Forgive me if I'm not . . . Maybe it was a terribly silly . . . You said I was cold, so I up and kissed you . . . Only I see it came out silly . . ."

Lise laughed and hid her face in her hands.

"And in that dress!" escaped her in the midst of her laughter, but she suddenly stopped laughing and became all serious, almost severe.

"Well, Alyosha, we must put off kissing, because neither of us knows how to do it yet, and we still have a long time to wait," she ended suddenly. "You'd better tell me why you're taking me—such a fool, such a sick little fool, and you so intelligent, so intellectual, so observant? Ah, Alyosha, I'm terribly happy, because I'm not worthy of you at all!"

"You are, Lise. In a few days I'll be leaving the monastery for good. Going out into the world, one ought to get married, that I know. And so he told me. Who better could I have than you . . . and who else but you would have me? I've already thought it over. First, you've known me since childhood, and second, you have very many abilities that are not in me at all. Your soul is lighter than mine; above all, you are more innocent than I am, and I've already touched many, many things . . . Ah, you don't know it, but I, too, am a Karamazov! What matter if you laugh and joke, and at me, too? On the contrary, laugh—I'm so glad of it . . . But you laugh like a little girl, and inside you think like a martyr . . ."

"A martyr? How so?"

"Yes, Lise, your question just now: aren't we contemptuous of that wretched man, dissecting his soul like that—that was a martyr's question . . . you see, I can't express it at all, but someone in whom such questions arise is capable of suffering. Sitting in your chair, you must already have thought a lot . . ."

"Alyosha, give me your hand, why are you taking it away?" Lise said in a voice somehow flat, weakened from happiness. "Listen, Alyosha, what are you going to wear when you leave the monastery, what kind of clothes? Don't laugh, don't be angry, it's very, very important for me."

"I haven't thought about clothes yet, Lise, but I'll wear whatever you like."

"I want you to have a dark blue velvet jacket, a white piqué waistcoat, and a gray soft felt hat . . . Tell me, did you really believe that I didn't love you this morning, when I renounced my letter from yesterday?"

"No, I didn't believe it."

"Oh, impossible man, incorrigible!"

"You see, I knew that you . . . seemed to love me, but I pretended to believe that you didn't love me, so that you would feel . . . more comfortable . . ."

"Worse still! The worst and best of all. Alyosha, I love you terribly. Today, when you were about to come, I bet myself: I'll ask him for yesterday's letter, and if he calmly takes it out and gives it to me (as might always be expected of him), that will mean that he doesn't love me at all, feels nothing, and is simply a silly and unworthy boy, and I am ruined. But you left the letter in your cell, and that encouraged me: isn't it true that you left it in the cell because you anticipated that I would demand the letter back, so that you wouldn't have to give it back? It's true, isn't it?"

"Oh, Lise, it's not true at all, because the letter is with me now, and it was with me then, too, in this pocket. Here it is."

Laughing, Alyosha took the letter out and showed it to her from afar.

"Only I won't give it to you, I'll hold it up for you to see."

"What? So you lied to me then? You, a monk, lied?"

"Perhaps I lied," Alyosha went on laughing. "I lied so as not to give you back the letter. It is very dear to me," he added suddenly with strong feeling, blushing again, "it will be so forever, and I will never give it to anyone!"

Lise looked at him with admiration.

"Alyosha," she murmured again, "look out the door, see if mama is eavesdropping."

"Very well, Lise, I will look, only wouldn't it be better not to look? Why suspect your mother of such meanness?"

"Meanness? What meanness? That she's eavesdropping on her daughter is her right, it's not meanness," Lise flared up. "And you may rest assured, Alexei Fyodorovich, that when I myself am a mother and have a daughter like me, I shall certainly eavesdrop on her."

"Really, Lise? That's not good."

"Oh, my God, what's mean about it? If it were an ordinary social conversation and I eavesdropped, that would be mean, but when her own daughter has locked herself up with a young man . . . Listen, Alyosha, I want you to know that I will spy on you, too, as soon as we are married, and I also want you to know that I will open all your letters and read everything . . . So be forewarned . . ."

"Yes, of course, if that is . . . ," muttered Alyosha, "only it's not good . . ."

"Ah, what contempt! Alyosha, dear, let's not quarrel from the very first moment—it's better if I tell you the whole truth: of course it's very bad to eavesdrop, and of course I am wrong and you are right, but I will eavesdrop anyway."

"Do, then. You won't spy out anything of the sort in me," Alyosha laughed.

"And, Alyosha, will you submit to me? This, too, ought to be decided beforehand."

"I will, certainly, with the greatest pleasure, only not in the most important things. If you disagree with me about the most important things, I will still do as duty tells me."

"That's how it should be. And you should know that I, too, on the contrary, am not only ready to submit to you in the most important things, but will also yield to you in everything, and I will give you my oath on it right now—in everything and for my whole life," Lise cried out fervently, "and happily, happily! What's more, I swear to you that I shall never eavesdrop on you, not once ever, nor shall I read even one of your letters, for you are right and I am not. And though I shall want terribly to eavesdrop, I know it, I still shan't do it, because you consider it ignoble. You are like my providence now . . . Listen, Alexei Fyodorovich, why have you been so sad these days, both yesterday and today? I know you have cares, great troubles, but I see that you have some special sadness besides, perhaps some secret one, don't you?"

"Yes, Lise, I have a secret one, too," Alyosha said sadly. "I can see that you love me if you've guessed that."

"What is this sadness? About what? Can you tell me?" Lise pleaded timidly.

"I'll tell you later, Lise . . . later . . . ," Alyosha became embarrassed. "Now perhaps you wouldn't understand it. And perhaps I wouldn't be able to explain it myself."

"Besides, I know that your brothers and your father are tormenting you."

"Yes, my brothers, too," said Alyosha, as if thinking to himself.

"I don't like your brother Ivan Fyodorovich, Alyosha," Lise suddenly remarked.

Alyosha noted her remark with a certain surprise, but did not take it up.

"My brothers are destroying themselves," he went on, "my father, too. And they're destroying others with them. This is the 'earthy force of the Karamazovs,' as Father Paissy put it the other day—earthy and violent, raw . . . Whether the Spirit of God is moving over that force—even that I do not know. I only know that I myself am a Karamazov . . . I am a monk, a monk? Am I a monk, Lise? Didn't you say somehow a moment ago that I was a monk?"

"Yes, I said that."

"And, look, maybe I don't even believe in God."

"You don't believe? What's the matter with you?" Lise asked softly and cautiously. But Alyosha did not answer. There was, in these too-sudden words, something too mysterious and too subjective, perhaps not clear to himself, but that undoubtedly tormented him.

"And now, on top of all that, my friend is going, the first of men in the world is leaving the earth! If you knew, if you knew, Lise, how bound I am, how welded my soul is to this man! And now I shall be left alone . . . I will come to you, Lise . . . Henceforth we will be together . . ."

"Yes, together, together! From now on, always together, for the whole of our lives. Listen, kiss me, I allow you to."

Alyosha kissed her.

"Well, go now, Christ be with you!" (and she made a cross over him). "Go *to him*, quickly, while he is alive. I see that I've delayed you cruelly. I will pray today for him and for you. Alyosha, we shall be happy! We shall be happy, shan't we?"

"It seems we shall be, Lise."

On parting from Lise, Alyosha chose not to go and see Madame Khokhlakov, and he was about to leave the house without saying good-bye to her. But as soon as he opened the door and went to the stairs, Madame Khokhlakov appeared before him from nowhere. Alyosha could tell from her very first words that she had been waiting there for him on purpose.

"Alexei Fyodorovich, this is terrible. It's a child's trifles and all nonsense. I hope you won't take it into your head to dream . . . Foolishness, foolishness, and more foolishness!" she pounced on him.

"Only don't say that to her," said Alyosha, "or she will get upset, and that is bad for her now."

"Sensible words from a sensible young man. Shall I take it that you agreed with her only because, out of compassion for her sickly condition, you did not want to anger her by contradicting her?"

"Oh, no, not at all, I spoke perfectly seriously with her," Alyosha declared firmly.

"Seriousness is impossible, unthinkable here, and first of all let me tell you that now I will not receive you again, not even once, and second, I will go away and take her with me."

"But why?" said Alyosha. "It's still so far off, we'll have to wait perhaps a year and a half."

"Ah, Alexei Fyodorovich, that's true, of course, and in a year and a half you will quarrel and break up with her a thousand times. But I'm so unhappy, so unhappy! Perhaps it's all a trifle, but it is a great blow to me. Now I'm like Famusov in the last scene, you are Chatsky, and she is Sophia,[1] and just imagine, I ran out here to the stairs on purpose to meet you, and there, too, all the fatal things take place on the stairs. I heard everything, I almost fell over. This explains the horrors of that whole night and all these recent hysterics! For the daughter—love, and for the mother—death. Go lie in your coffin. Now, the second and most important thing: what is this letter she wrote to you? Show it to me at once, at once!"

"No, there's no need. Tell me, how is Katerina Ivanovna's health? I very much need to know."

"She's still delirious, she hasn't come to herself; her aunts are here and do nothing but say 'Ah' and put on airs in front of me, and Herzenstube came and got so frightened that I didn't know what to do with him or how to save him, I even thought of sending for a doctor. He was taken away in my carriage. And suddenly, to crown it all, suddenly you, with this letter! True, it won't be for a year and a half. In the name of all that's great and holy, in the name of your dying elder, show me the letter, Alexei Fyodorovich, show me, her mother! Hold it up, if you wish, and I shall read it from your hand."

"No, I won't show it to you, Katerina Osipovna, even with her permission I would not show it to you. I'll come tomorrow, and, if you wish, I'll discuss many things with you, but now—farewell!"

And Alyosha ran downstairs into the street.

Chapter 2

Smerdyakov with a Guitar

Besides, he had no time. A thought flashed through him as he was saying good-bye to Lise—a thought about how he might contrive, now, to catch his brother Dmitri, who was apparently hiding from him. It was getting late, already past two in the afternoon. With his whole being Alyosha felt drawn to the monastery, to his "great" dying man, but the need to see his brother Dmitri outweighed everything: with each hour the conviction kept growing in Alyosha's mind that an inevitable, terrible catastrophe was about to occur. What precisely the catastrophe consisted in, and what he would say at that moment to his brother, he himself would perhaps have been unable to define. "Let my benefactor die without me, but at least I won't have to reproach myself all my life that I might have saved something and did not, but passed by, in a hurry to get home. In doing so, I shall be acting in accordance with his great word . . ."

His plan consisted in taking his brother Dmitri unawares—namely, by climbing over the same wattle fence as yesterday, getting into the garden, and planting himself in that gazebo. "If he's not there," Alyosha thought, "then, without telling either Foma or the landladies, I'll hide in the gazebo until evening, if need be. If he's still keeping watch for Grushenka's visit, most likely he'll come to the gazebo . . ." By the way, Alyosha did not give too much thought to the details of the plan, but decided to carry it out, even if it meant he would not get back to the monastery that day . . .

Everything went without hindrance: he climbed over the wattle fence at almost the same spot as the day before and secretly stole into the gazebo. He did not want to be observed: both the landlady and Foma (if he was there) might be on his brother's side and obey his orders, and therefore either not let Alyosha into the garden or forewarn his brother in good time that he was being sought and asked for. There was no one in the gazebo. Alyosha sat in the same place as the day before and began to wait. He looked around the gazebo, and for some reason it seemed to him much more decrepit than before; this time it seemed quite wretched to him. The day, by the way, was as fine as the day before. On the green table a circle was imprinted from yesterday's glass of cognac, which must have spilled over. Empty and profitless thoughts, as always during a tedious time of waiting, crept into his head: for example, why, as he had come in now, had he sat precisely in the very same place as the day before, and not in some other place? Finally he became very sad, sad from anxious uncertainty. But he had not been sitting there for even a quarter of an hour when suddenly, from somewhere very close by, came the strum of a guitar. Some people were sitting, or had just sat down, about twenty paces away, certainly not more, somewhere in the bushes. Alyosha suddenly had a flash of recollection that the day before, when he had left his brother and gone out of the gazebo, he had seen, or there flashed before him, as it were, to the left, near the fence, a low, old green garden bench among the bushes. The visitors, therefore, must just have sat down on it. But who were they? A single male voice suddenly sang a verse in a sweet falsetto, accompanying himself on the guitar:

> An invincible power
> Binds me to my flower.
> Lord have me-e-e-ercy
> On her and me!
> On her and me!
> On her and me![1]

The voice stopped. A lackey tenor, with a lackey trill. Another voice, female this time, suddenly said caressingly and timidly, as it were, but still in a very mincing manner:

"And why, Pavel Fyodorovich, have you been staying away from us so much? Why do you keep neglecting us?"

"Not at all, miss," a man's voice answered, politely enough, but above all with firm and insistent dignity. Apparently the man had the upper hand and the woman was flirting with him. "The man seems to be Smerdyakov," thought Alyosha, "judging by his voice at least. And the lady must be the daughter of the house, the one who came from Moscow, wears a dress with a train, and goes to get soup from Marfa Ignatievna . . ."

"I like any verses terribly, if it's nicely put together," the female voice went on. "Why don't you go on?"

The voice sang again:

> More than all a king's wealth
> Is my dear one's good health.
> Lord have me-e-e-ercy
> On her and me!
> On her and me!
> On her and me!

"Last time it came out even better," remarked the female voice. "After the king's wealth, you sang: 'Is my honey's good health.' It came out more tender. You must have forgotten today."

"Verse is nonsense, miss," Smerdyakov said curtly.

"Oh, no, I do so like a bit of verse."

"As far as verse goes, miss, essentially it's nonsense. Consider for yourself: who on earth talks in rhymes? And if we all started talking in rhymes, even by order of the authorities, how much would get said, miss? Verse is no good, Maria Kondratievna."

"You're so smart about everything! How did you ever amount to all that?" the female voice was growing more and more caressing.

"I could have done even better, miss, and I'd know a lot more, if it wasn't for my destiny ever since childhood. I'd have killed a man in a duel with a pistol for calling me low-born, because I came from Stinking Lizaveta without a father, and they were shoving that in my face in Moscow, it spread there thanks to Grigory Vasilievich. Grigory Vasilievich reproaches me for rebelling against my nativity: 'You opened her matrix,' he says.[2] I don't know about her matrix, but I'd have let them kill me in the womb, so as not to come out into the world at all, miss. They used to say in the market, and your mama, too, started telling me, with her great indelicacy, that she went around with her hair in a Polish plait and was *a wee bit* under five feet tall. Why say *a wee bit* when you can simply say 'a little' like everyone else? She wanted to make it tearful, but those are peasant tears, miss, so to speak, those are real peasant feelings. Can a Russian peasant have feelings comparably to an educated man? With such lack of education, he can't have any feelings at all. Ever since my childhood, whenever I hear this 'wee bit,' I want to throw myself at the wall. I hate all of Russia, Maria Kondratievna."

"If you were a military cadet or a fine young hussar, you wouldn't talk that way, you'd draw your sword and start defending all of Russia."

"I not only have no wish to be a fine military hussar, Maria Kondratievna, but I wish, on the contrary, for the abolition of all soldiers."

"And when the enemy comes, who will defend us?"

"But there's no need to at all, miss. In the year twelve there was a great invasion by the emperor Napoleon of France, the first, the father of the present one,[3] and it would have been good if we had been subjected then by those same Frenchmen: an intelligent nation would have subjected a very stupid one, miss, and joined it to itself. There would be quite a different order of things then, miss."

"Why, as if theirs are so much better than ours! I wouldn't trade a certain gallant I know for three of the youngest Englishmen," Maria Kondratievna said tenderly, no doubt accompanying her words at that moment with a most languid look.

"Folks have their preferences, miss."

"And you yourself are just like a foreigner, just like a real noble foreigner, I'll tell you so for all that I'm blushing."

"When it comes to depravity, if you want to know, theirs and ours are no different. They're all rogues, only theirs walks around in patent leather boots, and our swine stinks in his poverty and sees nothing wrong with it. The Russian people need thrashing, miss, as Fyodor Pavlovich rightly said yesterday, though he's a madman, he and all his children, miss."

"But you respect Ivan Fyodorovich, you said so yourself."

"And he made reference to me that I'm a stinking lackey. He considers me as maybe rebelling, but he's mistaken, miss. If I had just so much in my pocket, I'd have left long ago. Dmitri Fyodorovich is worse than any lackey, in his behavior, and in his intelligence, and in his poverty, miss, and he's not fit for anything, but, on the contrary, he gets honor from everybody. I may be only a broth-maker, but if I'm lucky I can open a café-restaurant in Moscow, on the Petrovka.[4] Because I cook *specialités*, and no one in Moscow except foreigners can serve *specialités*. Dmitri Fyodorovich is a ragamuffin, but if he were to challenge the biggest count's son to a duel, he would accept, miss, and how is he any better than me? Because he's a lot stupider than me. He's blown so much money, and for nothing, miss."

"I think duels are so nice," Maria Kondratievna suddenly remarked.

"How so, miss?"

"It's so scary and brave, especially when fine young officers with pistols in their hands are shooting at each other because of some lady friend. Just like a picture. Oh, if only they let girls watch, I'd like terribly to see one."

"It's fine when he's doing the aiming, but when it's his mug that's being aimed at, there's the stupidest feeling, miss. You'd run away from the place, Maria Kondratievna."

"Do you mean you would run away?"

But Smerdyakov did not deign to answer. After a moment's silence there came another strum, and the falsetto poured out the last verse:

> I don't care what you say
> For I'm going away,
> I'll be happy and free
> In the big citee!
> And I won't grieve,
> No, I'll never grieve,
> I don't plan ever to grieve.

Here something unexpected happened: Alyosha suddenly sneezed. The people on the bench hushed at once. Alyosha got up and walked in their direction. It was indeed Smerdyakov, dressed up, pomaded, perhaps even curled, in patent leather shoes. The guitar lay on the bench. The lady was Maria Kondratievna, the landlady's daughter; she was wearing a light blue dress with a train two yards long; she was still a young girl, and would have been pretty if her face had not been so round and so terribly freckled.

"Will my brother Dmitri be back soon?" Alyosha asked as calmly as he could.

Smerdyakov slowly rose from the bench; Maria Kondratievna rose, too.

"Why should I be informed as to Dmitri Fyodorovich? It's not as if I were his keeper," Smerdyakov answered quietly, distinctly, and superciliously.

"But I just asked if you knew," Alyosha explained.

"I know nothing of his whereabouts, and have no wish to know, sir."

"But my brother precisely told me that it is you who let him know about everything that goes on in the house, and have promised to let him know when Agrafena Alexandrovna comes."

Smerdyakov slowly and imperturbably raised his eyes to him.

"And how were you pleased to get in this time, since the gates here have been latched for an hour already?" he asked, looking fixedly at Alyosha.

"I got in over the fence from the lane and went straight to the gazebo. I hope you will excuse me for that," he addressed Maria Kondratievna, "I was in a hurry to get hold of my brother."

"Ah, how should we take offense at you," drawled Maria Kondratievna, flattered by Alyosha's apology, "since Dmitri Fyodorovich, too, often goes to the gazebo in the same manner, we don't even know it and there he is sitting in the gazebo."

"I am trying very hard to find him now, I very much wish to see him, or to find out from you where he is now. Believe me, it's a matter of great importance for him."

"He doesn't keep us notified," babbled Maria Kondratievna.

"Even though I come here as an acquaintance," Smerdyakov began again, "even here the gentleman harasses me cruelly with his ceaseless inquiries about the master; well, he says, how are things there, who comes and who goes, and can I tell him anything else? Twice he even threatened me with death."

"With death?" Alyosha asked in surprise.

"But that would constitute nothing for him, sir, given his character, which you yourself had the honor of observing yesterday. If I miss Agrafena Alexandrovna, and she spends the night here, he says, you won't live long, you first. I'm very afraid of him, sir, and if I wasn't even more afraid, I'd have to report him to the town authorities. God even knows what he may produce."

"The other day he said to him, 'I'll grind you in a mortar,'" Maria Kondratievna added.

"Well, if it's in a mortar, it may just be talk . . . ," Alyosha remarked. "If I could see him now, I might say something about that, too . . ."

"There's only one thing I can tell you," Smerdyakov suddenly seemed to make up his mind. "I come here sometimes as a customary neighborly acquaintance, and why shouldn't I, sir? On the other hand, today at daybreak Ivan Fyodorovich sent me to his lodgings, on his Lake Street, without a letter, sir, so that in words Dmitri Fyodorovich should come to the local tavern, on the square, to have dinner together. I went, sir, but I didn't find Dmitri Fyodorovich at home, and it was just eight o'clock. 'He's been and gone,' his landlords informed me, in those very words. As if they had some kind of conspiracy, sir, a mutual one. And now, maybe at this very moment he's sitting in that tavern with his brother Ivan Fyodorovich, because Ivan Fyodorovich did not come home for dinner, and Fyodor Pavlovich finished his dinner alone an hour ago, and then lay down to sleep. I earnestly request, however, that you not tell him anything about me and what I've told you, because he'd kill me for nothing, sir."

"My brother Ivan invited Dmitri to a tavern today?" Alyosha quickly asked again.

"Right, sir."

"To the 'Metropolis,' on the square?"

"That's the one, sir."

"It's quite possible!" Alyosha exclaimed in great excitement. "Thank you, Smerdyakov, that is important news, I shall go there now."

"Don't give me away, sir," Smerdyakov called after him.

"Oh, no, I'll come to the tavern as if by chance, don't worry."

"But where are you going? Let me open the gate for you," cried Maria Kondratievna.

"No, it's closer this way, I'll climb over the fence."

The news shook Alyosha terribly. He set off for the tavern. It would be improper for him to enter the tavern dressed as he was, but he could inquire on the stairs and ask them to come out. Just as he reached the tavern, however, a window suddenly opened and his brother Ivan himself shouted down to him:

"Alyosha, can you come in here, or not? I'd be awfully obliged."

"Certainly I can, only I'm not sure, the way I'm dressed . . ."

"But I have a private room. Go to the porch, I'll run down and meet you . . ."

A minute later Alyosha was sitting next to his brother. Ivan was alone, and was having dinner.

Chapter 3

The Brothers Get Acquainted

Ivan was not, however, in a private room. It was simply a place at the window separated by screens, but those who sat behind the screens still could not be seen by others. It was the front room, the first, with a sideboard along the wall. Waiters kept darting across it every moment. There was only one customer, a little old man, a retired officer, and he was drinking tea in the corner. But in the other rooms of the tavern there was all the usual tavern bustle, voices calling, beer bottles popping, billiard balls clicking, a barrel organ droning. Alyosha knew that Ivan hardly ever went to this tavern, and was no lover of taverns generally; therefore he must have turned up here, Alyosha thought, precisely by appointment, to meet with his brother Dmitri. And yet there was no brother Dmitri.

"I'll order some fish soup for you, or something—you don't live on tea alone, do you?" cried Ivan, apparently terribly pleased that he had managed to lure Alyosha. He himself had already finished dinner and was having tea.

"I'll have fish soup, and then tea, I'm hungry," Alyosha said cheerfully.

"And cherry preserve? They have it here. Do you remember how you loved cherry preserve at Polenov's when you were little?"

"You remember that? I'll have preserve, too, I still love it."

Ivan rang for the waiter and ordered fish soup, tea, and preserve.

"I remember everything, Alyosha, I remember you till you were eleven, I was nearly fifteen then. Fifteen and eleven, it's such a difference that brothers of those ages are never friends. I don't even know if I loved you. When I left for Moscow, in the first years I didn't even think of you at all. Later, when you got to Moscow yourself, it seems to me that we met only once somewhere. And now it's already the fourth month that I've been living here, and so far you and I have not exchanged a single word. I'm leaving tomorrow, and I was sitting here now, wondering how I could see you to say good-bye, and you came walking along."

"So you wished very much to see me?"

"Very much. I want to get acquainted with you once and for all, and I want you to get acquainted with me. And with that, to say good-bye. I think it's best to get acquainted before parting. I saw how you kept looking at me all these three months, there was a certain ceaseless expectation in your eyes, and that is something I cannot bear, which is why I never approached you. But in the end I learned to respect you: this little man stands his ground, I thought. Observe that I'm speaking seriously, though I may be laughing. You do stand your ground, don't you? I love people who stand their ground, whatever they may stand upon, and even if they're such little boys as you are. In the end, your expectant look did not disgust me at all; on the contrary, I finally came to love your expectant look . . . You seem to love me for some reason, Alyosha?"

"I do love you, Ivan. Our brother Dmitri says of you: Ivan is a grave. I say: Ivan is a riddle. You are still a riddle to me, but I've already understood something about you, though only since this morning!"

"What is it?" Ivan laughed.

"You won't be angry?" Alyosha laughed, too.

"Well?"

"That you are just a young man, exactly like all other young men of twenty-three—yes, a young, very young, fresh and nice boy, still green, in fact! Well, are you very offended?"

"On the contrary, you've struck me with a coincidence!" Ivan cried gaily and ardently. "Would you believe that after our meeting today at her place, I have been thinking to myself about just that, my twenty-three-year-old greenness, and suddenly you guessed it exactly, and began with that very thing. I've been sitting here now, and do you know what I was saying to myself? If I did not believe in life, if I were to lose faith in the woman I love, if I were to lose faith in the order of things, even if I were to become convinced, on the contrary, that everything is a disorderly, damned, and perhaps devilish chaos, if I were struck even by all the horrors of human disillusionment—still I would want to live, and as long as I have bent to this cup, I will not tear myself from it until I've drunk it all! However, by the age of thirty, I will probably drop the cup, even if I haven't emptied it, and walk away . . . I don't know where. But until my thirtieth year, I know this for certain, my youth will overcome everything—all disillusionment, all aversion to life. I've asked myself many times: is there such despair in the world as could overcome this wild and perhaps indecent thirst for life in me, and have decided that apparently there is not—that is, once again, until my thirtieth year, after which I myself shall want no more, so it seems to me. Some snotty-nosed, consumptive moralists, poets especially, often call this thirst for life base. True, it's a feature of the Karamazovs, to some extent, this thirst for life despite all; it must be sitting in you, too; but why is it base? There is still an awful lot of centripetal force on our planet, Alyosha. I want to live, and I do live, even if it be against logic. Though I do not believe in the order of things, still the sticky little leaves that come out in the spring[1] are dear to me, the blue sky is dear to me, some people are dear to me, whom one loves sometimes, would you believe it, without even knowing why; some human deeds are dear to me, which one has perhaps long ceased believing in, but still honors with one's heart, out of old habit. Here, they've brought your fish soup—help yourself. It's good fish soup, they make it well. I want to go to Europe, Alyosha, I'll go straight from here. Of course I know that I will only be going to a graveyard, but to the most, the most precious graveyard, that's the thing! The precious dead lie there, each stone over them speaks of such ardent past life, of such passionate faith in their deeds, their truth, their struggle, and their science, that I—this I know beforehand—will fall to the ground and kiss those stones and weep over them—being wholeheartedly convinced, at the same time, that it has all long been a graveyard and nothing more. And I will not weep from despair, but simply because I will be happy in my shed tears. I will be drunk with my own tenderness. Sticky spring leaves, the blue sky—I love them, that's all! Such things you love not with your mind, not with logic, but with your insides, your guts, you love your first young strength . . . Do you understand any of this blather, Alyoshka, or not?" Ivan suddenly laughed.

"I understand it all too well, Ivan: to want to love with your insides, your guts—you said it beautifully, and I'm terribly glad that you want so much to live," Alyosha exclaimed. "I think that everyone should love life before everything else in the world."

"Love life more than its meaning?"

"Certainly, love it before logic, as you say, certainly before logic, and only then will I also understand its meaning. That is how I've long imagined it. Half your work is done and acquired, Ivan: you love life. Now you need only apply yourself to the second half, and you are saved."

"You're already saving me, though maybe I wasn't perishing. And what does this second half consist of?"

"Resurrecting your dead, who may never have died. Now give me some tea. I'm glad we're talking, Ivan."

"I see you're feeling inspired. I'm terribly fond of such *professions de foi*[2] from such . . . novices. You're a firm man, Alexei. Is it true that you want to leave the monastery?"

"Yes, it's true. My elder is sending me into the world."

"So we'll see each other in the world, we'll meet before my thirtieth year, when I will begin to tear myself away from the cup. Now, father doesn't want to tear himself away from his cup until he's seventy, he's even dreaming of eighty, he said so himself, and he means it all too seriously, though he is a buffoon. He stands on his sensuality, also as on a rock . . . though after thirty years, indeed, there may be nothing else to stand on . . . But still, seventy is base; thirty is better: it's possible to preserve 'a tinge of nobility'[3] while duping oneself. Have you seen Dmitri today?"

"No, I haven't, but I did see Smerdyakov." And Alyosha told his brother quickly and in detail about his meeting with Smerdyakov. Ivan suddenly began listening very anxiously, and even asked him to repeat certain things.

"Only he asked me not to tell brother Dmitri what he had said about him," Alyosha added.

Ivan frowned and lapsed into thought.

"Are you frowning because of Smerdyakov?" asked Alyosha.

"Yes, because of him. Devil take him. Dmitri I really did want to see, but now there's no need . . . ," Ivan spoke reluctantly.

"Are you really leaving so soon, brother?"

"Yes."

"What about Dmitri and father? How will it end between them?" Alyosha said anxiously.

"Don't drag that out again! What have I got to do with it? Am I my brother Dmitri's keeper or something?" Ivan snapped irritably, but suddenly smiled somehow bitterly. "Cain's answer to God about his murdered brother, eh?

Maybe that's what you're thinking at the moment? But, devil take it, I can't really stay on here as their keeper! I've finished my affairs and I'm leaving. Don't think that I'm jealous of Dmitri and have been trying all these three months to win over his beauty Katerina Ivanovna! Damn it, I had my own affairs. I've finished my affairs and I'm leaving. I just finished my affairs today, as you witnessed."

"You mean today at Katerina Ivanovna's?"

"Yes, and I'm done with it all at once. And why not? What do I care about Dmitri? Dmitri has nothing to do with it. I had my own affairs with Katerina Ivanovna. You know yourself, on the contrary, that Dmitri behaved as if he were conspiring with me. I never asked, not at all, but he himself solemnly handed her over to me, with his blessing. It all smacks of the ludicrous! No, Alyosha, no, if only you knew how light I feel now! I was sitting here eating my dinner and, believe me, I almost wanted to order champagne to celebrate my first hour of freedom. Pah! half a year almost—and suddenly at once, I got rid of it all at once. Did I suspect, even yesterday, that it would cost me nothing to end it if I wanted?"

"Are you talking about your love, Ivan?"

"Love, if you wish, yes, I fell in love with a young lady, an institute girl. I tormented myself over her, and she tormented me. I sat over her . . . and suddenly it all blew away. This morning I spoke inspiredly, then I left—and burst out laughing, do you believe it? No, I'm speaking literally."

"You're also speaking quite cheerfully, now," Alyosha remarked, looking closely at his face, which indeed had suddenly turned cheerful.

"But how could I know that I didn't love her at all! Heh, heh! And it turns out that I didn't. Yet I liked her so! How I liked her even today, as I was reciting my speech. And, you know, even now I like her terribly, and at the same time it's so easy to leave her. Do you think it's all fanfaronade?"

"No. Only maybe it wasn't love."

"Alyoshka," laughed Ivan, "don't get into arguments about love! It's unseemly for you. But this morning, this morning, ai! how you jumped into it! I keep forgetting to kiss you for it . . . And how she tormented me! I was sitting next to a strain, truly! Ah, she knew that I loved her! And she loved me, not Dmitri," Ivan cheerfully insisted. "Dmitri is only a strain. Everything I said to her today is the very truth. But the thing is, the most important thing is, that she'll need maybe fifteen or twenty years to realize that she doesn't love Dmitri at all, and loves only me, whom she torments. And maybe she'll never realize it, even despite today's lesson. So much the better: I got up and left forever. By the way, how is she now? What happened after I left?"

Alyosha told him about the hysterics and that she was now apparently unconscious and delirious.

"And Khokhlakov isn't lying?"

"It seems not."

"I'll have to find out. No one, by the way, ever died of hysterics. Let her have hysterics, God loved woman when he sent her hysterics. I won't go there at all. Why get myself into that again!"

"Yet you told her this morning that she never loved you."

"I said it on purpose. Alyoshka, why don't I call for champagne, let's drink to my freedom. No, if only you knew how glad I am!"

"No, brother, we'd better not drink," Alyosha said suddenly, "besides, I feel somehow sad."

"Yes, you've been sad for a long time, I noticed it long ago."

"So you're definitely leaving tomorrow morning?"

"Morning? I didn't say morning . . . But, after all, maybe in the morning. Would you believe that I dined here today only to avoid dining with the old man, he's become so loathsome to me. If it were just him alone, I would have left long ago. And why do you worry so much about my leaving? You and I still have God knows how long before I go. A whole eternity of time, immortality!"

"What eternity, if you're leaving tomorrow?"

"But what does that matter to you and me?" Ivan laughed. "We still have time for our talk, for what brought us together here. Why do you look surprised? Tell me, what did we meet here for? To talk about loving Katerina Ivanovna, or about the old man and Dmitri? About going abroad? About the fatal situation in Russia? About the emperor Napoleon? Was it really for that?"

"No, not that."

"So you know yourself what for. Some people need one thing, but we green youths need another, we need first of all to resolve the everlasting questions, that is what concerns us. All of young Russia is talking now only about the eternal questions. Precisely now, just when all the old men have suddenly gotten into practical questions. Why have you been looking at me so expectantly for these three months? In order to ask me: 'And how believest thou, if thou believest anything at all?'[4] That is what your three months of looking come down to, is it not, Alexei Fyodorovich?"

"Maybe so," Alyosha smiled. "You're not laughing at me now, brother?"

"Me, laughing? I wouldn't want to upset my little brother who has been looking at me for three months with so much expectation. Look me in the eye,

Alyosha: I'm exactly the same little boy as you are, except that I'm not a novice. How have Russian boys handled things up to now? Some of them, that is. Take, for instance, some stinking local tavern. They meet there and settle down in a corner. They've never seen each other before in their whole lives, and when they walk out of the tavern, they won't see each other again for forty years. Well, then, what are they going to argue about, seizing this moment in the tavern? About none other than the universal questions: is there a God, is there immortality? And those who do not believe in God, well, they will talk about socialism and anarchism, about transforming the whole of mankind according to a new order, but it's the same damned thing, the questions are all the same, only from the other end. And many, many of the most original Russian boys do nothing but talk about the eternal questions, now, in our time. Isn't it so?"

"Yes, for real Russians the questions of the existence of God and immortality, or, as you just said, the same questions from the other end, are of course first and foremost, and they should be," Alyosha spoke, looking intently at his brother with the same quiet and searching smile.

"You see, Alyosha, sometimes it's not at all smart to be a Russian, but still it's even impossible to imagine anything more foolish than what Russian boys are doing now. Though I'm terribly fond of one Russian boy named Alyoshka."

"Nicely rounded off," Alyosha laughed suddenly.

"Now, tell me where to begin, give the order yourself—with God? The existence of God? Or what?"

"Begin with whatever you like, even 'from the other end.' You did proclaim yesterday at father's that there is no God," Alyosha looked searchingly at his brother.

"I said that on purpose yesterday, at dinner with the old man, just to tease you, and I saw how your eyes glowed. But now I don't mind at all discussing things with you, and I say it very seriously. I want to get close to you, Alyosha, because I have no friends. I want to try. Well, imagine that perhaps I, too, accept God," Ivan laughed, "that comes as a surprise to you, eh?"

"Yes, of course, unless you're joking again."

"'Joking.' They said yesterday at the elder's that I was joking. You see, my dear, there was in the eighteenth century an old sinner who stated that if God did not exist, he would have to be invented: *S'il n'existait pas Dieu, il faudrait l'inventer.*[5] And man has, indeed, invented God. And the strange thing, the wonder would not be that God really exists, the wonder is that such a notion—the notion of the necessity of God—could creep into the head of such a wild and wicked animal as man—so holy, so moving, so wise a notion, which does man such great honor. As for me, I long ago decided not to think about whether man created God or God created man. Naturally, I will not run through all the modern axioms laid down by Russian boys on the subject, which are all absolutely derived from European hypotheses; because what is a hypothesis there immediately becomes an axiom for a Russian boy, and that is true not only of boys but perhaps of their professors as well, since Russian professors today are quite often the same Russian boys. And therefore I will avoid all hypotheses. What task are you and I faced with now? My task is to explain to you as quickly as possible my essence, that is, what sort of man I am, what I believe in, and what I hope for, is that right? And therefore I declare that I accept God pure and simple. But this, however, needs to be noted: if God exists and if he indeed created the earth, then, as we know perfectly well, he created it in accordance with Euclidean geometry, and he created human reason with a conception of only three dimensions of space. At the same time there were and are even now geometers and philosophers, even some of the most outstanding among them, who doubt that the whole universe, or, even more broadly, the whole of being, was created purely in accordance with Euclidean geometry; they even dare to dream that two parallel lines, which according to Euclid cannot possibly meet on earth, may perhaps meet somewhere in infinity. I, my dear, have come to the conclusion that if I cannot understand even that, then it is not for me to understand about God. I humbly confess that I do not have any ability to resolve such questions, I have a Euclidean mind, an earthly mind, and therefore it is not for us to resolve things that are not of this world. And I advise you never to think about it, Alyosha my friend, and most especially about whether God exists or not. All such questions are completely unsuitable to a mind created with a concept of only three dimensions. And so, I accept God, not only willingly, but moreover I also accept his wisdom and his purpose, which are completely unknown to us; I believe in order, in the meaning of life, I believe in eternal harmony, in which we are all supposed to merge, I believe in the Word for whom the universe is yearning, and who himself was 'with God,' who himself is God, and so on, and so on and so forth, to infinity.[6] Many words have been invented on the subject. It seems I'm already on a good path, eh? And now imagine that in the final outcome I do not accept this world of God's, I do not admit it at all, though I know it exists. It's not God that I do not accept, you understand, it is this world of God's, created by God, that I do not accept and cannot agree to accept. With one reservation: I have a childlike conviction that the sufferings will be healed and smoothed over, that the whole offensive comedy of human contradictions will disappear like a pitiful mirage, a vile concoction of man's Euclidean mind, feeble and puny as an atom, and that ultimately, at the world's finale, in the moment of eternal harmony, there will occur and be revealed something so precious that it will suffice for all hearts, to allay all indignation, to redeem all human villainy, all bloodshed; it will suffice not only to make forgiveness possible, but also to justify everything that has happened with men—let this, let all of this come true and be revealed, but I do not accept it and do not want to accept it! Let the parallel lines even meet before my own eyes: I shall look and say, yes, they meet, and still I will not accept it. That is my essence, Alyosha, that is my thesis. I say it to you in all seriousness. I purposely started this talk of ours as stupidly as possible, but I arrived at my confession, because my confession is all you need. You did not need to know about God, you only needed to know what your beloved brother lives by. And I've told you."

Ivan ended his long tirade suddenly with a sort of special and unexpected feeling.

"And why did you start out 'as stupidly as possible'?" Alyosha asked, looking at him thoughtfully.

"Well, first, for the sake of Russianism, let's say: Russian conversations on these subjects are all conducted as stupidly as possible. And second, then, the stupider, the more to the point. The stupider, the clearer. Stupidity is brief and guileless, while reason hedges and hides. Reason is a scoundrel, stupidity is direct and honest. I brought the case around to my despair, and the more stupidly I've presented it, the more it's to my advantage."

"Will you explain to me why you 'do not accept the world'?" said Alyosha.

"Of course I'll explain, it's no secret, that's what I've been leading up to. My dear little brother, it's not that I want to corrupt you and push you off your foundation; perhaps I want to be healed by you," Ivan suddenly smiled just like a meek little boy. Never before had Alyosha seen him smile that way.

Chapter 4

Rebellion

"I must make an admission," Ivan began. "I never could understand how it's possible to love one's neighbors. In my opinion, it is precisely one's neighbors that one cannot possibly love. Perhaps if they weren't so nigh . . . I read sometime, somewhere about 'John the Merciful' (some saint) that when a hungry and frozen passerby came to him and asked to be made warm, he lay down with him in bed, embraced him, and began breathing into his mouth, which was foul and festering with some terrible disease.[1] I'm convinced that he did it with the strain of a lie, out of love enforced by duty, out of self-imposed penance. If we're to come to love a man, the man himself should stay hidden, because as soon as he shows his face—love vanishes."

"The elder Zosima has spoken of that more than once," Alyosha remarked. "He also says that a man's face often prevents many people, who are as yet inexperienced in love, from loving him. But there is still much love in mankind, almost like Christ's love, I know that, Ivan . . ."

"Well, I don't know it yet, and I cannot understand it, nor can a numberless multitude of other people along with me. The question is whether this comes from bad qualities in people, or is inherent in their nature. In my opinion, Christ's love for people is in its kind a miracle impossible on earth. True, he was God. But we are not gods. Let's say that I, for example, am capable of profound suffering, but another man will never be able to know the degree of my suffering, because he is another and not me, and besides, a man is rarely willing to acknowledge someone else as a sufferer (as if it were a kind of distinction). And why won't he acknowledge it, do you think? Because I, for example, have a bad smell, or a foolish face, or once stepped on his foot. Besides, there is suffering and suffering: some benefactor of mine may still allow a humiliating suffering, which humiliates me—hunger, for example; but a slightly higher suffering—for an idea, for example—no, that he will not allow, save perhaps on rare occasions, because he will look at me and suddenly see that my face is not at all the kind of face that, he fancies, a man should have who suffers, for example, for such and such an idea. And so he at once deprives me of his benefactions, and not even from the wickedness of his heart. Beggars, especially noble beggars, should never show themselves in the street; they should ask for alms through the newspapers. It's still possible to love one's neighbor abstractly, and even occasionally from a distance, but hardly ever up close. If it were all as it is on stage, in a ballet, where beggars, when they appear, come in silken rags and tattered lace and ask for alms dancing gracefully, well, then it would still be possible to admire them. To admire, but still not to love. But enough of that. I simply wanted to put you in my perspective. I meant to talk about the suffering of mankind in general, but better let us dwell only on the suffering of children. That will reduce the scope of my argument about ten times, but even so it's better if we keep to children. The more unprofitable for me, of course. But, first, one can love children even up close, even dirty or homely children (it seems to me, however, that children are never homely). Second, I will not speak of grown-ups because, apart from the fact that they are disgusting and do not deserve love, they also have retribution: they ate the apple, and knew good and evil, and became 'as gods.'[2]

And they still go on eating it. But little children have not eaten anything and are not yet guilty of anything. Do you love children, Alyosha? I know you love them, and you'll understand why I want to speak only of them now. If they, too, suffer terribly on earth, it is, of course, for their fathers; they are punished for their fathers who ate the apple—but that is reasoning from another world; for the human heart here on earth it is incomprehensible. It is impossible that a blameless one should suffer for another, and such a blameless one! Marvel at me, Alyosha—I, too, love children terribly. And observe, that cruel people—passionate, carnivorous, Karamazovian—sometimes love children very much. Children, while they are still children, up to the age of seven, for example, are terribly remote from grown-up people, as if they were different beings, of a different nature. I knew a robber in prison: he happened, in the course of his career, while slaughtering whole families in the houses he broke into and robbed at night, to have put the knife to several children as well. But he showed a strange affection for them while he was in prison. He spent all his time at the window, watching the children playing in the prison yard. He trained one little boy to come to his window, and the boy got to be very friendly with him . . . Do you know why I'm saying all this, Alyosha? I somehow have a headache, and I feel sad."

"You have a strange look as you speak," Alyosha observed anxiously, "as if you were in some kind of madness."

"By the way, a Bulgarian I met recently in Moscow," Ivan Fyodorovich went on, as if he were not listening to his brother, "told me how the Turks and Circassians there, in Bulgaria, have been committing atrocities everywhere, fearing a general uprising of the Slavs—they burn, kill, rape women and children, they nail prisoners by the ears to fences and leave them like that until morning, and in the morning they hang them—and so on, it's impossible to imagine it all. Indeed, people speak sometimes about the 'animal' cruelty of man, but that is terribly unjust and offensive to animals, no animal could ever be so cruel as a man, so artfully, so artistically cruel. A tiger simply gnaws and tears, that is all he can do. It would never occur to him to nail people by their ears overnight, even if he were able to do it. These Turks, among other things, have also taken a delight in torturing children, starting with cutting them out of their mothers' wombs with a dagger, and ending with tossing nursing infants up in the air and catching them on their bayonets before their mothers' eyes. The main delight comes from doing it before their mothers' eyes. But here is a picture that I found very interesting. Imagine a nursing infant in the arms of its trembling mother, surrounded by Turks. They've thought up an amusing trick: they fondle the baby, they laugh to make it laugh, and they succeed—the baby laughs. At that moment a Turk aims a pistol at it, four inches from its face. The baby laughs gleefully, reaches out its little hands to grab the pistol, and suddenly the artist pulls the trigger right in its face and shatters its little head . . . Artistic, isn't it? By the way, they say the Turks are very fond of sweets."

"What are you driving at, brother?" Alyosha asked.

"I think that if the devil does not exist, and man has therefore created him, he has created him in his own image and likeness."

"As well as God, then."

"You're a remarkably good 'implorator of unholy suits,' as Polonius says in *Hamlet*,"[3] Ivan laughed. "So you caught me, but let it be, I'm glad. A nice God you've got, if man created him in his image and likeness.[4] You asked me what I was driving at: you see, I'm an amateur and collector of certain little facts; I copy them down from newspapers and stories, from wherever, and save them—would you believe it?—certain kinds of little anecdotes. I already have a nice collection of them. The Turks, of course, are in it, but they're foreigners. I have native specimens as well, even better than the Turkish ones. You know, with us it's beating, the birch and the lash, that's our national way: with us nailed ears are unthinkable, we're Europeans after all, but the birch, the lash—that is ours and cannot be taken from us. Abroad they apparently no longer do any beating nowadays; either their morals have been purified or they've passed such laws that apparently one man no longer dares to whip another; but they've rewarded themselves with something else to make up for it, something as purely national as our way, so national that it is apparently impossible for us, though, by the way, it seems to be taking root here, especially since the time of the religious movement in our higher society. I have a lovely pamphlet, translated from the French, telling of how quite recently, only five years ago, in Geneva, a villain and murderer named Richard was executed—a lad of twenty-three, I believe, who repented and turned to the Christian faith at the foot of the scaffold. This Richard was someone's illegitimate child; at the age of six he was *presented* by his parents to some Swiss mountain shepherds, who brought him up to work for them. He grew up among them like a little wild beast; the shepherds taught him nothing; on the contrary, by the time he was seven, they were already sending him out to tend the flocks in the cold and wet, with almost no clothes and almost nothing to eat. And, of course, none of them stopped to think or repent of doing so; on the contrary, they considered themselves entirely within their rights, for Richard had been presented to them as an object, and they did not even think it necessary to feed him. Richard himself testified that in those years, like the prodigal son in the Gospel, he wanted terribly to eat at least the mash given to the pigs being fattened for market, but he was not given even that and was beaten when he stole from the pigs, and thus he spent his whole childhood and his youth, until he grew up and, having gathered strength, went out to steal for himself. The savage began earning money as a day laborer in Geneva, spent his earnings on drink, lived like a monster, and ended by killing some old man and robbing him. He was caught, tried, and condemned to death. They don't sentimentalize over there. So then in prison he was immediately surrounded by pastors and members of various Christian brotherhoods, philanthropic ladies, and so on. In prison they taught him to read and write, began expounding the Gospel to him, exhorted him, persuaded him, pushed him, pestered him, urged him, and finally he himself solemnly confessed his crime. He repented, he wrote to the court himself saying that he was a monster, and that at last he had been deemed worthy of being illumined by the Lord and of receiving grace. All of Geneva was stirred, all of pious and philanthropic Geneva. All that was lofty and well-bred rushed to him in prison; Richard was kissed, embraced: 'You are our brother, grace has descended upon you!' And Richard himself simply wept with emotion: 'Yes, grace has descended upon me! Before, through all my childhood and youth, I was glad to eat swine's food, and now grace has descended upon me, too, I am dying in the Lord!' 'Yes, yes, Richard, die in the Lord, you have shed blood and must die in the Lord. Though it's not your fault that you knew nothing of the Lord when you envied the swine their food and were beaten for stealing it (which was very bad, for it is forbidden to steal), but still you have shed blood and must die.' And so the last day came. Limp Richard weeps and all the while keeps repeating: 'This is the best day of my life, I am going to the Lord!' 'Yes,' cry the pastors, the judges, and the philanthropic ladies, 'this is your happiest day, for you are going to the Lord!' And it's all moving towards the scaffold, in carriages and on foot, following the cart of shame that is bearing Richard. They arrive at the scaffold. 'Die, brother,' they call out to Richard, 'die in the Lord, for grace has descended upon you, too!' And so, covered with the kisses of his brothers, brother Richard is dragged up onto the scaffold, laid down on the guillotine, and his head is whacked off in brotherly fashion, forasmuch as grace has descended upon him, too. No, it's quite typical. This little pamphlet was translated into Russian by some Russian Lutheranizing philanthropists from high society and sent out gratis with newspapers and other publications for the enlightenment of the Russian people. This thing about Richard is so good because it's national. Though for us it's absurd to cut our brother's head off only because he's become our brother and grace has descended upon him, still, I repeat, we have our own ways, which are almost as good. We have our historical, direct, and intimate delight in the torture of beating. Nekrasov has a poem describing a peasant flogging a horse on its eyes with a knout, 'on its meek eyes."[5] We've all seen that; that is Russianism. He describes a weak nag, harnessed with too heavy a load, that gets stuck in the mud with her cart and is unable to pull it out. The peasant beats her, beats her savagely, beats her finally not knowing what he's doing; drunk with beating, he flogs her painfully, repeatedly: 'Pull, though you have no strength, pull, though you die!' The little nag strains, and now he begins flogging her, flogging the defenseless creature on her weeping, her 'meek eyes.' Beside herself, she strains and pulls the cart out, trembling all over, not breathing, moving somehow sideways, with a sort of skipping motion, somehow unnaturally and shamefully—it's horrible in Nekrasov. But that's only a horse; God gave us horses so that we could flog them. So the Tartars instructed us,[6] and they left us the knout as a reminder. But people, too, can be flogged. And so, an intelligent, educated gentleman and his lady flog their own daughter, a child of seven, with a birch—I have it written down in detail. The papa is glad that the birch is covered with little twigs, 'it will smart more,' he says, and so he starts 'smarting' his own daughter. I know for certain that there are floggers who get more excited with every stroke, to the point of sensuality, literal sensuality, more and more, progressively, with each new stroke. They flog for one minute, they flog for five minutes, they flog for ten minutes—longer, harder, faster, sharper. The child is crying, the child finally cannot cry, she has no breath left: 'Papa, papa, dear papa!' The case, through some devilishly improper accident, comes to court. A lawyer is hired. Among the Russian people, lawyers have long been called 'hired consciences.' The lawyer shouts in his client's defense. 'The case,' he says, 'is quite simple, domestic, and ordinary: a father flogged his daughter, and, to the shame of our times, it has come to court!' The convinced jury retires and brings in a verdict of 'not guilty.' The public roars with delight that the torturer has been acquitted. Ahh, if I'd been there, I'd have yelled out a suggestion that they establish a scholarship in honor of the torturer . . . ! Lovely pictures. But about little children I can do even better, I've collected a great, great deal about Russian children, Alyosha. A little girl, five years old, is hated by her father and mother, 'most honorable and official people, educated and well-bred.'[7] You see, once again I positively maintain that this peculiar quality exists in much of mankind—this love of torturing children, but only children. These same torturers look upon all other examples of humankind even mildly and benevolently, being educated and humane Europeans, but they have a great love of torturing children, they even love children in that sense. It is precisely the defenselessness of these creatures that tempts the torturers, the angelic trustfulness of the child, who has nowhere to turn and no one to turn to—that is what enflames the vile blood of the torturer. There is, of course, a beast hidden in every man, a beast of rage, a beast of sensual inflammability at the cries of the tormented victim, an unrestrained beast let off the chain, a beast of diseases acquired in debauchery—gout, rotten liver, and so on. These educated parents subjected the poor five-year-old girl to every possible torture. They beat her, flogged her, kicked her, not knowing why themselves, until her whole body was nothing but bruises; finally they attained the height of finesse: in the freezing cold, they locked her all night in the outhouse, because she wouldn't ask to get up and go in the middle of the night (as if a five-year-old child sleeping its sound angelic sleep could have learned to ask by that age)—for that they smeared her face with her excrement and made her eat the excrement, and it was her mother, her mother who made her! And this mother could sleep while her poor little child was moaning all night in that vile place! Can you understand that a small creature, who cannot even comprehend what is being done to her, in a vile place, in the dark and the cold, beats herself on her strained little chest with her tiny fist and weeps with her anguished, gentle, meek tears for 'dear God' to protect her—can you understand such nonsense, my friend and my brother, my godly and humble novice, can you understand why this nonsense is needed and created? Without it, they say, man could not even have lived on earth, for he would not have known good and evil. Who wants to know this damned good and evil at such a price? The whole world of knowledge is not worth the tears of that little child to 'dear God.' I'm not talking about the suffering of grown-ups, they ate the apple and to hell with them, let the devil take them all, but these little ones! I'm tormenting you, Alyoshka, you don't look yourself. I'll stop if you wish."

"Never mind, I want to suffer, too," Alyosha murmured.

"One more picture, just one more, for curiosity, because it's so typical, and above all I just read it in one of the collections of our old documents, the *Archive*, *Antiquities*, or somewhere, I'll have to check the reference, I even forget where I read it.[8] It was in the darkest days of serfdom, back at the beginning of the century—and long live the liberator of the people![9] There was a general at the beginning of the century, a general with high connections and a very wealthy landowner, the sort of man (indeed, even then they seem to have been very few) who, on retiring from the army, feels all but certain that his service has earned him the power of life and death over his subjects. There were such men in those days. So this general settled on his estate of two thousand souls, swaggered around, treated his lesser neighbors as his spongers and buffoons. He had hundreds of dogs in his kennels and nearly a hundred handlers, all in livery, all on horseback. And so one day a house-serf, a little boy, only eight years old, threw a stone while he was playing and hurt the paw of the general's favorite hound. 'Why is my favorite dog limping?' It was reported to him that this boy had thrown a stone at her and hurt her paw. 'So it was you,' the general looked the boy up and down. 'Take him!' They took him, took him from his mother, and locked him up for the night. In the morning, at dawn, the general rode out in full dress for the hunt, mounted on his horse, surrounded by spongers, dogs, handlers, huntsmen, all on horseback. The house-serfs are gathered for their edification, the guilty boy's mother in front of them all. The boy is led out of the lockup. A gloomy, cold, misty autumn day, a great day for hunting. The general orders them to undress the boy; the child is stripped naked, he shivers, he's crazy with fear, he doesn't dare make a peep . . . 'Drive him!' the general commands. The huntsmen shout, 'Run, run!' The boy runs . . . 'Sic him!' screams the general and looses the whole pack of wolfhounds on him. He hunted him down before his mother's eyes, and the dogs tore the child to pieces . . . ! I believe the general was later declared incompetent to administer his estates. Well . . . what to do with him? Shoot him? Shoot him for our moral satisfaction? Speak, Alyoshka!"

"Shoot him!" Alyosha said softly, looking up at his brother with a sort of pale, twisted smile.

"Bravo!" Ivan yelled in a sort of rapture. "If even you say so, then . . . A fine monk you are! See what a little devil is sitting in your heart, Alyoshka Karamazov!"

"What I said is absurd, but . . ."

"That's just it, that 'but . . . ,'" Ivan was shouting. "I tell you, novice, that absurdities are all too necessary on earth. The world stands on absurdities, and without them perhaps nothing at all would happen. We know what we know!"

"What do you know?"

"I don't understand anything," Ivan went on as if in delirium, "and I no longer want to understand anything. I want to stick to the fact. I made up my mind long ago not to understand. If I wanted to understand something, I would immediately have to betray the fact, but I've made up my mind to stick to the fact . . ."

"Why are you testing me?" Alyosha exclaimed with a rueful strain. "Will you finally tell me?"

"Of course I'll tell you, that's just what I've been leading up to. You are dear to me, I don't want to let you slip, and I won't give you up to your Zosima."

Ivan was silent for a moment; his face suddenly became very sad.

"Listen to me: I took children only so as to make it more obvious. About all the other human tears that have soaked the whole earth through, from crust to core, I don't say a word, I've purposely narrowed down my theme. I am a bedbug, and I confess in all humility that I can understand nothing of why it's all arranged as it is. So people themselves are to blame: they were given paradise, they wanted freedom, and stole fire from heaven,[10] knowing that they would become unhappy—so why pity them? Oh, with my pathetic, earthly, Euclidean mind, I know only that there is suffering, that none are to blame, that all things follow simply and directly one from another, that everything flows and finds its level—but that is all just Euclidean gibberish, of course I know that, and of course I cannot consent to live by it! What do I care that none are to blame and that I know it—I need retribution, otherwise I will destroy myself. And retribution not somewhere and sometime in infinity, but here and now, on earth, so that I see it myself. I have believed, and I want to see for myself, and if I am dead by that time, let them resurrect me, because it will be too unfair if it all takes place without me. Is it possible that I've suffered so that I, together with my evil deeds and sufferings, should be manure for someone's future harmony? I want to see with my own eyes the hind lie down with the lion,[11] and the murdered man rise up and embrace his murderer. I want to be there when everyone suddenly finds out what it was all for. All religions in the world are based on this desire, and I am a believer. But then there are the children, and what am I going to do with them? That is the question I cannot resolve. For the hundredth time I repeat: there are hosts of questions, but I've taken only the children, because here what I need to say is irrefutably clear. Listen: if everyone must suffer, in order to buy eternal harmony with their suffering, pray tell me what have children got to do with it? It's quite incomprehensible why they should have to suffer, and why they should buy harmony with their suffering. Why do they get thrown on the pile, to manure someone's future harmony with themselves? I understand solidarity in sin among men; solidarity in retribution I also understand; but what solidarity in sin do little children have? And if it is really true that they, too, are in solidarity with their fathers in all the fathers' evildoings, that truth certainly is not of this world and is incomprehensible to me. Some joker will say, perhaps, that in any case the child will grow up and have time enough to sin, but there's this boy who didn't grow up but was torn apart by dogs at the age of eight. Oh, Alyosha, I'm not blaspheming! I do understand how the universe will tremble when all in heaven and under the earth merge in one voice of praise, and all that lives and has lived cries out: 'Just art thou, O Lord, for thy ways are revealed!'[12] Oh, yes, when the mother and the torturer whose hounds tore her son to pieces embrace each other, and all three cry out with tears: 'Just art thou, O Lord,' then of course the crown of knowledge will have come and everything will be explained. But there is the hitch: that is what I cannot accept. And while I am on earth, I hasten to take my own measures. You see, Alyosha, it may well be that if I live until that moment, or rise again in order to see it, I myself will perhaps cry out with all the rest, looking at the mother embracing her child's tormentor: 'Just art thou, O Lord!' but I do not want to cry out with them. While there's still time, I hasten to defend myself against it, and therefore I absolutely renounce all higher harmony. It is not worth one little tear of even that one tormented child who beat her chest with her little fist and prayed to 'dear God' in a stinking outhouse with her unredeemed tears! Not worth it, because her tears remained unredeemed. They must be redeemed, otherwise there can be no harmony. But how, how will you redeem them? Is it possible? Can they be redeemed by being avenged? But what do I care if they are avenged, what do I care if the tormentors are in hell, what can hell set right here, if these ones have already been tormented? And where is the harmony, if there is hell? I want to forgive, and I want to embrace, I don't want more suffering. And if the suffering of children goes to make up the sum of suffering needed to buy truth, then I assert beforehand that the whole of truth is not worth such a price. I do not, finally, want the mother to embrace the tormentor who let his dogs tear her son to pieces! She dare not forgive him! Let her forgive him for herself, if she wants to, let her forgive the tormentor her immeasurable maternal suffering; but she has no right to forgive the suffering of her child who was torn to pieces, she dare not forgive the tormentor, even if the child himself were to forgive him! And if that is so, if they dare not forgive, then where is the harmony? Is there in the whole world a being who could and would have the right to forgive? I don't want harmony, for love of mankind I don't want it. I want to remain with unrequited suffering. I'd rather remain with my unrequited suffering and my unquenched indignation, *even if I am wrong*. Besides, they have put too high a price on harmony; we can't afford to pay so much for admission. And therefore I hasten to return my ticket.[13] And it is my duty, if only as an honest man, to return it as far ahead of time as possible. Which is what I am doing. It's not that I don't accept God, Alyosha, I just most respectfully return him the ticket."

"That is rebellion," Alyosha said softly, dropping his eyes.

"Rebellion? I don't like hearing such a word from you," Ivan said with feeling. "One cannot live by rebellion, and I want to live. Tell me straight out, I call on you—answer me: imagine that you yourself are building the edifice of human destiny with the object of making people happy in the finale, of giving them peace and rest at last, but for that you must inevitably and unavoidably torture just one tiny creature, that same child who was beating her chest with her little fist, and raise your edifice on the foundation of her unrequited tears—would you agree to be the architect on such conditions? Tell me the truth."

"No, I would not agree," Alyosha said softly.

"And can you admit the idea that the people for whom you are building would agree to accept their happiness on the unjustified blood of a tortured child, and having accepted it, to remain forever happy?"

"No, I cannot admit it. Brother," Alyosha said suddenly, his eyes beginning to flash, "you asked just now if there is in the whole world a being who could and would have the right to forgive. But there is such a being, and he can forgive everything, forgive all *and for all*,[14] because he himself gave his innocent blood for all and for everything. You've forgotten about him, but it is on him that the structure is being built, and it is to him that they will cry out: 'Just art thou, O Lord, for thy ways have been revealed!' "

"Ah, yes, the 'only sinless One'[15] and his blood! No, I have not forgotten about him; on the contrary, I've been wondering all the while why you hadn't brought him up for so long, because in discussions your people usually trot him out first thing. You know, Alyosha—don't laugh!—I composed a poem once, about a year ago. If you can waste ten more minutes on me, I'll tell it to you."

"You wrote a poem?"

"Oh, no, I didn't write it," Ivan laughed, "I've never composed two lines of verse in my whole life. But I made up this poem and memorized it. I made it up in great fervor. You'll be my first reader—I mean, listener. Why, indeed, should an author lose even one listener?" Ivan grinned. "Shall I tell it or not?"

"I'm listening carefully," said Alyosha.

"My poem is called 'The Grand Inquisitor'—an absurd thing, but I want you to hear it."

Chapter 5

The Grand Inquisitor

"But here, too, it's impossible to do without a preface, a literary preface, that is—pah!" Ivan laughed, "and what sort of writer am I! You see, my action takes place in the sixteenth century, and back then—by the way, you must have learned this in school—back then it was customary in poetic works to bring higher powers down to earth. I don't need to mention Dante. In France, court clerks, as well as monks in the monasteries, gave whole performances in which they brought the Madonna, angels, saints, Christ, and God himself on stage. At the time it was all done quite artlessly. In Victor Hugo's *Notre*

Dame de Paris, in the Paris of Louis XI, to honor the birth of the French dauphin, an edifying performance is given free of charge for the people in the city hall, entitled *Le bon jugement de la très sainte et gracieuse Vierge Marie*,[1] in which she herself appears in person and pronounces her *bon jugement*. With us in Moscow, in pre-Petrine antiquity,[2] much the same kind of dramatic performances, especially from the Old Testament, were given from time to time; but, besides dramatic performances, there were many stories and 'verses' floating around the world in which saints, angels, and all the powers of heaven took part as needed. In our monasteries such poems were translated, recopied, even composed—and when?—under the Tartars. There is, for example, one little monastery poem (from the Greek, of course): *The Mother of God Visits the Torments*,[3] with scenes of a boldness not inferior to Dante's. The Mother of God visits hell and the Archangel Michael guides her through 'the torments.' She sees sinners and their sufferings. Among them, by the way, there is a most amusing class of sinners in a burning lake: some of them sink so far down into the lake that they can no longer come up again, and 'these God forgets'—an expression of extraordinary depth and force. And so the Mother of God, shocked and weeping, falls before the throne of God and asks pardon for everyone in hell, everyone she has seen there, without distinction. Her conversation with God is immensely interesting. She pleads, she won't go away, and when God points out to her the nail-pierced hands and feet of her Son and asks: 'How can I forgive his tormentors?' she bids all the saints, all the martyrs, all the angels and archangels to fall down together with her and plead for the pardon of all without discrimination. In the end she extorts from God a cessation of torments every year, from Holy Friday to Pentecost, and the sinners in hell at once thank the Lord and cry out to him: 'Just art thou, O Lord, who hast judged so.' Well, my little poem would have been of the same kind if it had appeared back then. He comes onstage in it; actually, he says nothing in the poem, he just appears and passes on. Fifteen centuries have gone by since he gave the promise to come in his Kingdom, fifteen centuries since his prophet wrote: 'Behold, I come quickly.'[4] 'Of that day and that hour knoweth not even the Son, but only my heavenly Father,'[5] as he himself declared while still on earth. But mankind awaits him with the same faith and the same tender emotion. Oh, even with greater faith, for fifteen centuries have gone by since men ceased to receive pledges from heaven:

> Believe what the heart tells you,
> For heaven offers no pledge.[6]

Only faith in what the heart tells you! True, there were also many miracles then. There were saints who performed miraculous healings; to some righteous men, according to their biographies, the Queen of Heaven herself came down. But the devil never rests, and there had already arisen in mankind some doubt as to the authenticity of these miracles. Just then, in the north, in Germany, a horrible new heresy appeared.[7] A great star, 'like a lamp' (that is, the Church), 'fell upon the fountains of waters, and they were made bitter.'[8] These heretics began blasphemously denying miracles. But those who still believed became all the more ardent in their belief. The tears of mankind rose up to him as before, they waited for him, loved him, hoped in him, yearned to suffer and die for him as before . . . And for so many centuries mankind had been pleading with faith and fire: 'God our Lord, reveal thyself to us,'[9] for so many centuries they had been calling out to him, that he in his immeasurable compassion desired to descend to those who were pleading. He had descended even before then, he had visited some righteous men, martyrs, and holy hermits while they were still on earth, as is written in their 'lives.' Our own Tyutchev, who deeply believed in the truth of his words, proclaimed that:

> Bent under the burden of the Cross,
> The King of Heaven in the form of a slave
> Walked the length and breadth of you,
> Blessing you, my native land.[10]

It must needs have been so, let me tell you. And so he desired to appear to people if only for a moment—to his tormented, suffering people, rank with sin but loving him like children. My action is set in Spain, in Seville, in the most horrible time of the Inquisition, when fires blazed every day to the glory of God, and

> In the splendid auto-da-fé
> Evil heretics were burnt.[11]

Oh, of course, this was not that coming in which he will appear, according to his promise, at the end of time, in all his heavenly glory, and which will be as sudden 'as the lightning that shineth out of the east unto the west.'[12] No, he desired to visit his children if only for a moment, and precisely where the fires of the heretics had begun to crackle. In his infinite mercy he walked once again among men, in the same human image in which he had walked for three years among men fifteen centuries earlier. He came down to the 'scorched squares'[13] of a southern town where just the day before, in a 'splendid auto-da-fé,' in the presence of the king, the court, knights, cardinals, and the loveliest court ladies, before the teeming populace of all Seville, the Cardinal Grand Inquisitor had burned almost a hundred heretics at once *ad majorem gloriam*

Dei.[14] He appeared quietly, inconspicuously, but, strange to say, everyone recognized him. This could be one of the best passages in the poem, I mean, why it is exactly that they recognize him. People are drawn to him by an invincible force, they flock to him, surround him, follow him. He passes silently among them with a quiet smile of infinite compassion. The sun of love shines in his heart, rays of Light, Enlightenment, and Power stream from his eyes and, pouring over the people, shake their hearts with responding love. He stretches forth his hands to them, blesses them, and from the touch of him, even only of his garments, comes a healing power. Here an old man, blind from childhood, calls out from the crowd: 'Lord, heal me so that I, too, can see you,' and it is as if the scales fell from his eyes, and the blind man sees him. People weep and kiss the earth he walks upon. Children throw down flowers before him, sing and cry 'Hosanna!' to him. 'It's he, it's really he,' everyone repeats, 'it must be he, it can be no one but he.' He stops at the porch of the Seville cathedral at the very moment when a child's little, open, white coffin is being brought in with weeping: in it lies a seven-year-old girl, the only daughter of a noble citizen. The dead child is covered with flowers. 'He will raise your child,' people in the crowd shout to the weeping mother. The cathedral padre, who has come out to meet the coffin, looks perplexed and frowns. Suddenly a wail comes from the dead child's mother. She throws herself down at his feet: 'If it is you, then raise my child!' she exclaims, stretching her hands out to him. The procession halts, the little coffin is lowered down onto the porch at his feet. He looks with compassion and his lips once again softly utter: '*Talitha cumi*'—'and the damsel arose.'[15] The girl rises in her coffin, sits up and, smiling, looks around her in wide-eyed astonishment. She is still holding the bunch of white roses with which she had been lying in the coffin. There is a commotion among the people, cries, weeping, and at this very moment the Cardinal Grand Inquisitor himself crosses the square in front of the cathedral. He is an old man, almost ninety, tall and straight, with a gaunt face and sunken eyes, from which a glitter still shines like a fiery spark. Oh, he is not wearing his magnificent cardinal's robes in which he had displayed himself to the people the day before, when the enemies of the Roman faith were burned—no, at this moment he is wearing only his old, coarse monastic cassock. He is followed at a certain distance by his grim assistants and slaves, and by the 'holy' guard. At the sight of the crowd he stops and watches from afar. He has seen everything, seen the coffin set down at his feet, seen the girl rise, and his face darkens. He scowls with his thick, gray eyebrows, and his eyes shine with a sinister fire. He stretches forth his finger and orders the guard to take him. And such is his power, so tamed, submissive, and tremblingly obedient to his will are the people, that the crowd immediately parts before the guard, and they, amidst the deathly silence that has suddenly fallen, lay their hands on him and lead him away. As one man the crowd immediately bows to the ground before the aged Inquisitor, who silently blesses the people and moves on. The guard lead their prisoner to the small, gloomy, vaulted prison in the old building of the holy court, and lock him there. The day is over, the Seville night comes, dark, hot, and 'breathless.' The air is 'fragrant with laurel and lemon.'[16] In the deep darkness, the iron door of the prison suddenly opens, and the old Grand Inquisitor himself slowly enters carrying a lamp. He is alone, the door is immediately locked behind him. He stands in the entrance and for a long time, for a minute or two, gazes into his face. At last he quietly approaches, sets the lamp on the table, and says to him: 'Is it you? You?' But receiving no answer, he quickly adds: 'Do not answer, be silent. After all, what could you say? I know too well what you would say. And you have no right to add anything to what you already said once. Why, then, have you come to interfere with us? For you have come to interfere with us and you know it yourself. But do you know what will happen tomorrow? I do not know who you are, and I do not want to know: whether it is you, or only his likeness; but tomorrow I shall condemn you and burn you at the stake as the most evil of heretics, and the very people who today kissed your feet, tomorrow, at a nod from me, will rush to heap the coals up around your stake, do you know that? Yes, perhaps you do know it,' he added, pondering deeply, never for a moment taking his eyes from his prisoner."

"I don't quite understand what this is, Ivan," Alyosha, who all the while had been listening silently, smiled. "Is it boundless fantasy, or some mistake on the old man's part, some impossible *qui pro quo*?"[17]

"Assume it's the latter, if you like," Ivan laughed, "if you're so spoiled by modern realism and can't stand anything fantastic—if you want it to be *qui pro quo*, let it be. Of course," he laughed again, "the man is ninety years old, and might have lost his mind long ago over his idea. He might have been struck by the prisoner's appearance. It might, finally, have been simple delirium, the vision of a ninety-year-old man nearing death, and who is excited, besides, by the auto-da-fé of a hundred burnt heretics the day before. But isn't it all the same to you and me whether it's *qui pro quo* or boundless fantasy? The only thing is that the old man needs to speak out, that finally after all his ninety years, he speaks out, and says aloud all that he has been silent about for ninety years."

"And the prisoner is silent, too? Just looks at him without saying a word?"

"But that must be so in any case," Ivan laughed again. "The old man himself points out to him that he has no right to add anything to what has already been said once. That, if you like, is the most basic feature of Roman Catholicism, in my opinion at least: 'Everything,' they say, 'has been handed over by you to the pope, therefore everything now belongs to the pope, and you may as well not come at all now, or at least don't interfere with us for the time being.' They not only speak this way, they also write this way, at least the Jesuits do. I've read it in their theologians myself. 'Have you the right to proclaim to us even one of the mysteries of that world from which you have come?' my old man asks him, and answers the question himself: 'No, you have not, so as not to add to what has already been said once, and so as not to deprive people of freedom, for which you stood so firmly when you were on earth. Anything you proclaim anew will encroach upon the freedom of men's faith, for it will come as a miracle, and the freedom of their faith was the dearest of all things to you, even then, one and a half thousand years ago. Was it not you who so often said then: "I want to make you free"?[18] But now you have seen these "free" men,' the old man suddenly adds with a pensive smile. 'Yes, this work has cost us dearly,' he goes on, looking sternly at him, 'but we have finally finished this work in your name. For fifteen hundred years we have been at pains over this freedom, but now it is finished, and well finished. You do not believe that it is well finished? You look at me meekly and do not deign even to be indignant with me. Know, then, that now, precisely now, these people are more certain than ever before that they are completely free, and at the same time they themselves have brought us their freedom and obediently laid it at our feet. It is our doing, but is it what you wanted? This sort of freedom?' "

"Again I don't understand," Alyosha interrupted. "Is he being ironic? Is he laughing?"

"Not in the least. He precisely lays it to his and his colleagues' credit that they have finally overcome freedom, and have done so in order to make people happy. 'For only now' (he is referring, of course, to the Inquisition) 'has it become possible to think for the first time about human happiness. Man was made a rebel; can rebels be happy? You were warned,' he says to him, 'you had no lack of warnings and indications, but you did not heed the warnings, you rejected the only way of arranging for human happiness, but fortunately, on your departure, you handed the work over to us. You promised, you established with your word, you gave us the right to bind and loose,[19] and surely you cannot even think of taking this right away from us now. Why, then, have you come to interfere with us?' "

"What does it mean, that he had no lack of warnings and indications?" Alyosha asked.

"You see, that is the main thing that the old man needs to speak about.

" 'The dread and intelligent spirit, the spirit of self-destruction and non-being,' the old man goes on, 'the great spirit spoke with you in the wilderness, and it has been passed on to us in books that he supposedly "tempted" you.[20] Did he really? And was it possible to say anything more true than what he proclaimed to you in his three questions, which you rejected, and which the books refer to as "temptations"? And at the same time, if ever a real, thundering miracle was performed on earth, it was on that day, the day of those three temptations. The miracle lay precisely in the appearance of those three questions. If it were possible to imagine, just as a trial and an example, that those three questions of the dread spirit had been lost from the books without a trace, and it was necessary that they be restored, thought up and invented anew, to be put back into the books, and to that end all the wise men on earth—rulers, high priests, scholars, philosophers, poets—were brought together and given this task: to think up, to invent three questions such as would not only correspond to the scale of the event, but, moreover, would express in three words, in three human phrases only, the entire future history of the world and mankind—do you think that all the combined wisdom of the earth could think up anything faintly resembling in force and depth those three questions that were actually presented to you then by the powerful and intelligent spirit in the wilderness? By the questions alone, simply by the miracle of their appearance, one can see that one is dealing with a mind not human and transient but eternal and absolute. For in these three questions all of subsequent human history is as if brought together into a single whole and foretold; three images are revealed that will take in all the insoluble historical contradictions of human nature over all the earth. This could not have been seen so well at the time, for the future was unknown, but now that fifteen centuries have gone by, we can see that in these three questions everything was so precisely divined and foretold, and has proved so completely true, that to add to them or subtract anything from them is impossible.

" 'Decide yourself who was right: you or the one who questioned you then? Recall the first question; its meaning, though not literally, was this: "You want to go into the world, and you are going empty-handed, with some promise of freedom, which they in their simplicity and innate lawlessness cannot even comprehend, which they dread and fear—for nothing has ever been more insufferable for man and for human society than freedom! But do you see these stones in this bare, scorching desert? Turn them into bread and mankind will run after you like sheep, grateful and obedient, though eternally trembling lest you withdraw your hand and your loaves cease for them." But you did not want to deprive man of freedom and rejected the offer, for what sort of freedom is it, you reasoned, if obedience is bought with loaves of bread? You objected that man does not live by bread alone, but do you know that in the name of this very earthly bread, the spirit of the earth will rise against you and fight with you and defeat you, and everyone will follow him exclaiming: "Who can compare to this beast, for he has given us fire from heaven!"[21] Do you know that centuries will pass and mankind will proclaim with the mouth of its wisdom and science that there is no crime, and therefore no sin, but only hungry men? "Feed them first, then ask virtue of them!"—that is what they will write on the banner they raise against you, and by which your temple will be destroyed. In place of your temple a new edifice will be raised, the terrible Tower of Babel will be raised again,[22] and though, like the former one, this one will not be completed either, still you could have avoided this new tower and shortened people's suffering by a thousand years—for it is to us they will come after suffering for a thousand years with their tower! They will seek us out again, underground, in catacombs, hiding (for again we shall be persecuted and tortured), they will find us and cry out: "Feed us, for those who promised us fire from heaven did not give it." And then we shall finish building their tower, for only he who feeds them will finish it, and only we shall feed them, in your name, for we shall lie that it is in your name. Oh, never, never will they feed themselves without us! No science will give them bread as long as they remain free, but in the end they will lay their freedom at our feet and say to us: "Better that you enslave us, but feed us." They will finally understand that freedom and earthly bread in plenty for everyone are inconceivable together, for never, never will they be able to share among themselves. They will also be convinced that they are forever incapable of being free, because they are feeble, depraved, nonentities and rebels. You promised them heavenly bread, but, I repeat again, can it compare with earthly bread in the eyes of the weak, eternally depraved, and eternally ignoble human race? And if in the name of heavenly bread thousands and tens of thousands will follow you, what will become of the millions and tens of thousands of millions of creatures who will not be strong enough to forgo earthly bread for the sake of the heavenly? Is it that only the tens of thousands of the great and strong are dear to you, and the remaining millions, numerous as the sands of the sea, weak but loving you, should serve only as material for the great and the strong? No, the weak, too, are dear to us. They are depraved and rebels, but in the end it is they who will become obedient. They will marvel at us, and look upon us as gods, because we, standing at their head, have agreed to suffer freedom and to rule over them—so terrible will it become for them in the end to be free! But we shall say that we are obedient to you and rule in your name. We shall deceive them again, for this time we shall not allow you to come to us. This deceit will constitute our suffering, for we shall have to lie. This is what that first question in the wilderness meant, and this is what you rejected in the name of freedom, which you placed above everything. And yet this question contains the great mystery of this world. Had you accepted the "loaves," you would have answered the universal and everlasting anguish of man as an individual being, and of the whole of mankind together, namely: "before whom shall I bow down?" There is no more ceaseless or tormenting care for man, as long as he remains free, than to find someone to bow down to as soon as possible. But man seeks to bow down before that which is indisputable, so indisputable that all men at once would agree to the universal worship of it. For the care of these pitiful creatures is not just to find something before which I or some other man can bow down, but to find something that everyone else will also believe in and bow down to, for it must needs be *all together*. And this need for *communality* of worship is the chief torment of each man individually, and of mankind as a whole, from the beginning of the ages. In the cause of universal worship, they have destroyed each other with the sword. They have made gods and called upon each other: "Abandon your gods and come and worship ours, otherwise death to you and your gods!" And so it will be until the end of the world, even when all gods have disappeared from the earth: they will still fall down before idols. You knew, you could not but know, this essential mystery of human nature, but you rejected the only absolute banner, which was offered to you to make all men bow down to you indisputably—the banner of earthly bread; and you rejected it in the name of freedom and heavenly bread. Now see what you did next. And all again in the name of freedom! I tell you that man has no more tormenting care than to find someone to whom he can hand over as quickly as possible that gift of freedom with which the miserable creature is born. But he alone can take over the freedom of men who appeases their conscience. With bread you were given an indisputable banner: give man bread and he will bow down to you, for there is nothing more indisputable than bread. But if at the same time someone else takes over his conscience—oh, then he will even throw down your bread and follow him who has seduced his conscience. In this you were right. For the mystery of man's being is not only in living, but in what one lives for. Without a firm idea of what he lives for, man will not consent to live and will sooner destroy himself than remain on earth, even if there is bread all around him. That is so, but what came of it? Instead of taking over men's freedom, you increased it still more for them! Did you forget that peace and even death are dearer to man than free choice in the knowledge of good and evil? There is nothing more seductive for man than the freedom of his conscience, but there is nothing more tormenting either. And so, instead of a firm foundation for appeasing human conscience once and for all, you chose everything that was unusual, enigmatic, and indefinite, you chose everything that was beyond men's strength, and thereby acted as if you did not love them at all—and who did this? He who came to give his life for them! Instead of taking over men's freedom, you increased it and forever burdened the kingdom of the human soul with its torments. You desired the free love of man, that he should follow you freely, seduced and captivated by you. Instead of the firm ancient law,[23] man had henceforth to decide for himself, with a free heart, what is good and what is evil, having only your image before him as a guide—but did it not occur to you that he would eventually reject and dispute even your image and your truth if he was oppressed by so terrible a burden as freedom of choice? They will finally cry out that the truth is not in you, for it was impossible to leave them in greater confusion and torment than you did, abandoning them to so many cares and insoluble problems. Thus you yourself laid the foundation for the destruction of your own kingdom, and do not blame anyone else for it. Yet is this what was offered you? There are three powers, only three powers on earth, capable of conquering and holding captive forever the conscience of these feeble rebels, for their own happiness—these powers are miracle, mystery, and authority. You rejected the first, the second, and the third, and gave yourself as an example of that. When the dread and wise spirit set you on a pinnacle of the Temple and said to you: "If you would know whether or not you are the Son of God, cast yourself down; for it is written of him, that the angels will bear him up, and he will not fall or be hurt, and then you will know whether you are the Son of God, and will prove what faith you have in your Father."[24] But you heard and rejected the offer and did not yield and did not throw yourself down. Oh, of course, in this you acted proudly and magnificently, like God, but mankind, that weak, rebellious tribe—are they gods? Oh, you knew then that if you made just one step, just one movement towards throwing yourself down, you would immediately have tempted the Lord and would have lost all faith in him and been dashed against the earth you came to save, and the intelligent spirit who was tempting you would rejoice. But, I repeat, are there many like you? And, indeed, could you possibly have assumed, even for a moment, that mankind, too, would be strong enough for such a temptation? Is that how human nature was created—to reject the miracle, and in those terrible moments of life, the moments of the most terrible, essential, and tormenting questions of the soul, to remain only with the free decision of the heart? Oh, you knew that your deed would be preserved in books, would reach the depths of the ages and the utmost limits of the earth, and you hoped that, following you, man, too, would remain with God, having no need of miracles. But you did not know that as soon as man rejects miracles, he will at once reject God as well, for man seeks not so much God as miracles. And since man cannot bear to be left without miracles, he will go and create new miracles for himself, his own miracles this time, and will bow down to the miracles of quacks, or women's magic, though he be rebellious, heretical, and godless a hundred times over. You did not come down from the cross when they shouted to you, mocking and reviling you: "Come down from the cross and we will believe that it is you."[25] You did not come down because, again, you did not want to enslave man by a miracle and thirsted for faith that is free, not miraculous. You thirsted for love that is free, and not for the servile raptures of a slave before a power that has left him permanently terrified. But here, too, you overestimated mankind, for, of course, they are slaves, though they were created rebels. Behold and judge, now that fifteen centuries have passed, take a look at them: whom have you raised up to yourself? I swear, man is created weaker and baser than you thought him! How, how can he ever accomplish the same things as you? Respecting him so much, you behaved as if you had ceased to be compassionate, because you demanded too much of him—and who did this? He who loved him more than himself! Respecting him less, you would have demanded less of him, and that would be closer to love, for his burden would be lighter. He is weak and mean. What matter that he now rebels everywhere against our power, and takes pride in this rebellion? The pride of a child and a schoolboy! They are little children, who rebel in class and drive out the teacher. But there will also come an end to the children's delight, and it will cost them dearly. They will tear down the temples and drench the earth with blood. But finally the foolish children will understand that although they are rebels, they are feeble rebels, who cannot endure their own rebellion. Pouring out their foolish tears, they will finally acknowledge that he who created them rebels no doubt intended to laugh at them. They will say it in despair, and what they say will be a blasphemy that will make them even more unhappy, for human nature cannot bear blasphemy and in the end always takes revenge for it. And so, turmoil, confusion, and unhappiness—these are the present lot of mankind, after you suffered so much for their freedom! Your great prophet tells in a vision and an allegory that he saw all those who took part in the first resurrection and that they were twelve thousand from each tribe.[26] But even if there were so many, they, too, were not like men, as it were, but gods. They endured your cross, they endured scores of years of hungry and naked wilderness, eating locusts and roots,[27] and of course you can point with pride to these children of freedom, of free love, of free and magnificent sacrifice in your name. But remember that there were only several thousand of them, and they were gods. What of the rest? Is it the fault of the rest of feeble mankind that they could not endure what the mighty endured? Is it the fault of the weak soul that it is unable to contain such terrible gifts? Can it be that you indeed came only to the chosen ones and for the chosen ones? But if so, there is a mystery here, and we cannot understand it. And if it is a mystery, then we, too, had the right to preach mystery and to teach them that it is not the free choice of the heart that matters, and not love, but the mystery, which they must blindly obey, even setting aside their own conscience. And so we did. We corrected your deed and based it on *miracle*, *mystery*, and *authority*. And mankind rejoiced that they were once more led like sheep, and that at last such a terrible gift, which had brought them so much suffering, had been taken from their hearts. Tell me, were we right in teaching and doing so? Have we not, indeed, loved mankind, in so humbly recognizing their impotence, in so lovingly alleviating their burden and allowing their feeble nature even to sin, with our permission? Why have you come to interfere with us now? And why are you looking at me so silently and understandingly with your meek eyes? Be angry! I do not want your love, for I do not love you. And what can I hide from you? Do I not know with whom I am speaking? What I have to tell you is all known to you already, I can read it in your eyes. And is it for me to hide our secret from you? Perhaps you precisely want to hear it from my lips. Listen, then: we are not with you, but with *him*, that is our secret! For a long time now—eight centuries already—we have not been with you, but with *him*. Exactly eight centuries ago we took from him what you so indignantly rejected,[28] that last gift he offered you when he showed you all the kingdoms of the earth: we took Rome and the sword of Caesar from him, and proclaimed ourselves sole rulers of the earth, the only rulers, though we have not yet succeeded in bringing our cause to its full conclusion. But whose fault is that? Oh, this work is still in its very beginnings, but it has begun. There is still long to wait before its completion, and the earth still has much to suffer, but we shall accomplish it and we shall be caesars, and then we shall think about the universal happiness of mankind. And yet you could have taken the sword of Caesar even then. Why did you reject that last gift? Had you accepted that third counsel of the mighty spirit, you would have furnished all that man seeks on earth, that is: someone to bow down to, someone to take over his conscience, and a means for uniting everyone at last into a common, concordant, and incontestable anthill—for the need for universal union is the third and last torment of men. Mankind in its entirety has always yearned to arrange things so that they must be universal. There have been many great nations with great histories, but the higher these nations stood, the unhappier they were, for they were more strongly aware than others of the need for a universal union of mankind. Great conquerors, Tamerlanes and Genghis Khans, swept over the earth like a whirlwind, yearning to conquer the cosmos, but they, too, expressed, albeit unconsciously, the same great need of mankind for universal and general union. Had you accepted the world and Caesar's purple, you would have founded a universal kingdom and granted universal peace. For who shall possess mankind if not those who possess their conscience and give them their bread? And so we took Caesar's sword, and in taking it, of course, we rejected you and followed *him*. Oh, there will be centuries more of the lawlessness of free reason, of their science and anthropophagy—for, having begun to build their Tower of Babel without us, they will end in anthropophagy. And it is then that the beast will come crawling to us and lick our feet and spatter them with tears of blood from its eyes. And we shall sit upon the beast and raise the cup, and on it will be written: "Mystery!"[29] But then, and then only, will the kingdom of peace and happiness come for mankind. You are proud of your chosen ones, but you have only your chosen ones, while we will pacify all. And there is still more: how many among those chosen ones, the strong ones who might have become chosen ones, have finally grown tired of waiting for you, and have brought and will yet bring the powers of their spirit and the ardor of their hearts to another field, and will end by raising their *free* banner against you! But you raised that banner yourself. With us everyone will be happy, and they will no longer rebel or destroy each other, as in your freedom, everywhere. Oh, we shall convince them that they will only become free when they resign their freedom to us, and submit to us. Will we be right, do you think, or will we be lying? They themselves will be convinced that we are right, for they will remember to what horrors of slavery and confusion your freedom led them. Freedom, free reason, and science will lead them into such a maze, and confront them with such miracles and insoluble mysteries, that some of them, unruly and ferocious, will exterminate themselves; others, unruly but feeble, will exterminate each other; and the remaining third, feeble and wretched, will crawl to our feet and cry out to us: "Yes, you were right, you alone possess his mystery, and we are coming back to you—save us from ourselves." Receiving bread from us, they will see clearly, of course, that we take from them the bread they have procured with their own hands, in order to distribute it among them, without any miracle; they will see that we have not turned stones into bread; but, indeed, more than over the bread itself, they will rejoice over taking it from our hands! For they will remember only too well that before, without us, the very bread they procured for themselves turned to stones in their hands, and when they came back to us, the very stones in their hands turned to bread. Too well, far too well, will they appreciate what it means to submit once and for all! And until men understand this, they will be unhappy. Who contributed most of all to this lack of understanding, tell me? Who broke up the flock and scattered it upon paths unknown? But the flock will gather again, and again submit, and this time once and for all. Then we shall give them quiet, humble happiness, the happiness of feeble creatures, such as they were created. Oh, we shall finally convince them not to be proud, for you raised them up and thereby taught them pride; we shall prove to them that they are feeble, that they are only pitiful children, but that a child's happiness is sweeter than any other. They will become timid and look to us and cling to us in fear, like chicks to a hen. They will marvel and stand in awe of us and be proud that we are so powerful and so intelligent as to have been able to subdue such a tempestuous flock of thousands of millions. They will tremble limply before our wrath, their minds will grow timid, their eyes will become as tearful as children's or women's, but just as readily at a gesture from us they will pass over to gaiety and laughter, to bright joy and happy children's song. Yes, we will make them work, but in the hours free from labor we will arrange their lives like a children's game, with children's songs, choruses, and innocent dancing. Oh, we will allow them to sin, too; they are weak and powerless, and they will love us like children for allowing them to sin. We will tell them that every sin will be redeemed if it is committed with our permission; and that we allow them to sin because we love them, and as for the punishment for these sins, very well, we take it upon ourselves. And we will take it upon ourselves, and they will adore us as benefactors, who have borne their sins before God. And they will have no secrets from us. We will allow or forbid them to live with their wives and mistresses, to have or not to have children—all depending on their obedience—and they will submit to us gladly and joyfully. The most tormenting secrets of their conscience—all, all they will bring to us, and we will decide all things, and they will joyfully believe our decision, because it will deliver them from their great care and their present terrible torments of personal and free decision. And everyone will be happy, all the millions of creatures, except for the hundred thousand of those who govern them. For only we, we who keep the mystery, only we shall be unhappy. There will be thousands of millions of happy babes, and a hundred thousand sufferers who have taken upon themselves the curse of the knowledge of good and evil. Peacefully they will die, peacefully they will expire in your name, and beyond the grave they will find only death. But we will keep the secret, and for their own happiness we will entice them with a heavenly and eternal reward. For even if there were anything in the next world, it would not, of course, be for such as they. It is said and prophesied that you will come and once more be victorious, you will come with your chosen ones, with your proud and mighty ones, but we will say that they saved only themselves, while we have saved everyone. It is said that the harlot who sits upon the beast and holds *mystery* in her hands will be disgraced, that the feeble will rebel again, that they will tear her purple and strip bare her "loathsome" body.[30] But then I will stand up and point out to you the thousands of millions of happy babes who do not know sin. And we, who took their sins upon ourselves for their happiness, we will stand before you and say: "Judge us if you can and dare." Know that I am not afraid of you. Know that I, too, was in the wilderness, and I, too, ate locusts and roots; that I, too, blessed freedom, with which you have blessed mankind, and I, too, was preparing to enter the number of your chosen ones, the number of the strong and mighty, with a thirst "that the number be complete."[31] But I awoke and did not want to serve madness. I returned and joined the host of those who have *corrected your deed*. I left the proud and returned to the humble, for the happiness of the humble. What I am telling you will come true, and our kingdom will be established. Tomorrow, I repeat, you will see this obedient flock, which at my first gesture will rush to heap hot coals around your stake, at which I shall burn you for having come to interfere with us. For if anyone has ever deserved our stake, it is you. Tomorrow I shall burn you. *Dixi*.' "[32]

Ivan stopped. He was flushed from speaking, and from speaking with such enthusiasm; but when he finished, he suddenly smiled.

Alyosha, who all the while had listened to him silently, though towards the end, in great agitation, he had started many times to interrupt his brother's speech but obviously restrained himself, suddenly spoke as if tearing himself loose.

"But . . . that's absurd!" he cried, blushing. "Your poem praises Jesus, it doesn't revile him . . . as you meant it to. And who will believe you about freedom? Is that, is that any way to understand it? It's a far cry from the Orthodox idea . . . It's Rome, and not even the whole of Rome, that isn't true—they're the worst of Catholicism, the Inquisitors, the Jesuits . . . ! But there could not even possibly be such a fantastic person as your Inquisitor. What sins do they take on themselves? Who are these bearers of the mystery who took some sort of curse upon themselves for men's happiness? Has anyone ever seen them? We know the Jesuits, bad things are said about them, but are they what you have there? They're not that, not that at all . . . They're simply a Roman army, for a future universal earthly kingdom, with the emperor—the pontiff of Rome—at their head . . . that's their ideal, but without any mysteries or lofty sadness . . . Simply the lust for power, for filthy earthly lucre,[33] enslavement . . . a sort of future serfdom with them as the landowners . . . that's all they have. Maybe they don't even believe in God. Your suffering Inquisitor is only a fantasy . . ."

"But wait, wait," Ivan was laughing, "don't get so excited. A fantasy, you say? Let it be. Of course it's a fantasy. But still, let me ask: do you really think that this whole Catholic movement of the past few centuries is really nothing but the lust for power only for the sake of filthy lucre? Did Father Paissy teach you that?"

"No, no, on the contrary, Father Paissy once even said something like what you . . . but not like that, of course, not at all like that," Alyosha suddenly recollected himself.

"A precious bit of information, however, despite your 'not at all like that.' I ask you specifically: why should your Jesuits and Inquisitors have joined together only for material wicked lucre? Why can't there happen to be among them at least one sufferer who is tormented by great sadness and loves mankind? Look, suppose that one among all those who desire only material and filthy lucre, that one of them, at least, is like my old Inquisitor, who himself ate roots in the desert and raved, overcoming his flesh, in order to make himself free and perfect, but who still loved mankind all his life, and suddenly opened his eyes and saw that there is no great moral blessedness in achieving perfection of the will only to become convinced, at the same time, that millions of the rest of God's creatures have been set up only for mockery, that they will never be strong enough to manage their freedom, that from such pitiful rebels will never come giants to complete the tower, that it was not for such geese that the great idealist had his dream of harmony. Having understood all that, he returned and joined . . . the intelligent people. Couldn't this have happened?"

"Whom did he join? What intelligent people?" Alyosha exclaimed, almost passionately. "They are not so very intelligent, nor do they have any great mysteries and secrets . . . Except maybe for godlessness, that's their whole secret. Your Inquisitor doesn't believe in God, that's his whole secret!"

"What of it! At last you've understood. Yes, indeed, that alone is the whole secret, but is it not suffering, if only for such a man as he, who has wasted his whole life on a great deed in the wilderness and still has not been cured of his love for mankind? In his declining years he comes to the clear conviction that only the counsels of the great and dread spirit could at least somehow organize the feeble rebels, 'the unfinished, trial creatures created in mockery,' in a tolerable way. And so, convinced of that, he sees that one must follow the directives of the intelligent spirit, the dread spirit of death and destruction, and to that end accept lies and deceit, and lead people, consciously now, to death and destruction, deceiving them, moreover, all along the way, so that they somehow do not notice where they are being led, so that at least on the way these pitiful, blind men consider themselves happy. And deceive them, notice, in the name of him in whose ideal the old man believed so passionately all his life! Is that not a misfortune? And if even one such man, at least, finds himself at the head of that whole army 'lusting for power only for the sake of filthy lucre,' is one such man, at least, not enough to make a tragedy? Moreover, one such man standing at its head would be enough to bring out finally the real ruling idea of the whole Roman cause, with all its armies and Jesuits—the highest idea of this cause. I tell you outright that I firmly believe that this one man has never been lacking among those standing at the head of the movement. Who knows, perhaps such 'ones' have even been found among the Roman pontiffs. Who knows, maybe this accursed old man, who loves mankind so stubbornly in his own way, exists even now, in the form of a great host of such old men, and by no means accidentally, but in concert, as a secret union, organized long ago for the purpose of keeping the mystery, of keeping it from unhappy and feeble mankind with the aim of making them happy. It surely exists, and it should be so. I imagine that even the Masons have something like this mystery as their basis,[34] and that Catholics hate the Masons so much because they see them as competitors, breaking up the unity of the idea, whereas there should be one flock and one shepherd . . . However, the way I'm defending my thought makes me seem like an author who did not stand up to your criticism. Enough of that."

"Maybe you're a Mason yourself!" suddenly escaped from Alyosha. "You don't believe in God," he added, this time with great sorrow. Besides, it seemed to him that his brother was looking at him mockingly. "And how does your poem end," he asked suddenly, staring at the ground, "or was that the end?"

"I was going to end it like this: when the Inquisitor fell silent, he waited some time for his prisoner to reply. His silence weighed on him. He had seen how the captive listened to him all the while intently and calmly, looking him straight in the eye, and apparently not wishing to contradict anything. The old man would have liked him to say something, even something bitter, terrible. But suddenly he approaches the old man in silence and gently kisses him on his bloodless, ninety-year-old lips. That is the whole answer. The old man shudders. Something stirs at the corners of his mouth; he walks to the door, opens it, and says to him: 'Go and do not come again . . . do not come at all . . . never, never!' And he lets him out into the 'dark squares of the city.'[35] The prisoner goes away."

"And the old man?"

"The kiss burns in his heart, but the old man holds to his former idea."

"And you with him!" Alyosha exclaimed ruefully. Ivan laughed.

"But it's nonsense, Alyosha, it's just the muddled poem of a muddled student who never wrote two lines of verse. Why are you taking it so seriously? You don't think I'll go straight to the Jesuits now, to join the host of those who are correcting his deed! Good lord, what do I care? As I told you: I just want to drag on until I'm thirty, and then—smash the cup on the floor!"

"And the sticky little leaves, and the precious graves, and the blue sky, and the woman you love! How will you live, what will you love them with?" Alyosha exclaimed ruefully. "Is it possible, with such hell in your heart and in your head? No, you're precisely going in order to join them . . . and if not, you'll kill yourself, you won't endure it!"

"There is a force that will endure everything," said Ivan, this time with a cold smirk.

"What force?"

"The Karamazov force . . . the force of the Karamazov baseness."

"To drown in depravity, to stifle your soul with corruption, is that it?"

"That, too, perhaps . . . only until my thirtieth year maybe I'll escape it, and then . . ."

"How will you escape it? By means of what? With your thoughts, it's impossible."

"Again, in Karamazov fashion."

"You mean 'everything is permitted'? Everything is permitted, is that right, is it?"

Ivan frowned, and suddenly turned somehow strangely pale.

"Ah, you caught that little remark yesterday, which offended Miusov so much . . . and that brother Dmitri so naively popped up and rephrased?" he grinned crookedly. "Yes, perhaps 'everything is permitted,' since the word has already been spoken. I do not renounce it. And Mitenka's version is not so bad."

Alyosha was looking at him silently.

"I thought, brother, that when I left here I'd have you, at least, in all the world," Ivan suddenly spoke with unexpected feeling, "but now I see that in your heart, too, there is no room for me, my dear hermit. The formula, 'everything is permitted,' I will not renounce, and what then? Will you renounce me for that? Will you?"

Alyosha stood up, went over to him in silence, and gently kissed him on the lips.

"Literary theft!" Ivan cried, suddenly going into some kind of rapture. "You stole that from my poem! Thank you, however. Get up, Alyosha, let's go, it's time we both did."

They went out, but stopped on the porch of the tavern.

"So, Alyosha," Ivan spoke in a firm voice, "if, indeed, I hold out for the sticky little leaves, I shall love them only remembering you. It's enough for me that you are here somewhere, and I shall not stop wanting to live. Is that enough for you? If you wish, you can take it as a declaration of love. And now you go right, I'll go left—and enough, you hear, enough.[36] I mean, even if I don't go away tomorrow (but it seems I certainly shall), and we somehow meet again, not another word to me on any of these subjects. An urgent request. And with regard to brother Dmitri, too, I ask you particularly, do not ever even mention him to me again," he suddenly added irritably. "It's all exhausted, it's all talked out, isn't it? And in return for that, I will also make you a promise: when I'm thirty and want 'to smash the cup on the floor,' then, wherever you may be, I will still come to talk things over with you once more . . . even from America, I assure you. I will make a point of it. It will also be very interesting to have a look at you by then, to see what's become of you. Rather a solemn promise, you see. And indeed, perhaps we're saying good-bye for some seven or ten years. Well, go now to your Pater Seraphicus;[37] he's dying, and if he dies without you, you may be angry with me for having kept you. Good-bye, kiss me once more—so—and now go . . ."

Ivan turned suddenly and went his way without looking back. It was similar to the way his brother Dmitri had left Alyosha the day before, though the day before it was something quite different. This strange little observation flashed like an arrow through the sad mind of Alyosha, sad and sorrowful at that moment. He waited a little, looking after his brother. For some reason he suddenly noticed that his brother Ivan somehow swayed as he walked, and that his right shoulder, seen from behind, appeared lower than his left. He had never noticed it before. But suddenly he, too, turned and almost ran to the monastery. It was already getting quite dark, and he felt almost frightened; something new was growing in him, which he would have been unable to explain. The wind rose again as it had yesterday, and the centuries-old pine trees rustled gloomily around him as he entered the hermitage woods. He was almost running. "Pater Seraphicus—he got that name from somewhere—but where?" flashed through Alyosha's mind. "Ivan, poor Ivan, when shall I see you again . . . ? Lord, here's the hermitage! Yes, yes, that's him, Pater Seraphicus, he will save me . . . from him, and forever!"

Several times, later in his life, in great perplexity, he wondered how he could suddenly, after parting with his brother Ivan, so completely forget about his brother Dmitri, when he had resolved that morning, only a few hours earlier, that he must find him, and would not leave until he did, even if it meant not returning to the monastery that night.

Chapter 6

A Rather Obscure One for the Moment

And Ivan Fyodorovich, on parting from Alyosha, went home to Fyodor Pavlovich's house. But, strangely, an unbearable anguish suddenly came over him, and, moreover, the closer he came to home, the worse it grew with every step. The strangeness lay not in the anguish itself, but in the fact that Ivan Fyodorovich simply could not define what the anguish consisted of. He had often felt anguish before, and it would be no wonder if it came at such a moment, when he was preparing, the very next day, having suddenly broken with everything that had drawn him there, to make another sharp turn, entering upon a new, completely unknown path, again quite as lonely as before, having much hope, but not knowing for what, expecting much, too much, from life, but unable himself to define anything either in his expectations or even in his desires. And yet at that moment, though the anguish of the new and unknown was indeed in his soul, he was tormented by something quite different. "Can it be loathing for my father's house?" he thought to himself. "Very likely. I'm so sick of it, and though today I shall cross that vile threshold for the last time, still it makes me sick . . ." But no, that was not it. Was it the parting with Alyosha and the conversation he had had with him? "For so many years I was silent with the whole world and did not deign to speak, and suddenly I spewed out so much gibberish!" Indeed, it could have been the youthful vexation of youthful inexperience and youthful vanity, vexation at having been unable to speak his mind, especially with such a being as Alyosha, on whom he undoubtedly counted a great deal in his heart. Of course there was that, too, that is, this vexation, there even had to be, but it was not that either, not that at all. "Anguish to the point of nausea, yet it's beyond me to say what I want. Perhaps I shouldn't think . . ."

Ivan Fyodorovich tried "not to think," but that, too, was no use. Above all, this anguish was vexing and annoyed him by the fact that it had some sort of accidental, completely external appearance; this he felt. Somewhere some being or object was standing and sticking up, just as when something sometimes sticks up in front of one's eye and one doesn't notice it for a long time, being busy or in heated conversation, and meanwhile one is clearly annoyed, almost suffering, and at last it dawns on one to remove the offending object, often quite trifling and ridiculous, something left in the wrong place, a handkerchief dropped on the floor, a book not put back in the bookcase, or whatever. At last, in a very bad and irritated state of mind, Ivan Fyodorovich reached his father's house, and suddenly, glancing at the gate from about fifty paces away, he at once realized what was tormenting and worrying him so.

On the bench by the gate, idly enjoying the cool of the evening, sat the lackey Smerdyakov, and Ivan Fyodorovich realized at the first sight of him that the lackey Smerdyakov was also sitting in his soul, and that it was precisely this man that his soul could not bear. It all suddenly became bright and clear. Earlier, with Alyosha's story of his encounter with Smerdyakov, something gloomy and disgusting had suddenly pierced his heart and immediately evoked a reciprocal malice. Later, during their conversation, Smerdyakov was temporarily forgotten, but remained in his soul nonetheless, and as soon as Ivan Fyodorovich parted with Alyosha and headed for home alone, the forgotten feeling at once began suddenly and quickly to reemerge. "But can it be that this worthless scoundrel troubles me so much!" he thought with unbearable malice.

It so happened that Ivan Fyodorovich had recently begun taking an intense dislike to the man, especially over the past few days. He had even begun to notice his growing feeling almost of hatred for this creature. Perhaps the process of hatred had intensified so precisely because at first, when Ivan Fyodorovich had just come to our town, things had gone quite differently. Then, Ivan Fyodorovich had suddenly taken some special interest in Smerdyakov, found him even very original. He got him accustomed to talking with him, always marveling, however, at a certain incoherence, or, better, a certain restiveness in his mind, unable to understand what it was that could so constantly and persistently trouble "this contemplator."[1] They talked about philosophical questions and even about why the light shone on the first day, while the sun, moon, and stars were created only on the fourth day, and how this should be understood; but Ivan Fyodorovich was soon convinced that the sun, moon, and stars were not the point at all, that while the sun, moon, and stars might be an interesting subject, for Smerdyakov it was of completely third-rate importance, and that he was after something quite different. Be it one way or the other, in any event a boundless vanity began to appear and betray itself, an injured vanity besides. Ivan Fyodorovich did not like that at all. Here his loathing began. Then disorder came to the house, Grushenka appeared, the episodes with his brother Dmitri began, there were troubles of all sorts—they talked about that, too, but though Smerdyakov always entered into these conversations with great excitement, once again it was impossible to discover what he himself wanted. One might even marvel at the illogic and incoherence of some of his wishes, which came out involuntarily and always with the same vagueness. Smerdyakov kept inquiring, asking certain indirect, apparently farfetched questions, but why—he never explained, and usually, at the most heated moment of his questioning, he would suddenly fall silent or switch to something quite different. But in the end the thing that finally most irritated Ivan Fyodorovich and filled him with such loathing was a sort of loathsome and peculiar familiarity, which Smerdyakov began displaying towards him more and more markedly. Not that he allowed himself any impoliteness; on the contrary, he always spoke with the greatest respect; but nonetheless things worked out in such a way that Smerdyakov apparently, God knows why, finally came to consider himself somehow in league, as it were, with Ivan Fyodorovich, always spoke in such tones as to suggest that there was already something agreed to and kept secret, as it were, between the two of them, something once spoken on both sides, which was known only to the two of them and was even incomprehensible to the other mortals milling around them. For a long time, however, Ivan Fyodorovich did not understand this real reason for his increasing loathing, and only very recently had he finally managed to grasp what it was. With a feeling of squeamishness and irritation, he was now about to walk through the gate silently and without looking at Smerdyakov; but Smerdyakov got up from the bench, and by that one gesture Ivan Fyodorovich perceived at once that he wished to have a special conversation with him. Ivan Fyodorovich looked at him and stopped, and the fact that he suddenly stopped like that, and did not pass by as he had wished to do a moment before, so infuriated him that he began to shake. With rage and loathing he looked at Smerdyakov's wasted, eunuch's physiognomy with its strands of hair brushed forward at the temples and a fluffed-up little tuft on top. His slightly squinting left eye winked and smirked as if to say: "What's the hurry? You won't pass me by. You know that we two intelligent men have something to talk over." Ivan Fyodorovich was shaking:

"Get away, scoundrel! I'm no friend of yours, you fool!" was about to fly out of his mouth, but to his great amazement what did fly out of his mouth was something quite different.

"How is papa, asleep or awake?" he said softly and humbly, to his own surprise, and suddenly, also to his own surprise, sat down on the bench. For a moment he was almost frightened—he remembered it afterwards. Smerdyakov stood in front of him, his hands behind his back, looking at him confidently, almost sternly.

"Still asleep, sir," he said unhurriedly. ("You see, you yourself spoke first, not I.") "I'm surprised at you, sir," he added after a short pause, lowering his eyes somehow demurely, moving his right foot forward, and playing with the toe of his patent leather boot.

"Why are you surprised at me?" Ivan asked abruptly and severely, doing his utmost to restrain himself, and suddenly he realized with loathing that he felt the most intense curiosity, and that nothing could induce him to leave before it was satisfied.

"Why won't you go to Chermashnya, sir?" Smerdyakov suddenly glanced up and smiled familiarly. "And why I'm smiling, you yourself should understand, if you're an intelligent man," his squinting left eye seemed to say.

"Why should I go to Chermashnya?" Ivan Fyodorovich said in surprise.

Smerdyakov paused again.

"Even Fyodor Pavlovich himself has begged you so to do it, sir," he said at last, unhurriedly and as if he attached no value to his answer: I'm getting off with a third-rate explanation, just so as to say something.

"What the devil do you want? Speak more clearly!" Ivan Fyodorovich cried at last angrily, passing from humility to rudeness.

Smerdyakov put his right foot together with his left, straightened up, but continued looking at him with the same calmness and the same little smile.

"Essentially nothing, sir . . . just making conversation . . ."

There was another pause. They were silent for about a minute. Ivan Fyodorovich knew that now he ought to rise up and be angry, and Smerdyakov stood in front of him as if he were waiting: "Now we'll see whether you get angry or not." So at least it seemed to Ivan Fyodorovich. At last he swung forward in order to get up. Smerdyakov caught the moment precisely.

"My position, sir, is terrible, Ivan Fyodorovich, I don't even know how to help myself," he suddenly said firmly and distinctly, with a sigh on the last word. Ivan Fyodorovich at once sat down again.

"They're both quite crazy, sir, they've both gone as far as childishness, sir," Smerdyakov went on. "I mean your father and your brother, sir, Dmitri Fyodorovich. He'll get up now, Fyodor Pavlovich will, and begin pestering me every minute: 'Why hasn't she come? How is it she hasn't come?' and it will go on until midnight, even past midnight. And if Agrafena Alexandrovna doesn't come (because she may have no intention of ever coming at all, sir), then he'll jump on me again tomorrow morning: 'Why didn't she come? Tell me why, and when will she come?'—just as if I stood to blame for that all before him. On the other hand, there's this matter, sir, that just as soon as it turns dusk, and even before, your good brother arrives at our neighbors', with a weapon in his hands. 'Listen, you rogue, you broth-maker,' he says, 'if you miss her and don't let me know when she comes—I'll kill you first of all.' The night goes by, and in the morning, he, too, like Fyodor Pavlovich, starts tormenting me with his torments: 'Why didn't she come? Will she be here soon?' and again it's as if I stood to blame before him, sir, because his lady didn't come. And both of them, sir, keep getting angrier and angrier with every day and every hour, so that I sometimes think of taking my own life, sir, from fear. I can't trust them, sir."

"And why did you get mixed up in it? Why did you begin carrying tales to Dmitri Fyodorovich?" Ivan Fyodorovich said irritably.

"How could I not get mixed up in it, sir? And I didn't get mixed up in it at all, if you want to know with complete exactitude, sir. I kept quiet from the very beginning, I was afraid to object, and the gentleman himself appointed me to be his servant Licharda.[2] And since then all he says to me is: 'I'll kill you, you rogue, if you miss her!' I suppose for certain, sir, that a long attack of the falling sickness will come on me tomorrow."

"What do you mean, a long attack?"

"A long sort of attack, sir, extremely long. Several hours, sir, maybe even a day or two. Once it went on for three days, I fell out of the attic that time. It would stop shaking me, and then it would start again; and for all three days I couldn't get into my right mind. Fyodor Pavlovich sent for Herzenstube, the local doctor, sir, and he put ice on my head and used some other remedy . . . I could have died, sir."

"But they say that with the falling sickness you can't know beforehand that an attack will come at such and such a time. What makes you say you'll have one tomorrow?" Ivan Fyodorovich inquired with peculiar and irritable curiosity.

"That's right, sir, you can't know beforehand."

"Besides, you fell from the attic that time."

"I climb up to the attic every day, sir. I could fall from the attic tomorrow, too. Or if not from the attic, then I might fall into the cellar, sir, I go to the cellar every day, too, with my duties, sir."

Ivan Fyodorovich gave him a long look.

"I see, you're just driveling, and I'm afraid I don't understand you," he said softly but somehow menacingly. "You mean you're going to pretend to have a three-day attack of the falling sickness tomorrow, eh?"

Smerdyakov, who was staring at the ground and again playing with his right toe, moved his right foot back, put his left foot forward instead, raised his eyes, and, smirking, said:

"Even if I could do such a thing, sir—that is, pretend, sir—and since for an experienced man it would be easy enough to do, then in that case, too, I would have every right to use such a means to save my life from death; for if I'm lying sick, then even if Agrafena Alexandrovna comes to his father, he can't ask a sick man: 'Why didn't you inform me?' He'd be ashamed to."

"What the devil!" Ivan Fyodorovich suddenly flung out, his face twisted with malice. "Why are you so afraid for your life? My brother Dmitri's threats are all just passionate talk, nothing more. He won't kill you; he'll kill, but not you!"

"He'd kill me like a fly, sir, me first of all. And even more than that, I'm afraid of something else: that I'll be considered in his accomplice when he commits some absurdity over his father."

"Why would they consider you his accomplice?"

"They'll consider me his accomplice because I informed him about the signals, in great secrecy, sir."

"What signals? Who did you inform? Devil take you, speak more clearly!"

"I must confess fully," Smerdyakov drawled with pedantic composure, "that I have a secret here with Fyodor Pavlovich. As you yourself have the honor of knowing (if you do have the honor of knowing it), for the past few days now, as soon as night comes, or just evening, he immediately locks himself in. Lately you've been going upstairs early, and yesterday you didn't go anywhere at all, sir, and therefore maybe you don't know how carefully he's begun locking himself in for the night. And even if Grigory Vasilievich himself was to come, he'd open the door for him, sir, only if he was sure of his voice. But Grigory Vasilievich won't come, sir, because I'm the only one who waits on him now in his room, sir—that's how he arranged it ever since he started this to-do with Agrafena Alexandrovna, and for the night, I, too, now retire, on his directions, and go and sleep in the cottage, provided I don't sleep before midnight, but keep watch, get up and walk around the yard, and wait for Agrafena Alexandrovna to come, sir, because he's been waiting for her like a crazy man for the past few days. And he reasons like this, sir: she's afraid of him, he says, of Dmitri Fyodorovich (he calls him Mitka), and therefore she will come late at night, by the back way; you watch out for her, he says, until midnight or later. And if she comes, run to the door and knock, on the door or on the garden window, first two times slowly, like this: one, two; then three times more quickly: tap-tap-tap. Then, he says, I'll know at once that she's there and will quietly open the door to you. The other signal he gave me in case something urgent happens: first twice quickly, tap-tap, then a pause, then one much stronger tap. Then he'll know that something sudden has happened and I need very bad to see him, and he'll open up and I'll come in and report. It's all in case Agrafena Alexandrovna might not come herself, but sends a message about something; Dmitri Fyodorovich might come, too, besides, so I should also inform him if he's around. He's real frightened of Dmitri Fyodorovich, so that even if Agrafena Alexandrovna has already come and he's locked himself up with her, and meanwhile Dmitri Fyodorovich turns up somewhere around, then, in that case, it is my duty to report it to him at once without fail, by three knocks, so that the first signal of five knocks means 'Agrafena Alexandrovna is here,' and the second signal of three knocks means 'Really have to see you'—that's how he himself taught me and explained them each several times, with examples. And since in the whole universe only he and I, sir, know about these signals, he'll come doubtless and not calling out any names (he's afraid of calling out loud) and open the door. And these same signals have now become known to Dmitri Fyodorovich."

"Become known? You told him? How dared you?"

"It's this same fear, sir. And how could I dare hold it back from him, sir? Dmitri Fyodorovich kept pressing me every day: 'You're deceiving me, what are you hiding from me? I'll break both your legs!' That's when I informed him about these same secret signals, so that at least he could see my servility and be satisfied that I'm not deceiving him and report to him in every way."

"If you think he'll use these signals to try and get in, you mustn't let him in."

"But if I was to be laid up with a fit, sir, then how could I stop him from coming in, even if I dared to stop him, sir, seeing how desperate he is?"

"How the devil can you be so sure you'll have a fit, devil take you! Are you laughing at me?"

"Would I dare laugh at you, sir, and do you think I feel up to laughing with all this fear? I anticipate that a falling fit will come on me, I have this anticipation, it will come from fear alone, sir."

"What the devil! If you're laid up then Grigory will keep watch! Warn Grigory beforehand, he certainly won't let him in."

"By no means would I dare tell Grigory Vasilievich about the signals without the master's orders, sir. And concerning Grigory Vasilievich hearing and not letting him in, he's come down sick today, ever since yesterday, and Marfa Ignatievna is going to give him the treatment tomorrow. They just decided on it. This treatment of theirs is rather curious, sir: Marfa Ignatievna knows this infusion, and always keeps it on hand, a strong one, with some herb in it—it's her secret, sir. And with this secret medicine she treats Grigory Vasilievich about three times a year, when his whole lower back goes out—he has something like a paralysis, sir, about three times a year. Then Marfa Ignatievna takes a towel, soaks it in this infusion, and rubs his whole back with it for half an hour, till it's dry and even gets quite red and swollen, sir, and then she gives him what's left in the bottle to drink, with some prayer, sir, not all of it, though, because on this rare occasion she leaves a small amount for herself as well, sir, and also drinks it. And neither of them, I can tell you, is used to drinking, and they drop down right there and fall fast asleep for a long time, sir; and when Grigory Vasilievich wakes up after that, he almost always feels good, and Marfa Ignatievna, she wakes up after that and always has a headache, sir. And so, if Marfa Ignatievna fulfills this same intention tomorrow, sir, it's not likely they'll be able to hear anything and not let Dmitri Fyodorovich in. They'll be asleep, sir."

"What drivel! And it will all come together just like that, as if on purpose: your falling fit, and the two of them unconscious!" cried Ivan Fyodorovich. "Or are you going to arrange it that way?" suddenly escaped him, and he frowned menacingly.

"How could I arrange it, sir . . . ? And why would I arrange it, if everything here depends on Dmitri Fyodorovich alone, sir, and only on his thoughts . . . ? If he wants to commit anything, he'll commit it, sir, and if not, I won't bring him on purpose and push him into his father's room."

"And why should he go to father, especially on the sly, if, as you say yourself, Agrafena Alexandrovna won't come at all?" Ivan Fyodorovich continued, turning pale with anger. "You say yourself, and I, too, have felt sure all along, that the old man is just dreaming, and that that creature would never come to him. Why, then, should Dmitri burst in on the old man if she doesn't come? Speak! I want to know what you think."

"If you please, sir, you know yourself why he will come, you don't need to know what I think. He'll come just because he's angry, or because he's suspicious, on account of my sickness, for example, he'll begin wondering, he'll get impatient and come to have a look through the rooms like he did yesterday, to see if maybe she didn't sneak by him and get in. He is also perfectly informed that Fyodor Pavlovich has a big envelope prepared, and there are three thousand roubles sealed up in it, with three seals, sir, tied round with a ribbon and addressed by his own hand: 'To my angel Grushenka, if she wants to come,' and after that, three days later, he added: 'and to my chicky.' So that's what's so dubious, sir."

"Nonsense!" cried Ivan Fyodorovich, almost in a rage. "Dmitri won't come to steal money and kill his father on top of it. He might have killed him yesterday over Grushenka, like a wild, angry fool, but he won't go and steal!"

"He needs money very bad, sir, he's in great extremities, Ivan Fyodorovich. You don't even know how bad he needs it," Smerdyakov explained with perfect composure and remarkable distinctness. "Besides, he considers that same three thousand, sir, as if it was his own, and he told me so himself: 'My father,' he said, 'still owes me exactly three thousand.' And on top of all that, Ivan Fyodorovich, consider also a certain pure truth, sir: it's almost a sure thing, one must say, sir, that Agrafena Alexandrovna, if only she wants to, could definitely get him to marry her, I mean the master himself, Fyodor Pavlovich, sir, if only she wants to—well, and maybe she'll want to, sir. I'm just saying that she won't come, but maybe she'll want even more, sir, I mean to become the mistress right off. I know myself that her merchant Samsonov told her in all sincerity that it would even be quite a clever deal, and laughed as he said it. And she's quite clever in her mind, sir. Why should she marry such a pauper as Dmitri Fyodorovich, sir? And so, taking that, now consider for yourself, Ivan Fyodorovich, that then there will be nothing at all left either for Dmitri Fyodorovich, or even for you, sir, along with your brother Alexei Fyodorovich, after your father's death, not a rouble, sir, because Agrafena Alexandrovna will marry him in order to get it all down in her name and transfer whatever capital there is to herself, sir. But if your father was to die now, while none of that has happened, sir, then each one of you would get a sure forty thousand all at once, even Dmitri Fyodorovich, whom he hates so much, because he hasn't made his will, sir . . . All of that is known perfectly well to Dmitri Fyodorovich . . ."

Something became twisted, as it were, and twitched in Ivan Fyodorovich's face. He suddenly blushed.

"And why, after all that," he suddenly interrupted Smerdyakov, "do you advise me to go to Chermashnya? What do you mean to say by that? I'll go, and that is what will happen here?" Ivan Fyodorovich was breathing with difficulty.

"Exactly right, sir," Smerdyakov said quietly and reasonably, but keeping his eyes fixed on Ivan Fyodorovich.

"Exactly right?" Ivan Fyodorovich repeated, trying hard to restrain himself, and his eyes flashed menacingly.

"I said it because I felt bad for you. In your place, if it were me, I'd leave the whole thing right now . . . rather than sit next to such business, sir . . . ," Smerdyakov replied, looking at Ivan Fyodorovich's flashing eyes with an air of great candor. Both were silent for a time.

"It seems you're a perfect idiot, and, no doubt . . . a terrible scoundrel!" Ivan Fyodorovich suddenly got up from the bench. He was about to walk straight through the gate, but suddenly stopped and turned to Smerdyakov. Something strange happened: all of a sudden, as if in a convulsion, Ivan Fyodorovich bit his lip, clenched his fists, and in another moment would certainly have thrown himself on Smerdyakov. The latter, at any rate, noticed it at the same moment, gave a start, and shrank back with his whole body. But the moment passed favorably for Smerdyakov, and Ivan Fyodorovich silently but in some perplexity, as it were, turned towards the gate.

"I am leaving for Moscow tomorrow, if you want to know—early tomorrow morning—and that's it!" he said suddenly, with malice, loudly and distinctly, wondering afterwards why he had felt any need to tell this to Smerdyakov.

"That's for the best, sir," the latter put in, as if it was just what he had been waiting for. "The only thing is that they might trouble you from here in Moscow, by telegraph, sir, in some such case."

Ivan Fyodorovich stopped again and again turned quickly to Smerdyakov. But with the latter, too, something seemed to happen. All his familiarity and casualness instantly dropped away; his whole face expressed extreme attention and expectation, but timid and obsequious now: "Don't you want to say something more? Don't you want to add anything?" could be read in the intent look he fixed on Ivan Fyodorovich.

"And wouldn't they also summon me from Chermashnya . . . in some such case?" Ivan Fyodorovich suddenly yelled, raising his voice terribly for some unknown reason.

"Also from Chermashnya, sir . . . they'll trouble you there, sir . . . ," Smerdyakov muttered almost in a whisper, as if taken aback, but continuing to look intently, very intently, straight into Ivan Fyodorovich's eyes.

"Only Moscow is further and Chermashnya is nearer—so are you worried about my travel expenses when you insist on Chermashnya, or about my having to make such a long detour?"

"Exactly right, sir . . . ," Smerdyakov muttered in a faltering voice now, with a hideous smile, again convulsively preparing to jump back just in time. But Ivan Fyodorovich, much to Smerdyakov's surprise, suddenly laughed and walked quickly through the gate, still laughing. Anyone seeing his face would certainly have concluded that he was not laughing at all out of merriment. And for the life of him he himself could not have explained what was happening to him at that moment. He moved and walked as if in spasms.

Chapter 7

"It's Always Interesting to Talk with an Intelligent Man"

And he spoke the same way. Having met Fyodor Pavlovich in the front hall, just as he came in, he suddenly cried out to him, waving his arms: "Upstairs, to my room, not now, good-bye," and walked past, trying not even to look at his father. Very possibly the old man was too hateful to him at that moment, but such an unceremonious display of animosity came as a surprise even to Fyodor Pavlovich. And indeed the old man was apparently in a hurry to tell him something, for which purpose he had come out to meet him in the front hall; but, greeted with such courtesy, he stood silently, with a sneering look, following his boy with his eyes until he disappeared up the stairs.

"What's with him?" he quickly asked Smerdyakov, who came in after Ivan Fyodorovich.

"He's angry about something, sir, who knows what," the servant muttered evasively.

"Ah, the devil! Let him be angry! Bring the samovar and clear out. Hurry up! Anything new?"

Then came all kinds of questions of the sort Smerdyakov had just complained of to Ivan Fyodorovich—that is, all to do with the expected lady visitor, which questions we shall omit here. Half an hour later the house was locked up and the crazy old fool was wandering through his rooms alone, in trembling expectation every moment of the five prearranged knocks, glancing from time to time at the dark windows and seeing nothing in them but night.

It was already very late, but Ivan Fyodorovich was still awake and pondering. That night he went to bed late, at about two. But we will not relate the whole train of his thought, nor is it time yet for us to enter into this soul—this soul will have its turn. And even if we should try to relate something, it would be very hard to do, because there were no thoughts, but something very indefinite, and, above all, too excited. He himself felt that he had lost his bearings. He was also tormented by various strange and almost entirely unexpected desires; for example, already after midnight, he suddenly felt an insistent and unbearable urge to go downstairs, unlock the door, go out to the servants' cottage, and give Smerdyakov a beating; but if you had asked him why, he would have been decidedly unable to give even one precise reason, save perhaps that this lackey had become hateful to him, as if he had offended him more gravely than anyone else in the world. On the other hand, more than once during the night his soul was seized by some inexplicable and humiliating timidity, which—he could feel it—even suddenly robbed him, as it were, of his physical strength. His head ached and he was giddy. Something hateful was gnawing his soul, as if he were about to take revenge on someone. He even hated Alyosha, recalling that day's conversation; at moments he hated himself very much as well. He almost forgot to think of Katerina Ivanovna, and afterwards was greatly surprised at that, the more so as he distinctly remembered how, just the morning before, when he had boasted so sweepingly at Katerina Ivanovna's that he was leaving the next day for Moscow, at the same moment in his soul he had whispered to himself: "That's nonsense, you won't go, it won't be so easy to tear yourself away as you're bragging now." Remembering this night long afterwards, Ivan Fyodorovich recalled with particular disgust how he suddenly would get up from the sofa and quietly, as though terribly afraid of being seen, open the door, go out to the head of the stairs, and listen to Fyodor Pavlovich moving around below, wandering through the downstairs rooms—he would listen for a long time, five minutes at a stretch, with a sort of strange curiosity, holding his breath, his heart pounding—and why he was doing all that, what he was listening for, he, of course, did not know himself. All his life afterwards he referred to this "action" as "loathsome," and all his life, deep in himself, in the inmost part of his soul, he considered it the basest action of his whole life. For Fyodor Pavlovich himself he did not even feel any hatred during those minutes, but was simply overwhelmingly curious about how he was wandering around down there, what approximately he could be doing now in his rooms, guessing and pondering how he might glance at the dark windows down there and suddenly stop in the middle of the room, waiting, waiting to hear if anyone knocked. Perhaps twice Ivan Fyodorovich went out to the stairs in this pursuit. When all became quiet and Fyodor Pavlovich had gone to bed, at about two o'clock, Ivan Fyodorovich, too, went to bed with a firm desire to fall asleep quickly, for he felt terribly exhausted. And indeed he suddenly fell fast asleep and slept dreamlessly, but he woke up early, at about seven o'clock, when it was already light. On opening his eyes, to his amazement, he suddenly felt in himself the surge of some remarkable energy; he jumped up quickly, dressed quickly, took out his suitcase, and without a pause hurriedly began packing it. He had gotten his linen back from the washerwoman just the previous morning. Ivan Fyodorovich even smiled at the thought that it had all worked out so well, that there was nothing to delay his sudden departure. And the departure indeed turned out to be sudden. Though Ivan

Fyodorovich had said the day before (to Katerina Ivanovna, Alyosha, and then Smerdyakov) that he would be leaving the next day, by the time he went to bed he remembered very well that he was not even thinking about his departure, at least he never imagined that his first impulse, on waking up in the morning, would be to rush and pack his suitcase. At last the suitcase and bag were ready. It was about nine o'clock when Marfa Ignatievna came upstairs to him with her usual daily question: "Will you be pleased to have tea in your room, or will you come downstairs?" Ivan Fyodorovich came downstairs, looking almost gay, though there was in him, in his words and gestures, something scattered and hasty, as it were. He greeted his father affably and even inquired especially about his health, and then, without waiting for his father to finish his reply, at once announced that he was leaving for Moscow in an hour, for good, and asked that the horses be sent for. The old man listened to the announcement with no sign of surprise, and quite indecently forgot to feel any grief at his boy's departure; instead he suddenly got into a great flutter, having just incidentally remembered some urgent business of his own.

"Ah, you! What a fellow! Couldn't have told me yesterday . . . well, no matter, we'll settle it now. Do me a great favor, old man, stop off at Chermashnya. You just have to turn left at the Volovya station, just eight short miles and you're in Chermashnya."

"I can't, for pity's sake! It's fifty miles to the railway, and the train leaves for Moscow at seven in the evening—I barely have time to make it."

"You'll make it tomorrow, or the day after, but turn off to Chermashnya today. What will it cost you to placate your father! If I hadn't been kept here, I'd have shot over there and back myself long ago, because the deal there is an urgent and special one, but now isn't the right time for me . . . You see, I have a woodlot there, two parcels, in Begichev and Dyachkina, on waste lands. The Maslovs, the old man and his son, merchants, are offering only eight thousand for it, to cut the timber, and just last year a buyer turned up who offered twelve thousand, but he wasn't local, that's the catch. Because there's no dealing among the locals now: the Maslovs—father and son, worth a hundred thousand—have got everybody in their fist: you take whatever they offer, and none of the locals dares to compete with them. And suddenly the priest at Ilyinskoye wrote me last Thursday that Gorstkin has come along, another little merchant, I know him, but the precious thing is that he's not a local, he comes from Pogrebovo, which means he's not afraid of the Maslovs, because he isn't local. Eleven thousand he says he'll give for the lot, do you hear? But the priest writes that he'll only be staying on for another week. So suppose you go and settle it with him . . ."

"Write to the priest; he'll settle it with him."

"He can't do it, that's the thing. This priest has no eye for business. He pure gold, I'd hand him twenty thousand right now for safekeeping, withou a receipt, but he has no eye at all, as if he weren't even a man, a crow could tric him. And he's a learned man, just think of it! This Gorstkin looks like a pea ant, wears a blue coat, only in character he's a complete scoundrel, that's th trouble for us: he lies, there's the catch. Sometimes he lies so much that yo wonder, why is he doing it? Two years ago he lied that his wife was dead an that he'd already married another one, and, imagine, not a word of it was tru his wife never died, she's still alive and beats him once every three days. S we've got to find out whether he's lying now, too, or really wants to buy an is offering eleven thousand."

"But there's no use sending me; I have no eye either."

"No, no, you'll do fine, because I'm going to tell you all his signs, Gors kin's, I mean; I've been dealing with him from way back. You see, you mus watch his beard; he has a red, ugly, thin little beard. If his beard shakes and h looks angry when he talks—good, it means he's telling the truth, he wants do business; but if he strokes his beard with his left hand and chuckles to him self—no good, he's swindling, he's going to cheat you. Never watch his eye you can't tell anything from his eyes, they're murky water, he's a rogue—bu watch his beard. I'll give you a note for him, and you show it. His name i Gorstkin, only it's not Gorstkin but Lyagavy, so don't tell him he's Lyagavy o he'll get offended.[1] If you settle with him and see that it's all right, send me note at once. Just write: 'He's not lying.' Insist on eleven thousand; you ca knock off a thousand, but not more. Think: from eight to eleven, it's a differ ence of three thousand. It's as if I just picked up three thousand, finding buyer is hard, and I need money desperately. Let me know if it's serious, the I'll shoot over and back myself, I'll snatch some time somehow. Why driv over there now, if the priest is only imagining things? Well, will you go o not?"

"Spare me, eh? I have no time."

"Ahh, do it for your father, I won't forget it! You have no hearts, any of you that's what! Will a day or two make any difference? Where are you off to— Venice? Your Venice won't fall apart in two days. I'd send Alyoshka, but Al yoshka's no use in such matters. It's because you're an intelligent man—don I know that? You're not a timber dealer, but you have a good eye. The onl thing is to see whether the man is talking seriously or not. Watch his beard, tell you: if his little beard shakes, it's serious."

"So you yourself are pushing me to this damned Chermashnya, eh?" Iva Fyodorovich cried with a malicious grin.

Fyodor Pavlovich did not perceive or did not want to perceive the malice, but he did catch the grin.

"You'll go, then, you'll go? I'll scribble a note for you right now."

"I don't know if I'll go, I don't know, I'll decide on the way."

"Why on the way? Decide now. Decide, my dear! Make the deal, write me two lines, give the note to the priest, and he'll send it to me at once. Then off to Venice—I won't keep you any longer. The priest will deliver you to the Volovya station with his own horses . . ."

The old man was simply delighted; he scribbled the note, the horses were sent for, cognac was served with a bite to eat. When the old man was pleased, he always became effusive, but this time he restrained himself, as it were. For instance, he did not say a single word about Dmitri Fyodorovich. And he was quite unmoved by the parting. He even seemed to have run out of things to talk about, and Ivan Fyodorovich was very much aware of it: "He's sick of me really," he thought to himself. Only when they were already saying good-bye on the porch did the old man begin to flutter about, as it were, and try to start kissing. But Ivan Fyodorovich quickly gave him his hand to shake, obviously backing away from the kisses. The old man understood at once and immediately checked himself.

"Well, God be with you, God be with you!" he kept repeating from the porch. "Will you come back again in this lifetime? Well, do come, I'll always be glad to see you. Well, so Christ be with you!"

Ivan Fyodorovich got into the carriage.

"Farewell, Ivan! Don't hold any grudges!" the father cried for the last time.

The whole household came out to see him off: Smerdyakov, Marfa, and Grigory. Ivan Fyodorovich presented each of them with ten roubles. When he was already seated in the carriage, Smerdyakov ran up to straighten the rug.

"You see . . . I'm going to Chermashnya . . . ," somehow suddenly escaped from Ivan Fyodorovich; again, as the day before, it flew out by itself, accompanied by a kind of nervous chuckle. He kept remembering it for a long time afterwards.

"So it's true what they say, that it's always interesting to talk with an intelligent man," Smerdyakov replied firmly, giving Ivan Fyodorovich a penetrating look.

The carriage started and raced off. All was vague in the traveler's soul, but he greedily looked around him at the fields, the hills, the trees, a flock of geese flying high above him in the clear sky. Suddenly he felt so well. He tried to strike up a conversation with the coachman, and found something in the peasant's reply terribly interesting, but a moment later he realized that it had all flown over his head and, in fact, he had not understood what the peasant had replied. He fell silent; it was good just as it was: clean, fresh, cool air; a clear sky. The images of Alyosha and Katerina Ivanovna flashed through his mind; but he gently smiled and gently blew at the dear shadows, and they flew away: "Their time will come," he thought. They covered the distance to the next station quickly, changed horses, and raced on to Volovya. "Why is it interesting to talk with an intelligent man? What did he mean by that?" the thought suddenly took his breath away. "And why did I report to him that I was going to Chermashnya?" They pulled up at the Volovya station. Ivan Fyodorovich got out of the carriage and was surrounded by coachmen. They haggled over the ride to Chermashnya, eight miles by country road, in a hired carriage. He told them to harness up. He went into the station house, looked around, glanced at the stationmaster's wife, and suddenly walked back out on the porch.

"Forget about Chermashnya, brothers. Am I too late to get to the railway by seven o'clock?"

"We'll just make it. Shall we harness up?"

"At once. Will one of you be in town tomorrow?"

"Yes, sure, Mitri here will be."

"Can you do me a favor, Mitri? Stop and see my father, Fyodor Pavlovich Karamazov, and tell him that I didn't go to Chermashnya. Can you do that?"

"Why not? I'll stop by. I've known Fyodor Pavlovich for a long time."

"Here's a tip for you; I don't suppose you'll get anything from him . . . ," Ivan Fyodorovich laughed gaily.

"True enough, I won't," Mitri laughed, too. "Thank you, sir, I'll be sure to do it . . ."

At seven o'clock in the evening Ivan Fyodorovich boarded the train and flew towards Moscow. "Away with all the past, I'm through with the old world forever, and may I never hear another word or echo from it; to the new world, to new places, and no looking back!" But instead of delight, such darkness suddenly descended on his soul, and such grief gnawed at his heart, as he had never known before in the whole of his life. He sat thinking all night; the train flew on, and only at daybreak, entering Moscow, did he suddenly come to, as it were.

"I am a scoundrel," he whispered to himself.

And Fyodor Pavlovich, having seen his boy off, was left feeling very pleased. For all of two hours he felt almost happy and sat sipping cognac; but suddenly there occurred a most annoying and unpleasant circumstance for everyone in the house, which instantly plunged Fyodor Pavlovich into great confusion: Smerdyakov went to the cellar for something and fell in from the top step. Fortunately, Marfa Ignatievna happened to be in the yard at the moment and heard it in time. She did not see the fall, but she did hear the cry, a special, strange cry, long familiar to her—the cry of an epileptic falling into a fit. Whether the fit had come on him as he was going down the stairs, so that of course he would have fallen unconscious at once, or whether, on the contrary, the fall and concussion had caused the fit in Smerdyakov, who was a known epileptic, was impossible to figure out; but he was found in the cellar, in cramps and convulsions, writhing and foaming at the mouth. At first they thought he must have broken something, an arm or a leg, and injured himself, but "God preserved him," as Marfa Ignatievna put it: nothing of the sort had happened, and the only difficulty lay in getting him up and out of the cellar into the daylight. But they asked for help from some neighbors and somehow managed to accomplish it. Fyodor Pavlovich was present at this ceremony and lent a hand, obviously frightened and lost, as it were. The sick man, however, did not regain consciousness: the fits would let up for a time, but they kept coming back, and everyone concluded that the same thing would happen as the year before when he had accidentally fallen from the attic. They remembered that then they had applied ice to his head. Some ice was found in the cellar and Marfa Ignatievna arranged things, and towards evening Fyodor Pavlovich sent for Dr. Herzenstube, which doctor arrived at once. Having examined the patient thoroughly (he was the most thorough and attentive doctor in the whole district, an elderly and most venerable man), he concluded that the fit was an extraordinary one and "might threaten a danger," and that meanwhile he, Herzenstube, does not fully understand it yet, but if by tomorrow morning the present remedies have not helped, he will venture to try others. The sick man was put to bed in the cottage, in a small room next to the quarters of Grigory and Marfa Ignatievna. For the rest of the day, Fyodor Pavlovich suffered one disaster after another: Marfa Ignatievna cooked dinner, and the soup, compared with Smerdyakov's cooking, came out "like swill," while the chicken was so dry that teeth could not chew it. In reply to the bitter, though just, reproaches of her master, Marfa Ignatievna objected that the chicken was a very old one to begin with, and that she had never been to cooking school. Towards evening another care cropped up: it was reported to Fyodor Pavlovich that Grigory, who had fallen ill two days before, was now almost completely bedridden with his lower back out. Fyodor Pavlovich finished tea as early as possible and locked himself up alone in the house. He was in terrible and anxious expectation. It so happened that he expected Grushenka's arrival almost certainly that very evening; at least he had gotten from Smerdyakov, still early that morning, almost an assurance that "she has now undoubtedly promised to arrive, sir." The irrepressible old man's heart was beating anxiously; he paced his empty rooms and listened. He had to be on the alert: Dmitri Fyodorovich could be watching out for her somewhere, and when she knocked at the window (Smerdyakov had assured Fyodor Pavlovich two days before that he had told her where and how to knock), he would have to open the door as quickly as possible and by no means keep her waiting in the entryway even for a second, or else, God forbid, she might become frightened and run away. It was bothersome for Fyodor Pavlovich, but never had his heart bathed in sweeter hopes: for it was possible to say almost for certain that this time she would surely come . . . !

BOOK VI: THE RUSSIAN MONK

Chapter 1

The Elder Zosima and His Visitors

When Alyosha, with anxiety and pain in his heart, entered the elder's cell, he stopped almost in amazement: instead of a dying sick man, perhaps already unconscious, as he had feared to find him, he suddenly saw him sitting in an armchair, his face, though worn out from weakness, cheerful and gay, surrounded by visitors and engaging with them in quiet and bright conversation. However, he had gotten up from bed not more than a quarter of an hour before Alyosha arrived; his visitors had gathered in his cell earlier and waited for him to wake, trusting in the firm assurance of Father Paissy that "the teacher will undoubtedly get up, in order to converse once more with those dear to his heart, as he himself said, and as he himself promised in the morning." Father Paissy believed firmly in this promise, and in every word of the departing elder, so much so that if he had seen him already quite unconscious and even no longer breathing, but had his promise that he would arise once more and say farewell to him, he would perhaps not have believed even death itself and would have kept expecting the dying man to come to and fulfill what had been promised. And that morning, as he was falling asleep, the elder Zosima had said positively to him: "I shall not die before I have once more drunk deeply of conversation with you, beloved of my heart, before I have looked upon your dear faces and poured out my soul to you once more." Those who gathered for this, probably the last of the elder's talks, were his most faithful friends from long ago. There were four of them: the hieromonks Father Iosif and Father Paissy, the hieromonk Father Mikhail, superior of the hermitage, not yet a very old man, far from very learned, of humble origin, but firm in spirit, with inviolable and simple faith, of stern appearance, but pervaded by a deep tenderness of heart, though he obviously concealed his tenderness even to the point of some sort of shame. The fourth visitor was quite old, a simple little monk from the poorest peasantry, Brother Anfim, all but illiterate, quiet and taciturn, rarely speaking to anyone, the humblest of the humble, who had the look of a man who has been permanently frightened by something great and awesome that was more than his mind could sustain. The elder Zosima very much loved this, as it were, trembling man, and throughout his life treated him with unusual respect, though throughout his life he had perhaps said fewer words to him than to anyone else, despite the fact that he had once spent many years traveling with him all over holy Russia. That was now very long ago, about forty years before, when the elder Zosima first began his monastic effort in a poor, little-known monastery in Kostroma, and when, soon after that, he went to accompany Father Anfim on his journeys collecting donations for their poor Kostroma monastery. Host and visitors all settled in the elder's second room, where his bed stood, a very small room, as was pointed out earlier, so that the four of them (not counting the novice Porfiry, who remained standing) had barely enough room to place themselves around the elder's armchair on chairs brought from the first room. Dusk was falling; the room was lighted by oil-lamps and wax candles before the icons. When he saw Alyosha, who became embarrassed as he entered and stopped in the doorway, the elder joyfully smiled to him and held out his hand:

"Greetings, my quiet one, greetings, my dear, so you've come. I knew you would come."

Alyosha went up to him, prostrated before him, and began to weep. Something was bursting from his heart, his soul was trembling, he wanted to sob.

"Come now, don't weep over me yet," smiled the elder, laying his right hand on his head, "you see, I am sitting and talking, perhaps I'll live twenty years more, as that woman wished me yesterday, that kind, dear woman from Vyshegorye, with the girl Lizaveta in her arms. Remember, O Lord, both the mother and the girl Lizaveta!" He crossed himself. "Porfiry, did you take her offering where I told you?"

He was remembering the sixty kopecks donated by the cheerful worshipper the day before, to be given "to someone poorer than I am." Such offerings are made as a penance, taken upon oneself voluntarily for one reason or another, and always from money gained by one's own labor. That same evening the elder had sent Porfiry to one of our townspeople, a widow with several children, who had recently lost everything in a fire and afterwards went begging. Porfiry hastened to report that it had been done, and that he had given the money, as he was instructed, "from an unknown benefactress."

"Stand up, my dear," the elder continued to Alyosha, "let me look at you. Have you been with your people, did you see your brother?"

It seemed strange to Alyosha that he should ask so firmly and precisely about just one of his brothers—but which one? Perhaps it was for that same brother that he had sent him away both yesterday and today.

"I saw one of my brothers," Alyosha replied.

"I mean the one from yesterday, the older one, before whom I bowed to the ground."

"I saw him only yesterday; today I simply couldn't find him," said Alyosha.

"Make haste and find him, go again tomorrow and make haste, leave everything and make haste. Perhaps you'll still be able to prevent something terrible. I bowed yesterday to his great future suffering."

He suddenly fell silent and seemed to lapse into thought. His words were strange. Father Iosif, a witness to the elder's bow the day before, exchanged glances with Father Paissy. Alyosha could not help himself:

"Father and teacher," he spoke in great excitement, "your words are too vague . . . What is this suffering that awaits him?"

"Do not be curious. Yesterday I seemed to see something terrible . . . as if his eyes yesterday expressed his whole fate. He had a certain look . . . so that I was immediately horrified in my heart at what this man was preparing for himself. Once or twice in my life I've seen people with the same expression in their faces . . . as if it portrayed the whole fate of the person, and that fate, alas, came about. I sent you to him, Alexei, because I thought your brotherly countenance would help him. But everything is from the Lord, and all our fates as well. 'Except a corn of wheat fall into the ground and die, it abideth alone: but if it die, it bringeth forth much fruit.' Remember that. And you, Alexei, I have blessed in my thoughts many times in my life for your face, know that," the elder said with a quiet smile. "Thus I think of you: you will go forth from these walls, but you will sojourn in the world like a monk. You will have many opponents, but your very enemies will love you. Life will bring you many misfortunes, but through them you will be happy, and you will bless life and cause others to bless it—which is the most important thing. That is how you are. My fathers and teachers," he turned to his visitors with a tender smile, "till this day I have never said even to him why the face of this youth is so dear to my soul. Only now do I say: his face has been, as it were, a reminder and a prophecy for me. At the dawn of my days, when still a little child, I had an older brother who died in his youth, before my eyes, being only seventeen years old. And later, making my way through life, I gradually came to see that this brother was, as it were, a pointer and a destination from above in my fate, for if he had not appeared in my life, if he had not been at all, then never, perhaps, as I think, would I have entered monastic orders and set out upon this precious path. That first appearance was still in my childhood, and now, on the decline of my path, a repetition of him, as it were, appeared before my eyes. It is a wonder, fathers and teachers, that while he does not resemble him very much in appearance, but only slightly, Alexei seemed to me to resemble him so much spiritually that many times I have actually taken him, as it were, for that youth, my brother, come to me mysteriously at the end of my way, for a certain remembrance and perception, so that I was even surprised at myself and this strange fancy of mine. Do you hear, Porfiry?" he turned to the novice who served him. "Many times I have seen you look distressed, as it were, that I should love Alexei more than you. Now you know why it was so, but I love you, too, know that, and I have grieved many times at your distress. And to you, my dear visitors, I wish to speak of this youth, my brother, for there has been no appearance in my life more precious than this one, more prophetic and moving. My heart feels tender, and at this moment I am contemplating my whole life as if I were living it all anew . . ."

Here I must note that this last talk of the elder with those who visited him on the last day of his life has been partly preserved in writing. Alexei Fyodorovich Karamazov wrote it down from memory some time after the elder's death. But whether it was just that conversation, or he added to it in his notes from former conversations with his teacher as well, I cannot determine. Besides, in these notes the whole speech of the elder goes on continuously, as it were, as if he were recounting his life in the form of a narrative, addressing his friends, whereas undoubtedly, according to later reports, it in fact went somewhat differently, for the conversation that evening was general, and though the visitors rarely interrupted their host, still they did speak for themselves, intervening in the talk, perhaps even imparting and telling something of their own; besides, there could hardly have been such continuity in the narration, because the elder sometimes became breathless, lost his voice, and even lay down on his bed to rest, though he did not fall asleep, and the visitors did not leave their places. Once or twice the conversation was interrupted by readings from the Gospel, Father Paissy doing the reading. It is also remarkable, however, that not one of them supposed he would die that same night, the less so as on this last evening of his life, after a day of sound sleep, he suddenly seemed to have found new strength in himself, which sustained him through all this long conversation with his friends. It was as though a last loving effort sustained this incredible animation in him, but only for a short time, for his life ceased suddenly . . . But of that later. At this point I want to make clear that I have preferred, rather than recounting all the details of the conversation, to limit myself to the elder's story according to the manuscript of Alexei Fyodorovich Karamazov. It will be shorter and not so tedious, though, of course, I repeat, Alyosha also took much from previous conversations and put it all together.

Chapter 2

From the Life of the Hieromonk and Elder Zosima, Departed in God, Composed from His Own Words by Alexei Fyodorovich Karamazov

BIOGRAPHICAL INFORMATION

(a) Of the Elder Zosima's Young Brother

Beloved fathers and teachers, I was born in a remote northern province, in the town of V——, of a noble father, but not of the high nobility, and not of very high rank. He died when I was only two years old, and I do not remember him at all. He left my mother a small wooden house and some capital, not a big sum, but enough to keep her and her children without want. And mother had only the two of us: myself, Zinovy, and my older brother, Markel. He was about eight years older than I, hot-tempered and irritable by nature, but kind, not given to mockery, and strangely silent, especially at home with me, mother, and the servants. He was a good student, but did not make friends with his schoolmates, though he did not quarrel with them either, at least not that our mother remembered. Half a year before his death, when he was already past seventeen, he took to visiting a certain solitary man of our town, a political exile it seems, exiled to our town from Moscow for freethinking. This exile was a great scholar and distinguished philosopher at the university. For some reason he came to love Markel and welcomed his visits. The young man spent whole evenings with him, and did so through the whole winter, until the exile was called back to government service in Petersburg, at his own request, for he had his protectors. The Great Lent came,[1] but Markel did not want to fast, swore and laughed at it: "It's all nonsense, there isn't any God," so that he horrified mother and the servants, and me, too, his little brother, for though I was only nine years old, when I heard those words I was very much afraid. Our servants were all serfs, four of them, all bought in the name of a landowner we knew. I also remember how mother sold one of the four, the cook Anfimia, who was lame and elderly, for sixty paper roubles, and hired a free woman in her place. And so, in the sixth week of Lent, my brother suddenly grew worse—he had always been unhealthy, with bad lungs, of weak constitution and inclined to consumption; he was tall, but thin and sickly, ye of quite pleasing countenance. Perhaps he had caught a cold or something, i any case the doctor came and soon whispered to mother that his consump tion was of the galloping sort, and that he would not live through spring Mother started weeping, she started asking my brother cautiously (more so a not to alarm him) to observe Lent and take communion of the divine and hol mysteries, because he was then still on his feet. Hearing that, he became angr and swore at God's Church, but still he grew thoughtful: he understood a once that he was dangerously ill, and that that was why his mother was urgin him, while he was still strong enough, to go to church and receive commu nion. Though he knew himself that he had been sick for a long time, and al ready a year before had once said coolly at the table, to mother and me: "I'r not long for this world among you, I may not live another year," and now i was as if he had foretold it. About three days went by, and then came Hol Week.[2] And on Tuesday morning my brother started keeping the fast an going to church. "I'm doing it only for your sake, mother, to give you joy an peace," he said to her. Mother wept from joy, and also from grief: "His en must be near, if there is suddenly such a change in him." But he did not go t church for long, he took to his bed, so that he had to confess and receive com munion at home. The days grew bright, clear, fragrant—Easter was late tha year. All night, I remember, he used to cough, slept badly, but in the mornin he would always get dressed and try to sit in an armchair. So I remember hir he sits, quiet and meek, he smiles, he is sick but his countenance is glad, joy ful. He was utterly changed in spirit—such a wondrous change had suddenl begun in him! Our old nanny would come into his room: "Dear, let me ligh the lamp in front of your icon." And before, he would never let her, he eve used to blow it out. "Light it, my dear, light it, what a monster I was to forbi you before! You pray to God as you light the icon lamp, and I pray, rejoicin at you. So we are praying to the same God." These words seemed strange to us and mother used to go to her room and weep, but when she went to him sh wiped her eyes and put on a cheerful face. "Mother, don't weep, my dear," h would say, "I still have a long time to live, a long time to rejoice with you, an life, life is gladsome, joyful!" "Ah, my dear, what sort of gladness is there fo you, if you burn with fever all night and cough as if your lungs were about t burst?" "Mama," he answered her, "do not weep, life is paradise, and we are al in paradise, but we do not want to know it, and if we did want to know it, to morrow there would be paradise the world over." And everyone marveled a his words, he spoke so strangely and so decisively; everyone was moved an wept. Acquaintances came to visit us: "My beloved," he would say, "my dea ones, how have I deserved your love, why do you love such a one as I, and hov is it that I did not know it, that I did not appreciate it before?" When the servants came in, he told them time and again: "My beloved, my dear ones, why do you serve me, am I worthy of being served? If God were to have mercy on me and let me live, I would begin serving you, for we must all serve each other." Mother listened and shook her head: "My dear, it's your illness that makes you talk like that." "Mama, my joy," he said, "it is not possible for there to be no masters and servants, but let me also be the servant of my servants, the same as they are to me. And I shall also tell you, dear mother, that each of us is guilty in everything before everyone, and I most of all." At that mother even smiled, she wept and smiled: "How can it be," she said, "that you are the most guilty before everyone? There are murderers and robbers, and how have you managed to sin so that you should accuse yourself most of all?" "Dear mother, heart of my heart," he said (he had then begun saying such unexpected, endearing words), "heart of my heart, my joyful one, you must know that verily each of us is guilty before everyone, for everyone and everything. I do not know how to explain it to you, but I feel it so strongly that it pains me. And how could we have lived before, getting angry, and not knowing anything?" Thus he awoke every day with more and more tenderness, rejoicing and all atremble with love. The doctor would come—the old German Eisenschmidt used to come to us: "Well, what do you think, doctor, shall I live one more day in the world?" he would joke with him. "Not just one day, you will live many days," the doctor would answer, "you will live months and years, too." "But what are years, what are months!" he would exclaim. "Why count the days, when even one day is enough for a man to know all happiness. My dears, why do we quarrel, boast before each other, remember each other's offenses? Let us go to the garden, let us walk and play and love and praise and kiss each other, and bless our life." "He's not long for this world, your son," the doctor said to mother as she saw him to the porch, "from sickness he is falling into madness." The windows of his room looked onto the garden, and our garden was very shady, with old trees, the spring buds were already swelling on the branches, the early birds arrived, chattering, singing through his windows. And suddenly, looking at them and admiring them, he began to ask their forgiveness, too: "Birds of God, joyful birds, you, too, must forgive me, because I have also sinned before you." None of us could understand it then, but he was weeping with joy: "Yes," he said, "there was so much of God's glory around me: birds, trees, meadows, sky, and I alone lived in shame, I alone dishonored everything, and did not notice the beauty and glory of it at all." "You take too many sins upon yourself," mother used to weep. "Dear mother, my joy, I am weeping from gladness, not from grief; I want to be guilty before them, only I cannot explain it to you, for I do not even know how to love them.

Let me be sinful before everyone, but so that everyone will forgive me, and that is paradise. Am I not in paradise now?"

And there was much more that I cannot recall or set down. I remember once I came into his room alone, when no one was with him. It was a bright evening, the sun was setting and lit up the whole room with its slanting rays. He beckoned when he saw me, I went over to him, he took me by the shoulders with both hands, looked tenderly, lovingly into my face; he did not say anything, he simply looked at me like that for about a minute: "Well," he said, "go now, play, live for me!" I walked out then and went to play. And later in life I remembered many times, with tears now, how he told me to live for him. He spoke many more such wondrous and beautiful words, though we could not understand them then. He died in the third week after Easter, conscious, and though he had already stopped speaking, he did not change to his very last hour: he looked joyfully, with gladness in his eyes, seeking us with his eyes, smiling to us, calling us. There was much talk even in town about his end. It all shook me then, but not deeply, though I cried very much when he was being buried. I was young, a child, but it all remained indelibly in my heart, the feeling was hidden there. It all had to rise up and respond in due time. And so it did.

(b) Of Holy Scripture in the Life of Father Zosima

We were left alone then, mother and I. Soon some good acquaintances advised her: look, you have only one boy left, and you are not poor, you have money, so why don't you send your son to Petersburg, as others do, for staying here you may be depriving him of a distinguished future. And they put it into my mother's head to take me to Petersburg to the Cadet Corps, so that later I could enter the Imperial Guard. Mother hesitated a long time: how could she part with her last son? But nevertheless she made up her mind to it, though not without many tears, thinking it would contribute to my happiness. She took me to Petersburg and had me enrolled, and after that I never saw her again; for she died three years later, and during all those three years she grieved and trembled over us both. From my parental home I brought only precious memories, for no memories are more precious to a man than those of his earliest childhood in his parental home, and that is almost always so, a long as there is even a little bit of love and unity in the family. But from a very bad family, too, one can keep precious memories, if only one's soul know how to seek out what is precious. With my memories of home I count also m memories of sacred history, which I, though only a child in my parenta home, was very curious to know. I had a book of sacred history then, with beautiful pictures, entitled *One Hundred and Four Sacred Stories from the Old and New Testaments*, and I was learning to read with it.[3] It is still lying here on my shelf, I keep it as a precious reminder. But I remember how, even before I learned to read, a certain spiritual perception visited me for the first time, when I was just eight years old. Mother took me to church by myself (I do not remember where my brother was then), during Holy Week, to the Monday liturgy. It was a clear day, and, remembering it now, I seem to see again the incense rising from the censer and quietly ascending upwards, and from above, through a narrow window in the cupola, God's rays pouring down upon us in the church, and the incense rising up to them in waves, as if dissolving into them. I looked with deep tenderness, and for the first time in my life I consciously received the first seed of the word of God in my soul. A young man walked out into the middle of the church with a big book, so big that it seemed to me he even had difficulty carrying it, and he placed it on the analogion,[4] opened it, and began to read, and suddenly, then, for the first time I understood something, for the first time in my life I understood what was read in God's church. There was a man in the land of Uz,[5] rightful and pious, and he had so much wealth, so many camels, so many sheep and asses, and his children made merry, and he loved them very much and beseeched God for them: for it may be that they have sinned in their merrymaking. Now Satan goes up before God together with the sons of God, and says to the Lord that he has walked all over the earth and under the earth. "And have you seen my servant Job?" God asks him. And God boasted before Satan, pointing to his great and holy servant. And Satan smiled at God's words: "Hand him over to me and you shall see that your servant will begin to murmur and will curse your name." And God handed over his righteous man, whom he loved so, to Satan, and Satan smote his children and his cattle, and scattered his wealth, all suddenly, as if with divine lightning, and Job rent his garments and threw himself to the ground and cried out: "Naked came I out of my mother's womb, and naked shall I return into the earth: the Lord gave and the Lord has taken away: blessed be the name of the Lord henceforth and forevermore!"[6] Fathers and teachers, bear with these tears of mine—for it is as if my whole childhood were rising again before me, and I am breathing now as I breathed then with my eight-year-old little breast, and feel, as I did then, astonishment, confusion, and joy. And the camels, which then so took my fancy, and Satan, who spoke thus with God, and God, who gave his servant over to ruin, and his servant crying out: "Blessed be thy name, albeit thou chastise me"—and then the soft and sweet singing in the church: "Let my prayer arise . . . ," and again the incense from the priest's censer, and the kneeling prayer![7] Since then—even just yesterday I turned to it—I cannot read this most holy story without tears.

And so much in it is great, mysterious, inconceivable! Later I heard the word of the scoffers and blasphemers, proud words: how could the Lord hand ove the most beloved of his saints for Satan to play with him, to take away his chil dren, to smite him with disease and sores so that he scraped the pus from hi wounds with a potsherd, and all for what? Only so as to boast before Satan "See what my saint can suffer for my sake!" But what is great here is this ver mystery—that the passing earthly image and eternal truth here touched eac other. In the face of earthly truth, the enacting of eternal truth is accom plished. Here the Creator, as in the first days of creation, crowning each da with praise: "That which I have created is good," looks at Job and again praise his creation. And Job, praising God, does not only serve him, but will als serve his whole creation, from generation to generation and unto ages o ages,[8] for to this he was destined. Lord, what a book, what lessons! What book is the Holy Scripture, what miracle, what power are given to man wit it! Like a carven image of the world, and of man, and of human characters and everything is named and set forth unto ages of ages. And so many mys teries resolved and revealed: God restores Job again, gives him wealth anew once more many years pass, and he has new children, different ones, and h loves them—Oh, Lord, one thinks, "but how could he so love those nev ones, when his former children are no more, when he has lost them? Remem bering them, was it possible for him to be fully happy, as he had been before with the new ones, however dear they might be to him?" But it is possible, i is possible: the old grief, by a great mystery of human life, gradually passe into quiet, tender joy; instead of young, ebullient blood comes a mild, seren old age: I bless the sun's rising each day and my heart sings to it as before, bu now I love its setting even more, its long slanting rays, and with them quiet mild, tender memories, dear images from the whole of a long and blesse life—and over all is God's truth, moving, reconciling, all-forgiving! My life i coming to an end, I know and sense it, but I feel with every day that is left m how my earthly life is already touching a new, infinite, unknown, but swift approaching life, anticipating which my soul trembles with rapture, my min is radiant, and my heart weeps joyfully . . . Friends and teachers, I hav heard more than once, and it has become even louder in recent days, that ou priests of God, the village priests most of all, are complaining tearfully an everywhere at their poor pay and their humiliation, and assert directly, eve in print—I have read it myself—that they are now supposedly unable to ex pound the Scriptures for people because of their poor pay, and if Lutheran and heretics come now and begin to steal away their flock, let them steal i away, because, they say, we are so poorly paid. Lord! I say to myself, may Go give them more of this pay that is so precious to them (for their complaint i just, too), but truly I tell you: half the blame is ours, if it is anyone's. For even if he has no time, even if he says rightly that he is oppressed all the time by work and church services,[9] still it is not quite all the time, still he does have at least one hour out of the whole week when he can remember God. And the work is not year-round. If at first he were to gather just the children in his house, once a week, in the evening, the fathers would hear about it and begin to come. Oh, there's no need to build a mansion for such a purpose, you can receive them simply in your cottage; do not fear, they will not dirty your cottage, you will have them only for an hour. Were he to open this book and begin reading without clever words and without pretension, without putting himself above them, but tenderly and meekly, rejoicing that you are reading to them, and that they are listening to you and understand you; loving these words yourself, and only stopping every once in a while to explain some word that a simple person would not understand—do not worry, they will understand everything, the Orthodox heart will understand everything! Read to them of Abraham and Sarah, of Isaac and Rebecca, of how Jacob went to Laban, and wrestled with the Lord in his dream, and said, "How dreadful is this place!"[10]—and you will strike the pious mind of the simple man. Read to them, and especially to the children, of how certain brothers sold their own brother into slavery, the dear youth Joseph,[11] a dreamer and a great prophet, and told their father that a wild beast had torn him, showing him his bloodstained garments. Read how afterwards the brothers went to Egypt for bread, and Joseph, now a great courtier, unrecognized by them, tormented them, accused them, seized his brother Benjamin, and all the while loving them: "I love you, and loving you, I torment you." For all his life he constantly remembered how they had sold him to the merchants, somewhere in the hot steppe, by a well, and how he, wringing his hands, had wept and begged his brothers not to sell him into slavery in a strange land, and now, seeing them after so many years, he again loved them beyond measure, but oppressed and tormented them even as he loved them. Finally, unable to bear the torment of his own heart, he goes away, throws himself on his bed, and weeps; then he wipes his face and comes back bright and shining, and announces to them: "Brothers, I am Joseph, your brother!" Let him read further how the aged Jacob rejoiced when he learned that his dear boy was still alive, and went down into Egypt, even abandoning the land of his fathers, and died in a strange land, having uttered unto ages of ages in his testament the great word that dwelt mysteriously in his meek and timorous heart all his life, that from his descendants, from Judah, would come the great hope of the world, its reconciler and savior![12] Fathers and teachers, forgive me and do not be angry that I am talking like a little child of what you have long known, which you could teach me a hundred times more artfully and graciously. I am only speaking from rapture, and forgive my tears, for I love this book! Let him, the priest of God, weep too, and he will see how the hearts of his listeners will be shaken in response to him. Only a little, a tiny seed is needed: let him cast it into the soul of a simple man, and it will not die, it will live in his soul all his life, hiding there amidst the darkness, amidst the stench of his sins, as a bright point, as a great reminder. And there is no need, no need of much explaining and teaching, he will understand everything simply. Do you think that a simple man will not understand? Try reading to him, further, the touching and moving story of beautiful Esther and the arrogant Vashti; or the wondrous tale of the prophet Jonah in the belly of the whale. Nor should you forget the parables of the Lord, chosen mainly from the Gospel of Luke (that is what I did), and then Saul's speech from the Acts of the Apostles (that is a must, a must),[13] and finally also from the Lives of the Saints, at least the life of Alexei, the man of God,[14] and of the greatest of the great, the joyful sufferer, God-seer, and Christ-bearer, our mother Mary of Egypt[15]—and you will pierce his heart with these simple tales, and it will only take an hour a week, notwithstanding his poor pay, just one hour. And he will see that our people are merciful and grateful and will repay him a hundredfold; remembering the priest's zeal and his tender words, they will volunteer to help with his work, and in his house, and will reward him with more respect than before—and thus his pay will be increased. It is such a simple matter that sometimes we are even afraid to say it for fear of being laughed at, and yet how right it is! Whoever does not believe in God will not believe in the people of God. But he who believes in the people of God will also see their holiness, even if he did not believe in it at all before. Only the people and their future spiritual power will convert our atheists, who have severed themselves from their own land. And what is the word of Christ without an example? The people will perish without the word of God, for their souls thirst for his word and for every beautiful perception. In my youth, way back, almost forty years ago, Father Anfim and I walked all over Russia collecting alms for our monastery, and once spent the night by a big, navigable river, on the bank, with some fishermen, and we were joined by a comely young man, who appeared to be about eighteen years old; he was hurrying to get to his workplace the next day, where he pulled a merchant's barge with a rope. I saw with what a tender and clear gaze he looked before him. It was a bright, still, warm July night, the river was wide, a refreshing mist rose from it, once in a while a fish would splash softly, the birds fell silent, all was quiet, gracious, all praying to God. And only the two of us, myself and this young man, were still awake, and we got to talking about the beauty of this world of God's, and about its great mystery. For each blade of grass, each little bug, ant, golden bee, knows its way amazingly; being without reason, they witness to the divine mystery, they ceaselessly enact it. And I could see that the good lad's heart was burning. He told me how he loved the forest and the forest birds; he was a birdcatcher, he knew their every call, and could lure any bird; "I don't know of anything better than the forest," he said, "though all things are good." "Truly," I answered him, "all things are good and splendid, because all is truth. Look at the horse," I said to him, "that great animal that stands so close to man, or the ox, that nourishes him and works for him, so downcast and pensive, look at their faces: what meekness, what affection for man, who often beats them mercilessly, what mildness, what trustfulness, and what beauty are in that face. It is even touching to know that there is no sin upon them, for everything is perfect, everything except man is sinless, and Christ is with them even before us." "But can it be that they, too, have Christ?" the lad asked. "How could it be otherwise," I said to him, "for the Word is for all, all creation and all creatures, every little leaf is striving towards the Word, sings glory to God, weeps to Christ, unbeknownst to itself, doing so through the mystery of its sinless life. There, in the forest," I said to him, "the fearsome bear wanders, terrible and ferocious, and not at all guilty for that." And I told him of how a bear had once come to a great saint, who was saving his soul in the forest, in a little cell, and the great saint felt tenderness for him, fearlessly went out to him and gave him a piece of bread, as if to say: "Go, and Christ be with you." And the fierce beast went away obediently and meekly without doing any harm.[16] The lad was moved that the bear had gone away without doing any harm, and that Christ was with him, too. "Ah," he said, "how good it is, how good and wonderful is all that is God's!" He sat deep in thought, quietly and sweetly. I could see that he understood. And he fell into an easy, sinless sleep beside me. God bless youth! And I prayed for him before going to sleep myself. Lord, send peace and light to thy people!

(c) Recollections of the Adolescence and Youth of the Elder Zosima While Still in the World. The Duel

I was in the Cadet Corps in Petersburg for a long time, almost eight years, and with my new education I stifled many of my childhood impressions, though I did not forget anything. Instead I took up so many new habits and even opinions that I transformed into an almost wild, cruel, and absurd creature. I acquired the polish of courtesy and worldly manners, together with the French language, but we all regarded the soldiers who served us in the Corps as perfect brutes, and I did the same. I most of all, perhaps, because of all my comrades I was the most susceptible to everything. When we graduated as officers, we were ready to shed our blood for the injured honor of our regiment, but hardly one of us knew what real honor is, and if anyone had found out, he would have been the first to laugh at it at once. We were all but proud of our drunkenness, debauchery, and bravado. I would not say we were wicked; they were all good young men, but they behaved wickedly, and I most of all. The chief thing was that I had come into my own money, and with that I threw myself into a life of pleasure, with all the impetuousness of youth, without restraint, under full sail. The wonder is that I also read books then, and even with great pleasure; the one book I almost never opened at that time was the Bible; though I never parted with it either, but carried it everywhere with me; I truly kept this book, without knowing it myself, "for the day and the hour, and the month and the year."[17] Having thus been in the service for about four years, I eventually found myself in the town of K——, where our regiment was stationed at the time. The local society was diverse, numerous, and fun-loving, hospitable and wealthy, and I was well received everywhere, for I was always of a fun-loving nature, and had the reputation, besides, of being far from poor, which is not unimportant in society. And then a circumstance occurred that was the start of everything. I formed an attachment to a young and wonderful girl, intelligent and worthy, of noble and shining character, the daughter of reputable parents. They were people of high standing, wealthy, influential, powerful, and they received me with affection and cordiality. And so I fancied that the girl favored me in her heart—my own heart was set aflame by this dream. Later I perceived and realized fully that I was perhaps not so greatly in love with her at all, but simply respected her intelligence and lofty character, as one could not fail to do. Selfishness, however, prevented me from offering her my hand at the time: it seemed a hard and fearful thing to part with the temptations of a depraved and free bachelor's life at such an early age, and with money in my pocket besides. Yet I did drop some hints. In all events, I postponed any decisive step for a short while. Then suddenly I happened to be ordered to another district for two months. I came back two months later and suddenly discovered that the girl had already married a local landowner, a wealthy man, older than I but still young, who had connections in the capital and with the best society, which I did not have, a very amiable man, and, moreover, an educated one, while, as for education, I had none at all. I was so struck by this unexpected event that my mind even became clouded. And the chief thing was, as I learned only then, that this young landowner had long been her fiancé, and that I myself had met him many times in their house but had noticed nothing, being blinded by my own merits. And that was what offended me most of all: how was it possible that almost everyone knew, and I alone knew nothing? And suddenly I felt an unbearable anger. Red-faced, I began to recall how many times I had almost declared my love to her, and as she had not stopped me or warned me then, I therefore concluded that she had been laughing at me. Later, of course, I realized and remembered that she had not been laughing in the least, but, on the contrary, had broken off such conversations with a jest and turned to other topics instead—but at the time I could not realize that and began to burn with revenge. I am astonished to recall how extremely heavy and loathsome this revenge and wrath were for me, because, having an easy character, I could not stay angry with anyone for long, and therefore had to incite myself artificially, as it were, and in the end became ugly and absurd. I waited for the right moment, and once at a big gathering I suddenly managed to insult my "rival," seemingly for a quite unrelated reason, jeering at his opinion about an important event of that time—it was 1826[18]—and I managed, so people said, to do it wittily and cleverly. After which I forced him to a talk, and in that talk treated him so rudely that he accepted my challenge despite the enormous differences between us, for I was younger than he, insignificant, and of low rank. Afterwards I learned with certainty that he had accepted my challenge also from a feeling of jealousy, as it were: he had been a little jealous of me on account of his wife even before, when she was still his fiancée, and now he thought that if she learned he had suffered an insult from me and had not dared to challenge me, she might unwillingly despise him and her love might be shaken. I quickly found a second, a comrade of mine, a lieutenant in our regiment. At that time, though duels were strictly forbidden, there was even a fashion for them, as it were, among the military—thus do barbaric prejudices sometimes spring up and thrive. It was the end of June, and our meeting was appointed for the next day, outside town, at seven o'clock in the morning—and here truly something fateful, as it were, happened to me. Having returned home in the evening, ferocious and ugly, I got angry with my orderly Afanasy and struck him twice in the face with all my might, so that his face was all bloody. He had not been long in my service, and I had had occasion to strike him before, yet never with such beastly cruelty. And believe me, my dears, though it was forty years ago, I still remember it with shame and anguish. I went to bed, slept for about three hours, woke up, day was breaking. Suddenly I got up, I did not want to sleep any longer, I went to the window, opened it, it looked onto the garden—I watched the sun rising, the weather was warm, beautiful, the birds began to chime. Why is it, I thought, that I feel something, as it were, mean and shameful in my soul? Is it because I am going to shed blood? No, I thought, it doesn't seem to be that. Is it because I am afraid of death, afraid to be killed? No, not that, not that at all . . . And suddenly I understood at once what it was: it was because I had beaten Afanasy the night before! I suddenly pictured it all as if it were happening over again. he is standing before me, and I strike him in the face with all my might, and he keeps his arms at his sides, head erect, eyes staring straight ahead as if he were at attention; he winces at each blow, and does not even dare raise a hand to shield himself—this is what a man can be brought to, a man beating his fellow man! What a crime! It was as if a sharp needle went through my soul. I stood as if dazed, and the sun was shining, the leaves were rejoicing, glistening, and the birds, the birds were praising God . . . I covered my face with my hands, fell on my bed, and burst into sobs. And then I remembered my brother Markel, and his words to the servants before his death: "My good ones, my dears, why are you serving me, why do you love me, and am I worthy of being served?" "Yes, am I worthy?" suddenly leaped into my mind. Indeed, how did I deserve that another man, just like me, the image and likeness of God, should serve me? This question then pierced my mind for the first time in my life. "Mother, heart of my heart, truly each of us is guilty before everyone and for everyone, only people do not know it, and if they knew it, the world would at once become paradise." "Lord," I wept and thought, "can that possibly not be true? Indeed, I am perhaps the most guilty of all, and the worst of all men in the world as well!" And suddenly the whole truth appeared to me in its full enlightenment: what was I setting out to do? I was setting out to kill a kind, intelligent, noble man, who was not at fault before me in any way, thereby depriving his wife of happiness forever, tormenting and killing her. I lay there flat on my bed, my face pressed into the pillow, not noticing how the time passed. Suddenly my comrade, the lieutenant, came in with the pistols to fetch me: "Ah," he said, "it's good you're up already, let's be off, it's time." I began rushing about, quite at a loss, but still we went out to the carriage. "Wait a bit," I said to him, "I must run back in for a moment, I've forgotten my purse." I ran back into the house alone, straight to Afanasy's room: "Afanasy," I said, "yesterday I struck you twice in the face. Forgive me," I said. He started as if he were afraid, and I saw that it was not enough, not enough; and suddenly, just as I was, epaulettes and all, I threw myself at his feet with my forehead to the ground: "Forgive me!" I said. At that he was completely astounded: "Your honor, my dear master, but how can you . . . I'm not worthy . . . ," and he suddenly began weeping himself, just as I had done shortly before, covered his face with both hands, turned to the window, and began shaking all over with tears. And I ran back out to my comrade, jumped into the carriage, and shouted: "Drive!" "Have you ever seen a winner?" I cried to him. "Here is one, right in front of you!" Such rapture was in me, I was laughing, talking, talking all the way, I don't remember what I was talking about. He looked at me: "Hey, you're a good man, brother, I can see you won't dishonor the regiment." So we came to the place, and they were already there waiting for us. They set us twelve paces apart, the first shot was his—I stood cheerfully before him, face to face, without batting an eye, looking at him lovingly, because I knew what I was going to do. He fired. The shot just grazed my cheek a little, and nicked my ear. "Thank God," I shouted, "you didn't kill a man!" And I seized my pistol, turned around, and sent it hurtling up into the trees: "That's where you belong!" I shouted. I turned to my adversary: "My dear sir," I said, "forgive a foolish young man, for it is my own fault that I offended you and have now made you shoot at me. I am ten times worse than you, if not more. Tell that to the person you honor most in the world." As soon as I said it, all three of them started yelling at me: "I beg your pardon," my adversary said, even getting angry, "if you did not want to fight, why did you trouble me?" "Yesterday I was still a fool, but today I've grown wiser," I answered him cheerfully. "As for yesterday, I believe you," he said, "but about today, from your opinion, it is hard to believe you." "Bravo," I cried to him, clapping my hands, "I agree with that, too, I deserved it!" "My dear sir, will you shoot or not?" "I will not, and you may shoot again if you wish, only it would be better if you didn't." The seconds were also shouting, especially mine: "What? Disgracing the regiment? Asking forgiveness in the middle of a duel? If only I'd known!" Then I stood before them all, no longer laughing: "My gentlemen," I said, "is it so surprising now, in our time, to meet a man who has repented of his foolishness and confesses his guilt publicly?" "But not in the middle of a duel!" my second shouted again. "But that's just it," I replied, "that is just what is so surprising, because I ought to have confessed as soon as we arrived here, even before his shot, without leading him into great and mortal sin, but we have arranged everything in the world so repugnantly that to do so was nearly impossible, for only now that I have stood up to his shot from twelve paces can my words mean something for him, but had I done it before his shot, as soon as we arrived, then people would simply say: he's a coward, he's afraid of a pistol, there's no point in listening to him. Gentlemen," I cried suddenly from the bottom of my heart, "look at the divine gifts around us: the clear sky, the fresh air, the tender grass, the birds, nature is beautiful and sinless, and we, we alone, are godless and foolish, and do not understand that life is paradise, for we need only wish to understand, and it will come at once in all its beauty, and we shall embrace each other and weep . . . " I wanted to go on but I could not, so much sweetness, so much youngness even took my breath away, and in my heart there was such happiness as I had never felt before in all my life. "That is all very sensible and pious," my adversary said to me, "and you're an original man, in any case." "Laugh," I said to him, laughing myself, "but later you will praise me." "But,"

he said, "I am ready to praise you even now. I will give you my hand, if yo
wish, for it seems you are indeed a sincere man." "No," I said, "not now, b
later when I've become better and deserve your respect, then give me you
hand and you will do well." We returned home, my second scolding me all th
way, while I kept kissing him. My comrades all heard about it at once and m
to pass judgment on me that same day: "He has dishonored the regiment
they said, "he must resign his commission." I had my defenders as well: "H
did stand up to the shot," they said. "Yes, but he was afraid of the other sho
and asked forgiveness in the middle of the duel." "But if he was afraid of th
other shots," my defenders objected, "he would have fired his own pistol firs
before asking forgiveness, but he threw it into the trees still loaded—n
there's something else here, something original." I listened and looked
them cheerfully. "My dearest friends and comrades," I said, "do not wor
about whether or not I should resign my commission, because I have alrea
done so, I turned in my papers today, at the office, this morning, and when m
discharge comes through, I shall go into a monastery at once, for that is wh
I resigned my commission." No sooner had I said this than all of them, to
man, burst out laughing: "But you should have told us so in the first place, th
explains everything, we can't pass judgment on a monk," they laughed, the
could not stop, yet they laughed not at all derisively, but tenderly, cheerful
they all loved me suddenly, even my most fervent accusers, and for the rest
that month, until my discharge came through, they kept making much of m
"Here comes our monk!" they would say. And each of them had a kind wo
for me, they tried to talk me out of it, they even pitied me: "What are you doi
to yourself?" "No," they would say, "he is brave, he stood up to the shot, ar
he could have fired his own pistol, but he had a dream the night before that h
should become a monk, that's why he did it." Almost exactly the same thin
happened with the local society. They had paid no particular attention to m
before, though they received me cordially, but now they suddenly found o
and began vying with each other to invite me: they laughed at me, and yet th
loved me. I will note here that though everyone was talking openly about o
duel, the authorities dismissed the case, because my adversary was a close re
ative of our general, and since the thing had ended bloodlessly, more like
joke, and, finally, as I had also resigned my commission, they chose to co
sider it indeed as a joke. And I then began to speak out quite fearlessly, despi
their laughter, for their laughter was kindly after all, not malicious. All the
conversations generally took place on social evenings, in the company of l
dies; it was the women who liked to listen to me then, and who made the m
listen. "But how is it possible that I am guilty for everyone," they would
laugh in my face, "well, for instance, can I be guilty for you?" "But how c

ɔu even understand it," I would answer, "if the whole world has long since ɔne off on a different path, and if we consider what is a veritable lie to be the uth, and demand the same lie from others? Here for once in my life I have :ted sincerely, and what then? I've become a sort of holy fool for you all, and ıough you've come to love me, you still laugh at me." "But how can we help ›ving someone like you?" the mistress of the house said to me, laughing, and ıere was a large crowd there. Suddenly I saw, standing up among the ladies, ıat same young woman over whom I had started the duel and whom until so :cently I had intended as my fiancée. And I had not noticed that she had just rived at the party. She stood up, came over to me, and held out her hand: ıllow me to tell you," she said, "that I will be the first not to laugh at you, and ıat, on the contrary, it is with tears that I thank you and declare my respect r you for what you did." Then her husband came over, and then suddenly eryone drifted towards me and all but kissed me. I was filled with joy, but ost of all I suddenly noticed one gentleman, an elderly man, who also came › to me, and whom I already knew by name, though I had not made his :quaintance and had never even exchanged a word with him until that ening.

(d) The Mysterious Visitor

e had been an official in our town for a long time, held a prominent position, ıs universally respected, wealthy, well known for his philanthropy, had do- :ted considerable sums for an almshouse and an orphanage, and besides at did many good deeds in private, without publicity, all of which became ıown later, after his death. He was about fifty years old and of almost stern pearance; he was taciturn; he had been married for no more than ten years a wife who was still young and who had borne him three still-small chil- en. And so I was sitting at home the next evening when suddenly my door ›ened and this very gentleman walked in.

It should be noted that I was no longer living in my old quarters then, but d moved, as soon as I turned in my resignation, to different rooms, rented t by the old widow of an official, and including her servant, for I had moved these lodgings for one reason only, that on the same day that I returned ›m the duel I had sent Afanasy back to his company, being ashamed to look n in the face after the way I had behaved with him that morning—so far is unprepared man of the world inclined to be ashamed even of the most :hteous act.

"For several days now," the gentleman said upon entering, "I have been lis- ıing to you in various houses with great curiosity, and wanted finally to

make your personal acquaintance, in order to talk with you in more detai
Can you do me such a great service, my dear sir?" "I can," I said, "with th
greatest pleasure, and I would even consider it a special honor." I said this
and yet I was almost frightened, so strong was the impression he made on m
that first time. For though people listened to me and were curious, no one ha
yet come up to me with such a serious and stern inner look. And this man ha
even come to my own rooms. He sat down. "I see there is great strength c
character in you," he went on, "for you were not afraid to serve the truth i
such an affair, though for the sake of your truth you risked suffering genera
contempt." "Your praise of me is perhaps rather exaggerated," I said to hin
"No, it is not exaggerated," he replied. "Believe me, to accomplish such an ac
is far more difficult than you think. As a matter of fact," he went on, "I wa
struck precisely by that, and because of that I have come to see you. Describ
for me, if you do not disdain my perhaps quite indecent curiosity, exactl
what you felt at that moment, when you decided to ask forgiveness during th
duel—can you remember? Do not regard my question as frivolous; on th
contrary, I have my own secret purpose in asking such a question, which
shall probably explain to you in the future, if God wills that we become mor
closely acquainted."

All the while he was speaking, I looked him straight in the face and suc
denly felt the greatest trust in him, and, besides that, an extraordinary cur
osity on my own part, for I sensed that he had some sort of special secret in h
soul.

"You ask exactly what I felt at that moment when I asked forgiveness of m
adversary," I replied, "but I had better tell you from the beginning what I hav
not yet told to anyone else," and I told him all that had happened betwee
Afanasy and me, and how I had bowed to the ground before him. "From th
you can see for yourself," I concluded, "that it was easier for me during th
duel, for I had already started at home, and once I set out on that path, the re
went not only without difficulty but even joyfully and happily."

He listened and looked kindly at me: "That is all extremely interesting," h
said. "I shall come and see you again and again." And after that he took to vi
iting me almost every evening. And we should have become very close frienc
if he had spoken to me about himself as well. But he said hardly a word abou
himself, but only kept asking me about myself. In spite of that, I came to lov
him very much, and trusted him completely with all my feelings, for
thought: why do I need his secrets, when I can see even without that that h
is a righteous man? Besides, he is such a serious man, and we are not the sam
age, yet he keeps coming to me and does not disdain my youth. And I learne
much that was useful from him, for he was a man of lofty mind. "That life

ıradise," he said to me suddenly, "I have been thinking about for a long ne"—and suddenly added, "that is all I think about." He looked at me, smilg. "I am convinced of it," he said, "more than you are; you shall find out why ter on." I listened and thought to myself: "Surely he wants to reveal someing to me." "Paradise," he said, "is hidden in each one of us, it is concealed thin me, too, right now, and if I wish, it will come for me in reality, tomorw even, and for the rest of my life." I looked at him: he was speaking with nderness and looking at me mysteriously, as if questioning me. "And," he ent on, "as for each man being guilty before all and for all, besides his own ıs, your reasoning about that is quite correct, and it is surprising that you uld suddenly embrace this thought so fully. And indeed it is true that when ople understand this thought, the Kingdom of Heaven will come to them, longer in a dream but in reality." "But when will this come true?" I exıimed to him ruefully. "And will it ever come true? Is it not just a dream?" h," he said, "now you do not believe it, you preach it and do not believe it urself. Know, then, that this dream, as you call it, will undoubtedly come ıe, believe it, though not now, for every action has its law. This is a matter the soul, a psychological matter. In order to make the world over anew, ople themselves must turn onto a different path psychically. Until one has deed become the brother of all, there will be no brotherhood. No science or f-interest will ever enable people to share their property and their rights ıong themselves without offense. Each will always think his share too ıall, and they will keep murmuring, they will envy and destroy one another. u ask when it will come true. It will come true, but first the period of human *lation* must conclude." "What isolation?" I asked him. "That which is now gning everywhere, especially in our age, but it is not all concluded yet, its m has not come. For everyone now strives most of all to separate his pern, wishing to experience the fullness of life within himself, and yet what mes of all his efforts is not the fullness of life but full suicide, for instead of fullness of self-definition, they fall into complete isolation. For all men in r age are separated into units, each seeks seclusion in his own hole, each thdraws from the others, hides himself, and hides what he has, and ends by shing himself away from people and pushing people away from himself. accumulates wealth in solitude, thinking: how strong, how secure I am w; and does not see, madman as he is, that the more he accumulates, the ore he sinks into suicidal impotence. For he is accustomed to relying only himself, he has separated his unit from the whole, he has accustomed his ıl to not believing in people's help, in people or in mankind, and now only mbles lest his money and his acquired privileges perish. Everywhere now human mind has begun laughably not to understand that a man's true security lies not in his own solitary effort, but in the general wholeness of h manity. But there must needs come a term to this horrible isolation, an everyone will all at once realize how unnaturally they have separated them selves one from another. Such will be the spirit of the time, and they will b astonished that they sat in darkness for so long, and did not see the light. The the sign of the Son of Man will appear in the heavens[19] . . . But until then w must keep hold of the banner, and every once in a while, if only individuall a man must suddenly set an example, and draw the soul from its isolation f an act of brotherly communion, though it be with the rank of holy fool. S that the great thought does not die . . ."

In such fervent and rapturous conversations we spent one evening aft another. I even abandoned society and began visiting people much less fr quently; besides, I was beginning to go out of fashion. I say that not in co demnation, for people went on loving me and receiving me cheerfully, b still one must admit that fashion is indeed the great queen of society. As f my mysterious visitor, I came finally to regard him with admiration, for, b sides enjoying his intelligence, I began to feel that he was nursing some sc of design in himself, and was perhaps preparing for a great deed. Perhaps h liked it, too, that I did not express any curiosity about his secret, and did n question him either directly or through hints. But at last I noticed that he hi self seemed to be longing to reveal something to me. In any case this becan quite apparent about a month after the start of his visits. "Do you know," h once asked me, "that there is great curiosity in town about the two of u People marvel that I come to see you so often; but let them marvel, for *so everything will be explained.*" Sometimes a great agitation suddenly came ov him, and on such occasions he almost always would get up and leave. An sometimes he would look at me long and piercingly, as it were—I wou think, "Now he is going to say something," but suddenly he would catch hi self and start talking about something familiar and ordinary. He also began complain frequently of headaches. And then one day, even quite unexpe edly, after talking long and fervently, I saw him suddenly grow pale, his fa became quite twisted, and he stared straight at me.

"What's the matter?" I said, "are you ill?"

He had been complaining precisely of a headache.

"I . . . do you know . . . I killed a person."

He said it and smiled, and his face was white as chalk. "Why is he smiling the thought suddenly pierced my heart even before I had understood an thing. I turned pale myself.

"What are you saying?" I cried to him.

"You see," he replied, still with a pale smile, "how much it cost me to say t rst word. Now I have said it, and, it seems, have set out on the path. I shall eep on."

For a while I did not believe him, nor did I believe him at once, but only af-r he had come to me for three days and told me everything in detail. I ought he was mad, but ended finally by being convinced clearly, to my great ief and astonishment. He had committed a great and terrible crime fourteen ars earlier, over a wealthy lady, young and beautiful, a landowner's widow, ho kept her own house in our town. Feeling great love for her, he made her declaration of his love, and tried to persuade her to marry him. But she had ready given her heart to another man, an officer of noble birth and high nk, who was then away on campaign, but whom she expected soon to re-rn to her. She rejected his proposal and asked him to stop visiting her. He d stop visiting her, but knowing the layout of her house, he came to her by ealth one night from the garden, over the roof, with great boldness, risking scovery. But, as so often happens, crimes committed with extraordinary ldness are more likely to succeed than any others. Having entered the attic rough a dormer window, he went down to her apartments by the little attic airway, knowing that, because of the servants' negligence, the door at the ot of the stairway was not always locked. He hoped for such carelessness is time, and was not disappointed. Stealing into her apartments, he made s way through the darkness to her bedroom, where an icon lamp was burn-g. Her two maids, as if on purpose, had gone secretly, without asking per-ssion, to a birthday party at a neighbor's house on the same street. The her menservants and maids slept in the servants' quarters or in the kitchen the ground floor. At the sight of the sleeping woman, passion flared up in m, and then his heart was seized by vengeful, jealous anger, and forgetting mself, like a drunk man, he went up to her and plunged a knife straight into r heart, so that she did not even cry out. Then, with infernal and criminal lculation, he arranged things so that the blame would fall on the servants: did not scruple to take her purse; with her keys, taken from under her pil-v, he opened her bureau and took certain things from it, precisely as an ig-rant servant would have done, leaving the valuable papers and taking only oney; he took some of the larger gold objects and neglected smaller objects at were ten times more valuable. He also took something for himself as a epsake, but of that later. Having carried out this horrible deed, he left by the me way he had come. Neither the next day, when the alarm was raised, nor er in his whole life afterwards, did it occur to anyone to suspect the real cul-t! Besides, no one knew of his love for her, for he had always been of tac-rn and unsociable character and had no friend to whom he confided his ıl. He was considered merely an acquaintance of the murdered woman,

and not a very close one at that, for he had not even called on her for the pas
two weeks. Her serf Pyotr was the immediate suspect, and circumstances a
came together just then to confirm the suspicion, for this servant knew, an
the dead woman had made no secret of it, that she intended to send him to th
army, to fulfill her quota of peasant recruits, because he had no family an
besides, was badly behaved. He had been heard, angry and drunk, in a tavern
threatening to kill her. And two days before her death he had run away an
lived somewhere in town, no one knew where. The very day after the murde
he was found on the road just outside town, dead drunk, with a knife in hi
pocket and, what's more, with his right palm for some reason stained wit
blood. He insisted that his nose had been bleeding, but no one believed him
The maids confessed that they had gone to a party, and that the front door ha
been left unlocked until their return. And on top of that there were many sim
ilar indications, on the basis of which they seized the innocent servant. H
was arrested, and proceedings were started, but just a week later the arreste
man came down with a fever and died unconscious in the hospital. Thus th
case was closed, handed over to the will of God, and everyone—the judge
the authorities, and society at large—remained convinced that the crime ha
been committed by no one other than the dead servant. And after that th
punishment began.

The mysterious visitor, by now my friend, divulged to me that at first h
had even suffered no remorse at all. He did suffer for a long time, not fro
that, but from regret that he had killed the woman he loved, that she was n
more, that having killed her, he had killed his love, while the fire of passic
was still in his veins. But he gave almost no thought then to the blood he ha
shed, to the murder of a human being. The idea that his victim might have b
come another man's wife seemed impossible to him, and thus for a long tim
he was convinced in his conscience that he could not have acted otherwis
The arrest of the servant caused him some anguish at first, but the speedy il
ness and then death of the arrested man set his mind at ease, for by all ev
dence he had died (so he reasoned then) not from the arrest or from fear, b
from the chill he had caught precisely during his fugitive days, when he ha
lain, dead drunk, all night on the damp ground. And the stolen articles an
money troubled him little, because (he kept reasoning in the same way) th
theft had been committed not for gain but to divert suspicion elsewhere. Th
sum stolen was insignificant, and he soon donated the entire sum and eve
much more for the almshouse that was being established in our town. He di
so on purpose to ease his conscience regarding the theft, and, remarkably, h
did indeed feel eased for a time, even for a long time—he told me so himse

Then he threw himself into great official activity, took upon himself a troublesome and difficult assignment, which occupied him for about two years, and, being of strong character, almost forgot what had happened; and when he did remember, he tried not to give it any thought. He also threw himself into philanthropic work, gave and organized a great deal in our town, became known in the capitals, was elected a member of philanthropic societies in Moscow and Petersburg. Nevertheless, he fell to brooding at last, and the torment was more than he was able to bear. Just then he became attracted to a wonderful and sensible girl, and in a short time he married her, dreaming that marriage would dispel his solitary anguish, and that, entering upon a new path and zealously fulfilling his duty towards wife and children, he would escape his old memories altogether. But what happened was exactly the opposite of this expectation. Already in the first month of marriage, a ceaseless thought began troubling him: "So my wife loves me, but what if she found out?" When she became pregnant with their first child and told him of it, he suddenly became troubled: "I am giving life, but I have taken a life." They had children: "How dare I love, teach, and raise them, how shall I speak to them of virtue: I have shed blood." They were wonderful children, one longed to caress them: "And I cannot look at their innocent, bright faces; I am unworthy." Finally the blood of the murdered victim began to appear to him, menacingly and bitterly, her destroyed young life, her blood crying out for revenge. He began to have horrible dreams. But, being stouthearted, he endured the torment for a long time: "I shall atone for it all with my secret torment." But that hope, too, was vain: the longer it went on, the more intense his suffering grew. He came to be respected in society for his philanthropic activity, though everyone was afraid of his stern and gloomy character, but the more respected he became, the more unbearable it was for him. He confessed to me that he had thought of killing himself. But instead of that he began to picture a different dream—a dream he at first considered impossible and insane, but which stuck so fast to his heart that he was unable to shake it off. His dream was this: he would rise up, go out in front of people, and tell them all that he had killed a person. For about three years he lived with this dream, he kept picturing it in various forms. Finally he came to believe with his whole heart that, having told his crime, he would undoubtedly heal his soul and find peace once and for all. But, believing that, he felt terror in his heart, for how could it be carried out? And suddenly there occurred that incident at my duel. "Looking at you, I have now made up my mind." I looked at him.

"Is it possible," I cried to him, clasping my hands, "that such a small incident should generate such resolution in you?"

"My resolution has been generating for three years," he replied, "and your incident only gave it a push. Looking at you, I reproached myself and envied you," he said this to me even with severity.

"But no one will believe you," I observed to him, "it was fourteen years ago."

"I have proofs, great proofs. I will present them."

I wept then, and kissed him.

"Decide one thing, just one thing, for me!" he said (as if everything now depended on me). "My wife, my children! My wife may die of grief, and my children, even if they are not stripped of rank and property, my children will become a convict's children, and that forever. And what a memory, what a memory I shall leave in their hearts!"

I was silent.

"And how to part with them, to leave them forever? For it will be forever, forever!"

I sat silently whispering a prayer to myself. Finally I got up, I was frightened.

"Well?" he looked at me.

"Go," I said, "tell them. All will pass, the truth alone will remain. Your children, when they grow up, will understand how much magnanimity there was in your great resolution."

He left me then, as if he had indeed made up his mind to it. Yet he still kept coming to me for more than two weeks, every evening, preparing himself, still unable to make up his mind. He tormented my heart. One time he would come determinedly and say with deep feeling:

"I know that paradise will come to me, will come at once, the moment I tell. For fourteen years I have been in hell. I want to suffer. I will embrace suffering and begin to live. One can go through the world with a lie, but there is no going back. Now I do not dare to love not only my neighbor, but even my own children. Lord, but perhaps my children really will understand the cost of my suffering and will not condemn me! The Lord is not in power but in truth."

"Everyone will understand your deed," I said to him, "if not now, they will understand later, for you will have served the truth, not earthly truth, but a higher one . . ."

And he would go away seeming comforted, and the next day he would suddenly come again, malicious, pale, and say mockingly:

"Each time I come in, you look at me with such curiosity: 'What, you still have not told?' Wait, do not despise me so much. It is not as easy to do as you may think. Perhaps I shall not do it at all. You would not go and denounce me then, would you, eh?"

Yet not only would I have been afraid to look at him with senseless curiosity, I was even afraid to glance at him. This torment made me ill, and my soul was full of tears. I was even unable to sleep at night.

"I have just now come from my wife," he went on. "Do you understand what a wife is? My children, as I was leaving, called out to me: 'Good-bye, papa, come back soon and read to us from *The Children's Reader*.' No, you do not understand that! No one is the wiser for another man's troubles."

His eyes flashed, his lips trembled. Suddenly he struck the table with his fist so that the things on it jumped—he was such a mild man, it was the first time he had done anything like that.

"But is there any need?" he exclaimed, "is there any necessity? No one was condemned, no one was sent to hard labor because of me, the servant died of illness. And I have been punished by my sufferings for the blood I shed. And they will not believe me at all, they will not believe one of my proofs. Is there any need to tell, is there any need? I am ready to suffer still, all my life, for the blood I have shed, only so as not to strike at my wife and children. Would it be just to ruin them along with myself? Are we not mistaken? Where is the truth here? And will people know this truth, will they appreciate it, will they respect it?"

"Lord!" I thought to myself, "he thinks about people's respect at such a moment!" And I felt so much pity for him then that I believe I would have shared his lot if it would have made it easier for him. I could see that he was nearly in a frenzy. I was horrified, having understood by then, not with reason alone but with my living soul, how great was the cost of such a resolution.

"Decide my fate!" he exclaimed again.

"Go and tell," I whispered to him. There was little voice left in me, but I whispered it firmly. Then I took the Gospel from the table, the Russian translation,[20] and showed him John, chapter 12, verse 24:

"Verily, verily, I say unto you, except a corn of wheat fall into the ground and die, it abideth alone: but if it die, it bringeth forth much fruit." I had read this verse just before he came.

He read it.

"True," he said, and smiled bitterly. "Yes, in these books," he said, after a pause, "one finds all sorts of terrible things. It is easy to shove them under someone's nose. Who wrote them, were they human beings?"

"The Holy Spirit wrote them," I said.

"It's easy for you to babble," he smiled again, but this time almost hatefully. I again took the book, opened it to a different place, and showed him the Epistle to the Hebrews, chapter 10, verse 31. He read: "It is a fearful thing to fall into the hands of the living God."

He read it and threw the book aside. He even began trembling all over.

"A fearful verse," he said. "You picked a good one, I must say." He got up from his chair. "So," he said, "farewell, I may not come again . . . we'll see each other in paradise. Well, it has been fourteen years since I 'fell into the hands of the living God,' that is the right way to describe these fourteen years. Tomorrow I shall ask those hands to let me go . . ."

I wanted to embrace him and kiss him, but I did not dare—so contorted was his face, and so heavy his expression. He left. "Lord," I thought, "what awaits the man!" Then I threw myself on my knees before the icon and wept for him to the most holy Mother of God, our swift intercessor and helper. I spent half an hour praying in tears, and it was already late, about midnight. Suddenly I saw the door open, and he came in again. I was amazed.

"Where have you been?" I asked him.

"I seem to have forgotten something . . . ," he said, "my handkerchief, I think . . . Well, even if I have not forgotten anything, let me sit down . . ."

He sat down in a chair. I stood over him. "You sit down, too," he said. I sat down. We sat for about two minutes; he looked at me fixedly and suddenly smiled—I remembered that—then got up, embraced me firmly, and kissed me . . .

"Remember, friend," he said, "how I came back to you this time—do you hear? Remember it!"

It was the first time he had called me "friend." Then he left. "Tomorrow," I thought.

And so it happened. I had not even known that evening that his birthday was the very next day. For I had not gone out over the past few days, and therefore could not have found out from anyone. Each year on that day he gave a big party; the whole town would come to it. They came this time, too. And so, after dinner, he stepped into the middle of the room with a paper in his hand—a formal statement to the authorities. And since the authorities were right there, he read the paper right then to the whole gathering. It contained a full account of the entire crime in all its details. "As an outcast, I cast myself out from among people. God has visited me," he concluded the paper, "I want to embrace suffering!" Right then he brought out and placed on the table all the things he fancied would prove his crime and had been keeping for fourteen years: the gold objects belonging to the murdered woman, which he had stolen to divert suspicion from himself; her locket and cross, taken from around her neck—the locket containing a portrait of her fiancé; a notebook and, finally, two letters: one from her fiancé, informing her of his imminent arrival, and her unfinished reply to his letter, left on the table to be sent to the post office the next day. He had taken both letters—but why? Why had he ept them for fourteen years instead of destroying them as evidence? And hat happened then: everyone was astonished and horrified, and no one anted to believe it, though they listened with great curiosity, but as to a sick an, and a few days later it was all quite decided among them, the verdict eing that the unfortunate man had gone mad. The authorities and the court ould not avoid starting proceedings, but they also held back: though the ar- cles and letters he produced did make them think, here, too, it was decided at even if the documents proved to be authentic, a final accusation could ot be pronounced on the basis of these documents alone. And the articles he ight have obtained from the woman herself, as her acquaintance and ustee. I heard, however, that the authenticity of the articles was later veri- ed by many acquaintances and relatives of the murdered woman, and that ere were no doubts about that. But, again, the case was destined to be left nfinished. Within five days everyone knew that the sufferer had become ill nd that they feared for his life. What the nature of his illness was, I cannot xplain; it was said that he had a heart ailment; but it became known that the tending physicians, at his wife's insistence, also examined his psychological ondition, and reached the verdict that madness was indeed present. I be- ayed nothing, though they came running to question me, but when I wished visit him, I was prohibited for a long time, mainly by his wife: "It was you ho upset him," she said to me, "he was gloomy anyway, and over the past ear everyone noticed his unusual anxiety and strange actions; then you ame along and ruined him, you and your endless reading at him did it; he ever left you for a whole month." And then not only his wife but everyone in wn fell upon me and accused me: "It is all your fault," they said. I kept silent, nd was glad in my soul, for I saw the undoubted mercy of God towards him ho had risen against himself and punished himself. I could not believe in his adness. At last they allowed me to see him, he had demanded it insistently order to say farewell to me. I went in and saw at once that not only his days ut even his hours were numbered. He was weak, yellow, his hands trembled, e gasped for breath, but his look was tender and joyful.

"It is finished!" he said to me. "I have long been yearning to see you, why dn't you come?"

I did not tell him that I had not been allowed to see him.

"God has pitied me and is calling me to himself. I know I am dying, but I el joy and peace for the first time after so many years. I at once felt paradise my soul, as soon as I had done what I had to do. Now I dare to love my chil- ren and kiss them. No one believes me, neither my wife nor the judges; my hildren will never believe me either. In that I see the mercy of God towards y children. I shall die and for them my name will remain untainted. And now I am looking towards God, my heart rejoices as in paradise . . . I have done my duty . . ."

He could not speak, he was gasping for breath, ardently pressing my hand, looking at me fervently. But our conversation was not long, his wife was constantly peeking in at us. Still he managed to whisper to me:

"Do you remember how I came to you again, at midnight? I told you to remember it. Do you know why I came? I came to kill you!"

I started.

"I went out from you then into the darkness, I wandered about the streets struggling with myself. And suddenly I hated you so much that my heart could barely stand it. 'Now,' I thought, 'he alone binds me and is my judge, now I cannot renounce my punishment tomorrow, for he knows everything.' Not that I was afraid you would turn me in (the idea never occurred to me), but I thought: 'How can I face him if I do not turn myself in?' And even if you had been in a faraway land, but still alive, the thought that you were alive and knew everything, and were judging me, would in any case have been unbearable. I hated you as if you were the cause of it all and to blame for it all. I came back to you then; I remembered that there was a dagger lying on your table. I sat down, and asked you to sit down, and thought for a whole minute. If I had killed you, I would have perished for that murder in any case, even if I did not tell about my previous crime. But I did not think of that at all, and did not want to think of it at that moment. I simply hated you and wished with all my might to revenge myself on you for everything. But my Lord defeated the devil in my heart. Know, however, that you have never been closer to death."

A week later he died. The whole town followed his coffin to the grave. The archpriest made a heartfelt speech. They bemoaned the terrible illness that had ended his days. But once he was buried, the whole town rose up against me and even stopped receiving me. It is true that some, a few at first, and then more and more, came to believe in the truth of his testimony and began visiting me all the time, questioning me with great curiosity and joy: for men love the fall of the righteous man and his disgrace. But I kept silent and soon quit the town altogether, and five months later I was deemed worthy by the Lord God to step onto a firm and goodly path, blessing the unseen finger that pointed my way so clearly. And every day, down to this very day, I have remembered the long-suffering servant of God, Mikhail, in my prayers.

Chapter 3

From Talks and Homilies of the Elder Zosima

(e) Some Words about the Russian Monk and His Possible Significance

athers and teachers, what is a monk? In the enlightened world of today, this
ord is now uttered in mockery by some, and by others even as a term of
use. And it gets worse and worse. True, ah, true, among monks there are
any parasites, pleasure-seekers, sensualists, and insolent vagabonds. Edu-
ted men of the world point this out, saying: "You are idlers, useless mem-
rs of society, shameless beggars, living on the labor of others." And yet
nong monks so many are humble and meek, thirsting for solitude and fer-
nt prayer in peace. People point less often to these monks, and even pass
em over in silence, and how surprised they would be if I were to say that
om these meek ones, thirsting for solitary prayer, will perhaps come once
ain the salvation of the Russian land! For truly they are made ready in peace
or the day and the hour, and the month and the year."[1] Meanwhile, in their
litude they keep the image of Christ fair and undistorted, in the purity of
od's truth, from the time of the ancient fathers, apostles, and martyrs, and
hen the need arises they will reveal it to the wavering truth of the world.
his is a great thought. This star will shine forth from the East.[2]

Thus I think of the monk, and can my thinking be false? can it be arrogant?
ok at the worldly and at the whole world that exalts itself above the people
God: are the image of God and his truth not distorted in it? They have sci-
nce, and in science only that which is subject to the senses. But the spiritual
orld, the higher half of man's being, is altogether rejected, banished with a
rt of triumph, even with hatred. The world has proclaimed freedom, es-
cially of late, but what do we see in this freedom of theirs: only slavery and
icide! For the world says: "You have needs, therefore satisfy them, for you
ve the same rights as the noblest and richest men. Do not be afraid to satisfy
em, but even increase them"—this is the current teaching of the world. And
this they see freedom. But what comes of this right to increase one's needs?
r the rich, *isolation* and spiritual suicide; for the poor, envy and murder, for
ey have been given rights, but have not yet been shown any way of satis-
ing their needs. We are assured that the world is becoming more and more
ited, is being formed into brotherly communion, by the shortening of dis-
nces, by the transmitting of thoughts through the air. Alas, do not believe in
ch a union of people. Taking freedom to mean the increase and prompt sat-

isfaction of needs, they distort their own nature, for they generate man
meaningless and foolish desires, habits, and the most absurd fancies in them
selves. They live only for mutual envy, for pleasure-seeking and self-displa
To have dinners, horses, carriages, rank, and slaves to serve them is now cor
sidered such a necessity that for the sake of it, to satisfy it, they will sacrific
life, honor, the love of mankind, and will even kill themselves if they are ur
able to satisfy it. We see the same thing in those who are not rich, while th
poor, so far, simply drown their unsatisfied needs and envy in drink. But soo
they will get drunk on blood instead of wine, they are being led to that. I as
you: is such a man free? I knew one "fighter for an idea" who told me himse
that when he was deprived of tobacco in prison, he was so tormented by th
deprivation that he almost went and betrayed his "idea," just so that the
would give him some tobacco. And such a man says: "I am going to fight fc
mankind." Well, how far will such a man get, and what is he good for? Perhap
some quick action, but he will not endure for long. And no wonder that i
stead of freedom they have fallen into slavery, and instead of serving brotl
erly love and human unity, they have fallen, on the contrary, into *disunity* an
isolation, as my mysterious visitor and teacher used to tell me in my youtl
And therefore the idea of serving mankind, of the brotherhood and onenes
of people, is fading more and more in the world, and indeed the idea now eve
meets with mockery, for how can one drop one's habits, where will this slav
go now that he is so accustomed to satisfying the innumerable needs he hin
self has invented? He is isolated, and what does he care about the whole? The
have succeeded in amassing more and more things, but have less and less jo

Very different is the monastic way. Obedience, fasting, and prayer a
laughed at, yet they alone constitute the way to real and true freedom: I cu
away my superfluous and unnecessary needs, through obedience I humbl
and chasten my vain and proud will, and thereby, with God's help, attain fre
dom of spirit, and with that, spiritual rejoicing! Which of the two is more ca
pable of upholding and serving a great idea—the isolated rich man or or
who is liberated from the tyranny of things and habits? The monk is r
proached for his isolation: "You isolate yourself in order to save your soul b
hind monastery walls, but you forget the brotherly ministry to mankind." W
shall see, however, who is more zealous in loving his brothers. For it is the
who are isolated, not we, but they do not see it. Of old from our midst cam
leaders of the people, and can they not come now as well? Our own humb
and meek ones, fasters and keepers of silence, will arise and go forth for
great deed. The salvation of Russia is from the people. And the Russian mo
astery has been with the people from time immemorial. If the people are is
lated, we, too, are isolated. The people believe as we do, but an unbelievir

leader will accomplish nothing in our Russia, even though he be sincere of heart and ingenious of mind. Remember that. The people will confront the atheist and overcome him, and there will be one Orthodox Russia. Watch over the people, therefore, and keep a watch on their hearts. Guide them in peace. Such is your monastic endeavor, for this is a God-bearing people.

(f) Some Words about Masters and Servants and Whether It Is Possible for Them to Become Brothers in Spirit

God knows there is sin among the people, too. And the flame of corruption is even visibly increasing by the hour, working down from above. Isolation is coming to the people as well: there are kulaks and commune-eaters;[3] the merchant now wants more and more honors, longs to show himself an educated man, though he has not the least education, and to that end basely scorns ancient customs, and is even ashamed of the faith of his fathers. He likes visiting princes, though he himself is only a peasant gone bad. The people are festering with drink and cannot leave off. And what cruelty towards their families, their wives, even their children, all from drunkenness! I have even seen ten-year-old children in the factories: frail, sickly, stooped, and already depraved. The stuffy workshop, work all day long, depraved talk, and wine, wine—is that what the soul of such a little child needs? He needs sunshine, children's games, bright examples all around, and to be given at least a drop of love. Let there be none of that, monks, let there be no torture of children; rise up and preach it at once, at once! But God will save Russia, for though the simple man is depraved, and can no longer refrain from rank sin, still he knows that his rank sin is cursed by God and that he does badly in sinning. So our people still believe tirelessly in truth, acknowledge God, weep tenderly. Not so their betters. These, following science, want to make a just order for themselves by reason alone, but without Christ now, not as before, and they have already proclaimed that there is no crime, there is no sin. And in their own terms, that is correct: for if you have no God, what crime is there to speak of? In Europe the people are rising up against the rich with force, and popular leaders everywhere are leading them to bloodshed and teaching them that their wrath is righteous. But "their wrath is accursed, for it is cruel."[4] Yet the Lord will save Russia, as he has saved her many times before. Salvation will come from the people, from their faith and their humility. Fathers and teachers, watch over the faith of the people—and this is no dream: all my life I have been struck by the true and gracious dignity in our great people, I have seen it, I can testify to it myself, I have seen it and marveled at it, seen it even in spite of the rank sins and beggarly appearance of our people. They are not servile, and that after two centuries of serfdom. They are free in appearance and manner, yet without any offense. And not vengeful, not envious. "You are noble, you are rich, you are intelligent and talented, very well, God bless you. I honor you, but I know that I, too, am a man. By honoring you without envy, I show my human dignity before you." Verily, though they do not say it (for they cannot say it yet), that is how they *act*, I have seen it myself, I have experienced it, and would you believe that the poorer and lower our Russian man is, the more one notices this gracious truth in him, for the rich among them, the kulaks and commune-eaters, are already corrupted in great numbers, and much, oh, so much of that came about because of our negligence and oversight! But God will save his people, for Russia is great in her humility. I dream of seeing our future, and seem to see it clearly already: for it will come to pass that even the most corrupt of our rich men will finally be ashamed of his riches before the poor man, and the poor man, seeing his humility, will understand and yield to him in joy, and will respond with kindness to his gracious shame. Believe me, it will finally be so: things are heading that way. Equality is only in man's spiritual dignity, and only among us will that be understood. Where there are brothers, there will be brotherhood; but before brotherhood they will never share among themselves. Let us preserve the image of Christ, that it may shine forth like a precious diamond to the whole world . . . So be it, so be it!

Fathers and teachers, a moving incident happened to me once. In my wanderings I met one day, in the provincial capital of K——, my former orderly, Afanasy. It was then already eight years since I had parted with him. He saw me by chance in the marketplace, recognized me, ran over to me, and God, how delighted he was to see me! He rushed up to me: "My dear master, is it you? Can it really be you?" He took me home. He had left the army by then, was married, and had two small children. They supported themselves by hawking wares in the marketplace. His room was poor, but clean, joyful. He sat me down, lit the samovar, sent for his wife, as if my appearance was somehow a festive occasion. He brought the children to me: "Bless them, father." "Is it for me to bless them?" I replied. "I am a simple and humble monk, I shall pray to God for them; and for you, Afanasy Pavlovich, I have prayed to God always, every day, since that very day, for I tell you, it all came about because of you." And I explained it to him as far as I could. And what do you think: the man looked at me and still could not imagine that I, his former master, an officer, could be there before him as I was, and dressed as I was. He even wept. "Why are you weeping?" I said to him. "Better rejoice for me in your soul, my dear, my unforgettable man, for my path is a bright and joyful one." He did not say much, but kept sighing and shaking his head over me tenderly. "And where is your wealth?" he asked. "I gave it to the monastery," I replied, "we live in common." After tea I was saying good-bye to them when he suddenly produced fifty kopecks as a donation to the monastery, and then slipped another fifty kopecks hurriedly into my hand: "This is for you, father, maybe you'll need it in your travels and wanderings." I accepted his fifty kopecks, bowed to him and his wife, and left rejoicing, thinking as I went: "Here are the two of us, he at home and I on the road, both no doubt sighing and smiling joyfully, in the gladness of our hearts, shaking our heads when we recall how God granted us this meeting." I never saw him again after that. I was his master, and he was my servant, and now, as we kissed each other lovingly and in spiritual tenderness, a great human communion took place between us. I have given it much thought, and now I reason thus: Is it so far beyond reach of the mind that this great and openhearted communion might in due time take place everywhere among our Russian people? I believe that it will take place, and that the time is near.

And about servants I will add the following: formerly, as a young man, I would often get angry with servants: "The cook made it too hot, the orderly did not brush my clothes." And then suddenly there shone on me my dear brother's thought, which I had heard from him in my childhood: "Am I worthy, such as I am, that another should serve me, and that, because he is poor and untaught, I should order him about?" And I marveled then that the simplest, most self-evident thoughts should come so late to our minds. The world cannot do without servants, but see to it that your servant is freer in spirit than if he were not a servant. And why can I not be the servant of my servant, and in such wise that he even sees it, and without any pride on my part, or any disbelief on his? Why can my servant not be like my own kin, so that I may finally receive him into my family, and rejoice for it? This may be accomplished even now, but it will serve as the foundation for the magnificent communion of mankind in the future, when a man will not seek servants for himself, and will not wish to turn his fellow men into servants, as now, but, on the contrary, will wish with all his strength to become himself the servant of all, in accordance with the Gospel.[5] And is it only a dream, that in the end man will find his joy in deeds of enlightenment and mercy alone, and not in cruel pleasures as now—in gluttony, fornication, ostentation, boasting, and envious rivalry with one another? I firmly believe not, and that the time is near. People laugh and ask: when will the time come, and does it look as if it will ever come? But I think that with Christ we shall bring about this great deed. And how many ideas there have been on the earth, in human history, that were unthinkable even ten years earlier, and that would suddenly appear when their mysterious time had come and sweep over all the earth! So it will be with us as well, and our people will shine forth to the world, and all men will say: "The stone which the builders rejected has become the head of the corner."[6] And the scoffers will themselves be asked: "If ours is a dream, then when will you raise up your edifice and make a just order for yourselves by your own reason, without Christ?" Even if they themselves affirm, on the contrary, that it is they who are moving towards communion, then indeed only the simplest of them believe it, so that one may even be astonished at such simplicity. Verily, there is more dreamy fantasy in them than in us. They hope to make a just order for themselves, but, having rejected Christ, they will end by drenching the earth with blood, for blood calls to blood, and he who draws the sword will perish by the sword.[7] And were it not for Christ's covenant, they would annihilate one another down to the last two men on earth. And these last two, in their pride, would not be able to restrain each other either, so that the last would annihilate the next to last, and then himself as well. And so it would come to pass, were it not for Christ's covenant, that for the sake of the meek and the humble this thing will be shortened.[8] I began while still in my officer's uniform, after my duel, to speak about servants at social gatherings, and everyone, I remember, kept marveling at me: "What?" they said, "shall we sit our servants on the sofa and offer them tea?" "Why not," I would say, "at least once in a while?" Then everyone laughed. Their question was frivolous, and my answer vague, yet I think there was some truth in it.

(g) Of Prayer, Love, and the Touching of Other Worlds

Young man, do not forget to pray. Each time you pray, if you do so sincerely, there will be the flash of a new feeling in it, and a new thought as well, one you did not know before, which will give you fresh courage; and you will understand that prayer is education. Remember also: every day and whenever you can, repeat within yourself: "Lord, have mercy upon all who come before you today." For every hour and every moment thousands of people leave their life on this earth, and their souls come before the Lord—and so many of them part with the earth in isolation, unknown to anyone, in sadness and sorrow that no one will mourn for them, or even know whether they had lived or not. And so, perhaps from the other end of the earth, your prayer for his repose will rise up to the Lord, though you did not know him at all, nor he you. How moving it is for his soul, coming in fear before the Lord, to feel at that moment that someone is praying for him, too, that there is still a human being on earth who loves him. And God, too, will look upon you both with more mercy, for if even you so pitied him, how much more will he who is infinitely more merciful and loving than you are. And he will forgive him for your sake.

Brothers, do not be afraid of men's sin, love man also in his sin, for this likeness of God's love is the height of love on earth. Love all of God's creation, both the whole of it and every grain of sand. Love every leaf, every ray of God's light. Love animals, love plants, love each thing. If you love each thing, you will perceive the mystery of God in things. Once you have perceived it, you will begin tirelessly to perceive more and more of it every day. And you will come at last to love the whole world with an entire, universal love. Love the animals: God gave them the rudiments of thought and an untroubled joy. Do not trouble it, do not torment them, do not take their joy from them, do not go against God's purpose. Man, do not exalt yourself above the animals: they are sinless, and you, you with your grandeur, fester the earth by your appearance on it, and leave your festering trace behind you—alas, almost every one of us does! Love children especially, for they, too, are sinless, like angels, and live to bring us to tenderness and the purification of our hearts and as a sort of example for us. Woe to him who offends a child. I was taught to love little children by Father Anfim: during our wanderings, this dear and silent man used to spend the little half-kopecks given us as alms on gingerbreads and candies, and hand them out to them. He could not pass by children without his soul being shaken: such is the man.

One may stand perplexed before some thought, especially seeing men's sin, asking oneself: "Shall I take it by force, or by humble love?" Always resolve to take it by humble love. If you so resolve once and for all, you will be able to overcome the whole world. A loving humility is a terrible power, the most powerful of all, nothing compares with it. Keep company with yourself and look to yourself every day and hour, every minute, that your image be ever gracious. See, here you have passed by a small child, passed by in anger, with a foul word, with a wrathful soul; you perhaps did not notice the child, but he saw you, and your unsightly and impious image has remained in his defenseless heart. You did not know it, but you may thereby have planted a bad seed in him, and it may grow, and all because you did not restrain yourself before the child, because you did not nurture in yourself a heedful, active love. Brothers, love is a teacher, but one must know how to acquire it, for it is difficult to acquire, it is dearly bought, by long work over a long time, for one ought to love not for a chance moment but for all time. Anyone, even a wicked man, can love by chance. My young brother asked forgiveness of the birds: it seems senseless, yet it is right, for all is like an ocean, all flows and connects; touch it in one place and it echoes at the other end of the world. Let it be madness to ask forgiveness of the birds, still it would be easier for the birds, and for a child, and for any animal near you, if you yourself were more gracious than you are now, if only by a drop, still it would be easier. All is like an ocean, I say to you. Tormented by universal love, you, too, would then start praying to the birds, as if in a sort of ecstasy, and entreat them to forgive you your sin. Cherish this ecstasy, however senseless it may seem to people.

My friends, ask gladness from God. Be glad as children, as birds in the sky. And let man's sin not disturb you in your efforts, do not fear that it will dampen your endeavor and keep it from being fulfilled, do not say, "Sin is strong, impiety is strong, the bad environment is strong, and we are lonely and powerless, the bad environment will dampen us and keep our good endeavor from being fulfilled." Flee from such despondency, my children! There is only one salvation for you: take yourself up, and make yourself responsible for all the sins of men. For indeed it is so, my friend, and the moment you make yourself sincerely responsible for everything and everyone, you will see at once that it is really so, that it is you who are guilty on behalf of all and for all. Whereas by shifting your own laziness and powerlessness onto others, you will end by sharing in Satan's pride and murmuring against God. I think thus of Satan's pride: it is difficult for us on earth to comprehend it, and therefore, how easy it is to fall into error and partake of it, thinking, moreover, that we are doing something great and beautiful.[9] And there is much in the strongest feelings and impulses of our nature that we cannot comprehend while on earth; do not be tempted by that, either, and do not think it can serve you as a justification for anything, for the eternal judge will demand of you that which you could comprehend, not that which you could not—you will be convinced of that, for then you will see all things aright and no longer argue. But on earth we are indeed wandering, as it were, and did we not have the precious image of Christ before us, we would perish and be altogether lost, like the race of men before the flood. Much on earth is concealed from us,[10] but in place of it we have been granted a secret, mysterious sense of our living bond with the other world, with the higher heavenly world, and the roots of our thoughts and feelings are not here but in other worlds. That is why philosophers say it is impossible on earth to conceive the essence of things. God took seeds from other worlds and sowed them on this earth, and raised up his garden; and everything that could sprout sprouted, but it lives and grows only through its sense of being in touch with other mysterious worlds; if this sense is weakened or destroyed in you, that which has grown up in you dies. Then you become indifferent to life, and even come to hate it. So I think.

(h) Can One Be the Judge of One's Fellow Creatures? Of Faith to the End

Remember especially that you cannot be the judge of anyone.[11] For there can be no judge of a criminal on earth until the judge knows that he, too, is a criminal, exactly the same as the one who stands before him, and that he is perhaps most guilty of all for the crime of the one standing before him. When he understands this, then he will be able to be a judge. However mad that may seem, it is true. For if I myself were righteous, perhaps there would be no criminal standing before me now. If you are able to take upon yourself the crime of the criminal who stands before you and whom you are judging in your heart, do so at once, and suffer for him yourself, and let him go without reproach. And even if the law sets you up as a judge, then, too, act in this spirit as far as you can, for he will go away and condemn himself more harshly than you would condemn him. And if, having received your kiss, he goes away unmoved and laughing at you, do not be tempted by that either: it means that his time has not yet come, but it will come in due course; and if it does not come, no matter: if not he, then another will know, and suffer, and judge, and accuse himself, and the truth will be made full. Believe it, believe it without doubt, for in this lies all hope and all the faith of the saints.

Work tirelessly. If, as you are going to sleep at night, you remember: "I did not do what I ought to have done," arise at once and do it. If you are surrounded by spiteful and callous people who do not want to listen to you, fall down before them and ask their forgiveness, for the guilt is yours, too, that they do not want to listen to you. And if you cannot speak with the embittered, serve them silently and in humility, never losing hope. And if everyone abandons you and drives you out by force, then, when you are left alone, fall down on the earth and kiss it and water it with your tears, and the earth will bring forth fruit from your tears, even though no one has seen or heard you in your solitude. Have faith to the end, even if it should happen that all on earth are corrupted and you alone remain faithful: make your offering even so, and praise God, you who are the only one left. And if there are two of you who come together thus, there is already a whole world, a world of living love; embrace each other in tenderness and give praise to the Lord: for his truth has been made full, if only in the two of you.

If you yourself have sinned, and are sorrowful even unto death for your sins, or for your sudden sin, rejoice for the other, rejoice for the righteous one, rejoice that though you have sinned, he still is righteous and has not sinned.

If the wickedness of people arouses indignation and insurmountable grief in you, to the point that you desire to revenge yourself upon the wicked, fear that feeling most of all; go at once and seek torments for yourself, as if you yourself were guilty of their wickedness. Take these torments upon yourself and suffer them, and your heart will be eased, and you will understand that you, too, are guilty, for you might have shone to the wicked, even like the only sinless One,[12] but you did not. If you had shone, your light would have lighted the way for others, and the one who did wickedness would perhaps not have done so in your light. And even if you do shine, but see that people are not saved even with your light, remain steadfast, and do not doubt the power of the heavenly light; believe that if they are not saved now, they will be saved later. And if they are not saved, their sons will be saved, for your light will not die, even when you are dead. The righteous man departs, but his light remains. People are always saved after the death of him who saved them. The generation of men does not welcome its prophets and kills them, but men love their martyrs and venerate those they have tortured to death. Your work is for the whole, your deed is for the future. Never seek a reward, for great is your reward on earth without that: your spiritual joy, which only the righteous obtain. Nor should you fear the noble and powerful, but be wise and ever gracious. Know measure, know the time, learn these things. When you are alone, pray. Love to throw yourself down on the earth and kiss it. Kiss the earth and love it, tirelessly, insatiably, love all men, love all things, seek this rapture and ecstasy. Water the earth with the tears of your joy, and love those tears. Do not be ashamed of this ecstasy, treasure it, for it is a gift from God, a great gift, and it is not given to many, but to those who are chosen.

(i) *Of Hell and Hell Fire: A Mystical Discourse*

Fathers and teachers, I ask myself: "What is hell?" And I answer thus: "The suffering of being no longer able to love."[13] Once in infinite existence, measured neither by time nor by space, a certain spiritual being, through his appearance on earth, was granted the ability to say to himself: "I am and I love." Once, once only, he was given a moment of active, *living* love, and for that he was given earthly life with its times and seasons. And what then? This fortunate being rejected the invaluable gift, did not value it, did not love it, looked upon it with scorn, and was left unmoved by it. This being, having departed the earth, sees Abraham's bosom, and talks with Abraham, as is shown us in the parable of the rich man and Lazarus,[14] and he beholds paradise, and could rise up to the Lord, but his torment is precisely to rise up to the Lord without having loved, to touch those who loved him—him who disdained their love. For he sees clearly and says to himself: "Now I have knowledge, and though I thirst to love, there will be no great deed in my love, no sacrifice, for my earthly life is over, and Abraham will not come with a drop of living water (that is, with a renewed gift of the former life, earthly and active) to cool the flame of the thirst for spiritual love that is burning me now, since I scorned it on earth; life is over, and time will be no more![15] Though I would gladly give my life for others, it is not possible now, for the life I could have sacrificed for love is gone, and there is now an abyss between that life and this existence."

People speak of the material flames of hell. I do not explore this mystery, and I fear it, but I think that if there were material flames, truly people would be glad to have them, for, as I fancy, in material torment they might forget, at least for a moment, their far more terrible spiritual torment. And yet it is impossible to take this spiritual torment from them, for this torment is not external but is within them. And were it possible to take it from them, then, I think, their unhappiness would be even greater because of it. For though the righteous would forgive them from paradise, seeing their torments, and call them to themselves, loving them boundlessly, they would thereby only increase their torments, for they would arouse in them an even stronger flame of thirst for reciprocal, active, and grateful love, which is no longer possible. Nevertheless, in the timidity of my heart I think that the very awareness of this impossibility would serve in the end to relieve them, for, having accepted the love of the righteous together with the impossibility of requiting it, in this obedience and act of humility they would attain at last to a certain image, as it were, of the active love they scorned on earth, and an action somewhat similar to it . . . I regret, my brothers and friends, that I cannot express it clearly. But woe to those who have destroyed themselves on earth, woe to the suicides! I think there can be no one unhappier than they. We are told that it is a sin to pray to God for them, and outwardly the Church rejects them, as it were, but in the secret of my soul I think that one may pray for them as well.[16] Christ will not be angered by love. Within myself, all my life, I have prayed for them, I confess it to you, fathers and teachers, and still pray every day.

Oh, there are those who remain proud and fierce even in hell, in spite of their certain knowledge and contemplation of irrefutable truth; there are terrible ones, wholly in communion with Satan and his proud spirit. For them hell is voluntary and insatiable; they are sufferers by their own will. For they have cursed themselves by cursing God and life. They feed on their wicked pride, as if a hungry man in the desert were to start sucking his own blood from his body.[17] But they are insatiable unto ages of ages, and reject forgiveness, and curse God who calls to them. They cannot look upon the living God without hatred, and demand that there be no God of life, that God destroy himself and all his creation. And they will burn eternally in the fire of their wrath, thirsting for death and nonexistence. But they will not find death . . .

Here ends the manuscript of Alexei Fyodorovich Karamazov. I repeat: it is incomplete and fragmentary. The biographical information, for example, embraces only the elder's early youth. From his homilies and opinions, much that had apparently been said at different times and for various reasons is brought together, as if into a single whole. What was said by the elder in those last hours proper of his life is not all precisely outlined, but only a notion is given of the spirit and nature of that conversation as compared with what Alexei Fyodorovich's manuscript contains from earlier homilies. The elder's death indeed came quite unexpectedly. For though all who had gathered around him on that last evening fully realized that his death was near, still it was impossible to imagine that it would come so suddenly; on the contrary, his friends, as I have already observed, seeing him apparently so cheerful and talkative that night, were even convinced that there had been a noticeable improvement in his health, be it only for a short time. Even five minutes before the end, as they told later with surprise, it was impossible to foresee anything. He suddenly seemed to feel a most acute pain in his chest, turned pale, and pressed his hands firmly to his heart. They all rose from their seats and rushed towards him; but he—suffering, but still looking at them with a smile—silently lowered himself from his armchair to the floor and knelt, then bowed down with his face to the ground, stretched out his arms, and, as if in joyful ecstasy, kissing the earth and praying (as he himself taught), quietly and joyfully gave up his soul to God. The news of his death spread immediately through the hermitage and reached the monastery. Those closest to the newly departed, and those whose duty it was by rank, began to prepare his body according to the ancient rite, and all the brothers gathered in the church. And still before dawn, as rumor later had it, the news about the newly departed reached town. By morning almost the whole town was talking of the event, and a multitude of townspeople poured into the monastery. But we shall speak of that in the next book, and here shall only add beforehand that the day was not yet over when something occurred that was so unexpected for everyone, and so strange, disturbing, and bewildering, as it were, from the impression it made within the monastery and in town, that even now, after so many years, a very vivid memory of that day, so disturbing for many, is still preserved in our town . . .

PART III

Chapter 1

The Odor of Corruption

The body of the deceased schēmahieromonk Father Zosima was prepared for burial according to the established rite.[1] As is known, the bodies of monks and schēmamonks are not washed. "When any monk departs to the Lord," says the Great Prayer Book, "the *uchinnenyi* [that is, the monk appointed to the task] shall wipe his body with warm water, first making the sign of the cross with a *guba* [that is, a Greek sponge] on the forehead of the deceased, on his chest, hands, feet, and knees, and no more than that." Father Paissy himself performed all of this over the deceased. After wiping him, he clothed him in monastic garb and wrapped him in his cloak; to do this, he slit the cloak somewhat, according to the rule, so as to wrap it crosswise. On his head he put a cowl with an eight-pointed cross.[2] The cowl was left open, and the face of the deceased was covered with a black *aer*.[3] In his hands was placed an icon of the Savior. Arrayed thus, towards morning he was transferred to the coffin (which had been prepared long since). They intended to leave the coffin in the cell (in the large front room, the same room in which the deceased elder received the brothers and lay visitors) for the whole day. As the deceased was a hieromonk of the highest rank, not the Psalter but the Gospel had to be read over him by hieromonks and hierodeacons. The reading was begun, immediately after the service for the dead, by Father Iosif; Father Paissy, who wished to read himself later in the day and all night, was meanwhile very busy and preoccupied, together with the superior of the hermitage, for something extraordinary, some unheard-of and "unseemly" excitement and impatient expectation, suddenly began to appear more and more among the monastery brothers and the lay visitors who came in crowds from the monastery guest houses and from town. Both the Father Superior and Father Paissy made every possible effort to calm this vain excitement. Well into daylight people began arriving from town, some even bringing their sick, children especially—just as if they had been waiting purposely for this moment, apparently in hopes of an immediate healing power, which, according to their faith, should not be slow to appear. Only now did it appear how accustomed people had become in our parts to considering the deceased elder, while he was still alive, an unquestionable and great saint. And those who came were far from being all peasants. This great expectation among the faithful, so hastily and nakedly displayed, even impatiently and all but demandingly, seemed to Father Paissy an unquestionable temptation, and though he had long anticipated it, still it in fact went beyond his expectations. Meeting the excited ones among the monks, he even began to reprimand them: "Such and so instant an expectation of something great," he would tell them, "is levity, possible only among worldly people; it is not fitting for us." But he was little heeded, and Father Paissy noticed it uneasily, notwithstanding that he himself (were one to recall the whole truth), though he was indignant at these too-impatient expectations and saw levity and vanity in them, still secretly, within himself, in the depths of his soul, shared almost the same expectations as the excited ones, which fact he could not but admit to himself. Nevertheless certain encounters were particularly unpleasant for him, awakening great doubts in him by some sort of foreboding. In the crowd pressing into the cell of the deceased, he noticed with disgust in his soul (for which he at once reproached himself) the presence, for example, of Rakitin, or the distant visitor, the Obdorsk monk, who was still staying at the monastery, both of whom Father Paissy suddenly considered for some reason suspicious—though they were not the only ones who could be pointed to in that sense. Among all the excited ones, the Obdorsk monk stood out as the busiest; he could be seen everywhere, in all places: he asked questions everywhere, listened everywhere, whispered everywhere with a sort of specially mysterious look. The expression on his face was most impatient, and as if already annoyed that the expected thing should be so long in coming. As for Rakitin, it was discovered later that he had turned up so early at the monastery on a special errand from Madame Khokhlakov. The moment she awoke and learned about the deceased, this kind but weak-willed woman, who could not be admitted to the hermitage herself, was suddenly filled with such impetuous curiosity that she at once dispatched Rakitin to the hermitage in her stead, to observe everything and report to her immediately in writing, about every half-hour, on *everything that happens*. She considered Rakitin a most devout and religious young man—so skillful was he in manipulating everyone and presenting himself to everyone according to the wishes of each, whenever he saw the least advantage for himself. The day was clear and bright, and there were many pilgrims crowded among the hermitage graves, which were scattered all over the grounds, though mainly clustered near the church. Going about the hermitage, Father Paissy suddenly remembered Alyosha, and that he had not seen him for a long time, perhaps not since the night before. And as soon as he remembered him, he noticed him at once, in the furthest corner of the hermitage, near the wall, sitting on the grave of a monk long since departed who was famous for his deeds. He sat with his back to the hermitage, facing the wall, as if hiding behind the tombstone. Coming close to him, Father Paissy saw that he had covered his face with both hands and was weeping, silently but bitterly, his whole body shaking with sobs. Father Paissy stood over him for a while.

"Enough, dear son, enough, my friend," he said at last with deep feeling. "What is it? You should rejoice and not weep. Don't you know that this is the greatest of *his* days? Where is he now, at this moment—only think of that!"

Alyosha glanced up at him, uncovering his face, which was swollen with tears like a little child's, but turned away at once without saying a word and again hid his face in his hands.

"Ah, perhaps it's just as well," Father Paissy said thoughtfully, "perhaps you should weep, Christ has sent you these tears." And he added, to himself now, "Your tender tears are a relief for your soul and will serve to gladden your dear heart." And he moved away from Alyosha, thinking of him with love. He hastened to go, incidentally, because he felt that, looking at him, he might start weeping himself. Meanwhile time went on, the monastic services and services for the dead continued in due order. Father Paissy again replaced Father Iosif by the coffin, and again took over the reading of the Gospel from him. But it was not yet three o'clock in the afternoon when something occurred that I have already mentioned at the end of the previous book, something so little expected by any of us, and so contrary to the general hope, that, I repeat, a detailed and frivolous account of this occurrence has been remembered with great vividness in our town and all the neighborhood even to the present day. Here again I will add, speaking for myself personally, that I find it almost loathsome to recall this frivolous and tempting occurrence, essentially quite insignificant and natural, and I would, of course, omit all mention of it from my story, if it had not influenced in the strongest and most definite way the soul and heart of the main, *though future*, hero of my story, Alyosha, causing, as it were, a crisis and upheaval in his soul, which shook his mind but also ultimately strengthened it for the whole of his life, and towards a definite purpose.

And so, back to the story. When, still before dawn, the body of the elder, prepared for burial, was placed in the coffin and carried out to the front room, the former reception room, a question arose among those attending the coffin: should they open the windows in the room? But this question, uttered cursorily and casually by someone, went unanswered and almost unnoticed—unless it was noticed, and even then privately, by some of those present, only in the sense that to expect corruption and the odor of corruption from the body of such a deceased was a perfect absurdity, even deserving of pity (if not laughter) with regard to the thoughtlessness and little faith of the one who had uttered the question. For quite the opposite was expected. Then, shortly after noon, something began that was first noticed by those coming in and going out only silently and within themselves, and even with an apparent fear of communicating the thought that was beginning to form in them, but which by three o'clock in the afternoon had manifested itself so clearly and undeniably that news of it spread instantly all over the hermitage and among all the pilgrims visiting the hermitage, at once penetrated the monastery as well and threw all the monks into consternation, and, finally, in a very short time, reached town and stirred up everyone there, both believers and unbelievers. The unbelievers rejoiced; as for the believers, some of them rejoiced even more than the unbelievers, for "people love the fall of the righteous man and his disgrace," as the deceased elder himself had pronounced in one of his homilies. The thing was that little by little, but more and more noticeably, an odor of corruption had begun to issue from the coffin, which by three o'clock in the afternoon was all too clearly evident and kept gradually increasing. Not for a long time had there been, nor was it possible to recall in the entire past life of our monastery, such temptation, so coarsely unbridled, and even impossible under any other circumstances, as was displayed immediately after this occurrence even among the monks themselves. Recalling that whole day in detail later on, and even after many years, some of our sensible monks were still amazed and horrified at how this temptation could then have reached such proportions. For before then it had also happened that monks of very righteous life, whose righteousness was in all men's eyes, God-fearing elders, had died, and even so, from their humble coffins, too, there had come an odor of corruption, appearing quite naturally as in all dead men, yet this did not produce any temptation, or even the least excitement. Of course there were some among the deceased of old whose memory was still kept alive in our monastery, and whose remains, according to tradition, had shown no corruption, which fact influenced the brothers movingly and mysteriously, and remained in their memory as a gracious and wondrous thing, and the promise of a still greater future glory from their tombs, if only, by God's will, the time for that were to come. Among these was especially preserved the memory of the elder Job, who lived to be a hundred and five, a famous ascetic, a great faster and keeper of silence, who had departed long ago, in the second decade of this century, and whose grave was pointed out with special and extreme respect to all pilgrims on their first visit, with the mysterious mention of some great expectations. (It was on this same grave that Father Paissy had found Alyosha sitting that morning.) Besides this long-since-departed elder, a similar memory was kept alive of the great schēmahieromonk, the elder Father Varsonofy, who had departed comparatively recently—the one whom Father Zosima had succeeded as elder, and who, in his lifetime, was considered definitely a holy fool by all the pilgrims who visited the monastery. Tradition maintained that these two both lay in their coffins as if alive and were buried without any corruption in them, and that their faces even brightened, as it were, in the coffin. And some even recalled insistently that one could sense an unmistakable fragrance coming from their bodies. Yet, even with such impressive memories, it would still be difficult to explain the direct cause of such a frivolous, absurd, and malicious phenomenon as occurred at the coffin of the elder Zosima. For my part, personally I suppose that in this case a number of things came together simultaneously, that a number of different causes combined their influence. One of these, for instance, was the inveterate hostility to the institution of elders, as a pernicious innovation, that was deeply hidden in the minds of many monks in the monastery. Then, of course, and above all, there was envy of the dead man's holiness, so firmly established while he lived that it was even forbidden, as it were, to question it. For, though the late elder had attracted many to himself, not so much by miracles as by love, and had built up around himself, as it were, a whole world of those who loved him, nevertheless, and still more so, by the same means he generated many who envied him, and hence became his bitter enemies, both open and secret, and not only among the monastics, but even among laymen. He never harmed anyone, for example, but then, "Why is he considered so holy?" And the gradual repetition of that one question finally generated a whole abyss of the most insatiable spite. Which is why I think that many, having noticed the odor of corruption coming from his body, and that so soon—for not even a day had passed since his death—were immensely pleased; just as among those devoted to the elder, who until then had honored him, there were at once found some who were all but insulted and personally offended by this occurrence. The gradual development of the matter went as follows.

No sooner had the corruption begun to reveal itself than one had only to look at the faces of the monks entering the cell of the deceased to see why they were coming. They would go in, stand for a while, and then leave, hastening to confirm the news to the others waiting in a crowd outside. Some of those waiting would sorrowfully nod their heads, but others did not even wish to conceal their joy, so obviously shining in their spiteful eyes. And no one reproached them any longer, no one raised a good voice, which is even a wonder, for those devoted to the deceased elder were still a majority in the monastery; yet, apparently, the Lord himself this time allowed the minority to prevail temporarily. Lay visitors, more particularly the educated sort, soon began coming to the cell to spy in the same way. Few of the simple people went in, though there were many of them crowding at the gates of the hermitage. There is no denying that precisely after three o'clock the influx of lay visitors grew considerably, and precisely as the result of the tempting news. Those who would not, perhaps, have come that day at all, and had no thought of coming, now deliberately put in an appearance, some high-ranking people among them. However, there was as yet no outward breach of good order, and Father Paissy, with a stern face, continued reading the Gospel aloud, firmly and distinctly, as if he did not notice what was happening, though he had long since noticed something unusual. But then he, too, began hearing voices, subdued at first, but gradually growing firm and confident. "Clearly God's judgment is not as man's," Father Paissy suddenly heard. The first to utter it was a layman, a town functionary, an elderly man, and, as far as anyone knew, quite a pious one; but, in uttering this aloud, he merely repeated what the monks had long been repeating in one another's ears. They had long ago uttered this despairing word, and the worst of it was that with almost every minute a certain triumph appeared and grew around this word. Soon, however, good order itself began to be violated, and it was as if everyone felt somehow entitled to violate it. "Why should *this* have happened?" some of the monks began to say, at first as if with regret. "He had a small, dry body, just skin and bones—where can the smell be coming from?" "Then it's a deliberate sign from God," others added hastily, and their opinion was accepted without argument and at once, for they indicated further that even though it was only natural for there to be a smell, as with any deceased sinner, still it should have come forth later, after a day at least, not with such obvious haste, but "this one has forestalled nature," and so there was nothing else in it but God and his deliberate finger. A sign. This argument struck irrefutably. The meek father hieromonk Iosif, the librarian, a favorite of the deceased, tried to object to some of the maligners, saying that "it is not so everywhere," and that there was no Orthodox dogma that the bodies of righteous men are necessarily incorruptible, it was only an opinion, and even in the most Orthodox countries, on Mount Athos for example, they are not so embarrassed by the odor of corruption, and it is not bodily incorruptibility that is regarded as the main sign of the glorification of the saved, but the color of their bones after their bodies have lain in the ground many years and even decayed in it, and "if the bones are found to be yellow like wax, that is the first sign that the Lord has glorified the righteous deceased; and if they are found to be not yellow but black, it means that the Lord has not deemed him worthy of his glory—that is how it is on Athos, a great place, where Orthodoxy from of old has been preserved inviolate and in shining purity," Father Iosif concluded. But the words of the humble father flew by without leaving any impression, and even evoked a mocking rebuff: "That's all learning and innovation, nothing worth listening to," the monks decided among themselves. "We stick to the old ways; who cares what innovations they come up with; should we copy them all?" added others. "We've had as many holy fathers as they have. They sit there under the Turks and have forgotten everything. Their Orthodoxy has long been clouded, and they don't have any bells," the greatest scoffers put in. Father Iosif walked away sorrowfully, the more so as he had not expressed his opinion very firmly, but as if he himself had little faith. But he foresaw with perplexity that something very unseemly was beginning and that disobedience itself was rearing its head. Little by little, after Father Iosif, all other reasonable voices fell silent. And it somehow happened that everyone who loved the deceased elder and accepted the institution of elders with loving obedience suddenly became terribly frightened of something, and when they met they only glanced timidly into each other's faces. The enemies of the institution of elders as a novelty proudly raised their heads: "Not only was there no odor from the late elder Varsonofy, but he even exuded a fragrance," they recalled maliciously, "but of that he was deemed worthy not as an elder, but as a righteous man." And after that, denunciations and even accusations poured down upon the newly departed elder: "He taught unrighteousness; he taught that life is great joy and not tearful humility," some of the more muddleheaded said. "He held fashionable beliefs, he did not accept the material fire of hell," added others, even more muddleheaded than the first. "He was not strict in fasting, allowed himself sweets, had cherry preserve with his tea, and liked it very much, ladies used to send it to him. What is a monk doing giving tea parties?" came from some of the envious. "He sat in pride," the most malicious cruelly recalled, "he considered himself a saint; when people knelt before him, he took it as his due." "He abused the sacrament of confession," the most ardent opponents of the institution of elders added in a malicious whisper, and among these were some of the oldest and most strictly pious of the monks, true adepts of fasting and silence, who had kept silent while the deceased was alive but now suddenly opened their mouths, which in itself was terrible, because their words had a strong influence on the young and as yet unfirm monks. The Obdorsk visitor, the little monk from St. Sylvester's, also listened to them attentively, sighing deeply and nodding his head: "Yes, apparently Father Ferapont judged rightly yesterday," he kept thinking to himself, and just then Father Ferapont appeared; he emerged as if precisely to aggravate the shock.

I have already mentioned that he rarely left his little wooden cell in the apiary, did not even go to church for long stretches of time, and that this was blinked at because he was supposedly a holy fool, not to be bound by the general rule. But to tell the whole truth, all this was blinked at even from a sort of necessity. For it was somehow even shameful to insist on burdening with the general rule so great an ascetic, who fasted and kept silence and prayed night and day (he even fell asleep on his knees), if he himself did not want to submit to it. "He is holier than any of us, and what he does is more difficult than following the rule," the monks would have said in that case, "and if he does not go to church, it means he knows himself when to go, he has his own rule." Because of the likelihood of such murmuring and temptation, Father Ferapont was left in peace. As everyone knew, Father Ferapont intensely disliked Father Zosima; and then the news reached him in his little cell that "God's judgment is not as man's, and that it has even forestalled nature." We may suppose that one of the first to run and bring him the news was the Obdorsk visitor, who had been to see him the day before, and who the day before had left him in terror. I have also mentioned that Father Paissy, who stood firmly and immovably reading over the coffin, though he could not hear or see what was taking place outside the cell, had unerringly divined all its essentials in his heart, for he knew his milieu thoroughly. But he was not dismayed, and waited fearlessly for all that might still take place, with a piercing gaze looking ahead to the outcome of the disturbance, which was already present to his mental eye. Then suddenly an extraordinary noise in the front hall, which clearly violated good order, struck his ear. The door was flung open and Father Ferapont appeared on the threshold. Behind him, as one could glimpse and even plainly see from the cell, many monks who accompanied him were crowding at the foot of the porch, and many laymen along with them. This company did not enter the cell, however, and did not come up on the porch, but stopped and waited to see what Father Ferapont would say and do next, for they suspected, even with a certain fear, despite all their boldness, that he had not come for nothing. Having stopped on the threshold, Father Ferapont lifted up his arms, and from under his right arm peeped the keen and curious little eyes of the Obdorsk visitor, the only one who could not keep himself from running up the stairs after Father Ferapont, for he was greatly curious. Apart from him, all the others, on the contrary, drew further back in sudden fear the moment the door was so noisily flung open. Lifting up his hands, Father Ferapont suddenly yelled:

"Casting will I cast out!" and facing all four directions in turn, he at once began making crosses with his hand at the walls and the four corners of the cell. Those who accompanied Father Ferapont understood this action at once; for they knew that he always did the same wherever he went, and that he would not sit down or say a word before driving out the unclean spirits.

"Get thee hence, Satan! Get thee hence, Satan!" he repeated with each sign of the cross. "Casting will I cast out!" he yelled again. He was wearing his coarse habit, girded with a rope. His bare chest overgrown with gray hair appeared from under his hempen shirt. He had nothing at all on his feet. As soon as he started waving his arms, the heavy chains he wore under his habit began shaking and clanking. Father Paissy interrupted his reading, stepped forward, and stood waiting in front of him.

"Wherefore have you come, worthy father? Wherefore do you violate good order? Wherefore do you trouble the humble flock?" he said at last, looking at him sternly.

"Whyfor have I come? Whyfor do you ask? How believest thou?"[4] Father Ferapont cried in his holy folly. "I came forth to drive out your guests here, the foul devils. I want to see how many you've stored up without me. I want to sweep them out with a birch broom."

"You drive out the unclean one, and it is perhaps him that you serve," Father Paissy went on fearlessly. "And who can say of himself, 'I am holy'? Can you, father?"

"I am foul, not holy. I would not sit in an armchair, I would not desire to be worshipped like an idol!" Father Ferapont thundered. "Now people are destroying the holy faith. The deceased, your saint here," he turned to the crowd, pointing at the coffin with his finger, "denied devils. He gave purgatives against devils. So they've bred here like spiders in the corners. And on this day he got himself stunk. In this we see a great sign from God."

Indeed, it had once happened in Father Zosima's lifetime. One of the monks began seeing unclean spirits, at first in his dreams and then also in reality. And when, in great fear, he divulged this to the elder, the latter advised him to pray without ceasing and fast zealously. But when that did not help either, he advised him, without abandoning his fasting and prayer, to take a certain medicine. Many found this a temptation and spoke of it among themselves, shaking their heads—Father Ferapont most of all, whom some slanderers had hastened to inform at once of the "extraordinary" instructions the elder had given in this particular case.

"Get thee hence, father!" Father Paissy spoke commandingly. "It is not for men to judge, but for God. Perhaps we see here such a 'sign' as neither I, nor you, nor any man is capable of understanding. Get thee hence, father, and do not trouble the flock!" he repeated insistently.

"He did not keep the fasts according to his monastic rank, therefore this sign has come. That's plain enough, it's a sin to conceal it!" The fanatic, maddened by his zeal, got himself going and would not be still. "He loved candies, the ladies used to bring him candies in their pockets, he was a tea sipper, a glutton, filling his stomach with sweets and his mind with arrogant thoughts . . . That is why he suffers this shame . . ."

"Frivolous are your words, father!" Father Paissy also raised his voice. "I marvel at your fasting and ascetic life, but frivolous are your words, as if spoken by some worldly youth, callow and inconstant of mind. Therefore get thee hence, father, I command you," Father Paissy thundered in conclusion.

"I will get hence," said Father Ferapont, as if somewhat taken aback, but not abandoning his spite. "You learned ones! In great wisdom you exalt yourselves above my nothingness. I came here illiterate, and here forgot what I did know, the Lord himself has protected me, his little one, from your wisdom . . ."

Father Paissy stood over him and waited firmly. Father Ferapont was silent for a short time; then, suddenly rueful, he put his right hand to his cheek and spoke in a singsong, looking at the coffin of the deceased elder:

"Tomorrow they will sing 'My Helper and Defender' over him—a glorious canon—and over me when I croak just 'What Earthly Joy'—a little song," he said tearfully and piteously.[5] "You are proud and puffed up! Empty is this place!" he suddenly yelled like a madman, and, waving his hand, turned quickly, and quickly went down the steps from the porch. The crowd awaiting him below hesitated: some followed him at once, but others lingered, for the cell was still open and Father Paissy, who had come out to the porch after Father Ferapont, was standing and watching. But the raging old man was not finished yet: going about twenty steps off, he suddenly turned towards the setting sun, raised both arms, and, as if he had been cut down, collapsed on the ground with a great cry:

"My Lord has conquered! Christ has conquered with the setting sun!" he cried out frenziedly, lifting up his hands to the sun, and, falling face down on the ground, he sobbed loudly like a little child, shaking all over with tears and spreading his arms on the ground. Now everyone rushed to him, there were exclamations, responsive sobs . . . Some kind of frenzy seized them all.

"It is he who is holy! It is he who is righteous!" voices exclaimed, quite fearlessly now. "It is he who should be made an elder," others added spitefully.

"He would not be made an elder . . . he would refuse . . . he would not serve a cursed innovation . . . he would not ape their foolery," other voices put in at once, and it was hard to imagine where it would end, but at that moment the bell rang calling them to church. They all suddenly began crossing themselves. Father Ferapont also got up, and, protecting himself with the sign of the cross, went to his cell without looking back, still uttering exclamations, but now quite incoherently. Some few drifted after him, but the majority began to disperse, hurrying to the service. Father Paissy handed over the reading to Father Iosif and went down. He could not be shaken by the frenzied cries of fanatics, but his heart was suddenly saddened and anguished by something in particular, and he felt it. He stopped and suddenly asked himself, "Why do I feel such sadness, almost to the point of dejection?" and perceived at once with surprise that this sudden sadness was evidently owing to a very small and particular cause: it happened that in the crowd milling about the entrance to the cell, among the rest of the excited ones, he had also noticed Alyosha, and he remembered that, seeing him there, he had at once felt, as it were, a pain in his heart. "Can it be that this young one means so much to my heart now?" he suddenly asked himself in surprise. At that moment Alyosha was just passing by him, as if hurrying somewhere, but not in the direction of the church. Their eyes met. Alyosha quickly turned away and dropped his eyes to the ground, and just from the look of the young man, Father Paissy could guess what a great change was taking place in him at that moment.

"Have you, too, fallen into temptation?" Father Paissy exclaimed suddenly. "Can it be that you, too, are with those of little faith?" he added ruefully.

Alyosha stopped and glanced somehow indefinitely at Father Paissy, but again quickly turned away and dropped his eyes to the ground. He stood sideways, not facing his questioner. Father Paissy observed him attentively.

"Where are you hurrying to? The bell is ringing for the service," he asked again, but Alyosha once more gave no answer.

"Or are you leaving the hermitage? Without permission? Without a blessing?"

Alyosha suddenly gave a twisted smile, raised his eyes strangely, very strangely, to the inquiring father, the one to whom, at his death, his former guide, the former master of his heart and mind, his beloved elder, had entrusted him, and suddenly, still without answering, waved his hand as if he cared nothing even about respect, and with quick steps walked towards the gates of the hermitage.

"But you will come back!" Father Paissy whispered, looking after him with rueful surprise.

Chapter 2

An Opportune Moment

Of course Father Paissy was not mistaken when he decided that his "dear boy" would come back, and perhaps even perceived (if not completely, yet perspicaciously) the true meaning of the mood of Alyosha's soul. Nevertheless I shall frankly admit that it would be very difficult for me now to convey clearly the precise meaning of this strange and uncertain moment in the life of the hero of my story, whom I love so much and who is still so young. To the rueful question Father Paissy addressed to Alyosha: "Or are you, too, with those of little faith?"—I could, of course, answer firmly for Alyosha: "No, he is not with those of little faith." Moreover, it was even quite the opposite: all his dismay arose precisely because his faith was so great. But dismay there was, it did arise, and it was so tormenting that even later, long afterwards, Alyosha considered this rueful day one of the most painful and fatal days of his life. If I were asked directly: "Could all this anguish and such great perturbation have arisen in him only because, instead of beginning at once to produce healings, the body of his elder, on the contrary, showed signs of early corruption?" I would answer without hesitation: "Yes, indeed it was so." I would only ask the reader not to be in too great a hurry to laugh at my young man's pure heart. Not only have I no intention of apologizing for him, of excusing and justifying his simple faith on account of his youth, for instance, or the little progress he had made formerly in the study of science, and so on and so forth, but I will do the opposite and declare firmly that I sincerely respect the nature of his heart. No doubt some other young man, who takes his heart's impressions more prudently, who has already learned how to love not ardently but just lukewarmly, whose thoughts, though correct, are too reasonable (and therefore cheap) for his age, such a young man, I say, would avoid what happened to my young man, but in certain cases, really, it is more honorable to yield to some passion, however unwise, if it springs from great love, than not to yield to it at all. Still more so in youth, for a young man who is constantly too reasonable is suspect and of too cheap a price—that is my opinion! "But," reasonable people may exclaim at this point, "not every young man can believe in such prejudices, and your young man is no example for others." To this I again reply: yes, my young man believed, believed piously and unshakably, but still I do not apologize for him.

You see, though I declared above (and perhaps too hastily) that I was not going to explain, excuse, or justify my hero, I find that it is still necessary, for the further comprehension of my story, to understand certain things. I will say this much: it was not a matter of miracles. It was not an expectation of miracles, frivolous in its impatience. Alyosha did not need miracles then for the triumph of certain convictions (it was not that at all), nor so that some sort of former, preconceived idea would quickly triumph over another—oh, no, by no means: in all this, and above all else, in the first place, there stood before him the person, and only the person—the person of his beloved elder, the person of that righteous man whom he revered to the point of adoration. That was just it, that the entirety of the love for "all and all" that lay hidden in his young and pure heart, then and during the whole previous year, was at times as if wholly concentrated, perhaps even incorrectly, mainly on just one being, at least in the strongest impulses of his heart—on his beloved elder, now deceased. True, this being had stood before him as an indisputable ideal for so long that all his youthful powers and all their yearning could not but turn to this ideal exclusively, in some moments even to the forgetting of "all and all." (He himself remembered later that on that painful day he quite forgot his brother Dmitri, about whom he had been so worried and grieved the day before; he also forgot to take the two hundred roubles to Ilyushechka's father, as he had also so fervently intended to do the day before.) Again, it was not miracles he needed, but only a "higher justice," which, as he believed, had been violated—it was this that wounded his heart so cruelly and suddenly. And what matter if, in the course of events, this "justice" had assumed in Alyosha's expectations the form of those miracles expected immediately from the remains of his adored former teacher? Everyone in the monastery thought and expected the same, even those whose minds Alyosha revered, Father Paissy himself, for example, and so Alyosha, not troubling himself with any doubts, clothed his dreams in the same form as all the others. And it had been settled thus in his heart for a long time, through the whole year of his life in the monastery, and his heart had acquired the habit of expecting it. But it was justice, justice he thirsted for, not simply miracles! And now he who, according to his hope, was to have been exalted higher than anyone in the whole world, this very man, instead of receiving the glory that was due him, was suddenly thrown down and disgraced! Why? Who had decreed it? Who could have judged so? These were the questions that immediately tormented his inexperienced and virgin heart. He could not bear without insult, even without bitterness of heart, that this most righteous of righteous men should be given over to such derisive and spiteful jeering from a crowd so frivolous and so far beneath him. Let there be no miracles, let nothing miraculous be revealed, let that which was expected immediately not come to pass, but why should there be this ignominy, why should this shame be permitted, why this hasty corruption, which "forestalled nature," as the spiteful monks were saying? Why this "sign" which they now so triumphantly brought forth together with Father Ferapont, and why did they believe they had any right to bring it forth? Where was Providence and its finger? Why did it hide its finger "at the most necessary moment" (Alyosha thought), as if wanting to submit itself to the blind, mute, merciless laws of nature?

That was why Alyosha's heart was bleeding, and of course, as I have already said, here first of all was the person he loved more than anything in the world, and this very person was "disgraced," this very person was "defamed"! Let this murmuring of my young man be thoughtless and rash, but I repeat again for the third time (granting beforehand that it is also perhaps thoughtless of me to do so): I am glad that at such a moment my young man turned out to be not so reasonable; the time will come for an intelligent man to be reasonable, but if at such an exceptional moment there is no love to be found in a young man's heart, then when will it come? I must not, however, fail to mention in this connection a certain strange phenomenon that did, if only momentarily, reveal itself in Alyosha's mind at this fatal and confused moment. This new *something* that appeared and flashed consisted of a certain tormenting impression from his conversation with his brother Ivan the day before, which Alyosha now kept recalling. Precisely now. Oh, not that any of his basic, so to speak elemental, beliefs were shaken in his soul. He loved his God and believed in him steadfastly, though he suddenly murmured against him. Yet some vague but tormenting and evil impression from the recollection of the previous day's conversation with his brother Ivan now suddenly stirred again in his soul, demanding more and more to come to the surface. It was already quite dark when Rakitin, passing through the pine grove from the hermitage to the monastery, suddenly noticed Alyosha lying face down on the ground under a tree, motionless and as if asleep. He went up and called him by name.

"Is that you, Alexei? Can it be that . . . ," he began, astonished, but stopped without finishing. He was going to say, "Can it be that you've *come to this*?" Alyosha did not glance up at him, but from a slight movement Rakitin guessed at once that he had heard and understood him.

"What's the matter with you?" he went on in surprise, but the surprise on his face was already beginning to be supplanted by a smile that turned more and more sarcastic.

"Listen, I've been looking for you for over two hours. You suddenly disappeared from the place. What are you doing here? What is all this blessed nonsense? Look at me, at least . . ."

Alyosha raised his head, sat up, and leaned his back against the tree. He was not crying, but his face wore an expression of suffering, and there was irritation in his eyes. He did not look at Rakitin, incidentally, but somewhere aside.

"You know, you've quite changed countenance. No more of that old, notorious meekness of yours. Are you angry with somebody, or what? Offended?"

"Leave me alone!" Alyosha said suddenly, still without looking at him, and waved his hand wearily.

"Oho, so that's how we are now! We're snappish, just like other mortals! And we used to be an angel! Well, Alyoshka, you surprise me, do you know that? I mean it. It's a long time since anything here has surprised me. Still, I did always consider you an educated man . . ."

Alyosha finally looked at him, but somehow distractedly, as if he still scarcely understood him.

"Can it be just because your old man got himself stunk? Can it be that you seriously believed he'd start pulling off miracles?" Rakitin exclaimed, passing again to the most genuine amazement.

"I believed, I believe, and I want to believe, and I will believe, and what more do you want!" Alyosha cried irritably.

"Precisely nothing, my dear. Ah, the devil! But even thirteen-year-old schoolboys don't believe such things anymore! Still . . . ah, the devil . . . So you've gotten angry with your God now, you've rebelled: they passed you over for promotion, you didn't get a medal for the feast day! Ah, you!"

Alyosha gave Rakitin a long look, his eyes somehow narrowed, and something flashed in them . . . but not anger at Rakitin.

"I do not rebel against my God, I simply 'do not accept his world,' " Alyosha suddenly smiled crookedly.

"What do you mean, you don't accept his world?" Rakitin thought over his reply for a moment. "What sort of gibberish is that?"

Alyosha did not answer.

"Well, enough talk of trifles, now to business: did you eat anything today?"

"I don't remember . . . I think I did."

"By the looks of you, you need fortifying. What a sorry sight! You didn't sleep last night, so I hear, you had a meeting. And then all this fuss and muss . . . I bet you had nothing but a piece of blessed bread to chew on. I've got a hunk of sausage here in my pocket, I brought it from town just in case, because I was coming here, only you probably won't . . ."

"Let's have your sausage."

"Aha! So that's how it is! Real rebellion, barricades and all! Well, brother, that's not to be sneered at! Let's go to my place . . . I'd love a shot of vodka right now, I'm dead tired. You wouldn't go so far as to have vodka . . . or would you?"

"Let's have your vodka."

"Say! Amazing, brother!" Rakitin rolled his eyes. "Well, one way or the other, vodka or sausage, it's a brave thing, a fine thing, not to be missed! Let's go!"

Alyosha silently got up from the ground and went after Rakitin.

"If your brother Vanechka could see it, wouldn't he be surprised! By the way, your good brother Ivan Fyodorovich went off to Moscow this morning, did you know that?"

"Yes," Alyosha said indifferently, and suddenly the image of his brother Dmitri flashed through his mind, but only flashed, and though it reminded him of something, some urgent business, which could not be put off even a minute longer, some duty, some terrible responsibility, this recollection did not make any impression on him, did not reach his heart, it flitted through his memory and was forgotten. But long afterwards Alyosha kept remembering it.

"Your dear brother Vanechka once pronounced me a 'giftless liberal windbag.' And you, too, could not help letting me know once that I was 'dishonest' . . . Very well! Now we'll see how gifted and honest you are" (Rakitin finished the phrase to himself, in a whisper). "Bah, listen!" he raised his voice again, "let's bypass the monastery and take the path straight to town . . . Hmm. By the way, I need to stop and see Khokhlakov. Imagine, I wrote her a report about all that happened, and just think, she replied at once with a note, in pencil (the lady simply loves writing notes), that she 'would not have expected *such conduct* from such a venerable old man as Father Zosima'! That's what she wrote: 'such conduct'! She was angry, too; ah, you all . . . ! Wait!" he cried again all at once, stopped suddenly, and, taking Alyosha by the shoulder, made him stop, too.

"You know, Alyoshka," he looked searchingly in his eyes, entirely absorbed by the impression of the sudden new thought that had shone upon him, and though ostensibly laughing, he was apparently afraid to voice this sudden new thought of his, so hard was it still for him to believe the surprising and quite unexpected mood in which he saw Alyosha now, "Alyoshka, do you know the best place of all for us to go now?" he finally said timidly and ingratiatingly.

"It makes no difference . . . wherever you like."

"Let's go to Grushenka's, eh? Will you go?" Rakitin finally uttered, all atremble with timid expectancy.

"Let's go to Grushenka's," Alyosha replied calmly and at once, and this was so unexpected for Rakitin—that is, this prompt and calm assent—that he almost jumped back.

"W-well . . . ! Now . . . !" he shouted in amazement, and suddenly, grasping Alyosha firmly by the arm, he led him quickly along the path, still terribly fearful that his determination might disappear. They walked in silence; Rakitin was even afraid to start talking.

"And how glad she'll be, how glad . . . ," he muttered, and fell silent again. It was not at all to make Grushenka glad that he was leading Alyosha to her; he was a serious man and never undertook anything without the aim of profiting from it. His aim this time was twofold: first, a revengeful one—that is, to see "the disgrace of the righteous man," the probable "fall" of Alyosha "from the saints to the sinners," which he was already savoring in anticipation—and second, he had in mind a material aim as well, one rather profitable for himself, of which more shall be said below.

"Well, if such a moment has come along," he thought gaily and maliciously to himself, "then we'd better just catch it by the scruff of the neck, the moment, I mean, because it's very opportune for us."

Chapter 3

An Onion

Grushenka lived in the busiest part of town, near the cathedral square, in a house belonging to the widow of the merchant Morozov, from whom she rented a small wooden cottage. The widow's house was large, stone, two-storied, old, and extremely unattractive. The owner, an old woman, lived a secluded life there with her two nieces, also quite elderly spinsters. She had no need to rent the cottage in her backyard, but everyone knew that she had taken Grushenka as her tenant (already four years since) only to please her relative, the merchant Samsonov, who was openly Grushenka's patron. It was said that in placing his "favorite" with the widow Morozov, the jealous old man had originally had in view the old woman's keen eye, to keep watch over the new tenant's behavior. But the keen eye soon turned out to be unnecessary, and in the end the widow Morozov rarely even met Grushenka and finally stopped bothering her altogether with her surveillance. True, it had already been four years since the old man had brought the timid, shy, eighteen-year-old girl, delicate, thin, pensive, and sad, to this house from the provincial capital, and since then much water had flowed under the bridge. All the same, the biography of this girl was only slightly and inconsistently known in our town; nor had anything been learned more recently, even at a time when a great many people began to be interested in the "beauty" Agrafena Alexandrovna had become in four years. There were only rumors that as a seventeen-year-old girl she had been deceived by someone, allegedly some officer, and then abandoned by him forthwith. The officer left, and was soon married somewhere, and Grushenka remained in poverty and disgrace. It was said, however, that though Grushenka had indeed been taken up from poverty by her old man, she was from an honorable family and came in some way from the clergy, being the daughter of a retired deacon or something of the sort. Thus, in four years, from the sensitive, offended, and pitiful orphan, there emerged a red-cheeked, full-bodied Russian beauty, a woman of bold and determined character, proud and insolent, knowing the value of money, acquisitive, tight-fisted, and cautious, who by hook or crook had already succeeded, so they said, in knocking together a little fortune of her own. Everyone was convinced of one thing: that Grushenka was hard to get, and that apart from the old man, her patron, there was not yet a single man in all those four years who could boast of her favors. This was a firm fact, for not a few aspirants had turned up, especially over the past two years, to obtain those favors. But all attempts were in vain; and some of the suitors were even forced to beat a comical and shameful retreat, after the firm and mocking rebuff dealt them by the strong-willed young lady. It was also known that the young lady especially during the past year, had gotten into what is known as "*gescheft*," and that she had proved herself extraordinarily able in this respect, so that i the end many started calling her a real Jew. Not that she lent money on in terest, but it was known, for example, that for some time, together with Fyo dor Pavlovich Karamazov, she had indeed been busily buying up promissory notes for next to nothing, ten kopecks to the rouble, and later made a roubl to ten kopecks on some of them. The ailing Samsonov, who in the past yea had lost the use of his swollen legs, a widower, a tyrant over his two grow sons, a man of great wealth, stingy and implacable, fell, however, under th strong influence of his protégée, whom he had at first kept in an iron grip, o a short leash, on "lenten fare," as some wags said at the time. But Grushenk had succeeded in emancipating herself, having inspired in him, however, boundless trust regarding her fidelity. This old man, a great businessma (now long deceased), was also of remarkable character, tight-fisted above a and hard as flint, and though Grushenka so struck him that he even could no live without her (in the past two years, for example, it had really been so), h

till did not allot her a large, considerable fortune, and even if she had threat-
ned to abandon him altogether, he would still have remained implacable. In-
tead he allotted her a small sum, and even that, when it became known, was
surprise to everyone. "You're a sharp woman," he said to her, giving her
bout eight thousand roubles, "you'll make out for yourself; but know this,
hat apart from your yearly allowance, as usual, you'll get no more from me
efore I die, and I will leave you nothing in my will." And he kept his word: he
lied and left everything to his sons, whom he had kept about him all his life
n the level of servants, with their wives and children, and made no mention
f Grushenka in his will. All of this became known afterwards. But he helped
Grushenka a great deal with advice on how to manage "her own money" and
rought "business" her way. When Fyodor Pavlovich Karamazov, who orig-
nally was connected with Grushenka with regard to some chance "*gescheft*,"
nded quite unexpectedly to himself by falling head over heels in love with
er and nearly losing his reason, old Samsonov, who by then already had one
oot in the grave, chuckled greatly. It is remarkable that Grushenka, through-
ut their acquaintance, was fully and even, as it were, cordially frank with her
ld man, and apparently with no one else in the whole world. Most recently,
when Dmitri Fyodorovich had also appeared suddenly with his love, the old
nan had stopped chuckling. On the contrary, one day he seriously and
ternly advised Grushenka: "If you must choose between the two of them, fa-
her and son, choose the old man, only in such a way, however, that the old
coundrel is certain to marry you, and makes over at least some of his money
n advance. And don't hobnob with the captain, nothing good will come of it."
These were the very words to Grushenka from the old voluptuary, who al-
eady felt himself near death and indeed died five months after giving this advice. I will also note in passing that although many in our town knew about
he absurd and ugly rivalry at that time between the Karamazovs, father and
on, the object of which was Grushenka, few then understood the true mean-
ng of her relations with the two of them, the old man and the son. Even Gru-
henka's two serving women (after the catastrophe, of which we shall speak
urther on, broke out) later testified in court that Agrafena Alexandrovna re-
eived Dmitri Fyodorovich only out of fear, because, they said, "he threat-
ned to kill her." She had two serving women, one a very old cook, from her
parents' household, ailing and nearly deaf, and the other her granddaughter,
a pert young girl, about twenty years old, Grushenka's maid. Grushenka lived
very frugally and in quite poor surroundings. There were only three rooms in
her cottage, furnished by the landlady with old mahogany furniture in the
fashion of the twenties. When Rakitin and Alyosha arrived, it was already
dusk, but there were no lights in the rooms. Grushenka was lying down in her

drawing room on her big, clumsy sofa with its imitation mahogany back, har
and upholstered with leather that had long since become worn and full
holes. Under her head were two white down pillows from her bed. She wa
lying stretched out on her back, motionless, with both hands behind h
head. She was dressed up as though she were expecting someone, in a blac
silk dress, with a delicate lace fichu on her head, which was very becoming
her; the lace shawl thrown around her shoulders was pinned with a massiv
gold brooch. She precisely was expecting someone, lying as if in anguish an
impatience, with a somewhat pale face, with hot lips and eyes, impatient
tapping the arm of the sofa with her right toe. The moment Rakitin and A
yosha appeared, a slight commotion took place: from the front hall they hear
Grushenka jump up quickly from the sofa and suddenly cry out in fear: "Wh
is it?" But the visitors were met by the maid, who at once replied to her mi
tress:

"It's not him, miss, it's some others, they're all right."

"What's the matter with her?" Rakitin muttered as he led Alyosha by th
arm into the drawing room. Grushenka stood by the sofa, still looking frigh
ened. A thick coil of her dark brown braid escaped suddenly from under th
fichu and fell over her right shoulder, but she did not notice it and did not tuc
it back until she had peered into her visitors' faces and recognized them.

"Ah, it's you, Rakitka? You got me all frightened. Who did you bring? Wh
is that with you? Lord, look who he's brought!" she exclaimed as she mac
out Alyosha's face.

"Send for some candles!" Rakitin said with the casual air of a very close ac
quaintance and intimate, who even has the right to give orders in the hous

"Candles . . . of course, candles . . . Fenya, fetch him a candle . . . Wel
you chose a fine time to bring him!" she exclaimed again, nodding at Alyosh
and turning to the mirror, she began to tuck up her braid with both hands. Sh
seemed displeased.

"Why, is something wrong?" Rakitin asked, instantly almost offended.

"You frightened me, Rakitka, that's what," Grushenka turned to Alyosh
with a smile. "Don't be afraid of me, Alyosha darling, I'm awfully glad to se
you, my so-unexpected visitor. But you, Rakitka, you frightened me:
thought it was Mitya forcing his way in. You see, I tricked him this afternoo
I made him swear to believe me, and then I lied to him. I told him I was goin
to be with Kuzma Kuzmich, my old man, all evening, counting the mone
with him till late at night. I go every week and spend a whole evening settlin
accounts with him. We lock ourselves in: he clicks away on the abacus, and
sit and write it down in the books—I'm the only one he trusts. Mitya believe

I'd be there, but I've locked myself up in my house and sit here waiting for a message. How could Fenya have let you in! Fenya, Fenya! Run out to the gate, open it, and look around, see if the captain is there anywhere. Maybe he's hiding and spying on me, I'm scared to death!"

"No one's there, Agrafena Alexandrovna, I just looked, and I keep peeking through the crack all the time, because I'm in fear and trembling myself."

"Are the shutters fastened, Fenya? And the curtains should be drawn—there!" she drew the heavy curtains herself, "or he might see the light and come flying in. I'm afraid of your brother Mitya today, Alyosha." Grushenka was speaking loudly, and though she was worried, she also seemed almost in a sort of ecstasy.

"Why are you so afraid of Mitenka today?" Rakitin inquired. "You don't seem to be timid with him, he dances to your tune."

"I told you, I'm expecting a message, a certain golden message, so it would be better now if there were no Mitenka around at all. Besides, he didn't believe I was going to see Kuzma Kuzmich, I feel it. He must be sitting there in the garden now, behind Fyodor Pavlovich's house, watching for me. And if he's sat himself down there, then he won't come here—so much the better! And I really did run over to see Kuzma Kuzmich, Mitya took me there himself, I told him I'd stay till midnight, and that he must come at midnight to take me home. He left, and I stayed at the old man's for about ten minutes and came back here again—oh, was I scared, I ran so as not to meet him."

"And why are you so spruced up? What a curious little cap you've got on!"

"You're much too curious yourself, Rakitin! I told you, I'm expecting a certain message. When it comes, I'll jump up and fly away, and that will be the last you ever see of me. So I'm all dressed and ready to go."

"Where will you fly to?"

"Ask me no questions, I'll tell you no lies."

"Just look at her! Happy all over . . . I've never seen you like this. Decked out as if for a ball," Rakitin looked her up and down.

"A lot you know about balls."

"And you?"

"I saw a ball once. Two years ago Kuzma Kuzmich's son got married, and I watched from the gallery. But why am I talking with you, Rakitka, when such a prince is standing here? What a visitor! Alyosha, darling, I look at you and can't believe it—Lord, how can you be here? To tell the truth, I never dreamed, I never expected, and till now I never believed you would come. Though it's not the right moment, still I'm awfully glad to see you! Sit down on the sofa, here, like that, my young moon. Really, I still can't come to my senses . . . Ah, Rakitka, why didn't you bring him yesterday, or the day before . . . ! Well, I'm glad all the same. Maybe it's even better that it's now, at such a moment, and not two days ago . . ."

She came over friskily, sat down next to Alyosha on the sofa, and looked at him decidedly with admiration. She really was glad, she was not lying when she said so. Her eyes were shining, her lips laughing, but good-naturedly, gaily. Alyosha never expected to see such a kind expression on her face . . . He had seldom met her until the day before, had formed a horrifying notion of her, and had been so terribly shocked the day before by her vicious and perfidious escapade with Katerina Ivanovna, that he was very surprised now suddenly to see in her, as it were, quite a different and unexpected being. And however weighed down he was by his own grief, his eyes involuntarily rested on her with attention. Her whole manner also seemed to have changed for the better since the day before: there was almost no trace of that sugary inflection, of those pampered and affected movements . . . everything was simple, simple-hearted, her movements were quick, direct, trusting, but she was very excited.

"Oh, Lord, such things keep coming true today, really," she began prattling again. "And why I'm so glad of you, Alyosha, I don't know myself. If you asked, I couldn't say."

"'You really don't know why you're glad?" Rakitin grinned. "There must have been some reason why you kept pestering me to bring him, bring him, all the time."

"I had a different reason before, but that's gone now, it's not the right moment. I'll feed you now, that's what. I've become kind now, Rakitka. Do sit down, Rakitka, why are you standing? Ah, you are sitting down? Never fear, Rakitushka will always look out for himself. Now he's sitting across from us, Alyosha, and feeling offended because I didn't ask him to sit down before you. My Rakitka is touchy, oh, so touchy!" Grushenka laughed. "Don't be angry, Rakitka, I'm feeling kind today. But why are you sitting there so sadly, Alyoshechka, or are you afraid of me?" she looked into his eyes with mocking gaiety.

"He has a grief. He didn't get promoted," Rakitin said in a deep voice.

"What do you mean, promoted?"

"His elder got smelly."

"What do you mean, 'smelly'? You're spewing a lot of nonsense, you just want to say something nasty. Shut up, fool. Will you let me sit on your lap, Alyosha—like this!" And all at once she sprang up suddenly and, laughing, leaped onto his knees like an affectionate cat, tenderly embracing his neck with her right arm. "I'll cheer you up, my pious boy! No, really, will you let me sit on your lap for a little, you won't be angry? Tell me—I'll jump off."

Alyosha was silent. He sat afraid to move; he heard her say: "Tell me—I'll jump off," but did not answer, as if he were frozen. Yet what was happening in him was not what might have been expected, or what might have been imagined, for example, by Rakitin, who was watching carnivorously from where he sat. The great grief in his soul absorbed all the feelings his heart might have conceived, and if he had been able at that moment to give himself a full accounting, he would have understood that he was now wearing the strongest armor against any seduction and temptation. Nevertheless, despite all the vague unaccountability of his state of soul and all the grief that was weighing on him, he still could not help marveling at a new and strange sensation that was awakening in his heart: this woman, this "horrible" woman, not only did not arouse in him the fear he had felt before, the fear that used to spring up in him every time he thought of a woman, if such a thought flashed through his soul, but, on the contrary, this woman, of whom he was afraid most of all, who was sitting on his knees and embracing him, now aroused in him suddenly quite a different, unexpected, and special feeling, the feeling of some remarkable, great, and most pure-hearted curiosity, and without any fear now, without a trace of his former terror—that was the main thing, and it could not but surprise him.

"Stop babbling nonsense," Rakitin cried. "You'd better bring us champagne, you owe it to me, you know!"

"It's true, I owe it to him. I promised him champagne, Alyosha, on top of everything else, if he brought you to me. Let's have champagne, I'll drink, too! Fenya, Fenya, bring us champagne, the bottle Mitya left, run quickly. Though I'm stingy, I'll stand you a bottle—not you, Rakitka, you're a mushroom, but he is a prince! And though my soul is full of something else now, I'll drink with you all the same, I want to be naughty!"

"But what is this moment of yours, and what, may I ask, is this message, or is it a secret?" Rakitin put in again with curiosity, pretending as hard as he could that he did not notice the barbs that kept coming at him.

"Eh, it's no secret, and you know it yourself," Grushenka suddenly said worriedly, turning to look at Rakitin and leaning back a little from Alyosha, though she stayed seated on his lap with her arm around his neck. "The officer is coming, Rakitin, my officer is coming!"

"I heard he was coming, but is he so nearby?"

"He's at Mokroye now, he'll send me a messenger from there, he wrote me so, the letter came just today. I'm sitting here waiting for the messenger."

"Aha! But why in Mokroye?"

"It's a long story, I've told you enough."

"Take that, Mitenka—ai, ai! Does he know?"

"Know? He doesn't know anything. If he found out, he'd kill me. But now I'm not afraid at all, I'm not afraid of his knife now. Shut up, Rakitin, don't remind me of Dmitri Fyodorovich: he's turned my heart to mush. And I don't want to think about anything right now. But I can think about Alyoshechka, I'm looking at Alyoshechka . . . Smile at me, darling, cheer up, smile at my foolishness, at my joy . . . He smiled, he smiled! What a tender look! You know, Alyosha, I keep thinking you must be angry with me because of two days ago, because of the young lady. I was a bitch, that's what . . . Only it's still good that it happened that way. It was bad, and it was good," Grushenka suddenly smiled meaningly, and a cruel little line suddenly flashed in her smile. "Mitya says she shouted: 'She should be flogged!' I must really have offended her. She invited me, wanted to win me over, to seduce me with her chocolate . . . No, it's good that it happened that way," she smiled again. "But I'm still afraid you're angry . . ."

"Really," Rakitin suddenly put in again with serious surprise, "she's really afraid of you, Alyosha, chicken that you are."

"To you he's a chicken, Rakitin, that's what . . . because you have no conscience, that's what! You see, I love him with my soul, that's what! Do you believe me, Alyosha, that I love you with all my soul?"

"Ah, shameless! She's confessing her love for you, Alexei!"

"Why not? I do love him."

"And the officer? And the golden message from Mokroye?"

"That's one thing, and this is another."

"Just like a woman!"

"Don't make me angry, Rakitka," Grushenka caught him up hotly. "That is one thing, and this is another. I love Alyosha differently. It's true I had sly thoughts about you, Alyosha. I'm a low woman, I'm a violent woman, yet there are moments, Alyosha, when I look upon you as my conscience. I keep thinking: 'How a man like him must despise a bad woman like me.' I thought the same thing two days ago, as I was running home from the young lady's. I noticed you long ago, Alyosha, and Mitya knows, I told him. And Mitya understands. Will you believe, Alyosha, really I look at you sometimes and feel ashamed, ashamed of myself . . . And I don't know, I don't remember how it was that I started thinking about you, or when it was . . ."

Fenya came in and placed a tray on the table, with an uncorked bottle of champagne and three full glasses on it.

"Here's the champagne!" Rakitin cried. "You're excited, Agrafena Alexandrovna, and beside yourself. You'll drink a glass and start dancing. Ehh, even this they couldn't get right," he added, examining the champagne. "The old woman poured it in the kitchen, and they brought the bottle without the cork, and it's warm. Well, let's have it anyway."

He went up to the table, took a glass, drank it in one gulp, and poured himself another.

"One doesn't bump into champagne too often," he said, licking his chops. "Hey, Alyosha, take a glass, prove yourself. What are we going to drink to? To the gates of paradise? Grusha, take a glass, drink with us to the gates of paradise."

"What gates of paradise?"

She took her glass. Alyosha took his, sipped at it, and set the glass down again.

"No, I'd better not," he smiled quietly.

"But you boasted . . . !" Rakitin cried.

"Then I won't drink either," Grushenka cut in, "I don't want to anyway. Drink the whole bottle yourself, Rakitka. If Alyosha drinks, I'll drink, too."

"What sentimental slop!" Rakitin taunted. "And sitting on his lap all the while! Granted he has his grief, but what have you got? He rebelled against his God, he was going to gobble sausage . . ."

"Why so?"

"His elder died today, the elder Zosima, the saint."

"The elder Zosima died!" Grushenka exclaimed. "Oh, Lord, I didn't know!" She crossed herself piously. "Lord, but what am I doing now, sitting on his lap!" She suddenly gave a start as if in fright, jumped off his knees at once, and sat down on the sofa. Alyosha gave her a long, surprised look, and something seemed to light up in his face.

"Rakitin," he suddenly said loudly and firmly, "don't taunt me with having rebelled against my God. I don't want to hold any anger against you, and therefore you be kinder, too. I've lost such a treasure as you never had, and you cannot judge me now. You'd do better to look here, at her: did you see how she spared me? I came here looking for a wicked soul—I was drawn to that, because I was low and wicked myself, but I found a true sister, I found a treasure—a loving soul . . . She spared me just now . . . I'm speaking of you, Agrafena Alexandrovna. You restored my soul just now."

Alyosha was breathless and his lips began to tremble. He stopped.

"Really saved you, did she!" Rakitin laughed spitefully. "Yet she was going to eat you up, do you know that?"

"Stop, Rakitka!" Grushenka suddenly jumped up. "Be still, both of you. I'll tell you everything now: you be still, Alyosha, because I feel ashamed of hearing such words from you, because I'm wicked, not good—that's how I am. And you, Rakitka, be still because you're lying. I did have such a low thought, of eating him up, but now you're lying, it's quite different now . . . and I don't want to hear any more from you, Rakitka!" Grushenka spoke all this with unusual excitement.

"Look at them—both senseless!" Rakitin hissed, staring at them both in amazement. "It's crazy, I feel like I'm in a madhouse. They've both gone soft, they'll start crying in a minute!"

"I will start crying, I will start crying!" Grushenka kept repeating. "He called me his sister, I'll never forget it! Just know one thing, Rakitka, I may be wicked, but still I gave an onion."

"An onion? Ah, the devil, they really have gone crazy!"

Rakitin was surprised at their exaltation, which offended and annoyed him, though he should have realized that everything had just come together for them both in such a way that their souls were shaken, which does not happen very often in life. But Rakitin, who could be quite sensitive in understanding everything that concerned himself, was quite crude in understanding the feelings and sensations of his neighbors—partly because of his youthful inexperience, and partly because of his great egoism.

"You see, Alyoshechka," Grushenka turned to him, laughing nervously, "I'm boasting to Rakitka that I gave an onion, but I'm not boasting to you, I'll tell you about it for a different reason. It's just a fable, but a good fable, I heard it when I was still a child, from my Matryona who cooks for me now. It goes like this: Once upon a time there was a woman, and she was wicked as wicked could be, and she died. And not one good deed was left behind her. The devils took her and threw her into the lake of fire. And her guardian angel stood thinking: what good deed of hers can I remember to tell God? Then he remembered and said to God: once she pulled up an onion and gave it to a beggar woman. And God answered: now take that same onion, hold it out to her in the lake, let her take hold of it, and pull, and if you pull her out of the lake, she can go to paradise, but if the onion breaks, she can stay where she is. The angel ran to the woman and held out the onion to her: here, woman, he said, take hold of it and I'll pull. And he began pulling carefully, and had almost pulled her all the way out, when other sinners in the lake saw her being pulled out and all began holding on to her so as to be pulled out with her. But the woman was wicked as wicked could be, and she began to kick them with her feet: 'It's me who's getting pulled out, not you; it's my onion, not yours.' No sooner did she say it than the onion broke. And the woman fell back into the lake and is burning there to this day. And the angel wept and went away.[2] That's the fable, Alyosha, I know it by heart, because I myself am that wicked woman. I boasted to Rakitin that I gave an onion, but I'll say it differently to you: in my whole life I've given *just one* little onion, that's how much good I've done. And don't praise me after that, Alyosha, don't think I'm good, I'm wicked, wicked as can be, and if you praise me you'll make me ashamed. Ah, let me confess everything: listen, Alyosha, I wanted so much to lure you here and pestered Rakitin so much that I even promised him twenty-five roubles if he'd bring you to me. No, wait, Rakitka!" She went briskly to the table, opened a drawer, got out a purse, and from the purse took a twenty-five-rouble bill.

"What nonsense! What nonsense!" exclaimed Rakitin, taken aback.

"I owe it to you, Rakitka, take it, you won't refuse, you asked for it yourself," and she flung the bill at him.

"Why refuse?" Rakitin said in a deep voice, visibly ashamed, but disguising his embarrassment with swagger. "It will truly come in handy; fools exist for the intelligent man's profit."

"And now keep still, Rakitka, what I'm going to say now is not for your ears. Sit there in the corner and keep still, you don't love us, so keep still."

"What's there to love you for?" Rakitin snarled, no longer concealing his spite. He put the twenty-five roubles in his pocket, and was decidedly ashamed before Alyosha. He had planned on being paid later, so that Alyosha would not know, but now shame made him angry. Up to that moment he had found it more politic not to contradict Grushenka too much, despite all her barbs, since she obviously had some sort of power over him. But now he, too, got angry:

"One loves for some reason, and what has either of you done for me?"

"You should love for no reason, like Alyosha."

"How does he love you? What has he shown you, that you're making such a fuss about it?"

Grushenka stood in the middle of the room; she spoke heatedly, and hysterical notes could be heard in her voice.

"Keep still, Rakitka, you don't understand anything about us! And don't you dare speak familiarly with me again, I forbid it. You're too bold, that's what! Sit in the corner like my lackey and keep still. And now, Alyosha, I will tell the whole, pure truth to you alone, so that you can see what a creature I am! I tell it to you, not to Rakitka. I wanted to ruin you, I was quite determined, that is the great truth: I wanted it so much that I bribed Rakitka with money to bring you. And why did I want it so much? You knew nothing, Alyosha, you used to turn away from me, you'd walk by me with your eyes on the ground, but I looked at you a hundred times before, I began asking everyone about you. Your face stayed in my heart: 'He despises me,' I thought, 'he doesn't even want to look at me.' And finally such a feeling took hold of me that I was surprised at myself: why should I be afraid of a boy like him? I'll eat him up and laugh. I was so angry! Believe me, no one here dares to say or think they can come to Agrafena Alexandrovna for that bad thing; I have only the old man here, I'm bought and sold to him, Satan married us, but there's no one else. Yet looking at you, I was determined: I'll eat him up. Eat him up and laugh. See what a wicked bitch I am, and you called me your sister! Now the man who wronged me has come, I'm sitting here waiting for his message. Do you know what this man has been to me? It's five years since Kuzma brought me here—I used to sit hiding from people, so that people wouldn't see or hear me, a silly slip of a girl, sitting and crying, not sleeping all night, thinking: 'Where is he now, the man who wronged me? He must be laughing at me with some other woman, and what won't I do to him, if only I ever see him, if only I meet him: I'll make him pay! How I'll make him pay!' At night, in the dark, I sobbed into the pillow and kept thinking it all over, I tore my heart on purpose, to ease it with spite: 'How I'll make him pay, oh, how I will!' I would sometimes even scream in the darkness. Then I would suddenly remember that I was not going to do anything to him, but that he was laughing at me now, or maybe had quite forgotten me, just didn't remember, and then I would throw myself from my bed onto the floor, flooding myself with helpless tears, and shake and shake till dawn. In the morning I would get up worse than a dog, ready to tear the whole world apart. And then you know what: I began saving money, became merciless, grew fat—and do you think I got any smarter? Not a bit. No one sees it, no one in the whole universe knows it, but when the dark of night falls, I sometimes lie just as I used to, as a young girl, five years ago, gnashing my teeth and crying all night, thinking: 'I'll show him, oh, yes, I'll show him!' Do you hear what I'm saying? Now try to understand me: a month ago I suddenly received this letter: he's coming, his wife died, he wants to see me. It took my breath away. Lord, I suddenly thought: what if he comes and whistles for me, calls me, and I just crawl to him like a little dog, guilty and beaten! I thought of it and couldn't believe myself: 'Am I so base? Will I just run to him?' And I've been so angry with myself all this month that it's even worse than five years ago. Now you see how violent, how wild I am, Alyosha, I've spoken out the whole truth to you! I've been toying with Mitya so as not to run to the other one. Keep still, Rakitin, it's not for you to judge me, I'm not telling it to you. Before you came I was lying here waiting, thinking, deciding my whole fate, and you will never know what was in my heart. No, Alyosha, tell your young lady not to be angry for two days ago. . . ! No one in the whole world knows how I feel now, or can know . . . Because maybe I'll take a knife with me today, I haven't decided yet . . ."

And having uttered this "pathetic" phrase, Grushenka suddenly could not help herself; she broke off, covered her face with her hands, threw herself onto the sofa, into the pillows, and sobbed like a little child. Alyosha stood up and went over to Rakitin.

"Misha," he said, "don't be angry. You're offended with her, but don't be angry. Did you hear her just now? One cannot ask so much of a human soul, one should be more merciful . . ."

Alyosha said this from an unrestrainable impulse of his heart. He had to speak out and he turned to Rakitin. If there had been no Rakitin, he would have begun exclaiming to himself. But Rakitin looked at him with a sneer, and Alyosha suddenly stopped.

"They just loaded you with your elder, and now you've fired your elder off at me, Alyoshenka, little man of God,"[3] Rakitin said with a hateful smile.

"Don't laugh, Rakitin, don't sneer, don't speak of the deceased: he is higher than anyone who has ever lived!" Alyosha cried with tears in his voice. "I stood up to speak to you not as a judge but as the lowliest of the accused. Who am I compared with her? I came here seeking my own ruin, saying: 'Who cares, who cares?' because of my faintheartedness; but she, after five years of torment, as soon as someone comes and speaks a sincere word to her, forgives everything, forgets everything, and weeps! The man who wronged her has come back, he is calling her, and she forgives him everything, and hastens to him with joy, and she won't take a knife, she won't! No, I am not like that. I don't know whether you are like that, Misha, but I am not like that! I learned this lesson today, just now . . . She is higher in love than we are . . . Have you ever heard her speak before of what she just told now? No, you have not; if you had, you would have understood everything long ago . . . and the other woman, who was offended two days ago, she, too, must forgive! And she will forgive if she knows . . . and she will know . . . This soul is not reconciled yet, it must be spared . . . maybe there is a treasure in this soul . . ."

Alyosha fell silent, because his breath failed him. Rakitin, despite all his anger, watched in amazement. He had never expected such a tirade from the quiet Alyosha.

"Quite a lawyer we've got here! Have you fallen in love with her or something? You win, Agrafena Alexandrovna, our ascetic is really in love with you!" he shouted with an insolent laugh.

Grushenka raised her head from the pillow and looked at Alyosha; a tender smile shone on her face, somehow suddenly swollen with tears.

"Let him be, Alyosha, my cherub, you see how he is, he's not worth talking to. Mikhail Osipovich," she turned to Rakitin, "I was about to ask your forgiveness for having been rude to you, but now I don't want to. Alyosha, come here and sit down," she beckoned to him with a joyful smile, "sit down, so, and tell me," she took his hand, smiling, and peered into his face, "you tell me: do I love this man or not? The one who wronged me, do I love him or not? I was lying here in the dark before you came, and kept asking my heart: do I love this man or not? Deliver me, Alyosha, the time has come; it shall be as you decide. Should I forgive him or not?"

"But you've already forgiven him," Alyosha said, smiling.

"Yes, I've forgiven him," Grushenka said meaningly. "What a base heart! To my base heart!" She suddenly snatched a glass from the table, drank it in one gulp, held it up, and smashed it as hard as she could on the floor. The glass shattered and tinkled. A certain cruel line flashed in her smile.

"Or maybe I haven't forgiven him yet," she said somehow menacingly, dropping her eyes to the ground, as though she were alone, talking to herself. "Maybe my heart is only getting ready to forgive him. I still have to struggle with my heart. You see, Alyosha, I've grown terribly fond of my tears over these five years . . . Maybe I've come to love only my wrong, and not him at all!"

"I'd hate to be in his skin!" Rakitin hissed.

"And you won't be, Rakitka, you'll never be in his skin. You'll make shoes for me, Rakitka, that's what I'll have you do, and you'll never get a woman like me . . . Maybe he won't either . . ."

"No? Then why all this finery?" Rakitin taunted her slyly.

"Don't reproach me with my finery, Rakitka, you don't know the whole of my heart yet! If I choose, I'll tear it off right now, I'll tear it off this very minute!" she cried in a ringing voice. "You don't know why I need this finery, Rakitka! Maybe I'll go up to him and say: 'Did you ever see me like this?' He left a seventeen-year-old, skinny, consumptive crybaby. I'll sit down beside him, I'll seduce him, I'll set him on fire: 'Take a good look at me now, my dear sir, because that's all you'll get—for there's many a slip twixt the cup and the lip!' Maybe that's why I need this finery, Rakitka," Grushenka finished with a malicious little laugh. "I'm violent, Alyosha, I'm wild. I'll tear off my finery, I'll maim myself, my beauty, I'll burn my face, and slash it with a knife, and go begging. If I choose, I won't go anywhere or to anyone; if I choose, I'll send everything back to Kuzma tomorrow, all his presents, and all his money, and go and work all my life as a charwoman . . . ! You think I won't do it, Rakitka, you think I won't dare to do it? I will, I will do it, I can do it now, only don't annoy me . . . and I'll get rid of that one, a fig for him, he won't get me!"

She shouted these last words hysterically, but again could not help herself, covered her face with her hands, threw herself onto the pillow, and again shook with sobs. Rakitin stood up.

"Time to go," he said, "it's late, they won't let us into the monastery."

Grushenka leaped to her feet.

"You're not going to leave, Alyosha!" she exclaimed in sorrowful amazement. "But what are you doing to me? You stirred me all up, tormented me, and now for another night I'll be left alone again!"

"What do you want him to do, spend the night here? He can if he wants to! I can go by myself!" Rakitin joked caustically.

"Keep still, you wicked soul," Grushenka shouted furiously at him, "you never said anything like what he came and told me."

"Just what did he tell you?" Rakitin grumbled irritably.

"I don't know, I don't know what he told me, my heart heard it, he wrung my heart . . . He's the first to pity me, and the only one, that's what! Why didn't you come before, you cherub," she suddenly fell on her knees to him, as if beside herself. "All my life I've been waiting for such a one as you, I knew someone like that would come and forgive me. I believed that someone would love me, a dirty woman, not only for my shame . . . !"

"What did I do for you?" Alyosha answered with a tender smile, and he bent down to her and gently took her hands. "I just gave you an onion, one little onion, that's all, that's all . . . !"

Having said that, he himself started weeping. At the same moment there was a sudden noise at the doorway, someone came into the front hall; Grushenka jumped up, looking terribly frightened. Fenya rushed noisily into the room, shouting:

"My lady, my dear, my lady, a messenger has ridden up," she exclaimed joyfully and breathlessly. "A carriage has come for you from Mokroye, Timofei the coachman with a troika, they're changing horses right now . . . The letter, the letter, my lady, here's the letter!"

She was holding the letter in her hand, waving it in the air all the while she was shouting. Grushenka snatched the letter from her and brought it near the candle. It was just a note, a few lines, and she read it in a moment.

"He's calling me!" she cried, quite pale, her face twisted in a painful smile. "He's whistling! Crawl, little dog!"

Only for one moment did she hesitate; suddenly the blood rushed to her head and brought fire to her cheeks.

"I'm going!" she suddenly exclaimed. "Oh, my five years! Farewell, everyone! Farewell, Alyosha, my fate is decided . . . Go, go, all of you, go away, I don't want to see you . . . ! Grushenka is flying to a new life . . . Rakitka, don't you think ill of me either. Maybe I'm going to my death! Ah, I feel drunk!"

She left them suddenly and ran to her bedroom.

"Well, she can't be bothered with us now!" Rakitin growled. "Let's go, or there may be more of this female screaming, I'm sick of these tearful screams . . ."

Alyosha mechanically allowed himself to be led out. The carriage stood in the yard, the horses were being unharnessed, people were bustling about with lanterns. A fresh troika was being led in through the open gate. But just as Alyosha and Rakitin were stepping off the porch, the window of Grushenka's bedroom suddenly opened, and she called after Alyosha in a ringing voice:

"Alyoshechka, bow to your brother Mitenka for me, and tell him not to think ill of me, his wicked woman. And tell him, too, that I said: 'Grushenka has fallen to a scoundrel, and not to you, a noble man!' And add this, too, that Grushenka loved him for one hour, just for one hour she loved him—and from now on he should remember that hour all his life; tell him, that is what Grushenka bids you forever."

She finished in a voice full of weeping. The window slammed shut.

"Hm, hm!" Rakitin grunted, laughing. "She does in your brother Mitenka and then tells him to remember all his life. What a carnivore!"

Alyosha made no reply, as if he had not heard; he walked briskly beside Rakitin, apparently in a great hurry; he walked mechanically, his mind apparently elsewhere. Rakitin was suddenly stung, as if someone had touched him on an open wound. He had been expecting something quite different when he brought Grushenka and Alyosha together; what had happened was something other than what he had wanted so much.

"He's a Pole, this officer of hers," he spoke again, restraining himself, "and he's not even an officer now, he served as a customs clerk in Siberia, somewhere on the Chinese border, just some runty little Polack. They say he lost his job. Now he's heard that Grushenka has some money, so he's come back—that's the whole miracle."

Again it was as if Alyosha did not hear. Rakitin could not help himself:

"So you converted a sinful woman?" he laughed spitefully to Alyosha. "Turned a harlot onto the path of truth? Drove out the seven devils, eh?[4] So here's where today's expected miracles took place!"

"Stop it, Rakitin," Alyosha replied with suffering in his soul.

"And now you 'despise' me for those twenty-five roubles? You think I sold a true friend. But you're not Christ, and I'm not Judas."

"Ah, Rakitin, I assure you I'd forgotten all about that," Alyosha exclaimed, "you've reminded me of it yourself . . ."

But now Rakitin finally got mad.

"The devil take you one and all!" he suddenly yelled. "Why the devil did I have anything to do with you! I don't even want to know you anymore. Go by yourself, there's your road!"

And turning abruptly into another street, he left Alyosha alone in the dark. Alyosha walked out of town, and went across the fields to the monastery.

Chapter 4

Cana of Galilee

It was very late by monastery rules when Alyosha came to the hermitage. The gatekeeper let him in by a special entrance. It had already struck nine, the hour of general rest and quiet, after such a troubled day for them all. Alyosha timidly opened the door and entered the elder's cell, where his coffin now stood. There was no one in the cell but Father Paissy, who was alone reading the Gospel over the coffin, and the young novice Porfiry, who, worn out from the previous night's conversation and the day's commotion, slept a sound young sleep on the floor in the next room. Father Paissy, though he had heard Alyosha come in, did not even look up at him. Alyosha turned to the right of the door, went to the corner, knelt, and began to pray. His soul was overflowing, but somehow vaguely, and no single sensation stood out, making itself felt too much; on the contrary, one followed another in a sort of slow and calm rotation. But there was sweetness in his heart, and, strangely, Alyosha was not surprised at that. Again he saw this coffin before him, and this dead man all covered up in it, who had been so precious to him, but in his soul there was none of that weeping, gnawing, tormenting pity that had been there earlier, in the morning. Now, as he entered, he fell down before the coffin as if it were a holy thing, but joy, joy was shining in his mind and in his heart. The window of the cell was open, the air was fresh and rather cool—"the smell must have become even worse if they decided to open the window," Alyosha thought. But even this thought about the putrid odor, which only recently had seemed to him so terrible and inglorious, did not now stir up any of his former anguish and indignation. He quietly began praying, but soon felt that he was praying almost mechanically. Fragments of thoughts flashed in his soul, catching fire like little stars and dying out at once to give way to others, yet there reigned in his soul something whole, firm, assuaging, and he was conscious of it himself. He would ardently begin a prayer, he wanted so much to give thanks and to love . . . But, having begun the prayer, he would suddenly pass to something else, lapse into thought, and forget both his prayer and what had interrupted it. He tried listening to what Father Paissy was reading, but, being very worn out, he began little by little to doze off . . .

"*And the third day there was a marriage in Cana of Galilee,*" read Father Paissy, "*and the mother of Jesus was there: and both Jesus was called, and his disciples, to the marriage.*"[1]

"Marriage? What was that . . . marriage . . . ?" swept like a whirlwind through Alyosha's mind. "There is happiness for her, too . . . She went to the feast . . . No, she didn't take a knife, she didn't take a knife, that was only a 'pathetic' phrase . . . Well, one should forgive pathetic phrases, one must. Pathetic phrases ease the soul, without them men's grief would be too heavy. Rakitin walked off into the alley. As long as Rakitin thinks about his grudges he will always walk off into some alley . . . But the road . . . the road is wide, straight, bright, crystal, and the sun is at the end of it . . . Ah? . . . what are they reading?"

"*And when they wanted wine, the mother of Jesus saith unto him, They have no wine . . . ,*" Alyosha overheard.

"Ah, yes, I've been missing it and I didn't want to miss it, I love that passage: it's Cana of Galilee, the first miracle . . . Ah, that miracle, ah, that lovely miracle! Not grief, but men's joy Christ visited when he worked his first miracle, he helped men's joy . . . 'He who loves men, loves their joy . . .' The dead man used to repeat it all the time, it was one of his main thoughts . . . One cannot live without joy, says Mitya . . . Yes, Mitya . . . All that is true and beautiful is always full of all-forgiveness—that, too, he used to say . . ."

"*. . . Jesus saith unto her, Woman, what have I to do with thee? mine hour is not yet come. His mother saith unto the servants, Whatsoever he saith unto you, do it.*"

"Do it . . . Joy, the joy of some poor, very poor people . . . Why, of course they were poor, if there wasn't even enough wine for the wedding. Historians write that the people living around the lake of Gennesaret and in all those parts were the poorest people imaginable . . .[2] And the other great heart of the other great being, who was right there, too, his mother, knew that he came down then not just for his great and awful deed, but that his heart was also open to the simple, artless merrymaking of some uncouth, uncouth but guileless beings, who lovingly invited him to their poor marriage feast. 'Mine hour is not yet come,' he says with a quiet smile (he must have smiled meekly to her) . . . Indeed, was it to increase the wine at poor weddings that he came down to earth? Yet he went and did what she asked . . . Ah, he's reading again."

"*. . . Jesus saith unto them, Fill the waterpots with water. And they filled them up to the brim. And he saith unto them, Draw out now, and bear unto the governor of the feast. And they bare it. When the ruler of the feast had tasted the water that was made wine, and knew not whence it was (but the servants which drew the water knew), the governor of the feast called the bridegroom, and saith unto him, Every man at the beginning doth set forth good wine; and when men have well drunk, then that which is worse: but thou hast kept the good wine until now.*"

"But what's this? what's this? Why are the walls of the room opening out? Ah, yes . . . this is the marriage, the wedding feast . . . yes, of course. Here are the guests, here the newlyweds, and the festive crowd, and . . . where is the wise ruler of the feast? But who is this? Who? Again the room is opening out . . . Who is getting up from the big table? What . . . ? Is he here, too? Why, he is in the coffin . . . But here, too . . . He has gotten up, he's seen me, he's coming over . . . Lord!"

Yes, to him, to him he came, the little wizened old man with fine wrinkles on his face, joyful and quietly laughing. Now there was no coffin anymore, and he was wearing the same clothes as the day before, when he sat with them and visitors gathered around him. His face was all uncovered and his eyes were radiant. Can it be that he, too, is at the banquet, that he, too, has been called to the marriage in Cana of Galilee . . . ?

"I, too, my dear, I, too, have been called, called and chosen," the quiet voice spoke over him. "Why are you hiding here, out of sight . . . ? Come and join us."

His voice, the elder Zosima's voice . . . How could it be anyone else, since he was calling? The elder raised Alyosha a little with his hand, and Alyosha got up from his knees.

"We are rejoicing," the little wizened man continued, "we are drinking new wine, the wine of a new and great joy. See how many guests there are? Here are the bridegroom and the bride, here is the wise ruler of the feast, tasting the new wine. Why are you marveling at me? I gave a little onion, and so I am here. And there are many here who only gave an onion, only one little onion . . . What are our deeds? And you, quiet one, you, my meek boy, today you, too, were able to give a little onion to a woman who hungered. Begin, my dear, begin, my meek one, to do your work! And do you see our Sun, do you see him?"

"I'm afraid . . . I don't dare to look," whispered Alyosha.

"Do not be afraid of him. Awful is his greatness before us, terrible is his loftiness, yet he is boundlessly merciful, he became like us out of love, and he is rejoicing with us, transforming water into wine, that the joy of the guests may not end. He is waiting for new guests, he is ceaselessly calling new guests, now and unto ages of ages. See, they are bringing the new wine, the vessels are being brought in . . ."

Something burned in Alyosha's heart, something suddenly filled him almost painfully, tears of rapture nearly burst from his soul . . . He stretched out his hands, gave a short cry, and woke up . . .

Again the coffin, the open window, and the quiet, solemn, distinct reading of the Gospel. But Alyosha no longer listened to what was being read. Strangely, he had fallen asleep on his knees, but now he was standing, and suddenly, as if torn from his place, with three firm, quick steps, he went up to the coffin. He even brushed Father Paissy with his shoulder without noticing it. The latter raised his eyes from the book for a moment, but looked away again at once, realizing that something strange was happening with the boy. For about half a minute Alyosha gazed at the coffin, at the covered up, motionless dead man stretched out with an icon on his chest and the cowl with an eight-pointed cross on his head. A moment ago he had heard his voice, and this voice was still sounding in his ears. He listened, waiting to hear more . . . but suddenly turned abruptly and walked out of the cell.

He did not stop on the porch, either, but went quickly down the steps. Filled with rapture, his soul yearned for freedom, space, vastness. Over him the heavenly dome, full of quiet, shining stars, hung boundlessly. From the zenith to the horizon the still-dim Milky Way stretched its double strand. Night, fresh and quiet, almost unstirring, enveloped the earth. The white towers and golden domes of the church gleamed in the sapphire sky. The luxuriant autumn flowers in the flowerbeds near the house had fallen asleep until morning. The silence of the earth seemed to merge with the silence of the heavens, the mystery of the earth touched the mystery of the stars . . . Alyosha stood gazing and suddenly, as if he had been cut down, threw himself to the earth.

He did not know why he was embracing it, he did not try to understand why he longed so irresistibly to kiss it, to kiss all of it, but he was kissing it, weeping, sobbing, and watering it with his tears, and he vowed ecstatically to love it, to love it unto ages of ages. "Water the earth with the tears of your joy, and love those tears . . . ," rang in his soul. What was he weeping for? Oh, in his rapture he wept even for the stars that shone on him from the abyss, and "he was not ashamed of this ecstasy." It was as if threads from all those innumerable worlds of God all came together in his soul, and it was trembling all over, "touching other worlds." He wanted to forgive everyone and for everything, and to ask forgiveness, oh, not for himself! but for all and for everything, "as others are asking for me," rang again in his soul. But with each noment he felt clearly and almost tangibly something as firm and immovable s this heavenly vault descend into his soul. Some sort of idea, as it were, was oming to reign in his mind—now for the whole of his life and unto ages of ges. He fell to the earth a weak youth and rose up a fighter, steadfast for the est of his life, and he knew it and felt it suddenly, in that very moment of his cstasy. Never, never in all his life would Alyosha forget that moment. "Some- ne visited my soul in that hour," he would say afterwards, with firm belief in is words . . .

Three days later he left the monastery, which was also in accordance with he words of his late elder, who had bidden him to "sojourn in the world."

BOOK VIII: MITYA

Chapter 1
Kuzma Samsonov

But Dmitri Fyodorovich, to whom Grushenka, flying to her new life, had "ordered" her last farewell sent and whom she bade remember forever the one hour of her love, unaware as he was of what had happened with her, was at that moment also running around in terrible disarray. For the past two days he had been in such an unimaginable state that, as he himself said afterwards, he might well have come down with brain fever. Alyosha had been unable to find him the morning before, and that same day his brother Ivan had been unable to arrange a meeting with him in the tavern. The owners of the little apartment he lived in covered his traces, as he had ordered them to do. And he, in those two days, had literally been rushing in all directions, "struggling with his fate and trying to save himself," as he put it afterwards, and had even flown out of town for a few hours on some urgent business, though he was afraid to leave Grushenka unwatched even for a moment. All of this was found out later in the most detailed and documented form, but here we shall outline only the most necessary facts from the history of those two terrible days of his life, which preceded the horrible catastrophe that broke so suddenly upon his fate.

Grushenka, though it was true that she had loved him genuinely and sincerely for one little hour, at the same time would torment him quite cruelly and mercilessly. The worst thing was that he could make out nothing of her intentions; it was impossible to coax them out of her either with tenderness or by force: she would not give in, and would only become angry and turn her back on him altogether—that he understood clearly at the time. He then suspected, quite correctly, that she herself was caught in some sort of struggle, in some sort of extraordinary indecision, trying to make up her mind and unable to make it up, and he therefore supposed with a sinking heart, and not groundlessly, that at moments she must simply hate him and his passion. Perhaps that was the case, but what precisely Grushenka was anguished about, he still did not understand. So far as he was concerned, the whole tormenting question formed itself into just two definitions: "Either him, Mitya, or Fyodor Pavlovich." Here, incidentally, one firm fact must be noted: he was quite certain that Fyodor Pavlovich would be sure to offer Grushenka (if he had not offered her already) a lawful marriage, and did not believe for a moment that the old voluptuary hoped to get off for a mere three thousand. This Mitya deduced from his knowledge of Grushenka and her character. Which was why it could sometimes seem to him that all of Grushenka's torment, and all her indecision, came simply from the fact that she did not know which of them to choose, and which of them would be the more profitable for her. Strangely enough, in those days he did not even think of thinking about the imminent return of "the officer"—that is, the fatal man in Grushenka's life, whose arrival she awaited with such fear and agitation. True, in the past few days Grushenka had been quite silent with him on the subject. Nevertheless, he had been fully informed by her of the letter she had received a month earlier from her former seducer, and he had also been partly informed of the content of the letter. In a wicked moment, Grushenka had shown him the letter, but, to her surprise, he placed very little value on this letter. And it would be quite difficult to explain why: perhaps simply because he was so oppressed by all the ugliness and horror of his struggle with his own father for this woman that he could not even imagine anything more terrible or dangerous for himself, at least not at that time. He simply did not believe in this fiancé who had suddenly sprung from somewhere after a five-year disappearance, much less that he would soon arrive. And this first letter from "the officer," which was shown to Mitenka, itself spoke quite uncertainly about the coming of this new rival: it was a very vague letter, very grandiloquent, and full of nothing but sentimentality. It should be noted that at the time Grushenka concealed from him the last lines of the letter, which spoke with more certainty about his return. Besides, Mitenka later recalled that at that moment he had detected, as it were, some involuntary and proud contempt for this missive from Siberia on the part of Grushenka herself. After that, Grushenka told Mitenka nothing about any of her subsequent dealings with this new rival. So it happened that little by little he even quite forgot about the officer. He thought only that whatever the outcome and whatever turn the affair might take, his impending final clash with Fyodor Pavlovich was too near and must be resolved before anything else. With a sinking soul he waited every moment for Grushenka's decision and kept thinking that it would occur as if unexpectedly, by inspiration. Suddenly she would tell him: "Take me, I'm yours forever," and it would all be over: he would snatch her up and take her to the end of the world at once. Oh, at once, take her far away, as far as possible, if not to the end of the world, then somewhere to the end of Russia, marry her there, and settle down with her incognito, so that no one would know anything about them, not here, not there, not anywhere. Then, oh, then a totally new life would begin at once! He dreamed of this other, this renewed and now "virtuous" life ("it must, it must be virtuous") ceaselessly and feverishly. He thirsted for this resurrection and renewal. The vile bog he had gotten stuck in of his own will burdened him too much, and, like a great many men in such cases, he believed most of all in a change of place: if only it weren't for these people, if only it weren't for these circumstances, if only one could fly away from this cursed place—then everything would be reborn! That was what he believed in and what he longed for.

But that would only be in the case of the first, *happy* solution to the question. There was another solution; he imagined a different and terrible ending. She suddenly says to him: "Go, I've just reached an agreement with Fyodor Pavlovich and shall marry him, you're no longer needed"—and then . . . but then . . . Incidentally, Mitya did not know what would happen then, until the very last hour he did not know, we must clear him of that. He had no definite intentions, the crime had not been thought out. He just watched, spied, and suffered, while preparing himself only for the first, happy ending to his fate. He even drove away all other thoughts. But here quite a different torment began, here arose a quite new and unrelated, but equally fatal and insoluble, circumstance.

Namely, if she should say to him: "I'm yours, take me away," how was he to take her away? Where would he get the means, the money to do it? Just at that time he had exhausted all his income from Fyodor Pavlovich's handouts, which until then had continued nonstop for so many years. Of course Grushenka had money, but on this point Mitya suddenly turned out to be terribly proud: he wanted to take her away himself, to start the new life with her on his own money, not on hers; he could not even imagine himself taking money from her and suffered at the thought to the point of painful revulsion. I will not enlarge upon this fact, or analyze it, I will only note that such was the cast of his soul at the moment. All of this might well have proceeded indirectly and unwittingly, as it were, from the secret suffering of his conscience over Katerina Ivanovna's money, which he had thievishly appropriated: "I am a scoundrel before one woman, and I'll prove at once to be a scoundrel before the other," he thought then, as he himself confessed later, "and Grushenka, if she finds out, will not want such a scoundrel." And so, where to find the means, where to find this fatal money? Otherwise all was lost, and nothing would happen, "for the sole reason that there wasn't enough money—oh, shame!"

To anticipate: the thing was that he perhaps knew where to get the money, he perhaps knew where it lay. I will not go into details just now, as it will all become clear later; but what his main trouble consisted of, I will say, albeit vaguely: in order to take this money that was lying somewhere, in order *to have the right* to take it, it was necessary beforehand to return the three thousand to Katerina Ivanovna—otherwise, "I am a pickpocket, I am a scoundrel, and I do not want to begin a new life as a scoundrel," Mitya decided, and therefore he decided to turn the whole world upside down, if need be, but to be sure to return the three thousand to Katerina Ivanovna at all costs and *before all else*. The final working out of this decision took place in him, so to speak, in the last hours of his life—that is, starting from his last meeting with Alyosha, two days before, in the evening, on the road, after Grushenka had insulted Katerina Ivanovna, and Mitya, having listened to Alyosha's account of it, admitted that he was a scoundrel and asked that Katerina Ivanovna be told so "if it's any comfort to her." Right then, that night, after parting with his brother, he had felt in his frenzy that it would be better even "to kill and rob someone, but repay his debt to Katya." "Better to stand as a murderer and a thief before that robbed and murdered man and before everyone, and go to Siberia, than that Katya should have the right to say I betrayed her and then stole money from her, and with that money ran away with Grushenka to start a virtuous life! That I cannot do!" Thus spoke Mitya, gnashing his teeth, and he might well have imagined at times that he would end up with brain fever. But meanwhile he went on struggling . . .

Strangely enough, it would seem that after such a decision nothing was left for him but despair; for how could one suddenly come up with so much money, especially such a pauper as he? Nevertheless, to the very end he kept hoping that he would get the three thousand, that the money would come to him, that it would somehow fly down to him by itself, from the sky no less. But that is precisely how things happen with people like Dmitri Fyodorovich, who all their lives know only how to spend and squander inherited money that they got without any effort, but have no idea of how money is earned. The most fantastic whirlwind arose in his head just after he had parted with Alyosha two days before, and confused all his thoughts. Thus it came about that he started with the wildest enterprise. Yes, perhaps with such people, precisely in such situations, it is the most impossible and fantastic enterprises that seem to offer the best possibilities. He suddenly decided to go to the merchant Samsonov, Grushenka's patron, to offer him a "plan," to obtain from him for this "plan" the entire sum he needed at once; he had not the slightest doubt about the commercial aspects of his plan, but doubted only how Samsonov himself might view his escapade if he chose to look beyond its commercial aspects. Though Mitya knew the merchant by sight, he was not acquainted with him and had never once spoken to him. But for some reason the conviction had settled in him, even much earlier, that this old profligate, now with one foot in the grave, might not be at all averse at the moment to Grushenka somehow arranging her life honorably and marrying "a trustworthy man." And that he not only would not resist, but even wished it himself, and would further it if the occasion should arise. He also concluded, either from rumors or from something Grushenka had said, that the old man might prefer him for Grushenka over Fyodor Pavlovich. Perhaps to many readers of our story the expectation of such help and the intention of taking his fiancée from the hand of her patron, so to speak, were much too crude and unscrupulous on Dmitri Fyodorovich's part. I can only note that Mitya thought of Grushenka's past as definitively passed. He looked upon that past with infinite compassion, and decided with all the fire of his passion that once Grushenka told him she loved him and would marry him, a completely new Grushenka would begin at once, and together with her a completely new Dmitri Fyodorovich, with no vices now, but with virtues only: they would forgive each other and start their life quite anew. As for Kuzma Samsonov, he considered him a fatal man in Grushenka's life, in that former, swallowed-up past, whom, however, she had never loved, and who—this above all—was now also "passed," done with, so that he was no longer there at all. And besides, Mitya could not even regard him as a man now, because it was known to all and sundry in town that he was an ailing wreck, who maintained only fatherly relations, so to speak, with Grushenka, and not at all on the same terms as before, and that it had been so for a long time, almost a year. In any case, there was much simple-heartedness here on Mitya's part, for with all his vices this was a very simple-hearted man. Because of his simple-heartedness, by the way, he was seriously convinced that old Kuzma, preparing to depart to another world, felt sincerely repentant for his past with Grushenka, and that she had no more faithful patron and friend than this already-harmless old man.

The day after his conversation with Alyosha in the fields, following which he had hardly slept the whole night, Mitya appeared at Samsonov's house at about ten o'clock in the morning and asked to be announced. The house was old, gloomy, spacious, two-storied, with outbuildings and a cottage in the yard. On the ground floor lived Samsonov's two married sons with their families, his elderly sister, and one unmarried daughter. The cottage housed his two clerks, one of whom also had a large family. Both his children and his clerks were cramped in their quarters, but the old man occupied the upper floor by himself and would not share it even with his daughter, who looked after him and at regular hours or at his irregular summons had each time to run up to him from downstairs, despite her chronic shortness of breath. This "upstairs" consisted of a number of large formal rooms, furnished in the merchant style of old, with long, dull rows of clumsy mahogany armchairs and sidechairs along the walls, with crystal chandeliers in dust covers, and sullen mirrors between the windows. All these rooms stood completely empty and uninhabited, because the sick old man huddled himself in one little room, his remote and tiny bedroom, where he was waited on by an old woman in a kerchief and a "lad" who resided on a bench in the front hall. Because of his swollen legs, the old man was almost entirely unable to walk, and only rarely got up from his leather chair, when the old woman, holding him under the arms, would take him once or twice around the room. He was severe and taciturn even with this old woman. When the arrival of "the captain" was announced to him, he at once gave orders not to admit him. But Mitya insisted and asked to be announced a second time. Kuzma Kuzmich questioned the lad in detail: how did he look, was he drunk, was he making trouble? The answer was "sober, but won't go away." The old man again refused to admit him. Then Mitya, who had foreseen as much, and therefore had purposely brought paper and pencil with him, wrote clearly on the piece of paper the words: "On most important business closely concerning Agrafena Alexandrovna," and sent it to the old man. Having thought a little, the old man told the lad to show the visitor to the drawing room, and sent the old woman downstairs with an order for his younger son to report upstairs at once. This younger son, a man over six feet tall and of enormous strength, who shaved his beard and dressed in German fashion (Samsonov himself wore a caftan and had a beard), came immediately and without a word. They all trembled before their father. The father sent for this stalwart not so much from fear of the captain (he was no coward) as simply to have him there, just in case, if he should need a witness. Accompanied by his son, who supported him under the arm, and by the lad, he finally came sailing into the drawing room. One may suppose he felt a certain rather strong curiosity. This drawing room where Mitya was waiting was a huge, dreary, killingly depressing room, with windows on both sides, a gallery, "marbled" walls, and three huge crystal chandeliers in dust covers. Mitya was sitting on a little chair by the entrance, awaiting his fate with nervous impatience. When the old man appeared at the opposite door, about twenty yards away from Mitya's chair, he jumped up suddenly and went to meet him with his long, firm, military stride. Mitya was respectably dressed in a buttoned frock coat, was holding a round hat, and wearing black leather gloves, exactly as three days before in the monastery, at the elder's, at the family meeting with Fyodor Pavlovich and his brothers. The old man stood solemnly and sternly waiting for him, and Mitya felt at once that he was examining him thoroughly as he approached. Mitya was also struck by the face of Kuzma Kuzmich, which had become extremely swollen recently: his lower lip, which had always been thick, now looked like a kind of drooping pancake. He bowed solemnly and silently to his guest, motioned him to an armchair near the sofa, and, leaning on his son's arm, with painful groans began slowly lowering himself onto the sofa facing Mitya, who, seeing his painful exertions immediately felt remorse in his heart, sensible of his present insignificance before this so solemn personage whom he had ventured to disturb.

"What do you want of me, sir?" the old man, having finally seated himself, said slowly, distinctly, sternly, but courteously.

Mitya gave a start, jumped up, and sat down again. Then all at once he began speaking loudly, quickly, nervously, gesticulating and decidedly in a frenzy. Here obviously was a man at the end of his rope, facing ruin and looking for a last way out, and if he did not find it, he might just go and drown himself. All this old Samsonov probably understood instantly, though his face remained unchanged and cold as an idol's.

"The most honorable Kuzma Kuzmich has doubtless already heard more than once of my disputes with my father, Fyodor Pavlovich Karamazov, who robbed me of my inheritance after my own mother . . . because the whole town is chattering about it . . . because here everyone chatters about things they shouldn't . . . And besides, it might also have come to you from Grushenka . . . I beg your pardon: from Agrafena Alexandrovna . . . from Agrafena Alexandrovna who is so greatly respected and so greatly honored by me . . ." Thus Mitya began, and broke off at the first sentence. However, we will not quote his whole speech word for word, but will only give a summary of it. The thing was, he said, that three months ago, he, Mitya, had purposefully consulted (he precisely said "purposefully," not "purposely") a lawyer in the provincial capital, "a famous lawyer, Kuzma Kuzmich, Pavel Pavlovich Korneplodov, perhaps you've heard of him, sir? A vast brain, almost the mind of a statesman . . . he knows you, too . . . he has the highest opinion . . . ," Mitya broke off again. But these gaps did not deter Mitya, he immediately leaped over them and rushed ahead. This same Korneplodov, after questioning him in detail and examining all the documents Mitya could present to him (about the documents Mitya spoke vaguely, and became particularly hurried at this point), opined that with regard to the village of Chermashnya, which should, he said, belong to him, Mitya, from his mother, it would indeed be possible to start a court action and knock the pins out from under the old hooligan . . . "because it's impossible that all doors are locked, and the law knows all the loopholes." In a word, he might hope for as much as an additional six thousand from Fyodor Pavlovich, maybe even seven, because after all Chermashnya is worth not less than twenty-five thousand—that is, certainly twenty-eight, "thirty, in fact, thirty, Kuzma Kuzmich, and just imagine, I never got even seventeen out of that cruel man . . . !" And then, he said, I, Mitya, dropped the whole business, because I can't deal with the law, and when I came here, I was dumbstruck by a countersuit (here Mitya became confused again, and again leaped abruptly ahead): and so, most honorable Kuzma Kuzmich, he said, how would you like to take over all my claims against that monster, and give me just three thousand . . . You can't lose in any case, I swear it on my honor, and quite the opposite, you could make six or seven thousand instead of three . . . And above all it must be settled "this same day." "I'll . . . at the notary, is it, or whatever . . . In a word, I'm ready for anything, I'll supply all the documents you want, I'll sign anything . . . and we could draw up the paper right now, and if possible, if only it were possible, this morning . . . You could let me have the three thousand . . . because who else is a capitalist in this little town if not you . . . and you would save me from . . . in a word, you would save my poor head for a most honorable deed, for a most lofty deed, one might say . . . for I cherish the most honorable feelings for a certain person, whom you know only too well, sir, and for whom you have a fatherly concern. Otherwise I wouldn't have come, if it wasn't fatherly. And here three men are at loggerheads, if you like, because fate is a grisly thing, Kuzma Kuzmich! Realism, Kuzma Kuzmich, realism! And since you should have been counted out long ago, there are two heads left, as I put it, awkwardly perhaps, but I'm not a literary man. That is, one of the heads is mine, and the other—that monster's. So choose: me or the monster? Everything is in your hands now—three fates and two lots . . . Forgive me, I've gotten confused, but you understand . . . I can see by your venerable eyes that you understand . . . And if you don't understand, I'll drown myself today, that's it!"

Mitya broke off his absurd speech with "that's it," and jumping up from his seat, awaited the answer to his stupid offer. At the last phrase, he felt suddenly and hopelessly that everything had fallen through, and, above all, that he had produced a lot of terrible drivel. "Strange, on my way here it all seemed fine, and now it's all drivel!" suddenly flashed through his hopeless head. All the while he was talking, the old man sat motionlessly and watched him with an icy expression in his eyes. However, after keeping him in suspense for a moment, Kuzma Kuzmich at last declared in the most resolute and cheerless tone:

"Excuse me, sir, we do not engage in that kind of business."

Mitya suddenly felt his legs give way under him.

"What am I to do now, Kuzma Kuzmich?" he murmured, with a pale smile. "I'm done for now, don't you think?"

"Excuse me, sir . . ."

Mitya went on standing, staring fixedly at the old man, and suddenly noticed a slight movement in his face. He gave a start.

"You see, sir, such business is not in our line," the old man said slowly, "there would be courts, lawyers, all kinds of trouble! But there is a man for that, if you like you can try him . . ."

"My God, who is he . . . ! You're my resurrection, Kuzma Kuzmich," Mitya began babbling suddenly.

"He's not a local man, the one I mean, and he's not here now. He's from peasants, he trades in timber, he's called Lyagavy.[1] He's been bargaining for a year with Fyodor Pavlovich over that woodlot in Chermashnya, but they can't agree on a price, as perhaps you've heard. Now he's come back again and is staying with the priest in Ilyinskoye, about eight miles or so from Volovya station, in the village of Ilyinskoye. He also wrote here, to me, about the same business—that is, concerning the woodlot—asking my advice. Fyodor Pavlovich himself wants to go and see him. So if you were to get there ahead of Fyodor Pavlovich, and make Lyagavy the same offer you made me, he might just . . ."

"A brilliant idea!" Mitya interrupted ecstatically. "It's made for him, just made for him! He's bargaining, the price is too high, and here is this document of ownership just made for him, ha, ha, ha!" Mitya burst into his clipped, wooden laugh, so unexpectedly that even Samsonov jerked his head.

"How can I thank you, Kuzma Kuzmich," Mitya was bubbling over.

"It's nothing, sir," Samsonov inclined his head.

"But you don't realize, you've saved me, oh, I was drawn to you by some presentiment . . . And so, off to that priest!"

"No thanks are necessary, sir."

"I hasten, I fly! I've abused your health. I will remember it always—it's a Russian man saying it to you, Kuzma Kuzmich, a R-r-russian man!"

"Well, sir."

Mitya seized his hand to shake it, but something malicious flashed in the old man's eyes. Mitya drew his hand back, and at once reproached himself for his suspicion. "He must be tired . . . ," flashed through his mind.

"For her! For her, Kuzma Kuzmich! You understand it's for her!" he roared suddenly to the rafters, then bowed, turned around sharply, and with the same long, quick strides walked to the door without looking back. He was trembling with delight. "Everything was on the verge of ruin, and my guardian angel saved me," raced through his mind. "And if such a businessman as this old man (a most honorable old man, and what bearing!) has pointed out this course, then . . . then this course must surely be a winner. I'll fly immediately. I'll be back before nightfall, by nightfall, but the thing will be won. Can the old man have been laughing at me?" Thus Mitya exclaimed, striding back to his lodgings, and of course to his mind it could not have appeared otherwise; that is, either it was businesslike advice, and from such a businessman, who knows business and knows this Lyagavy (strange name!), or—or the old man was laughing at him! Alas! only the second of these thoughts was true. Later, much later, when the whole catastrophe had already taken place, old Samsonov himself admitted, laughing, that he had made a fool of the "captain." This was a spiteful, cold, and sarcastic man, full of morbid antipathies as well. Whether it was the rapturous look of the captain, the foolish conviction of this "wastrel and spendthrift" that he, Samsonov, might fall for something as wild as his "plan," or jealousy over Grushenka, in whose name this "madcap" came with such a wild thing, asking for money—I cannot say what precisely prompted the old man at the time, but when Mitya stood before him, feeling his legs give way, and exclaimed senselessly that he was done for—at that moment the old man looked upon him with boundless spite and decided to make a fool of him. Once Mitya had left, Kuzma Kuzmich, livid with spite, turned to his son and told him to give orders that not a hair of that ragamuffin was to be seen in the future, that he was not even to be allowed into the yard, or else . . .

He did not finish his threat, but even his son, who had often seen him angry, jumped in fear. For a whole hour afterwards the old man was even shaking all over with spite, and by evening he had fallen ill and sent for a "leech."

Chapter 2

Lyagavy

So he had to go "at a gallop," and yet he had no money, not a kopeck, for horses—that is, he had forty kopecks, but that was all, all that remained from so many years of former prosperity! But at home he had an old silver watch that had long since stopped running. He grabbed it and took it to a watchmaker, a Jew, who had his shop in the marketplace. The Jew gave him six roubles for it. "I didn't expect even that much!" cried the delighted Mitya (he still went on being delighted), grabbed his six roubles and ran home. At home he added to the sum, borrowing three roubles from his landlords, who gave it to him gladly, though it was their last money—so much did they love him. Mitya, in his rapturous state, revealed to them at once that his fate was being decided, and told them, in a terrible hurry of course, almost the whole of his "plan," which he had just presented to Samsonov, then Samsonov's decision, his future hopes, and so on and so forth. His landlords even before then had been initiated into many of his secrets, which was why they looked upon him as one of *their own*, not at all as a proud gentleman. Having thus collected nine roubles, Mitya sent for post horses going to Volovya station. But in this way the fact came to be remembered and noted that "on the eve of a certain event, at noon, Mitya did not have a kopeck, and that, in order to get money, he sold his watch and borrowed three roubles from his landlords, all in the presence of witnesses."

I note this fact beforehand; why I do so will become clear later.

Although, as he galloped to Volovya station, Mitya was beaming with joyful anticipation that he was at last about to finish and have done with "all these affairs," he was nevertheless also trembling with fear: what would happen with Grushenka now, in his absence? What if precisely today she should at last decide to go to Fyodor Pavlovich? That was why he had left without telling her and ordered his landlords under no circumstances to reveal where he was going if anyone should come asking for him. "I must get back, I must get back by this evening," he kept saying, as he jolted along in the wagon, "and maybe even drag this Lyagavy here . . . to execute this deed . . ." So Mitya dreamed, with a sinking soul, but, alas, his dreams were not at all destined to come true according to his "plan."

First of all, he was late, having set out on a back road from Volovya station. Instead of eight miles, it turned out to be twelve. Second, he did not find the Ilyinskoye priest at home; he was away in a neighboring village. It was almost dark by the time Mitya located him, having driven to this neighboring village with the same, already exhausted, horses. The priest, a timid, tender-looking little man, explained to him at once that though this Lyagavy had been staying with him at first, he was now in Sukhoy Possyolok, and would be spending the night in the forester's hut, because he was buying timber there too. To Mitya's urgent requests to take him to Lyagavy at once and "thereby save him, so to speak," the priest, though hesitant at first, finally agreed to go with him to Sukhoy Possyolok, apparently out of curiosity; but, as bad luck would have it, he suggested that they go "afoot," since it was only "a wee bit more" than half a mile. Mitya naturally agreed and set off with his long strides, so that the poor priest almost had to run to keep up. He was not yet old, and was a very cautious little man. Mitya also began speaking with him at once about his plans, hotly and nervously demanded advice concerning Lyagavy, and talked all the way. The priest listened attentively, but gave little advice. He responded evasively to Mitya's questions: "I don't know, oh, I don't know, how am I to know that," and so on. When Mitya began speaking about his disputes with his father over the inheritance, the priest was even frightened, because he stood in some sort of dependent relation to Fyodor Pavlovich. However, he did ask in surprise why Mitya called this peasant trader Gorstkin by the name of Lyagavy, and made a point of explaining to him that though the man was indeed Lyagavy, he was also not Lyagavy, because he took bitter offense at the name, and that he must be called Gorstkin, "otherwise you won't get anywhere with him, and he won't even listen," the priest concluded. Mitya was slightly and briefly surprised, and explained that Samsonov himself had referred to the man that way. On hearing of this circumstance, the priest at once changed the subject, though he would have done better to explain then and there to Dmitri Fyodorovich what he suspected: that if Samsonov himself had sent him to this peasant calling him Lyagavy, did he not do it in mockery for some reason, and wasn't there something wrong here? But Mitya had no time to pause over "such trifles." He rushed, he strode along, and only when they reached Sukhoy Possyolok did he realize that they had gone not half a mile, not a mile, but a good mile and a half. This annoyed him, but he let it pass. They went into the hut. The forester, an acquaintance of the priest, occupied half of the hut, and in the other, the good half, on the opposite side of the entryway, Gorstkin was staying. They went into this good room and lighted a tallow candle. The room was overheated. The samovar on the pine table had gone out; there were also a tray with cups, an empty bottle of rum, an almost empty quart bottle of vodka, and some crusts of white bread. The visitor himself lay stretched out on a bench, his coat bunched up under his head for a pillow, snoring heavily. Mitya stood perplexed. "Of course I must wake him up; my business is too important, I've hurried so, I'm in a hurry to get back today," Mitya became alarmed; but the priest and the forester stood silently without expressing their opinion. Mitya went over himself and began shaking him, quite energetically, but the sleeping man would not wake up. "He's drunk," Mitya decided, "but what am I to do, Lord, what am I to do!" And suddenly, in terrible impatience, he began tugging the sleeping man by the arms and legs, rolling his head back and forth, lifting him up and sitting him on the bench, yet after prolonged exertions, all he accomplished was that the man began mumbling absurdly and uttering strong but inarticulate oaths.

"No, you'd better wait," the priest finally pronounced, "he's obviously in no condition."

"Been drinking all day," the forester echoed.

"Oh, God!" Mitya kept exclaiming, "if only you knew how necessary it is, and what despair I'm in now!"

"No, you'd better wait till morning," the priest repeated.

"Till morning? But, merciful God, that's impossible!" And in his despair he was about to rush at the drunk man to wake him, but stopped at once, realizing that all efforts were useless. The priest was silent, the sleepy forester was gloomy.

"What terrible tragedies realism inflicts on people," Mitya uttered in complete despair. Sweat was streaming down his face. Seizing the moment, the priest quite reasonably explained that even if they succeeded in waking the sleeping man up, still, in his drunken state, he would not be fit for any conversation, "and you have important business, so it would be safer to leave it till morning . . ." Mitya spread his arms helplessly and agreed.

"I'll stay here, father, with a lighted candle, and try to catch the right moment. When he wakes up, I'll begin . . . I'll pay you for the candle," he turned to the forester, "and for the night's lodging, too; you'll remember Dmitri Karamazov. Only I don't know what to do with you, father: where will you sleep?"

"No, I'd better go back to my place, sir. I'll take his mare and go," he pointed to the forester. "And now, farewell, sir, I hope you get full satisfaction."

So it was settled. The priest rode off on the mare, happy to have escaped at last, but still shaking his head in perplexity and wondering whether first thing next day he ought not to inform his benefactor Fyodor Pavlovich of this curious incident, "or else, worse luck, he may find out, get angry, and stop his favors." The forester, having scratched himself, silently went back to his room, and Mitya sat on the bench, waiting, as he put it, to catch the right moment. Deep anguish, like a heavy fog, enveloped his soul. Deep, terrible anguish! He sat and thought, but could not think anything through. The candle flickered, a cricket chirped, it was becoming unbearably stuffy in the overheated room. He suddenly imagined a garden, a lane behind the garden, the door of his father's house secretly opening, and Grushenka running in through the door . . . He jumped up from the bench.

"A tragedy!" he said, grinding his teeth, and mechanically going over to the sleeping man, he began looking at his face. He was a lean man, not yet old, with a very oblong face, light brown curly hair, and a long, thin, reddish beard, wearing a cotton shirt and a black waistcoat, from the pocket of which the chain of a silver watch peeped out. Mitya examined his physiognomy with terrible hatred, and for some reason the most hateful thing was his curly hair. Above all it was unbearably vexing that he, Mitya, should be standing there over him with his urgent business, having sacrificed so much, having left so much behind, utterly exhausted, while this parasite, "on whom my entire fate now depends, goes on snoring as if nothing were wrong, as if he came from another planet." "Oh, the irony of fate!" Mitya exclaimed, and suddenly losing his head altogether, he again tried frantically to rouse the drunken peasant. He began rousing him in a kind of rage, pulled him, pushed him, even beat him, but, having labored over him for about five minutes, again with no results, he went back to his bench in helpless despair and sat down.

"Stupid, stupid!" Mitya kept exclaiming, "and . . . how dishonorable it all is!" he suddenly added for some reason. He was getting a terrible headache. "Why not drop it? Go away altogether?" flashed through his mind. "Oh, no, not before morning. On purpose, I'll stay on purpose! Why did I come, after all? And I have no means of leaving, how can I leave here now? Oh, absurd!"

His head, however, was aching more and more. He sat without moving and had no recollection of how he dozed off and suddenly fell asleep sitting up. He must have slept for two hours or more. He was awakened by an unbearable pain in his head, so unbearable he could have screamed. It hammered at his temples, the top of his head throbbed; having come to, it was a long time before he was able to regain full consciousness and understand what had happened to him. He finally realized that the overheated room was full of fumes, and that he might even have died. And the drunken peasant still lay there and snored; the candle guttered and was about to go out. Mitya shouted and rushed staggering across the hallway to the forester's room. The forester woke up quickly, but on hearing that the other room was full of fumes, though he went to take care of it, he accepted the fact with strange indifference, which sorely surprised Mitya.

"But he's dead, he's dead, and now . . . what now?" Mitya kept shouting before him in a frenzy.

They opened the door, flung the windows wide, undamped the flue; Mitya brought a bucket of water from the hallway, wet his own head first, and then, finding some rag, dipped it in the water and put it to Lyagavy's head. The forester continued to treat the whole event somehow even disdainfully, and after opening the window, said sullenly: "That'll do," and went back to bed, leaving Mitya with a lighted iron lantern. Mitya fussed over the fume-poisoned drunkard for about half an hour, kept wetting his head, and seriously intended not to sleep for the rest of the night, but he became exhausted, sat down for a moment to catch his breath, instantly closed his eyes, then unconsciously stretched out on the bench and fell at once into a dead sleep.

He woke up terribly late. It was already approximately nine o'clock in the morning. The sun was shining brightly through the two windows of the hut. The curly-headed peasant of the night before was sitting on a bench, already dressed in his long-waisted coat. Before him stood a fresh samovar and a fresh quart bottle. The old one from the day before was empty, and the new one was more than half gone. Mitya jumped up and instantly realized that the cursed peasant was drunk again, deeply and irretrievably drunk. He stared wide-eyed at him for a moment. The peasant kept glancing at him silently and slyly, with a sort of offensive composure, even with a sort of derisive haughtiness, as Mitya fancied. He rushed up to him.

"Allow me, you see . . . I . . . you've probably heard from the forester there in the other room: I am Lieutenant Dmitri Karamazov, old Karamazov's son, from whom you are buying a woodlot . . ."

"That's a lie!" the peasant suddenly rapped out firmly and calmly.

"A lie? If you please, you do know Fyodor Pavlovich?"

"I don't please to know any Fyodor Pavlovich of yours," the peasant said, moving his tongue somehow heavily.

"A woodlot, you're buying a woodlot from him; wake up, come to your senses! Father Pavel Ilyinsky brought me here . . . You wrote to Samsonov, and he sent me to you . . . ," Mitya spoke breathlessly.

"A l-lie!" Lyagavy again rapped out.

Mitya's legs went cold.

"For pity's sake, this isn't a joke! You're a bit drunk, perhaps. But anyway you can speak, you can understand . . . otherwise . . . otherwise I don't understand anything!"

"You're a dyer!"

"For pity's sake, I'm Karamazov, Dmitri Karamazov, I have an offer to make you . . . a profitable offer . . . quite profitable . . . about that same woodlot."

The peasant was stroking his beard solemnly.

"No, you contracted for the job and turned out to be a cheat. You're a cheat!"

"You're mistaken, I assure you!" Mitya was wringing his hands in despair. The peasant kept stroking his beard and suddenly narrowed his eyes slyly.

"No, you show me one thing: show me where there's a law that allows people to play dirty tricks, do you hear? You're a cheat, understand?"

Mitya glumly stepped back, and suddenly it was as though "something hit him on the head," as he himself put it later. In an instant a sort of illumination came to him, "a light shone and I perceived everything." He stood dumbfounded, wondering how he, an intelligent man after all, could have given in to such foolishness, could have been sucked into such an adventure, and kept on with it all for nearly a whole day and night, worrying over this Lyagavy, wetting his head . . . "Well, the man is drunk, drunk out of his mind, and he'll go on drinking for another week—what is there to wait for? And what if

Samsonov sent me here on purpose? And what if she . . . Oh, God, what have I done . . . !"

The peasant sat watching him and chuckled. On another occasion Mitya might have killed the fool in a rage, but now he himself became weak as a child. He quietly walked over to the bench, took his coat, silently put it on, and went out of the room. He did not find the forester in the other room; no one was there. He took fifty kopecks in change from his pocket and put it on the table, for the night's lodging, the candle, and the trouble. Stepping out of the hut, he saw nothing but forest all around. He walked at random, not even remembering whether to turn right or left from the hut; hurrying there with the priest the night before, he had not noticed the way. There was no vengeance in his soul for anyone, not even Samsonov. He strode along a narrow forest path, senselessly, lost, with his "lost idea," not caring where he was going. A passing child might have knocked him down, so strengthless had he suddenly become in soul and body. Somehow he nevertheless got out of the forest: suddenly before him spread a boundless expanse of bare, harvested fields. "What despair, what death all around!" he kept saying as he strode on and on.

He was saved by some passers-by: a coachman was taking an old merchant over the back road. When they drew up with him, Mitya asked the way, and it turned out that they, too, were going to Volovya. After some negotiating, they agreed to take Mitya along. They arrived three hours later. At Volovya station Mitya immediately ordered post horses to town, and suddenly realized that he was impossibly hungry. While the horses were being harnessed, some fried eggs were fixed for him. He ate them instantly, ate a whole big hunk of bread, ate some sausage that turned up, and drank three glasses of vodka. Having refreshed himself, he cheered up and his soul brightened again. He flew down the road, urging the coachman on, and suddenly arrived at a new, and this time "immutable," plan for obtaining "that accursed money" before evening. "And to think that a man's fate should be ruined because of a worthless three thousand roubles!" he exclaimed contemptuously. "I'll have done with it today!" And had it not been for ceaselessly thinking of Grushenka and whether anything had happened with her, he would perhaps have become quite happy again. But the thought of her stabbed his soul every moment like a sharp knife. They arrived at last, and Mitya ran at once to Grushenka.

Chapter 3

Gold Mines

This was precisely the visit from Mitya of which Grushenka had told Rakitin with such fear. She was then expecting her "messenger," and was very glad that Mitya had not come either the day before or that day, hoping that perchance, God willing, he would not come before her departure, when suddenly he descended upon her. The rest we know: in order to get him off her hands, she persuaded him at once to take her to Kuzma Samsonov's, where she said it was terribly necessary for her to go to "count the money," and when Mitya promptly took her, she made him promise, as she said good-bye to him at Kuzma's gate, to come for her after eleven and take her home again. Mitya was also pleased with this order: "If she's sitting at Kuzma's, she won't go to Fyodor Pavlovich . . . if only she's not lying," he added at once. But from what he could see, she was not lying. His jealousy was precisely of such a sort that, separated from the beloved woman, he at once invented all kinds of horrors about what was happening with her, and how she had gone and "betrayed" him; but, running back to her, shaken, crushed, convinced irretrievably that she had managed to betray him, with the first look at her face, at the gay, laughing, tender face of this woman, his spirits would at once revive, he would at once lose all suspicion, and with joyful shame reproach himself for his jealousy. Having accompanied Grushenka, he rushed home. Oh, he still somehow had to do so much that day! But at least he felt relieved. "Only I must find out quickly from Smerdyakov whether anything happened last night, whether, God forbid, she went to Fyodor Pavlovich!" raced through his head. And so, in just the time it took him to run home, jealousy had already begun stirring again in his restless heart.

Jealousy! "Othello is not jealous, he is trustful," Pushkin observed,[1] and this one observation already testifies to the remarkable depth of our great poet's mind. Othello's soul is simply shattered and his whole world view clouded because *his ideal is destroyed*. Othello will not hide, spy, peep: he is trustful. On the contrary, he had to be led, prompted, roused with great effort to make him even think of betrayal. A truly jealous man is not like that. It is impossible to imagine all the shame and moral degradation a jealous man can tolerate without the least remorse. And it is not that they are all trite and dirty souls. On the contrary, it is possible to have a lofty heart, to love purely, to be full of self-sacrifice, and at the same time to hide under tables, to bribe the meanest people, and live with the nastiest filth of spying and eavesdropping. Othello could in no way be reconciled with betrayal—not that he could not forgive, but he could not be reconciled—though his soul was gentle and innocent as a babe's. Not so the truly jealous man: it is hard to imagine what some jealous men can tolerate and be reconciled to, and what they can forgive! Jealous men forgive sooner than anyone else, and all women know it. The jealous man (having first made a terrible scene, of course) can and will very promptly forgive, for example, a nearly proven betrayal, the embraces and kisses he has seen himself, if, for example, at the same time he can somehow be convinced that this was "the last time" and that his rival will disappear from that moment on, that he will go to the end of the earth, or that he himself will take her away somewhere, to some place where this terrible rival will never come. Of course, the reconciliation will only last an hour, because even if the rival has indeed disappeared, tomorrow he will invent another, a new one, and become jealous of this new one. And one may ask what is the good of a love that must constantly be spied on, and what is the worth of a love that needs to be guarded so intensely? But that is something the truly jealous will never understand, though at the same time there happen, indeed, to be lofty hearts among them. It is also remarkable that these same lofty-hearted men, while standing in some sort of closet, eavesdropping and spying, though they understand clearly "in their lofty hearts" all the shame they have gotten into of their own will, nevertheless, at least for that moment, while standing in that closet, will not feel any pangs of remorse. Mitya's jealousy disappeared at the sight of Grushenka, and for a moment he became trustful and noble, and even despised himself for his bad feelings. But this meant only that his love for this woman consisted in something much higher than he himself supposed and not in passion alone, not merely in that "curve of the body" he had explained to Alyosha. But when Grushenka disappeared, Mitya at once began again to suspect in her all the baseness and perfidy of betrayal. And for that he felt no pangs of remorse.

And so jealousy was again seething in him. He had to hurry in any case. First of all he needed at least a little money to get by on. The previous day's nine roubles had been almost entirely spent on the trip, and without money, as everyone knows, one cannot take a step. But that morning, in the wagon, along with his new plan, he had also thought of how to find some money to get by on. He had a pair of fine dueling pistols with cartridges, and if he had not pawned them yet, it was because he loved them more than anything else he owned. Some time before, in the "Metropolis," he had struck up a slight acquaintance with a certain young official and had learned somehow, also in the

tavern, that this official, a bachelor of no small means, had a passion for weap
ons, bought pistols, revolvers, daggers, hung them on the wall, showed ther
to his acquaintances, boasted of them, was expert at explaining the working
of the revolver, loading, firing, and so on. Without thinking twice, Mitya wer
straight to him and offered to pawn the pistols to him for ten roubles. The de
lighted official tried to persuade him to sell them outright, but Mitya woul
not agree, so the man handed him ten roubles, declaring that he would no
think of accepting any interest. They parted friends. Mitya was in a hurry; h
raced off to behind Fyodor Pavlovich's, to his gazebo, in order to send quickl
for Smerdyakov. In this way, again, the fact emerged that only three or fou
hours before a certain incident, of which I shall speak below, Mitya did no
have a kopeck, and pawned his dearest possession for ten roubles, wherea
three hours later he suddenly had thousands in his hands . . . But I antic
pate.

At Maria Kondratievna's (next door to Fyodor Pavlovich) the new
awaited him of Smerdyakov's illness, which struck and dismayed him greatly
He listened to the story of the fall into the cellar, then of the falling fit, the doc
tor's visit, Fyodor Pavlovich's concern; he was also interested to learn that hi
brother Ivan Fyodorovich had gone off to Moscow that morning. "He mus
have passed through Volovya ahead of me," Dmitri Fyodorovich thought, bu
Smerdyakov troubled him terribly: "What now? Who will keep watch? Wh
will bring me word?" Greedily he began inquiring of the women whether the
had noticed anything the previous evening. They knew very well what he wa
trying to find out and reassured him completely: no one had come, Ivan Fyo
dorovich had spent the night there, "everything was in perfect order." Mity
began to think. Undoubtedly he had to be on watch today, too, but where—
here, or at Samsonov's gate? Both here and there, he decided, depending o
the situation, but meanwhile, meanwhile . . . What faced him now was tha
morning's "plan," the new and this time certain plan, which he had though
up in the wagon, the carrying out of which could not be put off any longer. Mi
tya decided to sacrifice an hour to it: "In an hour I'll settle everything, find ou
everything, and then—then first of all to Samsonov's house, to see whethe
Grushenka is there, then immediately back here, stay here till eleven, the
again to Samsonov's to take her home." That was what he decided.

He flew home, washed, combed his hair, brushed his clothes, got dressed
and went to see Madame Khokhlakov. Alas, his "plan" lay there. He had mad
up his mind to borrow the three thousand from this lady. Moreover, sud
denly, somehow unexpectedly, he had acquired a remarkable certainty tha
she would not refuse him. It may be wondered why, given such certainty, h
had not gone there first, to his own society, so to speak, but had gone instea

to Samsonov, a man of alien caste, with whom he did not even know how to speak. But the thing was that for the past month he had almost broken off relations with Madame Khokhlakov, and even before then had been only slightly acquainted with her, and, moreover, he knew very well that she could not stand him. The lady had detested him from the beginning, simply because he was Katerina Ivanovna's fiancé, whereas she, for some reason, suddenly wanted Katerina Ivanovna to drop him and marry "the dear, chivalrously educated Ivan Fyodorovich, who has such beautiful manners." Mitya's manners she detested. Mitya even laughed at her and had said of her once that this lady "is as bold and lively as she is uneducated." And so that morning, in the wagon, he had been illumined by a most brilliant idea: "If she is so much against my marrying Katerina Ivanovna, and against it to such a degree" (he knew it was almost to the point of hysterics), "then why should she deny me the three thousand now, when this money would precisely enable me to leave Katya and clear out of here forever? These spoiled high-up ladies, if they take it into their heads to want something, will spare nothing to get their way. Besides, she's so rich," Mitya reasoned. As for the "plan" itself, it was all the same as before, that is, the offer of his rights to Chermashnya, but now with no commercial purpose, as with Samsonov the day before, not trying to tempt this lady, like Samsonov the day before, with the prospect of picking up twice the sum, about six or seven thousand, but merely as an honorable pledge for the borrowed money. Mitya went into ecstasies developing his new idea, but that is what always happened to him in all his undertakings, all his sudden decisions. He gave himself passionately to every new idea. Nevertheless, as he stepped onto the porch of Madame Khokhlakov's house, he suddenly felt a chill of horror run down his spine: only at that second did he realize fully and now with mathematical clarity that this was his last hope, that if this should fall through, there was nothing left in the world but "to kill and rob someone for the three thousand, and that's all . . ." It was half past seven when he rang the bell.

At first things seemed to smile on him: he was received at once, with remarkable promptness, as soon as he was announced. "Just as if she were expecting me," flashed through Mitya's mind, and then suddenly, as soon as he was shown into the drawing room, the hostess all but ran in and declared directly that she had been expecting him . . .

"I was expecting you, expecting you! I could not even think you would come to me, you must agree, and yet I was expecting you—just marvel at my instinct, Dmitri Fyodorovich, all morning I felt certain you would come today."

"That is indeed amazing, madame," Mitya uttered, sitting down clumsily, "but . . . I've come on extremely important business . . . the most important business, for me, that is, madame, for me alone, and I am in a hurry . . ."

"I know you have the most important business, Dmitri Fyodorovich, here there's no question of presentiments, no retrograde pretense to miracles (have you heard about the elder Zosima?), this, this is mathematics: you could not fail to come after all that's happened with Katerina Ivanovna, you could not, you simply could not, it's mathematics."

"The realism of actual life, madame, that's what it is! Allow me, however, to explain . . ."

"Realism precisely, Dmitri Fyodorovich. I'm all for realism now, I've been taught a good lesson about miracles. Have you heard that Zosima died?"

"No, madame, this is the first I've heard of it," Mitya was a little surprised. Alyosha's image flashed through his mind.

"Last night, and just imagine . . ."

"Madame," Mitya interrupted, "I can imagine only that I am in a most desperate position, and that if you do not help me, everything will fall through, and I will fall through first of all. Forgive the triviality of the expression, but I feel hot, I am in a fever . . ."

"I know, I know you're in a fever, I know everything, and you could hardly be in any other state of spirit, and whatever you may say, I know everything beforehand. I took your fate into consideration long ago, Dmitri Fyodorovich, I've been following it, studying it . . . Oh, believe me, I am an experienced doctor of souls, Dmitri Fyodorovich."

"Madame, if you are an experienced doctor, I am an experienced patient," Mitya forced himself into pleasantry, "and I have a feeling that if you have been following my fate as you say, you will help it in its ruination, but for that allow me, finally, to explain the plan with which I've ventured to come . . . and what I expect from you . . . I've come, madame . . ."

"Don't explain, it's secondary. As for helping, you will not be the first I've helped, Dmitri Fyodorovich. You've probably heard about my cousin, Madame Belmesov, her husband was ruined, he fell through, as you so characteristically expressed it, Dmitri Fyodorovich, and what did I do . . . ? I sent him into horse-breeding, and now he's flourishing. Do you have any notion of horse-breeding, Dmitri Fyodorovich?"

"Not the slightest, madame—oh, madame, not the slightest!" Mitya exclaimed in nervous impatience, and even rose from his seat. "I only beg you, madame, to listen to me, allow me just two minutes to speak freely, so that I can first of all explain everything to you, the whole project with which I have come. Besides, I'm short of time, I'm in a terrible hurry!" Mitya shouted hysterically, feeling that she was about to start talking again and hoping to outshout her. "I've come in despair . . . in the last degree of despair, to ask you to lend me money, three thousand, but to lend it on a sure, on the surest pledge, madame, on the surest security! Only let me explain . . ."

"All of that later, later!" Madame Khokhlakov waved her hand at him in turn, "and whatever you are going to say, I know it all beforehand, I've already told you that. You are asking for a certain sum, you need three thousand, but I will give you more, infinitely more, I will save you, Dmitri Fyodorovich, but you must do as I say!"

Mitya reared up from his seat again.

"Madame, can you possibly be so kind!" he cried with extreme feeling. "Oh, Lord, you've saved me. You are saving a man from a violent death, madame, from a bullet . . . My eternal gratitude . . ."

"I will give you more, infinitely more than three thousand!" Madame Khokhlakov cried, gazing at Mitya's rapture with a beaming smile.

"Infinitely? But I don't need so much. All that's necessary is that fatal three thousand, and I, for my part, am prepared to guarantee the sum to you, with infinite gratitude, and I've come to offer you a plan that . . ."

"Enough, Dmitri Fyodorovich, it's said and done," Madame Khokhlakov spoke abruptly, with the virtuous triumph of a benefactress. "I've promised to save you, and I will save you. I will save you as I did Belmesov. What do you think about gold mines, Dmitri Fyodorovich?"

"Gold mines, madame! I've never thought anything about them."

"But I have thought for you! I've thought and thought about it! I've been watching you for a whole month with that in mind. I've looked at you a hundred times as you walked by, saying to myself: here is an energetic man who must go to the mines. I even studied your gait and decided: this man will find many mines."

"From my gait, madame?" Mitya smiled.

"And why not from your gait? What, do you deny that it's possible to tell a man's character from his gait, Dmitri Fyodorovich? Natural science confirms it. Oh, I'm a realist now, Dmitri Fyodorovich. From this day on, after all that story in the monastery, which upset me so, I'm a complete realist, and want to throw myself into practical activity. I am cured. Enough! as Turgenev said."[2]

"But, madame, this three thousand, which you have so generously promised to lend me . . ."

"You will get it, Dmitri Fyodorovich," Madame Khokhlakov at once cut him short, "you may consider it as good as in your pocket, and not three thousand, but three million, Dmitri Fyodorovich, and in no time! I shall tell you your idea: you will discover mines, make millions, return and become an active figure, and you will stir us, too, leading us towards the good. Should everything be left to the Jews? You'll build buildings, start various enterprises. You will help the poor, and they will bless you. This is the age of railroads, Dmitri Fyodorovich. You will become known and indispensable to the Ministry of Finance, which is in such need now. The decline of the paper rouble allows me no sleep, Dmitri Fyodorovich, few know this side of me . . ."

"Madame, madame!" Dmitri Fyodorovich again interrupted with a certain uneasy foreboding. "Perhaps I will really and truly follow your advice, your sound advice, and go there, perhaps . . . to these mines . . . we can talk more about it . . . I'll come again . . . even many times . . . but about this three thousand, which you have so generously . . . Oh, it would set me free today if possible . . . That is, you see, I don't have any time now, not a moment . . ."

"Enough, Dmitri Fyodorovich, enough!" Madame Khokhlakov interrupted insistently. "The question is: are you going to the mines or not? Have you fully decided? Answer mathematically."

"I will go, madame, later . . . I'll go wherever you like, madame, but now . . ."

"Wait, then!" cried Madame Khokhlakov, and, jumping up, she rushed to her magnificent bureau with numerous little drawers and began pulling out one drawer after another, looking for something and in a terrible hurry.

"The three thousand!" Mitya's heart froze, "and just like that, without any papers, without any deed . . . oh, but how gentlemanly! A splendid woman, if only she weren't so talkative . . ."

"Here!" Madame Khokhlakov cried joyfully, coming back to Mitya. "Here is what I was looking for!"

It was a tiny silver icon on a string, of the kind sometimes worn around the neck together with a cross.

"It's from Kiev, Dmitri Fyodorovich," she continued reverently, "from the relics of the great martyr Varvara.[3] Allow me personally to put it around your neck and thereby bless you for a new life and new deeds."

And she indeed put the icon around his neck and began tucking it in. Mitya, in great embarrassment, leaned forward and tried to help her, and finally got the icon past his tie and collar and onto his chest.

"Now you can go!" Madame Khokhlakov uttered, solemnly resuming her seat.

"Madame, I am so touched . . . I don't know how to thank . . . for such kindness, but . . . if you knew how precious time is to me now . . . ! That sum, which I am so much expecting from your generosity . . . Oh, madame, since you are so kind, so touchingly generous to me," Mitya suddenly exclaimed inspiredly, "allow me to reveal to you . . . what you, however, have long known . . . that I love a certain person here . . . I've betrayed Katya . . . Katerina Ivanovna, I mean. Oh, I was inhuman and dishonorable towards her, but here I've come to love another . . . a woman you perhaps despise, madame, for you already know everything, but whom I absolutely cannot part with, absolutely, and therefore, now, this three thousand . . ."

"Part with everything, Dmitri Fyodorovich!" Madame Khokhlakov interrupted him in the most determined tone. "Everything, women especially. Your goal is the mines, and there's no need to take women there. Later, when you return in wealth and glory, you will find a companion for your heart in the highest society. She will be a modern girl, educated and without prejudices. By then the women's question, which is just beginning now, will have ripened, and a new woman will appear . . ."

"Madame, that's not it, not it . . . ," Dmitri Fyodorovich clasped his hands imploringly.

"That is it, Dmitri Fyodorovich, that is precisely what you need, what you thirst for, without knowing it. I am no stranger to the present women's question, Dmitri Fyodorovich. The development of women and even a political role for women in the nearest future—that is my ideal. I myself have a daughter, Dmitri Fyodorovich, and few know this side of me. I wrote in this regard to the writer Shchedrin. This writer has shown me so much, so much about the woman's vocation, that last year I sent him an anonymous letter of two lines: 'I embrace you and kiss you, my writer, for the contemporary woman: carry on.' And I signed it: 'A mother.' I almost wrote 'a contemporary mother,' but I hesitated, and then decided just to be a mother: it has more moral beauty, Dmitri Fyodorovich, and besides, the word 'contemporary' would have reminded him of *The Contemporary*—a bitter recollection for him, owing to our censorship . . .[4] Oh, my God, what's the matter with you?"

"Madame," Mitya jumped up at last, clasping his hands in helpless supplication, "you will make me weep, madame, if you keep putting off what you have so generously . . ."

"Weep, Dmitri Fyodorovich, weep! Such feelings are beautiful . . . and with such a path before you! Tears will ease you, afterwards you will return and rejoice. You will come galloping to me on purpose from Siberia, to rejoice with me . . ."

"But allow me, too," Mitya suddenly yelled, "for the last time I implore you, tell me, am I to have this promised sum from you today? And if not, precisely when should I come for it?"

"What sum, Dmitri Fyodorovich?"

"The three thousand you promised . . . which you so generously . . ."

"Three thousand? You mean roubles? Oh, no, I haven't got three thousand," Madame Khokhlakov spoke with a sort of quiet surprise. Mitya was stupefied . . .

"Then why . . . just . . . you said . . . you even said it was as good as in my pocket . . ."

"Oh, no, you misunderstood me, Dmitri Fyodorovich. In that case, you misunderstood me. I was talking about the mines . . . It's true I promised you more, infinitely more than three thousand, I recall it all now, but I was only thinking about the mines."

"And the money? The three thousand?" Dmitri Fyodorovich exclaimed absurdly.

"Oh, if you meant money, I don't have it. I don't have any money at all now, Dmitri Fyodorovich, just now I'm fighting with my manager, and the other day I myself borrowed five hundred roubles from Miusov. No, no, I have no money. And you know, Dmitri Fyodorovich, even if I had, I would not give it to you. First, I never lend to anyone. Lending means quarreling. But to you, to you especially I would not give anything, out of love for you I would not give anything, in order to save you I would not give anything, because you need only one thing: mines, mines, mines . . . !"

"Ah, devil take . . . !" Mitya suddenly roared, and banged his fist on the table with all his might.

"Aiee!" Khokhlakov cried in fear and flew to the other end of the drawing room.

Mitya spat and with quick steps walked out of the room, out of the house, into the street, into the darkness! He walked like a madman, beating himself on the chest, on that very place on his chest where he had beaten himself two days before, with Alyosha, when he had seen him for the last time, in the evening, in the darkness, on the road. What this beating on the chest, *on that spot*, meant, and what he intended to signify by it—so far was a secret that no one else in the world knew, which he had not revealed then even to Alyosha, but for him that secret concealed more than shame, it concealed ruin and suicide, for so he had determined if he were unable to obtain the three thousand to pay back Katerina Ivanovna and thereby lift from his chest, "from that place on his chest," the shame he carried there, which weighed so heavily on his conscience. All this will be perfectly well explained to the reader later on, but now, after his last hope had disappeared, this man, physically so strong, having gone a few steps from Madame Khokhlakov's house, suddenly dissolved in tears like a little child. He walked on, unconsciously wiping his tears away with his fist. Thus he came out into the square and suddenly felt that he had bumped into something with his full weight. He heard the squeaking howl of some little old woman whom he had almost knocked over.

"Lord, he nearly killed me! What are you stomping around here for, hooligan!"

"What, is it you?" Mitya cried, recognizing the old woman in the darkness. It was the same old serving-woman who served Kuzma Samsonov, and whom Mitya had noticed only too well the day before.

"And you, who are you, my dear?" the old woman said in quite a different voice. "I can't make you out in the dark."

"You live at Kuzma Kuzmich's, you're a servant there?"

"That's so, my dear, I've just run over to Prokhorich's . . . But how is it I still don't recognize you?"

"Tell me, granny, is Agrafena Alexandrovna there now?" Mitya asked, beside himself with impatience. "I took her there some time ago."

"She was, my dear, she came, she stayed for a while and left."

"What? Left?" cried Mitya. "When?"

"Right then she left, she only stayed for a minute, told Kuzma Kuzmich some story, made him laugh, and ran away."

"You're lying, damn you!" yelled Mitya.

"Aiee!" cried the little old woman, but Mitya's tracks were already cold; he ran as fast as he could to the widow Morozov's house. It was exactly at the same time that Grushenka drove off to Mokroye, not more than a quarter of an hour after her departure. Fenya was sitting in the kitchen with her grandmother, the cook Matryona, when the "captain" suddenly ran in. Seeing him, Fenya screamed to high heaven.

"You're screaming?" Mitya yelled. "Where is she?" And without giving the terror-stricken Fenya time to say a word, he suddenly collapsed at her feet:

"Fenya, for the sake of our Lord Jesus Christ, tell me where she is!"

"My dear, I know nothing, dear Dmitri Fyodorovich, I know nothing, even if you kill me, I know nothing," Fenya began swearing and crossing herself. "You took her yourself . . ."

"She came back . . . !"

"She didn't, my dear, I swear to God she didn't!"

"You're lying," roared Mitya. "I can see by how scared you are, you know where she is . . . !"

He dashed out. The frightened Fenya was glad to have gotten off so easily, but she knew very well that he simply had no time, otherwise it would have gone badly for her. But as he ran out, he still surprised both Fenya and old Matryona by a most unexpected act: on the table stood a brass mortar with a pestle in it, a small brass pestle, only seven inches long. As he was running out, having already opened the door with one hand, Mitya suddenly, without stopping, snatched the pestle from the mortar with his other hand, shoved it into his side pocket, and made off with it.

"Oh, Lord," Fenya clasped her hands, "he'll kill somebody!"

Chapter 4

In the Dark

Where did he run to? But of course: "Where could she be if not with Fyodor Pavlovich? She ran straight to him from Samsonov's, it's all clear now. The whole intrigue, the whole deception is obvious now . . ." All this flew like a whirlwind through his head. He did not even run over to Maria Kondratievna's yard: "No need to go there, no need at all . . . mustn't cause any alarm . . . they'll all play and betray at once . . . Maria Kondratievna is obviously in on the conspiracy, Smerdyakov, too, they've all been bought!" A different plan took shape in him: he ran down a lane, making a long detour around Fyodor Pavlovich's house, ran along Dmitrovsky Street, then ran across the footbridge, and came straight to the solitary back lane, empty and uninhabited, bordered on one side by the wattle fence of the neighbor's garden, and on the other by the strong, high fence surrounding Fyodor Pavlovich's garden. There he chose a spot that seemed, according to the story he had heard, to be the same spot where Stinking Lizaveta had once climbed over the fence. "If she could climb over," the thought flashed, God knows why, through his head, "surely I can climb over." He jumped, and indeed managed at once to grasp the top of the fence with his hands, then he pulled himself up energetically, climbed right to the top, and sat astride the fence. There was a little bathhouse nearby in the garden, but from the fence the lighted windows of the house could also be seen. "Just as I thought, there's a light in the old man's bedroom—she's there!" and he jumped down from the fence into the garden. Though he knew that Grigory was sick, and that Smerdyakov, perhaps, was indeed sick as well, and that there was no one to hear him, he instinctively hid himself, stood stock still, and began listening. But there was dead silence and, as if on purpose, complete stillness, not a breath of wind.

"And naught but the silence whispers,"[1] the little verse for some reason flashed through his head, "that is, if no one heard me jump over; and it seems no one did." Having paused for a minute, he quietly walked across the garden over the grass; he walked for a long time, skirting the trees and bushes, concealing each step, listening himself to each of his own steps. It took him about five minutes to reach the lighted window. He remembered that there, right under the window, there were several large, high, thick bushes of elder and snowball. The door from the house into the garden on the left side of the house was locked—he purposely and carefully checked it as he passed by. At last he reached the bushes and hid behind them. He held his breath. "I must wait now," he thought, "till they reassure themselves, in case they heard my footsteps and are listening . . . if only I don't cough, or sneeze . . ."

He waited for about two minutes, but his heart was pounding terribly, and he felt at moments as if he were suffocating. "No, my heart won't stop pounding," he thought, "I can't wait any longer." He was standing behind a bush in the shadow; the front part of the bush was lighted from the window. "Snowball berries, how red they are!" he whispered, not knowing why. Quietly, with careful, noiseless steps, he approached the window and stood on tiptoe. Before him lay the whole of Fyodor Pavlovich's bedroom. It was a small room, divided all the way across by red screens, "Chinese," as Fyodor Pavlovich called them. "Chinese" raced through Mitya's mind, "and behind the screens—Grushenka." He began examining Fyodor Pavlovich. He was wearing his new striped silk dressing gown, which Mitya had never seen on him before, tied with a tassled cord also of silk. Clean, stylish linen, a fine Dutch shirt with gold studs, peeped out from under the collar of the gown. On his head Fyodor Pavlovich had the same red bandage Alyosha had seen him wearing. "All dressed up," thought Mitya. Fyodor Pavlovich stood near the window, apparently deep in thought; suddenly he jerked his head up, listened for a moment, and, having heard nothing, went over to the table, poured half a glass of cognac from a decanter, and drank it. Then he heaved a deep sigh, paused again for a moment, absentmindedly went up to the mirror on the wall between the windows, lifted the red bandage from his forehead a little with his right hand, and began to examine his scrapes and bruises, which had still not gone away. "He's alone," thought Mitya, "most likely he's alone." Fyodor Pavlovich stepped away from the mirror, suddenly turned to the window, and looked out. Mitya instantly jumped back into the shadow.

"Maybe she's behind the screen, maybe she's already asleep," the thought needled his heart. Fyodor Pavlovich stepped away from the window. "He was looking for her from the window, so she must not be there: why else would he stare into the dark . . . ? So he's eaten up with impatience . . ." Mitya at once jumped closer and began looking through the window again. The old man was now sitting at the table, obviously feeling dejected. Finally he leaned on his elbow and put his right hand to his cheek. Mitya stared greedily.

"Alone, alone!" he again repeated. "If she were here, his face would be different." Strangely, some weird and unreasonable vexation suddenly boiled up in his heart because she was not there. "Not because she's not here," Mitya reasoned and corrected himself at once, "but because I have no way of knowing for certain whether she's here or not." Mitya himself later recalled that his mind at that moment was remarkably clear and took in everything to the last detail, grasped every smallest feature. But anguish, the anguish of ignorance and indecision, was growing in his heart with exceeding rapidity. "Is she here, finally, or is she not?" boiled angrily in his heart. And he suddenly made up his mind, reached out his hand, and tapped softly on the windowpane. He tapped out the signal agreed upon between the old man and Smerdyakov: twice slowly, then three times more quickly, tap-tap-tap—the signal meaning "Grushenka is here." The old man gave a start, jerked his head up, jumped quickly to his feet, and rushed to the window. Mitya jumped back into the shadow. Fyodor Pavlovich opened the window and stuck his head all the way out.

"Grushenka, is it you? Is it you?" he said in a sort of trembling half-whisper. "Where are you, sweetie, my little angel, where are you?" He was terribly excited; he was breathless.

"Alone!" Mitya decided.

"But where are you?" the old man cried again, and stuck his head out even further, stuck it out to the shoulders, looking in all directions, right and left. "Come here; I have a little present waiting for you; come, I'll show you . . .!"

"He means the envelope with the three thousand," flashed through Mitya's mind.

"But where are you . . . ? At the door? I'll open at once . . ."

And the old man leaned almost all the way out the window, looking to the right, in the direction of the garden gate, and peering into the darkness. In another second he would surely run to open the door, without waiting for any answer from Grushenka. Mitya watched from the side, and did not move. The whole of the old man's profile, which he found so loathsome, the whole of his drooping Adam's apple, his hooked nose, smiling in sweet expectation, his lips—all was brightly lit from the left by the slanting light of the lamp shining from the room. Terrible, furious anger suddenly boiled up in Mitya's heart: "There he was, his rival, his tormentor, the tormentor of his life!" It was a surge of that same sudden, vengeful, and furious anger of which he had spoken, as if in anticipation, to Alyosha during their conversation in the gazebo four days earlier, in response to Alyosha's question, "How can you say you will kill father?"

"I don't know, I don't know," he had said then. "Maybe I won't kill him, and maybe I will. I'm afraid that his face *at that moment* will suddenly become hateful to me. I hate his Adam's apple, his nose, his eyes, his shameless sneer. I feel a personal loathing. I'm afraid of that, I may not be able to help myself . . ."

The personal loathing was increasing unbearably. Mitya was beside himself, and suddenly he snatched the brass pestle from his pocket . . ."

. . . .

God was watching over me then," Mitya used to say afterwards: just at that time, the sick Grigory Vasilievich woke up on his bed. Towards evening of that day he had performed upon himself the famous treatment Smerdyakov had described to Ivan Fyodorovich—that is, with his wife's help he had rubbed himself all over with some secret, very strong infusion made from vodka, and had drunk the rest while his wife whispered "a certain prayer" over him, after which he lay down to sleep. Marfa Ignatievna also partook, and, being a nondrinker, fell into a dead sleep next to her husband. But then, quite unexpectedly, Grigory suddenly woke up in the middle of the night, thought for a moment, and, though he at once felt a burning pain in the small of his back, sat up in bed. Again he thought something over, got up, and dressed hurriedly. Perhaps he felt pangs of conscience for sleeping while the house was left unguarded "at such a perilous time." Smerdyakov, broken by the falling sickness, lay in the next room without moving. Marfa Ignatievna did not stir. "She's gone feeble," Grigory Vasilievich thought, glancing at her, and, groaning, went out onto the porch. Of course he only wanted to take a look from the porch, for he was quite unable to walk, the pain in his lower back and right leg was unbearable. But just then he remembered that he had not locked the garden gate that evening. He was a most precise and punctilious man, a man of established order and age-old habit. Limping and cringing with pain, he went down the porch steps and walked out towards the garden. Yes, indeed, the gate was wide open. Mechanically he stepped into the garden: perhaps he fancied something, perhaps he heard some noise, but, glancing to the left, he saw his master's window open, and the window was now empty, no one was peering out of it. "Why is it open? It's not summertime!" Grigory thought, and suddenly, just at that very moment, he caught a glimpse of something unusual right in front of him in the garden. About forty paces away from him a man seemed to be running in the darkness, some shadow was moving very quickly. "Lord!" said Grigory, and, forgetting himself and the pain in the small of his back, he rushed to intercept the running man. He took a short cut, obviously knowing the garden better than the running man; the latter was heading for the bathhouse, ran behind the bathhouse, dashed for the wall . . . Grigory kept his eyes on him and ran, forgetting himself. He reached the fence just as the fugitive was climbing over it. Beside himself, Grigory yelled, rushed forward, and clutched his leg with both hands.

Just so, his forebodings had not deceived him; he recognized the man, it was him, the "monster," the "parricide"!

"Parricide!" the old man shouted for all the neighborhood to hear, but that was all he had time to shout; suddenly he fell as if struck by a thunderbolt. Mitya jumped back down into the garden and bent over the stricken man. There was a brass pestle in Mitya's hand, and he threw it mechanically into the grass. The pestle fell two paces away from Grigory, not in the grass, however, but on a footpath, in a most conspicuous place. For a few seconds he examined the prostrate figure before him. The old man's head was all covered with blood; Mitya reached out his hand and began feeling it. Afterwards he clearly recalled that at that moment he had wanted terribly "to find out for certain" whether he had cracked the old man's skull or merely "dazed" him with the pestle. But the blood was flowing, flowing terribly, and instantly poured its hot stream over Mitya's trembling fingers. He remembered snatching from his pocket the new white handkerchief he had provided himself with for his visit to Madame Khokhlakov, and putting it to the old man's head, senselessly trying to wipe the blood from his forehead and face. But the handkerchief instantly became soaked with blood as well. "Lord, why am I doing this?" Mitya suddenly came to his senses. "If I've cracked his skull, how can I tell now . . . ? And what difference does it make?" he suddenly added hopelessly. "If I've killed him, I've killed him . . . You came a cropper, old man, now lie there!" he said aloud, and suddenly dashed for the fence, jumped over it into the lane, and started running. The blood-soaked handkerchief was crumpled in his right fist, and as he ran he stuffed it into the back pocket of his coat. He was running like mad, and the few rare passers-by he met in the darkness, in the streets of the town, remembered afterwards how they had met a wildly running man that night. He was flying again to the house of the widow Morozov. Fenya had rushed to the head porter, Nazar Ivanovich, just after he left, and begun begging him "by Christ God not to let the captain in again either today or tomorrow." Nazar Ivanovich listened and agreed, but, as bad luck would have it, he went upstairs to his mistress, who had suddenly summoned him, and on his way, having met his nephew, a lad about twenty years old who had just come from the village, he told him to stay in the yard, but forgot to tell him about the captain. Mitya ran up to the gate and knocked. The lad recognized him instantly: Mitya had already tipped him several times. He at once opened the gate for him, let him in, and with a cheerful smile courteously hastened to inform him that "Agrafena Alexandrovna is not at home at the moment, sir."

"Where is she, Prokhor?" Mitya stopped suddenly.

"She left about two hours ago, with Timofei, for Mokroye."

"Why?" Mitya cried.

"That I can't say, sir. To see some officer. Someone invited her there and sent horses . . ."

Mitya left him and ran like a madman for Fenya.

Chapter 5

A Sudden Decision

She was sitting in the kitchen with her grandmother; both were preparing to go to bed. Relying on Nazar Ivanovich, they had once again not locked the doors. Mitya ran in, rushed at Fenya, and seized her tightly by the throat.

"Talk now! Where is she? Who is she with in Mokroye?" he shouted in a frenzy.

Both women shrieked.

"Aie! I'll tell you. Aie, Dmitri Fyodorovich, dear, I'll tell you all right now, I won't hide anything," Fenya rattled out, frightened to death. "She went to Mokroye to see the officer."

"What officer?" Mitya shouted.

"Her former officer, the same one from before, from five years ago, who left her and went away," Fenya rattled out in the same patter.

Dmitri Fyodorovich relaxed his grip on her throat and let his hands fall. He stood before her, speechless and pale as death, but one could see from his eyes that he had understood everything at once, everything, everything all at once, at half a word, had understood it to the last detail and figured it all out. It was not for poor Fenya, of course, to notice at that moment whether he had understood or not. She sat on the chest where she had been sitting when he ran in, and remained like that, trembling all over, holding her hands out in front of her as if trying to protect herself, and froze in that position. She stared at him fixedly, her eyes terrified, her pupils dilated with fear. Worse still, both his hands were stained with blood. On the way, as he was running, he must have touched his forehead with them, wiping the sweat from his face, so that he left red patches of smeared blood both on his forehead and on his right cheek. Fenya was on the verge of hysterics, and the old cook jumped up, staring crazily, and nearly passed out. Dmitri Fyodorovich stood for a moment, then suddenly dropped mechanically into a chair next to Fenya.

He sat there, not pondering exactly, but as if in fear, as if in some kind of stupor. But everything was clear as day: this officer—he knew about him, he knew everything perfectly well, knew it from Grushenka herself, knew that a month ago a letter had come from him. So for a month, for a whole month this affair had been going on in deep secret from him, up to the present arrival of this new man, and he had not even given him a thought! But how could he, how could he not give him a thought? Why had he simply forgotten about the officer, forgotten the moment he learned of him? That was the question that stood before him like some sort of bogey. And he indeed contemplated this bogey in fear, in cold fear.

But suddenly he began speaking gently and meekly with Fenya, like a gentle and affectionate child, as if he had quite forgotten that he had just frightened, offended, and tormented her so much. He suddenly began questioning Fenya with great and, in his position, even surprising precision. And Fenya, though she gazed wildly at his bloodstained hands, also began answering each of his questions with surprising readiness and haste, as if she were even hastening to lay the whole "truthful truth" before him. Little by little, and even with a sort of joy, she began giving him all the details, not wishing in the least to torment him, but as if she were hastening, with all her heart, to please him as much as she could. She also told him to the last detail about that day, the visit of Rakitin and Alyosha, how she, Fenya, had kept watch, how her mistress had driven off, and that she had called from the window to Alyosha to bow to him, Mitenka, and tell him he should "remember forever how she had loved him for one hour." Hearing of the bow, Mitya suddenly grinned and a blush came to his pale cheeks. At that same moment, Fenya, now not the least bit afraid of her curiosity, said to him:

"But your hands, Dmitri Fyodorovich, they're all covered with blood!"

"Yes," Mitya answered mechanically, looked distractedly at his hands, and immediately forgot about them and about Fenya's question. Again he sank into silence. Some twenty minutes had already passed since he ran in. His initial fear was gone, but he was evidently now totally possessed by some new, inflexible resolve. He suddenly stood up and smiled pensively.

"What has happened to you, sir?" Fenya said, pointing again at his hands; said with regret, as if she were now the person closest to him in his grief.

Mitya again looked at his hands.

"That's blood, Fenya," he said, looking at her with a strange expression.

"that is human blood, and, my God, why was it shed? But . . . Fenya . . . there is a fence here" (he looked at her as though he were setting her a riddle), "a high fence, and fearful to look at, but . . . tomorrow at dawn, when 'the sun soars aloft,' Mitenka will jump over that fence . . . You don't understand about the fence, Fenya, but never mind . . . it doesn't matter, tomorrow you will hear and understand everything . . . and now, farewell! I won't interfere, I'll remove myself, I'll know how to remove myself. Live, my joy . . . you loved me for one little hour, so remember Mitenka Karamazov forever . . . She always called me Mitenka, remember?"

And with those words he suddenly walked out of the kitchen. Fenya was almost more frightened by this exit than she had been earlier when he ran in and fell upon her.

Exactly ten minutes later, Dmitri Fyodorovich walked into the rooms of the young official, Pyotr Ilyich Perkhotin, to whom he had pawned his pistols earlier that day. It was then half past eight, and Pyotr Ilyich, having had his tea at home, had just dressed himself once more in his frock coat in order to set off to the "Metropolis" for a game of billiards. Mitya caught him as he was going out. Seeing him and his bloodstained face, the young man cried out:

"Lord! What's with you?"

"So," Mitya said quickly, "I've come for my pistols and brought you the money. Many thanks. I'm in a hurry, Pyotr Ilyich, please make it fast."

Pyotr Ilyich grew more and more surprised: in Mitya's hand he suddenly noticed a pile of money, and, what was more, he had walked in holding this pile as no one in the world holds money and comes walking in with it: he had all the bills in his right hand, and was holding his hand, as if for show, straight out in front of him. A boy, the official's servant, who had met Mitya in the hallway, recounted later that he had walked through the front door just like that, with the money in his hand, which means that he had also been walking through the streets like that, carrying the money before him in his right hand. It was all in iridescent hundred-rouble bills, and he was holding them with his bloodied fingers. Afterwards, to the further questioning of certain interested persons as to how much money there was, Pyotr Ilyich replied that it was difficult to tell then by eye, maybe two thousand, maybe three, but it was a big, "hefty" wad. Dmitri Fyodorovich, as Perkhotin also testified later, "was not quite himself, as it were, not that he was drunk, but he seemed to be in some sort of ecstasy, quite distracted, and at the same time apparently concentrated, as if he were thinking about something, getting at something, but could not make up his mind. He was in a great hurry, responded abruptly in a very strange manner, and at moments seemed not grieved at all but even cheerful."

"But what is it, what's happened?" Pyotr Ilyich shouted again, staring wildly at his visitor. "How did you get so covered with blood? Did you fall? Look!"

He seized Mitya by the elbow and placed him in front of a mirror. Mitya saw his bloodstained face, gave a start, and frowned wrathfully.

"Ah, the devil! Just what I need," he muttered angrily, quickly shifted the bills from his right hand to his left, and convulsively snatched the handkerchief from his pocket. But the handkerchief, too, turned out to be all covered with blood (it was the same handkerchief he had used to wipe Grigory's head and face): there was hardly a white spot left on it, and it had not merely begun to dry, but had stiffened into a ball and refused to be unfolded. Mitya angrily flung it to the floor.

"Eh, the devil! Have you got some rag . . . to wipe myself off . . . ?"

"So you're only stained, you're not wounded? Then you'd better wash," Pyotr Ilyich answered. "There's the basin, let me help you."

"The basin? Good . . . only where am I going to put this?" With quite a strange sort of bewilderment he pointed at his wad of bills, looking questioningly at Pyotr Ilyich, as if the latter had to decide where he should put his own money.

"Put it in your pocket, or here on the table—nothing will happen to it."

"In my pocket? Yes, my pocket. Good . . . No, you see, it's all nonsense!" he cried, as if suddenly coming out of his distraction. "Look: first let's finish this business, the pistols, I mean, give them back to me, and here's your money . . . because I really, really must . . . and I have no time, no time at all . . ."

And taking the topmost hundred-rouble bill from the wad, he handed it to the official.

"But I don't have any change," the latter remarked, "don't you have something smaller?"

"No," Mitya said, glancing at the money again, and, as if uncertain of his words, he peeled back the first two or three bills with his fingers. "No, they're all the same," he added, and again looked questioningly at Pyotr Ilyich.

"How did you get so rich?" the latter asked. "Wait, I'll have my boy run over to Plotnikov's. They close late—maybe they'll change it. Hey, Misha!" he shouted into the hallway.

"To Plotnikov's shop—splendid!" Mitya, too, shouted, as if some thought had struck him. "Misha," he turned to the boy as he came in, "look, run over to Plotnikov's and tell them that Dmitri Fyodorovich sends them his respects and will come himself shortly . . . But listen, listen: tell them to have some champagne ready when he comes, three dozen bottles, let's say, and packed the same way as when I went to Mokroye . . . I bought four dozen that time," he turned suddenly to Pyotr Ilyich. "Don't worry, Misha, they'll know what I mean," he turned back to the boy. "And listen: some cheese, too, some Strasbourg pâté, smoked whitefish, ham, caviar, and everything, everything, whatever they've got, up to a hundred roubles, or a hundred and twenty, like the other time . . . And listen: they mustn't forget some sweets, candies, pears, watermelons—two, three, maybe four—well, no, one watermelon is enough, but there must be chocolate, sour balls, fruit-drops, toffee—well, all the same things they packed for me to take to Mokroye that time, it should come to about three hundred roubles with the champagne . . . It must be exactly the same this time. Try to remember, Misha, if you are Misha . . . His name is Misha, isn't it?" he again turned to Pyotr Ilyich.

"But wait," Pyotr Ilyich interrupted, staring at him and listening worriedly, "you'd better go yourself, then you can tell them, he'll get it all wrong."

"He will, I can see, he'll get it all wrong! Eh, Misha, and I was about to give you a kiss for your services. If you keep it all straight, you'll get ten roubles, now off with you . . . Champagne above all, let them break out the champagne, and some cognac, and red wine, and white wine, and all the rest, like the other time . . . They'll remember how it was."

"But listen to me!" Pyotr Ilyich interrupted, now with impatience. "I said, let him just run over to change the money and tell them not to lock up, and then you can go and talk to them yourself . . . Give me your bill. Off you go, Misha, shake a leg!" Pyotr Ilyich seemed to chase Misha out deliberately, because the boy was standing in front of the visitor, staring goggle-eyed at his bloody face and bloodstained hands, with a bunch of money in his trembling fingers, and just stood gaping in amazement and fear, probably grasping little of what Mitya was telling him to do.

"Well, now let's go and wash," Pyotr Ilyich said sternly. "Put the money on the table, or in your pocket . . . That's it, now come along. And take your frock coat off."

And he began helping him to take off his frock coat, but suddenly he cried out again:

"Look, there's blood on your coat, too!"

"It . . . it's not the coat. Only a little bit on the sleeve . . . And then just here, where the handkerchief was. It soaked through the pocket. I sat down on it at Fenya's and the blood soaked through," Mitya explained at once with surprising trustfulness. Pyotr Ilyich listened, frowning.

"How on earth did you get like this? You must have had a fight with someone," he muttered.

They began to wash. Pyotr Ilyich held the jug and poured water. Mitya hurried and did not soap his hands well. (His hands were trembling, as Pyotr Ilyich recalled afterwards.) Pyotr Ilyich at once ordered him to use more soap and scrub harder. It was as if, at that moment, he was gaining more and more of an upper hand over Mitya. Let us note in passing that the young man was not of a timid nature.

"Look, you didn't clean under your nails; now scrub your face, here, on the temples, by your ear . . . Will you go in that shirt? Where are you going? Look, the whole right cuff is bloody."

"Yes, bloody," Mitya remarked, examining the cuff of his shirt.

"Change your shirt, then."

"No time. Look, I'll just . . . ," Mitya went on with the same trustfulness, wiping his face and hands now and putting on his frock coat, "I'll just tuck the edge of the sleeve in here, and it won't show under the coat . . . See!"

"Tell me, now, how on earth did you get like this? Did you have a fight with someone? Was it in the tavern, like the other time? It wasn't that captain again—the one you beat and dragged around?" Pyotr Ilyich recalled as if in reproach. "Did you beat someone else . . . or kill him, possibly?"

"Nonsense!" said Mitya.

"Why nonsense?"

"Never mind," Mitya said, and suddenly grinned. "I just ran down a little old woman in the square."

"Ran down? A little old woman?"

"An old man!" Mitya shouted, looking Pyotr Ilyich straight in the face, laughing, and shouting at him as if he were deaf.

"Ah, devil take it—an old man, an old woman . . . Did you kill somebody?"

"We made peace. Had a fight, then made peace. Somewhere. We parted friends. Some fool . . . he's forgiven me . . . surely he's forgiven me by now . . . If he'd gotten up, he wouldn't have forgiven me," Mitya suddenly winked, "only, you know, devil take him, do you hear, Pyotr Ilyich, devil take him! Never mind! No more now!" Mitya snapped resolutely.

"I mean, why go getting into trouble with everybody . . . like the other time with that captain, over some trifle . . . You've had a fight, and now you're going off on a spree—that's just like you! Three dozen bottles of champagne—what do you need so much for?"

"Bravo! Now give me the pistols. By God, I have no time. I'd like to chat with you, my dear, but I have no time. And there's no need, it's too late for talking. Ah! Where's the money, where did I put it?" he cried, and began feeling in all his pockets.

"You put it on the table . . . yourself . . . there it is. Did you forget? Really, money is like trash or water for you. Here are your pistols. Strange, at six o'clock you pawned them for ten roubles, and now look how many thousands you've got. Must be two, or three?"

"Must be three!" Mitya laughed, putting the money into the side pocket of his trousers.

"You'll lose it that way. Have you got a gold mine or something?"

"A mine? A gold mine!" Mitya shouted at the top of his lungs, and burst out laughing. "Do you want to go to the gold mines, Perkhotin? There's a lady here who'll fork out three thousand on the spot if you'll agree to go. She did it for me, she likes gold mines so much! You know Madame Khokhlakov?"

"Not personally, but I've heard about her and seen her. Did she really give you three thousand? Just forked it out like that?" Pyotr Ilyich looked doubtful.

"Go there tomorrow, when the sun soars aloft, when the ever-youthful Phoebus soars aloft,[1] praising and glorifying God, go to her, to Khokhlakov, and ask her yourself if she forked me out three thousand or not. See what she says."

"I don't know what terms you're on . . . since you say it so positively, I suppose she did . . . And you grabbed the money, and instead of Siberia, you're going on a spree . . . But where are you really off to, eh?"

"Mokroye."

"Mokroye? But it's night!"

"Mastriuk had it all, Mastriuk had a fall,"[2] Mitya said suddenly.

"What do you mean, a fall? You've got thousands!"

"I'm not talking about thousands. To hell with thousands! I'm talking about a woman's heart:

> Gullible is the heart of woman,
> Ever-changing and full of vice.

I agree with Ulysses, it was he who said that."[3]

"I don't understand you."

"You think I'm drunk?"

"Not drunk, worse than that."

"I'm drunk in spirit, Pyotr Ilyich, drunk in spirit, and enough, enough . . ."

"What are you doing, loading the pistol?"

"Loading the pistol."

Indeed, having opened the pistol case, Mitya uncapped the powder horn, carefully poured in some powder, and rammed the charge home. Then he took a bullet and, before dropping it in, held it up in two fingers near the candle.

"What are you looking at the bullet for?" Pyotr Ilyich watched him with uneasy curiosity.

"Just a whim. Now, if you had decided to blow your brains out, would you look at the bullet before you loaded the pistol, or not?"

"Why look at it?"

"It will go into my brain, so it's interesting to see what it's like . . . Ah, anyway, it's all nonsense, a moment's nonsense. There, that's done," he added, having dropped the bullet in and rammed the wadding in after it. "Nonsense, my dear Pyotr Ilyich, it's all nonsense, and if you only knew what nonsense it is! Now give me a piece of paper."

"Here's some paper."

"No, smooth, clean, for writing. That's it." And having snatched a pen from the table, Mitya quickly wrote two lines on the piece of paper, folded it in half twice, and put it in his waistcoat pocket. He put the pistols back in their case, locked it with a little key, and took the case in his hands. Then he looked at Pyotr Ilyich and gave him a long, meaning smile.

"Let's go now," he said.

"Go where? No, wait . . . So you're thinking about putting it into your brain, the bullet, I mean . . . ?" Pyotr Ilyich asked uneasily.

"The bullet? Nonsense! I want to live, I love life! Believe me. I love golden-haired Phoebus and his hot light . . . My dear Pyotr Ilyich, do you know how to remove yourself?"

"What do you mean, remove myself?"

"To make way. To make way for one you hold dear, and for one you hate. And so that the one you hate becomes dear to you—to make way like that! And to say to them: God be with you, go, pass by, while I . . ."

"While you . . . ?"

"Enough. Let's go."

"By God, I'll tell someone," Pyotr Ilyich looked at him, "to keep you from going there. Why do you need to go to Mokroye now?"

"There's a woman there, a woman, and let that be enough for you, Pyotr Ilyich, drop it!"

"Listen, even though you're a savage, somehow I've always liked you . . . That's why I worry."

"Thank you, brother. I'm a savage, you say. Savages, savages! That's something I keep repeating: savages! Ah, yes, here's Misha, I forgot about him."

Misha came in, puffing, with a wad of small bills, and reported that "they all got a move on" at Plotnikov's and were running around with bottles, and fish, and tea—everything would be ready shortly. Mitya snatched a ten-rouble note and gave it to Pyotr Ilyich, and he tossed another ten-rouble note to Misha.

"Don't you dare!" Pyotr Ilyich cried. "Not in my house. Anyway, it's a harmful indulgence. Hide your money away, put it here, why throw it around? Tomorrow you'll need it, and it's me you'll come to asking for ten roubles. Why do you keep stuffing it into your side pocket? You're going to lose it!"

"Listen, my dear fellow, let's go to Mokroye together!"

"Why should I go?"

"Listen, let's open a bottle now, and we'll drink to life! I want to have a drink, and I want above all to have a drink with you. I've never drunk with you, have I?"

"Fine, let's go to the tavern, I'm on my way there myself."

"No time for the tavern, better at Plotnikov's shop, in the back room. Now, do you want me to ask you a riddle?"

"Ask."

Mitya took the piece of paper from his waistcoat pocket, unfolded it, and held it up. There was written on it in his large, clear hand:

"For my whole life I punish myself, I punish my whole life!"

"Really, I'm going to tell someone, I will go now and tell someone," Pyotr Ilyich said, having read the paper.

"You won't have time, my dear, let's have a drink, come on!"

Plotnikov's shop was only about two doors away from Pyotr Ilyich, at the corner of the street. It was the main grocery store in our town, owned by wealthy merchants, and in fact not bad at all. They had everything any store in the capital would have, all kinds of groceries: wines "bottled by Eliseyev brothers," fruit, cigars, tea, sugar, coffee, and so on. There were always three clerks on duty, and two boys to run around with deliveries. Though things had gone poorly in our parts, landowners had left, trade had slackened, yet the grocery business flourished as before, and even got better and better every year: purchasers for such goods were never lacking. Mitya was awaited with impatience at the shop. They remembered only too well how three or four weeks earlier he had bought in the same way, all at once, all kinds of goods and wines, for several hundred roubles in cash (they would not, of course, have given him anything on credit); they remembered that he had a whole wad of money sticking out of his hand, just as now, and was throwing it around for nothing, without bargaining, without thinking and without wishing to think why he needed such a quantity of goods, wines, and so forth. Afterwards the whole town was saying that he had driven off to Mokroye with Grushenka then, "squandered three thousand at once in a night and a day, and came back from the spree without a kopeck, naked as the day he was born." He had roused a whole camp of gypsies that time (they were in our neighborhood then), who in two days, while he was drunk, relieved him of an untold amount of money and drank an untold quantity of expensive wine. They said, laughing at Mitya, that in Mokroye he had drowned the cloddish peasants in champagne and stuffed their women and girls with candies and Strasbourg pâté. They also laughed, especially in the tavern, over Mitya's own frank and public confession (of course, they did not laugh in his face; it was rather dangerous to laugh in his face) that all he got from Grushenka for the whole "escapade" was that "she let him kiss her little foot, and would not let him go any further."

When Mitya and Pyotr Ilyich arrived at the shop, they found a cart ready at the door, covered with a rug, harnessed to a troika with bells and chimes, and the coachman Andrei awaiting Mitya. In the shop they had nearly finished "putting up" one box of goods and were only waiting for Mitya's appearance to nail it shut and load it on the cart. Pyotr Ilyich was surprised.

"How did you manage to get a troika?" he asked Mitya.

"I met him, Andrei, as I was running to your place, and told him to drive straight here to the shop. Why waste time! Last time I went with Timofei, but now Timofei said bye-bye and went off ahead of me with a certain enchantress. Will we be very late, Andrei?"

"They'll get there only an hour before us, if that, just an hour before!" Andrei hastily responded."I harnessed Timofei up, I know how he drives. His driving's not our driving, Dmitri Fyodorovich, not by a long shot. They won't make it even an hour before us!" Andrei, a lean fellow with reddish hair, not yet old, dressed in a long peasant coat and with a caftan over his arm, added enthusiastically.

"I'll give you fifty roubles for vodka if you're only an hour behind them."

"I guarantee you an hour, Dmitri Fyodorovich. An hour, hah! They won't even be half an hour ahead of us!"

Though Mitya began bustling about, making arrangements, he spoke and gave commands somehow strangely, at random and out of order. He began one thing and forgot to finish it. Pyotr Ilyich found it necessary to step in and help matters along.

"It should come to four hundred roubles, not less than four hundred roubles, just like the other time," Mitya commanded. "Four dozen bottles of champagne, not a bottle less."

"Why do you need so much? What for? Stop!" Pyotr Ilyich yelled. "What's this box? What's in it? Four hundred roubles' worth?"

The bustling shop clerks explained to him at once, in sugary tones, that this first box contained only a half dozen bottles of champagne and "all sorts of indispensable starters," such as appetizers, candies, fruit-drops, and so on. And that the main "provision" would be packed and sent separately that same hour, just as the other time, in a special cart, also drawn by a troika, and would get there in good time, "perhaps only an hour behind Dmitri Fyodorovich."

"No more than an hour, no more than an hour, and put in as much candy and toffee as you can—the girls there love it," Mitya hotly insisted.

"Toffee is one thing, but four dozen bottles—why do you need so much? One dozen is enough," Pyotr Ilyich was almost angry now. He started bargaining, demanded to see the bill, would not be silenced. He saved, however, only a hundred roubles. They settled on delivering three hundred roubles' worth of goods.

"Ah, devil take you!" Pyotr Ilyich cried, as if suddenly thinking better of it. "What do I care? Throw your money away, since you got it for nothing!"

"Come along, my economist, come along, don't be angry," Mitya dragged him into the back room of the shop. "They're going to bring us a bottle here, we'll have a sip. Eh, Pyotr Ilyich, let's go together, because you're a dear man, just the sort I like."

Mitya sat down on a little wicker chair in front of a tiny table covered with a most filthy tablecloth. Pyotr Ilyich squeezed in opposite him, and the champagne appeared at once. The offer was made to serve the gentlemen oysters, "foremost oysters, the latest arrivals."

"Devil take your oysters, I don't eat them, bring us nothing," Pyotr Ilyich snarled almost angrily.

"No time for oysters," Mitya remarked, "and I have no appetite. You know, my friend," he suddenly said with feeling, "I've never liked all this disorder."

"Who likes it? Three dozen bottles, for peasants? Good Lord, anyone would explode!"

"I don't mean that. I mean a higher order. There is no order in me, no higher order . . . But . . . that's all over, nothing to grieve about. Too late, devil take it! My whole life has been disorder, and I must put it in order. Punning, am I?"

"You're not punning, you're raving."

> "Glory to the Highest in the world,
> Glory to the Highest in me!

That verse once burst from my soul, not a verse but a tear, I wrote it myself . . . not, by the way, that time when I was dragging the captain by his beard . . ."

"Why mention him all of a sudden?"

"Why him all of a sudden? Nonsense! Everything ends, everything comes out even; a line—and a sum total."

"I keep thinking about your pistols, really."

"The pistols are nonsense, too! Drink and stop imagining things. I love life, I've grown to love life too much, so much it's disgusting. Enough! To life, my dear, let us drink to life, I offer a toast to life! Why am I so pleased with myself? I'm base, but I'm pleased with myself, and yet it pains me to be base and still pleased with myself. I bless creation, I'm ready right now to bless God and his creation, but . . . I must exterminate one foul insect, so that it will not crawl around spoiling life for others . . . Let us drink to life, dear brother! What can be more precious than life! Nothing, nothing! To life, and to one queen of queens."

"To life, then, and maybe to your queen as well."

They emptied their glasses. Mitya, though rapturous and expansive, was somehow sad. As though some insuperable and heavy care stood over him.

"Misha . . . was it your Misha who just came in? Misha, my dear Misha, come here, drink a glass for me, to the golden-haired Phoebus of tomorrow . . ."

"Not him!" Pyotr Ilyich cried irritably.

"No, please, let him. I want him to."

"Ahh . . .!"

Misha drank his glass, bowed, and ran out.

"He'll remember it better," Mitya observed. "A woman, I love a woman! What is woman? The queen of the earth! Sad, I feel sad, Pyotr Ilyich. Do you remember Hamlet? 'I am sad, so sad, Horatio . . . Ach, poor Yorick!'[4] It is I, perhaps, who am Yorick. Yorick now, that is, and later—the skull."

Pyotr Ilyich listened silently; Mitya also fell silent for a time.

"What kind of dog is that?" he suddenly asked the sales clerk distractedly, noticing a pretty little lapdog with black eyes in the corner.

"It's the mistress's, Varvara Alexeyevna's, lapdog," the sales clerk replied. "She brought him here today and forgot him. We must take him back to her."

"I saw one like it . . . in the regiment . . . ," Mitya said pensively, "only that one had a broken hind leg . . . Incidentally, Pyotr Ilyich, I wanted to ask you: have you ever stolen anything in your life?"

"What sort of question is that?"

"No, I'm just asking. From someone's pocket, you see, someone else's property? I don't mean government money, everyone steals government money, and of course you, too . . ."

"Go to the devil."

"I mean someone else's property: right from their pocket or purse, eh?"

"I once stole twenty kopecks from my mother, from the table, when I was nine years old. Took it on the sly and clutched it in my fist."

"And then what?"

"Then nothing. I kept it for three days, felt ashamed, confessed, and gave it back."

"And then what?"

"Naturally I got a whipping. Why, you haven't stolen anything, have you?"

"I have," Mitya winked slyly.

"What have you stolen?" Pyotr Ilyich became curious.

"Twenty kopecks from my mother, when I was nine, I gave it back in three days." Having said this, Mitya suddenly rose from his seat.

"Dmitri Fyodorovich, shouldn't we hurry up?" Andrei suddenly called from the door of the shop.

"Ready? Let's go!" Mitya got into a flutter. "Yet one last tale and then[5] . . . give Andrei a glass of vodka for the road now! And a shot of cognac along with it! This box" (the pistol case) "goes under my seat. Farewell, Pyotr Ilyich, think kindly of me."

"But you're coming back tomorrow?"

"Certainly."

"Will you be so kind as to settle the bill now, sir?" the sales clerk ran up.

"Ah, yes, the bill! Certainly!"

He again snatched the wad of money from his pocket, took three hundred-rouble bills from the top, tossed them on the counter, and walked hurriedly out of the shop. Everyone followed after him, bowing and sending him off with salutations and best wishes. Andrei grunted from the cognac he had just drunk and jumped up on the box. But as Mitya was about to take his seat, Fenya suddenly appeared quite unexpectedly before him. She came running up, out of breath, shouting, clasping her hands before him, and plopped down at his feet:

"Dear sir, Dmitri Fyodorovich, my dear, don't harm my mistress! And I told you everything . . . ! And don't harm him either, he's her former one! He'll marry Agrafena Alexandrovna now, that's what he came from Siberia for . . . Dear sir, Dmitri Fyodorovich, my dear, don't harm anyone's life!"

"Aha, so that's it! I see what you're up to now!" Perkhotin muttered to himself. "It's all clear now, no mistake about it. Dmitri Fyodorovich, give me back the pistols at once, if you want to be a man," he exclaimed aloud to Mitya, "do you hear me, Dmitri!"

"The pistols? Wait, my dear, I'll toss them into a puddle on the way," Mitya replied. "Fenya, get up, don't lie there in front of me. Mitya won't do any more harm, he won't harm anyone anymore, the foolish man. And something else, Fenya," he shouted to her, already seated in the cart, "I hurt you earlier, so forgive me and have mercy, I'm a scoundrel, forgive me . . . And if you won't forgive me, it doesn't matter. Because now nothing matters! Get going, Andrei, fly off, quickly!"

Andrei got going; the bells jingled.

"Farewell, Pyotr Ilyich! For you, for you is my last tear . . . !"

"He's not drunk, but what drivel he's spouting!" Pyotr Ilyich thought, watching him go. He almost made up his mind to stay and keep an eye on the loading of the cart (also with a troika) with the rest of the goods and wine, suspecting that Mitya would be cheated and robbed, but suddenly, getting angry with himself, he spat and went to his tavern to play billiards.

"A nice fellow, but a fool . . . ," he muttered to himself as he went. "I've heard about some officer, Grushenka's 'former' one. Well, if he's come now . . . Ah, those pistols! Eh, the devil, I'm not his nursemaid, am I? Go ahead! Anyway, nothing will happen. Loudmouths, that's all they are. They get drunk and fight, fight and make peace. They don't mean business. 'Remove myself,' 'punish myself'—what is all that? Nothing will happen! He's shouted in the same style a thousand times, drunk, in the tavern. Now he's not drunk. 'Drunk in spirit'—these scoundrels love style. I'm not his nursemaid, am I? He must have had a fight, his whole mug was covered with blood. But who with? I'll find out in the tavern. And that bloodstained handkerchief . . . Pah, the devil, he left it on my floor . . . But who cares?"

He arrived at the tavern in the foulest of humors, and at once got a game going. The game cheered him up. He played another, and suddenly began telling one of his partners that Dmitri Karamazov had money again, as much as three thousand, he had seen it himself, and that he had gone off to Mokroye again, on a spree with Grushenka. The listeners received his news with almost unexpected curiosity. And they all began to talk, not laughing, but somehow with strange seriousness. They even stopped playing.

"Three thousand? Where did he get three thousand?"

More questions were asked. The news about Madame Khokhlakov was received skeptically.

"Could he have robbed the old man, do you think?"

"Three thousand? Something's not right."

"He was boasting out loud that he'd kill his father, everyone here heard it. He talked precisely about three thousand . . ."

Pyotr Ilyich listened and suddenly started answering their questions drily and sparingly. He did not say a word about the blood on Mitya's hands and face, though on his way there he had been planning to mention it. They began a third game, gradually the talk about Mitya died away; but, having finished the third game, Pyotr Ilyich did not wish to play any more, put down his cue, and, without taking supper, as had been his intention, left the tavern. As he walked out into the square, he stopped in perplexity, and even marveled at himself. He suddenly realized that he was just about to go to Fyodor Pavlovich's house, to find out if anything had happened. "On account of the nonsense it will all turn out to be, I shall wake up someone else's household and cause a scandal. Pah, the devil, I'm not their nursemaid, am I?"

In the foulest humor, he went straight home, but suddenly remembered Fenya: "Eh, the devil, I should have asked her then," he thought with annoyance, "then I'd know everything." And the most impatient and stubborn desire to talk with her and find things out suddenly began burning in him, so much so that, halfway home, he turned sharply towards the widow Morozov's house, where Grushenka lived. Coming up to the gates, he knocked, and the knock breaking the stillness of the night again seemed suddenly to sober him and anger him. Besides, no one answered, everyone in the house was asleep. "Here, too, I'll cause a scandal!" he thought, now with a sort of suffering in his soul, but instead of finally going away, he suddenly began knocking again with all his might. The racket could be heard all up and down the street. "No, I'll keep knocking until they answer, I will!" he muttered, getting more and more enraged each time he knocked, and at the same time banging still louder on the gate.

Chapter 6

Here I Come!

Dmitri Fyodorovich flew over the road. Mokroye was some fifteen miles away, but Andrei's troika galloped so fast that they could make it in an hour and a quarter. It was as if the swift ride suddenly refreshed Mitya. The air was fresh and rather cool; big stars shone in the clear sky. This was the same night, perhaps the same hour, when Alyosha threw himself to the earth "vowing ecstatically to love it unto ages of ages." But Mitya's soul was troubled, very troubled, and though many things now tormented his soul, at this moment his whole being yearned irresistibly for her, for his queen, to whom he was flying in order to look at her for the last time. I will say just one thing: his heart did not argue even for a moment. I shall not be believed, perhaps, if I say that this jealous man did not feel the least jealousy towards this new man, this new rival who had sprung up from nowhere, this "officer." If some other man had appeared, he would at once have become jealous, and would perhaps again have drenched his terrible hands with blood, but towards this man, "her first," he felt no jealous hatred as he flew along in his troika, nor even any hostility—though it is true he had not yet seen him. "This is beyond dispute, this is his right and hers; this is her first love, which in five years she has not forgotten; so she has loved only him these five years, and I—what am I doing here? Why am I here, and what for? Step aside, Mitya, make way! And what am I now? It's all finished now, even without the officer, even if he hadn't come at all, it would still be finished . . ."

In some such words he might have set forth his feelings, if he had been able to reason. But at the moment he could no longer reason. All his present resolve had been born then, at Fenya's, from her first words, without reasoning, in an instant, had been felt at once and accepted as a whole with all its consequences. And yet, despite the attained resolve, his soul was troubled, troubled to the point of suffering: even his resolve did not bring him peace. Too much stood behind him and tormented him. And at moments it seemed strange to him: he had already written his own sentence with pen and paper: "I punish myself and my life"; and the paper was there, ready, in his pocket; the pistol was already loaded, he had already decided how he would greet the first hot ray of "golden-haired Phoebus" in the morning, and yet it was impossible to square accounts with the past, with all that stood behind him and tormented him, he felt it to the point of suffering, and the thought of it pierced his soul with despair. There was a moment on the way when he suddenly wanted to stop Andrei, jump out of the cart, take his loaded pistol, and finish everything without waiting for dawn. But this moment flew by like a spark. And the troika went flying on, "devouring space," and the closer he came to his goal, the more powerfully the thought of her again, of her alone, took his breath away and drove all the other terrible phantoms from his heart. Oh, he wanted so much to look at her, if only briefly, if only from afar! "She is with *him* now, so I will only look at how she is with him, with her former sweetheart, that is all I want." And never before had such love for this woman, so fatal for his destiny, risen in his breast, such a new feeling, never experienced before, a feeling unexpected even to himself, tender to the point of prayer, to the point of vanishing before her. "And I will vanish!" he said suddenly, in a fit of hysterical rapture.

They had been galloping for almost an hour. Mitya was silent, and Andrei, though he was a talkative fellow, had not said a word yet either, as though he were wary of talking, and only urged on his "nags," his lean but spirited bay troika. Then suddenly, in terrible agitation, Mitya exclaimed:

"Andrei! What if they're asleep?"

The thought suddenly came into his head; it had not occurred to him before.

"It's very possible they've gone to bed, Dmitri Fyodorovich."

Mitya frowned painfully: what, indeed, if he was flying there . . . with such feelings . . . and they were asleep . . . and she, too, perhaps was sleeping right there . . . ? An angry feeling boiled up in his heart.

"Drive, Andrei, whip them up, Andrei, faster!" he shouted in a frenzy.

"And maybe they haven't gone to bed yet," Andrei reasoned, after a pause. "Timofei was telling me there were a lot of them there . . ."

"At the station?"

"Not at the station, at Plastunov's, at the inn, it's a way station, too."

"I know; but what do you mean by a lot? How many? Who are they?" Mitya heaved himself forward, terribly alarmed by the unexpected news.

"Timofei said they're all gentlemen: two from town, I don't know who, but Timofei said two of them were locals, and those two others, the visitors, maybe there's more, I didn't ask him exactly. He said they sat down to play cards."

"To play cards?"

"So maybe they're not asleep if they've started playing cards. Not likely, since it's only eleven o'clock, if that."

"Drive, Andrei, drive!" Mitya cried again, nervously.

"Can I ask you something, sir?" Andrei began again after a pause. "Only I'm afraid it'll make you angry, sir."

"What is it?"

"Just now Fedosya Markovna fell at your feet, begging you not to harm her mistress, or anyone else . . . so, sir, well, I'm driving you there . . . Forgive me, sir, maybe I've said something foolish, because of my conscience."

Mitya suddenly seized his shoulders from behind.

"Are you a coachman? A coachman?" he began frenziedly.

"A coachman . . ."

"Then you know you have to make way. If you're a coachman, what do you do, not make way for people? Just run them down? Look out, I'm coming! No, coachman, do not run them down! You must not run anyone down, you must not spoil people's lives; and if you have spoiled someone's life—punish yourself . . . if you've ever spoiled, if you've ever harmed someone's life—punish yourself and go away."

All this burst from Mitya as if in complete hysterics. Andrei, though he was surprised at the gentleman, kept up the conversation.

"That's true, dear Dmitri Fyodorovich, you're right there, one mustn't run a man down, or torment him, or any other creature either, for every creature has been created, a horse, for example, because there's people that just barrel on regardless, some of us coachmen, let's say . . . And there's no holding him back, he just keeps pushing on, pushing right on."

"To hell?" Mitya suddenly interrupted, and burst into his abrupt, unexpected laugh. "Andrei, you simple soul," again he seized him firmly by the shoulders, "tell me: will Dmitri Fyodorovich Karamazov go to hell or not? What do you think?"

"I don't know, my dear, it depends on you, because you are . . . You see, sir, when the Son of God was crucified on the cross and died, he went straight from the cross to hell and freed all the sinners suffering there. And hell groaned because it thought it wouldn't have any more sinners coming. And the Lord said to hell: 'Do not groan, O hell, for all kinds of mighty ones, rulers, great judges, and rich men will come to you from all parts, and you will be as full as ever, unto ages of ages, till the time when I come again.' That's right, that's what he said . . ."[1]

"A popular legend—splendid! Whip up the left one, Andrei!"

"That's who hell is meant for, sir," Andrei whipped up the left one, "and you, sir, are just like a little child to us . . . that's how we look at you . . . And though you're one to get angry, that you are, sir, the Lord will forgive you for your simple heart."

"And you, will you forgive me, Andrei?"

"Why should I forgive you, you never did anything to me."

"No, for everyone, for everyone, will you alone, right now, this moment, here on the road, forgive me for everyone? Speak, my simple soul!"

"Ah, sir! I'm even afraid to be driving you, you talk so strange somehow . . ."

But Mitya did not hear. He was frantically praying, whispering wildly to himself.

"Lord, take me in all my lawlessness, but do not judge me. Let me pass without your judgment . . . Do not judge me, for I have condemned myself; do not judge me, for I love you, Lord! I am loathsome, but I love you: if you send me to hell, even there I will love you, and from there I will cry that I love you unto ages of ages . . . But let me also finish with loving . . . finish here and now with loving, for five hours only, till your hot ray . . . For I love the queen of my soul. I love her and cannot not love her. You see all of me. I will gallop up, I will fall before her: you are right to pass me by . . . Farewell and forget your victim, never trouble yourself!"

"Mokroye!" cried Andrei, pointing ahead with his whip.

Through the pale darkness of night suddenly appeared a solid black mass of buildings spread over a vast space. The population of the village of Mokroye was two thousand souls, but at that hour they were all asleep, and only a few lights gleamed here and there in the darkness.

"Drive, drive, Andrei, I'm coming!" Mitya exclaimed as if in fever.

"They're not asleep!" Andrei said again, pointing with his whip to Plastunov's inn, which stood just at the entrance and in which all six street windows were brightly lit.

"Not asleep!" Mitya echoed happily. "Make it rattle, Andrei, gallop, ring the bells, drive up with a clatter. Let everybody know who's come! I'm coming! Me! Here I come!" Mitya kept exclaiming frenziedly.

Andrei put the exhausted troika to a gallop, and indeed drove up to the high porch with a clatter and reined in his steaming, half-suffocated horses. Mitya jumped from the cart just as the innkeeper, who was in fact on his way to bed, peered out from the porch, curious who could just have driven up like that.

"Is it you, Trifon Borisich?"

The innkeeper bent forward, peered, ran headlong down the steps, and rushed up to his guest in servile rapture.

"My dear Dmitri Fyodorovich! Do we meet again?"

This Trifon Borisich was a thickset and robust man of medium height, with a somewhat fleshy face, of stern and implacable appearance, especially with the Mokroye peasants, but endowed with the ability to change his expression to one of the utmost servility whenever he smelled a profit. He went about dressed in Russian style, in a peasant blouse and a long, full-skirted coat, had quite a bit of money, but also constantly dreamed of a higher role. He had more than half of the peasants in his clutches, everyone was in debt to him. He rented land from the landowners, and had also bought some himself, and the peasants worked this land for him in return for their debts, which they could never pay back. He was a widower and had four grown-up daughters; one was already a widow and lived with him with her two little ones, his granddaughters, working for him as a charwoman. Another of his peasant daughters was married to an official, who had risen from being a petty clerk, and one could see on the wall in one of the rooms of the inn, among the family photographs, also a miniature photograph of this little official in his uniform and official epaulettes. The two younger daughters, on feast days or when going visiting, would put on light blue or green dresses of fashionable cut, tight-fitting behind and with three feet of train, but the very next morning, as on any other day, they would get up at dawn, sweep the rooms with birch brooms in their hands, take the garbage out, and clear away the trash left by the lodgers. Despite the thousands he had already made, Trifon Borisich took great pleasure in fleecing a lodger on a spree, and, recalling that not quite a month ago he had profited from Dmitri Fyodorovich in one day, during his spree with Grushenka, to the tune of more than two hundred roubles, if not three, he now greeted him joyfully and eagerly, scenting his prey again just by the way Mitya drove up to the porch.

"My dear Dmitri Fyodorovich, will you be our guest again?"

"Wait, Trifon Borisich," Mitya began, "first things first: where is she?"

"Agrafena Alexandrovna?" the innkeeper understood at once, peering alertly into Mitya's face. "She's here, too . . . staying . . ."

"With whom? With whom?"

"Some visitors passing through, sir . . . One is an official, must be a Pole from the way he talks, it was he who sent horses for her from here; the other one is a friend of his, or a fellow traveler, who can tell? They're both in civilian clothes . . ."

"What, are they on a spree? Are they rich?"

"Spree, nothing! They're small fry, Dmitri Fyodorovich."

"Small? And the others?"

"They're from town, two gentlemen . . . They were on their way back from Cherny and stopped here. One of them, the young one, must be a relative of Mr. Miusov's, only I forget his name . . . and the other one you know, too, I suppose: the landowner Maximov; he went on a pilgrimage to your monastery, he says, and now he's going around with this young relative of Mr. Miusov's . . ."

"And that's all?"

"That's all."

"Stop, listen, Trifon Borisich, now tell me the most important thing: what about her, how is she?"

"She just arrived, and now she's sitting with them."

"Happy? Laughing?"

"No, she doesn't seem to be laughing much. She's sitting there quite bored; she was combing the young man's hair."

"The Pole's? The officer's?"

"He's no young man, and no officer either, not at all; no, sir, not his but this nephew of Miusov's, the young man . . . I just can't remember his name."

"Kalganov?"

"Exactly—Kalganov."

"Good, I'll see for myself. Are they playing cards?"

"They played for a while, then they stopped and had tea. The official ordered liqueurs."

"Stop, Trifon Borisich, stop, my dear soul, I'll see for myself. Now answer the most important thing: are there any gypsies around?"

"There's been no word of gypsies at all lately, Dmitri Fyodorovich, the authorities chased them away, but there are Jews hereabouts, in Rozhdestvenskaya, they play cymbals and fiddles, you can send for them even now. They'll come."

"Send for them, do send for them!" Mitya cried. "And you can wake up the girls like the other time, Maria especially, and Stepanida, Arina. Two hundred roubles for the chorus!"

"For that money I'll wake up the whole village, though they've probably all dropped off by now. But are they worth such pampering, our peasants, or the girls, Dmitri Fyodorovich? To lay out so much for such coarseness and crudeness? It's not for our peasant to smoke cigars—and you did give them out. They all stink, the bandits. And the girls have lice, every last one of them. Why spend so much? I'll wake up my daughters for you for nothing, they just went to bed, I'll kick them in the backside and make them sing for you. Last time you gave the peasants champagne to drink, agh!"

Trifon Borisich had no call to feel sorry for Mitya: he himself had hidden half a dozen bottles of champagne from him last time, and had picked up a hundred-rouble bill from under the table and clutched it in his fist. And in his fist it remained.

"I ran through more than one thousand that time, do you remember, Trifon Borisich?"

"You did, my dear, how could I forget it? Must have been three thousand you left here."

"So, I've come with as much again, do you see?"

And he took out his wad of money and held it right under the innkeeper's nose.

"Now listen and understand: in an hour the wine will arrive, appetizers, pâté, and candies—send everything upstairs at once. That box in Andrei's cart should also go upstairs at once, open it and serve the champagne immediately . . . And above all, the girls, the girls, and especially Maria . . ."

He turned back to the cart and took the case with the pistols from under the seat.

"Your pay, Andrei, take it! Fifteen roubles for the troika, and fifty for vodka . . . for your willingness, your love . . . Remember the honorable Karamazov!"

"I'm afraid, your honor . . . ," Andrei hesitated. "Give me five roubles for a tip, if you like, but I won't take more. Trifon Borisich, be my witness. Forgive my foolish words . . ."

"What are you afraid of?" Mitya looked him up and down. "To hell with you, then!" he cried, tossing him five roubles. "Now, Trifon Borisich, take me in quietly and let me first have a look at them all, so that they don't notice me. Where are they, in the blue room?"

Trifon Borisich looked warily at Mitya, but at once obediently did as he was told: he carefully led him to the front hall, and himself went into the first large room, adjacent to the one in which the guests were sitting, and removed the candle. Then he quietly led Mitya in and put him in a corner, in the darkness, from where he could freely watch the company without being seen by them. But Mitya did not look for long, and could not simply look: he saw her, and his heart began to pound, his head swam. She was sitting at the end of the table, in an armchair, and next to her, on a sofa, sat Kalganov, a pretty and still very young man; she was holding him by the hand and seemed to be laughing, and he, without looking at her, was saying something loudly, apparently irritably, to Maximov, who sat across the table from Grushenka. Maximov was laughing very much at something. *He* sat on the sofa, and next to the sofa, on a chair by the wall, was some other stranger. The one on the sofa sat casually, smoking a pipe, and it flashed through Mitya that he was a sort of plumpish, broad-faced little man, who must be short and seemed to be angry about something. His companion, the other stranger, appeared to Mitya to be exceedingly tall; but he could make out nothing more. His breath failed him. Unable to stand still a moment longer, he put the case on a chest and, turning cold and with a sinking heart, walked straight into the blue room among them.

"Aie!" Grushenka shrieked in fear, noticing him first.

Chapter 7

The Former and Indisputable One

Mitya, with his long, quick strides, went right up to the table.

"Gentlemen," he began loudly, almost shouting, but stammering at each word, "it's . . . it's nothing! Don't be afraid," he exclaimed, "it's really nothing, nothing," he suddenly turned to Grushenka, who was leaning towards Kalganov in her armchair, firmly clutching his hand. "I . . . I am traveling, too. I'll stay till morning. Gentlemen, may a passing traveler . . . stay with you till morning? Only till morning, for the last time, in this same room?"

These final words he addressed to the fat little man with the pipe who was sitting on the sofa. The latter imposingly removed the pipe from his lips and observed sternly:

"*Panie*,[1] this is a private gathering. There are other rooms."

"But it's you, Dmitri Fyodorovich! But what's the matter?" Kalganov responded suddenly. "But do sit down with us! Good evening!"

"Good evening, my dear . . . and priceless fellow! I've always respected you . . . ," Mitya joyfully and impetuously responded, holding his hand out to him at once across the table.

"Aie, what a grip! You've quite broken my fingers," Kalganov laughed.

"He always shakes hands like that, always!" Grushenka responded gaily, still with a timid smile, seeming suddenly convinced by the looks of Mitya that he was not going to start a brawl, but peering at him with terrible curiosity and still uneasily. There was something in him that struck her greatly, and she had not at all expected that he would come in like that and speak like that at such a moment.

"Good evening, sir," the landowner Maximov responded sweetly from the left. Mitya rushed over to him as well:

"Good evening, you're here, too, I'm so glad you're here, too! Gentlemen, gentlemen, I . . . ," he turned again to the *pan* with the pipe, evidently taking him to be the most important person present, "I came flying here . . . I wanted to spend my last day and my last hour in this room, in this very room, where I once adored . . . my queen . . . ! Forgive me, *panie*!" he cried frantically. "I came flying, and I made a vow . . . Oh, don't be afraid, it's my last night! Let us drink for peace, *panie*! Wine will be served presently . . . I brought this." Suddenly, for some reason, he pulled out his wad of money. "Allow me, *panie*! I want music, noise, racket, everything just as before . . . And the worm, the useless worm, will crawl away over the earth and be no more! On my last night I will commemorate the day of my joy . . . !"

He was almost breathless; there was much, much that he wanted to say, but only odd exclamations flew out. The *pan* gazed motionlessly at him, at his wad of money, gazed at Grushenka, and was clearly bewildered.

"If my *królowa* permits . . . ," he started to say.

"What's a *królowa*, a queen or what?"[2] Grushenka suddenly interrupted. "It makes me laugh the way you all talk. Sit down, Mitya, what are you talking about? Don't frighten me, please. You aren't going to frighten me, are you? If you aren't, then I'm glad to see you . . ."

"Me? Me frighten you?" Mitya suddenly cried, throwing up his hands. "Oh, pass me by, go your way, I won't hinder you . . . !" And suddenly, quite unexpectedly for everyone, and certainly also for himself, he flung himself down on a chair and dissolved in tears, his head turned away to the opposite wall, and his arms firmly grasping the back of the chair as though embracing it.

"Now, now, is that any way to behave?" Grushenka exclaimed reproachfully. "That's just how he used to be when he came visiting me—he'd suddenly start talking, and I wouldn't understand a thing. Then once he began crying just like that, and now again—shame on you! What are you crying for? *As if you had anything to cry about!*" she suddenly added mysteriously, emphasizing her words with a sort of irritation.

"I . . . I'm not crying . . . Well, good evening!" he turned around instantly on his chair and suddenly laughed, not his abrupt, wooden laugh, but a sort of long, nervous, inaudible, and shaking laugh.

"What, again . . . ? Come on, cheer up, cheer up!" Grushenka urged him. "I'm very glad you've come, very glad, Mitya, do you hear that? I am very glad. I want him to sit here with us," she said imperiously, as if addressing everyone, though her words were obviously aimed at the man sitting on the sofa. "I want it, I want it! And if he leaves, I will leave, too, that's what!" she added, her eyes suddenly flashing.

"Whatever my queen pleases is the law!" the *pan* said, gallantly kissing Grushenka's hand. "You, *panie*, I ask to join our company!" he addressed Mitya courteously. Mitya jumped up a little again, obviously intending to break once more into a tirade, but something else came out.

"Let's drink, *panie*!" he stopped short suddenly instead of making a speech. Everyone laughed.

"Lord! I thought he was going to start talking again," Grushenka exclaimed nervously. "Listen, Mitya," she added insistently, "don't jump up any more, and it's lovely that you've brought champagne. I'll drink some myself, I can't stand liqueur. The best thing is that you yourself have come, it's such a bore . . . Are you on a spree again, or what? Do put your money in your pocket! Where did you get so much?"

Mitya, still holding in his hand the crumpled bank notes, which had been very well noticed by everyone, especially by the Poles, quickly and embarrassedly thrust them into his pocket. He blushed. At that same moment, the innkeeper brought an open bottle of champagne on a tray, with glasses. Mitya seized the bottle, but was so confused that he forgot what to do with it. Kalganov finally took it from him and poured the wine.

"Another bottle, another!" Mitya cried to the innkeeper, and, forgetting to clink glasses with the *pan* whom he had just so solemnly invited to drink for peace, suddenly drained his whole glass by himself, without waiting for anyone else. His whole face suddenly changed. Instead of the solemn and tragic expression he was wearing when he entered, something childlike, as it were, appeared in him. He seemed suddenly to have humbled and diminished himself. He looked timidly and joyfully at everyone, giggling nervously and frequently, with the grateful look of a guilty pup that has been patted and let in again. He seemed to have forgotten everything and looked at everyone around him admiringly, with a childish smile. He looked at Grushenka, laughing continually, and moved his chair up next to her armchair. Gradually he made out the two Poles, though he could make little sense of them. The *pan* on the sofa struck him by his bearing, his Polish accent, and, above all, his pipe. "Well, what of it? It's good that he smokes a pipe," Mitya contemplated. The *pan*'s nearly forty-year-old face, somewhat flabby, with a tiny little nose, under which appeared a pair of the thinnest little pointed moustaches, dyed and insolent, so far had not aroused the least question in Mitya. Even the *pan*'s quite wretched wig, made in Siberia, with the hair stupidly brushed forward on the temples, did not particularly strike him: "So, if there's a wig, that's how it should be," he went on contemplating blissfully. As for the other *pan* sitting by the wall, who was younger than the *pan* on the sofa, and was looking impudently and defiantly at the whole company, listening with silent disdain to the general conversation, he, in turn, struck Mitya only by his great height, terribly disproportionate to the *pan* sitting on the sofa. "About six foot six standing up," flashed through Mitya's head. It also flashed in him that this tall *pan* was most likely the friend and henchman of the *pan* on the sofa, "his bodyguard," so to speak, and that the little *pan* with the pipe of course gave orders to the tall *pan*. But all this, too, seemed terribly good and indisputable to Mitya. All rivalry had ceased in the little pup. He did not yet understand anything about Grushenka and the mysterious tone of some of her phrases; he only understood, trembling with his whole heart, that she had treated him tenderly, that she had "forgiven" him and sat him down next to her. He was beside himself with delight seeing her take a sip of wine from her glass. Suddenly, however, the silence of the company seemed to strike him, and he began looking around at everyone, his eyes expecting something: "Why are we just sitting here, why don't we get something started, gentlemen?" his grinning eyes seemed to say.

"It's him, he keeps telling lies, and we keep laughing," Kalganov suddenly began, as if guessing Mitya's thought, and he pointed at Maximov.

Mitya swiftly fixed his eyes on Kalganov and then at once on Maximov.

"Lies?" he burst into his abrupt, wooden laughter, at once becoming happy about something. "Ha, ha!"

"Yes. Imagine, he maintains that in the twenties our entire cavalry allegedly married Polish women; but that's awful nonsense, isn't it?"

"Polish women?" Mitya chimed in, now decidedly delighted.

Kalganov well understood Mitya's relations with Grushenka; he had also guessed about the *pan*; but all that did not interest him very much, and perhaps did not interest him at all: what interested him most was Maximov. He had turned up there with Maximov by chance, and met the Poles for the first time in his life there at the inn. As for Grushenka, he had known her previously and once even visited her with someone; she had not liked him then. But now she kept glancing at him very tenderly; before Mitya arrived she had even caressed him, but he remained somehow insensible. He was a young man, not more than twenty years old, stylishly dressed, with a very sweet, pale face, and with beautiful, thick, light brown hair. And set in this pale face were a pair of lovely light blue eyes, with an intelligent and sometimes deep expression, even beyond his age, notwithstanding that the young man sometimes spoke and looked just like a child, and was not at all embarrassed by it, being quite aware of it himself. Generally, he was very original, even whimsical, though always kind. Occasionally something fixed and stubborn flashed in the expression of his face: he looked at you, listened, and all the while kept dreaming about something of his own. At times he would become sluggish and lazy, at others he would suddenly get excited, often apparently for the most trivial reason.

"Imagine, I've been taking him around with me for four days now," he went on, drawing the words out a little, lazily, as it were, but quite naturally, and without any foppery. "Ever since the day your brother pushed him out of the carriage and sent him flying, remember? That made me very interested in him then, and I took him to the village with me, but now he keeps telling such lies that I'm ashamed to be with him. I'm taking him back . . ."

"The *pan* has never seen a Polish *pani*, and says what is not possible," the *pan* with the pipe observed to Maximov.

The *pan* with the pipe spoke Russian quite well, much better, at least, than he pretended. If he happened to use Russian words, he distorted them in a Polish manner.

"But I was married to a Polish *pani* myself, sir," Maximov giggled in reply.

"And did you also serve in the cavalry? You were talking about the cavalry. But you're no cavalryman," Kalganov immediately mixed in.

"No, indeed, he's no cavalryman! Ha, ha!" cried Mitya, who was listening greedily and quickly shifting his questioning glance to each speaker in turn, as if he expected to hear God knows what from each of them.

"No, you see, sir," Maximov turned to him, "I mean, sir, that those young Polish girls . . . pretty girls, sir . . . as soon as they'd danced a mazurka with one of our uhlans . . . as soon as she'd danced a mazurka with him, she'd jump on his lap like a little cat, sir . . . a little white cat, sir . . . and the *pan* father and the *pani* mother see it and allow it . . . allow it, sir . . . and the next day the uhlan would go and offer his hand . . . like that, sir . . . offer his hand, hee, hee!" Maximov ended with a giggle.

"The *pan* is a *łajdak*!"[3] the tall *pan* on the chair suddenly growled and crossed one leg over the other. All that caught Mitya's eye was his enormous greased boot with its thick and dirty sole. Generally, the clothing of both *pans* was rather grimy.

"So it's *łajdak* now! Why is he calling names?" Grushenka suddenly became angry.

"Pani Agrippina,[4] what the *pan* saw in the Polish land were peasant women, not noble ladies," the *pan* with the pipe observed to Grushenka.

"You can bet on that!" the tall *pan* on the chair snapped contemptuously.

"Really! Let him talk! People talk, why interfere with them? It's fun to be with them," Grushenka snarled.

"I am not interfering, *pani*," the *pan* in the wig observed significantly, with a prolonged look at Grushenka, and, lapsing into an imposing silence, began sucking on his pipe again.

"But no, no, what the *pan* just said is right," Kalganov got excited again, as if the matter involved were God knows how important. "He hasn't been to Poland, how can he talk about Poland? You didn't get married in Poland, did you?"

"No, sir, in Smolensk province. But, anyway, an uhlan brought her from Poland, sir, I mean my future spouse, sir, with her *pani* mother, and her aunt, and yet another female relation with a grown-up son, right from Poland . . . and let me have her. He was one of our sublieutenants, a very nice young man. First he wanted to marry her himself, but he didn't because she turned out to be lame . . ."

"So you married a lame woman?" Kalganov exclaimed.

"A lame woman, sir. They both deceived me a little bit then and concealed it. I thought she was skipping . . . she kept skipping all the time, and I thought it was from high spirits . . ."

"From joy that she was marrying you?" Kalganov yelled in a ringing, childlike voice.

"Yes, sir, from joy. And the reason turned out to be quite different, sir. Later, when we got married, that same evening after the church service, she confessed and asked my forgiveness with great feeling. She once jumped over a puddle in her young years, she said, and injured her little foot, hee, hee, hee!"

Kalganov simply dissolved in the most childlike laughter and almost collapsed on the sofa. Grushenka laughed, too. Mitya was in perfect bliss.

"You know, you know, he's telling the truth now, he's not lying anymore!" Kalganov exclaimed, addressing Mitya. "And you know, he was married twice—it's his first wife he's talking about—and his second wife, you know, ran away and is still alive, did you know that?"

"She did?" Mitya quickly turned to Maximov, his face expressing remarkable amazement.

"Yes, sir, she ran away, I've had that unpleasantness," Maximov confirmed humbly. "With a certain monsieur, sir. And the worst of it was that beforehand she first of all transferred my whole village to her name alone. You're an educated man, she said, you can always earn your keep. So she left me flat. A venerable bishop once observed to me: your first wife was lame, and the second too lightfooted, hee, hee!"

"Listen, listen!" Kalganov was really bubbling over, "even if he's lying—and he lies all the time—he's lying so as to give pleasure to us all: that's not mean, is it? You know, sometimes I love him. He's awfully mean, but naturally so, eh? Don't you think? Other people are mean for some reason, to get some profit from it, but he just does it naturally . . . Imagine, for instance, he claims (he was arguing about it yesterday all the while we were driving) that Gogol wrote about him in *Dead Souls*.[5] Remember, there's a landowner Maximov, and Nozdryov thrashes him and is taken to court 'for inflicting personal injury on the landowner Maximov with a birch while in a drunken condition'—do you remember? Imagine, now, he claims that was him, that it was he who was thrashed! But how can it be? Chichikov was traveling around in the twenties at the latest, the beginning of the twenties, so the dates don't fit at all. He couldn't have been thrashed then. He really couldn't, could he?"

It was hard to conceive why Kalganov was so excited, but his excitement was genuine. Mitya entered wholeheartedly into his interests.

"Well, what if he was thrashed!" he cried with a loud laugh.

"Not really thrashed, but just so," Maximov suddenly put in.

"How 'so'? Thrashed, or not thrashed?"

"*Która godzina, panie* (What time is it)?" the *pan* with the pipe addressed the tall *pan* on the chair with a bored look. The latter shrugged his shoulders in reply: neither of them had a watch.

"Why not talk? Let other people talk, too. You mean if you're bored, no one should talk?" Grushenka roused herself again, apparently provoking him on purpose. For the first time, as it were, something flashed through Mitya's mind. This time the *pan* replied with obvious irritation.

"*Pani*, I do not contradict, I do not say anything."

"All right, then. And you, go on with your story," Grushenka cried to Maximov. "Why are you all silent?"

"But there's really nothing to tell, because it's all foolishness," Maximov picked up at once with obvious pleasure, mincing a bit, "and in Gogol it's all just allegorical, because he made all the names allegorical: Nozdryov really wasn't Nozdryov but Nosov, and Kuvshinnikov doesn't bear any resemblance, because he was Shkvornyev. And Fenardi was indeed Fenardi, only he wasn't an Italian but a Russian, Petrov, sirs, and Mamzelle Fenardi was a pretty one, with pretty legs in tights, sirs, a short little skirt all-over sequins, and she made pirouettes, only not for four hours but just for four minutes, sirs . . . and seduced everyone . . ."

"What were you thrashed for, what did they thrash you for?" Kalganov kept on shouting.

"For Piron, sir," Maximov replied.[6]

"What Piron?" cried Mitya.

"The famous French writer Piron, sirs. We were all drinking wine then, a big company, in a tavern, at that fair. They invited me, and first of all I started reciting epigrams: 'Is it you, Boileau, in that furbelow?'[7] And Boileau answers that he's going to a masquerade, meaning to the bathhouse, sirs, hee, hee—so they took it personally. Then I hastened to tell them another one, very well known to all educated people, a sarcastic one, sirs:

> You're Sappho, I'm Phaon, agreed.
> But there's one thing still troubling me:
> You don't know your way to the sea.[8]

At that they got even more offended and began scolding me indecently, and I, unfortunately, tried to make things better by telling them a very educated anecdote about Piron, how he wasn't accepted into the French Academy, and in revenge wrote his own epitaph for his gravestone:

> Çi-gît Piron qui ne fut rien,
> Pas même académicien.[9]

Then they up and thrashed me."

"But what for, what for?"

"For my education. A man can be thrashed for all sorts of reasons," Maximov summed up meekly and sententiously.

"Eh, enough, it's all bad, I don't want to listen, I thought there would be some fun in it," Grushenka suddenly cut them off. Mitya, thrown into a flutter, stopped laughing at once. The tall *pan* rose to his feet and, with the haughty look of a man bored by company unsuited to him, began pacing from one corner to the other, holding his hands behind his back.

"Look at him pacing!" Grushenka glanced at him contemptuously. Mitya began to worry; besides, he noticed that the *pan* on the sofa kept glancing at him irritably.

"*Pan*," Mitya cried, "let us drink, *panie*! And the other *pan*, too: let us drink, *panowie*!" In a second he moved three glasses together and poured champagne.

"To Poland, *panowie*, I drink to your Poland, to the Polish land!" Mitya exclaimed.[10]

"*Bardzo mi to miło, panie, wypijem* (That is very nice, *panie*, let us drink)," the *pan* on the sofa said gravely and benevolently, taking his glass.

"And the other *pan*, what's his name? Hey, Excellency, take a glass!" Mitya fussed.

"Pan Vrublevsky," the *pan* on the sofa prompted.

Pan Vrublevsky came swinging up to the table and, standing, accepted his glass.

"To Poland, *panowie*, hurrah!" Mitya shouted, raising his glass.

All three men drank. Mitya seized the bottle and immediately poured three more glasses.

"Now to Russia, *panowie*, and let us be brothers!"

"Pour some for us," said Grushenka, "I'll drink to Russia, too."

"So will I," said Kalganov.

"I wouldn't mind, either, sirs . . . to our dear Russia, our old granny," Maximov joined in, giggling.

"Everyone, everyone!" cried Mitya. "Innkeeper, more bottles!"

The three remaining bottles that Mitya had brought were produced. Mitya poured.

"To Russia, hurrah!" he proclaimed again. Everyone drank except the *pans*, and Grushenka finished her glass at one gulp. The *panowie* did not even touch theirs.

"What about you, *panowie*?" Mitya exclaimed. "Is that how you are?"

Pan Vrublevsky took his glass, raised it, and pronounced in a booming voice:

"To Russia within her borders before 1772!"[11]

"*Oto bardzo pięknie* (Now that's better)*!*" shouted the other *pan*, and they both drained their glasses.

"You're both fools, *panowie*!" suddenly escaped from Mitya.

"*Pa-nie!*" both *pans* shouted threateningly, turning on Mitya like fighting cocks. Pan Vrublevsky especially was boiling.

"*Ale nie można nie mieć słabości do swojego kraju* (Can a man not love his own land)*?*" he proclaimed.

"Silence! No quarreling! There are to be no quarrels!" Grushenka cried commandingly and stamped her foot on the floor. Her face was flushed, her eyes gleaming. The glass she had just drunk was telling on her. Mitya got terribly frightened.

"*Panowie*, forgive me! It was my fault, I'll stop. Vrublevsky, Pan Vrublevsky, I'll stop . . . !"

"You keep quiet at least, sit down, you silly man!" Grushenka snarled at him with spiteful vexation.

They all sat down, they all fell silent, they all looked at one another.

"Gentlemen, I am the cause of everything!" Mitya began again, grasping nothing from Grushenka's exclamation. "Why are we all sitting here? What shall we do . . . for some fun, for some more fun?"

"Ah, it really isn't terribly much fun," Kalganov mumbled lazily.

"Why not a little game of baccarat like before, sirs . . . ?" Maximov suddenly tittered.

"Baccarat? Splendid!" Mitya picked up, "if only the *pans* . . ."

"*Późno, panie!*" the *pan* on the sofa responded as though reluctantly.

"True," Pan Vrublevsky agreed.

" 'Puzhno'? What does 'puzhno' mean?" asked Grushenka.

"It means late, *pani*, the hour is late," the *pan* on the sofa explained.

"For them it's always late, for them it's always impossible!" Grushenka almost shrieked in vexation. "They're bored sitting here, so they want everyone else to be bored, too. Before you came, Mitya, they just sat here saying nothing, puffing themselves up in front of me . . ."

"My goddess!" cried the *pan* on the sofa, "it shall be as you say. *Widzę niełaskę i jestem smutny* (I see you are ill disposed towards me and it makes me sad). *Jestem gotów* (I am ready), *panie*," he concluded, turning to Mitya.

"Begin, *panie*!" Mitya picked up, snatching his money from his pocket and laying out two hundred-rouble bills on the table.

"I want to lose a lot to you, *pan*. Take the cards. Make the bank."

"We should get cards from the innkeeper," the short *pan* said gravely and emphatically.

"*To najlepszy sposób* (It's the best way)," Pan Vrublevsky seconded.

"From the innkeeper? Very good, I understand, let them be from the innkeeper, that's fine, *panowie*! Cards!" Mitya called to the innkeeper.

The innkeeper brought an unopened deck of cards and announced to Mitya that the girls were already gathering, that the Jews with cymbals would probably arrive soon as well, and that the troika with provisions had not arrived yet. Mitya jumped up from the table and ran into the next room to make arrangements at once. But there were only three girls, and no Maria yet. And he himself did not know what arrangements to make, or why he had run out: he only gave orders for them to take some treats, some candies and toffees from the box and give them to the girls. "And some vodka for Andrei, some vodka for Andrei," he added hastily, "I offended Andrei!" Here Maximov, who came running after him, suddenly touched his shoulder.

"Give me five roubles," he whispered to Mitya, "I'd like to chance a little baccarat, too, hee, hee!"

"Wonderful! Splendid! Here, take ten!" he again pulled all the money from his pocket and found ten roubles. "And if you lose, come again, come again . . ."

"Very well, sir," Maximov whispered joyfully, and he ran back to the room. Mitya also returned at once and apologized for keeping them waiting. The *pans* had already sat down and opened the deck. They looked much more amiable, almost friendly. The *pan* on the sofa lit up a new pipe and prepared to deal; there was even a sort of solemn look on his face.

"Take seats, *panowie*," Pan Vrublevsky announced.

"No, I won't play anymore," replied Kalganov. "I've already lost fifty roubles to them."

"The *pan* was unlucky, the *pan* may be luckier this time," the *pan* on the sofa observed in his direction.

"How much is in the bank? Enough to cover?" Mitya was getting excited.

"That depends, *panie*, maybe a hundred, maybe two, as much as you want to stake."

"A million!" Mitya guffawed.

"The *pan* captain has perhaps heard of Pan Podvysotsky?"[12]

"What Podvysotsky?"

"There is a gaming house in Warsaw, and anyone who comes can stake against the bank. Podvysotsky comes, sees a thousand złoty, and stakes the bank. The banker says, 'Panie Podvysotsky, are you putting up the money, or your honor?' 'My honor, *panie*,' says Podvysotsky. 'So much the better, *panie*.' The banker deals, Podvysotsky wins and reaches for the thousand złoty. 'Here, *panie*,' says the banker, and he pulls out a drawer and gives him a million, 'take it, *panie*, you have won it!' There was a million in the bank. 'I did not know that,' says Podvysotsky. 'Panie Podvysotsky,' says the banker, 'you pledged your honor, and we pledged ours.' Podvysotsky took the million."

"That's not true," said Kalganov.

"Panie Kalganov, one does not say such things in decent company."

"As if a Polish gambler would give away a million!" Mitya exclaimed, but immediately checked himself. "Forgive me, *panie*, my fault, my fault again, of ourse he would give it away, on his *gonor*, on his Polish honor![13] See how ell I speak Polish, ha, ha! Here, ten roubles on the jack."

"And I put one little rouble on the queen, the queen of hearts, the pretty ing, the little *panienochka*,[14] hee, hee!" Maximov giggled, producing his ueen; and moving right up to the table, as though trying to conceal it from eryone, he hurriedly crossed himself under the table. Mitya won. The roue also won.

"Twenty-five!" cried Mitya.

"Another rouble, a little stake, a simple little stake," Maximov muttered lissfully, terribly happy to have won a rouble.

"Lost!" cried Mitya. "Double on the seven!"

The double, too, was lost.

"Stop!" Kalganov said suddenly.

"Double! Double!" Mitya kept doubling his stakes, and every time he douled a card, it lost. But the roubles kept winning.

"Double!" Mitya roared furiously.

"You've lost two hundred, *panie*. Will you stake another two hundred?" the *an* on the sofa inquired.

"What, two hundred already! Here's another two hundred! The whole two undred on the double!" and pulling the money from his pocket, Mitya threw own two hundred roubles on the queen, but Kalganov suddenly covered it ith his hand.

"Enough!" he cried in his ringing voice.

"What do you mean?" Mitya stared at him.

"Enough, I won't let you! You won't play anymore!"

"Why?"

"Because. Just spit and come away, that's why. I won't let you play any nore!"

Mitya looked at him in amazement.

"Quit, Mitya. Maybe he's right; you've lost a lot as it is," Grushenka, too, aid, with a strange note in her voice. Both *pans* suddenly rose to their feet, ooking terribly offended.

"*Żartujesz* (Are you joking), *panie?*" the little *pan* said, looking sternly at Kalganov.

"*Yak sen poważasz to robić, panie* (How dare you do that)*!*" Pan Vrublevsky lso roared at Kalganov.

"Don't you dare, don't you dare shout!" Grushenka shouted. "You turkey ocks!"

Mitya looked at each of them in turn; then something in Grushenka's face suddenly struck him, and at the same moment something quite new flashed through his mind—a strange new thought!

"Pani Agrippina!" the little *pan*, all flushed with defiance, began speaking, when Mitya suddenly came up to him and slapped him on the shoulder.

"A word with you, Excellency."

"*Czego chcesz, panie* (What do you want)?"

"Let's step into the other room, over there; I have some nice news for you, the best news, you'll be pleased to hear it."

The little *pan* was surprised and looked warily at Mitya. However, he agreed at once, but on the firm condition that Pan Vrublevsky also come with them.

"The bodyguard? Let him come, we need him, too! He must come, in fact!" Mitya exclaimed. "March, *panowie*!"

"Where are you going?" Grushenka asked anxiously.

"We'll be back in a moment," Mitya replied. A certain boldness, a certain unexpected cheerfulness flashed in his face; it was quite a different look from the one he had when he entered the same room an hour earlier. He led the *panowie* into the room at the right, not the big one where the chorus of girls was gathering and the table was being laid, but a bedroom, where there were trunks and boxes and two big beds with a pile of cotton pillows on each. There was a candle burning on a little wooden table in the very corner. The *pan* and Mitya sat down at this table, facing each other, while the enormous Pan Vrublevsky stood to one side of them, his hands behind his back. The *pans* looked stern, but were obviously curious.

"*Czym moge sluzyc panu* (What can I do for the *pan*)?" the little *pan* prattled.

"Here's what, *panie*, I won't waste words: take this money," he pulled out his bank notes, "if you want three thousand, take it and go wherever you like."

The *pan* acquired a keen look, he was all eyes, he fixed his gaze on Mitya's face.

"*Trzy tysiące, panie* (Three thousand, *panie*)?" he exchanged glances with Vrublevsky.

"*Trzy, panowie, trzy!* Listen, *panie*, I see you're a reasonable man. Take three thousand and go to the devil, and don't forget Vrublevsky—do you hear? But now, this minute, and forever, do you understand, *panie*, you'll walk out this door forever. What have you got in there—an overcoat, a fur coat? I'll bring it out to you. The troika will be harnessed for you this very moment and—good-bye, *panie*! Eh?"

Mitya waited confidently for an answer. He had no doubts. Something extremely resolute flashed in the *pan*'s face.

"And the roubles, *panie*?"

"We'll do it this way, *panie*: I'll give you five hundred roubles right now, for the coachman and as a first installment, and two thousand five hundred will come tomorrow in town—I swear on my honor, I'll dig it up somewhere!" Mitya cried.

The Poles exchanged glances again. The *pan*'s expression took a turn for the worse.

"Seven hundred, seven hundred, not five, right now, this minute, in your hands!" Mitya upped his offer, sensing that things were not going well. "What's the matter, *pan*? You don't believe me? I'm not going to give you all three thousand at once. I'd give it to you, and you'd go back to her tomorrow . . . And I don't have the whole three thousand with me, I have it at home, in town," Mitya babbled weakly, losing heart with each word, "by God, I have it, hidden . . . "

In an instant a sense of extraordinary dignity shone on the little *pan*'s face. "*Czy nie potrzebujesz jeszcze czego* (Is there anything else you'd like)?" he asked ironically. "*Pfui! Ah, pfui* (Shame on you)!" And he spat. Pan Vrublevsky also spat.

"You spit, *panie*, because," Mitya spoke as one in despair, realizing that all was over, "because you hope to get more from Grushenka. You're a couple of capons, that's what!"

"*Jestem do żywego dotknięty* (That is a mortal insult)!" the little *pan* suddenly turned red as a lobster, and briskly, in terrible indignation, as though unwilling to listen any longer, walked out of the room. Vrublevsky went swinging after him, and Mitya, confused and at a loss, followed them out. He was afraid of Grushenka, he anticipated that the *pan* would now make an uproar. And that, indeed, is what happened. The *pan* walked into the room and stood theatrically before Grushenka.

"*Pani Agrippina, jestem do żywego dotknięty!*" he began exclaiming, but Grushenka suddenly seemed to lose all patience, as if she had been touched on her sorest spot.

"Russian, speak Russian, not a word of Polish!" she shouted at him. "You used to speak Russian, did you forget it in five years?" She was all flushed with anger.

"Pani Agrippina . . ."

"I am Agrafena, I am Grushenka, speak Russian or I won't listen to you!" The *pan* was panting with *gonor*, and in broken Russian quickly and pompously declared:

"Pani Agrafena, I came to forget the past and to forgive it, to forget what has happened until today . . ."

"Forgive? You mean you came to forgive *me*?" Grushenka interrupted and jumped up from her seat.

"Just so, *pani*, I am not pusillanimous, I am magnanimous. But I was surprised when I saw your lovers. Pan Mitya, in the other room, offered me three thousand to depart. I spat in the *pan*'s face."

"What? He offered you money for me?" Grushenka cried hysterically. "Is it true, Mitya? How dare you! Am I for sale?"

"*Panie, panie*," Mitya cried out, "she is pure, she is shining, and I have never been her lover! It's a lie . . ."

"How dare you defend me to him," Grushenka went on shouting. "I have been pure not out of virtue, and not from fear of Kuzma, but in order to stand proudly before him and have the right to call him a scoundrel when I met him. But did he really not take your money?"

"He was, he was taking it!" Mitya exclaimed. "Only he wanted all three thousand at once, and I offered him just seven hundred down."

"But of course: he heard I had money, so he came to marry me!"

"Pani Agrippina," cried the *pan*, "I am a knight, a nobleman, not a *łajdak*. I arrived to take you for my wife, but I see a new *pani*, not as she was before, but wanton and shameless."

"Ah, go back where you came from! I'll order them to throw you out right now, and they will!" Grushenka cried in a rage. "I was a fool, a fool to torment myself for five years! And I didn't torment myself because of him at all, I tormented myself out of spite! And this isn't him at all! Was he like that? This one's more like his father! Where did you get such a wig? He was a falcon, and this one is a drake. He laughed and sang songs to me . . . And I, I have been shedding tears for five years, cursed fool that I am, mean, shameless!"

She fell onto her armchair and covered her face with her hands. At that moment the chorus of Mokroye girls, finally assembled in the next room to the left, suddenly burst into a rollicking dance song.

"This is Sodom!" Pan Vrublevsky suddenly bellowed. "Innkeeper, throw these shameless people out!"

The innkeeper, who had been peeking curiously through the door for a long time already, hearing shouts and seeing that his guests were quarreling, came into the room at once.

"What are you yelling about? Shut your trap!" he addressed Vrublevsky with a sort of discourtesy that was even impossible to explain.

"Swine!" roared Pan Vrublevsky.

"Swine, am I? And what sort of cards have you just been playing with? I gave you a deck and you hid it! You were playing with marked cards! I can pack you off to Siberia for marked cards, do you know that, it's the same as bad money . . ." And going over to the sofa, he put his fingers between the cushion and the back and pulled out an unopened deck of cards.

"Here's my deck, unopened!" He held it up and showed it all around. "From there I saw him shove my deck behind the cushion and put his own in place of it—you're not a *pan*, you're a cheat!"

"And I saw the other *pan* palm a card twice," cried Kalganov.

"Ah, what shame, what shame!" exclaimed Grushenka, clasping her hands and genuinely blushing with shame. "Lord, what he's come to!"

"And I thought so, too!" shouted Mitya. But he had barely spoken when Pan Vrublevsky, embarrassed and infuriated, turned to Grushenka and, shaking his fist at her, shouted:

"Public slut!" But he had barely exclaimed it when Mitya flew at him, seized him with both hands, lifted him up in the air, and in an instant carried him out of the room into the bedroom on the right, the one where he had just taken the two *pans*.

"I left him there on the floor!" he announced, returning at once, breathless with excitement. "He's struggling, the scum, but there's no chance he'll get out . . . !" He closed one half of the door, and holding the other wide open, he called out to the little *pan*:

"Excellency, would you care to follow him? If you please!"

"Mitri Fyodorovich, my dear," exclaimed Trifon Borisich, "take back the money you lost to them! It's the same as if they'd stolen it from you."

"I don't want my fifty roubles back," Kalganov suddenly answered.

"And I don't want my two hundred!" exclaimed Mitya. "Not for anything will I take it back, let him keep it as a consolation."

"Bravo, Mitya! Well done!" cried Grushenka, and a terribly malicious note rang in her exclamation. The little *pan*, purple with fury, yet by no means losing his stateliness, started for the door, but stopped and suddenly said, addressing Grushenka:

"*Pani, jeśli chcesz iść za mną, idźmy; jeśli nie—bywaj zdrowa* (*Pani*, if you want to come with me, come; if not—farewell)*!*"

And pompously, puffing with ambition and indignation, he went through the door. The man had character: after all that had taken place, he did not lose hope that the *pani* would follow after him—so highly did he value himself. Mitya slammed the door behind him.

"Lock it with a key," said Kalganov. But the lock clicked from the other side; they had locked themselves in.

"Bravo!" Grushenka cried again, mercilessly and maliciously. "Bravo! And good riddance!"

Chapter 8
Delirium

What began then was almost an orgy, a feast of feasts. Grushenka was the first to call for wine: "I want to drink, I want to get quite drunk, like before—remember, Mitya, remember how we were coming to know each other then?" Mitya himself was as if in delirium, anticipating "his happiness." Grushenka, incidentally, kept chasing him away from her all the while: "Go, enjoy yourself, tell them to dance, everyone should enjoy themselves, sing 'Dance cottage, dance stove' like before!"[1] she kept exclaiming. She was terribly excited. And Mitya would run to give orders. The chorus gathered in the next room. The room they had been sitting in so far was small in any case; it was divided in two by a cotton curtain, behind which, again, there was an enormous bed with a plump down mattress and a pile of the same sort of cotton pillows. Indeed, in all four "good" rooms of the house, there were beds everywhere. Grushenka settled herself just by the door; Mitya brought her an armchair: she had sat in the same place "then," on the day of their first spree, and from there had watched the chorus and the dancing. The girls who gathered were the same as then; the Jews with fiddles and zithers arrived, and finally the long-awaited troika arrived with its cart full of wines and provisions. Mitya bustled about. Uninvited guests came to watch, peasant men and women who had already gone to sleep but woke up sensing an unheard-of entertainment, like that of a month before. Mitya greeted and embraced those he knew, recalling their faces; he uncorked bottles and poured for all comers. Champagne was popular only with the girls; the men preferred rum and cognac and especially hot punch. Mitya ordered hot chocolate for all the girls, and three samovars to be kept boiling all night so that everyone who came could have tea or punch: whoever wants to can help himself. In a word, something disorderly and absurd began, but Mitya was in his natural element, as it were, and the more absurd it all became, the more his spirits rose. If some peasant had asked him for money at that moment, he would at once have pulled out his whole wad and started giving it away right and left without counting. That is probably why, in order to protect Mitya, the innkeeper Trifon Borisich, who seemed to have quite given up any thought of going to sleep that night, and who nevertheless drank little (he only had one glass of punch), was almost constantly scurrying around him, vigilantly looking out, in his own way, for

Mitya's interests. When necessary, he intervened in a friendly and servile manner, reasoning with him, not letting him, as he had "then," present the peasants with "cigarettes and Rhine wine" or, God forbid, with money, and was highly indignant that the girls were drinking liqueur and eating candy: "There's nothing but lice there, Mitri Fyodorovich," he would say, "I'd give them a knee in the backside, every one of them, and tell them to count it an honor—that's what they're like!" Mitya again remembered Andrei and ordered punch to be sent out to him. "I offended him before," he kept saying in a weak and tender voice. Kalganov did not want to drink at first, and very much disliked the girls' chorus, but after drinking two more glasses of champagne, he became terribly happy, paced about the rooms, laughed, and praised everyone and everything, songs and music. Maximov, blissful and tipsy, never left his side. Grushenka, who was also beginning to get drunk, kept pointing at Kalganov and saying to Mitya: "What a darling he is, what a wonderful boy!" And Mitya would run in rapture to kiss Kalganov and Maximov. Oh, he was expecting so much; she had not yet said anything to him, she obviously put off saying anything on purpose, and only glanced at him from time to time with caressing but ardent eyes. Finally she suddenly caught him fast by the hand and pulled him forcefully to herself. She was then sitting in the armchair by the door.

"How you walked in tonight, eh? How you walked in . . . ! I was so frightened. So you wanted to give me up to him, hm? Did you really?"

"I didn't want to ruin your happiness!" Mitya prattled blissfully. But she did not even need his answer.

"Now go . . . enjoy yourself," she chased him away again, "and don't cry, I'll call you back."

He would run off, and she would begin listening to the songs and watching the dancing again, following him with her eyes wherever he went, but after a quarter of an hour she would call him again, and he would again come running to her.

"Here, sit beside me now. Tell me, how did you hear about me yesterday, that I had come here? Who told you first?"

And Mitya would start telling her everything, incoherently, disconnectedly, feverishly, yet he spoke strangely, often suddenly frowning and breaking off.

"Why are you frowning?" she asked.

"It's nothing . . . I left a man sick there. I'd give ten years of my life for him to recover, just to know he'd recover!"

"Well, if he's sick, God help him! Were you really going to shoot yourself tomorrow? What a silly man! But why? I love such men, reckless men, like you," she prattled to him with a somewhat heavy tongue. "So you're ready to do anything for me? Eh? But were you really going to shoot yourself tomorrow, you little fool? No, wait now, tomorrow maybe I'll have something to tell you . . . not today, but tomorrow. And you'd like it to be today? No, today I don't want to . . . Go now, go, enjoy yourself."

Once, however, she called him over with a worried and perplexed look.

"Why are you sad? I can see you're sad . . . Yes, I see it," she added, peering sharply into his eyes. "Though you're kissing peasants and shouting in there, still I can see something. No, enjoy yourself. I'm enjoying myself, you enjoy yourself, too . . . I love someone here—guess who . . . ? Ah, look: my boy fell asleep, he's had too much, the dear."

She was referring to Kalganov: he had indeed had too much, and fell asleep for a moment sitting on the sofa. He fell asleep not only from drink; for some reason he suddenly felt sad, or "bored," as he put it. Towards the end he was also greatly disheartened by the girls' songs, which, as the drinking party wore on, gradually became rather non-lenten and licentious. And their dancing, too: two girls dressed themselves up as bears, and Stepanida, a pert girl with a stick in her hand, acted as their keeper and began "showing" them. "Faster, Maria," she cried, "or I'll use the stick!" The bears finally rolled on the floor somehow quite indecently, amid the loud laughter of the closely packed audience of peasants and their women. "Well, let them, let them," Grushenka kept saying sententiously, with a blissful look on her face, "how often do they have fun like this, so why shouldn't people enjoy themselves?" Kalganov looked as if he had soiled himself with something. "It's all swinishness, all this populism," he observed, drawing aside, "it's all spring revels, when they keep watch on the sun through the summer night." He especially disliked one "new" song with a perky dance tune,[2] where they sang of how a master rode around searching out the girls:

> And all the girls the master sought:
> Would they love him, or would they not?

But the girls decided they would not love the master:

> For he will beat me cruelly,
> And love like that is not for me.

Then along comes a gypsy:

> And all the girls the gypsy sought:
> Would they love him, or would they not?

But they would not give their love to the gypsy either:

For he'll turn out to be a thief,
And that, I'm sure, will bring me grief.

Many more people come in the same way, searching out the girls, even a soldier:

And all the girls the soldier sought:
Would they love him, or would they not?

But the soldier is rejected with contempt:

The soldier-boy will pack his kit
And drag me with him through . . .

There followed a most unprintable rhyme, sung quite openly, which caused a furore in the audience. The matter finally ended with a merchant:

And all the girls the merchant sought:
Would they love him, or would they not?

And it turns out that they will love him very much, because, they say:

The merchant will have gold in store,
I'll be his queen forevermore.

Kalganov even got angry.

"That song is no older than yesterday," he observed aloud, "and who is it writes such things for them? All they need is for a railroad man or a Jew to come seeking the girls: they'd win out over all of them." And, almost offended, he declared then and there that he was bored, sat down on the sofa, and suddenly dozed off. His pretty face turned somewhat pale and fell back on the cushion of the sofa.

"Look how pretty he is," Grushenka said, drawing Mitya over to him. "I was combing his hair earlier; it's like flax, and so thick . . ."

And, leaning over him tenderly, she kissed him on the forehead. Kalganov opened his eyes at once, looked at her, rose a little, and, with a most worried look, asked: "Where is Maximov?"

"That's who he wants," laughed Grushenka. "Do sit with me for a minute. Mitya, run and fetch his Maximov."

Maximov, it turned out, now never left the girls, and only ran off from time to time to pour himself some liqueur, or some chocolate, of which he had had two cups. His little face had turned red, his nose was purple, his eyes were moist and sweet. He ran up to them and announced that he was about to dance the *sabotière* "to a certain little tune."

"You see, I learned all these well-bred society dances when I was a young boy . . ."[3]

"Well, go, go with him, Mitya; I'll watch how he dances from here."

"And me, too, I'll go and watch, too," exclaimed Kalganov, rejecting in the most naive way Grushenka's offer to sit with him. And they all went to watch. Maximov indeed danced his dance, but produced no special admiration in anyone, except for Mitya. The whole dance consisted in a sort of hopping and twisting aside of the feet, soles up, and with every hop Maximov slapped the sole of his foot with his hand. Kalganov did not like it at all, but Mitya even kissed the dancer.

"Well, thank you, you're probably tired out, what do you have your eye on: would you like some candy, eh? How about a cigar?"

"A cigarette, sir."

"Would you like a drink?"

"Some of that liqueur, sir . . . Are there any chocolates, sir?"

"There, on the table, a whole pile of them, take whatever you want, you dear fellow!"

"No, sir, I'd like one with vanilla . . . they're for old folks, sir . . . Hee, hee!"

"No, brother, that's one kind we haven't got."

"Listen!" the old man suddenly leaned close to Mitya's ear. "This girl Mariushka—hee, hee—could I possibly make her acquaintance, would you be so kind . . . ?"

"So that's what you're after! No, brother, it won't do!"

"I don't mean any harm, sir," Maximov whispered dejectedly.

"All right, all right. They only come here to sing and dance, brother, but still . . . ah, the devil! wait a while . . . Eat for now, eat, drink, enjoy yourself. Do you need money?"

"Maybe later, sir," Maximov smiled.

"All right, all right . . ."

Mitya's head was burning. He walked out to the hallway and on to the upper wooden veranda, which ran part way around the inner side of the building, overlooking the courtyard. The fresh air revived him. He stood alone in the darkness, in a corner, and suddenly clutched his head with both hands. His scattered thoughts suddenly came together, his sensations merged, and the result of it all was light. A terrible, awful light! "If I'm going to shoot myself, what better time than now?" swept through his mind. "Go and get the pistol, bring it out here, and end everything in this dark and dingy corner." For almost a minute he stood undecided. Shame lay behind him that evening as he was flying there, the theft he had already committed, carried out, and the blood, that blood . . . ! But it had been easier for him then, oh, much easier! Everything had been finished then: he had lost her, given her up, she had died for him, disappeared—oh, his sentence seemed lighter then, at least it appeared inevitable, necessary, for why should he remain in the world? And now? Was it the same now as then? Now at least one ghost, one bogey was out of the way: the "former one," this indisputable and fatal man of hers, had vanished without a trace. The terrible ghost had suddenly turned into something so small, so comical; it was carried to the bedroom and locked up. It would never return. She was ashamed, and by her eyes he could now see clearly whom she loved. So now all he had to do was live, but . . . but he could not live, he could not, oh, damnation! "God, restore him who was struck down at the fence! Let this terrible cup pass from me![4] You worked miracles, O Lord, for sinners just like me! And what, what if the old man is alive? Oh, then I will remove the shame of the remaining disgrace, I will return the stolen money, I'll give it back, I'll dig it up somewhere . . . There will be no trace of shame left, except forever in my heart! But no, no, oh, fainthearted, impossible dreams! Oh, damnation!"

Yet it was as if a ray of some bright hope shone on him in the darkness. He tore himself away and rushed inside—to her, to her again, his queen forever! "Isn't one hour, one minute of her love worth the rest of my life, even in the torments of disgrace?" This wild question seized his heart. "To her, to her alone, to see her, to hear her, and not to think of anything, to forget everything, if only for this one night, for one hour, for one moment!" Still on the veranda, just at the door, he ran into the innkeeper, Trifon Borisich. He looked gloomy and worried, and seemed to be coming to find him.

"What is it, Borisich? Are you looking for me?"

"No, sir, not you," the innkeeper seemed suddenly taken aback. "Why should I be looking for you? And you . . . where were you, sir?"

"Why are you so glum? Are you angry? Wait a bit, you'll get to bed soon . . . What time is it?"

"It must be three by now. Maybe even past three."

"We'll stop, we'll stop."

"Don't mention it, it's nothing, sir. As long as you like, sir . . ."

"What's with him?" Mitya thought fleetingly, and ran into the room where the girls were dancing. But she was not there. She was not in the blue room, either; only Kalganov was dozing on the sofa. Mitya peeked behind the curtain—she was there. She was sitting in the corner, on a chest, her head and arms leaning on the bed beside her, crying bitterly, trying very hard to hold back and stifle her sobs so that no one would hear her. Seeing Mitya, she beckoned to him, and when he ran over to her, she caught him firmly by the hand.

"Mitya, Mitya, I did love him!" she began in a whisper. "I loved him so, all these five years, all, all this while! Did I love him, or only my spite? No, him! Oh, him! It's a lie that I loved only my spite and not him! Mitya, I was just seventeen then, he was so tender with me, so merry, he sang me songs . . . Or did he only seem that way to me, to a foolish girl . . . ? And now, Lord, it's not the same man, not him at all. And it's not his face, not his at all. I didn't even recognize his face. I was driving here with Timofei and kept thinking, all the way I kept thinking: 'How shall I meet him, what shall I say, how shall we look at each other . . . ?' My soul was frozen, and then it was as if he emptied a bucket of slops on me. He talks like a schoolmaster: it's all so learned, so pompous, he greeted me so pompously I didn't know what to do. I couldn't get a word in. At first I thought he was embarrassed in front of the other one, the tall one. I sat looking at them and thought: why is it I don't know how to speak with him now? You know, it's his wife that did it to him, the one he married then, after he dropped me . . . She's the one that changed him. What shame, Mitya! Oh, I'm ashamed, Mitya, ashamed, so ashamed for my whole life! Cursed, cursed be those five years, cursed!" And again she dissolved in tears, yet without letting go of Mitya's hand, holding on to it firmly.

"Mitya, my dear, wait, don't go, I want to tell you something," she whispered, and suddenly looked up at him. "Listen, tell me whom I love? I love one man here. Who is it? You tell me." A smile lighted on her face swollen with tears, her eyes shone in the semidarkness. "Tonight a falcon walked in, and my heart sank inside me. 'You fool, this is the one you love,' my heart whispered to me at once. You walked in and brightened everything. 'What is he afraid of?' I thought. And you really were afraid, quite afraid, you couldn't speak. 'He's not afraid of them—how can he be afraid of anyone? It's me he's afraid of, just me.' But Fenya did tell you, you little fool, how I shouted to Alyosha out the window that I loved Mitenka for one hour, and am now going off to love . . . another. Mitya, Mitya, how could I be such a fool to think I could love another after you! Do you forgive me, Mitya? Do you forgive me or not? Do you love me? Do you?"

She jumped up and grasped him by the shoulders with both hands. Mute with rapture, Mitya gazed into her eyes, at her face, her smile, and suddenly, embracing her firmly, began kissing her.

"Will you forgive me for tormenting you? I tormented all of you from spite.

I drove that old man out of his mind on purpose, just from spite . . . Do you remember how you once drank at my place and broke the glass? I remembered it, and today I, too, broke a glass as I drank to 'my base heart.' Mitya, my falcon, why aren't you kissing me? You kissed me once and tore yourself away, to look, to listen . . . Why listen to me! Kiss me, kiss me harder, like this! Let's love, if we're going to love! I'll be your slave now, your lifelong slave! It's sweet to be a slave . . . ! Kiss me! Beat me, torment me, do something to me . . . Oh, how I deserve to be tormented . . . Stop! Wait, not now, I don't want it to be like that . . . ," she suddenly pushed him away. "Go, Mitka, I'll drink wine now, I want to get drunk, I'm going to get drunk and dance, I want to, I want to!"

She broke away from him and went out through the curtain. Mitya followed after her like a drunk man. "Come what may, whatever happens now, I'll give the whole world for one minute," flashed through his head. Grushenka indeed drank another glass of champagne at one gulp and suddenly became very tipsy. She sat in her former place, in the armchair, with a blissful smile. Her cheeks were glowing, her lips were burning, her bright eyes turned bleary, her passionate gaze beckoned. Even Kalganov felt a stab in his heart and went up to her.

"Did you feel how I kissed you while you were sleeping?" she babbled to him. "I'm drunk now, that's what . . . And you, aren't you drunk? And why isn't Mitya drinking? Why aren't you drinking, Mitya? I drank and you're not drinking . . ."

"I'm drunk! Drunk anyway . . . drunk with you, and now I'm going to get drunk with wine." He drank another glass and—he found it strange himself—only this last glass made him drunk, suddenly drunk, though until then he had been sober, he remembered that. From then on everything began whirling around him as in delirium. He walked, laughed, talked with everyone, all oblivious of himself, as it were. Only one fixed and burning feeling made itself known in him every moment, "like a hot coal in my heart," as he recalled afterwards. He would go over to her, sit down by her, look at her, listen to her . . . And she became terribly talkative, kept calling everyone to her, would suddenly beckon to some girl from the chorus, the girl would come over, and she would sometimes kiss her and let her go, or sometimes make the sign of the cross over her. Another minute and she would have been in tears. She was also greatly amused by the "little old fellow," as she called Maximov. He ran up to her every other minute to kiss her hands, "and each little finger," and in the end danced one more dance to an old song, which he sang himself. He danced with particular ardor to the refrain:

The piggy goes oink, oink, oink,
The calfy goes moo, moo, moo,
The ducky goes quack, quack, quack
And the goosey goes goo, goo, goo.
Then little henny walks in the door,
Cluck, cluck, she says, and cluck once more,
Ai, ai, she clucked once more![5]

"Give him something, Mitya," Grushenka said, "give him a present, he's poor. Ah, the poor, the insulted . . . ! You know, Mitya, I will go into a convent. No, really, someday I will. Alyosha said something to me today that I'll never forget . . . Yes . . . But today let's dance. Tomorrow the convent, but today we'll dance. I want to be naughty, good people, what of it, God will forgive. If I were God I'd forgive all people: 'My dear sinners, from now on I forgive you all.' And I'll go and ask forgiveness: 'Forgive me, good people, I'm a foolish woman, that's what.' I'm a beast, that's what. But I want to pray. I gave an onion. Wicked as I am, I want to pray! Mitya, let them dance, don't interfere. Everyone in the world is good, every one of them. The world is a good place. We may be bad, but the world is a good place. We're bad and good, both bad and good . . . No, tell me, let me ask you, all of you come here and I'll ask you; tell me this, all of you: why am I so good? I am good, I'm very good . . . Tell me, then: why am I so good?" Thus Grushenka babbled on, getting more and more drunk, and finally declared outright that she now wanted to dance herself. She got up from her armchair and staggered. "Mitya, don't give me any more wine, not even if I ask. Wine doesn't bring peace. Everything is spinning, the stove and everything. I want to dance. Let everybody watch how I dance . . . how well and wonderfully I dance . . ."

The intention was serious: she took a white cambric handkerchief from her pocket and held it by one corner in her right hand, to wave while she danced. Mitya began bustling, the girls' chorus fell silent, preparing to burst into a dancing song at the first signal. Maximov, learning that Grushenka herself was going to dance, squealed with delight and began hopping in front of her, singing:

Its legs are naught, its sides are taut,
And its little tail's all in a curl.[6]

But Grushenka chased him away with a wave of her handkerchief.

"Shoo! Mitya, why aren't they coming? Let everyone come . . . to watch. Call them, too . . . the locked-up ones . . . What did you lock them up for? Tell them I'm dancing, let them watch me, too . . ."

Mitya swept drunkenly to the locked door and began knocking for the *pans* with his fist.

"Hey, you . . . Podvysotskys! Come out, she's going to dance, she's calling you."

"*Łajdak!*" one of the *pans* shouted in reply.

"And you are a *podłajdak*![7] A petty little Polish scoundrel, that's what you are!"

"You should stop deriding Poland," Kalganov, who had also drunk more than his fill, remarked sententiously.

"Quiet, boy! If I call him a scoundrel, it doesn't mean I'm calling all of Poland a scoundrel. One *łajdak* doesn't make a Poland. Keep quiet, pretty boy, eat your candy."

"Ah, what people! As if they weren't even human beings. Why won't they make peace?" said Grushenka, and she stepped out to dance. The chorus broke into "Ah, hallway, my hallway!"[8] Grushenka threw back her head, half opened her lips, smiled, waved the handkerchief, and suddenly, swaying badly, stopped perplexed in the middle of the room.

"I feel weak . . . ," she said in a sort of exhausted voice. "Forgive me, I feel weak, I can't . . . I'm sorry . . ."

She bowed to the chorus, and then began bowing on all sides.

"I'm sorry . . . Forgive me . . ."

"She's had a drop, the lady, the pretty lady's had a drop," voices were heard saying.

"She's drunk," Maximov explained, giggling, to the girls.

"Mitya, help me . . . take me, Mitya," Grushenka said weakly. Mitya rushed to her, picked her up, and ran behind the curtain with his precious booty. "Well, now I really shall leave," thought Kalganov, and going out of the blue room, he closed both halves of the door behind him. But the feast in the main room went thundering on, and thundered all the more. Mitya laid Grushenka on the bed and pressed his lips to hers in a kiss.

"Don't touch me," she murmured to him in a pleading voice, "don't touch me, I'm not yours yet . . . I said I was yours, but don't touch me . . . spare me . . . We mustn't do it with them here, in the next room. He is here. It's vile here . . ."

"I obey! I wouldn't dream . . . I revere . . . !" Mitya muttered. "Yes, it's vile here, oh, unspeakably." And without letting her out of his embrace, he knelt on the floor by the bed.

"I know, though you're a beast, you're still noble," Grushenka spoke with difficulty. "We should do it honestly . . . from now on it will be honest . . . and we should be honest, and we should be good, not beasts but good . . .

Take me away, take me far away, do you hear . . . ? I don't want to be here, I want to be far, far away . . ."

"Oh, yes, yes, we must!" Mitya pressed her in his arms. "I'll take you, we'll fly away . . . Oh, I'd give my whole life now for one year, if only I knew about that blood!"

"What blood?" Grushenka repeated in bewilderment.

"Nothing!" Mitya growled. "Grusha, you want it to be honest, but I am a thief. I stole money from Katka . . . What shame, what shame!"

"From Katka? You mean the young lady? No, you didn't steal anything. Give it back to her, take it from me . . . Why are you shouting? All that's mine is yours now. What do we care about money? We'll just throw it away on a spree . . . It's bound to be so with the likes of us. And you and I had better go work on the land. I want to scrape the earth with my hands. We must work, do you hear? Alyosha said so. I won't be a mistress to you, I'll be faithful, I'll be your slave, I'll work for you. We'll both go to the young lady, we'll bow to her and ask her forgiveness, and go away. And if she doesn't forgive us, we'll go away anyway. And you can give her back her money, and love me . . . And not love her. Do not love her any more. If you love her, I'll strangle her . . . I'll put out both her eyes with a needle . . ."

"I love you, you alone, I'll love you in Siberia . . ."

"Why in Siberia? But why not, I'll go to Siberia if you like, it's all the same . . . we'll work . . . there's snow in Siberia . . . I like driving over snow . . . and there should be a little sleigh bell . . . Do you hear a bell ringing . . . ? Where is that little bell ringing? People are driving . . . now it's stopped."

She closed her eyes helplessly, and suddenly seemed to fall asleep for a moment. A bell had indeed been ringing somewhere far away, and suddenly stopped ringing. Mitya lowered his head onto her breast. He did not notice how the bell stopped ringing, nor did he notice how the singing suddenly stopped as well, and instead of songs and drunken racket, a dead silence fell suddenly, as it were, over the whole house. Grushenka opened her eyes.

"What, was I asleep? Yes . . . the bell . . . I fell asleep and had a dream that I was driving over the snow . . . a bell was ringing, and I was dozing. It seemed I was driving with someone very dear to me—with you. Far, far away . . . I was embracing you and kissing you, pressing close to you, as if I were cold, and the snow was glistening . . . You know how snow glistens at night, and there's a new moon, and you feel as if you're not on earth . . . I woke up, and my dear was beside me—how good . . ."

"Beside you," Mitya murmured, kissing her dress, her breast, her hands.

And suddenly a strange fancy struck him: he fancied that she was looking straight ahead, not at him, not into his eyes, but over his head, intently and with a strange fixity. Surprise, almost fear, suddenly showed on her face.

"Mitya, who is that looking at us from there?" she whispered suddenly. Mitya turned and saw that someone had indeed parted the curtains and was apparently trying to make them out. More than one person, it seemed. He jumped up and quickly went towards the intruder.

"Here, come out here, please," someone's voice said to him, not loudly, but firmly and insistently.

Mitya stepped from behind the curtain and stood still. The whole room was full of people, not those who had been there before, but quite new ones. A momentary shiver ran down his spine, and he drew back. He recognized all these people instantly. The tall, plump old man in a coat and a service cap with a cockade was the district police commissioner, Mikhail Makarich. And the trim, "consumptive" fop, "always in such well-polished boots," was the deputy prosecutor. "He has a chronometer worth four hundred roubles, he showed it to me." And the short young man in spectacles . . . Mitya simply could not remember his last name, but he knew him, too, he had seen him: he was an attorney, a district attorney "from the Jurisprudence,"[9] recently arrived. And that one—the deputy commissioner, Mavriky Mavrikich—he knew him, he was an acquaintance. And the ones with badges, what were they doing here? And the other two, peasants . . . And Kalganov and Trifon Borisich there in the doorway . . .

"Gentlemen . . . What is it, gentlemen?" Mitya started to say, but suddenly, as if beside himself, as if not of himself at all, he exclaimed loudly, at the top of his lungs:

"I un-der-stand!"

The young man in spectacles suddenly came forward and, stepping up to Mitya, began in a dignified manner, though a little hurriedly, as it were:

"We must have . . . in short, would you kindly come over here, to the sofa . . . It is of the utmost necessity that we have a word with you."

"The old man!" Mitya cried in a frenzy, "the old man and his blood . . . ! I un-der-stand!"

And as if cut down, he fell more than sat on a chair standing nearby.

"You understand? He understands! Parricide and monster, your old father's blood cries out against you!" the old district police commissioner suddenly roared, going up to Mitya. He was beside himself, turned purple, and was shaking all over.

"But this is impossible!" cried the short young man. "Mikhail Makarich,

Mikhail Makarich! Not like that, not like that, sir . . . ! I ask you to allow me to speak alone . . . I would never have expected such an episode from you . . ."

"But this is delirium, gentlemen, delirium!" the police commissioner kept exclaiming. "Look at him: in the middle of the night, with a disreputable wench, covered with his father's blood . . . Delirium! Delirium!"

"I beg you as strongly as I can, dear Mikhail Makarich, to restrain your feelings for the moment," the deputy prosecutor whispered rapidly to the old man, "otherwise I shall have to resort to . . ."

But the short attorney did not let him finish; he turned to Mitya and firmly, loudly, and gravely declared:

"Retired Lieutenant Karamazov, sir, it is my duty to inform you that you are charged with the murder of your father, Fyodor Pavlovich Karamazov, which took place this night . . ."

He said something more, and the prosecutor, too, seemed to add something, but Mitya, though he listened, no longer understood them. With wild eyes he stared around at them all . . .

BOOK IX: THE PRELIMINARY INVESTIGATION

Chapter 1

The Start of the Official Perkhotin's Career

Pyotr Ilyich Perkhotin, whom we left knocking with all his might at the well-locked gates of the widow Morozov's house, in the end, of course, was finally successful. Hearing such furious knocking at the gate, Fenya, who had been so frightened two hours before, and who was still too excited and "thinking" too much to dare go to bed, became frightened once more almost to the point of hysterics: she fancied that it was Dmitri Fyodorovich knocking again (though she herself had seen him drive off), because no one else but he would knock so "boldly." She rushed to the awakened porter, who had heard the knocking and was already on his way to the gate, and began begging him not to open. But the porter made inquiries of the person who was knocking, and learning who he was, and that he wanted to see Fedosya Markovna on a very important matter, finally decided to open the gates for him. Going to the same kitchen with Fedosya Markovna—and she "on account of her doubts" prevailed upon Pyotr Ilyich to allow the porter to come with them—Pyotr Ilyich started questioning her and at once hit upon the most important fact: namely, that Dmitri Fyodorovich, as he ran off to look for Grushenka, had snatched the pestle from the mortar, and returned later without the pestle but with his hands covered with blood: "And the blood was still dripping, it kept dripping and dripping!" Fenya exclaimed, her distraught imagination apparently having invented this horrible detail. But Pyotr Ilyich had also seen those bloody hands himself, though the blood was not dripping, and had himself helped to wash them, and the question was not how soon the blood had dried, but where exactly Dmitri Fyodorovich had run with the pestle—that is, was it certain he had gone to Fyodor Pavlovich's, and what might be the grounds for such a positive inference? Perkhotin thoroughly emphasized this point, and though he did not find out anything definite as a result, he still became almost convinced that Dmitri Fyodorovich could not have run anywhere else but to his parent's house, and that, consequently, *something* must have happened there. "And when he came back," Fenya added excitedly, "and I told him everything, I began asking him: 'Dmitri Fyodorovich, my dear, why are your hands covered with blood?' and he answered me that it was human blood, and that he had just killed a man—he simply admitted it, he simply confessed it all to me, and suddenly ran out like a madman. I sat down and started thinking: where has he run off to like a madman? He'll go to Mokroye, I was thinking, and kill my mistress there. So I ran out to go to his place and beg him not to kill my mistress, but at Plotnikov's shop I saw that he was already leaving and that his hands weren't covered with blood anymore." (Fenya had noticed this and remembered it.) The old woman, Fenya's grandmother, confirmed all her granddaughter's statements as far as she could. Having asked a few more questions, Pyotr Ilyich left the house even more troubled and worried than when he had entered it.

One would think that the most immediate and direct thing for him to do now would be to go to Fyodor Pavlovich's house and find out if anything had happened, and, if so, what exactly, and being convinced beyond any doubt only then to go to the police commissioner, as Pyotr Ilyich had firmly resolved to do. But the night was dark, the gates of Fyodor Pavlovich's house were strong, he would have to knock again, and he was only distantly acquainted with Fyodor Pavlovich—and so he would have to keep knocking until he was heard and the gates were opened, and what if suddenly nothing had happened at all, and a jeering Fyodor Pavlovich were to go all over town tomorrow telling jokes about how a stranger, the official Perkhotin, had forced his way into his house at midnight in order to find out if anyone had murdered him. A scandal! And there was nothing in the world Pyotr Ilyich feared more than a scandal. Nevertheless he was moved by so strong a feeling that, having angrily stamped his foot on the ground and given himself another scolding he at once rushed on his way again, not to Fyodor Pavlovich's now, but to Madame Khokhlakov's. If she, he thought, would answer just one question whether or not she had given Dmitri Fyodorovich three thousand at such and such a time, then, in case the answer was negative, he would go straight to the police commissioner, without going to Fyodor Pavlovich; otherwise he would put everything off until tomorrow and go back home. Here, of course, it is immediately obvious that the young man's decision to go at night, at almost eleven o'clock, to the house of a society lady who was a complete stranger to him, and perhaps get her out of bed, in order to ask her an—under the circumstances—astonishing question, was perhaps much more likely to cause a scandal than going to Fyodor Pavlovich. But it sometimes happens that way—especially in such cases—with the decisions of the most precise and phlegmatic people. And at the moment Pyotr Ilyich was far from phlegmatic. He remembered afterwards all his life how the irresistible anxiety that gradually took possession of him finally became so painful that it carried him along even against his will. Naturally, he kept scolding himself all the way, in-any case, for going to this lady, but "I'll go through with it, I'll go through with it!" he repeated for the tenth time, clenching his teeth, and he did as he intended—he went through with it.

It was exactly eleven o'clock when he came to Madame Khokhlakov's house. He was promptly let into the yard, but to his question: "Is the lady asleep, or has she not gone to bed yet?" the porter could give no precise answer, beyond saying that at that hour people usually go to bed. "Ask to be announced upstairs; if the lady wants to receive you, she will; if she won't—she won't." Pyotr Ilyich went up to the door, but there things became more difficult. The lackey did not want to announce him, and finally called the maid. Pyotr Ilyich politely but insistently asked her to inform the lady that a town official, Perkhotin, had come on special business, and were the business not so important, he would not have ventured to come—"inform her precisely, precisely in those words," he asked the maid. She left. He stood waiting in the front hall. Madame Khokhlakov, though not yet asleep, had already retired to her bedroom. She had been upset since Mitya's visit and now anticipated that she would not get through the night without the migraine that was usual for her in such cases. On hearing the maid's report, she was surprised, and yet she irritably told her to refuse, though the unexpected visit at such an hour of a "town official" quite unknown to her greatly piqued her woman's curiosity. But this time Pyotr Ilyich was stubborn as a mule: hearing the refusal, he once again asked the maid very insistently to inform her mistress and tell her precisely "in these very words" that he had come "on extremely important business, and that the lady herself might regret it later if she did not receive him now." "It was like throwing myself off a mountain," as he afterwards recounted. The maid, having looked him over in surprise, went to announce him again. Madame Khokhlakov was amazed, thought for a moment, inquired about his appearance, and learned that "he was very properly dressed, young, and so polite." Let us note parenthetically and in passing that Pyotr Ilyich was quite a handsome young man, and was aware of it himself. Madame Khokhlakov decided to come out. She was already in her dressing gown and slippers, but she threw a black shawl over her shoulders. "The official" was shown into the drawing room, the very room where she had just recently received Mitya. The hostess came to meet her visitor with a sternly inquiring look and, without inviting him to sit down, began straight off with a question: "What is it you want?"

"I have ventured to trouble you, madame, in connection with our mutual acquaintance Dmitri Fyodorovich Karamazov," Perkhotin began, but as soon as he spoke this name, his hostess's face suddenly showed the greatest irritation. She all but shrieked and furiously interrupted him:

"How long, how long must I be tormented by that awful man?" she cried in frenzy. "How dare you, my dear sir, how could you venture to disturb a lady not of your acquaintance, in her own house, and at such an hour . . . and come to her to speak of a man who, right here, in this very drawing room, just three hours ago, came to murder me, stamped his feet, and walked out as no one walks out of a decent house. Let me tell you, my dear sir, that I will lodge a complaint against you, I will not stand for it, now kindly leave my house at once . . . I am a mother, I shall . . . I . . . I . . ."

"Murder! So he wanted to murder you, too?"

"Why, did he already murder someone else?" Madame Khokhlakov asked impetuously.

"Be so good, madame, as to listen for only half a minute, and I shall explain everything in two words," Perkhotin answered firmly. "Today, at five o'clock in the afternoon, Mr. Karamazov borrowed ten roubles from me as a friend, and I know for certain that he had no money, yet this same day, at nine o'clock, he walked into my rooms holding out for all to see a wad of hundred-rouble bills, approximately two or even three thousand roubles. His hands and face were all covered with blood, and it appeared as if he were mad. To my question as to where he got so much money, he replied with precision that he had just received it from you, and that you had loaned him the sum of three thousand roubles to go, he said, to the gold mines . . ."

Madame Khokhlakov's face suddenly acquired a look of extraordinary and morbid excitement.

"Oh, God! He's murdered his old father!" she cried out, clasping her hands. "I gave him no money, none! Oh, run, run . . . ! Not a word more! Save the old man, run to his father, run!"

"I beg your pardon, madame, so you did not give him any money? You firmly recall that you did not give him any?"

"I did not! I did not! I refused him because he was unable to appreciate it. He walked out furious and stamped his feet. He rushed at me, but I jumped aside . . . And I shall also tell you, as a man from whom I now have no intention of concealing anything, that he even spat at me, can you imagine it? But why are you standing? Ah, do sit down . . . Forgive me, I . . . Or, no, run, run, you must run and save the unfortunate old man from a horrible death!"

"But if he has already killed him?"

"Ah, my God, of course! What are we going to do now? What do you think we should do now?"

Meanwhile she sat Pyotr Ilyich down, and sat down herself facing him. Pyotr Ilyich gave her a brief but rather clear account of the affair, at least that part of the affair he himself had witnessed earlier; he also told her of his visit to Fenya, and mentioned the news of the pestle. All these details struck the agitated lady no end, so that she kept crying out and covering her eyes with her hands . . .

"Imagine, I foresaw it all! I am endowed with this property: whatever I imagine always happens. How often, how often have I looked at that terrible man and thought: here is a man who will end up by murdering me. And now it's happened . . . That is, if he hasn't killed me now, but only his father, it is most likely because the hand of God is obviously protecting me, and, besides, he was ashamed to murder me because I myself, here on this very spot, put an icon around his neck with a relic of the great martyr Varvara . . . How close I was to death at that moment! I went up to him, quite close, and he stretched out his neck to me! You know, Pyotr Ilyich (forgive me, you did say your name was Pyotr Ilyich?) . . . you know, I do not believe in miracles, but this icon and this obvious miracle with me now—it astounds me, and I'm beginning to believe in anything again. Have you heard about the elder Zosima . . . ? Ah, anyway, I don't know what I'm saying . . . And imagine, even with the icon on his neck, he still spat at me . . . Of course, he only spat, he didn't murder me, and . . . and . . . so that's where he galloped off to! But what of us, where shall we go now, what do you think?"

Pyotr Ilyich stood up and announced that he would now go directly to the police commissioner and tell him everything, and let him do as he thinks best.

"Ah, he is a wonderful, wonderful man, I know Mikhail Makarovich. Of course, go precisely to him. How resourceful you are, Pyotr Ilyich, and what a good idea you've come up with; you know, in your place I'd never have been able to come up with that!"

"All the more so in that I, too, am well acquainted with the commissioner," observed Pyotr Ilyich, still standing and evidently wishing somehow to tear himself away from the impetuous lady, who would not let him say good-bye to her and leave.

"And you know, you know," she went on prattling, "you must come back and tell me what you see and learn . . . and what they find out . . . and what they will decide about him, and where they will condemn him to. Tell me, we don't have capital punishment, do we? But you must come, even if it's three o'clock in the morning, even if it's four, even half past four . . . Tell them to wake me up, to shake me if I don't get up . . . Oh, God, but I'll never be able to fall asleep. You know, why don't I go with you myself?"

"N-no, madame, but if you would now write three lines with your own hand, just in case, saying that you did not give Dmitri Fyodorovich any money, it might not be amiss . . . just in case . . ."

"Certainly!" the delighted Madame Khokhlakov leaped to her bureau.

"And you know, you amaze me, you simply astound me with your resourcefulness and your skill in these matters . . . Are you in service here? I'm so pleased to know you're in service here . . ."

And while she spoke, she quickly inscribed the following three lines in a large hand on a half sheet of writing paper:

> Never in my life did I lend the unfortunate Dmitri Fyodorovich Karamazov (for he is unfortunate now, in any case) the sum of three thousand roubles today, or any other money, never, never! I swear to it by all that is holy in our world.
>
> *Khokhlakov*

"Here is the note!" she turned quickly to Pyotr Ilyich. "Go now and save. It is a great deed on your part."

And she crossed him three times. She even ran out to see him to the front hall.

"How grateful I am to you! You wouldn't believe how grateful I am to you now, for having come to me first. How is it we've never met? I shall be flattered to receive you in my house in the future. And how pleased I am to know that you're in service here . . . and with your precision, your resourcefulness . . . They must appreciate you, they must finally understand you, and whatever I can do for you, believe me . . . Oh, I love young people so! I am in love with young people. Young people—they are the foundation for all of today's suffering Russia, her only hope . . . Oh, go, go . . . !"

But Pyotr Ilyich had already run out, otherwise she would not have let him go so soon. All the same, Madame Khokhlakov made quite a pleasant impression on him, which even somewhat softened his alarm at getting involved in such a bad affair. Tastes are extremely divergent, that is a known fact. "She's not as old as all that," he thought with pleasure. "On the contrary, I might have taken her for her own daughter."

As for Madame Khokhlakov, she was simply enchanted with the young man. "Such skill, such exactitude, and in so young a man, in our time, and all that with such manners and appearance! And yet they say our modern young men cannot do anything, but here's an example for you," and so on and so forth. So that she simply forgot all about the "terrible incident," and only on the point of going to bed did she suddenly recall again "how close she had been to death." "Ah," she said, "it's terrible, terrible!" and at once fell into a sound and sweet sleep. By the way, I would not go into such petty and incidental details if the eccentric encounter I have just described, between a young official and a widow not all that old, had not afterwards served as the foundation for the whole life's career of that precise and accurate young man, which is still recalled with astonishment in our town, and of which we, too, shall perhaps have a special word to say, once we have concluded our long story of the Karamazov brothers.

Chapter 2

The Alarm

Our district commissioner of police, Mikhail Makarovich Makarov, a retired lieutenant colonel, redesignated a state councillor,[1] was a widower and a good man. He had come to us only three years earlier, but had already won general sympathy, mainly because he "knew how to bring society together." His house was never without guests, and it seemed he would have been unable to live without them. He had to have guests to dinner every day, even if only two, even if only one, but without guests he would not sit down to eat. He gave formal dinners, too, under all sorts of pretexts, sometimes even the most unexpected. The food he served, though not refined, was abundant, the cabbage pies were excellent, and the wines made up in quantity for what they lacked in quality. In the front room stood a billiard table, surrounded by quite decent furnishings; that is, there were even paintings of English racehorses in black frames on the walls, which, as everyone knows, constitute a necessary adornment of any billiard room in a bachelor's house. Every evening there was a card game, even if only at one table. But quite often all the best society of our town, including mamas and young girls, would get together there for a dance. Mikhail Makarovich, though a widower, lived as a family man, with his already long-widowed daughter, who in turn was the mother of two girls, Mikhail Makarovich's granddaughters. The girls were grown up by then and had finished their education; they were of not-unattractive appearance, of cheerful character, and though everyone knew that they would bring no dowries, they still drew our young men of society to their grandfather's house. In his official capacity, Mikhail Makarovich was none too bright, but he did his job no worse than many others. To tell the truth, he was rather an uneducated man, and even a bit carefree with respect to a clear understanding of the limits of his administrative power. Not that he did not fully comprehend some of the reforms of the present reign, but he understood them with certain, sometimes quite conspicuous, mistakes, and not at all because he was somehow especially incapable, but simply because of his carefree nature, because he never got around to looking into them. "I have the soul of a military man, not a civilian," he said of himself. He still did not seem to have acquired a firm and definite idea even of the exact principles of the peasant reform, and learned of them, so to speak, from year to year, increasing his knowledge practically and unwittingly, though, by the way, he himself was a landowner. Pyotr Ilyich knew with certainty that he was sure to meet some guests at Mikhail Makarovich's that evening, only he did not know exactly whom. Meanwhile, at that very moment, the prosecutor and our district doctor Varvinsky, a young man who had just come to us from Petersburg, after brilliantly completing his studies at the Petersburg Medical Academy, were sitting there playing whist. The prosecutor, Ippolit Kirillovich—the deputy prosecutor, that is, but we all called him the prosecutor—was a special man among us, not old, still only about thirty-five, but much inclined to consumption, and married, besides, to a rather fat and childless lady; he was proud and irritable, and yet of quite considerable intelligence, and even a kind soul. It appeared the whole trouble with his character was that he had a somewhat higher opinion of himself than his real virtues warranted. And that was why he constantly seemed restless. Besides, there were in him certain lofty and even artistic pretensions—for example, to psychologism, to a special knowledge of the human soul, to a special gift of comprehending the criminal and his crime. In this sense he considered himself somewhat ill treated and passed over in his service, and was forever persuaded that they were unable to appreciate him in higher spheres and that he had enemies. In his gloomier moments he even threatened to desert to the defense side of criminal law. The unexpected case of the Karamazov parricide thoroughly shook him, as it were: "A case like this could become known all over Russia." But I am getting ahead of myself.

In the next room, with the girls, there also sat our young district attorney, Nikolai Parfenovich Nelyudov, who had come to our town from Petersburg only two months earlier. Afterwards everyone talked of it and even marveled that all these persons should have come together as if on purpose, on the evening of the "crime," in the house of the executive authority. Yet it was a perfectly simple thing and happened quite naturally: it was the second day that Ippolit Kirillovich's wife had had a toothache, and he absolutely had to flee somewhere from her groaning; as for the doctor, by his very nature he could do nothing of an evening but play cards. And Nikolai Parfenovich Nelyudov had already been planning for three days to visit Mikhail Makarovich that evening, inadvertently, so to speak, in order suddenly and perfidiously to startle the older girl, Olga Mikhailovna, with the fact that he knew her secret, that he knew it was her birthday and that she had decided purposely to conceal it from our society, so as not to have to invite people for dancing. Much laughter was in store, much hinting at her age, that she was supposedly afraid to reveal it, that he, now being in possession of her secret, would tell everyone tomorrow, and so on and so forth. The dear young man was very naughty in this respect; our ladies in fact called him a naughty boy, and he seemed to like it very much. However, he was of quite good society, good family, good upbringing, and good feelings, a bon vivant but quite an innocent one, and always proper. Physically, he was short and of weak, delicate constitution. Several extremely large rings always flashed on his thin and pale fingers. When performing his duties, he became remarkably solemn, as though he conceived of his significance and responsibility as sacred. He was especially good at throwing murderers and other low-class criminals off guard in interrogations, and actually aroused in them, if not respect for himself, at least a certain astonishment.

When Pyotr Ilyich entered the commissioner's house, he was simply astounded: he suddenly saw that they knew everything already. Indeed, they had abandoned their cards, they all stood arguing, and even Nikolai Parfenovich came running from the young ladies with a most pugnacious and impetuous look on his face. Pyotr Ilyich was met with the astounding news that old Fyodor Pavlovich had really and truly been murdered in his house that evening, murdered and robbed. It had been learned just a moment before, in the following way.

Marfa Ignatievna—the wife of Grigory, who had been struck down at the fence—though she was fast asleep in her bed and might have gone on sleeping like that until morning, nevertheless suddenly woke up. Conducive to that end was a terrible epileptic scream from Smerdyakov, who lay unconscious in the next room—that scream with which his fits of falling sickness always began, and that always, all her life, frightened Marfa Ignatievna terribly and had a morbid effect on her. She simply never could get used to it. Half awake, she jumped up and, almost beside herself, rushed to Smerdyakov in his little room. It was dark there; she could only hear that the sick man had begun struggling and gasping horribly. Marfa Ignatievna screamed herself and began calling her husband, but suddenly realized that when she had gotten up Grigory seemed not to be in the bed. She ran back and felt in the bed again, but it was indeed empty. So he had gone out, but where? She ran to the porch and timidly called him. She got no answer, of course, but instead she heard, in the night's silence, some groans, which seemed to be coming from somewhere far away in the garden. She listened; the groans were repeated, and it became clear that they were indeed coming from the garden. "Lord, just like with Stinking Lizaveta!" flashed through her distraught head. She went timidly down the steps and saw that the garden gate was open. "He must be there, the poor dear," she thought, going up to the gate, and suddenly she clearly heard Grigory calling her, crying out: "Marfa, Marfa!" in a weak, wailing, woeful voice. "Lord, keep us from disaster," Marfa Ignatievna whispered and rushed towards the voice, and in that way she found Grigory. But she found him not by the fence, not on the spot where he had been struck down, but about twenty paces away. Later it turned out that, having come to his senses, he had begun crawling, and probably crawled for a long while, losing consciousness and passing out several times more. She noticed at once that he was all covered with blood, and at that began screaming to high heaven. Grigory kept muttering softly and incoherently: "He killed . . . father . . . killed . . . stop shouting, fool . . . run, tell . . ." But Marfa Ignatievna would not quiet down and went on screaming, and suddenly, seeing that the master's window was open and there was light inside, she ran to it and began calling Fyodor Pavlovich. But, looking through the window, she saw a terrible sight: the master was lying on his back on the floor, not moving. The front of his light-colored dressing gown and his white shirt were soaked with blood. A candle on the table shed a bright light on the blood and on the motionless, dead face of Fyodor Pavlovich. Now horrified to the last degree, Marfa Ignatievna rushed away from the window, ran out of the garden, unlocked the gates, and ran like mad through the back lane to her neighbor, Maria Kondratievna. Both neighbors, mother and daughter, were asleep by then, but at Marfa Ignatievna's urgent and frenzied shouting and knocking on the shutters, they woke up and jumped to the window. Marfa Ignatievna, shrieking and shouting, conveyed the essentials, however incoherently, and called for help. As it happened, that night the wandering Foma was staying with them. They roused him at once, and all three ran to the scene of the crime. On the way, Maria Kondratievna managed to recall that earlier, before nine o'clock, she had heard a terrible and piercing cry from their garden, which could be heard all over the neighborhood—and this certainly was precisely the cry of Grigory as he caught hold of the leg of Dmitri Fyodorovich, who was already sitting astride the fence, and cried out: "Parricide!" "Some one person shouted and suddenly stopped," Maria Kondratievna testified as she ran. Having come to the place where Grigory lay, the two women, with the help of Foma, carried him to the cottage. They lighted a candle and saw that Smerdyakov had still not calmed down but was struggling in his little room, his eyes crossed and foam running from his lips. Grigory's head was washed with water and vinegar; the water brought him back to his full senses, and he asked at once: "Has the master been killed?" The two women and Foma then went to the master's and this time saw, as they entered the garden, that not only the window but the door to the garden was wide open, whereas for the whole past week the master had been locking himself up securely in the evening, every night, and would not allow even Grigory to knock for him under any circumstances. Seeing the door open, all of them, the two women and Foma, were afraid to go to the master's room, "for fear something might come of it afterwards." Grigory, when they came back, told them to run at once to the police commissioner himself. It was at this point that Maria Kondratievna ran and gave the alarm to everyone at the commissioner's house. She preceded Pyotr Ilyich's arrival by only five minutes, so that he came not just with his own guesses and conclusions, but as an obvious witness, whose story even further confirmed the general surmise as to the identity of the criminal (which he, by the way, in the bottom of his heart, till this last moment, still refused to believe).

It was decided to act energetically. The assistant police chief was immediately ordered to round up as many as four witnesses, and, following all the rules, which I am not going to describe here, they penetrated Fyodor Pavlovich's house and carried out an investigation on the spot. The district doctor, a hot and new man, all but invited himself to accompany the commissioner, the prosecutor, and the district attorney. I will give only a brief outline: Fyodor Pavlovich turned out to be thoroughly murdered, his head having been smashed in, but with what?—most likely with the same weapon with which Grigory had also been struck later. And just then they found the weapon, having heard from Grigory, to whom all possible medical help was administered, a quite coherent, though weakly and falteringly uttered, account of how he had been struck down. They began searching near the fence with a lantern and found the brass pestle, thrown right on the garden path for all to see. No unusual disorder was noted in the room where Fyodor Pavlovich was lying, but behind the screen near his bed they picked up a big envelope from the floor, made of heavy paper, of official size, inscribed: "A little treat of three thousand roubles for my angel Grushenka, if she wants to come," and below that was added, most likely later, by Fyodor Pavlovich himself: "And to my chicky." There were three big seals of red wax on the envelope, but it had already been torn open and was empty: the money was gone. They also found on the floor a narrow pink ribbon with which the envelope had been tied. One circumstance among others in Pyotr Ilyich's evidence made an extraordinary impression on the prosecutor and the district attorney: namely, his guess that Dmitri Fyodorovich would certainly shoot himself towards dawn, that he had resolved to do it, spoken of it to Pyotr Ilyich, loaded his pistol, and so on and so forth. And that when he, Pyotr Ilyich, still unwilling to believe him, had threatened to go and tell someone to prevent the suicide, Mitya had answered him, grinning: "You won't have time." It followed that they had to hurry there, to Mokroye, in order to catch the criminal before he perhaps really decided to shoot himself. "That's clear, that's clear!" the prosecutor kept repeating in great excitement, "that's just how it is with such hotheads: tomorrow I'll kill myself, but before I die—a spree!" The story of his taking a lot of wine and provisions from the shop aroused the prosecutor even more. "Do you remember, gentlemen, that fellow who killed the merchant Olsufyev, robbed him of fifteen hundred, and went at once to have his hair curled, and then, without even hiding the money very well, almost holding it in his hand in the same way, went to the girls?" They were detained, however, by the investigation, the search of Fyodor Pavlovich's house, the paperwork, and so on. All this needed time, and therefore they sent to Mokroye, two hours ahead of them, the deputy commissioner, Mavriky Mavrikievich Shmertsov, who had come to town just the previous morning to collect his salary. Mavriky Mavrikievich was instructed to go to Mokroye and, without raising any alarm, to keep watch on the "criminal" tirelessly until the arrival of the proper authorities, as well as to procure witnesses, deputies, and so on and so forth. And all this Mavriky Mavrikievich did, preserving his incognito, and initiating only Trifon Borisovich, his old acquaintance, and then only partially, into the secret of the affair. This coincided precisely with the time when Mitya met the innkeeper in the darkness on the porch looking for him and at once noticed a sudden change in Trifon Borisovich's face and tone. Thus neither Mitya nor anyone else knew that he was being watched; his case with the pistols had long since been spirited away by Trifon Borisovich and hidden in some safe place. And only after four o'clock in the morning, almost at dawn, did all the authorities arrive, the police commissioner, the prosecutor, and the district attorney, in two carriages drawn by two troikas. The doctor stayed behind in Fyodor Pavlovich's house with the object of performing a postmortem in the morning on the body of the murdered man, but above all he had become particularly interested in the condition of the sick servant Smerdyakov: "Such severe and protracted fits of the falling sickness, recurring uninterruptedly over two days, are rarely met with: this case belongs to science," he said excitedly to his departing companions, and they laughingly congratulated him on his find. At the same time the prosecutor and the district attorney remembered very clearly the doctor adding in a most definite tone that Smerdyakov would not live till morning.

Now, after a long but, I believe, necessary explanation, we have returned precisely to that moment of our story at which we stopped in the previous book.

Chapter 3

The Soul's Journey through Torments. The First Torment

And so Mitya was sitting and staring around with wild eyes at those present, without understanding what was being said to him.[1] Suddenly he rose, threw up his hands, and cried loudly:

"Not guilty! Of that blood I am not guilty! Of my father's blood I am not guilty . . . I wanted to kill him, but I'm not guilty. Not me!"

But no sooner had he cried it than Grushenka jumped out from behind the curtains and simply collapsed at the feet of the police commissioner.

"It's me, me, the cursed one, I am guilty!" she cried in a heartrending howl, all in tears, stretching her arms out to everyone, "it's because of me that he killed him . . . ! I tormented him and drove him to it! I tormented that poor old dead man, too, out of spite, and drove things to this! I am the guilty one, first and most of all, I am the guilty one!"

"Yes, you are the guilty one! You are the chief criminal! You are violent, you are depraved, you are the guilty one, you most of all," screamed the commissioner, shaking his finger at her, but this time he was quickly and resolutely suppressed. The prosecutor even seized him with both arms.

"This is entirely out of order, Mikhail Makarovich," he cried, "you are positively hindering the investigation . . . ruining the whole thing . . . ," he was all but choking.

"Measures, measures, we must take measures!" Nikolai Parfenovich, too, began seething terribly, "otherwise it's positively impossible . . . !"

"Judge us together!" Grushenka went on exclaiming frenziedly, still on her knees. "Punish us together, I'll go with him now even to execution!"

"Grusha, my life, my blood, my holy one!" Mitya threw himself on his knees beside her and caught her tightly in his arms. "Don't believe her," he shouted, "she's not guilty of anything, of any blood, or anything!"

He remembered afterwards that several men pulled him away from her by force, that she was suddenly taken out, and that when he came to his senses he was already sitting at the table. Beside him and behind him stood people with badges. On the sofa across the table from him, Nikolai Parfenovich, the district attorney, sat trying to persuade him to sip some water from a glass that stood on the table: "It will refresh you, it will calm you down, you needn't be afraid, you needn't worry," he kept adding with extreme politeness. And Mitya, as he remembered, suddenly became terribly interested in his big rings, one with an amethyst, and another with a bright yellow stone, transparent and of a most wonderful brilliance. And for a long time afterwards he recalled with surprise how these rings irresistibly drew his eye even through all those terrible hours of interrogation, so that for some reason he was unable to tear himself away and forget them as something quite unsuitable in his position. On the left, at Mitya's side, where Maximov had been sitting at the start of the evening, the prosecutor now sat down, and to Mitya's right, where Grushenka had been, a pink-cheeked young man settled himself, dressed in a rather threadbare sort of hunting jacket, and in front of him appeared an inkstand and some paper. He turned out to be the district attorney's clerk, who had come with him. The police commissioner now stood near the window, at the other end of the room, next to Kalganov, who was sitting in a chair by the same window.

"Drink some water!" the district attorney gently repeated for the tenth time.

"I drank some, gentlemen, I drank some . . . but . . . come, gentlemen, crush me, punish me, decide my fate!" Mitya exclaimed, staring with horribly fixed, bulging eyes at the district attorney.

"So you positively assert that you are not guilty of the death of your father, Fyodor Pavlovich?" the district attorney asked gently but insistently.

"Not guilty! I'm guilty of other blood, of another old man's blood, but not of my father's. And I weep for it! I killed, I killed the old man, killed him and struck him down . . . But it's hard to have to answer for that blood with this other blood, this terrible blood, which I'm not guilty of . . . A terrible accusation, gentlemen, as if you'd stunned me on the head! But who killed my father, who killed him? Who could have killed him if not me? It's a wonder, an absurdity, an impossibility . . . !"

"Yes, who could have killed him . . . ," the district attorney began, but the prosecutor, Ippolit Kirillovich (the deputy prosecutor, but for the sake of brevity we, too, shall call him the prosecutor), exchanging glances with the district attorney, said, turning to Mitya:

"You needn't worry about the old servant, Grigory Vasiliev. I can tell you that he is alive, he has recovered, and despite the severe beating inflicted by you, according to his and now to your own evidence, it seems he will undoubtedly live, at least in the doctor's opinion."

"Alive? So he's alive!" Mitya suddenly shouted, clasping his hands. His whole face lit up. "Lord, I thank you for this greatest miracle, which you have done for me, a sinner and evildoer, according to my prayer! Yes, yes, it's according to my prayer, I was praying all night!" And he crossed himself three times. He was nearly breathless.

"And it is from this same Grigory that we have received such significant evidence regarding you, that . . . ," the prosecutor went on, but Mitya suddenly jumped up from his chair.

"One moment, gentlemen, for God's sake, just one moment; I'll run to her . . ."

"Sorry! Right now it's quite impossible!" Nikolai Parfenovich almost shrieked, and he, too, jumped to his feet. The men with badges laid hold of Mitya; however, he sat down on the chair himself . . .

"What a pity, gentlemen! I wanted to see her for just one moment . . . I wanted to announce to her that this blood that was gnawing at my heart all night has been washed away, has disappeared, and I am no longer a murderer! She is my fiancée, gentlemen!" he suddenly spoke ecstatically and reverently, looking around at them all. "Oh, thank you, gentlemen! Oh, how you've restored, how you've resurrected me in a moment . . . ! That old man—he carried me in his arms, gentlemen, he washed me in a tub when I was a three-year-old child and abandoned by everyone, he was my own father . . . !"

"And so you . . . ," the district attorney began.

"Sorry, gentlemen, sorry, just one more minute," Mitya interrupted, putting both elbows on the table and covering his face with his hands, "let me collect myself a little, let me catch my breath, gentlemen. It's all terribly shocking, terribly—a man is not a drumskin, gentlemen!"

"Have some more water," muttered Nikolai Parfenovich.

Mitya took his hands away from his face and laughed. His look was cheerful; he had quite changed, as it were, in a moment. And his whole tone was changed: here now sat a man once again the equal of all these men, of all these previous acquaintances of his, exactly as if they had all come together the day before, when nothing had happened yet, somewhere at a social gathering. Let us note, incidentally, that when he first came to our town, Mitya was warmly received at the commissioner's house, but later, especially during the last month, Mitya hardly ever visited him, and the commissioner, meeting him in the street, for example, frowned deeply and bowed to him only out of politeness, which circumstance Mitya noted very well. His acquaintance with the prosecutor was even more distant, but to the prosecutor's wife, a nervous and fantastic lady, he sometimes paid visits, most respectful visits, by the way, himself not even quite knowing why he was calling on her, and she always received him kindly, taking an interest in him for some reason, until quite recently. He had not yet had time to make the acquaintance of the district attorney, though he had met him and even spoken with him once or twice, both times about the female sex.

"You, Nikolai Parfenovich, are, I can see, a most skillful investigator," Mitya suddenly laughed gaily, "but now I will help you myself. Oh, gentlemen I am resurrected . . . and do not take it amiss that I address you so casually and directly. Besides, I'm a little drunk, that I will frankly admit. I believe I had the honor . . . the honor and the pleasure of meeting you, Nikolai Parfenovich, at the home of my relation, Miusov . . . Gentlemen, gentlemen, I do not claim to be equal, I quite understand who I am now, as I sit here before you. A horrible suspicion hangs over me . . . if Grigory has given evidence regarding me . . . then of course, oh, of course it hangs over me! Horrible, horrible—I quite understand! But—to business, gentlemen, I'm ready, and now we'll make short work of it, because, listen, listen, gentlemen. You see, if I know I am not guilty, then of course we can make short work of it! Can't we? Can't we?"

Mitya spoke much and quickly, nervously and expansively, and as if he decidedly took his listeners for his best friends.

"So, for the present we shall write down that you radically deny the accusation brought against you," Nikolai Parfenovich pronounced imposingly, and, turning to the clerk, he dictated in a low voice what he was to write down.

"Write down? You want to write it down? Well, write it down then, I consent, I give my full consent, gentlemen . . . Only, you see . . . Wait, wait, write it down like this: 'Of violence—guilty; of inflicting a savage beating on a poor old man—guilty.' And then, within himself, too, inside, in the bottom of his heart, he is guilty—but there's no need to write that down," he turned suddenly to the clerk, "that is my private life, gentlemen, that doesn't concern you now, the bottom of my heart, I mean . . . But of the murder of his old father—not guilty! It's a wild idea! It's an utterly wild idea . . . ! I'll prove it to you and you'll be convinced immediately. You'll laugh, gentlemen, you'll roar with laughter at your own suspicion . . . !"

"Calm yourself, Dmitri Fyodorovich," the district attorney reminded him, apparently as if he wished to subdue the frenzied man with his own calmness. "Before continuing the interrogation, I should like, if only you will agree to answer, to hear from you a confirmation of the fact that you seem to have disliked the late Fyodor Pavlovich, and were in some sort of permanent dispute with him . . . Here, in any case, a quarter of an hour ago, I believe you were pleased to say that you even wanted to kill him: 'I did not kill him,' you exclaimed, 'but I wanted to kill him!' "

"I exclaimed that? Ah, maybe I did, gentlemen! Yes, unfortunately I wanted to kill him, wanted to many times . . . unfortunately, unfortunately!"

"You wanted to. Would you be willing to explain what principles in fact guided you in this hatred for the person of your parent?"

"What's there to explain, gentlemen!" Mitya shrugged gloomily, looking down. "I've never hidden my feelings, the whole town knows of it—everyone in the tavern knows. Recently, in the monastery, I announced it in the elder Zosima's cell . . . That same day, in the evening, I beat my father and nearly killed him, and swore in front of witnesses that I would come back and kill him . . . Oh, there's a thousand witnesses! I've been shouting for the whole month, everyone is a witness . . . ! The fact is right there, the fact speaks, it cries out, but—feelings, gentlemen, feelings are something else. You see, gentlemen," Mitya frowned, "it seems to me that you have no right to question me about my feelings. You are empowered, I understand that, but this is my business, my inner business, an intimate thing, but . . . since I haven't hidden my feelings before . . . in the tavern, for instance, but have talked of it to all and sundry, so I won't . . . I won't make a secret of it now, either. You see, gentlemen, I quite understand that in that case there is horrible evidence against me: I told everyone I would kill him, and suddenly he is killed: who else but me in that case? Ha, ha! I don't blame you, gentlemen, I don't blame you at all. I'm struck to the epidermis myself, because who, finally, did kill him in that case, if not me? Isn't that so? If not me, then who, who? Gentlemen," he suddenly exclaimed, "I want to know, I even demand it of you, gentlemen: where was he killed? How was he killed, with what and how? Tell me," he asked quickly, looking around at the prosecutor and the district attorney.

"We found him lying on his back, on the floor of his study, with his head smashed in," the prosecutor said.

"How horrible, gentlemen!" Mitya suddenly shuddered, and leaning his elbow on the table, he covered his face with his right hand.

"Let us continue," Nikolai Parfenovich interrupted. "What, then, guided you in your feeling of hatred? I believe you have announced publicly that it was a feeling of jealousy?"

"Yes, jealousy, and not only jealousy."

"Disputes about money?"

"Yes, about money, too."

"The dispute seems to have been over three thousand roubles, allegedly due you as part of your inheritance?"

"Three thousand, hah! It was more, more," Mitya heaved himself up, "more than six, more than ten, maybe. I told everyone, I shouted it to everyone! But I decided to let it go, to settle for three thousand. I desperately needed that three thousand . . . so the envelope with three thousand which I knew was under his pillow, waiting for Grushenka, I considered definitely as stolen from me, that's what, gentlemen, I considered it mine, just as if it was my own property . . ."

The prosecutor exchanged meaningful glances with the district attorney and managed to wink at him unobserved.

"We shall come back to that subject later," the district attorney said at once "For now, allow me to take note of precisely this little point and write it down that you considered the money in that envelope as your own property."

"Write it down, gentlemen, I quite understand that it is one more piece of evidence against me, but I'm not afraid of evidence and even testify against myself. Do you hear, against myself! You see, gentlemen, you seem to be taking me for quite a different man from what I am," he suddenly added, glumly and sadly. "It is a noble man you are speaking with, a most noble person; above all—do not lose sight of this—a man who has done a world of mean things, but who always was and remained a most noble person, as a person, inside, in his depths, well, in short, I don't know how to say it . . . This is precisely what has tormented me all my life, that I thirsted for nobility, that I was, so to speak, a sufferer for nobility, seeking it with a lantern, Diogenes' lantern,[2] and meanwhile all my life I've been doing only dirty things, as we all do, gentlemen . . . I mean, me alone, gentlemen, not all but me alone, I made a mistake, me alone, alone . . . ! Gentlemen, my head aches," he winced with pain. "You see, gentlemen, I did not like his appearance, it was somehow dishonorable, boastful, trampling on all that's holy, mockery and unbelief, loathsome, loathsome! But now that he's dead, I think differently."

"How differently?"

"Not differently, but I'm sorry I hated him so much."

"You feel repentant?"

"No, not really repentant, don't write that down. I'm not good myself, gentlemen, that's the thing, I'm not so beautiful myself, and therefore I had no right to consider him repulsive, that's the thing. Perhaps you can write that down."

Having said this, Mitya suddenly became extremely sad. Gradually, for some time now, as he answered the district attorney's questions, he had been growing more and more gloomy. And suddenly, just at that moment, another unexpected scene broke out. It so happened that, though Grushenka had been removed, she had not been taken very far, only to the third room down from the blue room in which the interrogation was now going on. It was a small room with one window, just beyond the big room where they had been dancing and feasting during the night. There she sat, and so far the only one with her was Maximov, who was terribly shocked, terribly frightened, and clung to her as if seeking salvation at her side. Some peasant with a badge on his chest stood at their door. Grushenka was weeping, and then suddenly, when the grief came too near her soul, she jumped up, clasped her hands, and, crying "Woe, woe is me!" in a loud wail, rushed out of the room to him, to her Mitya, so unexpectedly that no one had time to stop her. Mitya, hearing her wail, shuddered all over, jumped up, gave a shout, and, as if forgetting himself, rushed headlong to meet her. But again they were not allowed to come together, though they had already caught sight of each other. He was seized firmly by the arms: he struggled, tried to break loose, it took three or four men to hold him. She, too, was seized, and he saw her shouting and stretching out her arms to him as they drew her away. When the scene was over, he came to himself again in the same place, across the table from the district attorney, and was shouting at them:

"What do you want with her? Why do you torment her? She's innocent, innocent . . . !"

The prosecutor and the district attorney were trying to talk sense into him. This took some time, about ten minutes; at last Mikhail Makarovich, who had stepped out, came hurriedly into the room, and in a loud, excited voice said to the prosecutor:

"She has been removed, she is downstairs; but will you permit me, gentlemen, to say just one word to this unfortunate man? In your presence, gentlemen, in your presence!"

"As you wish, Mikhail Makarovich," the district attorney answered, "in the present case we have nothing to say against it."

"Listen, Dmitri Fyodorovich, my dear fellow," Mikhail Makarovich began, turning to Mitya, his whole troubled face expressing warm, almost fatherly compassion for the unfortunate man, "I myself took your Agrafena Alexandrovna downstairs and handed her over to the innkeeper's daughters, and that old man, Maximov, is there and never leaves her now, and I talked with her, do you hear? I talked with her and calmed her down, I impressed upon her that you need to clear yourself and so she mustn't interfere, mustn't drive you to despair, otherwise you may get confused and give wrong evidence against yourself, you see? Well, in short, I talked with her and she saw. She's a smart woman, brother, she's kind, she wanted to kiss these old hands of mine, she asked me to help you. She sent me here herself to tell you that you mustn't worry about her, and it would be a good thing, my dear, it would be a good thing if I went and told her that you're not worried and are comforted about her. So you see, you mustn't worry. I'm guilty before her, she's a Christian soul, yes, gentlemen, she's a meek soul and not guilty of anything. Well, what shall I tell her, Dmitri Fyodorovich, are you going to be quiet or not?"

The kindly man said much more than was necessary, but Grushenka's grief, such human grief, had penetrated his kind soul, and tears even brimmed in his eyes. Mitya jumped up and rushed to him.

"Forgive me, gentlemen, allow me, oh, allow me!" he cried out. "You are an angelic soul, an angelic soul, Mikhail Makarovich, I thank you for her! I will, I will be quiet, I will be cheerful, tell her in the infinite kindness of your soul that I am cheerful, cheerful, I'll even start laughing now, knowing that she has such a guardian angel as you. I'll finish with all of this now, and the moment I'm free, I'll go to her at once, she'll see, she must wait! Gentlemen," he suddenly turned to the prosecutor and the district attorney, "I will now open and pour out my whole soul to you, we will finish with this in a moment, finish it cheerfully—in the end we'll have a good laugh, won't we? But, gentlemen, this woman is the queen of my soul! Oh, allow me to say it, this is something I'm going to reveal to you . . . I can see I'm with the noblest men: she is my light, my holy one, and if only you knew! Did you hear her cry: 'I'll go with you—even to execution'? And what have I, a naked beggar, given her, why such love for me, am I—a clumsy and shameful creature with a shameful face—worthy of such love, that she should go to hard labor with me? She just laid herself at your feet for me, she, a proud woman and not guilty of anything! How can I not adore her, not cry out, not long for her, as I do now? Oh, gentlemen, forgive me! But now, now I'm comforted!"

And he sank down and, covering his face with both hands, burst into sobs. But they were happy tears. He collected himself at once. The old commissioner was very pleased, and so the jurists seemed to be, too: they felt that the interrogation was now entering a new phase. Having sent the commissioner off, Mitya became quite cheerful.

"Well, gentlemen, now I am yours, yours completely. And . . . if only it weren't for all these small details, we would come to an understanding at once. Again I'm talking about small details. I'm yours, gentlemen, but, I swear, we must have mutual trust—you in me, and I in you—otherwise we'll never finish. I'm saying it for your sake. To business, gentlemen, to business, and above all don't go digging around in my soul so much, don't torment it with trifles, but keep to the point, to the facts, and I'll satisfy you at once. Devil take the small details!"

So Mitya exclaimed. The interrogation began again.

Chapter 4

The Second Torment

"You would not believe how encouraged we are, Dmitri Fyodorovich, by this readiness of yours . . . ," Nikolai Parfenovich started saying, with an animated look and with visible pleasure shining in his big, protruding, pale gray, and, by the way, extremely myopic eyes, from which he had just removed his spectacles a moment before. "And you have made a very just observation concerning our mutual confidentiality, without which it is sometimes even impossible to proceed in matters of such importance, in the case and sense that the suspected person indeed wishes, hopes, and is able to vindicate himself. For our part, we shall do everything possible, and you have already been able to see how we are conducting this case . . . Do you approve, Ippolit Kirillovich?" he suddenly turned to the prosecutor.

"Oh, indubitably," the prosecutor approved, though somewhat drily compared with Nikolai Parfenovich's outburst.

I will note once and for all that the newly arrived Nikolai Parfenovich, from the very beginning of his career among us, felt a marked respect for our Ippolit Kirillovich, the prosecutor, and became almost heart-to-heart friends with him. He was almost the only man who believed without reservation in the remarkable psychological and oratorical talents of our "passed-over" Ippolit Kirillovich, and also fully believed that he had indeed been passed over. He had heard of him while still in Petersburg. And in turn the young Nikolai Parfenovich happened to be the only man in the whole world whom our "passed-over" prosecutor came sincerely to love. On the way there they had had time to set up a few things and make arrangements for the impending case, and now, at the table, the sharp little mind of Nikolai Parfenovich caught on the wing and understood every indication, every movement in the face of his older colleague, from half a word, a look, a wink of the eye.

"Gentlemen, give me leave to tell my own story and do not interrupt me with trifles, and I will lay it all out for you in no time," Mitya was seething.

"Excellent, sir. Thank you. But before we go on to hear your account, allow me simply to mention one more little fact, of great interest for us, namely, the ten roubles you borrowed yesterday, at around five o'clock, by pawning your pistols to your friend Pyotr Ilyich Perkhotin."

"I pawned them, gentlemen, I pawned them for ten roubles, that's all.

What of it? As soon as I got back to town from my trip, I pawned them at once."

"Got back? So you left town?"

"I did, gentlemen, I went thirty miles out of town, didn't you know that?"

The prosecutor and Nikolai Parfenovich exchanged glances.

"Suppose you begin your story with a systematic description of your whole day yesterday, starting from the morning? Let us know, for example, why you left town, and precisely when you went and came back . . . and all these facts . . ."

"But you should have asked me that from the very beginning," Mitya laughed loudly, "and, if you please, I should start not from yesterday but from the day before yesterday, from that morning; then you'll understand where, how, and why I went or drove. The day before yesterday, gentlemen, I went to a local merchant, Samsonov, to borrow three thousand roubles from him on the best security—a sudden itch, gentlemen, a sudden itch . . ."

"Allow me to interrupt you," the prosecutor interjected politely, "why did you so suddenly need precisely that amount, that is, three thousand roubles?"

"Eh, gentlemen, why pick on such little things: how, when, and why, and precisely this much money and not that much, and all that claptrap . . . if you keep on, it'll take you three volumes and an epilogue to cram it all in."

All this Mitya said with the good-natured but impatient familiarity of a man who wishes to tell the whole truth and is full of the best intentions.

"Gentlemen," he caught himself, as it were, "don't murmur against me for my bristliness. I ask you again: believe once more that I feel the utmost respect and fully understand the situation. And don't think that I'm drunk. I've sobered up now. And it would be no hindrance if I were drunk, because:

Sober and wise, he's stupid,
Drunk and stupid, he's wise.

That's how I am. Ha, ha! I see, by the way, that it's not proper for me to be cracking jokes with you yet—that is, before we've explained everything. Allow me to keep my dignity. I quite understand the present difference: I'm still sitting before you as a criminal, and, therefore, unequal to you in the highest degree, and your duty is to watch me: you really can't pat me on the back for Grigory, one certainly can't go breaking old men's heads with impunity, you'll probably try me and lock me up for, what, six months or a year in the penitentiary for that, or, I don't know, whatever the sentence would be—but without loss of rights, it will be without loss of rights, won't it, prosecutor? And so, gentlemen, I quite understand this difference . . . But you must also agree that you could confuse even God himself with such questions: where I

tepped, how I stepped, when I stepped, what I stepped in? I'll get confused
hat way, and you'll pick up every dropped stitch and write it down at once,
and what will come of it? Nothing will come of it! And finally, since I've al-
eady begun telling my tale, I'll finish it now, and you, gentlemen, being most
noble and highly educated, will forgive me. I'll end precisely with a request:
you, gentlemen, must unlearn this official method of interrogation, I mean,
first you begin, say, with something measly and insignificant: how did you get
up, what did you eat, how did you spit, and 'having lulled the criminal's attention,' you suddenly catch him with a stunning question: 'Whom did you
kill, whom did you rob?' Ha, ha! That's your official method, that's your rule,
hat's what all your cleverness is based on! You can lull peasants with your
cleverness, but not me. I understand the system, I was in the service myself,
ha, ha, ha! You're not angry, are you, gentlemen? You'll forgive my boldness?"
he cried, looking at them with almost surprising good-naturedness. "Mitka
Karamazov said it, so it's excusable, because what would be inexcusable in an
intelligent man is excusable in Mitka! Ha, ha!"

Nikolai Parfenovich listened and laughed, too. The prosecutor, though he
did not laugh, was studying Mitya intently, without taking his eyes off him, as
f not wishing to miss the least word, the least movement, the least twitch of
he least little line on his face.

"Incidentally, that is how we began with you from the beginning," Nikolai
Parfenovich replied, still laughing, "not confusing you with questions about
how you got up in the morning and what you ate, but beginning even from
what is all too essential."

"I understand, I understood and appreciated it, and I appreciate still more
your present kindness to me, which is unprecedented, worthy of the noblest
souls. We are three noble men come together here, and let everything with us
be on the footing of mutual trust between educated and worldly men, bound
by nobility and honor. In any case, allow me to look upon you as my best
friends in this moment of my life, in this moment when my honor is humiliated! That's no offense to you, is it, gentlemen?"

"On the contrary, you've expressed it all quite beautifully, Dmitri Fyodorovich," Nikolai Parfenovich gravely and approvingly agreed.

"And away with little details, gentlemen, with all these pettifogging details," Mitya delightedly exclaimed, "otherwise the devil knows what will
come of it, isn't that so?"

"I will follow your sensible advice completely," the prosecutor suddenly
mixed in, addressing Mitya. "However, I still do not withdraw my question. It
is all too essentially necessary for us to know why precisely you needed such
an amount—that is, precisely three thousand."

"Why I needed it? Well, for this and that . . . well, to repay a debt."

"To whom, precisely?"

"That I positively refuse to tell you, gentlemen! You see, it's not that I cannot tell you, or don't dare, or am afraid, because it's all a paltry matter and perfectly trifling, no, but I won't tell you on principle: it's my private life, and I will not allow you to invade my private life. That is my principle. Your question is irrelevant to the case, and whatever is irrelevant to the case is my private life! I wanted to repay a debt, a debt of honor, but to whom I won't say."

"Allow us to write that down," said the prosecutor.

"As you wish. Write down this: that I just won't say. Write, gentlemen, that I would even consider it dishonorable to say. You've got lots of time for writing, haven't you?"

"Allow me, dear sir, to caution you and remind you once more, in case you are still unaware of it," the prosecutor said with particular and rather stern impressiveness, "that you have every right not to answer the questions that are put to you now, and we, on the contrary, have no right to extort answers from you, if you decline to answer for one reason or another. That is a matter of your personal consideration. On the other hand, in such a situation, it is our business to point out to you and explain the full extent of the harm you will be doing yourself by refusing to give this or that evidence. At which point I ask you to continue."

"Gentlemen, I'm not angry . . . I . . . ," Mitya started mumbling, somewhat taken aback by this reprimand, "you see, gentlemen, this Samsonov to whom I went then . . ."

We shall not, of course, reproduce his detailed account of what is already known to the reader. The narrator was impatient to tell everything in the smallest particulars, and at the same time to get through it quickly. But his evidence was being written down as he gave it, and he therefore had necessarily to be stopped. Dmitri Fyodorovich objected but submitted, was angry, but so far good-naturedly. True, from time to time he cried out, "Gentlemen, this would exasperate the Lord God himself!" or "Gentlemen, do you know you're irritating me for nothing?" but despite his exclamations, he still preserved his friendly and expansive mood. Thus he told them how Samsonov had "hoodwinked" him two days before. (He now realized fully that he had been hoodwinked then.) The sale of the watch for six roubles in order to get money for the road, which was still completely unknown to the district attorney and the prosecutor, at once aroused their greatest interest, and, to Mitya's boundless indignation, they found it necessary to record this fact in detail, seeing in it a second confirmation of the circumstance that even a day before he had been almost without a kopeck. Little by little Mitya was becoming gloomy. Then, having described his trip to Lyagavy, the night spent in the fume-poisoned hut, and so on, he brought his story as far as his return to town, where he began on his own, without being specially asked, to describe in detail his jealous torments over Grushenka. He was listened to silently and attentively; they particularly went into the circumstance of his having long ago set up his lookout for Grushenka going to Fyodor Pavlovich in Maria Kondratievna's backyard, and of Smerdyakov's bringing him information: this was much noticed and written down. Of his jealousy he spoke ardently and extensively, and though inwardly ashamed at displaying his most intimate feelings, so to speak, "for general disgrace," he obviously tried to overcome his shame for the sake of being truthful. The indifferent sternness of the district attorney's and, especially, the prosecutor's eyes, which they kept fixed on him during his account, disconcerted him in the end rather strongly: "This boy, Nikolai Parfenovich, with whom I exchanged some silly remarks about women only a few days ago, and this sickly prosecutor are not worthy of my telling them this," flashed sadly through his mind. "Oh, shame! 'Be patient, humble, hold thy peace,' "[1] he concluded his thoughts with this line of verse, but still collected himself again in order to go on. Having come to the part about Madame Khokhlakov, he even brightened up again, and was even about to tell a certain recent anecdote, unrelated to the case, concerning the good lady, but the district attorney stopped him and politely suggested that they pass on "to more essential things." Finally, having described his despair and told them of that moment when, as he walked out of Madame Khokhlakov's, he had even had the thought of "quickly putting a knife into someone, just to get the three thousand," he was stopped again, and it was recorded that "he wanted to put a knife into someone." Mitya let them write it down without protest. Finally he came to the point in the story when he suddenly found out that Grushenka had deceived him and left Samsonov's just after he brought her there, though she had told him she would stay until midnight. "If I didn't kill this Fenya right then, gentlemen, it was only because I had no time," suddenly escaped him at this place in the story. And this, too, was carefully written down. Mitya waited gloomily and was beginning to tell how he ran to his father's garden, when the district attorney suddenly stopped him, and, opening his large briefcase, which lay beside him on the sofa, took out of it a brass pestle.

"Are you familiar with this object?" he showed it to Mitya.

"Ah, yes!" Mitya grinned gloomily, "indeed I am! Let me see it . . . Or don't, devil take it!"

"You forgot to mention it," the district attorney observed.

"Ah, the devil! I wouldn't hide it from you, we certainly couldn't get along without it, don't you agree? It just escaped my memory."

"Be so good, then, as to tell us in detail how you came to arm yourself with it."

"I'll be so good, if you wish, gentlemen."

And Mitya told how he took the pestle and ran.

"But what purpose did you have in mind in arming yourself with such an implement?"

"What purpose? No purpose! I just grabbed it and ran."

"But why, if there was no purpose?"

Mitya was seething with vexation. He looked fixedly at the "boy" and grinned gloomily and maliciously. The thing was that he felt more and more ashamed at having just told "such people" the story of his jealousy, so sincerely and with such effusion.

"I spit on the pestle," suddenly escaped him.

"Even so, sir."

"So I grabbed it to keep off the dogs. Or because it was dark . . . Or just in case."

"And have you always been in the habit of taking some weapon with you when going out at night, since you are so afraid of the dark?"

"Agh, the devil, pah! Gentlemen, it's literally impossible to talk to you!" Mitya cried out in the utmost annoyance, and turning to the clerk, all red with anger, with a sort of frenzied note in his voice, quickly said to him:

"Take this down right now . . . right now . . . 'that I grabbed the pestle in order to run and kill my father, Fyodor Pavlovich . . . by hitting him on the head'! Well, are you content now, gentlemen? Does that ease your hearts?" he said, staring defiantly at the prosecutor and the district attorney.

"We realize only too well that you have given such evidence just now because you are annoyed with us and vexed by the questions we put to you, which you regard as petty, and which in essence are quite essential," the prosecutor answered him drily.

"But for pity's sake, gentlemen! So I took the pestle . . . So, what does one pick things up for in such cases? I don't know. I snatched it and ran. That's all. Shame on you, gentlemen—*passons*, or I swear I won't say anything more!"

He leaned his elbow on the table and propped his head in his hand. He was sitting sideways to them, looking at the wall, and trying to overcome the bad feeling inside him. In fact, he really had a terrible urge to stand up and declare that he was not going to say another word, "even if you should take me out and hang me."

"You see, gentlemen," he suddenly spoke, overcoming himself with difficulty, "you see. I'm listening to you and imagining . . . You see, sometimes I dream a dream in my sleep . . . one particular dream, and I often dream it, it keeps repeating itself, that someone is chasing me, someone I'm terribly afraid of is chasing me in the darkness, at night, looking for me, and I'm hiding from him somewhere behind a door or a wardrobe, hiding in a humiliating way, and moreover he knows perfectly well where I'm hiding, but he seems to pretend not to know where I am on purpose, in order to torment me longer, in order to revel in my fear . . . That's what you are doing now! It's just the same!"

"Is that the sort of dreams you have?" the prosecutor inquired.

"Yes, I have such dreams . . . Why, do you want to write it down?" Mitya grinned crookedly.

"No, sir, I do not want to write it down, but still you do have curious dreams."

"This time it's not a dream! Realism, gentlemen, the realism of actual life! I'm the wolf, you're the hunters—so hunt the wolf down."

"You shouldn't make such comparisons . . . ," Nikolai Parfenovich began very gently.

"Why shouldn't I, gentlemen, why shouldn't I!" Mitya boiled up again, though he had apparently unburdened his soul with this outburst of sudden anger and was growing kinder again with every word. "You may disbelieve a criminal or a prisoner in the dock whom you're tormenting with your questions, but to disbelieve the noblest man, gentlemen, the noblest impulses of the soul (I cry it boldly!)—no! that you cannot do . . . you even have no right to . . . but—

> . . . heart, hold thy peace,
> Be patient, humble, hold thy peace!

Well, shall I go on?" he broke off gloomily.

"Of course, if you'd be so good," replied Nikolai Parfenovich.

Chapter 5

The Third Torment

Though Mitya began speaking sternly, he apparently was trying all the more not to forget or skip over the least detail in his account. He told how he had jumped over the fence into his father's garden, how he went up to the window, and, finally, everything that took place under the window. Clearly, precisely, as though hammering it out, he spoke of the feelings that had troubled him during those moments in the garden, when he had wanted so terribly to know whether Grushenka was with his father or not. But, strangely, this time both the prosecutor and the district attorney somehow listened with terrible reserve, looked at him drily, asked far fewer questions. Mitya could gather nothing from their faces. "They're angry and offended," he thought, "well, devil take them!" When he told how he finally made up his mind to give his father the *signal* that Grushenka had come, so that he would open the window, the prosecutor and the district attorney paid no attention to the word "signal," as if they had no idea at all of the word's significance here; Mitya even noticed it. When he finally came to the moment when, seeing his father leaning out of the window, hatred boiled up in him and he snatched the pestle from his pocket, he suddenly stopped as if on purpose. He sat and looked at the wall, knowing they both had their eyes glued to him.

"Well, sir," said the district attorney, "so you snatched out the weapon and . . . and what then?"

"Then? Oh, then I killed him . . . smashed him on the head and split his skull. That's your version, is it!" he suddenly flashed his eyes. All the wrath that had almost died out in him suddenly rose up in his soul with extraordinary force.

"Ours," Nikolai Parfenovich repeated, "well, and what is yours?"

Mitya lowered his eyes and was silent for a long time.

"My version, gentlemen, my version is this," he began softly. "Whether it was someone's tears, or God heard my mother's prayers, or a bright spirit kissed me at that moment, I don't know—but the devil was overcome. I dashed away from the window and ran to the fence . . . Father got frightened. He caught sight of me then for the first time, cried out, and jumped back from the window—I remember that very well. And I ran through the garden to the fence . . . it was here that Grigory caught up with me, when I was already sitting on the fence . . ."

At this point he finally raised his eyes to his listeners. They seemed to be looking at him with completely untroubled attention. A sort of twinge of indignation went through Mitya's soul.

"But I see right now you're laughing at me, gentlemen!" he suddenly interrupted.

"Why would you draw such a conclusion?" Nikolai Parfenovich remarked.

"You don't believe a word of it, that's why! I quite understand that I've come to the main point: the old man is now lying there with his head smashed in, and I—having tragically described how I wanted to kill him and how I already snatched out the pestle—I suddenly run away from the window . . . A poem! In verse! Take the good man's word for it! Ha, ha! You are scoffers, gentlemen!"

And he swung his whole body around on the chair so hard that the chair creaked.

"And did you notice," the prosecutor began suddenly, as if paying no attention to Mitya's excitement, "did you notice, when you ran away from the window, whether the door to the garden, at the other end of the house, was open or not?"

"No, it was not open."

"It was not?"

"On the contrary, it was shut. Who could have opened it? Bah, the door—wait!" he suddenly seemed to collect himself and all but jumped up. "Did you find the door open?"

"Open."

"But who could have opened it, if you didn't open it yourselves?" Mitya was suddenly terribly surprised.

"The door was open, and your father's murderer undoubtedly went in through that door and, having committed the murder, went out through the same door," the prosecutor spoke slowly and distinctly, as though hammering out each word. "It is perfectly clear to us. The murder obviously took place in the room, *and not through the window*, which is positively clear from the investigation carried out, from the position of the body, and everything else. There can be no doubt of that circumstance."

Mitya was terribly astounded.

"But that's impossible, gentlemen!" he cried out, completely at a loss. "I . . . I didn't go in . . . I tell you positively, with exactness, that the door was shut all the while I was in the garden and when I ran out of the garden. I just stood outside the window and saw him in the window, and that's all, that's all . . . I remember it down to the last moment. And even if I didn't remember, I know it anyway, because the *signals* were known only to me and Smerdyakov, and to him, the dead man, and without the signals he wouldn't have opened the door to anyone in the world."

"Signals? What kind of signals?" the prosecutor said with greedy, almost hysterical curiosity, and instantly lost all his reserved demeanor. He asked as if creeping up timidly. He scented an important fact, still unknown to him, and at once felt great fear that Mitya might not be willing to reveal it fully.

"So you didn't even know?" Mitya winked at him, smiling mockingly and spitefully. "And what if I won't tell you? Who will you find out from then? Only the dead man knew about the signals, and me, and Smerdyakov, that's all, and heaven knew, too, but it won't tell you. And it's a curious little fact, one could build devil knows what on it, ha, ha! Take comfort, gentlemen, I'll reveal it to you. You've got foolishness in your minds. You don't know with whom you're dealing! You're dealing with a suspect who gives evidence against himself, who gives evidence that does him harm! Yes, sirs, for I am a knight of honor and you are not!"

The prosecutor swallowed all these pills; he was simply trembling with impatience to know about the new fact. Mitya gave them a precise and extensive account of everything to do with the signals invented by Fyodor Pavlovich for Smerdyakov, told them precisely what each knock on the window meant, even knocked out the signals on the table, and when asked by Nikolai Parfenovich whether it meant that he, Mitya, when he knocked on the old man's window, had used precisely the signal meaning "Grushenka has come," answered exactly that, yes, he had used precisely the signal meaning "Grushenka has come."

"There you are, now build your tower!" Mitya broke off, and again turned away from them in contempt.

"And only your deceased parent, you, and the servant Smerdyakov knew about these signals? And no one else?" Nikolai Parfenovich inquired once again.

"Yes, the servant Smerdyakov, and heaven, too. Write that down about heaven, too; it's worth writing down. And you'll have need of God yourselves."

Of course, they began writing it down, but while they were writing, the prosecutor, as if stumbling quite unexpectedly onto a new thought, suddenly said:

"But if Smerdyakov also knew about these signals, and you radically deny all accusations of your father's death, then was it not he who, having given the agreed signal, got your father to unlock the door for him, and then . . . committed the crime?"

Mitya gave him a deeply mocking and at the same time terribly hateful look. He stared at him long and silently, until the prosecutor began blinking his eyes.

"Caught the fox again!" Mitya spoke finally. "Pinched the rascal by the tail, heh, heh! I see right through you, prosecutor! You thought I'd jump up at once, snatch your prompting, and shout at the top of my lungs: 'Aie, it's Smerdyakov, he's the murderer!' Admit that's what you thought, admit it, and then I'll go on."

But the prosecutor admitted nothing. He was silent and waited.

"You're mistaken, I will not shout against Smerdyakov!" said Mitya.

"And you do not even suspect him at all?"

"Do you suspect him?"

"He is one of our suspects."

Mitya planted his eyes on the floor.

"Joking aside," he said gloomily, "listen: from the very beginning, almost from the moment when I ran out to you from behind the curtains tonight, this thought already flashed through me: 'Smerdyakov!' All the while I was sitting here at the table, shouting that I was not guilty of blood, I kept thinking: 'Smerdyakov!' And Smerdyakov would not let go of my soul. Finally, just now I suddenly had the same thought: 'Smerdyakov,' but only for a second; immediately, right next to it, came the thought: 'No, not Smerdyakov!' It's not his doing, gentlemen."

"In that case, do you suspect yet another person?" Nikolai Parfenovich asked guardedly.

"I don't know who or what person, the hand of heaven or Satan, but . . . not Smerdyakov!" Mitya snapped out resolutely.

"But why do you maintain so firmly and with such insistence that he is not the one?"

"From conviction. From impression. Because Smerdyakov is a man of the most abject nature and a coward. Not just a coward, but a conjunction of all cowardice in the world taken together, walking on two legs. He was born of a chicken. Every time he talked with me, he trembled for fear I might kill him, though I never even raised my hand. He fell at my feet and wept, he kissed these very boots of mine, literally, begging me not to 'scare' him. 'Scare,' do you hear?—what sort of word is that? And I even gave him presents. He's a sickly, epileptic, feebleminded chicken, who could be thrashed by an eight-year-old boy. What sort of a character is that? No, not Smerdyakov, gentlemen—and he doesn't care about money either, he never would take my presents . . . Anyway, why would he kill the old man? You see, he may be his son, his natural son, do you know that?"

"We have heard that legend. But after all, you, too, are your father's son, and yet you told everyone you wanted to kill him."

"A rock through my own window! And a low one, a nasty one! I'm not afraid. Oh, gentlemen, how mean of you to say that to my face! Mean, because I myself said it to you. I not only wanted to kill him, but I could well have killed him, and I voluntarily heaped it upon myself that I almost killed him! But I didn't kill him, my guardian angel saved me—that's what you haven't taken into consideration . . . And that is what makes it mean, mean! Because I didn't kill him, I didn't, I didn't! Do you hear, prosecutor: I didn't!"

He almost choked. Not once during the whole investigation had he been so agitated.

"And what has he told you, gentlemen—Smerdyakov, I mean?" he suddenly concluded, after a silence. "May I ask you that?"

"You may ask us anything," the prosecutor replied with a cold and stern look, "anything concerning the factual side of the case, and it is our duty, I repeat, to satisfy your every question. We found the servant Smerdyakov, about whom you inquire, lying unconscious in his bed with a very severe attack of the falling sickness, which had recurred perhaps ten times in succession. The doctor who was with us examined the sick man and told us he might not even live till morning."

"Well, in that case the devil killed my father!" suddenly escaped from Mitya, as if even up to that minute he had been asking himself: "Smerdyakov, or not Smerdyakov?"

"We shall return to this fact again," Nikolai Parfenovich resolved, "and now wouldn't you like to go on with your evidence?"

Mitya asked for a rest. It was politely granted. Having rested, he began to go on. But it was obviously difficult for him. He was worn out, insulted, and morally shaken. Besides, the prosecutor, now quite intentionally, began irritating him every moment by pestering him with "details." As soon as Mitya described how, sitting astride the fence, he had hit Grigory, who was clutching his left leg, on the head with the pestle, and then jumped down at once to the stricken man, the prosecutor stopped him and asked him to describe in greater detail how he was sitting on the fence. Mitya was surprised.

"Well, like this, astride it, one leg here, the other there . . ."

"And the pestle?"

"The pestle was in my hand."

"Not in your pocket? You remember such a detail? So, then you must have swung hard?"

"I must have swung hard—but what do you need that for?"

"Why don't you sit on the chair exactly as you were sitting on the fence then, and act out for us visually, for the sake of clarification, how and where you swung, in what direction?"

"You're not mocking me, are you?" Mitya asked, glancing haughtily at his interrogator, but the latter did not even bat an eye. Mitya turned convulsively, sat astride the chair, and swung his arm:

"That's how I hit him! That's how I killed him! Anything else?"

"Thank you. Now may I trouble you to explain why, in fact, you jumped down, with what purpose, and what, in fact, you had in mind?"

"Ah, the devil . . . I jumped down to the stricken man . . . I don't know why!"

"Even though you were so agitated? And running away?"

"Yes, agitated and running away."

"Did you want to help him?"

"Help him, hah . . . ! Well, maybe also to help him, I forget."

"You forgot yourself? That is, you were even somehow unconscious?"

"Oh, no, not unconscious at all, I remember everything. To the last shred. I jumped down to look at him and wiped the blood off with my handkerchief."

"We have seen your handkerchief. Did you hope to bring the man you struck back to life?"

"I don't know if I hoped anything. I simply wanted to make sure if he was alive or not."

"Ah, you wanted to make sure? Well, and so?"

"I'm not a doctor, I couldn't tell. I ran away thinking I'd killed him, but he recovered."

"Wonderful, sir," the prosecutor concluded. "Thank you. That is just what I wanted. Be so good as to continue."

Alas, it did not even occur to Mitya to tell them, though he remembered it, that he had jumped down out of pity, and that standing over the murdered man he had even uttered a few pathetic words: "You came a cropper, old man—there's no help for it—now lie there." But the prosecutor drew just one conclusion, that the man would only have jumped down "at such a moment and in such agitation," with the purpose of making completely sure whether the sole witness to his crime was alive or not. And what strength, consequently, what resolution, cold-bloodedness, and calculation the man possessed even at such a moment . . . and so on and so forth. The prosecutor was pleased: "I irritated the morbid fellow with 'details' and he gave himself away."

Painfully, Mitya went on. But again he was stopped at once, this time by Nikolai Parfenovich:

"How could you have run to the servant, Fedosya Markov, with your hands and, as it turned out later, your face so covered with blood?"

"But I didn't notice at the time that there was any blood on me!" Mitya answered.

"That's plausible, it does happen that way," the prosecutor exchanged looks with Nikolai Parfenovich.

"I precisely didn't notice—beautiful, prosecutor," Mitya, too, suddenly approved. But next came the story of Mitya's sudden decision "to remove himself" and "make way for the happy ones." And now it was quite impossible for him to bring himself to lay bare his heart, as before, and tell them about "the queen of his soul." It sickened him in the face of these cold people, who "bit at him like bedbugs." Therefore, to their repeated questions, he declared briefly and sharply:

"So I decided to kill myself. Why should I go on living? Naturally that jumped into the picture. Her offender arrived, the former, indisputable one, and he came riding to her with love, after five years, to end the offense with legal marriage. So I realized that it was all over for me . . . And behind me was disgrace, and that blood, Grigory's blood . . . Why live? So I went to redeem the pawned pistols, to load them, and to put a bullet into my sconce at dawn . . ."

"And feast the night before?"

"And feast the night before. Eh, the devil, let's get it over with quicker, gentlemen. I was certainly going to shoot myself, not far from here, just outside town, and I would have disposed of myself at about five o'clock in the morning—I had a note all prepared in my pocket, I wrote it at Perkhotin's when I loaded the pistol. Here it is, read it. I'm not telling it for you!" he suddenly added contemptuously. He threw the piece of paper from his waistcoat pocket onto the table in front of them; the investigators read it with curiosity, and, as is customary, filed it away.

"And you still did not think of washing your hands even as you entered Mr. Perkhotin's? In other words, you were not afraid of arousing suspicion?"

"What suspicion? Suspicion or not, all the same I'd have driven here and shot myself at five o'clock, and there would have been no time to do anything about it. If it weren't for what happened to my father, you wouldn't have found anything out and come here. Oh, the devil did it, the devil killed my father, and the devil let you find out so soon! How on earth did you get here so soon? It's a wonder, fantastic!"

"Mr. Perkhotin told us that when you came to him, you were holding your money . . . a lot of money . . . a wad of hundred-rouble bills . . . in your hands . . . your blood-stained hands, and that the servant boy also saw it!"

"Yes, gentlemen, that's true, I remember."

"Now one little question arises. Would you mind informing us," Nikolai Parfenovich began with extreme gentleness, "as to where you suddenly got so much money, when it appears from the evidence, even from the simple reckoning of time, that you did not stop at your own lodgings?"

The prosecutor winced slightly at the bluntness with which the question had been put, but he did not interrupt Nikolai Parfenovich.

"No, I didn't stop at my lodgings," Mitya replied, apparently very calmly, but dropping his eyes.

"Allow me, in that case, to repeat the question," Nikolai Parfenovich continued, somehow creeping up. "Where could you have gotten such a sum all at once, when, by your own admission, at five o'clock that same afternoon you . . ."

"Needed ten roubles, and pawned my pistols to Perkhotin, then went to Khokhlakov for three thousand, which she didn't give me, and so on, and all the rest of it," Mitya interrupted sharply. "So, yes, gentlemen, I needed money, and then suddenly thousands appeared, eh? You know, gentlemen, you're both afraid now: what if he won't tell us where he got it? And so it is: I won't tell you, gentlemen, you've guessed right, you'll never know," Mitya suddenly hammered out with great determination. The investigators fell silent for a moment.

"Understand, Mr. Karamazov, that it is an essential necessity that we know this," Nikolai Parfenovich said softly and humbly.

"I understand, but I still won't tell you."

The prosecutor intervened and again reminded him that a man under interrogation was of course at liberty not to answer questions if he thought it more beneficial, and so on, but in view of the harm the suspect might do himself by keeping silent, and especially in view of questions of such importance as . . .

"And so on, gentlemen, and so on! Enough, I've heard the whole harangue before!" Mitya again interrupted. "I myself understand the importance of the matter and what the most essential point is, and I still won't tell you."

"What is it to us, sir? It's not our business, but yours. You will only be harming yourself," Nikolai Parfenovich remarked nervously.

"You see, gentlemen, joking aside," Mitya raised his eyes and looked at them both steadily, "from the very beginning I had a feeling we would be at loggerheads on this point. But when I first started giving evidence today, that was all in a fog of things to come, it was all floating out there, and I was even so naive as to make a suggestion of 'mutual trust between us.' Now I see for myself that there could be no such trust, because we were bound to come to this cursed fence! Well, so we've come to it! It's impossible, that's all! I don't blame you, by the way, it's also impossible for you to take my word for it, I quite understand that."

He fell gloomily silent.

"But could you not, without in the least violating your determination to keep silent on this main point, could you not at the same time give us at least some slight hint as to precisely what sort of compelling motives might force you to keep silent at a moment so dangerous for you in your evidence?"

Mitya smiled sadly and somehow pensively.

"I am much kinder than you think, gentlemen, and I will tell you my reasons, and give you that hint, though you're not worthy of it. I keep silent, gentlemen, because it involves a disgrace for me. The answer to the question of where I got this money contains such a disgrace for me as could not be compared even with killing and robbing my father, if I had killed and robbed him. That is why I cannot speak. Because of the disgrace. What, gentlemen, are you going to write that down?"

"Yes, we shall write it down," Nikolai Parfenovich muttered.

"You shouldn't be writing it down—about the 'disgrace,' I mean. I only gave you that evidence out of the goodness of my soul, but I didn't have to do it, I gave it to you as a gift, so to speak, but you pick up every stitch. Well, write, write whatever you want," he concluded contemptuously and with distaste. "I'm not afraid of you, and . . . I'm proud before you."

"And would you tell us what sort of disgrace it might be?" muttered Nikolai Parfenovich.

The prosecutor winced terribly.

"No, no, *c'est fini*, don't bother. There's no need dirtying myself. I've already dirtied myself enough on you. You're not worthy, you or anyone else . . . Enough, gentlemen, drop it."

This was said all too resolutely. Nikolai Parfenovich stopped insisting, but he saw at once from the glance of Ippolit Kirillovich that he had not yet lost hope.

"Could you not at least state how much money was in your hands when you came with it to Mr. Perkhotin's—that is, exactly how many roubles?"

"I cannot state that either."

"I believe you made some statement to Mr. Perkhotin about three thousand that you supposedly got from Madame Khokhlakov?"

"Maybe I did. Enough, gentlemen, I won't tell you how much."

"In that case, will you kindly describe how you came here and all that you did when you came?"

"Oh, ask the local people about that. Or, no, maybe I will tell you."

He told them, but we shall not give his story here. It was dry, brief. He did not speak at all about the raptures of his love. He did tell, however, how the resolve to shoot himself abandoned him "in the face of new facts." He told it without giving motives, without going into details. And this time the investigators did not bother him much: it was clear that for them the main point now lay elsewhere.

"We shall check all that, we shall come back to everything when we question the witnesses, which will be done, of course, in your presence," Nikolai Parfenovich concluded the interrogation. "And now allow me to make a request of you, that you lay out here on the table all the things you have in your possession, especially all the money you now have."

"Money, gentlemen? By all means, I understand the need for it. I'm even surprised you didn't ask sooner. True, I wasn't going anywhere, I'm sitting in plain sight of everyone. Well, here it is, my money, here, count it, take it, that's all, I think."

He took everything out of his pockets, even the change; he pulled two twenty-kopeck pieces from the side pocket of his waistcoat. They counted the money, which came to eight hundred and thirty-six roubles and forty kopecks.

"And that's all?" asked the district attorney.

"All."

"You were so good as to tell us, giving your evidence just now, that you spent three hundred roubles at Plotnikov's shop, gave ten to Perkhotin, twenty to the coachman, lost two hundred in a card game here, so then . . ."

Nikolai Parfenovich totaled it all up. Mitya willingly helped. They remembered every kopeck and added it to the reckoning. Nikolai Parfenovich made a quick calculation.

"It follows that you originally had about fifteen hundred roubles, if we include this eight hundred."

"It follows," Mitya snapped.

"Why, then, does everyone claim there was much more?"

"Let them claim it."

"But you also claimed it yourself."

"I also claimed it."

"We shall still check it against the evidence of other persons who have not yet been questioned; don't worry about your money, it will be kept in a proper place and will be at your disposal at the end of . . . of what is now beginning . . . if it proves, or rather if we prove, so to speak, that you have an undisputed right to it. Well, sir, and now . . ."

Nikolai Parfenovich suddenly got up and firmly announced to Mitya that he was "obliged and duty-bound" to conduct a most thorough and minute examination "of your clothes and everything else . . ."

"As you wish, gentlemen, I'll turn all my pockets out, if you like."

And indeed he began turning his pockets out.

"It will even be necessary for you to take off your clothes."

"What? Undress? Pah, the devil! You can search me like this, isn't that possible?"

"Utterly impossible, Dmitri Fyodorovich. You must take your clothes off."

"As you will," Mitya gloomily submitted, "only, please, not here—behind the curtains. Who will do the examining?"

"Behind the curtains, of course," Nikolai Parfenovich inclined his head in a token of consent. His little face even wore an expression of unusual importance.

Chapter 6

The Prosecutor Catches Mitya

There began something quite unexpected and astonishing for Mitya. He could not at all have supposed, even a moment before, that anyone could treat him, Mitya Karamazov, like that! Above all there was something humiliating in it, and something "haughty and contemptuous towards him" on their part. To take off his coat would be nothing, but they asked him to undress further. And they did not merely ask, but, in fact, they ordered; he understood it perfectly. Out of pride and contempt he submitted completely, without a word. Along with Nikolai Parfenovich, the prosecutor also went behind the curtains, and there were several peasants as well, "for strength, of course," thought Mitya, "and maybe for something else."

"What, must I take my shirt off, too?" he asked sharply, but Nikolai Parfenovich did not answer: together with the prosecutor, he was absorbed in examining the coat, the trousers, the waistcoat, and the cap, and one could see that they were both very interested in examining them. "They don't stand on any ceremony," flashed through Mitya's mind, "they don't even observe the necessary politeness."

"I'm asking you for the second time: must I take my shirt off or not?" he said even more sharply and irritably.

"Don't worry, we'll let you know," Nikolai Parfenovich replied somehow even overbearingly. At least it seemed so to Mitya.

Meanwhile between the district attorney and the prosecutor a solicitous debate was going on in half whispers. Huge spots of blood, dry, stiff, and not softened very much yet, were found on the coat, especially on the left flap at the back. Also on the trousers. Furthermore, Nikolai Parfenovich, with his own hands, in the presence of witnesses, felt along the collar, cuffs, and all the seams of the coat and trousers with his fingers, evidently looking for something—money, of course. Above all, they did not conceal from Mitya the suspicion that he could and would have sewn money into his clothes. "As if they really were dealing with a thief, not an officer," Mitya growled to himself. And they were telling each other their thoughts in his presence, with a frankness that verged on strangeness. For example, the clerk, who also ended up behind the curtains, fussing about and assisting, drew Nikolai Parfenovich's attention to the cap, which was also felt over: "Do you remember Gridenko the scrivener, sir," he remarked, "who came in the summer to pick up the wages for the whole office, and announced when he got back that he had lost the money while drunk—and where did they find it? In this same piping, in his cap, sir—the hundred-rouble bills were rolled up and sewn into the piping." The fact about Gridenko was remembered very well by both the district attorney and the prosecutor, and therefore Mitya's cap, too, was set aside, and it was decided that all of that would have to be seriously reexamined later, and all the clothes as well.

"I beg your pardon," Nikolai Parfenovich suddenly cried, noticing the tucked-under right cuff of Mitya's right shirt sleeve, all stained with blood, "I beg your pardon, sir—is that blood?"

"Blood," snapped Mitya.

"That is, whose blood, sir . . . and why is it tucked under?"

Mitya told him how he had stained the cuff fussing over Grigory, and how he had tucked it under when he washed his hands at Perkhotin's.

"We shall have to take your shirt, too, it's very important . . . as material evidence." Mitya flushed and became furious.

"What, am I to stay naked?" he cried.

"Don't worry . . . We'll do something about it . . . and meanwhile may I also trouble you to take off your socks?"

"You must be joking! Is it really so necessary?" Mitya flashed his eyes.

"This is no time for joking," Nikolai Parfenovich parried sternly.

"Well, if you need it . . . I . . . ," Mitya muttered, and having sat down on the bed, he began taking his socks off. He felt unbearably awkward: everyone else was dressed, and he was undressed, and—strangely—undressed, he himself seemed to feel guilty before them, and, above all, he was almost ready to agree that he had indeed suddenly become lower than all of them, and that they now had every right to despise him. "If everyone is undressed, it's not shameful, but when only one is undressed and the others are all looking—it's a disgrace!" flashed again and again through his mind. "It's like a dream, I've dreamed of being disgraced like this." But to take his socks off was even painful for him: they were not very clean, nor were his underclothes, and now everyone could see it. And above all he did not like his own feet; all his life for some reason he had found both his big toes ugly, especially the right one with its crude, flat toenail, somehow curved under, and now they would all see it. This unbearable shame suddenly made him, deliberately now, even more rude. He tore his shirt off.

"Would you like to look anywhere else, if you're not ashamed to?"

"No, sir, not just now."

"So, what, am I to stay naked like this?" he added fiercely.

"Yes, it is necessary just now . . . May I trouble you to sit down here for now, you can take a blanket from the bed and wrap yourself, and I . . . I'll see to everything."

All the articles were shown to the witnesses, the report of the examination was drawn up, and Nikolai Parfenovich finally went out, and the clothes were taken out after him. Ippolit Kirillovich also went out. Only the peasants remained with Mitya, and stood silently, not taking their eyes off him. Mitya wrapped himself in a blanket; he was cold. His bare feet stuck out, and he kept trying unsuccessfully to pull the blanket over them so as to cover them. Nikolai Parfenovich did not come back for a long time, "painfully long." "He treats me like a pup," Mitya ground his teeth. "That rotten prosecutor left, too, must be from contempt, he got disgusted looking at a naked man." Mitya still supposed that his clothes would be examined elsewhere and then brought back. How great was his indignation when Nikolai Parfenovich suddenly returned with quite different clothes, brought in after him by a peasant.

"Well, here are some clothes for you," he said casually, apparently quite pleased with the success of his expedition. "Mr. Kalganov has donated them for this curious occasion, as well as a clean shirt for you. Fortunately, he happened to have it all in his suitcase. You may keep your own underwear and socks."

Mitya boiled over.

"I don't want other people's clothes!" he thundered. "Give me mine!"

"Impossible."

"Give me mine! Devil take Kalganov, him and his clothes!"

They reasoned with him for a long time. Anyway, they somehow calmed him down. They convinced him that his own clothes, being stained with blood, must "join the collection of material evidence," and to leave them on him "no longer even fell within their rights . . . in view of how the case might end." Mitya somehow finally understood this. He lapsed into a gloomy silence and began hurriedly getting dressed. He merely observed, as he was putting the clothes on, that they were more costly than his old ones, and that he did not want "to gain by it." And besides, "they're embarrassingly tight. Shall I play the buffoon in them . . . for your pleasure?"

Again he was convinced that here, too, he was exaggerating, that Mr. Kalganov, though taller than he, was only slightly taller, so that only the trousers might be a trifle long. But the coat did turn out to be narrow in the shoulders.

"Devil take it, I can hardly even button it," Mitya growled again. "Do me a favor, please tell Mr. Kalganov right now that I did not ask him for his clothes, and that I've been gotten up like a buffoon."

"He understands that very well, and he is sorry . . . not sorry about his clothes, that is, but, as a matter of fact, about this whole case . . . ," Nikolai Parfenovich mumbled.

"I spit on his 'sorry'! Well, where to now? Or do I go on sitting here?"

He was asked to go back to "that room." He went back, sullen with anger, trying not to look at anyone. He felt himself utterly disgraced in another man's clothes, even before those peasants and Trifon Borisovich, whose face for some reason flashed in the doorway and disappeared. "He came to have a look at the mummer," thought Mitya. He sat down on his former chair. He had the illusion of something nightmarish and absurd; it seemed to him he was not in his right mind.

"Well, what now, do you start flogging me with a birch, or what? There's nothing else left," he gnashed out, addressing the prosecutor. He no longer wanted even to turn towards Nikolai Parfenovich, as though he did not deign to speak with him. "He examined my socks too closely, and had them turned inside out, the scoundrel—he did it on purpose, to show everyone how dirty my underwear is!"

"Well, now we'll have to proceed to the interrogation of the witnesses," said Nikolai Parfenovich, as if in answer to Dmitri Fyodorovich's question.

"Yes," the prosecutor said thoughtfully, as if he, too, was pondering something.

"We have done all we could in your interest, Dmitri Fyodorovich," Nikolai Parfenovich continued, "but having received such a radical refusal on your part to give us any explanation concerning the sources of the sum found in your possession, we, at this point . . ."

"What's the stone in that ring?" Mitya suddenly interrupted, as if coming out of some sort of reverie, pointing to one of the three large rings that adorned Nikolai Parfenovich's right hand.

"Ring?" Nikolai Parfenovich repeated in surprise.

"Yes, that one . . . with the little veins in it, on your middle finger—what stone is that?" Mitya insisted somehow irritably, like a stubborn child.

"It's a smoky topaz," Nikolai Parfenovich smiled, "would you like to look at it? I'll take it off . . ."

"No, no, don't take it off," Mitya cried fiercely, suddenly coming to his senses, and angry with himself. "Don't take it off, there's no need . . . Ah, the devil . . . Gentlemen, you've befouled my soul! Can you possibly think I'd conceal it from you if I really killed my father? That I'd hedge, and lie, and hide? No, Dmitri Karamazov is not like that, he couldn't bear it, and if I were guilty, I swear, I wouldn't have waited for you to come here, or for the sun to rise, as I originally intended, I'd have destroyed myself even before, without waiting for dawn! I feel that in myself now. I've found out more in this one cursed night than I'd have learned in twenty years of living . . . ! And would I have been this way, would I have been this way on this night, and at this moment, sitting with you now, would I be talking like this, would I be moving like this, would I look at you and at the world like this, if I really were a parricide, when even the inadvertent killing of Grigory gave me no rest all night—not from fear, oh! not just from fear of your punishment! The disgrace of it! And you want me to reveal and tell about yet another new meanness of mine, yet another new disgrace, to such scoffers as you, who do not see anything and do not believe anything, blind moles and scoffers, even if it would save me from your accusation? Better penal servitude! The one who opened the door to my father's room and went in through that door is the one who killed him, he is the one who robbed him. Who he is, I am at a loss and at pains to say, but he is not Dmitri Karamazov, know that—and that is all I can tell you, and enough, stop badgering me . . . Exile me, hang me, but don't irritate me any more. I am silent. Call your witnesses!"

Mitya spoke his sudden monologue as if he were fully and finally determined to keep silent from then on. The prosecutor was watching him the whole time, and, as soon as he fell silent, suddenly said with the coldest and calmest air, as if it were the most ordinary thing:

"Incidentally, it is precisely with regard to that open door you have just mentioned that we can inform you, precisely now, of a highly curious piece of evidence, of the greatest importance for you and for us, supplied by Grigory Vasiliev, the old man you injured. On regaining consciousness, he clearly and emphatically told us, in answer to our inquiries, that when, coming out on the porch and hearing some noise in the garden, he decided to go into the garden through the gate, which was standing open; having gone into the garden, but before he noticed you running in the darkness, as you have told us already, away from the open window in which you saw your father, he, Grigory, glancing to the left and indeed noticing the open window, noticed at the same time that the door, much closer to him, was also wide open, that door of which you have stated that it remained shut all the while you were in the garden. I shall not conceal from you that Vasiliev himself firmly concludes and testifies that you must have run out of that door, though of course he did not see you run out with his own eyes, but noticed you for the first time when you were some distance away, in the middle of the garden, running in the direction of the fence . . ."

Mitya had already leaped from his chair halfway through the speech.

"Nonsense!" he suddenly yelled in frenzy, "a bold-faced lie! He could not have seen the door open then, because it was shut . . . He's lying . . . !"

"I consider it my duty to repeat to you that his testimony is firm. He has no hesitation. He stands upon it. We asked him several more times."

"Precisely, I asked him several more times!" Nikolai Parfenovich hotly confirmed.

"Not true, not true! It's either a slander against me or a madman's hallucination," Mitya went on shouting. "He simply imagined it in his delirium, all bloody, wounded, on regaining consciousness . . . So he's raving."

"Yes, sir, but he noticed the open door not when he regained consciousness from his wound, but already before then, when he was just going into the garden from the cottage."

"But it's not true, not true, it cannot be! He's slandering me out of malice . . . He couldn't have seen it . . . I didn't run out the door," Mitya was gasping for breath.

The prosecutor turned to Nikolai Parfenovich and said imposingly:

"Show him."

"Is this object familiar to you?" Nikolai Parfenovich suddenly placed on the table a large, official-sized envelope of thick paper, on which three intact seals could still be seen. The envelope itself was empty and torn open at one end. Mitya stared wide-eyed at it.

"That . . . that should be father's envelope," he muttered, "the one with the three thousand roubles . . . and it should have 'for my chicky' written on it . . . allow me . . . yes, look: three thousand," he cried out, "three thousand, you see?"

"Of course we see, sir, but we did not find the money in it, it was empty and lying on the floor, near the bed, behind the screen."

For a few seconds Mitya stood as if stunned.

"Gentlemen, it's Smerdyakov!" he suddenly shouted with all his might. "He killed him, he robbed him! He's the only one who knew where the old man hid the envelope . . . It's him, it's clear now!"

"But you also knew about the envelope and that it was under the pillow."

"I never knew: I've never seen it before, I'm seeing it now for the first time, I just heard about it from Smerdyakov . . . He's the only one who knew where the old man kept it hidden, I didn't know . . . ," Mitya was completely breathless.

"And yet you yourself told us just now that the envelope was under your deceased father's pillow. You precisely said under the pillow, which means you did know where it was."

"We have it written down!" Nikolai Parfenovich confirmed.

"Nonsense, absurdity! I had no idea it was under the pillow. And maybe it wasn't under the pillow at all . . . It was a random guess that it was under the pillow . . . What does Smerdyakov say? Did you ask him where it was? What does Smerdyakov say? That's the most important thing . . . And I deliberately told lies against myself . . . I lied to you that it was under the pillow, without thinking, and now you . . . Ah, you know, something just comes out of your mouth, and you tell a lie. But only Smerdyakov knew, just Smerdyakov alone, and no one else . . . ! He didn't even reveal to me where it was! So it's him, it's him; there's no question he killed him, it's clear as day to me now," Mitya kept exclaiming more and more frenziedly, repeating himself incoherently, growing impassioned and bitter. "You must understand that and arrest him quickly, quickly . . . Precisely he killed him, after I ran away and while Grigory was lying unconscious, it's clear now . . . He gave the signals, and father opened the door for him . . . Because he alone knew the signals, and without the signals father wouldn't have opened the door for anyone . . ."

"But again you are forgetting one circumstance," the prosecutor observed, still with the same restraint, but now, as it were, triumphantly, "that there was no need to give the signals if the door was already open, when you were still there, while you were still in the garden . . ."

"The door, the door," Mitya muttered, staring speechlessly at the prosecutor, and he sank down weakly on his chair again. Everyone fell silent.

"Yes, the door . . . ! It's a phantom! God is against me!" he exclaimed, staring before him with an altogether vacant look.

"So you see," the prosecutor spoke imposingly, "and judge for yourself now, Dmitri Fyodorovich: on one side there is this evidence of the open door from which you ran out, which overwhelms both you and us. And, on the other side, your inexplicable, persistent, and almost obdurate silence with regard to the source of the money that suddenly appeared in your hands, when only three hours prior to that sum, according to your own testimony, you pawned your pistols to get a mere ten roubles! In view of all this, decide for yourself: what should we believe, and where does it leave us? And do not hold a grudge against us for being 'cold cynics and scoffers' who are incapable of believing in the noble impulses of your soul . . . Try, on the contrary, to understand our position as well . . ."

Mitya was inconceivably agitated; he turned pale.

"All right!" he suddenly exclaimed, "I will reveal my secret to you, reveal where I got the money . . . ! I will reveal my disgrace, so as not to blame either you or myself later on . . ."

"And you may believe, Dmitri Fyodorovich," Nikolai Parfenovich added, in a sort of tenderly joyful little voice, "that any sincere and full confession you make precisely at this moment, may afterwards contribute towards an immeasurable alleviation of your fate, and, moreover, may even . . ."

But the prosecutor nudged him slightly under the table, and he managed to stop himself in time. Mitya, to tell the truth, was not listening to him.

Chapter 7

Mitya's Great Secret. Met with Hisses

"Gentlemen," he began in the same agitation, "the money . . . I want to confess completely . . . the money was *mine*."

The prosecutor and the district attorney even pulled long faces: this was not at all what they expected.

"How can that be," murmured Nikolai Parfenovich, "when at five o'clock in the afternoon, by your own admission . . ."

"Eh, devil take five o'clock in the afternoon and my own admission, that's not the point now! The money was mine, mine, that is, my stolen money . . . not mine, that is, but stolen, stolen by me, and it was fifteen hundred, and I had it with me, I had it with me all the while . . ."

"But where did you get it?"

"From around my neck, gentlemen, I got it from around my neck, from this very neck of mine . . . It was here on my neck, sewn up in a rag and hanging on my neck; for a long time, a month already, I was carrying it on my neck with shame and disgrace!"

"But who did you . . . appropriate it from?"

"Were you about to say 'steal'? Let's not mince words now. Yes, I consider it the same as if I'd stolen it—'appropriated,' indeed, if you wish, but in my view I stole it. And last evening I stole it altogether."

"Last evening? But you just said it was a month ago that you . . . obtained it!"

"Yes, but not from my father, not from my father, don't worry, I stole it not from my father, but from her. Let me speak and don't interrupt. It's hard. You see: a month ago, Katerina Ivanovna Verkhovtsev, my former fiancée, sent for me . . . Do you know her?"

"Of course, sir, good heavens!"

"I know you know her. The noblest soul, the noblest of the noble, but who has hated me for a long time, oh, a long, long time . . . and rightly so, rightly so!"

"Katerina Ivanovna?" the district attorney asked in surprise. The prosecutor also stared terribly.

"Oh, do not utter her name in vain! I'm a scoundrel to bring her into it. Yes, I saw that she hated me . . . long ago . . . from the very first, from that time in my rooms, already then . . . But enough, enough, you're even unworthy to know of that, there's no need at all . . . All you need to know is that she sent for me a month ago, handed me three thousand to send to her sister and some other relative in Moscow (as if she couldn't have sent it herself!), and I . . . it was precisely at that fatal moment of my life when I . . . well, in a word, when I had just fallen in love with the other one, *her*, the present one, she's sitting downstairs now, Grushenka . . . I carried her off here, to Mokroye, and in two days here I squandered half of that cursed three thousand, that is, fifteen hundred, and the other half I kept on me. Well, so the fifteen hundred that I kept, I wore here on my neck, in place of an amulet, and yesterday I got it out and squandered it. The eight hundred roubles left are now in your hands, Nikolai Parfenovich, that's what's left of yesterday's fifteen hundred."

"I beg your pardon, but how can that be, when you squandered three thousand here a month ago, not fifteen hundred, and everyone knows it?"

"Who knows it? Who counted? Did I let anyone count it?"

"Good heavens, but you yourself told everyone that you squandered exactly three thousand then."

"True, I said it. I said it to the whole town, and the whole town said it, and everyone thought so, and here in Mokroye everyone thought the same, that it was three thousand. Yet I only squandered fifteen hundred, not three thousand, and the other fifteen hundred I sewed into an amulet; that's how it was, gentlemen, and that's where yesterday's money came from . . ."

"It's almost miraculous . . . ," murmured Nikolai Parfenovich.

"Allow me to ask," the prosecutor spoke finally, "if there is someone at least whom you informed of this circumstance . . . that is, that you kept this fifteen hundred with you then, a month ago?"

"I told no one."

"That's strange. No one at all, can it really be?"

"No one at all. Nobody and no one."

"But why such reticence? What moved you to make such a secret of it? Let me explain myself more precisely: you have finally told us your secret, so 'disgraceful,' as you say, though as a matter of fact—I mean, of course, only relatively speaking—this action—namely, that is, the appropriation of another person's three thousand roubles, and, no doubt, only temporarily—this action, in my opinion at least, is simply a highly thoughtless action, but not so disgraceful, considering, moreover, your character . . . Well, let us say it is even a highly discreditable action, I agree, but still discreditable is not disgraceful . . . What I'm driving at, in fact, is that during this month many people have already guessed about Miss Verkhovtsev's three thousand, which you have spent, even without your confession—I have heard this legend myself . . . Mikhail Makarovich, for instance, has also heard it. So that, ultimately, it is almost not a legend anymore, but the gossip of the whole town. Moreover, there are signs that you yourself, if I am not mistaken, confessed it to someone or other—namely, that is, that this money came from Miss Verkhovtsev . . . And therefore I am all the more surprised that until now, that is, until this very present moment, you have attached such extraordinary secrecy to this fifteen hundred, which, as you say, you set aside, even connecting this secret of yours with some kind of horror . . . It is incredible that such a secret should cost you such torment in confessing it . . . for you were just shouting that penal servitude would be better than confessing it . . ."

The prosecutor fell silent. He was flushed. He did not conceal his vexation, almost spite, and poured out all he had stored up, not even caring about the beauty of his style, that is, confusedly and almost incoherently.

"The disgrace lay not in the fifteen hundred, but in my separating that fifteen hundred from the three thousand," Mitya spoke firmly.

"But what," the prosecutor smiled irritably, "what precisely is disgraceful about your having chosen to set aside half of the three thousand that you had already discreditably, or, if you wish, disgracefully taken? That you appropriated the three thousand is the main thing, not how you disposed of it. Incidentally, why exactly did you dispose of it that way, I mean, set aside that half? What for, with what purpose in mind—can you explain that to us?"

"Oh, but gentlemen, it is in that purpose that the whole force lies!" Mitya exclaimed. "I set it aside out of baseness—that is, out of calculation, because calculation in this case is baseness . . . And this baseness went on for a whole month!"

"Incomprehensible."

"You surprise me. But, anyway, let me explain further; perhaps it really is incomprehensible. Try to follow me. You see, I appropriate three thousand, entrusted to my honor, I go on a spree with it, I squander it all, the next morning I go to her and say: 'Katya, I'm sorry, I squandered your three thousand'—well, is that nice? No, it's not nice, it's dishonest, cowardly, I'm a beast, a man with no more self-restraint than a beast, right, am I right? But still not a thief! Not an outright thief, not outright, you'll agree! I squandered it, but I did not steal it! Now a second, even more favorable case—follow me, or I may get confused again—I'm somehow giddy—so, the second case: I go on a spree and spend only fifteen hundred out of the three thousand—half, in other words. The next day I go to her and bring her the other half: 'Katya, take this half back from me, a villain and a thoughtless scoundrel, because I've already squandered one half, therefore I'll also squander the other, so put me out of harm's way!' Well, what am I in that case? Whatever you like, a beast, a scoundrel, but not a thief, not finally a thief, because if I were a thief, I'd have appropriated the other half as well and certainly not have brought it back. She would see at once that if he's brought her the one half, he'll also bring her the rest, the part he squandered, he'll spend his life looking for it, he'll work, but he will find it and give it back. Thus, a scoundrel, but not a thief, not a thief, anything you like, but not a thief!"

"There is some difference, I grant you," the prosecutor smiled coldly. "But still it's strange that you see it as such a fatal difference."

"Yes, I see it as a fatal difference! Any man can be, and perhaps is, a scoundrel, but not any man can be a thief, only an arch-scoundrel can be that. Well, I'm not very good at these subtleties . . . But still, a thief is more of a scoundrel than a scoundrel, that is my conviction. Listen: I carry the money on me for a whole month, even tomorrow I can decide to give it back, and then I'm not a scoundrel, but I can't decide, that's the thing, though I keep deciding every day, though I push myself every day: 'Decide, you scoundrel, decide,' and yet I can't decide for a whole month, that's the thing! Is that nice? What do you think, is it nice?"

"I grant you it is not very nice, I can understand that perfectly, and I do not dispute it," the prosecutor answered with reserve. "And generally let us set aside any altercation concerning these subtleties and distinctions, and, if you please, come back to the point. And the point is that you have not yet explained to us, though we did ask, why you originally made such a division of the three thousand—that is, squandered one half and set aside the other half? Precisely what, properly speaking, did you set it aside for; and how, properly speaking, did you intend to use this separate fifteen hundred? I insist upon this question, Dmitri Fyodorovich."

"Ah, yes, indeed!" cried Mitya, slapping himself on the forehead. "Forgive me, I'm tormenting you and not explaining the main thing, otherwise you'd understand it at once, because it is in this purpose, in this purpose, that the whole disgrace lies! You see, it was the old man, the dead man, he kept troubling Agrafena Alexandrovna, and I was jealous, I thought then that she was hesitating between me and him; and so I kept thinking each day: what if there suddenly comes a decision from her, what if she gets tired of tormenting me and suddenly says to me, 'I love you and not him, take me away to the end of the earth.' And all I have is some small change; how will I take her, what will I do then—it's all over for me. I didn't know her then, I didn't understand, I thought she wanted money and that she'd never forgive me my poverty. And so I slyly counted out half of the three thousand and sewed it up with needle and thread, in cold blood, I sewed it up calculatingly, I sewed it up even before I went drinking, and then, when I had sewn it up, I went and got drunk on the other half! It took a scoundrel to do that, sir! Do you understand now?"

The prosecutor burst into loud laughter, as did the district attorney.

"In my opinion it is even sensible and moral that you restrained yourself and did not squander it all," Nikolai Parfenovich tittered, "because what's wrong with that, sir?"

"That I stole, that's what! Oh, God, you horrify me with your lack of understanding! All the while I carried that fifteen hundred sewn up on my chest, I kept saying to myself every day and every hour: 'You are a thief, you are a thief!' And that's why I raged all month, that's why I fought in the tavern, that's why I beat my father, because I felt I was a thief! I could not bring myself, I did not dare to reveal anything about the fifteen hundred even to Alyosha, my brother: so much did I feel myself a scoundrel and a pickpocket. But know that all the while I carried it, every day and every hour, I kept saying to myself at the same time: 'No, Dmitri Fyodorovich, perhaps you're not yet a thief.' Why? Precisely because you can go tomorrow and give the fifteen hundred back to Katya. And only yesterday did I decide to tear the amulet off my neck, on my way from Fenya to Perkhotin, for until that moment I couldn't decide, and as soon as I tore it off, at that moment I became a final and indisputable thief, a thief and a dishonest man for the rest of my life. Why? Because along with the amulet, my dream of going to Katya and saying: 'I am a scoundrel, but not a thief,' was also torn up! Do you understand now, do you understand!"

"Why did you decide to do it precisely last evening?" Nikolai Parfenovich interrupted.

"Why? A funny question! Because I had condemned myself to death, at five o'clock in the morning, here, at dawn: 'It's all the same how I die,' I thought, 'as a scoundrel or as a noble man!' But not so, it turned out not to be all the same! Believe me, gentlemen, what tormented me most this night was not that I had killed the old servant, and that I was threatened with Siberia, and all of that when?—when my love had been crowned and heaven was open to me again! Oh, that was a torment, but not so great, still not so great as the cursed awareness that I had finally torn that cursed money off my chest and spent it, and therefore was now a final thief! Oh, gentlemen, I repeat to you in my heart's blood: I learned a lot this night! I learned that it is impossible not only to live a scoundrel, but also to die a scoundrel . . . No, gentlemen, one must die honestly . . . !"

Mitya was pale. His face had a wasted and worn-out look, despite his intense excitement.

"I am beginning to understand you, Dmitri Fyodorovich," the prosecutor drawled softly and even somehow compassionately, "but, be it as you say, still, in my opinion it is just nerves . . . your overwrought nerves, that's all, sir. And why, for instance, to spare yourself so much torment over almost a whole month, would you not go and return the fifteen hundred to the person who entrusted it to you, and then, having talked things over with her, why, in view of your situation at the time, which you describe as being so terrible, would you not try the solution that so naturally comes to mind—I mean, after nobly confessing your errors to her, why not ask her for the sum needed for your expenses, which she, with her generous heart, seeing how upset you were, of course would not refuse you, especially with some written agreement, or, finally, at least with the same security you offered to the merchant Samsonov and Madame Khokhlakov? I suppose you still consider that security to be of value?"

Mitya suddenly blushed.

"Do you really consider me such a downright scoundrel? You can't possibly be serious . . . !" he said indignantly, looking the prosecutor in the eye, as if he could not believe what he had heard.

"I assure you I am serious . . . Why do you think I am not?" The prosecutor, in turn, was also surprised.

"Oh, how base that would be! Gentlemen, you're tormenting me, do you know that? As you wish, I'll tell you everything, so be it, I will now confess all my infernality to you, just to put you to shame, and you yourselves will be surprised at what baseness a combination of human feelings can sink to. Know, then, that I already had that solution in mind, the very one you were just talking about, prosecutor! Yes, gentlemen, I, too, had that thought during this cursed month, so that I almost resolved to go to Katya, so base I was! But to go to her, to announce my betrayal to her, and for that betrayal, to carry through that betrayal, for the future expenses of that betrayal, to ask money (to ask, do you hear, to ask!) from her, from Katya, and immediately run off with another woman, with her rival, with her hater and offender—my God, you're out of your mind, prosecutor!"

"Out of my mind or not, of course, in the heat of the moment, I did fail to consider . . . this matter of female jealousy . . . if indeed there is a question of jealousy here, as you affirm . . . yes, perhaps there is something of the sort," the prosecutor grinned.

"But it would be such an abomination!" Mitya pounded the table fiercely with his fist, "it would stink so much, I can't tell you! And do you know that she might have given me the money, and she would have given it, she certainly would have given it, she would have given it out of vengeance, for the pleasure of revenge, she would have given it out of contempt for me, because she, too, is an infernal soul, and a woman of great wrath! And I'd have taken the money, oh, I'd have taken it, I would, and then all my life . . . oh, God! Forgive me, gentlemen, I'm shouting so because I had this idea only recently, only two days ago, that night when I was worrying over Lyagavy, and then yesterday, yes, also yesterday, all day yesterday, I remember it, till this very accident . . ."

"Till what accident?" Nikolai Parfenovich put in with curiosity, but Mitya did not hear him.

"I've made a terrible confession to you," he concluded gloomily. "Do appreciate it, gentlemen. And it's not enough, not enough to appreciate it, you must not just appreciate it, it should also be precious to you, and if not, if this, too, goes past your souls, then it means you really do not respect me, gentlemen, I tell you that, and I will die of shame at having confessed to such men as you! Oh, I will shoot myself! And I can see, I can see already that you don't believe me! What, are you going to write this down, too?" he cried, frightened now.

"But what you have just said," Nikolai Parfenovich was looking at him in surprise, "that is, that until the very last hour you still thought of going to Miss

Verkhovtsev to ask for this sum . . . I assure you that this evidence is very important for us, Dmitri Fyodorovich, this whole story, that is . . . and especially important for you, especially for you."

"Have mercy, gentlemen," Mitya clasped his hands, "at least leave that out, for shame! I have, so to speak, torn my soul asunder before you, and you take advantage of it and go rummaging with your fingers in both halves of the torn spot . . . Oh, God!"

He covered his face with his hands in despair.

"Do not upset yourself, Dmitri Fyodorovich," the prosecutor concluded, "everything that has been written down here will be read over to you afterwards, and whatever you disagree with will be changed as you say, but now I shall repeat one little question for the third time: is it possible that indeed no one, really no one at all, heard from you about this money you sewed into the amulet? I must say I find that almost impossible to imagine."

"No one, no one, I told you, or else you've understood nothing! Leave me alone!"

"As you wish, sir, the matter will have to be clarified, but there is still time enough for that, yet meanwhile consider: we have perhaps dozens of testimonies that precisely you yourself were spreading and even shouted everywhere about the three thousand you had spent, three thousand and not fifteen hundred, and now, too, with the appearance of yesterday's money, you also let many people understand that once again you had brought three thousand with you . . ."

"Not dozens, you've got hundreds of testimonies, two hundred testimonies, two hundred people heard it, a thousand heard it!" Mitya exclaimed.

"Well, so you see, sir, everyone says it. Does the word *everyone* mean anything?"

"It means nothing, I lied, and everyone started lying after me."

"And what need did you have to 'lie,' as you put it?"

"Devil knows. Maybe in order to boast . . . well . . . about squandering so much money . . . Or maybe in order to forget about the money I had sewn up . . . yes, that's exactly why . . . ah, the devil . . . how many times must you ask me? So I lied, and that's it, I lied once and then I didn't want to correct it. Why does a man lie sometimes?"

"That is very difficult to say, Dmitri Fyodorovich, why a man lies," the prosecutor said imposingly. "Tell me, however: this amulet, as you call it, that you wore on your neck—was it big?"

"No, not big."

"What size was it, for instance?"

"Fold a hundred-rouble bill in half—that's the size for you."

"Hadn't you better show us the scraps of it? You must have them somewhere."

"Ah, the devil . . . what foolishness . . . I don't know where they are."

"I beg your pardon, but where and when did you take it off your neck? According to your own testimony, you did not stop at home."

"When I left Fenya and was going to Perkhotin's, on the way I tore the money off my neck and took it out."

"In the dark?"

"Should I have had a candle? I did it with my fingers in a second."

"Without scissors, in the street?"

"In the square, I think. And why scissors? It was a worn-out rag, it tore at once."

"What did you do with it then?"

"I dropped it right there."

"Where, exactly?"

"In the square, in the square somewhere. Devil knows where in the square! What do you need that for?"

"It is extremely important, Dmitri Fyodorovich: material evidence in your favor, why can't you understand that? And who helped you to sew it up a month ago?"

"No one did. I sewed it myself."

"You know how to sew?"

"A soldier has to know how to sew. It didn't take any special skill."

"And where did you get the material, the rag, that is, into which you sewed it?"

"Are you joking?"

"By no means, Dmitri Fyodorovich. This is no time for joking."

"I don't remember where I got the rag, I got it somewhere."

"I should think one would remember that."

"By God, I don't remember, maybe I tore some piece of my linen."

"That is very interesting: the piece might be found tomorrow in your lodgings, perhaps a shirt with a bit torn off of it. What sort of rag was it, cotton or linen?"

"Devil knows what it was. Wait . . . I think I didn't tear it off anything. It was calico . . . I think I sewed it up in my landlady's bonnet."

"Your landlady's bonnet?"

"Yes, I filched it from her."

"What's that? Filched?"

"You see, I remember I did once filch a bonnet for a rag, or maybe to wipe a pen. I took it without asking, because it wasn't good for anything, I had the scraps lying about, and then this fifteen hundred, so I went and sewed it . . . I think I sewed it precisely in those rags. Worthless old calico, washed a thousand times."

"And you remember that firmly now?"

"I don't know how firmly. I think it was a bonnet. But to hell with it!"

"In that case your landlady might at least remember finding it missing?"

"Not at all, she never missed it. It was an old rag, I tell you, an old rag, not worth a kopeck."

"And the needle, where did you get the needle and thread?"

"I quit, I won't go on! Enough!" Mitya finally got angry.

"Then, too, it's strange that you should forget so completely just where you dropped this . . . amulet in the square."

"So, order them to sweep the square tomorrow, maybe you'll find it," Mitya smirked. "Enough, gentlemen, enough," he finished in a weary voice. "I see very well that you don't believe me! Not a word, not a bit! It's my fault, not yours, I shouldn't have stuck my neck out. Why, why did I defile myself by confessing my secret! And you think it's funny, I can see by your eyes. You drove me to it, prosecutor! Sing your hymn, if you can . . . Damn you, tormentors!"

He bent his head and covered his face with his hands. The prosecutor and the district attorney were silent. After a moment, he raised his head and looked at them somehow vacantly. His face expressed an already complete, already irreversible despair, and he, somehow gently, fell silent, sat, and seemed hardly aware of himself. Meanwhile they had to finish their business: it was urgent that they move on to the interrogation of the witnesses. It was already eight o'clock in the morning. The candles had long been extinguished. Mikhail Makarovich and Kalganov, who kept coming in and out of the room during the interrogation, now both went out. The prosecutor and the district attorney also looked extremely tired. The morning brought bad weather, the sky was all overcast and it was pouring rain. Mitya gazed vacantly at the windows.

"May I look out?" he suddenly asked Nikolai Parfenovich.

"Oh, as much as you like," the latter replied.

Mitya rose and went over to the window. Rain was lashing the small greenish windowpanes. Just under the window a muddy road could be seen, and further off, in the rainy dimness, rows of black, poor, unsightly cottages, which seemed to have turned even blacker and poorer in the rain. Mitya remembered "golden-haired Phoebus" and how he had wanted to shoot himself at his first ray. "It might be better on a morning like this," he grinned, and, suddenly, with a downward wave of his hand, turned to his "tormentors."

"Gentlemen!" he exclaimed, "I'm lost, I can see that. But she? Tell me about her, I beg you, can it be that she, too, will be lost with me? She's innocent, she was out of her mind when she shouted last night about being 'guilty of everything.' She is guilty of nothing, nothing! All this night, sitting with you, I've been grieving . . . Won't you, can't you tell me what you're going to do with her now?"

"You can be decidedly reassured in that regard, Dmitri Fyodorovich," the prosecutor replied at once, and with obvious haste. "So far we have no significant motives for troubling in any way the person in whom you are so interested. It will turn out the same, I hope, as the case develops further . . . On the contrary, for our part we shall do everything possible in that sense. Be completely reassured."

"I thank you, gentlemen. I knew you were still honest and just men, in spite of everything. You've taken a burden from my soul . . . Well, what do we do now? I'm ready."

"Now, sir, we'll have to speed things up. It's urgent that we move on to the interrogation of the witnesses. This must all take place in your presence, to be sure, and therefore . . ."

"Why don't we have some tea first?" Nikolai Parfenovich interrupted. "I think by now we deserve it."

It was decided that if there was tea ready downstairs (for Mikhail Makarovich had certainly gone "for a cup of tea"), they would have some tea and then "carry on, carry on." And they would put off real tea and "a little something" until they had a free moment. Tea was indeed found downstairs, and was quickly brought upstairs. Mitya at first refused the cup Nikolai Parfenovich kindly offered him, but then asked for it himself and greedily drank it. Generally he looked even somehow surprisingly worn out. What, one might have thought, would one night of carousing mean for a man of such strength, even coupled with the strongest sensations? Yet he himself felt that he could hardly hold himself upright, and at times everything seemed to start swimming and turning before his eyes. "A little more and I'll probably start raving," he thought to himself.

Chapter 8

The Evidence of the Witnesses. The Wee One

The interrogation of the witnesses began. But we shall not continue our story in the same detail as we have maintained up to now. And therefore we shall omit how Nikolai Parfenovich impressed upon each witness called that he should give evidence truthfully and conscientiously, and that later he would have to repeat his evidence under oath; and how, finally, each witness was required to sign the transcript of his evidence, and so on and so forth. We shall note only one thing, that the main point to which the interrogators directed all their attention was predominantly the same question of the three thousand roubles—that is, whether it had been three thousand or fifteen hundred the first time, when Dmitri Fyodorovich gave his first party there, at Mokroye, a month ago, and three thousand or fifteen hundred yesterday, when Dmitri Fyodorovich gave his second party. Alas, all the evidence from first to last turned out to be against Mitya, and none in his favor, and some of the evidence even introduced new, almost astounding facts in refutation of his evidence. The first to be interrogated was Trifon Borisich. He came before the interrogators without a trace of fear; on the contrary, with a look of stern and severe indignation at the accused, thereby undoubtedly imparting to himself an air of extreme truthfulness and self-respect. He spoke little and with reserve, waiting for each question, answering precisely and deliberately. He testified firmly and without hesitation that the amount spent a month ago could not possibly have been less than three thousand, that all the peasants there would testify to having heard about the three thousand from "Mitri Fyodorovich" himself: "Look how much he threw away on the gypsy girls alone. It must have been over a thousand just on them."

"Probably not even five hundred," Mitya observed gloomily in response, "only I wasn't counting at the time, I was drunk, more's the pity . . ."

Mitya was now sitting to one side, his back to the curtains, listening gloomily, with a sad and tired look, as if to say: "Eh, tell them whatever you like, it makes no difference now!"

"Over a thousand went to them, Mitri Fyodorovich," Trifon Borisovich countered firmly. "You were throwing it away for nothing, and they were picking it up. They're pilfering folk, cheats, horse thieves, they were driven away from here, otherwise they'd testify themselves to how much they profited from you. I saw the amount you had in your hands myself—I didn't count it, you didn't let me, that's true, but I could tell by eye, and I remember it was much more than fifteen hundred . . . Fifteen hundred, hah! I've seen money enough, I can tell . . ."

As for the amount yesterday, Trifon Borisich testified outright that Dmitri Fyodorovich himself had announced to him, as soon as he dismounted, that he had brought three thousand.

"Come now, did I say that, Trifon Borisich," Mitya objected, "did I really announce so positively that I had brought three thousand?"

"You did, Mitri Fyodorovich. You said it in front of Andrei. Andrei's still here, he hasn't gone yet, call him in. And in the main room there, when you were giving treats to the chorus, you shouted right out that you were leaving your sixth thousand here—including the ones before, that's what it means. Stepan and Semyon heard it, and Pyotr Fomich Kalganov was standing next to you then, maybe the gentleman also remembers . . ."

The evidence concerning the sixth thousand was received with remarkable impression by the interrogators. They liked the new version: three and three makes six, meaning that three thousand then and three thousand now would take care of all six, the result was clear.

All the peasants pointed out by Trifon Borisovich were interrogated, Stepan and Semyon, the coachman Andrei, and Pyotr Fomich Kalganov. The peasants and the coachman confirmed without hesitation the evidence of Trifon Borisich. Besides that, special note was taken, in his own words, of Andrei's conversation with Mitya on the way there, about "where do you think I, Dmitri Fyodorovich, will go: to heaven or hell? And will I be forgiven in that world or not?" The "psychologist" Ippolit Kirillovich listened to it all with a subtle smile, and in the end recommended that this evidence about where Dmitri Fyodorovich would go should be "filed with the case."

The summoned Kalganov came in reluctantly, sullen and peevish, and spoke with the prosecutor and Nikolai Parfenovich as if he were seeing them for the first time in his life, whereas they were long-standing and everyday acquaintances. He began by saying that he "knows nothing of it and does not want to know." But it turned out that he, too, had heard about the sixth thousand, and admitted that he had been standing nearby at that moment. In his view, Mitya had "I don't know how much money" in his hands. With regard to the Poles cheating at cards, he testified in the affirmative. He also explained in reply to repeated questions, that once the Poles were banished, Mitya's affairs with Agrafena Alexandrovna changed for the better, and that she herself had said she loved him. About Agrafena Alexandrovna he expressed himself with reserve and respect, as if she were a lady of the best society, and did not once allow himself to call her "Grushenka." Despite the repugnance the young man obviously felt at giving evidence, Ippolit Kirillovich interrogated him for a long time, and from him alone learned all the details of what constituted Mitya's "romance," so to speak, that night. Mitya did not once stop Kalganov. At last the young man was dismissed, and he withdrew with unconcealed indignation.

The Poles were interrogated as well. Though they had tried to go to sleep in their little room, they had not slept all night, and, with the arrival of the authorities, had hastened to get dressed and put themselves in order, realizing that they would certainly be sent for. They made their appearance with dignity, though not without a certain fear. The chief one—that is, the little *pan*—turned out to be a retired official of the twelfth grade,[1] had served in Siberia as a veterinarian, and his last name was Pan Mussyalovich. And Pan Vrublevsky turned out to be a free-lance dentist—in Russian, a tooth doctor. Both of them, upon entering the room, despite the questions put to them by Nikolai Parfenovich, at once began addressing their answers to Mikhail Makarovich, who was standing to one side, through ignorance taking him to be the person of highest rank and authority there, and addressing him at every word as "Panie Colonel." And only after several times, and on instructions from Mikhail Makarovich himself, did they realize that they ought to address their answers only to Nikolai Parfenovich. It turned out that they could speak Russian quite correctly, except perhaps for the pronunciation of some words. About his relations with Grushenka, past and present, Pan Mussyalovich began declaiming hotly and proudly, so that Mitya lost his temper at once and shouted that he would not allow "the scoundrel" to talk like that in his presence. Pan Mussyalovich instantly called attention to the word "scoundrel" and asked that it be put in the record. Mitya flew into a rage.

"And a scoundrel he is! A scoundrel! Put it down, and put down that in spite of the record I'm still shouting that he's a scoundrel!" he shouted.

Nikolai Parfenovich, though he did put it in the record, also displayed, on this unpleasant occasion, a most praiseworthy efficiency and administrative skill: after severely reprimanding Mitya, he at once put an end to all further inquiry into the romantic side of the case and quickly moved on to the essential. And there emerged as essential a particular piece of evidence from the *pans*, which aroused unusual curiosity in the investigators: namely, how Mitya, in that little room, had been trying to bribe Pan Mussyalovich and had offered to buy him out for three thousand, with the understanding that he would give him seven hundred roubles on the spot and the remaining twenty-three hundred "tomorrow morning, in town," swearing on his word of honor, and declaring that he did not have so much money with him there, in Mokroye, but that the money was in town. Mitya remarked, in the heat of the moment, that he had not said he would certainly pay it in town tomorrow morning, but Pan Vrublevsky confirmed the evidence, and Mitya himself, after thinking for a minute, glumly agreed that it must have been as the *pans* said, that he was excited then and might well have said it. The prosecutor simply fastened on this evidence: it was becoming clear to the investigation (as was indeed concluded afterwards) that half or a part of the three thousand that had come into Mitya's hands might indeed have been hidden somewhere in town, or perhaps even somewhere there, in Mokroye, thus clarifying the circumstance, so ticklish for the investigation, that only eight hundred roubles had been found in Mitya's possession—the one circumstance, though the only one and rather negligible at that, that so far had been some sort of evidence in Mitya's favor. But now this only evidence in his favor was breaking down. To the prosecutor's question as to where he would have found the remaining twenty-three hundred to give to the *pan* the next day, if he himself asserted that he had only fifteen hundred, though he had assured the *pan* on his word of honor, Mitya firmly replied that he intended to offer the "little Polack" not the money, but a formal deed for his rights to the Chermashnya estate, the very same rights he had offered to Samsonov and Madame Khokhlakov. The prosecutor even smiled at the "innocence of the ruse."

"And you think he would have agreed to take these 'rights' instead of twenty-three hundred roubles in cash?"

"Certainly he would have agreed," Mitya snapped hotly. "My God, he might have got not just two, but four, even six thousand out of it! He'd immediately gather his little lawyers together, little Polacks and Yids, and they'd take the old man not just for three thousand but for the whole of Chermashnya."

Naturally, the evidence of Pan Mussyalovich was entered into the record in the fullest detail. With that, the *pans* were dismissed. As for the fact of their cheating at cards, it was barely mentioned; Nikolai Parfenovich was grateful enough to them as it was, and did not want to bother them with trifles, especially since it was all just an idle, drunken quarrel over cards, and nothing more. All sorts of carousing and scandalousness had gone on that night . . . So the money, two hundred roubles, simply stayed in the Poles' pockets.

Then the little old man, Maximov, was called. He came in timidly, approached with small steps, looked disheveled and very sad. He had been downstairs all the while, huddled next to Grushenka, sitting silently with her, and "every now and then he'd start whimpering over her, wiping his eyes with a blue-checkered handkerchief," as Mikhail Makarovich reported afterwards. So that she herself had to quiet and comfort him. The old man confessed at once, and with tears, that he was sorry but he had borrowed "ten roubles, sirs, on account of my poverty, sirs," from Dmitri Fyodorovich, and that he was ready to return it . . . To the direct question of Nikolai Parfenovich, whether he had noticed exactly how much money Dmitri Fyodorovich had in his hands, since he had had a close view of the money in his hands when he was borrowing from him, Maximov answered in the most decisive manner that it was "twenty thousand, sir."

"Have you ever seen twenty thousand anywhere before?" Nikolai Parfenovich asked, smiling.

"Of course I have, sir, when my wife mortgaged my little village, only it wasn't twenty thousand, it was seven, sir. And she only let me see it from far off, she was boasting to me. It was a very big bundle, sir, all hundred-rouble bills. And Dmitri Fyodorovich, too, had all hundred-rouble bills . . ."

He was soon dismissed. Finally it came to be Grushenka's turn. The investigators were obviously apprehensive of the impression her appearance would make on Dmitri Fyodorovich, and Nikolai Parfenovich even muttered a few words of admonition to him, but Mitya silently bent his head in reply, letting him know that "there would be no disturbance." Grushenka was led in by Mikhail Makarovich himself. She entered with a stern and sullen face, looking almost calm, and quietly sat down on the chair offered her facing Nikolai Parfenovich. She was very pale, she seemed to be cold, and kept wrapping herself tightly in her beautiful black shawl. In fact, she was then beginning to have a slight feverish chill—the start of a long illness that first came over her that night. Her stern look, her direct and serious eyes and calm manner produced quite a favorable impression on everyone. Nikolai Parfenovich even got somewhat "carried away" at once. He himself admitted, talking about it afterwards in one place or another, that he had only then perceived how "good-looking" this woman was, and that before, the few times he had seen her, he had always regarded her as something of a "provincial hetaera." "She has the manners of the highest society," he once blurted out rapturously in some ladies' circle. But this was received with the utmost indignation, and he was at once dubbed "a naughty boy" for it, which pleased him no end. As she entered the room, Grushenka seemed to give only a passing glance to Mitya, who in turn looked at her anxiously, but her appearance immediately reassured him. After the first obligatory questions and admonitions, Nikolai Parfenovich, hesitating a little, but nonetheless maintaining a most courteous air, asked her: "What had been her relations with the retired lieutenant Dmitri Fyodorovich Karamazov?" To which Grushenka quietly and firmly replied:

"He was my acquaintance, I received him during the past month as an acquaintance."

To further inquisitive questions she declared directly and with complete frankness, that though she had liked him "at times," she had not been in love with him, but had been enticing him "in my vile wickedness," as well as the "old man," that she had seen how jealous Mitya was of Fyodor Pavlovich and of everyone, but it only amused her. And she had never meant to go to Fyodor Pavlovich, but was just laughing at him. "All that month I couldn't be bothered with either of them; I was expecting another man, one who was guilty before me . . . But I think," she concluded, "that there is no need for you to ask about that, or for me to answer you, because that is my particular business."

And Nikolai Parfenovich immediately did just that: once again he stopped insisting on "romantic" points, and moved directly on to the serious one—that is, to the same and chief question concerning the three thousand. Grushenka confirmed that three thousand roubles had indeed been spent in Mokroye a month before, and that though she had not counted the money herself, she had heard from Dmitri Fyodorovich that it was three thousand roubles.

"Did he say it to you privately, or in someone else's presence, or did you only hear him say it to others around you?" the prosecutor inquired at once.

To which Grushenka replied that she had heard it in other people's presence, had heard him say it to others, and had also heard it privately from Mitya himself.

"Did he say it to you once or many times in private?" the prosecutor inquired again, and learned that Grushenka had heard it many times.

Ippolit Kirillovich was very pleased with this evidence. Further questioning revealed that Grushenka knew where the money had come from and that Dmitri Fyodorovich had taken it from Katerina Ivanovna.

"And did you ever once hear that the money squandered a month ago was not three thousand but less, and that Dmitri Fyodorovich had kept fully half of it for himself?"

"No, I never heard that," Grushenka testified.

It was further discovered that Mitya, on the contrary, had often told her during that month that he did not have a kopeck. "He kept waiting for what he would get from his father," Grushenka concluded.

"And did he ever say before you . . . somehow in passing, or in irritation," Nikolai Parfenovich suddenly struck, "that he intended to make an attempt on his father's life?"

"Ah, yes, he did!" sighed Grushenka.

"Once or several times?"

"He mentioned it several times, always in a fit of anger."

"And did you believe he would go through with it?"

"No, I never believed it!" she replied firmly. "I trusted in his nobility."

"Gentlemen, allow me," Mitya suddenly cried, "allow me to say just one word to Agrafena Alexandrovna in your presence."

"Say it," Nikolai Parfenovich consented.

"Agrafena Alexandrovna," Mitya rose a little from his chair, "believe God and me: I am not guilty of the blood of my father who was killed last night!"

Having said this, Mitya again sat down on his chair. Grushenka rose a little, looked towards the icon, and piously crossed herself.

"Glory be to God!" she said in an ardent, emotional voice, and turning to Nikolai Parfenovich before sitting down, she added: "What he has just said you must believe! I know him: when he babbles, he babbles, whether it's for fun or out of stubbornness, but if it's something against his conscience, he will never deceive you. He will speak the truth directly, you must believe that!"

"Thank you, Agrafena Alexandrovna, you have given my soul new courage!" Mitya responded in a trembling voice.

To the questions about yesterday's money she replied that she did not know how much there was, but had heard him say to many people yesterday that he had brought three thousand with him. And with regard to where he had got the money, he had told her privately that he had "stolen" it from Katerina Ivanovna, to which she had replied that he had not stolen it and that the money must be given back tomorrow. To the prosecutor's insistent question as to which money he said he had stolen from Katerina Ivanovna—yesterday's, or the three thousand spent there a month ago—she stated that he was speaking of the money from a month ago, that that was how she had understood him.

Grushenka was finally dismissed, Nikolai Parfenovich impetuously announcing to her that she could even return to town at once, and that if he, for his part, could be of any assistance to her, for example, in connection with the horses, or if, for example, she wished to be accompanied, then he . . . for his part . . .

"I humbly thank you," Grushenka bowed to him, "I'll go with that little old man, the landowner, I'll take him back with me, but meanwhile I'll wait downstairs, with your permission, until you decide here about Dmitri Fyodorovich."

She went out. Mitya was calm and even looked quite encouraged, but only for a moment. Some strange physical powerlessness was gradually overwhelming him. His eyes kept closing with fatigue. The interrogation of the witnesses finally came to an end. They moved on to the final editing of the transcript. Mitya got up, went from his chair to the corner, near the curtain, lay down on a large chest covered with a rug, and was asleep in a second. He had a strange sort of dream, somehow entirely out of place and out of time. It seemed he was driving somewhere in the steppe, in a place where he had served once long ago; he is being driven through the slush by a peasant, in a cart with a pair of horses. And it seems to Mitya that he is cold, it is the beginning of November, and snow is pouring down in big, wet flakes that melt as soon as they touch the ground. And the peasant is driving briskly, waving his whip nicely, he has a long, fair beard, and he is not an old man, maybe around fifty, dressed in a gray peasant coat. And there is a village nearby—black, black huts, and half of the huts are burnt, just charred beams sticking up. And at the edge of the village there are peasant women standing along the road, many women, a long line of them, all of them thin, wasted, their faces a sort of brown color. Especially that one at the end—such a bony one, tall, looking as if she were forty, but she may be only twenty, with a long, thin face, and in her arms a baby is crying, and her breasts must be all dried up, not a drop of milk in them. And the baby is crying, crying, reaching out its bare little arms, its little fists somehow all blue from the cold.

"Why are they crying? Why are they crying?" Mitya asks, flying past them at a great clip.

"The wee one," the driver answers, "it's the wee one crying." And Mitya is struck that he has said it in his own peasant way: "the wee one," and not "the baby." And he likes it that the peasant has said "wee one": there seems to be more pity in it.

"But why is it crying?" Mitya insists, as if he were foolish, "why are its little arms bare, why don't they wrap it up?"

"The wee one's cold, its clothes are frozen, they don't keep it warm."

"But why is it so? Why?" foolish Mitya will not leave off.

"They're poor, burnt out, they've got no bread, they're begging for their burnt-down place."

"No, no," Mitya still seems not to understand, "tell me: why are these burnt-out mothers standing here, why are the people poor, why is the wee one poor, why is the steppe bare, why don't they embrace and kiss, why don't they sing joyful songs, why are they blackened with such black misery, why don't they feed the wee one?"

And he feels within himself that, though his questions have no reason or sense, he still certainly wants to ask in just that way, and he should ask in just that way. And he also feels a tenderness such as he has never known before surging up in his heart, he wants to weep, he wants to do something for them all, so that the wee one will no longer cry, so that the blackened, dried-up mother of the wee one will not cry either, so that there will be no more tears in anyone from that moment on, and it must be done at once, at once, without delay and despite everything, with all his Karamazov unrestraint.

"And I am with you, too, I won't leave you now, I will go with you for the rest of my life," the dear, deeply felt words of Grushenka came from somewhere near him. And his whole heart blazed up and turned towards some sort of light, and he wanted to live and live, to go on and on along some path, towards the new, beckoning light, and to hurry, hurry, right now, at once!

"What? Where?" he exclaims, opening his eyes and sitting up on the chest, as if he were just coming out of a faint, and smiling brightly. Over him stands Nikolai Parfenovich, inviting him to listen to the transcript and sign it. Mitya guessed that he had slept for an hour or more, but he did not listen to Nikolai Parfenovich. It suddenly struck him that there was a pillow under his head, which, however, had not been there when he had sunk down powerlessly on the chest.

"Who put that pillow under my head? What good person did it?" he exclaimed with a sort of rapturous gratitude, in a sort of tear-filled voice, as though God knows what kindness had been shown him. The good man remained unidentified even later—perhaps one of the witnesses, or even Nikolai Parfenovich's clerk, had arranged that a pillow be put under his head, out of compassion—but his whole soul was as if shaken with tears. He went up to the table and declared that he would sign whatever they wanted.

"I had a good dream, gentlemen," he said somehow strangely, with a sort of new face, as if lit up with joy.

Chapter 9

Mitya Is Taken Away

When the transcript had been signed, Nikolai Parfenovich solemnly addressed the accused and read to him a "Resolution," setting forth that on such and such a day, of such and such a year, in such and such a place, having interrogated so and so (that is, Mitya), accused of such and such (all the charges were carefully enumerated), and insofar as the accused, while declaring himself not guilty of any of the crimes imputed to him, has brought forth nothing to vindicate himself, whereas the witnesses (so and so) and the circumstances (such and such) show him to be guilty in the highest degree, the district attorney of such and such district court, in accordance with such and such paragraphs of the *Criminal Code*, etc., hereby resolves: to commit so and so (Mitya) to such and such prison, in order to deprive him of all means of evading investigation and trial; to inform the accused of this fact; to forward a copy of this resolution to the deputy prosecutor, etc., etc. In short, Mitya was informed that from that moment on he was a prisoner, and that he would now be driven to town, where he would be locked up in a very unpleasant place. Mitya, having listened attentively, merely shrugged.

"Well, gentlemen, I don't blame you, I'm ready . . . I understand that you have no other choice."

Nikolai Parfenovich gently explained to him that he would be taken away at once by the deputy commissioner, Mavriky Mavrikievich, who happened to be there at the moment . . .

"Wait," Mitya interrupted suddenly, and with some irrepressible feeling he spoke, addressing everyone in the room. "Gentlemen, we are all cruel, we are all monsters, we all make people weep, mothers and nursing babies, but of all—let it be settled here and now—of all, I am the lowest vermin! So be it! Every day of my life I've been beating my breast and promising to reform, and every day I've done the same vile things. I understand now that for men such as I a blow is needed, a blow of fate, to catch them as with a noose and bind them by an external force. Never, never would I have risen by myself! But the thunder has struck.[1] I accept the torment of accusation and of my disgrace before all, I want to suffer and be purified by suffering! And perhaps I will be purified, eh, gentlemen? But hear me, all the same, for the last time: I am not guilty of my father's blood! I accept punishment not because I killed him, but because I wanted to kill him, and might well have killed him . . . But even so I intend to fight you, and I am letting you know it. I will fight you to the very end, and then let God decide! Farewell, gentlemen, do not be angry that I shouted at you during the interrogation—oh, I was still so foolish then . . . Another moment and I'll be a prisoner, but now, for the last time, while he is still a free man, Dmitri Karamazov offers you his hand. Saying farewell to you, I say it to all men . . . !"

His voice trembled and he did, indeed, offer his hand, but Nikolai Parfenovich, who was nearest to him, somehow suddenly, with an almost convulsive sort of movement, hid his hands behind him. Mitya noticed it at once and was startled. He immediately let fall his proffered hand.

"The investigation is not over yet," Nikolai Parfenovich muttered, somewhat embarrassed. "We shall continue it in town, and I, of course, for my part, am prepared to wish you all luck . . . in your acquittal . . . And you personally, Dmitri Fyodorovich, I have always been inclined to regard as a man, so to speak, more unfortunate than guilty . . . All of us here, if I may be so bold as to express myself on behalf of all, all of us are prepared to recognize you as a young man who is noble in principle, though one, alas, carried away by certain passions to a somewhat inordinate degree . . ."

Nikolai Parfenovich's little figure became, towards the end of his speech, a most perfect embodiment of stateliness. It flashed through Mitya's mind that this "boy" was now going to take him by the arm, lead him to the other corner, and start up their recent conversation about "girls" again. But all sorts of extraneous and unrelated thoughts sometimes flash even through the mind of a criminal who is being led out to execution.

"Gentlemen, you are kind, you are humane—may I see *her*, to say farewell for the last time?" asked Mitya.

"Certainly, but in view . . . in short, it is impossible now except in the presence . . ."

"Please do be present!"

Grushenka was brought in, but the farewell was brief, just a few words, hardly satisfying to Nikolai Parfenovich. Grushenka made a low bow to Mitya.

"I've told you that I am yours, and I will be yours, I will go with you forever, wherever they doom you to go. Farewell, guiltless man, who have been your own ruin."

Her lips trembled, tears flowed from her eyes.

"Forgive me, Grusha, for my love, that I've ruined you, too, with my love!"

Mitya wanted to say something more, but suddenly stopped himself short and walked out. He was immediately surrounded by people who kept a close eye on him. At the foot of the porch, where he had driven up with such a clatter in Andrei's troika the day before, two carts already stood waiting. Mavriky Mavrikievich, a squat, thickset man with a flabby face, was annoyed with something, some sudden new disorder, and was shouting angrily. He invited Mitya somehow too sternly to get into the cart. "He had quite a different face before, when I used to stand him drinks in the tavern," Mitya thought as he was getting in. Trifon Borisovich also came down from the porch. People, peasants, women, coachmen crowded at the gates; everyone stared at Mitya.

"Farewell and forgive, God's people!" Mitya suddenly cried to them from the cart.

"And you forgive us," two or three voices were heard.

"You, too, Trifon Borisich, farewell and forgive!"

But Trifon Borisich did not even turn his head, perhaps he was too busy. He, too, was bustling about and shouting for some reason. It turned out that things were not quite in order yet with the second cart, in which two deputies were to accompany Mavriky Mavrikievich. The little peasant who had been hired to drive the second troika was pulling on his coat and stoutly protesting that it was not him but Akim who had to drive. But Akim was not there; they ran to get him; the little peasant insisted and begged them to wait.

"Look what kind of people we've got, Mavriky Mavrikievich, no shame at all!" Trifon Borisich exclaimed. "Akim gave you twenty-five kopecks the day before yesterday, you spent it on drink, and now you're shouting. I'm really surprised you're so good-natured with our base peasants, Mavriky Mavrikievich, I can tell you that!"

"But what do we need a second troika for?" Mitya intervened. "Let's go in one, Mavriky Mavrikievich, I assure you I won't make trouble, I won't run away from you, old fellow—why the escort?"

"Kindly learn how to address me, sir, if you don't know already; I'm not your 'old fellow,' kindly do not be so familiar, and save your advice for some other time . . . ," Mavriky Mavrikievich snapped fiercely at Mitya all of a sudden, as if glad to vent his heart.

Mitya said no more. He blushed all over. A moment later he suddenly felt very cold. It had stopped raining, but the dull sky was still overcast, and a sharp wind was blowing straight in his face. "Have I caught a chill or something?" Mitya thought, twitching his shoulders. At last Mavriky Mavrikievich also got into the cart, sat down heavily, broadly, and, as if without noticing it, gave Mitya a strong shove with his body. True, he was out of sorts and intensely disliked the task entrusted to him.

"Farewell, Trifon Borisich!" Mitya called out again, and felt himself that this time he had called out not from good-naturedness but from spite, against his will. But Trifon Borisich stood proudly, both hands behind his back, staring straight at Mitya with a stern and angry look, and made no reply.

"Farewell, Dmitri Fyodorovich, farewell!" the voice of Kalganov, who popped up from somewhere, was suddenly heard. Running over to the cart, he offered his hand to Mitya. He had no cap on. Mitya just managed to seize and shake his hand.

"Farewell, you dear man, I won't forget this magnanimity!" he exclaimed ardently. But the cart started, and their hands were parted. The bell jingled—Mitya was taken away.

Kalganov ran back into the front hall, sat down in a corner, bent his head, covered his face with his hands, and began to cry. He sat like that and cried for a long time—cried as though he were still a little boy and not a man of twenty.

Oh, he believed almost completely in Mitya's guilt! "What are these people what sort of people can there be after this!" he kept exclaiming incoherently in bitter dejection, almost in despair. At that moment he did not even want to live in the world. "Is it worth it, is it worth it!" the grieved young man kept exclaiming.

PART IV

BOOK X: BOYS

Chapter 1

Kolya Krasotkin

The beginning of November. We had eleven degrees of frost, and with that came sheet ice. During the night a bit of dry snow had fallen on the frozen ground, and the wind, "dry and sharp,"[1] lifted it up and blew it over the dreary streets of our little town and especially over the marketplace. The morning was dull, but it had stopped snowing. Near the marketplace, close to Plotnikov's shop, stood a small house, very clean both inside and out, belonging to the widow of the official Krasotkin. Provincial secretary Krasotkin had died long ago, almost fourteen years before, but his widow, thirty years old and still a comely little lady, was alive and lived "on her own means" in her clean little house. She lived honestly and timidly, was of tender but quite cheerful character. She had lost her husband when she was eighteen, after living with him only for about a year and having just borne him a son. Since then, since the very day of his death, she had devoted herself entirely to the upbringing of her treasure, her boy Kolya, and though she had loved him to distraction all those fourteen years, she had of course endured incomparably more suffering than joy on account of him, trembling and dying of fear almost every day lest he become ill, catch cold, be naughty, climb on a chair and fall off, and so on and so forth. When Kolya started going to school and then to our high school, his mother threw herself into studying all the subjects with him, in order to help him and tutor him in his lessons, threw herself into acquaintances with his teachers and their wives, was sweet even to Kolya's schoolboy friends, fawning on them so that they would not touch Kolya, would not laugh at him or beat him. She went so far that the boys indeed began laughing at him because of her and began teasing him for being a mama's boy. But the lad knew how to stand up for himself. He was a brave boy, "terrifically strong," according to the rumor spread about him and quickly established in his class; agile, persistent in character, bold and enterprising in spirit. He was a good student, and there was even a rumor that in both mathematics and world history he could show up the teacher, Dardanelov, himself. Yet, though he looked down on everyone and turned up his nose at them, the boy was still a good friend and not overly conceited. He accepted the schoolboys' respect as his due, but behaved in a comradely way. Above all, he knew where to draw the line, could restrain himself when need be, and in relation to the authorities never overstepped that final and inscrutable limit beyond which a misdeed turns into disorder, rebellion, and lawlessness, and can no longer be tolerated. Yet he never minded getting into mischief at the first opportunity, any more than the worst boy, not so much for the sake of mischief as to do something whimsical, eccentric, to add some "extra spice," to dazzle, to show off. Above all, he was extremely vain. He even managed to make his mama submit to him and treated her almost despotically. And she submitted, oh, she had submitted long ago, and the only thing she simply could not bear was the thought that the boy "had little love for her." She imagined all the time that Kolya was "unfeeling" towards her, and there were occasions when, flooding herself with hysterical tears, she would begin to reproach him with his coldness. The boy did not like it, and the more heartfelt effusions she demanded of him, the more unyielding he became, as if deliberately. Yet it was not deliberate on his part, but involuntary—such was his nature. His mother was mistaken: he loved her very much, only he did not like "sentimental slop," as he said in his schoolboy's language. His father had left behind a bookcase in which a few books were kept; Kolya loved reading and had already read several of them on his own. His mother was not troubled by that, and only marveled sometimes at how the boy, instead of going out to play, would spend hours standing by the bookcase poring over some book. And it was thus that Kolya had read certain things that he should not have been given to read at his age. Of late, in any case, though the boy did not like to overstep a certain line in his pranks, there began to be some pranks that genuinely frightened his mother—not immoral ones, true, but desperate, daredevilish. Just that summer, in July, during the holidays, it so happened that the mama and her boy had gone to spend a week in another district, forty-five miles away, with a distant relative whose husband worked at a railway station (the same station, the one closest to our town, from which Ivan Fyodorovich Karamazov left for Moscow a month later). There Kolya began by looking over the railroad in detail, studying the procedures, realizing that he would be able to show off his new knowledge among the boys in his school. But just then a few other boys turned up with whom he made friends; some of them lived at the station, others in the neighborhood—about six or seven youths altogether, between twelve and fifteen years old, and two of them happened to be from our town. The boys played together, pulled pranks together, until on the fourth or fifth day of the visit at the station the foolish youngsters made up a most impossible wager, for two roubles—that is: Kolya, who was almost the youngest of all and was therefore somewhat despised by the older boys, out of vanity or reckless bravado, offered to lie face down between the rails that night when the eleven o'clock train came, and to lie there without moving while the train passed over him at full steam. It is true that a preliminary examination had been carried out, which showed that it was indeed possible to stretch out and flatten oneself down between the rails, so that the train, of course, would pass over without touching the person lying there, but still, how would it feel to lie there! Kolya firmly maintained that he would do it. At first they laughed at him, called him a liar, a braggart, but that only egged him on even more. Above all, those fifteen-year-olds turned up their noses too much, and did not even want to be friends with him at first, but regarded him as "a little boy," which was insufferably offensive. And so it was decided to go that evening to a spot about half a mile from the station, so that the train would have time to get up full speed after pulling out of the station. The boys met together. It was a moonless night, not just dark but almost pitch black. When the time came, Kolya lay down between the rails. The other five boys who were in on the wager waited with sinking hearts, and finally with fear and remorse, below the embankment, in the bushes near the road. At last there came the chugging of the train pulling out of the station. Two red lights flashed through the darkness, they heard the thunder of the approaching monster. "Run, run away from the rails!" the boys, dying with terror, shouted to Kolya from the bushes, but it was too late: the train loomed up and flew by. The boys rushed to Kolya: he lay without moving. They began pulling at him, lifting him up. Suddenly he rose and went silently down the embankment. When he got down he announced that he had pretended to be unconscious on purpose to frighten them, but the truth was that he had indeed fainted, as he himself later confessed long afterwards to his mama. Thus his reputation as a "desperado" was finally established forever. He returned home to the station white as a sheet. The next day he fell slightly ill with a nervous fever, but was in terribly joyful spirits, pleased and delighted. The incident became known in our town, though not at once, penetrated the high school, and reached the authorities. But at this point Kolya's mama rushed to plead with the authorities on her boy's behalf, and in the end got Dardanelov, a respected and influential teacher, to stand up and speak for him, and the case was set aside, as if it had never happened. This Dardanelov, a bachelor and not yet an old man, had for many years been passionately in love with Mrs. Krasotkin, and once already, about a year before, had ventured, most reverently, and sinking with fear and delicacy, to offer her his hand; but she flatly refused him, considering that acceptance would be a betrayal of her boy, though Dardanelov, from certain mysterious signs, even had, perhaps, some right to dream that he was not altogether repugnant to the lovely, but too chaste and sensitive, widow. Kolya's mad prank seemed to have broken the ice, and Dardanelov, in return for his intercession, received a hint with regard to his hopes, though a very remote one; but Dardanelov himself was a miracle of purity and sensitivity, and therefore it sufficed at the time for the fullness of his happiness. He loved the boy, though he would have considered it humiliating to seek his favor, and in class he treated him sternly and demandingly. But Kolya also kept him at a respectful distance, prepared his lessons excellently, was second in his class, addressed Dardanelov drily, and the whole class firmly believed that Kolya was so strong in world history that he could even "show up" Dardanelov himself. And indeed Kolya had once asked him the question "Who founded Troy?"—to which Dardanelov gave only a general answer about peoples, their movements and migrations, about the remoteness of the times, about fable telling, but who precisely had founded Troy—that is, precisely which persons—he could not say, and even found the question for some reason an idle and groundless one. But this only left the boys convinced that Dardanelov did not know who had founded Troy. As for Kolya, he had learned about the founders of Troy in Smaragdov,[2] whose history was in the bookcase left by his father. The upshot of it was that all the boys became interested finally in who precisely had founded Troy, but Krasotkin would not give away his secret, and the glory of his knowledge remained unshakably his own.

After the incident on the railway, a certain change took place in Kolya's relations with his mother. When Anna Fyodorovna (Krasotkin's widow) learned of her boy's deed, she almost went out of her mind with horror. She had such terrible hysterical fits, which continued intermittently for several days, that Kolya, now seriously frightened, gave her his solemn word of honor that such pranks would never be repeated. He swore on his knees before an icon and he swore by his father's memory, as Mrs. Krasotkin demanded, and the "manly" Kolya himself burst into tears like a six-year-old boy, from "feelings," and all that day both mother and son kept falling into each other's arms, sobbing and shaking. The next day Kolya woke up as "unfeeling" as ever, yet he grew more silent, more modest, more stern, more thoughtful. True, about a month and a half later, he was again caught in a prank, and his name even became known to our justice of the peace, but this was a prank of a very different sort, even a silly and funny one, and it turned out that he had not perpetrated it himself, but just happened to be mixed up in it. But of that another time. His mother went on trembling and suffering, and Dardanelov's hopes increased more and more in measure with her anxiety. It should be noted that Kolya understood and figured out this side of Dardanelov, and, naturally, deeply despised him for his "feelings"; previously he had even been tactless enough to display his contempt before his mother, remotely hinting to her that he understood what Dardanelov was up to. But after the incident on the railway, he changed his behavior in this respect as well: he allowed himself no more hints, not even the remotest, and began to speak more respectfully of Dardanelov in his mother's presence, which the sensitive Anna Fyodorovna understood at once with boundless gratitude in her heart, but at the same time, the slightest, most inadvertent mention of Dardanelov, even from some unaccustomed guest, if it was in Kolya's presence, would make her blush all over with embarrassment, like a rose. And at such moments Kolya would either look frowning out the window, or study his face in the tips of his boots, or shout fiercely for Perezvon, a rather big, shaggy, and mangy dog he had acquired somewhere about a month before, dragged home, and for some reason kept secretly indoors, not showing him to any of his friends. He tyrannized over him terribly, teaching him all sorts of tricks and skills, and drove the poor dog so far that he howled in his absence, when he was away at school, and when he came home, squealed with delight, jumped madly, stood on his hind legs, fell down and played dead, and so on; in short, he did all the tricks he had been taught, not on command, but solely from the ardor of his rapturous feelings and grateful heart.

Incidentally, I have forgotten even to mention that Kolya Krasotkin was the same one whom the boy Ilyusha, already known to the reader, son of the retired captain Snegiryov, stabbed in the thigh with a penknife, defending his father, whom the schoolboys taunted with "whiskbroom."

Chapter 2

Kids

And so on that cold and wintry November morning, the boy Kolya Krasotkin was sitting at home. It was Sunday, and there was no school. But the clock had just struck eleven and he absolutely had to go out "on very important business," and yet there he was, left alone in the whole house and decidedly in charge of it, because it so happened that all of its elder inhabitants were away, owing to some urgent and singular circumstance. There was only one other apartment in the widow Krasotkin's house, two little rooms across the hall from the widow's apartment, which she rented out, and which were occupied by a doctor's wife with two small children. This doctor's wife was the same age as Anna Fyodorovna, and a great friend of hers, while the doctor himself had gone off somewhere about a year before, first to Orenburg, then to Tashkent, and nothing had been heard of him for the past six months, so that had it not been for the friendship of Mrs. Krasotkin, which somewhat softened the grief of the doctor's abandoned wife, she would decidedly have drowned herself in the tears of that grief. And now it so happened, as if to crown all the adversities of fate, that Katerina, the doctor's wife's only maid, suddenly, and quite unexpectedly for her mistress, announced to her that very night, on Saturday, that she intended to give birth to a baby the next morning. How it happened that no one had noticed it before struck everyone as almost miraculous. The amazed doctor's wife judged it best, while there was still time, to take Katerina to an establishment kept by a midwife in our town, suitable for such occasions. Since she highly valued her maid, she put her plan into action at once, took her there, and moreover stayed there with her. Later, in the morning, for some reason there was need for all the friendly participation and help of Mrs. Krasotkin herself, who on such an occasion could ask someone for something and wield a certain influence. Thus both ladies were absent, and as for Mrs. Krasotkin's own maid, Agafya, she had gone to the market, and thus Kolya found himself for a time the keeper and guardian of the "squirts"—that is, the doctor's wife's little boy and girl, who were left all alone. Kolya was not afraid of guarding the house; besides he had Perezvon, who was ordered to lie down and "stay" under the bench in the front hall, and, precisely for that reason, every time Kolya, who kept pacing the rooms, came out to the hall, he shook his head and gave two firm and ingratiating thumps on the floor with his tail, but, alas, the summoning whistle did not come. Kolya would give the miserable dog a severe look, and again the dog would obediently freeze. But if anything troubled Kolya, it was the "squirts." He naturally looked with the deepest contempt upon the unexpected adventure with Katerina, but the orphaned squirts he loved very much, and he had already brought them some children's book. The older of the two, the girl Nastya, was eight and knew how to read, and the younger squirt, the seven-year-old boy, Kostya, liked it very much when Nastya read to him. Naturally, Krasotkin knew more interesting ways of entertaining them—for instance, by standing them side by side and playing soldiers, or hiding all over the house. He had done it more than once before and did not consider it beneath him, so that the rumor had even spread in his class that Krasotkin played "horses" at home with his little tenants, prancing and tossing his head like an outrunner, but Krasotkin proudly parried the accusation, putting forward the argument that "in our day" it would indeed be disgraceful to play "horses" with one's peers, with thirteen-year-olds, but that he did so with the "squirts" because he loved them, and no one should dare call him to account for his feelings. And how the two "squirts" adored him! But this was no time for games. He was faced with some very important business of his own, which somehow even appeared almost mysterious, and meanwhile time was passing, and Agafya, with whom he could have left the children, still refused to come back from the market. He had already gone across the hall several times, opened the door to the other apartment, and looked in anxiously at the "squirts," who, on his orders, were sitting there with a book, and, each time he opened the door, gave him big, silent smiles, expecting him to come in and do something wonderful and amusing. But Kolya was troubled in his soul and would not go in. Finally it struck eleven and he decided firmly and ultimately that if in ten minutes that "cursed" Agafya had not come back, he would leave without waiting for her, of course making the "squirts" give their word that they would not be scared without him, would not get into mischief, and would not cry from fear. With that thought in mind, he put on his padded winter coat with some kind of sealskin collar, slung his bag over his shoulder, and, despite his mother's oft-repeated pleadings that he not go out "in such cold" without his galoshes, merely glanced at them in disdain, passing through the hall, and went out in just his boots. Perezvon, as soon as he saw him with his coat on, began thumping the floor still harder with his tail, nervously twitching all over, and even uttered a pitiful howl, but Kolya, seeing such passionate yearning in his dog, decided it was bad discipline, and kept him longer, though just a moment longer, under the bench, and only as he was opening the door to the hall did he suddenly whistle for him. The dog jumped up madly and began leaping ecstatically in front of him. Kolya crossed the hall and opened the "squirts'" door. They were both still sitting at the table, not reading now, but arguing heatedly about something. The children often argued with each other about various provocative matters of life, and Nastya, being older, always had the upper hand; and Kostya, if he did not agree with her, almost always went to appeal to Kolya Krasotkin, and whatever he decided remained the ultimate verdict for all sides. This time the argument between the "squirts" somewhat interested Krasotkin, and he stopped in the doorway to listen. The children saw he was listening and carried on their dispute with even greater enthusiasm.

"I'll never, ever believe," Nastya ardently prattled, "that midwives find little babies in the vegetable garden, between the cabbage rows. It's winter now and there aren't any cabbage rows, and the midwife couldn't have brought Katerina a baby girl."

"Whe-ew!" Kolya whistled to himself.

"Or maybe it's like this: they do bring them from somewhere, but only when people get married."

Kostya stared at Nastya, listened gravely, and pondered.

"Nastya, what a fool you are," he said at last, firmly and without excitement. "Where could Katerina get a baby if she's not married?"

Nastya grew terribly excited.

"You don't understand anything," she cut him short irritably. "Maybe she had a husband, but he's in prison now, so she went and had a baby."

"But is her husband in prison?" the staid Kostya inquired gravely.

"Or else," Nastya swiftly interrupted, completely abandoning and forgetting her first hypothesis, "she hasn't got a husband, you're right about that, but she wants to get married, so she started thinking how to get married, and she kept thinking and thinking, and she thought so much that now she got a baby instead."

"Well, maybe," agreed the utterly defeated Kostya, "but you didn't say that before, so how could I know?"

"Well, kids," said Kolya, taking a step into the room, "you're dangerous people, I see!"

"And Perezvon, too?" Kostya grinned, and began snapping his fingers and calling Perezvon.

"I'm in trouble, squirts," Krasotkin began importantly, "and you've got to help me: of course Agafya must have broken her leg, since she's not back yet, that's signed and sealed, but I have to leave. Will you let me go or not?"

The children worriedly exchanged looks, their grinning faces showed signs of anxiety. However, they still did not quite understand what was wanted of them.

"You won't get into mischief while I'm gone? You won't climb on the cupboard and break your leg? You won't cry from fear if you're left alone?"

Terrible grief showed on the children's faces.

"And to make up for it I'll show you a little something—it's a little brass cannon that shoots with real powder."

The children's faces brightened at once.

"Show us the little cannon," Kostya said, beaming all over.

Krasotkin thrust his hand into his bag, pulled out a little bronze cannon, and placed it on the table.

"'Show us, show us!' Look, it has little wheels," he drove the toy along the table, "and it can shoot. Load it with small shot and it shoots."

"And can it kill somebody?"

"It can kill everybody, you just have to aim it," and Krasotkin explained how to put in the powder and roll in the shot, showed the little hole for the primer, and explained to them that there was such a thing as recoil. The children listened with terrible curiosity. What particularly struck their imagination was that there was such a thing as recoil.

"And have you got some powder?" Nastya inquired.

"I have."

"Show us the powder, too," she whined with an imploring smile.

Krasotkin again went into his bag, and took out of it a small bottle, which indeed contained some real powder, and a folded paper, which turned out to have a few pellets of shot in it. He even opened the bottle and poured a little powder out in his palm.

"So long as there's no fire around, or it would explode and kill us all," Krasotkin warned, for the sake of effect.

The children gazed at the powder with an awestruck fear, which only increased their pleasure. But Kostya liked the shot better.

"Does shot burn?" he inquired.

"Shot does not burn."

"Give me some shot," he said in a pleading voice.

"I'll give you a little, here, take it, only don't show it to your mother before I come back, or she may think it's powder, and she'll die of fear and give you a whipping."

"Mama never beats us," Nastya observed at once.

"I know, I just said it for the beauty of the style. And you should never deceive your mama, except this once—till I come back. Well, squirts, can I go or not? Are you going to cry from fear without me?"

"We w-will c-cry," Kostya whined, already preparing to cry.

"We will, we really will cry!" Nastya added in a frightened patter.

"Oh, children, children, how perilous are your years.[1] So, there's nothing to be done, chicks, I'll have to stay with you I don't know how long. And the time, the time, oof!"

"Tell Perezvon to play dead," Kostya asked.

"Well, nothing to be done, I'll have to resort to Perezvon. *Ici*, Perezvon!" And Kolya began giving orders to the dog, and he began doing all his tricks. He was a shaggy dog, the size of any ordinary mongrel, with a sort of blue gray coat. He was blind in his right eye, and his left ear for some reason had a nick in it. He squealed and jumped, stood and walked on his hind legs, threw himself on his back with all four legs in the air and lay motionless as if dead. During this last trick the door opened and Agafya, Mrs. Krasotkin's fat maid, a pockmarked woman of about forty, appeared on the threshold, returning from the market with a paper bag full of groceries in her hand. She stood with the bag perched on her left hand and began watching the dog. Kolya, however eagerly he had been waiting for Agafya, did not interrupt the performance, and having kept Perezvon dead for a certain length of time, finally whistled: the dog jumped up and began leaping for joy at having fulfilled his duty.

"Some dog that is!" Agafya said didactically.

"Why are you late, female sex?" Krasotkin asked sternly.

"Female sex yourself, pipsqueak."

"Pipsqueak?"

"Yes, pipsqueak. What's it to you if I'm late? If I'm late I must have had good reason," Agafya muttered, as she started bustling about the stove, not at all in a displeased or angry voice, but, on the contrary, sounding very pleased, as if she were glad of the chance to exchange quips with her cheerful young master.

"Listen, you frivolous old woman," Krasotkin began, rising from the sofa, "will you swear to me by all that's holy in this world, and something else besides, that you will keep a constant eye on the squirts in my absence? I'm going out."

"Why should I go swearing to you?" Agafya laughed. "I'll look after them anyway."

"No, not unless you swear by the eternal salvation of your soul. Otherwise I won't go."

"Don't go, then. I don't care. It's freezing out; stay home."

"Squirts," Kolya turned to the children, "this woman will stay with you till I come back, or till your mama comes, because she, too, should have been back long ago. And furthermore she will give you lunch. Will you fix them something, Agafya?"

"Could be."

"Good-bye, chicks, I'm going with an easy heart. And you, granny," he said, imposingly and in a low voice, as he passed by Agafya, "spare their young years, don't go telling them all your old wives' nonsense about Katerina. *Ici*, Perezvon!"

"And you know where you can go!" Agafya snarled, this time in earnest. "Funny boy! Ought to be whipped yourself for such talk, that's what."

Chapter 3

A Schoolboy

But Kolya was no longer listening. At last he was able to leave. He walked out the gate, looked around, hunched his shoulders, and having said "Freezing!" set off straight down the street and then turned right down a lane to the market square. When he reached the next to the last house before the square, he stopped at the gate, pulled a whistle out of his pocket, and whistled with all his might, as if giving a prearranged signal. He did not have to wait more than a minute—a ruddy-cheeked boy of about eleven years old suddenly ran out to him through the gate, also wearing a warm, clean, and even stylish coat. This was the Smurov boy, who was in the preparatory class (whereas Kolya Krasotkin was two years ahead), the son of a well-to-do official, whose parents evidently would not allow him to go around with Krasotkin, a notoriously desperate prankster, so that this time Smurov obviously had escaped on the sly. This Smurov, if the reader has not forgotten, was one of the group of boys who were throwing stones at Ilyusha across the ditch two months before, and had told Alyosha Karamazov then about Ilyusha.

"I've been waiting a whole hour for you, Krasotkin," Smurov said with a determined look, and the boys strode off towards the square.

"I'm late," Krasotkin replied. "Circumstances arose. They won't whip you for being with me?"

"Lord, no, they never whip me! So you've brought Perezvon?"

"Perezvon, too!"

"He's going there, too?"

"He's going, too."

"Ah, if only it was Zhuchka!"

"Impossible. Zhuchka does not exist. Zhuchka has vanished in the darkness of the unknown."

"Ah, couldn't we do it?" Smurov suddenly stopped for a moment. "Ilyusha did say that Zhuchka was shaggy, and gray and smoky, just like Perezvon—couldn't we tell him it's really Zhuchka? Maybe he'll even believe it?"

"Schoolboy, do not stoop to lying, first; and second, not even for a good cause. And above all, I hope you didn't tell them anything about my coming."

"God forbid, I know what I'm doing. But you won't comfort him with Perezvon," sighed Smurov. "You know, his father, the captain, I mean, the whiskbroom, told us he was going to bring him a puppy today, a real mastiff, with a black nose; he thinks he can comfort Ilyusha with it, only it's not likely."

"And Ilyusha himself—how is he?"

"Ah, he's bad, bad! I think he has consumption. He's quite conscious, only he keeps breathing, breathing, it's not healthy the way he breathes. The other day he asked to be walked around the room, they put his boots on, he tried to walk but kept falling down. 'Ah,' he said, 'I told you my old boots were no good, papa, even before I had trouble walking in them.' He thought he was stumbling because of his boots, but it was simply weakness. He won't live another week. Herzenstube keeps coming. They're rich again now, they've got a lot of money."

"Swindlers."

"Who are swindlers?"

"Doctors, and all medical scum, generally speaking, and, naturally, in particular as well. I reject medicine. A useless institution. But I'm still looking into all that. Anyway, what are these sentimentalities you've got going? Seems like your whole class is sitting there."

"Not the whole class, but about ten of us always go there, every day. It's all right."

"What surprises me in all this is the role of Alexei Karamazov: his brother is going on trial tomorrow or the day after for such a crime, and he still finds so much time for sentimentalizing with boys!"

"There isn't any sentimentalizing in it. You yourself are going now to make peace with Ilyusha."

"To make peace? A funny expression. Incidentally, I allow no one to analyze my actions."

"And Ilyusha will be so glad to see you! He doesn't even dream that you're coming. Why, why wouldn't you come for such a long time?" Smurov exclaimed with sudden ardor.

"That's my business, my dear boy, not yours. I am going on my own, because such is my will, while you were all dragged there by Alexei Karamazov, so there's a difference. And how do you know, maybe I'm not going to make peace at all? Silly expression!"

"It wasn't Karamazov at all, not him at all. Some of us just started going there by ourselves, of course with Karamazov at first. And there was never anything like that, nothing silly. First one of us went, then another. His father was terribly glad to see us. You know, he'll just go out of his mind if Ilyusha dies. He can see Ilyusha's going to die. But he's so glad about us, that we made peace with Ilyusha. Ilyusha asked about you, but he didn't add anything more. He just asks, and that's all. His father will go out of his mind, or hang himself. He's acted crazy before. You know, he's a noble man, and that was all a mistake. It was the fault of that murderer, the one who gave him the beating."

"Still, Karamazov is a riddle to me. I could have made his acquaintance long ago, but I like to be proud in certain cases. Besides, I've formed an opinion of him that still has to be verified and explained."

Kolya fell imposingly silent; so did Smurov. Smurov, of course, stood in awe of Kolya Krasotkin and did not dare even think of rivaling him. And now he was terribly curious, because Kolya had explained that he was going "on his own," and so there must be some riddle in the fact that Kolya had suddenly decided to go, and precisely on that day. They were crossing the market square, which at that hour was filled with farm wagons and lots of live fowl. Town women were selling rolls, thread, and so forth, under their shed roofs. In our town, such Sunday markets are naively called fairs, and there are many such fairs during the year. Perezvon ran along in the merriest spirits, constantly straying to right and left to smell something here and there. When he met other dogs, he sniffed them with remarkable zeal, according to all canine rules.

"I like observing realism, Smurov," Kolya suddenly spoke. "Have you noticed how dogs sniff each other when they meet? It must be some general law of their nature."

"Yes, and a funny one, too."

"In fact, it is not a funny one, you're wrong there. Nothing is funny in nature, however it may seem to man with his prejudices. If dogs could reason and criticize, they would undoubtedly find as much that is funny to them in the social relations of humans, their masters—if not far more; I repeat, because I am convinced of it, that there is far more foolishness in us. That is Rakitin's thought, a remarkable thought. I am a socialist, Smurov."

"And what is a socialist?" asked Smurov.

"It's when everyone is equal, everyone has property in common, there are no marriages, and each one has whatever religion and laws he likes, and all the rest. You're not grown up enough for that yet, you're too young. It is cold, by the way."

"Yes. Twelve degrees of frost. My father just looked at the thermometer."

"And have you noticed, Smurov, that in the middle of winter, when there are fifteen or even eighteen degrees of frost, it doesn't seem as cold as it does now, for example, in the beginning of winter, if there's suddenly an unexpected cold snap, like now, of twelve degrees, especially when there isn't much snow. It means people aren't used to it yet. Everything is habit with people, everything, even state and political relations. Habit is the chief motive force. What a funny peasant, by the way."

Kolya pointed to a stalwart peasant in a sheepskin coat, with a good-natured face, who was standing beside his wagon clapping his hands in their mittens to keep them warm. His long, light brown beard was all hoary with frost.

"The peasant's got his beard frozen!" Kolya cried loudly and pertly as he passed by him.

"Many have got their beards frozen," the peasant uttered calmly and sententiously in reply.

"Don't pick on him," Smurov remarked.

"It's all right, he won't be angry, he's a nice fellow. Good-bye, Matvey."

"Good-bye."

"Are you really Matvey?"

"I am. Didn't you know?"

"No, I just said it."

"Well, I declare. You must be one of them schoolboys."

"One of them schoolboys."

"And what, do they whip you?"

"Not really, so-so."

"Does it hurt?"

"It can."

"E-eh, that's life!" the peasant sighed from the bottom of his heart.

"Good-bye, Matvey."

"Good-bye. You're a nice lad, that's what."

The boys walked on.

"A good peasant," Kolya began saying to Smurov. "I like talking with the people, and am always glad to do them justice."

"Why did you lie about them whipping us at school?" asked Smurov.

"But I had to comfort him."

"How so?"

"You know, Smurov, I don't like it when people keep asking questions, when they don't understand the first time. Some things can't even be explained. A peasant's notion is that schoolboys are whipped and ought to be whipped: what kind of schoolboy is he, if he isn't whipped? And if I were suddenly to tell him that they don't whip us in our school, it would upset him. Anyway, you don't understand these things. One has to know how to talk with the people."

"Only please don't pick on them, or there'll be another incident like that time with the goose."

"Are you afraid?"

"Don't laugh, Kolya. I am afraid, by God. My father will be terribly angry. I'm strictly forbidden to go around with you."

"Don't worry, nothing will happen this time. Hello, Natasha," he shouted to one of the market women under the shed.

"Natasha, is it? My name's Maria," the woman, who was still far from old, replied in a shrill voice.

"Maria! How nice! Good-bye."

"Ah, the scamp! Knee-high to a mushroom and he's at it already!"

"No time, I have no time for you now, tell me next Sunday," Kolya waved his hand at her, as if he was not bothering her but she him.

"What am I going to tell you next Sunday? I'm not pestering you, you're pestering me, you rascal," Maria went on shouting, "you ought to be whipped, that's what, you're a famous offender, that's what!"

There was laughter among the other market women, who were selling things from their stands next to Maria, when suddenly, from under the arcade of shops nearby, for no reason at all an irritated man jumped out, who looked like a shop clerk, but a stranger, not one of our tradesmen, in a long blue caftan and a visored cap, a young man, with dark brown, curly hair and a long, pale, slightly pockmarked face. He was somehow absurdly agitated, and at once began threatening Kolya with his fist.

"I know you," he kept exclaiming irritably, "I know you!"

Kolya stared fixedly at him. He was unable to recall when he could have had any quarrel with this man. But he had had so many quarrels in the streets that he could not remember them all.

"So you know me?" he asked ironically.

"I know you! I know you!" the tradesman kept repeating like a fool.

"So much the better for you. But I am in a hurry. Good-bye."

"You're still up to your tricks?" the tradesman shouted. "Up to your tricks again? I know you! So you're up to your tricks again?"

"It's none of your business, brother, what tricks I'm up to," Kolya said, stopping and continuing to examine him.

"None of my business, is it?"

"That's right, it's none of your business."

"And whose is it? Whose? Well, whose?"

"It's Trifon Nikitich's business now, brother, not yours."

"What Trifon Nikitich?" the fellow stared at Kolya in foolish surprise, though still with the same excitement. Kolya solemnly looked him up and down.

"Have you been to the Church of the Ascension?" he suddenly asked him sternly and insistently.

"What Ascension? Why? No, I haven't," the fellow was a bit taken aback.

"Do you know Sabaneyev?" Kolya went on, still more insistently and sternly.

"What Sabaneyev? No, I don't know him."

"Devil take you, then!" Kolya suddenly snapped, and turning sharply to the right, quickly went his way as if scorning even to speak with such a dolt who does not even know Sabaneyev.

"Hey, wait! What Sabaneyev?" the fellow came to his senses and again got all excited. "What's he talking about?" he suddenly turned to the market women, staring foolishly at them.

The women burst out laughing.

"A clever boy," one of them said.

"What, what Sabaneyev did he mean?" the fellow kept repeating frenziedly, waving his right hand.

"Ah, it must be the Sabaneyev that worked for the Kuzmichevs, must be that one," one woman suddenly understood.

The fellow stared wildly at her.

"For the Kuz-mi-chevs?" another woman repeated. "He's no Trifon. That one's Kuzma, not Trifon, and the boy said Trifon Nikitich, so it's somebody else."

"No, he's no Trifon, and he's no Sabaneyev either, he's Chizhov," a third woman suddenly joined in, who up to then had been silent and listening seriously. "His name's Alexei Ivanich. Alexei Ivanich Chizhov."

"That's right, he is Chizhov," a fourth woman confirmed emphatically.

The stunned fellow kept looking from one woman to another.

"But why did he ask me, why did he ask me, good people?" he kept exclaiming, now almost in despair. " 'Do you know Sabaneyev?' Devil knows who Sabaneyev is!"

"What a muddlehead! Didn't you hear, it's not Sabaneyev, it's Chizhov, Alexei Ivanich Chizhov, that's who!" one of the market women shouted at him imposingly.

"What Chizhov? Who is he? Tell me, if you know."

"A tall, snot-nosed fellow, he used to sit in the marketplace last summer."

"What the hell do I need your Chizhov for, eh, good people?"

"How do I know what the hell you need Chizhov for?"

"Who knows what you need him for?" another woman joined in. "You should know what you need him for, it's you doing all the squawking. He was speaking to you, not to us, fool that you are. So you really don't know him?"

"Who?"

"Chizhov."

"Ah, devil take Chizhov, and you along with him! I'll give him a thrashing, that's what! He was laughing at me!"

"You'll give Chizhov a thrashing? More likely he'll give you one! You're a fool, that's what!"

"Not Chizhov, not Chizhov, you wicked, nasty woman, I'll thrash the boy, that's what! Let me have him, let me have him—he was laughing at me!"

The women all roared with laughter. And Kolya was already far off, strutting along with a triumphant expression on his face. Smurov walked beside him, looking back at the group shouting far behind them. He, too, was having a good time, though he still feared getting into some scandal with Kolya.

"What Sabaneyev were you asking him about?" he asked Kolya, guessing what the answer would be.

"How do I know? They'll go on shouting till nighttime now. I like stirring up fools in all strata of society. There stands another dolt, that peasant there. People say, 'There's no one stupider than a stupid Frenchman,' but note how the Russian physiognomy betrays itself. Isn't it written all over that peasant's face that he's a fool, eh?"

"Leave him alone, Kolya. Let's keep going."

"No, now that I've gotten started, I wouldn't stop for the world. Hey! Good morning, peasant!"

A burly peasant, who was slowly passing by and seemed to have had a drop to drink already, with a round, simple face and a beard streaked with gray, raised his head and looked at the lad.

"Well, good morning, if you're not joking," he answered unhurriedly.

"And if I am joking?" laughed Kolya.

"Joke then, if you're joking, and God be with you. Never mind, it's allowed. A man can always have his joke."

"Sorry, brother, I was joking."

"So, God will forgive you."

"But you, do you forgive me?"

"That I do. Run along now."

"Look here, you seem to be a smart peasant."

"Smarter than you," the peasant replied unexpectedly, and with the same air of importance.

"That's unlikely," Kolya was somewhat taken aback.

"It's the truth I'm telling you."

"Well, maybe it is."

"So there, brother."

"Good-bye, peasant."

"Good-bye."

"Peasants differ," Kolya observed to Smurov after some silence. "How was I to know I'd run into a smart one? I'm always prepared to recognize intelligence in the people."

Far away the cathedral clock struck half past eleven. The boys began to hurry, and covered the rest of the still quite long way to Captain Snegiryov's house quickly and now almost without speaking. Twenty paces from the house, Kolya stopped and told Smurov to go on ahead and call Karamazov out to meet him there.

"For some preliminary sniffing," he observed to Smurov.

"But why call him out?" Smurov tried to object. "Just go in, they'll be terribly glad to see you. Why do you want to get acquainted in the freezing cold?"

"It's for me to know why I need him here, in the freezing cold," Kolya snapped despotically (as he was terribly fond of doing with these "little boys"), and Smurov ran to carry out the order.

Chapter 4

Zhuchka

Kolya leaned against the fence with an important look on his face and began waiting for Alyosha to appear. Yes, he had long been wanting to meet him. He had heard a lot about him from the boys, but so far had always ostensibly displayed an air of scornful indifference whenever anyone spoke to him about Alyosha, and even "criticized" him as he listened to what was told about him. But within himself he wanted very, very much to make his acquaintance; there was something sympathetic and attractive in all the stories he had heard about Alyosha. Thus, the present moment was an important one; first of all he must not disgrace himself, he must show his independence: "Otherwise he'll think I'm thirteen, and take me for the same sort as those boys. What does he find in those boys anyway? I'll ask him once we've become friends. Too bad I'm so short, though. Tuzikov is younger than I am, but he's half a head taller. Still, I have an intelligent face; I'm not good-looking, I know my face is disgusting, but it's an intelligent face. I also mustn't give myself away too much, otherwise, if I start right out with embraces, maybe he'll think . . . Pfui, how disgusting if he was to think . . ."

Such were Kolya's worries, while he did his best to assume the most independent look. Above all, what tormented him was his small stature, not so much his "disgusting" face as his stature. At home, on the wall in one corner, there was a little pencil mark showing his height, which he had put there a year before, and since then, every two months, he would go excitedly to measure himself and see how much he had grown. But, alas, he grew terribly little, and that at times would bring him simply to despair. As for his face, it was not "disgusting" at all; on the contrary, it was quite comely, fair, pale, and freckled. His small but lively gray eyes had a brave look and would often light up with emotion. His cheekbones were somewhat broad, his lips were small, not too thick, but very red; his nose was small and decidedly upturned: "Quite snub-nosed, quite snub-nosed!" Kolya muttered to himself whenever he looked in the mirror, and he always went away from the mirror with indignation. "And it's not much of an intelligent face either," he sometimes thought, doubting even that. Still, it must not be thought that worrying about his face and height absorbed his whole soul. On the contrary, however painful those moments before the mirror were, he would quickly forget them, and for a long time, "giving himself wholly to ideas and to real life," as he himself defined his activity.

Alyosha soon appeared and hurriedly came up to Kolya; Kolya could see even from several paces away that Alyosha's face was somehow quite joyful. "Can it be he's so glad to see me?" Kolya thought with pleasure. Here, incidentally, we must note that Alyosha had changed very much since we last saw him: he had thrown off his cassock and was now wearing a finely tailored coat and a soft, round hat, and his hair was cut short. All of this lent him charm, and, indeed, he looked very handsome. His comely face always had a cheerful look, but this cheerfulness was somehow quiet and calm. To Kolya's surprise, Alyosha came out to him dressed just as he was, without an overcoat; obviously he had rushed to meet him. He held out his hand to Kolya at once.

"Here you are at last, we've been waiting for you so!"

"There were reasons, which you will learn of in a moment. In any case, I am glad to make your acquaintance. I have long been waiting for an opportunity, and have heard a lot," Kolya mumbled, slightly out of breath.

"But you and I would have become acquainted anyway, I've heard a lot about you myself; it's here, to this place, you've been slow in coming."

"Tell me, how are things here?"

"Ilyusha is very bad, he will certainly die."

"Really? You must agree, Karamazov, that medicine is vile," Kolya exclaimed ardently.

"Ilyusha has mentioned you often, very often, you know, even in his sleep, in delirium. Evidently you were very, very dear to him before . . . that incident . . . with the penknife. There's another reason besides . . . Tell me, is this your dog?"

"Yes. Perezvon."

"Not Zhuchka?" Alyosha looked pitifully into Kolya's eyes. "She just vanished like that?"

"I know you'd all like to have Zhuchka, I've heard all about it," Kolya smiled mysteriously. "Listen, Karamazov, I'll explain the whole business to you, I came mainly for that purpose, that was why I called you outside, to explain the whole affair to you ahead of time, before we go in," he began animatedly. "You see, Karamazov, Ilyusha entered the preparatory class last spring. Well, everybody knows the preparatory class—little boys, kids. They immediately started picking on Ilyusha. I'm two classes ahead, and naturally looked on from a distance, as an outsider. I saw that the boy was small, weak, but he didn't submit, he even fought with them—a proud boy, his eyes flashing. I like that kind. And they went after him worse than ever. The main thing was that he had such shabby clothes then, and his pants were riding up, and his boots had holes in them. They picked on that, too. Humiliated him. No, that I didn't like, I stepped in and made it hot for them. I beat them up—and they adore me, do you know that, Karamazov?" Kolya boasted effusively. "And I like kids generally. I've got two chicks on my neck at home now, in fact they made me late today. So, after that they stopped beating Ilyusha, and I took him under my protection. I saw he was a proud boy, I can tell you how proud he is, but in the end he gave himself up to me like a slave, obeyed my every order, listened to me as though I were God, tried to copy me. In the breaks between classes he would come running to me at once and we would walk together. On Sundays, too. In our school they laugh when an older boy makes friends with a little one on such footing, but that is a prejudice. It suits my fancy, and that's enough, don't you think? I was teaching him, developing him—tell me, why shouldn't I develop him, if I like him? And you did befriend all these kids, Karamazov, which means you want to influence the young generation, develop them, be useful, no? And I admit, this trait of your character, which I knew only from hearsay, interested me most of all. But to business: I noticed that a sort of tenderness, sensitivity, was developing in the boy, and, you know, I am decidedly the enemy of all sentimental slop, and have been since the day I was born. Moreover, there were contradictions: he was proud, but devoted to me like a slave—devoted to me like a slave, yet suddenly his eyes would flash and he wouldn't even want to agree with me, he'd argue, beat on the wall. I used to put forward various ideas sometimes: it wasn't that he disagreed with the ideas, I could see that he was simply rebelling against me personally, because I responded coldly to his sentimentalities. And so, the more sentimental he became, the colder I was, in order to season him; I did it on purpose, because it's my conviction. I had in mind to discipline his character, to shape him up, to create a person . . . well, and so . . . you'll understand me, naturally, from half a word. Suddenly I noticed he was troubled for a day, for two, three days, that he was grieving, not over sentiments now, but something else, something stronger, higher. What's the tragedy, I wondered. I pressed him and found out this: he had somehow managed to make friends with Smerdyakov, your late father's lackey (your father was still alive then), and he had taught the little fool a silly trick—that is, a beastly trick, a vile trick—to take a piece of bread, the soft part, stick a pin in it, and toss it to some yard dog, the kind that's so hungry it will swallow whatever it gets without chewing it, and then watch what happens. And so they fixed up such a morsel and threw it to that very same shaggy Zhuchka that so much fuss is being made over now, a yard dog from the sort of house where they simply never fed her and she just barked at the wind all day long. (Do you like that silly barking, Karamazov? I can't stand it.) She rushed for it, swallowed it, and started squealing, turning round and round, then broke into a run, still squealing as she ran, and disappeared—so Ilyusha described it to me himself. He was crying as he told me, crying, clinging to me, shaking: 'She squealed and ran, she squealed and ran,' he just kept repeating it, the picture really struck him. Well, I could see he felt remorse. I took it seriously. Above all I wanted to discipline him for the previous things, so that, I confess, I cheated here, I pretended to be more indignant than maybe I really was: 'You have committed a base deed,' I said, 'you are a scoundrel. Of course, I will not give you away, but for the time being I am breaking relations with you. I will think it over and let you know through Smurov' (the same boy who came with me today; he's always been devoted to me) 'whether I will continue relations with you hereafter, or will drop you forever as a scoundrel.' That struck him terribly. I'll admit I felt right then that I might be treating him too harshly, but what could I do, it was how I thought at the time. A day later I sent Smurov to him with the message from me that I was 'not talking' with him any more, that's what we say when two friends break relations with each other. Secretly I just meant to give him the silent treatment for a few days, and then, seeing his repentance, to offer him my hand again. That was my firm intention. But what do you think: he listened to Smurov, and suddenly his eyes flashed. 'Tell Krasotkin from me,' he shouted, 'that now I'm going to throw bread with pins in it to all the dogs, all of them, all!' 'Aha,' I thought, 'he's got a free little spirit in him, this will have to be smoked out,' and I began showing complete contempt for him, turning away whenever I met him, or smiling ironically. And then suddenly that incident with his father took place—the whiskbroom, I mean—remember? You should understand that he was already prepared beforehand to be terribly vexed. Seeing that I had dropped him, the boys all fell on him, taunting him: 'Whiskbroom! Whiskbroom!' It was then that the battles started between them, which I'm terribly sorry about, because it seems they beat him badly once. Then once he attacked them all in the street as they were coming out of school, and I happened to be standing ten steps away, looking at him. And, I swear, I don't remember laughing then; on the contrary, I was feeling very, very sorry for him; another moment and I'd have rushed to defend him. But then he suddenly met my eyes: what he imagined I don't know, but he pulled out a penknife, rushed at me, and stuck it into my thigh, here, on my right leg. I didn't move, I must admit I can be brave sometimes, Karamazov, I just looked at him with contempt, as if to say: 'Wouldn't you like to do it again, in return for all my friendship? I'm at your service.' But he didn't stab me a second time, he couldn't stand it, got scared himself, dropped the knife, burst into sobs, and ran away. Naturally, I did not go and squeal on him, and I told everybody to keep quiet about it so that the authorities wouldn't find out; even my mother I told only after it was all healed—and the wound was a trifling one, just a scratch. Then I heard he'd been throwing stones that same day, and bit your finger—but you understand what state he was in! Well, what can I say, I acted foolishly: when he got sick, I didn't go to forgive him—that is, to make peace—and now I regret it. But I had special reasons then. Well, that's the whole story . . . only I guess I did act foolishly . . ."

"Ah, what a pity," Alyosha exclaimed with feeling, "that I didn't know about the relations between you before, or I'd have come long ago and asked you to go and see him with me. Would you believe that he talked about you in his fever, in delirium, when he was sick? I didn't even know how dear you were to him! And can it be, can it be that you never found that Zhuchka? His father and all the boys were searching all over town. Would you believe that three times, since he got sick, I've heard him say in tears to his father: 'I'm sick because I killed Zhuchka, papa, God is punishing me for it'—and he won't give up the idea! If only we could find that Zhuchka now and show him that she's not dead, that she's alive, he might just be resurrected by the joy of it. We've all had our hopes on you."

"Tell me, what reason did you have to hope that I would find Zhuchka—that is, that precisely I would be the one to find her?" Kolya asked with great curiosity. "Why did you count precisely on me and not on someone else?"

"There was some rumor that you were looking for her, and that when you found her, you would bring her. Smurov said something like that. Most of all, we keep trying to assure him that Zhuchka is alive, that she's been seen somewhere. The boys found a live hare someplace, but he just looked at it, smiled faintly, and asked us to let it go in the fields. And so we did. Just now his father came home and brought him a mastiff pup, he also got it someplace, he wanted to comfort him, but it seems to have made things even worse . . ."

"Another thing, Karamazov: what about his father? I know him, but how would you define him: a buffoon, a clown?"

"Ah, no, there are people who feel deeply but are somehow beaten down. Their buffoonery is something like a spiteful irony against those to whom they dare not speak the truth directly because of a long-standing, humiliating timidity before them. Believe me, Krasotkin, such buffoonery is sometimes extremely tragic. For him, now, everything on earth has come together in Ilyusha, and if Ilyusha dies, he will either go out of his mind from grief or take his own life. I'm almost convinced of it when I look at him now!"

"I understand you, Karamazov, I see that you know human nature," Kolya added with feeling.

"And so, when I saw you with a dog, I immediately thought you must be bringing that Zhuchka."

"Wait, Karamazov, maybe we'll still find her, but this one—this one is Perezvon. I'll let him into the room now, and maybe he'll cheer Ilyusha up more than the mastiff. Wait, Karamazov, you're going to find something out now. Ah, my God, but I'm keeping you out here!" Kolya suddenly cried. "You're just wearing a jacket in such cold, and I'm keeping you—see, see what an egoist I am! Oh, we're all egoists, Karamazov!"

"Don't worry; it's cold, true, but I don't catch cold easily. Let's go, however. By the way, what is your name? I know it's Kolya, but the rest?"

"Nikolai, Nikolai Ivanov Krasotkin, or, as they say in official jargon, son of Krasotkin," Kolya laughed at something, but suddenly added: "Naturally, I hate the name Nikolai."

"But why?"

"Trivial, official-sounding . . ."

"You're going on thirteen?" Alyosha asked.

"No, fourteen, in two weeks I'll be fourteen, quite soon. I'll confess one weakness to you beforehand, Karamazov, to you alone, for the sake of our new acquaintance, so that you can see the whole of my character at once: I hate being asked my age, more than hate it . . . and finally, another thing, there's a slanderous rumor going around about me, that I played robbers with the preparatory class last week. That I played with them is actually true, but that I played for myself, for my own pleasure, is decidedly slander. I have reason to think it may have reached your ears, but I played not for myself, but for the kids, because they couldn't think up anything without me. And people here are always spreading nonsense. This town lives on gossip, I assure you."

"And even if you did play for your own pleasure, what of it?"

"Well, even if I did . . . But you don't play hobbyhorse, do you?"

"You should reason like this," Alyosha smiled. "Adults, for instance, go to the theater, and in the theater, too, all sorts of heroic adventures are acted out, sometimes also with robbers and battles—and isn't that the same thing, in its own way, of course? And a game of war among youngsters during a period of recreation, or a game of robbers—that, too, is a sort of nascent art, an emerging need for art in a young soul, and these games are sometimes even better conceived than theater performances, with the only difference that people go to the theater to look at the actors, and here young people are themselves the actors. But it's only natural."

"You think so? Is that your conviction?" Kolya was looking at him intently. "You know, you've said a very interesting thought; I'll set my mind to it when I get home. I admit, I did suspect it would be possible to learn something from you. I've come to learn from you, Karamazov," Kolya concluded in an emotional and effusive voice.

"And I from you," Alyosha smiled, pressing his hand.

Kolya was extremely pleased with Alyosha. It struck him that Alyosha was to the highest degree on an equal footing with him, and spoke with him as with "the most adult" person.

"I'm going to show you a stunt now, Karamazov, also a theater performance," he laughed nervously, "that's what I came for."

"Let's stop at the landlady's first, on the left; we all leave our coats there, because it's crowded and hot in the room."

"Oh, I've just come for a moment, I'll go in and keep my coat on. Perezvon will stay here in the entryway and play dead. *Ici*, Perezvon, *couche*, and play dead! See, he's dead. I'll go in first, check out the situation, and then at the right moment I'll whistle: *Ici*, Perezvon! And you'll see, he'll come rushing in like mad. Only Smurov must not forget to open the door at that moment. I'll arrange it, and you'll see a real stunt . . ."

Chapter 5

At Ilyusha's Bedside

The room, already familiar to us, in which the family of our acquaintance retired captain Snegiryov lived was at that moment both stuffy and crowded with a numerous gathering of visitors. This time several boys were sitting with Ilyusha, and though all of them were ready, like Smurov, to deny that it was Alyosha who had reconciled and brought them together with Ilyusha, still it was so. His whole art in this case lay in getting them together one by one, without "sentimental slop," but as if quite unintentionally and inadvertently. And this brought enormous relief to Ilyusha in his suffering. Seeing an almost tender friendship and concern for him in all these boys, his former enemies, he was very touched. Only Krasotkin was missing, and this lay as a terrible burden on his heart. If in Ilyushechka's bitter memories there was any that was most bitter, it was precisely the whole episode with Krasotkin, once his sole friend and protector, whom he had then attacked with a knife. So, too, thought the smart lad Smurov (who was the first to come and be reconciled with Ilyusha). But when Smurov remotely mentioned that Alyosha wanted to come and see him "on a certain matter," Krasotkin at once broke in and cut it short, charging Smurov to inform "Karamazov" immediately that he knew how to act himself, that he asked for no one's advice, and that if he did go to see the sick boy, he would decide himself when to go, because he had "his own considerations." That was still about two weeks before this Sunday. And that was why Alyosha had not gone in person to see him, as he had intended. Yet, though he waited a little, he nevertheless sent Smurov to Krasotkin once again, and then a third time. But both times Krasotkin responded with a most impatient and abrupt refusal, asking him to tell Alyosha that if he came in person to get him, then just for that he would never go to see Ilyusha, and that he did not want to be bothered any more. Smurov himself had not known even up to the very last day that Kolya had decided to go and see Ilyusha that morning, and it had only been the previous evening that Kolya, as he was saying good-bye to Smurov, suddenly told him brusquely to wait for him at home the next morning, because he was going to the Snegiryovs' with him, warning him, however, that he must not dare inform anyone of his coming, because he wanted to arrive unexpectedly. Smurov obeyed. And his hope that Krasotkin would bring the lost Zhuchka, Smurov based on a few words he dropped in passing, "that they were all asses if they couldn't find the dog, provided it was alive." But when Smurov, waiting for the right moment, timidly hinted to Krasotkin what he had guessed about the dog, the latter suddenly became terribly angry: "What an ass I'd be to go looking for other people's dogs all over town, when I've got my Perezvon! And who would even dream that a dog could survive after swallowing a pin? It's sentimental slop, that's all!"

Meanwhile, for almost two weeks Ilyusha had not left his little bed in the corner near the icons. And he had not gone to classes since the time he had met Alyosha and bitten his finger. Incidentally, it was on that same day that he had become sick, though for another month he was somehow able occasionally to walk around the room and entryway when he occasionally got up from his bed. Finally he grew quite weak, so that he could not move without his father's help. His father trembled over him, even stopped drinking entirely, became almost crazy from fear that his boy would die, and often, especially after leading him around the room by the arm and putting him back to bed, would run out to the entryway, to a dark corner, and, leaning his forehead against the wall, would begin to weep, shaking and sobbing uncontrollably, stifling his voice so that his sobs would not be heard by Ilyushechka.

Then, coming back into the room, he would usually start amusing and comforting his dear boy with something, would tell him stories, funny jokes, or mimic various funny people he had chanced to meet, even imitating animals with their funny howls or cries. But Ilyusha disliked it very much when his father clowned and presented himself as a buffoon. Though the boy tried not to show that he found it unpleasant, it pained his heart to realize that his father was socially humiliated, and he never for a moment forgot the "whiskbroom" and that "terrible day." Ninochka, Ilyushechka's crippled, quiet, and meek sister, also did not like it when their father started clowning (as for Varvara Nikolaevna, she had long since returned to the university in Petersburg), but the half-witted mama was greatly amused, and laughed heartily when her husband began acting something out or making funny gestures. It was the only thing that could comfort her, and the rest of the time she spent grumbling and complaining constantly that everyone had forgotten her now, that no one respected her, that they offended her, and so on and so forth. But in the very last few days, she, too, had quite changed, as it were. She began looking frequently at Ilyusha in his little corner, and grew thoughtful. She grew much more silent, quiet, and if she began to cry, it was softly, so as not to be heard. With bitter perplexity, the captain noticed this change in her. At first she did not like the boys' visits, which only made her angry, but later their cheerful voices and stories began to amuse her, too, and in the end she liked it so much that, if the boys had stopped coming, she would sorely have missed them. When the children told something or started playing, she laughed and clapped her hands. She would call some of them over and kiss them. She came especially to love the boy Smurov. As for the captain, the appearance in his lodgings of children who had come to entertain Ilyusha from the very beginning filled his soul with rapturous joy, and even with hope that Ilyusha would stop being sad now, and would perhaps recover sooner because of it. Until very recently, he never doubted, not for a single moment, despite all his fear for Ilyusha, that his boy would suddenly recover. He met the little guests with reverence, hovered around them, waited on them, was ready to give them rides on his back, and indeed even started giving them rides, but Ilyusha did not like these games and they were abandoned. He began buying treats for them, gingerbread, nuts, served tea, made sandwiches. It should be noted that all this time he was never without money. He had accepted the two hundred roubles from Katerina Ivanovna, exactly as Alyosha predicted. And then

Katerina Ivanovna, learning in more detail about their situation and about Ilyusha's illness, visited their home herself, became acquainted with the whole family, and even managed to charm the captain's half-witted wife. Since then she had been unstinting in her help to them; and the captain, overwhelmed with terror at the thought that his boy might die, forgot his former hauteur and humbly accepted her alms. All this while Dr. Herzenstube, at Katerina Ivanovna's invitation, kept coming to see the sick boy, but little good came of his visits, and he simply stuffed him full of medications. But, on the other hand, they were expecting at the captain's that day—that is, that same Sunday morning—a new doctor, visiting from Moscow, who was considered a celebrity there. Katerina Ivanovna had written specially and invited him from Moscow for a large sum—not for Ilyushechka, but for another purpose, of which more will be said below in the proper place, but since he had come anyway, she asked him to see Ilyushechka as well, and the captain had been forewarned. But he did not at all anticipate the arrival of Kolya Krasotkin, though he had long wished for a visit, finally, from this boy who was the cause of such torment to his Ilyushechka. At the moment when Krasotkin opened the door and appeared in the room, everyone, the captain and all the boys, was crowded around the sick boy's bed, looking at the tiny mastiff pup, just brought in, that had been born just the day before, but had been ordered by the captain a week earlier to amuse and comfort Ilyushechka, who kept grieving over the vanished and, of course, by now dead Zhuchka. But though Ilyusha, who had already heard and knew three days before that he was to be given a little dog, and not simply a dog but a real mastiff (which, of course, was terribly important), had, from fine and delicate feeling, expressed joy at the present, still everyone, both his father and the boys, could see clearly that the new dog stirred perhaps even more strongly in his heart the memory of the unfortunate Zhuchka, whom he had tormented to death. The puppy lay and fumbled about at his side, and he, with a sickly smile, was stroking it with his thin, pale, withered little hand; one could see that he even liked the dog, but still . . . it was not Zhuchka, Zhuchka was not there, but if there could be both Zhuchka and the puppy together, then there would be complete happiness!

"Krasotkin!" one of the boys suddenly cried, the first to notice that Kolya had come in. There was visible excitement, the boys stepped back and stood on either side of the little bed, so that suddenly Ilyushechka was in full view. The captain rushed impetuously to meet Kolya.

"Come in, come in . . . dear guest!" he prattled to him. "Ilyushechka, Mr. Krasotkin has come to see you . . ."

But Krasotkin, having given him a quick handshake, at once also displayed his extraordinary knowledge of social propriety. Immediately and before anything else, he addressed the captain's wife, sitting in her chair (who just at that moment was terribly displeased and was grumbling because the boys were standing in front of Ilyusha's bed and would not let her look at the new dog), and with extraordinary courtesy bent before her, and then, turning to Ninochka, gave her, as a lady, the same sort of bow. This courteous behavior made a remarkably pleasing impression on the sick lady.

"One can always tell at once a well-bred young man," she spoke loudly, spreading her arms, "not like our other visitors: they come riding in on each other."

"How do you mean, mama, how do they come riding in on each other?" the captain murmured, tenderly but still a little apprehensive about "mama."

"They just ride right in. One sits on another's shoulders in the entryway, and they come riding in like that, to see respectable people. What sort of visitor is that?"

"But who, who came in like that, mama, who was it?"

"This boy came riding in on that boy today, and this one on that one . . ."

But Kolya was already standing by Ilyusha's little bed. The sick boy turned visibly pale. He rose on his bed and looked very, very attentively at Kolya. It was two months since Kolya had seen his former little friend, and he suddenly stopped before him, completely struck: he could not even have imagined seeing such a thin and yellow little face, such eyes, which burned with fever and seemed to have become terribly big, such thin arms. With sorrowful surprise he noticed how heavily and rapidly Ilyusha breathed, how dry his lips were. He took a step towards him, gave him his hand, and, almost completely at a loss, said:

"Well, so, old man . . . how are you?"

But his voice broke, he could not muster enough nonchalance, his face somehow suddenly twitched, and something trembled around his lips. Ilyusha kept smiling wanly, still unable to say a word. Kolya suddenly reached out and for some reason stroked Ilyusha's hair with his hand.

"Never mind!" he murmured softly to him, perhaps to encourage him, or else not knowing himself why he said it. They were silent for another minute.

"What's this, a new puppy?" Kolya suddenly asked, in a most unfeeling voice.

"Ye-e-es!" Ilyusha answered in a long whisper, breathlessly.

"A black nose means he's a fierce sort, a watchdog," Kolya observed imposingly and firmly, as if everything had to do precisely with the puppy and its black nose. But the main thing was that he was still trying with all his might to overcome the emotion he felt and not to start crying like a "little boy," and still could not overcome it. "When he grows up, you'll have to keep him on a chain, I can tell you that."

"He'll be huge!" one boy in the group exclaimed.

"He sure will, he's a mastiff, huge, like this, big as a calf," several voices were suddenly heard.

"Big as a calf, a real calf," the captain jumped over to them. "I picked one like that on purpose, the fiercest, and his parents are huge, too, and really fierce, this high off the ground . . . Sit down, sir, here on Ilyusha's bed, or else on the bench here. Welcome, our dear guest, our long-awaited guest . . . Did you come with Alexei Fyodorovich, sir?"

Krasotkin sat down on the bed at Ilyusha's feet. Though he had perhaps prepared a way of casually beginning the conversation while coming there, he had now decidedly lost the thread.

"No . . . I came with Perezvon . . . I have a dog now, named Perezvon. A Slavic name. He's waiting outside . . . A whistle from me, and he'll come flying in. I came with a dog, too," he suddenly turned to Ilyusha. "Do you remember Zhuchka, old man?" he suddenly hit him with the question.

Ilyushechka's face twisted. He looked with suffering at Kolya. Alyosha, who was standing by the door, frowned and shook his head at Kolya on the sly that he should not begin talking about Zhuchka, but he either did not notice or did not want to notice.

"Where is . . . Zhuchka?" Ilyusha asked in a strained voice.

"Well, brother, your Zhuchka—whe-ew! Your Zhuchka's a goner!"

Ilyusha said nothing, but once more looked very, very attentively at Kolya. Alyosha, catching Kolya's eye, again shook his head as hard as he could, but again Kolya looked away and pretended not to notice.

"She ran off somewhere and died. How could she not, after such an appetizer," Kolya slashed mercilessly, at the same time becoming breathless himself for some reason. "But I've got Perezvon instead . . . A Slavic name . . . I've brought him for you . . ."

"Don't!" Ilyushechka suddenly said.

"No, no, I will, you must see . . . It will amuse you. I brought him on purpose . . . he's as shaggy as she was . . . Will you permit me, madame, to call my dog here?" he suddenly addressed Mrs. Snegiryov, now quite inconceivably excited.

"Don't, don't!" exclaimed Ilyusha, with a rueful strain in his voice. His eyes burned with reproach.

"Perhaps, sir," the captain suddenly darted up from the chest by the wall, where he had just sat down, "perhaps, sir . . . some other time, sir . . . ," he prattled, but Kolya, persisting unrestrainably and in haste, suddenly shouted to Smurov: "Smurov, open the door!" and the moment Smurov opened it, he blew his whistle. Perezvon dashed headlong into the room.

"Up, Perezvon, on your hind legs! On your hind legs!" Kolya shouted, jumping from his seat, and the dog, getting on its hind legs, stood straight up right in front of Ilyusha's bed. Something took place that no one expected: Ilyusha started, and suddenly made a great lunge forward, bent down to Perezvon, and, as if frozen, looked at him.

"It's . . . Zhuchka!" he cried out suddenly, his voice cracked with suffering and happiness.

"Who else did you think it was?" Krasotkin shouted with all his might, in a ringing, happy voice, and bending down to the dog, he seized him and lifted him up to Ilyusha.

"Look, old man, you see, he's lost one eye, and there's a little nick on his left ear, exactly the marks you described to me. I found him by those marks! I found him right then, very quickly. He didn't belong to anybody, he didn't belong to anybody!" he explained, quickly turning to the captain, to his wife, to Alyosha, and then back to Ilyusha. "He lived in the Fedotovs' backyard, made his home there, but they didn't feed him, he's a runaway, he ran away from some village . . . So I found him . . . You see, old man, it means he didn't swallow your piece of bread that time. If he had, he'd surely have died, surely! It means he managed to spit it out, since he's alive now. And you didn't even notice him spit it out. He spat it out, but it still pricked his tongue, that's why he squealed then. He was running and squealing, and you thought he'd swallowed it completely. He must really have squealed, because dogs have very tender skin in their mouths . . . more tender than a man's, much more tender!" Kolya exclaimed frenziedly, his face flushed and beaming with rapture.

And Ilyusha could not even speak. White as a sheet, he stared open-mouthed at Kolya, his big eyes somehow bulging terribly. And if the unsuspecting Krasotkin had only known what a tormenting and killing effect such a moment could have on the sick boy's health, he would never have dared pull such a trick as he just had. But perhaps the only one in the room who did realize it was Alyosha. As for the captain, he seemed to have turned into a very little boy.

"Zhuchka! So it's Zhuchka?" he kept crying out in a blissful voice. "Ilyushechka, it's Zhuchka, your Zhuchka! Mama, it's Zhuchka!" he all but wept.

"And I never guessed!" Smurov exclaimed ruefully. "That's Krasotkin! I said he'd find Zhuchka, and he did find her!"

"He did find her!" someone else joyfully echoed.

"Bravo, Krasotkin!" a third voice rang out.

"Bravo, bravo!" the boys all cried and began to applaud.

"But wait, wait," Krasotkin made an effort to outshout them all, "let me tell you how it happened, what counts is how it happened, not anything else! Because I found him, dragged him home and hid him immediately, and locked up the house, and I didn't show him to anyone till the very last day. Only Smurov found out two weeks ago, but I assured him it was Perezvon and he never suspected, and in the meantime I taught Zhuchka all kinds of clever things, you should see, you should just see what tricks he can do! I taught him so as to bring him to you, old man, already sleek and well-trained, and say: here, old man, look at your Zhuchka now! If you've got a little piece of beef, he'll show you a trick now that will make you fall down laughing—beef, a little piece, have you got any?"

The captain dashed impetuously across the hall to the landlady's room, where his food was also prepared. And Kolya, not to lose precious time, in a desperate hurry, cried "Play dead!" to Perezvon. Perezvon suddenly spun around, lay on his back, and stayed stock still with all four legs in the air. The boys all laughed, Ilyusha watched with the same suffering smile, but "mama" liked the way Perezvon died more than anyone. She burst out laughing at the dog and began snapping her fingers and calling:

"Perezvon, Perezvon!"

"He won't get up, not for anything, not for anything," Kolya shouted, triumphant and justly proud. "The whole world can shout all it wants, but if I shout, he'll jump up at once! *Ici*, Perezvon!"

The dog jumped up and began leaping and squealing with joy. The captain ran in with a piece of boiled beef.

"It's not hot, is it?" Kolya inquired hastily, in a businesslike manner, taking the piece. "No, it's not—because dogs don't like hot things. Look, everyone, Ilyushechka, look, come on, look, look, old man, why aren't you looking? I brought him, and he doesn't look!"

The new trick consisted in getting the dog to stand motionlessly with his nose held out, and putting the tasty piece of beef right on the tip of it. The unfortunate dog had to stand without moving, with the meat on his nose, for as long as the master ordered, not moving, not budging, even for half an hour. But Perezvon was kept only for a brief moment.

"Fetch!" cried Kolya, and in a second the piece flew from Perezvon's nose into his mouth. The audience, naturally, expressed rapturous amazement.

"And can it be, can it be that you refused to come all this time only in order to train the dog!" Alyosha exclaimed with involuntary reproach.

"That's precisely the reason," Kolya shouted in the most naive way. "I wanted to show him in all his glory!"

"Perezvon! Perezvon!" Ilyusha suddenly began snapping his thin fingers, calling the dog.

"What do you want? Let him jump up on the bed himself. *Ici*, Perezvon!"

Kolya patted the bed, and Perezvon flew like an arrow up to Ilyusha. The boy impetuously hugged his head with both arms, and in return Perezvon immediately gave him a lick on the cheek. Ilyusha pressed himself to the dog, stretched out on his bed, and hid his face from them all in its shaggy fur.

"Lord, Lord!" the captain kept exclaiming.

Kolya sat down again on Ilyusha's bed.

"Ilyusha, there's something else I can show you. I've brought you a little cannon. Remember, I told you one time about this cannon, and you said: 'Ah, I wish I could see it!' So, now I've brought it."

And Kolya hurriedly pulled the little bronze cannon out of his bag. He was hurrying because he himself was very happy: another time he would have waited until the effect produced by Perezvon had worn off, but now he hastened on, heedless of all self-control: "You're already happy as it is, well, here's some more happiness for you!" He himself was in complete ecstasy.

"I spotted this thing for you long ago at the official Morozov's—for you, old man, for you. It was just sitting there uselessly, he got it from his brother, so I traded him a book for it, *A Kinsman of Mahomet, or Healing Folly*,[1] that was in my papa's bookcase. It's a dirty book, published in Moscow a hundred years ago, even before there was any censorship, and just the sort of thing Morozov loves. He even thanked me . . ."

Kolya held the cannon up in his hand before them all, so that they could all see and delight in it. Ilyusha rose a little, and, still hugging Perezvon with his right arm, studied the toy with admiration. The effect reached its peak when Kolya announced that he had powder as well, and that it would be possible to fire the cannon right then, "if it wouldn't be too upsetting for the ladies." "Mama" immediately asked to have a closer look at the cannon, which was granted at once. She liked the little bronze cannon on wheels terribly much and began rolling it across her knees. To the request for permission to fire it, she responded with full consent, having no notion, however, of what she had been asked. Kolya produced the powder and the shot. The captain, as a former military man, saw to the loading himself, poured in a very small quantity of powder, and asked to save the shot for some other time. The cannon was put on the floor, the barrel aimed into empty space, three grains of powder were squeezed into the touch-hole, and it was set off with a match. There was a most spectacular bang. Mama jumped at first, but immediately laughed with joy. The boys gazed in speechless triumph, but most blissfully happy was the captain as he looked at Ilyusha. Kolya took the little cannon and at once presented it to Ilyusha, together with the powder and shot.

"It's for you, for you! I got it for you long ago," he repeated once more, in the fullness of happiness.

"Ah, give it to me! No, you'd better give the little cannon to me!" mama suddenly began begging like a little girl. Her face wore an expression of sad anxiety for fear they would not give it to her. Kolya was embarrassed. The captain became anxiously worried.

"Mama, mama!" he jumped over to her, "the cannon is yours, yours, but let Ilyusha keep it, because it's his present, but it's the same as if it was yours, Ilyushechka will always let you play with it, it can belong to both of you, both . . ."

"No, I don't want it to be both of ours, no, I want it to be just mine and not Ilyusha's," mama went on, getting ready to cry in earnest.

"Take it, mama, here, take it!" Ilyusha suddenly cried. "Krasotkin, may I give it to mama?" he suddenly turned to Krasotkin with a pleading look, as if he were afraid Krasotkin might be offended if he gave his present to someone else.

"Perfectly possible!" Krasotkin agreed at once, and, taking the little cannon from Ilyusha, he himself handed it to mama with a most polite bow. She even burst into tears, she was so moved.

"Ilyushechka, dear, he loves his dear mama!" she exclaimed tenderly, and immediately began rolling the cannon across her knees again.

"Mama, let me kiss your hand," her husband jumped close to her and at once carried out his intention.

"And if anyone is the nicest young man of all, it's this kind boy!" the grateful lady said, pointing to Krasotkin.

"And I'll bring you as much powder as you want, Ilyusha. We make our own powder now. Borovikov found out the ingredients: twenty-four parts saltpeter, ten parts sulphur, and six of birch charcoal; grind it all together, add some water, mix it into a paste, and rub it through a sieve—and you've got powder."

"Smurov already told me about your powder, only papa says it's not real powder," Ilyusha replied.

"What do you mean, not real?" Kolya blushed. "It burns all right. However, I don't know . . ."

"No, sir, it's nothing, sir," the captain suddenly jumped over to them with a guilty look. "I did say that real powder is not made like that, but it's nothing, you can do it like that, sir."

"I don't know, you know better. We burned it in a stone pomade jar, it burned well, it all burned away, there was only a little soot left. And that was just the paste, but if you rub it through a sieve . . . However, you know better, I don't know . . . And Bulkin got a whipping from his father because of our powder, did you hear?" he suddenly addressed Ilyusha.

"I did," Ilyusha replied. He was listening to Kolya with infinite curiosity and delight.

"We made a whole bottle of powder, he kept it under his bed. His father saw it. It might explode, he said. And he whipped him right then and there. He wanted to make a complaint about me to the school. Now they won't let him have anything to do with me, no one is allowed to have anything to do with me now. Smurov isn't allowed either, I've become notorious with everybody; they say I'm a 'desperado,'" Kolya grinned scornfully. "It all started with the railway."

"Ah, we've also heard about that exploit of yours!" exclaimed the captain. "How did you manage to lie there through it? And can it be that you weren't afraid at all while you were lying under the train? Weren't you scared, sir?"

The captain was fawning terribly on Kolya.

"N-not particularly!" Kolya replied nonchalantly. "What really botched my reputation around here was that cursed goose," he again turned to Ilyusha. But though he put on a nonchalant air while he was talking, he still could not control himself and was continually thrown off pitch, as it were.

"Ah, I've heard about the goose, too!" Ilyusha laughed, beaming all over. "They told me about it, but I didn't understand, did they really take you in front of the judge?"

"It was the most brainless, the most insignificant thing, from which, as usual here, they concocted a whole mountain," Kolya began casually. "I was going across the market square one day, and they'd just driven in some geese. I stopped and looked at the geese. Suddenly a local fellow, Vishnyakov, he's working as an errand boy for Plotnikov's now, looked at me and said: 'What are you looking at the geese for?' I looked at him: the fellow was no more than twenty, a stupid, round mug, I never reject the people, you know. I like to be with the people . . . We lag behind the people—that is an axiom—you seem to be laughing, Karamazov?"

"No, God forbid, I'm listening carefully," Alyosha replied with a most guileless look, and the insecure Kolya was immediately reassured.

"My theory, Karamazov, is clear and simple," he at once hurried joyfully on again, "I believe in the people and am always glad to do them justice, but I'm by no means for spoiling them, that is a *sine qua* . . . Yes, about the goose. So I turned to the fool and answered him: 'I'm thinking about what the goose might be thinking about.' He gave me a completely stupid look: 'And what,' he said, 'is the goose thinking about?' 'Do you see that cart full of oats?' I said. 'The oats are spilling from the sack, and the goose has stretched his neck out right under the wheel and is pecking up the grains—do you see?' 'I see all right,' he said. 'Well,' I said, 'if the cart rolled forward a bit now—would it break the goose's neck or not?' 'Sure it would,' he said, and he was already grinning from ear to ear, he was melting all over. 'So let's do it, man, come on.' 'Yeah, let's do it,' he said. And it was easy enough to set up: he stood near the bridle on the sly, and I stood beside the cart to direct the goose. And the peasant got distracted just then, he was talking with someone, so that I didn't even have to direct: the goose stretched his neck out to get the oats, under the cart, right under the wheel. I winked at the fellow, he gave a tug, and—cr-r-ack, the wheel rolled right across the middle of the goose's neck. But it just so happened that at that very second all the peasants saw us, and they all started squawking at once: 'You did it on purpose!' 'No, I didn't.' 'Yes, you did!' Then they squawked: 'To the justice of the peace with him!' They took me along, too: 'You were there, you helped him, the whole marketplace knows you!' And indeed, for some reason the whole marketplace does know me," Kolya added vainly. "We all went to the justice of the peace, and they brought the goose along, too. I could see that my fellow was afraid; he started howling, really, howling like a woman. And the poultryman was shouting: 'You could run over all the geese in the market that way!' Well, of course there were witnesses. The justice wrapped it up in no time: the poultryman got a rouble for the goose, and the fellow got the goose. And he was never to allow himself such jokes in the future. And the fellow kept howling like a woman: 'It wasn't me, he made me do it,' and he pointed at me. I answered with complete equanimity that I had by no means made him do it, that I had merely stated the basic idea and was speaking only hypothetically. Judge Nefedov chuckled, and was immediately angry with himself for having chuckled: 'I shall send a report to your authorities at once,' he said to me, 'so that in future you will not fall into such hypotheses instead of sitting over your books and learning your lessons.' He didn't report to the authorities, it was a joke, but the thing got around and reached the ears of the authorities anyway: we have long ears here! The classics teacher, Kolbasnikov, was particularly incensed, but Dardanelov stood up for me again. And Kolbasnikov is mad at everybody now, like a green ass. You must have heard he got married, Ilyusha, picked up a thousand roubles in dowry from the Mikhailovs, and the bride is a real eyesore, first-rate and to the last degree. The boys in the third class immediately wrote an epigram:

> The class was astonished to discover
> The slob Kolbasnikov is a lover.

And so on, very funny, I'll bring it to you later. I will say nothing about Dardanelov: he's a man of learning, decidedly a man of learning. I respect his kind, and not at all because he stood up for me . . ."

"But you still showed him up over who founded Troy!" Smurov suddenly interjected, being decidedly proud of Krasotkin at the moment. He liked the story about the goose very much.

"Did you really show him up?" the captain joined in fawningly. "Over who founded Troy, sir? We heard about that, that you showed him up. Ilyushechka told me right then, sir . . ."

"He knows everything, papa, better than any of us!" Ilyushechka also joined in. "He only pretends to be like that, but he's the first student in every subject . . ."

Ilyusha looked at Kolya with boundless happiness.

"Well, it's all nonsense about Troy, trifles. I myself consider it an idle question," Kolya responded with prideful modesty. He was now perfectly on pitch, though he was still somewhat worried: he felt that he was overly excited, and that he had told about the goose, for example, too openheartedly, while Alyosha had kept silent all through the story and looked serious, so that it gradually began to rankle the vain boy: "Is he silent because he despises me, thinking that I'm seeking his praise? If so, if he dares to think so, then I . . ."

"I consider it decidedly an idle question," he proudly broke off once again.

"I know who founded Troy," one boy suddenly spoke quite unexpectedly. He had said almost nothing till then, was silent and obviously shy, a very pretty-looking boy, about eleven years old, by the name of Kartashov. He was sitting just next to the door. Kolya gave him a surprised and imposing look. The thing was that the question of who precisely founded Troy had decidedly become a great secret in all the classes, and in order to penetrate it one had to read Smaragdov. But no one except Kolya had a copy of Smaragdov. And so one day when Kolya's back was turned, the boy Kartashov had quickly and slyly opened Smaragdov, which lay among Kolya's books, and lighted just on the passage discussing the founders of Troy. That had been some time ago, but he was somehow embarrassed and could not bring himself to reveal publicly that he, too, knew who had founded Troy, for fear something might come of it and Kolya might somehow confound him. But now, suddenly, for some reason he could not refrain from saying it. He had been wanting to for a long time.

"Well, who did?" Kolya turned to him arrogantly and condescendingly, having already seen from the boy's face that he indeed did know, and, of course, preparing himself at once for all the consequences. What is known as a dissonance came into the general mood.

"Troy was founded by Teucer, Dardanus, Ilius, and Tros," the boy rapped out at once, and instantly blushed all over, blushed so much that it was pitiful to see. But all the boys stared fixedly at him, stared for a whole minute, and then suddenly all those staring eyes turned at once to Kolya. He stood looking the bold boy up and down with disdainful equanimity.

"And in what sense did they found it?" he deigned at last to speak. "What generally is meant by the founding of a city or a state? Did each of them come and lay a brick, or what?"

There was laughter. The guilty boy turned from pink to crimson. He was silent, he was on the verge of tears. Kolya kept him like that for another minute.

"If one is to speak of such historical events as the founding of a nation, one must first know what it means," he uttered distinctly, severely, by way of admonition. "I, in any case, do not regard these old wives' tales as important, and generally I do not have much respect for world history," he suddenly added nonchalantly, now addressing everyone present.

"World history, sir?" the captain inquired suddenly with some sort of fear.

"Yes, world history. It is the study of the succession of human follies, and nothing more. I only respect mathematics and natural science," Kolya swaggered, and glanced at Alyosha: his was the only opinion in the room that he feared. But Alyosha was still as silent and serious as before. If Alyosha had said anything now, the matter would have ended there, but Alyosha did not respond, and "his silence could well be contemptuous," and at that Kolya became quite vexed.

"And also these classical languages we have now: simply madness, nothing more . . . Again you seem to disagree with me, Karamazov?"

"I disagree," Alyosha smiled restrainedly.

"Classical languages, if you want my full opinion about them—it's a police measure, that's the sole purpose for introducing them," again Kolya gradually became breathless, "they were introduced because they're boring, and because they dull one's faculties. It was boring already, so how to make it even more boring? It was muddled already, so how to make it even more muddled? And so they thought up the classical languages. That is my full opinion of them, and I hope I shall never change it," Kolya ended sharply. Flushed spots appeared on both his cheeks.

"That's true," Smurov, who had been listening diligently, suddenly agreed in a ringing and convinced voice.

"And he's first in Latin himself!" one boy in the crowd cried.

"Yes, papa, he says that, and he's first in the class in Latin," Ilyusha echoed.

"What of it?" Kolya found it necessary to defend himself, though the praise also pleased him very much. "I grind away at Latin because I have to, because

I promised my mother I'd finish school, and I think that whatever one does one ought to do well, but in my soul I deeply despise classicism and all that baseness . . . You don't agree, Karamazov?"

"Why 'baseness'?" Alyosha smiled again.

"But, good heavens, the classics have been translated into all languages, therefore there was absolutely no need for Latin in order to study the classics, they needed it only as a police measure and to dull one's faculties. Wouldn't you call that baseness?"

"But who taught you all that?" exclaimed Alyosha, at last surprised.[2]

"First of all, I myself am capable of understanding without being taught, and second, let me inform you that the very thing I just explained about the classics being translated, our teacher, Kolbasnikov, said himself to the whole third class . . ."

"The doctor has come!" Ninochka, who had been silent all the while, suddenly exclaimed.

Indeed, a carriage belonging to Madame Khokhlakov drove up to the gates of the house. The captain, who had been expecting the doctor all morning, madly rushed out to meet him. Mama pulled herself together and assumed an important air. Alyosha went over to Ilyusha and began straightening his pillow. Ninochka anxiously watched from her armchair as he straightened the little bed. The boys began saying good-bye hastily, some of them promised to stop by in the evening. Kolya called Perezvon, and he jumped down from the bed.

"I'm not leaving, I'm not," Kolya said hurriedly to Ilyusha, "I'll wait in the entryway and come back when the doctor leaves, I'll bring Perezvon back."

But the doctor was already coming in—an imposing figure in a bearskin coat, with long, dark side-whiskers and a gleamingly shaven chin. Having stepped across the threshold, he suddenly stopped as if taken aback: he must have thought he had come to the wrong place. "What's this? Where am I?" he muttered, without doffing his fur coat or his sealskin hat with its sealskin visor. The crowd, the poverty of the room, the laundry hanging on a line in the corner bewildered him. The captain bent double before him.

"It's here you were coming, sir, it's here, sir," he kept muttering servilely, "you've come here, sir, to my place, come to my place, sir . . ."

"Sne-gi-ryov?" the doctor pronounced loudly and importantly. "Mr. Snegiryov—is that you?"

"It's me, sir."

"Ah!"

The doctor once again looked squeamishly around the room and threw off his fur coat. An important decoration hanging on his neck flashed in everyone's eyes. The captain caught the coat in midair, and the doctor took off his hat.

"Where is the patient?" he asked loudly and emphatically.

Chapter 6

Precocity

What do you think the doctor will say to him?" Kolya rattled out. "What a disgusting mug, by the way, don't you agree? I can't stand medicine!"

"Ilyusha will die. That seems certain to me now," Alyosha replied sadly.

"Swindlers! Medicine is a swindle! I'm glad, however, to have met you, Karamazov. I've long wanted to meet you. Only it's too bad we've met so sadly . . ."

Kolya would have liked very much to say something even more ardent, more expansive, but something seemed to cramp him. Alyosha noticed it, smiled, and pressed his hand.

"I've long learned to respect the rare person in you," Kolya muttered again, faltering and becoming confused. "I've heard you are a mystic and were in the monastery. I know you are a mystic, but . . . that didn't stop me. The touch of reality will cure you . . . With natures like yours, it can't be otherwise."

"What do you mean by 'a mystic'? Cure me of what?" Alyosha was a little surprised.

"Well, God and all that."

"What, don't you believe in God?"

"On the contrary, I have nothing against God. Of course God is only a hypothesis . . . but . . . I admit, he is necessary, for the sake of order . . . for the order of the world and so on . . . and if there were no God, he would have to be invented,"[1] Kolya added, beginning to blush. He suddenly fancied that Alyosha might be thinking he wanted to show off his knowledge and prove how "adult" he was. "And I don't want to show off my knowledge at all," Kolya thought indignantly. And he suddenly became quite vexed.

"I'll admit, I can't stand entering into all these debates," he snapped. "It's possible to love mankind even without believing in God, don't you think? Voltaire did not believe in God, but he loved mankind, didn't he?" ("Again, again!" he thought to himself.)

"Voltaire believed in God, but very little, it seems, and it seems he also loved mankind very little," Alyosha said softly, restrainedly, and quite naturally, as if he were talking to someone of the same age or even older than himself. Kolya was struck precisely by Alyosha's uncertainty, as it were, in his opinion of Voltaire, and that he seemed to leave it precisely up to him, little Kolya, to resolve the question.

"So you've read Voltaire?" Alyosha concluded.

"No, I can't say I've read him . . . I've read *Candide*,[2] though, in a Russian translation . . . an old, clumsy translation, very funny . . ." ("Again, again!")

"And did you understand it?"

"Oh, yes, everything . . . I mean . . . why do you think I wouldn't understand it? Of course there are lots of salacious things in it . . . But of course I'm capable of understanding that it's a philosophical novel, written in order to put forward an idea . . . ," Kolya was now completely muddled. "I'm a socialist, Karamazov, I am an incorrigible socialist," he suddenly broke off for no reason at all.

"A socialist?" Alyosha laughed. "But how have you had time? You're still only thirteen, I think?"

Kolya cringed.

"First of all, I'm fourteen, not thirteen, fourteen in two weeks," he flushed deeply, "and second, I absolutely do not understand what my age has to do with it. The point is what my convictions are, not how old I am, isn't it?"

"When you're older, you will see yourself what significance age has upon convictions. It also occurred to me that you were using words that weren't yours," Alyosha replied calmly and modestly, but Kolya hotly interrupted him.

"For God's sake, you want obedience and mysticism. You must agree, for instance, that the Christian faith has only served the rich and noble, so as to keep the lower classes in slavery, isn't that so?"

"Ah, I know where you read that, and I knew someone must have been teaching you!" Alyosha exclaimed.

"For God's sake, why must have I read it? And no one has taught me at all. I myself am capable . . . And, if you like, I'm not against Christ. He was a very humane person, and if he was living in our time, he would go straight to join the revolutionaries, and perhaps would play a conspicuous part . . . It's even certain he would."

"But where, where did you get all that? What kind of fool have you been dealing with?" Alyosha exclaimed.

"For God's sake, the truth can't be hidden! Of course, I often talk with Mr. Rakitin about a certain matter, but . . . Old Belinsky used to say the same thing, they say."

"Belinsky? I don't remember. He never wrote it anywhere."

"Maybe he didn't write it, but they say he said it. I heard it from a certain . . . ah, the devil . . . !"

"And have you read Belinsky?"

"In fact . . . no . . . I haven't exactly read him, but . . . the part about Tatiana, why she didn't go with Onegin, I did read."[3]

"What? Why she didn't go with Onegin? Can it be that you already . . . understand that?"

"For God's sake, you seem to take me for the boy Smurov," Kolya grinned irritably. "By the way, please don't think I'm such a revolutionary. I quite often disagree with Mr. Rakitin. If I speak about Tatiana, it's not at all to say that I'm for women's emancipation. I acknowledge that woman is a subordinate creature and must obey. *Les femmes tricottent*,[4] as Napoleon said," Kolya smirked for some reason, "and at least here I fully share the conviction of that pseudo great man. I also think, for example, that to flee the fatherland for America is a base thing, worse than base—it's foolish. Why go to America, if one can also be of much use to mankind here? Precisely now. There's a whole mass of fruitful activity. That was my answer."

"Answer? Who did you answer? Has someone already invited you to America?"

"I must admit they were urging me, but I declined. Naturally that's between us, Karamazov, not a word to anyone, do you hear? It's only for you. I have no desire to fall into the kindly clutches of the Third Department and take lessons at the Chain Bridge.

> You will never forget
> The house near the Chain Bridge!

Do you remember? Splendid! What are you laughing at? Do you think it's all lies?" ("And what if he finds out that there's only that one issue of *The Bell* in my father's bookcase, and that I never read any more than that?" Kolya thought fleetingly, but with a shudder.)[5]

"Oh, no, I'm not laughing, and I don't at all think you've been lying to me. That's just it, I don't think so because all of that, alas, is quite true! Well, and Pushkin, tell me, have you read him, have you read *Onegin* . . . ? You just mentioned Tatiana."

"No, I haven't read it, but I intend to. I have no prejudices, Karamazov. I want to hear both sides. Why do you ask?"

"I just wondered."

"Tell me, Karamazov, do you despise me terribly?" Kolya suddenly blurted out, and he drew himself up straight before Alyosha, as if positioning himself. "Kindly tell me, without beating around the bush."

"I despise you?" Alyosha looked at him with surprise. "But what for? I'm only sad that such a lovely nature as yours, which has not yet begun to live, should already be perverted by all this crude nonsense."

"Don't worry about my nature," Kolya interrupted, not without some smugness, "but it's true that I'm insecure. Stupidly insecure, crudely insecure. You just smiled, and I thought you seemed to . . ."

"Ah, I smiled at something quite different. You see, what I smiled at was this: I recently read a comment by a foreigner, a German, who used to live in Russia, about our young students these days. 'Show a Russian schoolboy a chart of the heavens,' he writes, 'of which hitherto he had no idea at all, and the next day he will return the chart to you with corrections.' No knowledge and boundless conceit—that's what the German meant to say about the Russian schoolboy."

"Ah, but he's absolutely right!" Krasotkin suddenly burst out laughing. "*Verissimo*, exactly! Bravo, German! However, the Kraut didn't look at the good side, what do you think? Conceit—so be it, it comes from youth, it will correct itself, if there's any need for correction, but, on the other hand, an independent spirit, almost from childhood, a boldness of thought and conviction, and not the spirit of those sausage-makers groveling before the authorities . . . But still, the German put it well! Bravo, German! Though the Germans still ought to be strangled. They may be good at science there, but they still ought to be strangled . . ."

"Strangled? Why?" Alyosha smiled.

"Well, maybe I was just mouthing off, I agree. Sometimes I'm a terrible child, and when I'm pleased about something, I can't restrain myself, I'm ready to mouth all kinds of nonsense. Listen, though, here we are chatting about trifles, and that doctor seems to have got stuck in there for a long time. Though maybe he's examining 'mama' too, and that crippled Ninochka. You know, I like that Ninochka. She suddenly whispered to me as I was going out: 'Why didn't you come before?' And in such a voice, so reproachful! I think she's terribly kind and pathetic."

"Yes, yes! When you've come more often, you'll see what sort of being she is. It's very good for you to get to know such beings, in order to learn to value many other things besides, which you will learn precisely from knowing these beings," Alyosha observed warmly. "That will remake you more than anything."

"Oh, how sorry I am and how I scold myself for not coming sooner!" Kolya exclaimed with bitter feeling.

"Yes, it's a great pity. You saw for yourself what a joyful impression you made on the poor child! And how he grieved as he waited for you!"

"Don't tell me! You're just rubbing it in! It serves me right, though: it was vanity that kept me from coming, egoistic vanity and base despotism, which

I haven't been able to get rid of all my life, though all my life I've been trying to break myself. I'm a scoundrel in many ways, Karamazov, I see it now!"

"No, you have a lovely nature, though it's been perverted, and I fully understand how you could have such an influence on this noble and morbidly sensitive boy!" Alyosha replied ardently.

"And you say that to me!" Kolya cried, "and just imagine, I thought—several times already since I came here today—I thought you despised me! If only you knew how I value your opinion!"

"But can it be that you really are so insecure? At your age? Well, imagine, I was thinking just that, as I watched you telling stories there in the room, that you must be very insecure."

"You thought that? What an eye you have, really, you see, you see! I bet it was when I was telling about the goose. Precisely at that moment I imagined you must deeply despise me for being in such a hurry to show what a fine fellow I was, and I even hated you for it and began talking drivel. Then I imagined (it was here, just now) when I was saying: 'If there were no God, he would have to be invented,' that I was in too great a hurry to show off my education, especially since I got the phrase out of a book. But I swear to you, I was in a hurry to show off, not out of vanity, but just, I don't know, for the joy of it, by God, as if for the joy of it . . . though it's an extremely disgraceful quality in a man to go throwing himself on everyone's neck out of joy. I know that. But now instead I'm convinced that you don't despise me, that I invented it all myself. Oh, Karamazov, I'm profoundly unhappy. Sometimes I imagine God knows what, that everyone is laughing at me, the whole world, and then I . . . then I'm quite ready to destroy the whole order of things."

"And you torment the people around you," Alyosha smiled.

"And I torment the people around me, especially my mother. Tell me, Karamazov, am I very ridiculous now?"

"But don't think about it, don't think about it at all!" Alyosha exclaimed. "And what does it mean—ridiculous? What does it matter how many times a man is or seems to be ridiculous? Besides, nowadays almost all capable people are terribly afraid of being ridiculous, and are miserable because of it. I'm only surprised that you've begun to feel it so early, though, by the way, I've been noticing it for a long time, and not in you alone. Nowadays even children almost are already beginning to suffer from it. It's almost a madness. The devil has incarnated himself in this vanity and crept into a whole generation—precisely the devil," Alyosha added, not smiling at all, as Kolya, who was looking at him intently, thought for a moment. "You are like everyone else," Alyosha concluded, "that is, like a great many others, only you ought not to be like everyone else, that's what."

"Even if everyone is like that?"

"Yes, even if everyone is like that. You be the only one who is not like that. And in fact you're not like everyone else: you weren't ashamed just now to confess bad and even ridiculous things about yourself. Who would confess such things nowadays? No one, and people have even stopped feeling any need for self-judgment. So do not be like everyone else; even if you are the only one left who is not like that, still do not be like that."

"Splendid! I was not mistaken in you. You know how to give comfort. Oh, how I've yearned for you, Karamazov, how long I've been seeking to meet you! Can it be that you also thought about me? You said just now that you were thinking about me?"

"Yes, I had heard about you and also thought about you . . . and if it's partly vanity that makes you ask, it doesn't matter."

"You know, Karamazov, our talk is something like a declaration of love," Kolya said in a sort of limp and bashful voice. "That's not ridiculous, is it?"

"Not ridiculous at all, and even if it were ridiculous, it still wouldn't matter, because it's good," Alyosha smiled brightly.

"And you know, Karamazov, you must admit that you yourself feel a little ashamed with me now . . . I can see it in your eyes," Kolya smiled somehow slyly, but also with almost a sort of happiness.

"Ashamed of what?"

"Why did you blush, then?"

"But it was you who made me blush!" Alyosha laughed, and indeed blushed all over. "Well, yes, a little ashamed, God knows why, I don't know . . . ," he muttered, even almost embarrassed.

"Oh, how I love you and value you right now, precisely because you, too, are ashamed of something with me! Because you're just like me!" Kolya exclaimed, decidedly in ecstasy. His cheeks were flushed, his eyes shining.

"Listen, Kolya, by the way, you are going to be a very unhappy man in your life," Alyosha suddenly said for some reason.

"I know, I know. How do you know all that beforehand!" Kolya confirmed at once.

"But on the whole you will bless life all the same."

"Precisely! Hurrah! You're a prophet. Oh, we will become close, Karamazov. You know, what delights me most of all is that you treat me absolutely as an equal. And we're not equal, no, not equal, you are higher! But we will become close. You know, all this past month I've been saying to myself: 'He and I will either become close friends at once and forever, or from the first we'll part as mortal enemies!' "

"And surely you already loved me as you said it!" Alyosha was laughing happily.

"I did, I loved you terribly, I loved you, and I was dreaming about you! But how do you know everything beforehand? Hah, here's the doctor. Lord, what's he going to say? Look at his face!"

Chapter 7
Ilyusha

The doctor was just coming out of the room, already wrapped up in his fur coat and with his hat on his head. His face was almost angry and squeamish, as if he were afraid of dirtying himself on something. He gave a cursory look around the entryway and glanced sternly at Alyosha and Kolya. Alyosha waved to the coachman from the doorway, and the carriage that had brought the doctor drove up to the front door. The captain rushed out after the doctor and, bending low, almost writhing before him, stopped him to get his final word. The poor man looked completely crushed, his eyes were frightened.

"Your Excellency, your Excellency . . . can it be . . . ?" he began, and could not finish, but simply clasped his hands in despair, though still making a last plea to the doctor with his eyes, as if a word from the doctor now might indeed change the poor boy's sentence.

"What can I do? I am not God," the doctor replied in a casual, though habitually imposing, voice.

"Doctor . . . your Excellency . . . and will it be soon, soon?"

"Be pre-pared for any-thing," the doctor pronounced, emphasizing each syllable, and, lowering his eyes, he himself prepared to step across the threshold to the carriage.

"Your Excellency, for Christ's sake!" the captain, frightened, stopped him again. "Your Excellency! . . . isn't there anything, can it be that nothing, nothing at all can save . . . ?"

"It no longer de-pends on me," the doctor spoke impatiently, "but, however, hmm," he suddenly paused, "if you could, for example . . . con-vey . . . your patient . . . at once and without the least delay" (the doctor uttered the words "at once and without the least delay" not so much sternly as almost angrily, so that the captain was even startled) "to Sy-ra-cuse, then . . . as a result of the new, fa-vor-able cli-ma-tic conditions . . . there might, perhaps, be . . ."

"To Syracuse!" the captain cried, as if he still understood nothing.

"Syracuse—it's in Sicily," Kolya suddenly snapped loudly, by way of explanation. The doctor looked at him.

"To Sicily! Good Lord, your Excellency," the captain was at a loss. "But haven't you seen?" he pointed to his surroundings with both hands. "And mama, and the family?"

"N-no, the family should go, not to Sicily, but to the Caucasus, in early spring . . . your daughter to the Caucasus, and your wife . . . after a course of treatments with the waters—also in the Caucasus, in view of her rheumatism . . . should immediately afterwards be con-veyed to Paris, to the clinic of the psy-chi-a-trist Le-pel-le-tier, I can give you a note to him, and then there might, perhaps, be . . ."

"Doctor, doctor! But don't you see!" the captain again waved his hands, pointing in despair at the bare log walls of the entryway.

"Ah, that is not my business," the doctor grinned, "I have merely said what sci-ence can say to your questions about last measures. As for the rest . . . to my regret . . ."

"Don't worry, leech, my dog won't bite you," Kolya cut in abruptly, having noticed the doctor's somewhat anxious look at Perezvon, who was standing in the doorway. An angry note rang in Kolya's voice. And he used the word "leech" instead of "doctor" *on purpose*, as he declared afterwards, and "meant it as an insult."

"What did you say?" the doctor threw back his head and stared at Kolya in surprise. "Who is this?" he suddenly turned to Alyosha, as if asking him for an explanation.

"This is Perezvon's master, leech, don't worry about my humble self," Kolya snapped again.

"Swan?" the doctor repeated, not understanding what "Perezvon" meant.

"Yes, as in zvon-song. Good-bye, leech, see you in Syracuse."

"Wh-ho is he? Who, who?" the doctor suddenly became terribly excited.

"A local schoolboy, doctor, he's a prankster, don't pay any attention to him," Alyosha rattled out, frowning. "Kolya, be still!" he cried to Krasotkin. "Pay no attention to him, doctor," he repeated, this time more impatiently.

"Whip-ped, he ought to be whip-ped!" the doctor, who for some reason was utterly infuriated, began stamping his feet.

"On the other hand, leech, my Perezvon may just bite!" Kolya said in a trembling voice, turning pale, his eyes flashing. "*Ici*, Perezvon!"

"Kolya, if you say another word, I'll break with you forever," Alyosha cried peremptorily.

"Leech, there is only one person in the whole world who can tell Nikolai

Krasotkin what to do—this is the man," Kolya pointed to Alyosha. "I obey him. Good-bye!"

He tore himself from his place, opened the door, and quickly went into the room. Perezvon dashed after him. The doctor stood stupefied, as it were, for another five seconds, looking at Alyosha, then suddenly spat and quickly went out to the carriage, repeating loudly: "This-s is, this-s is, this-s is . . . I don't know what this-s is!" The captain rushed to help him into the carriage. Alyosha followed Kolya into the room. He was already standing by Ilyusha's bed. Ilyusha was holding him by the hand and calling his papa. In a moment the captain, too, returned.

"Papa, papa, come here . . . we . . . ," Ilyusha prattled in great excitement, but, apparently unable to go on, suddenly thrust both his thin arms out and, as firmly as he could, embraced the two of them, Kolya and his papa, uniting them in one embrace and pressing himself to them. The captain suddenly began shaking all over with silent sobs, and Kolya's lips and chin started trembling.

"Papa, papa! I'm so sorry for you, papa!" Ilyusha moaned bitterly.

"Ilyushechka . . . darling . . . the doctor said . . . you'll get well . . . we'll be happy . . . the doctor . . . ," the captain started to say.

"Ah, papa! I know what the new doctor told you about me . . . I could see!" Ilyusha exclaimed, and again firmly, with all his strength, he pressed them both to himself, hiding his face on his papa's shoulder.

"Papa, don't cry . . . and when I die, you get some nice boy, another one . . . choose from all of them, a nice one, call him Ilyusha, and love him instead of me . . ."

"Shut up, old man, you'll get well!" Krasotkin suddenly shouted as if he were angry.

"And don't ever forget me, papa," Ilyusha went on, "visit my grave . . . and one more thing, papa, you must bury me by the big stone where we used to go for our walks, and visit me there with Krasotkin, in the evenings . . . And Perezvon . . . And I'll be waiting for you . . . Papa, papa!"

His voice broke off. All three embraced one another and were silent now. Ninochka, too, wept quietly in her chair, and suddenly, seeing everyone crying, the mother also dissolved in tears.

"Ilyushechka! Ilyushechka!" she kept exclaiming.

Krasotkin suddenly freed himself from Ilyusha's embrace.

"Good-bye, old man, my mother's expecting me for dinner," he spoke quickly. "Too bad I didn't warn her! She'll be really worried . . . But after dinner I'll come right back, for the whole day, for the whole evening, and I'll tell you so many things, so many things! And I'll bring Perezvon—I'll have to take him with me now, because without me he'll howl and bother you—good-bye!"

And he ran out to the entryway. He did not want to cry, but in the hall he started crying all the same. Alyosha found him in that state.

"Kolya, you absolutely must keep your word and come, otherwise he'll grieve terribly," Alyosha said emphatically.

"Absolutely! Oh, how I curse myself for not coming before," Kolya muttered, crying and no longer embarrassed to be crying. At that moment the captain all but jumped out of the room and at once closed the door behind him. His face was frenzied, his lips trembled. He stood facing the two young men and threw up his arms.

"I don't want a nice boy! I don't want another boy!" he whispered in a wild whisper, clenching his teeth. "If I forget thee, O Jerusalem, let my tongue cleave . . ."[1]

He broke off as if he were choking, and sank helplessly on his knees in front of the wooden bench. Pressing his head with both fists, he began sobbing, shrieking somehow absurdly, restraining himself as much as he could, however, so that his shrieks would not be heard in the room. Kolya ran out to the street.

"Good-bye, Karamazov! And you, are you coming back?" he cried sharply and angrily to Alyosha.

"I'll certainly come back in the evening."

"What was that he said about Jerusalem . . . ? What was it?"

"It's from the Bible: 'If I forget thee, O Jerusalem,' meaning if I forget all that's most precious to me, if I exchange it for anything, may I be struck . . ."

"Enough, I understand! So, make sure you come! *Ici*, Perezvon!" he shouted quite fiercely to the dog, and strode home with long, quick strides.

Chapter 1

At Grushenka's

lyosha made his way towards Cathedral Square, to the house of the widow orozov, to see Grushenka. Early that morning she had sent Fenya to him vith an urgent request that he come. Having questioned Fenya, Alyosha ound out that her mistress had been in some great and particular alarm ever ince the previous day. During the two months following Mitya's arrest, Al-osha had often visited the widow Morozov's, both at his own urging and on rrands for Mitya. Some three days after Mitya's arrest, Grushenka had be-ome quite ill and was sick for almost five weeks. For one of those five weeks he lay unconscious. Her face was greatly changed, she had become thin and allow, though for almost two weeks she had already been able to go out. But n Alyosha's opinion her face had become even more attractive, as it were, and e loved meeting her eyes when he entered her room. Something firm and ware seemed to have settled in her eyes. Some spiritual turnabout told in her; certain steadfast, humble, but good and irrevocable resolution appeared. A mall vertical wrinkle came to her forehead, between her eyebrows, giving er dear face a look of thoughtfulness concentrated upon itself, which was ven almost severe at first glance. There was no trace, for example, of her for-ner frivolity. Alyosha found it strange, too, that despite all the misfortune hat had befallen the poor woman, engaged to a fiancé arrested on accusation f a terrible crime almost at the very moment she had become engaged to him, despite her illness afterwards, and the threat of the almost inevitable verdict to come, Grushenka still had not lost her former youthful gaiety. In her once proud eyes there now shone a certain gentleness, although . . . although from time to time, nevertheless, those eyes blazed once again with a sort of ominous fire, whenever a certain old anxiety visited her, which not only had not abated, but had even grown stronger in her heart. The object of that anx-iety was ever the same: Katerina Ivanovna, whom Grushenka even spoke of in her delirium when she was still lying sick. Alyosha understood that she was terribly jealous of her because of Mitya, the prisoner Mitya, despite the fact that Katerina Ivanovna had not once visited him in prison, though she could have done so whenever she liked. All of this turned into a somewhat difficult problem for Alyosha, because Grushenka opened her heart to him alone and constantly asked his advice; and sometimes he was utterly unable to tell her anything.

Preoccupied, he entered her apartment. She was home by then; it was half an hour since she had come back from seeing Mitya, and by the quick movement with which she jumped up from the armchair at the table to greet him, he concluded that she had been waiting for him with great impatience. There were cards on the table, and a game of "fools" had been dealt out. On the leather sofa on the other side of the table a bed had been made up on which Maximov, obviously ill and weak, though smiling sweetly, reclined in a dressing gown and cotton nightcap. Having returned with Grushenka from Mokroye about two months before, the homeless old man had simply stayed on with her and by her and never left. When he arrived with her that day in the rain and slush, drenched and frightened, he sat down on the sofa and stared at her silently with a timid, imploring smile. Grushenka, who was in terrible grief and in the first stages of a fever, and was so taken up with various troubles that she almost forgot about him for the first half hour after her arrival—suddenly looked at him somehow attentively: he giggled at her in a pathetic and lost way. She called Fenya and told her to give him something to eat. All that day he sat in the same place almost without stirring; when it grew dark and the shutters were closed, Fenya asked her mistress:

"Well, miss, is he going to stay the night?"

"Yes, make up a bed for him on the sofa," Grushenka replied.

Questioning him in more detail, Grushenka learned that he indeed had nowhere at all to go just then, and that "my benefactor, Mr. Kalganov, announced to me straight out that he would no longer receive me, and gave me five roubles." "Well, stay then, God help you," Grushenka decided in anguish, giving him a compassionate smile. The old man cringed at her smile, and his lips trembled with grateful weeping. And so the wandering sponger had remained with her ever since. Even during her illness he did not leave. Fenya and her mother, Grushenka's cook, did not turn him out, but continued to feed him and make up his bed on the sofa. Later, Grushenka even got used to him, and, coming back from seeing Mitya (whom, as soon as she felt a bit better, she at once began visiting, even before she was fully recovered), in order to kill her anguish she would sit down and start talking with "Maximushka" about all sorts of trifles, just so as not to think about her grief. It turned out that the old man could occasionally come up with some story or other, so that finally he even became necessary to her. Apart from Alyosha, who did not come every day, however, and never stayed long, Grushenka received almost no one. By then her old man, the merchant, was terribly ill, "on the way out," as people said in town, and indeed he died only a week after Mitya's trial. Three weeks before his death, feeling that the finale was near, he at last summoned his sons upstairs, with their wives and children, and told them not to leave him thereafter. As for Grushenka, from that same moment he gave strict orders not to admit her, and to tell her if she came: "He wishes you a long and happy life, and asks you to forget him completely." Grushenka sent almost every day, however, to inquire about his health.

"You've come at last!" she cried, throwing down the cards and joyfully greeting Alyosha, "and Maximushka's been scaring me that you might not come after all. Ah, how I need you! Sit down at the table; well, what will you have, some coffee?"

"Why not?" said Alyosha, sitting down at the table. "I'm very hungry."

"So there. Fenya, Fenya, some coffee!" cried Grushenka. "I've had it ready for a long time, waiting for you. Bring some pirozhki, too, and make sure they're hot. No, listen, Alyosha, I had a big storm over those pirozhki today. I took them to the prison for him, and would you believe it, he threw them back at me and wouldn't eat them. He even flung one on the floor and trampled on it. So I said: 'I'll leave them with the guard; if you don't eat them by evening, it means you're feeding on your own venomous wickedness!' and with that I left. We really quarreled again, do you believe it? Each time I go, we quarrel."

Grushenka poured it all out in her excitement. Maximov, having at once grown timid, smiled and dropped his eyes.

"But what did you quarrel about this time?" asked Alyosha.

"I didn't even expect it! Imagine, he got jealous over my 'former' one: 'Why are you keeping him?' he said. 'So you've started keeping him, have you?' He gets jealous all the time, jealous over me! He gets jealous eating and sleeping. Once last week he even got jealous of Kuzma."

"But he knew about the 'former' one, didn't he?"

"What can I say? He's known about him from the very beginning right down to this day, and today he suddenly gets up and starts scolding me. It's shameful even to tell what he was saying. Fool! Rakitka came to see him as I was leaving. Maybe it's Rakitka who has been baiting him, eh? What do you think?" she added as if absentmindedly.

"He loves you, that's what, he loves you very much. And he's worried now, too."

"How could he not be worried, the trial is tomorrow. I went to say something to him about tomorrow, because, Alyosha, I'm afraid even to think about what will happen tomorrow! You say he's worried, but how about me! And he talks about the Pole! What a fool! Well, there's no fear he'll get jealous of Maximushka here."

"My spouse was also very jealous over me, ma'am," Maximov put a little word in.

"Over you, really?" Grushenka laughed despite herself. "Who was she jealous of?"

"The chambermaids, ma'am."

"Eh, keep still, Maximushka, it's no time for laughing now. I even feel angry. Don't ogle the pirozhki, you won't get any, they're not good for you, and you won't get your little drop either. Must I bother with him, too? Really, it's like running an almshouse," she laughed.

"I am unworthy of your benefactions, ma'am, I am nothing, ma'am," Maximov said in a tearful little voice. "You'd do better to lavish your benefactions on those who are more useful than I am, ma'am."

"Ahh, everyone is useful, Maximushka, and how can anyone say who is more useful? I wish that Pole wasn't here at all, Alyosha, you know, he decided to get sick today. I visited him, too. And now I'm going to send him some pirozhki on purpose, I didn't send him any, but Mitya accused me of it, so now I'll send some on purpose, on purpose! Ah, here's Fenya with a letter! Well, just as I thought, it's from the Poles again, asking for money again."

Pan Mussyalovich had indeed sent an extremely long and, as was his custom, flowery letter, in which he asked for a loan of three roubles. The letter was accompanied by a receipt and a note promising payment within three months; Pan Vrublevsky also signed the receipt. Grushenka had already received many such letters from her "former" one, all with such receipts. It started with her recovery, about two weeks before. She knew, however, that both *pans* had also come during her illness to inquire about her health. The first letter Grushenka had received was long, on stationery of large format, sealed with a big family crest, and terribly obscure and flowery, so that she read only halfway through and dropped it without having understood a thing. And she could hardly be bothered with letters then. The first letter was followed the next day by a second one, in which Pan Mussyalovich asked for a loan of two thousand roubles for a very short term. This letter Grushenka also left unanswered. After that a whole series of letters followed, one letter a day, all equally pompous and flowery, but in which the amount requested, gradually diminishing, went down to a hundred roubles, to twenty-five roubles, to ten roubles, and finally Grushenka suddenly received a letter in which the two *pans* asked her for only one rouble, and enclosed a receipt which they both had signed. Then Grushenka suddenly felt sorry for them, and at dusk he herself ran over to see the *pan*. She found the two Poles in terrible, almost bject poverty, without food, without firewood, without cigarettes, in debt to heir landlady. The two hundred roubles they had won from Mitya at Mo-roye had quickly disappeared somewhere. Grushenka found it surprising, owever, that both *pans* met her with haughty pomposity and independence, vith the greatest ceremony, with high-flown speeches. Grushenka merely aughed and gave her "former" one ten roubles. That time she had laughingly old Mitya about it, and he was not jealous at all. But from then on the *pans* ad kept hold of Grushenka, bombarding her daily with letters asking for noney, and each time she sent them a little. And suddenly that day Mitya de-ided to become fiercely jealous.

"Like a fool I stopped at his place, too, just for a moment, on my way to see Mitya, because he, too, has gotten sick—my former *pan*, I mean," Grushenka egan again, fussing and hurrying, "so I laughed and told Mitya about it: magine, I said, my Pole decided to sing me his old songs on the guitar, he hought I'd get all sentimental and marry him. And Mitya jumped up curs-ng . . . So I'm just going to send some pirozhki to the *pans*! Did they send that same girl, Fenya? Here, give her three roubles and wrap up a dozen or so pirozhki in paper, and tell her to take them, and you, Alyosha, be sure to tell Mitya that I sent pirozhki to them."

"I wouldn't tell him for anything," Alyosha said, smiling.

"Eh, you think he's suffering; but he gets jealous on purpose, and in fact he doesn't really care," Grushenka said bitterly.

"What do you mean, on purpose?" asked Alyosha.

"You are a silly one, Alyoshenka, that's what, you don't understand any-thing about it, for all your intelligence, that's what. What hurts me is not that he's jealous of me, such as I am; it would hurt me if he wasn't jealous at all. I'm like that. I wouldn't be hurt by his jealousy, I also have a cruel heart, I can be jealous myself. No, what hurts me is that he doesn't love me at all and is being jealous *on purpose* now, that's what. I'm not blind, I can see! He suddenly started telling me about her, about Katka: she's this and she's that, she wrote and invited a doctor from Moscow for him, for the trial, she did it to save him, she also invited the best lawyer, the most learned one. It means he loves her, if he starts praising her right to my face, the brazen-face! He feels guilty to-wards me, and so he pesters me in order to make me guiltier than he is and put all the blame on me alone: 'You were with the Pole before me,' he means, 'so I'm allowed to do it with Katka.' That's what it is! He wants to put all the blame on me alone. He pesters me on purpose, I tell you, on purpose, only I . . ."

Grushenka did not finish saying what she would do. She covered her eyes with her handkerchief and burst into tears.

"He does not love Katerina Ivanovna," Alyosha said firmly.

"Well, I'll soon find out whether he loves her or not," Grushenka said, with a menacing note in her voice, taking the handkerchief from her eyes. Her face became distorted. Alyosha was grieved to see her face, which had been meek and quietly joyful, suddenly become sullen and wicked.

"Enough of this foolishness," she suddenly snapped, "I did not call you here for that at all. Alyosha, darling, tomorrow, what will happen tomorrow? That's what torments me! And I'm the only one it torments! I look at everyone, and no one is thinking about it, no one wants to have anything to do with it. Do you at least think about it? They're going to judge him tomorrow! Tell me, how are they going to judge him there? It was the lackey who killed him, the lackey! Lord! Can it be that they'll condemn him instead of the lackey, and no one will stand up for him? They haven't even bothered the lackey at all, have they?"

"He was closely questioned," Alyosha observed thoughtfully, "but they all concluded that it wasn't him. Now he's lying in bed very sick. He's been sick ever since that falling fit. Really sick," Alyosha added.

"Lord, but why don't you go to this lawyer yourself and tell him the whole business in private? They say he was invited from Petersburg for three thousand."

"The three of us put up the three thousand—my brother Ivan and I, and Katerina Ivanovna—and the doctor was called in from Moscow for two thousand by her alone. The lawyer Fetyukovich would have charged more, but the case has become known all over Russia, they're talking about it in all the newspapers and magazines, so Fetyukovich agreed to come more for the sake of glory, because the case has become so famous. I saw him yesterday."

"Well, what? Did you tell him?" Grushenka asked hastily.

"He listened to me and said nothing. He said he had already formed a certain opinion. But he promised to take my words into consideration."

"What? Into consideration? They're swindlers! They'll ruin him! And the doctor, why did that woman call in the doctor?"

"As an expert. They want to establish that my brother is crazy and killed in a fit of madness, not knowing what he was doing," Alyosha smiled quietly, "only my brother won't agree to it."

"Ah, but it would be true, if he were the murderer!" Grushenka exclaimed. "He was crazy then, completely crazy, and it's I who am to blame, base creature that I am! Only he didn't kill him, he didn't! And they all say he killed him, the whole town. Even Fenya, even she gave such evidence that it comes out as if he killed him. And in the shop, and that official, and earlier in the tavern people heard him! Everyone is against him, everyone is squawking."

"Yes, the evidence has multiplied terribly," Alyosha observed glumly.

"And Grigory, Grigory Vasilievich, he, too, stands by his story that the door was open, that he saw it, he just sticks to it and won't be budged, I ran over to see him, I talked with him myself! And he's cursing on top of it."

"Yes, that is perhaps the strongest evidence against my brother," Alyosha said.

"And as for Mitya being crazy, that's just what he is now, too," Grushenka suddenly began with a particularly worried and mysterious sort of look. "You know, Alyoshenka, I've wanted to tell you about it for a long time: I visit him every day and simply wonder. Tell me what you think: do you know what he's started talking about now? He talks and talks—and I can't understand a thing, I think it must be something intelligent and I'm just stupid, I can't understand it; but he's suddenly started talking about a wee one—that is, about some baby. 'Why is the wee one poor?' he says. 'For that wee one I'll go to Siberia now, I'm not a murderer, but I must go to Siberia!' What does he mean, what wee one? I didn't understand a thing. I just started crying as he was speaking, because he spoke so well, and he was crying himself, and I started crying, and suddenly he kissed me and made the sign of the cross over me. What is it, Alyosha, tell me, what is this 'wee one'?"

"It's Rakitin, for some reason he's taken to visiting him," Alyosha smiled, "although . . . that is not from Rakitin. I didn't go to see him yesterday; today I shall."

"No, it's not Rakitka, it's his brother Ivan Fyodorovich upsetting him, he keeps going to see him, that's what . . . ," Grushenka said, and suddenly stopped short. Alyosha stared at her as if stunned.

"Keeps going? Has he really gone to see him? Mitya himself told me Ivan had not come once."

"Well . . . well, there I've done it. Blurted it out!" Grushenka exclaimed in embarrassment, turning crimson all over. "Wait, Alyosha, don't say anything. Since I've blurted it out, so be it, I'll tell you the whole truth: he went to see him twice, the first time as soon as he arrived—he came galloping here at once from Moscow, I hadn't had time to get sick yet—and the second time a week ago. He told Mitya not to tell you about it, by any means, and not to tell anyone, because he had come in secret."

Alyosha sat deep in thought, pondering something. The news obviously struck him.

"Brother Ivan does not speak about Mitya's case with me," he said slowly, "and generally over these two months he has spoken very little with me, and when I went to see him, he was always displeased that I had come, so I haven't been to see him for three weeks now. Hmm . . . If he went a week ago, then . . . some sort of change has indeed come over Mitya this week . . ."

"A change, a change!" Grushenka quickly joined in. "They have a secret, they have a secret! Mitya told me himself there was a secret, and, you know, it's such a secret that Mitya can't even calm down. He was cheerful before, and he's cheerful now, too, only, you know, when he starts shaking his head like that, and pacing the room, and pulling the hair on his temple with his right finger, then I know something is troubling his soul . . . I know it . . . ! He used to be cheerful; well, but he was cheerful today, too!"

"Didn't you say he was worried?"

"But he's worried and still cheerful. He keeps getting worried for just a moment, and then he's cheerful, and then suddenly he's worried again. And you know, Alyosha, I keep marveling at him: there's such a fright ahead of him, and he sometimes laughs at such trifles, as if he were a child himself."

"And it's true that he asked you not to tell me about Ivan? He actually said: don't tell him?"

"He actually said: don't tell him. It's you he's most afraid of—Mitya, I mean. Because there's a secret here, he himself said there's a secret . . . Alyosha, darling, go and try to worm their secret out of him, and come and tell me," Grushenka started up and implored him suddenly, "resolve it for me, poor woman, so that I know my cursed lot! That's why I sent for you."

"So you think it's something to do with you? But then he wouldn't have mentioned the secret in front of you."

"I don't know. Maybe he wants to tell me but doesn't dare. He's warning me. There's a secret, he says, but what secret he doesn't say."

"What do you think yourself?"

"What can I think? It's the end of me, that's what I think. The three of them have prepared an end for me, because Katka is in on it. It's all Katka, it all comes from her. 'She's this and she's that' means that I'm not. He's saying it beforehand, he's warning me beforehand. He's planning to leave me, that's the whole secret! The three of them thought it up—Mitka, Katka, and Ivan Fyodorovich. Alyosha, I've been wanting to ask you for a long time: a week ago he suddenly revealed to me that Ivan is in love with Katka, because he goes to see her often. Was he telling me the truth or not? Tell me honestly, stab me in the heart!"

"I won't lie to you. Ivan is not in love with Katerina Ivanovna, that is what I think."

"That's what I immediately thought! He's lying to me, brazenly, that's what! And he's being jealous now so that he can blame me later. He's a fool, he can't cover his traces, he's so open . . . But I'll show him, I'll show him! 'You believe I killed him,' he said—he said it to me, to me, he reproached me with that! God help him! But you just wait, that Katka will get it from me at the trial! I'll have a little something to say there . . . I'll say everything there!"

And again she cried bitterly.

"This much I can tell you firmly, Grushenka," Alyosha said, rising, "first, that he loves you, loves you more than anyone in the world, and only you, believe me when I say it. I know. I really know. The second thing I will tell you is that I am not going to try and worm the secret out of him, but if he tells me himself today, I'll tell him straight out that I have promised to tell you. Then I'll come to you this very day and tell you. Only . . . it seems to me . . . Katerina Ivanovna has nothing to do with it, and the secret is about something else. That is certainly so. It doesn't look at all as if it has to do with Katerina Ivanovna, so it seems to me. Good-bye for now!"

Alyosha pressed her hand. Grushenka was still crying. He saw that she had very little faith in his consolations, but it was good enough even so that she had vented her grief, that she had spoken herself out. He was sorry to leave her in such a state, but he was in a rush. He still had much to do ahead of him.

Chapter 2

An Ailing Little Foot

The first thing he had to do was at Madame Khokhlakov's house, and he hurried there to get it over with as quickly as possible and not be late for Mitya. Madame Khokhlakov had been a bit unwell for the past three weeks: her foot had become swollen for some reason, and though she did not stay in bed, she spent the day reclining on the couch in her boudoir, dressed in an attractive, but decent, deshabille. Alyosha once noted to himself with an innocent smile that, despite her illness, Madame Khokhlakov had become almost dressy—all sorts of lace caps, bows, little bed-jackets appeared—and he imagined he knew why, though he tried to chase such idle thoughts from his mind. Among other guests, Madame Khokhlakov had been visited over the past two months by the young man Perkhotin. Alyosha had not come to call for four days, and, on entering the house, hastened to go straight to Liza, as it was with her that he had to do, since Liza had sent her maid to him the day before with an urgent request that he come to her at once "about a very important circumstance," which, for certain reasons, aroused Alyosha's interest. But while the maid was gone to announce him to Liza, Madame Khokhlakov learned of his arrival from someone and sent at once asking him to come to her "for just a moment." Alyosha decided it would be better to satisfy the mother's request first, or she would keep sending to Liza every minute while he was with her. Madame Khokhlakov was lying on her couch, dressed somehow especially festively and obviously in a state of extreme nervous excitement. She greeted Alyosha with cries of rapture.

"Ages, ages, it's such ages since I've seen you! A whole week, for pity's sake, ah, but no, you were here just four days ago, on Wednesday. You've come to see Lise, I'm sure you wanted to go straight to her, tiptoeing so that I wouldn't hear. Dear, dear Alexei Fyodorovich, if you knew how I worry about her! But of that later. Of that later—though it's the most important thing. Dear Alexei Fyodorovich, I trust you with my Liza completely. After the elder Zosima's death—God rest his soul!" (she crossed herself) "—after him I've regarded you as a monk, though you do look lovely in your new suit. Where did you find such a tailor here? But no, no, that's not the main thing—of that later. Forgive me if I sometimes call you Alyosha, I'm an old woman, all is allowed me," she smiled coyly, "but of that later, too. The main thing is not to forget the main thing. Please remind me if I get confused; you should say: 'And what about the main thing?' Ah, how do I know what the main thing is now! Ever since Lise took back her promise—a child's promise, Alexei Fyodorovich—to marry you, you've understood of course that it was all just the playful, childish fantasy of a sick girl, who had sat for so long in a chair—thank God she's walking now. That new doctor Katya invited from Moscow for that unfortunate brother of yours, who tomorrow . . . But why speak of tomorrow! I die just at the thought of tomorrow! Mainly of curiosity . . . In short, that doctor was here yesterday and saw Lise . . . I paid him fifty roubles for the visit. But that's not it, again that's not it . . . You see, now I'm completely confused. I rush. Why do I rush? I don't know. It's terrible how I've stopped knowing these days. Everything's got mixed up for me into some kind of lump. I'm afraid you'll be so bored you'll just go running out my door and leave not a trace behind. Oh, my God! Why are we sitting here and—coffee, first of all—Yulia, Glafira, coffee!"

Alyosha hastened to thank her and announced that he had just had coffee.

"With whom?"

"With Agrafena Alexandrovna."

"With . . . with that woman! Ah, it's she who has ruined everybody, but in fact I don't know, they say she's become a saint, though it's a bit late. She'd better have done it before, when it was needed, but what's the use of it now? Hush, hush, Alexei Fyodorovich, because there's so much I want to say that I'm afraid I won't say anything. This terrible trial . . . I must go, I am preparing myself, I'll be carried in in a chair, and anyway I'll be able to sit, there will be people with me, and, you know, I'm one of the witnesses. How am I going to speak, how am I going to speak? I don't know what I shall say. I shall have to take an oath, that's so, isn't it?"

"That is so, but I don't think you will be able to go."

"I can sit; ah, you're confusing me! This trial, this wild act, and then everyone goes to Siberia, others get married, and it all happens so quickly, so quickly, and everything is changing, and in the end there's nothing, everyone is old and has one foot in the grave. Well, let it be, I'm tired. This Katya—*cette charmante personne*, she's shattered all my hopes: now she'll follow your one brother to Siberia, and your other brother will follow her and live in the next town, and they'll all torment one another. It drives me crazy, and above all, the publicity: they've written about it a million times in all the Petersburg and Moscow newspapers. Ah, yes, imagine, they also wrote about me, that I was your brother's 'dear friend,' I don't want to say a naughty word, but imagine, just imagine!"

"It can't be! Where and how did they write it?"

"I'll show you right now. I received it yesterday and read it yesterday. Here, in the newspaper *Rumors*, from Petersburg. These *Rumors* just started coming out this year, I'm terribly fond of rumors, so I subscribed, and now I've been paid back for it, this is the sort of rumors they turned out to be. Here, this passage, read it."

And she handed Alyosha a page from a newspaper that had been under her pillow.

She was not really upset, but somehow all in pieces, and it was perhaps possible that everything had indeed become mixed into a lump in her head. The newspaper item was a typical one and, of course, must have had a rather ticklish effect on her, but, fortunately, at that moment she was perhaps unable to concentrate on any one point, and could therefore even forget about the newspaper in a moment and jump on to something quite different. Alyosha had known for some time that the rumor of a terrible trial had spread everywhere throughout Russia, and, God, what wild reports and articles he had read in the course of those two months, along with other, accurate items, about his brother, about the Karamazovs in general, and even about himself. In one newspaper it was even stated that he had become a monk from fear, following his brother's crime, and gone into seclusion; this was denied in another, where it was written that, on the contrary, he and his elder Zosima had robbed the monastery cash box and "skipped from the monastery." Today's item in the newspaper *Rumors* was entitled "From Skotoprigonyevsk"[1] (alas, that is the name of our town; I have been concealing it all this time) "Concerning the Trial of Karamazov." It was brief, and there was no direct mention of Madame Khokhlakov, and generally all the names were concealed. It was simply reported that the criminal whose forthcoming trial was causing so much noise was a retired army officer, of an insolent sort, an idler and serf-owner, who devoted all his time to amorous affairs, and had a particular influence with certain "bored and solitary ladies." And that one such lady, "a bored widow," rather girlish, though she already had a grown-up daughter, took such a fancy to him that only two hours before the crime she had offered him three thousand roubles if he would run away with her at once to the gold mines. But the villain still preferred better to kill his father and rob him precisely of three thousand, counting on doing it with impunity, rather than drag himself off to Siberia with the forty-year-old charms of his bored lady. This playful communication ended, quite properly, with noble indignation at the immorality of parricide and the former serfdom. Having read it with curiosity, Alyosha folded the page and handed it back to Madame Khokhlakov.

"Well, who else is it but me?" she started prattling again. "It's me, I offered him gold mines almost an hour before, and suddenly those 'forty-year-old charms'! But it wasn't that! He says it on purpose! May the eternal judge forgive him those forty-year-old charms, as I forgive him, but this . . . do you know who it is? It's your friend Rakitin."

"Perhaps," said Alyosha, "though I've heard nothing about it."

"It's him, him, and no 'perhaps'! Because I turned him out . . . Do you know that whole story?"

"I know you suggested that he not visit you in the future, but precisely why, I haven't heard . . . at least, not from you."

"Ah, so you heard it from him! And what, does he abuse me, does he abuse me very much?"

"Yes, he abuses you, but he abuses everybody. But why you closed your door to him—that he didn't tell me. And in fact I see him very seldom. We are not friends."

"Well, then I'll reveal it all to you and—since there's no help for it—I'll confess, because there's a point here that may be my own fault. Just a tiny, little point, the tiniest, so tiny it may not even exist. You see, my dear," Madame Khokhlakov suddenly acquired a sort of playful look, and a lovely, though mysterious, little smile flashed on her lips, "you see, I suspect . . . you'll forgive me, Alyosha, I'm speaking to you as a mother . . . oh, no, no, on the contrary, I'm speaking to you now as my father . . . because mother doesn't fit here at all . . . Well, just as to Father Zosima in confession, that's the most accurate, that fits very well: I did just call you a monk—well, so that poor young man, your friend Rakitin (oh, God, I simply cannot be angry with him! I'm angry and cross, but not very much), in short, that frivolous young man, just imagine, suddenly seems to have decided to fall in love with me. I only noticed it later, suddenly, but at first, that is, about a month ago, he started visiting me more often, almost every day, though we were acquainted before then. I didn't suspect a thing . . . and then suddenly it dawned on me, as it were, and I began noticing, to my surprise. You know, two months ago I began to receive that modest, nice, and worthy young man Pyotr Ilyich Perkhotin, who is in service here. You've met him so many times yourself. A worthy, serious man, isn't it so? He comes once every three days, not every day (though why not every day?), and is always so well dressed, and generally I like young people, Alyosha, talented, modest, like you, and he has almost the mind of a statesman, he speaks so nicely, I shall certainly, certainly put in a word for him. He is a future diplomat. He all but saved me from death on that horrible day, when he came to me at night. Well, and then your friend Rakitin always comes in such boots, and drags them on the carpet . . . in short, he even began dropping some hints, and suddenly once, as he was leaving, he squeezed my hand terribly. As soon as he squeezed my hand, my foot suddenly started to hurt. He had met Pyotr Ilyich in my house before, and would you believe it, he was constantly nagging him, nagging him, just grumbling at him for some reason. I used to look at the two of them, when they got together, and laugh to myself. Then suddenly, as I was sitting alone, that is, no, I was already lying down then, suddenly, as I was lying alone, Mikhail Ivanovich came and, imagine, brought me a poem of his, a very short one, on my ailing foot, that is, he described my ailing foot in the poem. Wait, how did it go?

> This little foot, this little foot,
> Is hurting now a little bit . . .

or something like that—I can never remember poetry—I have it here—but I'll show it to you later, it's charming, charming, and, you know, it's not just about my foot, it's edifying, too, with a charming idea, only I've forgotten it, in short, it's just right for an album. Well, naturally I thanked him, and he was obviously flattered. I had only just thanked him when Pyotr Ilyich also came in, and Mikhail Ivanovich suddenly looked black as night. I could see that Pyotr Ilyich had hampered him in something, because Mikhail Ivanovich certainly wanted to say something right after the poem, I already anticipated it, and then Pyotr Ilyich walked in. I suddenly showed Pyotr Ilyich the poem, and didn't tell him who wrote it. But I'm sure, I'm sure he guessed at once, though he still hasn't admitted it and says he didn't guess; but he says it on purpose. Pyotr Ilyich immediately laughed and started criticizing: worthless doggerel, he said, some seminarian must have written it—and you know, he said it with such passion, such passion! Here your friend, instead of laughing, suddenly got completely furious . . . Lord, I thought, they're going to start fighting. 'I wrote it,' he said. 'I wrote it as a joke,' he said, 'because I consider it base to write poetry . . . Only my poem is good. They want to set up a monument to your Pushkin for women's little feet,[2] but my poem has a tendency, and you,' he said, 'are a serf-owner; you have no humaneness at all,' he said, 'you don't feel any of today's enlightened feelings, progress hasn't touched you; you are an official,' he said, 'and you take bribes!' At that point I began shouting and pleading with them. And Pyotr Ilyich, you know, is not timid at all, and he suddenly assumed the most noble tone: he looked at him mockingly, listened, and apologized: 'I did not know,' he said. 'If I had known, I should not have said it, I should have praised it,' he said . . . 'Poets,' he said, 'are all so irritable . . .' In short, it was that sort of taunting in the guise of the most noble tone. He himself explained to me later that he was just taunting him, and I thought he was in earnest. Only suddenly I was lying there, just as I am before you now, and I thought: would it be noble, or would it not, if I suddenly turned Mikhail Ivanovich out for shouting so rudely at a guest in my house? And, would you believe it, I lay there, I closed my eyes and thought: would it or would it not be noble, and I couldn't decide, and I was tormented, tormented, and my heart was pounding: should I shout, or shouldn't I? One voice said: shout, and the other said: no, don't shout! And no sooner had that other voice spoken than I suddenly shouted and suddenly fainted. Well, naturally there was a commotion. I suddenly stood up and said to Mikhail Ivanovich: 'It grieves me to say this to you, but I no longer wish to receive you in my house.' So I turned him out. Ah, Alexei Fyodorovich! I know myself that I did a bad thing, it was all a lie, I wasn't angry with him at all, but I suddenly—the main thing is, I suddenly fancied that it would be so nice, that scene . . . Only, believe me, it was quite a natural scene, because I even burst into tears, and cried for several days afterwards, and then suddenly after dinner I forgot it all. So he stopped coming, it's been two weeks now, and I wondered: will he really not come ever again? That was just yesterday, and suddenly in the evening these *Rumors* came. I read it and gasped, who could have written it, he wrote it, he went home that time, sat down—and wrote it; he sent it—they printed it. Because it happened two weeks ago. Only, Alyosha, it's terrible what I'm saying, and I'm not at all saying what I should be saying! Ah, it comes out by itself!"

"Today I need terribly to get to see my brother in time," Alyosha attempted to murmur.

"Precisely, precisely! You've reminded me of everything! Listen, what is a fit of passion?"

"A fit of passion?" Alyosha said in surprise.

"A legal fit of passion. A fit of passion for which they forgive everything. Whatever you do—you're immediately forgiven."

"But what are you talking about?"

"I'll tell you: this Katya . . . ah, she's a dear, dear creature, only I can't tell who she's in love with. She was sitting here the other day, and I couldn't get anything out of her. The more so as she's begun talking to me so superficially now, in short, it's all about my health and nothing more, and she even adopts such a tone, so I said to myself: well, never mind, God be with you . . . Ah, yes, so about this fit of passion: the doctor has come. You do know that the doctor has come? But of course you know, the one who can recognize crazy people, you invited him yourself—that is, not you but Katya. It's all Katya! So, look: a man sits there and he's not crazy at all, only suddenly he has a fit of passion. He may be fully conscious and know what he's doing, but at the same time he's in a fit of passion. And so, apparently, Dmitri Fyodorovich also had a fit of passion. They found out about the fit of passion as soon as they opened the new law courts. It's a blessing of the new courts. The doctor was here and questioned me about that evening, I mean about the gold mines: 'How was he then?' he said. Of course it was a fit of passion—he came in shouting: 'Money, money, three thousand, give me three thousand,' and then went and suddenly killed. 'I don't want to,' he said, 'I don't want to kill,' and suddenly he killed. And so, just for that he'll be forgiven, because he tried to resist, and then killed."

"But he did not kill," Alyosha interrupted a bit sharply. Worry and impatience were overcoming him more and more.

"I know, it was that old man, Grigory . . ."

"What? Grigory?" Alyosha cried.

"Yes, yes, it was Grigory. After Dmitri Fyodorovich hit him, he lay there for a while, then got up, saw the door open, went in, and killed Fyodor Pavlovich."

"But why, why?"

"He had a fit of passion. After Dmitri Fyodorovich hit him on the head, he came to, had a fit of passion, and went and killed him. And if he says he didn't kill him, then maybe he just doesn't remember. Only, you see: it would be better, so much better, if it were Dmitri Fyodorovich who killed him. And that's how it was, though I say it was Grigory, it was certainly Dmitri Fyodorovich, and that's much, much better! Oh, not better because a son killed his father, I'm not praising that; on the contrary, children should honor their parents; but still it's better if it was he, because then there's nothing to weep about, because he was beside himself when he did it, or, rather, he was within himself, but didn't know what was happening to him. No, let them forgive him; it's so humane, and everyone will see this blessing of the new courts, and I didn't even know about it, but they say it has existed for a long time, and when I found out yesterday, I was so struck that I wanted to send for you at once; and afterwards, if they forgive him, then right after the trial he'll come here for dinner, and I'll invite acquaintances, and we shall drink to the new courts. I don't think he's dangerous; besides, I'll invite a lot of guests, so it will always be possible to remove him if he does anything; and later he can become a justice of the peace somewhere in another town, or something like that, because those who have suffered some misfortune themselves are the best judges of all. And moreover, who isn't in a fit of passion these days—you, me, we're all in a fit of passion, there are so many examples: a man sits singing some old song, and suddenly something annoys him, he takes out a gun and shoots whoever happens to be there, and then they all forgive him. I read it recently, and all the doctors confirmed it. The doctors confirm nowadays, they confirm everything. Good heavens, my Lise is in a fit of passion, I wept just yesterday on her account, and the day before yesterday, and today I realized that she's simply in a fit of passion. Oh, Lise upsets me so! I think she's gone quite mad. Why did she send for you? Did she send for you, or did you come by yourself?"

"Yes, she sent for me, and I shall go to her now," Alyosha made a resolute attempt to stand up.

"Ah, dear, dear Alexei Fyodorovich, perhaps that is the main thing," Madame Khokhlakov cried, and suddenly burst into tears. "God knows I sincerely trust you with Lise, and it doesn't matter that she sent for you in secret from her mother. But, forgive me, I cannot with the same ease trust my daughter to your brother, Ivan Fyodorovich, though I continue to regard him as a most chivalrous young man. And, imagine, he suddenly visited Lise, and I knew nothing about it."

"What? How? When?" Alyosha was terribly surprised. He did not sit down again, but listened standing.

"I shall tell you, that is perhaps why I called you here, because otherwise I don't know why I called you here. It was like this: Ivan Fyodorovich has been to see me only twice since his return from Moscow; the first time he came as an acquaintance, to visit me; the other time, this was just recently, Katya was here, and he came over because he found out she was here. I, naturally, have never claimed he should visit often, knowing how many troubles he had without that—*vous comprenez, cette affaire et la mort terrible de votre papa*[3]—only I suddenly learned that he had come again, not to me but to Lise, it was about six days ago, he came, stayed for five minutes, and left. And I learned of it a whole three days later from Glafira, so it was quite a shock to me. I summoned Lise at once, and she laughed: 'He thought you were asleep,' she said, 'and came to ask me about your health.' Of course that's how it was. Only Lise, Lise—oh, God, how she upsets me! Imagine, one night suddenly—it was four days ago, just after you were here last time and left—suddenly that night she had hysterics, shouting, shrieking! Why is it I never have hysterics? Then hysterics the next day, and again the third day, and yesterday, and then yesterday this fit of passion. And she suddenly shouted at me: 'I hate Ivan Fyodorovich, I demand that you not receive him, that you forbid him the house!' I was astounded, it was so sudden, and I objected to her: 'Why on earth should I not receive such a worthy young man, and such a learned one besides, and with such misfortunes, because all these stories—certainly they're a misfortune, there's nothing fortunate about them, is there?' She suddenly burst out laughing at my words, and, you know, so impudently. Well, I was glad, thinking I had made her laugh and now the hysterics would go away, all the more so as I myself wanted to stop receiving Ivan Fyodorovich, because of these strange visits without my consent, and to demand an explanation. Only suddenly this morning, Liza woke up and got angry with Yulia, and, imagine, slapped her in the face. But this is monstrous, I am always formal with my maids. And suddenly an hour later she was embracing Yulia and kissing her feet. And she sent to tell me that she would not come to me at all and would never come to me thereafter, and when I dragged myself to her, she rushed to kiss me and weep, and as she was kissing me, she pushed me out without saying a word, so that I didn't find out anything. Now, dear Alexei Fyodorovich, all my hopes are on you, and, of course, the fate of my whole life is in your hands. I simply ask you to go to Lise, find out everything from her, as only you can do, and come and tell me—me, her mother, because you understand I shall die, I shall simply die, if this all goes on, or else I shall run away. I can bear it no longer, I have patience, but I may lose it, and then . . . and then there will be horrors. Ah, my God, here is Pyotr Ilyich at last!" Madame Khokhlakov cried, brightening up all over, as she saw Pyotr Ilyich Perkhotin come in. "You're late, late! Well, what is it, sit down, speak, decide my fate, what about this lawyer? Where are you going, Alexei Fyodorovich?"

"To Lise."

"Ah, yes! But you won't forget, you won't forget what I asked you? It's a matter of fate, of fate!"

"Of course I won't forget, if only I can . . . but I'm so late," Alyosha muttered, hastily retreating.

"No, come for certain, for certain, and no 'if I can,' otherwise I'll die!" Madame Khokhlakov called after him, but Alyosha had already left the room.

Chapter 3

A Little Demon

When he entered Liza's room, he found her half-reclining in her former chair, in which she had been wheeled around while she was as yet unable to walk. She did not make a move to meet him, but fixed him with her alert, sharp eyes. Her eyes were somewhat feverish, her face was pale and yellow. Alyosha was amazed at how much she had changed in three days; she had even lost weight. She did not hold out her hand to him. He touched her thin, long fingers, which lay motionless on her dress, then silently sat down facing her.

"I know you're in a hurry to get to the prison," Liza said sharply, "and my mother has just kept you for two hours telling you about me and Yulia."

"How did you find out?" asked Alyosha.

"I was eavesdropping. Why are you staring at me? If I want to eavesdrop, I'll eavesdrop, there's nothing wrong with it. I'm not asking forgiveness."

"Are you upset about something?"

"On the contrary, I am very pleased. I've just been thinking over for the thirtieth time how good it is that I refused you and am not going to be your wife. You're unfit to be a husband: I'd marry you, and suddenly give you a note to take to someone I'd have fallen in love with after you, and you would take it and make sure to deliver it, and even bring back the reply. And you'd be forty years old and still carrying such notes."

She suddenly laughed.

"There is something wicked and guileless about you at the same time," Alyosha smiled at her.

"What's guileless is that I'm not ashamed with you. Moreover, not only am I not ashamed, but I do not want to be ashamed, precisely before you, precisely with you. Alyosha, why don't I respect you? I love you very much, but I don't respect you. If I respected you, I wouldn't talk like this without being ashamed, would I?"

"That's true."

"And do you believe that I'm not ashamed with you?"

"No, I don't."

Liza again laughed nervously; she was talking rapidly, quickly.

"I sent some candy to your brother, Dmitri Fyodorovich, in prison. Alyosha, you know, you are so nice! I will love you terribly for allowing me not to love you so soon."

"Why did you send for me today, Lise?"

"I wanted to tell you a wish of mine. I want someone to torment me, to marry me and then torment me, deceive me, leave me and go away. I don't want to be happy!"

"You've come to love disorder?"

"Ah, I want disorder. I keep wanting to set fire to the house. I imagine how I'll sneak up and set fire to it on the sly, it must be on the sly. They'll try to put it out, but it will go on burning. And I'll know and say nothing. Ah, what foolishness! And so boring!"

She waved her hand in disgust.

"It's your rich life," Alyosha said softly.

"Why, is it better to be poor?"

"Yes, it is."

"Your deceased monk filled you with all that. It's not true. Let me be rich and everyone else poor, I'll eat candy and drink cream, and I won't give any to any of them. Ah, don't speak, don't say anything," she waved her hand, though Alyosha had not even opened his mouth, "you've told me all that before, I know it all by heart. Boring. If I'm ever poor, I'll kill somebody—and maybe I'll kill somebody even if I'm rich—why just sit there? But, you know, what I want is to reap, to reap the rye. I'll marry you, and you'll become a peasant, a real peasant, we'll keep a colt, would you like that? Do you know Kalganov?"

"Yes."

"He walks about and dreams. He says: why live in reality, it's better to dream. One can dream up the gayest things, but to live is boring. And yet he's going to marry soon, he's even made me a declaration of love. Do you know how to spin a top?"

"Yes."

"Well, he's like a top: spin him and set him down and then whip, whip, whip: I'll marry him and keep him spinning all his life. Are you ashamed to sit with me?"

"No."

"You're terribly angry that I don't talk about holy things. I don't want to be holy. What will they do in that world for the greatest sin? You must know exactly."

"God will judge," Alyosha was studying her intently.

"That's just how I want it to be. I'll come, and they will judge me, and suddenly I'll laugh them all in the face. I want terribly to set fire to the house, Alyosha, to our house—you still don't believe me?"

"Why shouldn't I? There are even children, about twelve years old, who want very much to set fire to something, and they do set fire to things. It's a sort of illness."

"That's wrong, wrong; maybe there are children, but that's not what I'm talking about."

"You take evil for good, it's a momentary crisis, perhaps it comes from your former illness."

"So, after all, you do despise me! I just don't want to do good, I want to do evil, and illness has nothing to do with it."

"Why do evil?"

"So that there will be nothing left anywhere. Ah, how good it would be if there were nothing left! You know, Alyosha, I sometimes think about doing an awful lot of evil, all sorts of nasty things, and I'd be doing them on the sly for a long time, and suddenly everyone would find out. They would all surround me and point their fingers at me, and I would look at them all. That would be very pleasant. Why would it be so pleasant, Alyosha?"

"Who knows? The need to smash something good, or, as you said, to set fire to something. That also happens."

"But I'm not just saying it, I'll do it, too."

"I believe you."

"Ah, how I love you for saying you believe me. And you're not lying at all, not at all. But maybe you think I'm saying all this on purpose, just to tease you?"

"No, I don't think that . . . though maybe there's a little of that need, too."

"There is a little. I can never lie to you," she said, her eyes flashing with some sort of fire.

Alyosha was struck most of all by her seriousness: not a shadow of laughter or playfulness was left on her face, though before gaiety and playfulness had not abandoned her even in her most "serious" moments.

"There are moments when people love crime," Alyosha said pensively.

"Yes, yes! You've spoken my own thought, they love it, they all love it, and love it always, not just at 'moments.' You know, it's as if at some point they all agreed to lie about it, and have been lying about it ever since. They all say they hate what's bad, but secretly they all love it."

"And are you still reading bad books?"

"Yes. Mama reads them and hides them under her pillow, and I steal them."

"Aren't you ashamed to be ruining yourself?"

"I want to ruin myself. There's a boy here, and he lay down under the rails while a train rode over him. Lucky boy! Listen, your brother is on trial now for killing his father, and they all love it that he killed his father."

"They love it that he killed his father?"

"They love it, they all love it! Everyone says it's terrible, but secretly they all love it terribly. I'm the first to love it."

"There's some truth in what you say about everyone," Alyosha said softly.

"Ah, what thoughts you have!" Liza shrieked with delight, "and you a monk! You wouldn't believe how I respect you, Alyosha, for never lying. Ah, I'll tell you a funny dream of mine: sometimes I have a dream about devils, it seems to be night, I'm in my room with a candle, and suddenly there are devils everywhere, in all the corners, and under the tables, and they open the door, and outside the door there's a crowd of them, and they want to come in and grab me. And they're coming close, they're about to grab me. But I suddenly cross myself and they all draw back, afraid, only they don't quite go away, they stand by the door and in the corners, waiting. And suddenly I have a terrible desire to start abusing God out loud, and so I start abusing him, and they suddenly rush at me again in a crowd, they're so glad, and they're grabbing me again, and I suddenly cross myself again—and they all draw back. It's such terrible fun; it takes my breath away."

"I've sometimes had the same dream," Alyosha said suddenly.

"Really?" Liza cried out in surprise. "Listen, Alyosha, don't laugh, this is terribly important: is it possible for two different people to have one and the same dream?"

"It must be."

"Alyosha, I'm telling you, this is terribly important," Liza went on in some sort of extreme amazement. "It's not the dream that's important, but that you could have the same dream I had. You never lie, so don't lie now either: is it true? You're not joking?"

"It's true."

Liza was terribly struck by something and sat silently for half a minute.

"Alyosha, do come to see me, come to see me more often," she spoke suddenly in a pleading voice.

"I'll always come to see you, all my life," Alyosha answered firmly.

"I tell this to you alone," Liza began again. "Only to myself, and also to you. You alone in the whole world. And rather to you than to myself. And I'm not at all ashamed with you. Alyosha, why am I not at all ashamed with you, not at all? Alyosha, is it true that Jews steal children on Passover and kill them?"

"I don't know."

"I have a book here, I read in it about some trial somewhere, and that a Jew first cut off all the fingers of a four-year-old boy, and then crucified him on the wall, nailed him with nails and crucified him, and then said at his trial that the boy died quickly, in four hours. Quickly! He said the boy was moaning, that he kept moaning, and he stood and admired it. That's good!"

"Good?"

"Good. Sometimes I imagine that it was I who crucified him. He hangs there moaning, and I sit down facing him, eating pineapple compote. I like pineapple compote very much. Do you?"

Alyosha was silent and looked at her. Her pale yellow face suddenly became distorted, her eyes lit up.

"You know, after I read about that Jew, I shook with tears the whole night. I kept imagining how the child cried and moaned (four-year-old boys already understand), and I couldn't get the thought of the compote out of my mind. In the morning I sent a letter to a certain man, telling him that he *must* come and see me. He came and I suddenly told him about the boy, and the compote, I told him *everything*, *everything*, and said it was 'good.' He suddenly laughed and said it was indeed good. Then he got up and left. He stayed only five minutes. Did he despise me, did he? Speak, speak, Alyosha, did he despise me or not?" she sat up straight on the couch, flashing her eyes.

"Tell me," Alyosha said with agitation, "did you yourself send for him, for this man?"

"Yes, I did."

"You sent him a letter?"

"Yes."

"To ask him just about that, about the child?"

"No, not about that at all, not at all. But as soon as he came, I immediately asked him about that. He answered, laughed, got up and left."

"The man treated you honorably," Alyosha said softly.

"And despised me? Laughed at me?"

"No, because he may believe in the pineapple compote himself. He's also very sick now, Lise."

"Yes, he does believe in it!" Liza flashed her eyes.

"He doesn't despise anyone," Alyosha went on, "he simply doesn't believe anyone. And since he doesn't believe them, he also, of course, despises them."

"That means me, too? Me?"

"You, too."

"That's good," Liza somehow rasped. "When he walked out laughing, I felt it was good to be despised. The boy with his fingers cut off is good, and to be despised is good . . ."

And she laughed in Alyosha's face, somehow wickedly and feverishly.

"You know, Alyosha, you know, I'd like to . . . Alyosha, save me!" she suddenly jumped up from the couch, rushed to him, and held him tightly in her arms. "Save me," she almost groaned. "Would I tell anyone in the world what I told you? But I told you the truth, the truth, the truth! I'll kill myself, because everything is so loathsome to me! I don't want to live, because everything is so loathsome to me. Everything is so loathsome, so loathsome! Alyosha, why, why don't you love me at all!" she finished in a frenzy.

"No, I do love you!" Alyosha answered ardently.

"And will you weep for me? Will you?"

"I will."

"Not because I didn't want to be your wife, but just weep for me, just so?"

"I will."

"Thank you! I need only your tears. And as for all the rest, let them punish me and trample me with their feet, all, all of them, without *any* exception! Because I don't love anyone. Do you hear, not a-ny-one! On the contrary, I hate them! Go, Alyosha, it's time you went to your brother!" she suddenly tore herself away from him.

"But how can I leave you like this?" Alyosha said, almost afraid.

"Go to your brother, they'll shut the prison, go, here's your hat! Kiss Mitya for me, go, go!"

And she pushed Alyosha out the door almost by force. He looked at her with rueful perplexity, when suddenly he felt a letter in his right hand, a small letter, tightly folded and sealed. He looked and at once read the address: "To Ivan Fyodorovich Karamazov." He glanced quickly at Liza. Her face became almost menacing.

"Give it to him, be sure to give it to him!" she ordered frenziedly, shaking all over, "today, at once! Otherwise I will poison myself! That's why I sent for you!"

And she quickly slammed the door. The lock clicked. Alyosha put the letter in his pocket and went straight to the stairs without stopping to see Madame Khokhlakov, having even forgotten about her. And Liza, as soon as Alyosha was gone, unlocked the door at once, opened it a little, put her finger into the chink, and, slamming the door, crushed it with all her might. Ten seconds later, having released her hand, she went quietly and slowly to her chair, sat straight up in it, and began looking intently at her blackened finger and the blood oozing from under the nail. Her lips trembled, and she whispered very quickly to herself:

"Mean, mean, mean, mean!"

Chapter 4

A Hymn and a Secret

It was already quite late (and how long is a November day?) when Alyosha rang at the prison gate. It was even beginning to get dark. But Alyosha knew he would be allowed to see Mitya without hindrance. Such things are the same in our town as everywhere else. At first, of course, after the conclusion of the whole preliminary investigation, access to Mitya on the part of his relations and certain other persons was hedged by certain necessary formalities, but after a while, though these formalities were not exactly relaxed, certain exceptions somehow established themselves, at least for some of Mitya's visitors. So much so that sometimes their meetings with the prisoner in the specially designated room even took place almost one-to-one. However, there were very few such visitors: only Grushenka, Alyosha, and Rakitin. But Grushenka was very much in favor with the police commissioner, Mikhail Makarovich. His shouting at her in Mokroye weighed on the old man's heart. Afterwards, having learned the essentials, he completely changed his thinking about her. And, strangely, though he was firmly convinced of Mitya's crime, since the moment of his imprisonment he had come to look on him more and more leniently: "He was probably a man of good soul, and then came to grief like a Swede at Poltava,[1] from drinking and disorder!" His initial horror gave place in his heart to some sort of pity. As for Alyosha, the commissioner loved him very much and had already known him for a long time, and Rakitin, who later took to visiting the prisoner very often, was one of the closest acquaintances of "the commissioner's misses," as he called them, and was daily to be found hanging about their house. And he gave lessons in the home of the prison warden, a good-natured old man, though a seasoned veteran. Alyosha, again, was also a special and old acquaintance of the warden's, who loved to talk with him generally about "wisdom."[2] Ivan Fyodorovich, for example, was not really respected by the warden, but was actually even feared, above all for his opinions, though the warden himself was a great philosopher, "having gotten there by his own reason," of course. But he felt some sort of irresistible sympathy for Alyosha. During the past year the old man had set himself to reading the Apocryphal Gospels,[3] and reported his impressions every other moment to his young friend. Earlier he had even gone to visit him in the monastery and had spent long hours talking with him and with the hieromonks. In short, even if Alyosha was late coming to the prison, he had only to go to the warden and the matter was always settled. Besides, everyone in the prison, down to the last guard, was used to Alyosha. And the sentries, of course, would not interfere as long as the authorities had given their permission. Mitya, when he was summoned, would always come down from his little cell to the place designated for visits. Just as he entered the room, Alyosha ran into Rakitin, who was taking leave of Mitya. Both were talking loudly. Mitya, seeing him out, was laughing heartily at something, and Rakitin seemed to be grumbling. Rakitin, especially of late, did not like meeting Alyosha, hardly spoke to him, and even greeted him with difficulty. Now, seeing Alyosha come in, he frowned more than usual and looked the other way, as if totally absorbed in buttoning his big, warm coat with its fur collar. Then he immediately began looking for his umbrella.

"Mustn't forget my things," he muttered, just to say something.

"Don't forget anyone else's things either!" Mitya joked, and promptly guffawed at his own joke. Rakitin instantly flared up.

"Tell that to your Karamazovs, your serf-owning spawn, not to Rakitin!" he cried suddenly, beginning to shake with anger.

"What's the matter? I was joking!" cried Mitya. "Pah, the devil! They're all like that," he turned to Alyosha, nodding towards the quickly departing Rakitin. "He was sitting here laughing, feeling fine, and now suddenly he boils over! He didn't even nod to you, have you really quarreled or something? And why so late? I wasn't only expecting you, I've been thirsting for you all morning. But never mind! We'll make up for it!"

"Why has he taken to coming so often? Are you friends with him now, or what?" Alyosha asked, also nodding towards the door through which Rakitin had cleared out.

"Me, friends with Mikhail? No, not really. Why would I be, the swine! He considers me . . . a scoundrel. And he doesn't understand jokes—that's the main trouble with them. They never understand jokes. Their souls are dry, flat and dry, like the prison walls when I was looking at them as I drove up that day. But he's an intelligent man, intelligent. Well, Alexei, my head will roll now!"

He sat down on the bench and sat Alyosha down next to him.

"Yes, tomorrow is the trial. You mean you really have no hope at all, brother?" Alyosha said with a timid feeling.

"What are you talking about?" Mitya looked at him somehow indefinitely. "Ah, yes, the trial! Devil take it! Up to now we've been talking about trifles, about this trial and all, and I haven't said a word to you about the most important thing. Yes, tomorrow is the trial, but I didn't say my head would roll because of the trial. It's not my head that will roll, but what was in my head. Why are you looking at me with such criticism on your face?"

"What are you talking about, Mitya?"

"Ideas, ideas, that's what! Ethics. What is ethics?"

"Ethics?" Alyosha said in surprise.

"Yes, what is it, some sort of science?"

"Yes, there is such a science . . . only . . . I must confess I can't explain to you what sort of science it is."

"Rakitin knows. Rakitin knows a lot, devil take him! He won't become a monk. He's going to go to Petersburg. There, he says, he'll get into the department of criticism, but with a noble tendency. Why not? He can be useful and make a career. Oof, how good they are at making careers! Devil take ethics! But I am lost, Alexei, I'm lost, you man of God! I love you more than anyone. My heart trembles at you, that's what. Who is this Carl Bernard?"

"Carl Bernard?" Again Alyosha was surprised.

"No, not Carl, wait, I've got it wrong: Claude Bernard.[4] What is it? Chemistry or something?"

"He must be a scientist," Alyosha replied, "only I confess I'm not able to say much about him either. I've just heard he's a scientist, but what kind I don't know."

"Well, devil take him, I don't know either," Mitya swore. "Some scoundrel, most likely. They're all scoundrels. But Rakitin will squeeze himself in, he'll squeeze himself through some crack—another Bernard. Oof, these Bernards! How they breed!"

"But what's the matter with you?" Alyosha asked insistently.

"He wants to write an article about me, about my case, and begin his role in literature that way, that's why he keeps coming, he explained it to me himself. He wants something with a tendency: 'It was impossible for him not to kill, he was a victim of his environment,' and so on, he explained it to me. It will have a tinge of socialism, he says. So, devil take him, let it have a tinge, it's all the same to me. He doesn't like brother Ivan, he hates him, you're not in favor with him either. Well, and I don't throw him out because he's an intelligent man. He puts on airs too much, however. I was telling him just now: 'The Karamazovs are not scoundrels, but philosophers, because all real Russians are philosophers, and you, even though you've studied, are not a philosopher, you're a stinking churl.' He laughed, maliciously. And I said to him: *de thoughtibus non est disputandum*[5]—a good joke? At least I, too, have joined classicism," Mitya suddenly guffawed.

"But why are you lost? What were you just saying?" Alyosha interrupted.

"Why am I lost? Hm! The fact is . . . on the whole . . . I'm sorry for God, that's why!"

"What do you mean, sorry for God?"

"Imagine: it's all there in the nerves, in the head, there are these nerves in the brain (devil take them!) . . . there are little sorts of tails, these nerves have little tails, well, and when they start trembling there . . . that is, you see, I look at something with my eyes, like this, and they start trembling, these little tails . . . and when they tremble, an image appears, not at once, but in a moment, it takes a second, and then a certain moment appears, as it were, that is, not a moment—devil take the moment—but an image, that is, an object or an event, well, devil take it—and that's why I contemplate, and then think . . . because of the little tails, and not at all because I have a soul or am some sort of image and likeness,[6] that's all foolishness. Mikhail explained it to me, brother, just yesterday, and it was as if I got burnt. It's magnificent, Alyosha, this science! The new man will come, I quite understand that . . . . And yet, I'm sorry for God!"

"Well, that's good enough," said Alyosha.

"That I'm sorry for God? Chemistry, brother, chemistry! Move over a little, Your Reverence, there's no help for it, chemistry's coming! And Rakitin doesn't like God, oof, how he doesn't! That's the sore spot in all of them! But they conceal it. They lie. They pretend. 'What, are you going to push for that in the department of criticism?' I asked. 'Well, they won't let me do it openly,' he said, and laughed. 'But,' I asked, 'how will man be after that? Without God and the future life? It means everything is permitted now, one can do anything?' 'Didn't you know?' he said. And he laughed. 'Everything is permitted to the intelligent man,' he said. 'The intelligent man knows how to catch crayfish, but you killed and fouled it up,' he said, 'and now you're rotting in prison!' He said that to me. A natural-born swine! I once used to throw the likes of him out—well, and now I listen to them. He does talk a lot of sense, after all. He writes intelligently, too. About a week ago he started reading me an article, I wrote down three lines of it on purpose; wait, here it is."

Mitya hurriedly pulled a piece of paper from his waistcoat pocket and read:

" 'In order to resolve this question it is necessary, first of all, to put one's person in conflict with one's actuality.' Do you understand that?"

"No, I don't," said Alyosha.

He was watching Mitya and listened to him with curiosity.

"I don't understand it either. Obscure and vague, but intelligent. 'Everybody writes like that now,' he says, 'because it's that sort of environment . . .' They're afraid of the environment. He also writes verses, the scoundrel, he celebrated Khokhlakov's little foot, ha, ha, ha!"

"So I've heard," said Alyosha.

"You have? And have you heard the jingle itself?"

"No."

"I have it; here, I'll read it to you. You don't know, I never told you, but there's a whole story here. The swindler! Three weeks ago he decided to tease me: 'You fouled it up, like a fool,' he said, 'for the sake of three thousand, but I'll grab a hundred and fifty thousand, marry a certain widow, and buy a stone house in Petersburg.' And he told me he was offering his attentions to Khokhlakov, and that she, who wasn't very smart to begin with, had lost her mind altogether by the age of forty. 'But she's very sentimental,' he said, 'so that's how I'll bring it off with her. I'll marry her, take her to Petersburg, and start a newspaper there.' And he had such nasty, sensual drool on his lips—drooling not over Khokhlakov, but over the hundred and fifty thousand. And he convinced me, he convinced me; he kept coming to see me every day; she's weakening, he said. He was beaming with joy. And then suddenly he was turned out: Perkhotin, Pyotr Ilyich, got the upper hand, good fellow! I mean, I really could kiss the foolish woman for turning him out! So it was while he was coming to see me that he also wrote this jingle. 'For the first time in my life,' he said, 'I've dirtied my hands writing poetry, for the sake of seduction—that is, for the sake of a useful cause. If I get the capital away from the foolish woman, then I can be of civic use.' Because they have a civic excuse for every abomination! 'And anyway,' he said, 'I've done a better job of writing than your Pushkin, because I managed to stick civic woes even into a foolish jingle.' What he says about Pushkin I quite understand. After all, maybe he really was a capable man, but all he wrote about was little feet! And how proud he was of his little jingles! Such vanity they have, such vanity! 'For the Recovery of My Object's Ailing Little Foot'—that's the title he came up with—a nimble fellow!

Ah, what a charming little foot,
But what a swelling has come to 't!
Tho' doctors visit, bringing balm,
They only seem to do it harm.

I do not long for little feet—
Let Pushkin sing them if he please:
My longing's for a head that's sweet
But does not comprehend ideas.

It used to comprehend a bit;
The little foot's distracted it!
Oh, little foot, if you'd but mend,
The little head might comprehend.[7]

"A swine, a pure swine, but he's written it playfully, the scoundrel! And he really did stick in his 'civic' idea. And how mad he was when he got turned out. He was gnashing!"

"He's already had his revenge," said Alyosha. "He wrote an article about Madame Khokhlakov."

And Alyosha told him hastily about the article in the newspaper *Rumors*.

"That's him, him!" Mitya confirmed, frowning. "It's him! These articles . . . how well I know . . . I mean, so many base things have already been written, about Grusha, for instance . . . ! And about the other one, about Katya . . . Hm!"

He walked worriedly around the room.

"Brother, I can't stay with you long," Alyosha said, after a pause. "Tomorrow will be a terrible, great day for you: divine judgment will be passed on you . . . and so it surprises me that you're walking around, talking about God knows what instead of anything that matters . . ."

"No, don't be surprised," Mitya hotly interrupted. "What should I talk about—that stinking dog, or what? About the murderer? We've talked enough about that, you and I. No more talk about the stinking son of Stinking Lizaveta! God will kill him, you'll see. Keep still!"

Excited, he went up to Alyosha and suddenly kissed him. His eyes lit up.

"Rakitin wouldn't understand this," he began, all in a sort of rapture, as it were, "but you, you will understand everything. That's why I've been thirsting for you. You see, for a long time I've been wanting to say many things to you here, within these peeling walls, but I've kept silent about the most important thing: the time didn't seem to have come yet. I've been waiting till this last time to pour out my soul to you. Brother, in these past two months I've sensed a new man in me, a new man has arisen in me! He was shut up inside me, but if it weren't for this thunderbolt, he never would have appeared. Frightening! What do I care if I spend twenty years pounding out iron ore in the mines, I'm not afraid of that at all, but I'm afraid of something else now: that this risen man not depart from me! Even there, in the mines, underground, you can find a human heart in the convict and murderer standing next to you, and you can be close to him, because there, too, it's possible to live, and love, and suffer! You can revive and resurrect the frozen heart in this convict, you can look after him for years, and finally bring up from the cave into the light a soul that is lofty now, a suffering consciousness, you can revive an angel, resurrect a hero! And there are many of them, there are hundreds, and we're all guilty for them! Why did I have a dream about a 'wee one' at such a moment? 'Why is the wee one poor?' It was a prophecy to me at that moment! It's for the 'wee one' that I will go. Because everyone is guilty for everyone else. For all the 'wee ones,' because there are little children and big children. All people are 'wee ones.' And I'll go for all of them, because there must be someone who will go for all of them. I didn't kill father, but I must go. I accept! All of this came to me here . . . within these peeling walls. And there are many, there are hundreds of them, underground, with hammers in their hands. Oh, yes, we'll be in chains, and there will be no freedom, but then, in our great grief, we will arise once more into joy, without which it's not possible for man to live, or for God to be, for God gives joy, it's his prerogative, a great one . . . Lord, let man dissolve in prayer! How would I be there underground without God? Rakitin's lying: if God is driven from the earth, we'll meet him underground! It's impossible for a convict to be without God, even more impossible than for a non-convict! And then from the depths of the earth, we, the men underground, will start singing a tragic hymn to God, in whom there is joy! Hail to God and his joy! I love him!"

Mitya was almost breathless uttering his wild speech. He grew pale, his lips trembled, tears poured from his eyes.

"No, life is full, there is life underground, too!" he began again. "You wouldn't believe, Alexei, how I want to live now, what thirst to exist and be conscious has been born in me precisely within these peeling walls! Rakitin doesn't understand it, all he wants is to build his house and rent out rooms, but I was waiting for you. And besides, what is suffering? I'm not afraid of it, even if it's numberless. I'm not afraid of it now; I was before. You know, maybe I won't even give any answers in court . . . And it seems to me there's so much strength in me now that I can overcome everything, all sufferings, only in order to say and tell myself every moment: I am! In a thousand torments—I am; writhing under torture—but I am. Locked up in a tower, but still I exist, I see the sun, and if I don't see the sun, still I know it *is*. And the whole of life is there—in knowing that the sun *is*. Alyosha, my cherub, all these philosophies are killing me, devil take them! Brother Ivan . . ."

"What about brother Ivan?" Alyosha tried to interrupt, but Mitya did not hear.

"You see, before I didn't have any of these doubts, but they were all hiding in me. Maybe I was drinking and fighting and raging, just because unknown ideas were storming inside me. I was fighting to quell them within me, to tame them, to subdue them. Brother Ivan is not Rakitin, he hides his idea. Brother Ivan is a sphinx; he's silent, silent all the time. And I'm tormented by God. Tormented only by that. What if he doesn't exist? What if Rakitin is right, that it's an artificial idea of mankind? So then, if he doesn't exist, man is chief of the earth, of the universe. Splendid! Only how is he going to be virtuous without God? A good question! I keep thinking about it. Because whom will he love then—man, I mean? To whom will he be thankful, to whom will he sing the hymn? Rakitin laughs. Rakitin says it's possible to love mankind even without God. Well, only a snotty little shrimp can affirm such a thing, but I can't understand it. Life is simple for Rakitin: 'You'd do better to worry about extending man's civil rights,' he told me today, 'or at least about not letting the price of beef go up; you'd render your love for mankind more simply and directly that way than with any philosophies.' But I came back at him: 'And without God,' I said, 'you'll hike up the price of beef yourself, if the chance comes your way, and make a rouble on every kopeck.' He got angry. Because what is virtue?—answer me that, Alexei. I have one virtue and a Chinese has another—so it's a relative thing. Or not? Not relative? Insidious question! You mustn't laugh if I tell you that I didn't sleep for two nights because of it. I just keep wondering now how people can live and think nothing about these things. Vanity! Ivan does not have God. He has his idea. Not on my scale. But he's silent. I think he's a freemason. I asked him—he's silent. I hoped to drink from the waters of his source—he's silent. Only once did he say something."

"What did he say?" Alyosha picked up hastily.

"I said to him: 'Then everything is permitted, in that case?' He frowned: 'Fyodor Pavlovich, our papa, was a little pig,' he said, 'but his thinking was right.' That's what he came back with. That's all he ever said. It's even neater than Rakitin."

"Yes," Alyosha bitterly confirmed. "When was he here?"

"That can wait, there's something else now. I've said almost nothing to you about Ivan so far. I've been putting it off till last. When this thing is over with me here, and they give me my sentence, then I'll tell you certain things, I'll tell you everything. There's one terrible matter here . . . And you'll be my judge in this matter. But for now don't even get into it, for now—hush. You were talking about tomorrow, about the trial, but, would you believe it, I don't know a thing."

"Have you talked with that lawyer?"

"Forget the lawyer! I talked with him about everything. He's a smooth Petersburg swindler. A Bernard! He just doesn't believe a pennyworth of what I say. He thinks I killed him, can you imagine? I see it. I asked him, 'In that case, why have you come to defend me?' To hell with them. They've called in a doctor, too, they want to prove I'm crazy. I won't have it! Katerina Ivanovna wants to do 'her duty' to the end. What an effort!" Mitya smiled bitterly. "A cat! A cruel heart! And she knows what I said about her in Mokroye then, that she's a woman of 'great wrath'! They told her. Yes, the evidence has multiplied like the sands of the sea! Grigory stands by his; Grigory is honest, but he's a fool. Many people are honest simply because they're fools. That's Rakitin's notion. Grigory is my enemy. Certain people it's better to have as enemies than as friends. I'm referring to Katerina Ivanovna. I'm afraid, oh, I'm afraid she'll tell in court about that bow to the ground after the forty-five hundred! She'll pay me back to the uttermost farthing.[8] I don't want her sacrifice! They'll put me to shame in court! I'll endure it somehow. Go to her, Alyosha, ask her not to say it in court. Or is it impossible? Ah, the devil, it makes no difference, I'll endure! And I'm not sorry for her. She's asking for it. Let the thief get his beating. I'll have my say, Alexei," again he smiled bitterly. "Only . . . only Grusha, Grusha . . . Lord! Why should she take such suffering on herself?" he suddenly exclaimed, in tears. "Grusha is killing me, the thought of her is killing me, killing me! She was here today . . ."

"She told me. She was very upset by you today."

"I know. Devil take me and my character. I got jealous! I repented as I was letting her go, I kissed her. I didn't ask her forgiveness."

"Why didn't you?" exclaimed Alyosha.

Mitya suddenly laughed almost gaily.

"God save you, dear boy, from ever asking forgiveness for your guilt from a woman you love! Especially from a woman you love, no matter how guilty you are before her! Because a woman—devil knows what a woman is, brother, I'm a good judge of that at least! Try going and confessing your guilt to her; say, 'I'm guilty, forgive me, pardon me,' and right then and there you'll be showered with reproaches! She'll never forgive you directly and simply, she'll humble you in the dust, she'll take away things that weren't even there, she'll take everything, she'll forget nothing, she'll add things of her own, and only then will she forgive you. And that's the best of them, the best! She'll scrape up the last scraps and heap them on your head—such bloodthirstiness just sits in them, I tell you, in all of them, to the last one, those angels without whom it's even impossible for us to live! You see, my dear, I'll tell you frankly and simply: every decent man ought to be under the heel of some woman at least. That's my conviction; not a conviction, but a feeling. A man ought to be magnanimous, and that's no stain on a man. It's no stain even on a hero, even on Caesar! Well, but still don't go asking forgiveness, not ever, not for anything. Remember that rule: it was taught you by your brother Mitya, who perished because of women. No, I'd better restore myself in Grusha's eyes some other way, without forgiveness. I revere her, Alexei, revere her! Only she doesn't see it, no, it's still not enough love for her. And she frets me, she frets me with her love. Before was nothing! Before it was just her infernal curves that fretted me, but now I've taken her whole soul into my soul, and through her I've become a man! Will they let us be married? Without that I'll die of jealousy. I keep imagining something every day . . . What did she say to you about me?"

Alyosha repeated everything Grushenka had told him earlier. Mitya listened closely, asked about many things, and was left feeling pleased.

"So she's not angry that I'm jealous," he exclaimed. "A real woman! 'I have a cruel heart myself.' Oof, I love such cruel women, though I can't stand it when anyone's jealous over me, I can't stand it! We will fight. But love—oh, I will love her infinitely. Will they let us be married? Do they let convicts marry? A good question. And I can't live without her . . . ."

Mitya walked glumly around the room. The room was getting almost dark. Suddenly he became terribly worried.

"A secret, so she says there's a secret? She says the three of us are conspiring against her, and she says 'Katka' is mixed up in it? No, Grushenka old girl, that's not it. You've missed your mark this time, you've missed your silly female mark! Alyosha, darling—ah, well, why not? I'll reveal our secret to you!"

He looked around, quickly went up to Alyosha, who was standing before him, and whispered to him with a mysterious air, though in fact no one could hear them: the old guard was nodding on his bench in the corner, and not a word could reach the sentries.

"I'll reveal our whole secret to you!" Mitya began whispering hastily. "I was going to reveal it later, because how could I decide to do anything without you? You are everything to me. Though I say that Ivan is the highest of us, you are my cherub. Only your decision will decide it. Maybe it's you who are the highest man, and not Ivan. You see, here it's a matter of conscience, a matter of the highest conscience—a secret that is so important that I cannot deal with it myself and have put everything off for you. And it's still too early to decide, because the sentence must come first: the sentence will be given, and then you will decide my fate. Don't decide now: I'll tell you now, you will listen, but don't decide. Stand and be silent. I won't reveal everything to you. I'll tell you only the idea, without details, and you be silent. Not a question, not a movement, agreed? But anyway, Lord, what am I going to do about your eyes? I'm afraid your eyes will tell me your decision even if you are silent. Oof, I'm afraid! Alyosha, listen: brother Ivan suggests that I *escape*. I'm not telling you the details: everything has been foreseen, everything can be arranged. Be silent, don't decide. To America with Grusha. I really can't live without Grusha! What if they won't let her join me there? Do they let convicts marry? Brother Ivan says they don't. And without Grusha what will I do under the ground with my sledgehammer? I'll take the sledgehammer and smash my own head with it! On the other hand, what about my conscience? I'll be running away from suffering! I was shown a path—and I rejected the path; there was a way of purification—I did an about-face. Ivan says that a man 'with good inclinations' can be of more use in America than under the ground. Well, and where will our underground hymn take place? Forget America, America means vanity again! And there's a lot of swindling in America, too, I think. To run away from crucifixion! I'm talking to you, Alexei, because you alone can understand this, and no one else, for the others it's foolishness, raving—all that I was telling you about the hymn. They'll say, he's lost his mind, or else he's a fool. But I haven't lost my mind, and I'm not a fool either. Ivan, too, understands about the hymn, oof, he understands—only he doesn't respond to it, he's silent. He doesn't believe in the hymn. Don't speak, don't speak: I see your look: you've already decided! Don't decide, spare me, I can't live without Grusha, wait for the trial!"

Mitya ended as if in a frenzy. He held Alyosha by the shoulders with both hands, and simply fixed his eyes with his yearning, feverish look.

"Do they let convicts marry?" he repeated for the third time, in a pleading voice.

Alyosha listened with extreme surprise and was deeply shaken.

"Tell me one thing," he said, "does Ivan insist on it very much, and who was the first to come up with it?"

"He, he came up with it, he insists on it! For a while he wouldn't come to see me, and then he suddenly came a week ago and began straight off with it. He's terribly insistent. He doesn't ask, he orders. He has no doubt I'll obey, though I turned my heart inside out for him, as I did for you, and talked about the hymn. He told me how he would arrange it, he's gathered all the information, but of that later. He wants it to the point of hysterics. The main thing is the money: ten thousand for the escape, he says, and twenty thousand for America, and with ten thousand, he says, we'll arrange a splendid escape."

"And he asked you by no means to tell me?" Alyosha asked again.

"By no means to tell anyone, and you above all: not to tell you for anything! He's surely afraid that you'll stand before me as my conscience. Don't tell him I told you. Oof, don't tell him!"

"You're right," Alyosha decided, "it's impossible to decide before the sentence. After the trial you will decide yourself; you'll find a new man in yourself then, and he will decide."

"A new man, or a Bernard, and he will decide Bernard-wise! Because I think I'm a contemptible Bernard myself!" Mitya grinned bitterly.

"But can it be, brother, can it be that you have no hope of acquittal?"

Mitya shrugged convulsively and shook his head.

"Alyosha, darling, it's time for you to go!" he suddenly hurried. "The warden's shouting in the yard, he'll be here soon. It's late for us, it's not in order. Embrace me quickly, kiss me, cross me, darling, cross me for tomorrow's cross . . ."

They embraced and kissed each other.

"And Ivan," Mitya spoke suddenly, "suggests I escape, but then he believes I killed father!"

A sad smile forced itself to his lips.

"Did you ask him if he believes it?" Alyosha asked.

"No, I didn't ask him. I wanted to ask him, but I couldn't, I lacked the strength. But anyway I can see it in his eyes. Well, good-bye!"

They hastily kissed each other again, and Alyosha was already going out when Mitya suddenly called him back.

"Stand in front of me, like this."

And again he firmly grasped Alyosha by the shoulders with both hands. His face suddenly became quite pale, so that it was terribly noticeable in the near-darkness. His lips twisted, his eyes were fixed on Alyosha.

"Alyosha, tell me the complete truth, as before the Lord God: do you believe I killed father or not? You, you yourself, do you believe it or not? The complete truth, don't lie!" he cried to him frenziedly.

Alyosha reeled, as it were, and his heart—he could feel it—seemed pierced by some sharp thing.

"No, don't, what are you . . . ," he murmured, as if at a loss.

"The whole truth, the whole, don't lie!" Mitya repeated.

"Never for a single moment have I believed that you are the murderer," the trembling voice suddenly burst from Alyosha's breast, and he raised his right hand as if calling on God to witness his words. Mitya's whole face instantly lit up with bliss.

"Thank you!" he uttered slowly, as if sighing after a swoon. "Now you've revived me . . . Would you believe it, up to now I was afraid to ask you, even you, you! Well, go, go! You've strengthened me for tomorrow, God bless you! Well, go, love Ivan!" was the last word that burst from Mitya.

Alyosha walked out all in tears. Such a degree of insecurity in Mitya, such a degree of mistrust even of him, of Alyosha—all of this suddenly opened up before Alyosha such an abyss of ineluctable grief and despair in the soul of his unfortunate brother as he had not suspected before. Deep, infinite compassion suddenly took hold of him and at once tormented him. His pierced heart ached terribly. "Love Ivan!"—he suddenly recalled Mitya's parting words. And he was on his way to Ivan. Since morning he had needed terribly to see Ivan. Ivan tormented him no less than Mitya, and now, after his meeting with his brother, more than ever.

Chapter 5

Not You! Not You!

On the way to Ivan he had to pass by the house where Katerina Ivanovna was staying. There was light in the windows. He suddenly stopped and decided to go in. It was more than a week since he had seen Katerina Ivanovna. But it just occurred to him that Ivan might be with her now, especially on the eve of such a day. He rang and was starting up the stairs, dimly lit by a Chinese lantern, when he saw a man coming down in whom, as they drew near each other, he recognized his brother. He was then just leaving Katerina Ivanovna's.

"Ah, it's only you," Ivan Fyodorovich said drily. "Well, good-bye. Are you coming to see her?"

"Yes."

"I don't recommend it; she's 'agitated,' and you will upset her even more."

"No, no!" a voice suddenly cried from above, from the instantly opened door. "Alexei Fyodorovich, are you coming from him?"

"Yes, I was just there."

"Did he ask you to tell me anything? Come in, Alyosha, and you, Ivan Fyodorovich, you must, must come back. Do you hear me!"

Such an imperious note sounded in Katya's voice that Ivan Fyodorovich, after hesitating a moment, decided after all to go upstairs again with Alyosha.

"She was eavesdropping!" he whispered irritably to himself, but Alyosha heard it.

"Allow me to keep my coat on," Ivan Fyodorovich said as he entered the drawing room. "And I won't sit down. I won't stay more than a minute."

"Sit down, Alexei Fyodorovich," Katerina Ivanovna said, while she herself remained standing. She had changed little during this time, but her dark eyes gleamed with an ominous fire. Alyosha remembered afterwards that she had seemed extremely good-looking to him at that moment.

"Well, what did he ask you to tell me?"

"Only one thing," Alyosha said, looking directly in her face, "that you should spare yourself and not give any evidence in court . . . ," he faltered a little, "of what happened between you . . . at the time of your first acquaintance . . . in that town . . ."

"Ah, about bowing down for the money!" she joined in with a bitter laugh.

"And what, is he afraid for himself or for me—eh? He said I should spare—but whom? Him, or myself? Tell me, Alexei Fyodorovich."

Alyosha was watching intently, trying to understand her.

"Both yourself and him," he spoke softly.

"So!" she snapped somehow viciously, and suddenly blushed. "You do not know me yet, Alexei Fyodorovich," she said menacingly, "and I do not know myself yet. Perhaps you will want to trample me underfoot after tomorrow's questioning."

"You will testify honestly," said Alyosha, "that's all that's necessary."

"Women are often dishonest," she snarled. "Just an hour ago I was thinking how afraid I am to touch that monster . . . like a viper . . . but no, he's still a human being for me! But is he a murderer? Is he the murderer?" she exclaimed hysterically, all of a sudden, turning quickly to Ivan Fyodorovich. Alyosha understood at once that she had already asked Ivan Fyodorovich the same question, perhaps only a moment before he arrived, and not for the first but for the hundredth time, and that they had ended by quarreling.

"I've been to see Smerdyakov . . . It was you, you who convinced me that he is a parricide. I believed only you, my dear!" she went on, still addressing Ivan Fyodorovich. The latter smiled as if with difficulty. Alyosha was startled to hear this "my dear." He would not even have suspected they were on such terms.[1]

"Well, enough, in any case," Ivan snapped. "I'm going. I'll come tomorrow." And turning at once, he left the room and went straight to the stairs. Katerina Ivanovna, with a sort of imperious gesture, suddenly seized Alyosha by both hands.

"Go after him! Catch up with him! Don't leave him alone for a minute!" she whispered rapidly. "He's mad. Did you know he's gone mad? He has a fever, a nervous fever! The doctor told me. Go, run after him . . ."

Alyosha jumped up and rushed after Ivan Fyodorovich. He was not even fifty paces away.

"What do you want?" he suddenly turned to Alyosha, seeing that he was catching up with him. "She told you to run after me because I'm crazy. I know it all by heart," he added irritably.

"She's mistaken, of course, but she's right that you are ill," said Alyosha. "I was looking at your face just now, when we were there; you look very ill, really, Ivan!"

Ivan walked on without stopping. Alyosha followed him.

"And do you know, Alexei Fyodorovich, just how one loses one's mind?" Ivan asked in a voice suddenly quite soft, quite unirritated now, in which suddenly the most ingenuous curiosity could be heard.

"No, I don't know; I suppose there are many different kinds of madness."

"And can one observe oneself losing one's mind?"

"I think it must be impossible to watch oneself in such a case," Alyosha answered with surprise. Ivan fell silent for half a minute.

"If you want to talk to me about something, please change the subject," he said suddenly.

"Here, so that I don't forget, is a letter for you," Alyosha said timidly, and, pulling Liza's letter from his pocket, he handed it to him. Just then they came up to a streetlamp. Ivan recognized the hand at once.

"Ah, it's from that little demon!" he laughed maliciously, and, without unsealing the envelope, he suddenly tore it into several pieces and tossed them to the wind. The scraps flew all over.

"She's not yet sixteen, I believe, and already offering herself!" he said contemptuously, and started down the street again.

"What do you mean, offering herself?" Alyosha exclaimed.

"You know, the way loose women offer themselves."

"No, no, Ivan, don't say that!" Alyosha pleaded ruefully and ardently. "She's a child, you're offending a child! She's ill, she's very ill; she, too, may be losing her mind . . . I had no choice but to give you her letter . . . I wanted, on the contrary, to hear something from you . . . to save her."

"You'll hear nothing from me. If she's a child, I'm not her nanny. Keep still, Alexei. Don't go on. I'm not even thinking about it."

They again fell silent for a minute or so.

"She'll be praying all night now to the Mother of God, to show her how to act at the trial tomorrow," he suddenly spoke again, sharply and spitefully.

"You . . . you mean Katerina Ivanovna?"

"Yes. Whether to come as Mitenka's savior, or as his destroyer. She will pray for her soul to be illumined. She doesn't know yet, you see, she hasn't managed to prepare herself. She, too, takes me for a nanny, she wants me to coo over her!"

"Katerina Ivanovna loves you, brother," Alyosha said sorrowfully.

"Maybe. Only I don't fancy her."

"She's suffering. Why, then, do you . . . sometimes . . . say things to her that give her hope?" Alyosha went on, with timid reproach. "I know you used to give her hope—forgive me for talking like this," he added.

"I cannot act as I ought to here, break it off and tell her directly!" Ivan said irritably. "I must wait until they pass sentence on the murderer. If I break off with her now, she'll take vengeance on me by destroying the scoundrel in court tomorrow, because she hates him and she knows she hates him. There are nothing but lies here, lie upon lie! But now, as long as I haven't broken off with her, she still has hopes, and will not destroy the monster, knowing how much I want to get him out of trouble. Oh, when will that cursed sentence come!"

The words "murderer" and "monster" echoed painfully in Alyosha's heart.

"But in what way can she destroy our brother?" he asked, pondering Ivan's words. "What testimony can she give that would destroy Mitya outright?"

"You don't know about it yet. She has hold of a document, in Mitenka's own hand, which proves mathematically that he killed Fyodor Pavlovich."

"That can't be!" Alyosha exclaimed.

"Why can't it? I've read it myself."

"There can be no such document!" Alyosha repeated hotly. "There cannot be, because he is not the murderer. It was not he who murdered father, not he!"

Ivan Fyodorovich suddenly stopped.

"Then who is the murderer, in your opinion?" he asked somehow with obvious coldness,[2] and a certain haughty note even sounded in the tone of the question.

"You know who," Alyosha said softly, and with emotion.

"Who? You mean that fable about the mad epileptic idiot? About Smerdyakov?"

Alyosha suddenly felt himself trembling all over.

"You know who," escaped him helplessly. He was breathless.

"Who? Who?" Ivan cried almost fiercely now. All his reserve suddenly vanished.

"I know only one thing," Alyosha said, still in the same near whisper. "It was *not you* who killed father."

"'Not you'! What do you mean by 'not you'?" Ivan was dumbfounded.

"It was not you who killed father, not you!" Alyosha repeated firmly.

The silence lasted for about half a minute.

"But I know very well it was not me—are you raving?" Ivan said with a pale and crooked grin. His eyes were fastened, as it were, on Alyosha. The two were again standing under a streetlamp.

"No, Ivan, you've told yourself several times that you were the murderer."

"When did I . . . ? I was in Moscow . . . When did I say so?" Ivan stammered, completely at a loss.

"You've said it to yourself many times while you were alone during these two horrible months," Alyosha continued as softly and distinctly as before. But he was now speaking not of himself, as it were, not of his own will, but obeying some sort of irresistible command. "You've accused yourself and confessed to yourself that you and you alone are the murderer. But it was not you who killed him, you are mistaken, the murderer was not you, do you hear, it was not you! God has sent me to tell you that."

They both fell silent. For a whole, long minute the silence continued. They both stood there looking into each other's eyes. They were both pale. Suddenly Ivan began shaking all over and gripped Alyosha hard by the shoulder.

"You were in my room!" he uttered in a rasping whisper. "You were in my room at night when he came . . . Confess . . . you saw him, didn't you?"

"Who are you talking about . . . Mitya?" Alyosha asked in bewilderment.

"Not him—devil take the monster!" Ivan shouted frenziedly. "Can you possibly know that he's been coming to me? How did you find out? Speak!"

"Who is *he*? I don't know who you're talking about," Alyosha murmured, frightened now.

"No, you do know . . . otherwise how could you . . . it's impossible that you don't know . . ."

But suddenly he seemed to check himself. He stood and seemed to be thinking something over. A strange grin twisted his lips.

"Brother," Alyosha began again, in a trembling voice, "I've said this to you because you will believe my word, I know it. I've spoken this word to you for the whole of your life: it was *not you*! Do you hear? For the whole of your life. And it is God who has put it into my heart to say this to you, even if you were to hate me forever after . . ."

But Ivan Fyodorovich had now apparently managed to regain control of himself.

"Alexei Fyodorovich," he spoke with a cold smile, "I cannot bear prophets and epileptics, messengers from God especially, you know that only too well. From this moment on I am breaking with you, and, I suppose, forever. I ask you to leave me this instant, at this very crossroads. Besides, your way home is down this lane. Beware especially of coming to me today! Do you hear?"

He turned and walked straight off, with firm steps, not looking back.

"Brother," Alyosha called after him, "if anything happens to you today, think of me first of all . . . !"

But Ivan did not answer. Alyosha stood at the crossroads under the streetlamp until Ivan disappeared completely into the darkness. Then he turned down the lane and slowly made his way home. He and Ivan lived separately, in different lodgings: neither of them wanted to live in the now empty house of Fyodor Pavlovich. Alyosha rented a furnished room with a family of tradespeople; and Ivan Fyodorovich lived quite far from him, and occupied a spacious and rather comfortable apartment in the wing of a good house belonging to the well-to-do widow of an official. But his only servant in the whole wing was an ancient, completely deaf old woman, rheumatic all over, who went to bed at six o'clock in the evening and got up at six o'clock in the morning. Ivan Fyodorovich had become undemanding to a strange degree during those two months and liked very much to be left completely alone. He even tidied the one room he occupied himself; as for the other rooms in his lodgings, he rarely even went into them. Having come up to the gates of his house, and with his hand already on the bell, he stopped. He felt himself still trembling all over with a spiteful trembling. He suddenly let go of the bell, spat, turned around, and quickly went off again to quite a different, opposite end of town, about a mile and a half from his apartment, to a tiny, lopsided log house, the present lodgings of Maria Kondratievna, formerly Fyodor Pavlovich's neighbor, who used to come to Fyodor Pavlovich's kitchen to get soup and to whom Smerdyakov, in those days, used to sing his songs and play on the guitar. She had sold her former house, and now lived with her mother in what was almost a hut, and the sick, nearly dying Smerdyakov had been living with them ever since Fyodor Pavlovich's death. It was to him that Ivan Fyodorovich now directed his steps, drawn by a sudden and irresistible consideration.

Chapter 6

The First Meeting with Smerdyakov

This was now the third time that Ivan Fyodorovich had gone to talk with Smerdyakov since his return from Moscow. The first time he had seen him and spoken with him after the catastrophe was immediately upon the day of his arrival; then he had visited him once more two weeks later. But after this second time, he stopped his meetings with Smerdyakov, so that now he had not seen him, and had scarcely heard anything about him, for more than a month. Ivan Fyodorovich had returned from Moscow only on the fifth day following his father's death, so that he did not even find him in his coffin: the burial took place just the day before he arrived. The reason for Ivan Fyodorovich's delay was that Alyosha, not knowing his precise address in Moscow, had resorted to Katerina Ivanovna to send the telegram, and she, being equally ignorant of his actual address, had sent the telegram to her sister and aunt, reckoning that Ivan Fyodorovich would go to see them as soon as he arrived in Moscow. But he had gone to see them only on the fourth day after his arrival, and, having read the telegram, he at once, of course, came flying back here. The first one he met was Alyosha, but after talking with him, he was greatly amazed to find that he refused even to suspect Mitya and pointed directly to Smerdyakov as the murderer, contrary to all other opinions in our town. Having then met with the police commissioner and the prosecutor, having learned the details of the accusation and the arrest, he was still more surprised at Alyosha, and ascribed his opinion to his highly aroused brotherly feeling and compassion for Mitya, whom, as Ivan knew, Alyosha loved very much. Incidentally, let us say just two words once and for all about Ivan's feelings towards his brother Dmitri Fyodorovich: he decidedly disliked him, and the most he occasionally felt for him was compassion, but even then mixed with great contempt, reaching the point of squeamishness. The whole of Mitya, even his whole figure, was extremely unsympathetic to him. Katerina Ivanovna's love for him Ivan regarded with indignation. Nonetheless he also met with the imprisoned Mitya on the day of his arrival, and this meeting not only did not weaken his conviction of Mitya's guilt, but even strengthened it. He found his brother agitated, morbidly excited. Mitya was verbose, but absentminded and scattered, spoke very abruptly, accused Smerdyakov, and was terribly confused. Most of all he kept referring to those same three thousand roubles that the deceased had "stolen" from him. "The money was mine, it was mine," Mitya kept repeating, "even if I had stolen it, I'd be right." He contested almost none of the evidence against him, and when he did interpret facts in his favor, again he did so quite inconsistently and absurdly—generally as though he did not even wish to justify himself at all before Ivan or anyone else; on the contrary, he was angry, proudly scanted the accusations, cursed and seethed. He merely laughed contemptuously at Grigory's evidence about the open door, and insisted it was "the devil who opened it." But he could not present any coherent explanation of this fact. He even managed to insult Ivan Fyodorovich in this first meeting, telling him abruptly that he was not to be suspected or questioned by those who themselves assert that "everything is permitted." Generally on this occasion he was very unfriendly to Ivan Fyodorovich. It was right after this meeting with Mitya that Ivan Fyodorovich went to see Smerdyakov.

While still on the train, flying back from Moscow, he kept thinking about Smerdyakov and his last conversation with him the evening before his departure. There was much in it that perplexed him, much that seemed suspicious. But when he gave his evidence to the investigator, Ivan Fyodorovich kept silent about that conversation for the time being. He put everything off until he had seen Smerdyakov. The latter was then in the local hospital. In reply to Ivan Fyodorovich's insistent questions, Dr. Herzenstube and Dr. Varvinsky, whom Ivan Fyodorovich met in the hospital, stated firmly that Smerdyakov's falling sickness was indubitable, and were even surprised at the question: "Could he have been shamming on the day of the catastrophe?" They gave him to understand that the fit was even an exceptional one, that it had persisted and recurred over several days, so that the patient's life was decidedly in danger, and that only now, after the measures taken, was it possible to say affirmatively that the patient would live, though it was very possible (Dr. Herzenstube added) that his reason would remain partially unsettled "if not for life, then for a rather long time." To Ivan Fyodorovich's impatient asking whether "that means he's now mad?" the reply was "not in the full sense of the word, but some abnormalities can be noticed." Ivan Fyodorovich decided to find out for himself what these abnormalities were. In the hospital he was admitted at once as a visitor. Smerdyakov was in a separate ward, lying on a cot. Just next to him was another cot taken up by a local tradesman, paralyzed and all swollen with dropsy, who was obviously going to die in a day or two; he would not interfere with the conversation. Smerdyakov grinned mistrustfully when he saw Ivan Fyodorovich, and in the first moment even seemed to become timorous. That at least is what flashed through Ivan Fyodorovich's mind. But it was a momentary thing; for the rest of the time, on the contrary, Smerdyakov almost struck him by his composure. From the very first sight of him, Ivan Fyodorovich was convinced beyond doubt of his complete and extremely ill condition: he was very weak, spoke slowly, and seemed to have difficulty moving his tongue; he had become very thin and yellow. All through the twenty minutes of the visit, he complained of a headache and of pain in all his limbs. His dry eunuch's face seemed to have become very small, his side-whiskers were disheveled, and instead of a tuft, only a thin little wisp of hair stuck up on his head. But his left eye, which squinted and seemed to be hinting at something, betrayed the former Smerdyakov. "It's always interesting to talk with an intelligent man"—Ivan Fyodorovich immediately recalled. He sat down on a stool at his feet. Smerdyakov painfully shifted his whole body on the bed, but did not speak first; he kept silent, and looked now as if he were not even particularly interested.

"Can you talk to me?" Ivan Fyodorovich asked. "I won't tire you too much."

"I can, sir," Smerdyakov murmured in a weak voice. "Did you come long ago, sir?" he added condescendingly, as though encouraging a shy visitor.

"Just today . . . To deal with this mess here."

Smerdyakov sighed.

"Why are you sighing? You knew, didn't you?" Ivan Fyodorovich blurted right out.

Smerdyakov remained sedately silent for a while.

"How could I not know, sir? It was clear beforehand. Only who could know it would turn out like this?"

"What would turn out? Don't hedge! Didn't you foretell that you'd have a falling fit just as you went to the cellar? You precisely indicated the cellar."

"Did you testify to that at the interrogation?" Smerdyakov calmly inquired.

Ivan Fyodorovich suddenly became angry.

"No, I did not, but I certainly shall testify to it. You have a lot to explain to me right now, brother, and let me tell you, my dear, that I shall not let myself be toyed with!"

"And why should I want to toy like that, sir, when all my hope is in you alone, as if you were the Lord God, sir!" Smerdyakov said, still in the same calm way, and merely closing his eyes for a moment.

"First of all," Ivan Fyodorovich began, "I know that a falling fit cannot be predicted beforehand. I've made inquiries, don't try to hedge. It's not possible to predict the day and the hour. How is it, then, that you predicted both the day and the hour to me, and the cellar on top of that? How could you know beforehand that you would fall in a fit precisely into that cellar, unless you shammed the fit on purpose?"

"I had to go to the cellar in any case, sir, even several times a day, sir," Smerdyakov drawled unhurriedly. "Just the same as I fell out of the attic a year ago, sir. It's certainly true, sir, that one can't predict the day and the hour of a falling fit, but one can always have a presentiment."

"But you did predict the day and the hour!"

"Concerning my falling fit, sir, you'd best inquire of the local doctors, sir, whether it was a real one or not a real one—I have nothing more to tell you on that subject."

"And the cellar? How did you foresee the cellar?"

"You and your cellar, sir! As I was going down to the cellar that day, I was in fear and doubt; and mostly in fear, because, having lost you, I had no one else in the whole world to expect any protection from. And there I was climbing down into that cellar, thinking: 'It will come now, it will strike me, am I going to fall in or not?' and from this same doubt I was seized by the throat by this same inevitable spasm, sir . . . well, and so I fell in. All these things and all the previous conversation with you, sir, on the eve of that day, in the evening by the gate, sir, how I informed you then of my fear and about the cellar, sir—all that I gave out in detail to mister Dr. Herzenstube and the investigator, Nikolai Parfenovich, and he wrote it all into the record, sir. And the local doctor, Mr. Varvinsky, he especially insisted to them all that this happened precisely from the thought, that is, from this same insecurity, 'am I going to fall, or not?' And there it was waiting to get me. And they wrote down, sir, that it certainly must have happened like that, that is, for the sole reason of my fear, sir."

Having said this, Smerdyakov drew a deep breath, as though suffering from fatigue.

"So you stated all that in your evidence?" Ivan Fyodorovich asked, somewhat taken aback. He had been about to scare him with the threat of reporting their earlier conversation, when it turned out that he had already reported everything himself.

"What should I be afraid of? Let them write down all the real truth," Smerdyakov said firmly.

"And you told them every word of our conversation at the gate?"

"No, not really every word, sir."

"And that you could sham a falling fit, as you boasted then—did you tell them that?"

"No, I didn't say that either, sir."

"Now tell me, why were you sending me to Chermashnya then?"

"I was afraid you'd leave for Moscow; Chermashnya is closer, after all, sir."

"Lies! You were asking me to leave yourself: go, you said, get out of harm's way."

"I said it out of sole friendship for you then, and heartfelt devotion, anticipating calamity in the house, sir, feeling pity for you. Only I pitied myself more than you, sir. That's why I said: get out of harm's way, so you'd understand that things were going to be bad at home, and you'd stay to protect your parent."

"You should have been more direct, fool!" Ivan Fyodorovich suddenly flared up.

"How could I be more direct then, sir? It was just fear alone speaking in me, and besides you might have been angry. Of course I might have been wary lest Dmitri Fyodorovich cause some scandal and take away that same money, because he regarded it as if it was his, but who could know it would end with such a murder? I thought he would simply steal those three thousand roubles that were lying under the master's mattress, in an envelope, sir, but he went and killed him. And you, too, how could you possibly have guessed, sir?"

"But if you yourself say it was impossible to guess, how could I have guessed it and stayed? Why are you confusing things?" Ivan Fyodorovich said, pondering.

"You could have guessed just because I was sending you to Chermashnya, and not to Moscow, sir."

"What could be guessed from that?"

Smerdyakov seemed very tired and again was silent for about a minute.

"Thereby you could have guessed, sir, that if I was dissuading you from

Moscow to Chermashnya, it meant I wanted your presence closer by, because Moscow is far away, and Dmitri Fyodorovich, seeing you were not so far away, wouldn't be so encouraged. Besides, in case anything happened, you could come with greater swiftness to protect me, for I myself pointed out Grigory Vasilievich's illness to you, and also that I was afraid of the falling sickness. And having explained to you about those knocks by which one could get in to the deceased, and that through me they were all known to Dmitri Fyodorovich, I thought you would guess yourself that he would be certain to commit something, and not only would not go to Chermashnya, but would stay altogether."

"He talks quite coherently," Ivan Fyodorovich thought, "even though he mumbles; what is this unsettling of his faculties Herzenstube was referring to?"

"You're dodging me, devil take you!" he exclaimed, getting angry.

"And I must admit that I thought you had already guessed it quite well then," Smerdyakov parried with a most guileless air.

"If I had guessed, I would have stayed!" Ivan Fyodorovich shouted, flaring up again.

"Well, sir, and I thought you'd guessed everything, and were just getting as quick as possible out of harm's way, so as to run off somewhere, saving yourself out of fear, sir."

"You thought everyone was as much a coward as you?"

"Forgive me, sir, I thought you were like I am."

"Of course, I should have guessed," Ivan was agitated, "and indeed I was beginning to guess at some loathsomeness on your part . . . Only you're lying, lying again," he cried out, suddenly recalling. "Do you remember how you came up to the carriage then and said to me: 'It's always interesting to talk with an intelligent man'? Since you praised me, doesn't it mean you were glad I was leaving?"

Smerdyakov sighed again and yet again. Color seemed to come to his face.

"If I was glad," he said, somewhat breathlessly, "it was only for the reason that you agreed to go not to Moscow but to Chermashnya. Because it's closer, after all; only I spoke those words then not as praise but as a reproach, sir. You failed to make it out, sir."

"Reproach for what?"

"That anticipating such a calamity, sir, you were abandoning your own parent and did not want to protect us, because they could have hauled me in anytime for that three thousand, for having stolen it, sir."

"Devil take you!" Ivan swore again. "Wait: did you tell the district attorney and the prosecutor about those signals, those knocks?"

"I told it all just as it was, sir."

Again Ivan Fyodorovich was inwardly surprised.

"If I was thinking of anything then," he began again, "it was only of some loathsomeness on your part. Dmitri might kill, but that he would steal—I did not believe at the time . . . But I was prepared for any loathsomeness on your part. You told me yourself that you could sham a falling fit—why did you tell me that?"

"For the sole reason of my simple-heartedness. And I've never shammed a falling fit on purpose in my life, I only said it so as to boast to you. Just foolishness, sir. I loved you very much then, and acted in all simplicity."

"My brother accuses you directly of the murder and the robbery."

"And what else has he got left to do?" Smerdyakov grinned bitterly. "And who will believe him after all that evidence? Grigory Vasilievich did see the open door, and there you have it, sir. Well, what can I say, God be with him! He's trembling, trying to save himself . . ."

He was calmly silent for a while, and suddenly, as if realizing something, added:

"There's this, sir, yet another thing: he wants to shift the blame, so that it was my doing, sir—I've heard that already, sir—but just take this other thing, that I'm an expert at shamming the falling sickness: but would I have told you beforehand that I could sham it if I really had any plot against your parent then? If I was plotting such a murder, could I possibly be such a fool as to tell such evidence against myself beforehand, and tell it to his own son, for pity's sake, sir! Does that resemble a probability? As if that could happen, sir; no, on the contrary, not ever at all, sir. No one can hear this conversation between us now, except that same Providence, sir, but if you informed the prosecutor and Nikolai Parfenovich, you could thereby ultimately defend me, sir: because what kind of villain is so simple-hearted beforehand? They may well consider all that, sir."

"Listen," Ivan Fyodorovich, struck by Smerdyakov's last argument, rose from his seat, interrupting the conversation, "I do not suspect you at all and even consider it ridiculous to accuse you . . . on the contrary, I am grateful to you for reassuring me. I am leaving now, but I shall come again. Meanwhile, good-bye; get well. Perhaps there's something you need?"

"I'm grateful in all things, sir. Marfa Ignatievna doesn't forget me, sir, and assists me in everything, if there's ever anything I need, according to her usual goodness. Good people visit every day."

"Good-bye. Incidentally, I won't mention that you know how to sham . . . and I advise you not to testify to it," Ivan said suddenly for some reason.

"I understand ver-ry well, sir. And since you won't testify about that, sir, I also will not report the whole of our conversation by the gate that time . . ."

What happened then was that Ivan Fyodorovich suddenly went out, and only when he had already gone about ten steps down the corridor did he suddenly feel that Smerdyakov's last phrase contained some offensive meaning. He was about to turn back, but the impulse left him, and having said "Foolishness!" he quickly walked out of the hospital. He felt above all that he was indeed reassured, and precisely by the circumstance that the guilty one was not Smerdyakov but his brother Mitya, though it might seem that it should have been the opposite. Why this was so, he did not want to analyze then, he even felt disgusted at rummaging in his feelings. He wanted sooner to forget something, as it were. Then, during the next few days, when he had more closely and thoroughly acquainted himself with all the evidence weighing against him, he became completely convinced of Mitya's guilt. There was the evidence of the most insignificant people, yet almost astounding in itself, Fenya's and her mother's, for example. To say nothing of Perkhotin, the tavern, Plotnikov's shop, the witnesses at Mokroye. Above all, the details weighed against him. The news of the secret "knocks" struck the district attorney and the prosecutor almost to the same degree as Grigory's evidence about the open door. In reply to Ivan Fyodorovich's question, Grigory's wife, Marfa Ignatievna, told him directly that Smerdyakov had been lying all night behind the partition, "less than three steps from our bed," and that, though she herself was a sound sleeper, she had awakened many times hearing him moaning there: "He moaned all the time, moaned constantly." When he spoke with Herzenstube and told him of his doubts, that Smerdyakov did not seem mad to him at all but simply weak, he only evoked a thin little smile in the old man. "And do you know what he is especially doing now?" he asked Ivan Fyodorovich. "He is learning French vocables by heart; he has a notebook under his pillow, and someone has written out French words for him in Russian letters, heh, heh, heh!" Ivan Fyodorovich finally dismissed all doubts. He could not even think of his brother Dmitri now without loathing. One thing was strange, though: Alyosha kept stubbornly insisting that Dmitri was not the murderer, and that "in all probability" it was Smerdyakov. Ivan had always felt that Alyosha's opinion was very high for him, and therefore he was quite puzzled by him now. It was also strange that Alyosha did not try to talk with him about Mitya, and never began such conversations himself, but merely answered Ivan's questions. This Ivan Fyodorovich noticed very well. However, at the time he was much diverted by an altogether extraneous circumstance: in the very first days after his return from Moscow, he gave himself wholly and irrevocably to his fiery and mad passion for Katerina Ivanovna. This is not the proper place to begin speaking of this new passion of Ivan Fyodorovich's, which later affected his whole life: it could all serve as the plot for another story, for a different novel, which I do not even know that I shall ever undertake. But, all the same, even now I cannot pass over in silence that when Ivan Fyodorovich, as I have already described, leaving Katerina Ivanovna's with Alyosha at night, said to him: "But I don't fancy her," he was lying terribly at that moment: he loved her madly, though it was true that at times he also hated her so much that he could even have killed her. Many causes came together here: all shaken by what had happened with Mitya, she threw herself at Ivan Fyodorovich, when he returned to her, as if he were somehow her savior. She was wounded, insulted, humiliated in her feelings. And here the man who had loved her so much even before—oh, she knew it only too well—had appeared again, the man whose mind and heart she always placed so far above herself. But the strict girl did not sacrifice herself entirely, despite all the Karamazovian unrestraint of her lover's desires and all his charm for her. At the same time she constantly tormented herself with remorse for having betrayed Mitya, and in terrible, quarreling moments with Ivan (and there were many of them), she used to tell him so outright. It was this that, in talking with Alyosha, he had called "lie upon lie." Of course there was indeed much lying here, and that annoyed Ivan Fyodorovich most of all . . . but of all that later. In short, he almost forgot about Smerdyakov for a time. And yet, two weeks after his first visit to him, the same strange thoughts as before began tormenting him again. Suffice it to say that he began asking himself constantly why, on his last night in Fyodor Pavlovich's house, before his departure, he had gone out silently to the stairs, like a thief, and listened for what his father was doing down below. Why had he recalled it later with such loathing, why had he suddenly felt such anguish the next morning on the road, why had he said to himself on reaching Moscow: "I am a scoundrel"? And then it once occurred to him that because of all these tormenting thoughts, he was perhaps even ready to forget Katerina Ivanovna, so strongly had they suddenly taken possession of him again! Just as this occurred to him, he met Alyosha in the street. He stopped him at once and suddenly asked him a question:

"Do you remember when Dmitri burst into the house after dinner and beat father, and I then said to you in the yard that I reserved 'the right to wish' for myself—tell me, did you think then that I wished for father's death?"

"I did think so," Alyosha answered softly.

"You were right, by the way, there was nothing to guess at. But didn't you also think then that I was precisely wishing for 'viper to eat viper'—that is, precisely for Dmitri to kill father, and the sooner the better . . . and that I myself would not even mind helping him along?"

Alyosha turned slightly pale and looked silently into his brother's eyes.

"Speak!" Ivan exclaimed. "I want with all my strength to know what you thought then. I need it; the truth, the truth!" He was breathing heavily, already looking at Alyosha with some sort of malice beforehand.

"Forgive me, I did think that, too, at the time," Alyosha whispered, and fell silent, without adding even a single "mitigating circumstance."

"Thanks!" Ivan snapped, turned from Alyosha, and quickly went his way. Since then, Alyosha had noticed that his brother Ivan somehow abruptly began to shun him and even seemed to have begun to dislike him, so that later Alyosha himself stopped visiting him. But at that moment, just after that meeting with him, Ivan Fyodorovich, without going home, suddenly made his way to Smerdyakov again.

Chapter 7

The Second Visit to Smerdyakov

Smerdyakov had already been discharged from the hospital by then. Ivan Fyodorovich knew his new lodgings: precisely in that lopsided little log house with its two rooms separated by a hallway. Maria Kondratievna was living in one room with her mother, and Smerdyakov in the other by himself. God knows on what terms he lived with them: was he paying, or did he live there free? Later it was supposed that he had moved in with them as Maria Kondratievna's fiancé and meanwhile lived with them free. Both mother and daughter respected him greatly and looked upon him as a superior person compared with themselves. Having knocked until the door was opened to him, Ivan Fyodorovich went into the hallway and, on Maria Kondratievna's directions, turned left and walked straight into the "good room" occupied by Smerdyakov. The stove in that room was a tiled one, and it was very well heated. The walls were adorned with blue wallpaper, all tattered, it is true, and behind it, in the cracks, cockroaches swarmed in terrible numbers, so that there was an incessant rustling. The furniture was negligible: two benches along the walls and two chairs by the table. But the table, though it was a simple wooden one, was nevertheless covered by a tablecloth with random pink designs. There was a pot of geraniums in each of the two little windows. In the corner was an icon stand with icons. On the table stood a small, badly dented copper samovar and a tray with two cups. But Smerdyakov was already finished with his tea and the samovar had gone out . . . He himself was sitting at the table on a bench, looking into a notebook and writing something with a pen. A bottle of ink stood by him, as well as a low, cast-iron candlestick with, incidentally, a stearine candle. Ivan Fyodorovich concluded at once from Smerdyakov's face that he had recovered completely from his illness. His face was fresher, fuller, his tuft was fluffed up, his side-whiskers were slicked down. He was sitting in a gaily colored quilted dressing gown, which, however, was rather worn and quite ragged. On his nose he had a pair of spectacles, which Ivan Fyodorovich had never seen on him before. This most trifling circumstance suddenly made Ivan Fyodorovich even doubly angry, as it were: "Such a creature, and in spectacles to boot!" Smerdyakov slowly raised his head and peered intently through the spectacles at his visitor; then he slowly removed them and raised himself a little from the bench, but somehow not altogether respectfully, somehow even lazily, with the sole purpose of observing only the most necessary courtesy, which it is almost impossible to do without. All of this instantly flashed through Ivan, and he at once grasped and noted it all, and most of all the look in Smerdyakov's eyes, decidedly malicious, unfriendly, and even haughty: "Why are you hanging about here," it seemed to say, "didn't we already settle everything before? Why have you come again?" Ivan Fyodorovich could barely contain himself:

"It's hot in here," he said, still standing, and unbuttoned his coat.

"Take it off, sir," Smerdyakov allowed.

Ivan Fyodorovich took his coat off and threw it on a bench, took a chair with his trembling hands, quickly moved it to the table, and sat down. Smerdyakov managed to sit down on his bench ahead of him.

"First of all, are we alone?" Ivan Fyodorovich asked sternly and abruptly. "Won't they hear us in there?"

"No one will hear anything, sir. You saw yourself: there's a hallway."

"Listen, my friend, what was that remark you came out with as I was leaving you at the hospital, that if I said nothing about you being an expert at shamming the falling sickness, then you also would not tell the district attorney about the whole of our conversation at the gate that time? What *whole*? What could you mean by that? Were you threatening me or what? Have I entered into some league with you or what? Am I afraid of you or what?"

Ivan Fyodorovich uttered this quite in a rage, obviously and purposely letting it be known that he scorned all deviousness, all beating around the bush, and was playing an open hand. Smerdyakov's eyes flashed maliciously, his left eye began winking, and at once, though, as was his custom, with measure and reserve, he gave his answer—as if to say, "You want us to come clean, here's some cleanness for you."

"This is what I meant then, and this is why I said it then: that you, having known beforehand about the murder of your own parent, left him then as a sacrifice; and so as people wouldn't conclude anything bad about your feelings because of that, and maybe about various other things as well—that's what I was promising not to tell the authorities."

Though Smerdyakov spoke unhurriedly and was apparently in control of himself, all the same there was something hard and insistent, malicious and insolently defiant in his voice. He stared boldly at Ivan Fyodorovich, who was even dazed for the first moment.

"How? What? Are you out of your mind?"

"I'm perfectly in my mind, sir."

"But did I *know* about the murder then?" Ivan Fyodorovich cried out at last, and brought his fist down hard on the table. "What is the meaning of 'various other things'? Speak, scoundrel!"

Smerdyakov was silent and went on studying Ivan Fyodorovich with the same insolent look.

"Speak, you stinking scum, what 'various other things'?" the latter screamed.

"And by 'various other things' just now, I meant that maybe you yourself were even wishing very much for your parent's death then."

Ivan Fyodorovich jumped up and hit him as hard as he could on the shoulder with his fist, so that he rocked back towards the wall. In an instant his whole face was flooded with tears, and saying, "Shame on you, sir, to strike a weak man!" he suddenly covered his eyes with his blue-checkered and completely sodden handkerchief and sank into quiet, tearful weeping. About a minute passed.

"Enough! Stop it!" Ivan Fyodorovich finally said peremptorily, sitting down on the chair again. "Don't drive me out of all patience."

Smerdyakov took the rag from his eyes. Every line on his puckered face spoke of the offense he had just endured.

"So, you scoundrel, you thought I was at one with Dmitri in wanting to kill father?"

"I didn't know your thoughts then, sir," Smerdyakov said in an injured voice, "and that was why I stopped you then, as you were coming in the gate, in order to test you on that same point, sir."

"To test what? What?"

"Precisely that same circumstance: whether you did or did not want your parent to be killed soon."

What aroused Ivan Fyodorovich's indignation most of all was this insistent, insolent tone, which Smerdyakov stubbornly refused to give up.

"You killed him!" he exclaimed suddenly.

Smerdyakov grinned contemptuously.

"That I did not kill him, you yourself know for certain. And I'd have thought that for an intelligent man there was no more to be said about it."

"But why, why did you have such a suspicion about me then?"

"From fear only, sir, as you already know. Because I was in such a state then, all shaking from fear, that I suspected everybody. And I decided to test you, sir, because I thought that if you, too, wanted the same thing as your brother, then it would be the end of the whole business, and I'd perish, too, like a fly."

"Listen, you said something else two weeks ago."

"It was the same thing I had in mind when I spoke with you in the hospital, only I thought you'd understand without so many words, and that you yourself didn't want to talk straight out, being a most intelligent man, sir."

"Is that so! But answer me, answer, I insist: precisely how could I then have instilled such a base suspicion about myself into your mean soul?"

"As for killing—you, personally, could never have done it, sir, and you didn't want to do it either; but as for wanting someone else to kill—that you did want."

"And he says it so calmly, so calmly! But why should I want it, why in hell should I have wanted it?"

"What do you mean, why in hell, sir? What about the inheritance, sir?" Smerdyakov picked up venomously and even somehow vindictively. "After your parent, you, each of you three good brothers, would then get nearly forty thousand, and maybe even more, sir, but if Fyodor Pavlovich was to marry that same lady, Agrafena Alexandrovna, she would surely transfer all the capital to herself, right after the wedding, because she's not at all stupid, sir, so that your parent wouldn't even leave you two roubles, for all three of you good brothers. And was marriage so far off, sir? Only a hair's breadth, sir: the lady had only to beckon to him with her little finger, and he'd have run after her to church at once with his tongue hanging out."

Ivan Fyodorovich painfully managed to restrain himself.

"All right," he said at last, "you see I didn't jump up, I didn't beat you, I didn't kill you. Go on: so, according to you, I meant brother Dmitri to do it, I was counting on him?"

"How could you not count on him, sir; if he killed him, then he'd be deprived of all rights of nobility, of rank and property, and be sent to Siberia, sir. And then his share, sir, after your parent, would be left for you and your brother, Alexei Fyodorovich, equally, sir, meaning not forty then but sixty thousand for each of you, sir. So you surely must have been counting on Dmitri Fyodorovich!"

"What I suffer from you! Listen, scoundrel: if I had been counting on anyone then, it would most certainly have been you and not Dmitri, and, I swear, I even did anticipate some sort of loathsomeness from you . . . at the time . . . I remember my impression!"

"And I, too, thought for a moment then that you were counting on me as well," Smerdyakov grinned sarcastically, "so that you thereby gave yourself away even more to me, because if you were anticipating on me and you left all the same, it was just as if you told me thereby: you can kill my parent, I won't prevent you."

"Scoundrel! So that's how you understood it!"

"It was all from that same Chermashnya, sir. For pity's sake! You were going to Moscow, and refused all your parent's pleas to go to Chermashnya, sir! And after just one foolish word from me, you suddenly agreed, sir! And why did you have to agree to Chermashnya? If you went to Chermashnya instead of Moscow for no reason, after one word from me, then it means you expected something from me."

"No, I swear I did not!" Ivan yelled, gnashing his teeth.

"What do you mean 'no,' sir? On the contrary, after such words from me then, you, being your parent's son, ought first of all to have reported me to the police and given me a thrashing, sir . . . at least slapped me in the mug right there, but you, for pity's sake, sir, on the contrary, without getting the least bit angry, at once amicably fulfilled everything exactly according to my rather foolish word, sir, and left—which was altogether absurd, sir, for you ought to have stayed to protect your parent's life . . . How could I not conclude?"

Ivan sat scowling, leaning convulsively with both fists on his knees.

"Yes, it's a pity I didn't slap you in the mug," he grinned bitterly. "I couldn't have dragged you to the police then—who would have believed me, and what did I have to show them? But as for your mug . . . ach, it's a pity it didn't occur to me; though beating is forbidden, I'd have made hash out of your ugly snout."

Smerdyakov looked at him almost with delight.

"In the ordinary occasions of life," he spoke in that complacently doctrinaire tone in which he used to argue about religion with Grigory Vasilievich and tease him while they were standing at Fyodor Pavlovich's table, "in the ordinary occasions of life, mug-slapping is indeed forbidden by law nowadays, and everyone has stopped such beatings, sir, but in distinctive cases of life, not only among us but all over the world, be it even the most complete French republic, beatings do go on all the same, as in the time of Adam and Eve, sir, and there will be no stop to it, sir, but even then, in a distinctive case, you did not dare, sir."

"What are you doing studying French vocables?" Ivan nodded towards the notebook on the table.

"And why shouldn't I be studying them, sir, so as to further my education thereby, supposing that some day I myself may chance to be in those happy parts of Europe."

"Listen, monster," Ivan's eyes started flashing, and he was shaking all over, "I am not afraid of your accusations, give whatever evidence you like against me, and if I haven't beaten you to death right now, it is only because I suspect you of this crime, and I shall have you in court. I shall unmask you yet!"

"And in my opinion you'd better keep silent, sir. Because what can you tell about me, in view of my complete innocence, and who will believe you? And if you begin, then I, too, will tell everything, sir, for how could I not defend myself?"

"Do you think I'm afraid of you now?"

"Maybe in court they won't believe all the words I was just telling you, sir, but among the public they will believe, sir, and you will be ashamed, sir."

"So once again: 'It's always interesting to talk with an intelligent man'—eh?" Ivan snarled.

"Right on the mark, if I may say so, sir. So be intelligent, sir."

Ivan Fyodorovich stood up all trembling with indignation, put his coat on, and no longer replying to Smerdyakov, not even looking at him, quickly left the cottage. The fresh evening air refreshed him. The moon was shining brightly in the sky. A terrible nightmare of thoughts and feelings seethed in his soul. "Go and denounce Smerdyakov right now? But denounce him for what: he's innocent all the same. On the contrary, he will accuse me. Why, indeed, did I go to Chermashnya then? Why? Why?" Ivan Fyodorovich kept asking. "Yes, of course, I was expecting something, he's right . . . " And again for the hundredth time he recalled how, on that last night at his father's, he had eavesdropped from the stairs, but this time he recalled it with such suffering that he even stopped in his tracks as if pierced through: "Yes, that is what I expected, it's true! I wanted the murder, I precisely wanted it! Did I want the murder, did I . . . ? I must kill Smerdyakov . . . ! If I don't dare kill Smerdyakov now, life is not worth living . . . !" Without going home, Ivan Fyodorovich then went straight to Katerina Ivanovna and frightened her by his appearance: he seemed insane. He told her the whole of his conversation with Smerdyakov, down to the last little detail. He could not be calmed, no matter how she talked to him; he kept pacing the room and spoke abruptly, strangely. Finally he sat down, put his elbows on the table, rested his head in both hands, and uttered a strange aphorism:

"If it was not Dmitri but Smerdyakov who killed father, then, of course, I am solidary with him, because I put him up to it. Whether I did put him up to it—I don't know yet. But if it was he who killed him, and not Dmitri, then, of course, I am a murderer, too."

Hearing this, Katerina Ivanovna silently rose from her seat, went to her desk, opened a box standing on it, took out a piece of paper, and placed it before Ivan. This piece of paper was the same document of which Ivan Fyodorovich later told Alyosha, calling it "a mathematical proof" that brother Dmitri had killed their father. It was a letter to Katerina Ivanovna, written by Mitya in a drunken state the same evening he had met Alyosha in the fields on his way back to the monastery, after the scene in Katerina Ivanovna's house when Grushenka had insulted her. Then, having parted with Alyosha, Mitya rushed to Grushenka; it is not known whether he saw her or not, but towards nightfall he turned up at the "Metropolis" tavern, where he got properly drunk. Once drunk, he called for pen and paper, and penned an important document against himself. It was a frenzied, verbose, and incoherent letter—precisely "drunk." It was the same as when a drunken man comes home and begins telling his wife or someone in the house, with remarkable ardor, how he has just been insulted; what a scoundrel his insulter is; what a fine man, on the contrary, he himself is; and how he is going to show that scoundrel—and it is all so long, long, incoherent, and agitated, with pounding of fists on the table, with drunken tears. The paper they gave him for the letter in the tavern was a dirty scrap of some ordinary writing paper, of poor quality, on the back of which some bill had been written. Apparently there was not space enough for drunken verbosity, and Mitya not only filled all the margins with writing, but even wrote the last lines across the rest of the letter. The content of the letter was as follows:

> Fatal Katya! Tomorrow I will get money and give you back your three thousand, and farewell, woman of great wrath, but farewell, too, my love! Let us end it! Tomorrow I'll try to get it from all people, and if I don't get it from people, I give you my word of honor, I will go to my father and smash his head in and take it from under his pillow, if only Ivan goes away. I may go to hard labor, but I will give you back the three thousand. And—farewell to you. I bow to you, to the ground, for I am a scoundrel before you. Forgive me. No, better not forgive, it will be easier for me and for you! Better hard labor than your love, for I love another, and you've found out too much about her today to be able to forgive. I will kill my thief. I will go away from you all, to the East, so as not to know anyone. From *her* as well, for you are not my only tormentor, but she is, too. Farewell!
>
> P.S. I am writing a curse, yet I adore you! I hear it in my heart. One string is left, and it sings. Better to tear my heart asunder! I will kill myself, but that dog first. I'll tear the three thousand from him and throw it to you. Though I'm a scoundrel before you, I am not a thief! Wait for the three thousand. Under the dog's mattress, with a pink ribbon. I am not a thief, but I will kill my thief. Katya, don't look contemptuous: Dmitri is not a thief, he is a mur-

derer! He's killed his father and ruined himself in order to stand up and not have to endure your pride. And not to love you.

P.P.S. I kiss your feet, farewell!

P.P.P.S. Katya, pray to God they give me the money. Then there won't be blood on me, but otherwise—blood there will be! Kill me!

Your slave and enemy,
D. Karamazov.

When Ivan finished reading the "document," he stood up, convinced. So his brother was the murderer, and not Smerdyakov. Not Smerdyakov, and therefore not he, Ivan. This letter suddenly assumed a mathematical significance in his eyes. There could be no further doubt for him now of Mitya's guilt. Incidentally, the suspicion never occurred to Ivan that Mitya might have done the murder together with Smerdyakov; besides, it did not fit the facts. Ivan was set completely at ease. The next morning he recalled Smerdyakov and his jeers merely with contempt. A few days later he was even surprised that he could have been so painfully offended by his suspicions. He resolved to despise him and forget him. And so a month passed. He no longer made any inquiries about Smerdyakov, but a couple of times he heard in passing that he was very ill and not in his right mind. "He'll end in madness," the young doctor, Varvinsky, once said of him, and Ivan remembered it. During the last week of that month, Ivan himself began to feel very bad. He had already gone to consult the doctor from Moscow, invited by Katerina Ivanovna, who arrived just before the trial. And precisely at the same time his relations with Katerina Ivanovna intensified to the utmost. The two were some sort of enemies in love with each other. Katerina Ivanovna's reversions to Mitya, momentary but strong, now drove Ivan to perfect rage. It is strange that until the very last scene at Katerina Ivanovna's, which we have already described, when Alyosha came to her from seeing Mitya, he, Ivan, had never once heard any doubts of Mitya's guilt from her during that whole month, despite all her "reversions" to him, which he hated so much. It was also remarkable that, though he felt he hated Mitya more and more every day, he understood at the same time that he hated him not because of Katya's "reversions" to him, but precisely *because he had killed their father*! He himself felt it and was fully aware of it. Nevertheless, some ten days before the trial, he went to Mitya and offered him a plan of escape—a plan apparently already conceived long ago. Here, apart from the main reason prompting him to take such a step, the cause also lay in a certain unhealing scratch left on his heart by one little remark of Smerdyakov's, that it was supposedly in his, Ivan's, interest that his brother be convicted, because then the amount of the inheritance for himself and Alyosha would go up from forty to sixty thousand. He decided to sacrifice thirty thousand from his own portion to arrange for Mitya's escape. Coming back from seeing him then, he felt terribly sad and confused: he suddenly began to feel that he wanted this escape not only so as to sacrifice the thirty thousand to it, and thus heal the scratch, but also for some other reason. "Is it because in my soul I'm just as much a murderer?" he asked himself. Something remote, but burning, stung his soul. Above all, his pride suffered greatly all that month, but of that later . . . When, after his conversation with Alyosha, he stood with his hand on the bell of his apartment and suddenly decided to go to Smerdyakov, Ivan Fyodorovich was obeying some peculiar indignation that suddenly boiled up in his breast. He suddenly recalled how Katerina Ivanovna had just exclaimed to him in Alyosha's presence: "It was you, you alone, who convinced me that he" (that is, Mitya) "is the murderer!" Recalling it, Ivan was dumbfounded: never in his life had he assured her that Mitya was the murderer, on the contrary, he had actually suspected himself before her when he came to her from Smerdyakov. On the contrary, it was she, *she* who had then laid the "document" before him and proved his brother's guilt! And suddenly it was she who exclaimed: "I myself went to see Smerdyakov!" Went when? Ivan knew nothing of it. So she was not so sure of Mitya's guilt! And what could Smerdyakov have told her? What, what precisely did he tell her? Terrible wrath began burning in his heart. He did not understand how he could have missed those words of hers half an hour ago and not shouted right then. He let go of the bell and set out for Smerdyakov. "This time maybe I'll kill him," he thought on the way.

Chapter 8

The Third and Last Meeting with Smerdyakov

He was only halfway there when a sharp, dry wind arose, the same as early that morning, and fine, thick, dry snow began pouring down. It fell on the earth without sticking to it, the wind whirled it about, and soon a perfect blizzard arose. We have almost no streetlamps in the part of town where Smerdyakov was living. Ivan Fyodorovich strode through the darkness without noticing the blizzard, finding his way instinctively. His head ached and there was a painful throbbing in his temples. His hands were cramped, he could feel it. Some distance from Maria Kondratievna's house, Ivan Fyodorovich suddenly met with a solitary drunk little peasant in a patched coat, who was walking in zigzags, grumbling and cursing, and then would suddenly stop cursing and begin to sing in a hoarse, drunken voice:

Ah, Vanka's gone to Petersburg
And I'll not wait for him![1]

But he stopped each time at the second line, again began cursing someone, and then struck up the same song again. Ivan Fyodorovich had long been feeling an intense hatred for him, before he even thought about him, and suddenly he became aware of him. He at once felt an irresistible desire to bring his fist down on the little peasant. Just at that moment they came abreast of each other, and the little peasant, staggering badly, suddenly lurched full force into Ivan. The latter furiously shoved him away. The little peasant flew back and crashed like a log against the frozen ground, let out just one painful groan: "O-oh!" and was still. Ivan stepped up to him. He lay flat on his back, quite motionless, unconscious. "He'll freeze!" Ivan thought, and strode off again to Smerdyakov.

Still in the hallway, Maria Kondratievna, who ran out with a candle in her hand to open the door, began whispering to him that Pavel Fyodorovich (that is, Smerdyakov) was very, very sick, sir, not sick in bed, sir, but as if he's not in his right mind, sir, and even told her to take the tea away, he didn't want any.

"What, is he violent or something?" Ivan Fyodorovich asked rudely.

"Oh, no, it's the opposite, he's very quiet, sir, only don't talk to him for too long . . . ," Maria Kondratievna begged.

Ivan Fyodorovich opened the door and stepped into the room.

It was as well heated as the last time, but some changes could be noticed in the room: one of the side benches had been taken out, and a big, old leather sofa of imitation mahogany had appeared in its place. A bed had been made up on it, with quite clean white pillows. On the bed sat Smerdyakov, wearing the same dressing gown. The table had been moved in front of the sofa, so that there was now very little space in the room. On the table lay a thick book covered in yellow paper, but Smerdyakov was not reading it, he seemed to be sitting and doing nothing. He met Ivan Fyodorovich with a long, silent look, and was apparently not at all surprised at his coming. His face was changed, he had become very thin and yellow. His eyes were sunken, his lower eyelids had turned blue.

"But you really are sick?" Ivan Fyodorovich stopped. "I won't keep you long, I won't even take my coat off. Is there anywhere to sit?"

He went around the table, moved a chair up to it, and sat down.

"So you stare and say nothing? I've come with just one question, and I swear I won't leave without an answer: did the lady Katerina Ivanovna come to see you?"

There was a long silence during which Smerdyakov kept looking calmly at Ivan, but suddenly he waved his hand and turned his face away from him.

"What is it?" Ivan exclaimed.

"Nothing."

"What nothing?"

"So she came, so what do you care? Leave me alone, sir."

"No, I won't leave you alone! Tell me, when was it?"

"I even forgot to remember about her," Smerdyakov grinned contemptuously, and suddenly turned his face to Ivan again, fixing him with a sort of wildly hateful look, the same look as he had at their meeting a month earlier.

"You seem to be sick yourself, your face is all pinched, you look awful," he said to Ivan.

"Never mind my health, answer the question."

"And why have your eyes become yellow? The whites are quite yellow. Are you suffering greatly or what?"

He grinned contemptuously, and suddenly laughed outright.

"Listen, I said I won't leave here without an answer!" Ivan cried in terrible irritation.

"Why are you bothering me, sir? Why are you tormenting me?" Smerdyakov said with suffering.

"Eh, the devil! I don't care about you. Answer the question and I'll leave at once."

"I have nothing to answer you!" Smerdyakov dropped his eyes again.

"I assure you I shall make you answer!"

"Why do you keep worrying?" Smerdyakov suddenly stared at him, not so much with contempt now as almost with a sort of repugnance. "Is it because the trial starts tomorrow? But nothing will happen to you, be assured of that, finally! Go home, sleep peacefully, don't fear anything."

"I don't understand you . . . what could I have to fear tomorrow?" Ivan spoke in surprise, and suddenly some sort of fear indeed blew cold on his soul. Smerdyakov measured him with his eyes.

"You don't un-der-stand?" he drawled reproachfully. "Why would an intelligent man want to put on such an act?"

Ivan gazed at him silently. The unexpected tone in which his former lackey now addressed him, full of quite unheard-of arrogance, was unusual in itself. There had been no such tone even at their last meeting.

"I'm telling you, you have nothing to fear. I won't say anything against you, there's no evidence. Look, his hands are trembling. Why are your fingers moving like that? Go home, *it was not you that killed him.*"

Ivan gave a start; he remembered Alyosha.

"I know it was not me . . . ," he began to murmur.

"You know?" Smerdyakov picked up again.

Ivan jumped up and seized him by the shoulder.

"Tell all, viper! Tell all!"

Smerdyakov was not in the least frightened. He merely fastened his eyes on him with insane hatred.

"Well, it was you who killed him in that case," he whispered furiously.

Ivan sank onto his chair as if he had just figured something out. He grinned maliciously.

"You're still talking about that? The same as last time?"

"But last time, too, you stood there and understood everything, and you understand it now."

"I understand only that you are crazy."

"Doesn't a man get tired of it? Here we are, just the two of us, so what's the use of putting on such an act, trying to fool each other? Or do you still want to shift it all onto me, right to my face? You killed him, you are the main killer, and I was just your minion, your faithful servant Licharda,[2] and I performed the deed according to your word."

"Performed? Was it you that killed him?" Ivan went cold.

Something shook, as it were, in his brain, and he began shivering all over with cold little shivers. Now Smerdyakov in turn looked at him in surprise: he probably was struck, at last, by the genuineness of Ivan's fear.

"You mean you really didn't know anything?" he murmured mistrustfully, looking him in the eye with a crooked grin.

Ivan kept staring at him; he seemed to have lost his tongue.

Ah, Vanka's gone to Petersburg
And I'll not wait for him—

suddenly rang in his head.

"You know what: I'm afraid you're a dream, a ghost sitting there in front of me," he murmured.

"There's no ghost, sir, besides the two of us, sir, and some third one. No doubt he's here now, that third one, between the two of us."

"Who is it? Who is here? What third one?" Ivan Fyodorovich said fearfully, looking around, his eyes hastily searching for someone in all the corners.

"That third one is God, sir, Providence itself, sir, it's right here with us now, sir, only don't look for it, you won't find it."

"It's a lie that you killed him!" Ivan shouted in a rage. "You're either crazy, or you're taunting me like the last time!"

Smerdyakov kept watching him inquisitively, as before, with no trace of fear. He still could not manage to get over his mistrust, he still thought Ivan "knew everything" and was merely pretending in order to "shift it all onto him, right to his face."

"Just a moment, sir," he finally said in a weak voice, and suddenly pulled his left leg from under the table and began rolling up his trouser. The leg turned out to have a long white stocking on it, and a slipper. Unhurriedly, Smerdyakov removed the garter and thrust his hand far down into the stocking. Ivan Fyodorovich stared at him and suddenly began shaking with convulsive fear.

"Madman!" he shouted, and, jumping quickly from his seat, he reeled backwards so that his back struck the wall and was as if glued to it, drawn up tight as a string. He looked at Smerdyakov with insane horror. The latter, not in the least disturbed by his fear, kept fishing around in his stocking as if he were trying to get hold of something and pull it out. Finally he got hold of it and began to pull. Ivan Fyodorovich saw that it was some papers, or a bundle of papers. Smerdyakov pulled it out and placed it on the table.

"Here, sir," he said softly.

"What?" Ivan answered, shaking.

"Take a look, if you please, sir," Smerdyakov said, just as softly.

Ivan stepped to the table, took the bundle, and began to unwrap it, but suddenly jerked his hands back as if he had touched some loathsome, horrible viper.

"Your fingers are trembling, sir, you've got a cramp," Smerdyakov observed, and he slowly unwrapped the bundle himself. Under the wrapping were found three packets of iridescent hundred-rouble bills.

"It's all there, sir, all three thousand, no need to count it. Have it, sir," he invited Ivan, nodding towards the money. Ivan sank onto the chair. He was white as a sheet.

"You frightened me . . . with that stocking . . . ," he said, grinning somehow strangely.

"Can it possibly be that you didn't know till now?" Smerdyakov asked once again.

"No, I didn't. I kept thinking it was Dmitri. Brother! Brother! Ah!" he suddenly seized his head with both hands. "Listen: did you kill him alone? Without my brother, or with him?"

"Just only with you, sir; together with you, sir, and Dmitri Fyodorovich is as innocent as could be, sir."

"All right, all right . . . We'll get to me later. Why do I keep trembling . . . I can't get a word out."

"You used to be brave once, sir, you used to say 'Everything is permitted,' sir, and now you've got so frightened!" Smerdyakov murmured, marveling. "Would you like some lemonade? I'll tell them to bring it, sir. It's very refreshing. Only I must cover that up first, sir."

And he nodded again towards the money. He made a move to get up and call for Maria Kondratievna from the doorway to make some lemonade and bring it to them, but, looking for something to cover the money with, so that she would not see it, he first pulled out his handkerchief, but, as it again turned out to be completely sodden, he then took from the table that thick, yellow book, the only one lying on it, the one Ivan had noticed as he came in, and placed it on top of the bills. The title of the book was *The Homilies of Our Father among the Saints, Isaac the Syrian.*[3] Ivan Fyodorovich read it mechanically.

"I don't want any lemonade," he said. "We'll get to me later. Sit down and tell me: how did you do it? Tell everything . . ."

"You should at least take your coat off, sir, or you'll get all sweaty."

Ivan Fyodorovich, as though he had only just thought of it, tore his coat off and threw it on the bench without getting up.

"Speak, please, speak!"

He seemed to calm down. He waited, with the assurance that Smerdyakov would now tell him *everything*.

"About how it was done, sir?" Smerdyakov sighed. "It was done in the most natural manner, sir, according to those same words of yours."

"We'll get to my words later," Ivan interrupted again, not shouting as before, but uttering the words firmly and as if with complete self-possession. "Just tell me in detail how you did it. Step by step. Don't leave anything out. The details, above all, the details. I beg you."

"You left, and then I fell into the cellar, sir . . ."

"In a falling fit, or were you shamming?"

"Of course I was shamming, sir. It was all a sham. I went quietly down the stairs, sir, to the very bottom, and lay down quietly, sir, and after I lay down, I started yelling. And I kept thrashing while they were taking me out."

"Wait! You were shamming all the while, even later, and in the hospital?"

"By no means, sir. The very next day, in the morning, still before the hospital, a real one struck me, and such a strong one, there hasn't been one like it for many years. I was completely unconscious for two days."

"All right, all right, go on."

"They put me on that cot, sir, and I knew it would be behind the partition, sir, because on every occasion when I was sick, Marfa Ignatievna always put me for the night behind the partition in her room, sir. She's always been tender to me since my very birth, sir. During the night I kept moaning, only softly, sir. I kept expecting Dmitri Fyodorovich."

"Expecting what, that he'd visit you?"

"Why would he visit me? I expected him to come to the house, for I had no doubt at all that he would arrive that same night, for, being deprived of me and not having any information, he would surely have to get to the house over the fence, as he knew how to, sir, and commit whatever it was."

"And what if he didn't come?"

"Then nothing would happen, sir. I wouldn't dare without him."

"All right, all right . . . speak more clearly, don't hurry, and above all—don't omit anything!"

"I was expecting him to kill Fyodor Pavlovich, sir . . . that was bound to be, sir. Because I'd already prepared him for it . . . in those last few days, sir . . . and the main thing was that those signals became known to him. Given his suspiciousness and the rage he'd stored up over those days, he was sure to use the signals to get right into the house, sir. It was sure to be. I was just expecting him, sir."

"Wait," Ivan interrupted, "if he killed him, he'd take the money and go off with it; wouldn't you have reasoned precisely that way? What would you get out of it then? I don't see."

"But he never would have found the money, sir. I only instructed him that the money was under the mattress. But it wasn't true, sir. At first it was in the box, that's how it was, sir. And then I instructed Fyodor Pavlovich, since he trusted only me of all mankind, to transfer that same package with the money to the corner behind the icons, because no one would ever think of looking there, especially if he was in a hurry. And so that package lay there in the corner, behind the icons, sir. And to keep it under the mattress would even be ridiculous, the box at least had a lock on it. And everyone here now believes it was under the mattress. Foolish reasoning, sir. And so, if Dmitri Fyodorovich committed that same murder, then, having found nothing, he would either run away in a hurry, sir, afraid of every rustle, as always happens with murderers, or he'd be arrested, sir. So then, either the next day, or even that same night, sir, I could always get behind the icons and take that same money, sir, and it would all have fallen on Dmitri Fyodorovich. I could always hope for that."

"Well, and what if he didn't kill him, but only gave him a beating?"

"If he didn't kill him, then of course I wouldn't dare take the money, and it would all be in vain. But there was also the calculation that he might beat him unconscious, and meanwhile I'd have time to take the money, and then afterwards I would report to Fyodor Pavlovich that it was none other than Dmitri Fyodorovich who had beaten him and carried off the money."

"Wait . . . I'm getting confused. So it was Dmitri who killed him after all, and you just took the money?"

"No, it wasn't him that killed him, sir. Look, even now I could tell you he was the murderer . . . but I don't want to lie to you now, because . . . because if, as I see now, you really didn't understand anything before this, and weren't pretending so as to shift your obvious guilt onto me right to my face, still you are guilty of everything, sir, because you knew about the murder, and you told me to kill him, sir, and, knowing everything, you left. Therefore I want to prove it to your face tonight that in all this the chief murderer is you alone, sir, and I'm just not the real chief one, though I did kill him. It's you who are the most lawful murderer!"

"Why, why am I the murderer? Oh, God!" Ivan finally could not bear it, forgetting that he had put off all talk of himself to the end of the conversation. "Is it still that same Chermashnya? Wait, speak, why did you need my consent, if you did take Chermashnya for consent? How will you explain that now?"

"Being confident of your consent, I'd know you wouldn't come back and start yelling because of that lost three thousand, in case the authorities suspected me for some reason instead of Dmitri Fyodorovich, or that I was Dmitri Fyodorovich's accomplice; on the contrary, you'd protect me from the others . . . And the inheritance, when you got it, you might even reward me sometime later, during the whole rest of your life to come, because, after all, you'd have had the pleasure of getting that inheritance through me, otherwise, what with marrying Agrafena Alexandrovna, all you'd get is a fig."

"Ah! So you intended to torment me afterwards, all the rest of my life!" Ivan growled. "And what if I hadn't left then, but had turned you in?"

"What could you turn me in for? That I put you up to Chermashnya? But that's foolishness, sir. Besides, after our conversation you could either go or stay. If you stayed, then nothing would happen, I'd simply know, sir, that you didn't want this business, and I wouldn't undertake anything. But since you did go, it meant you were assuring me that you wouldn't dare turn me over to the court and would forgive me the three thousand. And you wouldn't be able to persecute me at all afterwards, because in that case I'd tell everything in court, sir, that is, not that I stole or killed—I wouldn't say that—but that it was you who put me up to stealing and killing, only I didn't agree. That's why I needed your consent then, so that you couldn't corner me with anything afterwards, sir, because where would you get any proof of that, but I could always corner you, sir, by revealing how much you desired your parent's death, and I give you my word—the public would all believe me, and you'd be ashamed for the rest of your life."

"So I did, I did desire it, did I?" Ivan growled again.

"You undoubtedly did, sir, and by your consent then you silently allowed me that business, sir," Smerdyakov looked firmly at Ivan. He was very weak and spoke softly and wearily, but something inner and hidden was firing him up, he apparently had some sort of intention. Ivan could sense it.

"Go on," he said to him, "go on with that night."

"So, to go on, sir. I lay there and thought I heard the master cry out. And before that, Grigory Vasilievich suddenly got up and stepped out and suddenly shouted, and then all was still, dark. So I was lying there waiting, with my heart pounding, I could hardly stand it. Finally I got up and went, sir—I saw the master's left window to the garden open, so I took another step to the left, sir, to listen whether he was alive in there or not, and I heard the master stirring about and groaning, which meant he was alive, sir. Ech, I thought! I went up to the window, called to the master: 'It's me,' I said. And he called to me: 'He was here, he was here, he ran away!' That is, Dmitri Fyodorovich, sir. 'He killed Grigory!' 'Where?' I whispered to him. 'There, in the corner,' he pointed, also in a whisper. 'Wait,' I said. I went to have a look in the corner, and stumbled over Grigory Vasilievich, lying near the wall, all covered with blood, unconscious. 'So it's true, Dmitri Fyodorovich was here,' jumped into my mind at once, and I at once decided to finish it all right then and there, sir, since even if Grigory Vasilievich was still alive, he wouldn't see anything while he was unconscious. The only risk was that Marfa Ignatievna might suddenly wake up. I felt it at that moment, only this desire got such a hold on me, it even took my breath away. I went up to the master's window again and said: 'She's here, she's come, Agrafena Alexandrovna is here, she wants to get in.' He got all startled, just like a baby. 'Here where? Where?' he kept gasping, and he still didn't believe it. 'She's standing right here,' I said, 'open up!' He looked at me through the window, believing it and not believing it, but he was afraid to open the door—it's me he's afraid of, I thought. And here's a funny thing: I suddenly decided to knock those same signals on the window, right in front of his eyes, meaning Grushenka was there: he didn't seem to believe words, but as soon as I knocked the signals, he ran at once to open the door. He opened it. I tried to go in, but he stood and blocked my way with his body. 'Where is she, where is she?' he looked at me and trembled. Well, I thought, that's bad, if he's so afraid of me! And my legs even went limp from fear that he wouldn't let me in, or would shout, or else that Marfa Ignatievna would come running, or whatever, I don't remember anymore, but I must have stood pale in front of him then. I whispered to him: 'But she's there, right there, under the window,' I said, 'how is it you didn't see her?' 'Bring her here, bring her here!' 'But she's afraid,' I said, 'she got scared by the shouting, she's hiding in the bushes, go and call her yourself from the study,' I said. He ran there, went up to the window, put a candle in the window. 'Grushenka,' he called, 'Grushenka, are you here?' He called her, but he didn't want to lean out the window, he didn't want to move away from me, from that same fear, because he was very afraid of me and therefore didn't dare move away from me. 'But there she is,' I said (I went up to the window and leaned all the way out), 'there she is in the bushes, smiling to you, see?' He suddenly believed it, he just started shaking, because he really was very much in love with her, sir, and he leaned all the way out the window. Then I grabbed that same cast-iron paperweight, the one on his desk—remember, sir?—it must weigh all of three pounds, and I swung and hit him from behind on the top of the head with the corner of it. He didn't even cry out. He just sank down suddenly, and I hit him one more time, and then a third time. The third time I felt I smashed his skull. He suddenly fell on his back, face up, all bloody. I looked myself over: there was no blood on me, it didn't splatter, I wiped the paperweight off, put it back, went behind the icons, took the money out of the envelope, dropped the envelope on the floor, and that pink ribbon next to it. I went out to the garden shaking all over. I went straight to that apple tree, the one with the hole in it—you know that hole, I'd chosen it long ago, there was already a rag and some paper in it, I'd prepared it long ago; I wrapped the whole sum in paper, then in the rag, and shoved it way down. And it stayed there for more than two weeks, that same sum, sir, I took it out later, after the hospital. I went back to my bed, lay down, and thought in fear: 'Now if Grigory Vasilievich is killed altogether, things thereby could turn out very badly, but if he's not killed and comes round again, then it will turn out really well, because he'll be a witness that Dmitri Fyodorovich was there, and so it was he who killed him and took the money, sir.' Then I began groaning, from doubt and impatience, in order to waken Marfa Ignatievna the sooner. She got up finally, was about to rush to me, but as soon as she suddenly saw that Grigory Vasilievich wasn't there, she ran out, and I heard her screaming in the garden. So then, sir, that all started for the whole night, and I no longer worried about it all."

The narrator stopped. Ivan had listened to him all the while in deathly silence, without stirring, without taking his eyes off him. And Smerdyakov, as he was telling his story, merely glanced at him occasionally, but most of the time looked aside. By the end he had evidently become agitated himself and was breathing heavily. Sweat broke out on his face. It was impossible to tell, however, whether he felt repentant or what.

"Wait," Ivan picked up, putting things together. "What about the door? If he only opened the door for you, then how could Grigory have seen it open before you? Because he did see it before you?"

Remarkably, Ivan asked this in a most peaceful voice, even in quite a different tone, not at all angry, so that if someone had opened the door at that moment and looked in at them from the doorway, he would certainly have concluded that they were sitting and talking peaceably about some ordinary, though interesting, subject.

"Concerning the door, and that Grigory Vasilievich supposedly saw it open, he only fancied it was so," Smerdyakov grinned crookedly. "Because he is not a man, let me tell you, but just like a stubborn mule, sir: he didn't see it, but he fancied he saw it—and you'll never be able to shake him, sir. It was just a great piece of luck for you and me that he thought it up, because Dmitri Fyodorovich will undoubtedly be thoroughly convicted after that."

"Listen," Ivan Fyodorovich said, as if he were beginning to get lost again and were trying hard to figure something out, "listen . . . I wanted to ask you many other things, but I've forgotten . . . I get confused and forget everything . . . Ah! Tell me just this one thing: why did you open the envelope and leave it there on the floor? Why didn't you simply take it, envelope and all . . . ? As you were telling it, it seemed to me you were speaking of the envelope as if that was how it should have been done . . . but why, I don't understand . . ."

"That I did for a certain reason, sir. Because if it was a man who knew and was familiar, like me, for example, who had seen that money himself beforehand, and maybe wrapped it in the envelope himself, and watched with his own eyes while it was sealed and addressed, then why on earth would such a man, if, for example, it was he who killed him, unseal the envelope after the murder, and in such a flurry besides, knowing quite for certain anyway that the money was sure to be in that envelope, sir? On the contrary, if the thief was like me, for example, he'd simply shove the envelope in his pocket without opening it in the least, and make his getaway as fast as he could, sir. Now Dmitri Fyodorovich is quite another thing: he knew about the envelope only from hearsay, he never saw it, and so supposing, for example, he took it from under the mattress, he'd open it right away to find out if that same money was really there. And he'd throw the envelope down, having no time by then to consider that he was leaving evidence behind, because he's an unaccustomed thief, sir, and before that never stole anything obviously, because he's a born nobleman, sir, and even if he did decide to steal this time, it was not precisely to steal, as it were, but only to get his own back, since he gave the whole town preliminary notice of it, and boasted out loud beforehand in front of everybody that he would go and take his property back from Fyodor Pavlovich. In my interrogation, I told this same thought to the prosecutor, not quite clearly, but, on the contrary, as if I were leading him to it by a hint, as if I didn't understand it myself, and as if he had thought it up, and not that I'd prompted him, sir—and Mr. Prosecutor even started drooling over that same hint of mine, sir . . ."

"But can you possibly have thought of all that right there on the spot?" Ivan Fyodorovich exclaimed, beside himself with astonishment. He again looked fearfully at Smerdyakov.

"For pity's sake, sir, how could I have thought it all up in such a flurry? It was all thought out beforehand."

"Well . . . well, then the devil himself helped you!" Ivan Fyodorovich exclaimed again. "No, you're not stupid, you're much more intelligent than I thought . . ."

He rose, obviously intending to walk about the room. He was in terrible anguish. But as the table was in his way and he could barely squeeze between the table and the wall, he merely turned on the spot and sat down again. Perhaps it irritated him suddenly that he had not managed to walk about, for he suddenly shouted almost in his former frenzy:

"Listen, you wretched, despicable man! Do you understand that if I haven't killed you so far, it's only because I'm keeping you to answer in court tomorrow. God knows," Ivan held up his hand, "perhaps I, too, was guilty, perhaps I really had a secret desire that my father . . . die, but I swear to you that I was not as guilty as you think, and perhaps I did not put you up to it at all. No, no, I did not! But, anyway, I shall give evidence against myself tomorrow, in court, I've decided! I shall tell everything, everything. But we shall appear together! And whatever you say against me in court, whatever evidence you give—I accept, and I am not afraid of you; I myself shall confirm it all! But you, too, must confess to the court! You must, you must, we shall go together! So it will be!"

Ivan said this solemnly and energetically, and one could tell just from his flashing eyes that it would be so.

"You're sick, I see, sir, you're very sick, sir. Your eyes, sir, are quite yellow," Smerdyakov said, but without any mockery, even as if with condolence.

"We shall go together!" Ivan repeated, "and if you won't go, I alone shall confess anyway."

Smerdyakov was silent for a while, as if he were pondering.

"None of that will be, sir, and you will not go, sir," he finally decided categorically.

"You don't know me!" Ivan exclaimed reproachfully.

"It will be too shameful for you, sir, if you confess everything about yourself. And moreover it will be useless, quite useless, sir, because I will certainly say right out that I never told you any such thing, sir, and that you're either in some sort of sickness (and it does look that way, sir), or else you really pitied your brother so much that you were sacrificing yourself, and you invented all that against me since you've considered me like a fly all your life anyway, and not like a man. And who will believe you, and what evidence, what single piece of evidence have you got?"

"Listen, you showed me that money, of course, in order to convince me."

Smerdyakov removed Isaac the Syrian from the money and set it aside.

"Take the money with you, sir, take it away," Smerdyakov sighed.

"Of course I shall take it away! But why are you giving it back to me, if you killed because of it?" Ivan looked at him in great surprise.

"I've got no use at all for it, sir," Smerdyakov said in a trembling voice, waving his hand. "There was such a former thought, sir, that I could begin a life on such money in Moscow, or even more so abroad, I did have such a dream, sir, and even more so as 'everything is permitted.' It was true what you taught me, sir, because you told me a lot about that then: because if there's no infinite God, then there's no virtue either, and no need of it at all. It was true. That's how I reasoned."

"Did you figure it out for yourself?" Ivan grinned crookedly.

"With your guidance, sir."

"So now you've come to believe in God, since you're giving back the money?"

"No, sir, I haven't come to believe, sir," whispered Smerdyakov.

"Why are you giving it back then?"

"Enough . . . it's no use, sir!" Smerdyakov again waved his hand. "You yourself kept saying then that everything was permitted, so why are you so troubled now, you yourself, sir? You even want to go and give evidence against yourself . . . Only there will be nothing of the sort! You won't go and give evidence!" Smerdyakov decided again, firmly and with conviction.

"You'll see!" said Ivan.

"It can't be. You're too intelligent, sir. You love money, that I know, sir, you also love respect, because you're very proud, you love women's charms exceedingly, and most of all you love living in peaceful prosperity, without bowing to anyone—that you love most of all, sir. You won't want to ruin your life forever by taking such shame upon yourself in court. You're like Fyodor Pavlovich most of all, it's you of all his children who came out resembling him most, having the same soul as him, sir."

"You're not stupid," Ivan said as if struck; the blood rushed to his face. "I used to think you were stupid. You're serious now!" he remarked, suddenly looking at Smerdyakov in some new way.

"It was your pride made you think I was stupid. Do have the money, sir."

Ivan took all three packets of bills and shoved them into his pocket without wrapping them in anything.

"I'll show them to the court tomorrow," he said.

"No one there will believe you, sir, seeing as you've got enough money of your own, now, so you just took it out of your box and brought it, sir."

Ivan rose from his seat.

"I repeat to you, that if I haven't killed you, it's only because I need you for tomorrow, remember that, don't forget it!"

"Well, so kill me, sir. Kill me now," Smerdyakov suddenly said strangely, looking strangely at Ivan. "You won't dare do that either, sir," he added, with a bitter smirk, "you won't dare do anything, you former brave man, sir!"

"Until tomorrow!" Ivan cried, and made a move to go.

"Wait . . . show it to me one more time."

Ivan took the money out and showed it to him. Smerdyakov looked at it for about ten seconds.

"Well, go," he said, waving his hand. "Ivan Fyodorovich!" he suddenly called after him again.

"What is it?" Ivan turned, already walking out.

"Farewell, sir!"

"Until tomorrow!" Ivan cried again, and walked out of the cottage.

The blizzard was still going on. He walked briskly for the first few steps, but suddenly began staggering, as it were. "It's something physical," he thought, and grinned. It was as if a sort of joy now descended into his soul. He felt an infinite firmness in himself: the end to his hesitations, which had tormented him so terribly all through those last days! The decision was taken, "and now will not be changed," he thought with happiness. At that moment he suddenly stumbled against something and nearly fell. Having stopped, he made out at his feet the little peasant he had struck down, who was still lying in the same spot, unconscious and not moving. The blizzard had all but covered his face. Ivan suddenly pulled him up and took him on his back. Seeing light in a cottage to the right, he went over, knocked on the shutters, and when the tradesman who owned the house answered, asked him to help him carry the peasant to the police station, with the promise that he would give him three roubles at once for it. The tradesman got ready and came out. I will not describe in detail how Ivan Fyodorovich then managed to achieve his goal and get the peasant installed in the police station and have him examined immediately by a doctor, while he once again provided liberally "for the expenses." I will say only that the affair took him almost a whole hour. But Ivan Fyodorovich was left feeling very pleased. His thoughts were expanding and working. "If my decision for tomorrow had not been taken so firmly," he suddenly thought with delight, "I would not have stayed for a whole hour arranging things for the little peasant, I would simply have passed him by and not cared a damn whether he froze . . . I'm quite capable of observing myself, incidentally," he thought at the same moment, with even greater delight, "and they all decided I was losing my mind!" As he reached his house, he stopped all at once under a sudden question: "And shouldn't I go to the prosecutor right now at once and tell him everything?" He resolved the question by turning towards his house again: "Tomorrow everything together!" he whispered to himself, and, strangely, almost all his joy, all his self-content vanished in a moment. And as he entered his room, something icy suddenly touched his heart, like a recollection, or, rather, a reminder, of something loathsome and tormenting that was precisely in that room now, presently, and had been there before. He sank wearily onto his sofa. The old woman brought him the samovar, he made tea, but did not touch it; he dismissed the woman till morning. He sat on the sofa feeling dizzy. He felt himself sick and strengthless. He was beginning to fall asleep, but got up nervously and paced the room to drive sleep away. At moments he fancied that he seemed delirious. But it was not sickness that occupied him most of all; when he sat down again he began looking around from time to time, as if searching for something. This happened several times. Finally his eyes focused intently on one spot. Ivan grinned, but an angry flush covered his face. He sat where he was for a long time, his head propped firmly on both hands, but still looking sideways at the former spot, at the sofa standing against the opposite wall. Apparently something there, some object, irritated him, troubled him, tormented him.

Chapter 9

The Devil. Ivan Fyodorovich's Nightmare

I am not a doctor, but nevertheless I feel the moment has come when it is decidedly necessary for me to explain to the reader at least something of the nature of Ivan Fyodorovich's illness. Getting ahead of myself, I will say only one thing: he was, that evening, precisely just on the verge of brain fever, which finally took complete possession of his organism, long in disorder but stubbornly refusing to succumb. Though I know nothing of medicine, I will venture the suggestion that he had indeed succeeded, perhaps, by a terrible effort of will, in postponing his illness for a time, hoping, of course, to overcome it completely. He knew he was not well, but he was loath to be ill at that time, during those approaching fatal moments of his life; he had to be personally present, to speak his word boldly and resolutely, and "vindicate himself to himself." However, he did once visit the new doctor who had come from Moscow, invited by Katerina Ivanovna owing to a fantasy of hers, which I have already mentioned above. The doctor, having listened to him and examined him, concluded that he was indeed suffering from something like a brain disorder, as it were, and was not at all surprised at a certain confession that he made to him, though not without repugnance. "In your condition hallucinations are quite possible," the doctor decided, "though they should be verified . . . but generally it is necessary to begin serious treatment without a moment's delay, otherwise things will go badly." But Ivan Fyodorovich, having left the doctor, did not follow up this sensible advice, and treated the idea of treatment with disregard: "I'm up and about, I'm still strong enough, if I collapse it's another matter, then anyone who likes can treat me," he decided, with a wave of the hand. And so he was sitting there now, almost aware of being delirious, and, as I have already said, peering persistently at some object on the sofa against the opposite wall. Someone suddenly turned out to be sitting there, though God knows how he had got in, because he had not been in the room when Ivan Fyodorovich came back from seeing Smerdyakov. It was some gentleman, or, rather, a certain type of Russian gentleman, no longer young, *qui frisait la cinquantaine*,[1] as the French say, with not too much gray in his dark, rather long, and still thick hair, and with a pointed beard. He was wearing a sort of brown jacket, evidently from the best of tailors, but already shabby, made approximately three years ago and already completely out of fashion, such as no well-to-do man of society had been seen in for at least two years. His linen, his long, scarflike necktie, all was just what every stylish gentleman would wear, but, on closer inspection, the linen was a bit dirty and the wide scarf was quite threadbare. The visitor's checkered trousers fitted perfectly, but again they were too light and somehow too narrow, of a style no one wore any longer, as was the soft, downy white hat the visitor had brought with him, though it was entirely the wrong season. In short, he gave the appearance of decency on rather slender means. The gentleman looked as though he belonged to the category of former idle landowners that flourished in the time of serfdom; had obviously seen the world and decent society, had once had connections and perhaps had them still, but, after the gay life of his youth and the recent abolition of serfdom, had gradually fallen into poverty and become a sort of sponger, in bon ton, as it were, knocking about among good old acquaintances, and received by them for his easy, agreeable nature, and also considering that he was, after all, a decent man, who could even be invited to sit at the table in any company, though, of course, in a humble place. Such spongers, gentlemen of agreeable nature, who can tell a story or two and play a hand of cards, and who decidedly dislike having any tasks thrust upon them, are usually single, either bachelors or widowers, and if they have children, the children are always brought up somewhere far away, by some aunts, whom the gentleman hardly ever mentions in decent company, as though somewhat ashamed of such relations. They gradually become estranged from their children altogether, occasionally receiving letters from them on their birthday or at Christmas, and sometimes even answering them. The unexpected visitor's physiognomy was not so much good-humored as, again, agreeable and ready, depending on the circumstances, for any amiable expression. He did not have a watch, but he had a tortoiseshell lorgnette on a black ribbon. On the middle finger of his right hand there was displayed a massive gold ring with an inexpensive opal. Ivan Fyodorovich was spitefully silent and did not want to begin talking. The visitor sat and waited precisely like a sponger who had just come down from upstairs, from the room assigned to him, to keep his host company at tea, but was humbly silent, since the host was preoccupied and scowling at the thought of something; but who was ready for any amiable conversation as soon as the host would begin it. Suddenly his face seemed to express some unexpected concern.

"Listen," he began to Ivan Fyodorovich, "forgive me, it's just a reminder: didn't you go to Smerdyakov to find out about Katerina Ivanovna? Yet you left without finding out anything about her, you must have forgotten . . ."

"Ah, yes!" suddenly escaped from Ivan, and his face darkened with worry, "yes, I forgot . . . Anyway, it's all the same now, all till tomorrow," he muttered to himself. "As for you," he turned irritably to his visitor, "I'd have remembered it myself in a moment, because that's exactly what has been causing me such anguish! Why did you have to come out with it? Do you think I'll simply believe you prompted me and not that I remembered it myself?"

"Don't believe it then," the gentleman smiled sweetly, "what good is faith by force? Besides, proofs are no help to faith, especially material proofs. Thomas believed not because he saw the risen Christ but because he wanted to believe even before that.[2] Spiritualists, for example . . . I like them so much . . . imagine, they think they're serving faith because devils show their little horns to them from the other world. 'This,' they say, 'is a material proof, so to speak, that the other world exists.' The other world and material proofs, la-di-da! And, after all, who knows whether proof of the devil is also a proof of God? I want to join an idealist society and form an opposition within it: 'I'm a realist,' I'll say, 'not a materialist,' heh, heh!"

"Listen," Ivan Fyodorovich suddenly got up from the table. "I seem to be delirious now . . . and of course I am delirious . . . you can lie as much as you like, it's all the same to me! You won't put me into a rage, as you did last time. Only I'm ashamed of something . . . I feel like pacing the room . . . I sometimes don't see you, and don't even hear your voice, as last time, but I always guess what you're driveling, because *it is I, I myself who am talking, and not you*! Only I don't know whether I was asleep last time or actually saw you. I am now going to wet a towel with cold water and put it to my head, and maybe you'll evaporate."

Ivan Fyodorovich went to the corner, took a towel, carried out his intention, and with the wet towel on his head began pacing up and down the room.

"I'm glad we can be so informal with each other," the visitor tried to begin.

"Fool," Ivan laughed, "what, should I call you 'sir' or something? I feel fine now, only there's a pain in my temple . . . and in the top of my head . . . only please don't philosophize, as you did last time. Tell some pleasant lies, if you can't clear out. Gossip, since you're a sponger, go ahead and gossip. Why am I stuck with such a nightmare! But I'm not afraid of you. I will overcome you. They won't take me to the madhouse!"

"*C'est charmant*—sponger! Yes, that is precisely my aspect. What am I on earth if not a sponger? Incidentally, I'm a little surprised listening to you: by God, it seems you're gradually beginning to take me for something real, and not just your fantasy, as you insisted last time . . ."

"Not for a single moment do I take you for the real truth," Ivan cried, somehow even furiously. "You are a lie, you are my illness, you are a ghost. Only I don't know how to destroy you, and I see I'll have to suffer through it for a while. You are my hallucination. You are the embodiment of myself, but of just one side of me . . . of my thoughts and feelings, but only the most loathsome and stupid of them. From that angle you could even be interesting to me, if I had time to bother with you . . ."

"I beg your pardon, I'm going to catch you now: earlier, under the streetlamp, when you jumped on Alyosha and shouted: 'You learned it from him! How do you know that *he* has been coming to me?' You were thinking of me then. It means that for one little moment you believed, you did believe that I really am," the gentleman laughed softly.

"Yes, that was a lapse of character . . . but I couldn't believe in you. I don't know whether I was asleep or awake the last time. Perhaps I only saw you in my sleep and not in reality at all."

"And why were you so severe with him today, with Alyosha, I mean? He's a dear boy; I owe him one for the elder Zosima."

"Shut up about Alyosha! How dare you, you lackey!" Ivan laughed again.

"You laugh while you're abusing me—a good sign. By the way, you're much more amiable with me today than you were last time, and I know why: that great decision . . ."

"Shut up about my decision!" Ivan cried ferociously.

"I understand, I understand, *c'est noble*, *c'est charmant*, you go to defend your brother tomorrow, and you sacrifice yourself . . . *c'est chevaleresque*."[3]

"Shut up or I'll kick you!"

"I'd be glad of it in a way, because my goal would then be achieved: if it comes to kicks, that means you must believe in my realism, because one doesn't kick a ghost. Joking aside: it's all the same to me, abuse me if you like, but still it would be better to be a bit more polite, even with me. Fool, lackey—what sort of talk is that?"

"By abusing you, I'm abusing myself!" Ivan laughed again. "You are me, myself, only with a different mug. You precisely say what I already think . . . and you're not capable of telling me anything new!"

"If my thoughts agree with yours, it only does me honor," the gentleman said with dignity and tact.

"You just pick out all my bad thoughts, and above all the stupid ones. You are stupid and banal. You are terribly stupid. No, I can't endure you! What am I to do, what am I to do!" Ivan gnashed his teeth.

"My friend, I still want to be a gentleman, and to be accepted as such," the visitor began in a fit of some sort of purely spongerish, good-natured, and already-yielding ambition. "I am poor, but . . . I won't say very honest, but . . . in society it is generally accepted as an axiom that I am a fallen angel. By God, I can't imagine how I could ever have been an angel. If I ever was one, it was so long ago that it's no sin to have forgotten it. Now I only value my reputation as a decent man and get along as best I can, trying to be agreeable. I sincerely love people—oh, so much of what has been said about me is slander! Here, when I move in with people from time to time, my life gets to be somewhat real, as it were, and I like that most of all. Because, like you, I myself suffer from the fantastic, and that is why I love your earthly realism. Here you have it all outlined, here you have the formula, here you have geometry, and with us it's all indeterminate equations! I walk about here and dream. I love to dream. Besides, on earth I become superstitious—don't laugh, please: that is precisely what I like, that I become superstitious. Here I take on all your habits: I've come to love going to the public baths, can you imagine that? I love having a steam bath with merchants and priests. My dream is to become incarnate, but so that it's final, irrevocable, in some fat, two-hundred-and-fifty-pound merchant's wife, and to believe everything she believes. My ideal is to go into a church and light a candle with a pure heart—by God, it's true. That would put an end to my sufferings. I've also come to love getting medical treatment here: there was smallpox going around this spring, so I went to the foundling hospital and had myself inoculated against smallpox—if only you knew how pleased I was that day: I donated ten roubles for our brother Slavs . . . ![4] But you're not listening. You know, you seem rather out of sorts tonight," the gentleman paused for a moment. "I know you went to see that doctor yesterday . . . well, how is your health? What did the doctor say?"

"Fool!" snapped Ivan.

"And aren't you a smart one! So you're abusing me again? I'm just asking, not really out of sympathy. You don't have to answer. And now this rheumatism's come back . . ."

"Fool," Ivan repeated.

"You keep saying the same thing, but I caught such rheumatism last year that I still remember it."

"The devil with rheumatism?"

"Why not, if I sometimes become incarnate? Once incarnate, I accept the consequences. Satan *sum et nihil humanum a me alienum puto*."[5]

"How's that? Satan *sum et nihil humanum* . . . not too bad for the devil!"

"I'm glad I've finally pleased you."

"And you didn't get that from me," Ivan suddenly stopped as if in amazement, "that never entered my head—how strange . . ."

"*C'est de nouveau, n'est-ce pas?*[6] This time I'll be honest and explain to you. Listen: in dreams and especially in nightmares, well, let's say as a result of indigestion or whatever, a man sometimes sees such artistic dreams, such complex and real actuality, such events, or even a whole world of events, woven into such a plot, with such unexpected details, beginning from your highest manifestations down to the last shirt button, as I swear even Leo Tolstoy couldn't invent; and, by the way, it's not writers who occasionally see such dreams, but quite the most ordinary people, officials, journalists, priests . . . There's even a whole problem concerning this: one government minister even confessed to me himself that all his best ideas come to him when he's asleep. Well, and so it is now. Though I am your hallucination, even so, as in a nightmare, I say original things, such as have never entered your head before, so that I'm not repeating your thoughts at all, and yet I am merely your nightmare and nothing more."

"Lies. Your goal is precisely to convince me that you are in yourself and are not my nightmare, and so now you yourself assert that you're a dream."

"My friend, today I've adopted a special method, I'll explain it to you later. Wait, where was I? Oh, yes, so I caught a cold, only not here, but there . . ."

"There where? Tell me, are you going to stay long, couldn't you go away?" Ivan exclaimed almost in despair. He stopped pacing, sat down on the sofa, rested his elbows on the table again, and clutched his head with both hands. He tore the wet towel off and threw it aside in vexation: obviously it did not help.

"Your nerves are unstrung," the gentleman remarked, with a casually familiar and yet perfectly amiable air, "you're angry with me even for the fact that I could catch cold, whereas it happened in the most natural way. I was then hurrying to a diplomatic soirée at the home of a most highly placed Petersburg lady, who had designs on a ministry. Well, evening dress, white tie, gloves—and yet I was God knows where, and to get to your earth I still had to fly through space . . . of course it only takes a moment, but then a sun's ray takes a full eight minutes, and, imagine, in a dinner jacket, with an open vest. Spirits don't freeze, but when one's incarnate, then . . . in short, it was flighty of me, I just set out, and in those spaces, I mean, the ether, the waters above the firmament,[7] it's so freezing cold . . . that is, don't talk about freezing—you can't call it freezing anymore, just imagine: a hundred and fifty degrees below zero! You know how village girls amuse themselves: they ask some unsuspecting novice to lick an axe at thirty degrees below zero; the tongue instantly sticks to it, and the dolt has to tear it away so that it bleeds; and that's just at thirty below, but at a hundred and fifty, I suppose, if you just touched your finger to an axe, there would be no more finger, that is . . . that is, if there happened to be an axe . . ."

"And could there happen to be an axe?" Ivan Fyodorovich suddenly interrupted, absently and disgustedly. He was trying with all his might not to believe in his delirium and not to fall into complete insanity.

"An axe?" the visitor repeated in surprise.

"Yes, what would an axe be doing there?" Ivan Fyodorovich cried with a sort of fierce and persistent stubbornness.

"What would an axe be doing in space? *Quelle idée!* If it got far enough away, I suppose it would begin flying around the earth, without knowing why, like a satellite. The astronomers would calculate the rising and setting of the axe, Gattsuk would introduce it into the calendar,[8] and that's all."

"You are stupid, you are terribly stupid!" Ivan said cantankerously. "Put more intelligence into your lies, or I won't listen. You want to overcome me with realism, to convince me that you are, but I don't want to believe that you are! I won't believe it!!"

"But I'm not lying, it's all true; unfortunately, the truth is hardly ever witty.

You, I can see, are decidedly expecting something great from me, and perhaps even beautiful.[9] That's a pity, because I give only what I can . . ."

"Stop philosophizing, you ass!"

"How philosophize, when my whole right side was numb, and I was moaning and groaning. I called on the entire medical profession: they diagnose beautifully, they tell you all that's wrong with you one-two-three, but they can't cure you. There happened to be one enthusiastic little student: even if you die, he said, at least you'll have a thorough knowledge of what disease you died of! Then, too, they have this way of sending you to specialists: we will give you our diagnosis, they say, then go to such and such a specialist and he will cure you. I tell you, the old-fashioned doctor who treated all diseases has completely disappeared, now there are only specialists, and they advertise all the time in the newspapers. If your nose hurts, they send you to Paris: there's a European specialist there, he treats noses. You go to Paris, he examines your nose: I can treat only your right nostril, he says, I don't treat left nostrils, it's not my specialty, but after me, go to Vienna, there's a separate specialist there who will finish treating your left nostril. What is one to do? I resorted to folk remedies, one German doctor advised me to take a steam bath and rub myself with honey and salt. I did it, only for the chance of having an extra bath: I got myself all sticky, and to no avail. In desperation I wrote to Count Mattei in Milan; he sent me a book and some drops, God help him. And imagine, what cured me was Hoff's extract of malt! I accidentally bought some, drank a glass and a half, and could even have danced—everything went away. I was absolutely determined to thank him publicly in the newspapers, the feeling of gratitude was crying out in me, but, imagine, that led to another story: not one publisher would take it! 'It would be too retrograde, no one will believe it, *le diable n'existe point*.'[10] They advised me to publish it anonymously. Well, what good is a 'thank you' if it's anonymous? I had a laugh with the clerks: 'In our day,' I said, 'what's retrograde is believing in God; but I am the devil, it's all right to believe in me.' 'We understand,' they said, 'who doesn't believe in the devil? But all the same we can't do it, it might harm our tendency. Or perhaps only as a joke?' Well, I thought, as a joke it wouldn't be very witty. So they simply didn't publish it. And would you believe that it still weighs on my heart? My best feelings, gratitude, for example, are formally forbidden solely because of my social position."

"Up to his neck in philosophy again!" Ivan snarled hatefully.

"God preserve me from that, but one can't help complaining sometimes. I am a slandered man. Even you tell me I'm stupid every other minute. It shows how young you are. My friend, the point is not just intelligence! I have a naturally kind and cheerful heart, 'and various little vaudevilles, I, too . . .' You seem to take me decidedly for some gray-haired Khlestakov,[11] and yet my fate is far more serious. By some pre-temporal assignment, which I have never been able to figure out, I am appointed 'to negate,' whereas I am sincerely kind and totally unable to negate. No, they say, go and negate, without negation there will be no criticism, and what sort of journal has no 'criticism section'? Without criticism, there would be nothing but 'Hosannah.' But 'Hosannah' alone is not enough for life, it is necessary that this 'Hosannah' pass through the crucible of doubt, and so on, in the same vein. I don't meddle with any of that, by the way, I didn't create it, and I can't answer for it. So they chose themselves a scapegoat, they made me write for the criticism section, and life came about. We understand this comedy: I, for instance, demand simply and directly that I be destroyed. No, they say, live, because without you there would be nothing. If everything on earth were sensible, nothing would happen. Without you there would be no events, and there must be events. And so I serve grudgingly, for the sake of events, and I do the unreasonable on orders. People take this whole comedy for something serious, despite all their undeniable intelligence. That is their tragedy. Well, they suffer, of course, but . . . still they live, they live really, not in fantasy; for suffering is life. Without suffering, what pleasure would there be in it—everything would turn into an endless prayer service: holy, but a bit dull. And me? I suffer, and still I do not live. I am an *x* in an indeterminate equation. I am some sort of ghost of life who has lost all ends and beginnings, and I've finally even forgotten what to call myself. You're laughing . . . no, you're not laughing, you're angry again. You're eternally angry, you want reason only, but I will repeat to you once more that I would give all of that life beyond the stars, all ranks and honors, only to be incarnated in the soul of a two-hundred-and-fifty-pound merchant's wife and light candles to God."

"So you don't believe in God, then?" Ivan grinned hatefully.

"Well, how shall I put it—that is, if you're serious . . ."

"Is there a God, or not?" Ivan cried again with fierce insistence.

"Ah, so you are serious? By God, my dear, I just don't know—there's a great answer for you!"

"You don't know, yet you see God? No, you are not in yourself, you are *me*, *me* and nothing else! You are trash, you are my fantasy!"

"Let's say I'm of one philosophy with you, if you like, that would be correct. *Je pense donc je suis*,[12] I'm quite sure of that, but all the rest around me, all those worlds, God, even Satan himself—for me all that is unproven, whether it exists in itself, or is only my emanation, a consistent development of my *I*, which exists pre-temporally and uniquely . . . in short, I hasten to stop, because you look as if you're about to jump up and start fighting."

"Better tell me some funny anecdote!" Ivan said sickly.

"There is an anecdote, and precisely on our subject—that is, not an anecdote but more of a legend. You reproach me with unbelief: 'You see, but you don't believe.' But, my friend, I am not alone in that, all of us there are stirred up now, and it all comes from your science. While there were still just atoms, five senses, four elements, well, then it all still stayed together anyhow. They had atoms in the ancient world, too. But when we found out that you had discovered your 'chemical molecule,' and 'protoplasm,' and devil knows what else—then we put our tails between our legs. A real muddle set in; above all—superstition, gossip (we have as much gossip as you do, even a bit more); and, finally, denunciations as well (we, too, have a certain department where such 'information' is received).[13] And so there is this wild legend, which goes back to our middle ages—not yours but ours—and no one believes it except for two-hundred-and-fifty-pound merchants' wives—that is, again, not your merchants' wives but ours. Everything that you have, we have as well; I'm revealing one of our secrets to you, out of friendship, though it's forbidden. This legend is about paradise. There was, they say, a certain thinker and philosopher here on your earth, who 'rejected all—laws, conscience, faith,'[14] and, above all, the future life. He died and thought he'd go straight into darkness and death, but no—there was the future life before him. He was amazed and indignant: 'This,' he said, 'goes against my convictions.' So for that he was sentenced . . . I mean, you see, I beg your pardon, I'm repeating what I heard, it's just a legend . . . you see, he was sentenced to walk in darkness a quadrillion kilometers (we also use kilometers now), and once he finished that quadrillion, the doors of paradise would be opened to him and he would be forgiven everything."

"And what other torments have you got in that world, besides the quadrillion?" Ivan interrupted with some strange animation.

"What other torments? Ah, don't even ask: before it was one thing and another, but now it's mostly the moral sort, 'remorse of conscience' and all that nonsense. That also started because of you, from the 'mellowing of your mores.'[15] Well, and who benefited? The unscrupulous benefited, because what is remorse of conscience to a man who has no conscience at all? Decent people who still had some conscience and honor left suffered instead . . . There you have it—reforms on unprepared ground, and copied from foreign institutions as well—nothing but harm! The good old fire was much better. Well, so this man sentenced to the quadrillion stood a while, looked, and then lay down across the road: 'I don't want to go, I refuse to go on principle!' Take the soul of an enlightened Russian atheist and mix it with the soul of the prophet Jonah, who sulked in the belly of a whale for three days and three nights—you'll get the character of this thinker lying in the road."

"And what was he lying on?"

"Well, there must have been something there. Or are you laughing?"

"Bravo!" cried Ivan, still with the same strange animation. He was listening now with unexpected curiosity. "Well, so is he still lying there?"

"The point is that he isn't. He lay there for nearly a thousand years, and then got up and started walking."

"What an ass!" Ivan exclaimed, bursting into nervous laughter, still apparently trying hard to figure something out. "Isn't it all the same whether he lies there forever or walks a quadrillion kilometers? It must be about a billion years' walk!"

"Much more, even. If we had a pencil and paper, we could work it out. But he arrived long ago, and this is where the anecdote begins."

"Arrived! But where did he get a billion years?"

"You keep thinking about our present earth! But our present earth may have repeated itself a billion times; it died out, let's say, got covered with ice, cracked, fell to pieces, broke down into its original components, again there were the waters above the firmament, then again a comet, again the sun, again the earth from the sun—all this development may already have been repeated an infinite number of times, and always in the same way, to the last detail. A most unspeakable bore . . ."

"Go on, what happened when he arrived?"

"The moment the doors of paradise were opened and he went in, before he had even been there two seconds—and that by the watch, the watch (though I should think that on the way his watch would long ago have broken down into its component elements in his pocket)—before he had been there two seconds, he exclaimed that for those two seconds it would be worth walking not just a quadrillion kilometers, but a quadrillion quadrillion, even raised to the quadrillionth power! In short, he sang 'Hosannah' and oversweetened it so much that some persons there, of a nobler cast of mind, did not even want to shake hands with him at first: he jumped over to the conservatives a bit too precipitously. The Russian character. I repeat: it's a legend. Take it for what it's worth. That's the sort of ideas current among us on all these subjects."

"Caught you!" Ivan cried out with almost childish glee, as if he had now finally remembered something. "That anecdote about the quadrillion years—I made it up myself! I was seventeen years old then, I was in high school . . . I made up that anecdote then and told it to a friend of mine, his last name was Korovkin, it was in Moscow . . . It's such a typical anecdote that I couldn't have gotten it from anywhere. I almost forgot it . . . but now I've unconsciously recalled it—recalled it myself, not because you told it to me! Just as one sometimes recalls a thousand things unconsciously, even when one is being taken out to be executed . . . I've remembered it in a dream. You are my dream! You're a dream, you don't exist!"

"Judging by the enthusiasm with which you deny me," the gentleman laughed, "I'm convinced that you do believe in me all the same."

"Not in the least! Not for a hundredth part do I believe in you!"

"But for a thousandth part you do believe. Homeopathic doses are perhaps the strongest. Admit that you do believe, let's say for a ten-thousandth part . . ."

"Not for one moment!" Ivan cried in a rage. "And, by the way, I should like to believe in you!" he suddenly added strangely.

"Aha! Quite a confession, really! But I am kind, I will help you here, too. Listen, it is I who have caught you, not you me! I deliberately told you your own anecdote, which you had forgotten, so that you would finally lose faith in me."

"Lies! The purpose of your appearance is to convince me that you are."

"Precisely. But hesitation, anxiety, the struggle between belief and disbelief—all that is sometimes such a torment for a conscientious man like yourself, that it's better to hang oneself. Precisely because I knew you had a tiny bit of belief in me, I let in some final disbelief, by telling you that anecdote. I'm leading you alternately between belief and disbelief, and I have my own purpose in doing so. A new method, sir: when you've completely lost faith in me, then you'll immediately start convincing me to my face that I am not a dream but a reality—I know you now; and then my goal will be achieved. And it is a noble goal. I will sow just a tiny seed of faith in you, and from it an oak will grow—and such an oak that you, sitting in that oak, will want to join 'the desert fathers and the blameless women';[16] because secretly you want that ver-ry, ver-ry much, you will dine on locusts, you will drag yourself to the desert to seek salvation!"

"So, you scoundrel, you're troubling yourself over the salvation of my soul?"

"One needs to do a good deed sometimes, at least. But I see you're angry with me, really angry!"

"Buffoon! And have you ever tempted them, the ones who eat locusts and pray for seventeen years in the barren desert, and get overgrown with moss?"

"My dear, I've done nothing else. One forgets the whole world and all worlds, and clings to such a one, because a diamond like that is just too precious; one such soul is sometimes worth a whole constellation—we have our own arithmetic. It's a precious victory! And some of them, by God, are not inferior to you in development, though you won't believe it: they can contemplate such abysses of belief and disbelief at one and the same moment that, really, it sometimes seems that another hair's breadth and a man would fall in 'heel-over-headed,' as the actor Gorbunov says."[17]

"So, what? They put your nose out of joint?"

"My friend," the visitor observed sententiously, "it's sometimes better to have your nose put out of joint than to have no nose at all, as one afflicted marquis (he must have been treated by a specialist) uttered not long ago in confession to his Jesuit spiritual director. I was present—it was just lovely. 'Give me back my nose!' he said, beating his breast. 'My son,' the priest hedged, 'through the inscrutable decrees of Providence everything has its recompense, and a visible calamity sometimes brings with it a great, if invisible, profit. If a harsh fate has deprived you of your nose, your profit is that now for the rest of your life no one will dare tell you that you have had your nose put out of joint.' 'Holy father, that's no consolation!' the desperate man exclaimed. 'On the contrary, I'd be delighted to have my nose put out of joint every day of my life, if only it were where it belonged!' 'My son,' the priest sighed, 'one cannot demand all blessings at once. That is to murmur against Providence, which even here has not forgotten you; for if you cry, as you have just cried, that you would gladly have your nose put out of joint for the rest of your life, in this your desire has already been fulfilled indirectly; for, having lost your nose, you have thereby, as it were, had your nose put out of joint all the same . . ."

"Pah, how stupid!" cried Ivan.

"My friend, I merely wanted to make you laugh, but I swear that is real Jesuit casuistry, and I swear it all happened word for word as I've told it to you. That was a recent incident, and it gave me a lot of trouble. The unfortunate young man went home and shot himself that same night; I was with him constantly up to the last moment . . . As for those little Jesuit confessional booths, that truly is my pet amusement in the sadder moments of life. Here's another incident for you, from just the other day. A girl comes to an old priest, a blonde, from Normandy, about twenty years old. Beautiful, buxom, all nature—enough to make your mouth water. She bends down and whispers her sin to the priest through the little hole. 'What, my daughter, can you have fallen again so soon . . . ?' the priest exclaims. 'O Sancta Maria, what's this I hear? With another man now? But how long will it go on? What shame!' '*Ah, mon père*,' the sinner replies, bathed in tears of repentance, '*ça lui fait tant de plaisir, et à moi si peu de peine!*'[18] Well, just imagine such an answer! At that even I backed off: it was the very cry of nature, which, if you like, is better than innocence itself. I remitted her sin on the spot and turned to leave, but I had to come back at once: I heard the priest arranging a rendezvous with her for that evening through the hole; the old man was solid as a rock, but he fell in an instant! It was nature, the truth of nature, claiming its own! What, are you turning your nose up again, are you angry again? I really don't know how to please you . . ."

"Leave me, you're throbbing in my brain like a persistent nightmare," Ivan groaned painfully, powerless before his apparition. "I'm bored with you, it's unbearable, agonizing! I'd give a lot to be able to get rid of you!"

"I repeat, moderate your demands, don't demand 'all that is great and beautiful'[19] of me, and we shall live in peace and harmony, you'll see," the gentleman said imposingly. "Indeed, you're angry with me that I have not appeared to you in some sort of red glow, 'in thunder and lightning,' with scorched wings, but have presented myself in such a modest form. You're insulted, first, in your aesthetic feelings, and, second, in your pride: how could such a banal devil come to such a great man? No, you've still got that romantic little streak in you, so derided by Belinsky.[20] It can't be helped, young man. This evening, as I was getting ready to come to you, I did think of appearing, for a joke, in the form of a retired Regular State Councillor who had served in the Caucasus, with the star of the Lion and Sun pinned to my frock coat, but I was decidedly afraid, because you'd have thrashed me just for daring to tack the Lion and Sun on my frock coat, instead of the North Star or Sirius at least.[21] And you keep saying how stupid I am. But, my God, I don't make any claims to being your equal in intelligence. Mephistopheles, when he comes to Faust, testifies of himself that he desires evil, yet does only good.[22] Well, let him do as he likes, it's quite the opposite with me. I am perhaps the only man in all of nature who loves the truth and sincerely desires good. I was there when the Word who died on the cross was ascending into heaven, carrying on his bosom the soul of the thief who was crucified to the right of him, I heard the joyful shrieks of the cherubim singing and shouting 'Hosannah,' and the thundering shout of rapture from the seraphim, which made heaven and all creation shake. And, I swear by all that's holy, I wanted to join the chorus and shout 'Hosannah' with everyone else. It was right on my lips, it was already bursting from my breast . . . you know, I'm very sensitive and artistically susceptible. But common sense—oh, it's the most unfortunate quality of my nature—kept me within due bounds even then, and I missed the moment! For what—I thought at that same moment—what will happen after my 'Hosannah'? Everything in the world will immediately be extinguished and no events will occur. And so, solely because of my official duty and my social position, I was forced to quash the good moment in myself and stay with my nasty tricks. Someone takes all the honor of the good for himself and only leaves me the nasty tricks. But I don't covet the honor of living as a moocher, I'm not ambitious. Why, of all beings in the world, am I alone condemned to be cursed by all decent people, and even to be kicked with boots, for, when I become incarnate, I must occasionally take such consequences as well? There's a secret here, I know, but they won't reveal this secret to me for anything, because then, having learned what it's all about, I might just roar 'Hosannah,' and the necessary minus would immediately disappear and sensibleness would set in all over the world, and with it, of course, the end of everything, even of newspapers and journals, because who would subscribe to them? I know that I will finally be reconciled, that I, too, will finish my quadrillion and be let in on the secret. But until that happens I sulk and grudgingly fulfill my purpose: to destroy thousands so that one may be saved. For instance, how many souls had to be destroyed, and honest reputations put to shame, in order to get just one righteous Job, with whom they baited me so wickedly in olden times! No, until the secret is revealed, two truths exist for me: one is theirs, from there, and so far completely unknown to me; the other is mine. And who knows which is preferable . . . Are you asleep?"

"What else?" Ivan groaned spitefully. "Everything in my nature that is stupid, long outlived, mulled over in my mind, flung away like carrion—you are now offering to me as some kind of news!"

"Displeased again! And I hoped you might even be charmed by such a literary rendition: that 'Hosannah' in heaven really didn't come out too badly, did it? And then that sarcastic tone, à la Heine,[23] eh? Don't you agree?"

"No, never have I been such a lackey! How could my soul produce such a lackey as you?"

"My friend, I know a most charming and dear young Russian gentleman: a thinker and a great lover of literature and other fine things, the author of a promising poem entitled 'The Grand Inquisitor' . . . It was him only that I had in mind."

"I forbid you to speak of 'The Grand Inquisitor,'" Ivan exclaimed, blushing all over with shame.

"Well, and what about the 'Geological Cataclysm'? Remember that? What a poem!"

"Shut up, or I'll kill you!"

"Kill me? No, excuse me, but I will have my say. I came in order to treat myself to that pleasure. Oh, I love the dreams of my friends—fervent, young, trembling with the thirst for life! 'There are new people now,' you decided last spring, as you were preparing to come here, 'they propose to destroy everything and begin with anthropophagy. Fools, they never asked me! In my opinion, there is no need to destroy anything, one need only destroy the idea of God in mankind, that's where the business should start! One should begin with that, with that—oh, blind men, of no understanding! Once mankind has renounced God, one and all (and I believe that this period, analogous to the geological periods, will come), then the entire old world view will fall of itself, without anthropophagy, and, above all, the entire former morality, and everything will be new. People will come together in order to take from life all that it can give, but, of course, for happiness and joy in this world only. Man will be exalted with the spirit of divine, titanic pride, and the man-god will appear. Man, his will and his science no longer limited, conquering nature every hour, will thereby every hour experience such lofty delight as will replace for him all his former hopes of heavenly delight. Each will know himself utterly mortal, without resurrection, and will accept death proudly and calmly, like a god. Out of pride he will understand that he should not murmur against the momentariness of life, and he will love his brother then without any reward. Love will satisfy only the moment of life, but the very awareness of its momentariness will increase its fire, inasmuch as previously it was diffused in hopes of an eternal love beyond the grave' . . . well, and so on and so on, in the same vein. Lovely!"

Ivan was sitting with his hands over his ears, looking down, but his whole body started trembling. The voice went on:

"'The question now,' my young thinker reflected, 'is whether or not it is possible for such a period ever to come. If it does come, then everything will be resolved and mankind will finally be settled. But since, in view of man's inveterate stupidity, it may not be settled for another thousand years, anyone who already knows the truth is permitted to settle things for himself, absolutely as he wishes, on the new principles. In this sense, "everything is permitted" to him. Moreover, since God and immortality do not exist in any case, even if this period should never come, the new man is allowed to become a man-god, though it be he alone in the whole world, and of course, in this new rank, to jump lightheartedly over any former moral obstacle of the former slave-man, if need be. There is no law for God! Where God stands—there is the place of God! Where I stand, there at once will be the foremost place . . . "everything is permitted," and that's that!' It's all very nice; only if one wants to swindle, why, I wonder, should one also need the sanction of truth? But such is the modern little Russian man: without such a sanction, he doesn't even dare to swindle, so much does he love the truth . . ."

The visitor spoke, obviously carried away by his own eloquence, raising his voice more and more, and glancing sidelong at his host; but he did not manage to finish: Ivan suddenly snatched a glass from the table and flung it at the orator.

"*Ah, mais c'est bête enfin!*"[24] the latter exclaimed, jumping up from the sofa and shaking the spatters of tea off himself. "He remembered Luther's inkstand![25] He considers me a dream and he throws glasses at a dream! Just like a woman! I knew you were only pretending to stop your ears and were really listening . . ."

Suddenly there came a firm, insistent knocking on the window from outside. Ivan Fyodorovich jumped up from the sofa.

"Listen, you'd better open," the visitor cried, "it's your brother Alyosha with the most unexpected and interesting news, I guarantee it!"

"Shut up, deceiver, I knew it was Alyosha without you, I had a presentiment of him, and of course he hasn't come for no reason, of course he has 'news'!" Ivan exclaimed frenziedly.

"But open, open to him. There's a blizzard out there, and he's your brother. *Monsieur sait-il le temps qu'il fait? C'est à ne pas mettre un chien dehors . . .*"[26]

The knocking continued. Ivan wanted to rush to the window; but something seemed suddenly to bind his legs and arms. He was straining as hard as he could to break his bonds, but in vain. The knocking on the window grew stronger and louder. At last the bonds broke and Ivan Fyodorovich jumped up from the sofa. He looked around wildly. The two candles were almost burnt down, the glass he had just thrown at his visitor stood before him on the table, and there was no one on the opposite sofa. The knocking on the window continued insistently, but not at all as loudly as he had just imagined in his dream, on the contrary, it was quite restrained.

"That was no dream! No, I swear it was no dream, it all just happened!" Ivan Fyodorovich cried, rushed to the window, and opened it.

"Alyosha, I told you not to come!" he cried fiercely to his brother. "Make it short: what do you want? Make it short, do you hear?"

"Smerdyakov hanged himself an hour ago," Alyosha answered from outside.

"Come to the porch, I'll open at once," Ivan said, and he went to open the door for Alyosha.

Chapter 10

"He Said That!"

Once inside, Alyosha told Ivan Fyodorovich that a little more than an hour ago Maria Kondratievna came running to his place and announced that Smerdyakov had taken his own life. "So I went into his room to clear away the samovar, and he was hanging from a nail in the wall." To Alyosha's question of whether she had reported it to the proper authorities, she replied that she had not reported to anyone, but "rushed straight to you first, and was running all the way." She looked crazy, Alyosha went on, and was shaking all over like a leaf. When Alyosha ran back with her to the cottage, he found Smerdyakov still hanging. There was a note on the table: "I exterminate my life by my own will and liking, so as not to blame anybody." Alyosha left the note on the table and went straight to the police commissioner, to whom he reported everything, "and from there straight to you," Alyosha concluded, looking intently into Ivan's face. All the while he was talking, he had not taken his eyes off him, as if very much struck by something in the expression of his face.

"Brother," he cried suddenly, "you must be terribly ill! You look and it's as if you don't understand what I'm saying."

"It's good that you've come," Ivan said, thoughtfully, as it were, seeming not to have heard Alyosha's exclamation. "I knew he had hanged himself."

"From whom?"

"I don't know from whom. But I knew. Did I know? Yes, he told me. He was just telling me."

Ivan stood in the middle of the room and spoke still with the same thoughtfulness, looking at the ground.

"Who is *he*?" Alyosha asked, automatically looking around.

"He slipped away."

Ivan raised his head and smiled gently:

"He got frightened of you, of you, a dove. You're a 'pure cherub.' Dmitri calls you a cherub. A cherub . . . The thundering shout of the seraphim's rapture! What is a seraph? Maybe a whole constellation. And maybe that whole constellation is just some chemical molecule . . . Is there a constellation of the Lion and Sun, do you know?"

"Sit down, brother!" Alyosha said in alarm. "For God's sake, sit down on the sofa. You're raving, lean on the pillow, there. Want a wet towel for your head? Wouldn't it make you feel better?"

"Give me that towel on the chair, I just threw it there."

"It's not there. Don't worry, I know where it is—here," said Alyosha, finding the clean, still folded and unused towel in the other corner of the room, near Ivan's dressing table. Ivan looked strangely at the towel; his memory seemed to come back to him all at once.

"Wait," he rose a little from the sofa, "just before, an hour ago, I took this towel from there and wetted it. I put it to my head, and then threw it down here . . . how can it be dry? I don't have another."

"You put the towel to your head?" Alyosha asked.

"Yes, and I paced the room, an hour ago . . . Why are the candles so burned down? What time is it?"

"Nearly twelve."

"No, no, no!" Ivan suddenly cried out, "it was not a dream! He was here, sitting here, on that sofa. As you were knocking on the window, I threw a glass at him . . . this one . . . Wait, I was asleep before, but this dream isn't a dream. It's happened before. I sometimes have dreams now, Alyosha . . . yet they're not dreams, but reality: I walk, talk, and see . . . yet I'm asleep. But he was sitting here, he came, he was there on that sofa . . . He's terribly stupid, Alyosha, terribly stupid," Ivan suddenly laughed and began pacing the room.

"Who is stupid? Who are you talking about, brother?" Alyosha asked again, sorrowfully.

"The devil! He's taken to visiting me. He's been here twice, even almost three times. He taunted me, saying I'm angry that he's simply a devil and not Satan, with scorched wings, with thunder and lightning. But he's not Satan, he's lying. He's an impostor. He's simply a devil, a rotten little devil. He goes to the public baths. Undress him and you're sure to find a tail, long and smooth as a Great Dane's, a good three feet long, brown . . . Alyosha, you're chilly, you were out in the snow, do you want some tea? What? It's cold? Shall I tell them to make some hot? *C'est à ne pas mettre un chien dehors* . . ."

Alyosha ran quickly to the sink, wetted the towel, persuaded Ivan to sit down again, and put the wet towel around his head. He sat down beside him.

"What were you saying earlier about Liza?" Ivan began again. (He was becoming very talkative.) "I like Liza. I said something nasty to you about her. I was lying, I like her . . . I'm afraid for Katya tomorrow, afraid most of all. For the future. She'll drop me tomorrow and trample me under her feet. She thinks I'm destroying Mitya out of jealousy over her! Yes, that's what she thinks! But no, it won't be! Tomorrow the cross, but not the gallows. No, I won't hang myself. Do you know, I'd never be able to take my own life, Alyosha! Is it out of baseness, or what? I'm not a coward. Out of thirst for life! How did I know Smerdyakov had hanged himself? But it was *he* who told me . . ."

"And you're firmly convinced that someone was sitting here?" Alyosha asked.

"On that sofa in the corner. You'd have chased him away. And you did chase him away: he disappeared as soon as you came. I love your face, Alyosha. Did you know that I love your face? And *he*—is me, Alyosha, me myself. All that's low, all that's mean and contemptible in me! Yes, I'm a 'romantic,' he noticed it . . . though it's a slander. He's terribly stupid, but he makes use of it. He's cunning, cunning as an animal, he knew how to infuriate me. He kept taunting me with believing in him and got me to listen to him that way. He hoodwinked me, like a boy. By the way, he told me a great deal that's true about myself. I would never have said it to myself. You know, Alyosha, you know," Ivan added, terribly seriously, and as if confidentially, "I would much prefer that he were really *he* and not I!"

"He has worn you out," Alyosha said, looking at his brother with compassion.

"He taunted me! And cleverly, you know, very cleverly: 'Conscience! What is conscience? I make it up myself. Why do I suffer then? Out of habit. Out of universal human habit over seven thousand years. So let us get out of the habit, and we shall be gods!' He said that, he said that!"

"And not you, not you!" Alyosha cried irrepressibly, looking brightly at his brother. "So never mind him, drop him, and forget about him! Let him take with him all that you curse now and never come back!"

"Yes, but he's evil! He laughed at me. He was impudent, Alyosha," Ivan said with a shudder of offense. "He slandered me, slandered me greatly. He lied about me to my face. 'Oh, you are going to perform a virtuous deed, you will announce that you killed your father, that the lackey killed your father at your suggestion . . . !' "

"Brother," Alyosha interrupted, "restrain yourself: you did not kill him. It's not true!"

"He says it, he, and he knows it: 'You are going to perform a virtuous deed, but you don't even believe in virtue—that's what makes you angry and torments you, that's why you're so vindictive.' He said it to me about myself, and he knows what he's saying . . ."

"You are saying it, not him!" Alyosha exclaimed ruefully, "and you're saying it because you're sick, delirious, tormenting yourself!"

"No, he knows what he's saying. You're going out of pride, he says, you'll stand up and say: 'I killed him, and you, why are you all shrinking in horror, you're lying! I despise your opinion, I despise your horror!' He said that about me, and suddenly he said: 'And, you know, you want them to praise you: he's a criminal, a murderer, but what magnanimous feelings he has, he wanted to save his brother and so he confessed!' Now that is a lie, Alyosha!" Ivan suddenly cried, flashing his eyes. "I don't want the stinking rabble to praise me. He lied about that, Alyosha, he lied, I swear to you! I threw a glass at him for that, and it smashed on his ugly snout."

"Brother, calm yourself, stop!" Alyosha pleaded.

"No, he knows how to torment, he's cruel," Ivan went on, not listening. "All along I had a presentiment of what he came for. 'Suppose you were to go out of pride,' he said, 'but still there would also be the hope that Smerdyakov would be convicted and sent to hard labor, that Mitya would be cleared, and you would be condemned only *morally*' (and then he laughed, do you hear!), 'and some would even praise you. But now Smerdyakov is dead, he's hanged himself—so who's going to believe just you alone there in court? But you'll go, you'll go, you'll still go, you've made up your mind to go. But, in that case, what are you going for?' I'm afraid, Alyosha, I can't bear such questions! Who dares ask me such questions!"

"Brother," Alyosha interrupted, sinking with fear, but still as if hoping to bring Ivan to reason, "how could he have talked of Smerdyakov's death with you before I came, if no one even knew of it yet, and there was no time for anyone to find out?"

"He talked of it," Ivan said firmly, not admitting any doubt. "He talked only of that, if you like. 'And one could understand it,' he said, 'if you believed in virtue: let them not believe me, I'm going for the sake of principle. But you are a little pig, like Fyodor Pavlovich, and what is virtue to you? Why drag yourself there if your sacrifice serves no purpose? Because you yourself don't know why you're going! Oh, you'd give a lot to know why you're going! And do you think you've really decided? No, you haven't decided yet. You'll sit all night trying to decide whether to go or not. But you will go all the same, and you know you will go, you know yourself that no matter how much you try to decide it, the decision no longer depends on you. You will go because you don't dare not to. Why you don't dare—you can guess for yourself, there's a riddle for you!' He got up and left. You came and he left. He called me a coward, Alyosha! *Le mot de l'énigme* is that I'm a coward![1] 'It's not for such eagles to soar above the earth!' He added that, he added that! And Smerdyakov said the same thing. He must be killed! Katya despises me, I've seen that already for a month, and Liza will also begin to despise me! 'You're going in order to be praised'—that's a beastly lie! And you, too, despise me, Alyosha. Now I'll start hating you again. I hate the monster, too, I hate the monster! I don't want to save the monster, let him rot at hard labor! He's singing a hymn! Oh, tomorrow I'll go, stand before them, and spit in all their faces!"

He jumped up in a frenzy, threw off the towel, and began pacing the room again. Alyosha recalled what he had just said: "It's as if I'm awake in my sleep . . . I walk, talk, and see, yet I'm asleep." That was precisely what seemed to be happening now. Alyosha stayed with him. The thought flashed in him to run and fetch a doctor, but he was afraid to leave his brother alone: there was no one to entrust him to. At last Ivan began gradually to lose all consciousness. He went on talking, talked incessantly, but now quite incoherently. He even enunciated his words poorly, and suddenly he staggered badly on his feet. But Alyosha managed to support him. Ivan allowed himself to be taken to bed. Alyosha somehow undressed him and laid him down. He sat over him for two hours more. The sick man lay fast asleep, without moving, breathing softly and evenly. Alyosha took a pillow and lay down on the sofa without undressing. As he was falling asleep he prayed for Mitya and Ivan. He was beginning to understand Ivan's illness: "The torments of a proud decision, a deep conscience!" God, in whom he did not believe, and his truth were overcoming his heart, which still did not want to submit. "Yes," it passed through Alyosha's head, which was already lying on the pillow, "yes, with Smerdyakov dead, no one will believe Ivan's testimony; but he will go and testify!" Alyosha smiled gently: "God will win!" he thought. "He will either rise into the light of truth, or . . . perish in hatred, taking revenge on himself and everyone for having served something he does not believe in," Alyosha added bitterly, and again prayed for Ivan.

BOOK XII: A JUDICIAL ERROR

Chapter 1

The Fatal Day

The day after the events just described, at ten o'clock in the morning, our district court opened its session and the trial of Dmitri Karamazov began.

I will say beforehand, and say emphatically, that I am far from considering myself capable of recounting all that took place in court, not only with the proper fullness, but even in the proper order. I keep thinking that if one were to recall everything and explain everything as one ought, it would fill a whole book, even quite a large one. Therefore let no one grumble if I tell only that which struck me personally and which I have especially remembered. I may have taken secondary things for the most important, and even overlooked the most prominent and necessary features . . . But anyway I see that it is better not to apologize. I shall do what I can, and my readers will see for themselves that I have done all I could.

And, first of all, before we enter the courtroom, I will mention something that especially surprised me that day. By the way, as it turned out later, it surprised not only me but everyone else as well. That is: everyone knew that this case interested a great many people, that everyone was burning with impatience for the trial to begin, that for the whole two months past there had been a great deal of discussion, supposition, exclamation, anticipation among our local society. Everyone also knew that the case had been publicized all over Russia, but even so they never imagined that it had shaken all and sundry to such a burning, such an intense degree, not only among us but everywhere, as became clear at the trial that day. By that day visitors had come to us not only from the provincial capital but from several other Russian cities, and lastly from Moscow and Petersburg. Lawyers came, several noble persons even came, and ladies as well. All the tickets were snapped up. For the most respected and noble of the men visitors, certain quite unusual seats were even reserved behind the table at which the judges sat: a whole row of chairs appeared there, occupied by various dignitaries—a thing never permitted before. There turned out to be an especially large number of ladies—our own and visitors—I would say even not less than half the entire public. The lawyers alone, who arrived from all over, turned out to be so numerous that no one knew where to put them, since the tickets had all been given out, begged, besought long ago. I myself saw a partition being temporarily and hastily set up at the end of the courtroom, behind the podium, where all these arriving lawyers were admitted, and they even considered themselves lucky to be able at least to stand there, because in order to make room, the chairs were removed from behind this partition, and the whole accumulated crowd stood through the whole "case" in a closely packed lump, shoulder to shoulder. Some of the ladies, especially among the visitors, appeared in the gallery of the courtroom extremely dressed up, but the majority of the ladies were not even thinking about dresses. Hysterical, greedy, almost morbid curiosity could be read on their faces. One of the most characteristic peculiarities of this whole society gathered in the courtroom, which must be pointed out, was that, as was later established by many observations, almost all the ladies, at least the great majority of them, favored Mitya and his acquittal. Mainly, perhaps, because an idea had been formed of him as a conqueror of women's hearts. It was known that two women rivals were to appear. One of them—that is, Katerina Ivanovna—especially interested everyone; a great many remarkable things were told about her, astonishing tales were told of her passion for Mitya despite his crime. Special mention was made of her pride (she paid visits to almost no one in our town), her "aristocratic connections." It was said that she intended to ask the government for permission to accompany the criminal into penal servitude and to marry him somewhere in the mines, underground. Awaited with no less excitement was the appearance in court of Grushenka, Katerina Ivanovna's rival. The meeting before the judges of two rivals—the proud, aristocratic girl, and the "hetaera"—was awaited with painful curiosity. Grushenka, by the way, was better known to our ladies than Katerina Ivanovna. Our ladies had seen her, "the destroyer of Fyodor Pavlovich and his unfortunate son," even before, and were all, almost as one, surprised that father and son could both fall in love to such an extent with such a "most common and even quite plain Russian tradeswoman." In short, there was much talk. I know positively that in our town itself several serious family quarrels even took place on account of Mitya. Many ladies quarreled hotly with their husbands owing to a difference of opinion about this whole terrible affair, and naturally, after that, all the husbands of these ladies arrived in court feeling not only ill disposed towards the defendant but even resentful of him. And generally it can be stated positively that the entire male contingent, as opposed to the ladies, was aroused against the defendant. One saw stern, scowling faces, some even quite angry, and not a few of them. It was also true that Mitya had managed to insult many of them personally during his stay in our town. Of course, some of the visitors were even almost merry and quite indifferent to Mitya's fate in itself, although, again, not to the case under consideration; everyone was concerned with its outcome, and the majority of the men decidedly wished to see the criminal punished, except perhaps for the lawyers, who cared not about the moral aspect of the case, but only, so to speak, about its contemporary legal aspect. Everyone was excited by the coming of the famous Fetyukovich. His talent was known everywhere, and this was not the first time he had come to the provinces to defend a celebrated criminal case. And after his defense such cases always became famous all over Russia and were remembered for a long time. There were several anecdotes going around concerning both our prosecutor and the presiding judge. It was said that our prosecutor trembled at the thought of meeting Fetyukovich, that they were old enemies from way back in Petersburg, from the beginning of their careers, that our vain Ippolit Kirillovich, who ever since Petersburg had always thought himself injured by someone, because his talents were not properly appreciated, had been resurrected in spirit by the Karamazov case and even dreamed of resurrecting his flagging career through it, and that his only fear was Fetyukovich. But the opinions concerning his trembling before Fetyukovich were not altogether just. Our prosecutor was not one of those characters who lose heart in the face of danger; he was, on the contrary, of the sort whose vanity grows and takes wing precisely in pace with the growing danger. And generally it must be noted that our prosecutor was too ardent and morbidly susceptible. He would put his whole soul into some case and conduct it as if his whole fate and his whole fortune depended on the outcome. In the legal world this gave rise to some laughter, for our prosecutor even achieved a certain renown precisely by this quality, if not everywhere, at least more widely than one might have supposed in view of his modest position in our court. The laughter was aimed especially at his passion for psychology. In my opinion they were all mistaken: as a man and as a character, our prosecutor seems to me to have been much more serious than many people supposed. But from his very first steps this ailing man was simply unable to show himself to advantage, either at the beginning of his career or afterwards for the rest of his life.

As for our presiding judge, one can simply say of him that he was an educated and humane man, with a practical knowledge of his task, and with the most modern ideas. He was rather vain, but not overly concerned with his career. His chief goal in life was to be a progressive man. He had a fortune and connections besides. He took, as it turned out later, a rather passionate view of the Karamazov case, but only in a general sense. He was concerned with the phenomenon, its classification, seeing it as a product of our social principles, as characteristic of the Russian element, and so on and so forth. But his attitude towards the personal character of the case, its tragedy, as well as towards the persons of the participants, beginning with the defendant, was rather indifferent and abstract, as, by the way, it perhaps ought to have been.

Long before the appearance of the judges, the courtroom was already packed. Our courtroom is the best hall in town, vast, lofty, resonant. To the right of the judges, who were placed on a sort of raised platform, a table and two rows of chairs were prepared for the jury. To the left was the place for the defendant and his attorney. In the center of the hall, close to the judges, stood a table with the "material evidence." On it lay Fyodor Pavlovich's bloodstained white silk dressing gown, the fatal brass pestle with which the supposed murder had been committed, Mitya's shirt with its bloodstained sleeve, his frock coat with bloodstains in the area of the pocket into which he had put his bloodsoaked handkerchief, that same handkerchief all stiff with blood and now quite yellow, the pistol Mitya had loaded at Perkhotin's in order to kill himself and that had been taken from him on the sly by Trifon Borisovich in Mokroye, the inscribed envelope that had contained the three thousand prepared for Grushenka, and the narrow pink ribbon that had been tied around it, and many other objects I no longer remember. At a certain distance farther back in the hall began the seats for the public, but in front of the balustrade stood several chairs for those witnesses who would remain in the courtroom after giving their evidence. At ten o'clock the members of the court appeared, consisting of the presiding judge, a second judge, and an honorary justice of the peace. Of course, the prosecutor also appeared at once. The presiding judge was a stocky, thick-set man, of less than average height, with a hemorrhoidal face, about fifty years old, his gray-streaked hair cut short, wearing a red ribbon—I do not remember of what order. To me, and not only to me but to everyone, the prosecutor looked somehow too pale, with an almost green face, which for some reason seemed suddenly to have grown very thin, perhaps overnight, since I had seen him just two days before looking quite himself. The presiding judge began by asking the marshal if all the jurors were present . . . I see, however, that I can no longer go on in this way, if only because there were many things I did not catch, others that I neglected to go into, still others that I forgot to remember, and, moreover, as I have said above, if I were to recall everything that was said and done, I literally would not have time or space. I know only that neither side—that is, neither the defense attorney nor the prosecutor—objected to very many of the jurors. But I do remember who the twelve jurors consisted of: four of our officials, two merchants, and six local peasants and tradesmen. In our society, I remember, long before the trial, the question was asked with some surprise, especially by the ladies: "Can it be that the fatal decision in such a subtle, complex, and psychological case is to be turned over to a bunch of officials, and even to peasants?" and "What will some ordinary official make of it, not to mention a peasant?" Indeed, all four of the officials who got on the jury were minor persons of low rank, gray-haired old men—only one of them was a little younger—scarcely known in our society, vegetating on meager salaries, with old wives, no doubt, whom they could not present anywhere, and each with a heap of children, perhaps even going barefoot; who at most found diversion in a little game of cards somewhere in their off hours, and who most assuredly had never read a single book. The two merchants, though of grave appearance, were somehow strangely silent and immobile; one of them was clean-shaven and dressed in German fashion; the other had a little gray beard and wore some medal around his neck on a red ribbon. There is nothing much to say about the tradesmen and peasants. Our Skotoprigonyevsk tradesmen are almost peasants themselves, they even handle the plow. Two of them were also in German dress, and perhaps for that reason looked dirtier and more unseemly than the other four. So that indeed the thought might well enter one's head, as it entered mine, for example, as soon as I took a look at them: "What can such people possibly grasp of such a case?" Nevertheless their faces made a certain strangely imposing and almost threatening impression; they were stern and frowning.

Finally the presiding judge announced the hearing of the case of the murder of the retired titular councillor Fyodor Pavlovich Karamazov—I do not quite remember how he put it then. The marshal was told to bring in the defendant, and so Mitya appeared. A hush came over the courtroom, one could have heard a fly buzz. I do not know about the others, but on me Mitya's looks made a most unpleasant impression. Above all, he appeared a terrible dandy, in a fresh new frock coat. I learned later that he had specially ordered himself a frock coat for that day from Moscow, from his former tailor, who had his measurements. He was wearing new black kid gloves and an elegant shirt. He walked in with his yard-long strides, looking straight and almost stiffly ahead of him, and took his seat with a most intrepid air. Right away, at once, the defense attorney, the famous Fetyukovich, also appeared, and a sort of subdued hum, as it were, swept through the courtroom. He was a tall, dry man, with long, thin legs, extremely long, pale, thin fingers, a clean-shaven face, modestly combed, rather short hair, and thin lips twisted now and then into something halfway between mockery and a smile. He looked about forty. His face would even have been pleasant had it not been for his eyes, which, in themselves small and inexpressive, were set so unusually close together that they were separated only by the thin bone of his thin, long-drawn nose. In short, his physiognomy had something sharply birdlike about it, which was striking. He was dressed in a frock coat and a white tie. I remember the presiding judge's first questions to Mitya—that is, about his name, social position, and so forth. Mitya answered sharply, but somehow in an unexpectedly loud voice, so that the judge even shook his head and looked at him almost in surprise. Then the list of persons called for questioning in court—that is, of witnesses and experts—was read. It was a long list; four of the witnesses were not present: Miusov, who was then already in Paris, but whose testimony had been taken during the preliminary investigation; Madame Khokhlakov and the landowner Maximov, for reasons of health; and Smerdyakov, on account of his sudden death, for which a police certificate was presented. The news about Smerdyakov caused a great stir and murmuring in the courtroom. Of course, many of the public knew nothing as yet about the sudden episode of his suicide. But most striking was Mitya's sudden outburst: as soon as the report on Smerdyakov was made, he exclaimed from his seat so that the whole courtroom could hear:

"The dog died like a dog!"

I remember how his attorney dashed over to him and how the judge addressed him, threatening to take stern measures if such an outburst were repeated. Abruptly, nodding his head, but with no show of repentance, Mitya repeated several times in a low voice to his attorney:

"I won't, I won't! It just came out! Not again!"

And of course this brief episode did not stand him in favor with the jurors or the public. His character was already showing and speaking for itself. And it was under this impression that the accusation was read by the clerk of the court.

It was rather brief, but thorough. Only the chiefest reasons were stated why so and so had been brought to court, why he should stand trial, and so on. Nevertheless it made a strong impression on me. The clerk read clearly, sonorously, distinctly. The whole tragedy seemed to unfold again before everyone, vivid, concentrated, lit by a fatal, inexorable light. I remember how, right after the reading, the prosecutor loudly and imposingly asked Mitya:

"Defendant, how do you plead, guilty or not guilty?"

Mitya suddenly rose from his seat:

"I plead guilty to drunkenness and depravity," he exclaimed, again in some unexpected, almost frenzied voice, "to idleness and debauchery. I intended to become an honest man ever after, precisely at the moment when fate cut me down! But of the death of the old man, my enemy and my father—I am not guilty! Of robbing him—no, no, not guilty, and I could not be guilty: Dmitri Karamazov is a scoundrel, but not a thief!"

Having cried this out, he sat down in his seat, visibly trembling all over.

The presiding judge again addressed him with a brief but edifying admonition that he should answer only what he was asked, and not get into irrelevant and frenzied exclamations. Then he ordered the examination to begin. All the witnesses were brought in to take the oath. It was then that I saw them all together. Incidentally, the defendant's brothers were permitted to testify without the oath. After being admonished by the priest and the presiding judge, the witnesses were led away and seated as far apart from one another as possible. Then they were called up one by one.

Chapter 2

Dangerous Witnesses

I do not know whether the witnesses for the prosecution and the defense were somehow divided into groups by the judge, or in precisely what order they were supposed to be called. All that must have been so. I know only that the witnesses for the prosecution were called first. I repeat, I do not intend to describe all the cross-examinations step by step. Besides, my description would also end up as partly superfluous, because, when the closing debate began, the whole course and meaning of all the evidence given and heard was brought, as it were, to a fine point, shown in a bright and characteristic light, in the speeches of the prosecutor and the defense attorney, and these two remarkable speeches I did write down in full, at least some parts of them, and will recount them in due time, as well as one extraordinary and quite unexpected episode that broke out all of a sudden, even before the closing debate, and undoubtedly influenced the dread and fatal outcome of the trial. I will note only that from the very first moments of the trial a certain peculiar characteristic of this "case" stood out clearly and was noticed by everyone—namely, the remarkable strength of the prosecution as compared with the means available to the defense. Everyone realized this at the first moment when, in this dread courtroom, the facts were focused and began falling together, and all the horror and blood began gradually to emerge. It perhaps became clear to everyone from the very outset that this was not a controversial case at all, that there were no doubts here, that essentially there was no need for any debate, that the debate would take place only for the sake of form, and that the criminal was guilty, clearly guilty, utterly guilty. I even think that the ladies, one and all, who yearned with such impatience for the acquittal of an interesting defendant, were at the same time fully convinced of his complete guilt. Moreover, I believe they would even have been upset if his guilt were not unquestionable, for in that case there would be no great effect at the denouement when the criminal was acquitted. And that he would be acquitted, all the ladies, strangely enough, remained utterly convinced almost to the very last moment: "He is guilty, but he will be acquitted because of humaneness, because of the new ideas, because of the new feelings that are going around nowadays," and so on and so forth. This was what brought them running there with such impatience. The men were mostly interested in the struggle between the prosecutor and the renowned Fetyukovich. Everyone was wondering and asking himself what even a talent like Fetyukovich's could do with such a lost case, not worth the candle—and therefore followed his deeds step by step with strained attention. But to the very end, to his very last speech, Fetyukovich remained an enigma to everyone. Experienced people suspected that he had a system, that he already had something worked out, that he had an aim in view, but it was almost impossible to guess what it was. His confidence and self-assurance, however, stared everyone in the face. Furthermore, everyone immediately noticed with pleasure that during his brief stay with us, in perhaps only three days' time, he had managed to become surprisingly well acquainted with the case, and had "mastered it in the finest detail." Afterwards people delighted in telling, for example, how he had been able to "take down" all the witnesses for the prosecution, to throw them off as much as possible, and, above all, to cast a slight taint on their moral reputations, thereby, of course, casting a slight taint on their evidence. It was supposed, however, that at the most he was doing it for sport, so to speak, for the sake of a certain juridical brilliance, in order to omit none of the conventional strategies of defense: for everyone was convinced that he could achieve no great and ultimate advantage by all these "slight taints," and that he probably knew it better than anyone, holding ready some idea of his own, some still hidden weapon of defense that he would suddenly reveal when the time came. But meanwhile, aware of his strength, he was frisking and playing, as it were. Thus, for example, during the questioning of Grigory Vasiliev, Fyodor Pavlovich's former valet, who had given the most fundamental evidence about "the door open to the garden," the defense attorney simply fastened upon him when it came his turn to ask questions. It should be noted that Grigory Vasilievich stood up in the courtroom not in the least embarrassed either by the grandeur of the court or by the presence of the huge audience listening to him, and appeared calm and all but majestic. He gave his testimony with as much assurance as if he had been talking alone with his Marfa Ignatievna, only perhaps more respectfully. It was impossible to throw him off. The prosecutor first questioned him at length about all the details of the Karamazov family. The family picture was vividly exposed to view. One could hear, one could see that the witness was a simple-hearted and impartial man. With all his deep respect for the memory of his former master, he still declared, for example, that he had been unjust to Mitya and "didn't bring the children up right. Lice would have eaten the little boy but for me," he added, telling of Mitya's childhood. "And it wasn't good for the father to do his son wrong over his mother's family estate." To the prosecutor's question as to what grounds he had for asserting that Fyodor Pavlovich had done his son wrong in their settlement, Grigory Vasilievich, to everyone's surprise, did not offer any solid facts at all, yet he stood by his statement that the settlement with the son was "unfair" and that there were certainly "several thousands left owing to him." I will note in passing that the prosecutor later posed this question of whether Fyodor Pavlovich had indeed paid Mitya something less than he owed him with special insistence to all the witnesses to whom he could pose it, not excepting Alyosha and Ivan Fyodorovich, but got no precise information from any of them; everyone confirmed the fact, yet no one could offer even the slightest clear proof. After Grigory described the scene at the table when Dmitri Fyodorovich had burst in and beaten his father, threatening to come back and kill him—a gloomy impression swept over the courtroom, the more so as the old servant spoke calmly, without unnecessary words, in his own peculiar language, and it came out as terribly eloquent. He observed that he was not angry at Mitya for hitting him in the face and knocking him down, and that he had forgiven him long ago. Of the late Smerdyakov he expressed the opinion, crossing himself, that he had been a capable fellow but stupid and oppressed by illness, and that, above all, he was a godless man, and had learned his godlessness from Fyodor Pavlovich and his elder son. But Smerdyakov's honesty he confirmed almost ardently, and told then and there how Smerdyakov, ages ago, had found the money his master had dropped, and instead of keeping it had brought it to his master, who "gave him a gold piece" as a reward, and thereafter began trusting him in all things. The open door to the garden he confirmed with stubborn insistence. However, he was questioned so much that I cannot even recall it all. Finally the questioning passed to the defense attorney, and he, first of all, began asking about the envelope in which Fyodor Pavlovich "supposedly" hid three thousand roubles for "a certain person." "Did you see it yourself—you, a man closely attendant on your master for so many years?" Grigory answered that he had not seen it and had never heard of such money from anyone, "until now when everyone started talking." This question about the envelope, Fetyukovich, for his part, posed to every witness he could put it to, with the same insistence as the prosecutor asked his question about the division of the estate, and also received just one answer from them all, that no one had seen the envelope, though a great many had heard of it. Everyone noticed the defense attorney's insistence on this question from the very beginning.

"Now, with your kind permission, I should like to ask you a question," Fetyukovich said suddenly and quite unexpectedly. "What were the ingredients of that balm, or, so to speak, that infusion, with which you rubbed your suffering lower back, in hopes thereby of being cured, that evening before going to bed, as we know from the preliminary investigation?"

Grigory looked dumbly at the questioner and, after a short silence, muttered:

"There was sage in it."

"Just sage? You don't recall anything else?"

"There was plantain, too."

"And pepper, perhaps?" Fetyukovich inquired further.

"And pepper."

"And so on. And all steeped in vodka?"

"In spirits."

A slight laugh flitted through the courtroom.

"So, in spirits no less. After rubbing your back, you drank the rest of the bottle with a certain pious prayer, known only to your wife, is that so?"

"I drank it."

"Approximately how much did you drink? Just approximately. A shot-glass or two?"

"About a tumbler."

"About a tumbler no less. Maybe even a tumbler and a half?"

Grigory fell silent. He seemed to have understood something.

"About a tumbler and a half of pure spirits—not bad at all, wouldn't you say? Enough to see 'the doors of heaven open,'[1] not to mention the door to the garden?"

Grigory remained silent. Again a slight laugh went through the courtroom. The judge stirred.

"Do you know for certain," Fetyukovich was biting deeper and deeper, "whether you were awake or not at the moment when you saw the door to the garden open?"

"I was standing on my feet."

"That's no proof that you were awake." (More and more laughter in the courtroom.) "Could you, for instance, have answered at that moment if someone had asked you something—say, for instance, what year it is?"

"That I don't know."

"And what year of the present era, what year of our Lord is it—do you know?"

Grigory stood looking bewildered, staring straight at his tormentor. It seemed strange indeed that he apparently did not know what year it was.

"But perhaps you do know how many fingers you have on your hand?"

"I am a subordinate man," Grigory suddenly said, loudly and distinctly. "If the authorities see fit to deride me, then I must endure it."

Fetyukovich was a little taken aback, as it were, but the presiding judge also intervened with a didactic reminder to the defense attorney that he ought to ask more appropriate questions. Fetyukovich, having listened, bowed with dignity, and announced that he had no further questions. Of course, both the public and the jury might be left with a small worm of doubt as to the testimony of a man for whom it was possible to "see the doors of heaven" in a certain state of medical treatment, and who, besides, did not know what year of our Lord it was; so that the attorney had nonetheless achieved his goal. But before Grigory stepped down another episode took place. The judge, addressing the defendant, asked whether he had anything to say concerning the present testimony.

"Except for the door, it's all true as he said," Mitya cried loudly. "For combing the lice out of my hair, I thank him; for forgiving me my blows, I thank him; the old man has been honest all his life, and was as faithful to my father as seven hundred poodles."

"Watch your words, defendant," the judge said sternly.

"I am not a poodle," Grigory also grumbled.

"Then I am, I am a poodle!" cried Mitya. "If he's offended, I take it upon myself and ask his forgiveness: I was a beast and cruel to him! I was cruel to Aesop, too."

"What Aesop?" the judge again picked up sternly.

"That Pierrot . . . my father, Fyodor Pavlovich."

The presiding judge repeated once again to Mitya, imposingly and most sternly now, that he should watch his words more carefully.

"You are harming yourself in the opinion of your judges."

In just the same rather clever way the defense attorney handled the questioning of the witness Rakitin. I will note that Rakitin was one of the most important witnesses and was undoubtedly valued by the prosecutor. It turned out that he knew everything, knew surprisingly much, had really been everywhere, seen everything, spoken with everyone, knew in the most detailed way the biography of Fyodor Pavlovich and of all the Karamazovs. True, he, too, had heard of the envelope with the three thousand only from Mitya himself. On the other hand, he described in detail Mitya's deeds in the "Metropolis" tavern, all his compromising words and gestures, and told the story of Captain Snegiryov's "whiskbroom." Concerning the particular point, whether Fyodor Pavlovich still owed Mitya anything after the settling of the estate, even Rakitin himself could indicate nothing specific and got off merely with commonplaces of a contemptuous nature: "Who could say which of them was to blame or calculate who owed what to whom, with all that muddled Karamazovism, in which no one could either define or understand himself?" The whole tragedy of the crime on trial he portrayed as resulting from the ingrained habits of serfdom and a Russia immersed in disorder and suffering from a lack of proper institutions. In short, he was allowed to speak out on certain matters. It was starting with this trial that Mr. Rakitin first declared himself and gained notice; the prosecutor knew that the witness was preparing an article for a magazine about the present crime, and in his closing statement (as we shall see below) he quoted several thoughts from this article, indicating that he was already familiar with it. The picture portrayed by the witness was a gloomy and fatal one, and greatly strengthened "the prosecution." Generally, Rakitin's presentation captivated the public by its independence of thought and the remarkable nobility of its flight. Two or three spontaneous bursts of applause were even heard—namely, at those passages where mention was made of serfdom and of Russia suffering from disorder. But Rakitin, being still a young man, made a little slip, which was at once superbly exploited by the defense attorney. Answering certain questions about Grushenka, he got carried away by his success, which he was certainly already aware of, and by the height of nobility to which he had soared, and allowed himself to refer to Agrafena Alexandrovna somewhat contemptuously as "the merchant Samsonov's kept woman." He would have given much afterwards to take that little phrase back, for it was picked up at once by Fetyukovich. And it was all because Rakitin simply never expected that he could have familiarized himself, in so short a time, with such intimate details of the case.

"Allow me to inquire," the defense attorney began, with a most amiable and even respectful smile, when it came his turn to ask questions, "whether you are not, indeed, the same Mr. Rakitin whose pamphlet *The Life of the Elder, Father Zosima, Fallen Asleep in God*, published by the diocesan authorities, full of profound and religious thoughts, and with an excellent and pious dedication to His Grace, I have recently had the great pleasure of reading?"

"I didn't write it for publication . . . they published it afterwards," Rakitin mumbled, as if suddenly taken aback by something, and almost ashamed.

"Oh, but that's wonderful! A thinker like you can, and even must, have a very broad attitude towards all social phenomena. Through the patronage of

His Grace, your most useful pamphlet was distributed and has been relatively beneficial . . . But what I mainly wanted to inquire about was this: you have just stated that you are a quite close acquaintance of Miss Svetlov?" (*Nota bene*: Grushenka's last name turned out to be "Svetlov." I learned it for the first time only that day, in the course of the trial.)

"I cannot answer for all my acquaintances . . . I am a young man . . . and who can answer for everyone he meets?" Rakitin simply blushed all over.

"I understand, I understand only too well!" exclaimed Fetyukovich, as if embarrassed himself, and as if hastening to apologize. "You, like anyone else, might be interested for your own part in the acquaintance of a young and beautiful woman who readily received the flower of local youth, but . . . I simply wanted to inquire: it is known to us that about two months ago Miss Svetlov was extremely eager to make the acquaintance of the youngest Karamazov, Alexei Fyodorovich, and just for bringing him to her, and precisely in the monastery attire he was then wearing, she promised you twenty-five roubles, to be handed over as soon as you brought him. And that, as we know, took place precisely on the evening of the day that ended in the tragic catastrophe that has led to the present trial. You brought Alexei Karamazov to Miss Svetlov, but . . . did you get the twenty-five-rouble reward from her—that is what I wanted to hear from you."

"It was a joke . . . I don't see why it should interest you. I took it for a joke . . . so as to give it back later . . ."

"You did take it, then. But you have not given it back yet . . . or have you?"

"It's nothing . . .," Rakitin muttered, "I cannot answer such questions . . . Of course I'll give it back."

The presiding judge intervened, but the defense attorney announced that he had finished questioning Mr. Rakitin. Mr. Rakitin left the stage somewhat besmirched. The impression of the lofty nobility of his speech was indeed spoiled, and Fetyukovich, following him with his eyes, seemed to be saying, intending it for the public: "So, there goes one of your noble accusers!" I remember that this, too, did not go by without an episode on Mitya's part: infuriated by the tone in which Rakitin referred to Grushenka, he suddenly cried out from his place: "Bernard!" And when, after all the questioning of Rakitin was over, the presiding judge addressed the defendant, asking him if he had any observations to make, Mitya shouted in a booming voice:

"He kept hitting me for loans, even in prison! A despicable Bernard and careerist, and he doesn't believe in God, he hoodwinked His Grace!"

Mitya, of course, was again brought to reason for the violence of his language, but that was the end of Mr. Rakitin. There was no luck with Captain Snegiryov's testimony either, but for an entirely different cause. He presented himself to the court all tattered, in dirty clothes, dirty boots, and, despite all precautions and preliminary "expertise," suddenly turned out to be quite drunk. Asked about the insult he had received from Mitya, he suddenly refused to answer.

"God be with him, sir. Ilyushechka told me not to. God will repay me there, sir."

"Who told you not to speak? Who are you referring to?"

"Ilyushechka, my little son. 'Papa, papa, how he humiliated you!' He said it by our stone. Now he's dying, sir . . ."

The captain suddenly burst into sobs and threw himself at the judge's feet. He was quickly taken out amid the laughter of the public. The effect prepared by the prosecutor did not come off at all.

The defense attorney continued using every possible means, and surprised people more and more by his familiarity with the smallest details of the case. Thus, for example, the testimony of Trifon Borisovich was on its way to producing a rather strong impression, and one certainly highly unfavorable to Mitya. He calculated precisely, almost on his fingers, that during his first visit to Mokroye about a month before the catastrophe, Mitya could not have spent less than three thousand, or "maybe just a tiny bit less. Think how much he threw to the gypsy girls alone! 'To fling kopecks down the street'—no, sir, he gave our lousy peasants twenty-five roubles at least, he wouldn't give less than that. And how much was simply stolen from him then, sir! Whoever stole certainly didn't sign for it; try catching a thief, when he himself was just throwing it around for nothing! Our people are robbers, they're not worried about their souls. And the girls, our village girls, what he spent on them! People have got rich since then, that's what, sir, and before there was just poverty." In short, he recalled each expense and worked it all out precisely, as on an abacus. Thus the supposition that only fifteen hundred had been spent, and the rest set aside in the amulet, became unthinkable. "I myself saw it, I saw three thousand to a kopeck in his hands, contemplated it with my own eyes, who knows about money if not me, sir!" Trifon Borisovich kept exclaiming, doing his best to please "authority." But when the defense attorney began his cross-examination, instead of actually trying to refute the testimony, he suddenly started talking about how the coachman Timofei and another peasant named Akim, during that first spree in Mokroye a month before the arrest, had picked up a hundred roubles that Mitya had dropped on the floor in his drunken state, and turned the money over to Trifon Borisovich, for which he gave them each a rouble. "Well, and did you then return the hundred roubles to Mr. Karamazov, or not?" Trifon Borisovich tried in every way to dodge the question, but after the peasants themselves testified, he was forced to admit to the found hundred roubles, adding only that he had at once religiously returned and restored everything to Dmitri Fyodorovich "in all honesty, and that he simply wasn't able to recall it himself, having been quite drunk at that time, sir." But since he had nonetheless denied finding the hundred roubles before the peasant witnesses were called, his testimony about returning the money to the drunken Mitya was naturally called very much in question. And so one of the most dangerous witnesses brought forward by the prosecution again left under suspicion and with his reputation rather besmirched. The same thing happened with the Poles: the two of them appeared looking proud and independent. They loudly testified, first, that they had both "served the Crown" and that "Pan Mitya" had offered them three thousand, to buy their honor, and they themselves had seen a great deal of money in his hands. Pan Mussyalovich introduced a terrible quantity of Polish words into his phrases, and, seeing that this only raised him in the eyes of the judge and the prosecutor, finally let his spirit soar and in the end started speaking entirely in Polish. But Fetyukovich caught them, too, in his snares: no matter how Trifon Borisovich, who was called up again, tried to hedge, he still had to confess that Pan Vrublevsky had switched the innkeeper's deck of cards for one of his own, and that Pan Mussyalovich had cheated while keeping the bank. This was also confirmed by Kalganov when his turn came to testify, and the two *pans* withdrew somewhat covered in shame, even amid public laughter.

Exactly the same thing happened with almost all the most dangerous witnesses. Fetyukovich succeeded in morally tainting each one of them and letting them go with their noses somewhat out of joint. Amateurs and lawyers were filled with admiration, and only wondered, again, what great and ultimate purpose all this could serve, for, I repeat, everyone felt that the accusation, which was growing and becoming ever more tragic, was irrefutable. But they waited, seeing by the assurance of "the great magician" that he himself was calm: "such a man" would not have come from Petersburg for nothing, nor was he such as to go back with nothing.

Chapter 3

Medical Expertise and One Pound of Nuts

Medical expertise was not much help to the defendant either. And Fetyukovich himself seemed not to be counting on it very much, as turned out later to be the case. Basically, it was introduced solely at the insistence of Katerina Ivanovna, who had purposely invited a famous doctor from Moscow. The defense, of course, could not lose anything by it, and at best might even gain something. What came of it, however, was partly even comic, as it were, owing to some disagreement among the doctors. The experts called were: the famous visiting doctor, then our own Dr. Herzenstube, and finally the young Dr. Varvinsky. The latter two were also called as regular witnesses by the prosecution. The first to give expert testimony was Dr. Herzenstube. He was an old man of seventy, gray-haired and bald, of medium height and sturdy build. Everyone in our town valued and respected him very much. He was a conscientious doctor, an excellent and pious man, some sort of Herrnhuter or "Moravian brother"[1]—I am not sure which. He had been with us for a very long time and behaved with the greatest dignity. He was kind and philanthropic, treated poor patients and peasants for nothing, visited their hovels and cottages himself, and left them money for medications, yet for all that he was stubborn as a mule. Once an idea had lodged itself in his head, it was impossible to shake it out of him. Incidentally, almost everyone in town knew by then that the famous visiting doctor, in the two or three days since his arrival, had allowed himself several extremely insulting comments with respect to Dr. Herzenstube's abilities. The thing was that, though the Moscow doctor charged no less than twenty-five roubles for a visit, some people in our town still rejoiced at the occasion of his coming, and, not sparing the money, rushed to him for advice. Previously all these sick people had, of course, been treated by Herzenstube, and now the famous doctor went around criticizing his treatment with extreme sharpness. In the end, coming to a sick person, he would ask straight off: "Well, who's been mucking about with you—Herzenstube? Heh, heh!" Dr. Herzenstube, of course, found out about all this. And so all three doctors appeared, one after the other, to be questioned. Dr. Herzenstube declared directly that "the mental abnormality of the defendant is self-evident." Then, having offered his considerations, which I omit here, he added that this abnormality could be perceived above all, not only in many of the defendant's former actions, but also now, even this very minute, and when asked to explain how it could be perceived now, this very minute, the old doctor, with all his simple-hearted directness, pointed out that the defendant, on entering the courtroom, "had, considering the circumstances, a remarkable and strange look, marched along like a soldier, and kept his eyes fixed straight in front of him, whereas it would have been more correct for him to look to the left where, among the public, the ladies were sitting, since he was a great admirer of the fair sex and ought to have thought very much about what the ladies would now be saying of him," the dear old man concluded in his peculiar language. It should be added that he spoke Russian readily and copiously, but somehow each of his phrases came out in German fashion, which, however, never embarrassed him, for all his life he had the weakness of considering his spoken Russian exemplary, "even better than with the Russians," and he was even very fond of quoting Russian proverbs, each time maintaining that Russian proverbs were the best and most expressive proverbs in the world. I will note, also, that in conversation, perhaps from some sort of absentmindedness, he often forgot the most ordinary words, which he knew perfectly well, but which for some reason suddenly slipped his mind. The same thing happened, incidentally, when he spoke German, and he would always start waving his hand in front of his face, as if seeking to catch the lost word, and no one could make him go on with what he was saying before the lost word was found. His observation that the defendant ought to have looked at the ladies as he came in drew some playful whispers from the public. All our ladies loved our dear old doctor very much, and also knew that he, a lifelong bachelor, a chaste and pious man, looked upon women as exalted and ideal beings. His unexpected observation therefore struck everyone as terribly strange.

The Moscow doctor, questioned in his turn, sharply and emphatically confirmed that he considered the defendant's mental condition abnormal, "even in the highest degree." He spoke at length and cleverly about "mania" and the "fit of passion," and concluded from all the assembled data that the defendant, before his arrest, as much as several days before, was undoubtedly suffering from a morbid fit of passion, and if he did commit the crime, even consciously, it was also almost involuntarily, being totally unable to fight the morbid moral fixation that possessed him. But, besides this fit of passion, the doctor also detected a mania that, in his words, promised to lead straight to complete insanity. (*N.B.* The words are my own; the doctor expressed himself in a very learned and special language.) "All his actions are contrary to common sense and logic," he continued. "I am not talking about what I did not see—that is, the crime itself and this whole catastrophe—but even the day before yesterday, during a conversation with me, he had an inexplicable, fixed look in his eyes. Unexpected laughter, when it was quite uncalled for. Incomprehensible, constant irritation; strange words: 'Bernard' and 'ethics,' and others that were uncalled for." But the doctor especially detected this mania in the defendant's inability even to speak of the three thousand roubles, of which he considered himself cheated, without extraordinary irritation, whereas he could recall and speak of all his other failures and offenses rather lightly. Finally, according to inquiries, it had been the same even before as well; each time the three thousand came up, he would fly almost into some sort of frenzy, and yet people said of him that he was disinterested and ungrasping. "And concerning the opinion of my learned colleague," the Moscow doctor added ironically, concluding his speech, "that the defendant, on entering the courtroom, ought to have been looking at the ladies and not straight in front of him, I shall only say that, apart from the playfulness of such a conclusion, it is, besides, also radically erroneous; for though I fully agree that the defendant, on entering the courtroom where his fate is to be decided, ought not to have looked so fixedly in front of him, and that this indeed can be considered a sign of his abnormal psychological condition at that moment, yet at the same time I assert that he ought not to have been looking to the left, at the ladies, but, on the contrary, precisely to the right, seeking out his defense attorney, in whose help all his hopes lie, and on whose defense his entire fate now depends." The doctor expressed his opinion decisively and emphatically. But the disagreement of the two learned experts became especially comical in light of the unexpected conclusion of Dr. Varvinsky, who was the last to be questioned. In his opinion the defendant, now as well as before, was in a perfectly normal condition, and although, before his arrest, he must have been in a very nervous and extremely excited state, this could have been owing to a number of quite obvious reasons: jealousy, wrath, continual drunkenness, and so on. But this nervous condition would not in itself imply any special "fit of passion" such as had just been discussed. As to which way the defendant ought to have been looking, to the left or to the right, on entering the courtroom, "in his humble opinion" the defendant, on entering the courtroom, ought to have looked straight in front of him, as in fact he did, because in front of him were sitting the presiding judge and the members of the court, on whom his entire fate now depended, "so that, by looking straight in front of him, he thereby precisely proved his perfectly normal state of mind at the present moment," the young doctor somewhat heatedly concluded his "humble" testimony.

"Bravo, leech!" Mitya cried from his place. "Precisely right!"

Mitya, of course, was cut short, but the young doctor's opinion had the most decisive influence both on the court and on the public, for, as it turned out later, everyone agreed with him. However, Dr. Herzenstube, when questioned as a witness, suddenly served quite unexpectedly in Mitya's favor. As an old-timer in town who had long known the Karamazov family, he furnished some evidence that was quite interesting for "the prosecution," but suddenly, as if he had just realized something, he added:

"And yet the poor young man might have had an incomparably better lot, for he was of good heart both in childhood and after childhood, for this I know. But the Russian proverb says: 'It is good when someone has one head, but when an intelligent man comes to visit, it is better still, for then there will be two heads and not just one . . .'"

"Two heads are better than one," the prosecutor prompted impatiently, being long familiar with the old man's habit of speaking in a slow, drawn-out fashion, without being embarrassed by the impression he produced or by the fact that he was making everyone wait for him, but, on the contrary, prizing all the more his potato-thick and always happily self-satisfied German wit. And the dear old man loved to be witty.

"Oh, y-yes, that's what I am saying," he picked up stubbornly, "two heads are much better than one head. But no one came to him with another head, and he even sent his own head for . . . How do you say, where did he send it? This word—where he sent his head—I've forgotten," he went on waving his hand in front of his eyes, "ah, yes, *spazieren*."

"For a walk?"

"Yes, for a walk, that's what I am saying. So his head went for a walk and came to some deep place where it lost itself. And yet he was a grateful and sensitive young man, oh, I remember him still as such a tiny boy, left alone in his father's backyard, where he was running in the dirt without any shoes and just one button on his little britches."

A certain note of sensitivity and emotion was suddenly heard in the honest old man's voice. Fetyukovich fairly started, as if anticipating something, and instantly hung on to it.

"Oh, yes, I myself was a young man then . . . I was . . . well, yes, I was then forty-five years old, and had just come here. And I felt pity for the boy then, and I asked myself: why shouldn't I buy him a pound of . . . well, yes, a pound of what? I forget what it's called . . . a pound of what children like so much, what is it—well, what is it . . . ?" the doctor again waved his hand. "It grows on a tree, they gather it and give it to everyone . . ."

"Apples?"

"Oh, n-n-no! A pound, a pound—apples come in dozens, not pounds . . . no, there are many of them, and they are all small, you put them in the mouth and cr-r-rack . . . !"

"Nuts?"

"Well, yes, nuts, that is what I am saying," the doctor confirmed in the calmest way, as if he had not even been searching for the word, "and I brought the boy a pound of nuts, because no one had ever yet brought the boy a pound of nuts, and I held up my finger and said to him: 'Boy! *Gott der Vater*,' and he laughed and said, '*Gott der Vater*.' '*Gott der Sohn*.' Again he laughed and said, '*Gott der Sohn*.' '*Gott der heilige Geist*.' Then he laughed again and said as well as he could, '*Gott der heilige Geist*.'[2] And I left. Two days later I was passing by and he called out to me himself: 'Hey, uncle, *Gott der Vater*, *Gott der Sohn*,' only he forgot '*Gott der heilige Geist*,' but I reminded him, and again I felt great pity for him. But he was taken away, and I did not see him anymore. And now after twenty-three years have gone by, I am sitting one morning in my study, and my head is already gray, and suddenly a blossoming young man comes in, whom I would never have recognized, but he held up his finger and said, laughing: '*Gott der Vater, Gott der Sohn, und Gott der heilige Geist!* I've just arrived, and have come to thank you for that pound of nuts; for no one bought me a pound of nuts before; you are the only one who ever bought me a pound of nuts.' And then I remembered my happy youth, and a poor boy in the yard without any shoes, and my heart turned over, and I said: 'You are a grateful young man, for all your life you have remembered that pound of nuts I brought you in your childhood.' And I embraced him and blessed him. And I wept. He was laughing, but he also wept . . . for a Russian quite often laughs when he ought to weep. But he wept, too, I saw it. And now, alas . . . !"

"And I'm weeping now, too, German, I'm weeping now, too, you man of God!" Mitya suddenly cried from his place.

In any event, this little anecdote produced a certain favorable impression on the public. But the major effect in Mitya's favor was produced by the testimony of Katerina Ivanovna, which I shall come to presently. And, generally, when the witnesses *à décharge*—that is, called by the defense—began to testify, fate seemed suddenly and even seriously to smile on Mitya and—what is most remarkable—to the surprise even of the defense itself. But before Katerina Ivanovna, Alyosha was questioned, and he suddenly recalled one fact that even looked like positive evidence against one most important point of the accusation.

Chapter 4

Fortune Smiles on Mitya

It came as a complete surprise even to Alyosha himself. He was called up without being under oath, and I remember that from the very first words of the examination all sides treated him with great gentleness and sympathy. One could see that his good fame had preceded him. Alyosha testified modestly and with reserve, but an ardent sympathy for his unfortunate brother kept obviously breaking through his testimony. In answer to one question, he outlined his brother's character as that of a man who, if he was indeed violent and carried away by his passions, was also noble, proud, and magnanimous, ready even for any sacrifice if it was wanted of him. He admitted, however, that in recent days his brother had been in an unbearable situation because of his passion for Grushenka, because of the rivalry with his father. But he indignantly rejected even the suggestion that his brother could have killed with the purpose of robbery, though he confessed that in Mitya's mind the three thousand roubles had turned almost into some sort of mania, that he regarded it as an inheritance left owing to him by his father, who had cheated him, and that, while he was a totally unmercenary man, he could not even begin speaking of that three thousand without rage and fury. Concerning the rivalry of the two "persons," as the prosecutor put it—that is, Grushenka and Katya—he answered evasively, and even preferred once or twice not to answer at all.

"Did your brother tell you, at least, that he intended to kill his father?" the prosecutor asked. "You may choose not to answer if you find it necessary," he added.

"He never said it directly," Alyosha replied.

"And how, then? Indirectly?"

"He once spoke to me of his personal loathing for father, and of his fear that . . . in an extreme moment . . . in a moment of loathing . . . he could, perhaps, even kill him."

"And did you believe it when you heard it?"

"I am afraid to say I did. But I was always convinced that at the fatal moment some higher feeling would always save him, as it did indeed save him, because it was *not he* who killed my father," Alyosha concluded firmly, in a loud voice, for all the courtroom to hear. The prosecutor gave a start, like a warhorse hearing the sound of trumpets.

"Rest assured that I fully believe in the complete sincerity of your conviction, and do not in the least connect it or assimilate it with love for your unfortunate brother. Your singular view of the whole tragic episode that took place in your family is already known to us from the preliminary investigation. I shall not conceal from you that it is original in the highest degree and contradicts all the other evidence obtained by the prosecution. And therefore at this point I must insist on asking you: what precisely were the facts that guided your thought and led you to a final conviction of your brother's innocence and, on the contrary, of the guilt of a certain other person to whom you pointed directly in the preliminary investigation?"

"In the preliminary investigation I simply answered questions," Alyosha said softly and calmly, "I did not come out and accuse Smerdyakov myself."

"But still you pointed to him?"

"I pointed to him from what my brother Dmitri said. Even before the interrogation I was told of what happened at his arrest, and how he himself had then pointed to Smerdyakov. I believe completely that my brother is innocent. And if it was not he who killed father, then . . ."

"Then it was Smerdyakov? But why Smerdyakov, precisely? And precisely why did you become so utterly convinced of your brother's innocence?"

"I could not but believe my brother. I know he would not lie to me. I saw by his face that he was not lying to me."

"Only by his face? That's all the proof you have?"

"I have no other proof."

"And concerning Smerdyakov's guilt, you have not the slightest proof to base it on, apart from your brother's words and the look on his face?"

"No, I do not have any other proof."

At that the prosecutor had no more questions. Alyosha's answers produced a most disappointing impression on the public. There had been some talk of Smerdyakov even before the trial, someone had heard something, someone had pointed to something, it was said that Alyosha had gathered some extraordinary proof in favor of his brother and of the lackey's guilt, and now—nothing, no proof, except for certain moral convictions quite natural in him as the defendant's brother.

But then Fetyukovich began his questioning. He asked precisely when it was that the defendant had told him, Alyosha, of his hatred for their father, and of being capable of killing him, whether he had said it, for example, at their last meeting before the catastrophe, and as Alyosha was answering, he suddenly seemed to jump, as if he had just then recalled and understood something:

"I now recall one circumstance I had quite forgotten; it was not at all clear to me then, but now . . ."

And Alyosha excitedly recalled, obviously having just suddenly hit upon the idea himself, how during his last meeting with Mitya, in the evening, by the tree, on the road to the monastery, Mitya, hitting himself on the chest, "on the upper part of the chest," repeated to him several times that he had a means of restoring his honor, and that this means was there, right there, on his chest . . . "At the time I thought, when he hit himself on the chest, that he was speaking of his heart," Alyosha went on, "that in his heart he might find the strength to escape some terrible disgrace that lay ahead of him, and that he did not dare confess even to me. I admit that right then I thought precisely that he was speaking of father, and that he was shuddering as if from shame at the thought of going to father and doing some violence to him, and yet precisely then he seemed to point at something on his chest, so that I remember precisely then some thought flashed through me that the heart isn't in that part of the chest at all, but lower down, while he was hitting himself much higher, here, right under his neck, and indicating that place. My thought seemed stupid to me then, but perhaps precisely then he was pointing to that amulet with the fifteen hundred roubles sewn up in it . . . !"

"Precisely!" Mitya suddenly shouted from his place. "It's true, Alyosha, true, I was pounding on it with my fist!"

Fetyukovich rushed to him in a flurry, begging him to calm down, and at the same time simply fastened on to Alyosha. Alyosha, carried away himself by his recollection, ardently voiced his supposition that the disgrace most likely lay precisely in the fact that, while he had these fifteen hundred roubles on him, which he could return to Katerina Ivanovna as half of what he owed her, he had nonetheless decided not to give her this half but to use it for something else—that is, to take Grushenka away, if she were willing . . .

"That's it, that's precisely it," Alyosha kept exclaiming in sudden agitation, "my brother precisely kept exclaiming to me then that he could remove half, half of the disgrace from himself at once (several times he said *half*!), but was so unfortunate in the weakness of his character that he would not do it . . . he knew beforehand that he could not, that he was not strong enough to do it!"

"And you firmly, clearly remember that he hit himself precisely in that place on his chest?" Fetyukovich questioned him greedily.

"Clearly and firmly, because I precisely thought then: why is he hitting himself up there, when the heart is lower down, and the thought immediately struck me as stupid . . . I remember that it struck me as stupid . . . it flashed through my mind. That's why I remembered it just now. And how could I have forgotten it all this time! He was pointing precisely to the amulet, showing that he had the means but that he would not return the fifteen hundred! And at his arrest in Mokroye he precisely cried out—I know this, I was told—that he considered it the most shameful thing in all his life that, having the means to pay back half (precisely half!) of his debt to Katerina Ivanovna and not be a thief to her, he still could not decide to do it, and preferred to remain a thief in her eyes rather than part with the money! And how he suffered, how he suffered over that debt!" Alyosha exclaimed in conclusion.

Naturally, the prosecutor also intervened. He asked Alyosha to describe it all once more, and insisted on asking several times whether the defendant, as he beat himself on the chest, in fact seemed to be pointing at something. Perhaps he was simply beating himself on the chest with his fist?

"No, not with his fist!" exclaimed Alyosha. "He was precisely pointing with his finger, and pointing here, very high . . . But how could I have forgotten it so completely till this very moment!"

The presiding judge turned to Mitya and asked what he had to say regarding the present testimony. Mitya confirmed that it had all happened precisely that way, that he had precisely been pointing at the fifteen hundred roubles that were on his chest, just below the neck, and that, of course, it was a disgrace, "a disgrace I do not repudiate, the most disgraceful act of my whole life!" Mitya cried out. "I could have returned it and I did not return it. I preferred better to remain a thief in her eyes, and did not return it, and the chief disgrace was that I knew beforehand that I wasn't going to return it! Alyosha is right! Thank you, Alyosha!"

With that the questioning of Alyosha ended. What was important and characteristic was precisely the circumstance that at least one fact had been found, at least one, shall we say, very small proof, almost just the hint of a proof, that nonetheless gave at least a drop of evidence that the amulet had actually existed, that it had contained the fifteen hundred, and that the defendant had not been lying at the preliminary investigation in Mokroye when he declared that the fifteen hundred "was mine." Alyosha was glad; all flushed, he proceeded to the place pointed out to him. He kept repeating to himself for a long time: "How did I forget! How could I forget! And how did I suddenly recall it only now!"

The questioning of Katerina Ivanovna began. The moment she appeared, something extraordinary swept through the courtroom. The ladies snatched up their lorgnettes and opera-glasses, the men began to stir, some stood in order to get a better view. Everyone asserted afterwards that Mitya suddenly went "white as a sheet" the moment she came in. All in black, she modestly and almost timidly approached the place pointed out to her. It was impossible to tell from her face if she was excited, but there was a gleam of resolution in her dark, gloomy eyes. Afterwards, it should be noted, a great many people declared that she was remarkably good-looking at that moment. She spoke softly but clearly, so that she could be heard throughout the courtroom. She expressed herself with extreme calmness, or at least with an effort to be calm. The presiding judge began his questions cautiously, with extreme respect, as though fearing to touch "certain strings" and deferring to great misfortune. But Katerina Ivanovna herself, from the very first words, declared firmly to one of the questions put to her that she had been engaged to be married to the defendant, "before he himself left me . . . ," she added softly. When asked about the three thousand roubles entrusted to Mitya to be sent by mail to her relations, she said firmly: "I did not give it to him to be mailed straight away; I sensed at the time that he very much needed money . . . that minute . . . I gave him the three thousand roubles on condition that he send it, if he would, within a month. There was no need for him to torment himself so much afterwards because of this debt . . ."

I am not repeating all the questions and all her answers exactly, I am only giving the basic sense of her testimony.

"I firmly believed that he would always be able to send the three thousand as soon as he got it from his father," she went on answering the questions. "I always believed in his disinterestedness and in his honesty . . . his high honesty . . . in matters of money. He firmly believed that he would get three thousand roubles from his father, and said so to me several times. I knew he was having a dispute with his father, and have always been and still am convinced that his father wronged him. I do not recall any threats against his father on his part. At least in my presence he never said anything, any threats. If he had come to me then, I would immediately have calmed his anxiety about the miserable three thousand he owed me, but he no longer came to me . . . and I myself . . . I was put in such a position . . . that I could not ask him to come . . . And besides, I had no right to be demanding of him about that debt," she suddenly added, and something resolute rang in her voice, "I myself once received a financial favor from him even greater than three thousand, and I accepted it, although I could not even foresee then that at least one day I might be able to repay him my debt . . ."

One seemed to feel a sort of challenge in the tone of her voice. Precisely at that moment the questioning was taken over by Fetyukovich.

"That was not here, but at the beginning of your acquaintance?" Fetyukovich picked up, approaching cautiously, having instantly sensed something favorable. (I will note parenthetically that in spite of the fact that he had been invited from Petersburg in part by Katerina Ivanovna herself, he knew nothing as yet about the episode of the five thousand given her by Mitya in that town, or about the "bow to the ground." She had concealed it and did not tell him of it! And that was surprising. One could suppose quite certainly that she herself did not know until the very last moment whether she would tell of this episode in court or not, and was waiting for some sort of inspiration.)

No, never shall I forget those moments! She began telling, she told *everything*, the whole episode Mitya had revealed to Alyosha, including the "bow to the ground," and the reasons, and about her father, and her appearance at Mitya's, and did not betray by a word, not by a single hint, that Mitya himself had suggested, through her sister, that they "send Katerina Ivanovna to him for the money." She magnanimously concealed it, and was not ashamed to present it as if she, she herself, had gone running to a young officer, on her own impulse, hoping for something . . . to beg him for money. This was something tremendous! I had chills and trembled as I listened; the courtroom was dead silent, grasping at every word. Here was an unparalleled thing, so that even from such an imperious and contemptuously proud girl as she was, such extremely frank testimony, such sacrifice, such self-immolation was almost impossible to expect. And for what, for whom? To save her betrayer and offender, at least somehow, at least slightly, to contribute to his salvation by creating a good impression in his favor! And indeed the image of an officer giving away his last five thousand roubles—all he had left in the world—and respectfully bowing to the innocent girl, made a rather sympathetic and attractive picture, but . . . how my heart ached! I sensed that what might come of it afterwards (and so it did, it did) was slander! Afterwards, all over town, it was said with a wicked snigger that the story was perhaps not entirely accurate—namely, at the point where the officer supposedly let the girl go "with just a respectful bow." It was hinted that something had been "left out" there. "And even if it wasn't left out, if it was all true," even our most respectable ladies said, "it still isn't clear that it was quite so noble for a girl to act in such a way even to save her father." And can it be that Katerina Ivanovna, with her intelligence, with her morbid perspicacity, did not anticipate that there would be such talk? She must have anticipated it, and still she determined to tell everything! Of course, all these dirty little doubts about the truth of the story arose only later, but in the first moment all were thoroughly shaken. As for the members of the court, they listened to Katerina Ivanovna in reverent and even, so to speak, bashful silence. The prosecutor did not allow himself any further questions on the subject. Fetyukovich bowed deeply to her. Oh, he was almost triumphant! Much had been gained: a man who, on a noble impulse, gives away his last five thousand roubles, and then the same man killing his father in the night with the purpose of robbing him of three thousand—there was something partly incongruous about it. Now Fetyukovich could at least eliminate the robbery. A certain new light suddenly poured over "the case." Something sympathetic emerged in Mitya's favor. As for him . . . it was said that once or twice during Katerina Ivanovna's testimony he jumped up from his place, then fell back on the bench again and covered his face with his hands. But when she had finished, he suddenly exclaimed in a sobbing voice, stretching his hands out to her:

"Katya, why have you ruined me!"

And he burst into loud sobs that could be heard all over the courtroom. However, he instantly restrained himself and again cried out:

"Now I am condemned!"

And then he froze in his place, as it were, clenching his teeth and crossing his arms tightly on his chest. Katerina Ivanovna remained in the courtroom and sat down on the chair pointed out to her. She was pale and kept her eyes cast down. Those who were near her said she trembled for a long time as if in fever. Grushenka appeared for questioning.

I am drawing near the catastrophe that, when it suddenly broke out, indeed perhaps ruined Mitya. For I am certain, and so is everyone else, and all the lawyers also said afterwards, that if it had not been for this episode, the criminal would at least have been given a lighter sentence. But of that presently. And first a few words about Grushenka.

She also came into the courtroom dressed all in black, with her beautiful black shawl over her shoulders. Smoothly, with her inaudible step, swaying slightly, as full-figured women sometimes walk, she approached the balustrade, looking steadily at the presiding judge, and never once glancing either right or left. In my opinion she was very good-looking at that moment, and not at all pale, as the ladies asserted afterwards. It was also asserted that she had a somehow concentrated and angry look. I simply think she was on edge and strongly sensible of the contemptuously curious eyes fixed upon her by our scandal-loving public. Hers was a proud character, which could not brook contempt—of the sort that, at the first suspicion of contempt from someone, at once flares up with wrath and the desire to strike back. With that, of course, there was also timidity, and an inner shame because of this timidity, so it was no wonder that she spoke unevenly—now angry, now contemptuous and overly rude, now suddenly with a sincere, heartfelt note of self-condemnation, self-accusation. But sometimes she spoke as if she were flying into some sort of abyss: "I don't care what comes of it, I'll say it anyway . . ." Concerning her acquaintance with Fyodor Pavlovich, she observed sharply: "There was nothing to it—is it my fault that he hung onto me?" And then, a minute later, she added: "It was all my fault, I was laughing at both of them—at the old man and at him—and drove them both to it. It all happened because of me." Somehow Samsonov came up: "That's nobody's business," she snarled at once, with a sort of insolent defiance. "He was my benefactor, he took me in barefoot when my relations threw me out of the house." The judge reminded her, quite courteously, by the way, that she should answer the questions directly, without getting into unnecessary details. Grushenka blushed, and her eyes flashed.

She had not seen the envelope with the money, and had only heard from "the villain" that Fyodor Pavlovich had some sort of envelope with three thousand in it. "Only it was all foolishness—I just laughed—I wouldn't have gone there for anything . . ."

"When you said 'the villain' just now, whom did you mean?" the prosecutor inquired.

"Why, the lackey, Smerdyakov, who killed his master and hanged himself last night."

Of course she was asked at once what grounds she had for such a definite accusation, but it turned out that she, too, had no grounds for it.

"Dmitri Fyodorovich told me so himself, and you can believe him. It was that man-stealer who ruined him, that's what; she alone is the cause of everything, that's what," Grushenka added, all shuddering from hatred, as it were, and a malicious note rang in her voice.

Again she was asked whom she was hinting at.

"At the young lady, at this Katerina Ivanovna here. She sent for me once, treated me to chocolate, wanted to charm me. She has little true shame in her, that's what . . ."

Here the presiding judge stopped her, quite sternly now, asking her to moderate her language. But the jealous woman's heart was already aflame and she was prepared even to hurl herself into the abyss . . .

"At the time of the arrest in the village of Mokroye," the prosecutor asked, recalling, "everyone saw and heard how you ran out of the other room, crying: 'I am guilty of it all, we'll go to penal servitude together!' Meaning that at that moment you were already certain he had killed his father?"

"I don't remember what my feelings were then," Grushenka replied. "Everyone was shouting that he had killed his father, so I felt that I was guilty, and that he had killed him because of me. But as soon as he said he was not guilty, I believed him at once, and I still believe him and shall always believe him: he's not the sort of man who would lie."

It was Fetyukovich's turn to ask questions. Incidentally, I remember him asking about Rakitin and the twenty-five roubles "for bringing Alexei Fyodorovich Karamazov to you."

"And why is it so surprising that he took the money?" Grushenka grinned with contemptuous spite. "He was forever coming to wheedle money out of me, sometimes he'd take up to thirty roubles a month, mostly for his own pleasures: he had enough money to eat and drink without me."

"And on what grounds were you so generous to Mr. Rakitin?" Fetyukovich picked up, ignoring the fact that the judge was stirring uneasily.

"But he's my cousin. My mother and his mother are sisters. Only he always begged me not to tell anyone here, because he was so ashamed of me."

This new fact came as a complete surprise to everyone, no one in the entire town knew of it, nor even in the monastery, not even Mitya knew it. It was said that Rakitin turned crimson from shame in his seat. Grushenka had found out somehow, even before she entered the courtroom, that he had testified against Mitya, and it made her angry. All of Mr. Rakitin's earlier speech, all its nobility, all its outbursts against serfdom, against the civil disorder of Russia—all of it was now finally scrapped and destroyed in the general opinion. Fetyukovich was pleased: once again it was a small godsend. But in general Grushenka was not questioned for very long, and, of course, she could not say anything especially new. She left a rather unpleasant impression on the public. Hundreds of contemptuous looks were fixed on her when, having finished her testimony, she went and sat down in the courtroom a good distance from Katerina Ivanovna. Mitya was silent throughout her questioning, as if turned to stone, his eyes fixed on the ground.

The next witness to appear was Ivan Fyodorovich.

Chapter 5

A Sudden Catastrophe

I will note that he had already been called once, ahead of Alyosha. But the marshal had reported to the presiding judge that, owing to sudden illness or an attack of some kind, the witness could not appear at that moment, but that as soon as he felt better he would be ready to give his testimony whenever they wanted. Somehow, by the way, no one heard this, and it became known only afterwards. His appearance at first went almost unnoticed: the main witnesses, especially the two rival women, had already been questioned; curiosity, for the time being, was satisfied. One could even sense some weariness in the public. They faced the prospect of listening to several more witnesses, who probably had nothing special to say in view of all that had already been said. And time was passing. Ivan Fyodorovich somehow approached remarkably slowly, not looking at anyone and even with his head bowed, as though gloomily pondering something. He was dressed impeccably, but his face produced a morbid impression, at least on me: there was in his face something, as it were, touched with clay, something resembling the face of a dying man. His eyes were dull; he raised them and looked slowly around the courtroom. Alyosha suddenly jumped up from his chair and groaned: aah! I remember it. But not many people caught that either.

The presiding judge began by saying that he was not under oath, that he could give evidence or withhold it, but that, of course, all testimony should be given in good conscience, etc., etc. Ivan Fyodorovich listened and looked at him dully; but suddenly his face began slowly spreading into a grin, and as soon as the judge, who looked at him in surprise, finished speaking, he suddenly burst into laughter.

"Well, anything else?" he asked loudly.

A hush came over the courtroom; something was sensed, as it were. The judge became uneasy.

"You . . . are perhaps still a bit unwell?" he said, looking around for the marshal.

"Don't worry, Your Honor, I'm well enough, and I have something curious to tell you," Ivan Fyodorovich suddenly replied, quite calmly and respectfully.

"You mean you have some specific information to present?" the judge went on, still mistrustfully.

Ivan Fyodorovich looked down, hesitated for a few seconds, and, raising his head again, stammered, as it were, in reply:

"No . . . I don't. Nothing special."

They began asking him questions. He replied somehow quite reluctantly, somehow with exaggerated brevity, even with a sort of repugnance, which increased more and more, though, by the way, his answers were still sensible. To many questions he pleaded ignorance. No, he did not know anything of his father's accountings with Dmitri Fyodorovich. "Nor was I concerned with it," he said. Yes, he had heard the defendant threaten to kill his father. Yes, he had heard about the money in the envelope from Smerdyakov . . .

"It's all the same thing over and over," he suddenly interrupted with a weary look. "I have nothing special to tell the court."

"I can see that you are not well, and I understand your feelings . . . ," the judge began.

He turned to the two parties, the prosecutor and the defense attorney, inviting them to ask questions if they thought it necessary, when suddenly Ivan Fyodorovich said in an exhausted voice:

"Let me go, Your Honor, I am feeling very ill."

And at that, without waiting for permission, he suddenly turned and started out of the courtroom. But having gone about four steps, he stopped as if suddenly pondering something, chuckled softly, and went back to his former place again.

"I'm like that peasant girl, Your Honor . . . you know how it goes: 'I'll jump if I want, and I won't if I don't.' They go after her with some sarafan or wedding skirt or whatever, asking her to jump up so they can tie it around her and take her to church to be married, and she says: 'I'll jump if I want, and I won't if I don't . . .' It's some sort of folk custom . . ."

"What do you mean to say by that?" the judge asked sternly.

"Here . . . ," Ivan Fyodorovich suddenly pulled out a wad of money, "here is the money . . . the same money that was in that envelope," he nodded towards the table with the material evidence, "and on account of which my father was murdered. Where shall I put it? Marshal, please hand it to him."

The marshal took the entire wad and handed it to the judge.

"How could this money possibly end up in your possession . . . if it is the same money?" the judge said in surprise.

"I got it from Smerdyakov, the murderer, yesterday. I visited him before he hanged himself. It was he who killed father, not my brother. He killed him, and killed him on my instructions . . . Who doesn't wish for his father's death . . . ?"

"Are you in your right mind?" inadvertently escaped from the judge.

"The thing is that I am precisely in my right mind . . . my vile mind, the same as you, and all these . . . m-mugs!" he suddenly turned to the public. "A murdered father, and they pretend to be frightened," he growled with fierce contempt. "They pull faces to each other. Liars! Everyone wants his father dead. Viper devours viper . . . If there were no parricide, they'd all get angry and go home in a foul temper . . . Circuses! 'Bread and circuses!'[1] And me, I'm a good one! Is there some water? Give me a drink, for Christ's sake!" he suddenly clutched his head.

The marshal at once approached him. Alyosha suddenly jumped up and shouted: "He's sick, don't believe him, he's delirious!" Katerina Ivanovna rose impetuously from her chair and, motionless with horror, looked at Ivan Fyodorovich. Mitya stood up and, with a sort of wild, twisted smile, looked and listened greedily to his brother.

"Calm yourselves, I'm not mad, I'm simply a murderer!" Ivan began again. "One really cannot expect eloquence from a murderer . . . ," he suddenly added for some reason, with a twisted laugh.

The prosecutor, visibly perturbed, leaned over to the presiding judge. The members of the court fidgeted and whispered among themselves. Fetyukovich pricked up his ears, listening attentively. The courtroom was frozen in expectation. The judge suddenly came to his senses, as it were.

"Witness, your words are incomprehensible and impossible in this place. Calm yourself if you can, and tell us . . . if you really have anything to tell. How can you confirm such a confession . . . if in fact you are not raving?"

"That's the trouble, I have no witnesses. That dog Smerdyakov won't send you evidence from the other world . . . in an envelope. You keep asking for envelopes, as if one wasn't enough. I have no witnesses . . . except one, perhaps," he smiled pensively.

"Who is your witness?"

"He's got a tail, Your Honor, you'd find him inadmissible! *Le diable n'existe point!*[2] Pay no mind to him, he's a wretched, paltry devil," he added, confidentially, as it were, and suddenly stopped laughing. "He's sure to be here somewhere, there, under the table with the material evidence, where else would he be sitting? You see, listen to me: I told him I would not keep silent, and he started telling me about the geological cataclysm . . . what rot! Well, set the monster free . . . he's begun his hymn, because he finds it all so easy. The same as if some drunken lout started bawling that 'Vanka's gone to Petersburg,' but I'd give a quadrillion quadrillion for two seconds of joy. You don't know me! Oh, how stupid this all is! Well, take me instead of him! I must have come for some reason . . . Why, why is everything in the world so stupid . . . !"

And again, slowly, pensively, as it were, he began looking around the courtroom. But by then all was astir. Alyosha rushed to him from his place, but the marshal had already seized Ivan Fyodorovich by the arm.

"What is the meaning of this?" Ivan Fyodorovich exclaimed, staring straight into the marshal's face, and suddenly, seizing him by the shoulders, he flung him violently to the floor. But the guards were already there, he was seized, and then he cried out with a frenzied cry.[3] And all the while he was being taken away, he kept shouting and crying out something incoherent.

Turmoil ensued. I do not remember everything in order, I was excited myself and could not follow. I know only that afterwards, when everything had quieted down, and everyone realized what had happened, the marshal got a telling off, though he thoroughly explained to the authorities that the witness had been well all along, that the doctor had examined him an hour ago when he felt slightly ill, but that before entering the courtroom he had spoken coherently, so that it was impossible to foresee anything; that he himself, on the contrary, had demanded and absolutely wanted to testify. But right after this scene, before everyone had at least somewhat calmed down and recovered, yet another scene broke out: Katerina Ivanovna had hysterics. She began sobbing, with loud shrieks, but would not leave, struggled and begged not to be taken away, and suddenly cried out to the judge:

"I have one more piece of evidence to give, at once . . . at once . . . ! Here is a paper, a letter . . . take it, read it quickly, quickly! It's a letter from that monster, that one, that one!" she was pointing at Mitya. "He killed his father, you'll see now, he writes to me how he's going to kill his father! And the other one is ill, ill, he's delirious! I've seen for three days that he's delirious!"

So she cried out, beside herself. The marshal took the paper she was holding out to the judge, and she, collapsing on her chair and covering her face, began sobbing convulsively and soundlessly, shaking all over and suppressing the slightest moan for fear of being put out of the courtroom. The paper she handed over was that same letter Mitya had written from the "Metropolis" tavern, which Ivan Fyodorovich referred to as a document of "mathematical" importance. Alas, it was acknowledged precisely as mathematical, and had it not been for this letter, Mitya would perhaps not have perished, or at least not have perished so terribly! I repeat, it was difficult to follow all the details. Even now I picture it as so much turmoil. The presiding judge must at once have communicated the new document to the court, the prosecutor, the defense attorney, the jury. I remember only how they began questioning the witness. To the question of whether she had calmed down, which the judge gently addressed to her, Katerina Ivanovna exclaimed impetuously:

"I am ready, ready! I am quite capable of answering you," she added, apparently still terribly afraid that for some reason she would not be listened to. She was asked to explain in more detail what this letter was and under what circumstances she had received it.

"I received it on the eve of the crime itself, but he wrote it the day before, in the tavern, which means two days before his crime—look, it's written on some sort of bill!" she cried breathlessly. "He hated me then, because he himself had done a base thing, going after that creature . . . and also because he owed me that three thousand . . . Oh, he felt bad about that three thousand because of his own baseness! The three thousand happened like this—I ask you, I beg you to listen to me: three weeks before he killed his father, he came to me in the morning. I knew he needed money, and knew what he needed it for—precisely, precisely to seduce that creature and take her away. I knew that he had already betrayed me, and wanted to abandon me, and I, I myself, handed him the money then, I myself offered it to him, supposedly to be sent to my sister in Moscow—and as I was handing it to him, I looked him in the face and said he could send it whenever he chose, 'even in a month.' How, how could he not understand that I was telling him right to his face: 'You need money to betray me with your creature, here is the money, I'm giving it to you myself, take it, if you're dishonorable enough to take it . . . !' I wanted to catch him out, and what then? He took it, he took it and went off and spent it with that creature there, in one night . . . But he saw, he saw that I knew everything, I assure you, he also saw that I was just testing him by giving him the money: would he be so dishonorable as to take it from me, or not? I looked into his eyes, and he looked into my eyes and saw everything, everything, and he took it, he took my money and went off with it!"

"True, Katya!" Mitya suddenly yelled. "I looked in your eyes, knowing that you were dishonoring me, and yet I took your money! Despise the scoundrel, all of you, despise me, I deserve it!"

"Defendant," cried the judge, "one more word and I'll order you to be removed."

"That money tormented him," Katya continued, hurrying convulsively, "he wanted to give it back to me, he wanted to, it's true, but he also needed money for that creature. So he killed his father, but he still did not give me back the money, but went with her to that village where he was seized. There he again squandered the money he had stolen from his father, whom he had killed. And the day before he killed his father, he wrote me that letter, he was drunk when he wrote it, I saw that at once, he wrote it out of spite, and knowing, knowing for certain that I wouldn't show the letter to anyone, even if he did kill him. Otherwise he wouldn't have written it. He knew I would not want to revenge myself and ruin him! But read it, read it closely, please, read it more closely and you'll see that he described everything in the letter, everything beforehand: how he would kill his father, and where he kept his money. Look, please don't miss this one phrase there: 'I will kill him, if only Ivan goes away.' So he thought it all out beforehand, how he was going to kill him," Katerina Ivanovna went on, gloatingly, and insidiously prompting the court. Oh, one could see that she had thoroughly examined this fatal letter and studied every little detail of it. "If he hadn't been drunk, he would never have written to me, but see how everything is described beforehand, everything exactly as he killed him afterwards, the whole program!"

So she went on exclaiming, beside herself, and, of course, heedless of all consequences for herself, though she had certainly foreseen them, perhaps as much as a month before, because even then, perhaps, shuddering with malice, she had imagined: "Why don't I read it in court?" And now it was as if she had thrown herself off the mountain. I seem to recall the clerk reading the letter aloud precisely at that moment, and it made a tremendous impression. Mitya was asked if he acknowledged the letter.

"It's mine, mine!" cried Mitya. "If I hadn't been drunk, I'd never have written it . . . ! We hated each other for many things, Katya, but I swear, I swear I loved you even as I hated you, and you—didn't!"

He sank back on his seat, wringing his hands in despair. The prosecutor and the defense attorney began cross-examining her, mainly in one sense: "What prompted you to withhold such a document till now and to testify previously in a completely different spirit and tone?"

"Yes, yes, I was lying before, it was all lies, against my honor and conscience, but then I wanted to save him, because he hated me so, and despised me so," Katya exclaimed wildly. "Oh, he despised me terribly, he despised me always, and you know, you know—he despised me from the very moment when I bowed at his feet for that money. I saw it . . . I felt it right then, at once, but for a long time I didn't believe myself. How many times I've read it in his eyes: 'Still, it was you who came to me that time.' Oh, he didn't understand, he didn't understand at all why I came running then, he can only imagine the basest reasons! He measured me by his own measure, he thought everyone was like him," Katya snarled fiercely, now in an utter frenzy. "And he wanted to marry me only because of the inheritance I received, that's why, that's why, I've always suspected that was why! Oh, he's a beast! He was sure I would go on trembling before him all my life out of shame for having come to him that time, and that he could despise me eternally and so hold himself above me—that's why he wanted to marry me! It's true, it's true! I tried to win him over with my love, love without end, I was even willing to endure his betrayal, but he understood nothing, nothing! And how could he understand anything! He's a monster! That letter I received only the next day, in the evening, they brought it to me from the tavern, and still that morning, still in the morning of that same day, I was willing to forgive him everything, everything, even his betrayal!"

The judge and the prosecutor tried, of course, to calm her down. I am sure that they were all, perhaps, ashamed to be taking advantage in such a way of her frenzy, and to be listening to such confessions. I remember hearing them say to her: "We understand how difficult it is for you, believe us, we are not unfeeling," and so on, and so on—and yet they did extract evidence from the raving, hysterical woman. She finally described with extraordinary clarity, which often shines through briefly even in moments of such an overwrought condition, how for those two whole months Ivan Fyodorovich had been driving himself nearly out of his mind over saving "the monster and murderer," his brother.

"He tormented himself," she exclaimed, "he kept trying to minimize his brother's guilt, confessing to me that he had not loved his father either, and perhaps had wished for his death himself. Oh, he has a deep, deep conscience! He tormented himself with his conscience! He revealed everything to me, everything, he would come to see me and talk with me every day as with his only friend. I have the honor of being his only friend!" she exclaimed suddenly, as if with some sort of defiance, and her eyes flashed. "Twice he went to see Smerdyakov. Once he came to me and said: 'If it wasn't my brother who killed him, but Smerdyakov' (because everyone here had been spreading this fable that Smerdyakov killed him), 'then perhaps I am guilty, too, because

Smerdyakov knew that I did not like my father, and perhaps thought I wished for my father's death.' Then I took out that letter and showed it to him, and he was totally convinced that his brother was the killer, and it totally overwhelmed him. He could not bear it that his own brother was a parricide! Already a week ago I saw that he had become ill from it. In the past few days, sitting with me, he was raving. I saw that he was losing his mind. He went about raving, he was seen like that in the streets. The visiting doctor, at my request, examined him the day before yesterday and told me that he was close to brain fever—all because of him, all because of the monster! And yesterday he learned that Smerdyakov had died—he was so struck by it that he's lost his mind . . . and all because of the monster, all to save the monster!"

Oh, to be sure, one can speak thus and confess thus only once in one's life—in the moment before death, for instance, mounting the scaffold. But it was precisely Katya's character and Katya's moment. It was the same impetuous Katya who had once rushed to a young libertine in order to save her father; the very same Katya who, proud and chaste, had just sacrificed herself and her maiden's honor before the whole public by telling of "Mitya's noble conduct," in order to soften at least somewhat the fate in store for him. So now, in just the same way, she again sacrificed herself, this time for another man, and perhaps only now, only that minute, did she feel and realize fully how dear this other man was to her! She sacrificed herself in fear for him, imagining suddenly that he had ruined himself with his testimony that he, and not his brother, was the killer, sacrificed herself in order to save him, his good name, his reputation! And yet a terrible thought flashed through one's mind: was she lying about Mitya in describing her former relations with him?—that was the question. No, no, she was not slandering him deliberately when she cried out that Mitya despised her for bowing to him! She believed it herself, she was deeply convinced, and had been perhaps from the moment of the bow itself, that the guileless Mitya, who adored her even then, was laughing at her and despised her. And only out of pride had she then attached herself to him with a hysterical and strained love, love out of wounded pride, a love that resembled not love but revenge. Oh, perhaps this strained love would have grown into real love, perhaps Katya wished for nothing else, but Mitya insulted her to the depths of her soul with his betrayal, and her soul did not forgive. The moment of revenge came unexpectedly, and everything that had been long and painfully accumulating in the offended woman's breast burst out all at once and, again, unexpectedly. She betrayed Mitya, but she betrayed herself as well! And, naturally, as soon as she had spoken it out, the tension broke, and shame overwhelmed her. Hysterics began again, she collapsed, sobbing and screaming. She was taken away. The moment she was taken out, Grushenka rushed to Mitya with a cry, so that there was no time to hold her back.

"Mitya!" she cried out, "your serpent has destroyed you! See, she's shown you what she is!" she shouted to the court, shaking with anger. At a sign from the judge, they seized her and attempted to remove her from the courtroom. She would not give in, fought and strained to reach Mitya. Mitya cried out and also strained to reach her. He was seized.

Yes, I suppose our lady spectators were left satisfied: the spectacle had been a rich one. Then I remember how the visiting Moscow doctor appeared. It seems that the presiding judge had sent the marshal out earlier with orders to render assistance to Ivan Fyodorovich. The doctor reported to the court that the sick man was suffering from a most dangerous attack of brain fever, and that he ought to be taken away at once. Questioned by the prosecutor and the defense attorney, he confirmed that the patient had come to him two days earlier, and that he had warned him then that brain fever was imminent, but that he had not wished to be treated. "And he was definitely not in a good state of mind, he confessed to me himself that he saw visions while awake, met various persons in the street who were already dead, and that Satan visited him every evening," the doctor concluded. Having given his testimony, the famous doctor withdrew. The letter produced by Katerina Ivanovna was added to the material evidence. After conferring, the court ruled that the investigation be continued and that both unexpected testimonies (Katerina Ivanovna's and Ivan Fyodorovich's) be entered into the record.

But I will not describe the rest of the examination. In any case, the testimony of the remaining witnesses was merely a repetition and confirmation of the previous testimony, though each with its characteristic peculiarities. But, I repeat, everything will be drawn together in the speech of the prosecutor, which I shall come to presently. Everyone was excited, everyone was electrified by the latest catastrophe and only waited with burning impatience for a quick denouement, the speeches of both sides and the verdict. Fetyukovich was visibly shaken by Katerina Ivanovna's evidence. But the prosecutor was triumphant. When the examination was over, an intermission in the proceedings was announced, which lasted for nearly an hour. Finally the presiding judge called for the closing debate. I believe it was precisely eight o'clock in the evening when our prosecutor, Ippolit Kirillovich, began his statement for the prosecution.

Chapter 6

The Prosecutor's Speech. Characterizations

Ippolit Kirillovich began his statement for the prosecution all nervously atremble, with a cold, sickly sweat on his forehead and temples, feeling alternately chilled and feverish all over. He said so afterwards himself. He considered this speech his chef d'oeuvre, the chef d'oeuvre of his whole life, his swan song. True, he died nine months later of acute consumption, so that indeed, as it turned out, he would have been right to compare himself to a swan singing its last song, had he anticipated his end beforehand. Into this speech he put his whole heart and all the intelligence he possessed, and unexpectedly proved that in him were hidden both civic feeling and the "accursed" questions,[1] insofar at least as our poor Ippolit Kirillovich could contain them in himself. Above all, his speech went over because it was sincere: he sincerely believed in the defendant's guilt; his accusation was not made to order, it was not merely dutiful, and, in calling for "revenge," he really was trembling with the desire to "save society." Even our ladies, ultimately hostile to Ippolit Kirillovich, nonetheless admitted the greatness of the impression made. He began in a cracked, faltering voice, but very soon his voice grew stronger and rang through the whole courtroom, and so to the end of his speech. But as soon as he finished it, he nearly fainted.

"Gentlemen of the jury," the prosecutor began, "the present case has resounded throughout all Russia. But what, one might think, is so surprising, what is so especially horrifying about it? For us, for us especially? We're so used to all that! And here is the real horror, that such dark affairs have almost ceased to horrify us! It is this, and not the isolated crime of one individual or another, that should horrify us: that we are so used to it. Where lie the reasons for our indifference, our lukewarm attitude towards such affairs, such signs of the times, which prophesy for us an unenviable future? In our cynicism, in an early exhaustion of mind and imagination in our society, so young and yet so prematurely decrepit? In our moral principles, shattered to their foundations, or, finally, in the fact that we, perhaps, are not even possessed of such moral principles at all? I do not mean to resolve these questions; nevertheless they are painful, and every citizen not only ought, but is even obliged, to suffer over them. Our budding, still timid press has all the same rendered some service to society, for without it we should never have learned, in any measure of fullness, of those horrors of unbridled will and moral degradation that it ceaselessly reports in its pages, to everyone, not merely to those who attend the sessions of the new open courts granted us by the present reign.[2] And what do we read almost daily? Oh, hourly we read of things before which the present case pales and seems almost something ordinary. But what is most important is that a great number of our Russian, our national, criminal cases bear witness precisely to something universal, to some general malaise that has taken root among us, and with which, as with universal evil, it is already very difficult to contend. Here we have a brilliant young officer of high society, just setting out on his life and career, who basely, stealthily, without any remorse, puts a knife into a petty official, in part his former benefactor, and his serving-woman, in order to steal his own promissory document, and the rest of the official's cash along with it: 'It will come in handy for my social pleasures and my future career.' Having stabbed them both to death, he leaves, putting pillows under the heads of the two corpses. Or again we have a young hero, all hung with medals for valor, who, like a robber on the highway, kills the mother of his chief and benefactor and, to urge his comrades on, assures them that 'she loves him like her own son, and will therefore follow all his advice and take no precautions.' Granted he is a monster, but now, in our time, I no longer dare say he is just an isolated monster. Another man may not kill, perhaps, but he will think and feel exactly the same way, in his heart he is just as dishonest as the first. In silence, alone with his conscience, perhaps he asks himself: 'What is honor, after all, and why this prejudice against shedding blood?' Perhaps people will cry out against me, and say of me that I am a morbid man, a hysterical man, that I am raving, exaggerating, slandering monstrously. Let them, let them—and, God, how I would be the first to rejoice! Oh, do not believe me, consider me a sick man, but still remember my words: for if only a tenth, only a twentieth part of what I say is true, even then it is terrible! Look, gentlemen, look at how our young men are shooting themselves—oh, without the least Hamletian question of 'what lies *beyond*,'[3] without a trace of such questions, as if this matter of our spirit, and all that awaits us beyond the grave, had been scrapped long ago in them, buried and covered with dust. Look, finally, at our depravity, at our sensualists. Fyodor Pavlovich, the unfortunate victim in the current trial, is almost an innocent babe next to some of them. And we all knew him, 'he lived among us' . . .[4] Yes, perhaps some day the foremost minds both here and in Europe will consider the psychology of Russian crime, for the subject is worthy of it. But this study will be taken up later on, at leisure, and when the whole tragic topsy-turveydom of our present moment has moved more into the background so that it will be possible to examine it more intelligently and more impartially than people like myself, for example, can do. For now we are either horrified or pretend that we are horrified, while, on the contrary, relishing the spectacle, like lovers of strong, eccentric sensations that stir our cynical and lazy idleness, or, finally, like little children waving the frightening ghosts away, and hiding our heads under the pillow until the frightening vision is gone, so as to forget it immediately afterwards in games and merriment. But should not we, too, some day begin to live soberly and thoughtfully; should not we, too, take a look at ourselves as a society; should not we, too, understand at least something of our social duty, or at least begin to understand? A great writer of the previous epoch, in the finale of the greatest of his works, personifying all of Russia as a bold Russian troika galloping towards an unknown goal, exclaims: 'Ah, troika, bird-troika, who invented you!'—and in proud rapture adds that all nations respectfully stand aside for this troika galloping by at breakneck speed. Let it be so, gentlemen, let them stand aside, respectfully or not, but in my sinful judgment the artistic genius ended like that either in a fit of innocently infantile sunnymindedness, or simply from fear of contemporary censorship. For if his troika were to be drawn by none but his own heroes, the Sobakeviches, Nozdryovs, and Chichikovs, then no matter who is sitting in the coachman's box, it would be impossible to arrive at anything sensible with such horses! And those were still former horses, a far cry from our own, ours are no comparison . . ."[5]

Here Ippolit Kirillovich's speech was interrupted by applause. They liked the liberalism of his depiction of the Russian troika. True, only two or three claps broke out, so that the presiding judge did not even find it necessary to address the public with a threat to "clear the court" and merely gave the clappers a stern look. But Ippolit Kirillovich was encouraged: never had he been applauded before! For so many years no one had wanted to listen to the man, and suddenly there came an opportunity to speak out for all Russia to hear!

"Indeed," he went on, "what is this Karamazov family that has suddenly gained such sad notoriety all over Russia? Perhaps I am greatly exaggerating, but it seems to me that certain basic, general elements of our modern-day educated society shine through, as it were, in the picture of this nice little family—oh, not all the elements, and they shine only microscopically, 'like to the sun in a small water-drop,'[6] yet something has been reflected, something has betrayed itself. Look at this wretched, unbridled, and depraved old man, this 'paterfamilias,' who has so sadly ended his existence. A nobleman by birth, starting out his career as a poor little sponger, who through an accidental and unexpected marriage grabs a small capital as a dowry, at first a petty cheat and flattering buffoon with a germ of mental capacity, a far from weak one, by the way, and above all a usurer. As the years go by—that is, as his capital grows—

he gets bolder. Self-deprecation and fawning disappear, only a jeering and wicked cynic and sensualist remains. The whole spiritual side has been scrapped, but there is an extraordinary thirst for life. In the end he sees nothing in life apart from sensual pleasure, and thus he teaches his children. Of the spiritual sort of fatherly duties—none at all. He laughs at them, he brings his little children up in the backyard and is glad when they are taken away from him. He even forgets about them altogether. The old man's whole moral rule is—*après moi le déluge*.[7] Everything contrary to the idea of a citizen, a complete, even hostile separation from society: 'Let the whole world burn, so long as I am all right.' And he is all right, he is perfectly content, he wants to live like that for another twenty or thirty years. He cheats his own son, and with the son's money, his maternal inheritance, which he does not want to give him, he takes his own son's mistress away. No, I have no intention of handing over the defense of the accused to the highly talented attorney from Petersburg. I myself can speak the truth, I myself understand the sum total of indignation he has stored up in his son's heart. But enough, enough of that unfortunate old man, he has his reward. Let us recall, however, that he is a father, and one of our modern-day fathers. Shall I offend society if I say that he is even one of many modern-day fathers? Alas, so many modern-day fathers simply do not speak their minds as cynically as this one did, for they are better bred, better educated, but essentially they are of almost the same philosophy as he. But allow that I am a pessimist, allow that I am. You will forgive me: that was our arrangement. Let us settle it beforehand: do not believe me, do not believe me, I shall speak, but do not believe me. But still let me speak my mind, still you may remember a little something of what I say. Now, however, we come to the children of this old man, this paterfamilias: one of them stands before us in the dock, we shall have much to say of him later; the others I shall mention only in passing. The elder of the two is one of our modern young men, brilliantly educated, with quite a powerful mind, who, however, no longer believes in anything, who has already scrapped and rejected much, too much in life, exactly as his father had done. We have all heard him, he was received amicably in our society. He did not conceal his opinions, even the opposite, quite the opposite, which now emboldens me to speak of him somewhat frankly, not as a private person, of course, but only as a member of the Karamazov family. Yesterday a certain sick idiot died here, on the outskirts of our town, by suicide; a person much involved in the present case, the former servant and, perhaps, illegitimate son of Fyodor Pavlovich, Smerdyakov. In the preliminary investigation he told me, with hysterical tears, how this young Karamazov, Ivan Fyodorovich, had horrified him with his spiritual unrestraint. 'Everything, according to him, is permitted, whatever there is in the world, and from now on nothing should be forbidden—that's what he kept teaching me about.' It seems that this thesis, which he was taught, ultimately caused the idiot to lose his mind, though, of course, his mental disorder was also affected by his falling sickness, and by this whole terrible catastrophe that had broken out in their house. But this idiot let drop one very, very curious remark, which would do honor even to a more intelligent observer, and that is why I am mentioning it now: 'If,' he said to me, 'any one of the sons most resembles Fyodor Pavlovich in character, it is him, Ivan Fyodorovich!' At this remark I shall interrupt the characterization I have begun, considering it indelicate to continue further. Oh, I do not want to draw any further conclusions and, like the raven, only croak ruin over a young fate. We have just seen, here in this hall, that the direct force of the truth still lives in his young heart, that the feeling of family loyalty has not yet been stifled in him by unbelief and moral cynicism, acquired more as an inheritance than through real mental suffering. Now the other son—oh, still a youth, pious and humble, who, in contrast to the dark, corrupting world view of his brother, seeks to cling to 'popular foundations,' so to speak, or to what goes by that clever name among us in certain theoretical corners of our thinking intelligentsia. He clung to the monastery, you see; he all but became a monk himself. In him, it seems to me, unconsciously, as it were, and so early on, there betrayed itself that timid despair that leads so many in our poor society, fearing its cynicism and depravity, and mistakenly ascribing all evil to European enlightenment, to throw themselves, as they put it, to the 'native soil,' so to speak, into the motherly embrace of the native earth, like children frightened by ghosts, who even at the dried-up breast of a paralyzed mother wish only to fall peacefully asleep and even to sleep for the rest of their lives, simply not to see the horrors that frighten them. For my part, I wish the good and gifted young man all the best, I hope that his youthful brightheartedness and yearning for popular foundations will not turn later, as so often happens, into dark mysticism on the moral side, and witless chauvinism on the civic side[8]—two qualities that perhaps threaten more evil for the nation than even the premature corruption owing to a falsely understood and gratuitously acquired European enlightenment from which his elder brother suffers."

Mysticism and chauvinism again drew two or three claps. And of course Ippolit Kirillovich had gotten carried away, and all this scarcely suited the present case, to say nothing of its being rather vague, but this consumptive and embittered man had too great a desire to speak his whole mind at least once in his life. It was said afterwards that in characterizing Ivan Fyodorovich, he had even been prompted by an indelicate feeling, because the young man had publicly snubbed him once or twice in argument, and Ippolit Kirillovich, remembering it, now desired to have his revenge. But I do not know that it is possible to draw such a conclusion. In any event, all this was merely a preamble, and further on the speech became more direct and to the point.

"But now we have the third son of this father of a modern-day family," Ippolit Kirillovich continued. "He is in the dock, he stands before us. Before us also stand his deeds, his life and acts: the hour has come, and everything has been unfolded, everything has been revealed. In contrast to the 'Europeanism' and the 'popular foundations' of his brothers, he seems to represent ingenuous Russia—oh, not all, not all, and God forbid it should be all! Yet she is here, our dear mother Russia, we can smell her, we can hear her. Oh, we are ingenuous, we are an amazing mixture of good and evil, we are lovers of enlightenment and Schiller, and at the same time we rage in taverns and tear out the beards of little drunkards, our tavern mates. Oh, we can also be good and beautiful, but only when we are feeling good and beautiful ourselves. We are, on the contrary, even possessed—precisely possessed—by the noblest ideals, but only on condition that they be attained by themselves, that they fall on our plate from the sky, and, above all, gratuitously, gratuitously, so that we need pay nothing for them. We like very much to get things, but terribly dislike having to pay for them, and so it is with everything. Oh, give us, give us all possible good things in life (precisely all, we won't settle for less) and, more particularly, do not obstruct our character in any way, and then we, too, will prove that we can be good and beautiful. We are not greedy, no, but give us money, more and more money, as much money as possible, and then you will see how generously, with what scorn for filthy lucre, we can throw it away in one night of unrestrained carousing. And if we are not given any money, we will show how we manage to get it anyway when we want it badly enough. But of that later—let us take things in order. First of all, we see a poor, neglected boy, 'in the backyard, without any shoes,' as it was just put by our venerable and respected citizen—alas, of foreign origin! Once more I repeat, I yield to no one in defending the accused. I am prosecutor, but also defender. Yes, we, too, are human and are able to weigh the influence on a man's character of the earliest impressions of childhood and the parental nest. But then the boy becomes a youth, a young man, an officer; for riotous conduct, for a challenge to a duel, he is exiled to one of the remote frontier towns of our bounteous Russia. There he serves, there he carouses, and of course a big ship needs a big sea. We need money, money above all, and so, after a long dispute, he and his father agree on a final six thousand, which is sent to him. Note that he signed this document, that this letter exists in which he all but renounces everything, and on payment of this six thousand ends his dispute with his father over the inheritance. Here occurs his encounter with a young girl of lofty character and development. Oh, I dare not repeat the details, you have only just heard them: here is honor, here is selflessness, I shall say no more. The image of a young man, thoughtless and depraved, who nonetheless bows to true nobility, to a lofty idea, flashed before us extremely sympathetically. But suddenly, after that, in this same courtroom, the other side of the coin followed quite unexpectedly. Again I dare not venture to guess, and will refrain from analyzing, why it followed thus. And yet there were reasons why it followed thus. This same person, all in tears from her long-concealed indignation, declares to us that he, he himself, was the first to despise her for her perhaps imprudent and impetuous, but all the same lofty and magnanimous impulse. It was in him, in this girl's fiancé, before anyone else, that this derisive smile flashed, which from him alone she could not endure. Knowing that he had already betrayed her (betrayed her in the prior conviction that now she must bear with him in everything, even in his betrayal), knowing this, she deliberately offers him three thousand roubles, and clearly, all too clearly, lets him understand that she is offering him money to betray her: 'Well, will you take it or not, will you be so cynical?' she says to him silently with her probing and accusing eyes. He looks at her, he understands her thoughts perfectly (he himself confessed here before you that he understood everything), and without reservation he appropriates the three thousand and squanders it in two days with his new sweetheart! What are we to believe, then? The first legend—the impulse of a lofty nobility giving its last worldly means and bowing down before virtue, or the other side of the coin, which is so repugnant? It is usually so in life that when there are two opposites one must look for truth in the middle; in the present case it is literally not so. Most likely in the first instance he was sincerely noble, and in the second just as sincerely base. Why? Precisely because we are of a broad, Karamazovian nature—and this is what I am driving at—capable of containing all possible opposites and of contemplating both abysses at once, the abyss above us, an abyss of lofty ideals, and the abyss beneath us, an abyss of the lowest and foulest degradation. Recall the brilliant thought expressed earlier by a young observer who has profoundly and closely contemplated the whole Karamazov family, Mr. Rakitin: 'A sense of the lowness of degradation is as necessary for these unbridled, unrestrained natures as the sense of the loftiest nobility'—and it is true: they precisely need this unnatural mixture, constantly and ceaselessly. Two abysses, two abysses, gentlemen, in one and the same moment—without that we are wretched and dissatisfied, our existence is incomplete. We are broad, broad as our whole mother Russia, we will embrace everything and get along with everything! Incidentally, gentlemen of the jury, we have now touched on these three thousand roubles, and I shall take the liberty of getting somewhat ahead of myself. Simply imagine him, this broad nature, having obtained this money—in such a way, through such shame, such disgrace, such uttermost humiliation—simply imagine him supposedly being capable that same day of setting aside half of it, of sewing it into an amulet, and being firm enough after that to carry it around his neck for a whole month, despite all temptations and extreme needs! Not while drinking riotously in the taverns, not when flying out of town to get, God knows from whom, the money he so badly needed to save his sweetheart from seduction by his rival, his own father—would he venture to touch this amulet. But if only precisely not to leave her to the seduction of the old man of whom he was so jealous, he ought to have opened his amulet and stayed home to keep relentless watch over his sweetheart, waiting for the moment when she would finally say to him: 'I am yours,' and he would fly off with her somewhere far away from the present fatal situation. But no, he would not touch his talisman, and on what pretext? The original pretext was, we have said, precisely so that when he was told: 'I am yours, take me wherever you like,' he would have the wherewithal to take her. But this first pretext, according to the defendant's own words, paled beside the second one. As long as I carry this money on myself, he said, 'I am a scoundrel, but not a thief,' for I can always go to my insulted fiancée and, laying before her this half of the whole sum I fraudulently appropriated, I can always say to her: 'You see, I squandered half of your money, and proved thereby that I am a weak and immoral man, a scoundrel if you like' (I am using the defendant's own language), 'but even if I am a scoundrel, I am still not a thief, for if I were a thief, I would not have brought you this remaining half of the money, but would have appropriated it as I did the first half.' An astonishing explanation of the fact! This most violent but weak man, who was unable to resist the temptation of accepting the three thousand roubles along with such disgrace—this same man suddenly finds in himself such stoic firmness that he can carry thousands of roubles around his neck without venturing to touch them! Is this even slightly congruous with the character we are analyzing? No, and I shall permit myself to tell you how the real Dmitri Karamazov would have acted in such a case, even if he had indeed decided to sew his money into an amulet. At the very first temptation—say, again to provide some entertainment for this same new sweetheart with whom he had already squandered the first half of the money—he would undo his amulet and take out, well, maybe just a hundred roubles to begin with, for why should he need to return exactly half, that is, fifteen hundred—fourteen hundred will do, it comes to the same thing: 'a scoundrel, but not a thief, because I've at least brought back fourteen hundred, and a thief would have taken it all and brought back nothing.' Then in a little while he would undo the amulet again, and take out a second hundred, then a third, then a fourth, and by no later than the end of the month he would have taken out all but the last hundred: so I'll bring back a hundred, it comes to the same thing: 'a scoundrel, but not a thief. I squandered twenty-nine hundred, but I've brought back one at least, a thief would not have done that.' And finally, having squandered all but the last hundred, he would look at that last hundred and say to himself: 'But there's really no point in giving a hundred back—why don't I squander this, too!' That is how the real Dmitri Karamazov, as we know him, would have acted. But as for the legend of this amulet—it is hard even to imagine anything more contrary to reality. One can suppose anything but that. But we shall come back to that later."

After mentioning in order everything the investigation had disclosed about the property dispute and the family relations between father and son, and having again and again drawn the conclusion that, from the facts available, there was not the slightest possibility of determining who had outdone whom or who had been done out of what in this question of the property division, Ippolit Kirillovich brought up the medical opinions concerning the three thousand roubles stuck as a fixed idea in Mitya's mind.

Chapter 7

A Historical Survey

"The medical experts strove to prove to us that the defendant is out of his mind and a maniac. I insist that he is precisely in his right mind, and so much the worse for him: had it not been his mind, he might have turned out to be much more intelligent. As for his being a maniac, I am prepared to agree, but precisely on one point only—that same point the experts indicated, precisely the defendant's view of the three thousand roubles supposedly left owing to him by his father. Nevertheless, it may be possible to find an incomparably closer point of view than his inclination to madness to explain the defendant's constant frenzy with regard to this money. For my part, I agree completely with the opinion of the young doctor who found that the defendant is and was in full and normal possession of his mental faculties, but has simply been exasperated and embittered. And that is just it: the object of the defendant's constant and frenzied bitterness consisted not in the three thousand, not in the sum itself, but in the fact that there was a special reason that provoked his wrath. That reason was—jealousy!"

Here Ippolit Kirillovich unfolded at length the whole picture of the defendant's fatal passion for Grushenka. He began from the very moment when the defendant went to "the young person" in order "to give her a beating"—in his own words, Ippolit Kirillovich commented—"but instead of beating her, he stays there at her feet—that is the beginning of this love. At the same time the old man, the defendant's father, also sets his eye on the same person—a coincidence both surprising and fatal, for both hearts caught fire suddenly, simultaneously, though they had met and known this person before—and both hearts caught fire with the most unrestrained, the most Karamazovian passion. Here we have her own confession: 'I laughed,' she says, 'at both of them.' Yes, she suddenly wanted to laugh at the two of them; she had not wanted to before, but now suddenly this intention flew into her mind—and the end of it was that they both fell conquered before her. The old man, who worshipped money as if it were God, at once prepared three thousand roubles if she would only just visit his abode, but was soon driven to the point where he would have considered it happiness to lay his name and all his property at her feet if only she would consent to become his lawful wife. For this we have firm evidence. As for the defendant, his tragedy is obvious, it stands before us. But such was this young person's 'game.' The seductress did not even give any hope to the unfortunate young man, for hope, real hope, was given him only at the very last moment, when he, kneeling before his tormentress, stretched out to her his hands already stained with the blood of his father and rival: precisely in that position he was arrested. 'Send me, send me to hard labor with him, I drove him to it, I am the guiltiest of all!'—this woman herself exclaimed, in sincere repentance, at the moment of his arrest. The talented young man who has taken it upon himself to write about the present case—the same Mr. Rakitin whom I have already mentioned—defines this heroine's character in a few concise and characteristic phrases: 'Early disappointment, early deception and fall, the treachery of a fiancé-seducer who abandoned her, then poverty, the curses of a respectable family, and, finally, the patronage of a rich old man, whom she herself incidentally regards even now as her benefactor. Anger was buried far too early in a young heart, which perhaps contained much good. What formed was a calculating, money-hoarding character. What formed was a derisive and vengeful attitude towards society.' After such a characterization one can understand how she might laugh at the two of them simply as a game, a vicious game. And so, during this month of hopeless love, of moral degradation, of betrayal of his fiancée, of appropriation of another person's money, which was entrusted to his honor—the defendant, on top of that, was driven almost to frenzy, almost to fury, by continual jealousy, and of whom—of his own father! Worst of all, the crazy old man was luring and seducing the object of his passion with the very three thousand that he regarded as his family money, his maternal inheritance, for which he reproached his father. Yes, I agree, this was hard to bear! Here even a mania might appear. The point was not the money, but that by means of this very money his happiness was being shattered with such loathsome cynicism!"

Ippolit Kirillovich then went on to tell how the thought of killing his father gradually emerged in the defendant, and traced it fact by fact.

"At first we only shout in the taverns—shout all that month. Oh, we love to live among people and to inform these people at once of everything, even our most infernal and dangerous ideas; we like sharing with people, and, who knows why, we demand immediately, on the spot, that these people respond to us at once with the fullest sympathy, enter into all our cares and concerns, nod in agreement with us, and never cross our humor. Otherwise we will get angry and wreck the whole tavern." (There followed the anecdote about Captain Snegiryov.) "Those who saw and heard the defendant during this month felt finally that these were not mere shouts and threats against his father, but that, considering the frenzied state he was in, the threats might become reality." (Here the prosecutor described the family meeting in the monastery, the conversations with Alyosha, and the ugly scene of violence in his father's house when the defendant burst in after dinner.) "I do not mean to assert emphatically," Ippolit Kirillovich continued, "that before this scene the defendant had already determined deliberately and premeditatedly to do away with his father by murdering him. Nevertheless the idea had already presented itself to him several times, and he deliberately contemplated it—for that we have facts, witnesses, and his own confession. I must admit, gentlemen of the jury," Ippolit Kirillovich added, "that even until today I was hesitant whether to ascribe to the defendant complete and conscious premeditation of the crime that was suggesting itself to him. I was firmly convinced that his soul had already contemplated many times the fatal moment ahead, but merely contemplated it, imagined it only as a possibility, without settling either on the time or the circumstances of its accomplishment. But I was hesitant only until today, until this fatal document was presented to the court today by Miss Verkhovtsev. You heard her exclamation yourselves, gentlemen: 'This is the plan, this is the program of the murder!'—thus she defined the unfortunate 'drunken' letter of the unfortunate defendant. And indeed this letter bears all the significance of a program and of premeditation. It was written two days before the crime, and thus we now know firmly that two days before accomplishing his horrible design, the defendant declared with an oath that if he did not get the money the next day, he would kill his father, so as to take the money from under his pillow, 'in the envelope with the red ribbon, if only Ivan goes away.' Do you hear: 'if only Ivan goes away'—so everything had been thought out, the circumstances had been weighed—and what then? It was all accomplished as written! Premeditation and deliberateness are beyond doubt, the crime was to be carried out for the purpose of robbery, that is stated directly, it is written and signed. The defendant does not deny his signature. I shall be told: it was written by a drunk man. But that diminishes nothing, it makes it all the more important: he wrote when drunk what he had planned when sober. Had he not planned it when sober, he would not have written about it when drunk. I shall perhaps be asked: why was he shouting about his intentions in the taverns? If a man determines to do such a thing *with premeditation*, he is silent and keeps it to himself. True, but he shouted when there was no plan or premeditation as yet, when just the desire alone was present, a yearning that was ripening. Later on he did not shout so much about it. On the evening when this letter was written, having gotten drunk in the 'Metropolis' tavern, he was silent, contrary to his custom, did not play billiards, sat apart, spoke to no one, and only chased a local shop clerk from his seat, but this he did almost unconsciously, from a habit of quarreling, which he could not do without anytime he entered a tavern. True, along with his final determination, the fear must have occurred to the defendant that he had shouted around town too much beforehand and that it would go a long way towards exposing and accusing him once he had carried out his plan. But there was no help for it, the fact of publication had been accomplished, it could not be taken back, and, after all, things had always worked out before, so they would work out now as well. We set our hopes on our lucky star, gentlemen! I must admit, furthermore, that he did a lot to get around the fatal moment, that he exerted much effort to avoid the bloody outcome. 'Tomorrow I'll ask all people for the three thousand,' as he writes in his peculiar language, 'and if I don't get it from people, blood will be shed.' Again it was written in a drunken state, and again in a sober state it was accomplished as written!"

Here Ippolit Kirillovich embarked on a detailed description of all Mitya's efforts to obtain the money, in order to avoid the crime. He described his adventures with Samsonov, his journey to Lyagavy—all of it documented. "Worn out, ridiculed, hungry, having sold his watch for the journey (but still keeping the fifteen hundred roubles on him—supposedly, oh, supposedly!), tortured by jealousy over the object of his love, whom he had left in town, suspecting that without him she would go to Fyodor Pavlovich, he finally returns to town. Thank God, she has not been with Fyodor Pavlovich! He himself takes her to her patron Samsonov. (Strangely, we are not jealous of Samsonov, and this is a rather typical psychological peculiarity of this case!) Then he races to his observation post 'in the backyard' and there—and there discovers that Smerdyakov is down with a falling fit, that the other servant is sick—the field is clear, and the 'signals' are in his hands—what a temptation! Nevertheless he still resists; he goes to Madame Khokhlakov, a temporary local resident greatly respected by us all. Having long felt compassion for his fate, this lady offers him the most reasonable advice: to drop all this carousing, this outrageous love affair, this idling in taverns, the fruitless waste of his young strength, and go to Siberia, to the gold mines: 'There is an outlet for your stormy strength, your romantic character yearning for adventure.'" Having described the outcome of that conversation, and the moment when the defendant suddenly received word that Grushenka had not stayed at Samsonov's at all, having described the instantaneous frenzy of the unfortunate, jealous, overwrought man at the thought that she had precisely deceived him and was now there, with Fyodor Pavlovich, Ippolit Kirillovich concluded by drawing attention to the fatal significance of chance: "If the maid had managed to tell him that his sweetheart was in Mokroye with the 'former' and 'indisputable' one—nothing would have happened. But she was overcome with fright, began vowing and swearing, and if the defendant did not kill her right then, it was only because he rushed headlong after his traitoress. But observe: beside himself as he may have been, he did take the brass pestle with him. Why precisely the pestle, why not some other weapon? But since we have been contemplating this picture for a whole month and preparing for it, the moment anything resembling a weapon flashes before us, we grab it as a weapon. And that some such object might serve as a weapon—this we have already been imagining for a whole month. That is why we recognized it so instantly and unquestionably as a weapon! Therefore it was by no means unconsciously, by no means inadvertently that he grabbed this fatal pestle. And now he is in his father's garden—the field is clear, no witnesses, the dead of night, darkness, and jealousy. The suspicion that she is there, with his rival, in his arms, and perhaps is laughing at him that very minute—takes his breath away. And not merely the suspicion—why talk of suspicion, when the deception is evident, obvious: she is there, in that room, where the light is coming from, she is with him behind the screen—and so the unfortunate man steals up to the window, respectfully peeks in, virtuously resigns himself, and sensibly departs, hastening to put trouble behind him, lest something dangerous and immoral happen—and we are asked to believe this, we who know the defendant's character, who understand what state of mind he was in, a state we know from the facts, and, above all, that he was in possession of the signals with which he could open the house at once and go in!" Here, apropos the "signals," Ippolit Kirillovich left off his accusatory speech for a time, finding it necessary to expatiate on Smerdyakov, so as to exhaust completely this whole parenthetic episode to do with suspecting Smerdyakov of the murder, and have done with the idea once and for all. He did so quite thoroughly, and everyone understood that, despite the contempt he showed for this suggestion, he still considered it very important.

Chapter 8

A Treatise on Smerdyakov

"First of all, where did the possibility of such a suspicion come from?" was the question with which Ippolit Kirillovich began. "The first one to cry out against Smerdyakov as the murderer was the defendant himself at the moment of his arrest, and yet, from that very first cry down to this very moment of the trial, he has failed to present even one fact to confirm his accusation—and not only no fact, but not even the ghost of a fact to any degree congruous with human reason. Then, the accusation is confirmed by only three persons: the defendant's two brothers and Miss Svetlov. Yet the defendant's older brother announced his suspicion only today, when he was ill, in a fit of unquestionable delirium and fever, while previously, for the whole two months, as is positively known to us, he fully shared the conviction of his brother's guilt and did not even attempt to object to the idea. But we shall go into that more particularly later on. Then, the defendant's younger brother announces to us today that he has no facts, not even the slightest, to support his notion of Smerdyakov's guilt, and that his conclusion is based only on the words of the defendant himself and 'the look on his face'—yes, this colossal proof was uttered twice today by his brother. And Miss Svetlov expressed herself perhaps even more colossally: 'Whatever the defendant tells you, you must believe, he's not the sort of man to lie.' That is the sum total of factual evidence against Smerdyakov produced by these three persons, who are only too interested in the defendant's fate. Nevertheless the accusation against Smerdyakov made its way and held out, and is still holding out—can you believe it, can you imagine it?"

Here Ippolit Kirillovich found it necessary to sketch briefly the character of the late Smerdyakov, "who put an end to his life in a fit of morbid delirium and madness." He portrayed him as a feebleminded man with the rudiments of some vague education, who was confused by philosophical ideas that were too much for his mind, and frightened by certain modern-day teachings on duty and obligation, extensively offered him in practice by the devil-may-care life of his late master, and perhaps also father, Fyodor Pavlovich, and in theory by various strange philosophical conversations with the master's elder son, Ivan Fyodorovich, who readily allowed himself this diversion—most likely out of boredom or a need for mockery that could find no better application. "He himself described to me the state of his soul during the last days of his life in his master's house," Ippolit Kirillovich explained, "but others, too, have given the same testimony: the defendant himself, his brother, even the servant Grigory, all those, that is, who must have known him quite well. Being oppressed, moreover, by the falling sickness, Smerdyakov was 'cowardly as a chicken.' 'He used to fall at my feet and kiss them,' the defendant told us at a time when he had not yet realized that such information was hardly beneficial to him. 'It's a chicken with falling sickness,' as he put it in his characteristic language. And it is him that the defendant (he testifies to it himself) chooses as his confidant, and bullies into agreeing to serve him as a spy and informer. In this capacity of domestic rat, he betrays his master, he tells the defendant both about the existence of the envelope with the money and about the signals that would enable one to get into the master's house—and how could he not tell! 'He'd kill me, sir, I just saw that he'd kill me, sir,' he kept saying in the interrogation, shaking and trembling even before us, notwithstanding that the tormentor who bullied him was then already under arrest and could no longer come and punish him. 'He suspected me every minute, sir; in fear and trembling, just to satisfy his wrath, I hastened to tell him about every secret, sir, just so he could see my innocence before him, sir, and let me go in peace with my life, sir.' These are his own words, I wrote them down and remembered them: 'He'd start yelling at me, and I'd just fall on my knees before him.' Being a highly honest young man by nature, and having thereby gained the trust of his master, who recognized this honesty in him when he returned the lost money, the unfortunate Smerdyakov was, one can only think, terribly tormented by remorse at his betrayal of his master, whom he loved as his benefactor. People severely afflicted with the falling sickness, according to the findings of the profoundest psychiatrists, are always inclined to constant and, of course, morbid self-accusation. They suffer from their 'guilt' for something and before someone, are tormented by pangs of conscience; often, even without any grounds, they exaggerate and even invent various guilts and crimes for themselves. And now one such individual, from fear and bullying, becomes guilty and criminal in reality. Moreover, he strongly anticipated that something bad might come of the circumstances taking shape before his eyes. When the elder son of Fyodor Pavlovich, Ivan Fyodorovich, was leaving for Moscow, just before the catastrophe, Smerdyakov begged him to stay, although, following his cowardly custom, he did not dare voice all his apprehensions clearly and categorically. He contented himself merely with hints, but these hints were not understood. It should be noted that he saw in Ivan Fyodorovich his protection, as it were, his guarantee, as it were, that as long as he stayed at home, no disaster would occur. Recall the phrase in the 'drunken' letter of Dmitri Karamazov: 'I'll kill the old man, if only Ivan goes away'; meaning that the presence of Ivan Fyodorovich seemed to everyone a guarantee of peace and order in the house, as it were. But then he leaves, and at once, scarcely an hour after the young master's departure, Smerdyakov comes down with a falling fit. That is perfectly understandable. It should be mentioned here that Smerdyakov, oppressed by fears and despair of a sort, during those last days especially felt in himself the possibility of an impending attack of the falling sickness, which before, too, had always come upon him in moments of moral tension and shock. It is, of course, impossible to foresee the day and hour of such an attack, but every epileptic can feel in himself beforehand a disposition towards an attack. This medical science tells us. And so, as soon as Ivan Fyodorovich quits the place, Smerdyakov, under the impression of his, so to speak, orphaned and defenseless state, goes to the cellar on a household errand, thinking as he starts down the stairs: 'Will I have a fit or not, and what if it comes now?' And so, precisely because of this mood, this insecurity, these questions, the spasm in the throat, which always precedes a falling fit, seizes him, and he topples headlong, unconscious, into the bottom of the cellar. And people manage to see something suspicious in this perfectly natural accident, some sort of clue, some sort of hint that he was *deliberately* pretending to be sick! But if it was deliberate, the question immediately arises: what for? Out of what calculation, with what aim? I am not speaking of medicine now; science lies, they say, science makes mistakes, the doctors were unable to distinguish truth from pretense—maybe so, maybe so, but all the same answer my question: why would he pretend? Could it be that, having planned the murder, he wanted in advance and at once to attract attention to himself in the house by having a fit? You see, gentlemen of the jury, there were five people in and around Fyodor Pavlovich's house on the night of the crime: first, Fyodor Pavlovich himself, but he could not have killed himself, that is clear; second, his servant Grigory, but he himself was almost killed; third, Grigory's wife, the serving-woman Marfa

Ignatieva, but it is simply shameful to imagine her as her master's murderer. Thus two people are left in view: the defendant, and Smerdyakov. But the defendant insists it was not he who killed his father, so Smerdyakov must have killed him, there is no other solution, for there is no one else to be found, there is no way to pick another murderer. Here, here then is the source of this 'cunning' and colossal accusation against the unfortunate idiot who yesterday took his own life! Precisely for the simple reason that there is no one else to pick! Were there at least a shadow, at least a suspicion of someone else, some sixth person, I am sure that in that case even the defendant himself would be ashamed to point to Smerdyakov, and would point to this sixth person instead, for to accuse Smerdyakov of this murder is utterly absurd.

"Let us lay aside psychology, gentlemen, let us lay aside medicine, let us lay aside even logic itself, let us turn just to the facts, simply to the facts alone, and let us see what the facts will tell us. Smerdyakov killed him, but how? Alone or together with the defendant? Let us first consider the first alternative—that is, that Smerdyakov was working alone. Of course, if he did kill him, it was with some object, for some sort of profit. But, not having even the shadow of a motive for murder such as the defendant had—that is, hatred, jealousy, and so on and so forth—Smerdyakov would undoubtedly have killed only for the sake of money, in order to appropriate precisely the three thousand roubles he had seen his master put into the envelope. And so, having planned the murder, he informs another person beforehand—a highly interested person, moreover, namely, the defendant—of all the circumstances to do with the money and the signals: where the envelope lay, what exactly was written on it, how it was tied, and above all, above all, he tells him about these 'signals' by which one can get into his master's house. Why does he do it? To betray himself straight off? Or so as to have a rival, who perhaps will want to get in and acquire the envelope himself? No, I shall be told, he did it out of fear. But how could that be? A man who did not shrink from planning such a fearless and beastly thing and then carrying it out, gives away information that he alone in the whole world knows, and that, if he had only kept silent about it, no one in the whole world would have found out? No, however cowardly the man might be, if he were planning such a thing, he would never tell anyone about the envelope and the signals, for that would mean giving himself away beforehand. He would deliberately invent something, some lie or other, if he absolutely had to give information, but he would be silent about that! On the contrary, I repeat, if he kept silent about the money at least, and then went and killed and appropriated the money for himself, no one in the whole world would in any case ever be able to accuse him of murder for the sake of robbery, because no one but he would have seen the money, no one else would have known it was there in the house. Even if he were accused, it would inevitably be thought that he had killed from some other motive. But since no one ever noticed any such motive in him before, and everyone saw, on the contrary, that he was loved by his master and honored with his trust, then of course he would be the last to be suspected, and the one to be suspected would be the one who had such motives, who himself shouted that he had such motives, who did not conceal them, who revealed them to everyone, in short, the one to be suspected would be the murdered man's son, Dmitri Fyodorovich. Smerdyakov would have committed the murder and robbery, and the son would be accused of it—surely this would be advantageous for Smerdyakov, the murderer? Well, and it is this son Dmitri that Smerdyakov, having planned the murder, tells beforehand about the money, the envelope, and the signals—how clear, how logical it is!

"The day of the murder planned by Smerdyakov comes, and so he goes tumbling into the cellar, shamming an attack of the falling sickness—what for? But, of course, so that first of all the servant Grigory, who was planning his treatment, seeing that there was absolutely no one to watch the house, would perhaps postpone his treatment and stand guard himself. Second, naturally, so that the master himself, seeing that no one was on guard, and being terribly afraid of his son's coming, which he did not conceal, would be twice as mistrustful and cautious. Finally, and above all, so that of course he, Smerdyakov, brought down by the fit, would at once be transferred from the kitchen, where he always slept apart from everyone and where he could come and go as he pleased, to the other end of the cottage, to Grigory's little room, behind the partition, three steps away from their own bed, as had always been done from time immemorial whenever he was brought down by the sickness, on the orders of his master and the tenderhearted Marfa Ignatievna. Of course, lying there behind the partition, he would most likely start groaning, in order to show himself truly sick, thereby waking them up throughout the night (as he did, according to the evidence of Grigory and his wife)—and all that, all that to make it more convenient for himself to get up suddenly and then kill his master!

"But, I shall be told, perhaps he pretended to be sick precisely so that no one would suspect him, and informed the defendant about the money and the signals precisely to tempt him into coming and killing him himself, and, don't you see, when he has killed him and leaves, taking the money with him, perhaps while doing so he will make some noise and clatter, awaking witnesses, and then, you see, Smerdyakov can also get up and go—well, what will he go and do? Why, he will precisely go and kill his master a second time, and a second time take the already-taken money. Do you laugh, gentlemen? Personally I am ashamed to make such suggestions, and yet, just imagine, this very thing is precisely what the defendant asserts: after me, he says, when I had already left the house, knocked Grigory down and raised the alarm, he got up, went in, killed, and robbed. I will not even ask how Smerdyakov could have calculated all this beforehand and foreknown it all as if on his fingers, I mean, that the furious and exasperated son would come with the sole purpose of peeking respectfully in the window, though he knew the signals, and then retreat, leaving him, Smerdyakov, with all the booty! Gentlemen, I put the question to you seriously: where is the moment when Smerdyakov committed his crime? Show me that moment, for without it there can be no accusation.

"But perhaps the falling fit was real. The sick man suddenly came to, heard a cry, went out—well, and what then? He looked around and said to himself: why don't I go and kill the master? But how would he know what was going on, what was happening there, if he had been lying unconscious up to then? No, gentlemen, fantasy, too, must have its limits.

" 'Well, sir,' subtle people will say, 'and what if the two were accomplices, what if they murdered him together and divided the money—what then?'

"Yes, indeed, that is a weighty suspicion, and, to begin with, there is colossal evidence to confirm it: one kills and takes all the labor upon himself, and the other accomplice lies on his back pretending to have a falling fit, precisely with the aim of arousing suspicion in everyone ahead of time, of alarming the master, of alarming Grigory. With what motives, I wonder, could the two accomplices have thought up precisely such an insane plan? But perhaps it was not at all an active complicity on Smerdyakov's part, but, so to speak, passive and suffering: perhaps the bullied Smerdyakov merely agreed not to resist the murder and, anticipating that he would be accused of allowing his master to be killed, of not shouting or resisting, negotiated with Dmitri Karamazov beforehand for permission to spend the time lying down as if in a falling fit, 'and you can go and kill him any way you like, it's none of my apples.' But even so, since this falling fit, again, would be bound to cause a commotion in the house, Dmitri Karamazov, foreseeing that, would by no means agree to such an arrangement. But suppose he did agree: in that case it would still come out that Dmitri Karamazov was the murderer, the direct murderer and instigator, while Smerdyakov would only be a passive participant, and not even a participant, but merely a conniver out of fear and against his will, as the court would surely discern—and yet what do we see? No sooner is the defendant arrested than he at once shifts all the blame onto Smerdyakov alone and accuses him *alone*. He does not accuse him as his accomplice, but him alone: he alone did it, he says, he killed him and robbed him, it is his handiwork! But what sort of accomplices are they, if they immediately start denouncing each other—no, that never happens. And notice the risk for Karamazov: he is the chief murderer, the other is not the chief one, he is merely a conniver, he was lying down behind the partition, and now he shifts it all onto the one lying down. But he, the one lying down, might get angry, and just for reasons of self-preservation alone might hasten to proclaim the real truth: we both participated, only I didn't kill him, I just went along and connived at it out of fear. For surely he, Smerdyakov, would be able to understand that the court would immediately perceive the degree of his guilt, and he could therefore reckon that if he were to be punished, it would be far less severely than the other one, the chief murderer, who wanted to shift it all onto him. Which means, then, that willy-nilly he would make a confession. This, however, we have not seen. Smerdyakov never so much as whispered about any complicity, despite the fact that the murderer firmly accused him, and kept pointing at him all along as the sole murderer. Moreover, it was Smerdyakov who revealed to the prosecution that *he himself* had informed the defendant of the envelope with the money and of the signals, and that without him he would never have known anything. If he was indeed an accomplice and guilty, would he inform the prosecution of it so lightly—that is, that he himself informed the defendant of all that? On the contrary, he would try to deny it, and would most certainly distort the facts and diminish them. But he did not distort and he did not diminish. Only an innocent man, who has no fear of being accused of complicity, would act that way. And so, yesterday, in a fit of morbid melancholy resulting from his falling sickness and the outbreak of this whole catastrophe, he hanged himself. And, hanging himself, he left a note, written in his own peculiar style: 'I exterminate myself by my own will and liking, so as not to blame anybody.' It would have cost him nothing to add: 'I am the murderer, not Karamazov.' But he did not add it: did he have enough conscience for the one thing, but not for the other?

"And now what? This afternoon money was brought into court, three thousand roubles—'the same,' we were told, 'that was here in this envelope, which is on the table with the material evidence; received yesterday from Smerdyakov,' we were told. But you yourselves, gentlemen of the jury, cannot have forgotten that sad picture. I will not go back over the details, but all the same I shall allow myself to make two or three observations, choosing from the most insignificant of them—precisely because they are insignificant, and so will not have occurred to everyone and might be forgotten. First, once again, we have Smerdyakov, yesterday, returning the money in remorse and hanging himself. (For without remorse he would not have returned the money.) And of course it was only yesterday evening that he confessed his crime for the first time to Ivan Karamazov, as Ivan Karamazov himself declared, otherwise why would he have been silent about it up to now? He confessed, then; but, I repeat once more, why did he not proclaim the whole truth to us in his dying note, knowing that the innocent defendant was going to his last judgment the very next day? The money alone is no proof. I, for example, and two other persons in this room, became acquainted with a certain fact quite by chance a week ago—namely, that Ivan Fyodorovich Karamazov sent two five-percent bank notes, for five thousand roubles each, that is, ten thousand in all, to the provincial capital to be cashed. All I mean to say is that anyone could happen to have money on a given day, and by producing three thousand one does not necessarily prove that it is the same money as lay precisely in some particular drawer or envelope. Finally, having received such important information from the real murderer yesterday, Ivan Karamazov kept still. Why did he not report it at once? Why did he put it off till the next morning? I suppose I have the right to guess why: his health had been unsettled for about a week, he himself confessed to the doctor and to those closest to him that he was having visions, meeting people who were already dead; on the verge of brain fever, which struck him precisely today, having learned unexpectedly of Smerdyakov's demise, he suddenly forms the following argument: 'The man is dead, he can be denounced, and I will save my brother. I have money: I'll take a wad of bills and say that Smerdyakov gave it to me before he died.' You will tell me it is dishonest; that even though the man is dead, it is still dishonest to lie, even to save a brother? Perhaps so, but what if he lied unconsciously, what if he himself imagined that it happened that way, his mind precisely being struck finally by the news of the lackey's sudden death? You did see that scene today, you saw what state the man was in. He stood here and spoke, but where was his mind? Today's testimony from a delirious man was followed by a document, the defendant's letter to Miss Verkhovtsev, written by him two days before he committed the crime, containing beforehand a detailed program of the crime. Why, then, are we looking for the program and its authors? It was accomplished exactly following this program, and accomplished by none other than its author. Yes, gentlemen of the jury, 'accomplished as written!' And in no case, in no case did we run respectfully and timidly from our father's window, being at the same time firmly convinced that our sweetheart was there with him. No, that is absurd and impossible. He went in and—finished the business. Very likely he killed him in exasperation, in anger, which flared up as soon as he looked at his foe and rival, but once he had killed him, which he probably did instantly, with one swing of the arm wielding the brass pestle, and made sure, after a thorough search, that she was not there, he still did not forget to slip his hand under the pillow and take the envelope with the money, the torn remains of which are lying here on the table with the material evidence. What I am getting at is that you should notice one circumstance, in my opinion a highly characteristic one. Were we dealing here with an experienced murderer, and precisely with a murderer whose sole purpose was robbery—well, would he have left the torn envelope on the floor, where it was found, next to the body? Were it Smerdyakov, for example, killing for the sake of robbery—why, he would simply have taken the whole envelope with him, without bothering in the least to open it over his victim's body; because he knew for certain that the money was in the envelope—it had been put there and sealed in his presence—and if he had taken the envelope away altogether, would anyone even know there had been a robbery? I ask you, gentlemen of the jury, would Smerdyakov have acted this way? Would he have left the envelope on the floor? No, that is precisely how a frenzied murderer would act, one who is not thinking well, a murderer who is not a thief, who has never stolen anything before, and who even now snatches the money from under the bed not as a thief stealing, but as someone taking his own back from the thief who has stolen it—for that is precisely the idea Dmitri Karamazov had of those three thousand roubles, which had become almost a mania with him. And so, taking hold of this envelope, which he has never seen before, he tears it open to make sure the money is there, then runs away with the money in his pocket, forgetting even to think that he is leaving behind a colossal accusation against himself in the form of a torn envelope lying on the floor. All because it was Karamazov, not Smerdyakov; he did not think, he did not see, and how could he! He runs away, he hears the shout of the servant overtaking him, the servant seizes him, stops him, and falls, struck down by the brass pestle. The defendant jumps down to him . . . out of pity. Imagine, he suddenly assures us that he jumped down to him then out of pity, out of compassion, in order to see if he could help him in some way. But was that any moment to be showing such compassion? No, he jumped down precisely in order to make sure that the only witness to his evil deed was no longer alive. Any other feeling, any other motive would be unnatural! Notice, he takes trouble over Grigory, he wipes his head with a handkerchief, and, convinced that he is dead, he runs, out of his senses, all covered with blood, there, to the house of his sweetheart—how did it not occur to him that he was covered with blood and would give himself away at once? But the defendant himself assures us that he never even noticed he was covered with blood; that is conceivable, that is very possible, that always happens with criminals in such moments. Devilish calculation in the one case, and in the other no discernment at all. But his only thought at that moment was of where *she* was. He had to find out quickly where she was, and so he runs to her place and learns some unexpected and colossal news: she has gone to Mokroye with her 'former,' 'indisputable' one!"

Chapter 9

Psychology at Full Steam. The Galloping Troika. The Finale of the Prosecutor's Speech

Having come thus far in his speech, Ippolit Kirillovich, who had evidently chosen a strictly historical method of accounting, which is a favorite resort of all nervous orators who purposely seek a strict framework in order to restrain their own impatient zeal—Ippolit Kirillovich expanded particularly on the "former" and "indisputable" one, and on this topic expressed several rather amusing thoughts. "Karamazov, who was jealous of everyone to the point of frenzy, suddenly and instantly collapses and vanishes, as it were, before the 'former' and 'indisputable' one. And it is all the more strange in that previously he had paid almost no attention to this new threat to himself, coming in the person of this, for him, unexpected rival. But his notion had always been that it was all still very far off, and a Karamazov always lives in the present moment. Most likely he even considered him a fiction. But having understood at once in his sick heart that the woman had perhaps been concealing this new rival, that she had deceived him that same day, precisely because this newly emerged rival, so far from being a fantasy or a fiction, constituted all for her—all her hopes in life—having instantly understood this, he resigned himself. Indeed, gentlemen of the jury, I cannot pass over in silence this sudden streak in the soul of the defendant, who seemed to be totally incapable of manifesting it; there suddenly arose in him an inexorable need for truth, a respect for woman, an acknowledgement of the rights of her heart, and when?—at the very moment when, because of her, he had stained his hands with his father's blood! It is also true that the spilt blood was at that moment already crying out for revenge, for he, having ruined his soul and all his earthly destiny, could not help feeling and asking himself at the same time: 'What does he mean and what could he mean *now* to her, to this being whom he loved more than his own soul, compared with this "former" and "indisputable" one, who had repented and returned to the woman he had ruined once, with new love, with honest offers, with the promise of a restored and now happy life? And he, unfortunate man, what could he give her *now*, what could he offer her?' Karamazov understood it all, he understood that all paths were closed to him by his crime, and that he was just a criminal under sentence and not a man with a life ahead of him! This thought crushed and destroyed him. And so he instantly fixes on a wild plan that, considering Karamazov's character, could not but seem to him the only and fatal way out of his terrible situation. This way out was suicide. He runs for his pistols, which he had pawned to the official Perkhotin, and at the same time, as he runs, he pulls all his money out of his pocket, for which he had just spattered his hands with his father's blood. Oh, money is what he needs most of all now: Karamazov dies, Karamazov shoots himself, this will be remembered! Not for nothing are we a poet, not for nothing have we been burning our life like a candle at both ends. 'To her, to her—and there, there I will put on a feast, a feast such as the world has never seen, to be remembered and talked about long after. Amid wild shouts, mad gypsy singing and dancing, we will raise a cup and toast the new happiness of the woman we adore, and then—right there, at her feet, we will blow our brains out before her, and punish our life! Some day she will remember Mitya Karamazov, she will see how Mitya loved her, she will feel sorry for Mitya!' There is a good deal of posturing here, of romantic frenzy, of wild Karamazovian unrestraint and sentimentality—yes, and also something else, gentlemen of the jury, something that cries out in the soul, that throbs incessantly in his mind, and poisons his heart unto death; this *something* is conscience, gentlemen of the jury, the judgment, the terrible pangs of conscience! But the pistol will reconcile everything, the pistol is the only way out, there is no other, and beyond—I do not know whether Karamazov thought at that moment of '*what lies beyond*'[1] or whether a Karamazov could think, in Hamlet fashion, of what lies beyond. No, gentlemen of the jury, they have their Hamlets, but so far we have only Karamazovs!"

Here Ippolit Kirillovich unfolded a most detailed picture of Mitya's preparations, the scene at Perkhotin's, at the shop, with the coachmen. He cited a quantity of words, phrases, gestures—all confirmed by witnesses—and the picture terribly swayed his listeners' convictions. What swayed them above all was the totality of the facts. The guilt of this frenzied, turbulent man, who no longer cared about himself, was set forth irrefutably. "There was no longer any reason for him to care about himself," Ippolit Kirillovich went on. "Two or three times he was on the verge of confessing outright, almost hinted at it, and stopped just short of telling all." (Here followed the testimony of the witnesses.) "He even shouted to the coachman on the way: 'Do you know you're driving a murderer!' But still he could not tell all: he had first to get to the village of Mokroye, and there finish the poem. What awaits the unfortunate man, however? The thing is that almost from his first moments in Mokroye, he sees and finally perceives fully that his 'indisputable' rival is perhaps not so indisputable, and that no congratulations for new happiness and no raised cups would either be wanted or accepted from him. But you already know the facts, gentlemen of the jury, from the court's investigation. Karamazov's triumph over his rival turned out to be beyond dispute, and here—oh, here his soul entered quite a new phase, even the most terrible of all his soul has lived through and will yet live through! One can positively admit, gentlemen of the jury," exclaimed Ippolit Kirillovich, "that outraged nature and the criminal heart revenge themselves more fully than any earthly justice! Moreover, justice and earthly punishment even alleviate the punishment of nature, are even necessary for the soul of the criminal in those moments as its salvation from despair, for I cannot even imagine the horror and the moral suffering of Karamazov when he discovered that she loved him, that for him she rejected her 'former' and 'indisputable' one, that she was calling him, him, 'Mitya,' to renewed life, promising him happiness, and all of that when? When everything was finished for him, and nothing was possible! Incidentally, I shall make one rather important observation in passing, to clarify the true essence of the defendant's situation at that moment: this woman, this love of his, until the very last minute, even until the very instant of his arrest, remained inaccessible to him, passionately desired but unattainable. Why, why did he not shoot himself right then, why did he abandon his original intent and even forget where his pistol was? It was precisely this passionate thirst for love and the hope of satisfying it right then and there that held him back. In a daze of revelry he fastened himself to his beloved, who reveled with him, more lovely and alluring for him than ever—he would not leave her side, he admired her, he melted away before her. This passionate thirst even managed for a moment to suppress not only his fear of arrest, but the very pangs of his conscience! For a moment, oh, only for a moment! I picture to myself the state of the criminal's soul at that time as an indisputable slavish submission to three elements that overwhelmed it completely: first, a state of drunkenness, daze and noise, feet pounding, singers wailing, and she, she, flushed with wine, singing and dancing, drunk and laughing to him! Second, the remote, encouraging dream that the fatal ending was still a long way off, was at least not near—perhaps only the next day, only in the morning, would they come and take him. Several hours, then—a long time, terribly long! One can think up a lot in several hours. He felt, as I picture it to myself, something similar to what a criminal feels on his way to execution, to the gallows: he still has to go down a long, long street, and at a slow pace, past thousands of people, then turn down another street, and only at the end of that other street—the terrible square! I precisely think that at the start of the procession the condemned man, sitting in the cart of shame, must feel precisely that there is still an endless life ahead of him. Now, however, the houses are going past, the cart is moving on—oh, that's nothing, it's still such a long way to the turn down the second street, and so he still looks cheerfully to right and left at those thousands of indifferently curious people whose eyes are fastened on him, and he still fancies he is the same sort of man as they are. But here comes the turn down the other street—oh, it's nothing, nothing, still a whole street to go. And no matter how many houses pass by, he will keep thinking: 'There are still a lot of houses left.' And so on to the very end, to the very square. So it was then, as I picture it to myself, with Karamazov. 'They haven't had enough time yet,' he thinks, 'it's still possible to find some way, oh, there's still time to invent a plan of defense, to think up a response, but now, now—she's so lovely now!' His soul is full of darkness and dread, but even so he manages to set aside half his money and hide it somewhere—otherwise I cannot explain to myself the disappearance of one whole half of the three thousand he had just taken from under his father's pillow. This was not his first time in Mokroye, he had once spent two days carousing there. He knew that big, old wooden house with all its sheds and porches. I precisely suppose that part of the money disappeared right then, and precisely in that house, not long before his arrest, into some crack, some crevice, under some floorboard, somewhere in a corner, under the roof—but why? You ask why? The catastrophe may come now, and of course we have not thought out how to meet it, we have had no time, and our head is throbbing, and we are drawn to *her*, but money?—money is necessary in all situations! A man with money is a man everywhere. Perhaps such calculation at such a moment appears unnatural to you? But does he not insist himself that a month earlier, also in a most anxious and fatal moment for him, he set apart half of the three thousand and sewed it into his amulet, and, of course, if that is not true, as we shall presently prove, still the idea is familiar to Karamazov, he did contemplate it. Moreover, when he later insisted to the investigator that he had set apart fifteen hundred in the amulet (which never existed), he perhaps invented this amulet that same instant, precisely because two hours earlier he had set apart half of his money and hidden it somewhere there in Mokroye, just in case, until morning, so as not to keep it with him, on a sudden inspiration. Two abysses, gentlemen of the jury, remember that Karamazov can contemplate two abysses, and both at the same time. We searched that house and found nothing. Perhaps the money is still there, or perhaps it disappeared the next day and is now with the defendant. In any case, he was arrested at her side, kneeling before her, she was lying on a bed, he was stretching out his hands to her, and was so oblivious of everything at that moment that he did not even hear the approach of those who arrested him. He had no time to prepare any response in his mind. Both he and his mind were caught unawares.

"And now he stands before his judges, before the arbiters of his fate. Gentlemen of the jury, there are moments when, in the exercise of our duty, we ourselves feel almost afraid before man, and afraid for man! These are the moments when one contemplates the animal terror of the criminal who already knows that all is lost but is still struggling, still intends to struggle with you. These are the moments when all the instincts of self-preservation rise up in him at once, and, trying to save himself, he looks at you with a piercing eye, questioning and suffering, he catches you and studies you, your face, your thoughts, waiting to see from which side you will strike, and instantly creates thousands of plans in his tremulous mind, but is still afraid to speak, afraid he will let something slip. These humiliating moments of the human soul, this journey through torments, this animal thirst for self-salvation, are terrible and sometimes evoke trepidation and commiseration even in an investigator! And so we then witnessed all that. At first he was stunned, and in his terror let drop a few words that gravely compromised him: 'Blood! I've deserved it!' But he quickly restrained himself. What to say, how to answer—none of this is prepared in him yet, but what is prepared in him is one unsubstantiated denial: 'I am not guilty of my father's death!' That is our fence for the time being, and there, behind the fence, perhaps we can set up something, some sort of barricade. He hastens to explain his first compromising exclamations, forestalling our questions, by saying he considers himself guilty only of the death of the servant Grigory. 'That blood I am guilty of, but who killed my father, gentlemen, who killed him? Who could have killed him *if not I*?' Do you hear that? He asks us, us, who came to him with the very same question! Do you hear that little phrase—'if not I'—running ahead of itself, its animal cunning, its naivety, its Karamazovian impatience? It was not I who killed him, do not even think it was I: 'I wanted to kill him, gentlemen, I wanted to kill him,' he hastens to admit (he is in a hurry, he is in a terrible hurry!), 'and yet I am not guilty, it was not I who killed him!' He concedes to us that he wanted to kill him, as if to say: you see how sincere I am, so you can all the sooner believe that I did not kill him. Oh, in such cases the criminal sometimes becomes incredibly careless and credulous. And here, quite inadvertently, as it were, the investigators suddenly asked him a most guileless question: 'Could it be Smerdyakov who killed him?' And the result was just as we expected: he became terribly angry that we had forestalled him and caught him unawares before he had time to prepare, to choose and catch the moment when it would be most plausible to bring up Smerdyakov. As is his nature, he at once rushed to the extreme and began assuring us with all his might that Smerdyakov could not have killed him, was incapable of killing him. But do not believe him, it was only a ruse: by no means, by no means was he giving up Smerdyakov; on the contrary, he still meant to bring him forward, because who else could he bring forward, but he would do it at some other moment, since for the time being the thing was spoiled. He would bring him forward only the next day, or even in a few days, picking the moment when he would cry out to us: 'You see, I myself rejected Smerdyakov more than you did, you remember that yourselves, but now I, too, am convinced: it was he who killed him, it could not be anyone else!' And with us, meanwhile, he falls into a gloomy and irritable denial, his anger and impatience prompting him, however, to a most inept and implausible explanation of how he looked into his father's window and then respectfully went away from the window. The main thing being that he does not yet know the circumstances, the scope of the evidence given by the recovered Grigory. We proceed to the examination and search of his person. The examination angers him, but also encourages him: the full three thousand is not found, only fifteen hundred. And, of course, only in this moment of angry silence and denial does the idea of the amulet jump into his head for the first time in his life. He himself undoubtedly sensed the utter incredibility of his invention, and he was at pains, at terrible pains, to make it more credible, to spin a whole plausible novel out of it. In such cases the first thing, the chief task of the investigators is to keep the criminal from preparing himself, to take him by surprise so that he speaks out his cherished ideas in all their revealing ingenuousness, implausibility, and inconsistency. And it is possible to make the criminal speak only by unexpectedly, inadvertently, as it were, informing him of some new fact, some circumstance of the case that has colossal significance, but that he previously had no notion of and could in no way have foreseen. We had kept this fact in readiness, oh, long in readiness: it was the evidence of the recovered servant Grigory about the open door through which the defendant had fled. He had completely forgotten about this door, and it never occurred to him that Grigory could have seen it. The effect was colossal. He jumped up and suddenly shouted to us: 'It was Smerdyakov who killed him, Smerdyakov!'—and thus revealed his cherished, his basic idea in its most implausible form, for Smerdyakov could have committed the murder only after he himself had struck Grigory down and run away. But when we told him that Grigory had seen the door open before he fell, and, on going out of his bedroom, had heard Smerdyakov groaning behind the partition—Karamazov was truly crushed. My collaborator, our esteemed and witty Nikolai Parfenovich, told me later that at that moment he pitied him to the point of tears. And this is the moment when, to make things better, he hastens to tell us about the notorious amulet: very well, I'll tell you my story! Gentlemen of the jury, I have already made known to you why I consider all this invention about money sewn into an amulet a month earlier not only an absurdity, but also the most implausible contrivance that could have been hit upon in this situation. If one bet on whether anything more implausible could be said or imagined, even then it would be impossible to invent anything worse than that. Here, above all, the triumphant novelist can be brought up short and demolished by details, those very details in which reality is always so rich, and which are always neglected by such unfortunate and unwilling authors, as if they were utterly insignificant and unnecessary trifles, if indeed they even occur to them. Oh, they cannot be bothered with that at the moment, their mind creates only the grandiose whole—and then someone dares suggest such a trifle to them! But that is where they get caught! The defendant is asked the question: 'Well, would you mind telling us where you got the cloth for your amulet, and who sewed it for you?' 'I sewed it myself.' 'And where did you get the cloth?' The defendant is now offended, he considers it almost offensively trifling, and believe me, he is sincere, sincere! But they are all like that. 'I tore it off my shirt.' 'Splendid, sir. That means that tomorrow we will find among your linen this shirt with a piece torn from it.' And, understand, gentlemen of the jury, that if only we had actually found this shirt (and how could we not have found it in his suitcase or chest of drawers, if such a shirt indeed existed?)—it would be a fact, a tangible fact in favor of the truth of his testimony! But this he is unable to understand. 'I don't remember, maybe it wasn't from my shirt, I sewed it up in my landlady's bonnet.' 'What sort of bonnet?' 'I took it from her, it was lying about, an old calico rag.' 'And you remember that firmly?' 'No, not firmly . . .' And he is angry, angry, and yet just think: how could one help remembering? In a man's most terrible moment, say, when he is being taken to his execution, it is precisely such trifles that stick in his memory. He will forget everything, but some green roof that flashes by on the way, or a jackdaw sitting on a cross—that he will remember. For he was hiding from the rest of the household while he sewed his amulet, he must remember the humiliation he suffered, needle in hand, for fear someone would come in and catch him; how at the first knock he would jump up and run behind the partition (there is a partition in his apartment) . . . But, gentlemen of the jury, why am I telling you all this, all these details, these trifles!" Ippolit Kirillovich suddenly exclaimed. "Precisely because the defendant has stubbornly insisted on all this absurdity up to this very minute! In the two whole months since that fatal night, he has not explained anything, he has not added even one real, clarifying circumstance to his earlier fantastic testimony; as if to say, that is all just trifles, you must believe me on my honor! Oh, we are glad to believe, we are eager to believe, even on his honor! What are we, jackals, eager for human blood? Give us, point out to us at least one fact in the defendant's favor, and we shall be glad—but a real, tangible fact, not his own brother's conclusion based on the defendant's facial expression, or pointing out that when he was beating himself on the chest, he must certainly have been pointing to the amulet, and in the dark no less. We shall be glad of this new fact, we shall be the first to renounce our accusation, we shall hasten to renounce it. But now justice cries out, and we insist, we cannot renounce anything." Here Ippolit Kirillovich moved on to the finale. He was as if in a fever, crying out for the spilt blood, the blood of a father murdered by his son "with the base purpose of robbery." He pointed firmly to the tragic and crying totality of the facts. "And whatever you are about to hear from the defendant's renowned and talented attorney," Ippolit Kirillovich could not refrain from saying, "whatever eloquent and moving words, aimed at your emotions, will resound here, remember still that at this moment you are in the sanctuary of our justice. Remember that you are the defenders of our truth, the defenders of our holy Russia, of her foundations, of her family, of all that is holy in her! Yes, here, at this moment, you represent Russia, and your verdict will resound not only in this courtroom but for all of Russia, and all of Russia will listen to you as to her defenders and judges, and will be either heartened or discouraged by your verdict. Then do not torment Russia and her expectations, our fateful troika is racing headlong, perhaps to its destruction. And all over Russia hands have long been held out and voices have been calling to halt its wild, impudent course. And if so far the other nations still stand aside for the troika galloping at breakneck speed, it is not at all, perhaps, out of respect, as the poet would have it, but simply from horror—mark that—from horror, and perhaps from loathing for her. And still it is good that they stand aside, but what if they should suddenly stop standing aside, and form into a solid wall before the speeding apparition, and themselves halt the mad course of our unbridledness, with a view to saving themselves, enlightenment, and civilization! We have already heard such anxious voices from Europe. They are already beginning to speak out. Do not tempt them, do not add to their ever-increasing hatred with a verdict justifying the murder of a father by his own son . . . !"

In a word, Ippolit Kirillovich, though very much carried away, still ended on a note of pathos—and, indeed, the impression he produced was extraordinary. He himself, having finished his speech, left hastily and, I repeat, nearly fainted in the next room. The courtroom did not applaud, but serious people were pleased. And if the ladies were not so pleased, they still admired such eloquence, the more so as they were not at all fearful of the consequences and waited for everything from Fetyukovich: "He will finally speak and, of course, overcome them all!" Everyone kept glancing at Mitya; he sat silently throughout the prosecutor's speech, clenching his fists, gritting his teeth, looking down. Only from time to time did he raise his head and listen. Especially when there was mention of Grushenka. When the prosecutor quoted Rakitin's opinion of her, a contemptuous and spiteful smile appeared on his face, and he said quite audibly: "Bernards!" When Ippolit Kirillovich told about interrogating him and tormenting him in Mokroye, Mitya raised his head and listened with terrible curiosity. At one point in the speech he even seemed about to jump up and shout something; he controlled himself, however, and merely shrugged his shoulders contemptuously. About this finale of the speech—namely, to do with the prosecutor's feats in Mokroye during the interrogation of the criminal—there was talk later among our society, and Ippolit Kirillovich was made fun of: "The man couldn't help boasting of his abilities," they said. The session was interrupted, but for a very short time, a quarter of an hour, twenty minutes at the most. There were exchanges and exclamations among the public. I recall some of them:

"A serious speech!" a gentleman in one group observed, frowning.

"Too wrapped up in psychology," another voice was heard.

"Yes, but all true, irrefutably true!"

"Yes, he's a master of it."

"Summed it all up."

"Us, too, he summed us up, too," a third voice joined in, "at the start of the speech, remember, that we're all the same as Fyodor Pavlovich?"

"And at the end, too. But that was all rubbish."

"There were some vague spots."

"Got a bit carried away."

"Unjust, unjust, sir."

"No, but anyway it was clever. The man waited for a long time, and finally he said it, heh, heh!"

"What will the defense attorney say?"

In another group:

"It wasn't very smart of him to prod the Petersburg fellow: 'aimed at your emotions,' remember?"

"Yes, that was awkward."

"Much too hasty."

"A nervous man, sir."

"We may laugh, but how about the defendant?"

"Yes, sir, how about Mitenka?"

"And what will the defense attorney say?"

In a third group:

"Which lady, the one with the lorgnette, the fat one, at the end?"

"Former wife of a general, a divorcée, I know her."

"That's the one, with the lorgnette."

"Trash."

"No, no, quite sprightly."

"The little blonde two seats away from her is better."

"Clever how they caught him at Mokroye, eh?"

"Yes, clever. And he had to tell it again. He's already told it all over town."

"And now he just couldn't resist. Vanity."

"An offended man, heh, heh!"

"Quick to take offense, too. And too much rhetoric, long phrases."

"And browbeating, did you notice how he kept browbeating us? Remember the troika? 'They have their Hamlets, but so far we have only Karamazovs!' That was clever."

"Courting liberalism. Afraid."

"He's also afraid of the defense attorney."

"Yes, what will Mr. Fetyukovich say?"

"Well, whatever he says, he won't get around our peasants."

"You don't think so?"

In a fourth group:

"But that was good about the troika, the part about the other nations."

"And it's true, remember, where he said the other nations won't wait."

"What do you mean?"

"In the English Parliament just last week one member stood up, to do with the nihilists, and asked the Ministry if it wasn't time to intervene in a barbarous nation, in order to educate us. It was him Ippolit meant, I know it was him. He talked about it last week."

"There's many a slip."

"What slip? Why many?"

"We'll close Kronstadt and not give them any bread.[2] Where will they get it?"

"And America? It's America now."

"Rubbish."

But the bell rang, all rushed to their places. Fetyukovich mounted the rostrum.

Chapter 10

The Defense Attorney's Speech. A Stick with Two Ends

All became hushed as the first words of the famous orator resounded. The whole room fixed their eyes on him. He began with extreme directness, simplicity, and conviction, but without the slightest presumption. Not the slightest attempt at eloquence, at notes of pathos, at words ringing with emotion. This was a man speaking within an intimate circle of sympathizers. His voice was beautiful, loud, and attractive, and even in this voice itself one seemed to hear something genuine and guileless. But everyone realized at once that the orator could suddenly rise to true pathos—and "strike the heart with an unutterable power."[1] He spoke perhaps less correctly than Ippolit Kirillovich, but without long phrases, and even more precisely. There was one thing the ladies did not quite like: he somehow kept bending forward, especially at the beginning of his speech, not really bowing, but as if he were rushing or flying at his listeners, and this he did by bending precisely, as it were, with half of his long back, as if a hinge were located midway down that long and narrow back that enabled it to bend almost at a right angle. He spoke somehow scatteredly at the beginning, as if without any system, snatching up facts at random, but in the end it all fell together. His speech could be divided into two halves: the first half was a critique, a refutation of the charges, at times malicious and sarcastic. But in the second half of the speech he seemed to change his tone and even his method, and all at once rose into pathos, and the courtroom seemed to be waiting for it and all began trembling with rapture. He went straight to work, and began by saying that although his practice was in Petersburg, this was not the first time he had visited the towns of Russia to defend a case, though he did so only when he was convinced of the defendant's innocence or anticipated it beforehand. "The same thing happened to me in the present case," he explained. "Even in the initial newspaper reports alone, I caught a glimpse of something that struck me greatly in favor of the defendant. In a word, I was interested first of all in a certain juridical fact, which appears often enough in legal practice, though never, it seems to me, so fully or with such characteristic peculiarities as in the present case. This fact I ought to formulate only in the finale of my speech, when I have finished my statement; however, I shall express my thought at the very beginning as well, for I have a weakness for going straight to the point, not storing up effects or sparing impressions. This may be improvident on my part, yet it is sincere. This thought of mine—my formula—is as follows: the overwhelming totality of the facts is against the defendant, and at the same time there is not one fact that will stand up to criticism, if it is considered separately, on its own! Following along through rumors and the newspapers, I was becoming more and more firmly set in my thought, when suddenly I received an invitation from the defendant's relatives to come and defend him. I hastened here at once, and here became finally convinced. It was in order to demolish this terrible totality of facts and show how undemonstrable and fantastic each separate accusing fact is, that I undertook the defense of this case."

Thus the defense attorney began, and suddenly he raised his voice:

"Gentlemen of the jury, I am a newcomer here. All impressions fell upon me without preconceived ideas. The defendant, a man of stormy and unbridled character, had not offended me to begin with, as he had perhaps a hundred persons in this town, which is why many are prejudiced against him beforehand. Of course, I also admit that the moral sense of local society has been justly aroused: the defendant is stormy and unbridled. Nonetheless he was received in local society; even in the family of the highly talented prosecutor he was warmly welcomed." (*Nota bene*: At these words two or three chuckles came from the public, quickly suppressed, but noticed by all. We all knew that the prosecutor had admitted Mitya to his house against his will, solely because for some reason he interested the prosecutor's wife—a highly virtuous and respectable, but fantastic and self-willed, lady, who in certain cases, for the most part trifling, loved to oppose her husband. Mitya, by the way, had visited their home rather infrequently.) "Nevertheless, I make so bold as to assume," the defense attorney went on, "that even in such an independent mind and just character as my opponent's, a somewhat erroneous prejudice against my unfortunate client might have formed. Oh, it's quite natural: the unfortunate man deserved all too well to be treated with prejudice. And an offended moral and, even more so, aesthetic sense is sometimes implacable. Of course, in the highly talented speech for the prosecution, we have all heard a strict analysis of the defendant's character and actions, a strictly critical attitude towards the case; and, above all, such psychological depths were demonstrated to explain the essence of the matter, that a penetration to those depths could by no means have taken place were there even the slightest amount of deliberate and malicious prejudice with regard to the person of the defendant. But there are things that are even worse, even more ruinous in such cases than the most malicious and preconceived attitude towards the matter. Namely, if we are, for example, possessed by a certain, so to speak, artistic game, by the need for artistic production, so to speak, the creation of a novel, especially seeing the wealth of psychological gifts with which God has endowed our abilities. While still in Petersburg, still only preparing to come here, I was warned—and I myself knew without any warning—that I would meet here as my opponent a profound and most subtle psychologist, who has long deserved special renown for this quality in our still young legal world. But psychology, gentlemen, though a profound thing, is still like a stick with two ends." (A chuckle from the public.) "Oh, you will of course forgive the triviality of my comparison; I am not a master of eloquent speaking. Here, however, is an example—I take the first I happen upon in the prosecutor's speech. The defendant, at night, in the garden, climbs the fence as he is fleeing, and strikes down with a brass pestle the servant who has seized him by the leg. Then he at once jumps back down into the garden and for a whole five minutes fusses over the fallen man, trying to see whether he has killed him or not. Now, not for anything will the prosecutor believe in the truthfulness of the defendant's testimony that he jumped down to the old man Grigory out of pity. 'No,' he says, 'how could there be such sensitivity at such a moment; this is unnatural; he jumped down precisely in order to make sure that the only witness to his evil deed was dead, and thereby testified that he had committed this evil deed, since he could not have jumped down into the garden for any other reason, inclination, or feeling.' There you have psychology; but let us take the same psychology and apply it to this case, only from the other end, and the result will be no less plausible. The murderer jumps down as a precaution, to make sure if the witness is alive or not, and yet, according to the words of the prosecutor himself, he had just left in the study of his father, whom he had murdered, a colossal piece of evidence against himself in the form of a torn envelope on which it was written that it contained three thousand roubles. 'Were he to have taken this envelope with him, no one in the whole world would have learned that the envelope existed, or the money inside it, and that the defendant had therefore robbed the money.' These are the prosecutor's own words. Well, so you see, on the one hand the man was not cautious enough, he lost his head, got frightened, and ran away leaving evidence on the floor, but when two minutes later he strikes and kills another man, then all at once the most heartless and calculating sense of caution comes to our service. But so, let it be so: it is, shall we say, the subtlety of psychology that under certain circumstances I instantly become bloodthirsty and sharp-eyed as a Caucasian eagle, and the next moment as blind and timid as a worthless mole. But if I am so bloodthirsty and cruelly calculating that, having killed, I jump down only to see if the witness against me is alive or not, do you think I would fuss over this new victim of mine for a whole five minutes, allowing, perhaps, for new witnesses? Why soak the handkerchief, wiping blood from the fallen man's head, so that this handkerchief can later serve as evidence against me? No, if we really are so calculating and hard-hearted, would it not be better, having jumped down, simply to whack the fallen servant on the head again and again with the same pestle, so as to kill him finally, and, having eradicated the witness, to put all worry out of our mind? And, lastly, I jump down in order to see whether the witness against me is alive or dead, and right there on the path I leave another witness—namely, this very pestle that I took from the two women, both of whom can later recognize the pestle as theirs and testify that I took it from their house. And it's not that I forgot it on the path, dropped it in distraction, in confusion: no, we precisely threw our weapon away, because it was found about fifteen paces from the spot where Grigory was struck down. The question is, why did we do that? But we did it precisely because we felt bitter at having killed a man, an old servant, and therefore in vexation, with a curse, we threw the pestle away as a murderous weapon, it could not be otherwise, or why throw it with such force? And if we could feel pain and pity at having killed a man, it is of course because we did not kill our father: if he had killed his father, he would not have jumped down to another fallen man out of pity, in that case there would be a different feeling, in that case we would not be bothered with pity but would think about self-salvation, that is certainly so. On the contrary, I repeat, we would have smashed his skull finally, and not fussed over him for five minutes. There was room for pity and kind feeling precisely because our conscience was clear to begin with. Here, then, is a different psychology. I myself, gentlemen of the jury, have resorted to psychology now, in order to demonstrate that one can draw whatever conclusions one likes from it. It all depends on whose hands it is in. Psychology prompts novels even from the most serious people, and quite unintentionally. I am speaking of excessive psychology, gentlemen of the jury, of a certain abuse of it."

Here again approving chuckles came from the public, all directed at the prosecutor. I shall not give the entire speech of the defense attorney in detail, but shall only take some parts of it, some of its most salient points.

Chapter 11

There Was No Money. There Was No Robbery

There was one point that even struck everyone in the defense attorney's speech—namely, his complete denial of the existence of the fatal three thousand roubles, and thus also of the possibility of their robbery.

"Gentlemen of the jury," the defense attorney began, "one most characteristic peculiarity will strike any fresh and unprejudiced person in this case—namely, the charge of robbery, and at the same time the complete impossibility of pointing in fact to what precisely was robbed. Money, they say, was robbed—namely, three thousand roubles—but whether this money actually existed, nobody knows. Consider: first of all, how did we learn of the three thousand, and who actually saw it? The only one who saw it and pointed out that it was wrapped in the envelope with the inscription was the servant Smerdyakov. He told this information to the defendant and to his brother Ivan Fyodorovich still prior to the catastrophe. It was also made known to Miss Svetlov. Yet none of these three persons saw the money, again only Smerdyakov saw it, but here the question naturally arises: if the money really existed and Smerdyakov saw it, when was the last time he saw it? And what if his master took the money from under the bed and put it back in the box without telling him? Notice, according to Smerdyakov the money was under the bed, under the mattress; the defendant would have had to pull it from under the mattress, and yet the bed was not rumpled at all, that has been carefully noted in the record. How could the defendant leave the bed entirely unrumpled, and, moreover, not stain with his still bloody hands the fresh, fine bed linen that had just been put on it purposely for the occasion? But, you will say, what about the envelope on the floor? It is worth saying a few words about this envelope. I was even somewhat surprised just now: the highly talented prosecutor, when he began speaking of this envelope, suddenly declared of it himself—do you hear, gentlemen, himself—namely, in that part of his speech where he points out the absurdity of the suggestion that Smerdyakov was the murderer: 'Were it not for this envelope, had it not been left on the floor as evidence, had the robber taken it with him, no one in the whole world would have learned that the envelope existed, or the money inside it, and that the defendant had therefore robbed the money.' Thus it is solely because of this torn scrap of paper with the inscription on it, as even the prosecutor himself admits, that the defendant has been accused of robbery, 'otherwise no one would know that there had been a robbery, nor perhaps that there had been any money either.' But can the simple fact that this scrap of paper was lying on the floor possibly be proof that it once contained money and that this money had been robbed? 'But,' they will reply, 'Smerdyakov did see it in the envelope,' but when, when did he last see it?—that is my question. I spoke with Smerdyakov, and he told me that he had seen it two days before the catastrophe! But why can I not suppose at least some such circumstance, for example, as that old Fyodor Pavlovich, having locked himself in the house, in impatient, hysterical expectation of his beloved, might suddenly decide, having nothing better to do, to take the envelope and unseal it. 'An envelope is just an envelope,' he might think, 'why should she believe me? If I show her a wad of hundred-rouble bills, that will really work, it will make her mouth water'—and so he tears open the envelope, takes out the money, and throws the envelope on the floor with the imperious gesture of an owner, and certainly not afraid of any evidence. Listen, gentlemen of the jury, could anything be more possible than such a speculation and such a fact? Why is it impossible? But if at least something of the sort could have taken place, then the charge of robbery is wiped out of itself: there was no money, therefore there was no robbery. If the envelope lying on the floor is evidence that there was once money in it, then why may I not assert the opposite—namely, that the envelope was lying on the floor precisely because it no longer contained any money, the money having been taken out of it previously by the owner himself? 'Yes, but in that case where did the money go, if Fyodor Pavlovich took it out of the envelope himself; it was not found when his house was searched?' First, part of the money was found in his box, and second, might he not have taken it out that morning, or even the day before, and made some other use of it, paid it out, sent it away, might he not, finally, have changed his thinking, the very basis of his plan of action, and that without finding it at all necessary to report first to Smerdyakov? And if even the mere possibility of such a speculation exists, then how can it be asserted so insistently and so firmly that the defendant committed the murder with the purpose of robbery, and indeed that the robbery existed? We thereby enter the realm of novels. If one asserts that such and such a thing was robbed, one must needs point to this thing, or at least prove indisputably that it existed. Yet no one even saw it. Not long ago in Petersburg a young man, hardly more than a boy, eighteen years old, a little peddler with a tray, went into a money changer's shop in broad daylight with an axe, and with extraordinary, typical boldness killed the shopkeeper and carried off fifteen hundred roubles. About five hours later he was arrested, and except for fifteen roubles that he had already managed to spend, the entire fifteen hundred was found on him. Moreover, the shop clerk, who returned to the shop after the murder, informed the police not only of the amount stolen, but also of what sort of money it consisted—that is, so many hundred-rouble bills, so many fifties, so many tens, so many gold coins and precisely which ones—and then precisely the same bills and coins were found on the arrested murderer. On top of that there followed a full and frank confession from the murderer that he had killed the man and taken that very money. This, gentlemen of the jury, is what I call evidence! Here I know, I see, I touch the money, and I cannot say that it does not or never did exist. Is that so in the present case? And yet it is a matter of life and death, of a man's fate. 'So it is,' they will say, 'but that night he was carousing, throwing money away, he was found with fifteen hundred roubles—where did he get it?' But precisely because only fifteen hundred was found, and the other half of the sum could not be located or discovered anywhere, precisely this fact proves that the money could be quite different, that it may never have been in any envelope at all. By the reckoning of time (quite strict here), it has been determined and demonstrated by the preliminary investigation that the defendant, when he ran from the serving-women to the official Perkhotin, did not stop at his place, and did not stop anywhere else, and afterwards was constantly in the presence of other people, and therefore could not have separated half of the three thousand and hidden it somewhere in town. Precisely this consideration caused the prosecutor to assume that the money was hidden somewhere in a crevice in the village of Mokroye. And why not in the dungeons of the castle of Udolpho,[1] gentlemen? Is it not a fantastic, is it not a novelistic suggestion? And, notice, let just this one assumption—that is, that the money is hidden in Mokroye—be demolished, and the whole charge of robbery is blown sky-high, for where is it, what has become of this fifteen hundred? By what miracle did it disappear, if it has been proved that the defendant did not stop anywhere? And with such novels we are prepared to ruin a human life! They will say: 'Still, he was unable to explain where he got the fifteen hundred that was found on him; moreover, everyone knew that before that night he had no money.' But who, in fact, knew that? The defendant has given clear and firm testimony to where he got the money, and, if I may say so, gentlemen of the jury, if I may say so—there neither can nor ever could be anything more plausible than this testimony, nor more in keeping with the defendant's character and soul. The prosecution liked its own novel: a man of weak will, who determined to take the three thousand so shamingly offered him by his fiancée, could not, they say, have separated half of it and sewn it into an amulet; on the contrary, even if he did, he would open it every two days and peel off a hundred, and thus run through it all in a month. Remember, this was all told here in a tone that would brook no objections. Well, and what if the thing went quite differently, what if you have created a novel around quite a different person? That's just it, you have created a different person! It will perhaps be objected: 'There are witnesses that the whole three thousand he took from Miss Verkhovtsev was squandered in the village of Mokroye a month before the catastrophe, at one go, to the last kopeck, so that he could not have set aside half of it.' But who are these witnesses? The degree of trustworthiness of these witnesses has already displayed itself in court. Besides, a crust always looks bigger in another man's hand. Lastly, not one of these witnesses counted the money himself, they merely judged by eye. Did not the witness Maximov testify that the defendant had twenty thousand in his hands? So, gentlemen of the jury, since psychology has two ends, allow me to apply the other end and let us see if it comes out the same.

"A month before the catastrophe, the defendant was entrusted by Miss Verkhovtsev with three thousand roubles to be sent by mail—but a question: is it true that it was entrusted to him in such shame and humiliation as was declared here today? In Miss Verkhovtsev's first testimony on the same subject, it came out differently, quite differently; and in her second testimony all we heard were cries of anger, revenge, cries of long-concealed hatred. But this alone, that the witness testified incorrectly in her first testimony, gives us the right to conclude that her second testimony may also be incorrect. The prosecutor 'does not wish, does not dare' (in his own words) to touch on this romance. So be it, I shall not touch on it either, but will only allow myself to observe that if a pure and highly virtuous person such as the highly esteemed Miss Verkhovtsev undoubtedly is, if such a person, I say, allows herself suddenly, all at once, in court, to change her first testimony with the direct aim of ruining the defendant, then it is clear that she has also not given this testimony impartially, coolheadedly. Can we be deprived of the right to conclude that a vengeful woman may have exaggerated many things? Yes, precisely exaggerated the shame and disgrace in which she offered the money. On the contrary, it was offered precisely in such a way that it could still be accepted, especially by such a light-minded man as our defendant. Above all, he still had it in his head then that he would soon receive the three thousand he reckoned was owing to him from his father. This was light-minded, but precisely because of his light-mindedness he was firmly convinced that his father would give it to him, that he would get it, and therefore would always be able to mail the money entrusted to him by Miss Verkhovtsev and settle his debt. But the prosecutor will in no way allow that on that same day, the day of the accusation, he was capable of separating half of the money entrusted to him and sewing it into an amulet: 'Such,' he says, 'is not his character, he could not have had such feelings.' But you yourself were shouting that Karamazov is broad, you yourself were shouting about the two extreme abysses Karamazov can contemplate. Karamazov is precisely of such a nature, with two sides, two abysses, as can stop amid the most unrestrained need of carousing if something strikes him on the other side. And the other side is love, precisely this new love that flared up in him like powder, and for this love he needs money, he has more need of it, oh! much more need of it even than of carousing with this same beloved. If she were to say to him: 'I am yours, I do not want Fyodor Pavlovich,' and he were to snatch her and take her away—then he would have to have some means of taking her away. This is more important than carousing. Could Karamazov fail to understand that? This is precisely what he was sick over, this care—what, then, is so incredible in his separating this money and stashing it away just in case? But now, however, time is passing, and Fyodor Pavlovich does not give the defendant his three thousand; on the contrary, he hears that he has allotted it precisely to luring away his beloved. 'If Fyodor Pavlovich does not give it back to me,' he thinks, 'I will come out as a thief before Katerina Ivanovna.' But now the thought is born in him that he will take this same fifteen hundred, which he is still carrying on him in the amulet, lay it before Miss Verkhovtsev, and say to her: 'I am a scoundrel, but not a thief.' So now he has a double reason to hold on to this fifteen hundred like the apple of his eye, and on no account to unstitch the amulet and peel off a hundred at a time. Why should you deny the defendant a sense of honor? No, he has a sense of honor, let's say a faulty one, let's say very often a mistaken one, but he has it, has it to the point of passion, and he has proved it. Now, however, the situation gets more complicated, the torments of jealousy reach the highest pitch, and the same questions, the two old questions, etch themselves more and more tormentingly in the defendant's fevered brain: 'If I give it back to Katerina Ivanovna, with what means will I take Grushenka away?' If he was raving so, getting drunk and storming in the taverns all that month, it is precisely, perhaps, because he felt bitter himself, it was more than he could bear. These two questions finally became so acute that they finally drove him to despair. He tried sending his younger brother to their father to ask one last time for the three thousand, but without waiting for an answer he burst in himself and ended by beating the old man in front of witnesses. After that, consequently, there is no one to get the money from, his beaten father will not give it. The evening of that same day he beats himself on the chest, precisely on the upper part of the chest, where the amulet was, and swears to his brother that he has the means not to be a scoundrel, but will still remain a scoundrel, because he foresees that he will not use this means, he will not have enough strength of soul, he will not have enough character. Why, why does the prosecution not believe the evidence of Alexei Karamazov, given so purely, so sincerely, so spontaneously and plausibly? Why, on the contrary, would they have me believe in money hidden in some crevice, in the dungeons of the castle of Udolpho? That same evening, after the conversation with his brother, the defendant writes this fatal letter, and now this letter is the most important, the most colossal evidence, convicting the defendant of robbery! 'I will ask all people, and if I don't get it from people, I will kill father and take it from under his mattress, in the envelope with the pink ribbon, if only Ivan goes away'—a complete program of the murder, they say; who else could it be? 'It was accomplished as written!' the prosecution exclaims. But, first of all, the letter is a drunken one, and written in terrible exasperation; second, about the envelope, again he is writing in Smerdyakov's words, because he did not see the envelope himself; and, third, maybe he wrote it, but was it accomplished as written, is there any proof of that? Did the defendant take the envelope from under the pillow, did he find the money, did it even exist? And was it money that the defendant went running for—remember, remember? He went running headlong, not to rob, but only to find out where she was, this woman who had crushed him—so it was not according to the program, not as written, that he went running there, that is, not for a premeditated robbery; he ran suddenly, impulsively, in a jealous rage! 'Yes,' they will say, 'but having come and killed him, he also took the money.' But did he kill him, finally, or not? The accusation of robbery I reject with indignation: there can be no accusation of robbery if it is impossible to point exactly to what precisely has been robbed—that is an axiom! But did he kill him, without the robbery, did he kill him? Is this proved? Is this not also a novel?"

Chapter 12

And There Was No Murder Either

"Forgive me, gentlemen of the jury, but there is a human life here, and we must be more careful. We have heard the prosecution testify that until the very last day, until today, until the day of the trial, even they hesitated to accuse the defendant of full and complete premeditation of the murder, hesitated until this same fatal 'drunken' letter was produced today in court. 'It was accomplished as written!' But again I repeat: he ran to her, for her, only to find out where she was. This is an indisputable fact. Had she been at home, he would not have run anywhere, he would have stayed with her, and would not have done what he promised in the letter. He ran impulsively and suddenly, and perhaps had no recollection at all of his 'drunken' letter. 'He took the pestle with him,' they say—and you will remember how an entire psychology was derived for us from this pestle alone: why he had to take this pestle as a weapon, to snatch it up as a weapon, and so on and so forth. A most ordinary thought comes to my mind here: what if this pestle had not been lying in plain sight, had not been on the shelf from which the defendant snatched it, but had been put away in a cupboard?—then it wouldn't have caught the defendant's eye, and he would have run off without a weapon, empty-handed, and so perhaps would not have killed anyone. How, then, can I possibly arrive at the conclusion that the pestle is a proof of arming and premeditating? Yes, but he shouted in the taverns that he was going to murder his father, and two days before, on the evening when he wrote his drunken letter, he was quiet and quarreled only with a shop clerk, 'because,' they say, 'Karamazov could not help quarreling.' To which I reply that if he was contemplating such a murder, had planned it, moreover, and written it out, he surely would not have quarreled with a shop clerk, and perhaps would not have stopped at the tavern at all, because a soul that has conceived such a thing seeks silence and self-effacement, seeks disappearance, not to be seen, not to be heard: 'Forget all about me if you can,' and that not only from calculation, but from instinct. Gentlemen of the jury, psychology has two ends, and we, too, are able to understand psychology. As for all this shouting in taverns for the whole month, oftentimes children or drunken idlers, leaving a tavern or quarreling with each other, shout: 'I'll kill you,' but they don't kill anyone. And this fatal letter—is it not also drunken exasperation, the shout of a man coming out of a tavern: 'I'll kill you, I'll kill you all!' Why not, why could it not be so? What makes this letter a fatal one; why, on the contrary, is it not funny? Precisely because the corpse of the murdered father has been found, because a witness saw the defendant in the garden, armed and running away, and was himself struck down by him—therefore it was all accomplished as written, and therefore the letter is not funny but fatal. Thank God, we have gotten to the point: 'Since he was in the garden, it means he also killed him.' On these two words—since he *was*, it also inevitably *means*—everything, the entire accusation, rests: 'He was, therefore it means.' And what if it does not *mean*, even though he was? Oh, I agree that the totality of the facts and the coincidence of the facts are indeed rather eloquent. Consider all these facts separately, however, without being impressed by their totality: why, for instance, will the prosecution in no way accept the truth of the defendant's testimony that he ran away from his father's window? Remember the sarcasms the prosecution allows itself concerning the respectfulness and 'pious' feelings that suddenly took hold of the murderer. And what if there actually was something of the sort—that is, if not respectfulness of feeling, then piety of feeling? 'My mother must have been praying for me at that moment,' the defendant testified at the investigation, and so he ran away as soon as he was convinced that Miss Svetlov was not in his father's house. 'But he could not have been convinced by looking through the window,' the prosecution objects to us. And why couldn't he? After all, the window was opened when the defendant gave the signals. Fyodor Pavlovich might have uttered some one word then, some cry might have escaped him—and the defendant might suddenly have been convinced that Miss Svetlov was not there. Why must we assume what we imagine, or imagine what we have assumed? In reality a thousand things can flash by, which escape the observation of the subtlest novelist. 'Yes, but Grigory saw the door open, therefore the defendant had certainly been in the house, and therefore he killed him.' About that door, gentlemen of the jury . . . You see, about that open door we have testimony from only one person, who was himself, however, in such a condition at the time . . . But suppose it was so, suppose the door was open, suppose the defendant denied it, lied about it from a sense of self-protection, quite understandable in his position; suppose so, suppose he got into the house, was in the house—well, what of it, why is it so inevitable that if he was, he also killed him? He might have burst in, run through the rooms, might have pushed his father aside, might even have hit his father, and then, convinced that Miss Svetlov was not there, he might have run away rejoicing that she was not there and that he had run away without killing his father. Perhaps he jumped down from the fence a moment later to help Grigory, whom he had struck down in his excitement, precisely because he was capable of a pure feeling, a feeling of compassion and pity, because he had run away from the temptation to kill his father, because he felt in himself a pure heart and the joy that he had not killed his father. With horrifying eloquence, the prosecutor describes to us the terrible state the defendant was in when love opened to him again, in the village of Mokroye, calling him to new life, and when it was no longer possible for him to love, because behind him lay the bloodstained corpse of his father, and beyond that corpse—punishment. Yet the prosecutor still assumes there was love, and has explained it according to his psychology: 'Drunkenness,' he says 'a criminal being taken to his execution, still a long time to wait,' and so on and so forth. But, I ask you again, have you not created a different character, Mr. Prosecutor? Is the defendant so coarse, is he so heartless that he could still think at that moment about love and about hedging before the court, if indeed the blood of his father lay upon him? No, no, and no! As soon as it became clear to him that she loved him, was calling him to her, promised him new happiness—oh, I swear, he should then have felt a double, a triple need to kill himself, and he would certainly have killed himself if he had had his father's corpse behind him! Oh, no, he would not have forgotten where his pistols lay! I know the defendant: the savage, stony heartlessness imputed to him by the prosecution is incompatible with his character. He would have killed himself, that is certain; he did not kill himself precisely because 'his mother prayed for him,' and his heart was guiltless of his father's blood. That night in Mokroye he suffered, he grieved only for the stricken old man Grigory, and prayed to God within himself that the old man would rise and recover, that his blow would not be fatal and punishment would pass him by. Why should we not accept such an interpretation of events? What firm proof have we that the defendant is lying to us? But there is his father's body, it will be pointed out to us again: he ran away, he did not kill him—then who did kill the old man?

"Here, I repeat, is the whole logic of the prosecution: who did kill him, if not he? There is no one to put in his place, they say. Is that so, gentlemen of the jury? Is it right, is it indeed so, that there is simply no one to put in his place? We heard the prosecution list on its fingers all those who were in or around the house that night. There were five of them. Three of the five, I agree, are completely irresponsible: these are the murdered man himself, old Grigory, and his wife. Thus the defendant and Smerdyakov are left, and so the prosecutor exclaims with pathos that the defendant is pointing to Smerdyakov because he has no one else to point to, because if there were some sixth person, even the ghost of some sixth person, the defendant would himself drop his charge against Smerdyakov, being ashamed of it, and point to this sixth person. But, gentlemen of the jury, what keeps me from drawing the opposite conclusion? We have two men: the defendant, and Smerdyakov—why can I not say that you accuse my client solely because you have no one else to accuse? And you have no one else only because, on an entirely preconceived notion, you began by excluding Smerdyakov from all suspicion. Yes, it's true, only the defendant, his two brothers, and Miss Svetlov point to Smerdyakov, and that is all. Yet there are some others who in fact also point to him: there is a certain, though vague, ferment of some question in society, some suspicion, some vague rumor can be heard, some expectation is felt to exist. Finally, there is the evidence of a certain juxtaposition of facts, rather characteristic, though, I admit, also rather vague: first, this fit of the falling sickness precisely on the day of the catastrophe, a fit that the prosecutor for some reason was forced to defend and uphold so strenuously. Then the sudden suicide of Smerdyakov on the eve of the trial. Then the no-less-sudden testimony from the elder of the defendant's brothers, today in court, who up to now believed in his brother's guilt, and who suddenly brought in the money and also pronounced, again, the name of Smerdyakov as the murderer! Oh, I am fully convinced, along with the court and the prosecution, that Ivan Karamazov is sick and in fever, that his testimony may indeed be a desperate attempt, conceived, moreover, in delirium, to save his brother by shifting the blame onto the dead man. But, still, Smerdyakov's name has been uttered, again there is the ring of something mysterious, as it were. Something seems to have been left unspoken here, gentlemen of the jury, and unfinished. Perhaps it will yet be spoken. But let us put that aside for now; that will come later. The court decided this afternoon to continue its session, but in the meantime, while waiting, I might incidentally make some remarks, for example, about the characterization of the late Smerdyakov, drawn with so much subtlety and so much talent by the prosecutor. For, astonished as I am by such talent, I cannot quite agree with the essence of the characterization. I visited Smerdyakov, I saw him and spoke with him, and on me he made an entirely different impression. His health was weak, it is true, but his character, his heart—oh, no, he was not at all such a weak man as the prosecution has made him out to be. I especially did not find any timidity in him, that timidity the prosecutor so characteristically described for us. As for guilelessness, there was nothing of the sort; on the contrary, I found a terrible mistrustfulness in him, behind a mask of naivety, and a mind capable of contemplating quite a lot. Oh! it was too guileless on the part of the prosecution to regard him as feebleminded. On me he made quite a definite impression: I left convinced that he was a decidedly spiteful being, enormously ambitious, vengeful, and burning with envy. I gathered some information: he hated his origin, was ashamed of it, and gnashed his teeth when he recalled that he was 'descended from Stinking Lizaveta.' He was irreverent towards the servant Grigory and his wife, who had been his childhood benefactors. He cursed Russia and laughed at her. He dreamed of going to France and remaking himself as a Frenchman. He used to talk about it often and said that he only lacked the means to do so. It seems to me that he loved no one but himself, and his respect for himself was peculiarly high. Enlightenment he regarded as good clothes, clean shirt fronts, and polished boots. Considering himself (and there are facts to support it) the illegitimate son of Fyodor Pavlovich, he might very well detest his position as compared with that of his master's legitimate children: everything goes to them, you see, and nothing to him; to them all the rights, to them the inheritance, while he is just a cook. He disclosed to me that he himself had helped Fyodor Pavlovich put the money in the envelope. The purpose of this sum—a sum that could have made his career—was, naturally, hateful to him. Besides, he saw three thousand roubles in bright, iridescent bills (I deliberately asked him about it). Oh, never show a proud and envious man a great deal of money at once—and this was the first time he had seen such a sum in one hand. The impression of the iridescent bundle might have had a morbid effect on his imagination, though at the time without any consequences. The highly talented prosecutor outlined for us with remarkable subtlety all the pros and cons of the assumption that Smerdyakov might be accused of the murder, and asked particularly: why did he need to sham a falling fit? Yes, but he may not have been shamming at all, the fit may have happened quite naturally, it may also have passed quite naturally, and the sick man may have come round again. Let's say, not that he recovered, but that at some point he came round and regained consciousness, as happens with the falling sickness. The prosecution asks: where is the moment when Smerdyakov committed the crime? But it is extremely easy to point out this moment. He could have come round, gotten up from a deep sleep (for he was just asleep: fits of the falling sickness are always followed by a deep sleep) precisely at the moment when old Grigory, having seized the fleeing defendant by the leg on the fence, shouted 'Parricide!' for the whole neighborhood to hear. It could have been this unusual cry, in the stillness, in the dark, that awakened Smerdyakov, who by that time might not have been sleeping very soundly: he might have begun to wake up naturally an hour earlier. Having gotten out of bed, he goes almost unconsciously and without any intention towards the shout, to see what it was. His head is in a sickly daze, his reason is still drowsy, but now he is in the garden, he goes up to the lighted window and hears the terrible news from his master, who, of course, was glad to see him. Reason at once lights up in his head. He finds out all the details from his frightened master. And now a thought gradually forms in his disordered and sick brain—terrible, but tempting and irresistibly logical: to kill him, take the three thousand, and afterwards shift it all onto his young master: who will be suspected now if not the young master, whom can they accuse if not the young master, so much evidence, and he was there? A terrible thirst for money, booty, might have taken his breath away, along with the notion of impunity. Oh, these unexpected and irresistible impulses so often come when a chance offers itself, and above all come unexpectedly to such murderers, who just a moment before had no idea they would want to kill! And so Smerdyakov could have gone into his master's room and accomplished his plan—with what, what weapon?—why, with the first stone he picked up in the garden. And what for, with what purpose? But three thousand, it's a whole career! Oh! I am not contradicting myself: the money may well have existed. And Smerdyakov may even have been the only one who knew where to find it, where exactly his master was keeping it. 'Well, and the wrapping for the money, the torn envelope on the floor?' Earlier, when the prosecutor was speaking about this envelope, and set forth his extremely subtle argument that only an unaccustomed thief would have left it on the floor—namely, a thief like Karamazov, and never one like Smerdyakov, who in no case would have left behind such evidence against himself—earlier, gentlemen of the jury, as I was listening, I suddenly felt I was hearing something extremely familiar. And just imagine, I did hear precisely the same argument, the same conjecture as to what Karamazov would have done with the envelope, just two days ago, from Smerdyakov himself. Moreover, he even struck me at the time: I precisely thought he was being falsely naive, heading me off, foisting this idea on me so that I would come up with the same argument myself, as if he were prompting me. Did he not prompt the prosecution, too, with this argument? Did he not foist it on to the highly talented prosecutor as well? They will say: what about the old woman, Grigory's wife? She did hear the sick man groaning just beside her all night. Yes, she heard him, but this argument is extremely flimsy. I knew a lady who complained bitterly that some mutt kept waking her up all night and would not let her sleep. And yet, as it turned out, the poor little dog had yapped only two or three times during the whole night. It's quite natural; a man is sleeping and suddenly hears a groan, he wakes up annoyed at being awakened, but immediately falls asleep again. Two hours later, another groan, he wakes up again and again falls asleep; finally, yet another groan, again in two hours, just three times during the night. In the morning the sleeping man gets up and complains that someone was groaning all night and constantly waking him up. But it must inevitably seem so to him; he slept, and does not remember the intervals of sleep, two hours each, but only the moments when he was awakened, and so it seems to him that he was being awakened all night. But why, why, the prosecution exclaims, did Smerdyakov not confess in his death note? 'He had enough conscience for the one thing,' they say, 'why not for the other?' Excuse me, but conscience implies repentance, and it may be that the suicide was not repentant but simply in despair. Despair and repentance are two totally different things. Despair can be malicious and implacable, and the suicide, as he was taking his life, may at that moment have felt twice as much hatred for those whom he had envied all his life. Gentlemen of the jury, beware of a judicial error! What, what is implausible in all that I have just presented and portrayed to you? Find the error in my account, find what is impossible, absurd. But if there is at least a shadow of possibility, a shadow of plausibility in my conjectures—withhold your sentence. And is there not more than a shadow here? I swear by all that's holy, I believe completely in the explanation of the murder I have just presented to you. And above all, above all, I am disturbed and beside myself from the very thought that out of the whole mass of facts that the prosecution has heaped upon the defendant, there is not one that is at least somewhat exact and irrefutable, and that the unfortunate man will perish merely from the totality of these facts. Yes, this totality is horrible; this blood, this blood dripping from his fingers, the blood-stained shirt, the dark night echoing with the shout of 'Parricide!' and the one who shouted falling with his head smashed, and then this mass of phrases, testimonies, gestures, cries—it has so much influence, it can sway one's convictions, but your convictions, gentlemen of the jury, can it sway your convictions? Remember, you are given an immense power, the power to bind and to loose.[1] But the greater the power, the more terrible its application! I do not renounce one iota of what I have just said, but suppose I did, suppose for a moment that I, too, agreed with the prosecution that my unfortunate client stained his hands with his father's blood. This is only a supposition, I repeat, I do not doubt his innocence for a moment, but let it be so, let me suppose that my defendant is guilty of parricide, yet, even allowing for such a supposition, hear what I say. I have it in my heart to speak out something more to you, for I also sense a great struggle in your hearts and minds . . . Forgive my speaking of your hearts and minds, gentlemen of the jury, but I want to be truthful and sincere to the end. Let us all be sincere . . ."

At this point the defense attorney was interrupted by rather loud applause. Indeed, he uttered his last words with such a sincere-sounding note that everyone felt he perhaps really had something to say, and that what he would say now was most important of all. But the presiding judge, hearing the applause, loudly threatened to "clear" the court if "such an instance" occurred again. Everything became hushed, and Fetyukovich began in a sort of new, heartfelt voice, quite unlike the one in which he had been speaking so far.

Chapter 13

An Adulterer of Thought

"It is not only the totality of the facts that ruins my client, gentlemen of the jury," he exclaimed, "no, my client is ruined, in reality, by just one fact: the corpse of his old father! Were it simply a homicide, you, too, would reject the accusation, in view of the insignificant, the unsubstantiated, the fantastic nature of the facts when they are each examined separately and not in their totality; at least you would hesitate to ruin a man's destiny merely because of your prejudice against him, which, alas, he has so richly deserved! But here we have not simply a homicide, but a parricide! This is impressive, and to such a degree that the very insignificance and unsubstantiatedness of the incriminating facts become not so insignificant and unsubstantiated, and that even in the most unprejudiced mind. Now, how can such a defendant be acquitted? And what if he did kill him and goes unpunished—that is what everyone feels in his heart, almost unwittingly, instinctively. Yes, it is a horrible thing to shed a father's blood—his blood who begot me, his blood who loved me, his life's blood who did not spare himself for me, who from childhood ached with my aches, who all his life suffered for my happiness and lived only in my joys, my successes! Oh, to kill such a father—who could even dream of it! Gentlemen of the jury, what is a father, a real father, what does this great word mean, what terribly great idea is contained in this appellation? We have just indicated something of what a true father is and ought to be. In the present case, with which all of us are now so involved, for which our souls ache—in the present case the father, the late Fyodor Pavlovich Karamazov, in no way fitted the idea of a father that has just spoken to our hearts. That is a calamity. Yes, indeed, some fathers are like a calamity. Let us examine this calamity more closely—we must not be afraid of anything, gentlemen of the jury, in view of the importance of the impending decision. We more especially ought not to be afraid now, or, so to speak, to wave certain ideas away, like children or frightened women, as the highly talented prosecutor happily expressed it. Yet in his ardent speech my esteemed opponent (my opponent even before I uttered my first word) exclaimed several times: 'No, I shall not turn over the defense of the accused to anyone, I shall not yield his defense to the defense attorney from Petersburg—I am both prosecutor and defender!' So he exclaimed several times, and yet he forgot to mention that if this terrible defendant was, for all of twenty-three years, so grateful just for one pound of nuts given him as a child by the only man who was ever nice to him in his paternal home, then, conversely, such a man could not fail to remember, for all those twenty-three years, how his father had him running around barefoot 'in the backyard, without any shoes, his little britches hanging by one button,' as the philanthropic Dr. Herzenstube put it. Oh, gentlemen of the jury, why need we examine this 'calamity' more closely, why repeat what everyone already knows! What did my client meet when he came home to his father? And why, why portray my client as heartless, as an egoist, a monster? He is unbridled, he is wild and stormy, that is why we are trying him now, but who is responsible for his destiny, who is responsible that for all his good inclinations, his noble, sensitive heart, he received such an absurd upbringing? Did anyone teach him any sense at all, has he been enlightened by learning, did anyone give him at least a little love in his childhood? My client grew up in God's keeping—that is, like a wild beast. Perhaps he longed to see his father after so many years of separation; perhaps a thousand times before then, recalling his childhood as if in sleep, he had driven away the loathsome ghosts of his childhood dreams, and longed with all his soul to vindicate his father and embrace him! And now what? He meets with nothing but cynical jeers, suspiciousness, and pettifoggery over the disputed money; all he hears daily, 'over the cognac,' are talk and worldly precepts that make him sick at heart; and, finally, he beholds his father stealing his mistress away from him, from his own son, and with the son's own money—oh, gentlemen of the jury, this is loathsome and cruel! And this same old man complains to everyone about the irreverence and cruelty of his son, besmirches him in society, injures him, slanders him, buys up his promissory notes in order to put him in jail! Gentlemen of the jury, these souls, these people who seem hardhearted, stormy, and unrestrained, people like my client, sometimes, and indeed most often, are extremely tenderhearted, only they keep it hidden. Do not laugh, do not laugh at my idea! Earlier the talented prosecutor laughed mercilessly at my client, pointing to his love for Schiller, his love for 'the beautiful and lofty.' I should not laugh at that if I were him, if I were a prosecutor! Yes, these hearts—oh, let me defend these hearts, which are so rarely and so wrongly understood—these hearts quite often thirst for what is tender, for what is beautiful and righteous, precisely the contrary, as it were, of themselves, of their storminess, their cruelty—thirst for it unconsciously, precisely thirst for it. Outwardly passionate and cruel, they are capable, for instance, of loving a woman to the point of torment, and inevitably with a lofty and spiritual love. Again, do not laugh at me: it most often happens precisely so with such natures! Only they are unable to conceal their passion, at times very coarse—and that is what strikes everyone, that is what everyone notices, and no one sees the inner man. On the contrary, all such passions are quickly spent, but at the side of a noble, beautiful being this apparently coarse and cruel man seeks renewal, seeks the chance to reform, to become better, to become lofty and honest—'lofty and beautiful,' much ridiculed though the phrase may be! I said earlier that I would not venture to touch on my client's romance with Miss Verkhovtsev. Yet I may allow myself half a word: what we heard earlier was not testimony, but only the cry of a frenzied and vengeful woman, and it is not for her, no, it is not for her to reproach him with betrayal, because she herself has betrayed him! If she had had a little time to think better of it, she would not have given such testimony! Oh, do not believe her, no, my client is not a 'monster,' as she called him! The crucified lover of mankind, as he was going to his cross, said: 'I am the good shepherd: the good shepherd giveth his life for the sheep, so that not one will be destroyed . . .'[1] Let us, too, not destroy a human soul! What is a father, I was asking just now, and exclaimed that it is a great word, a precious appellation. But, gentlemen of the jury, one must treat words honestly, and I shall allow myself to name a thing by the proper word, the proper appellation: such a father as the murdered old Karamazov cannot and does not deserve to be called a father. Love for a father that is not justified by the father is an absurdity, an impossibility. Love cannot be created out of nothing: only God creates out of nothing. 'Fathers, provoke not your children,' writes the apostle,[2] from a heart aflame with love. I quote these holy words now not for the sake of my client, but as a reminder to all fathers. Who has empowered me to teach fathers? No one. But as a man and a citizen I call out—*vivos voco!*[3] We are not long on this earth, we do many evil deeds and say many evil words. And therefore let us all seize the favorable moment of our being together in order to say a good word to each other as well. And so I do; while I am in this place, I make the best of my moment. Not in vain is this tribune given us by a higher will—from here we can be heard by the whole of Russia. I speak not only to fathers here, but to all fathers I cry out: 'Fathers, provoke not your children!' Let us first fulfill Christ's commandment ourselves, and only then let us expect the same of our children. Otherwise we are not fathers but enemies of our children, and they are not our children but our enemies, and we ourselves have made them our enemies! 'With what measure ye mete, it shall be measured to you'[4]—it is not I who say this, it is the Gospel precept: measure with the same measure as it is measured to you. How can we blame our children if they measure to us with our own measure? Recently in Finland a girl, a servant, was suspected of secretly giving birth to a baby. They began watching her, and in the attic of the house, in a corner, behind some bricks, found her chest, which no one knew about, opened it, and took out of it the little body of a newborn baby that she had killed. In the same chest were found two skeletons of babies she had given birth to previously and killed at the moment of birth, as she confessed. Gentlemen of the jury, was she a mother to her children? Yes, she gave birth to them, but was she a mother to them? Would any one of us dare pronounce over her the sacred name of mother? Let us be brave, gentlemen of the jury, let us even be bold, it is even our duty to be so in the present moment and not to be afraid of certain words and ideas, like Moscow merchants' wives who are afraid of 'metal' and 'brimstone.'[5] No, let us prove, on the contrary, that the progress of the past few years has touched our development as well, and let us say straight out: he who begets is not yet a father; a father is he who begets and proves worthy of it. Oh, of course, there is another meaning, another interpretation of the word 'father,' which insists that my father, though a monster, though a villain to his children, is still my father simply because he begot me. But this meaning is, so to speak, a mystical one, which I do not understand with my reason, but can only accept by faith, or, more precisely, *on faith*, like many other things that I do not understand, but that religion nonetheless tells me to believe. But in that case let it remain outside the sphere of real life. While within the sphere of real life, which not only has its rights, but itself imposes great obligations—within this sphere, if we wish to be humane, to be Christians finally, it is our duty and obligation to foster only those convictions that are justified by reason and experience, that have passed through the crucible of analysis, in a word, to act sensibly and not senselessly as in dreams or delirium, so as not to bring harm to a man, so as not to torment and ruin a man. Then, then it will be a real Christian deed, not only a mystical one, but a sensible and truly philanthropic deed . . ."

At this point loud applause broke out in many parts of the hall, but Fetyukovich even waved his hands, as if begging not to be interrupted and to be allowed to finish. Everything at once became hushed. The orator went on:

"Do you think, gentlemen of the jury, that such questions can pass our children by, let's say, if they are now adolescents, let's say, if they are now beginning to reason? No, they cannot, and let us not ask such impossible forbearance of them! The sight of an unworthy father, especially in comparison with other fathers, fathers worthy of their children, his own peers, involuntarily presents a young man with tormenting questions. To these questions he receives the conventional answer: 'He begot you, you are of his blood, that is why you must love him.' The young man involuntarily begins thinking: 'But did he love me when he was begetting me,' he asks, wondering more and more. 'Did he beget me for my own sake? He did not know me, not even my sex at that moment, the moment of passion, probably heated up with wine, and probably all he did for me was pass on to me an inclination to drink—so much for his good deeds . . . Why should I love him just because he begot me and then never loved me all my life?' Oh, perhaps to you these questions appear coarse, cruel, but do not demand impossible forbearance from a young mind: 'Drive nature out the door and it will fly back in the window'[6]—and above all, above all, let us not be afraid of 'metal' and 'brimstone,' let us decide the question as reason and the love of man dictate, and not as dictated by mystical notions. How decide it, then? Here is how: let the son stand before his father and ask him reasonably: 'Father, tell me, why should I love you? Father, prove to me that I should love you'—and if the father can, if he is able to answer and give him proof, then we have a real, normal family, established not just on mystical prejudice, but on reasonable, self-accountable, and strictly humane foundations. In the opposite case, if the father can give no proof—

the family is finished then and there: he is not a father to his son, and the son is free and has the right henceforth to look upon his father as a stranger and even as his enemy. Our tribune, gentlemen of the jury, should be a school of truth and sensible ideas."

Here the orator was interrupted by unrestrained, almost frenzied applause. Of course, the whole room did not applaud, but still about half the room applauded. Fathers and mothers applauded. From above, where the ladies were sitting, shrieks and cries could be heard. Handkerchiefs were waved. The presiding judge began ringing the bell as hard as he could. He was obviously annoyed with the behavior of the courtroom, but decidedly did not dare "clear" the court, as he had recently threatened to do: even the dignitaries, the old men with stars on their frock coats, who were sitting on special chairs behind the judges, were applauding and waving handkerchiefs to the orator, so that when the noise died down, the judge contented himself merely with repeating his strict promise to clear the court, and the triumphant and excited Fetyukovich began to go on with his speech.

"Gentlemen of the jury, you remember that terrible night of which so much has been said today, when the son climbed over the fence, got into his father's house, and finally stood face to face with the enemy and offender who begot him. I insist as strongly as I can—he did not come running for money then: the accusation of robbery is an absurdity, as I have already explained before. And he did not break into his house in order to kill him, oh, no: if that had been his premeditated intention, he would at least have seen to the weapon beforehand, but he grabbed the brass pestle instinctively, not knowing why himself. Suppose he did deceive his father with the signals, suppose he did get in—I have already said that I do not for a moment believe this legend, but very well, let us suppose it for the moment! Gentlemen of the jury, I swear to you by all that's holy, if it had not been his father but some other offender, then, having run through the rooms and made sure that the woman was not in the house, he would have run away as fast as he could, without doing his rival any harm; he might have hit him, pushed him aside, but that would be all, because he could not be bothered with that, he had no time, he had to find out where she was. But his father, his father—oh, it was all because of the sight of his father, his enemy, his offender, who had hated him from childhood, and now—his monstrous rival! A feeling of hatred took hold of him involuntarily, unrestrainably; to reason was impossible: everything surged up in a moment! It was madness and insanity, a fit of passion, but a natural fit of passion, avenging its eternal laws unrestrainably and unconsciously, like all things in nature. But even then the killer did not kill—I assert it, I cry it aloud—no, he merely swung the pestle in disgusted indignation, not wishing to kill, not knowing that he would kill. Had it not been for that fatal pestle in his hand, he would perhaps only have beaten his father, and not killed him. He did not know as he ran away whether the old man he had struck down was killed or not. Such a murder is not a murder. Such a murder is not a parricide, either. No, the murder of such a father cannot be called parricide. Such a murder can be considered parricide only out of prejudice! But was there, was there indeed any murder—again and again I call out to you from the bottom of my soul! Gentlemen of the jury, we shall condemn him, and then he will say to himself: 'These people did nothing for my destiny, my upbringing, my education, nothing to make me better, to make a man of me. These people did not give me to eat, they did not give me to drink, I lay naked in prison and they did not visit me,[7] and now they have exiled me to penal servitude. I am quits, I owe them nothing now, and I owe nothing to anyone unto ages of ages. They are wicked, and I shall be wicked. They are cruel, and I shall be cruel.' That is what he will say, gentlemen of the jury! And I swear: with your verdict you will only ease him, ease his conscience, he will curse the blood he has shed and not regret it. Along with that you will destroy the still-possible man in him, for he will remain wicked and blind for the rest of his life. No, if you want to punish him terribly, fearfully, with the most horrible punishment imaginable, but so as to save and restore his soul forever—then overwhelm him with your mercy! You will see, you will hear how his soul will tremble and be horrified: 'Is it for me to endure this mercy, for me to be granted so much love, and am I worthy of it?' he will exclaim! Oh, I know, I know that heart, it is a wild but noble heart, gentlemen of the jury. It will bow down before your deed, it thirsts for a great act of love, it will catch fire and resurrect forever. There are souls that in their narrowness blame the whole world. But overwhelm such a soul with mercy, give it love, and it will curse what it has done, for there are so many germs of good in it. The soul will expand and behold how merciful God is, and how beautiful and just people are. He will be horrified, he will be overwhelmed with repentance and the countless debt he must henceforth repay. And then he will not say, 'I am quits,' but will say, 'I am guilty before all people and am the least worthy of all people.' In tears of repentance and burning, suffering tenderness he will exclaim: 'People are better than I, for they wished not to ruin but to save me!' Oh, it is so easy for you to do it, this act of mercy, for in the absence of any evidence even slightly resembling the truth, it will be too difficult for you to say: 'Yes, guilty.' It is better to let ten who are guilty go, than to punish one who is innocent—do you hear, do you hear this majestic voice from the last century of our glorious history?[8] Is it for me, insignificant as I am, to remind you that the Russian courts exist not only for punishment but also for the salvation of the ruined man! Let other nations have the letter and punishment, we have the spirit and meaning, the salvation and regeneration of the lost. And if so, if such indeed are Russia and her courts, then—onward, Russia! And do not frighten us, oh, do not frighten us with your mad troikas, which all nations stand aside from in disgust! Not a mad troika, but a majestic Russian chariot will arrive solemnly and peacefully at its goal. In your hands is the fate of my client, in your hands is also the fate of our Russian truth. You will save it, you will champion it, you will prove that there are some to preserve it, that it is in good hands!"

Chapter 14

Our Peasants Stood Up for Themselves

Thus Fetyukovich concluded, and the rapture that burst from his listeners this time was unrestrainable, like a storm. To restrain it now was unthinkable: women wept, many of the men also wept, even two of the dignitaries shed tears. The presiding judge submitted and even delayed ringing his bell: "To trespass upon such enthusiasm would amount to trespassing upon something sacred," as our ladies cried afterwards. The orator himself was genuinely moved. And it was at such a moment that our Ippolit Kirillovich rose once more "to voice certain objections." He was met with hateful stares: "How? What's this? He still dares to object?" the ladies prattled. But even if all the ladies in the world, with the prosecutor's own wife at their head, had begun prattling, it would have been impossible to restrain him at that moment. He was pale, shaking with emotion; the first words, the first phrases he uttered were even incomprehensible; he was breathless, inarticulate, confused. However, he quickly recovered. But I shall quote only a few phrases from his second speech.

". . . We are reproached with having invented all sorts of novels. But what has the defense attorney offered if not novel upon novel? The only thing lacking is poetry. Fyodor Pavlovich, while waiting for his mistress, tears up the envelope and throws it on the floor. Even what he said on this remarkable occasion is quoted. Is this not a poem? And where is the proof that he took out the money, who heard what he was saying? The feebleminded idiot Smerdyakov, transformed into some sort of Byronic hero revenging himself upon society for his illegitimate birth—is this not a poem in the Byronic fashion?

And the son bursting into his father's house, killing him, and at the same time not killing him, this is not even a novel, not a poem, it is a sphinx posing riddles, which it, of course, will not solve itself. If he killed him, he killed him; how can it be that he killed him and yet did not kill him—who can understand that? Then it is announced to us that our tribune is the tribune of truth and sensible ideas, and so from this tribune of 'sensible ideas' an axiom resounds, accompanied by an oath, that to call the murder of a father parricide is simply a prejudice! But if parricide is a prejudice, and if every child ought to ask his father, 'Father, why should I love you?'—what will become of us, what will become of the foundations of society, where will the family end up? Parricide—don't you see, it's just the 'brimstone' of some Moscow merchant's wife? The most precious, the most sacred precepts concerning the purpose and future of the Russian courts are presented perversely and frivolously, only to achieve a certain end, to achieve the acquittal of that which cannot be acquitted. 'Oh, overwhelm him with mercy,' the defense attorney exclaims, and that is just what the criminal wants, and tomorrow everyone will see how overwhelmed he is! And is the defense attorney not being too modest in asking only for the defendant's acquittal? Why does he not ask that a fund be established in the parricide's name, in order to immortalize his deed for posterity and the younger generation? The Gospel and religion are corrected: it's all mysticism, he says, and ours is the only true Christianity, tested by the analysis of reason and sensible ideas. And so a false image of Christ is held up to us! '*With what measure ye mete, it shall be measured to you*,' the defense attorney exclaims, and concludes then and there that Christ commanded us to measure with the same measure as it is measured to us—and that from the tribune of truth and sensible ideas! We glance into the Gospel only on the eve of our speeches, in order to make a brilliant display of our familiarity with what is, after all, a rather original work, which may prove useful and serve for a certain effect, in good measure, all in good measure! Yet Christ tells us precisely not to do so, to beware of doing so, because that is what the wicked world does, whereas we must forgive and turn our cheek, and not measure with the same measure as our offenders measure to us. This is what our God taught us, and not that it is a prejudice to forbid children to kill their own fathers. And let us not, from the rostrum of truth and sensible ideas, correct the Gospel of our God, whom the defense attorney deems worthy of being called merely 'the crucified lover of mankind,' in opposition to the whole of Orthodox Russia, which calls out to him: 'For thou art our God . . . !' "[1]

Here the presiding judge intervened and checked the carried-away speaker, asking him not to exaggerate, to stay within proper bounds, and so on and so forth, everything presiding judges usually say in such cases. And the courtroom was restless as well. The public was stirring, even calling out in indignation. Fetyukovich did not even object; he stepped up, putting his hands to his heart, only to pronounce in an offended voice a few words full of dignity. He touched again, lightly and mockingly, on "novels" and "psychology," and at one point appropriately added: "Thou art angry, Jupiter, therefore thou art wrong,"[2] drawing numerous and approving chuckles from the public, for Ippolit Kirillovich in no way resembled Jupiter. Then, to the charge that he supposedly gave the younger generation permission to kill their fathers, Fetyukovich observed with profound dignity that he saw no need to reply. With regard to the "false image of Christ," and his not deeming Christ worthy to be called God, but calling him merely "the crucified lover of mankind," which is "contrary to Orthodoxy and should not be spoken from the tribune of truth and sensible ideas"—Fetyukovich hinted at "sinister intent" and said that in preparing to come here he had trusted at least that this tribune would be secure from accusations "dangerous to my person as a citizen and a loyal subject . . ." But at these words the presiding judge checked him as well, and Fetyukovich, with a bow, finished his response, followed by a general murmur of approval from the courtroom. And Ippolit Kirillovich, in the opinion of our ladies, was "crushed forever."

Then the defendant himself was given the opportunity to speak. Mitya stood up, but said little. He was terribly tired in body and in spirit. The look of strength and independence with which he had appeared in court that morning had all but vanished. He seemed to have experienced something that day for the rest of his life, which had taught and brought home to him something very important, something he had not understood before. His voice had grown weaker, he no longer shouted as earlier. Something new, resigned, defeated, and downcast could be heard in his words.

"What can I say, gentlemen of the jury! My judgment has come, I feel the right hand of God upon me. The end of the erring man! But I tell you as if I were confessing to God: 'No, of my father's blood I am not guilty!' For the last time I repeat: 'I did not kill him.' I erred, but I loved the good. Every moment I longed to reform, yet I lived like a wild beast. My thanks to the prosecutor, he said much about me that I did not know, but it is not true that I killed my father, the prosecutor is mistaken! My thanks also to the defense attorney, I wept listening to him, but it is not true that I killed my father, there was no need even to suppose it! And don't believe the doctors, I'm entirely in my right mind, only my soul is heavy. If you spare me, if you let me go—I will pray for you. I will become better, I give you my word, I give it before God. And if you condemn me—I will break the sword over my head myself, and kiss the broken pieces![3] But spare me, do not deprive me of my God, I know myself: I will murmur! My soul is heavy, gentlemen . . . spare me!"

He all but fell back in his seat, his voice broke, he barely managed to utter the last phrase. Then the court proceeded to pose the questions and asked for conclusions from both sides. But I omit the details here. At last the jury rose to retire for deliberation. The presiding judge was very tired, which is why his instructions to them were so weak: "Be impartial," he said, "do not be impressed by the eloquent words of the defense, and yet weigh carefully, remember that a great obligation rests upon you," and so on and so forth. The jury retired, and there came a break in the session. People could stand, move about, exchange their stored-up impressions, have a bite to eat at the buffet. It was very late, already about an hour past midnight, but no one wanted to leave. They were all so tense that rest was the last thing on their minds. They all waited with sinking hearts; though, incidentally, not everyone's heart was sinking. The ladies were simply hysterically impatient, but their hearts were untroubled: "Acquittal is inevitable." They were preparing themselves for the spectacular moment of general enthusiasm. I must admit that in the male half of the room, too, a great many were convinced of an inevitable acquittal. Some were glad, but others frowned, and still others simply hung their heads: they did not want acquittal! Fetyukovich, for his part, was firmly assured of success. He was surrounded, congratulated, fawned upon.

"There are," he said to one group, as was reported afterwards, "there are these invisible threads that bind the defense attorney and the jury together. They begin and can already be sensed during the speech. I felt them, they exist. Don't worry, the case is ours."

"I wonder what our peasants are going to say?" said one sullen, fat, pockmarked gentleman, a neighboring landowner, approaching a group of gentlemen conversing.

"But they're not all peasants. There are four officials among them."

"Yes, officials," a member of the district council said, joining them.

"And do you know Nazaryev, Prokhor Ivanovich, the merchant with the medal, the one on the jury?"

"What about him?"

"Palatial mind."

"But he never says a word."

"Never says a word, but so much the better. Your man from Petersburg has nothing to teach him; he could teach the whole of Petersburg himself. Twelve children, just think of it!"

"Good God, how can they possibly not acquit him?" cried one of our young officials in another group.

"He's sure to be acquitted," a resolute voice was heard.

"It would be a shame and a disgrace not to acquit him!" the official went on exclaiming. "Suppose he did kill him, but there are fathers and fathers! And, finally, he was in such a frenzy . . . Maybe he really did just swing the pestle and the old man fell down. Only it's too bad they dragged the lackey into it. That's just a ridiculous episode. If I were the defense attorney, I'd have said straight out: he killed him, but he's not guilty, and devil take you!"

"But that's just what he did, only he didn't say 'devil take you.'"

"No, Mikhail Semyonovich, but he nearly said it," a third little voice chimed in.

"Good God, gentlemen, didn't they acquit an actress, during Great Lent, who cut the throat of her lover's lawful wife?"*

"But she didn't finish cutting it."

"All the same, all the same, she started to!"

"And what he said about children! Splendid!"

"Splendid."

"And about mysticism, about mysticism, eh?"

"Mysticism nothing," someone else cried out, "think about Ippolit, think what his fate is going to be after this day! His wife is sure to scratch his eyes out tomorrow over Mitenka."

"Is she here?"

"Here, hah! If she were here, she'd have scratched his eyes out right here. She's at home with a toothache. Heh, heh, heh!"

"Heh, heh, heh!"

In a third group:

"It looks like Mitenka will be acquitted after all."

"Tomorrow, for all I know, he'll smash up the whole 'Metropolis,' he'll go on a ten-day binge."

"Ah, the devil you say!"

"The devil? Yes, the devil's in it all right, where else would he be if not here?"

"Eloquence aside, gentlemen, people can't be allowed to go breaking their fathers' heads with steelyards. Otherwise where will we end up?"

"The chariot, the chariot, remember that?"

"Yes, he made a chariot out of a dung cart."

"And tomorrow a dung cart out of a chariot, 'in good measure, all in good measure.'"

"Folks are clever nowadays. Do we have any truth in Russia, gentlemen, or is there none at all?"

But the bell rang. The jury deliberated for exactly an hour, not more, not less. A deep silence reigned as soon as the public resumed their seats. I remember how the jury filed into the courtroom. At last! I omit giving the questions point by point, besides I've forgotten them. I remember only the answer to the first and chief question of the presiding judge—that is, "Did he commit murder for the purpose of robbery, and with premeditation?" (I do not remember the text.) Everything became still. The foreman of the jury—namely, one of the officials, the youngest of them all—pronounced loudly and clearly, in the dead silence of the courtroom:

"Yes, guilty!"

And then it was the same on each point: guilty, yes, guilty, and that without the least extenuation! This really no one had expected, almost everyone was certain at least of extenuation. The dead silence of the courtroom remained unbroken, everyone seemed literally turned to stone—both those who longed for conviction and those who longed for acquittal. But this lasted only for the first moments. Then a terrible chaos broke loose. Many among the male public turned out to be very pleased. Some even rubbed their hands with unconcealed joy. The displeased ones seemed crushed; they shrugged, whispered, as if still unable to comprehend it. But, my God, what came over our ladies! I thought they might start a riot! At first they seemed not to believe their ears. Then, suddenly, exclamations were heard all over the courtroom: "What's that? What on earth is that?" They jumped up from their seats. They must have thought it could all be redone and reversed on the spot. At that moment Mitya suddenly rose and cried in a sort of rending voice, stretching his arms out before him:

"I swear by God and by his terrible judgment, I am not guilty of my father's blood! Katya, I forgive you! Brothers, friends, have pity on the other woman!"

He did not finish and broke into sobs heard all over the courtroom, in a voice, terrible, no longer his own, but somehow new, unexpected, which suddenly came to him from God knows where. In the gallery above, from the furthest corner, came a woman's piercing cry: it was Grushenka. She had begged someone earlier and had been let back into the courtroom before the attorneys began their debate. Mitya was taken away. The sentencing was put off until the next day. The whole courtroom rose in turmoil, but I did not stay and listen. I remember only a few exclamations from the porch on the way out.

"He'll get a twenty-year taste of the mines."

"Not less."

"Yes, sir, our peasants stood up for themselves."

"And finished off our Mitenka."

End of the Fourth and Last Part

EPILOGUE

Chapter 1

Plans to Save Mitya

On the fifth day after Mitya's trial, very early in the morning, before nine o'clock, Alyosha came to see Katerina Ivanovna, to make final arrangements in a certain business important for them both, and with an errand to her besides. She sat and talked with him in the same room where she had once received Grushenka; nearby, in the next room, lay Ivan Fyodorovich, in fever and unconscious. Immediately after the scene in court, Katerina Ivanovna had ordered the sick and unconscious Ivan Fyodorovich moved to her house, scorning any future and inevitable talk of society and its condemnation. One of the two relatives who lived with her left for Moscow just after the scene in court, the other remained. But even if both had left, Katerina Ivanovna would not have altered her decision and would have stayed to look after the sick man and sit by him day and night. He was treated by Varvinsky and Herzenstube; the Moscow doctor had gone back to Moscow, refusing to predict his opinion concerning the possible outcome of the illness. Though the remaining doctors encouraged Katerina Ivanovna and Alyosha, it was apparent that they were still unable to give any firm hope. Alyosha visited his sick brother twice a day. But this time he came on special, most troublesome business, and sensed how difficult it would be to begin talking about it, and yet he was in a hurry: he had other pressing business that same morning in a different place and had to rush. They had already been talking for about a quarter of an hour. Katerina Ivanovna was pale, very tired, and at the same time in a state of extreme, morbid agitation: she sensed why, among other things, Alyosha had come to her now.

"Don't worry about his decision," she told Alyosha with firm insistence. "One way or another, he will still come to this way out: he must escape! That unfortunate man, that hero of honor and conscience—not him, not Dmitri Fyodorovich, but the one lying behind this door, who sacrificed himself for his brother," Katya added with flashing eyes, "told me the whole plan of escape long ago. You know, he has already made contacts . . . I've already told you something . . . You see, it will probably take place at the third halt, when the party of convicts is taken to Siberia. Oh, it's still a long way off. Ivan Fyodorovich has been to see the head man at the third halting-place. But it's not known yet who will head the party, and it's impossible to find out beforehand. Tomorrow, perhaps, I'll show you the whole plan in detail; Ivan Fyodorovich left it with me the night before the trial, in case something . . . It was that same time, remember, when you found us quarreling that evening: he was just going downstairs, and when I saw you, I made him come back—remember? Do you know what we were quarreling about?"

"No, I don't," said Alyosha.

"Of course he concealed it from you then: it was precisely about this plan of escape. He had revealed all the main things to me three days earlier—that was when we began quarreling, and we went on quarreling for three days. We quarreled because, when he announced to me that if Dmitri Fyodorovich was convicted, he would flee abroad with that creature, I suddenly got furious—I won't tell you why, I don't know why myself . . . Oh, of course, because of that creature, I got furious because of that creature, and precisely because she, too, was going to flee abroad, together with Dmitri!" Katerina Ivanovna suddenly exclaimed, her lips trembling with wrath. "As soon as Ivan Fyodorovich saw how furious I was because of that creature, he immediately thought I was jealous of her over Dmitri, and that it meant I still loved Dmitri. And that led to our first quarrel. I did not want to give explanations, I could not ask forgiveness; it was hard for me to think that such a man could suspect me of still loving that . . . Even though I myself had already told him directly, long before, that I did not love Dmitri, but loved only him! I got furious with him only because I was so furious with that creature! Three days later, that evening when you came, he brought me a sealed envelope, to be opened at once in case something happened to him. Oh, he foresaw his illness! He revealed to me that the envelope contained details of the escape, and that if he should die or become dangerously ill, I must save Mitya alone. He left me money along with it, nearly ten thousand roubles—the same money the prosecutor mentioned in his speech, having learned somehow that he had sent it to be cashed. I was terribly struck that Ivan Fyodorovich, who was still jealous over me and still convinced that I loved Mitya, nonetheless did not abandon the idea of saving his brother, and entrusted me, me myself, with saving him! Oh, there was a sacrifice! No, you would not understand such self-sacrifice in all its fullness, Alexei Fyodorovich. I almost fell at his feet in reverence, but the thought suddenly occurred to me that he would take it simply as my joy at Mitya's being saved (and he certainly would have thought that), and I was so annoyed simply at the possibility of such an unjust thought on his part, that I became annoyed again, and instead of kissing his feet, I made another scene! Oh, how wretched I am! It's my character—a terrible, wretched character! Oh, one day you'll see: I'll do it, I'll bring it to such a point that he, too, will leave me for some other woman, someone easier to live with, as Dmitri did, but then . . . no, I couldn't bear it, I'd kill myself! And when you came then, and I called to you and told him to come back, when he came in with you then, the hateful, contemptuous look he suddenly gave me filled me with such wrath that—remember?—I suddenly cried to you that *he, he alone* had convinced me that his brother Dmitri was a murderer! I slandered him on purpose, in order to hurt him once more, but he never, never tried to convince me that his brother was a murderer, on the contrary, it was I, I who kept trying to convince him! Oh, my rage was the cause of everything, everything! It was I, I who brought on that cursed scene in court! He wanted to prove to me that he was noble, and that even though I might love his brother, he still would not destroy him out of revenge and jealousy. And so he stood up in court . . . I am the cause of it all, I alone am guilty!"

Never before had Katya made such confessions to Alyosha, and he felt that she had then reached precisely that degree of unbearable suffering when a proud heart painfully shatters its own pride and falls, overcome by grief. Oh, Alyosha knew yet another terrible reason for her present torment, no matter how she had concealed it from him all those days since Mitya had been convicted; but for some reason it would have been too painful for him if she had decided to lower herself so much as to begin talking with him herself, now, at that moment, about that reason. She was suffering over her "betrayal" in court, and Alyosha sensed that her conscience was urging her to confess, precisely to him, to Alyosha, with tears, with shrieks, with hysterics, beating on the floor. But he dreaded that moment and wished to spare the suffering woman. This made the errand on which he had come all the more difficult. He again began talking about Mitya.

"Never mind, never mind, don't worry about him!" Katya began again, sharply and stubbornly. "It's all momentary with him, I know him, I know his heart only too well. Rest assured, he'll agree to escape. And, above all, it's not right now; he still has time to make up his mind. Ivan Fyodorovich will be well by then, and will handle it all himself, so there will be nothing left for me to do. Don't worry, he'll agree to escape. He has already agreed: how can he part with that creature of his? Since they won't let her go to penal servitude, how can he not escape? He's afraid of you most of all, afraid you won't approve of his escape on moral grounds, but you must magnanimously *allow* him to do it, since your sanction here is so necessary," Katya added with venom. She paused briefly and grinned.

"He keeps talking there," she started again, "about some sort of hymns, about the cross he has to bear, about some sort of duty, I remember Ivan Fyodorovich told me a lot about it then, and if you knew how he spoke!" Katya suddenly exclaimed with irrepressible feeling. "If you knew how he loved the wretched man at that moment, as he was telling about him, and how he hated him, perhaps, at the same moment! And I, oh, I listened to his story and his tears with a scornful smile! Oh, the creature! Me, I'm the creature! I gave birth to this brain fever for him! And that man, that convict, is not prepared to suffer," Katya concluded with irritation, "how can such a man suffer? Such men never suffer!"

Some feeling of hatred and contemptuous loathing sounded in these words. And yet she had betrayed him. "Oh, well, perhaps it's because she feels so guilty towards him that she hates him at moments," Alyosha thought to himself. He hoped it was only "at moments." He caught the challenge in Katya's last words, but did not take it up.

"That is why I sent for you today, so that you would promise to convince him yourself. Or do you, too, consider it not honest to escape, not valiant, or whatever you call it . . . not Christian, or what?" Katya added with even more challenge.

"No, not at all. I'll tell him everything . . . ," Alyosha muttered. "He asks you to come and see him today," he blurted out suddenly, looking steadily in her eyes. She shuddered all over and drew back from him a little on the sofa.

"Me . . . is it possible?" she murmured, turning pale.

"It is and must be!" Alyosha began insistently, becoming animated. "He needs you very much, precisely now. I wouldn't mention the subject and torment you beforehand if it weren't necessary. He's ill, he seems mad, he keeps asking for you. He doesn't ask you to come and make peace, but just to show yourself in the doorway. A lot has happened to him since that day. He understands how incalculably guilty he is before you. He doesn't want your forgiveness: 'I cannot be forgiven,' he says it himself—but only that you show yourself in the doorway . . ."

"You suddenly . . . ," Katya stammered, "all these days I had a feeling you would come with that . . . I just knew he would ask for me . . . ! It's impossible!"

"It may be impossible, but do it. Remember, for the first time he's been struck by how he insulted you, for the first time in his life, he never grasped it so fully before! He says: if she refuses to come, then I 'will be unhappy for the rest of my life.' Do you hear? A man sentenced to twenty years of penal servitude still intends to be happy—isn't that pitiful? Think: you will be visiting a man who has been guiltlessly ruined," burst from Alyosha with a challenge, "his hands are clean, there is no blood on them! For the sake of his countless future sufferings, visit him now! Go, see him off into the darkness . . . stand in the doorway, that's all . . . You really must, *must* do it!" Alyosha concluded, emphasizing the word "must" with incredible force.

"I must, but . . . I can't," Katya nearly groaned, "he will look at me . . . I can't."

"Your eyes must meet. How will you live all your life if you don't bring yourself to do it now?"

"Better to suffer all my life."

"You must go, you *must* go," Alyosha again emphasized implacably.

"But why today, why now . . . ? I cannot leave a sick man . . ."

"You can for a moment, it will just be a moment. If you don't go, he will come down with brain fever by tonight. I wouldn't lie to you—have pity!"

"Have pity on me," Katya bitterly reproached him, and she started to cry.

"So you will go!" Alyosha said firmly, seeing her tears. "I'll go and tell him you're coming now."

"No, no, don't tell him!" Katya cried out in fear. "I will go, but don't tell him beforehand, because I'll go there but I may not go in . . . I don't know yet . . ."

Her voice broke off. She had difficulty breathing. Alyosha rose to leave.

"And what if I meet someone?" she suddenly said softly, turning pale again.

"That's why it needs to be now, so that you won't meet anyone. I assure you, no one will be there. We'll be waiting for you," he concluded insistently, and walked out of the room.

Chapter 2

For a Moment the Lie Became Truth

He rushed to the hospital where Mitya was now lying. Two days after the decision of the court, he had come down with nervous fever and was sent to our town hospital, to the section for convicts. But at the request of Alyosha and many others (Madame Khokhlakov, Liza, and so on), Dr. Varvinsky placed Mitya apart from the convicts, in the same little room where Smerdyakov had been. True, a sentry stood at the end of the corridor, and the window was barred, so that Varvinsky could rest easy concerning his indulgence, which was not quite legal, but he was a kind and compassionate young man. He understood that it was hard for a man like Mitya suddenly to step straight into the company of murderers and swindlers, and that he would have to get used to it first. Visits from relatives and acquaintances were permitted by the doctor, and by the warden, and even by the police commissioner, all underhandedly. But Mitya had been visited during those days only by Alyosha and Grushenka. Rakitin had tried twice to see him; but Mitya insistently asked Varvinsky not to let him in.

Alyosha found him sitting on a cot, in a hospital robe, a little feverish, his head wrapped in a towel moistened with water and vinegar. He glanced at the entering Alyosha with a vague look, and yet some sort of fear seemed to flash in this look.

Generally, since the day of the trial, he had become terribly pensive. Sometimes he would be silent for half an hour, apparently thinking ponderously and painfully about something, forgetting whoever was there. And if he roused himself from his pensiveness and began to speak, he would always somehow begin suddenly, and inevitably not with what he really ought to be saying. Sometimes he looked at his brother with suffering. It seemed to be easier for him with Grushenka than with Alyosha. True, he hardly said a word to her, but the moment she entered his whole face lit up with joy. Alyosha silently sat down next to him on the cot. This time he had been anxiously awaiting Alyosha, but he did not dare ask him anything. He considered it unthinkable that Katya would agree to come, and at the same time he felt that if she did not come, it would be something altogether impossible. Alyosha understood his feelings.

"This Trifon," Mitya began speaking nervously, "Borisich, I mean, has destroyed his whole inn, they say: he's taking up the floorboards, ripping out planks, they say he's broken his 'verander' to bits—looking for treasure all the time, for the money, the fifteen hundred the prosecutor said I'd hidden there. They say he started this lunacy as soon as he got back. Serves the swindler right! The guard here told me yesterday; he comes from there."

"Listen," said Alyosha, "she will come, but I don't know when, maybe today, maybe one of these days, that I don't know, but she will come, she will, it's certain."

Mitya started, was about to say something, but remained silent. The news affected him terribly. One could see that he painfully wanted to know the details of the conversation, but once again he was afraid to ask: anything cruel and contemptuous from Katya at that moment would have been like the stab of a knife.

"She told me this, by the way: that I must absolutely set your conscience at rest concerning the escape. Even if Ivan has not recovered by that time, she will take care of it herself."

"You already told me that," Mitya observed pensively.

"And you already passed it on to Grusha," observed Alyosha.

"Yes," Mitya confessed. "She won't come this morning," he looked timidly at his brother. "She will only come in the evening. She didn't say anything yesterday when I told her Katya was taking charge of it; but her lips twisted. She just whispered: 'Let her!' She understood the importance of it. I was afraid to dig any deeper. She does seem to understand now that the other one loves Ivan and not me."

"Does she?" escaped from Alyosha.

"Maybe she doesn't. Only she won't come this morning," Mitya hastened to stress again, "I gave her an errand . . . Listen, brother Ivan will surpass us all. It's for him to live, not us. He will recover."

"You know, though Katya trembles for him, she has almost no doubt that he will recover," said Alyosha.

"That means she's convinced he will die. It's fear that makes her so sure he'll recover."

"Our brother has a strong constitution. And I, too, have every hope that he will recover," Alyosha observed anxiously.

"Yes, he will recover. But she's convinced he will die. She has so much grief . . ."

There was silence. Something very important was tormenting Mitya.

"Alyosha, I love Grusha terribly," he said suddenly in a trembling, tear-filled voice.

"They won't let her go to you *there*," Alyosha picked up at once.

"And here's something else I wanted to tell you," Mitya continued in a suddenly ringing voice, "if they start beating me on the way, or *there*, I won't let them, I'll kill someone, and they'll shoot me. And it's for twenty years! They've already started talking down to me here. The guards talk down to me. I was lying here all last night judging myself: I'm not ready! Not strong enough to take it! I wanted to sing a 'hymn,' yet I can't stand the guards' talking down to me! I'd endure everything for Grusha, everything . . . except beatings, that is . . . But they won't let her go *there*."

Alyosha smiled quietly.

"Listen, brother, once and for all," he said, "here are my thoughts about it. And you know very well I won't lie to you. Listen, then: you're not ready, and such a cross is not for you. Moreover, unready as you are, you don't need such a great martyr's cross. If you had killed father, I would regret that you rejected your cross. But you're innocent, and such a cross is too much for you. You wanted to regenerate another man in yourself through suffering; I say just remember that other man always, all your life, and wherever you escape to—and that is enough for you. That you did not accept that great cross will only serve to make you feel a still greater duty in yourself, and through this constant feeling from now on, all your life, you will do more for your regeneration, perhaps, than if you went *there*. Because there you will not endure, you will begin to murmur, and in the end you may really say: 'I am quits.' The attorney was right about that. Heavy burdens are not for everyone, for some they are impossible . . . These are my thoughts, if you need them so much. If others had to answer for your escape—officers, soldiers—then I 'would not allow' you to flee," Alyosha smiled. "But they tell me and assure me (the head man there told Ivan himself) that if it's managed well, there won't be much penalty, and they can get off lightly. Of course, bribery is dishonest even in this case, but I wouldn't make myself a judge here for anything, since, as a matter of fact, if Ivan and Katya asked me to take charge of it for you, for example, I know I would go and bribe; I must tell you the whole truth here. And therefore I am no judge of you in how you yourself act. But know, too, that I will never condemn you. And it would be strange, wouldn't it, for me to be your judge in these things? Well, I think I've covered everything."

"But I will condemn myself!" exclaimed Mitya. "I will run away, that's already been decided without you: how could Mitka Karamazov not run away? But I will condemn myself in return, and sit there praying for my sin forever! This is how the Jesuits talk, right? The way you and I are talking now, eh?"

"Right," Alyosha smiled quietly.

"I love you for always telling the whole complete truth and never hiding anything!" Mitya exclaimed, laughing joyfully. "So I've caught my Alyoshka being a Jesuit! You deserve kissing for that, that's what! So, now listen to the rest, I'll unfold the remaining half of my soul to you. This is what I've thought up and decided: if I do run away, even with money and a passport, and even to America, I still take heart from the thought that I will not be running to any joy or happiness, but truly to another penal servitude, maybe no better than this one! No better, Alexei, I tell you truly, no better! This America, devil take it, I hate it already! So Grusha will be with me, but look at her: is she an American woman? She's Russian, every little bone of her is Russian, she'll pine for her native land, and I'll see all the time that she's pining away for my sake, that she has taken up such a cross for my sake, and what has she done wrong? And I, will I be able to stand the local rabble, though every last one of them may be better than I am? I hate this America even now! And maybe every last one of them is some sort of boundless machinist or whatever—but, devil take them, they're not my people, not of my soul! I love Russia, Alexei, I love the Russian God, though I myself am a scoundrel! But there I'll just croak!" he exclaimed suddenly, flashing his eyes. His voice was trembling with tears.

"So this is what I've decided, Alexei, listen!" he began again, suppressing his excitement. "Grusha and I will arrive there—and there we'll immediately set to work, digging the land, with the wild bears, in solitude, in some remote place. Surely there must be some remote places there. People say there are still redskins there, somewhere on the edge of the horizon, so we'll go to that edge, to the last Mohicans.[1] And we'll immediately start on the grammar, Grusha and I. Work and grammar—about three years like that. In three years we'll learn Engullish as well as any downright Englishman. And as soon as we've learned it—good-bye America! We'll flee here, to Russia, as American citizens. Don't worry, we won't come to this little town. We'll hide somewhere far away, in the north or the south. I'll have changed by then, and so will she; a doctor there, in America, will fabricate some kind of wart for me; it's not for nothing they're all mechanics. Or else I'll blind myself in one eye, let my beard grow a yard long, a gray beard (I'll go gray thinking of Russia), and maybe they won't recognize me. And if they do, worse luck, let them exile me, I don't care. Here, too, we'll dig the land somewhere in the wilderness, and I'll pretend to be an American all my life. But we will die in our native land. That's my plan, and it will not be changed. Do you approve?"

"I do," said Alyosha, not wishing to contradict him.

Mitya fell silent for a moment, and said suddenly:

"And how they set me up in court! They really set me up!"

"Even if they hadn't set you up, you'd have been convicted anyway," Alyosha said, sighing.

"Yes, the local public is sick of me! God help them, but it's a heavy thing!" Mitya groaned with suffering.

Again they fell silent for a moment.

"Put me out of my misery, Alyosha!" he exclaimed suddenly. "Is she coming now or not, tell me! What did she say? How did she say it?"

"She said she would come, but I don't know about today. It's really hard for her!" Alyosha looked timidly at his brother.

"Of course it is, of course it's hard for her! Alyosha, this is driving me crazy. Grusha keeps looking at me. She knows. Lord God, humble me: what am I asking for? I'm asking for Katya! Do I realize what I am asking? This impious Karamazov unrestraint! No, I'm not fit for suffering! A scoundrel, that says it all!"

"Here she is!" exclaimed Alyosha.

At that moment Katya suddenly appeared in the doorway. She stopped for a second, gazing at Mitya with a sort of lost expression. He jumped impetuously to his feet, a frightened look came to his face, he turned pale, but at once a shy, pleading smile flashed on his lips, and suddenly, irrepressibly, he reached out to Katya with both hands. Seeing this, she rushed impetuously to him. She seized his hands and almost by force sat him down on the bed, sat down beside him, and, still holding his hands, kept squeezing them strongly, convulsively. Several times they both tried to say something, but checked themselves and again sat silently, their eyes as if fastened on each other, gazing at each other with a strange smile; thus about two minutes passed.

"Have you forgiven or not?" Mitya murmured at last, and at the same moment, turning to Alyosha, his face distorted with joy, he cried to him:

"Do you hear what I'm asking, do you hear?"

"That's why I loved you, for your magnanimous heart!" escaped suddenly from Katya. "And you do not need my forgiveness, nor I yours; it's all the same whether you forgive or not, all my life you will remain a wound in my soul, and I in yours—that's how it should be . . . ," she stopped to catch her breath.

"Why have I come?" she began again, frenziedly and hastily. "To embrace your feet, to squeeze your hands, like this, till it hurts—remember how I used to squeeze them in Moscow?—to say to you that you are my God, my joy, to tell you that I love you madly," she nearly groaned from suffering, and suddenly, greedily pressed her lips to his hand. Tears streamed from her eyes.

Alyosha stood speechless and embarrassed; he had never expected to see what he was seeing.

"Love is gone, Mitya!" Katya began again, "but what is gone is painfully dear to me. Know that, for all eternity. But now, for one minute, let it be as it might have been," she prattled with a twisted smile, again looking joyfully into his eyes. "You now love another, I love another, but still I shall love you eternally, and you me, did you know that? Love me, do you hear, love me all your life!" she exclaimed with some sort of almost threatening tremor in her voice.

"I shall love you, and . . . you know, Katya," Mitya also began to speak, catching his breath at each word, "five days ago, that evening, you know, I loved you . . . When you collapsed, and they carried you out . . . All my life! It will be so, eternally so . . ."

Thus they prattled to each other, and their talk was frantic, almost senseless, and perhaps also not even truthful, but at that moment everything was truth, and they both utterly believed what they were saying.

"Katya," Mitya suddenly exclaimed, "do you believe I killed him? I know you don't believe it now, but then . . . when you were testifying . . . Did you, did you really believe it!"

"I did not believe it then either! I never believed it! I hated you, and suddenly I persuaded myself, for that moment . . . While I was testifying . . . I persuaded myself and believed it . . . and as soon as I finished testifying, I stopped believing it again. You must know all that. I forgot that I came here to punish myself!" she said with some suddenly quite new expression, quite unlike her prattling of love just a moment before.

"It's hard for you, woman!" suddenly escaped somehow quite unrestrainably from Mitya.

"Let me go," she whispered, "I'll come again, it's hard now . . . !"

She got up from her place, but suddenly gave a loud cry and drew back. All at once, though very quietly, Grushenka came into the room. No one was expecting her. Katya stepped swiftly towards the door, but, coming up with Grushenka, she suddenly stopped, turned white as chalk, and softly, almost in a whisper, moaned to her:

"Forgive me!"

The other woman stared her in the face and, pausing for a moment, answered in a venomous voice, poisoned with wickedness:

"We are wicked, sister, you and I! We're both wicked! It's not for us to forgive! Save him, and I'll pray to you all my life."

"You don't want to forgive!" Mitya cried to Grushenka with wild reproach.

"Don't worry, I'll save him for you!" Katya whispered quickly, and she ran out of the room.

"But how could you not forgive her, after she herself said 'Forgive me' to you?" Mitya again exclaimed bitterly.

"Mitya, do not dare to reproach her, you have no right!" Alyosha shouted hotly at his brother.

"It was her proud lips speaking, not her heart," Grushenka said with a sort of loathing. "If she delivers you—I'll forgive everything . . ."

She fell silent, as if she had quelled something in her soul. She still could not recover herself. She had come in, as it turned out later, quite by chance, suspecting nothing, and not at all expecting to meet what she met.

"Alyosha, run after her!" Mitya turned swiftly to his brother, "tell her . . . I don't know what . . . don't let her go away like that!"

"I'll come to you before evening!" cried Alyosha, and he ran after Katya. He caught up with her outside the hospital gate. She was walking briskly, hurrying, but as soon as Alyosha caught up with her, she quickly said to him:

"No, I cannot punish myself before that one! I said 'forgive me' to her because I wanted to punish myself to the end. She did not forgive . . . I love her for that!" Katya added in a distorted voice, and her eyes flashed with savage wickedness.

"My brother did not expect her at all," Alyosha began muttering, "he was sure she would not come . . ."

"No doubt. Let's drop it," she cut him short. "Listen: I can't go with you to the funeral now. I sent them flowers for the coffin. They still have money, I think. If need be, tell them that in the future I shall never abandon them . . . Well, leave me now, please leave me. You're late going there as it is, they're already ringing for the late service . . . Leave me, please!"

Chapter 3

Ilyushechka's Funeral. The Speech at the Stone

Indeed, he was late. They had waited for him and even decided finally to carry the pretty little coffin, all decked with flowers, to the church without him. It was the coffin of the poor little boy Ilyushechka. He had died two days after Mitya was sentenced. At the gate of the house Alyosha was met by the shouts of the boys, Ilyusha's comrades. They had been waiting impatiently for him and were glad that he had come at last. There were about twelve boys altogether, all with their satchels and shoulder bags. "Papa will cry, be with papa," was Ilyusha's dying wish, and the boys remembered it. At their head was Kolya Krasotkin.

"I'm so glad you've come, Karamazov!" he exclaimed, holding out his hand to Alyosha. "It's terrible here. Really, it's hard to watch. Snegiryov is not drunk, we know for certain he's had nothing to drink today, but it's as if he were drunk . . . I'm a strong man, but this is terrible. Karamazov, if I'm not keeping you, one more question, may I, before you go in?"

"What is it, Kolya?" Alyosha stopped for a moment.

"Is your brother innocent or guilty? Was it he who killed your father, or was it the lackey? As you say, so it will be. I've lost four nights' sleep over this idea."

"The lackey killed him, my brother is innocent," Alyosha replied.

"That's just what I say!" the boy Smurov suddenly cried.

"Thus he will perish an innocent victim for truth!" exclaimed Kolya. "But though he perish, he is happy! I am ready to envy him!"

"What do you mean? How can you be? And why?" exclaimed the surprised Alyosha.

"Oh, if only I, too, could some day offer myself as a sacrifice for truth!" Kolya said with enthusiasm.

"But not for such a cause, not with such disgrace, not with such horror!" said Alyosha.

"Of course . . . I should like to die for all mankind, and as for disgrace, it makes no difference: let our names perish. I respect your brother!"

"And so do I!" another boy suddenly and quite unexpectedly called out from the crowd, the same boy who had once announced that he knew who had founded Troy, and, just as he had done then, having called it out, he blushed up to his ears like a peony.

Alyosha went into the room. In a blue coffin decorated with white lace, his hands folded and his eyes closed, lay Ilyusha. The features of his emaciated face were hardly changed at all, and, strangely, there was almost no smell from the corpse. The expression of his face was serious and, as it were, pensive. His hands, folded crosswise, were especially beautiful, as if carved from marble. Flowers had been placed in his hands, and the whole coffin was adorned inside and out with flowers, sent at daybreak from Liza Khokhlakov. But flowers had also come from Katerina Ivanovna, and, as Alyosha opened the door, the captain, with a bunch of flowers in his trembling hands, was again strewing them over his dear boy. He barely glanced at Alyosha when he came in, nor did he want to look at anyone, not even at his mad, weeping wife, his "mama," who kept trying to stand up on her bad legs and have a closer look at her dead boy. But Ninochka had been picked up in her chair by the children and moved close to the coffin. She was sitting with her head pressed to it, and must also have been quietly weeping. Snegiryov's face looked animated but, as it were, bewildered, and at the same time embittered. There was something half crazed in his gestures, in the words that kept bursting from him. "Dear fellow, dear old fellow!" he exclaimed every moment, looking at Ilyusha. He had had the habit, when Ilyusha was still alive, of calling him tenderly: "Dear fellow, dear old fellow!"

"Papa, give me flowers, too, take one from his hands, that white one, and give it to me!" the mad "mama" asked, sobbing. Either she liked the little white rose in Ilyusha's hand very much, or else she wanted to take a flower from his hands as a keepsake, for she began tossing about, reaching out for the flower.

"I'm not giving anything, not to anybody!" Snegiryov exclaimed hard-heartedly. "They're his flowers, not yours. It's all his, nothing's yours!"

"Papa, give mother the flower!" Ninochka suddenly raised her face, wet with tears.

"I won't give anything, to her least of all! She didn't love him. She took his little cannon away from him that time, and he . . . gave it to her," the captain suddenly sobbed loudly, remembering how Ilyusha had let his mother have the little cannon. The poor, mad woman simply dissolved in quiet tears, covering her face with her hands. Finally, seeing that the father would not let the coffin go from him, but that it was time to carry it out, the boys suddenly crowded around the coffin and began to lift it up.

"I don't want him buried in the churchyard!" Snegiryov suddenly cried out. "I'll bury him by the stone, by our stone! Ilyusha told me to! I won't let you take him!"

Previously, too, over the past three days, he had been saying that he would bury him by the stone; but Alyosha, Krasotkin, the landlady, her sister, all the boys intervened.

"What an idea, to bury him by some heathenish stone, like some hanged man," the old landlady said sternly. "The ground in the churchyard has the cross on it. They'll pray for him there. You can hear singing from the church there, and the deacon is so clean-spoken and literal when he reads, it will all reach him every time, as if they were reading right over his grave."

The captain finally waved his hands as if to say: "Take him wherever you like!" The children picked up the coffin, but as they carried it past his mother, they stopped in front of her for a moment and set it down, so that she could say her farewells to Ilyusha. But, suddenly looking so closely at that dear little face, which for the past three days she had only seen from a distance, she began suddenly shaking all over, wagging her gray head back and forth hysterically above the coffin.

"Mama, cross him, bless him, kiss him," Ninochka cried to her. But she kept wagging her head like an automaton, and then, silently, her face twisted with burning grief, she suddenly began beating her breast with her fist. They moved on with the coffin. Ninochka pressed her lips to her dead brother's mouth for the last time as they carried it past her. Alyosha turned to the landlady as he was leaving the house and tried to ask her to look after those who were staying behind, but she would not even let him finish:

"I know, I know, I'll stay with them, we're Christians, too." The old woman wept as she said it.

It was not a far carry to the church, no more than about three hundred paces. The day had become clear, calm; it was frosty, but not very. The church bells were still ringing. Snegiryov, fussing and bewildered, ran after the coffin in his old, short, almost summer coat, bare-headed, with his old wide-brimmed felt hat in his hand. He was in some sort of insoluble anxiety, now reaching out suddenly to support the head of the coffin, which only interfered with the bearers, then running alongside to see if he could find a place for himself. A flower fell on the snow, and he simply rushed to pick it up, as if God knows what might come from the loss of this flower.

"The crust, we forgot the crust of bread," he exclaimed suddenly, terribly alarmed. But the boys reminded him at once that he had taken the crust earlier, and that it was in his pocket. He at once snatched it out of his pocket and, having made sure, calmed down.

"Ilyushechka told me, Ilyushechka," he exclaimed at once to Alyosha, "he was lying there one night, and I was sitting by him, and he suddenly told me: 'Papa, when they put the dirt on my grave, crumble a crust of bread on it so the sparrows will come, and I'll hear that they've come and be glad that I'm not lying alone.'"

"That's a very good thing," said Alyosha, "you must do it more often."

"Every day, every day!" the captain babbled, brightening all over, as it were.

At last they arrived at the church and set the coffin down in the middle of it. The boys all placed themselves around it and stood solemnly like that through the whole service. It was a very old church and rather poor, many of the icons were without settings, but one somehow prays better in such churches. During the liturgy Snegiryov seemed to calm down somewhat, though at times the same unconscious and, as it were, bewildered anxiety would break out in him: he would go up to the coffin to straighten the covering or the fillet,[1] and when a candle fell from the candle stand, he suddenly rushed to put it back and spent a terribly long time fussing with it. Then he calmed down again and stood quietly at the head of the coffin looking dumbly anxious and, as it were, perplexed. After the Epistle he suddenly whispered to Alyosha, who was standing beside him, that the reading had not been *done right*, but he did not explain what he meant. During the Cherubic Hymn he began to sing along, but stopped before the end and, kneeling down, touched his forehead to the stone floor of the church and remained lying like that for quite a long time. At last they began the funeral service; candles were distributed. The demented father began fussing about again, but the deeply moving, tremendous singing over the coffin awakened and shook his soul. He suddenly somehow shrank into himself and began weeping in quick, short sobs, stifling his voice at first, but towards the end sobbing loudly. When it came time to take leave of the dead and cover the coffin, he threw his arms around it as if to keep them from covering Ilyushechka, and began quickly, greedily, repeatedly kissing his dead boy on the mouth. They finally talked with him and were about to lead him down the steps when he suddenly reached out swiftly and snatched several flowers from the coffin. He looked at them and it was as if some new idea dawned on him, so that he seemed to forget the main thing for a moment. Gradually he fell into reverie, as it were, and did not resist when they lifted the coffin and carried it to the grave. It was just outside, in the churchyard, right next to the church, an expensive one; Katerina Ivanovna had paid for it. After the usual ritual, the gravediggers lowered the coffin. Snegiryov, with his flowers in his hand, leaned so far over the open grave that the boys caught hold of his coat in alarm and began pulling him back. But he no longer seemed to understand very well what was happening. When they began filling in the grave, he suddenly began pointing anxiously at the falling earth and even tried to say something, but no one could make it out, and he suddenly fell silent himself. Then he was reminded that he had to crumble the crust of bread, and he became terribly excited, pulled out the crust, and began crumbling it, scattering the pieces over the grave: "Fly down, birds, fly down, little sparrows!" he muttered anxiously. One of the boys tried to suggest to him that it must be awkward to crumble the bread with flowers in his hand, and that he should let someone else hold them for a time. But he would not give them up, even suddenly became afraid for his flowers, as if they wanted to take them from him altogether, and, after looking at the grave, as if making sure that everything had now been done and the crust had been crumbled, he suddenly, unexpectedly, and even quite calmly, turned and slowly walked home. Soon, however, his pace quickened, he was hurrying, almost running. The boys and Alyosha did not lag behind.

"Flowers for mama, flowers for mama! Mama has been hurt!" he suddenly started exclaiming. Someone shouted to him to put his hat on because it was cold, but hearing that, he flung his hat on the snow as if in anger and began repeating: "I don't want any hat, I don't want any hat!" The boy Smurov picked it up and carried it after him. All the boys were crying, Kolya and the boy who discovered Troy most of all, and though Smurov, with the captain's hat in his hand, was also crying terribly, he still managed, while almost running, to snatch up a piece of brick lying red on the snow-covered path and fling it at a flock of sparrows flying quickly by. He missed, of course, and went on running, crying. Halfway home, Snegiryov suddenly stopped, stood for half a minute as if struck by something, and suddenly, turning back to the church, started running towards the abandoned little grave. But the boys immediately caught up with him and seized him from all sides. Then, as if strengthless, as if he had been struck down, he fell on the snow, struggling, screaming, sobbing, and began crying out: "Ilyushechka, dear fellow, dear old fellow!" Alyosha and Kolya set about lifting him up, pleading with him, persuading him.

"Enough, captain, a brave man must endure," Kolya mumbled.

"And you'll ruin the flowers," Alyosha added, "and 'mama' is waiting for them, she's sitting there crying because you didn't give her any flowers from Ilyushechka this morning. Ilyusha's bed is still there . . ."

"Yes, yes, to mama!" Snegiryov suddenly remembered again. "They'll put the bed away, they'll put it away!" he added, as if fearing that they might indeed put it away, and he jumped up and ran for home again. But it was not far now, and they all came running up together. Snegiryov threw the door open and shouted to his wife, with whom he had quarreled so hardheartedly that morning.

"Mama, dear, Ilyushechka has sent you flowers, oh, poor crippled feet!" he cried, handing her the little bunch of flowers, frozen and broken from when he had just been struggling in the snow. But at that same moment he noticed Ilyusha's little boots standing side by side in the corner, in front of Ilyusha's bed, where the landlady had just neatly put them—old, stiff, scuffed, and patched little boots. Seeing them, he threw up his hands and simply rushed to them, fell on his knees, snatched up one boot, and, pressing his lips to it, began greedily kissing it, crying out: "Ilyushechka, dear fellow, dear old fellow, where are your little feet?"

"Where did you take him? Where did you take him?" the mad woman screamed in a rending voice. And then Ninochka also started sobbing. Kolya ran out of the room, the boys started going out after him. Finally Alyosha also went out after them. "Let them cry it through," he said to Kolya, "of course there's no use trying to comfort them now. Let's wait a minute and then go back."

"No, there's no use, it's terrible," Kolya agreed. "You know, Karamazov," he suddenly lowered his voice so that no one could hear, "I feel very sad, and if only it were possible to resurrect him, I'd give everything in the world!"

"Ah, so would I," said Alyosha.

"What do you think, Karamazov, should we come here tonight? He's sure to get drunk."

"Yes, he may get drunk. Just you and I will come, and that will be enough, to sit with them for an hour, with his mother and Ninochka; if we all come at once, we'll remind them of everything again," Alyosha advised.

"The landlady is setting the table for them now—for this memorial dinner or whatever, the priest will be there; shall we stay for that, Karamazov?"

"Certainly," said Alyosha.

"It's all so strange, Karamazov, such grief, and then pancakes all of a sudden—how unnatural it all is in our religion!"

"They're going to have salmon, too," the boy who discovered Troy remarked suddenly in a loud voice.

"I ask you seriously, Kartashov, not to interrupt anymore with your foolishness, especially when no one is talking to you or even cares to know of your existence," Kolya snapped irritably in his direction. The boy flushed deeply, but did not dare make any reply. Meanwhile they were all walking slowly along the path, and Smurov suddenly exclaimed:

"Here's Ilyusha's stone, the one they wanted to bury him under!"

They all silently stopped at the big stone. Alyosha looked and the whole picture of what Snegiryov had once told him about Ilyushechka, crying and embracing his father, exclaiming: "Papa, papa, how he humiliated you!" rose at once in his memory. Something shook, as it were, in his soul. With a serious and important look he gazed around at all those dear, bright faces of the schoolboys, Ilyusha's comrades, and suddenly said to them:

"Gentlemen, I should like to have a word with you, here, on this very spot."

The boys gathered around him and turned to him at once with attentive, expectant eyes.

"Gentlemen, we shall be parting soon. Right now I shall be with my two brothers for a while, one of whom is going into exile, and the other is lying near death. But soon I shall leave this town, perhaps for a very long time. And so we shall part, gentlemen. Let us agree here, by Ilyusha's stone, that we will never forget—first, Ilyushechka, and second, one another. And whatever may happen to us later in life, even if we do not meet for twenty years afterwards, let us always remember how we buried the poor boy, whom we once threw stones at—remember, there by the little bridge?—and whom afterwards we all came to love so much. He was a nice boy, a kind and brave boy, he felt honor and his father's bitter offense made him rise up. And so, first of all, let us remember him, gentlemen, all our lives. And even though we may be involved with the most important affairs, achieve distinction or fall into some great misfortune—all the same, let us never forget how good we once felt here, all together, united by such good and kind feelings as made us, too, for the time that we loved the poor boy, perhaps better than we actually are. My little doves—let me call you that—little doves, because you are very much like those pretty gray blue birds, now, at this moment, as I look at your kind, dear faces—my dear children, perhaps you will not understand what I am going to say to you, because I often speak very incomprehensibly, but still you will remember and some day agree with my words. You must know that there is nothing higher, or stronger, or sounder, or more useful afterwards in life, than some good memory, especially a memory from childhood, from the parental home. You hear a lot said about your education, yet some such beautiful, sacred memory, preserved from childhood, is perhaps the best education. If a man stores up many such memories to take into life, then he is saved for his whole life. And even if only one good memory remains with us in our hearts, that alone may serve some day for our salvation. Perhaps we will even become wicked later on, will even be unable to resist a bad action, will laugh at people's tears and at those who say, as Kolya exclaimed today: 'I want to suffer for all people'—perhaps we will scoff wickedly at such people. And yet, no matter how wicked we may be—and God preserve us from it—as soon as we remember how we buried Ilyusha, how we loved him in his last days, and how we've been talking just now, so much as friends, so together, by this stone, the most cruel and jeering man among us, if we should become so, will still not dare laugh within himself at how kind and good he was at this present moment! Moreover, perhaps just this memory alone will keep him from great evil, and he will think better of it and say: 'Yes, I was kind, brave, and honest then.' Let him laugh to himself, it's no matter, a man often laughs at what is kind and good; it just comes from thoughtlessness; but I assure you, gentlemen, that as soon as he laughs, he will say at once in his heart: 'No, it's a bad thing for me to laugh, because one should not laugh at that!' "

"It will certainly be so, Karamazov, I understand you, Karamazov!" Kolya exclaimed, his eyes flashing. The boys were stirred and also wanted to exclaim something, but restrained themselves, looking tenderly and attentively at the orator.

"I am speaking about the worst case, if we become bad," Alyosha went on, "but why should we become bad, gentlemen, isn't that true? Let us first of all and before all be kind, then honest, and then—let us never forget one another. I say it again. I give you my word, gentlemen, that for my part I will never forget any one of you; each face that is looking at me now, at this moment, I will remember, be it even after thirty years. Kolya said to Kartashov just now that we supposedly 'do not care to know of his existence.' But how can I forget that Kartashov exists and that he is no longer blushing now, as when he discovered Troy, but is looking at me with his nice, kind, happy eyes? Gentlemen, my dear gentlemen, let us all be as generous and brave as Ilyushechka, as intelligent, brave, and generous as Kolya (who will be much more intelligent when he grows up a little), and let us be as bashful, but smart and nice, as Kartashov. But why am I talking about these two? You are all dear to me, gentlemen, from now on I shall keep you all in my heart, and I ask you to keep me in your hearts, too! Well, and who has united us in this good, kind feeling, which we will remember and intend to remember always, all our lives, who, if not Ilyushechka, that good boy, that kind boy, that boy dear to us unto ages of ages! Let us never forget him, and may his memory be eternal and good in our hearts now and unto ages of ages!"[2]

"Yes, yes, eternal, eternal," all the boys cried in their ringing voices, with deep feeling in their faces.

"Let us remember his face, and his clothes, and his poor boots, and his little coffin, and his unfortunate, sinful father, and how he bravely rose up against the whole class for him!"

"We will, we will remember!" the boys cried again, "he was brave, he was kind!"

"Ah, how I loved him!" exclaimed Kolya.

"Ah, children, ah, dear friends, do not be afraid of life! How good life is when you do something good and rightful!"

"Yes, yes," the boys repeated ecstatically.

"Karamazov, we love you!" a voice, which seemed to be Kartashov's, exclaimed irrepressibly.

"We love you, we love you," everyone joined in. Many had tears shining in their eyes.

"Hurrah for Karamazov!" Kolya proclaimed ecstatically.

"And memory eternal for the dead boy!" Alyosha added again, with feeling.

"Memory eternal!" the boys again joined in.

"Karamazov!" cried Kolya, "can it really be true as religion says, that we shall all rise from the dead, and come to life, and see one another again, and everyone, and Ilyushechka?"

"Certainly we shall rise, certainly we shall see and gladly, joyfully tell one another all that has been," Alyosha replied, half laughing, half in ecstasy.

"Ah, how good that will be!" burst from Kolya.

"Well, and now let's end our speeches and go to his memorial dinner. Don't be disturbed that we'll be eating pancakes. It's an ancient, eternal thing, and there's good in that, too," laughed Alyosha. "Well, let's go! And we go like this now, hand in hand."

"And eternally so, all our lives hand in hand! Hurrah for Karamazov!" Kolya cried once more ecstatically, and once more all the boys joined in his exclamation.

NOTES

Biblical references, unless otherwise noted, are to the King James Version. Parenthetical references are to Victor Terras, *A Karamazov Companion: Commentary on the Genesis, Language, and Style of Dostoevsky's Novel* (Madison: University of Wisconsin Press, 1981). *The Brothers Karamazov* is abbreviated *B.K.* and sections are identified by part, book, and chapter numbers: for example, 1.3.2 signifies part 1, book 3, chapter 2.

Dedication

Anna Grigorievna Dostoevsky, née Snitkin (1846–1918), was Dostoevsky's second wife.

1.1.1 Fyodor Pavlovich Karamazov

1. *the chafings of a mind imprisoned*: quotation from Mikhail Lermontov's poem "Do not, do not believe yourself . . ." (1839).

2. *Now lettest thou* . . . : from the prayer of St. Simeon (Luke 2:29), read at Vespers in the Orthodox Church.

1.1.2 The First Son Sent Packing

1. *Proudhon and Bakunin*: Pierre-Joseph Proudhon (1809–65), French philosopher, a principal socialist theorist. Mikhail Bakunin (1814–76), Russian radical activist, a leader of the First International, later a major theorist of anarchism.

2. *February revolution* . . . : the three-day revolution in 1848 that ended the reign of Louis-Philippe and proclaimed the Second Republic.

3. *souls*: before the emancipation of the serfs in 1861, Russian estates were evaluated according to the number of "souls," or adult male serfs, living on them.

1.1.3 Second Marriage, Second Children

1. *provincial marshal of nobility*: the highest elective office in a province, before the reforms of the 1860s. Governors and administrators were appointed by the tsar.

2. *ecclesiastical courts*: courts exercising canon law rather than civil law. The Judicial Reform Act of 1864 raised the question of their continued existence, which was much debated in the press, by Dostoevsky among others.

1.1.4 The Third Son, Alyosha

1. *lover of mankind*: an epithet for Christ in many Orthodox prayers and liturgical exclamations.

2. *holy fools*: a "holy fool" (or "fool in God," or "fool for Christ"—*yurodivyi* in Russian) could be a harmless village idiot (cf. "Stinking Lizaveta," *B.K.* 1.3.2), but there are also saintly persons or ascetics whose saintliness is expressed as "folly." Holy fools of this sort were known early in Orthodox tradition. The term reappears several times in *B.K.*, notably in reference to Alyosha.

3. *Il faudrait les inventer*: "They would have to be invented." A variation of Voltaire's *Si Dieu n'existait pas, il faudrait l'inventer* ("If God did not exist, he would have to be invented").

4. *J'ai vu* . . . : "I saw the shade of a coachman scrubbing the shade of a carriage with the shade of a brush." A popular quotation from a seventeenth-century French parody of the *Aeneid* (book 6, the descent to the underworld) by Charles Perrault and others.

1.1.5 Elders

1. *Apostle Thomas*: John 20:24–29.
2. *Tower of Babel*: Genesis 11:1–9.
3. *If thou wilt be perfect . . .* : see Matthew 19:21, Mark 10:21, Luke 18:22.
4. *Sinai and Athos*: the monastery of St. Catherine in the Sinai and the many monasteries on Mt. Athos in Greece, both ancient and still active Orthodox monastic centers.
5. *Tartar yoke*: the period of Tartar domination of Russia (1237–1480); the Tartars, or Tatars, who invaded Russia from Central Asia, were of Turkish and Mongol origin.
6. *the fall of Constantinople*: Constantinople (Istanbul), capital of the Eastern Roman Empire and ecclesiastical center of Orthodoxy, fell to the Turks in 1453.
7. *Paissy Velichkovsky*: (1722–94), "the father of the Russian elders" (G. P. Fedotov, *The Russian Religious Mind* [Belmont, Mass., 1975], 2:394), canonized by the Russian Church in 1988. Dostoevsky owned a copy of the 1854 edition of his translation of the homilies of St. Isaac the Syrian, a seventh-century monk; the book is mentioned twice in *B.K.* St. Isaac, whose spiritual influence has been very great, seems also to have influenced Dostoevsky's elder Zosima, particularly in his reflections on hell and divine love (see Terras, pp. 22–23).
8. *Kozelskaya-Optina*: pilgrims of all classes visited this celebrated hermitage, among them Dostoevsky, who drew from it a number of details for the monastery in *B.K.* The elder Zosima is thought to be modeled in part on the elder Amvrosy of Optina (1812–91), canonized by the Russian Church in 1988, six months after the hermitage was restored to the Church by the Soviet authorities.
9. *All catechumens, depart*: an exclamation that occurs at a certain point in the Orthodox liturgy. A catechumen is a person preparing for baptism, hence not yet "in" the Church. The catechumens are asked to depart, only the "faithful" remaining for the Eucharist. This monk, by his disobedience, made himself "unfaithful"—hence his departure.
10. *Ecumenical Patriarch*: title of the Patriarch of Constantinople, the highest administrative authority of the Greek Orthodox Church and its exarchies.
11. *Who made me . . .* : see Luke 12:14.

1.2.1 They Arrive at the Monastery

1. *Un chevalier parfait*: "A perfect knight."
2. *von Sohn*: victim of an actual murder case in Petersburg in 1870.
3. *When in Rome . . .* : a substitute for the Russian saying Fyodor Pavlovich actually uses: "Don't take your *ordo* [monastic rule] to another monastery," which is more apropos.

1.2.2 The Old Buffoon

1. *hieromonks*: a hieromonk is a monk who is also a priest.
2. *schism*: the reforms of the patriarch Nikon (1605–81) caused a split, or "schism," in the Russian Orthodox Church, the "Old Believers" refusing to accept his changes.
3. *punctuality . . .* : a popular saying in Russia, attributed to Louis XVIII.
4. *Napravnik*: E. F. Napravnik (1839–1916), Russian composer, first *Kapellmeister*, or director, of the Mariinsky (now Kirov) Theater, the imperial opera and ballet theater in Petersburg.
5. *Diderot*: Denis Diderot (1713–84), French philosopher and writer, founder of the *Encyclopédie*, an atheist and materialist. He was invited to Russia in 1733 by the empress Catherine the Great (1729–96) and spent five months there.
6. *Metropolitan Platon*: (1737–1812), bishop of the "metropolis" of Moscow, a famous preacher and Church activist.
7. *The fool hath said . . .* : Psalms 14:1, 53:1.
8. *Princess Dashkova . . . and . . . Potiomkin*: Ekaterina Romanovna Dashkova

(1743–1810), writer, president of the Russian Academy, and a close friend of the empress Catherine. Grigory Alexandrovich Potiomkin (1739–91), general and statesman, the most famous and influential of Catherine's lovers.

9. *Blessed . . .* : Luke 11:27.

10. *Teacher . . . what should I do . . .* : see Luke 10:25, Mark 10:17, Matthew 19:16.

11. *father of a lie . . . son of a lie . . .* : see John 8:44, where the "father" refers to the devil. The phrase and its correction may be a first hint at later developments concerning Ivan.

12. *some holy wonder-worker . . .* : the reference is to St. Denis of Paris (third century A.D.); the source, however, is not the Lives of the Saints, but Voltaire, who tells this jesting story about St. Denis in the notes to his play *The Maid of Orleans* (1774).

13. *read from the Lives of the Saints . . .* : Miusov and his French informant are unaware (which is the point) that saints' lives are not read in the Orthodox liturgy.

1.2.3 Women of Faith

1. *three months short of three years old*: Dostoevsky's son Alexei died at this age in 1878.

2. *Rachel of old . . .* : Matthew 2:18 (quoting Jeremiah 31:15).

3. *Alexei, the man of God*: St. Alexis, a Greek anchorite who died around 412 A.D., is much loved in Russia, where he is known as "Alexei, the man of God." There is a folk legend of his life, from which Dostoevsky may have drawn. Alexei Karamazov is referred to several times as a "man of God."

4. *And there is more joy . . .* : see Luke 15:7.

1.2.4 A Lady of Little Faith

1. *Lise*: Madame Khokhlakov often uses this French form of her daughter's name, as do the narrator and Alyosha.

2. *burdock . . .* : words spoken by Bazarov, the atheist hero of Turgenev's *Fathers and Sons* (1862).

1.2.5 So Be It! So Be It!

1. *ecclesiastical courts*: see note 2 to page 16 in section 1.1.3 above.

2. *Ultramontanism*: the doctrine of absolute papal supremacy favored by members of the Italian party in the Roman Catholic Church, who were "across the mountains" (ultramontane) from their French opponents, the "Gallican" party. The controversy dates to the 1820s.

3. *a kingdom . . .* : see John 18:36 for the true sense of these words.

4. *holy gifts*: the consecrated bread and wine of the Eucharist.

5. *times and seasons*: see Acts 1:7, 1 Thessalonians 5:1–2.

6. *Pope Gregory the Seventh*: pontificate 1073–85; canonized. One of the greatest and most powerful of the popes of Rome, known for his struggle against the emperor Henry IV, whom he humbled at Canossa.

7. *third temptation of the devil*: the devil's third temptation of Christ; see Matthew 4:1–11. A foreshadowing of Ivan Karamazov's Grand Inquisitor.

8. *December revolution*: the coup d'état in 1851 that ended the French Second Republic; a year later Louis-Napoléon Bonaparte was made emperor.

1.2.6 Why Is Such a Man Alive!

1. *to set . . . in heaven*: a conflation of Colossians 3:2 and Philippians 3:20.

2. *regierender Graf von Moor*: "reigning Count von Moor." Friedrich Schiller (1759–1805) wrote his historical drama *The Robbers* in 1781. There are references to Schiller's

plays and poetry and to the notion from *The Robbers* of "the great and beautiful" all through B.K.

3. *Anna with swords*: the medal of the Order of St. Anne, a military and civil distinction; the swords indicate the colonel's military status. Decorations worn on the neck were not as "high" as decorations worn on the breast.

4. *across a handkerchief*: alludes to Schiller's play *Cabal and Love* (1784), in which such a challenge is made.

5. *her who loved much*: see Luke 7:47. The passage is grotesquely misinterpreted by Fyodor Pavlovich.

6. *the Church calendar*: a yearly listing of saints' and feast days; in this case it would not prove anything.

1.2.7 A Seminarist-Careerist

1. *obedience*: the term for a task imposed on a monk by his superior or spiritual director.

2. *what's the meaning of this dream*: a journalistic commonplace of the 1860s and 1870s, used by Dostoevsky's ideological adversary M. E. Saltykov-Shchedrin among others; a paraphrase of a line from Pushkin's "The Bridegroom": "Well then, what is your dream about?" It betrays Rakitin as a "liberal."

3. *Pushkin* . . . : several of Pushkin's poems celebrate women's "little feet," for which the liberals of the 1860s censured him. Rakitin himself will soon "sing" of a woman's feet (*B.K.* 4.11.2 and 4.11.4).

4. *On the one hand* . . . : Rakitin borrows this phrase from Saltykov-Shchedrin's *Unfinished Conversations*, pt. 1 (1873); again he labels himself (see Terras, p. 162).

5. *archimandrite*: superior of a monastery; now often honorary.

1.2.8 Scandal

1. *your noble reverence*: an absurdly incorrect way to address the superior of a monastery.

2. *von Sohn*: see note 2 to page 36 in section 1.2.1.

3. *plus de noblesse que de sincerité*: "more nobility than sincerity." And vice versa.

4. *the Holy Fathers*: Fyodor Pavlovich apparently believes that "secret confession" was instituted by the early fathers of the Church, which it was not.

5. *flagellationism*: the practice of self-flagellation as a way of purification from sin; never accepted by the Church.

6. *Synod*: a council of bishops instituted (contrary to canon law) by Peter the Great (1672–1725) to administer the Russian Orthodox Church, answerable to the tsar himself, who thus became the de facto head of the Church.

7. *Robbers*: see note 2 to page 71 in section 1.2.6.

8. *Eliseyev Brothers*: famous Petersburg provisioners. The shop has survived intact, is still a provisioners', and is often still referred to as Eliseyevs'.

9. *seven councils*: a hyperbolic reference to the seven "ecumenical councils" that were held between 325 and 787 A.D.

1.3.1 In the Servants' Quarters

1. *six fingers*: such malformations, to some minds, implied the work or even the presence of "unclean spirits." Hence Grigory later calls the child a "dragon."

2. *the Book of Job*: references to the Book of Job appear frequently in *B.K.* and are a key to one of its themes: the "justification of suffering," i.e., theodicy.

3. *Isaac the Syrian*: see note 7 to page 27 in section 1.1.5.

4. *Flagellants*: see note 5 to page 88 in section 1.2.8.

1.3.2 Stinking Lizaveta

1. *state councillor*: rank of the fifth grade in the civil service, corresponding to the military rank of colonel.

2. *Smerdyashchaya*: "Stinking [woman]" in Russian. Smerdyakov's name thus means roughly "[son] of the stinking one."

1.3.3 Confession. In Verse

1. *Glory* . . . : the verses are by Dmitri Fyodorovich himself.

2. *Do not believe* . . . : from "When from the Darkness of Error" (1865) by Nikolai Nekrasov (1821–78); one of Dostoevsky's favorite poems, about a rescued prostitute.

3. *the golden fish* . . . : allusion to the well-known folktale about the magic fish, of which Pushkin made a poetic version, "The Tale of the Fisherman and the Fish" (1833).

4. *O man* . . . : the line is Goethe's, from "The Divine" (1783).

5. *An die Freude*: Schiller's famous ode "To Joy" (1785), from which Dmitri will quote a little further on.

6. *And a ruddy-mugged Silenus* . . . : from "Bas-relief" (1842) by Apollon Maikov (1821–79), a friend of Dostoevsky's.

7. *Darkly hid in cave and cleft* . . . : stanzas 2–4 from Schiller's "Eleusinian Festival" (1798). The version here is adapted from an anonymous English translation of 1843, as is the version of the ode "To Joy" that follows.

8. *That men to man* . . . : from "Eleusinian Festival," stanza 7.

9. *Joy is the mainspring* . . . : Schiller's "To Joy," stanzas 4 and 3.

1.3.4 Confession. In Anecdotes

1. *Paul de Kock*: (1794–1871), French writer, author of innumerable novels depicting petit bourgeois life, some of which were considered risqué.

1.3.5 Confession. "Heels Up"

1. *There was sweet confusion* . . . : verses of unknown origin, possibly by Dostoevsky himself (Terras, p. 176).

2. *bring up my life from the Pit*: Jonah 2:6 (Revised Standard Version).

1.3.6 Smerdyakov

1. *Balaam's ass*: Numbers 22:30. The ass of the false prophet Balaam suddenly speaks to its master.

2. *The Lord God created* . . . : see Genesis 1:3–5, 14–17.

3. *falling sickness*: Dostoevsky prefers this old term for epilepsy.

4. *Evenings on a Farm near Dikanka*: the first book of tales by Nikolai Gogol (1809–52).

5. *Smaragdov's Universal History*: a common Russian textbook of the earlier nineteenth century.

6. *Kramskoy*: I. N. Kramskoy (1837–87), well-known Russian painter. *The Contemplator* was first exhibited in 1878.

1.3.7 Disputation

1. *a Russian soldier* . . . : an actual event, which Dostoevsky wrote about in his *Diary of a Writer* (1877).

2. *Jesuits*: popularly considered masters of casuistry.

3. *my fine young Jesuit*: in wording and rhythm, an ironic paraphrase of a line from Pushkin's *Tale of Tsar Saltan* (1831): "Greetings, my fine young prince."

4. *in the Scriptures* . . . : see Matthew 17:20, 21:21; Mark 11:23; Luke 17:6.

1.3.8 Over the Cognac

1. *For as you measure . . .* : see Matthew 7:2, Mark 4:24, Luke 6:38. Fyodor Pavlovich misquotes.

2. *Tout cela c'est de la cochonnerie*: "That's all swinishness."

3. *Best of all . . .* : after the emancipation of 1861, peasants had their own courts, alongside the official courts, and often used whipping as a punishment.

4. *il y a du Piron là-dedans*: "there's a bit of the Piron in him." Alexis Piron (1689–1773), French poet, the author of many songs, satires, and epigrams; witty, but often licentious.

5. *Arbenin*: protagonist of Mikhail Lermontov's play *Masquerade*; the protagonist of *A Hero of Our Time* (1840) is Pechorin.

1.3.11 One More Ruined Reputation

1. *all five*: Dmitri confuses the number of cardinal points with the number of continents, considered to be five in the nineteenth century.

2.4.1 Father Ferapont

1. *the rite of holy unction*: in the Orthodox Church, a sacrament of healing, consisting of anointing with oil and remission of sins, administered to the sick and the dying.

2. *on behalf of all and for all*: a liturgical formula often repeated or alluded to in *B.K.*

3. *falling asleep*: in Orthodox understanding, death is a "falling asleep in the Lord."

4. *prosphora*: a small, round yeast bread specially prepared for the sacrament of the Eucharist; the Greek word means "offering."

5. *blessed*: the Russian word *blazhennyi* can mean either "blessed" or "silly, odd," as in the English phrase "blessed idiot."

6. *Holy Week*: the last week of Lent, between Palm Sunday and Easter; each of the days is called "Great and Holy."

7. *Laodicea*: a council of the Church held in Laodicea (modern Latakia, Syria) in the mid fourth century A.D.

8. *Pentecost*: the feast celebrating the descent of the Holy Spirit on the apostles (Acts 2:1–4), fifty days after Easter.

9. *in the form of a dove*: the Holy Spirit appeared "like a dove" only once, at Christ's baptism in the Jordan (see Matthew 3:16, Mark 1:10, Luke 3:22).

10. *Elijah*: Luke 1:17 (Revised Standard Version).

11. *the gates of hell*: Matthew 16:18.

2.4.5 Strain in the Drawing Room

1. *Den Dank, Dame, begehr ich nicht*: "Madame, I want no thanks." From Schiller's ballad "The Glove" (1797).

2.4.6 Strain in the Cottage

1. *And in all nature . . .* : lines from Pushkin's poem "The Demon" (1823).

2. *Chernomazov*: Arina Petrovna inadvertently brings out the implicit meaning of Alyosha's surname: *cherny* is Russian for "black"; however, in the Turkish and Tartar languages, *kara* also means "black" (the root, *maz*, in Russian conveys the idea of "paint" or "smear").

2.5.1 A Betrothal

1. *Now I'm like Famusov . . .* : Famusov, Chatsky, and Sophia are characters in A. S. Griboyedov's celebrated comedy *Woe from Wit* (1824), in which the last scene takes place on a stairway.

2.5.2 Smerdyakov with a Guitar

1. *An invincible power* . . . : the Russian original was heard and written down by Dostoevsky in Moscow ca. 1839. Smerdyakov sings the last stanza a bit further on.
2. *You opened her matrix*: a biblical expression (see Exodus 13:2, 12; 34:19); Grigory often uses such language, and Smerdyakov has picked up some of it, e.g., "nativity" just before.
3. *father of the present one*: Napoleon I was the uncle, not the father, of Napoleon III.
4. *Petrovka*: a street in the center of Moscow.

2.5.3 The Brothers Get Acquainted

1. *sticky little leaves* . . . : allusion to Pushkin's poem "Chill Winds Still Blow" (1828).
2. *professions de foi*: "professions of faith."
3. *a tinge of nobility*: a borrowing from Pushkin's epigram "A tsar was once told . . ." (1825): "Flatterers, flatterers, try to preserve / A tinge of nobility even in your baseness."
4. *And how believest thou* . . . : this first half of Ivan's question comes from the Orthodox order for the consecration of a bishop; in response the bishop-elect recites the Creed.
5. *an old sinner* . . . : Voltaire. The quotation comes from his *Epistles*, 111, "To the Author of a New Book on the Three Impostors" (1769); cf. note 3 to page 24 in section 1.1.4.
6. *the Word* . . . : see John 1:1–2.

2.5.4 Rebellion

1. *John the Merciful*: a saint, patriarch of Alexandria (611–19). The episode comes, however, from Flaubert's "La Légende de Saint-Julien-l'Hospitalier" (1876), "Saint Julian the Merciful" in Turgenev's Russian translation (1877). Ivan significantly substitutes the name John (Ioann, in Russian, i.e., Ivan) for Julian: Flaubert's Julian is a parricide.
2. *they ate* . . . : see Genesis 3:5.
3. *as Polonius says* . . . : *Hamlet*, 1.3.129 (we have substituted an appropriate line from the passage Dostoevsky quotes in Russian translation).
4. *image and likeness*: here, as just earlier, Ivan plays perversely on Genesis 1:26 ("And God said, Let us make man in our image, after our likeness").
5. *on its meek eyes*: from "Before Evening," a poem from the cycle *About the Weather* (1859) by Nikolai Nekrasov.
6. *Tartars*: see note 5 to page 27 in section 1.1.5.
7. *A little girl* . . . : this and the preceding story are both based on actual court cases. Dostoevsky discussed the first at length in *Diary of a Writer* (1876); the defense attorney there, V. D. Spassovich, is thought to be a possible model for Fetyukovich in *B.K.*
8. *I even forget where I read it*: the story actually appeared in the *Russian Herald* (1877, no. 9), where *B.K.* was also published serially. The article was entitled "Memoirs of a Serf."
9. *the liberator of the people*: Alexander II, tsar from 1855 to 1881; the emancipation of the serfs was the most important of his many reforms.
10. *paradise* . . . *fire from heaven*: Ivan combines biblical and Greek motifs, the paradise of Genesis with the revolt of Prometheus, who "stole fire from heaven" against the will of Zeus.
11. *the hind lie down with the lion*: a variation on Isaiah 11:6, 65:25.
12. *Just art thou* . . . : a variation on several biblical passages: cf. Revelation 15:3–4, 16:7, 19:1–2; Psalm 119:137.
13. *I hasten to return my ticket*: allusion to Schiller's poem "Resignation" (1784).
14. *and for all*: echoes an Orthodox liturgical phrase (cf. note 2 to page 164 in section 2.4.1).
15. *the only sinless One*: Christ. The words come from the Hymn of the Resurrection sung at Matins in the Orthodox Church.

2.5.5 The Grand Inquisitor

1. *Le bon jugement* . . . : "The Compassionate Judgment of the Most Holy and Gracious Virgin Mary."

2. *pre-Petrine antiquity*: before the reign of Peter the Great, tsar of Muscovy (1682–1721), then emperor of Russia (1721–25), who moved the capital from Moscow to Petersburg.

3. *The Mother of God Visits* . . . : a Byzantine apocryphal legend, translated into Old Slavonic in the early Russian middle ages.

4. *I come quickly*: the "prophet" is St. John; see Revelation 3:11, 22:7, 12, 20.

5. *Of that day* . . . : see Mark 13:32, Matthew 24:36.

6. *Believe* . . . : from the last stanza of Schiller's poem "Sehnsucht" ("Yearning," 1801). The Russian version, translated here, differs considerably from the original.

7. *a horrible new heresy*: Lutheranism.

8. *A great star* . . . : misquotation of Revelation 8:10–11: the star Wormwood.

9. *God our Lord* . . . : the exclamation "God is the Lord, and has revealed himself to us" is sung at Matins and in the Divine Liturgy of the Orthodox Church. Ivan misunderstands the Old Slavonic (the language of the Russian Church) to the point of reversing its meaning—a not uncommon mistake.

10. *Bent under the burden* . . . : the last stanza of F. I. Tyutchev's poem "These poor villages . . ." (1855).

11. *In the splendid auto-da-fé* . . . : a somewhat altered quotation from A. I. Polezhayev's poem "Coriolanus" (1834). The Portuguese *auto da fé* means "a (judicial) act of faith," i.e., the carrying out of a sentence of the Inquisition, usually the public burning of a heretic.

12. *as the lightning* . . . : see Matthew 24:27, Luke 17:24.

13. *scorched squares*: also from Polezhayev's poem.

14. *ad majorem* . . . : "for the greater glory of God," the motto of the Jesuits (correctly *ad majorem Dei gloriam*).

15. *Talitha cumi*: "damsel arise" in Aramaic: Mark 5:40–42. Ivan bases this "second appearance" of Christ on Gospel accounts.

16. *fragrant with laurel and lemon*: an altered quotation from scene 2 of Pushkin's "The Stone Guest," a play on the Don Juan theme, set in Seville (one of Pushkin's "Little Tragedies").

17. *qui pro quo*: Latin legal term: "one for another," i.e., mistaken identity.

18. *I want to make you free*: see John 8:31–36.

19. *to bind and loose*: see Matthew 16:19.

20. *"tempted" you*: see Matthew 4:1–11, Luke 4:1–13.

21. *Who can compare* . . . : see Revelation 13:4, 13 (also note 10 to page 244 in section 2.5.4).

22. *Tower of Babel*: see note 2 to page 26 in section 1.1.5.

23. *Instead of the firm ancient law*: according to Christ's words in the Gospel (Matthew 5:17–18), he came not to replace but to fulfill the law given to Moses. The Inquisitor (or Ivan) overstates his case.

24. *If you would know* . . . : see Matthew 4:6. The text is misquoted, and the last two clauses are added.

25. *Come down* . . . : an abbreviated misquotation of Matthew 27:42 (see also Mark 15:32).

26. *Your great prophet* . . . : again, St. John (see Revelation 7:4–8).

27. *locusts and roots*: see Matthew 3:4, Mark 1:6; the allusion is to John the Baptist.

28. *Exactly eight centuries ago* . . . : in 755 A.D., eight centuries before the Inquisitor's time (mid sixteenth century), Pepin the Short, king of the Franks, took the Byzantine ex-

archate of Ravenna and the Pentapolis ("five cities": i.e., Rimini, Pesaro, Fano, Sinnigaglia, and Ancona) from the Lombards and turned the territories over to Pope Stephen II, thus initiating the secular power of the papacy.

29. *And it is then that the beast . . . "Mystery!"*: combines the Great Beast from Revelation 13 and 17 with lines from scene 2 of Pushkin's "Covetous Knight" (another of the "Little Tragedies"): "Submissive, timid, blood-bespattered crime / Comes crawling to my feet, licking my hand, / Looking me in the eye . . ." (see Terras, p. 235).

30. *It is said* . . . : see Revelation 17:15–16.

31. *that the number be complete*: see Revelation 6:11 (Revised Standard Version).

32. *Dixi*: "I have spoken."

33. *filthy earthly lucre*: see Titus 1:7.

34. *I imagine that even the Masons* . . . : Freemasons, a secret society of mutual aid and brotherhood who organized their first "grand lodge" in London in 1717 and from there spread to most parts of the world; considered heretical by the Orthodox and Roman Catholic churches.

35. *dark squares*: an altered quotation from Pushkin's poem "Remembrance" (1828).

36. *you go right, I'll go left* . . . : see perhaps Genesis 13:9. The left is the "sinister" side, associated with the devil, especially in depictions of the Last Judgment. Ivan hunches up his left shoulder in a moment; Smerdyakov often squints or winks with his left eye.

37. *Pater Seraphicus*: "Seraphic Father." An epithet applied to St. Francis of Assisi; also an allusion to Goethe's *Faust*, part 2, act 5, lines 11918–25. Ivan's sarcasm is not without respect.

2.5.6 A Rather Obscure One

1. *this contemplator*: see the end of *B.K.* 1.3.6.

2. *servant Licharda*: Licharda (a distortion of "Richard") is the faithful servant in *The Tale of Prince Bova*, a sixteenth-century Russian version of a medieval romance of French origin widely spread in Europe. Licharda is used by the evil queen in her plot to murder the king.

2.5.7 "It's Always Interesting"

1. *His name is Gorstkin* . . . : "Lyagavy," Gorstkin's nickname, means "bird dog."

2.6.2 From the Life of the Elder Zosima

1. *Great Lent*: the forty-day fast preceding Easter; called the "Great Lent" in the Orthodox Church to distinguish it from "lesser" fasts during the liturgical year.

2. *Holy Week*: see note 6 to page 168 in section 2.4.1.

3. *One Hundred and Four Sacred Stories* . . . : a Russian translation of a German collection of Bible stories edited by Johannes Hübner (1714). According to his wife, Dostoevsky had this book as a child and "learned to read with it."

4. *analogion*: (from Greek) lectern; a stand in the middle of the church on which the Bible is placed during readings.

5. *There was a man* . . . : the beginning of the Book of Job; here and in the following, Zosima paraphrases from memory.

6. *Naked came I* . . . : from Job, with some alterations: Zosima significantly adds "into the earth" and from habit concludes Job's words "blessed be the name of the Lord" with the liturgical formula "henceforth and forevermore" (the whole phrase is an exclamation repeated three times near the end of the Orthodox liturgy).

7. *Let my prayer arise* . . . : the full phrase is "Let my prayer arise in thy sight as in-

cense"; sung at Vespers during the censing of the church. In the services of Holy Week, people customarily kneel while the verses are sung. The Book of Job is read at Vespers on Holy Monday and Tuesday.

8. *unto ages of ages*: a liturgical formula (cf. the Latin *in saecula saeculorum*).

9. *work*: a parish priest would often have to do his own farming as well as serve his parish.

10. *Read to them of Abraham and Sarah* . . . : see Genesis 11–35. The words "How dreadful is this place" (Genesis 28:17) belong to the episode of Jacob's dream of the ladder, not that of his wrestling with the angel.

11. *Joseph*: Genesis 37–50.

12. *having uttered . . . the great word* . . . : Jacob's prophecy about Judah (Genesis 49:10) is regarded by Christians as referring to Christ.

13. *Saul's speech*: Acts 13:16–41.

14. *Alexei, the man of God*: see note 3 to page 50 in section 1.2.3.

15. *Mary of Egypt*: a fifth-century saint greatly venerated in Orthodoxy; a prostitute who became a Christian and spent forty-seven years in the desert in prayer and repentance.

16. *And I told him of how a bear* . . . : an episode from the life of St. Sergius of Radonezh (1314–99), one of the greatest figures in the history of the Russian Church, founder of an important monastery in Zagorsk, near Moscow.

17. *for the day and the hour* . . . : see Revelation 9:15.

18. *1826*: the "important event" must have been the Decembrist uprising of 14 December 1825, aimed at limiting the power of the tsar.

19. *Then the sign* . . . : see Matthew 24:30, Christ's words about his Second Coming.

20. *Russian translation*: the language of the Russian Church is Old Slavonic, not Russian. The New Testament was translated into Russian early in the nineteenth century.

2.6.3 Talks and Homilies

1. *for the day and the hour* . . . : see note 17 to page 296 in section 2.6.2.

2. *This star* . . . : see Matthew 2:2.

3. *kulaks and commune-eaters*: abusive terms for peasants who act against the communal life of the village for their own private gain. *Kulak* literally means "fist."

4. *their wrath* . . . : Genesis 49:7.

5. *in accordance with the Gospel*: see Matthew 20:25–26, 23:11; Mark 9:35, 10:43.

6. *The stone* . . . : see Matthew 21:42 (quoting Psalm 118:22–23); the passage is often quoted in Orthodox services.

7. *he who draws the sword* . . . : see Matthew 26:52.

8. *for the sake of the meek* . . . : see Matthew 24:22, Mark 13:20. Zosima alters the passage without distorting its meaning.

9. *great and beautiful*: see note 2 to page 71 in section 1.2.6.

10. *Much on earth* . . . : Victor Terras rightly considers the passage from here to the end of the sub-chapter to be "probably the master key to the philosophic interpretation, as well as to the structure," of *B.K.* (see Terras, p. 259).

11. *Remember especially* . . . : see Matthew 7:1–5.

12. *the only sinless One*: Christ (see also note 15 to page 246 in section 2.5.4).

13. *no longer able to love*: Zosima's thought here and in the long paragraph that follows is drawn from the homilies of St. Isaac the Syrian (see note 7 to page 27 in section 1.1.5), e.g., Homily 84 (Greek numbering).

14. *the rich man and Lazarus*: see Luke 16:19–31. "Abraham's bosom" is the place of blessed rest for the righteous.

15. *time will be no more*: see Revelation 10:6.

16. *one may pray for them as well*: suicide is considered among the greatest sins; the Church forbids the burial of suicides by established rites and does not hold memorial services for them. Zosima's broad notions of love and forgiveness are traced by some commentators to the teachings of St. Tikhon of Zadonsk (1724–83).

17. *sucking his own blood* . . . : an image from St. Isaac the Syrian, Homily 73 (Greek numbering).

3.7.1 The Odor of Corruption

1. *schēmahieromonk*: (from the Greek) a hieromonk who also wears a special vestment, or *schēma*, indicating a higher monastic degree calling for special ascetic discipline.

2. *eight-pointed cross*: the typical cross of the Russian Church.

3. *aer*: (from the Greek) a square of cloth used to cover the chalice and paten containing the holy gifts on the altar.

4. *How believest thou*: see note 4 to page 233 in section 2.5.3. Absurd in this context.

5. *Tomorrow they will sing* . . . : "As the body of a monk or schēmamonk is carried from his cell to the church, and after the funeral service to the cemetery, the *stikhera* [verses on biblical themes] 'What Earthly Joy' are sung. If the deceased was a schēmahieromonk, the canon 'My Helper and Defender' is sung" (Dostoevsky's note).

3.7.3 An Onion

1. *gescheft*: a Yiddish word that has entered Russian, meaning "a little business" or "shady dealing."

2. *And the angel wept* . . . : in a letter to his publisher, N. A. Lyubimov (16 September 1879), Dostoevsky refers to this "fable" as "a gem, taken down by me from a peasant woman."

3. *Alyoshenka, little man of God*: see note 3 to page 50 in section 1.2.3; the diminutive here is contemptuous.

4. *seven devils*: Rakitin is thinking of Mary Magdalene; see Mark 16:9, Luke 8:1–2.

3.7.4 Cana of Galilee

1. *Cana of Galilee*: see John 2:1–11. Father Paissy reads from this passage further on.

2. *the lake of Gennesaret*: the Sea of Galilee.

3.8.1 Kuzma Samsonov

1. *Lyagavy*: see note 1 to page 278 in section 2.5.7.

3.8.3 Gold Mines

1. *Pushkin observed*: in his *Table-Talk*, notes modeled on Hazlitt's *Table Talk* (1821), whose English title Pushkin borrowed; written during the 1830s, unpublished in the poet's lifetime.

2. *Enough*: refers to "Enough. A Fragment from the Notes of a Deceased Artist" (1865) by Turgenev, a piece Dostoevsky particularly disliked.

3. *Varvara*: St. Barbara, fourth-century virgin and martyr.

4. *I wrote in this regard* . . . : M. E. Saltykov-Shchedrin (1826–89), journalist, novelist, and satirist, was one of Dostoevsky's leading adversaries (see also note 2 to page 78 in section 1.2.7). *The Contemporary*, a journal founded by Pushkin in 1836, became an organ of Russian revolutionary democrats; it was closed by the authorities in 1866. Shchedrin was one of its editors for a time. Dostoevsky teases his opponents (as Turgenev earlier) by associating them with Madame Khokhlakov.

3.8.4 In the Dark

1. *And naught . . .* : from Pushkin's *Ruslan and Lyudmila* (1820); the line flashes through Mitya's mind in slightly altered form.

3.8.5 A Sudden Decision

1. *Phoebus*: Apollo, in his function as sun god.
2. *Mastriuk . . .* : quotation from the historical ballad "Mastriuk Temriukovich," in which Mastriuk has his clothes stolen while lying unconscious.
3. *Gullible . . .* : lines from F. Tyutchev's translation (1851) of Schiller's "Victory Banquet" ("Das Siegesfest," 1803), where the reference is to Clytemnestra.
4. *I am sad . . .* : Mitya is, of course, rewriting *Hamlet* here.
5. *Yet one last tale . . .* : cf. the first line of the monk Pimen's speech in Pushkin's historical tragedy *Boris Godunov* (1824–25), proverbial among Russians.

3.8.6 Here I Come!

1. *You see, sir, when the Son of God . . .* : one of many variations on the theme of hell in *B.K.* Andrei's version may derive from a popular verse legend, "The Dream of the Most Holy Mother of God," itself based on apocryphal accounts of Christ's descent into hell.

3.8.7 The Former and Indisputable One

1. *Panie*: Polish forms of address, as well as Polish words and phrases, appear throughout this chapter. *Pan* means "sir" or "gentleman." *Panie* (pronounced PAN-yeh) is the form of direct address for a gentleman, *pani* (PAN-ee) for a lady; *panowie* (pan-OH-vyeh) is the plural of *panie*. For the Polish phrases, Dostoevsky most often supplies his own translation in parentheses; we do the same.
2. *królowa . . .* : Grushenka is right; the word is close to the Russian *koroleva* ("queen").
3. *łajdak*: "scoundrel."
4. *Agrippina*: the Polish form of Agrafena.
5. *Dead Souls*: the reference is to an episode at the end of part 1, ch. 4 of Gogol's satirical masterpiece (1842).
6. *Piron*: see note 4 to page 135 in section 1.3.8.
7. *Is that you, Boileau . . .* : from an epigram by I. A. Krylov (1769–1844), on a bad translation of Nicolas Boileau's *Art poétique*.
8. *You're Sappho . . .* : an epigram by K. N. Batyushkov (1787–1855), on a bad woman poet; legend has it that Sappho died by throwing herself into the sea.
9. *Çi-gît Piron . . .* : "Here lies Piron who was nothing, / Not even an academician."
10. *To Poland . . .* : the action of *B.K.* is set in the mid 1860s, shortly after the Polish uprising of 1863; Mitya, as a former Russian officer, is making an unusually conciliatory gesture (see Terras, p. 303).
11. *To Russia . . .* : Pan Vrublevsky declines to be conciliatory. Russia, Prussia, and Austria partitioned Poland for the first time in 1772, a disaster that awakened the Polish national spirit.
12. *Pan Podvysotsky*: in a letter to his publisher, N. A. Lyubimov (16 November 1879), Dostoevsky notes that he had heard this same anecdote three separate times over the years.
13. *gonor*: Mitya uses the Polish word *honor* (pronounced *gonor* in Russian) rather than the Russian word *chest'*.
14. *panienochka*: Maximov makes a Russian diminutive of *pani*.

3.8.8 Delirium

1. *Dance cottage* . . . : from a popular Russian dance song.

2. *"new" song*: in a letter to his publisher (see note 12 to page 426 in section 3.8.7), Dostoevsky notes that he copied this song down himself "from real life" and calls it "an example of recent peasant creativity."

3. *You see, I learned* . . . : Maximov's self-mockery; the *sabotière* is a peasant clog-dance (French *sabot*, "clog").

4. *Let this terrible cup* . . . : see Matthew 26:39, Mark 14:36, Luke 22:42; referring to Christ's agony in Gethsemane.

5. *The piggy* . . . : refrain of several Russian folksongs.

6. *Its legs* . . . : from a riddle song.

7. *podłajdak*: Mitya adds a Russian prefix meaning *sub-* to the Polish word for "scoundrel."

8. *Ah, hallway* . . . : another popular dance song, about a peasant girl who defies her father out of love for a young man (see Terras, p. 310).

9. *the Jurisprudence*: the Imperial School of Jurisprudence in Petersburg.

3.9.2 The Alarm

1. *state councillor*: see note 1 to page 99 in section 1.3.2.

3.9.3 The First Torment

1. *The Soul's Journey through Torments*: according to a purely popular Christian notion, as a person's soul ascends towards heaven after death, it meets evil spirits that try to force it down to hell. Only the souls of the righteous avoid these "torments" (there are said to be twenty of them). The point here is that Mitya's soul, figuratively, is not merely suffering but rising; the "journey" is one of purification.

2. *Diogenes' lantern*: Diogenes the Cynic (404–323? B.C.), a Greek philosopher, is said to have gone about with a lantern in broad daylight, "looking for a man."

3.9.4 The Second Torment

1. *Be patient* . . . : an imprecise quotation from "Silentium" (1836), a famous poem by F. Tyutchev.

3.9.8 The Evidence of the Witnesses

1. *of the twelfth grade*: one of the lowest grades (there were fourteen) of the imperial civil service.

3.9.9 Mitya Is Taken Away

1. *the thunder has struck*: refers to a Russian proverb that Dostoevsky quotes in a letter to his publisher (see note 12 to page 426 in section 3.8.7): "Unless thunder strikes, a peasant won't cross himself."

4.10.1 Kolya Krasotkin

1. *dry and sharp*: from the poem "Before Rain" (1846) by Nikolai Nekrasov.

2. *Smaragdov*: see note 5 to page 125 in section 1.3.6.

4.10.2 Kids

1. *Oh, children* . . . : beginning of the fable "The Cock, the Cat, and the Mouse" (1802) by I. I. Dmitriev (1760–1837).

4.10.5 At Ilyusha's Bedside

1. *A Kinsman* . . . : a book translated from the French, published in Moscow in 1785.

2. *who taught you all that*: Kolya's ideas throughout his harangue are drawn from the liberal press of the time. Again, as with Madame Khokhlakov, Dostoevsky is teasing his opponents, here by reflecting their ideas through a schoolboy's mind. There is, of course, a serious point to it, connected with one of the major themes of *B.K.*, the influence of the word.

4.10.6 Precocity

1. *if there were no God* . . . : see note 3 to page 24 in section 1.1.4 and note 5 to page 234 in 2.5.3.

2. *Candide*: Voltaire's satirical-philosophical tale (1759).

3. *Belinsky* . . . *Onegin*: refers to the "Ninth Essay on Pushkin" (1844–45) by the influential liberal critic Vissarion Belinsky (1811–48). Onegin and Tatiana are the hero and heroine of Pushkin's novel in verse *Evgeny Onegin* (1823–31).

4. *Les femmes tricottent*: "Women are knitters."

5. *The Bell*: the two lines of verse Kolya quotes are from an anti-government satire that appeared in the émigré magazine *North Star* (no. 6, 1861) and elsewhere, but not in *The Bell*, published in London by Alexander Herzen (1812–70), where a sequel to it appeared. The "Third Department" was the imperial secret police, whose headquarters were near the Chain Bridge in Petersburg.

4.10.7 Ilyusha

1. *If I forget thee* . . . : see Psalm 137, "By the rivers of Babylon . . ."

4.11.2 An Ailing Little Foot

1. *Skotoprigonyevsk*: roughly "Cattle-roundup-ville."

2. *They want to set up* . . . : the question of a monument to Pushkin began to be discussed in the press in 1862; on 6 June 1880 the monument was finally unveiled. Dostoevsky gave a famous address on the occasion.

3. *vous comprenez* . . . : "you know, this business and the terrible death of your papa."

4.11.4 A Hymn and a Secret

1. *like a Swede at Poltava*: a common Russian saying; the original has "like a Swede," the "at Poltava" being implied. Charles XII of Sweden was roundly defeated at Poltava in 1709 by Peter the Great.

2. *wisdom*: in this context, the Old Slavonic word *premudrost'* (wisdom) most likely refers to the Scriptures.

3. *Apocryphal Gospels*: accounts of the life of Christ (such as the Gospels of Thomas or James) not accepted as canonical.

4. *Claude Bernard*: French physiologist (1813–78), whose *Introduction to the Study of Experimental Medicine* defined the basic principles of scientific research.

5. *de thoughtibus* . . . : Mitya's variation on the Latin saying *de gustibus non est disputandum* ("there is no arguing over taste").

6. *image and likeness*: see note 4 to page 239 in section 2.5.4.

7. *Ah, what a charming little foot* . . . : Dostoevsky's (not Rakitin's) jesting response to D. D. Minaev's parody of a poem by Pushkin. Minaev (1835–89) was a poet of civic themes.

8. *to the uttermost farthing*: see Matthew 5:26.

4.11.5 Not You! Not You!

1. *Alyosha was startled . . .* : Katerina Ivanovna suddenly addresses Ivan in the familiar second person singular, indicating greater intimacy than social conventions would have allowed them.

2. *with obvious coldness*: here Ivan suddenly addresses Alyosha in the formal second person plural.

4.11.8 The Third Meeting with Smerdyakov

1. *Ah, Vanka's gone . . .* : Vanka is a diminutive of Ivan. The song must unconsciously remind Ivan of his departure on the eve of the catastrophe (see Terras, p. 381).

2. *Licharda*: see note 2 to page 269 in section 2.5.6.

3. *The Homilies . . .* : see note 7 to page 27 in section 1.1.5.

4.11.9 The Devil

1. *qui frisait la cinquantaine*: "who was pushing fifty."

2. *Thomas believed . . .* : see note 1 to page 26 in section 1.1.5.

3. *c'est noble . . . c'est chivaleresque*: "it's noble, it's delightful . . . it's chivalrous."

4. *I donated ten roubles . . .* : that is, to a fund to help liberate Slavs under Turkish domination in the Balkans.

5. *Satan sum . . .* : the devil adapts a famous line from the Roman playwright Terence (190–159 B.C.): *homo sum, humani nihil a me alienum puto* ("I am a man, nothing human is alien to me").

6. *C'est de nouveau, n'est-ce pas?*: "That's something new, isn't it?"

7. *the waters above the firmament*: see Genesis 1:7.

8. *Gattsuk . . .* : A. A. Gattsuk (1832–91) was a Moscow publisher who published a yearly almanac in the 1870s and 1880s.

9. *great . . . beautiful*: see note 2 to page 71 in section 1.2.6.

10. *Le diable n'existe point*: "The devil does not exist."

11. *and various little vaudevilles . . . Khlestakov*: the quoted line is spoken by Khlestakov, the impostor-hero of Gogol's comedy *The Inspector-General* (1836).

12. *Je pense donc je suis*: "I think, therefore I am," the well-known phrase of the philosopher René Descartes (1596–1650).

13. *a certain department . . .* : see note 5 to page 555 in section 4.10.6.

14. *rejected all . . .* : the quoted words are spoken by Repetilov in Griboyedov's *Woe from Wit* (see note 1 to page 221 in section 2.5.1).

15. *the 'mellowing . . .'*: a commonplace in the eighteenth-century debate on the progress of civilization.

16. *the desert fathers . . .* : first line of a poem by Pushkin (1836) that goes on to paraphrase the fourth-century Prayer of St. Ephraim the Syrian, recited in weekday services during the Great Lent.

17. *the actor Gorbunov*: I. F. Gorbunov (1831–96), a personal friend of Dostoevsky, also a writer and talented improvisor.

18. *Ah, mon père . . .* : "Ah, father, it is such pleasure for him, and so little trouble for me." This witticism goes back to an anonymous epigram on the French actress Jeanne-Catherine Gaussain (1711–67).

19. *great and beautiful*: again, see note 2 to page 71 in section 1.2.6.

20. *Belinsky*: see note 3 to page 555 in section 4.10.6.

21. *I did think . . .* : Dostoevsky plays in this passage on the names of certain decorations and of certain publications: the "Lion and Sun" was a Persian order, which might be awarded to a Russian serving in the Caucasus; the "North Star" was a Swedish order, but

also a Russian radical almanac; "Sirius," the Dog Star, is also the hero of Voltaire's *Micromégas* (1752). The devil teases Ivan with being a liberal.

22. *Mephistopheles* . . . : see Goethe, *Faust*, part 1, lines 1335–36.

23. *à la Heine*: Heinrich Heine (1797–1856), German poet and essayist of irreverent wit.

24. *Ah, mais c'est bête enfin!*: "Ah, but how stupid, really!"

25. *Luther's inkstand*: it is said that Martin Luther (1483–1546) was tempted by the devil while translating the Bible and threw his inkstand at him.

26. *Monsieur sait-il* . . . : "Does the gentleman know what the weather is like? One wouldn't put a dog outside . . ." The first half of a joke, the punch line being: "Yes, but you are not a dog." The whole joke appears in Dostoevsky's notebooks of 1876–77.

4.11.10 "He Said That!"

1. *Le mot de l'énigme*: "the key to the riddle."

4.12.2 Dangerous Witnesses

1. *the doors of heaven open*: see Revelation 4:1.

4.12.3 Medical Expertise

1. *Herrnhuter or "Moravian Brother"*: the Herrnhuters emerged as a religious sect in eighteenth-century Saxony and subsequently spread to Russia. Their beliefs were rooted in the teachings of the fifteenth-century Moravian Brethren.

2. *Gott der Vater* . . . : Herzenstube teaches Mitya to say "God the Father, God the Son, and God the Holy Spirit" in German.

4.12.5 A Sudden Catastrophe

1. *Bread and circuses!*: in Latin, *panem et circenses*; bitter words addressed by the poet Juvenal (65?–128 A.D.) to the Romans of the decadent period (*Satires* 10.81).

2. *Le diable* . . . : see note 10 to page 641 in section 4.11.9.

3. *then he cried out with a frenzied cry*: a Hebraism reminiscent of the cries of those possessed by evil spirits; cf. Acts 8:6–7, Luke 8:28, Matthew 8:29, Mark 9:26.

4.12.6 The Prosecutor's Speech

1. *"accursed" questions*: God versus reason, human destiny, the future of Russia, and so forth; questions that concerned Dostoevsky himself (see Terras, p. 412).

2. *new open courts* . . . : the judicial reform of 1864 introduced public jury trials in Russia.

3. *least Hamletian question* . . . : refers to *Hamlet* 3.1.78; not a quotation.

4. *he lived among us*: first line of Pushkin's poem to the Polish poet Adam Mickiewicz (1798–1855).

5. *A great writer* . . . *comparison*: the line "Ah, troika . . ." comes from Gogol's *Dead Souls*; Sobakevich, Nozdryov, and Chichikov are the grotesque heroes of the novel.

6. *like to the sun* . . . : a line from the ode "God" (1784) by the great Russian poet G. R. Derzhavin (1743–1816).

7. *après moi le déluge*: "after me the flood," attributed to Louis XV, and also to his favorite, the Marquise de Pompadour.

8. *dark mysticism* . . . *witless chauvinism*: criticisms often leveled at Dostoevsky by his opponents, here treated good-humoredly.

4.12.9 The Finale of the Prosecutor's Speech

1. *what lies beyond*: see note 3 to page 694 in section 4.12.6.

2. *We'll close Kronstadt* . . . : island and port on the Gulf of Finland; in the nineteenth century Russia was a major exporter of wheat.

4.12.10 The Defense Attorney's Speech

1. *strike the heart* . . . : quotation from Pushkin's poem "Reply to Anonymous" (1830).

4.12.11 No Money. No Robbery

1. *Udolpho*: refers to *The Mysteries of Udolpho* (1794), a gothic novel by the English writer Ann Radcliffe (1764–1823), very popular in Russia in the earlier nineteenth century.

4.12.12 No Murder Either

1. *the power to bind and to loose*: see Matthew 16:19, 18:18; rather loosely applied by Fetyukovich.

4.12.13 An Adulterer of Thought

1. *The crucified lover of mankind* . . . : the quotation is a conflation of John 10:11, 14–15, with the last phrase added by Fetyukovich. On the epithet "lover of mankind," see note 1 to page 18 in section 1.1.4.

2. *Fathers, provoke not* . . . : cf. Colossians 3:21. Fetyukovich "adulters" by what he omits (see Colossians 3:20).

3. *vivos voco!*: "I call the living." From the epigraph to Schiller's "Song of the Bell," used in turn as an epigraph by the radical journal *The Bell* (see note 5 to page 555 in section 4.10.6).

4. *With what measure ye mete* . . . : see note 1 to page 133 in section 1.3.8; Fetyukovich goes on to reverse the meaning of this "precept."

5. *'metal' and 'brimstone'*: refers to a passage from the play *Hard Days* (1863) by Alexander Ostrovsky (1823–86), in which a merchant's wife is afraid to hear these biblical words.

6. *Drive nature out the door* . . . : quotation from a Russian translation of La Fontaine's "La Chatte metamorphosée en femme" (The cat changed into a woman), *Fables* 2.18.

7. *These people* . . . : see Matthew 25:35–43.

8. *It is better* . . . : the majestic voice is Peter the Great's; the words are a slightly altered quotation from his *Military Code* (1716).

4.12.14 Our Peasants Stood Up

1. *For Thou art our God* . . . : the phrase appears in many Orthodox prayers, particularly in the Hymn of the Resurrection sung at Matins.

2. *Thou art angry, Jupiter* . . . : a well-known saying in Russia. Its ultimate source is unknown, but a somewhat similar phrase occurs in a dialogue by the Greek satirist Lucian. See N. S. Ashukin and M. G. Ashukina, *Krylatye Slova* (Winged words) (Moscow, 1986), pp. 721–22.

3. *I will break the sword* . . . : a sword was broken over the condemned man's head in the ceremony known as "civil execution" (see Terras, p. 436). Dostoevsky underwent such an "execution" on 22 December 1849, and described it in a letter to his brother Mikhail written that same day.

4. *Good God, gentlemen* . . . : refers to an actual case, involving the actress A. B. Kairova, which Dostoevsky wrote about in his *Diary of a Writer* (May 1876).

Epilogue.2 The Lie Became Truth

1. *to the last Mohicans*: James Fenimore Cooper's novel *The Last of the Mohicans* (1826) was very popular in Russia; Dostoevsky owned a French translation of it.

Epilogue.3 Ilyushechka's Funeral

1. *fillet*: a narrow band with a prayer of absolution written on it, customarily placed on the head of the deceased in Russian funeral services.

2. *may his memory . . . ages of ages*: liturgical language echoing the service they have all just attended; the prayer "Memory Eternal," sung at the very end of the funeral service, refers to God's memory.

ABOUT THE INTRODUCER

Malcolm V. Jones is Professor of Slavonic Studies at the University of Nottingham and author of *Dostoyevsky, The Novel of Discord* and *Dostoyevsky After Bakhtin*.

ABOUT THE TRANSLATORS

RICHARD PEVEAR has published translations of Alain, Yves Bonnefoy, Alberto Savinio and Pavel Florensky as well as two books of poetry.

LARISSA VOLOKHONSKY has translated the work of prominent Orthodox theologians Alexander Schmemann and John Meyendorff.

Together they are known for their highly acclaimed translations of Dostoevsky's novels. Their translation of *The Brothers Karamazov* was awarded the PEN/Book-of-the-Month Club Prize.

Everyman's Library, founded in 1906 and relaunched in 1991, aims to offer the most complete library in the English language of the world's classics. Each volume is printed in a classic typeface on acid-free, cream-wove paper with a sewn full cloth binding.